THE BLACK LIZARD
BIG
BOOK OF
PULPS

THE BLACK LIZARD

BIG
BOOK OF
PULPS

Edited by

OTTO PENZLER

VINTAGE CRIME/BLACK LIZARD
Vintage Books
A Division of Random House, Inc.
New York

A VINTAGE CRIME/BLACK LIZARD ORIGINAL,
NOVEMBER 2007

Library of Congress Cataloging-in-Publication Data
The Black Lizard big book of pulps / edited by Otto Penzler.
p. cm.
ISBN 978-0-307-28048-0
1. Crime—Fiction. 2. Noir fiction, American. I. Penzler, Otto.
PS648.C7B585 2007
813'.087208—dc22
2007021103

Book design by Christopher M. Zucker

Printed in the United States of America
10 9 8 7 6 5 4 3 2 1

For Sally Owen
my irreplaceable colleague
with affection and gratitude
and
For Sheila Mitchell and H.R.F. Keating
my dear friends and hoteliers par excellence

CONTENTS

THE BLACK LIZARD

BIG
BOOK OF
PULPS

FOREWORD BY OTTO PENZLER

LIKE JAZZ, the hard-boiled private detective is entirely an American invention, and it was given life in the pages of pulp magazines. Pulp now is a nearly generic term, frequently misused to indicate hack work of inferior literary achievement. While that often may be accurate, pulp was not intended to describe literary excellence or lack thereof, but was derived from the word pulpwood, which is the very cheap paper that was used to produce popular magazines. These, in turn, were the offspring of "dime novels," mainly magazine-sized mystery, Western, and adventure novels produced for young or unsophisticated readers.

After World War I, the popularity of American pulpwood magazines increased rapidly, reaching their peak of success in the 1920s and 1930s, as more than 500 titles a month hit the newsstands. With their reasonable prices (mostly a dime or fifteen cents a copy), brilliantly colored covers depicting lurid and thrilling scenes, and a writing style that emphasized action and adventure above philosophizing and introspection, millions of copies of this new, uniquely American literature were sold every week.

At first, the magazines sought to publish something for all tastes, so a single issue might feature a Western story, an aviation adventure, a mystery, a science fiction tale, and a sports report. New titles came along and most of the old ones quickly morphed into special interest publications. The very first issues of *Black Mask*, for example, often had Western scenes on the covers, but by the mid 1920s it had become devoted almost entirely to mystery fiction.

While there were magazines designated to stories of railroads, jungle adventure, "spicy" stories, romance, horror, and any other subject that enterprising publishers thought would attract a readership, the most successful pulps were those featuring superheroes and detective fiction (with the notable exception of *Weird Tales*, the long-lived pulp devoted to fantasy and science fiction).

One of the elements that made the detective magazines so popular was the heroic figures in the center of the action. The hard-boiled cop or, especially, private detective was the idealization of the lone individual, representing justice and decency, pitted against virulent gangs, corrupt politicians, or other agencies who violated that sense of goodness with which most readers identified. The best of these crime-fighting tough guys became series characters, taking on one group of thugs after another, always emerging victorious in spite of the almost hopeless odds he (and these protagonists were almost always male) encountered.

Many of the most memorable of these protagonists became staples of *Black Mask, Detective Fiction Weekly, Dime Detective*, and the other major pulp publications. Dashiell Hammett's Continental Op, Carroll John Daly's Race Williams, Frank Gruber's Oliver Quade, Ramon Decolta's (Raoul Whitfield) Jo Gar, Norbert Davis's Max Latin, George Harmon Coxe's

Flash Casey, W. T. Ballard's Bill Lennox, Robert Reeves's Cellini Smith, and Frederick L. Nebel's Cardigan are just a few of the detectives who appeared month after month to the delight of a reading public whose appetite for this sort of no-nonsense, shoot-first-and-ask-questions-later fiction remained unsated until the end of the second World War.

Crimefighters in the pulps were seldom the sensitive type who understood that a difficult childhood or an unloving grandmother were responsible for the violence of the criminals with whom they came into contact. No, his role was to battle bad guys, and he did it without fear, without pity, and without remorse. It was a black-and-white world in the pulps, a simple conflict between the forces of goodness and virtue and those who sought to plunder, harm, and kill the innocent. In the pages of the pulps, and between the covers of this book, Good is triumphant over Evil. Perhaps that is the key to the enormous popularity they enjoyed for so many years. Depression-era crowds eagerly snatched up each new episode of their favorite crime-fighting protagonist, rooting for and identifying with the stalwart men of action and intellect.

In addition to the hero, there was another essential element in each adventure—a monstrous opponent. For a hero to be worthy of the name, it was utterly required that he do battle with a villain so despicable, so vile, so conscienceless that only a man of supreme strength of body and mind, and an incorruptible soul, could hope to emerge victorious. Here, in *The Crimes of Richmond City,* you will see the almost overwhelming odds faced by MacBride and Kennedy as they attempt to right the wrongs they are forced to encounter. Other detectives, in other tales, had no lesser difficulties to overcome.

The pulps were also home to a different kind of crook, and readers were able to identify with them, too. These larcenous entities were admittedly thieves, but not your common, or garden variety, robber.

Virtually all the thieves who became successful series characters in the pulps (and, indeed, in all of crime fiction) were Robin Hood–type crooks. They did not commit violent acts, and they stole from the rich. Not just any rich person, mind you, but always someone who had come by his fortune illicitly. This was an exceptionally agreeable manner of behaving during the Depression era, when literally millions of Americans were jobless, standing in slow-moving bread lines to procure minimal sustenance for themselves and their families. The impoverished multitudes blamed the actions of Wall Street brokers, bankers, big businessmen, and factory owners for their plight, so what could be more attractive than to see someone break into their posh apartments and crack their safes, or nick the diamond necklaces from the fat necks of their bloated wives? Furthermore, these crooks generally donated their swag to charity or to a worthy individual (after deducting a sufficient amount to ensure their own rather lavish lifestyle, of course).

Perhaps not strangely, but nevertheless in apparent contradiction to their chosen careers, a large percentage of these redistributionist thieves, after several successful adventures, become detectives. Often they are suspected of a murder or another crime which they did not commit, and so must discover the true culprit in order to exonerate themselves. In other instances, they have friends in the police department who need their help. A long tradition of criminals behaving in this manner predates the pulp era. The American master criminal, Frederick Irving Anderson's creation, the Infallible Godahl (not included in this collection because he did not appear in the pulps), was so brilliant that he planned and executed capers so meticulously that he was never arrested. Eventually, the police paid him a large stipend to not commit crimes, since they knew they could never catch him and wanted to avoid the embarrassment of seeing headlines with yet another successful burglary. It is left to your own ethical proclivities to determine whether you identify with the safecrackers, con men, burglars, and villains or with the police who are paid to catch them.

Women were not significant in the early years of the pulp magazines. Hulbert Footner's Rosika Storey was a successful character in the pages of *Argosy*, eventually appearing as the prime figure in six books beginning in the late 1920s, but she had little company. *Black Mask* seldom used stories in which women were featured, rarely bought stories by women writers, and never had a female series character. The major authors didn't mind writing about women; they merely wrote about them, sometimes with great prominence, as the catalyst for all the ensuing action. Also, in more cases than not, they were the victims, either innocents or bad girls who got what was coming to them (according to the murderer).

When girls (and they were usually called girls, or dolls, or, heaven help us, frails, or some term of endearment like honey or sugar or baby or cutie) took the role of detective, they tended to be acceptable to male readers mainly when they were assistants, girlfriends, or professional sidekicks, such as reporters. Their roles were predictable in most stories. If they weren't present as comic relief, they needed to be rescued. It would be impossible to calculate the number of pretty young things who were kidnapped or held hostage until our hero burst through a door on the last page to save her—often from a fate worse than death. One needs only to look at the colorful cover paintings that adorned the magazines for evidence of this cliché. It is a rare cover indeed that does not display a buxom beauty in a low-cut dress or sweater, frequently in tatters, being menaced by a thug or gang of thugs.

Some of the lesser pulps, those that paid even less than the standard penny a word, began to feature women in the second decade of the detective pulps, the 1930s, while those that sought an audience with racier material, such as *Gun Molls, Saucy Stories,* and *Spicy Detective,* had even more ample reason to feature them. In these pages, opportunities for placing luscious young beauties in grave peril of violation were rampant, providing titillation to young male readers who hid their ten-cent purchases inside newspapers or more respectable journals.

One role in crime fiction in which women have been featured with some regularity is as the criminals. The pages of the pulps are rich with female jewel thieves of a certain elegance who seem always to be in formal attire at a country house party or a penthouse soiree. They function largely in the same manner as their male counterparts, though they are often required to use their seductive beauty to escape capture. Tough broads appeared in later pulps, either as out-and-out hoodlums or, more frequently but no less dangerously, as gun molls for their gangster boyfriends.

All types of female detectives and crooks who first saw the light of day in pulp magazines appear in section three of this book. There are independent private investigators, assistants, rogues, victims, molls, police officers, and innocent bystanders. They are young and old, good looking and plain, funny and dour, brave and timid, violent and gentle, honest and crooked. In short, very much like their male counterparts.

While there is more than one way to judge the success of a pulp magazine, including longevity, circulation, and profitability, the undisputed champion in the area of having developed the greatest writers and having had the most long-lasting literary influence was *Black Mask,* and most of the stories in this collection were originally published in its pages. Had it done no more than publish Carroll John Daly's first story, *Black Mask* would have achieved immortality. On May 15, 1923, with the publication of "Three Gun Terry," the hard-boiled private eye made his first appearance, quickly followed by Daly's creation of Race Williams, the first series character in hard-boiled fiction.

While Daly was truly a hack writer devoid of literary pretension, aspiration, and ability, he laid the foundation for the form that continues to flourish to this day in the work of such writers as Robert B. Parker, Joe Gores, James Crumley, Bill Pronzini, Michael Connelly, and James Lee Burke (although the latter two employ series characters who are cops, they function in the same individualistic way that private investigators do, and frequently use the same smart-aleck speech patterns as their kindred freelancers do).

Dashiell Hammett produced his first Continental Op story for *Black Mask* later in the same year, and the future of the genre was secure, as the editors and the reading public quickly recognized that this was serious literature in the guise of popular fiction. Every significant writer of the pulp era worked for *Black Mask*, including Paul Cain, Horace McCoy, Frederick L. Nebel, Raoul Whitfield, Erle Stanley Gardner, Charles G. Booth, Roger Torrey, Norbert Davis, George Harmon Coxe, and, of course, the greatest of them all, Raymond Chandler.

It was the era between the two World Wars in which the pulps flourished, their garish covers enticing readers and their cheap prices providing mass entertainment through the years of the Great Depression. It has been widely stated that the advent of television tolled the death knell for the pulps, but it is not true. They were replaced by the creation and widespread popularity of paperback books, virtually unknown as a mass market commodity before World War II.

There is quotable prose in these pages, and characters that you will remember, and fascinating evocations of another time and place, but the writers mainly had the goal of entertaining readers when these stories were produced. No reasonable reader will ever complain that the stories are slow moving, that they lack action and conflict—in short, that they are dull. Many of the contributors to this book went on to successful writing careers in other arenas, including Hollywood, but here is the real stuff: stories written at breakneck speed and designed to be read the same way.

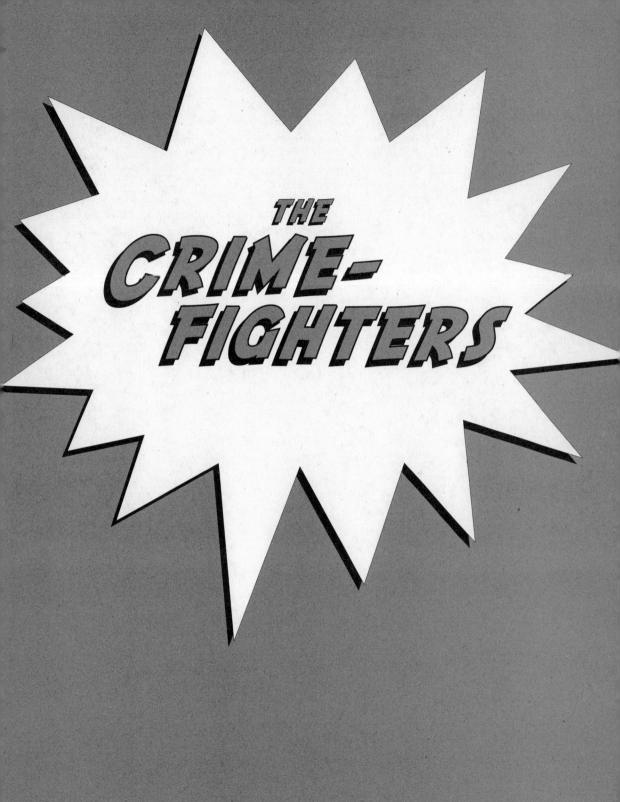

INTRODUCTION BY HARLAN COBEN

Dear Reader:

Oh man, do I envy you.

Welcome to the world of pulp fiction. If you have been here before, well, skip this introduction and dive in. You already have some idea of the delights that await. For the rest of you, I will keep this brief.

I know some writers who claim that they have never read pulp fiction. I put them in two classes. The larger group I call, for a lack of a better term, liars. Of course they have read pulp fiction. They may not know it. They may, because of the various connotations derived from the word "pulp," not want to admit it. But come on now.

Reading pulp fiction is a bit like, uh, something else. Ninety percent of the writers out there admit they do it. Ten percent lie about it.

The second group, the writers who really have never read pulp fiction (yes, I know this contradicts the last paragraph where I basically said one hundred percent read it, but go with me here)—these are writers the rest of us do not associate with. They have poor self-esteem. They had a troubled home life. They are not fun at parties.

Discovering pulp fiction now, right now, is a bit like finding a lost treasure. You are unearthing something that will entertain, enlighten, amuse, horrify, mangle, jangle, keep you riveted. Decades after they were written, these stories still manage to have an edge.

Edge. That might be the key for me. These stories still cut, still tear, still even shock a bit. These guys experimented. They wrote on the move. They wrote, like Shakespeare and Oscar Wilde, for money. They went places maybe they shouldn't have and we love them for it.

I like edge. I like it a lot. I think you will too.

Otto Penzler has carefully selected the greatest of the great from the history of pulp fiction. Legendary writers you've already heard of, like Dashiell Hammett, Erle Stanley Gardner, Cornell Woolrich, and Raymond Chandler, are here. Legendary writers that you should have heard of, like Frederick L. Nebel, Paul Cain, Carroll John Daly, George Harmon Coxe, Charles Booth, Leslie White, William Rollins, Norbert Davis, Horace McCoy, and Thomas Walsh, are also where they should be—with the greats.

In short: you got the goods here.

Finally, you have a great tour guide for this treasure hunt. Otto Penzler knows more about pulp fiction than pretty much anyone else I know. He also has self-esteem, a fine home life, and man, is he fun at parties.

Okay, put a bullet in this. I'm done. Turn the page, dammit. Start reading.

One, Two, Three

Paul Cain

ONE OF THE TRUE mystery men of pulp fiction, Paul Cain was discovered to be the pseudonym of the successful screenwriter Peter Ruric. Then, not so many years ago, it was further learned that even that name was a disguise for the author's actual name, George Carrol Sims (1902–1966).

His fame as a writer of crime fiction rests with a single novel, *Fast One* (1933), which Raymond Chandler called "some kind of high point in the ultra hard-boiled manner."

The novel had its genesis in a series of short stories published in *Black Mask*, beginning with "Fast One" in the March 1932 issue, followed by four other adventures of Gerry Kells and his alcoholic girlfriend, S. Granquist. Cain had been writing pulp stories in New York but moved to Los Angeles when Cary Grant began filming *Gambling Ship*, which was loosely based on these stories. The sale of the film to Hollywood inspired him to pull the stories together as a novel, which was both savaged by the review media at the time while praised by others. It sold few copies and he never wrote another.

He did write films, however, most famously *The Black Cat* (1934), about a Satanic cult, that starred Boris Karloff, with whom he became friends, as well as *Affairs of a Gentlemen* (1934), *Grand Central Murders* (1942), and *Mademoiselle Fifi* (1944).

"One, Two, Three" was first published in *Black Mask* in May 1933 and collected in his short story collection, *Seven Slayers* (1946).

One, Two, Three
Paul Cain

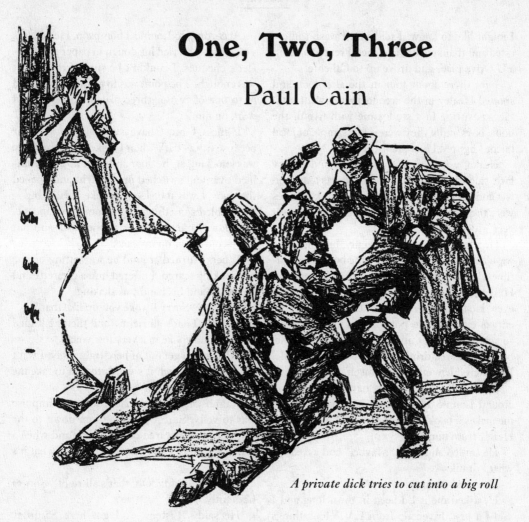

A private dick tries to cut into a big roll

'D BEEN IN Los Angeles waiting for this Healey to show for nearly a week. According to my steer, he'd taken a railroad company in Quebec for somewhere in the neighborhood of a hundred and fifty grand on a swarm of juggled options or something. That's a nice neighborhood.

My information said further that he was headed west and that he dearly loved to play cards. I do, too.

I'll take three off the top, please.

I missed him by about two hours in Chicago

and spent the day going around to all the ticket-officers, getting chummy with agents, finally found out Healey had bought a ticket to LA, so I fanned on out there and cooled.

Pass.

Sunday afternoon I ran into an op for Eastern Investigators, Inc., named Gard, in the lobby of the Roosevelt. We had a couple drinks and talked about this and that. He was on the Coast looking for a gent named Healey. He was cagey about who the client was, but Eastern handles mostly missing persons, divorces, stuff like that.

Monday morning Gard called me and said the Salt Lake branch of his outfit had located Healey in Caliente, Nevada. He said he thought

·5·

I might like to know. I told him I wasn't interested and thanked him and then I rented a car in a U Drive place and drove up to Caliente.

I got there about four in the afternoon and spotted Healey in the second joint I went into. He was sitting in a stud game with five of the home boys and if they were a fair sample of local talent I figured I had plenty of time.

Healey was a big man with a round cheery face, smooth pink skin. His mouth was loose and wet and his eyes were light blue. I think his eyes were the smallest I've ever seen. They were set very wide apart.

He won and lost pretty evenly, but the game wasn't worth a nickel. The home boys were old-timers and played close to their vests and Healey's luck was the only thing that kept him even. He finally scared two of them out of a seventy or eighty-dollar pot and that made him feel so good that he got up and came over to the the bar and ordered drinks for the boys at the table. He ordered lemonade for himself.

I said: "Excuse me, but haven't I seen you around Lonnie Thompson's in Detroit?" Lonnie makes a book and I had most of my dope on Healey from him.

He smiled and said: "Maybe," and asked me what I drank.

I ordered whiskey.

He asked me if I'd been in town long and I said I'd just driven up from LA to look things over and that things didn't look so hot and that I would probably drive back to LA that night or the next morning.

I bought him another lemonade and had another whiskey and we talked about Detroit. In a little while he went back to the table and sat down.

That was enough for a beginning. I had registered myself with him as one of the boys. I went out and drove a couple of blocks to the Pine Hotel and took a room. The Pine was practically the only hotel in town, but I flipped the register back a day or so and found Healey's name to make sure. Then I went up and washed and lay down to smoke a cigarette and figure out the details.

According to Lonnie Thompson, Healey was a cash boy—carried his dough in paper and traveler's cheques. I couldn't be sure of that but it was enough. The point was to get him to LA and in to one of two or three places where I could work on him.

I guess I must have slept almost an hour because it was dark when I woke up. Somebody was knocking at the door and I got up and stumbled over and switched on the light and opened the door. I was too sleepy to take Healey big— I mumbled something about coming in and sitting down, and went over to the basin and put some cold water on my face.

When I turned around he was sitting on the bed looking scared. I offered him a cigarette and he took it and his hand was shaking.

He said: "Sorry I woke you up like that."

I said: "That's all right," and then he leaned forward and spoke in a very low voice:

"I've got to get out of here right away. I want to know how much it's worth to you to take me down to Los Angeles."

I almost fell off the chair. My first impulse was to yell, "Sure," and drag him down to the car; but he was scared of something and when a man's scared is a swell time to find out what it's all about.

I stalled. I said: "Oh, that's all right," sort of hesitantly.

He said: "Listen. . . . I got here Saturday morning. I was going to stay here long enough to establish residence and then apply for one of those quick divorces, under the Nevada law.

"My wife has been on my tail six weeks with a blackmail gag," he went on. "She's here. When I got back to the hotel a little while ago she came into my room and put on an act."

I thought then I knew who Gard's client was.

"She came in this afternoon. She's got the room next to mine."

He was silent so long that I laughed a little and said: "So what?"

"I've got to duck, quick," he went on. "She's a bad actor. She came into my room and put on an act. She's got a guy with her that's supposed to be her brother and he's a bad actor, too. You said you were going to drive back to LA. I saw your name on the register when I came in and I thought you might take me along. I can't rent a car here and there isn't a train till midnight."

He pulled the biggest roll I ever saw out of his pocket and skimmed off a couple notes. "If it's a question of money . . ."

I shook my head with what I hoped was a suggestion of dignity. I said: "I'd decided to go back myself tonight. It will be a pleasure to take you, Mister Healey," and I got up and put on my coat. "How about your stuff?"

He looked blank until I said: "Luggage," and then he said: "That's all right—I'll leave it." He smiled again. "I travel light."

At the top of the stairs he whispered: "This is sure a big lift." Then he remembered that he had to sneak up to his room to get something and said he'd meet me at the car. I told him where it was. He said he'd paid his hotel bill.

I went on downstairs and checked out.

My car was wedged in between a Ford truck and a light-blue Chrysler roadster. There was plenty of room ahead of the roadster, so I went up and snapped off the hand-brake and pushed it ahead about eight feet. Then I got into my car and leaned back and waited.

The whole layout looked pretty bad, what with him scared to death of a deal he admitted was blackmail and all. He said he didn't want his luggage and then right on top of it, he had to go up to his room to get something. That would be taking a chance on running into the wife again. I wondered if she was his wife.

I couldn't figure out how a wife could blackmail a husband while she was jumping from state to state with a man who was "supposed" to be her brother; but then almost anything is possible in Nevada.

After about five minutes I began to get nervous. I opened the door of the car and stepped out on the side-walk, and as I closed the door there were five shots close together some place upstairs in the hotel.

I can take trouble or leave it alone; only I always take it. Like a sap, I went into the hotel.

The clerk was a big blond kid with glasses. He came out from behind the counter as I went in the door; we went upstairs together, two or three at a time.

There was a man in long woolly underwear standing in the corridor on the third floor and he pointed to a door and we went in. Healey was lying flat on his face in the middle of the room, and beyond him, close to the wall, was the body of a woman, also face downward.

The clerk turned a beautiful shade of green; he stood there staring at Healey. I went over and rolled the woman over on her back. She couldn't have been much over twenty-two or three; little, gray-eyed blonde. There was a knife in her side, under the arm. There was a .38 automatic near her outstretched hand. She was very dead.

The man in the woolly underwear peeked in and then hurried across the hall and into another room. I could hear him yelling the news to somebody there.

I went over and tapped the clerk on the shoulder and pointed at the girl. The clerk swallowed a couple of times, said: "Miss Mackay," and looked back at Healey. He was hypnotized by the way Healey's back looked. Hamburger.

Then about two dozen people came into the room all at once.

The sheriff had been in a pool-hall across the street. He rolled Healey over and said: "This is Mister Healey," as if he'd made a great discovery.

I said: "Uh-huh. He's been shot."

I guess the sheriff didn't like the way I said it very well. He glanced at the clerk and then asked me who I was. I told him my name and the clerk nodded and the sheriff scratched his head and went over and looked at the girl. I wanted to say that she'd been knifed, but I restrained myself.

Shaggy underwear was back with his pants on. He said he hadn't heard anything except somebody swearing and then, suddenly, the shots.

I asked him how long after the shots it had been when he came into the corridor and he said he wasn't sure, but it was somewhere around half a minute.

The first interesting thing that turned up was that it wasn't Healey's room—it was Miss Mackay's room. His was next door. That probably meant that Healey had deliberately gone into her room; that she hadn't surprised him in his room while he was getting something he'd forgotten.

Number two was that the knife was Healey's. Half a dozen people had seen him with it. It was an oversize jack-knife with a seven-inch blade—one of the kind that snaps open when you press a spring. Somebody said Healey had a habit of playing mumbletypeg with it when he was trying to out-sit a raise or scare somebody into splitting a pot.

Number three was the topper. The dough was gone. The sheriff and a couple of deputies searched Healey and went through both rooms with a fine-tooth comb. They weren't looking for big money because they didn't know about it; they were looking for evidence.

All they found on Healey were four hundred-dollar bills tucked into his watch pocket, and the usual keys, cigarettes, whatnot. There were no letters or papers of any kind. There was one big suitcase in his room and it was full of dirty clothes. The roll he'd flashed on me was gone.

In the next half-hour I found out a lot of things. The girl had come to the hotel alone. No one else had checked in that day, except myself. The door to the girl's room was about twenty feet from the top of the back stairs and there was a side-door to the hotel that they didn't lock until ten o'clock.

It looked like a cinch for the man Healey had told me about, the one who was supposed to be Miss Mackay's brother.

Healey had probably gone upstairs to take care of the girl. I knew that his being scared of her was on the level because I know bona-fide fear when I see it. She evidently had plenty on him. He'd arranged his getaway with me and

then gone up to carve the girl, shut her up forever.

The alleged brother had come in the side-door and had walked in on the knife act and opened up Healey's back with the automatic at about six feet.

Then he'd grabbed the roll and whatever else Healey had in his pocket that was of any value—maybe a book of traveler's cheques—had tossed the gun on the floor and screwed back down the back stairway and out the side-door. Something like that. It wasn't entirely plausible, but it was all I could figure right then.

By the time I'd figured that much out the sheriff had it all settled that Healey had knifed the girl and then she'd plugged him five times, in a ten-inch square in his back. With about three inches of steel in her heart.

That was what the sheriff said so I let it go. They didn't know about the brother and I didn't want to complicate their case for them. And I did want a chance to look for that roll without interference.

When I got out to the car the blue Chrysler was gone. That wasn't important except that I wondered who had been going away from the hotel when it looked like everybody in town was there or on the way there.

I didn't get much information at the station. The agent said he'd just come on duty; the telegraph operator had been there all afternoon but he was out to supper. I found him in a lunch-room across the street and he said there'd been a half-dozen or so people get off the afternoon train from Salt Lake; but the girl had been alone and he wasn't sure who the other people had been except three or four hometowners. That was no good.

I tried to find somebody else who had been in the station when the train came in but didn't have any luck. They couldn't remember.

I went back to the car and that made me think about the blue Chrysler again. It was just possible that the Mackay girl had come down from Salt Lake by rail, and the boyfriend or brother or whatever he was had driven down. It didn't look particularly sensible but it was an idea. Maybe they didn't want to appear to be traveling together or something.

I stopped at all the garages and gas-stations I could find but I couldn't get a line on the Chrysler. I went back to the hotel and looked at the register and found out that Miss Mackay had put down Chicago as her home, and I finagled around for a half hour and talked to the sheriff and the clerk and everybody who looked like they wanted to talk but I didn't get any more angles.

The sheriff said he'd wired Chicago because it looked like Healey and Miss Mackay were both from Chicago, and that he'd found a letter in one of Healey's old coats from a Chicago attorney. The letter was about a divorce, and the sheriff had a hunch that Miss Mackay was Mrs. Healey.

I had a sandwich and a piece of pie in the hotel restaurant and bundled up and went out and got in the car and started for LA.

I didn't get up till around eleven o'clock Tuesday morning. I had breakfast in my room and wired a connection in Chi to send me all he could get on Miss Mackay and her brother. I called the desk and got the number of Gard's room and on the way down stopped in to see him.

He was sitting in his nightshirt by the window, reading the morning papers. I sat down and asked him how he was enjoying his vacation and he said swell, and then he said: "I see by the papers that our friend Healey had an accident."

I nodded.

Gard clucked: "Tch, tch, tch. His wife will sure be cut up."

I smiled a little and said, "Uh-huh," and Gard looked up and said: "What the hell are you grinning about and what do you mean: Uh-huh?"

I told him that according to my paper Mrs. Healey was the lady who had rubbed Healey—the lady who was on her way back East in a box.

Gard shook his head intelligently and said: "Wrong. That one was an extra. Mrs. Healey is alive and kicking and one of the sweetest dishes God ever made."

I could see that he was going to get romantic

so I waited and he told me that Mrs. Healey had been the agency's client in the East and that she'd come in from Chicago Monday morning by plane and that he'd met her in the agency office, and then he went on for five or ten minutes about the color of her eyes and the way she wore her hair, and everything.

Gard was pretty much of a ladies' man. He told it with gestures.

Along with the poetry he worked in the information that Mrs. Healey, as he figured it, had had some trouble with Healey and that they'd split up and that she wanted to straighten it all out. That was the reason she'd wired the Salt Lake office of his agency to locate Healey. And almost as soon as they'd found Healey he'd shoved off for LA and the agency had wired her in Chicago to that effect. She'd arrived the morning Healey had been spotted in Caliente and had decided to wait in LA for him.

Gard said he had helped her find an apartment. He supposed the agency had called her up and told her that bad news about Healey. He acted like he was thinking a little while and then asked me if I didn't think he ought to go over and see if he could help her in any way. "Comfort her in her bereavement," was the way he put it.

I said: "Sure—we'll both go."

Gard didn't go for that very big, but I told him that my having been such a pal of Healey's made it all right.

We went.

Mrs. Healey turned out a great deal better than I had expected from Gard's glowing description. As a matter of fact she was swell. She was very dark, with dark blue eyes and blue-black hair; her clothes were very well done and her voice was cultivated, deep. When she acknowledged Gard's half-stammered introduction, inclined her head towards me and asked us to sit down, I saw that she had been crying.

Gard had done pretty well in the way of helping her find an apartment. It was a big luxurious duplex in the Garden Court on Kenmore.

I said we wanted her to know how sorry we were about it all and that I had known Healey in

Detroit, and if there was anything we could do—that sort of thing.

There wasn't much else to say. There wasn't much else said.

She asked Gard to forgive her for bothering him so much the previous evening with her calls, but that she'd been nervous and worried and kept thinking that maybe Healey had arrived in LA after the agency was closed and that she hadn't been notified. They'd been watching the trains of course.

Gard said that was all right and got red and stammered some more. He was stunned by the lady. So was I. She was a pip.

She said she thought she'd stay in California and she told us delicately that she'd made arrangements for Healey's body to be shipped to his folks in Detroit.

Finally I said we'd better go and Gard nodded and we got up. She thanked us again for coming and a maid helped us with our coats and we left.

Gard said he had to go downtown so I took a cab and went back to the hotel. There was a wire from Chicago:

JEWEL MACKAY TWO CONVICTIONS EXTORTION STOP WORKS WITH HUSBAND ARTHUR RAINES ALIAS J L MAXWELL STOP LEFT CHICAGO WEDNESDAY FOR LOS ANGELES WITH RAINES STOP DESCRIPTION MACKAY FOUR ELEVEN ONE HUNDRED TWO BLONDE GRAY EYES RAINES FIVE SIX ONE HUNDRED TWENTY-FIVE RED BROWN EYES STOP MAY LOCATE THROUGH BROTHER WILLIAM RAINES REAL ESTATE SOUTH LABREA REGARDS
ED.

I got the number of Raines' real estate office from the telephone book and took a cab and went down and looked it over. I didn't go in. Then I told the driver to take me to the Selwyn Apartments on Beverly Boulevard. That was the place the telephone book had listed as Raines' residence.

It took a half-hour of jabbering about spark plugs with the Bohunk in the Selwyn garage to find out that Mister Raines had gone out about ten o'clock with another gentleman, and what Mister Raines looked like and what kind of a car he drove. The gentleman who had been with him was tall—or maybe he was short. Or maybe it had been a lady. The Bohunk wasn't sure.

I jockeyed the cab around to a good spot in the cross street and went into the drug-store on the opposite corner and drank Coca-Colas. Along about the fifth Coca-Cola the car I was looking for pulled up in front of the Selwyn. A medium-sized middle-aged man who I figured to be the brother got out of the driver's seat and went into the apartment house. The other man in the car moved over into the driver's seat and started west on Beverly. By that time I was back in the cab and after him.

Of course I couldn't be sure it was Raines. It looked like a little man. I had to take that chance.

We followed the car out Beverly to Western, up Western. I wondered what had become of the blue Chrysler. Then we drew up close behind Raines' car at an intersection and I nearly fell out the window. The man in the car ahead turned around and looked back; we looked smack at one another for five seconds.

I'd seen him before! I'd seen him the night before in Miss Mackay's room at the Pine Hotel in Caliente! He'd been one of the raft of people who'd busted in with the sheriff and stood around ah-ing and oh-ing. The man had guts. He'd come in while Healey and the girl were still warm to see what a neat job he'd done.

The traffic bell rang and I knew he'd recognized me, too. He went across that intersection like a bat out of hell, up Western to Fountain.

He lost us on Fountain. I talked to my driver like a father. I got down on my knees and begged him to keep that car in sight. I called him all the Portuguese pet-names I could think of and made up a few new ones, but Raines ran away from us on Fountain.

On the way back to the hotel I stopped at the Hollywood Branch of the Automobile Club and had a friend of mine look up the license number of the car. Of course it was the brother's car, in the brother's name. That didn't get me anywhere. I was pretty sure Raines wouldn't go back to his brother's place now that he knew I'd spotted him; and it was a cinch he wouldn't use that car very long.

He didn't know what I wanted. He might figure me for a dick and scram out of LA—out of the country. I sat in my room at the hotel and thought soft thoughts about what a chump I'd been not to go to him directly when he'd stopped with his brother in front of the Selwyn, and the speed of taxicabs as compared to automobiles—things like that. It looked like the Healey case was all washed up as far as I was concerned.

I went out about five o'clock and walked. I walked down one side of Hollywood Boulevard to Bronson and back up the other side to Vine and went into the U Drive joint and rented the car again. I was nervous and jumpy and disgusted, and the best way for me to get over feeling that way is to drive it off.

I drove out through Cahuenga Pass a ways and then I had an idea and drove back to the Selwyn Apartments. The idea wasn't any good. William Raines told the clerk to send me up and he asked me what he could do for me and smiled and offered me a drink.

I said I wanted to get in touch with his brother on a deal that would do us both a lot of good. He said his brother was in Chicago and that he hadn't seen him for two years. I didn't tell him he was a liar. It wouldn't have done any good. I thanked him and went back down to the car.

I drove down to LA and had dinner in a Chinese place. Then I went back by the Santa Fe and found out about trains—I figured on going back to New York the next day.

On the way back to Hollywood I drove by the Garden Court. Not for any particular reason—I thought about Mrs. Healey and it wasn't much out of the way.

The blue Chrysler was sitting squarely across the street from the entrance.

I parked up the street a little way and got out and went back to be sure. I lit a match and looked at the card on the steering column; the car was registered to another U Drive place, downtown, on South Hope.

I went across the street and walked by the desk with my nose in the air. The Spick elevator boy didn't even look at the folded bill I slipped him, he grinned self-consciously and said that a little red-haired man had gone up to four just a couple minutes ago. Mrs. Healey was on four and there were only three apartments on a floor.

I listened at the door but could only hear a confused buzz that sounded like fast conversation. I turned the knob very slowly and put a little weight against the door. It was locked. I went down to the end of the hall and went out as quietly as possible through a double door to a fire-escape platform. By standing outside the railing and holding on with one hand and leaning far out I could see into the dining-room of Mrs. Healey's apartment, could see a couple inches of the door that led, as well as I could remember, into the drawing-room. It was closed.

There is nothing that makes you feel quite so simple as hanging on a fire-escape, trying to look into a window. Particularly when you can't see anything through the window. After a few minutes I gave it up and climbed back over the railing.

I half sat on the railing and tried to figure things out. What business would the guy who shot Healey have with Mrs. Healey? Did the blackmail angle that Raines and Mackay had held over Healey cover Mrs. Healey, too? Was Raines milking his lowdown for all it was worth? It was too deep for me.

I went back into the hall and listened at the door again. They were a little louder but not loud enough to do me any good. I went around a bend in the hall to what I figured to be the kitchen-door and gave it the slow turn and it opened. I mentally kicked myself for wasting time on the fire-escape, tip-toed into the dark kitchen and closed the door.

It suddenly occurred to me that I was in a quaint spot if somebody should come in. What the hell business did I have there! I fixed that, to myself, with some kind of vague slant about protecting Mrs. Healey and edged over to the door, through to the room I'd been looking into from the fire-escape.

The door into the drawing-room was one of those pasteboard arrangements that might just as well not be there. The first thing I heard was a small, suppressed scream like somebody had smacked a hand over somebody else's mouth, and then something like a piece of furniture being tipped over. It was a cinch someone was fighting in there, quietly—or as quietly as possible.

There wasn't much time to think about whether I was doing the right thing or not. If I'd thought about it I'd probably have been wrong, anyway. I turned the knob, swung the door open.

Mrs. Healey was standing against the far wall. She was standing flat against the wall with one hand up to her mouth. Her eyes were very wide.

There were two men locked together on the floor near the central table and as I came in they rolled over a turn or so and one broke away and scrambled to his feet. It was Raines. He dived after a nickel-plated revolver that was lying on the floor on the far side of the table, and the other man, who had risen to his knees, dived after it, too. The other man was Gard.

He beat Raines by a hair but Raines was on his feet; he kicked the gun out of Gard's hand, halfway across the room. Gard grabbed his leg and pulled him down and they went round and round again. They fought very quietly; all you could hear was the sound of heavy breathing and an occasional bump.

I went over and picked up the gun and stooped over the mess of arms and legs and picked out Raines' red head and took hold of the barrel of the gun. I took dead aim and let Raines have it back of the ear. He relaxed.

Gard got up slowly. He ran his fingers through his hair and jiggled his shoulders around to straighten his coat and grinned foolishly.

I said: "Fancy, meeting you here."

I turned around and looked at Mrs. Healey. She was still standing against the wall with her hand across her mouth. Then the ceiling fell down on top of my head and everything got dark very suddenly.

Darkness was around me when I opened my eyes, but I could see the outlines of a window and I could hear someone breathing somewhere near me. I don't know how long I was out. I sat up and my head felt like it was going to explode; I lay down again and closed my eyes.

After a while I tried it again and it was a little better. I crawled towards what I figured to be a door and ran into the wall and I got up on my feet and felt along the wall until I found the light switch.

Raines was lying in the same place I'd smacked him, but his hands and feet were tied with a length of clothes-line and there was a red, white and blue silk handkerchief jammed into his mouth. His eyes were open and he looked at me with an expression that I can only describe as bitter amusement.

Gard was lying belly-down on the floor near the door into the dining-room. He was the hard breather I'd heard in the darkness. He was still out.

I ungagged Raines and sat down. I kept having the feeling that my head was going to blow up. It was a very unpleasant feeling.

In a little while Raines got his jaws limbered up and started talking. The first thing he said was: "What a bright boy *you* turned out to be!" I was too sick to know very much about what that meant—or care.

He went on like that for some time, talking in a high, squeaky voice, and the idea gradually filtered through the large balloon-shaped ache that my head had turned into.

It seems that Raines and the Mackay gal had juggled Healey into a swell spot. One of their angles was that Healey, in an expansive moment, had entirely forgotten about Mrs. Healey and married Miss Mackay. They had a lot of material besides; everything from the Mann Act to mayhem. When he'd made the hundred and fifty grand lick in Quebec they'd jumped him in Chicago.

Healey had ducked out of Chi and they'd trailed him, first to Salt Lake, then to Caliente. Monday night, Raines had helped Mackay put on the act in the hotel that Healey had told me about.

Raines hadn't got off the train with her or checked into the hotel with her because they didn't want to be seen together in case anything went wrong, but he ducked up that handy back stairway and they'd given Healey the act, showing him exactly the color and size of the spot they had him on.

Then, when Healey came down to my room, Raines had gone down and planted across the street in case Healey tried to powder.

Raines hadn't been there five minutes before Mrs. Healey and a man rolled up in the blue Chrysler. Raines recognized Mrs. Healey because she'd spotted Healey with Miss Mackay and Raines in a cabaret in Chicago once and crowned Miss Mackay with a beer bottle. It seems Mrs. Healey was a nice quiet girl.

They parked in front of the hotel and the man went in a minute, probably to buy a cigar and get a peek at the register. Then he came out and talked to Mrs. Healey a little while and went back in the little alleyway that led to the side door. He was only there a minute; he probably found out that it was practical to go into the hotel that way and came back and told her.

Along about that time in Raines' yarn I woke up to the fact that he was referring to the man who was with Mrs. Healey as "this guy." I opened my eyes and looked at him and he was looking at Gard.

Gard had stayed in the car while Mrs. Healey went back through the alleyway and into the hotel. After a couple minutes he got nervous and got out and walked up the street a little ways, and Raines went across the street and went upstairs to find out what it was all about. That must have been about the time I was checking out.

Gard must have been coming back down the other side of the street and he saw me come out and finagle with his car and get into mine, and he

stayed away until hell started popping upstairs and I went into the hotel.

Raines stopped a minute. I got up and went over and rolled Gard over on his back. He groaned and opened his eyes and blinked up at me and then he sat up slowly and leaned against the wall.

Raines said Mrs. Healey must have tried Healey's door and then waited till Healey came up the front stairway after he left me, and she ducked around a corner and watched Healey go into Mackay's room. By that time Raines was at the top of the back stairway and he watched Mrs. Healey take a gun out of her bag and go down and listen at Miss Mackay's door. When Healey opened the door after whittling Mackay, she backed him into the room and closed the door. Raines said she probably told him a few pertinent truths about himself and relieved him of what was left of the hundred and fifty and then opened him up with the .38.

It was a swell spot for her, with the Mackay gal there with a knife in her heart. Raines said he figured she'd intended to rub Healey from the start, before he could divorce her—Healey had said she'd sworn to kill him, before he left Chicago. A nice quiet girl—Mrs. Healey. A lady.

She'd dodged Raines on the stairs and he'd chased her down to the car, but by that time Gard was back in the car with the engine running and they'd shoved off fast. Then Raines had come back up with the sheriff and his gang to look things over. That's where I'd seen him.

He'd taken the midnight train for LA and it had taken him all day Tuesday to locate Mrs. Healey. He'd been putting the screws on her and Gard for a split of the important money and Gard had gone into a wrestling number with him just before I arrived.

By the time Raines had got all that out of his system Gard was sitting up straight with his mouth open and his hands moving around fast and that dumb, thoughtful look on his face as if he wanted to say something. When Raines stopped to breathe, Gard said that the lady had talked him into driving her up to Caliente because she said she was too nervous to wait for Healey in LA—she said she had to see Healey and try to make their scrap up right away, or she'd have a nervous breakdown or something, and Gard—the big chump—fell for it.

He said he was the most surprised man in the world when the shooting started, and that when she came galloping down and they scrammed for LA she'd told him that she'd walked in on Mackay ventilating Healey, just like the sheriff said, and that Mackay had shot at her as she ran away. Gard had fallen for that, too. She had the poor sap hypnotized.

Gard knew I'd been up at Caliente, of course—he'd seen me; so when I walked into his place in the morning he'd figured I had some kind of slant on what it was all about and he'd taken me over to her place so they could put on their "comfort her in her bereavement" turn for my benefit.

Then, Tuesday night, when I'd walked in on the shakedown and knocked Raines out, Gard, who had had a load of what Raines had to say to Mrs. Healey and who half believed it, calculated that his best play was to take the air with her. He was too much mixed up in it to beat an accessory rap anyway, so he'd sapped me with a bookend and they'd tied Raines, who was coming to, and he'd helped her pack her things. They were going to light out for New Zealand or some quiet place like that; only she'd sneaked up behind him and smacked him down at the last minute. A lovely lady.

We all stopped talking about that time—Raines and Gard and me—and looked at one another.

Gard laughed. He squinted at me and said: "You looked silly when I clipped you with the bookend!"

Raines said: "You didn't look particularly intelligent when our girlfriend let *you* have it."

Gard snickered on the wrong side of his face and got up and went out into the kitchen for a drink of water. He found a bottle out there—almost a full fifth of White Horse. He brought it in, I untied Raines and we all had a snort.

I was thinking about what suckers we'd been, I'd popped Raines and Gard had popped me and Mrs. Healey had popped Gard—all of us. One, two, three. Tinker to Evers to Chance—only more so.

I think we were all pretty washed up with La Belle Healey. It was a cinch Gard wouldn't want any more of her. I don't know about Raines. But I know I didn't.

We finished the bottle and Raines snooped around and found a full one and we did a little business with that.

I didn't find out I had a concussion till next morning. I was a week and two days in the hospital at twenty dollars a day, and the doctor nicked me two-fifty. He'll get the rest of it when he catches me.

The whole Healey play, what with one thing and another, cost somewhere in the neighborhood of a grand. I got a lame skull and about two-bits' worth of fun out of it.

I pass.

The Creeping Siamese
Dashiell Hammett

THE ARGUMENT could be made that the most influential writer of the twentieth century was Dashiell Hammett. As writers turned from the orotund style of Henry James and his Victorian predecessors to lean and swift prose, later scholars have pointed to the undeniably profound force of Ernest Hemingway. But who influenced Hemingway? Hammett did.

Publishing dates are hard facts, not esoteric theories. Hammett's first Continental Op story appeared in *Black Mask* on October 1, 1923. The quintessential hard-boiled private eye appeared frequently in the ensuing years. Hemingway's first book, *In Our Time*, was published in Paris in a limited edition in 1924, and published in a tiny edition of 1,335 copies in the United States in October 1925, by which time Hammett was already well established and a highly popular regular contributor to the most important pulp magazine of its time.

In addition to the nameless operative of the Continental Detective Agency, Hammett (1894–1961) created Sam Spade, the hero of the most famous American detective novel ever written or filmed, *The Maltese Falcon*, which had been serialized in *Black Mask*, as were all of his novels excepting the last, *The Thin Man*.

Written at the height of his success and powers, "The Creeping Siamese" was published in *Black Mask* in March 1926, the year before he began to serialize his first novel, *Red Harvest*.

The Creeping Siamese

Dashiell Hammett

I

STANDING BESIDE THE CASHIER'S DESK in the front office of the Continental Detective Agency's San Francisco branch, I was watching Porter check up my expense account when the man came in. He was a tall man, raw-boned, hard-faced. Grey clothes bagged loosely from his wide shoulders. In the late afternoon sunlight that came through partially drawn blinds, his skin showed the color of new tan shoes.

He opened the door briskly, and then hesitated, standing in the doorway, holding the door open, turning the knob back and forth with one bony hand. There was no indecision in his face.

It was ugly and grim, and its expression was the expression of a man who is remembering something disagreeable.

Tommy Howd, our freckled and snub-nosed office boy, got up from his desk and went to the rail that divided the office.

"Do you—?" Tommy began, and jumped back.

The man had let go the doorknob. He crossed his long arms over his chest, each hand gripping a shoulder. His mouth stretched wide in a yawn that had nothing to do with relaxation. His mouth clicked shut. His lips snarled back from clenched yellow teeth.

"Hell!" he grunted, full of disgust, and pitched down on the floor.

· 16 ·

I heaved myself over the rail, stepped across his body, and went out into the corridor.

Four doors away, Agnes Braden, a plump woman of thirty-something who runs a public stenographic establishment, was going into her office.

"Miss Braden!" I called, and she turned, waiting for me to come up. "Did you see the man who just came in our office?"

"Yes." Curiosity put lights in her green eyes. "A tall man who came up in the elevator with me. Why?"

"Was he alone?"

"Yes. That is, he and I were the only ones who got off at this floor. Why?"

"Did you see anybody close to him?"

"No, though I didn't notice him in the elevator. Why?"

"Did he act funny?"

"Not that I noticed. Why?"

"Thanks. I'll drop in and tell you about it later."

I made a circuit of the corridors on our floor, finding nothing. The raw-boned man was still on the floor when I returned to the office, but he had been turned over on his back. He was as dead as I had thought. The Old Man, who had been examining him, straightened up as I came in. Porter was at the telephone, trying to get the police. Tommy Howd's eyes were blue half-dollars in a white face.

"Nothing in the corridors," I told the Old Man. "He came up in the elevator with Agnes Braden. She says he was alone, and she saw nobody close to him."

"Quite so." The Old Man's voice and smile were as pleasantly polite as if the corpse at his feet had been a part of the pattern in the carpet. Fifty years of sleuthing have left him with no more emotion than a pawnbroker. "He seems to have been stabbed in the left breast, a rather large wound that was staunched with this piece of silk"—one of his feet poked at a rumpled ball of red cloth on the floor—"which seems to be a sarong."

Today is never Tuesday to the Old Man: it *seems* to be Tuesday.

"On his person," he went on, "I have found some nine hundred dollars in bills of various denominations, and some silver; a gold watch and a pocket knife of English manufacture; a Japanese silver coin, 50 *sen;* tobacco, pipe and matches; a Southern Pacific timetable; two handkerchiefs without laundry marks; a pencil and several sheets of blank paper; four two-cent stamps; and a key labeled *Hotel Montgomery, Room 540.*

"His clothes seem to be new. No doubt we shall learn something from them when we make a more thorough examination, which I do not care to make until the police come. Meanwhile, you had better go to the Montgomery and see what you can learn there."

In the Hotel Montgomery's lobby the first man I ran into was the one I wanted: Pederson, the house copper, a blond-mustached ex-bartender who doesn't know any more about gum-shoeing than I do about saxophones, but who does know people and how to handle them, which is what his job calls for.

"Hullo!" he greeted me. "What's the score?"

"Six to one, Seattle, end of the fourth. Who's in 540, Pete?"

"They're not playing in Seattle, you chump! Portland! A man that hasn't got enough civic spirit to know where his team—"

"Stop it, Pete! I've got no time to be fooling with your childish pastimes. A man just dropped dead in our joint with one of your room-keys in his pocket—540."

Civic spirit went blooey in Pederson's face.

"540?" He stared at the ceiling. "That would be that fellow Rounds. Dropped dead, you say?"

"Dead. Tumbled down in the middle of the floor with a knife-cut in him. Who is this Rounds?"

"I couldn't tell you much off-hand. A big bony man with leathery skin. I wouldn't have noticed him excepting he was such a sour looking body."

"That's the bird. Let's look him up."

At the desk we learned that the man had arrived the day before, registering as H. R. Rounds, New York, and telling the clerk he expects to leave within three days. There was no record of mail or telephone calls for him. Nobody knew when he had gone out, since he had not left his key at the desk. Neither elevator boys nor bell-hops could tell us anything.

His room didn't add much to our knowledge. His baggage consisted of one pigskin bag, battered and scarred, and covered with the marks of labels that had been scraped off. It was locked, but traveling bags locks don't amount to much. This one held us up about five minutes.

Rounds' clothes—some in the bag, some in the closet—were neither many nor expensive, but they were all new. The washable stuff was without laundry marks. Everything was of popular makes, widely advertised brands that could be bought in any city in the country. There wasn't a piece of paper with anything written on it. There wasn't an identifying tag. There wasn't anything in the room to tell where Rounds had come from or why.

Pederson was peevish about it.

"I guess if he hadn't got killed he'd of beat us out of a week's bill! These guys that don't carry anything to identify 'em, and that don't leave their keys at the desk when they go out, ain't to be trusted too much!"

We had just finished our search when a bell-hop brought Detective Sergeant O'Gar, of the police department Homicide Detail, into the room.

"Been down to the Agency?" I asked him.

"Yeah, just came from there."

"What's new?"

O'Gar pushed back his wide-brimmed black village-constable's hat and scratched his bullet head.

"Not a heap. The doc says he was opened with a blade at least six inches long by a couple wide, and that he couldn't of lived two hours after he got the blade—most likely not more'n one. We didn't find any news on him. What've you got here?"

"His name is Rounds. He registered here yesterday from New York. His stuff is new, and there's nothing on any of it to tell us anything except that he didn't want to leave a trail. No letters, no memoranda, nothing. No blood, no signs of a row, in the room."

O'Gar turned to Pederson.

"Any brown men been around the hotel? Hindus or the like?"

"Not that I saw," the house copper said. "I'll find out for you."

"Then the red silk was a sarong?" I asked.

"And an expensive one," the detective sergeant said. "I saw a lot of 'em the four years I was soldiering on the islands, but I never saw as good a one as that."

"Who wears them?"

"Men and women in the Philippines, Borneo, Java, Sumatra, Malay Peninsula, parts of India."

"Is it your idea that whoever did the carving advertised himself by running around in the streets in a red petticoat?"

"Don't try to be funny!" he growled at me. "They're often enough twisted or folded up into sashes or girdles. And how do I know he was knifed in the street? For that matter, how do I know he wasn't cut down in your joint?"

"We always bury our victims without saying anything about 'em. Let's go down and give Pete a hand in the search for your brown men."

That angle was empty. Any brown men who had snooped around the hotel had been too good at it to be caught.

I telephoned the Old Man, telling him what I had learned—which didn't cost me much breath—and O'Gar and I spent the rest of the evening sharp-shooting around without ever getting on the target once. We questioned taxi-cab drivers, questioned the three Roundses listed in the telephone book, and our ignorance was as complete when we were through as when we started.

The morning papers, on the streets at a little after eight o'clock that evening, had the story as we knew it.

At eleven o'clock O'Gar and I called it a night, separating in the direction of our respective beds.

We didn't stay apart long.

II

I opened my eyes sitting on the side of my bed in the dim light of a moon that was just coming up, with the ringing telephone in my hand.

O'Gar's voice: "1856 Broadway! On the hump!"

"1856 Broadway," I repeated, and he hung up.

I finished waking up while I phoned for a taxicab, and then wrestled my clothes on. My watch told me it was 12:55 a.m. as I went downstairs. I hadn't been fifteen minutes in bed.

1856 Broadway was a three-story house set behind a pocket-size lawn in a row of like houses behind like lawns. The others were dark. 1856 shed light from every window, and from the open front door. A policeman stood in the vestibule.

"Hello, Mac! O'Gar here?"

"Just went in."

I walked into a brown and buff reception hall, and saw the detective sergeant going up the wide stairs.

"What's up?" I asked as I joined him.

"Don't know."

On the second floor we turned to the left, going into a library or sitting room that stretched across the front of the house.

A man in pajamas and bathrobe sat on a davenport there, with one bared leg stretched out on a chair in front of him. I recognized him when he nodded to me: Austin Richter, owner of a Market Street moving picture theater. He was a round-faced man of forty-five or so, partly bald, for whom the Agency had done some work a year or so before in connection with a ticket-seller who had departed without turning in the day's receipts.

In front of Richter a thin white-haired man with doctor written all over him stood looking at Richter's leg, which was wrapped in a bandage just below the knee. Beside the doctor, a tall woman in a fur-trimmed dressing-gown stood, a roll of gauze and a pair of scissors in her hands. A husky police corporal was writing in a note-book at a long narrow table, a thick hickory walking stick laying on the bright blue table cover at his elbow.

All of them looked around at us as we came into the room. The corporal got up and came over to us.

"I knew you were handling the Rounds job, sergeant, so I thought I'd best get word to you as soon as I heard they was brown men mixed up in this."

"Good work, Flynn," O'Gar said. "What happened here?"

"Burglary, or maybe only attempted burglary. They was four of them—crashed the kitchen door."

Richter was sitting up very straight, and his blue eyes were suddenly excited, as were the brown eyes of the woman.

"I beg your pardon," he said, "but is there—you mentioned brown men in connection with another affair—is there another?"

O'Gar looked at me.

"You haven't seen the morning papers?" I asked the theatre owner.

"No."

"Well, a man came into the Continental office late this afternoon, with a stab in his chest, and died there. Pressed against the wound, as if to stop the bleeding, was a sarong, which is where we got the brown men idea."

"His name?"

"Rounds, H. R. Rounds."

The name brought no recognition into Richter's eyes.

"A tall man, thin, with dark skin?" he asked. "In a grey suit?"

"All of that."

Richter twisted around to look at the woman.

"Molloy!" he exclaimed.

"Molloy!" she exclaimed.

"So you know him?"

Their faces came back toward me.

"Yes. He was here this afternoon. He left—"

Richter stopped, to turn to the woman again, questioningly.

"Yes, Austin," she said, putting gauze and scissors on the table, and sitting down beside him on the davenport. "Tell them."

He patted her hand and looked up at me again with the expression of a man who has seen a nice spot on which to lay down a heavy load.

"Sit down. It isn't a long story, but sit down."

We found ourselves chairs.

"Molloy—Sam Molloy—that is his name, or the name I have always known him by. He came here this afternoon. He'd either called up the theater or gone there, and they had told him I was home. I hadn't seen him for three years. We could see—both my wife and I—that there was something the matter with him when he came in.

"When I asked him, he said he'd been stabbed, by a Siamese, on his way here. He didn't seem to think the wound amounted to much, or pretended he didn't. He wouldn't let us fix it for him, or look at it. He said he'd go to a doctor after he left, after he'd got rid of the thing. That was what he had come to me for. He wanted me to hide it, to take care of it until he came for it again.

"He didn't talk much. He was in a hurry, and suffering. I didn't ask him any questions. I couldn't refuse him anything. I couldn't question him even though he as good as told us that it was illegal as well as dangerous. He saved our lives once—more than my wife's life—down in Mexico, where we first knew him. That was in 1916. We were caught down there during the Villa troubles. Molloy was running guns over the border, and he had enough influence with the bandits to have us released when it looked as if we were done for.

"So this time, when he wanted me to do something for him, I couldn't ask him about it. I said, 'Yes,' and he gave me the package. It wasn't a large package: about the size of—well—a loaf of bread, perhaps, but quite heavy for its size. It was wrapped in brown paper. We unwrapped it after he had gone, that is, we took the paper off. But the inner wrapping was of canvas, tied with silk cord, and sealed, so we didn't open that. We put it upstairs in the pack room, under a pile of old magazines.

"Then, at about a quarter to twelve tonight—I had only been in bed a few minutes, and hadn't gone to sleep yet—I heard a noise in here. I don't own a gun, and there's nothing you could properly call a weapon in the house, but that walking stick"—indicating the hickory stick on the table—"was in a closet in our bedroom. So I got that and came in here to see what the noise was.

"Right outside the bedroom door I ran into a man. I could see him better than he could see me, because this door was open and he showed against the window. He was between me and it, and the moonlight showed him fairly clear. I hit him with the stick, but didn't knock him down. He turned and ran in here. Foolishly, not thinking that he might not be alone, I ran after him. Another man shot me in the leg just as I came through the door.

"I fell, of course. While I was getting up, two of them came in with my wife between them. There were four of them. They were medium-sized men, brown-skinned, but not so dark. I took it for granted that they were Siamese, because Molloy had spoken of Siamese. They turned on the lights here, and one of them, who seemed to be the leader, asked me:

" 'Where is it?'

"His accent was pretty bad, but you could understand his words good enough. Of course I knew they were after what Molloy had left, but I pretended I didn't. They told me, or rather the leader did, that he knew it had been left here, but they called Molloy by another name—Dawson. I said I didn't know any Dawson, and nothing had been left here, and I tried to get them to tell me what they expected to find. They wouldn't though—they just called it 'it.'

"They talked among themselves, but of course I couldn't make out a word of what they were saying, and then three of them went out, leaving one here to guard us. He had a Luger pistol. We could hear the others moving around the house. The search must have lasted an hour. Then the one I took for the leader came in, and said something to our guard. Both of them looked quite elated.

" 'It is not wise if you will leave this room for many minutes,' the leader said to me, and they left us—both of them—closing the door behind them.

"I knew they were going, but I couldn't walk on this leg. From what the doctor says, I'll be lucky if I walk on it inside of a couple of months. I didn't want my wife to go out, and perhaps run into one of them before they'd got away, but she insisted on going. She found they'd gone, and she phoned the police, and then ran up to the pack room and found Molloy's package was gone."

"And this Molloy didn't give you any hint at all as to what was in the package?" O'Gar asked when Richter had finished.

"Not a word, except that it was something the Siamese were after."

"Did he know the Siamese who stabbed him?" I asked.

"I think so," Richter said slowly, "though I am not sure he said he did."

"Do you remember his words?"

"Not exactly, I'm afraid."

"I think I remember them," Mrs. Richter said. "My husband, Mr. Richter, asked him, 'What's the matter, Molloy? Are you hurt, or sick?'

"Molloy gave a little laugh, putting a hand on his chest, and said, 'Nothing much. I run into a Siamese who was looking for me on my way here, and got careless and let him scratch me. But I kept my little bundle!' And he laughed again, and patted the package."

"Did he say anything else about the Siamese?"

"Not directly," she replied, "though he did tell us to watch out for any Asiatics we saw around the neighborhood. He said he wouldn't leave the package if he thought it would make trouble for us, but that there was always a chance that something would go wrong, and we'd better be careful. And he told my husband"—nodding at Richter—"that the Siamese had been dogging

him for months, but now that he had a safe place for the package he was going to 'take them for a walk and forget to bring them back.' That was the way he put it."

"How much do you know about Molloy?"

"Not a great deal, I'm afraid," Richter took up the answering again. "He liked to talk about the places he had been and the things he had seen, but you couldn't get a word out of him about his own affairs. We met him first in Mexico, as I have told you, in 1916. After he saved us down there and got us away, we didn't see him again for nearly four years. He rang the bell one night, and came in for an hour or two. He was on his way to China, he said, and had a lot of business to attend to before he left the next day.

"Some months later I had a letter from him, from the Queen's Hotel in Kandy, asking me to send him a list of the importers and exporters in San Francisco. He wrote me a letter thanking me for the list, and I didn't hear from him again until he came to San Francisco for a week, about a year later. That was in 1921, I think.

"He was here for another week about a year after that, telling us that he had been in Brazil, but, as usual, not saying what he had been doing there. Some months later I had a letter from him, from Chicago, saying he would be here the following week. However, he didn't come. Instead, some time later, he wrote from Vladivostok, saying he hadn't been able to make it. Today was the first we'd heard of him since then."

"Where's his home? His people?"

"He always says he has neither. I've an idea he was born in England, though I don't know that he ever said so, or what made me think so."

"Got any more questions?" I asked O'Gar.

"No. Let's give the place the eye, and see if the Siamese left any leads behind 'em."

The eye we gave the house was thorough. We didn't split the territory between us, but went over everything together—everything from roof to cellar—every nook, drawer, corner.

The cellar did most for us: it was there, in the cold furnace, that we found the handful of black buttons and the fire-darkened garter clasps. But the upper floors hadn't been altogether worthless: in one room we had found the crumpled sales slip of an Oakland store, marked *1 table cover*, and in another room we had found no garters.

"Of course it's none of my business," I told Richter when O'Gar and I joined the others again, "but I think maybe if you plead self-defense you might get away with it."

He tried to jump up from the davenport, but his shot leg failed him.

The woman got up slowly.

"And maybe that would leave an out for you," O'Gar told her. "Why don't you try to persuade him?"

"Or maybe it would be better if you plead the self-defense," I suggested to her. "You could say that Richter ran to your help when your husband grabbed you, that your husband shot him and was turning his gun on you when you stabbed him. That would sound smooth enough."

"My husband?"

"Uh-huh, Mrs. Rounds-Molloy-Dawson. Your late husband, anyway."

Richter got his mouth far enough closed to get words out of it.

"What is the meaning of this damned nonsense?" he demanded.

"Them's harsh words to come from a fellow like you," O'Gar growled at him. "If this is nonsense, what do you make of that yarn you told us about creeping Siamese and mysterious bundles, and God knows what all?"

"Don't be too hard on him," I told O'Gar. "Being around movies all the time has poisoned his idea of what sounds plausible. If it hadn't, he'd have known better than to see a Siamese in the moonlight at 11:45, when the moon was just coming up at somewhere around 12:45, when you phoned me."

Richter stood up on his one good leg.

The husky police corporal stepped close to him.

"Hadn't I better frisk him, sergeant?"

O'Gar shook his bullet head.

"Waste of time. He's got nothing on him. They cleaned the place of weapons. The chances

are the lady dropped them in the bay when she rode over to Oakland to get a table cover to take the place of the sarong her husband carried away with him."

That shook the pair of them. Richter pretended he hadn't gulped, and the woman had a fight of it before she could make her eyes stay still on mine.

O'Gar struck while the iron was hot by bringing the buttons and garters clasps we had salvaged out of his pocket, and letting them trickle from one hand to another. That used up the last bit of the facts we had.

I threw a lie at them.

"Never me to knock the press, but you don't want to put too much confidence in what the papers say. For instance, a fellow might say a few pregnant words before he died, and the papers might say he didn't. A thing like that would confuse things."

The woman reared up her head and looked at O'Gar.

"May I speak to Austin alone?" she asked. "I don't mean out of your sight."

The detective sergeant scratched his head and looked at me. This letting your victims go into conference is always a ticklish business: they may decide to come clean, and then again, they may frame up a new out. On the other hand, if you don't let them, the chances are they get stubborn on you, and you can't get anything out of them. One way was as risky as another. I grinned at O'Gar and refused to make a suggestion. He could decide for himself, and, if he was wrong, I'd have him to dump the blame on. He scowled at me, and then nodded to the woman.

"You can go over into that corner and whisper together for a couple of minutes," he said, "but no foolishness."

She gave Richter the hickory stick, took his other arm, helped him hobble to a far corner, pulled a chair over there for him. He sat with his back to us. She stood behind him, leaning over his shoulder, so that both their faces were hidden from us.

O'Gar came closer to me.

"What do you think?" he muttered.

"I think they'll come through."

"That shot of yours about being Molloy's wife hit center. I missed that one. How'd you make it?"

"When she was telling us what Molloy had said about the Siamese she took pains both times she said 'my husband' to show that she meant Richter."

"So? Well—"

The whispering in the far corner had been getting louder, so that the s's had become sharp hisses. Now a clear emphatic sentence came from Richter's mouth.

"I'll be damned if I will!"

Both of them looked furtively over their shoulders, and they lowered their voices again, but not for long. The woman was apparently trying to persuade him to do something. He kept shaking his head. He put a hand on her arm. She pushed it away, and kept on whispering.

He said aloud, deliberately:

"Go ahead, if you want to be a fool. It's your neck. I didn't put the knife in him."

She jumped away from him, her eyes black blazes in a white face. O'Gar and I moved softly toward them.

"You rat!" she spat at Richter, and spun to face us.

"I killed him!" she cried. "This thing in the chair tried to and—"

Richter swung the hickory stick.

I jumped for it—missed—crashed into the back of his chair. Hickory stick, Richter, chair, and I sprawled together on the floor. The corporal helped me up. He and I picked Richter up and put him on the davenport again.

The woman's story poured out of her angry mouth:

"His name wasn't Molloy. It was Lange, Sam Lange. I married him in Providence in 1913 and went to China with him—to Canton, where he had a position with a steamship line. We didn't stay there long, because he got into some trouble through being mixed up in the revolution that year. After that we drifted around, mostly around Asia.

"We met this thing"—she pointed at the now sullenly quiet Richter—"in Singapore, in 1919, I think—right after the World War was over. His name is Holley, and Scotland Yard can tell you something about him. He had a proposition. He knew of a gem-bed in upper Burma, one of many that were hidden from the British when they took the country. He knew the natives who were working it, knew where they were hiding their gems.

"My husband went in with him, with two other men that were killed. They looted the natives' cache, and got away with a whole sackful of sapphires, topazes and even a few rubies. The two other men were killed by the natives and my husband was badly wounded.

"We didn't think he could live. We were hiding in a hut near the Yunnan border. Holley persuaded me to take the gems and run away with them. It looked as if Sam was done for, and if we stayed there long we'd be caught. I can't say that I was crazy about Sam anyway; he wasn't the kind you would be, after living with him for a while.

"So Holley and I took it and lit out. We had to use a lot of the stones to buy our way through Yunnan and Kwangsi and Kwangtung, but we made it. We got to San Francisco with enough to buy this house and the movie theater, and we've been here since. We've been honest since we came here, but I don't suppose that means anything. We had enough money to keep us comfortable.

"Today Sam showed up. We hadn't heard of him since we left him on his back in Burma. He said he'd been caught and jailed for three years. Then he'd got away, and had spent the other three hunting for us. He was that kind. He didn't want me back, but he did want money. He wanted everything we had. Holley lost his nerve. Instead of bargaining with Sam, he lost his head and tried to shoot him.

"Sam took his gun away from him and shot him in the leg. In the scuffle Sam had dropped a knife—a kris, I think. I picked it up, but he grabbed me just as I got it. I don't know how it happened. All I saw was Sam staggering back, holding his chest with both hands—and the kris shining red in my hand.

"Sam had dropped his gun. Holley got it and was all for shooting Sam, but I wouldn't let him. It happened in this room. I don't remember whether I gave Sam the sarong we used for a cover on the table or not. Anyway, he tried to stop the blood with it. He went away then, while I kept Holley from shooting him.

"I knew Sam wouldn't go to the police, but I didn't know what he'd do. And I knew he was hurt bad. If he dropped dead somewhere, the chances are he'd be traced here. I watched from a window as he went down the street, and nobody seemed to pay any attention to him, but he looked so conspicuously wounded to me that I thought everybody would be sure to remember him if it got into the papers that he had been found dead somewhere.

"Holley was even more scared than I. We couldn't run away, because he had a shot leg. So we made up that Siamese story, and I went over to Oakland, and bought the table cover to take the place of the sarong. We had some guns and even a few oriental knives and swords here. I wrapped them up in paper, breaking the swords, and dropped them off the ferry when I went to Oakland.

"When the morning papers came out we read what had happened, and then we went ahead with what we had planned. We burned the suit Holley had worn when he was shot, and his garters—because the pants had a bullet-hole in them, and the bullet had cut one garter. We fixed a hole in his pajama-leg, unbandaged his leg,—I had fixed it as well as I could,—and washed away the clotted blood until it began to bleed again. Then I gave the alarm."

She raised both hands in a gesture of finality and made a clucking sound with her tongue.

"And there you are," she said.

"You got anything to say?" I asked Holley, who was staring at his bandaged leg.

"To my lawyer," he said without looking up.

O'Gar spoke to the corporal.

"The wagon, Flynn."

Ten minutes later we were in the street, helping Holley and the woman into a police car.

Around the corner on the other side of the street came three brown-skinned men, apparently Malay sailors. The one in the middle seemed to be drunk, and the other two were supporting him. One of them had a package that could have held a bottle under his arm.

O'Gar looked from them to me and laughed.

"We wouldn't be doing a thing to those babies right now if we had fallen for that yarn, would we?" he whispered.

"Shut up, you, you big heap!" I growled back, nodding at Holley, who was in the car by now. "If that bird sees them he'll identify 'em as his Siamese, and God knows what a jury would make of it!"

We made the puzzled driver twist the car six blocks out of his way to be sure we'd miss the brown men. It was worth it, because nothing interfered with the twenty years apiece that Holley and Mrs. Lange drew.

Honest Money

Erle Stanley Gardner

IT IS THE NUMBERS that are so impressive when thinking about Erle Stanley Gardner. He created the most famous criminal defense attorney in literature, Perry Mason, when he published *The Case of the Velvet Claws* on March 1, 1933. He went on to produce eighty Mason novels which, in all editions, sold more than 300,000,000 copies.

The novels were the ultimate in formulaic genre fiction, with the lawyer taking on the role of detective to prove his client innocent at trial, turning to point a finger at the real culprit, who generally broke down and confessed. The television series based on the character, starring Raymond Burr, was enormously successful for nine years, running from September 21, 1957 to May 22, 1966, and showing in reruns pretty much ever since.

Before Perry Mason, however, there was Ken Corning, an equally hard-hitting, fearless, and incorruptible defense attorney who made his debut in *Black Mask* magazine in November 1932. Had he been named Perry Mason, and his secretary named Della Street instead of Helen Vail, it would be impossible to tell the difference between the two. "Honest Money" is the first story in the series.

Gardner (1889–1970) began his lengthy writing career in the pulps in *Breezy Stories* in 1921, eventually producing hundreds of short stories, countless articles, more than a hundred novels, and numerous nonfiction books on the law and, as a noted outdoorsman, on travel and environmental issues. At the time of his death, he was the bestselling writer in history.

Ken Corning, fighting young lawyer, tries to earn an honest living in a city of graft

Honest Money

Erle Stanley Gardner

THE CLOCK ON THE CITY hall was booming the hour of nine in the morning when Ken Corning pushed his way through the office door. On the frosted glass of that door appeared the words: *"Kenneth D. Corning, Attorney at Law—Enter."*

Ken Corning let his eye drift over the sign. It was gold leaf and untarnished. It was precisely thirty days since the sign painter had collected for the job, and the sign painter had collected as soon as his brush had finished the last letter of the last word of that sign.

The credit of young attorneys in York City wasn't of the best. This was particularly true of young lawyers who didn't seem to have an "in" with the administration.

Helen Vail was dusting her desk. She grinned at Ken.

He reached a hand to his inside pocket.

"Pay day," he said.

Her eyes glinted with a softness that held a touch of the maternal.

"Listen, Ken, let it go until you get started. I can hang on a while longer. . . ."

He took out a wallet, started spreading out ten-dollar bills. When he had counted out five of them, he pushed the pile over to her. There were two bills left in the wallet.

"Honest, Ken. . . ."

He pushed his way to the inside office. "Forget it," he said. "I told you we'd make it go. We haven't started to fight yet."

She followed him in, the money in her hand. Standing in the doorway, very erect, chin up, she waited for him to turn to meet her gaze.

The outer door of the entrance office made a noise.

She turned. Looking over her shoulder, Ken could see the big man who stood on the threshold. He looked as though his clothes had been filled with apply jelly. He quivered and jiggled like a jellyfish on a board. Fat encased him in layers, an unsubstantial, soft fat that seemed to be hanging to his bones with a grip that was but temporary.

His voice was thin and falsetto.

"I want to see the lawyer," he shrilled.

Helen turned on her heel, called over her shoulder: "All right, Mr. Corning. I'll enter up this retainer." To the man she said: "You'll have to wait. Mr. Corning's preparing an important brief. He'll see you in a minute or two."

The pneumatic door check swung the door to.

Ken Corning turned in his swivel-chair and sent swift hands to his tie. From the outer office sounded the furious clack of a typewriter. Three minutes passed. The roller of the machine made sounds as the paper was ripped from it. The door of the private office banged open. Helen Vail pushed her way in, in an ecstasy of haste, crinkling a legal paper in her hands.

"All ready for your signature," she said.

The pneumatic door check was swinging the door closed as Ken reached for the paper. On it had been written with the monotony of mechanical repetition, over and over: "Now is the time for all good men to come to the aid of the party."

The door completed its closing. The latch clicked.

"Get his name?" asked Ken.

"Sam Parks. He's nervous. It's a criminal case. I'd have kept him waiting longer, but he won't stand for it. He's looking at his watch—twice in the last sixty seconds."

Ken patted her hand.

"Okey. Good girl. Shoot him in."

Helen walked to the door, opened it, smiled sweetly. "You may come in now, Mr. Parks."

She held the door open. Ken could see the big man heaving his bulk free of the chair. He saw him blot out the light in the doorway as the girl stepped aside. He was signing a paper as the big man entered the office and paused. Ken kept his eyes on the paper until the door catch clicked. Then he looked up with a smile.

"Mr. Parks, is it?" he asked.

The big man grunted, waddled over to the chair which was placed so close to the new desk as to invite easy intimacy. He sat down, then, apparently feeling that the chair was too far away, started hitching it closer and closer to the desk. His voice was almost a shrill whisper.

"My wife," he said, "has been arrested."

Ken laid down the pen, looked professional.

"What," he asked, "is the charge?"

The big man's shrill voice rattled off a string of swift words: "Well, you see it was this way. We had a place, a little restaurant, and the officers came busting in without a warrant . . . tell me, can they come into a place without a warrant, that way?"

Ken replied crisply: "They did, didn't they?"

"Yes."

"Okey, then they can. They're not supposed to, but they did, they do and they can. What happened?"

"Well, that was about all. They claimed we were selling booze."

Ken's voice was sharp.

"Find any?"

"A little."

"How much?"

"Ten or fifteen gallons."

"Then they arrested you both?"

The fat man blinked glassy eyes.

"Just her. They didn't take me."

"Why?"

He fidgeted, and the layers of fat jiggled about.

"Well, we sort of outslicked 'em. There had

been a guy eating at one of the tables. He got wise as soon as the first man walked in on the raiding party. He ducked out the back. I sat down at his table and finished up his food. The wife pretended she didn't know me, and asked the officers if she could collect my bill before they took her. They said she could. I paid her fifty cents for the food and gave her a ten-cent tip. Then they closed up the place, took the booze away with 'em, and put me out. The wife said she ran the place alone."

Ken Corning twisted a pencil in his fingers.

"I'll want a retainer of a hundred and fifty dollars," he said, "and then I'll see what I can do and report."

The glassy eyes squinted.

"You ain't in with the gang here?"

"I'm a newcomer."

The man opened his coat, disclosed a wrinkled vest and shirt, soggy with perspiration. He pulled a leather wallet from an inside pocket and pulled out a hundred dollar bill and a fifty. The wallet was crammed with money. He tossed the money carelessly on the desk.

"The first thing to do," he said, "is to see the wife. Tell her you're going to represent her, see? Let her know I'm on the job, and tell her to keep a stiff upper lip, and to keep quiet, see? Tell her to keep quiet, see?"

Ken Corning folded the money, got to his feet, stood there, signifying that the interview was over.

"Come back when I send for you. Leave your name and address and your wife's name with the girl in the outer office so I can get my records straight. Leave a telephone number where you can be reached."

The man turned on the threshold.

"You ain't in with the ring?" he asked, and there was a note of anxiety in his voice.

Ken Corning reached for a law book, shook his head.

The pneumatic door clicked shut.

Ken set down the law book and fingered the money. He turned it over and over in his fingers. He cocked his head on one side, listening. After

a moment he heard the click of the outer door catch. Then Helen Vail was standing on the threshold of the inner office. Her eyes were starry.

Ken Corning waved the money.

"Start an account for that bird, and credit it with a hundred and fifty."

She was smiling at him when the door opened. Broad shoulders pushed their way across the outer office. From his desk, Ken could see the man as he crossed the outer office. Helen Vail barred the inner office door.

"Whom do you wish?" she asked.

The man laughed, pushed past her, walked directly to Ken Corning's desk. He flipped back a corner of his coat with a casual hand.

"Who," he asked, "was the guy that just left here, and what'd he want?"

Ken Corning pushed back the swivel-chair as he got to his feet.

"This," he said, "is my private office."

The broad shouldered man laughed. His face was coarse skinned, but the gray eyes had little lights in them that might have meant humor, or might have meant a love of conflict.

"Keep your shirt on, keep your shirt on," he said. "I'm Perkins from the booze detail. There was a speak knocked over last night. The woman who was running it tried to slip a bribe, and she's booked on a felony. That big guy was sitting in there, eating chow. He claimed he was a customer. I happened to see him come in here. He looked phoney, so I tagged along. I want to know what he wanted."

Ken Corning's voice was hard.

"This," he said, "is a law office, not an information bureau."

The gray eyes became brittle hard. The jaw jutted forward. Perkins crowded to the desk.

"Listen, guy," he said, "you're new here. Whether you're going to get along or not depends on whether you play ball or not. I asked you who that guy was. I asked because I wanted to know. . . ."

Corning moved free of the swivel-chair.

"You getting out?" he asked.

The lips of the broad shouldered man twisted in a sneer.

"So that's your line of chatter?"

"That's my line of chatter."

The man turned on his heel, strode towards the door. He turned with his hand on the knob.

"Try and get some favors out of the liquor detail!" he said.

Ken's tone was rasping. He stood with his feet planted wide apart, eyes glinting.

"I don't want favors," he said, "from anybody!"

The broad shouldered man walked from the office, heels pounding the floor. Slowly the automatic door check swung the door shut.

Ken was ready to leave his office, seeking an interview with his client at the jail, when the door of his private office framed the white features of Helen Vail.

"It's Mr. Dwight," she said.

"What is?"

"The man who just came in. Carl Dwight. He's outside. He wants to see you."

Ken whistled. "Show him in," he said.

She motioned towards the desk.

"Shall I get you some papers?"

"Not with him. He's a wise bird. He knows. Shoot him in."

Helen stood to one side of the door and beckoned. Carl Dwight came in. He walked with a slight limp. His lips were smiling. He had pale eyes that seemed covered with a thin white film, like boiled milk. Those eyes didn't smile. His skin was swarthy and oily. There was a cut on his forehead, a slight bruise on his left cheek bone.

He wasn't large, and yet he radiated a suggestion of ominous power. He said, crisply: "I'm busy. You're busy. You know of me. I know of you. I've had my eye on you for the last week or two. You're a likely looking young man. I want to give you a retainer. Here's five hundred dollars. That'll be for this month. There'll be five hundred dollars more coming next month, and the month after that."

His gloved hand laid an envelope on the desk.

Ken picked up the envelope. It was unsealed. There were five one hundred-dollar bills in it.

"What," asked Ken cautiously, "am I supposed to do?"

The gloved hand waved in an airy gesture.

"Just use your head," said Dwight. "I've got rather extensive interests here. You've probably heard of me, know who I am."

Ken Corning chose his words carefully.

"You," he said, "are reputed to be the head of the political machine in this county. You are reputed to be the man who tells the mayor what to do."

The filmed eyes blinked. The swarthy skinned man made clucking noises in his throat.

"That, of course, is an exaggeration, Mr. Corning. But I have interests in the county, interests which are rather extensive. Now you can sort of look out for those interests. And, by the way, there's a criminal case, the matter of a woman who was running rather a disreputable joint, gambling, hooch and all that. Parks was the name, I believe.

"Do you know, I think it might be rather a good thing to have that case disposed of rather rapidly. A plea of guilty, let us say. I'm certain you'll agree that it's a dead open and shut case. She tried to bribe an officer. There were witnesses. She gave him fifty dollars. Having such things aired in front of a jury don't do any good."

He got to his feet. The swarthy skin crinkled in a smile, a sallow, bilious smile. The filmed eyes regarded Ken Corning with the wisdom of a serpent.

"So now," he smirked, "we understand each other perfectly. I think you'll like it in York City, Corning."

Ken slowly got to his feet.

"Yes," he said, "I understand you perfectly. But you don't understand me, not by a long ways. Take back this damned money before I slap your face with it!"

Dwight teetered back and forth on his feet, made little clucking noises with his mouth.

"Like that, eh?" he said.

"Like that," agreed Corning.

Dwight sneered.

"You won't last long. You can't . . ."

He didn't finish. Ken Corning reached out with the envelope which he held by a corner, and slapped it across Dwight's mouth. The filmed eyes blazed into light. The mouth twisted in a snarl. Dwight snatched at the envelope, crammed it in his pocket, whirled and started to the door. He paused on the threshold.

"Wait," he said, significantly.

And Ken Corning, standing by his desk, feet braced wide apart, jaw thrust forward, said: "You're damned tooting I'll wait. I'll be waiting long after you think you're finished with me!"

The attorneys' room in the county jail was a dull, cheerless place. There was a long desk which ran down the center of the room. Above this desk was a heavy wire screen. The prisoner could sit on one side of the desk, the attorney on the other.

Esther Parks came into the room through the doorway which led to the cell corridor. Ken Corning watched her with interest. Her face was heavy, her walk plodding. She was a big woman, broad-hipped and big-shouldered. Her eyes were like oysters on a white plate.

She plowed her way forward.

The attendant who had charge of the room stood at the doorway, beyond earshot, but where he could see everything that went on in the room.

The woman sat down on the stool opposite Ken Corning. Her face was within three feet of his. Her big hands were folded upon the scarred wood of the long desk. The heavy screen separated them.

"Hello," she said.

Ken Corning kept his voice low pitched.

"Hello. I'm the attorney that your husband engaged to represent you. He thought you were just charged with unlawful possession of liquor. You're not. They've got you on the charge of offering a bribe to an officer. That's a felony."

He paused expectantly.

The woman said: "Uh-huh."

Ken stared into the oyster eyes.

"Well," he said, "I'm to do the best I can for you. Can we go to trial and beat the charge?"

The eyes didn't change expression. The heavy face rippled into dull speech.

"I was running a speak, me and Sam. We went in mostly for cheap food with drinks to sell to the right parties. I don't see why they had to pick on us. Everybody's doing it, that is, everybody anywhere round our neighborhood."

Ken frowned and shook his head.

"I'm telling you it isn't the liquor charge they've got you on. I could square that with a fine. It's the bribery charge. Can we beat that?"

The woman's voice was blurred in its accent, indifferent and stolid in tone.

"I don't know. I gave him the money. They all take the money. Twice before I've had men call on me and say they was the law. I've given 'em money. I gave this man money. Then he collared me. They didn't spot Sam. He sat down at a table and ate some grub."

Ken Corning made little drumming noises with the tips of his fingers. He regarded the woman through the wire mesh of the screen.

"Have they asked you for a statement?" he wanted to know.

A flicker of intelligence appeared in the pale, watery eyes.

"I ain't so dumb. I told 'em to wait until my lawyer showed up, then they could talk with him."

"Who was it?" asked Corning, "the one who wanted the statement?"

She moved her head in a gesture of slow negation.

"I dunno. Somebody from the Sheriff's office, or the District Attorney's office. He was a young fellow and he had a man with him that took down what I said in shorthand."

"What did you say?"

"Nothin'."

Corning squinted his eyes thoughtfully.

"How did it happen that they didn't spot Sam

as your husband? Usually when they make these raids they've had a stoolie go in and make a purchase or two. They have all the dope on where the stuff is kept and who runs the place."

The woman's head turned again, slowly, from side to side.

"I dunno. They just didn't spot Sam, that was all. I was behind the counter at the cash register. They came walkin' in. I think I heard somebody say 'There she is,' or 'That's her, now,' or somethin' like that. I didn't pay so much attention. They made the pinch, and I tried to hand 'em the dough.

"It was their fault I slipped 'em the money, too. One of the men held up the jug that had the hooch in it, and said: 'Well, sister, what are you goin' to do about this?' I seen he had me, dead to rights, so I opened the cash register, an' asked him if he'd listen to reason. He said he would. I slipped him the cash, an' then they said something to each other and told me to come along with them.

"Sam had got wise to what was goin' on, an' he'd gone over to the table an' was boltin' down food. I asked the law if I could close up the joint, take the cash an' collect from the gent at the table. They said I could, an' I did, an' that's all I know about it. They took me here."

Ken Corning clamped his mouth into a thin line.

"Then we've got to plead guilty," he said.

She shrugged her shoulders.

"That's your job. I dunno. I'm tellin' you what happened. I figured Sam would get a mouthpiece an' spring me."

Corning continued to drum with his fingers.

"Look here," he said, "there's something funny about this case. I'm going to keep a close mouth for a while, and see if I can find out what's back of it. You seem to be on the outs with the ring that's running the town. Do you know why?"

The big head shook slowly.

"Well," said Corning, "sit tight for a while. Don't talk to anyone. If anyone asks you any questions, no matter who it is, tell them to see your lawyer, Mr. Corning. Can you remember to do that?"

"Uh-huh."

"I'll have you arraigned and get bail set. Can you raise bail?"

"How much?"

"Maybe three thousand dollars?"

"No."

"Two thousand?"

"Maybe."

"Any property you could put up as security with a bail bond company for the purpose of getting them to issue a bail bond?"

"No. Just cash. We had a lease on the joint. It paid fair money. Lately it ain't been payin'."

Ken Corning got to his feet.

"All right," he said. "Sit tight. Remember what I told you. Don't talk. I'm going to see what I can do."

The attendant moved forward.

"This way," he said to the woman, in a voice that was a mechanical monotone.

Don Graves, the Deputy District Attorney in charge of the case of the People vs. Esther Parks, was almost totally bald, despite the fact that he was in his early thirties. His face ran to nose. The eyes on either side were round and lidless. He had a peculiar peering appearance like that of a startled anteater.

He turned the nose directly towards Ken Corning, so that the twin eyes bored unblinkingly into those of the attorney, and said: "We won't reduce the charge. She bribed an officer. That's a serious offense."

Ken kept his temper.

"That's a hard charge to prove, and you know as well as I do that the officer kept angling to get her to give him money. You get a jury of twelve people together, and some of 'em are going to think it's a hell of a note to send a woman to the pen because she had some hooch and an officer kept sticking his palm out at her. It's only natural to slip a man something when he makes a stall like that. That isn't being criminal. That's just human nature."

The deputy licked his lips with the tip of a pale tongue that seemed, somehow, to be utterly cold.

"The penal code don't say so, brother."

Ken Corning frowned.

"The penal code says lots of things—so does the Constitution."

Don Graves said: "Yeah," and made as though he'd turn away.

Corning raised his voice.

"Well, listen, about bail. If you'll suggest to the magistrate that bail be reduced to a thousand dollars cash, I think she can raise it."

Graves turned back to Corning, stared lidlessly at him.

"You heard what the magistrate said: ten thousand bucks cash, or twenty thousand bond."

Corning's rage flared up.

"A hell of a bail that is. You'd think the woman was guilty of a murder or something. If you don't know that these cheap dicks are sticking their palms out right and left and shaking down the people that run the little speaks, you're just plain crazy! You keep riding me around, and I'll take this jane before a jury and see what twelve men in a box have to say about the way you're getting so damned virtuous in York City all of a sudden."

The lidless eyes remained hard and peering.

"Go ahead," said Graves.

"I will!" snapped Corning.

Graves spoke as Ken Corning was halfway to the door.

"Tell you what I *will* do, Corning."

Corning paused, turned.

"Take her into court right away, plead her guilty as charged, and I'll ask to have a minimum sentence imposed."

Corning asked: "Fine or imprisonment?"

"Imprisonment," said Graves. "To hell with a fine."

Corning's retort was emphatic. "To hell with *you!*" he said, and slammed the door.

Helen Vail had the afternoon papers for him when he walked into his office.

"News?" she asked.

He grinned at her, took the papers, touched her fingertips as he took them, and suddenly patted her hand.

"Good girl," he said.

"Why?"

"Oh, I don't know. You just are."

"How about the case?"

"I don't know. There's something funny. You'd think the woman had done a murder or something. And Graves, that billiard ball guy with the snake eyes, told me he'd let me cop a minimum sentence if I'd rush her through the mill and make a plea."

Helen Vail's eyes were sympathetic.

"You mean send the woman to the pen because she slipped one of these dicks a little dough?"

"Exactly."

"What'd you tell him?"

Corning grinned.

"That, precious, is something your little shell-like ears shouldn't hear."

And he walked into the inner office, taking the papers with him. He sat in his swivel-chair, put his feet on the desk, turned to the sporting page, browsed through the headlines, turned back to the front page.

The telephone rang.

He called out to Miss Vail: "I've got it, Helen," and scooped the receiver to his ear, holding the newspaper in one hand, the telephone in the other.

The shrill, piping voice of Sam Parks came over the wire.

"Listen, is this Corning, the lawyer?"

"Yes."

"Okey. This is Parks. I was in to see you this morning about my wife. Listen, I know why they're trying to give her the works. I can't tell you over the telephone. I'm coming over. You be there?"

"Come right away," said Corning.

"Yeah!" shrilled Parks excitedly, and banged the receiver into place. Ken Corning hung up, turned to the paper. There was a frown creasing his forehead. He looked at his watch. It was five minutes to four. Street noises came up through the open window. The afternoon was warm, the air laden with the scents of late summer.

Ken's eyes drifted unseeingly to the front page of the newspaper. Why should so much stir be made over the matter of a commonplace woman in a third-grade speakeasy giving some money to an officer who held out his hand for it? Why should a raid be made on a place where the officers hadn't collected enough information to know who was running the place, and had let the husband slip through their fingers?

He stared at the newspaper, let his forehead crinkle in thought, and tried to fit the ends of the puzzle together.

Minutes passed.

The clock on the city hall boomed the hour of four, and the big gilt hands crept around until the minute hand marked the quarter hour.

There was the sound of a truck backfiring in the street,

Something came trebling up through the window, the scream of a child, or of a very frightened woman. Then there was the sound of rubber tires, skidding into a turn on pavement, the shout of a man.

There was a second silence, and then the noise made by many voices, the sound of feet running on cement. A siren wailed in the distance.

Ken Corning, lost in contemplation, did not interpret the significance of those sounds until the siren had become a scream, until the clanging bell of the ambulance sounded almost directly beneath his office window, and until the door of his private office opened and Helen Vail stared at him.

"There seems to have been a man hurt," she said.

Ken Corning put down the paper and went to the window. Helen put her hand on his shoulder as they leaned out. Corning was conscious of the touch of her hair against his cheek, the pressure of her hand on his shoulder. He slid his right arm out, around her waist.

They looked down upon the street.

There was no traffic. Such vehicles as were on the street were stalled. Men swarmed about like busy ants, moving in seething disorder. An ambulance was backing towards the curb. A uniformed officer was clearing a path for it. Stalled cars, their motors running, belched forth thin smoke films which made the air a light blue color.

A black circle of men were not moving. They were grouped about something which lay on the sidewalk. From that form there was a dark stain which had welled along the cement until it trickled in a thin, sluggish stream into the gutter.

The man was big and fat. He was lying on his back.

"Good heavens!" said the voice of Helen Vail, "it's the man who was in the office."

Ken Corning swung from the window. He reached the doorway of the private office in three strides, and gained the stairs. He went down them two at a time. He reached the sidewalk as the men were loading the stretcher. He pushed his way through the crowd. Men muttered comments, turned and stared at him, growled warnings to watch what he was doing. Corning paid no attention to them.

He reached the inner circle, saw the stretcher bearers heaving against the weight of the bulk that they strove to place in the ambulance.

Parks had been shot twice. To all appearances he was dead. The bullet holes welled a red trail which dripped from the stretcher. The eyes were half open and waxy. The skin was like discolored dough. The hands trailed limply at the ends of dangling arms.

One of the stretcher bearers spoke sharply.

"Give us a hand here, some of you guys!"

Ken Corning pushed through the circle as two of the spectators swirled forward. A uniformed officer also bent to give a lift. Corning asked a question: "Who saw it? How did it happen?"

Men stared at him with blank curiosity. He was hatless, wandering about asking how it had happened, and men regarded him as a part of the incident which had broken into the routine of their daily life. They watched him with that expression of impersonal curiosity with which fish in an aquarium stare at spectators who press against the glass tank.

On the fifth repetition of the question, a man gave an answer.

"I saw it. He drove up in an automobile and parked the car. He started walking along the street. The guy that shot him was in a roadster. He pulled right in to the curb, and he didn't drive away until he was sure the guy was dead. The first shot smacked him over. He shot again when the guy was on the cement. I seen him twitch when the second bullet struck!"

Corning led the man to one side.

"Drove up in a car, eh? Which car?"

He indicated the line of parked machines.

The witness shrugged his shoulders. "I ain't sure. I think it was the flivver over there. I remember that it was a car that had a smashed fender. You know, there wasn't no reason why I should notice him until . . ."

"Yes," said Corning, "I know. Now you want some advice?"

The man looked at him with curious eyes. "Huh?" he asked.

"Get away from here and don't tell your story to a soul. Go to headquarters, get the homicide squad's office and ask for Sergeant Home. He's on the square. Tell your story to him, and ask that your name be withheld. Otherwise, if you got a good look at the man that did the shooting, you might find yourself parked on a marble slab. Killers don't like witnesses."

The man's face paled. "Gee," he said; then, after an interval: "Gee whiz!"

He spun on his heel, started walking rapidly away. From time to time he glanced over his shoulder.

His tip gave Ken Corning the chance to be the first man to examine the light car with the bent fender.

He looked at the registration certificate which was strapped about the steering post of the car. That showed the machine was registered in the name of Esther Parks, and the address which was given was the same address as that of the place which had been raided when the woman was arrested.

Ken felt of the seat. It was still warm.

He noticed an afternoon newspaper lying on the floorboards. He picked it up. There was nothing else on the inside of the car to give any inkling as to who had driven or owned it. Ken felt in the flap pocket of the right-hand door. His groping fingers encountered a lady's handkerchief, a pair of pliers, the cap from an inner tube, and a bit of pasteboard. He pulled out the pasteboard.

It was red, bearing the insignia of the police department. It was, he found when he deciphered the scrawled lines which were placed in the printed blanks, a ticket for parking within fifteen feet of a fire hydrant on Seventh Street, between Madison and Harkley. The time was checked at three-forty-five, of that day.

Ken pocketed the ticket and walked around to the front of the car, inspecting the dent in the fender. There was but little paint left upon the nondescript car which Parks had been driving. That little paint had been cracked and chipped where the fender had crumpled. And, on the tip of that crumpled fender, was a spot of bright red enamel, evidently taken from the car with which the flivver had collided.

Ken examined the front of the springs, the radiator, found further evidences of a collision, further bits of red paint. The accident had evidently been very recent.

Aside from those things, there was nothing to indicate anything whatever about the occupant of the car, or the errand upon which it had been driven.

Ken walked to the curb, looked at the crowd which was commencing to move along under orders of the uniformed police. The traffic was moving now, crawling past at a snail's pace, horns blaring. An officer, accompanied by a woman, moved along the parked lane of cars, inspecting them.

Corning felt that this woman had seen the fat man emerge from a machine, but couldn't identify the machine. Ken let himself drift away with the scattering spectators. He walked around the block, and back to his office. He climbed the stairs, smiled at Helen Vail's white face.

"Was it . . . ?"

He nodded, passed into the inner office. She came and stood in the doorway. Ken smoothed out the newspaper he had taken from the car Parks had driven. He spread it out.

A knife had cut away a section of the front page.

"Was it because he came here?" asked Helen, mustering her courage.

Ken Corning reached for the other afternoon newspaper he had been reading when the sound of the shots had interrupted him. He nodded absently as he spread the two front pages out on the desk, one over the other.

The paper from the death car showed the page of the other paper through the opening where the knife had cut. That which had been cut out was a picture with a small paragraph or two below it.

Ken looked at the picture.

It showed a man with a square-cut chin, shell glasses, a firm, thin mouth, high cheek bones and a high forehead. Below it appeared the words *Mayor Appoints Harry B. Dike as New Head of Water Department.*

Corning read the few paragraphs appearing below the headlines of the accompanying news article. Those paragraphs recited the enviable record Harry B. Dike had enjoyed in connection with his own business enterprises and such civic activities as had claimed his time. It also mentioned that Dike was firmly opposed to the granting of contracts and concessions to those who enjoyed political pull, and that, in the future, the water department would be conducted upon a basis of efficiency with all work thrown open to the lowest responsible bidders, although the department would reserve the right to let private contracts.

The article sounded very promising. It gave the location of Dike's office in the Monadnock Building. The Monadnock Building was on Seventh Street, between Madison and Harkley.

Helen Vail watched Corning as he clamped his hat down on his forehead.

"Ken," she said, "you're going out . . . on this thing, into danger?"

Her face was a dead white. The eyes were starry and tender.

He laughed at her, saw the pale lips stiffen, quiver and tremble into the first sign of a sob, then lift into a half smile. He patted her shoulder, grinned at her.

"Listen, kid, I'm a newcomer here. I'm here to stay. Some of these chaps don't recognize that fact yet, that's all. It's time they did. I'm just going out and let a few of them know that when I hung out my shingle in this town I did it with my eyes open. I planted my feet here, and I'm staying here."

And he strode across the office, went through the outer door, made time to the street, caught a taxi. "Monadnock Building," he said, as he settled back against the cushions, "and make it snappy."

The cab lurched into motion.

"Man shot here a while back," said the communicative driver. "Raised hell with traffic."

Corning said: "Yeah," without interest and the conversaion languished. The cab swung in to the curb at Seventh Street, Corning paid the meter, consulted the directory of the Monadnock Building, found that Dike's office was on the seventh floor, and took the elevator up.

There was no one in the reception office except a typist who was tapping frantically at the keys of a noiseless typewriter, and a rather stern-faced but pretty secretary who sat stiffly behind a desk in the corner of the room, three telephones in front of her.

Corning walked to her, smiled.

"I'm anxious to get in touch with a man who was to have met me here earlier this afternoon, but I had a puncture and was delayed. He's a great big man, fat, about forty-eight, wearing a gray suit that's in need of pressing . . ."

Her voice was crisply efficient.

"You mean Mr. Parks. He's been here and gone."

Corning made a gesture of disappointment, but his mouth clamped shut to keep from showing his elation.

"Mr. Dike's in?"

"Yes. He's busy. You haven't an appointment?"

"No. Can you answer the question? What kind of a car does he drive?"

"A Cadillac. It's a sedan. Then he had a roadster, a Buick."

"Thanks. I think I'm interested in the Cadillac. It's a bright red, isn't it?"

"It's red, yes."

"I'm afraid I've got to disturb Mr. Dike. Tell him it's Mr. Corning, and that I'm in a hurry."

She shook her head.

"He's not to be disturbed. You haven't an appointment, and . . ."

Corning gained the door to the inner office in a swift stride, without waiting for her to finish the sentence.

"And I'm in a hurry," he said, and opened the door.

Harry B. Dike was even more dignified in his frosty appearance than the newspaper photograph would have indicated to a casual observer. The light glinted from the bald reaches of his high forehead. His eyes were steel gray and bored steadily out from behind his shell spectacles. He looked up from a desk which contained a sheaf of papers, stared at Corning and said: "Get out! I'm busy."

His eyes went down to the papers.

Corning walked across the room.

Dike didn't look up again. He was moving the point of a pencil along the typewritten lines of a document. "Get out," he said, "or I'll call a cop and have you thrown in for disturbing the peace. I've canceled my appointments. I don't want any life insurance, any books or a new automobile."

Corning sat down.

Dike scowled at him, banged the pencil down on his desk and reached for the telephone.

"I'm Kenneth D. Corning, attorney for Sam Parks, the man who called on you a little while earlier this afternoon," he said.

Dike dropped the telephone. His eyes widened, darkened, then became fixedly steady in gaze and expression. He said coldly: "What's that to me?"

"It has to do with your acceptance of the position of Superintendent of the Water Department," said Corning. "I think it would be far better for you to refuse the appointment—particularly in view of the fact that Parks was murdered about twenty minutes ago."

The face did not change by so much as a line.

"You mean that you think I had something to do with the murder?" asked Dike coldly.

Corning's tone was equally cold.

"Yes," he said.

The two men stared at each other.

"Corning," said Dike, as though trying to place the name. "A newcomer here, eh? I presume you're crazy. But if you've got anything to say, I'll listen."

Corning spoke, his tone dispassionate.

"He made the mistake of coming to you first. I presume he wanted a shakedown. When things didn't go to suit him here he called me. It was Dwight's men who put him on the spot. You probably weren't directly connected with it. You notified Dwight, that's all. You weren't entirely surprised to hear of the murder, but you hadn't exactly expected it."

Dike got to his feet.

"All right. You've had your say. Now get out."

Corning held his ground.

"You accept that position of Superintendent of the Water Department," he said, slowly and forcefully, "and I'll have you before the grand jury for murder."

Dike laughed scornfully.

"A man calls at my office. Later on he's found murdered. I have been sitting here all the time. Simply because he came here you think that I should give up my career, eh?"

Corning played his bluff.

"Forget it," he said. "I know what I'm doing. Parks talked before he died. It was on the road to the hospital. I rode with him in the ambulance."

That statement shook Dike's self-control. The eyes wavered. The mouth twitched. Then he gripped himself and was as granite once more.

"I presume he said I ran alongside his flivver and stabbed him!" he snorted.

Corning grinned.

"So you know it was a flivver, eh? Well, I'll tell you what he said. He said that he and his wife were out driving and that they had an automobile accident. The car that they ran into was your car. You were in it, and there was another man in it, Carl Dwight, the head of the machine that's milking the city of millions in graft money. The people had been demanding a change in the water department because of that very graft. The mayor made them a gesture by putting you in charge. You were supposed to put an end to the graft on water contracts. Yet you were out riding with Dwight, the man you were supposed to fight.

"You didn't get the man's name. But you found out about the woman. She was driving the car. You learned she was running a speakeasy. You thought it'd be a good plan to get her where her testimony wouldn't count. So Dwight raided her place and framed a felony rap on her. She didn't know the full significance of what she'd seen. You thought it'd be a good plan to forestall developments. The testimony of a convicted felon wouldn't go very far in a court of law."

Corning ceased talking. His fists were clenched, his eyes cold and steady.

Dike's gaze was equally steady.

"Corning," he said, "you are a very vigorous and impulsive young man. You are also either drunk or crazy. Get out and stay out."

Corning turned towards the door.

"I thought," he said, "that I would have the satisfaction of telling you what I know, and showing you that you can't gain anything by railroading this woman. Also you'll either resign your post, or you'll be mixed up in murder."

Dike scooped up the telephone.

"When you go out," he said, "tell my secretary to put the spring catch on the door. I don't want any more crazy guys busting in here."

Corning grinned at him.

"I'll put the catch on the door myself," he said, and pushed the thumb snap down, walked out and closed the door behind him. The typist paused in her pounding of the keys to watch him. The secretary stared with wide eyes. Corning walked to the corridor and took the elevator.

He stepped into a drug-store on the corner and called police headquarters. He asked for the homicide squad, and got Sergeant Home on the line.

"This," he said, "is a tip."

"What is?" gruffed the sergeant.

"What you're hearing. A man named Parks was killed this afternoon. He'd been driving a flivver that had collided with a red car. Harry B. Dike owns a red car that's been in a collision. Parks had been to call on Dike just before he got killed. Carl Dwight has been in some sort of a smash. There's a cut on his forehead, and he walks with a limp. Sam Parks has a wife, Esther. You've got her in jail right now on a felony charge."

Sergeant Home's voice betrayed his excitement.

"Tell me, who is this speaking? Where do you get that dope?"

Ken snapped his answer into the transmitter.

"Have a man you can trust at the *Columbino* at eight tonight. Have him wear a white carnation and sit near the front door. Look up the information I've given you in the meantime."

And Corning slammed the receiver back on the hook, waited a moment for a free line, and then called Harry Dike's office on the telephone. The line was busy. He called three times with the same result. The fourth time he got Dike on the line, after some argument with the secretary.

"Corning," he snapped crisply. "I'm giving you one last chance to get out of the tangle Dwight's got you in. I'll be at the *Columbino* tonight at eight. If you want to make a written statement and get out of the mess I won't put the screws down."

Dike's voice was smoothly suave.

"Kind of you, I'm sure, but I don't think I

care to see you there. However . . . where are you now?"

Corning laughed into the transmitter.

"Wouldn't you like to know!" he said, and hung up.

He waited in front of the drug-store, keeping in the background, yet being where he could watch the entrance to Dike's office building.

Carl Dwight didn't show up. But a speeding automobile, slamming into the curb at the fire hydrant, disgorged Perkins, the detective. Half a dozen minutes later a taxicab paused to let out Fred Granger, who was Dwight's right-hand man.

Perkins came out, almost on the run, within fifteen minutes. Granger didn't come out for half an hour. Dike followed him. Ten minutes after that, a police car bearing a detective stopped in front of the office building.

Ken Corning terminated his vigil, stepped into a barber shop, had a shave, hot towels, massage, haircut and shampoo. He was careful not to go near any of his regular haunts, or leave a trail which could be picked up.

The *Columbino* ran fairly wide open. Anyone could get in there who had the price. It went in somewhat for music, atmosphere and an aura of respectability. The liquor was very good.

It was early when Ken Corning walked into the place, exactly eight o'clock, and there were but few patrons, most of them eating. The dance floor would fill up later on, and by midnight the place would be going full blast.

A man in evening clothes, with a conspicuous white carnation in his buttonhole, had a table in the front of the place. Ken heaved a sigh as he saw that Home had investigated his tip, found out enough to go ahead on the lead.

Ken Corning ordered a full dinner with a cocktail at the start, a bottle of wine with the meal, a cordial afterwards. Momentarily he expected action, and the action did not come.

It was nine-fifteen when he reluctantly called for the waiter and paid the check. The man with the white carnation continued to sit by the door.

Evidently the powers that ruled the city had decided to ignore Ken Corning, and Ken was disquieted at the thought. Things were not turning out as he had anticipated.

The waiter was gone some little time. Ken waited for the change. The man in the dinner coat with white carnation looked at his watch, pursed his lips. Ken got the idea that this man had a definite time limit fixed. At nine-thirty, probably, he would leave.

The waiter returned.

"I beg your pardon," he said, "but the manager wants to see you in his office. There's a bit of trouble, sir."

Ken got to his feet, followed the waiter. He was walking lightly, his hands slightly away from his sides, his head carried alertly, eyes watchful.

The manager stared coldly from behind the desk.

The waiter turned to go. Ken thought that something brushed against his coat. He couldn't be sure. He glanced at the waiter's retreating back.

The manager said: "I'm sure it's a mistake, but it's something I'll have to investigate."

"What is?" asked Corning.

"This," said the manager, and placed on the desk in front of him the bill which Ken Corning had given the waiter. "It's counterfeit."

Ken laughed.

"Well," he said, "it happens that I can give a complete history of that bill. It was paid me this morning by way of retainer in a legal matter, in the presence of my secretary. What's more, I don't think it's counterfeit."

A door opened. A man stepped purposefully into the room.

The manager waved his hand.

"I'll let you discuss that with McGovern, of the Secret Service. You probably don't know it, but we've been flooded with clever counterfeits here the last week. McGovern has been waiting on call."

Ken turned to meet the man's eyes.

McGovern smiled, and the smile was frank.

"If you can tell me where you got it, that's all

I need to know," he said. "One look at you's enough to convince me *you're* no counterfeiter."

Ken smiled in return, then let the smile fade.

"Look here," he said, "this bill came from a client. I have an idea certain interests would like to frame something else on that client and his wife. The man is dead. The wife isn't—yet. I don't want to play into any frame-up. . . ."

The other smiled, waved his hand.

"Just a formality, but you'll have to tell me. You're dealing with the Federal Secret Service now. You won't find any political frame-ups with us. As a matter of form, would you mind letting me see the rest of your money?"

Ken laughed, reached in his coat, took out his wallet.

That wallet felt strangely bulky. He stared at it. It wasn't his wallet. It was crammed with currency. He made a move as though to put it back in his pocket. The Federal man whipped down a swift arm.

"Here," he said, "none of that. Acting funny ain't going to help you."

He grabbed the wallet, opened it, whistled.

There was a moment of silence.

"That," said Ken, "is not my wallet. I demand that the waiter who brought me in here be called. I want to have him searched. He slipped this wallet into my pocket and took mine out. He's a professional dip, and this is a plant."

The lip of the Federal man curled.

"Yeah," he said. "How often I've heard that one! You've got to come along. Want to go quietly, or would you rather make a fuss?"

Ken stared at the wallet.

"I'll go quietly if you'll pick up the waiter and take him along, too," said Ken.

The Federal turned to the manager.

"Who was it?" he asked.

"Frank," said the manager.

"Get him," said the Federal. "In the meantime I'll take this guy along in a cab. Come on. You can tell your story where it'll be appreciated. They don't pay me to listen, only to do things."

Ken went out through the cabaret.

The man in the dinner coat, who wore the white carnation, was looking at his watch with an air of finality. Ken walked rapidly so that he was a step or two ahead of McGovern. There were couples standing on the floor. Many of the tables were vacant. The music stopped when Ken was some twenty feet from the table occupied by the man in the dinner coat who wore the white carnation. There was a perfunctory spatter of applause and then couples stood, waiting, staring at the orchestra expectantly.

Ken Corning raised his voice and called over his shoulder to McGovern: "This is just a frame-up, because I've got some evidence in that Parks murder case."

McGovern spoke in an even, ominous tone. "Shut up!" he said.

Ken flashed a glance to the man who wore the white carnation. He was signaling a waiter for his check. There was nothing on his face to indicate that he had heard what Ken had said; or hearing, was in anywise concerned with it. The orchestra struck up an encore. As the couples started to twine and twist to the strains of the dance, Ken flashed a glance at McGovern, then at the man who wore the white carnation. The man was handing the waiter a bill. The waiter was pushing an oblong of pink pasteboard at him from which had been figured the items of the check. The man pushed away the pasteboard, made a sweeping gesture with his hand as though to indicate that the waiter should keep the change. Staring at his face, it was impossible for Ken to tell whether the man had hurried his exit because Ken was leaving, or whether he had simply grown tired of waiting, and decided to knock off for the day.

Behind him, McGovern said: "Get your hat and coat and don't try any funny business."

Ken moved up to the checking stand. A girl with a beautiful face flashed him a smile that was meant to be dazzling, but was only mechanical, took the square of pasteboard which he handed her and pushed Ken's hat out over the counter.

The man who wore the white carnation in his

dinner coat had evidently found some people he knew. He was chatting with them, a young man of about thirty, and a red-haired woman who could not have been over twenty-three. As he chatted, he reached up and plucked the white carnation from the dinner jacket, dropped it to the floor and stepped on it.

Ken said to McGovern: "Can I talk with you? Will you listen to reason?"

McGovern said: "Sure, I'll listen to any guy who wants to talk; only remember that anything you say will be used against you."

Ken lured him over to the far corner of the checking counter and said: "All right now, listen. I told you that this thing was a frame-up because I was a witness in the Parks case. You don't seem to be interested."

McGovern said: "Why should I be interested? That's a state case, I'm a Federal. You tell me where you got this counterfeit money from and where the plates are and I'll sit here and listen to you until daylight. But if you've got anything to say on the Parks case you can tell it to the state authorities—I'm not interested."

Ken fixed his eyes on McGovern and said: "Listen, suppose that I could show you that this man Parks had something on the administration and was going to keep Dike from accepting the position of Superintendent of the Water Department? Suppose I could show you that Carl Dwight is mixed up with Dike; that, in place of being enemies, those two fellows are working hand in glove regardless of all this newspaper talk about Dike wanting to clean up the graft. . . ."

McGovern took his arm above the elbow and gave him a push.

"Listen, guy, I told you I wasn't interested in all that stuff. Are you going to tell me where you got the plates or where you've got the rest of this queer cached?"

Ken Corning's eyes narrowed.

"Okey," he said, "I tried to give you the breaks and you wouldn't listen. Now I'll take a look at *your* credentials before I leave this place."

McGovern grinned easily and dropped his right hand to the side pocket.

"Gee," he said, "you sure are full of alibis and stalls. Come on and let's get going. This is all in the day's work with me and I want to get home and get my beauty sleep. You can stall all night, but you can't keep me from taking you to jail and booking you on a charge of possession of counterfeit money. If you want my authority, here it is."

Ken felt something hard prodding against his ribs. He glanced down to where the right hand of McGovern was holding the gun concealed by the right-hand side pocket of his coat. He said: "Oh, it's like that, is it?"

McGovern said: "Yes, guy, it's like that. You're going to take it and like it. Get started out of here. You've got counterfeit money in your possession and there are witnesses that you tried to pass it. You can either go quietly or you can get your insides blown out right here. Which is it going to be?"

Ken grinned and said: "Under the circumstances, I guess I'll go quietly."

McGovern said: "Now you're talking sense. You can't gain anything by talking any other way. I'm on the square and I'm going to take you in, but I ain't going to stand here all night and listen to a lot of hooey and I ain't going to have you pull any smart aleck stuff on me. Get started!"

Corning moved towards the door. He noticed that the man who had worn the white carnation was moving towards the door also and that the man who had been with the red-haired girl was walking with him. The red-haired girl moved off towards the left and went into the women's dressing room. The man who had worn the white carnation lit a cigarette. He seemed in no hurry. Ken Corning went out of the door painfully conscious of the pressure of the gun which was held against his ribs. The doorman looked at them and said: "Taxicab?"

McGovern shook his head and said: "No, I've got a car."

The big limousine which had been parked near the curb with motor running slid smoothly up to the front of the cabaret and stopped. The doorman started to open the door and McGovern spoke sharply: "That's all right," he said, "I'm a Federal dick and this man is a prisoner. He's desperate and may try to start something. Keep back, I'll handle this!"

He reached out and opened the door. His gun prodded Ken in the ribs. "Get in," he said.

Ken put his right foot on the running-board of the limousine. He could see two men seated in the back seat. They were grinning. Ken swung his body in a pivot, grabbing with his left hand at the gun which McGovern was holding against his ribs and pushing down with all his strength.

McGovern fired twice before Ken's fist connected with his jaw. Neither shot hit. Somebody shot from the interior of the limousine but the bullet hit the plate-glass window, shattered it into a thousand fragments and deflected. McGovern went down like a sack of cement. Ken swung himself on him and reached for the gun. Over his shoulder he could see the swirl of motion from the interior of the limousine. A man jumped to the running-board while Ken was still struggling for the possession of the gun. Ken heard him say: "All right, guy, take a load of this!"

Two shots roared out as though they had been one explosion. The man who had stood on the running-board of the limousine pitched forward and struck on his face. Ken jerked the gun from the pocket of McGovern and saw that the man in the dinner jacket was standing on the steps of the cabaret, an automatic in his hand. The man who had been with the red-haired girl was standing on the sidewalk a little bit to one side with a double-action revolver spouting fire. The doorman was running heavily, his gold-braided coat flapping grotesquely behind him. The limousine had lurched into motion. Somebody was rolling down the back window, which had not been shattered. Guns blazed over Ken's head. A bullet whistled past his cheek. The two men standing in the front of the cabaret answered the fire.

Ken got McGovern's gun in his hand and took a couple of shots at the limousine. He heard the bullets give forth a clinking sound as they struck against the metal of the body. The limousine swung far over to one side as it rounded the corner to the accompaniment of screaming tires.

The man in the dinner coat ran towards Ken as McGovern, recovering from the daze of Ken's blow, started to struggle to his feet.

Ken said: "Those men were trying to take me for a ride. This guy posed as a Federal agent . . ."

McGovern spoke up and said: "I am a Federal agent. This crook's been shoving the queer. He's got a wallet of phoney stuff on him right now."

The man in the dinner coat laughed and said: "Federal, hell! I know you, you're Jim Harper, and you've done time!"

A uniformed policeman, on beat, ran up. The man in the dinner coat spoke to him sharply: "All right, Bell. Get the crowd back. I'll handle what's left of this."

A curious crowd was commencing to form a ring around the men, and the uniformed policeman started to herd them back.

The man in the dinner coat said: "That's all right, buddy, I know this guy, he's a crook. You're a witness in the Parks case, huh?"

Ken Corning stared at him with round eyes and shook his head.

"No," he said, "I'm not a witness, I'm attorney for Mrs. Parks and I came here to meet a witness but he didn't show up."

The man in the dinner jacket stared at Ken Corning for a long five seconds. Then his right eyelid slowly closed in a solemn wink: "So," he said, "*that's* your story, eh?"

Ken Corning kept his face perfectly straight and his eyes perfectly steady. "That," he said, "is my story and I'm sticking to it. I'm not a witness, I'm a lawyer. I was to meet a witness here. These guys tried to keep me from meeting him, that's all."

The man in the dinner coat said: "Who were they? Would you recognize any of them if you saw them again?"

Ken Corning shook his head.

"No," he said, "the light wasn't good enough. I couldn't see them."

The man in the dinner coat turned to the fake Federal agent. Ken Corning slipped away. No one tried to stop him. There was the sound of a police siren, approaching fast, as he turned the corner.

Ken Corning walked into his office.

The morning sun streamed in at the east window. Helen Vail stared at him with eyes that were dark with emotion, warm with pride.

"Got your name in the papers, didn't you?"

He grinned at her.

"How about our client?" she asked.

He spread his hands, palm up, made a sweeping gesture.

"Gone. Case is closed, dismissed."

"And all we get then is the hundred and fifty dollar retainer?"

Ken nodded.

"That's all. The woman was driving the car. Her husband wasn't with her. I figured that he must have been, but he wasn't. Dike and Dwight had been having a secret meeting. They'd been out in the country at a roadhouse where they were safe. Coming back they were riding in the same car. Dike was driving and he was a little bit 'lickered.' The woman was driving the flivver and they had a smash. She was a little bit belligerent and insisted on taking down the license number of the automobile. They paid her for her damage but she acted a little suspicious so Dwight got the license number of her automobile and found out who she was. They knew that she was running a speak, and figured that she was too dumb to know what it was all about, but they wanted her out of the way, just the same. With the deal Dike was planning to pull, it would have been fatal if somebody had uncovered this woman as a witness, so Dwight decided that he'd get her convicted of a felony. That would have discredited her testimony if she'd ever been called as a witness.

"She probably was suspicious, because she told her husband about it. Nobody knows just how much she told him or how much he knew, but it's a cinch that he knew enough to put two

and two together when he saw Dike's picture in the paper with the blurb about his taking over the Water Department and eliminating graft."

Helen Vail watched him with wide eyes.

"Can we prove any of that?" she asked.

Ken Corning shook his head. "We can't prove anything," he said. "Wouldn't do us any good if we could. They've dismissed the case against the woman, released her from custody and she's gone. They probably made a deal with her, gave her some money and started her traveling."

"Why would they do that?" asked Helen Vail. "Her testimony is just as damaging now as it ever was."

Ken Corning smiled and motioned towards the morning paper.

"Read the news," he said, "and you'll notice that Dike has declined the appointment. He said that his private business was taking up too much of his time for him to make the sacrifice of accepting a public position."

Helen Vail blinked her eyes thoughtfully and said: "How about the people in the automobile— don't you know any of them?"

Ken Corning said: "You mean the ones who were trying to take me for a ride?"

She nodded her head.

Ken laughed and said: "Sure I do. Perkins was one of them. He was the detective who barged into the office here. He's a cheap heel who does dirty work for the Dwight machine."

"But," she said, "you told the officers that you couldn't recognize any of them."

Ken Corning laughed mirthlessly and said: "Of course I did. I'd never get anywhere trying to pin anything on Perkins. He'd produce an alibi and get acquitted. Then they'd turn around and prosecute me for perjury. I'm bucking a machine in this town, and the machine is well entrenched with a lot of money back of it. I'm not a fool!"

"How about the man who pretended to be a Federal officer?" she asked.

"He's got to take the rap. They've got the goods on him. They might have managed to make some sort of stall there, only I knew it was coming. I had worked the wallet that the waiter had planted on me out of my pocket. When they opened the door of the limousine I tossed the wallet in with my left hand before I grabbed at this guy's gun and socked him with my right."

She shuddered and said: "Oh, Ken, I don't like it."

He stood with his feet planted far apart, his jaw thrust forward, hands thrust into the pocket of his coat.

"I like it," he said, "and I'm going to make them like it. I'm going to bust this town wide open. They're going to stop me if they can. They'll try to frame me, try to take me for a ride, try to freeze me out. I'm going to stay! I'm going to be here after they're gone."

"But, Ken," she objected, "you've done all this work and risked your life and we only get a hundred and fifty dollars out of it."

Ken Corning nodded and laughed.

"A hundred and fifty dollars," he said, "and it's honest money."

Then he walked into his private office and the door clicked shut.

Helen Vail could hear him moving around in the inner office. He was whistling cheerfully as though he didn't have a care in the world.

She opened the drawer of her desk, took out a ledger which was innocent of entry, took a pen and wrote in a hand which trembled slightly: "People versus Parks—cash retainer $150.00."

Frost Rides Alone

Horace McCoy

A SOMEWHAT PROLIFIC author of pulp stories, primarily for *Black Mask*, Horace McCoy (1897–1955) is mainly remembered for his dark, tragic, and occasionally violent novels, several of which have been made into notable films.

A memorable work of noir fiction and a classic film is *They Shoot Horses, Don't They?* (1935), filmed in 1969 with Sydney Pollack as the director, which achieved its aim of illustrating the pain and hopelessness of the Great Depression, using a marathon dance contest as a metaphor, with the exhausting and pointless expenditure of energy for participants being analogous to the plight of the majority of Americans.

The film *The Turning Point* (1952), directed by William Dieterle, became the novel *Corruption City* in 1959; *Kiss Tomorrow Goodbye* (1948) starred James Cagney and was directed by Gordon Douglas when it was filmed in 1950; *No Pockets In a Shroud* (1937) was filmed in France in 1975; and *Scalpel* (1952) was filmed the following year as *Bad for Each Other*, the screenplay co-written by McCoy and directed by Irving Rapper. The only one of McCoy's novels to have no film version is *I Should Have Stayed Home* (1938), and McCoy's screenplay was published in 1978.

Captain Jerry Frost of the Texas (Air) Rangers made his debut in "Dirty Work" in *Black Mask* in September 1929; "Frost Rides Alone" was published in the March 1930 issue.

Frost Rides Alone

Horace McCoy

FROST FELT THAT HE and the woman were being followed, had been followed since they crossed the Border. As they emerged from the Plaza Madero and turned down the crooked street towards the Café Estrellita he became acutely aware that footsteps were proceeding in the same direction as himself and that the owner was trying to attract as little attention as possible.

To satisfy himself that he was not the victim of his own imagination, so often the case when he invaded old Mexico after nightfall, he halted briefly before a shop window, wherein baubles were exhibited, and whispered a caution to his companion. The moment they stopped the footfalls ceased. No one passed. Quite evidently someone was following.

Fully alive now, his nerves on edge, Frost spoke to his companion, and they walked on. In the distance he could see the lights of the Café Estrellita and outside the shadowy forms of customers at the sidewalk tables. Frost walked slowly, his ears strained, but did not look around. He was still being followed. Moreover, the number of steps behind him had increased. There were now two or three men. The street was narrow and the footsteps loud: overhead the stars blinked and from a hidden patio nearby there floated the dim tinkle of a guitar.

As the woman passed the dark, dank interiors she gave way to a swift rush of apprehension and took Frost's arm nervously. He leaned over and whispered: "Don't get excited, but I'd like to know if you can use a gun."

She moved her head closer. "I'm sort of jumpy," she apologized lamely, "but really, I can use a gun. Fact is—" her confidence returned "—I've got one." She patted her voluminous handbag. She went on lightly. "I haven't been a newspaper woman ten years without learning a few things."

Frost said, "Oh!" rather contritely, and steered her into the café without looking back at his pursuers.

La Estrellita was a little square room overcrowded with tables at which, outside and inside, sat perhaps half a hundred persons. The ceiling was almost obscured by cigarette smoke, and there was all the variety of noises commonly associated with Border joints. It was the hour when Algadon blazed with the specific intent of luring tourists, although the patronage here was now, as far as Frost determined in a hurried glance, mostly native.

At one end of the room was a bar at which two Mexicans were mixing drinks; behind them was the traditional frosted mirror and long rows of bottles. A square-shouldered, semi-bald man was busy plying a rag with what amounted to violence and one look at him left no doubt concerning his origin. He was one of those old-time American bartenders driven into Mexico by prohibition.

Glasses and spoons littered one end of the bar and near this end, on a raised platform, sat a quintet of native musicians languidly strumming their guitars. They simulated indifference, ennui, hoping to chisel a round of drinks from a sympathetic tourist. The house was bare of sympathy.

Frost led his companion inside and half way to the table he had mentally selected he recognized the unmistakable form of Ranger Captain George Stuart. Frost slowly passed Stuart's table and said under his breath:

"Don't look up, George. Just get set. Hell's fixing to pop."

The only indication Stuart heard was an almost imperceptible movement of his fingers as he knocked the ashes off his cigarette. Twenty years on the Border had given him perfect control of all his faculties, had deadened his emotions.

Frost went to a table near the end of the bar and helped his companion into a chair. Then he sat down, facing the room and glanced at George Stuart.

There passed a look of understanding. Stuart crossed his legs and as he did so slid his six-gun inside his thigh by means of his elbow. At that moment three men came through the doorway, looked hurriedly about the room and walked to a table near Frost. As they sat down their chairs scraped and the sounds were audible above the maudlin talk and the soporific music.

The three of them were young, Mexican in cast of countenance, with sharp faces and narrow eyes—of a general type with which the Border, from end to end, teems: shrewd, crafty wastrels who will turn any sort of a trick for any sort of a price.

Frost ordered two bottles of beer from a waiter, and looked at his companion.

"I'm afraid," he said, striving to be unconcerned, "I've got you into a mess—and the only way out is straight ahead."

"You think," she asked, inclining her head slightly, "those men—"

"I don't know," Frost said. "But I've got a sweet hunch you're liable to get a good story before this party ends. There's a window directly behind you. If—if anything happens, get out and keep going."

"You talk," she said, "as if you regretted bringing me."

Frost eyed her. "I never have regrets," he said, "they're cowardly. Just the same it didn't look this foggy when we started. If we tried to get out now we'd never live to reach the street."

"As bad as that?" She was smiling and the smile annoyed Frost. He didn't answer. He thought her question was stupid. Hell, of course it was bad. She had no business here. But that was the way with the newspaper tribe—all of them. Especially women. They thought that their profession was protection. Helen Stevens, however, seemed more officious than any other Frost had known. Probably, he presumed, because she was to author a series about Hell's Stepsons for an indubitably important organization, the Manhattan Syndicate, Inc. But, even then, Frost told himself again, this time bitterly, she had no business here.

Few spots on the Border are safe for a woman after dark; Algadon was no spot for a woman at any time. But Helen Stevens had insisted and as the final persuasive force she had even brought a letter from the Adjutant-General. And here she was.

It looked bad.

The waiter returned with the bottles and two glasses. He poured the drinks, placed the bottles on a tray, and started away.

"*Psst!*" said Frost. "*Deja los botella.*"

The waiter turned, surprised. "*Como?*"

"*Deja los botella!*" Frost repeated, more sharply.

The waiter lifted his eyes as if invoking divine compassion on the fool before him; and put the empty bottles back on the table. He moved away, slightly puzzled; but no more so than the newspaper woman.

"How odd!" she observed.

"Not at all," Frost said. "I've got a lot of funny little habits like that." He didn't feel it necessary to tell her experience had taught him there was nothing comparable to the efficiency of a beer bottle at close quarters; or that he had a deep-seated hunch it would be at close quarters soon.

He took a sip from his glass and looked at his companion. Her face was unworried, lovely. He thought of that moment on route to La Estrellita when she had, momentarily frightened, touched his arm. Her face betrayed no fear now—nor anything that remotely approached fear. From the tranquillity of her demeanor she might have been sitting in the refinement of an opera loge instead of a Mexican dive where the air was charged with expectancy. Frost felt, irreverently, that if he, accustomed to tension, was slightly ill at ease, she, unaccustomed to anything of the sort, should at least have shared a portion of that discomfort. It mildly annoyed him that she didn't.

She reached for the glass with her long fingers and as she lifted it she drummed her fingers lightly against the stem. Out of the corner of his eye Frost saw one of the three men who had followed him lean over and whisper to his comrades. He also saw George Stuart move forward in his chair, ready to get into action in a split second.

Helen Stevens was speaking in a dulcet voice. "Is this," she was saying, "typical of Border towns?"

"Is it possible," Frost countered, "that you are a stranger to Border towns?"

She laughed and her eyes beamed spiritedly. "Of course."

"In that case it's typical. Just the same," Frost went on, "I wish we hadn't come."

"Why?" she demanded. She seemed positively to be enjoying it. "I'm glad," she went on, rippling, "that I can see you against your proper background." She inclined her head. "Captain, I'm afraid you dramatize yourself fearfully."

For the second time in the past few minutes Frost was the victim of mixed emotions. She alternately stirred him and irritated him. Now he was in no mood for tea-room repartee.

"Please," he said, "let's not get personal." He contemplated that remark and decided it wasn't exactly what he wanted to say. It sounded flat. So he hurried on, "Miss Stevens, you mustn't get me wrong. Our men have been having a tough time along this river with an important gang. We are constantly expecting things to happen—anything. To you that may seem dramatic. But I am only cautious—" he lifted his eyes "—and thinking of you."

"You needn't," she said suddenly. "I'm all right."

Somehow he didn't quite think so. He was alarmed—rather definitely alarmed. Notwithstanding his attitude of indifference he felt that something was going to happen before they got out of La Estrellita. He knew the signs. It was the sort of a prelude that always traveled along in the same slot. Never any change. Had he been alone he could have forced the issue. But he was not alone. There was a woman with him—a personal charge. That sort of cramped his style. Jerry Frost had been in the habit of meeting trouble half-way.

Three men had followed him. Why? Footpads intent on robbing a tourist? He dismissed that thought. They knew very well who he was—should have known—and even if they didn't, George Stuart was there. Every man, woman and child in Algadon knew the rock-ribbed Stuart. He was part and parcel of the Border country. Men who stalk American game along the Rio with a Ranger within the same walls are bent on a mission more sinister than robbery.

Did they think Frost had on his person the valuable black book he got from Flash Singleton in the little episode at Jamestown—the little black book the gangster had carried, giving names and information? He didn't know. But there was a voice within him—a small, still voice that roused him to the alert. It bred expectancy. Helen Stevens had thought, and said so, that this was theatricality. Frost smiled reflectively. She could think what she damn well pleased. He had no fault to find with his intuition. It had saved him too often.

"Do you think," she whispered, "any of the gang is here now?"

"*No se,*" he shrugged. "They're everywhere."

"But I thought I'd read that Hell's Stepsons had broken it up."

He cast her what was intended to be a rueful grimace, but it hardly was that. "No," he admitted, "we've made only a small dent in it. We've caught only the little fish."

She moved again, this time her body. She placed her hand on Frost's wrist and swayed her head a little. "I hope," she said suddenly and, he thought, softly, "you get the big ones!"

Frost felt she was animated by deep sincerity, and as quickly as his suspicions had mounted they disappeared. They might have been dissipated by the touch of her hand, by the proximity of her lovely face, by the faint smile on her lips; but dissipated they most assuredly were. Helen Stevens was a good-looking woman of the type which has been vaguely classified as a man's woman. It had been a long time since such a creature had been as close to him. He became poignantly and swiftly aware that he had been missing something.

He patted her hand gratefully, sighed like a silly schoolboy and said: "I hope so, too."

There was a scuffling sound from the front of the house and a man got up unsteadily. After an hour he had become aware that the orchestra was not functioning well.

"*Una cancion!*" he cried. "*Canta!*"

"*Si, si,*" came the chorus.

The musicians on the platform be-stirred themselves and stroked the strings with a little more life than they had previously evidenced. They played a few bars as a vamp and then lifted their voices in a plaintive rendering of *La Cucaracha,* camp song of that immortal renegade—Villa.

They finished and were rewarded with loud applause. It was to be expected. *La Cucaracha* is a sort of provincial national air. It brought back flashing memories of the Chihuahua stable cleaner who later flung his defy in the teeth of the government: "*Que chico se me hace el mar para hacer un buche de agua . . .* I'll use the ocean to gargle!"

The lethargy in La Estrellita was falling away.

Frost looked at the table where the three men were sitting. They were, to him, plainly agitated.

Their heads bobbed excitedly, and one of them exchanged wise looks with the bartender. After that the bartender moved slowly down the rail with affected nonchalance. Frost pretended to be thoroughly immersed in his drink and his companion. But he was not too immersed in either.

Something was about to occur.

"Remember," he said aside to the woman, "the window is directly behind you. It looks like trouble is coming. Understand?"

"Perfectly," she said quietly. She reached for her bag, and opened it in her lap. Her hand slipped inside and closed about the butt of a gun. "Don't worry."

"I won't," he said. He meant it. The calmness and sureness of her decision relieved him. Again he admired her, found himself wondering what sort of a companion she would be in more agreeable surroundings.

One of the three Mexicans got up. The impression he meant to convey was drunkenness. Frost got no such impression.

He caught the eye of George Stuart and nodded. Stuart nodded likewise.

The Mexican started off between the tables, ostensibly intent on reaching the bar. He never got that far. He purposely stepped out of the way to trip against Frost's foot, almost falling to the floor. He righted himself and poured out a volume of Spanish; swept the glasses from the table.

Here it was. The big blow-off. Here it was. Frost had been waiting, taut as a bow-string.

He leaped from his chair and put all his power into a short uppercut that landed flush on the Mexican's chin and sent him reeling ten feet away against a table.

"Beat it!" he said to the woman.

His right hand went to his hip after his gun and his left hand groped for the empty bottle. But he had lost a precious few seconds. He turned to find himself looking down the blue barrels of two pistols held in the hands of the remaining pursuers. It was too late to draw his own weapon.

The career of Jerry Frost might have ended

on the spot had it not been for George Stuart. He had come from behind softly, but fast, and brought the butt of his gun down upon the head of one of the Mexicans. It was a terrific blow. The man groaned and fell to the floor. Stuart quickly threw his arms about the other's shoulders.

Frost availed himself of the lull to take a step backward and look for Helen Stevens. She was missing; and he had no time to speculate on where she was or how she got away. Through the door came five men, as tough looking as any Frost had ever seen. They were rushing forward recklessly, intent on but one purpose. Everybody in the room had risen by now, offering the quintet slight impediment.

Frost swung the beer bottle with all the force he could muster, and it crashed against the head of the man with whom Stuart was wrestling. The Mexican's cheek bone ripped through the skin as if by magic, and blood poured down his face. He instantly grew limp; and Stuart let him slide to the floor.

An unseen hand pressed the switch and La Estrellita was swept into darkness.

A pistol cracked, light blue and scarlet, and the bullet whistled by Frost's head. Pandemonium arose. Frost stepped to one side; not a moment too soon. The pistol barked again. From the flash Frost deduced he had been in direct line of fire. If—

There was a stampede towards the door. Frost lashed out in the dark, heard a grunt, and lashed out again. A third time he swung the beer bottle; this time it shattered. Spanish blasphemy ascended. La Estrellita was an inferno. Tables and chairs rattled, glasses crashed, and a loud voice shouted:

"*Luz! Luz!*"

Someone was calling for lights and it struck Frost that the sensible thing to do now was retreat before the lights went up. So he shouted for Stuart to follow him, ducked quickly, and moved towards the window. His escape was made difficult by the cursing, wedging mob. Everybody was fighting to get outside. Frost lunged with his fists, and a blow banged against

his jaw. He reeled, almost fell but came up swinging. Outside he could hear the shrill whistles of the police. The Mexican constabulary was calling, like no other police in the world, for order.

Frost set his teeth and flailed his arms. And every time they went out they struck something. He dived forward and some of the mob went down before the force of his body. He got up and climbed over, carrying others in his mad march to the exit.

He wanted to shout at Stuart again to let him know where he was, but even in that chaos of mind and flesh, Frost realized to cry out now would be to betray himself by his voice. So he fought his way slowly to the window.

He could see it as a rectangle of outside light a few feet ahead and he pushed and struggled and continued to swing. He thrilled to the power in his long arms and his fists . . . a form loomed in front of him in clear silhouette and he started a blow from the floor. His fist crashed against the blurred vision that was a head; there was a smothered exclamation, and the man went down.

Frost shifted his arms and got his pistol, and as he came near the window he swung again and again; then of a sudden he became aware that his legs were not moving. They were imprisoned in a human vise.

He fell forward.

But he did not hit the floor. He fell on top of several squirming bodies; and realized he had been pulled down in the confusion. Fearful lest he be trampled, he yanked himself up again by means of somebody's coat and was thankful he still had his pistol. He came to his knees, then full up, and, finding he had sufficient space to move his legs, kicked lustily at the form on the floor. There was an oath.

He reached for the window, anchored his hand and pulled. He finally made it. He climbed up and literally fell into the night. With the first intake of air he thought of the woman and Stuart.

Where were they? Safe? There had been, he reflected, but two pistol shots. So far as he could determine neither had found a mark. Mexican marksmanship is, notoriously, bad; their first love is the blade. And the blade is, generally, silent. Had? . . . The thought sent Frost into a rage. Still, Stuart was a veteran. He had been in hundreds of brawls . . . and yet. . . .

Regardless of everything now, Frost lifted his voice:

"George! George!"

As if in answer to his reckless cry, George Stuart tumbled through the window.

"Thank God!" Frost panted. "Hurt?"

"Nope!" Laconically. Then: "You?"

"Bruised." Then: "George, I've got to find the woman!"

They moved quickly across the street. The mêlée in the café continued. The police were puffing at their whistles and occasionally shouting in an official voice that did no good; there was general discord.

"In the meantime," George said, "we're in a fine shape to stop a slug or two. Let's step on it."

They walked rapidly towards the international bridge.

Stuart said, "Who the hell was that dame?"

"A newspaper woman the Old Man sent down—but I'd rather not talk about it."

"I don't blame you," Stuart said. "You had a swell idea—bringing her to this town. She damn near got us messed up."

"I know that now. But it could have been worse." He went on quietly, "You saved my life, George."

George Stuart rubbed his chin reflectively and pretended he didn't hear.

"Where do you suppose she went?" he asked.

"I tried to tell her what was coming," Frost said. "If she was smart she went across."

They had gone so far now the sounds in La Estrellita were but murmurs. Overhead the stars blinked on; once in a while the Rangers caught the music of guitars as an indolent part of Algadon, impervious to the excitement, sang on.

"Know those yeggs who started the fight?" Stuart asked, matching the strides of the long-legged flyer.

"Never saw 'em before," Frost said. "I guess they were hired by the gang. I wonder," he mused, "where it'll all end?"

Stuart had no answer for that one. They walked along silently.

"I hope," Frost went on, as if to himself, "she got back okey. I sort of had the idea she could look out for herself."

"Well," put in Stuart truculently, "she had a swell opportunity of doing that little thing tonight."

"And she wasn't bad looking," Frost went on in the same tone.

"Yeh—I saw that, too."

At the international boundary they exchanged pleasantries they did not feel with the customs officials. Frost asked for the woman. The officers said they were sorry, but no woman had passed into the States. Frost stoutly insisted they must be mistaken; they insisted just as stoutly they could not be.

George Stuart was familiar with their technique. He said, "Well?" to Frost in such a tone his meaning was clear.

"A mess," Frost exploded—"a first-class mess. God," he breathed, "if anything's happened . . . Well," resolutely, "I can't go back without her. That much is a cinch."

Stuart lighted a cigarette and said, "Anything you say, Jerry. Wanna take a look at La Estrellita?" thus leaving the plan of action to the flyer.

"It's not a question of wanting to, George. But the Old Man sent her—"

"Sure." Stuart turned to the officials and requested, with a trace of belligerence, that if the woman who had crossed with Frost returned she be detained. He then divested himself of certain pertinent remarks. "Jerry—you're the biggest damn fool I ever saw. You know how you stand around here," and, having unburdened himself, he again became the fighting man with a terse, "Hell, let's go!"

And with no more than that they swung back to La Estrellita, whence they had so recently and so narrowly escaped with their lives.

The café had quieted somewhat when they

returned. Stuart and Frost made their way inside. A few patrons had come back (a great many had never left), but many of the tables were over-turned and everywhere there were unmistakable signs of the fight, notwithstanding the expeditious work of the café's ubiquitous emergency corps. The five-man Mexican orchestra was back on the platform playing in the same listless fashion which forever characterizes their music. This was a bland lot of musicians. A brawl, a pistol fight, a knife duel—nothing to them. Every night was just another night.

Their hands on their hips, the Rangers stood inside the door of the café and returned glare for glare. There were low murmurs of recognition as they entered.

They summoned the proprietor.

"I know this guy Rasaplo," Stuart said. "Lemme do all the talking."

Rasaplo waddled up solicitously, portly after the vogue of Mexican café owners, with long mustachios and sagging jowls that could be either fierce or cherubic. At this moment he chose for them to be cherubic. He rubbed his hands as if Frost and Stuart were patron saints who had stepped from their *nichos,* and smiled broadly.

"*Señors,*" he said, "I am sorry—vair sorry." He looked from one face to the other, seeking some indication of official forgiveness. There was none. The Rangers stared at him and through him. Rasaplo quailed somewhat.

"Now lissen," Stuart said, his voice steely. "The *capitan* here brought a woman with him—*la mujer Americana. Ella desvaneca*—disappeared. *Sabe* what that means?"

Rasaplo's eyes widened in surprise. His whole person registered consternation. Great actors, those fellows. Rasaplo lifted his hands in horror.

"*Imposible!*" he managed. "Never in La Estrellita. Never! La Estrellita ees—"

"Yeh," Stuart cut in; "I know that speech backwards! La Estrellita is a little nursery where mommas leave their children." He clucked heatedly. "Nix on that patriotism stuff, Ras-aplo! Your dump ain't no different from any of the others along this creek. Now get this—the woman disappeared in here tonight—and she's got to be found. Tell me something before I—"

"But," Rasaplo wheezed, "I am in the back room when a gun go boom! and the place get dark. I know no more."

Stuart looked at Frost and nodded. "Well, in that case," he began, his meaning clear, "I guess we'll—"

Rasaplo said quickly, "Mebbe Pete know. Pete always know." He went briskly to the bar and engaged a bartender in conversation. He was the one Frost had seen moving down the rail before the lights went out. From the way the patrons eyed the scene the Rangers could tell they still were annoyed at having their evening interrupted. They were content, however, merely to stare.

But the bartender was mystified, too. There was no misinterpreting his gestures. He didn't know how the fight started, and he didn't remember any woman. All he knew was that after the lights went on again several natives were carried out, semi-conscious.

Rasaplo darted a swift look around, leaned over the bar a little farther, and something changed hands. Stuart and Frost both saw it at the same time. They went forward.

"Gimme that!" Stuart commanded.

Rasaplo grinned abashed, and handed over a letter. "They give it to the boy to mail," he said. "I do not know anything."

The letter was addressed to Captain Jerry Frost, Gentry, Texas, and there was a two-cent U.S. stamp in the corner. Frost ripped it open. A note on the back of a menu. It said:

"Thanks, Captain, for the woman."

It was written in that peculiar, flamboyant foreign style. Frost fingered it blankly and held it up for Stuart to see. Stuart said to Rasaplo: "Where's the waiter who got this?"

Rasaplo summoned a sleek servitor, who eyed Stuart and Frost with an expression that can only be called baleful.

"Who gave you this?" Frost held up the letter.

The waiter shrugged his shoulders to say he couldn't remember all the patrons; but made no answer.

"Who gave you this?" Frost repeated.

"I no remember," he said. "A man—" as if that would help.

Rasaplo inserted his broad bulk into the scene to give his employee whatever protection he could muster. "He know nothing," he said. "He get the letter and boom! the place go dark. Mebbe we get *miedo*—and no mail letter. But—" His voice, colorless, trailed off.

Stuart gestured disgustedly to Frost. For the time being they knew they were against a blank wall. Trying to elicit criminal information from some Mexicans can be—in some instances, is—nothing short of impossible. Indeed, some of them are so clumsy in trying to remain innocent they incriminate themselves.

The Rangers knew they could do no more; and, too, they were chancing further trouble by remaining in La Estrellita.

"Come on, let's go see the cops." On the way out Stuart went on: "But don't expect too much of the law here. It's quite probably the rottenest force in the world. Maybe, though—"

They went around the corner to the police station, and Frost soon learned that Stuart had properly classified the Algadon police. They said they hadn't the faintest idea what happened to the woman; moreover, they gave the impression, and it was true, that they weren't in the least interested. They were without the slightest degree of enthusiasm, and raised their brows superciliously to convey the thought that if the Rangers couldn't look out for their own women they shouldn't expect anyone else to.

Stuart said to Frost: "I'd like to sock this gang in the jaw."

Frost nodded abstractedly. He wasn't particularly concerned with that. It was the woman. His last hope, for the present, had fled. She had been his responsibility, his personal charge, and to return to Gentry without her likely would

cause complications. She could be one of a thousand places. He rephrased Stuart's words: he had been a damn fool.

And the Old Man. He'd raise hell. Well, what the hell? He'd just have to raise it; that was all. There wasn't anything they could do about it now. Anyway, it was partly his fault. He'd never brought her over if the Old Man hadn't written that letter. "Let her have a look at Algadon by night," he had said. The exact words. Let her have a look by night. . . . Well, she'd had one.

Frost damned his thoughts and turned to Stuart. "Should I have kept her there and taken a chance?" he asked. "Didn't I do the right thing when I told her to get out?"

"Sure," said Stuart broadly, consolingly. Under his breath he rasped: "I'd like to sock this gang in the nose!"

Back at the boundary the Customs officers said no woman had passed since Frost and Stuart were last there, and the Rangers swore roundly and stamped across the bridge. There were headed for the police department in Gentry.

Fifteen minutes later the telegraph wires of the Border country were humming a message, soon to be broadcast over the nation:

KIDNAPED IN ALGADON, MEXICO, ON THE NIGHT OF FEBRUARY ELEVENTH: WOMAN ANSWERING TO NAME OF HELEN STEVENS, REPRESENTATIVE OF MANHATTAN NEWSPAPER SYNDICATE OF NEW YORK CITY. ABOUT FIVE FEET FIVE INCHES, HUNDRED TEN POUNDS, LIGHT BROWN HAIR, BLUE EYES, TEETH UNMARKED, WEARING BROWN COAT AND SKIRT, FLAT-HEELED TWO-TONE SHOES. NOTIFY TEXAS AIR RANGERS, CAPTAIN JERRY FROST GENTRY, TEXAS.

Stuart and Frost then went to the barracks of Hell's Stepsons and dived into bed. George Stuart, again exhibiting remarkable mental control, went immediately to sleep.

Not so Frost. He rolled, pitched, tossed and fretted at his impotence.

Within seventy-two hours the Manhattan Syndicate, Inc., of New York City, had taken official cognizance of the disappearance of one of its representatives by bringing the matter to the attention of the ranking officer of the sovereign State of Texas. Powerfully allied, as are all important syndicates, it lost no time in applying all the pressure at its command.

Messages were exchanged and the austere Mexican government moved, as a gesture of courtesy, a detachment of *rurales* into Algadon. Nobody, of course, expected them to achieve results.

Helen Stevens had disappeared as completely as if the earth had swallowed her.

Yet the law, tank-like in its motion, rumbled on.

The spotlight was fixed on Hell's Stepsons, and its glare was not favorable. The spectacular work done in the past was forgotten.

On the fourth day after her disappearance there was a conference within the great, gilt-domed state capitol at Austin, in the inner office of the governor's suite. There were three men there: the Great Man himself, the Adjutant-General and Captain Frost.

"It is unfortunate," the Governor was saying; "most unfortunate." He was tapping his glasses against his chin: a dignified patriarch, product of the expansive state he represented—rugged, sincere and honest.

"Yes," the Adjutant-General agreed. He was commander of that crack constabulary, the Texas Rangers, the personification of the ideals of that brigade. Big and gaunt he was; you knew at a glance, the sort of an official who would, if needs be, climb into the saddle himself and take the trail.

"The woman," the Governor went on, "is well connected. We cannot, in any event, let up in the search."

"But, sir," mildly demurred the Adjutant-General, "we *are* trying. I feel," he went on,

"somewhat responsible in a personal sense. I insisted Captain Frost take her across."

"No," Frost said quickly; "the fault was mine."

"Well," the Governor declared, "whose fault it was is beside the point. We have got to do something at once."

"They're a tough lot," Frost mused. He spread his hands on the desk. He was, for obvious reasons, highly uncomfortable. "Gentlemen," he said, "I agree that we are being made to look bad. But what else can we do?"

"It has been my experience," said the Adjutant-General, "that this gang never strikes blindly. There always is a motive back of every crime. What was it in this case? Why did they kidnap Helen Stevens? Revenge? Hardly. Ransom?" He shook his head. "No—something else. Some reason we don't know yet."

Frost nodded. "If I had the slightest idea where she was," he said, "I'd go get her—no matter where that happened to be."

Silence.

Then the Governor said, "Perhaps we ought to ask for a bigger appropriation for the Ranger force. Increase them. Move some of them south." He looked sagacious. "The only bad feature about movement like that is the publicity. Our opponents always construe that as inefficiency. It gives them something to talk about. I dislike having this case noised around."

"Well," Frost said bluntly, "the only way to keep it in the family is to let me have a crack at it alone."

Then the unbelievable happened. The immense, carved door swung open noiselessly, and the Governor's secretary entered.

"I'm sorry, sir," he addressed the Great Man, "but I've a message for Captain Frost."

"For me?" Frost asked.

"Yes, sir—forwarded from Gentry."

The Governor said: "Come in, Leavell, come in."

The secretary walked to Captain Frost and handed him the message. Frost made no move to open it until the secretary had departed.

"May I—"

"Certainly," said the Governor.

A deep silence fell. Frost read the message without even a blink of the eye and passed it over the desk to the Governor.

He put on his glasses and read aloud:

COAST GUARD CUTTER FORTY-NINE
SIGHTED RUM-RUNNER CATHERINE B
LONGITUDE NINETY-SEVEN EAST LAT-
ITUDE TWENTY-SEVEN NEAR BROWNS-
VILLE WITH WOMAN ABOARD ANSWERING
DESCRIPTION STEVENS STOP CUT-
TER OUTDISTANCED STOP RUM BOAT
ONE OF FORMER AL THOMAS FLEET.
                                O'Neill.

The Governor removed his glasses and tapped them against his chin again. The Adjutant-General looked at Frost. Frost looked out the window.

"I sort of thought so," he soliloquized.

"Al Thomas," mused the Governor. "Who is that?"

"A gunman killed in a plane smash a couple of months ago after a dogfight with Hell's Step-sons," Frost replied. "His men seem to be carry-ing on."

" 'Cutter outdistanced,' " the Governor went on. "I wonder how—"

"Please, sir," Frost put in. He was on his feet now. Hours of inactivity, of recrimination, of criticism, rushed to a climax which crystallized his attitude. "Please, sir—I'd like to play this alone. Single-handed. It started mine and—" his voice was grim—"I'd like it to finish the same way. I don't want any help."

"But, Captain—" he began.

"Of course, Jerry," said the Adjutant-General in a placating voice. "You can't go streaking off like this!"

Frost raised his hand. His face was in a cast of resolve. "Please," he said again, firmly. He looked at the Adjutant-General and the Adjutant-General understood. "I've got to go it alone."

The Governor nodded; Frost saluted and went out.

As the door closed the Adjutant-General smiled and offered an observation to his chief. "I'd hate like hell to have him after me."

Coast Guard Cutter Forty-Nine's base was at Cor-pus Christi, and it was towards there that Frost turned when he hopped off from Austin. He was at Cuero in fifty minutes, stopping only long enough to wire Jimmy O'Neill that he was on his way and to notify Hans Traub he again was temporarily in command of the Air Rangers.

"I'm riding alone on the Stevens case," he telegraphed.

Two hours and fifty minutes after he had cir-cled the dome of the state capitol, he dipped into the airport at Corpus Christi and taxied his bat-tle plane into a hangar. He got O'Neill on the phone at the government docks.

"Coming right over, Jimmy."

"Great," said O'Neill. "Ox Clay is here. You'll like him."

Frost did like Ox Clay. That name ought to awaken memories of sporting page devotees because Ox Clay was pretty well known back in '21 and '22 when he was ripping football lines to shreds for the Middies: little, square-jawed, built like a bullet, and innumerable laugh wrin-kles around his eyes. "Hello, Jerry," he greeted the flyer. "I've heard so damn much about you I feel as if we're old friends."

"You're no stranger yourself." Frost returned. He said to O'Neill: "Well, Jimmy, I've just left one of those high and mighty confer-ences. Believe you me, Missus Frost's young son has got to do something and do it pronto. What's it all about?"

"Ox can tell you more than I can, Jerry. He was riding Forty-Nine himself."

"I'll say I was," Clay retorted with a grimace. "And the way that baby slipped away from Forty-Nine was nobody's business. We took a couple of shots—it wasn't good target practice. We only scared her faster."

"What about the woman?"

"I was getting to that. It's that Stevens

skirt—no two ways about it. They let us get pretty close—and then kidded us by pulling away. But nobody can tell me I didn't see her during those first few minutes—brown suit, brown hair—"

"Right!" said Frost. "Sounds like my little playmate. What about the boat?"

"Well, she used to belong to the Singleton outfit. Name's the *Catherine B*. Lately taken over by Thomas, and then his gang got it when you fellows rubbed him out. She's the prize of the Gulf, can store about three thousand cases and make close to forty knots. We've never got her because she's fast and then there are hundreds of little coves along the coast she ducks in when trouble appears. When we saw her she was heading to sea."

"We've got plenty of dope on that outfit," O'Neill said. "But so far it hasn't done us any good. We know they load on the stuff at Tampico, Vera Cruz and God knows where else—and about a hundred miles out they transfer it to the launches."

"I see," Frost said. "The launches don't dare get out farther than that?"

"Exactly," Clay put in. "They work close to the Mexican side. There must be five hundred coves between here and the Laguna de la Madre."

"If we could grab the *Catherine B*," O'Neill said; "we'd stop a lot of the smuggling. What's your idea about this, Jerry?"

"Well, I'm going to have a look for her," Frost said quietly.

They thought he was kidding.

"Bring your bathing suit?" Clay asked.

"I'm serious," Frost said.

"Really?" Incredulously.

"Hell, yes, Why not? I'll get pontoons and try to take her. She can't outrun my boat."

"It'd be suicide," said Clay, shaking his head.

Frost laughed. "Lissen, Ox—I admit it may seem funny to you, but it doesn't to me. Besides, I've *got* to do it. How am I going to know when I see her?"

"Easy," said Clay. "Brass taffrails. She's ebony black all over but for her taffrails. You can

see 'em rain or shine. She carries one funnel, looks perfect alow and aloft, has a heavy stern and her cutwater and bow lines are as pretty as I ever saw."

Frost laughed. "I don't get that conversation," he said. "But I did understand about the brass. I don't guess I can miss her."

"You can't," O'Neill said.

"Definitely made up your mind to go it alone?" asked Clay.

"Yep. Would it be possible for me to requisition silencers?"

Ox Clay swung open a drawer and took out two pistols fitted with longish muzzles. "Presto!" he said. He handed them to Frost. "I'll let you use mine."

Frost stared at them curiously. "This," he said, "is the first time I ever saw a silencer. Are they apt to jam?"

Clay grinned. "The first shots will be all right. After that you gamble. Hope they'll do you, Jerry. They're my contribution to your success."

Frost took an automatic out of his hip-holster and one from under his chamois jacket. He said: "I'll trade for the time being. Now one thing more and I'll blow a bugle over your grave. Will you phone Roland at the field that I'm on my way and be sure and be in."

"I'll phone, but don't think that gang on the *Catherine B* will be a pushover. It's a tough mob."

"I know." Frost shook hands with each of them. "Well," he said; "so long."

"So long. Good luck."

"Thanks."

He sheathed his pistols and walked out. Ox Clay looked at Jimmy O'Neill.

"Lotsa guts," he observed.

"You said it!"

Major Oliver Roland, commander of the flying field at Corpus Christi was a stout admirer of Jerry Frost personally and professionally, being a veteran airman himself, but he thought Frost's plan to take the air in an effort to locate the kidnaped woman was a wild idea.

"It's all wet," as he put it.

Frost said no.

"Ridiculous—and dangerous."

"Neither," Frost retorted crisply. "I can't afford to think of either one."

"You ought to." Sternly: "Just because you've had a lot of success along the Border you think you're invulnerable That makes you cocky and breeds overconfidence. You mustn't get that way."

Roland's tone was firm, but inoffensive, and Frost grinned. "I'm not overconfident. I've got good reasons not to be." He was thinking of that time not so long ago when he escaped in an enemy plane, to think he had the world by the tail on a down-hill pull, and was promptly shot down by his companions. "I'm not overconfident," he repeated. "But I am curious—curious as hell. It's up to me to get that woman—and with your help I intend to!"

Oliver Roland knew flyers. He looked into Frost's eyes—clear. He looked at his mouth—tight. He looked at his chin—square under pressure of the jaws. He decided the young man knew what he was doing.

"Very well," he surrendered. "Want a flying boat?"

"Nope, pontoons. Just pontoons. Will you fit me?"

Roland nodded. "On the condition that you forget where you got 'em."

"My memory's awful," Frost smiled.

It required little more than two hours to fit the pontoons and service the ship; and then the silver-winged bird cascaded through the Gulf of Mexico, left the water in a stream of fume, and turned its eager wings southward.

That bird was a fighting ship of the Texas Rangers, carried two thousand rounds of ammunition, a veteran pilot who had a brace of silencer-equipped pistols, and, what was infinitely more important, a stout heart.

Jerry Frost was riding alone. He climbed to fifteen thousand feet better to deaden the roar of his motor, and swung down the jagged coast line. The Gulf lay beneath, a somber expanse as far as his eyes could see, its surface rippling with whitecaps:

long, thin, broken lines like the foreground of an etching. Far down the lanes he could see the funnels of a boat which seemed to hang on the edge of the world, so slowly did it move.

The coast line was dotted with innumerable coves and the waves rolled against them to be broken into effervescence. Frost reflected that Ox Clay had been entirely correct. There were so many of these serrated sanctuaries which afforded natural shelter for the lawless they could well defy the maps. No cartographer possibly could have marked them all.

Frost rocketed down the coast line for a hundred miles and then veered over the Gulf in a wider flight. Already he had come to realize that finding the *Catherine B* out here was no sinecure for a young man who wanted action. There was, however, one consoling thought: he, at least, was in the air with a definite objective.

The *Catherine B* had been seen in Longitude 97 east and Latitude 27. He consulted the map on his board. That would be, as near as he could roughly estimate, fifty miles out of the Laguna de la Madre in a line with Rockport and Vera Cruz. Of course, she wouldn't be there now. But she had started—and there was a reason why. It was not, manifestly, chance. She was on her way to keep a rendezvous.

Frost kept cudgeling his brain seeking a motive for the kidnaping of Helen Stevens. It probably was the least remunerative thing the gang could have done. What could they hope to gain? Didn't they know they would only attract official attention? And that the less attention they attracted the more success would attend their missions?

It seemed, to Frost, inconsistent, imbecilic. But—they had her. He couldn't very well get away from that—they had her. And it was up to him.

It seemed simple. "Two and two," he said to his instrument board; "make four."

A long way out from the Mexican coast his eyes were caught by a tiny boat that was slipping through the water, leaving a long wake, and he deduced she must be running all of thirty knots.

Even from his height he knew the speed was unusual. His heart jumped. He came as close as he dared and maneuvered to get the sun on her. He looked closely. No brass reflection. A rum-runner, but, now, inconsequential. Frost was not interested.

He rolled back closer to the coast and maintained his vigil for thirty more minutes. Then he looked down and was surprised to see another boat. Bang, like that. He had been looking away for only a moment and when he gazed below the boat was there.

He thought probably the lowering sun was playing tricks on him, so he stared intently. No mistake. A boat. Speeding southwest; occasionally outlined against wide swells. If the first launch he saw was speeding there was no adjective for this one. She was, comparatively, doing more than that. And she looked capacious and businesslike now that he could see well. Worth investigating.

He turned the nose of his ship up and climbed. Over to the left was a perfect cirro-cumulus formation which invited him with its natural protection, and he went for it. As he took a gap in the fleece his eyes caught a reflection.

Brass!

The *Catherine B!*

He offered a silent prayer for the cloud bank and took a hurried compass reading. The course the boat was holding was in a straight line with Galveston. The big traffic route! But it could dare. It could show its stern to ninety-nine out of a hundred. . . .

Frost knew it would be fatal to attempt a landing now. Too much light yet. Something might happen. He thought about that rather sharply. An unknown grave in the Gulf was not appealing. That was the way Nungesser and Coli went. And Pedlar. And Erwin. Poor old Bill. There was a tug at Frost's throat. He had gone through many a dogfight with the Dallas ace. . . .

No, Frost knew, he couldn't go down now. Must wait. Hang back and wait for the dark. A big gamble then. A big gamble. Now it would be death.

He guessed the dusk was less than an hour away, but it was a bad guess. It was eighty minutes away and they were the longest eighty minutes Frost ever spent. Occasionally he stole through a rift in the bank to check his quarry to make sure it was within range. The *Catherine B* had now reduced its speed and was drifting idly: quite plainly at its trysting place.

Frost was forcibly struck by the profundity of the situation. Below was a rum boat a hundred miles at sea; above was a formation of clouds which concealed an eagle of justice. Soon that mass of clouds would part to disgorge a winged courier of the law. Why did those clouds happen—just happen to be there? Providence? Frost went off into an endless speculation about the omnipotence of the Creator.

And he found time to breathe a cautious prayer. Cautious because he had never done so openly. It struck him as cowardly. So he prayed quietly and cautiously.

He had decided to go down now in a few minutes.

The sun reached the end of the world, slid off the rim, and reached with long, tenuous fingers for a final hold, missed and fell into the lap of night. Frost was constantly amazed at the swiftness of the sunset; had always been amazed. Yet it is a source of indefinable joy to airmen to see the sun sink from the sky, for at fifteen thousand feet you seem pretty close to the heart of things. Frost probably always would be stirred by such manifestations, no matter how exigent the conditions under which he viewed them. They mildly disquieted him; made him wish he had been an artist.

"Hell," he said to his instrument board, "you're only a lousy airman. Get your head back into this cockpit!"

Night slipped up and five minutes later it was dark. Frost dropped out of the cloud bank among, it seemed, the fledgling stars which were timidly trying their wings, and looked for the *Catherine B*. The Gulf had lost the blackness so apparent in the sunlight and now had become opaque to a faint luminosity. A wayward light flickered below on deck. The light revealed the boat Frost had come to take—and he had determined to take it. Bellerophon felt the same way about the Chimaera.

Frost took off his gauntlet and slipped the silencer-equipped .38 into the seat beside him. Its touch comforted him, reassured him. Of a sudden he picked it up and pulled the trigger. No other sound broke above the throttled humming of the motor.

"Hot stuff!" he said to the sky. To the instrument board he said: "Well, here we go!"

He fell into a glide and kicked his switch off. It was his farewell to the air. Dropping fifteen thousand feet his motor would get cold, too cold to start again in an emergency. But, he told himself, there must be no emergency.

A quarter of a mile back he nosed up into a sort of drift, timing the distance with that weird sense all good flyers possess. And his landing was a tribute to long years of feeling his air. The premium he collected was munificent—his life. To have failed meant death.

The *Catherine B*, on the spot of its meeting, drooled in a wide circle, and as the little battle plane slowly moved by the stern, Frost could plainly read her markings:

CATHERINE B
GALVESTON

Frost kicked his rudder bar around and turned in towards the boat. He flattened out against its sides when he saw a spurt of flame and heard the crash of the report. The man shot from the rail amidships. Frost leveled his gun and fired. Then he quickly threw his anchor rope over the rail. There had been no far-carrying report from his gun, but the man dropped. He was out on the wing in a moment, over the rail in another, and had tied his ship off with a loop knot.

Attracted by the explosion, a husky fellow shoved half his bulk through the wheelhouse door and Frost saw him level his gun. The Ranger shot from the hip; the man collapsed in

the door and rolled on deck. He never knew what had hit him. Frost ran forward.

There was a scuffling sound aft and a man's head and shoulders appeared. He seemed to rise out of nowhere. But he was cautious, had come to investigate what he thought was a shot.

Frost tensed his muscles and gripped his pistol. He pressed himself close to the skylights as the man stepped out gingerly and came towards the wheel-house. He was roughly dressed. He had nearly reached Frost's side, when he stopped suddenly and sucked in his breath in a swift intake. He had seen the plane.

In a flash Frost was beside him. He rammed the gun into his ribs.

"One crack and off goes your head! Get down flat!"

Silently, the man obeyed. He stretched out an arm's length from the second man who had been shot.

Frost said tensely: "That guy is dead. You didn't hear my gun go off because it's got a silencer, see? Now answer my questions and answer 'em quick!"

"All right," the man grunted.

"How many on this tub?"

"Six."

"One of them a woman?"

"Two women."

"Two!"

Frost thought that over.

"What's this boat doing out here?"

"Meeting the *Mermaid* at midnight."

"Liquor?"

"Yep."

"Well, I'll have to give you the works to get you out of the way," Frost said grimly. He meant it. The man knew he meant it. The game had gone too far to take chances.

"I'm a Texas Ranger."

"I know," was the answer. "We been expecting you. But not like this. You're Frost."

"Expecting me?" Frost thought probably he hadn't heard aright.

"Sure. Catherine said you'd come."

"Who's Catherine?"

Flash's girl."

Frost rolled his tongue against his cheek. "Singleton?"

"Yep."

"I didn't know he had a girl."

"I'll say he had."

Frost hesitated, his mind in a turmoil. The man misconstrued the silence.

"You ain't gonna kill me?" he pleaded. "I'll do anything—"

"Okey," Frost said offhand. "Go over there and call the crew up here. And remember that I've killed two of this crew—and you'll be number three if you make a false move. I'll slug you right through the back of your head. Get up!"

The man walked to the poop ladder, Frost a step behind.

"Hey—Hans!" he yelled through his cupped hands.

Shortly there was a mumble from below.

"Come above and bring Marcelle with you. Hurry!"

Two men climbed out on deck and stood beside the ladder. They hardly were up before Frost stepped out from behind the man and leveled his gun. "Get up in a hurry!" he barked.

They slowly complied.

"Now," Frost went on tensely, "unless you do exactly as I say I'll kill you!"

He looked at the man called Hans. "Throw your gun away!"

The light was feeble, but Frost could see the man scowl. He made no move to comply; he merely grunted.

"Get that gun overboard!"

Still the man said nothing. One of those hard-boiled seamen.

Put-t!

The flame leaped from Frost's gun; there was a muttered oath and the man grabbed his shoulder and moaned, "I'm hit! I'm hit!"

"Get that gun overboard! The next time you stop it with your head!"

There was no mistaking the command now. Frost disliked to shoot the man, but this was no time to quibble. They must be impressed with his determination.

The man groaned and threw his gun overboard with the arm that was still serviceable.

"Get that hand back in the air! And you—throw that gun over! Now yours!"

The men discarded their pistols. Frost lined them up and backed them towards the hatch. "Unbatten it!" he commanded.

They did.

"Pile in!"

"What?"

"Pile in!"

"But, we'll—"

"In there!"

The wounded man called Hans was the last one down. The others aided him. They disappeared below the top, and Frost wrestled the hatch and battened it down as if heading for the open sea. Then he retrieved his pistol and moved to the wheelhouse. The man who lay on deck had been shot through the mouth, and evidently was a first officer. Frost noticed the wheel was chained, so he dragged the body against the skylights and went to the foredeck where he had glimpsed the first sailor.

He had pitched forward on his face, his gun at his feet. Before Frost stooped to inspect him, he kicked the gun across the deck into the water. Then he tugged the man over, saw he, too, was dead, and came back to the after companion. The night now had come on full. The stars were gleaming and a pale moon glowed off the starboard.

Frost went down the steps slowly. He walked along the passage and heard sounds of music, struggling to free itself of the confinement and get into the air. He could sense the struggle. He paused at the cabin door and listened. An electric gramaphone. Someone evidently was unworried. He rapped on the door.

It opened and he thrust his foot inside. He pried it open with his leg and entered, his gun drawn.

He faced a woman—and gasped.

"You!"

"You!"

His companion of La Estrellita!

Here—in full panoply, arrayed like a queen; against a background of luxury. For a moment he was nonplussed. A lot had happened. This was the crowning blow. He gradually recovered, and thought about the awkward picture he presented there with his pistol drawn.

"Miss Stevens," he coughed, embarrassed. "Er—"

"How do you do, Captain?" she said. "Sit down." Frost did so. "Do you find it helps the effect when you visit a young lady with drawn revolver?"

Frost grinned. "Well, I hardly expected to find you like this. I thought—"

"Yes," she beamed; "they are good to me, aren't they?"

She nonchalantly moved across the cabin to a wall telephone. He thought that rather an odd thing for a prisoner to do—telephone. That simple act brought the pieces of the puzzle together with a click. Frost had just been told there were two women on board. One he expected to find a prisoner—Helen Stevens. But this woman was no prisoner—

Catherine!

With pent-up fury he leaped from his chair and was beside her before she could get an answer. He snatched the telephone out of her hand and replaced it. He faced her, flushing with anger.

"Get away!" he said. "And I hope it won't be necessary for me to kill you!"

She lifted her face in a half sneer. "Well," she said, moving in a swagger, "how long do you think you can get away with this high-handed stuff?"

"Don't make me laugh," Frost said.

There was the sound of a knock on a door in another wall than that by which he had entered.

"Who's in there?" he demanded.

"Find out for yourself," she snapped.

"I will," he said. He observed her with something not unlike admiration. "So you're Catherine, eh?" He was a little taken aback.

Disappointed. Once he had had an adventure with her. Men do not easily forget such things. Now it all came back in a rush . . . her indifference to the danger in La Estrellita . . . the tapping of her fingers on the glass was a signal. . . .

He glared: "You tried to trap me, didn't you? Tried to get me killed?"

She laughed. "Why not? You bumped off the only man I ever loved, and for that I'm going to *get* you, Frost. What a pity those saps didn't kill you that night in Algadon!"

"Yes," he mused; "what a pity! You know—you're a damned attractive woman to be mixed up with a rotten gang like this."

"I'm going to stay mixed. You can't bluff me, Frost. I don't scare worth a damn."

"Maybe you don't. Oh, by the way; I neglected to tell you I locked three of your thugs in the hold. Also," this casually, "I had to bump off a couple of 'em. Now who's the woman in the other room?"

"Nobody. That is—"

"Get that door open, or I'll tear it down!"

She got up sullenly and unlocked the narrow door. Through it another woman stumbled, her hair disheveled, her clothes wrinkled, her face worried. She saw Frost and stopped short.

"It's all right," Frost said reassuringly, "I'm a policeman. Who are you?"

"I'm—"

"Don't you talk!" came the swift interruption. "This bum means no good." She tried to reach the woman's side, but Frost intervened.

"Never mind her," he said. "I'm Frost of the Rangers."

"Oh! Frost!" she murmured the words. "I'm Helen Stevens. I've been a prisoner for a week."

"Huh! Are you a newspaper woman?"

"Yes."

Frost grinned broadly, spread his legs and said: "Well, sit down, ladies, and get comfortable. This ought to be good."

Then it was that Frost observed both women were about the same height and build, and that the genuine Helen Stevens wore a brown ensemble similar to the one worn by his companion that night in La Estrellita. He began to see the light.

"A week ago," said Helen Stevens, "I was kidnaped in Jamestown, drugged and brought here. I don't know why. I never had an enemy in my life."

"There's no puzzle there," Frost said. "This jane here is the ex-sweetheart of an ex-racketeer who was allied with the Black Ship gang and bumped off by Hell's Stepsons. She wanted revenge on me; the way to get that was remove you and assume your identity." He smiled appreciatively. "That right, Mrs. Singleton?"

"You go to hell!"

"So," mused Helen Stevens, slightly more at ease, "you're Captain Frost. I was on my way to see you—had a letter from the Adjutant-General. It was stolen with my luggage!"

"I got it," Frost grinned. "You'll learn after a while that this is a high-powered gang you're dealing with."

Helen Stevens was surveying the broad figure of Jerry Frost, remembering tales of his prowess in the skies of France and in the jungles of Latin America—*El Beneficio* they called him then—surveying him in frank admiration.

"I think," Frost said, "it would be wise to get going. This boat has got a date I'd rather not keep. First, I'm afraid we'll have to tie up the hellcat."

The hellcat got to her feet, her eyes burning with passionate hatred, and leaped at Frost. She landed in his lap and they both went over backwards with the chair. His pistol rattled on the hardwood floor.

"Get that gun!" he yelled, a moment before she clawed at his face. She interposed a few choice oaths, and hammered Frost about the ears with her fists. They squirmed on the floor inelegantly until he managed to get a hammer-lock on her arm. She swore and cried out in pain.

"Pipe down and I'll let you go!" Frost said. "Otherwise I'll break it off." His eyes fell on the silk cord knotted around port hole draperies and he said to Helen Stevens, "Get that cord."

She untied it and brought it to him. Frost slipped it around the woman's wrists and tied her hands behind her. Then he took off his belt and strapped it tightly around her ankles. To complete the job he took out his handkerchief and crammed it in her mouth.

"Now," he said; "I need a bandage."

Helen Stevens did not hesitate. She lifted her dress, revealed a sheeny knee and a silk petticoat. She ripped it, jerked off a strip and handed it to Frost.

"Great stuff!" he said. "I'm beginning to think you'll do!"

"You're damned right I'll do!" she admitted.

Frost tied the gag and then stepped back to inspect his craftmanship. Apart from the woman's squirming, and nobody has ever invented a way to stop that, he had to confess it was very good.

"Not bad for a beginner," he observed.

The woman grunted and her eyes flashed. Frost picked her up and deposited her, none too carefully, on a lounge. He whispered in her ear: "Now we're going up to take the wheel." She grunted again, and in a fit of temper wriggled to the floor with a bang.

Frost looked at her loftily. "All right, baby—suit yourself."

Helen Stevens handed him his pistol and said: "Don't you think it would be wise to use the radio and let somebody know where we are?"

Frost slanted his head from side to side as if he had known her a century; decided she, too, was a fluffy bit of femininity. His light mood was sharpened by his success. "Another great idea," he said. "Let's have a look."

They came on deck together, he holding her hand. It was, like the night, warm and soft—he remembered snatches of books and stories he'd read about women . . . regal poise . . . generations of aristocrats to produce one like this . . . long lashes . . . and full red lips. . . . He even tried to recall some poetry.

He looked at her suddenly as if he knew she had read his thoughts. He was blushing. . . . She laughed. He laughed too—not knowing what else to do.

They entered the wheelhouse of the *Catherine B* as she rose on a long swell, poised herself, and settled into the valley of the Gulf. It was dark and quiet, only a light glowed from the compass box; Frost found the switch and pulled it. A light sprang into life at the top of the pilothouse.

On one side was the wireless and without further ado Frost seated himself and cut on the switch. The motor hummed, tiny sparks glowed, and he adjusted the head set. He tapped out a message hurriedly. Presently there was a light cracking sound in the headphone and he bent over his task. He finished and sat up.

"They're on their way," he said.

He took a look at the binnacle and moved to the chart table. "Now to figure out which way to go," he remarked. "I'd hate to wind up in Cuba." He studied the chart for a few silent minutes. Then he moved the wheel and unchained it. "Look," he said, "think you can hold this wheel on one-eighteen when I get her on that course?"

"Sure," she said, still the adventuress.

"I'll have a look around," Frost said. He went to the side of the box and yanked at the control. From somewhere in the boat's depth a bell tinkled. It slowly gained speed. Frost spun the wheel and held her circling until she was on the course he had determined upon as most likely to intercept the cutter he had summoned. Frost reached into his shoulder-holster and took out his other pistol. He laid it on the table beside her. "That's a .38," he said; "fitted with a silencer. And it's ready to blast." She nodded and he went out.

Frost noted that the *Catherine B* was holding steady at about half speed. He went to the rail and unloosed the rope that anchored his plane, snubbed it along the rail and finally tied it off the stern. Then he walked for'ard and went below through the fo'csle.

Helen Stevens, left alone on as weird an adventure as any newspaper woman ever had, gripped the wheel, her teeth clenched, and stared into that disk of white light that held the magic number, 118, wavering across a red line.

Some time later Frost emerged from the shadows of the deck-house and came forward into the wheelhouse wearing a wide smile.

"We're all alone but for the engineer," he said. "Now I'll take charge of that." He took the wheel, and she stood beside him and shivered.

"You might as well get comfortable," he said.

"I'm all right," she said. "I think this is a good time to begin that belated interview. Born?"

"Yes?"

She laughed. "Where?"

"I'd rather talk about you," Frost said. "How long are you going to be around Texas?"

"That depends."

"On what?"

"How long it takes to get this story."

"In that case——" he smiled.

And she smiled.

They probably would have been talking yet had not a siren sounded off the port side some two hours later. Frost rang the signal for power off and went out of the wheelhouse.

"Ahoy, there!"

"Who's there?"

"U.S. Coast Guard!"

"Okey! This is Frost—Texas Rangers!"

The cutter pulled up alongside, its fenders bumped and they lashed on. Half a dozen huskies vaulted the rails. The leader shifted his pistol to his right hand and came forward fast. Frost could see in the half-light he was some sort of an officer.

"Frost?"

"Right!"

"I'm Al Bennett." They shook hands. "We picked up your message. I radioed Clay in Corpus that I'd located you."

Thanks," said Frost. "Can you send a man over to take the wheel? I've got somebody in there who's just about washed up."

"Sure," said Bennett. "Bucko—on the wheel!"

The man saluted smartly and preceded Frost and Bennett into the wheelhouse.

"Miss Stevens this is Mr. Bennett, of the Coast Guard." Bennett nodded his head. "So you're the little girl who's been leading us such a merry chase?"

"I'm afraid so," she said. She took Frost's arm.

"Bennett, there's three of the crew in the hold—one winged. For'ard there's a man dead and beside the sky-light there's another one in the same fix. There is a woman below I had to tie up."

Bennett looked at him, his eyes wide.

"Say," he said, "is it possible you took this baby all alone?"

"It was a cinch." Lightly.

"Yeh? Well. I don't mind telling you the whole Coast Guard has been trying to land this bark for weeks."

"Will you," asked Frost, disregarding the praise, "see that we get into port okey?"

"You bet." He went to the door and spoke to the crew who had come over in the recent boarding. "Pass the word along for the cutter to shove off. You men stay aboard with me. We're going to Corpus." He came back to the wheel.

"We'll go below," Frost said. "Er—"

"Sure," said Bennett, grinning.

"Business," Frost went on. "She's getting—"

"Sure—"

But Frost, self-conscious, refused to let Bennett be diplomatic. Helen Stevens finally had to rush to the rescue. "I'm interviewing him," she explained.

Bennett laughed, full. "That's okey with me, Miss," he said. "But you'd better shove off. Ox Clay and Jimmy O'Neill are on their way out here."

Frost and the woman walked out—close together.

The moment they disappeared Bennett turned to the man at the wheel and said: "Ever hear of anything like it?"

"Beats me."

Bennett looked aft at the shadowy form that rose and fell behind like a phantom. It was Frost's battle plane.

"I guess," said Bennett, soberly, "a guy has got to be a little goofy to try something like this. It wouldn't work once in a hundred times. They must be right about that guy, Frost. I've read of those one-man cyclones, but I never saw one before."

"You said it," contributed the man at the wheel.

The *Catherine B*, in the firm hands of the Coast Guard, slipped on towards Corpus Christi with a grim greyhound of the Gulf for a convoy, and another on the way.

In four hours they would be in port.

Double Check
Thomas Walsh

NIGHTMARE IN MANHATTAN, Thomas Walsh's first novel, one of the most exciting police novels ever written, was rightly awarded the Edgar Allan Poe Award by the Mystery Writers of America as the Best First Mystery of 1950.

Walsh, however, had been writing for the pulps since 1933, and then wrote numerous stories for such better-paying "slicks" as *Collier's* and *The Saturday Evening Post,* as well as numerous contributions to *Ellery Queen's Mystery Magazine.* He won his second Edgar for the short story "Second Chance" in 1978.

When his prize-winning novel was made into a motion picture in the same year in which it was published, the title was changed to *Union Station,* clearly New York's Grand Central Station under a pseudonym. It was well-adapted from the printed page to the screen, losing none of its tension. The entire plot occurs within a 48-hour period and the notion of a deadline looming, while now a cliché of thriller movies, was still fresh when Walsh (1908–1984) wrote this, the first of his eleven novels.

He wrote a half-dozen stories for *Black Mask* in the 1930s, and "Double Check" was the first; it appeared in the issue of July 1933.

*A detective long on brains and a copper long on brawn
team up on a big-loot, murder case*

Double Check

Thomas Walsh

EVINE WAS A SMALL, slender man, thin-featured, and quick of manner. His hair and the wisp of mustache on his upper lip were deep black. His sharp eyes, wrinkled at the corners, watched the man across from him with a mixture of anxiety and forced lightness as he spoke.

"You must understand that I'm not taking it seriously," he said.

Flaherty nodded. He knew the type—money, position, pride and a manner that told nothing whatsoever of the man himself.

The banker's low voice went on more rapidly:

"I received the first letter two weeks ago. After that they kept coming at intervals of two or three days. Of course I paid them no attention—men in my profession are constantly getting letters of this type. Cranks, most of them. But yesterday they put in a phone call here to my office; it was then that I decided to send for the police. Professional advice, you know—" He smiled faintly with an uncertain upward curl of the lips.

Flaherty nodded. "The right thing to do," he said. "Have you got the letters?"

Devine turned slightly in his chair, pressing one of the white-disced buzzers at his side.

"Why, no. Unless Barrett—my secretary—kept them. I didn't imagine—"

A tall man with gray eyes, gray clothes, grayish-brown hair, came noiselessly through the door. He stared coldly at Flaherty after a brief nod.

"No," he answered, when Devine repeated the question. "Sorry—I threw them in the waste-paper basket; in fact, it seemed the best place for that kind of rubbish. I had no idea they were necessary."

Flaherty's lean young face soured. Snobby guy, he thought. "You should have saved them. Sometimes there's a lot to be got out of stuff like that. Hold any more." He turned back to Devine. "What did the phone call say?"

"It came in about noon. When I picked up the receiver there seemed to be two voices at the other end. But they were speaking too far away from the instrument for me to make out the words. Oh, yes—I think I got one; something like Ginger or Jigger. I took it for one of the men's names. When I said hello a voice replied: 'We're not fooling. Have the money by noon Thursday. No police. If you're ready to pay put an ad in the *Morning Herald* to Charlie. We'll let you know what to do with it.' Then they hung up."

"That all?" Flaherty asked, shortly. At the banker's nod he rose and gripped his hat. "Don't do anything until you hear from me; I'll phone you tonight. We might have to put that ad in the morning paper to get them. There's nothing to worry about."

Devine's thin features broke in a smile he couldn't quite control; his tongue tipped out nervously for an instant. "I'm not afraid, of course. I have no intention of paying. They can't frighten me like they would a little shopkeeper. I'll leave it in your hands, Mr. eh—Flaherty."

Flaherty didn't like that eh stuff so much as he went out. He slammed the door behind him and passed through the outer offices of the First Commercial Bank to the shaded crispness of a late September afternoon. His dark, small eyes flickered right and left along the street. Nothing to stuff like that, usually. Still—

He handed in his report at headquarters and was going down the stairs from the chief's office when he met Mike Martin coming up. Mike was big and paunchy, with a gruff voice and hands like fleshed mallets. Beside the younger, slimly muscled Flaherty he resembled a fat pug next a whippet.

Flaherty grabbed his arm and drew him into a niche by the elevator shaft. "Just the man, Mike. You're working with me on an extortion case. Old man's say-so."

"The old man's getting' smart," said Mike. "He musta wanted someone with brains on the job."

"Yeh," said Flaherty. "And he thought you'd pick up a little experience. It's Conrad Devine, head of the Commercial Bank."

Mike took a cigarette from Flaherty's pack and puffed slowly.

"Devine?" he said. "They're not picking smart. There's talk the Commercial's about to crash."

Flaherty grunted. "What bank ain't?" he said. "They called him up yesterday. He says he heard one of the names—it sounded like Jigger to him."

Mike spat thoughtfully into the corner of the wall. "Jigger? That might be Jigger Burns—been pretty quiet for a while now. But he don't figure in a case like this."

Flaherty said: "That's the way I got it. This ain't the Jigger's line. But anything'll do these days."

"Let's see," said Mike. "Jigger's a peter man—expert on nitro. He's cracked enough jackboxes to blow us to hell." He stared at Flaherty wide-eyed, without seeing him. "I saw him in Joe's place Monday night—fourteen minutes to eight. He was wearin' a blue suit, white spats, yella gloves—" Mike stopped admiringly. "Yella gloves! The old lady bought me some last Christmas, but I'm damned if I could ever wear 'em. I had to tell her they were lost. He was talkin' to Johnny Greco."

"You're fading," said Flaherty. "I didn't hear you mention his tie. What you got on Johnny Greco?"

"Tough," said Mike, spitting again. "Thirty-five; five feet eight; one sixty on the hoof; dark hair and eyes; scar on right eyebrow. Up twice for assault—once for homicide. Acquitted—no witnesses. He—"

"Can it," said Flaherty. "I know the ginny. Davis brought him in on a loft job last week, but had to drop him on a writ. He plays around with a Polack girl at the *Esplanade*. We could stop there this evenin' and pick him up."

Mike looked at his watch. "Make it nine," he said. "The old lady's havin' company, and she'll want me around for a bit."

"Run along," said Flaherty bitterly. "They oughta put married coppers on desk duty, with aprons and bibs. I'll bet you look sweet with a baby blue dishtowel spread on that belly of yours. What do you use to make your wash so white, Mr. Martin?"

"Honest to gawd," Mike scowled, "some day, Flaherty, I'm gonna lay you like a rug."

The long vertical sign threw a rush of dirty yellow light across the pavement. The lettering winked on and off rapidly: *Esplanade—Dancing 25c.*

Two dusty, fly-spattered doors gave into a hallway with shabbily carpeted stairs leading up. A quick rush of music, undertoned by voices and sudden, whirled-away gusts of laughter, swept against his ears as Flaherty stepped in, holding the door back for Mike Martin. Flaherty was neat and slender in a brown suit and wine-colored tie; behind him Mike was in gray, unpressed and shiny. His tie was crooked and his soft collar folded up in clumsy flabs.

Flaherty gritted his teeth. "You're the type, fella; watch the girls fightin' for you when we get upstairs. By —— a blind man miles off could tell you were a copper."

"They could," said Mike. "The old man mighta wanted a cop on the job as well as a jig-gollo. If I'd had my good suit back from the tailor's—"

"Yeh," said Flaherty. "I'll work inside. Stick by the door, Mike, and try to hide behind a cus-pidor. Come on."

Mike followed slowly up behind his partner's quick legs. At the stairhead Flaherty tossed a quarter to a girl in a window, and was passed through the turnstile by a tall, pimply faced man with glasses. A small anteroom, lit dimly by wall clusters of frosted red bulbs, and furnished with stuffed lounges and wood-backed settees, opened before him; past this the larger space of the ballroom spread from side to side of the building.

Flaherty pushed his way slowly along the side, looking over the crowd. He came back to the door, went around a second time, a third. After he smoked a cigarette and danced once with a plump brunette he walked out to where Mike was waiting in a chair near the door.

"No luck," he said. "Johnny and the Jigger aren't showing. Maybe they will be in later. We'd better stick."

Mike nodded. Time passed slowly. Now and again men came up the stairs and pushed through the turnstile, greeting the pimply faced guardian as they passed. Flaherty grew restless, lit one cigarette from another, took a few quick puffs and quenched them in the sand bowl at his feet.

They had been waiting almost an hour when a little sallow-faced man came up the stairs and went past them to the men's room. Mike jerked his head.

"Joey Helton, Flaherty. We can give him a try."

Flaherty nodded and followed him across the room to the door. Inside, the little man was washing his hands at the sink. He didn't turn as they entered but jumped quickly when Mike said: "Hello, Joey." The sharp rat's eyes flickered from one to the other, narrowed and beady.

Flaherty said, smiling thinly: "Hello, Joey. We got some news for Johnny the Greek. Seen him lately?"

"I ain't," said the little man. "What's the news?"

"He's been left a dirty pair of socks," said Flaherty. "We wanta see him about washin' them up. Try to remember, Joey."

The little man snarled suddenly. "To hell with you!" He stepped by them with a quick twist of his body for the door.

Flaherty's arm yanked him back, thrust the small body against the sink. "Easy, Joey. Three months without a sniff would soften you up."

Joey glanced at Mike's stony face, licked his lips weakly. He said: "All right. I don't know nothin' about the Greek; he's been comin' here pretty often, and hangin' out with that Polish skirt. That's all I see."

"That's all I want," said Flaherty. "You're a good boy, Joey. When you go out step up to the Polack and say something. But nothin' about this. Got it?"

"Yeh," said Joey. He straightened his tie sullenly and went out. A second later they followed.

Flaherty reached the edge of the dance-floor a yard behind the little man. He watched him thread a way through the crowd, stop before a tall blonde girl near the front. She nodded, turned away, and Joey went on again.

Flaherty went back to Mike. "I'm gonna call Devine," he said. "Stick here."

"Okey," said Mike. "I'll wait."

Flaherty went past the ticket-taker to a phone booth at one side. He thumbed through the book, got his number, dropped a nickel in the box. When he announced himself a man's voice said: "Just a moment, sir." He was trying to get a cigarette from his pack with one hand when a quick, staccato voice broke metallically in the earpiece.

"Mr. Flaherty?" Flaherty grinned a little; there was no eh stuff this time. Devine's voice quivered and ran up swiftly, like a child's. "I've got another message—by phone. They threaten to kill me tonight. They found out about you. My ——! You must get out here at once. If they—"

Flaherty got out his cigarette and scraped a match against the side of the booth. He said: "Don't get excited. We'll have some men out there in ten minutes, maybe less. They're trying to scare you into it. Don't worry."

He hung up. Scared as hell now, but tough enough this afternoon when the steam wasn't on. No guts, that kind. . . .

Mike was waiting for him. "Wanta hop out to Devine's?" Flaherty said. "Pick up a man on

your way. He's got the jitters—thinks they're gonna spot him tonight. I'll stick here; maybe I can get something from the Greek's girl. Call me when you get there."

Mike said: "Okey," and went out towards the stairs. Flaherty stepped on to the dance-floor and looked about. The girl Joey Helton had spoken to was off at one side, in a row of chairs reserved for hostesses. Flaherty walked across the floor and stopped before her. "Dancing this one?" he asked.

She nodded, looked up without interest. When the music started they glided out to the floor. She was as tall almost as Flaherty, with blonde, short-clipped hair, and a heavy sensuous mouth. Her eyes were dark blue, thick-lidded.

They danced on without speaking. When the number was over, Flaherty said: "Thanks. You can step, sweetheart. Have the next?"

She responded with a faint shrug of her bared shoulders. The lights dimmed down and a young man in the band laid aside his instrument, began to croon in a sleepy voice through a small megaphone.

She had a firm, supple curved body. She kept her head turned, eyes over his shoulder. He shifted, tightened his hold.

"You're nice," he said. "Me, I think so. Too nice to waste your time on greaseballs."

She didn't say anything for a moment; then she spoke from the side of her mouth, not turning her head. "Greaseballs?" she said.

"Sure," said Flaherty. "You know who I mean. The little ginny I saw you dancing with last night."

Her face swung up to his, whiffing with it a cheap reek of perfume across his nostrils. There was a faint mocking gleam under her mascaraed lashes.

"I was not here last night." Her voice was low, husky, with a thin blur of accent.

Flaherty laughed. "Musta been the night before. I see you with him a lot. Steady?"

She shrugged, humming the song the band played, deep in her throat.

"I get breaks like that," Flaherty said. "Any chance of ditchin' him for dinner tonight?"

"No," she said. "I got a sick mother."

"I know the song," Flaherty answered. "The old man ain't so well and you're keepin' the kid sister in a convent. All right, girlie; I'll see you again."

When the music was over he let her go back to her seat. She was meeting someone, probably; he'd have to take a chance on that being Johnny Greco. He resigned himself to wait, looking at his watch. Twenty minutes past ten; Mike's call would be due now.

He walked out to the anteroom and smoked a cigarette. When the phone in the booth tinkled he went across and into it before the pimply faced man could turn.

"Hello," he said.

"Flaherty?" Under Mike Martin's furred voice pulsed a ripple of excitement. "Better get out here quick, boy. Someone laid a pineapple in Devine's car. The chauffeur and him was blown to hell not five minutes ago."

Flaherty got a taxi at the corner and stared tense-eyed into the darkness during the ten-minute ride. What was coming off? Johnny Greco was no fool; neither was Jigger Burns. Bumping a guy was a dough job—they weren't in it for fun. Devine hadn't come through—they didn't give him time. Force of example, so that the next heavy man they touched wouldn't squawk? That, maybe. He wondered what Mike had seen.

The cab swung into the quiet darkness of Magnolia Avenue. Three blocks farther on, a knot of people huddled together under the pale glint of a street lamp. Lights gleamed from houses all about; hastily clad people grouped in doorways, called to each other in shrill tones from window to window.

Flaherty got out and paid the driver. "Wait ten minutes," he said.

Devine's house was set back from the road on a low terrace. Flaherty saw it as a large three-story building, with a curve of graveled driveway leading whitely up across the dark lawn. A thick hedge banked it on the street side; when Flaherty cut in through this on the driveway a uniformed figure stepped out before him. He was fishing for his badge when Mike Martin came out from the shadows.

"All right, Smith," he said. "Get the crowd away. It's up here, Flaherty."

They went up in silence to the top of the hill. Lights poured from the ground-floor windows, sending a flood of illumination across grass and shrubbery. Ragged curtain ends fluttered out through the smashed panes; the stoop to the porch sagged drunkenly, half of it toppled on its side and resting on the earth. The porch itself had been a Colonial affair, tall, white, with slim pillars and a curved portico. Three of the pillars were snapped off in the center, and at the right end a segment of roof hung down like a misshapen curtain.

The car squatted before the house, a foot away from the stoop. In the light it was a twisted and charred mass of grayish metal. The top was blown off, and fragments of glass from its windows littered the ground with little silver shreds of light. At the side nearest Flaherty the metal warped outward in a great hole.

"It's a morgue job," said Mike. "You couldn't identify either of them with a microscope."

Flaherty bent and looked inside. When he straightened, his face was grayish. "Cripes!" he said.

"Yes," said Mike. "Messy, hah?"

"Did you see it go up?"

Mike spat and nodded. "We'd just got here," he said. "I grabbed Smith at the station and we came out in the flivver. I didn't see anybody in the street. I told Smith to wait and crossed over. Then I saw a little guy in a top hat come down the stoop and get into the car."

Flaherty scowled at his feet. "Devine," he said. "I thought the damn' fool would know enough to stick inside."

"I heard the starter begin to purr—just for a second. Then I felt the pineapple bust loose. I didn't see anything—it slammed me back through the bushes like I was a laundry bag. When I got up here it was all over."

Flaherty lit a cigarette and tossed the match in the grass. For a second the flame scooped his lean, sharp face out of the shadow.

"They might have had it wired to the motor. But then why the hell didn't it blast out comin' from the garage? What was the chauffeur doin'? Did he leave the bus at all after bringin' it out?"

"I don't know," Mike answered. "I haven't had time to talk to the servants. They're so scared they're blubberin'. They got an English butler in there you should see, Flaherty. Gawd! He'll give the laundry a job this week."

"See what the chauffeur was doin'." Flaherty said. "You might get a tip questionin' the people around here. I'm goin' back for Johnny Greco and the Jigger. This is where the nitro came in, Mike."

Blocks distant a siren screamed. Flaherty tossed aside his cigarette.

"That's probably the old man. Devine was a big shot in this burg; he'll wanta know how come. I'll leave you get the congrats, Mike. So-long. I'll phone you at headquarters later."

Mike cursed bitterly. "You yella——" he said. "The old man will save some for you. I'll see to that."

At the corner Flaherty's taxi swerved to avoid the police car, then straightened out along Magnolia Avenue. They made good time; it was ten minutes past eleven by Flaherty's watch when they pulled up before the *Esplanade*.

The crowd inside was thicker, gayer, noisier. Flaherty sifted through the mob, passed to the anteroom, came back to the dance-floor. The blonde was nowhere in sight. He went out to the gate; to the pimply faced man on duty he said: "Where'd the tall blonde go? That Polack girl——"

The man shrugged. "She left ten minutes ago."

Flaherty cursed. "Where does she live?" he snapped.

"I'm not runnin' that kind of place," pimply face said. Behind the lenses his eyes were small and guarded. "There's plenty of blondes in there, guy."

Flaherty yanked him around; he said, hard-eyed: "Where does she live?"

Pimply face licked his lips uncertainly and then shot out his jaw. "What you lookin' for, guy? Trouble? I told you—"

"Yeh," said Flaherty. "I heard you the first time. I guess you ain't got the records. You're in a spot, fella. You know the regulations on joints like this."

Pimply face tried to hold his stare and failed. He said sullenly: "Sure I got the records. Wait a minute. I'll see."

He went across to the window, spoke to the girl inside, and came back with a small white filing slip in his hand. "Anna Brinski—213 Allington Place," he said, raising his eyes furtively to Flaherty's. "What's the trouble? Any—"

Flaherty let his words drift out without answering. He took the stairs three at a step and turned left at the door. Four blocks over, Allington Place emptied into the avenue: a narrow, darkly lit thoroughfare, with two parallel rows of cheap brownstone tenements leading down. He found 213 by counting off six houses from the corner; the numbers over the door, faded by time and weather, were indistinguishable in the gloom.

In the vestibule he struck a match, passing the flame over the bells. He read near the end: Anna Brinski, Apt. 43. The door swung back at his touch, admitting him to a narrow hall, palely lit.

He went up on his toes, two steps at a time, without sound. A radio moaned harshly in one of the flats, squawked with a sudden inrush of static as he passed; he caught fragments of voices, snores, the lingering thick odor of fried fish.

At the top of the flight a single bulb glowed weakly, shedding a wan light over the apartment doors. There were six on each floor; the one numbered three was in an angle near the front. When he got to the fourth landing Flaherty stopped and listened; he could hear nothing but the high querulous voice of a drunken woman below.

His footsteps patted on the oilcloth, slid off into the darkness with low echoes. He rapped sharply, twice, on the door of 43—there was no bell.

After a minute of quietness someone said inside: "Who's there?"

Flaherty said hoarsely: "Anna? Johnny sent me over. He can't meet you tonight. He's bein' tailed."

She said something short, bitterly. Flaherty grinned. When the door opened a crack he laid his body against it and pushed.

The room inside was brightly lit. There was a day-bed at one end, not yet made up, a messy dressing-table across from it, a tall floor-lamp with a torn shade near the window. The air was drenched with the brassy smell of burnt out cigarettes. Clothes littered the couch, poured over on to the floor; an open suitcase lay on the small center-table.

"So you're goin' away," said Flaherty, leaning against the door. "You shoulda let me know, Anna."

Her hair was down, stuck with curlers; she was wearing a sleazy dressing-gown. She smiled softly, but her eyes kept the same.

"The cheap bull," she said. "Where do you think?"

"No fun," said Flaherty. "I'm asking, Anna."

He locked the door behind him and went across to the hall at one end that led into the tiny kitchenette and bath. Both were empty.

He grinned coming back. "So Joey Helton squeaked to you after all. We'll have to mark him up a point."

She sat down on the couch and picked a cigarette from the heavy bronze smoking-stand at the side. "What do you want?" she said.

"Nothin' much," said Flaherty. "Where were you gonna meet Johnny Greco?"

She shrugged. Her gown slipped down and she pulled it up, lazily, with one hand. "I don't know him—this Johnny."

Flaherty's eyes narrowed. "You're wastin' your time on that stuff, sister. Where were you to meet him?"

She stared down at the cigarette in her hand without answering. Flaherty turned away from her and walked over to the suitcase. He thumbed through the flap in the top. He picked up the garments one by one, felt them through, dropped them to the floor. Her eyes changed color, darkened, in the cone of light from the lamp. She spat out something that Flaherty couldn't understand.

He stared at her for a second. "Don't say it in English," he said. "I'm the kind of guy that hasn't got any chivalry."

When the bag was empty he went over to the couch and reached down for the pocket-book she had tried to hide with her back. As he bent for it she was on him like a tigress, without warning. He snapped his elbow up under her chin, felt the jarring click of teeth coming together as her knee shot up viciously to his stomach, stabbing him with pain. He grabbed her wrist; his grasp tightened, twisted until she moaned suddenly and went soft in his arms. He dropped her roughly to the couch and picked up the bag.

"Any more?" he asked.

She lay staring up at him, her eyes blazing. After a minute Flaherty turned his attention to the bag. Two folded pink strips of paper were on top; he shook them out, dropping his eyes along the lines. "Los Angeles!" He whistled. "Gettin' out far, weren't you? The other one for Johnny—" He put them in his pocket. "Get dressed, kid; I'm gonna take you for a little ride downtown. I know a couple of guys there that have the knack of getting' questions answered."

She sat up sullenly, rubbing her wrists. He tossed her a dress from the heap and fished in his pockets for his cigarettes. He was taking them out when knuckles rapped quickly on the door.

Half into the dress she stopped, looked up. Her mouth opened. Flaherty's grasp yanked her head back in an instant.

"Quiet," he said softly. "It'll be better for you later, Anna."

The knuckles rapped again. In two steps Flaherty was by the door, swinging it back, hidden as it came. Anna stood motionless by the couch.

A tall, gray-clad man entered, his head jerking forward as he saw her. He spoke quickly, without breath. "Anna! It's all set. I—"

He might have heard Flaherty breathe. In the quick twist of his head under a lowered hat brim Flaherty could see nothing but lips and a sharp chin. He said, pushing the door to behind him: "Drop it, guy." The other snarled, his eyes wavering for an instant to Anna.

"You dirty little—"

Flaherty shot as the man's gun came out, dropping him limply, suddenly, like a pricked balloon. The short, sharp crash of the gun echoed back from the walls to a beating silence. Flaherty heard faintly the drunken woman still quarreling as he bent over the body.

"You've killed him," said Anna. Her voice was quiet enough. She stood by the bronze stand, the cigarette in her fingers drifting smoke lazily across her face.

Flaherty said nothing. He gripped the man's shoulders and swung him around back to Anna for a brief moment. At the sound of her rush behind him he straightened too late. On one knee as he brought the gun up he saw the light glinting dully on the edge of the bronze base. Then it crashed down in a vicious arc, before the dark glitter of her eyes. Flaherty fell forward across the dead man, his gun dropping from his hand, his mind whirling and lost in red-streaked confusion.

He was pulled back to consciousness slowly by a throbbing agony over his left ear. When he opened his eyes the light pierced them like tiny knives driving into his skull. He pushed the body away from him, got to his knees, his feet, stood swaying unsteadily as he looked around.

The lights in the room were still lit, but it was very quiet. Anna, of course, was gone. He went out to the kitchen and put his head under the faucet, letting the water pour coldly over his cheek. The skin was unbroken, but there was a lump that felt like an apple where the blow had landed.

After a minute he felt better; he dried off his face and returned to the living-room, looking at his watch. Quarter past twelve. He hadn't been out long; half hour maybe—not more. He

gripped the dead body and swung it over on its back.

He found himself looking at the thin, pale face of Barrett, the banker's secretary. There was a hole just over the bridge of his nose. Flaherty squatted on the floor, resting his body on his clenched hands. Barrett!

It came clearer to him in a while. Barrett and Anna—the two of them had framed it from the start. Then where did Johnny Greco and the Jigger come in? Had Anna been using Barrett all the time, ready to ring in the other two for the big prize?

He cursed his aching head. This mixed it up worse than ever. If Barrett was the brains he wouldn't have stood for the blow-up—not without the money. He'd be in a game like this once, for big stakes—but he wasn't the kind to risk it as a steady racket. He hadn't the guts. Then why had Devine been killed without a chance to get the money?

Flaherty couldn't figure it. Unless there was something more, something in back, something he hadn't come upon— He pushed back the dead man's coat and turned out his pockets. A wallet, dark leather, well used; a few bills, a letter, some cards; a slip of white paper, without inscription, marked in hasty handwriting— 1934. That was all.

He put the paper in his pocket, picked up the gun, and rose. He closed the door behind him, leaving the lights still lit and the dead eyes of Barrett staring glassily at the ceiling. The hall was pretty quiet as he descended. He wondered if anyone had heard the shot. Taken it for backfire if they had; it wouldn't be healthy to meddle in a joint like this.

He turned left on the pavement and headed for the avenue, grateful for the cool night air that swept over his forehead. He had almost reached the corner when a car turned in. It raced along smoothly, slowed as it passed him. He had an instant's warning in the split-second glitter of steel from the seat.

At his side a row of ashcans flanked the dark space of an area. He dropped to the ground, rolled over, heard the ting of the bullets, sharp and vicious, as they hit the metal cans. He turned quickly in the narrow space, fired twice. The car flashed under the lamps like a black monster, spitting four more stabs of orange from its side before it rounded the corner at the far end and roared away.

Windows slammed up and a man's voice shouted hoarsely. Flaherty rose from his shelter, brushing his pants carefully. It was getting hot now. They'd come back for him, sure enough; if he'd been out five minutes longer, there'd be two stiffs up there now instead of one. Why? What was coming off, so important that they had to get him out of the way?

It was Anna, of course. She was the only one who knew where he was. She had told Johnny, and he came back to finish the job. The game wasn't over yet, then. And whatever was going to happen they were afraid he would spoil—they thought that somehow, somewhere he'd gotten a tip. What the hell could it be?

It worried Flaherty. Did they take him for a sucker, potting at him like that? What was under his double-blanked eyes that he couldn't see?

Farther down the avenue there was an all-night drug-store. Flaherty went in and called headquarters; after a minute he was connected with Mike Martin.

He said: "Meet me at the corner of Lynch and Holland as soon as you can make it. Things are popping, Mike."

Outside again he waited in the darkened entrance of a jewelry store. Lynch Street, a thoroughfare of office buildings and stockbrokers' firms, stretched dark and silent before him, its blackness interspersed by scattered yellow pools from street lamps. The black bulk of Devine's bank squatted back from the pavement a half block away. Flaherty lit a cigarette and scowled at it. Things had moved fast in ten hours. Now—

A dull monstrous boom, a roll of thunder in a confined space, crashed in one wave down the avenue. A golden flare burst up and expired in an instant behind the glass doors of the Commercial bank.

Flaherty raced up the street, bringing his gun loose. A block away he heard the shrill pipe of a police whistle, and closer at hand the rasping squeal of car brakes. He swung around to see Mike Martin hop off a taxi running-board and rush to him across the sidewalk.

"Take the front," snapped Flaherty. "Don't go in. They've not had time to scatter."

He raced around the side of the building over the grass plot that rimmed it. A door gaped open in the rear, with the red bulb of a night-light on top. In its glow Flaherty saw that the yard, rimmed by a high stone fence in back, was empty. They had to get out the front way then, or around by the grass plot. And they couldn't have, yet. They were bottled.

He got inside, keeping to the shadows. A heavy puff of smoke was rising slowly from the center of the building's long room; as he advanced cautiously it thinned, faded slowly against the high stone ceiling. Between the book-keepers' desks in back and the glass partitioned cashiers' cages in front there was a wide, iron-gated alcove. The gate was open now, with the sprawled figure of a man before it.

Flaherty was motionless in the shadow, listening. He could hear nothing. Queer, this— They must have known the explosion would be heard, must have known—

After an irresolute moment he stepped over the dead man and into the lighted alcove, automatic ready before him. The huge steel door of the vault was flung outward against the wall, the center of it torn and twisted like paper by the charge. Flaherty gave it a glance and then went back to the watchman, rolling him over. An old, wizened face, not much expression now, a bullet hole through the back of his head. Flaherty got up and went softly to the back door.

Mike stood in the shadows outside, dropping his raised arm when he saw Flaherty.

"The man on beat came up. I left him at the front. See anything, Flaherty?"

Flaherty took a second before answering. "The watchman's stiff, Mike. He's been dead at least an hour. And the vault's been cleaned of cash."

"Hell," said Mike. "They couldn't have cleaned it; they didn't have time."

"No," said Flaherty. "They didn't have time, Mike—that's the funny part."

After a second he continued: "We haven't figured the thing right from the start. There's something in back of this we're not even sniffing. It don't hang together the way it is. If they wanted to rob the bank what did they kill Devine for? He wasn't in the way."

"I don't get you," said Mike. "It's open and shut to me. They bump off Devine but don't get the money. All right—they figure they're in and they might as well get somethin' out of it, so they lam back here and blow the vault. Jigger's opened ones a lot tougher than this cheesebox."

Flaherty said: "That's one way, Mike. But why did they clean the vault first and then blow it? That's the only answer—we both know they didn't have time after the charge went off. A guy would do that just for one reason; to make it look—" He stopped. After a breath he said: "Oh!" softly, and whistled.

Mike moved restlessly. "What the hell you gettin' at?"

"I was just wonderin'," said Flaherty, "how tall Jigger Burns is."

"He's a little guy. Not much over five five."

Flaherty grunted. "It's beginnin' to fit." From his upper vest pocket he took a small slip of paper and held it out to Mike. After a minute Mike handed it back. "1934? Don't mean nothin' to me."

Flaherty rapped out briefly the events of the night. When he had finished Mike said: "The secretary, hah? I'll be double damned."

"We ain't got much time. What do you think that number means?"

Mike pushed back his hat. "A street number, d'ye think—"

"Yeh," said Flaherty, "only there ain't a street name on it. It might be a post-office box only there ain't no key. Maybe it's next year."

Mike stirred uneasily. "Lay off," he said.

"Some day, honest to gawd, I'm gonna lay you like a rug."

Flaherty said: "I found it on Barrett's body. What's he carryin' it around for? Because it's something important—something he mustn't forget. Take it that way. Then he probably got to meet someone there tonight—they haven't much time—at 1934. It wouldn't be a street number; he'd know the house, and wouldn't hafta mark the number down on paper. You can't run out and hire a house in the middle of the night. Besides the getaway has to be fast, so it would be somethin' they could hire any time and leave when they wanted. What's left? A hotel room?"

"I was gonna say it," Mike answered. "If it's a hotel there's only two in town high enough for a number like that: The *Sherman* and the *Barrisford*."

Flaherty crushed the slip in his pocket. "There'll be a squad along any minute. Stay till they slow, Mike. Let them go through the place—they won't find anything. Then hop over to the *Sherman;* that's the nearest and busiest. The clerk'll know if I'm upstairs. If I'm not, try the *Barrisford*."

He left Mike and walked swiftly to the corner after a word to the policeman in front. Three blocks up and two over he entered the lobby of the hotel *Sherman*. From the restaurant in back, swift syncopated strains of dance music floated out, but the lobby itself was almost deserted.

The clerk at the desk was a slight, superior-looking person with a pale face and exquisite hands. When Flaherty flashed the badge his lower lip dropped. He said: "Oh—oh! Really, I hope—"

Flaherty fumbled for the paper. "You have nineteen floors, haven't you?"

The clerk looked relieved. "No," he said. "There are only eighteen. Of course—"

Flaherty stopped searching; he cursed and chewed his lip while the little man eyed him apprehensively. "How tall's the *Barrisford*?" he snapped.

"Sixteen, I believe. I know we're the biggest in town. Eight hundred rooms—"

Flaherty got out the paper and looked again. No mistake: 1934. That settled that. Telephone number—safe deposit vault, maybe? But how—

The clerk cleared his throat nervously. "It's funny," he said. "I don't know whether you— You see, we have to be careful, there are so many superstitious people. We haven't a floor numbered thirteen—we skipped it. Thirteen is fourteen and so on. We really have only eighteen floors though our room numbers run up to nineteen. Now if you—"

Flaherty, turning away, whirled back. "Who's in 1934? Get it quick. I want the key."

The clerk jumped at his voice. He came back from the inner office holding a key, his eyes worried.

"A gentleman registered this evening for that room—a Mr. Walker. Is there anything wrong? I can't let you have this without our man—"

Flaherty reached over and grabbed the key. "Who's your house dick—Gilmour? Send him up as soon as you locate him. Tell him to be careful—it won't be a picnic. There'll be shooting."

He headed across the lobby while the clerk said: "Oh—oh," faintly.

At the top floor Flaherty left the elevator and stepped into a long red carpeted corridor, empty and brightly lit. He looked at the room numbers and swung to his left.

Nineteen thirty-four was near the end of the hall. He stood outside, listening. No sound . . . He fitted the key in the lock and twisted the knob an inch at a time, softly. A tiny line of blackness appeared at the crack and Flaherty bent double, slipped through in a flash, silently.

Darkness netted him in, diffused faintly by two windows at the far side. He made out the dim white splotch of a bed to his right—nothing more in the light-blurred focus of his gaze. Nothing happened. He stood motionless an instant, surprised and uneasy, before turning to the wall for the light switch.

The faintest flicker of darkness moved from his left—in the same instant he felt a thin rush of air, and something hard, sharp-edged, crashed viciously into his wrist, knocking his gun to the floor. He dropped, feeling for it, as the lights overhead snapped on. A woman's leg flicked past his hand, kicking the revolver across the rug. Someone said in a soft, oily voice: "Hold it, Flaherty."

Flaherty got up slowly to his knees, his lips pressed tight against the pain in his wrist. There were three people in the room: Anna, behind him and to his left, Johnny the Greek near the door, automatic in hand, and a slender small man in a chair, bound to it and gagged.

Johnny's face, edged with a bluish bristle of beard, twisted in a leer. "Smart guy, Flaherty. Too bad we was expectin' you. Next time you're in a lobby look around. There's telephones."

"I shoulda thought of a lookout," said Flaherty. "But this don't help you, Johnny; I got the joint tied up in a knot. The outside's lousy with cops."

Johnny sneered. "Sez you. That stuff don't go, dick—you came into the lobby alone. Your pals'll be along, but that'll be too late to do you any good. We're about through here." His eyes flickered to Anna. "Behind him, kid." To Flaherty he said: "Get over to that chair, snappy."

Flaherty went over slowly and sat down, watching his face. There wasn't a chance. Johnny stared at him through narrow lids, his eyes small and hard like balls of black glass. Killer's eyes . . .

"I'll have to get some towels," Anna said. "They'll do for his arms." She moved back of him towards the bathroom.

The little man made sounds under his gag. Flaherty looked at him and saw a large head with blond, oddly streaked hair, pale eyes, clean shaven upper lip.

"What you want?" snarled Johnny. The sounds continued. He dropped one hand and loosened the gag. "Spit it quick, fella."

The little man breathed hoarsely once or twice before speaking. He looked at Flaherty and quickly away. His words were rapid, imploring.

"You've got the money—give me a chance to get free. I'll leave you downstairs. If he knows who I am—"

"I know you're Conrad Devine," said Flaherty. He was stalling for time. Where the hell were Gilmour and Mike Martin? If he could keep them here five minutes— "You shaved off your mustache and blondined your hair—not a very good job, but good enough to fool anybody who thought you were dead. And who wouldn't?"

The little man snarled savagely; he said to Johnny: "You see?"

"Sure," said Flaherty. "Your bank was on the rocks and you didn't have a nickel to save it. You thought you'd get what you could, so you framed this little racket with Barrett. The fact that you two birds got where you did in a bank is a laugh.

"Barrett knew Anna through going to the dance hall, and she got you in with Jigger Burns. You let Jigger in on it for a cut—you needed him for the bombs. You figured everything was as safe as Gibraltar—

"When I phoned tonight you made out you were scared, asked me to come right out. You cooked up some story for Jigger Burns—you were about the same size—and sent him out to your car when you saw the police flivver arrive. Fitted in one of your top hats, I was supposed to recognize your figger—I'd be too far away to see the face—watch you blown to hell, and give you a perfect alibi. Even the cops wouldn't be dumb enough to suspect a dead man.

"You mentioned Jigger to me at your office so I'd be lookin' for him. That made everything hotsy-totsy: you'd be livin' in another town with enough dough to last you the rest of your life, the police would be lookin' for a guy that was in a thousand bits, and I'd be left holdin' the bag. Yeh—"

Johnny said: "That ain't such a bad idea, Flaherty. I like to see cops holdin' the bag. We'll give you a start, Devine—but no breaks, guy! Let him loose, Anna."

There was a sudden quick flicker in Devine's eyes, instantly hid. Flaherty seeing it, said noth-ing. Anna came over in a moment with the tow-els and knelt behind Flaherty, pressing his arms together.

Flaherty continued to talk, while Devine stretched himself with a long sigh and went over to the bed, watched carefully by Johnny.

"I got the lead at your bank," Flaherty droned on. "The vault was blown after the money was taken. Why? To make it look like a strong-arm job. Whoever pulled it got in the back door with a key, murdered the watchman, and opened the vault with the combination. Then they set the time bomb and beat it. I got to thinkin' about you then, Devine. You had the keys and knew the combinations. There was talk your bank was crackin'; the body in the car couldn't be identi-fied. You didn't have any notes to show me— you were too smart to rib them yourself—"

"Shut up," snarled Johnny. "Got him fast, Anna?"

Flaherty laughed. "And at the end they gypped you, at that. When you got the dough and came back here to lie low for a couple of days before headin' out, the girl friend and Johnny fix you like a baby and take away the candy. Hell—"

The banker's pale eyes were slits of ice. His lips were frozen in a wrenched smile. "You're very clever," he said.

Anna yanked the toweling tight. As she began to fasten the knot Flaherty flexed his arms, push-ing her backward to the floor. Johnny came for-ward a step, not watching Devine, his eyes vicious. "Once more and I drop you, guy."

Flaherty got it then, watching the set, pinched-in face of Devine as his hand dropped to his overcoat pocket. Johnny had frisked him; had he frisked the topcoat on the bed? The damn' fool—Flaherty got his weight on his toes, ready to leap.

"Yeh," said Johnny. "Be a good boy. You ought—"

Anna screamed suddenly, seeing the sudden bulge in the banker's pocket.

"Johnny! He—"

Johnny whirled, opening his mouth. The

shot came before he could speak. He gave a puffy, choked grunt, fell flatly to the floor.

At the report Flaherty flung himself face downward behind the bed. Johnny was on the other side, moaning, his gun a foot away from his clenched hand. Flaherty wriggled forward, stretched his arm, grabbed the butt as darkness fell at a click over the room.

There was a rush of feet in the hall and confused shouts. Someone lunged furiously at the door; Flaherty heard Mike Martin's bull voice roaring.

Devine fired twice. The bullets dug splinters from the floor, flung them in Flaherty's face. Flaherty didn't shoot; he crouched back, watching the far wall.

In the darkness Anna kept screaming shrilly, terribly. There was a rustle of motion, a scraping, a sudden rush, before the pale square of the window on the far side was darkened by a slender figure. Flaherty could see it very clearly. He fired once.

The door to the hall crashed back, and a slit of light melted instantly into the greater brilliance of the ceiling bulbs. Mike was by the switch, covering the room. In the doorway stood Gilmour, the house detective, his fat face pale and flabby. "What the hell!" he said.

Flaherty got to his feet. "It's all right," he said. "The party's over, fella."

In the center of the room Anna was on her knees over Johnny, sobbing. The Greek didn't seem badly hurt; he sat up and stripped off his bloody coat, cursing sullenly under Gilmour's revolver.

On the other side a breeze from the open window puffed the curtains lightly past the figure of Devine that lay half across the sill. It didn't move.

Flaherty went over and lifted it back from the fire-escape, then reached out and pulled in the yellow leather bag Devine had pushed before him. Under two shirts on top, crisp piles of greenbacks were stacked row on row to the bottom.

Flaherty grunted, caressed them a second with his long fingers. "What a haul," he said. "And I'd have to be a copper."

Mike Martin's puffy red face showed over his shoulder. "What's all the shootin', Flaherty? Who the hell is that?"

"Ain't you heard?" said Flaherty. "It's Santa Claus."

Mike cursed. "Honest to gawd," he said, "some day, Flaherty, I'm gonna lay you like a rug."

Stag Party

Charles G. Booth

ONCE AN ENORMOUSLY successful novelist and writer of pulp stories, Charles G. Booth (1896–1949) is a name largely forgotten today, his fiction generally unread, while the films with which he was involved have taken on cult status and more.

He won an Academy Award for writing the best original story of the spy thriller, *The House on 92nd Street* (1945), an early work of documentary realism. His novel *Mr. Angel Comes Aboard* was filmed as *Johnny Angel* in 1945, a year after publication, and he wrote the novel *The General Died at Dawn,* which was filmed with Gary Cooper in 1936.

Born in Manchester, England, he emigrated to Canada before moving to Los Angeles in 1922, eventually becoming a contract writer for 20th Century Fox.

As with much of his fiction, "Stag Party" has a strong sense of place and evokes its time wonderfully. The hero, preparing for a showdown with gangsters in an underworld-run nightclub, dresses in his dinner jacket so that he'll look his best for the confrontation.

Originally published in the November 1933, issue of *Black Mask,* "Stag Party" is the first and longest of three novellas featuring McFee of the Blue Shield Detective Agency to be collected in one of the rarest private eye volumes of the 1940s, *Murder Strikes Thrice* (1946), published by the short-lived paperback publisher Bond.

Stag Party
Charles G. Booth

1

STIRRING HIS COFFEE McFee—Blue Shield Detective Agency—thought he had seen the girl somewhere. She had dull red hair. She had a subtle red mouth and experienced eyes with green lights in them. That was plenty. But over her provocative beauty, lay a hard sophistication as brightly polished as new nickel.

McFee said, "You ought to be in pictures."

"I've been in pictures." Her voice was husky. "That's where you've seen me."

"No, it isn't," McFee said. "Sit down. Coffee?"

"Black."

The girl let herself drop into the chair on the other side of the table. Her wrap fell back. She wore an evening gown of jade green velvet and a necklace of square-cut emeralds. Her eyes were guarded but urgent; desperate, perhaps.

Abruptly, she asked, "Do I look like a fool?"

"I dunno what a fool looks like." McFee finished his apple pie, sugared his coffee. His movements, the flow of his words, the level staring of his V-thatched, somber eyes were as precisely balanced as the timing of a clock. The girl was restlessly tapping the table pedestal with a green satin pump when McFee asked: Some'dy tell you I was here?"

"Jules—at the door. He's been with Cato's ever since I can remember."

A waiter came, drew the booth curtains, went away. McFee gave the girl a cigarette. A flame came into each of her eyes and she began to pelt him with little hard bullets of words.

"I am Irene Mayo. Rance Damon and I were dining here one night and Rance pointed you out. He said, 'That's McFee, the Blue Shield operative.' Jules told us you often dropped in for coffee around midnight—"

McFee muttered, "Coffee and Cato's apple pie."

"Yes. That's what Jules told us. And Rance said, 'Irene, if you ever run into a jam get McFee.' So I knew if you were here—"

"What sort of jam you in?"

"I don't know." The girl stared at the ruddy vitality of McFee, shivered. "Rance and I left my apartment—the St. Regis—around eleven. We were going to the Cockatoo for supper and some dancing, but we didn't get there."

"Pretty close," McFee said.

She nodded. "Rance had just turned into Carter, from Second, when he saw Sam Melrose—"

"That's funny," McFee said. He tapped a newspaper beside his coffee cup. "The Trib says Melrose is aboard Larry Knudson's yacht. Has been all week."

Irene Mayo flared out, "That's what Rance said. That's why he went after him. Melrose has been evading the Grand Jury ever since they opened up that Shelldon scandal. Rance said they couldn't serve him."

"I dunno that indicting him'll do any good,"

McFee muttered, frowning. "Sam took the town over when Gaylord rubbed out, and he's got his hooks in deep. Damon saw Melrose and went after him, you said—"

"Into the Gaiety Theatre. Rance parked on Second. The house was dark—after eleven—"

McFee cut in, "Melrose owns the Gaiety now."

"Rance told me. He said he'd be back in fifteen minutes—less, maybe. But he had to see Melrose." The girl's green eyes dilated a little. "I waited an hour and fifteen minutes. He didn't come back. I couldn't stand it any longer. I went to the lobby doors. They were locked. The box office was locked. I could see into the theatre. It was dark."

McFee said, "You tried the alley fire exits?"

"I didn't think of those. But why would Rance—"

The girl stared at McFee with terrified eyes. "Nothing can have happened—I mean, Melrose wouldn't dare—"

"I dunno, Sam Melrose—"

McFee saw the girl's red mouth lose its subtlety in the sharp twitching of the lip muscles. He stood up. "Put that coffee under your belt and stay here till I come back."

2

McFee crossed Third and went down Carter. A late street car rumbled somewhere along Brant, but the town was quiet. He walked fast for half a block.

Cato's had been at Third and Carter when the town was young and the Gaiety Theatre had billed Martin Thomas in Othello and William Gillette in Sherlock Holmes. That had been before business moved west and the corner had gone pawn shop and fire sale, and buttoned itself on to Chinatown. Second and Carter's had been McFee's nursery. Cato's hadn't moved because Signor Cato and Papa Dubois had known the value of tradition to the restaurant business, and because M. Papoulas, the present proprietor,

also knew it. But Cato's had kept its head up. The Gaiety had gone burleycue.

McFee tried the lobby doors. They were tight. The interior of the theatre was black. Light from the street seeped into the lobby. On the walls were life-sized tinted photographs of the girls. A legend under one of them said Mabel Leclair. She Knocked 'Em Cold on Broadway.

An alley separated the Gaiety Building from the Palace Hotel at Second. The Gaiety had two exit doors in the north side of the alley. On the south side the Palace had a service entrance. Instead of turning into the alley, McFee went to where Maggie O'Day had her ten-by-four hole-in-the-wall in the hotel building. She was putting her stock away. McFee bought a pack of cigarettes.

He said, "Seen Sam Melrose lately, Maggie?"

She was a little dark witch of a woman with rouged cheek bones and tragic purple-brown eyes. Like McFee and the Gaiety girls, she belonged to the picture. Always had. In the Gaiety's Olga Nethersole–melodrama days, she had played minor parts. That had been about the time the late Senator Gaylord was coming into power. Things had happened, and she had gone to singing in Sullivan's saloon on Second, until a street car accident had crippled her hip. Now she leaned on a crutch in her hole-in-the-wall and shook dice with the dicks and the Gaiety girls. Midnight or later she rolled herself home in a wheel chair she kept in the Gaiety alley.

"Sam's getting up in the world," the old woman answered.

"See him go into the Gaiety a while back?"

"Sam go into the Gaiety—" The old woman's voice thinned into silence. She stared at McFee. "It wasn't Sam I saw . . . It wasn't Sam—" And then, vehemently, "I can't be seeing everybody. . . ."

McFee said gently, "You better go home, Maggie."

He turned into the Gaiety alley, barked his shin against Maggie O'Day's wheel chair. He tried the nearer exit door. It was unbolted. The door creaked as McFee pulled on it. He slipped inside.

The darkness fell all around McFee. It had a hot, smothering touch. It plucked at his eyeballs. He chewed a cigarette, listened. Vague murmurings were audible. The sort of noises that haunt old theatres. Dead voices. . . . Sara Kendleton, Martin Thomas, Mrs. Fiske, Edwin South. But that sort of thing didn't touch McFee. He knew the Gaiety for the rattletrap barn it was and waited, his hat on the back of his head and his ears wide open.

Suddenly he was on his toes.

The sound coming towards him was a human sound. It came down the side aisle from the stage end. It was a rustling sound, like dead leaves in a wind; then it identified itself as the slow slurring of a body dragging exhaustedly over a flat surface. Against a wall. Over a floor. It stopped. The taut quietness that followed throttled McFee. A groan flowed through the darkness, a low strangling cough. The slurring sound was resumed. It was closer now, but there was a bitter-end exhaustion in it.

McFee, chewing his cigarette, felt at the gun and the flashlight in his pocket. He took three steps forward, his arms spread wide.

The man pitched forward and fell against his chest.

McFee slid him down to the floor of the aisle. The man's chest was wet. He felt a warm stickiness on his hands. He made light, spread it over the man's face. It was Rance Damon. His eyes were wide open, fixed in horror; his lips were bloodless. McFee felt at the heart.

Damon was dead.

McFee muttered, "He's been a while dying."

The hole was in the chest. A good deal of blood had flowed.

Damon was around thirty, a dark, debonair lad with straight hair as black as Maggie O'Day's had once been. His bright eloquence, the bold ardor of his restless eyes, had stepped him along. The late Senator Gaylord (Senator by courtesy) had placed him in the District Attorney's office. Damon had become a key man. You had to figure on him. But his mouth was lax.

"The boys'll have to plant a new in-man," McFee said. He sniffed the odor of gin. "Party,

I guess." And then, "Well, well! Rubbed out doing his little stunt!"

McFee had lifted Damon's left arm. The fingers clutched a tangle of five-century notes. Ten of them.

A trail of blood spots on the aisle floor led backstage. The wall was smeared where Damon had fought his way agonizingly along it. McFee followed the sign, back of the boxes, up a short stair, through a door into the backstage. A dingy curtain shut him off from the house. He stood under the drops, among a bedroom set, and waved his light. Damon had crawled across the stage into the wing, where a final resurgence of life lifted him up.

Entering the dressing room from which Damon had come, McFee saw high, fly-blown walls that pictured the evolution of the burley-cue girl. He had appreciated it on previous occasions. A quart bottle of gin, two-thirds empty, stood on a rickety dressing table, two glasses beside it. He did not touch them. A table lamp lay on the floor, broken. Dancing costumes lay about. A rug was turned up.

Make-up material had been swept off the dressing table—powder, crimson grease paint, lipstick, eyebrow buffer. The tube of grease paint had been stepped on by someone, burst open. The stuff smeared the floor. It looked like coagulated blood.

Near the door lay a .32 automatic pistol. One shell had been ejected.

McFee went back to the aisle.

Irene Mayo was kneeling beside the body.

3

McFee said, "I'm sorry, sister."

The cold beam of his torch made her eyes look enormous in her white, drawn face. Her mouth quivered. She pressed her hand against it, stifled a sob. But after a moment she said dully, "He would have been governor some day."

McFee answered moodily, "Damon had the makings." He stared down into the girl's uplifted eyes, at the purple shadows beneath them. The emeralds at her throat blazed coldly. He added, "If it's in a man's blood you can't stop him."

"Unless you kill him." The girl spoke passionately. "It's in me, too, but there's more than that in me. If it's the last thing I do—"

McFee cut in, "You saw Melrose?"

"No—" The girl hesitated, her eyes hardening. "But Rance saw him. Rance said—" Her eyes fell apprehensively. "I don't understand about that money—"

"Were you in love with Damon?"

"I don't know." She spoke slowly. "I liked him. He took me around a lot. He was a dear—yes, I did love him!" She rocked distractedly, said in a frenzy, "I'll spend every dollar I have to get Melrose."

"Good kid."

"Are you with me, McFee?"

Instead of replying, McFee put out his flash, said softly, "There's someone in the house."

The girl stood up, moved close to him, her wrap drawn tightly around her body. Her breath fanned McFee's cheeks. Neither of them moved. McFee pushed the girl flat against the wall.

"Stay here," he whispered.

"McFee—"

"Easy, sister."

McFee took off his shoes. He felt for his gun, went up the sloping aisle on the balls of his feet. A rustling sound became audible, quieted. He reached the top of the aisle, turned, felt his way towards the foyer. McFee sniffed. Perfume. Thick, too. He grinned, put away his gun. A door was on his right—the manager's office. He turned into the room.

McFee stopped. Someone was breathing heavily. He heard a sob—suppressed. A floor board creaked. McFee thought he located the woman. He took three steps forward, his arms wide apart, as when he had gone to meet Rance Damon. Caught the glitter of a necklace. As he flung one arm around the woman's neck, he slammed the other against her mouth and shut off her scream. She fought, but McFee held her.

He said softly, "One yip and I'll blow you in two."

The woman became quiet. McFee removed his hand.

"Lemme go, McFee," she said huskily.

"Leclair—swell! Anyb'dy else on the party?"

"Rance Damon—" The woman leaned on McFee's arm. "Oh, my God!" she wept. "Damon—that's all—"

Mabel Leclair's blond beauty was unconfined and too abundant. The petulant immaturity of her features ran at odds with the hardness in her round blue eyes. She presented a scanty negligee effect.

McFee asked, "That kind of a party?"

The woman's hands and negligee were bloody. She looked down at them and went sick. McFee directed the light into her eyes. "Sit down," he said. She fell moaning into a chair.

McFee snapped a desk lamp switch. The room contained a shabby desk, chairs, a safe, a water cooler and a couch. The dingy walls were a photograph album burleycue theme.

From the door Irene Mayo cried out, "She killed him—"

"I did not!" the Leclair woman screamed, and jumped up. "What you doing here? What'd I kill him for? We were having a party—oh—" The blood on her hands sickened her again. She wiped them on her negligee. She thrust her hands behind her back, shut her eyes, rocked her head. "Get me a drink," she whimpered, and fell into the chair.

"You had plenty, sister. What kind of party?"

"Just a party, McFee." She tried to smile wisely. "Rance dropped in to see me—"

Irene Mayo cut in, "That's a lie!"

"You think so?" The Leclair woman spoke wickedly. "Kid, I never seen the buttercup I couldn't pick. And I've picked 'em from Broadway west."

McFee said harshly, "Got anything to say before I call the cops?"

"Wait a minute, Handsome." The woman's eyes took fright again, but she seemed to be listening, too. "Lemme tell you. Rance was drinking some. Not much. I hadn't touched it. Honest, McFee—well, mebbe I had a coupla quick ones, but I wasn't lit. I'm telling you, McFee. I was standing in front of the dressing table. Rance was standing beside me, next to the couch. He heard some'dy on the stage. The door was open—the backstage was dark. Rance turned around. And that's when he got it. Right in the chest. I saw the flash—that's all. McFee, I'm telling you! He spun round—kind of. I caught him—" The woman shuddered, shut her eyes.

"Yes?" said McFee.

"He was bleeding—" She wrung her hands. "He slid out of my arms—slow. I thought he'd never drop. The look in his eyes knocked me cuckoo. I fainted. When I came to—" She covered her face.

"When you came to—"

"It was dark. We'd busted the lamp, falling. McFee, he wasn't dead. He was groaning somewhere. I lit a match. He'd dragged himself out backstage. He wouldn't quit crawling. I was scared to switch on the lights—" McFee's cold eyes alarmed the woman. She reiterated desperately. "I'm giving you the straight of it. Rance and me—"

"What you here for?"

"To phone the cops."

"Did you phone 'em?"

"No. You came in. I was scared stiff. I thought it might be Rance's murderer coming back—"

"Phone anyb'dy?"

"No." The woman stared at McFee, the listening look in her eyes. "I didn't phone anybody."

McFee said, "You're a liar." He picked up the desk telephone. The receiver was moist. Leclair stared at McFee. "Who'd you call?"

"Go roll your hoop."

Irene Mayo leaned against the wall, a little to the left of the door. Her eyes were tragic and scornful. McFee was about to unhook the telephone when she gestured warningly.

In the foyer a man said, "Put that telephone down, McFee."

Mabel Leclair laughed.

4

The man moved into the lane of light that flowed out of the office. It was Joe Metz, who ran the Spanish Shawl Club, a Melrose enterprise. McFee threw a glance at the red-headed girl. She seemed to understand what was in his mind.

McFee flung the telephone at the desk lamp. Glass shattered. The room went dark. Leclair screamed. McFee dropped behind the desk.

Joe Metz called, "You birds cover those exits. Smoke him, if you have to . . . McFee!"

The latter, feeling around for the telephone, said, "Speaking."

"I've got three of the boys with me. Nice boys. Boys you've played ball with—" Metz was inside the room now. "They don't wanna hurt you—"

McFee answered, "You'll have me crying pretty soon." Prone on his stomach, he found the instrument, put the receiver to his ear, his lips to the mouthpiece. "Tell me some more, Joe."

Central did not respond.

Mabel Leclair ejaculated, "He's got the telephone, Joe!"

"That's all right," Metz drawled. "I've cut the wire. How about sitting in a little game, McFee?"

"Speak your piece," McFee said, and then: "I got a gun on the door."

"Handsome, it's this way," Metz said. "Sam Melrose has named the next district attorney—Claude Dietrich. Now the Gaiety's a Melrose house and Sam don't want a deputy district attorney dying in it two months before election. So we gotta get Damon away. But that's not the half of it." Metz spoke with a careful spacing of his words. "Damon was in a position to get Sam something he hadda have, election coming on. So Sam turned Blondy loose on the boy—Sam has more swell ideas than a tabloid editor.

Damon was a nut for the frills. He fell for Leclair like a bucket of bricks. Blondy makes a deal with Damon. The boy's taken money before. Taking five grand from Blondy is duck soup—"

McFee said, "Five grand for what?"

"Oh, some photographs, an affidavit, a letter Melrose wrote, a coupla cancelled checks, some testimony from a lad that died—the usual junk."

"Grand Jury file on the Shelldon blow-off?" McFee asked.

"That's right—you're a good guy, McFee. The Grand Jury turned it over to the D.A. Melrose thought it ought to disappear."

"Lemme see," McFee said. "There's a murder tied up with the indictment, isn't there?"

"Sam'll beat that. But you know how it is, election coming on."

"Well, I haven't got it."

"Now, look here, McFee, you aren't in any shape to stand off me and the boys. Melrose wants that Grand Jury indictment."

McFee had begun to creep noiselessly towards Metz and the door. "Who give you the notion that I got it?"

Metz said coldly, "You gotta have it—or know where it is. Damon had the money and the Shelldon file in his hands when that .32 bumped him. He flopped into Blondy's arms. She threw a faint—" Metz interrupted himself to say, "There's places where women is swell, but a jam like that ain't one of 'em."

The Leclair woman cried, "You got your nerve! After what I been through—"

Metz laughed. "I've said there are places where women is swell." He proceeded swiftly. "When Blondy woke up Damon had the five grand in his fist, but the file was gone. She give me a bell at the Shawl. McFee, you got that Shelldon file, or you know where it is. Better play ball."

McFee said softly, "I'm covering you, Joe." And then, "You mean, I killed Damon?"

Metz answered carefully, "Damon don't count now. He isn't going to be found here. It don't matter who killed him. There's plenty

boys Melrose can plant when Dietrich is in. If you killed Damon, swell! You know your business. But you better not try bucking Melrose."

McFee moved some more.

He was in a spot. If Metz was bluffing, a Melrose heel had killed Damon, and the Melrose crowd had the Shelldon file. That would mean McFee knew too much and must become casualty No. 2. If Metz was not bluffing, he probably was convinced McFee had done the job and copped the file. Bad, too. And it left the question: Who shot Damon?

McFee asked, "Where's Melrose?"

"Aboard Larry Knudson's yacht," Metz answered smoothly.

McFee crept forward again.

The Leclair woman shrilled, "Joe! He's coming at you—"

5

Rising straight from his heels, a little to the right of Metz, McFee threw his left to where he thought the man's chin was, landed. Metz' head snapped back. The rest of him followed it. His gun spat flame. McFee steamed past. Metz cracked against the foyer wall.

Metz howled, "Watch those fire exits!"

"Lights!" another man yelled. "Where the hell—"

The Leclair woman screamed, "Backstage—" and then, "Look out for that redheaded tramp—"

McFee ran towards the north side aisle. McFee knew what he was doing. The switch was in the front of the house, off the backstage, north side. He was depending on the red-headed girl. They had a reasonable chance with the house dark—none if the lights came on.

Someone collided with an aisle seat. McFee jumped the man, struck bone with the nose of his gun. The man fell among the seats. He groaned, then shouted faintly, "Over here, you birds—"

Metz yelled, "The other aisle! Gun him, if he

jumps an exit— Some'dy find that damned light room—"

McFee found it. Hadn't he been a Gaiety usher when he was a kid? There were steel switch boxes on a wall. The master switch box was largest. He plucked out a couple of fuses. They heard him. They drummed after him. Sets snapped back as someone crossed the house.

McFee cleared the switch room door, a flash beam jumped up the stage stair, pranced around in the wing.

A man howled, "Now we got the ——"

Leclair screamed. "That red-headed witch—"

McFee ducked across the backstage. The light lost him. A door hinge creaked, and he knew what was troubling Leclair. Very swell!

But the others didn't hear Leclair. They didn't hear the red-headed girl opening the exit door. Somebody monkeyed in the switch room, but the house stayed dark. A couple of men collided in the backstage. McFee wasn't one of them. The light jack-rabbited around the wall, shied at McFee. He chased towards the south wing. A shot came after him.

Metz yelled, "Jump him, Tony—"

The flash beam plucked Tony Starke out of the north wing. Starke had been a pretty fair heavy, and he owned a gymnasium. He looked tremendous. McFee twisted sidewise and leaned on the canvas drop that shut the backstage off from the house. The canvas was rotten old. It ripped with a thin scream, spraying dust, as McFee fell through it.

Art Kline was on the runway that fronted the orchestra. Pretty nearly as big as Starke, Kline bounced for Joe Metz, at the Spanish Shawl and was famous for his hands. He had broken a man's neck with them. Kline pulled a fast jump over the orchestra and landed on top of McFee. They milled for a moment. Then Metz, coming through the ripped curtain, collided with them, and all three pitched into the orchestra, McFee on top.

Kline conked his head, but it didn't do him any harm. He and Metz held McFee. Metz

yelled for the flashlight. They milled some more, bone thudding on bone; then a door opened and they rolled down a short stair under the stage and hit a wall. The place smelled of stale beer and fried onions.

Leclair shrilled, "That red-headed tramp's gone for the coppers. I'm telling you—"

McFee was getting plenty now. The flash beam came. Monty Welch brought it. Welch was five feet four. He dealt blackjack at the Spanish Shawl and knew when every cop in the city paid his next mortgage installment. Tony Starke rolled in with him, sat on McFee's head.

Metz went through McFee's clothes, then said, "What you done with that Shelldon file?"

McFee said nothing. He didn't like it under Tony Starke's two hundred and twenty, but he still was figuring on the red-headed girl. The coppers could make it in three minutes flat—if they wanted to.

Monty Welch said in his whispering voice, "Gimme a cigarette and a match, Art. I'll open his trap—"

The Leclair woman showed up then. Tony Starke put the light on her. She wore an ermine coat pulled tight around her body. Leclair had brought the coat from Broadway. Somebody said she had traded a couple of letters for it. She said very quietly, "McFee's red-headed friend went for the cops while you birds was playing tag—"

Metz blurted, "What's that?"

"I been telling you—the tramp that was with him—"

Metz said huskily, "We got to get outta this." He sucked in his cheeks. His bulbous temples were wet and gleaming. "We take McFee. McFee'll talk later. Monty, you jam your gun in his kidneys. Hand it to him if he squawks. Tony, Art, carry Damon. I'll drive."

Kline and Starke hoisted McFee to his feet. Welch's gun made him step fast. They drummed up the stair. They climbed out of the orchestra, paraded up the center aisle, cut across to the south aisle by the seventh row. It was like a scene from an old Gaiety play.

As they clattered into the side aisle, a police siren wailed somewhere down Carter Street.

Metz said tersely, "We go through the Palace. Monty, fan that light—" And then, as Welch spread the beam on the aisle floor, "Cripes!"

They forgot McFee. His toe sent the flash whizzing out of Welch's hand. It shattered against the wall and darkness buried them. McFee sank back into the seat right behind him.

Metz howled, "Some'dy's been here—"

"I fell over him when I came in," Starke sobbed.

"Grab McFee—"

But the coppers were hammering on the foyer door, and they hadn't time to look for McFee, Metz said, "Scram!" They jumped through the fire exit, pushed through the Palace service door. Sam Melrose had taken over the Palace along with the Gaiety.

The coppers were coming down the alley.

McFee crawled out of a seat and spread his hands on the aisle floor, where he had left Damon's body. It wasn't there.

McFee leaned against the wall. He rolled a match in his ear. "That's funny," he said.

6

McFee felt a draft on his face. A man carefully let himself into the house. Two other men were behind him. The first man, Pete Hurley, of the homicide squad, spread a flash beam over the aisle floor. Hurley's hard hat sat on the back of his square head and he jiggled a cold cigarette between pouchy lips.

Hurley said bitterly, "Hello, Handsome."

"You got a pip this time." McFee sucked on a loose tooth, felt his jaw. "Tell one of your boys to fix a light. Here's a coupla fuses."

One of the men took the fuses, went away.

"Some'dy belled the desk and yelled 'Murder at the Gaiety,'" Hurley said querulously. He added cautiously, "Rance Damon. What's the dope?"

"Sweet," McFee answered, and stood up. "A box full of medals for Some'dy, and nob'dy

wanting to wear 'em." Wobbling, he put on his shoes. "Gimme a cigarette, Beautiful."

"I ain't looking for medals," Hurley said harshly. "Medals ain't safe in this town. Where's Damon?"

"Damon's dead. He went away. Ask Melrose's boys."

"Melrose's boys?"

"Joe Metz, Art Kline, Monty Welch, Tony Starke. It was good while it lasted." McFee lighted a cigarette, then spread out his hand. Lights began to go on. Hurley stared at McFee with his bitter, button eyes. McFee added presently, "Irene Mayo brought you boys."

"Who's this Mayo queen?"

"A nice little number. She's been in pictures. Likes to pull strings. She wanted Damon to be governor."

"You got that Shelldon file?"

"I didn't kill Damon, mister."

Hurley didn't look at McFee, as he said slowly, "The birds that shot Damon musta got away with him. You say Melrose's boys didn't take him away, so they didn't shoot him. That's reasonable ain't it?" He forced his uneasy, hostile eyes up to McFee's cold grin. "I said, that's reasonable, ain't it?"

"Anything's reasonable that's got to be," McFee answered.

Hurley's tone was sullen as he proceeded, "Melrose's boys is out then. How about that red-headed number. I mean—"

"You mean, did she carry Damon out in her stocking? No, Buttercup, she didn't. And if she didn't she couldn't have rubbed him out. That's reasonable, isn't it?"

Hurley's cigarette became still. "Mebbe there'll be a coupla medals in this after all—"

McFee said, "You can always sell 'em for hardware."

Hurley spread light upon the wet smear Damon's body had left. Sign indicated that the body had been dragged to the fire exit and out into the alley. There the sign ended.

Inside again, Hurley asked McFee, "Why don't that red-headed dame come back?"

"I guess she'd had plenty. You'll find her at

the St. Regis." He added dryly, "Melrose'll tell you where to find Leclair."

"I'll find Leclair." And then, impressively, "Melrose is aboard Knudson's yacht."

Hurley followed the blood drop down the aisle. Here and there on the drab wall were imprints of Damon's wet, red hands. They leaped at the eye. They implied a frantic striving, a dreadful frustration. The two dicks tailed Hurley, McFee trailed the three of them, chewing the end of his cigarette. They crossed the backstage, shoved into the dressing room.

Hurley looked the automatic over, put it down. He looked at the glasses and gin bottle, at the upset table lamp, at the squashed tube of crimson grease paint.

"Some'dy better change his shoes," Hurley muttered.

McFee said casually, "Leclair's shoes looked clean."

Hurley stared sourly at the picture album around the walls. "Burleycue ain't what she was. You need a pair of field glasses to see the jittering toothpicks that prance on the boards nowadays." Turning to one of his men he said, "Harry, go give Littner a bell. Tell him he'd better slide over. Tell him—" Hurley slanted his eyes at McFee. "Tell him we are in a spot."

Littner was Captain of Detectives.

Hurley chalked crosses on the floor, near the dressing table and close to the couch, to indicate where he and McFee thought Damon and Leclair had stood, when the shot was fired.

Littner and the Chief came first; then Larrabee, the District Attorney, and Atwell, a deputy coroner. Larrabee said it was too bad about Damon. Pretty nearly everybody said it was too bad and something ought to be done. When Larrabee heard about the Grand Jury Shelldon file he went white around the gills, and shut up. Larrabee was half and half about most things. He had Bright's Disease. That was why he wasn't going to run again. The camera boys stood up their flashlight set. The fingerprint lads prowled around with their brushes and powders. A flock of dicks were detailed to do this and that. Littner turned the pistol over to Wal-

ter Griggs, the ballistic expert. The newshawks came.

The Chief said to Littner, "Melrose is gonna be damn good and sore."

"He ought to be damn good and glad some'dy else lifted Damon," Littner muttered.

"You figure he needs an out?"

Littner said cautiously, "Melrose is aboard Knudson's yacht, isn't he?"

Littner ought to have been Chief of Police.

After a while, McFee said to Hurley, "I guess I'll go finish my coffee."

7

McFee walked up Carter to Third, stood there a minute, rolling a match in his ear. The block between Second and Third was full of police and county cars, but the rest of the town looked empty. It was three-fifteen. McFee had been in the Gaiety about two and a half hours. He saw a coupe parked half a block down Third and walked towards it.

Irene Mayo sat behind the wheel, smoking a cigarette. Her eyes were feverish. Her white face was posed above the deep fur of her wrap like a flower in a vase. She said huskily, "I thought you'd come."

"It takes a while," McFee answered. He got in beside her. "Thanks for giving the cops a bell."

"Did they hurt you?" She looked intently at him.

"Some'dy sat on my head."

The red-headed girl let in the clutch. They made a couple of righthand turns then a left.

McFee said, "Damon sold out, didn't he, sister?"

"Yes—" The word tore itself from Irene Mayo's lips. Her knuckles tightened on the wheel. "That blonde woman—"

"Hadn't it in him, I guess," McFee muttered.

She said in a brittle voice, "He could have been governor. I had what he needed . . . I could have given him—" She shivered, pressed her hand to her throat. "I don't blame Rance. A man is just so much—no more. But Melrose—Sam Melrose—" She uttered the name as if it poisoned her mouth. "Melrose knew how to break Rance. And he had Rance shot because he wasn't *sure*—" She stared straight ahead, her eyes as hard as bright new coins. "I'll make Sam Melrose wish he hadn't come to this town if it kills me to do it."

They drove some more.

"Some'dy took Damon's body away," McFee said.

"What did you say?"

McFee told her about it. "Damon must have been taken after you got away. There was a five minute interval before the cops came."

"What do the police think?"

"It isn't what they think—this is Melrose's town. They take the position that Melrose didn't have Damon blinked because it wasn't his boys carted Damon's body away. They say that means some'dy else killed Damon."

"Don't you see?" Her tone was stinging, vicious. "Those Melrose men had Rance taken while you were talking to that Leclair woman. When the police came, and they couldn't take you with them, they pretended Rance had vanished. They knew you'd tell the police. They knew the police—Melrose's police!—would use it for an 'out.' McFee—" She gripped his arm, her face terribly white, "you must see that! You don't believe what the police are only pretending to believe?"

They made a right-hand turn.

McFee put a cigarette in his mouth, said quietly, "Sister, you better lemme take the wheel. There's a car tailing us. They'll have more power than we have."

"They can't run us down."

"They can do anything in this town. And they will, if they think I got what they want. Slide over."

The girl said cooly, "Have you got what they want, McFee?"

A pair of white eyes grew large in the rear view mirror, McFee laid one hand on the wheel, slid the other around the girl's hips. His toe lifted her foot from the gas pedal. McFee said harshly, "Don't be a fool—this is serious." She yielded then and glided over his lap.

McFee jumped the car forward. It was a handy little bus, but it didn't have the steam. McFee made a left hand turn and they hit a through boulevard. The tail car showed its lights again. The lights grew bigger. A milk truck rattled past.

McFee let the coupe out, but the white eyes swelled.

McFee said, "This is your coupe?"

"Rance's."

"Where's your house?"

"Avalon. Eighteen hundred block. Avalon's about a mile beyond the next boulevard stop."

McFee looked at the girl out of slanted eyes. "I got a hunch they're out to wreck us. I know those birds. If they ride us down, it'll be as soon as we quit the boulevard."

Irene Mayo said passionately, "I don't know what they want, but nothing will make me believe Melrose didn't have Rance killed."

They approached the cross boulevard, doing fifty or so. The neon lights of an all-night filling station blazed on the opposite corner.

"I'd like to stand those lads on their heads," McFee muttered. He grinned, but his somber eyes were calculating as they looked at the girl. "I got a hunch. How much you good for, sister?"

"As much as you are."

He laughed a little. "Maybe we could get away, but I doubt it. If we waited somewhere, and phoned for a police bodyguard, they'd jump us before the cops could find us. I don't know but what we hadn't better try to stand 'em on their heads."

The girl said nothing. McFee ran the car up to the filling station oil pumps. Behind them, the brakes of the pursuing car made a high wailing sound and the car—a rakish black sedan—rocked to a standstill. It had not crossed the intersection.

"What's the street this side of Avalon?"

"Hawthorne."

"Trees on it?"

"Yes."

To the white-uniformed, freckle-faced lad who came running up, McFee said, "Gimme a five-gallon can of crankcase oil—Eastern. Step on it." McFee took out a jacknife, opened a blade. The lad reappeared, lugging the can of oil. McFee placed it on the seat, between himself and the red-headed girl. "Throw in five gallons of gas." He added to the girl, "Just to fool those birds," and drove his knife blade into the top of the can. Ripping around the edge, he muttered, "This is going to be dirty."

The girl's eyes became spheres of green light.

Oil slopped onto McFee's clothing, over the girl's wrap. The lad came back, McFee threw ten dollars at him.

"Keep the change, kid. And do this—" McFee impaled him with an oily forefinger. "Hop your telephone. Call police headquarters. Tell 'em, there's an accident on Hawthorne, north of Grand. Tell 'em to send a riot squad. Tell 'em McFee told you."

The boy blurted, "Anybody hurt?"

"There's going to be," McFee said as he jumped the car into the boulevard.

They hit fifty. The sedan behind them zoomed across the intersection, then settled down to tailing the coop from two blocks back.

Irene Mayo said tersely. "Avalon—three blocks."

McFee dropped to thirty. The car behind picked up. McFee made the right hand turn at Hawthorne. The street was narrow, a black tunnel of peppers and eucalypti.

McFee drove half a block, dropping to fifteen. He shifted off the crown of the street. He placed the red-headed girl's right hand on top of the wheel. She stared at him, her mouth a red gash in her white face. McFee bent back the top of the can. He caught the ragged edge nearest him with his left hand, thrust his right under the bottom of the can. The lights behind made a wide arc as the sedan swung crazily into Hawthorne.

Before the lights had quite straightened out, McFee heaved the can over the wheel and dumped the oil onto the crown of the road.

The oil ran in every direction. McFee flung the can into the trees. The sedan came roaring down Hawthorne, huge and devastating behind its tremendous lights. McFee shot the coupe ahead. He abruptly turned into a private driveway, shut off the lights.

The brakes of the big sedan screamed. The car staggered, ploughed towards the wet smear that oozed towards either curb of the narrow street. Someone in the car shouted thickly, hysterically.

The locked wheels of the sedan skidded into the oil.

McFee and Irene Mayo saw a big sedan slide sidewise on tortured rubber. Twice the car cut a complete circle at terrible speed, its lights slicing the darkness; then it leaped the opposite curb and snapped off a street light standard. Glass shattered. A wheel flew somewhere. The huge car lifted itself in a final spasm and fell on its side.

McFee said softly, "Very swell."

8

Windows were going up as McFee backed into Hawthorne. He turned on his lights. Somebody yelled at him. At the corner, he made a left hand turn; then a right hand at Avalon. He drove two blocks, and saw the St. Regis, a green light over its entrance, at the next corner. It was a fairly exclusive, small, three-story house with garages. He drove into an open garage.

"Not bad." He laughed and looked at the girl. She was leaning against his shoulder, very white. "Oh," said McFee. "Well."

He took out the ignition key. There were five keys on a ring. Sliding out of the coupe, he lifted the girl into his arms and carried her around to the front entrance. No one was about. The trees in the parking threw long shadows after him. A police siren wailed somewhere.

The letter-box directory indicated that Miss Mayo's apartment was No. 305. He carried her upstairs, reminded of an Olga Nethersole play he had seen at the Gaiety years ago. Heavy, wine-colored carpet covered the stairs and halls. Some potted palms stood around and looked at him.

At No. 305, McFee tried three of the keys before he got the door open. A little light from the corridor came in with McFee—enough for him to see a divan in the middle of the living room into which the small entrance hall opened. He laid the girl on it, snapped a floor lamp switch. The room had dim lights, soft rugs, lots of pillows, some books and a couple of pictures. A swell little shack for a lad to hang up his hat in.

One of the girl's green snakeskin slippers had become unbuckled. It fell off. McFee saw a long manila envelope fastened to the lining of her wrap with a safety pin. He chewed his knuckle, then unpinned the envelope. "Shelldon File" was penciled on its upper left-hand corner. The envelope was sealed. McFee stared hard at the girl. Her eyelashes rested on the shadows beneath her eyes. Slitting the top of the envelope, he looked into it. His expression became astonished. He smiled crookedly and put the envelope inside his waistcoat.

In the kitchen McFee got a glass of water. When he came back the girl was sitting up.

"How's it coming?" he asked.

"Nicely." Her eyes were amused but a little cold. "You must have done a gorgeous Sappho." She looked at her hands, at her wrap and gown. "That oil made a horrible mess. Do you suppose they are hurt?"

"You can give the hospital a bell in ten minutes."

She laughed uneasily. "Make yourself comfortable while I get into something else."

McFee was in a mess himself. He lit a cigarette. He began to walk up and down.

An ornamental mirror hung on the wall opposite the bedroom door. The girl had not closed the door and he saw her reflection in the mirror. She stood beside a table, a framed photograph clasped in her hands. Her expression and attitude were tragic and adoring. She pressed the photograph to her lips, held it there.

Her slender body drooped. She put the photograph down but continued to stare at it, her fingers pressed against her mouth. The photograph was of Rance Damon.

Irene Mayo slipped out of her green gown, when she reappeared some minutes later her eyes were subtle and untragic, and she wore lounging pajamas of green silk with a flowing red sash. She dropped onto the divan and laid her red head against a green pillow.

"You'd better use the bathroom, McFee," she told him.

The bathroom was finished in green and white tile and much nickel. He used a monogrammed hand towel on his oil splashed clothes. He washed his hands and face and combed his hair. Stared at his automatic meditatively, then stood it on its nose in his right hand coat pocket.

When McFee showed himself again, Irene Mayo had a bottle of gin and a couple of glasses on a small table.

"Straight is all I can do."

"You couldn't do better."

McFee sat down on the girl's left. The liquor made a gurgling sound. She poured until McFee said "yes," which wasn't immediately.

As he occupied himself with the glass, a blunt object jammed his ribs. He finished the liquor.

The girl said coldly, "Your own gun."

McFee asked, "What do you want?"

"That envelope." Her eyes were cold, too. "McFee, I went through Rance's pockets just before you came back and found me kneeling beside him. He had the Shelldon file. I took it. You have it. I want it back."

"What you want it for?"

"That's my business."

"Maybe I want it too."

"Don't be a fool." Her cheek bones began to burn. "I'll kill you if you don't give me that file."

"What'd the coppers say to that?"

"I'd tell them you wouldn't go home."

McFee smiled charmingly and unbuttoned his waistcoat. Still smiling, he handed her the envelope and said, "You better look at the catch."

Suspicious, she jumped up, backed to the other side of the room, still covering him with the .38, and shook the envelope. Sheets of folded paper slid out, fluttered onto the floor. They were blank.

The girl said furiously, "McFee, I'll give you just three seconds—"

"Use your bean," McFee said harshly. "You saw me unpin that envelope. You know where I been since—the kitchen, the bathroom. I haven't got anything in my clothes. "If you like, I'll take 'em off. Some'dy's give you the run-around."

She stared at him, the cold fury in her eyes turning to mortification. "I didn't look—I took it for granted— What an idiot you must think me!" she wept. And then, stamping angrily, "How do you explain this?"

McFee said, "I can think of a coupla answers." He helped himself appreciatively to the gin. "Number One: Leclair's putting the buzz on Melrose. She killed Damon, picked the meat out of the envelope, and left those blanks behind. Number Two: Damon had showed Leclair the file, but was trying to sell her the blanks." McFee set his glass down. "Here's another one: Mr. X, as the book writers call him, shot Damon and worked the switch. Don't ask me why. There's only one answer, sister."

"And Sam Melrose knows it!" Irene Mayo declared passionately.

She came towards McFee, her red sash swaying as she walked. Laughing a little, she sat down beside him, handed him the pistol. McFee took the cartridge clip out of his coat pocket, opened the magazine, shot the clip home. He set the safety.

Irene Mayo said, "Oh! You knew what I would do? You are clever—"

"Just an agency dick trying to get along," McFee answered softly.

She laid her head on the green pillow, her red mouth smiling.

"I didn't mean to," she murmured. And then, "Is your wife home, McFee?"

"Visiting her sister," he said.

After a while, McFee went away.

Down below McFee hopped the taxi he had called from Irene Mayo's apartment. He told the man to take him to the Manchester Arms, on Gerard Street. It was daylight.

At the Manchester, McFee paid the fare and went into the house, feeling for his keys. They were gone. "Metz!" he muttered, and explored his other pockets. Some letters and a note book he had had were gone. "I owe those lads a couple," he muttered.

McFee got a spare key off the building superintendent and walked up to his apartment on the fourth floor. He let himself into the entrance hall and pushed into the living room.

Joe Metz sat in a chair in front of the door. He had a .38 in his hand.

Metz said, "Hello, McFee."

McFee stood quite still. Metz's left cheek was strapped in adhesive tape from eye to mouth. His bulbous forehead was wet. Art Kline came out of the bathroom in his shirt sleeves. He was swart and squat, a barrel of a man. His nose and right forearm were plastered. The door behind McFee closed. Steel prodded his kidneys.

"Don't make any break, sap," said whispering Monty Welch.

McFee answered, "I thought I put you lads on ice."

"You bust Tony Starke's neck," Metz said.

Welch drove McFee forward. Metz stood up. The whites of his eyes showed. Art Kline shuffled across the room. He carried his hands as if they were paws. His eyes were fixed, reddish, minute.

Metz said, "Sit down."

McFee stared at the empty chair. It had wide wings. The three closed in upon him.

"Sit down, McFee."

The latter whirled quietly and crashed his right into Kline's swart jaw. The blow made a dull chopping sound. Kline hit a sofa against the wall. If he'd had anything less than a horse shoe in his jaw he'd have stayed there, but as the other two jumped McFee he bounced up, shook his head, dived in. McFee took a beating before they slammed him down into the chair. He rocked a moment, then threw himself forward and up. They slammed him back.

Art Kline smashed him terrifically in the mouth. McFee fell against the back of the chair. Metz began to go swiftly, thoroughly, through his clothes.

He said harshly, "McFee, what you done with that Shelldon file? What we just handed you is pie crust to what you'll get if you don't play ball."

"I haven't got it," McFee whispered.

Kline hit him again. McFee's mouth became bloody. He sat very still.

Metz said, "What you holding out for, goat? This is Melrose's town. You can't buck Sam. Come through, or I'll turn this coupla bear eaters loose."

Sick and raging, McFee blurted, "You bat-eyed kite, d'you think I'd be sitting here if I had it? I'd be down at the Trib spilling a story to Roy Cruikshank that'd put you gophers in your holes."

"Not if you were saving it until you thought you had enough to put the bell on Melrose." Metz unfolded a handkerchief, wiped his wet forehead, said slowly, "McFee, you must have that file. And if you have it, you're holding it with a notion of putting the bell on Sam. Nob'dy in this town'll live long enough to do that— I mean it both ways. But Sam wants that indictment killed, election coming on. Ten grand, McFee?"

"Go paddle your drum."

"Lemme work on him," Art Kline said. An impediment in his speech gummed up his voice. "I owe him a couple for Tony."

He went behind McFee's chair. He laid his tremendous hands on the top of it, flexed his powerful fingers. Whispering Monty Welch sat on the right arm of the chair. His patent leather-shod diminutive feet swung clear of the floor. Welch placed a cigarette between his lips, ignited it with a gem-studded lighter.

McFee waited.

Metz said, "They got no use for dicks in heaven."

McFee's mouth twitched. There was sweat in his eyes, on his cheekbones. He suddenly threw himself out of the chair and at Metz. The latter smacked him lightly across the head with his gun. McFee wobbled, fell back.

Metz said, "I'm waiting."

McFee did not answer. Welch dragged on his cigarette. The detached expression of his puckish face was unchanged as he held the red end a half inch from McFee's cheek. McFee slowly lifted his head. Art Kline laughed and slapped adhesive tape over McFee's mouth; then he caught McFee's wrists and began to bend his arms over the back of the chair.

Metz said, "Blow your whistle when it's plenty."

McFee threw himself around in the chair, but the steam had gone out of him. Metz and Welch held his legs. Kline leaned heavily, enthusiastically, on his arms. A seam in McFee's coat shoulder burst. His sinews cracked. His eyeballs came slowly out of their sockets.

Metz said, "Well?" anxiously.

McFee mumbled defiantly behind his taped lips.

"Funny about a guy's arm," Art Kline said.

To his downward pressure he added a sidewise motion. Welch drew his cigarette across McFee's corded throat. McFee's face turned green. His eyes rolled in a hot, white hate.

"This oughta do it," Art Kline said.

Someone knocked at the door.

McFee fell sidewise in his chair, his arm limp. Welch squeezed out his cigarette. Metz held up a hand, his thin white face oddly disconcerted. The other two nodded slowly. The knocking set up a reverberation in the room.

A soprano voice said lazily, "This is Roy Cruikshank, McFee. Pete Hurley's with me. The superintendent said you came in ten minutes ago. We are coming in with a pass key, if you don't open up." Placatingly, "Now be reasonable, Handsome—we got to get out the paper." Pete Hurley added querulously, "I wanna talk to you about that wrecked sedan on Hawthorne. Open the door!"

McFee lifted his head. He clawed at his taped lips, raised up in his chair. Art Kline smacked him down again.

"One peep outta you—"

Metz's agile eyes had been racing around the room. They jumped at Kline. "Cut that!" he said tersely. And then, in a loud voice, "I'm coming. We been in a little game."

Metz' eyes lighted on a tier of bookshelves. On the top shelf were some decks of cards and a box of poker chips. Beside the bookshelves stood a card table. Moving fast, Metz grabbed the table with one hand, cards and box of chips with the other. Monty Welch took them away from him.

"Set 'em up," Metz said.

In the kitchen on the sink were some glasses and a bottle of gin. Metz carried these into the living room. He placed them on the floor beside the card table, which Welch had set up in front of McFee's chair. McFee stared at Metz ironically. Art Kline stood over him, bewildered. Metz carefully upset the card table, spilling chips and cards. He threw some money on the floor.

Outside, Hurley shouted, "McFee, I told you t'open the door!" and rattled the handle.

"Maybe he's pulling his pants on," Roy Cruikshank said patiently.

"Don't get excited." Metz spoke irritably. "I'm coming." He ripped the tape off McFee's lips. "Tell 'em anything you please—it won't stick. Not in this town, it won't. We got all the alibis we need." To the other two he said, "McFee and Art tangled over a pair of jacks, see? Art laid him out."

Metz poured gin into a glass. He drank half of it, spilled the remainder on the carpet. He wiped his lips on a handkerchief and opened the door.

"Hello, Pete!" Metz said.

"Oh, it's you!" Hurley's bitter button eyes went tight in their sockets. He shoved past Metz, saying, "Where's McFee?"

Roy Cruikshank tailed him into the living room. Cruikshank was a slouching pink lad in his thirties. He had an egg-shaped stomach, evangelical hands and cynical, indolent eyes.

"Party," Cruikshank said lazily. "Well, well."

Hurley's hostile eyes made their calculations. Art Kline sat on the couch, nursing his jaw. Welch, leaning back in a chair near the table, squeezed five cards in his left hand, lighted a cigarette with his right. McFee's face was a mess.

"What happened, Handsome?" Hurley muttered.

McFee smiled with bruised lips. "Ask Metz."

"Art and McFee mixed over a pair of Jacks," Metz said with annoyed distinctness. "McFee smacked Art. Art laid him out."

"How long you been playing?"

"Half an hour."

Hurley flared out, "The superintendent told Roy and me—"

"It don't matter what the superintendent told you. McFee's been here half an hour. Coupla days ago, out to the Shawl, McFee said, 'Joe, why don't you and the boys drop in for a session some time? If the missus and me are out you'll find the key under the mat.' There's a lad for you! So we dropped in tonight—around two. We played rummy until McFee came."

Hurley looked at Welch and Kline. "That right?"

"Check."

"Me, too." Kline rubbed his jaw. "That guy packs a cannon in his kick."

Glinting amusement surfaced the dark violence in McFee's eyes. Hurley put a cigarette in his mouth, jiggled it angrily. Reddening, he said, "You heard these boys, McFee?"

"Sure!" McFee answered. "Gimme a drink, some'dy."

As Cruikshank handed McFee the glass a faint irritability stirred his cynical indolence. "Sure that's all, McFee?"

"That's all right now," McFee answered deliberately.

But Hurley had a couple of kicks left. To Metz he said vehemently, "I want the how of this Gaiety business."

"Some'dy phoned the Shawl," Metz replied cautiously. "Who was it, Art?"

"I dunno."

Metz waved his hand. "That's how it is, Pete. Tough, though. Damon was a nice kid. And Melrose is going to be damn good and sore."

Hurley suddenly became enraged. "You got your gall sitting there telling me—" He became inarticulate, his face a network of purple veins. "By God! This town—"

Metz asked quietly, "What you want to know, Pete?"

Hurley took out a handkerchief, wiped the palm of his hands, put it away. He said huskily, "I wanna know where you boys were between eleven and one."

"I'll tell you," Metz said confidingly. "We were having a little supper in Sam Melrose's rooms at the Shawl. Art, Monty, Tony, Max Beck, Fred Pope and me. Mabel Leclair put on a shimmy number. She left the Gaiety around eleven. One o'clock, Tony pulled out. He had a date. Art and Monty and me came here." Metz added lazily, "Anything else, Pete?"

Hurley's throat sounded dry as he said, "And that Leclair queen didn't hand Rance Damon five grand for the Shelldon file; and—"

"Why, Pete!"

"—You birds didn't walk Damon away with a hole in his chest—"

Metz asked Welch and Kline seriously. "Either you boys got Damon in your pockets?" And then, "Who's been giving you the run-around, Pete?"

Hurley glared at McFee. The latter said nothing. McFee's eyes were hot and violent, but he smiled with his lips and Hurley pulled his own eyes back into his head.

"And you ain't heard Tony Starke bust his neck in a smash on Hawthorne?"

"Gosh, no! How'd it happen?"

Hurley flared out disgustedly, "Mercy Hospital. He'll live."

Metz stood up. "We better go buy Tony a bouquet." He put on his hat. He buttoned his waistcoat. Art Kline got into his coat and shook down his trousers. Monty Welch carefully smoothed down his hair. Metz smiled. "Well, I'll be seeing you, McFee. We had a hot party."

As they reached the door Hurley said sourly, "The vice detail raids the Shawl tonight. Slattery and his boys. Midnight."

"Saturday's a swell date to knock over a roadhouse doing our business—"

"We got to make a play, ain't we? The Mayor's coming."

"Ohhh," said Metz. "Hizoner. Well!"

They went away.

9

Roy Cruikshank wrapped his evangelical hands around glassware and poured himself a drink. He set his hat on the back of his pink head. "Those lads were giving you the works, McFee?"

The latter jeered, "And why didn't I tell Hurley about it?" He flexed his shoulder muscles, began to walk the floor. "Why didn't I tell him those pansies tailed Mayo and me in that sedan to Hawthorne Street? Roy, I told Hurley plenty before I left the Gaiety."

Hurley blew up. "I mighta called the wagon, sure. And Morry Lasker'd have had 'em bailed out before I'd booked 'em at the desk. If it had come to court—which ain't likely—Metz and his lads'd have brought a sockful of alibis, and Lasker'd have given McFee the haw-haw for his tag-in-the-dark yarn. 'Y'honor-gen'lemen-the-jury, the witness admits the only light in the theater was that of an electric torch. How could he positively have identified my clients—'" Hurley jiggled his cigarette. "The papers'd pan the cops and the D. A. for not making it stick. And me out airing my pants."

The Tribune man crooned, "Now he's getting sore."

"Whatdayou want for two hundred bucks a month? If I can crack the Melrose drag, fine. If I pull a dud I lose my badge. Lookit Frank Ward. Chased Melrose doing seventy and give him a ticket. Frank lost his job—and five kids." Hurley jerked his hat over his eyes, stood up. "The Chief said to me, 'Hurley, you're a good copper. But don't get too good.' I ain't going to."

Hurley slammed the entrance door.

Putting a cigarette in the middle of his pink face, Roy Cruikshank said, "Hurley isn't a bad guy." He laughed from his belly up. "Tonight the vice detail raids Melrose's Spanish Shawl. The Mayor goes along. Metz has rolled up the bar and there's checkers in the gambling room. Hizoner drinks his lemonade and makes his little speech, entitled, Everything's Rosy in Our Town. Some'dy ought to give us a new deal."

McFee went into the bathroom. He swabbed his face with hot water, took a shower. He rubbed his shoulders with linament, got into clean pajamas, a bathrobe. He had a mouse under his left eye. His lips were bruised and broken. The hot violence still glinted on the surface of his eyes.

In the kitchen McFee prepared coffee, ham and eggs and flap-jacks; set the food on a tray with mess-gear. Cruikshank had righted the card table. He was dealing himself poker hands. "Boy!" said Cruikshank. They ate without talk, McFee believing in food first. Cruikshank was careless with his eggs. His neckties said so.

After they had cleaned up the tray, Cruikshank began to fool abstractedly with the cards. McFee suggested they cut for nickels. Cruikshank thought it a good idea until McFee had won around five dollars; then he muttered sourly, "I guess I've paid for my breakfast."

McFee said abruptly, "Who's the Trib backing for district attorney?"

"The Trib—" Cruikshank cut a ten-spade to McFee's heart-queen. "What you got on those girls, damn your hide—" He shoved across a chip. "The Trib—oh, yeah. Why, Jim Hughes, I guess. Jim's a good egg, and he'd give the county a break."

"Jim isn't bad," McFee admitted, "but Luke Addams is better; Luke knows the political set-up. Jim'd have to learn too much."

"Well, it don't matter who the Trib backs. Melrose has written the ticket—Dietrich. The Mayor endorses Dietrich and it's count 'em and weep."

McFee stacked chips. "Dietrich elected'll throw the county Melrose." He looked at Cruikshank, eyes cold. "That'll give him the county, City Hall and police machines. Larrabee is soft, but he's got church backing and while he's D.A. he's never been more than half Melrose's man."

"What's on your mind?"

"I'll tell you." McFee spoke harshly. "If Melrose's heels had kept their hands off me this morning, I'd have kept mine in my pants pocket. But they didn't." His words made a bitter, drumming sound. "So I'm out to give Melrose a ride."

"On what?"

"The Damon murder."

"You think he or his heels killed Damon?"

McFee said softly, "Can I make it look that way, you mean?"

"You got the City Hall hook-up to beat."

McFee shuffled the cards. "Littner might buy a ticket," he muttered. "Littner ought to be chief." He added thoughtfully. "Littner's going to be Chief." And then, "Roy, could you swing the Trib to Luke Addams, if you wanted to?"

"Mebbe." Cruikshank rubbed his plump hands on his fat thighs. "But I don't guess I want to. Jim Hughes—"

"Swell!" said McFee. "Roy, you owe me five- ten. I'll cut you for it against Luke Addams for D.A. Five-ten isn't high for a district attorney."

Cruikshank grinned. "Cut 'em first."

McFee turned up a four-diamond.

"If I don't beat that—" Cruikshank exulted. But his cut was a trey-heart.

"McFee, you lucky stiff, I got a hunch you're going to slam this across."

McFee said, "You owe me five-ten, Roy." He poured a couple of drinks. "To Luke Addams, the next D.A."

Cruikshank went away.

At his telephone McFee dialed Dresden 5216. He said, "Hello, Luke . . . McFee. Pin this in your hat: You are to be District Attorney . . ." Luke Addams laughed. So did McFee.

Then he hung up and went to bed.

McFee got up around twelve and stood under the shower. His eye was bad, his lips were puffy, but he felt better. As he dressed, the telephone rang.

Irene Mayo was calling.

McFee said, "Oh, pretty good . . . a couple of the boys dropped in. Nothing much . . ." And then, "How about some lunch, sister? . . . Cato's. Half an hour . . . Right."

McFee stopped at his office, in the Strauss Building and looked over the mail his secretary had laid on his desk. Out of a white envelope— five-and-ten stock—fell a triangular shaped scrap of drug store paper. On it, in crude characters, was printed:

Sam Melrose got the Shelldon file, you bet. He's going to work on it.

MR. INSIDE.

McFee stared at the note. "Well," he said finally, and went out.

At Cato's Irene Mayo waited in the booth McFee usually occupied. She wore a green felt beret, a string of pearls and a knitted green silk suit with white cuffs. Her eyes were smudgy, feverish in her taut face. She smiled, with a slow, subtle curving of her red lips.

McFee said, "Pretty nice."

"Not very nice," she answered. "Does your eye hurt?"

McFee grinned. "You ought to see the other lad . . . I suppose you had callers?"

She nodded. "Captain Littner and Mr. Hurley. They stayed about an hour, but I couldn't tell them anything they didn't know."

The red-headed girl ordered a roast. McFee said he was on a diet and took turtle soup, planked steak with mushrooms and apple pie. They talked a while. The girl presently fetched an envelope out of her vanity bag.

"That came this morning," she said.

The envelope was a replica of the one McFee had received. He took a swallow of coffee and shook a scrap of drug store paper out of the envelope. The crude printing on it was familiar.

You tell McFee Melrose got the Shelldon file at the Spanish Shawl.

MR. INSIDE.

The girl flared out, "Of course he's got it. And that means he had Rance shot. McFee—" She laid a cold hand on his, her eyes hot. "—I could kill Melrose—myself. It's in me to do it. Rance meant everything to me—I can't tell you—"

McFee said, "The Governor's lady."

She turned white. She whipped up her fork as if she was going to throw it at him. After a long moment she said coldly, "You mean I didn't love him—that I was just politically ambitious—"

"Oh, you loved him, sister."

"McFee, you are horrid." Tears started in her eyes. "But I don't care what you think. He'd have got there. I could have made him. He had appeal—the public—"

"What about the Leclair woman?" McFee asked.

Irene Mayo answered stonily, "She didn't count," and made patterns on the table cloth with her fork. "I loved him, but—I shouldn't have minded his blonde—much. A man is a man. Only the other thing *really* mattered—" The red-headed girl lifted her eyes to McFee's. "I am exposing myself, McFee. I did want to be—the Governor's lady. You'll think me mercenary. I don't care. I'd rather be that than dishonest. But Sam Melrose had to—" Her eyelids fell over the hate behind them, as she asked, "Who do you suppose 'Mr. Inside' is?"

"That doesn't make sense."

"Nothing makes sense."

"What does he mean by that sentence in your note, 'He's going to work on it?' "

"I been thinking about that," McFee said. "If Melrose has that Shelldon file he could do one of two things with it: Burn it, or work it over. By work it over, I mean change, substitute, lose in part, cut out, then send the file back with its kick gone. But we still got a good one to answer—" McFee stirred his coffee. "If Melrose has the file, what's he been chasing you and me all over the lot for?" He added after a moment. "The vice detail raids the Shawl tonight, by the way."

This appeared to interest Irene Mayo tremendously, but she stared at McFee silently while he wiped mushroom gravy off his lips and buttered a biscuit. "You said the Shelldon scandal wasn't big enough, in itself, to pull Melrose down, didn't you?"

McFee nodded. "You know what happened, don't you? Mike Shelldon was a big shot poker hound. Some'dy bumped him off in one of Melrose's joints—Melrose, maybe—but there isn't enough, if y'ask me."

"Wouldn't there be enough if it was definitely linked with the murder of Rance?"

"Yes."

"You just said the vice detail was going to raid the Shawl tonight. McFee—" She laid her hand on his. "—if Melrose has that file at the Shawl, and it should be found there—by the police—before witnesses—newspaper men—"

"Swell!" said McFee. "Some'dy'd have to do something then. But it isn't going to be, sister—"

"You don't know—" Her words came feverishly. "I'm not the sort of woman to sit down and wait. *I can't!* I've got to do something myself. McFee, take me out to the Shawl tonight. It's Saturday—there'll be a crowd—"

"If Sam has that file out there, you don't suppose it's lying around loose—"

"Of course I don't. But we might get a break. Things do break sometimes—unexpectedly. He knows what a gun is for, doesn't he?" she said, a little wildly. "He threatened us—we can threaten him—and if the police and some newspaper men are there—" She stared at McFee. She was very pale. She held her napkin in a ball between her clasped hands. "Not afraid, are you?"

McFee had finished his apple pie, sugared his second coffee.

"Got a hunch?"

"Yes."

"Well—" His eyes were amused. "Wrap

yourself around that food and I'll give you a bell tonight."

"McFee, you are a darling!"

"That's better than being Governor," he said.

After he had taken Irene Mayo to her car, McFee walked back along Third, turned down Carter. Some people were staring vacantly at the Gaiety Theater. A sign in the lobby said; HOUSE CLOSED TODAY. Across the exit alley hung a theater ladder. A cop on guard said, "Hello, McFee."

"Dirty job," McFee replied. He noticed that Maggie O'Day's hole-in-the-wall was shuttered. "That's funny," he muttered. "What happened to O'Day?"

"Search me," the cop said. "I been around Second and Carter twenty years and I never seen that old girl shut up before."

Rolling a match in his ear, McFee went down Second. He walked seven blocks and turned west on Finch, a street of ramshackle detached houses. Finch had been red light once; now it was colored. McFee stopped in front of a tall house with a crazy porch and a triangular wooden block at the curb. A pickaninny thumbed his nose at McFee.

McFee went along a broken cement walk to a drab side door. Two sloping boards with grooves in them led from the broken walk up to the door sill. McFee knocked. No one came. He was about to knock again when he sniffed the air. His eyes ran down the door. Folded newspaper showed between door bottom and sill. A keyhole was blocked. Moving fast, McFee pinched out his cigarette, picked up a piece of cement and shattered the window with it. He rammed the door with his shoulder. Lock and bolt gave and he fell into the room. A wave of combustible gas forced him back into the open, gagging.

A fat colored woman with a red handkerchief on her hair came up, running. She screamed.

McFee said, "Shut up. Go telephone the coppers." The harsh fury in his tones spun her around, goggle-eyed.

McFee drew air deep down into his lungs and

plunged into the gas-filled room. He shot up a window, hung his head outside, refilled his lungs. Facing inside he saw a gas heater, its cock wide open. Three cocks of a gas plate in one corner of the room were open. He shut off the gas flow and refreshed himself again.

Maggie O'Day lay in the middle of the floor. She lay on her side. Close against her was the wheel chair she had rolled herself home in for twenty years or more. But the last time she had come home she had come on her crutches.

Rance Damon's body was in the chair.

A rug tucked him into it. The five grand was still in his left hand. His right hung over the side of the chair, clutched in one of Maggie O'Day's weather-beaten bony ones.

McFee bent over the woman. He felt at her heart, lifted an eyelid. "Tough," he muttered. He went to the door and filled his lungs.

There were some rag rugs, a day bed, a couple of rocking chairs with antimacassars, a table, some framed pictures; near the gasplate was a wall cabinet. A door that led into the wall had been made tight with newspapers. Sheets of newspaper littered the floor.

A photograph of a large, fleshy, pallid man, still in his thirties, but already gross with high living, lay on the table. It was faded, had been taken perhaps thirty years before. The print had been torn in three, then carefully pieced together with adhesive tape.

McFee muttered, "The late Senator Gaylord." He chewed a knuckle, stared at the photograph, then looked at Damon and the woman. He said moodily, "Poor old girl!"

A bruise discolored Maggie O'Day's left temple. One of her crutches lay on the floor, behind the wheel chair. McFee saw something else then. He saw a red smear some two inches long on a sheet of newspaper on the floor in front of the wheel chair. He picked up the sheet, his eyes fixed and cold.

The smear was crimson grease paint.

McFee inspected Damon's shoes, the old woman's shoes. Neither pair was daubed with grease paint.

Very softly McFee said, "Pretty!"

A couple of coppers came. An assistant coroner, named Ridley, came.

Presently, Ridley said, "The old girl's been dead quite a while—ten or twelve hours. She cracked her head when she fell. It must have knocked her cold."

"Maybe some'dy cracked her first," McFee said.

"You mean, somebody else turned on the gas?"

10

A couple of hours later, McFee talked with Captain Littner, Chief of the Homicide Squad, in Littner's office, in police headquarters on Greer Street. Littner was a lean hairless man with an oval head and bleak eyes as clear as cold water. He had a political, a cautious mind.

"O'Day had a son," Littner said. "Some thirty years ago. But nobody knew—I mean, nobody was *sure*—what became of him. There was a lot of talk. Gaylord—" Littner rubbed his chin, looked at McFee.

"Sure," said McFee. "Gaylord. And now we got Melrose. You talked with Leclair yet?"

"Yes."

"Did she mention alibis?"

"Nine of them."

"Where'd you see her?"

"Melrose brought her in. He said he left the Scudder yacht late this morning." Littner was amused. "He guessed we better close the Gaiety awhile. And anyhow, Leclair was opening a dance act at the Spanish Shawl tonight. He guessed he owed Leclair a statement to the police—oh, beans!" said Captain Littner gently. "What a town!"

"You ought to be Chief, Littner," McFee said.

"Yes," Littner answered carefully. "We traced that .32—the one killed Damon. It belonged to Joe Metz."

McFee exclaimed, "Now, you don't tell me!"

"Joe said he hadn't much use of a .32 and he sold it to Damon in the Press Club, couple of weeks ago. Rance wanted it for someone, Joe said. Joe's got all the witnesses he needs—Carl Reder, Fred Pope, Wade Fiske. They say they saw Damon buy the gun, take it from Metz. Damon paid him fifteen dollars—" Littner smiled coldly. "Maybe he did."

McFee said abstractedly, "Maybe he did, at that." And then, "What do you think of this notion Damon's murderer bumped off O'Day because the old girl saw him leave the Gaiety?"

"We have that smear of grease paint."

"Grease paint isn't easy to clean up," McFee said, thoughtfully. "If it's on cloth—any sort of fabric, I guess—it isn't. Now if I'd killed some'dy and stepped in a mess of grease paint, I'd throw my shoes away."

"Where'd you throw 'em, McFee?"

"Well, I might throw 'em in some'dy's trash barrel. How's that?"

"Not bad." Littner made a note on a memorandum pad. "I'll put a detail on trash collection." He pulled his long jaw down. "McFee," he asked, "what about that red-headed girl?"

"Nice little number." McFee stood his hat on the back of his head. "A go-getter, and no better than she ought to be, maybe. Littner, if Leclair had dropped instead of Damon, I'd say Mayo could have done it. But she wanted Damon; she had a notion she could make him governor. Mayo wouldn't have shot Damon." Littner nodded, and McFee proceeded. "I got another idea. The vice detail's going to knock over the Shawl tonight—twelve p.m. Melrose'll be there— Metz, Leclair. The Mayor's billed to tell a bedtime story. How about it, Mr. Littner?"

Captain Littner said, "Beans!" He opened a cupboard in his desk. "What'll you have, McFee?"

"Rye," said McFee. "The trouble with you, Littner, is you don't wisecrack 'em enough. Lookit the Chief now—" He took the glass Littner handed him, pushed his forehead up, pulled it down. "Littner," he asked again, "how'd you like to be Chief?"

"The pay's good."

"You'd need plenty drag."

"Yes." Littner stared at McFee with a flicker of warmth in his eyes. "Yes, I'd need plenty of drag."

"Luke Addams is going to be District Attorney," McFee said. "We got to elect Luke first."

"Luke'd be a big help," Littner admitted.

McFee leaned close again. "Here's a question: If that Shelldon file should happen to be found in the Spanish Shawl tonight, what'd the Shelldon-Damon tie-up do to the Melrose organization?"

"Everything," Littner answered drily. "But it won't be."

McFee handed Littner the "Mr. Inside" notes. He told him where he'd got them and watched Littner over the end of his cigarette.

Littner said carefully, "Maybe I'll drop in at the Shawl around twelve." And then, "Help yourself."

"Thanks," said McFee.

It was five o'clock. McFee's car was in a garage on Fourth. He walked up to Carter, crossed Second. The cop was still on duty in the Gaiety alley. One of the lobby doors of the theater was open. A man with wide ears and a thick neck came out.

McFee said, "Hello, Harrigan."

"A swell dish you canaries handed me last night," the house manager said sourly.

"Lookit the publicity," McFee told him.

"What the hell! You pull a murder on me and the coppers close the house. I could have sold out at two bucks a seat if they'd give me a break."

"Why'n't you talk to Melrose?"

Harrigan muttered uneasily and put a cigar in his mouth. "Guess it ain't my picnic." McFee followed him towards the door and Harrigan said, "The show's closed, mister."

"There's a couple of points I want to check up."

"Go read a book."

McFee said, "There ought to be money in this for the house. If I give you a slant on what happened you ought to be able to hang an act on it when the coppers give you the go–sign. It'd sell big."

Harrigan looked at the end of his cigar. "A guy's gotta be careful," he mumbled; and then, "All right."

The backstage was dark. In Leclair's room, McFee turned on a wall bracket lamp. Light flowed out into the backstage. The couch stood against the wall. McFee stared at the crosses Hurley had chalked on the floor.

"Leclair was standing farthest from wall and couch," McFee muttered. "Damon was close against the couch—"

Harrigan cut in obliquely, "Leclair was out to the Shawl when Damon—if it was Damon— rubbed out."

"Oh, sure," McFee said solemnly. "Joe Metz and the boys said so. It was just a couple of ghosts I saw. Well, Mr. and Mrs. X, then. Mr. X flopped into Mrs. X's arms. They went down. Got a ball of string, Harrigan?"

The latter found string.

"Stand here," McFee said, and Harrigan set his No. 10's on the Mr. X cross. "Hold this against your chest."

McFee gave Harrigan the loose end of the string. Unrolling the ball as he went, he walked some twenty feet into the backstage, stopped and held the ball of string chest high. He stood on the south edge of the lane of light. The darkness of the backstage partly concealed him.

"The bullet must have traveled pretty well along the line of the string," McFee said. He added drily, "If there was any bullet—"

Slackening the line, McFee inspected a shallow horizontal groove, about an inch long, in the door jamb. The string had been level with the groove and about six inches to the right of it. McFee stared hard at the groove, twirled a match in his ear.

Backing up again, McFee said, "Put your dogs on the other cross."

Harrigan did so and the string grazed the groove. McFee said, "Swell!" and threw the ball at Harrigan. "Buy yourself a drink on me."

"Hey, wait a minute, fellah," Harrigan yelled. "You got me on by toes. What's the rest of it?"

McFee said, "Read it in the papers," and went out.

At Cato's, McFee ordered a Porterhouse steak smothered in onions. After his third coffee, he drove to his apartment. It was now eight o'clock. He looked up Irene Mayo's number and dialed Spring 2341. There was no response. McFee waited a little, then hung up.

He walked around the room, glaring at the Evening Tribune. The Trib said two killings in twenty-four hours was plenty and something ought to be done. McFee made a ball of the sheet. He carried the breakfast tray in to the kitchen. He put away the card table and poured himself a drink. He tried Irene Mayo's number again. No good.

McFee took a shower and got into his dinner clothes. He had wrecked four black ties when his telephone rang.

"Hello," McFee said. No one answered. "Hello, there—McFee talking."

He heard voices, vaguely familiar, but detached and distant and apparently not addressed to him. He embedded his ear in the receiver and waited, a fixed, hot look in his eyes.

The indistinct muttering continued until a voice suddenly cried, "You can't keep me here! I know where we are. We are in a house on Butte Street—I saw the name—Butte Street. Butte Street!"

It was Irene Mayo's voice that had ended on that desperate shrill note. Her voice had been thin and distant, but clear. McFee heard that muttering again.

And then, hysterically, "Don't touch me! I haven't got it—McFee—" A man laughed. A woman laughed.

McFee waited. His forehead was wet. He wiped it with a handkerchief. Gently replaced the receiver, and stood up. At his desk, McFee looked at a city map. He put a gun in his jacket pocket, and went down into the street.

As he got into his car, McFee said softly, "A house on Butte Street."

11

McFee drove towards the foothills that threw a possessive arm around the town, on the north. Here the streets went up and down like stair carpets and lost themselves in tangles of oaks and eucalypti. This neighborhood had been built up years before, then forgotten while the town grew westward. Most of the residences were scattered, set in small acreage, and exclusively hedged about. Street lights were few.

Butte, a tag-end street, one block long, ended in a canyon. McFee drove up, then down the street. There were only three houses on it. Two were dark. The third, at the end of the street, was a secretive-looking, one-story, rambling, redwood place. A cypress hedge enclosed the grounds. A side window glowed.

McFee left his car at the corner, across the road from the street lamp, and walked back.

He went up a cinder driveway, saw a garage, half filled by a dark-colored sedan. The lighted side window shone dimly in the black expanse of house and mantling trees. Curtains screened the windows. McFee could not see into the room, but he heard voices.

He heard Joe Metz' voice. He heard Joe Metz say, "Sister, we just begun to work on you—"

McFee found the back door locked. The house was built on the slope of the canyon. He saw a basement window on his left, below the level on which he stood. The light was on the other side of the house; the wind made a melancholy rustling in the trees. He came to a decision. Holding his soft felt hat against one of the small square panes of the cellar window, he struck the felt sharply with the nose of his gun. The brittle glass broke with a tinkling sound.

His arm inside the window, McFee found the hook. The window swung upward on hinges. McFee threw the beam of his flash inside the cellar room, let himself down into it. He saw a stair, went quietly up it, came to a door. It opened when he turned the handle and pushed against it. He left his shoes on the top step.

McFee found himself in a dark, square hall, redwood timbered. He heard voices, saw an open door with light somewhere beyond it. Through the door he entered a living room with a huge stone fireplace. The light and the voices came from a partly opened door, opposite the one through which he had just come.

As McFee approached this door, Monty Welch whispered, "Lemme at her, Joe—"

This room was the library. McFee saw Mabel Leclair in a black velvet gown, curled up on a divan, eating chocolates. Metz and Welch were bent over an arm chair in which Irene Mayo strained away from them in an attitude of terror. Joe Metz held her by the arm. Her eyes were enormous, frantic. She whimpered faintly. Her lips were taped. Welch burned a cigarette.

McFee said, "Quit that, Joe."

Monty Welch must have heard McFee first. He spun on his heel, white violence bursting through his professional calm. As McFee said "Joe," Welch fired from the pocket of his dinner jacket. He fired again, lurching toward McFee. The latter aimed, let go. Welch's shoulder bunched up, he screamed and went down. He threshed about, buried his face in the carpet.

Metz stood erect, his hands at his sides. McFee went towards him. Metz did not move or speak. His bulbous forehead gleamed. His lip muscles twitched. McFee took a long stride, a short one, and struck Metz a terrible blow in the mouth. It made a crunching sound and Metz hit the carpet. McFee pulled the adhesive tape from Irene Mayo's lips.

"McFee—" the red-headed girl sobbed. She rocked in the chair, began to rub her wrists.

"Sure," McFee said. "Take it easy."

Welch dragged himself across the floor. McFee toed his gun under the divan. Metz lay groaning. His mouth and the plaster strap on his cheek were a crimson mess. He held a handkerchief against it. Suddenly, he jerked out an automatic. McFee's unshod toe caught his wrist before he could fire. The gun shattered the glass front of a bookcase. McFee raised Metz by his lapels and flung him onto the divan, alongside

Mabel Leclair. The Leclair woman screamed and covered her face.

McFee searched all three of them for other weapons, found none.

"What give you the notion Miss Mayo had the Shelldon file, Joe?"

Metz blotted his wet lips, whispered, "She knows where it is—you, too—one of you—"

McFee cut in softly, "The gun killed Damon was yours, Joe."

"I sold it to Damon." Metz' bruised lips distorted his speech. "The boys saw me hand it him. I told Littner—"

"How about Damon handing it to Leclair?"

The blonde woman opened her mouth, but as McFee looked at her she closed it again with a gasping sound. McFee proceeded. "You went to Miss Mayo's apartment, I s'pose. That's kidnapping. We'll give Littner a bell."

The telephone stood on the table. McFee backed towards it. Metz stared after him, his eyes haggard above the red-spotted handkerchief against his lips. The blonde woman wept. Holding his shoulder, Monty Welch struggled to a sitting position, his lips gray.

The telephone was a dial instrument. Several magazines had been inserted under the receiver, so that while the receiver was on the hook, the hook was up. McFee laughed a little and looked at the red-headed girl. She nodded, her eyes hot with hate. As McFee seized the telephone, she got control of herself and caught his arm.

"What's on your mind, sister?"

"McFee, it's our turn now." She spoke feverishly. "These people aren't important. Melrose—Sam Melrose is. He's at the Shawl. The Leclair woman is opening a dance act there tonight. Well, she isn't—"

"What's that?"

Irene Mayo said deliberately, "Metz is going to phone Melrose that Leclair is too ill to appear. Shock—anything! And he's going to tell Melrose her red-headed friend, Zella Vasquez, is on her way out to take Leclair's place. Melrose—no one at the Spanish Shawl has seen me. If Metz telephones Melrose I'm coming he'll accept me as Leclair's friend. Why shouldn't he?" Irene Mayo hammered on the table. "McFee, you've got to make Metz telephone him—"

"Swelll!" McFee said.

"I won't!" Metz shouted thickly. "By God, if you lay a hand on me—"

McFee jerked him up and shook him into a shivering silence. He walked him backwards, slammed him down beside the table.

He said, "Metz, since half-past one this morning, you've been rocking the cradle. It's my turn now. Do as I tell you, or I'll spatter you over that wall. Grab that phone and tell Melrose Leclair is sick. Tell him Zella Vasquez, her red-headed side kick, is on her way out. And make it stick!"

Metz' Adam's apple ran up and down his throat. He rubbed his wet palms together, pulled the telephone towards him. He dialed Thorn 99238. He had to do it twice and then, huskily, "Mr. Melrose—tell him Metz calling."

McFee stuck his gun into the back of Metz' neck. He didn't say anything. Melrose helloed, and Metz began a pretty good job of doing as he had been told. When he weakened, McFee leaned on his gun and Metz picked up again. Melrose put some question about Zella Vasquez.

Metz answered carefully, "I dunno, Sam. Leclair says she's good—that oughta be plenty—" The blonde woman made blasphemous noises but subsided when McFee looked at her. Metz proceeded, "She's on her way, Sam . . ." Metz hung up. "What Melrose won't do to you for this, mister—"

McFee gave Irene Mayo his gun, said, "Watch him," and cut out a length of the telephone cord. He bound Metz' hands and corded them to the straight back of the chair in which he sat. Metz did not resist. His ankles McFee fastened to the legs of the chair with Metz' belt and a couple of handkerchiefs. Metz dripped sweat but said nothing. At the back of the house McFee found some clothesline. He sat Monty Welch on another straight backed chair and roped him to it. Welch had fainted. McFee slammed a third chair down in front of Mabel Leclair.

She screamed, "You ain't going to tie me up—"

McFee cut in, "I'll forget you're a lady, if you don't sit in that chair."

"Forget it anyhow," Irene Mayo said hotly.

As McFee was tying up the Leclair woman, she flared out, "Sam Melrose thinks you red-headed Shebas are particular arsenic."

"He's going to change his mind."

"You couldn't hold Rance Damon."

Vivid spots of color on her cheek bones, Irene Mayo slapped the blonde woman hard across the mouth, rocking her head backwards. Mabel Leclair went pale under her make-up, became inarticulate. The red-headed girl was throwing up the gun when McFee said, "That's plenty, sister."

McFee found a roll of adhesive tape on the table. He taped the lips of his prisoners. Metz he dragged into the hall, on the heels of his chair, and tumbled into a clothes closet. The door locked, he threw the key into the cellar and put on his shoes, he locked Monty Welch in the pantry; left Mabel Leclair in the library.

Irene Mayo said, "You do a good job, McFee."

He nodded. "That telephone stunt was slick."

She shuddered. "I was afraid you were out. They were getting some drinks. I knew it was the only chance— They thought I was shouting at them."

McFee stared at her. He said slowly, "Think you can put over that Zella Vasquez number?"

She smiled. "I've known lots of men, McFee."

"What you think you're going to get out of it?"

"I told you at lunch. If Melrose has that Shell-don file—if I should find it—or the police—You said they were raiding the Shawl—" She clasped her hands, whispered huskily, "Perhaps I'm a fool, but I can't help it. I can't help feeling some-thing's going to break—"

McFee muttered, "Let's get at it, then."

A clock in the hall showed nine-five as they went out.

They walked down Butte Street to McFee's car.

"I want to go home first," the girl said.

McFee smiled one-sidedly, answered, "Right."

At Irene Mayo's apartment, McFee poured himself a drink. He took the glass over to the telephone and called Roy Cruikshank, at the Tribune office, then Littner at headquarters. Ringing off, he pushed his face up and set his glass down. Near the telephone stood a portable typewriter. McFee took a chair and slid paper under the roller. He wrote for about ten minutes, then read what he had written, and put the paper inside his jacket pocket.

Irene Mayo came prancing out of the bed-room. She wore a green silk blouse, a blue velvet bolero, a frothy red skirt and a green sash. She looked like a red-headed Carmen. Snapping her fingers, she fell into McFee's arms. Her green eyes were veiled and humid.

McFee said, "Very nice," and kissed her. "If Melrose don't fall, I'll go peddling fleas to a dog circus."

It was nine-fifty. McFee drove fast. They took one of the beach boulevards, followed it a while, and turned north. Presently they made a west turn, then a northwest turn into a dirt road that ended in a grove of cypress trees. The trees were on a bluff high above a crashing beach, and garlands of red, green and blue lights hung against them. Crooked in the bright arm of the trees was a sprawling, dark-shingled building with gemlike windows. A horde of cars stood around. Music throbbed. People churned in a splatter of sound and color.

Irene Mayo said, "I'll go in alone. You come back later—" She added lightly, "If you care to."

McFee laughed and let her out. She ran under a canopy of colored lights and vanished through a door. An attendant ran towards McFee's car, but McFee reversed and roared down the road. At the intersection he parked long enough to smoke a couple of cigarettes before he put the car around.

He entered the Spanish Shawl at eleven-five.

12

At one end of the rowdy cafe floor a six-piece colored orchestra—Dutch Louie and his Pals—peddled hot music. The ebony lads looked livid and wet in the overhead yellow lights. A good crowd danced about. The closely regimented tables made a horseshoe about the patch of shining floor. Most of them were taken but Leo Ganns, the head waiter, found McFee one at the lower end of the room.

He ordered broiled lobster and coffee.

The music stopped and the floor emptied. McFee touched a match to a cigarette. The air was heavy with smoke and the odors of food. Some liquor was flowing. Two girls near McFee sat lopsided and very still. Dutch Louie began to shout through a megaphone in his mellow drawl. He ballyhooed one Zella Vasquez, red-headed Spanish dancer, who stood 'em on their ears in Havana, Cuba. "Yessir, ladies and gem'men, an' if you don't think she's got something you jest gotta have—"

Irene Mayo whirled onto the floor in her Spanish costume. Behind her came a dark, slick-looking number from the Argentine or Chicago, maybe. They did a fox trot, the ebony boys wailing "My Baby's a Red-head-too." After that, a tango. Then Irene Mayo went solo and turned in a sweet *la jota Aragonese*. As she frothed past McFee, her eyes bright with fever, rested on him without recognition. She threw herself into the dark number's arms, and the crowd stamped. They did another tango. McFee dug into his lobster. The crowd howled for more and got the hat dance.

Sam Melrose came smiling onto the floor. He was an olive-skinned man with an uneven mouth and grizzled hair parted in the middle. His face was old, his forehead was corded by deep lines that never smoothed out. He was thirty-eight.

The hat dance finished, Irene Mayo pin-wheeled towards Melrose. He caught her in his arms, kissed her, and whirled her off through a door. The house yelled its throat dry, but the red-headed girl did not return. The slick-looking number took the bows.

McFee said, "Not bad," and finished his coffee.

McFee strolled through a door which opened into a red-carpeted hall, pushed through a door in the wall opposite and joined half a dozen men drinking at a bar. The bar was a swivel arrangement that could be swung into the hall behind it on a couple of minutes' notice.

The barkeep said, "What'll you have, McFee?"

"Straight." As the barkeep set up his goods, McFee asked, "Comp'ny tonight, Ed?"

"I dunno," the man muttered.

McFee walked into the gaming room, which adjoined the bar. Roulette, black jack and craps were running. There were no windows in the room. The only entrance to it was from the bar. The games were at the lower end of the room, and it was possible to swing a false wall across the tables as quickly as the bar could be made to vanish. The device was superficial, but all the roadhouse ever had needed. Some twenty or thirty people were playing, their voices feverish and blurred. Now and then a word pattern emerged. "You pick 'em—we pay 'em . . . Get your money down . . . Six . . . point is six . . . twenty-one . . . throws a nine. Take your money . . ."

Art Kline stood near the crap dealer. He looked at McFee, flexed his shoulder muscles, looked away. It was twenty minutes of midnight.

Walking into the hall, McFee glanced down it to where Melrose had his rooms. A woman's voice lifted hysterically for an instant above the harsh overtones of the Shawl. Art Kline stuck his head into the hall. When he saw McFee, he pulled it back. McFee smiled coldly, waited a minute, then went past the bar to a side door.

It was light outside. He walked to the rear of the building. Here it was dark. Trees threw tall shadows. Light came from a curtained window behind some shrubbery. McFee glanced around, then pushed through the shrubbery. It plucked at his face and throat. The window curtains did not quite meet and he was able to see into the room. He saw a soft, intimate room and a floor with a yellow parchment shade. Irene Mayo reclined in a plush upholstered chair beneath the lamp. Sam Melrose sat on an arm of the chair.

The red-headed girl laughed provocatively. Melrose bent towards her. She pushed him away, her fingers on his lips. They talked a while, Melrose leaning attentively over the girl. McFee heard her slightly hysterical laugh and Melrose's bleak chuckle, but Dutch Louie and His Pals drowned out their conversation.

The room had three doors. One led into the hall, another opened into a small washroom, the third gave entrance from the business office. A red carpet covered the floor. An ornate flat-topped desk stood in one corner, a chair behind it, a cloak tree beside it. On the desk was a wire letter basket.

Melrose got up and went into the business office, closing the door behind him. Irene Mayo came sharply forward onto her feet. She stared at the closed door, an obsessed look on her face. She ran swiftly towards the ornate desk, bent over the wire basket. McFee saw a flat manila envelope in her hand, and muttered, "Swell!"

Someone behind him said, "We got you covered, McFee."

13

McFee turned slowly, his palms tight against his thighs. Three men in dinner jackets stood on the other side of the shrubbery, guns in their hands. One of them was Art Kline. An ascetic-looking man with disillusioned eyes and a plume of gray hair on his white forehead had addressed McFee. This was Fred Pope, who ran the Red Jacket, a Melrose enterprise.

Their faces gleamed a little. Their shirt fronts stood up like slabs of stone.

Fred Pope said, "Sam wants to talk to you, McFee."

"I had a notion he might."

"Come outta that."

McFee stepped into the triangular huddle the three men had made of their bodies. They took his gun away from him.

"Straight ahead," Pope said. "No monkey business."

A private door gave them access to the business office. There were comfortable chairs, a couple of mahogany desks, safe, telephone, and a filing cabinet. A desk lamp was lighted. The hall door opened and Sam Melrose entered, a cob-webby bottle in his hands.

When he saw McFee the lines that corded his forehead tightened until they looked like wires embedded in his skull. He set the bottle down, came towards McFee with quiet, quick steps. Fred Pope laughed, dropped into a chair. Kline and the other man laid their backs against the outer wall.

An electric clock on the filing cabinet indicated seven minutes of twelve.

Sam Melrose said, "McFee, I want that Grand Jury Shelldon file."

"Don't be a sap."

"What do you mean?"

"You got it already, Sam."

"McFee, you been handing my boys that line ever since they ran you down in the Gaiety this morning. I'm damn good and sick of it." Melrose's flat-surfaced eyes distended coldly. "But I'll give you a break. You shoved your nose into my business—got what I paid money for. All right—come through with that file and we quit even. You walk outta here. You go home. You forget everything you figured on remembering. And you let my business alone after this. When I get this town like I want it I'll throw some sugar your way. Where you put that file?"

McFee smiled, felt for a cigarette, put it in his mouth. He flipped a match at it. Anger puffed across Melrose's eyes, subsided. The two hard-faced men started forward, but fell back at Melrose's gesture.

The clock showed four minutes of twelve.

McFee said, "Lemme see, there's a murder tied up with that Shelldon blow-off, isn't there, Sam?"

"I can beat it."

"What's the idea, then?"

"It looks bad, election coming on. I want it outta the way."

"Wait a minute, Sam. You got Leclair to make a deal with Damon. Damon is dead. His mother is dead. And the old lady didn't turn on the gas—" McFee paused, considered the other indulgently. "Can you beat all that, Sam?"

Melrose cut in harshly, "My boys didn't rub out Damon and his mother."

"Well, you oughta know. If that Shelldon file don't turn up at the wrong time, maybe the tax-payers'll believe you. It's funny what taxpayers'll believe. But the Damon-O'Day murders and the Shelldon racket'd make a bad combination." McFee laughed. "That Shelldon file's getting pretty important, Sam."

Melrose said, "Ten grand, McFee?"

"I haven't got it."

"Listen, mister—" The lines that corded Melrose's frontal bone deepened again. "I dunno what you playing for, but if it's to put the bell on me you got the wrong cat by the tail. I'm running this town. I'm gonna keep on running it. Nob'dy can get to first base unless I say so. McFee—" he prodded the latter in the chest, "—I want that Shelldon file. If you don't come across my boys'll walk you out and leave you some place."

The clock said one minute of twelve.

Dragging on his cigarette, McFee muttered, "Well, I dunno—"

The telephone rang.

Melrose picked it up. He did not remove his eyes from McFee, as he said, "Melrose talking." . . . And then, "Yes, Joe . . . Yes, what's that? . . . McFee—That red-head—His side-kick—But you phoned—What? . . . A frame-up— . . . You dunno . . ." Melrose's violent eyes impaled McFee. The latter stood stiffly, sweat on his temples. Melrose said coldly, "I got both of 'em here—Oh, McFee'll talk—"

Comprehendingly, Art Kline, Fred Pope and the other man crowded McFee. As Melrose rang off, he said, "Watch McFee!" and jumped toward his private room, jerked the door open. His eyes were hot when he faced around. "She musta heard—Fred, that redhead's the Mayo woman. McFee brought her—a frame—Bring her back."

As Fred Pope went away, Melrose said quietly, "What's back of this Mayo woman coming here?"

"Some'dy's been kidding you, Sam."

"You gonna talk?"

"Nothing to talk about."

"Lemme work on him a while, Boss," Art Kline said.

It was two minutes after twelve.

McFee shook the sweat out of his eyes. Dutch Louie and His Pals were tearing a staccato jazz out of their horns. The music swelled, filled the house with crashing sound. But McFee could hear the ticking of his watch, the pounding of his heart.

"Listen to the music, Sam," he said.

Melrose shouted, "By God, McFee, if you won't talk my boys'll burn it out of your toes—"

McFee struck him in the mouth. As Melrose went backwards, Kline and the other men jumped in. They milled for a minute. McFee got home four or five good ones, but he was taking a beating when the music stopped. The house became completely quiet.

A police whistle shrilled out in the cafe room.

Melrose ejaculated, "The coppers! I for-got—" And then, "I'll fix those birds—" He checked himself, said less positively, "Art, you stay here—"

McFee cut in softly, "You can't do it." Melrose glared at him, dabbed a cut lip with a handkerchief. "Sam, you are in a spot. Littner and Cruikshank are out there. You didn't s'pose I'd walk in here without having my tail covered? I told Littner to look for me."

"Lotta good that'll do you," Melrose said harshly. To his men, "Take McFee down the beach—the shack. Keep him there till I come."

Art Kline stood behind McFee. "Get going,

sap," he said, in his gummed-up voice, and shoved metal into McFee's back.

As McFee moved towards the side door, Littner entered.

Melrose's eyes turned white. Kline and the other man stared at him, slid their guns away. Littner looked around with his cold water eyes, rubbed his long jaw.

"Hello, McFee," he said. "Sam."

"Littner," McFee said.

"Argument?"

"No," McFee answered. "Sam bit his lip. He was just going to open a bottle of bubbly." McFee walked to the desk, picked up the bottle Melrose had placed there. It was moist and cold. "Seventy-six. Elegant." He turned to Melrose. "Got a glass for Littner, Sam?"

Melrose stared at McFee, his flat eyes inflamed. He did not speak. A flood of sound, shot through with panic, filled the house. Women screamed, glassware shattered. Melrose wiped his mouth, felt at his throat, pulled in a long breath. Then he sullenly crossed to the filing cabinet and took three glasses, a corkscrew and a napkin out of the bottom drawer. McFee ceremoniously handed him the bottle. Melrose wiped the top of the bottle, wrapped the napkin around it. The cork popped. Melrose poured unsteadily.

McFee said, "To the next District Attorney." They drank.

Blood from Melrose's cut lip turned the "seventy-six" pink. He muttered blasphemously, held the napkin against his mouth. McFee hung his arm over Melrose's shoulders. A white heat played across the flat surfaces of Melrose's eyes.

McFee asked, "You got the Mayor out there, Littner?"

"Yes."

"Buy him a lemonade before you bring him in. Sam and I got business to do." McFee slapped Melrose's shoulder affectionately. "Five minutes, Littner."

McFee linked his arm in Melrose's. Melrose resisted him a moment, then let the other lead him towards the door of the inner room. Littner's eyes followed them, faintly ironical.

Art Kline and his companion glared angry bewilderment.

At the door, McFee said softly, "Tell your boys this is private, Sam."

Melrose muttered, "That stands."

McFee looked at Littner. "Maybe you better stick close. Some'dy might take a notion." Littner nodded.

McFee shut the door.

Melrose's face was yellow and wet. "What's your proposition?"

14

The room had a secretive intimacy that affronted the uncomplicated McFee, but he marched his somber eyes around it. The washroom door stood ajar. It had been shut when McFee had looked in through the window. His eyes dwelt on it a moment. Then he dug out the "Mr. Inside" notes and handed them to Melrose. "Take a look at these."

Melrose said thickly, "Would my boys have been tailing you all day, if I had that file here?"

"Sure you haven't got it here, Sam?"

"What you mean?"

McFee said slowly, "Littner and Roy are here to look for it. It'll make a swell story—if they find it in this room—A swell story, Sam—"

Comprehending, Melrose yelled, "You planted that file here! You and that readheaded tramp—What you done with it?" He dropped his hand into his jacket pocket. He pushed his face into McFee's, said in a low tone, "You find that file quick, or take it in the belly."

"Littner's out there, Sam."

Melrose breathed hard. He took his hand out of his pocket. He wiped sweat out of his eyes, rubbed his palms together. "I'll bust you for this, McFee." His eyes slid desperately around the room—chairs, desk, washroom, carpet.

McFee said, "Sit tight, Sam, or I'll call Littner."

Melrose began to walk the floor. He stopped abruptly, came to grips with himself. "Let 'em find it," he said huskily. "I can beat the rap."

"Think so?" McFee chewed a finger nail. "Damon wasn't so much, but O'Day was his mother. Nob'dy knew it until today. The old girl had about a million friends in this town and all of 'em are beginning to feel sorry for her. You know what people are when they begin feeling sorry. Think you got enough drag to beat the Damon-O'Day-Shelldon combination?"

"My boys didn't rub out Damon and O'Day."

"This is politics, Sam." McFee thumbed a match at a cigarette. "It isn't what a lad does or don't do—it's what his public'll stand for."

"How d'I know that file's planted here?"

"Call Littner—you'll know then."

"You found out who killed Damon?"

McFee answered carefully, "Maybe."

Melrose pulled up in front of McFee. "What you want?"

The racket on the cafe floor had dropped to a backlash of irritation and protest. A door opened. Littner spoke to someone. Joe Cruikshank's soprano answered. The Mayor's platform boom cut in.

McFee said, "Sam, you been running this town long enough. I'm going to take it away from you."

"Yes?"

"The Mayor's out there telling everybody what a good guy he is." McFee spoke softly, pulled out the paper he had typewritten at Irene Mayo's. "The Mayor's your man. Your money elected him, keeps him in the City Hall. This is an unsigned indorsement of Luke Addams' candidacy for District Attorney—"

"A lotta help that'll give him."

McFee said gently, "With the City Hall machine and the newspapers pulling for Addams we got a pretty good chance beating Dietrich. Addams in, we work for a new deal in the police hookup—Littner chief. But that's future. Sam, you are going to tell Hizoner to put his John Henry to this declaration of independence, or I give Littner the go sign." He smiled. "How 'bout it?"

Melrose raged, "I will not!" But he was shaken. "I'll see you—"

McFee cut in, "You want Littner to use his

search warrant? This is politics. I'm telling you."

Jerking at his wilted collar, Melrose walked to the window. McFee slanted his eyes at the washroom door. He kept them there until Melrose faced around.

"I can throw plenty sugar your way—"

McFee said, "You are going to need sugar, Sam."

Melrose opened his mouth, shut it without saying anything, pressed the heels of his hands into his eyes. When he dropped them, his eyes were crazy, and he came charging towards McFee with his hands clenched. Littner entered just then, a brown paper parcel under his arm. Roy Cruikshank was behind him. The Mayor boomed in the outer room. His handsome, silver head was visible for a moment before Cruikshank closed the door. Melrose shook his head, let his hands fall.

Littner sat down, laid the parcel on the floor beside him. He said nothing. His oval head, his cold water eyes said nothing. Cruikshank put a cigarette in his pink mouth, pulled his hat over his eyes and leaned against the wall.

"Do I get that file?" Melrose asked tonelessly.

McFee said, "Sorry. We got to have a guarantee the City Hall'll root hard enough." He added reluctantly, "But I'll give you a break, Sam. I'll show Littner who killed Damon and his mother."

Melrose wet his lips. "All right." McFee handed him the unsigned indorsement. He read it, turned it over, flared out, "None of my boys killed Damon. By God, McFee if this is another frame—"

McFee said, "I never framed anybody, Sam."

As Melrose went out and shut the door behind him, the Mayor's platform boom ceased. A low-toned, bitter argument began. Melrose's voice whiplashed, "I'm still running this town, Mr. Mayor."

McFee sat down. His eyes moved towards the washroom door, remained there a moment, came back. He wiped his face.

Littner said mildly, "Warm for the time of the year."

"It's some of that unusual weather," Cruikshank muttered under his hat brim.

"Maybe Sam'll buy us a highball," McFee said. He laughed softly, looked at the cherubic Cruikshank, at the politically minded Littner. "Politics is funny. The lad who don't have to put over more than a couple of dirty ones to pull three good members out the bag has a medal coming to him."

"Some'dy ought to pin a medal on you, Handsome," Cruikshank said.

"I'm not through with this town yet."

Melrose came in then, a dull burn on either wet cheek bone. He handed McFee the indorsement, sat down and shelved his chin on his chest. He did not speak, did not look at McFee. The latter examined the signature. A clock ticked loudly somewhere. In the next room the Mayor was booming, "Luke Addams is a man in whom I have the greatest confidence. It will be a pleasure—" Dutch Louie and His Pals whipped into a jazz.

Parading his eyes around the room, McFee blinked at the washroom door, let them idle on the ornate desk. He went to the desk, bent over the wire basket and looked through the papers in it. He stood erect and stared at the end of his cigarette. A couple of overcoats hung on the cloak tree, near the desk. McFee put a hand inside one of them and brought forth a long manila envelope with "Shelldon" penciled in one corner. The envelope was open. He glanced into it.

Melrose lifted his head. Rage had contracted his eye pupils, ground them to points of bitter, fierce light. He did not speak.

McFee handed Cruikshank the Shelldon file and the Mayor's indorsement. "Stick 'em in the Tribune vault a while," he said.

"Right," Cruikshank muttered.

15

Littner gave McFee the brown paper parcel. "No. 3 trash collection wagon brought them in," he said.

"Very nice," McFee answered. He sat down, the parcel on his knees. He looked at his watch. "Twelve-thirty-five. It's just twenty-four hours since a lady came to see me, at Cato's. She said the lad she was with, Rance Damon, had gone into the Gaiety about an hour before. She said he'd followed Sam Melrose—"

Melrose ejaculated, "He did not. I was on Scudder's yacht. I got all the alibis—" He stopped there, wiped his mouth on the napkin. "You birds got nothing on me."

McFee proceeded softly, "The lady and I got into the Gaiety. Damon had been shot. He died. Some'dy had stepped on a tube of grease paint. Crimson. Smeared it around. Damon's body walked out. I found it in Maggie O'Day's. Maggie was his mother. She had rolled him home in her wheel chair. Maggie was dead—gas. But there was a bruise on her head. Maybe she fell. Maybe she was slugged. I found a smear of crimson grease paint on a newspaper on the floor. There was no grease paint on Maggie's shoes or Damon's. Very well. I figured this way: The party killed Damon stepped on the tube of grease paint, in the dark, bust it open, got all smeared up. Grease paint is bad. Maggie saw that party beating it out the Gaiety. The party followed Maggie home, to see how come. Maggie accused the party of murdering her son and got slugged—with her own crutch, maybe. The gas was to make it look like suicide—grief. The party's shoe smeared the newspaper. The party didn't know it, went away. Now grease paint is hard to clean off fabric goods, and when the party saw what'd happened to a nice pair of shoes it looked like a good idea to get rid of 'em. Sounds easy. Only it isn't. Littner's men found 'em at the city trash collection dump."

McFee unrolled Littner's brown paper parcel. A pair of green satin pumps fell out. He held one of them up. The sole, instep, and right side of the pump were smeared with crimson grease paint.

Melrose blurted, "That lets my boys out."

McFee lighted a cigarette, looked at the match a while. "I said a lady came to see me at Cato's. She was wearing green satin pumps—

these pumps. When I took her home three hours later she was wearing green snakeskin slippers. She beat it out the Gaiety and phoned headquarters around 1:30. I picked her up on Third at 3:15—nearly two hours. That gave her plenty time to tail Maggie O'Day home, kill her, get back to the car, drive to her apartment—taking the Shelldon file with her—change her shoes, and get back to Third."

McFee rolled a match in his ear. "But I couldn't figure out why Irene Mayo killed Damon. Wasn't she going to make him Governor, herself the Governor's lady? So I went back to the Gaiety and ran a string along what looked like the bullet trajectory. There was a horizontal groove in the door jamb level with the line the bullet followed—"

A muffled, sobbing sound interrupted McFee and terminated in a wail of despair. McFee wiped his face and throat with a handkerchief. A bitter, silent moment went by.

McFee said deliberately, "Irene Mayo wrote those 'Mr. Inside' notes. She planted that Shelldon file here because Melrose's blonde had taken Damon with five grand. She wasn't with Damon last night. She tailed him down to the Gaiety. Melrose wasn't there. Slick little number. She tried to pull a fast one at her apartment this morning with a 'Shelldon' envelope full of blanks. Said she'd found it on Damon while I was in Leclair's room. Said it had fooled her. Well, she pretty near fooled me." McFee stared gloomily at his cigarette. "Damon must have given her that gun—Metz' gun. She didn't intend to kill him—the lad she was going to make Governor. No. She fired at Leclair. Because Leclair was gumming up the works. You can't figure women. The bullet ricochetted from the door jamb, took Damon—"

That tortured cry came again, McFee got up, walked towards the washroom door.

A pistol shot reverberated in the room.

McFee took three strides forward. The door leaned open. He caught the redheaded girl in his arms. He carried her to a chair, laid her in it. Littner, Melrose, Cruikshank stood around. People came rushing in, the Mayor booming . . .

McFee said, "I had a notion she'd do it." And then, huskily, "I never was much of a lad for hanging a woman."

The City of Hell!
Leslie T. White

BARELY REMEMBERED today, Leslie T. White (1901–1967) was a lifelong member of the law enforcement community, beginning as a ranger on some of the large private estates that dotted the landscape in the California of the early part of the twentieth century.

He moved to jobs in the sheriff's office and police department before becoming one of a few highly paid investigators attached to the District Attorney's office in Los Angeles, where he became a largely self-taught expert in fingerprinting, electronic eavesdropping, trailing suspects, photography, and other nascent tools of crime fighters.

He had headline-making experiences in the tong wars, battles with communists, helping to solve the Doheny murder mystery, and numerous other major criminal activities in California. These experiences served as the basis for his autobiography, *Me, Detective*, and such novels as *Homicide* (1937), *Harness Bull* (1937) and *The River of No Return* (1941).

His 1943 novel *5,000 Trojan Horses* was filmed in the same year by Warner as *Northern Pursuit* with a screenplay by Frank Gruber; it was directed by Raoul Walsh and starred Errol Flynn. Ten years later, *Harness Bull* was made into the famous motion picture *Vice Squad* (released in Great Britain as *The Girl in Room 17*) with a screenplay by Lawrence Roman; it was directed by Arnold Laven and starred Edward G. Robinson.

"The City of Hell!" was first published in *Black Mask* in October 1935.

The City of Hell!

Leslie T. White

Four honest cops and a city of gunmen and graft

 HE PIERCING SCREAMS of a woman filled the awed hollow of silence left void by the chatter of a sub-machine-gun and acted as a magnet of sound to suck the big squad car to the scene. Even before the police driver braked the hurtling machine to a full stop, Duane and Barnaby debouched from either side of the tonneau, balanced a moment on the running-boards, and hit the pavement running. Then while the doughty sergeant restrained the hysterical mother, Captain Barnaby went down on his baggy knees beside the broken little body.

It lay across the curb, feet and knees in the street, rag-covered torso flattened on the sidewalk: a tot of three, chubby, with light olive skin and eyes black as a starless night. There were three welling holes staggered across the tiny back and from somewhere beneath rivulets of scarlet inched along the dusty cement like accusing tentacles. A chubby little fist moved convulsively, aimlessly. Barnaby laid one of his great calloused hands over the baby hand, squeezed it, then looked up.

A sea of sullen faces met his frowning gaze; haunted faces with frightened eyes that stared. They formed a thick circle around him, ringing him in with the dead baby, with Sergeant Duane and the crazed mother whose agonized wails stabbed his consciousness.

"What happened here?" he demanded. "Come on, can't anybody speak?"

He saw they were afraid; their silence showed that. They stared dully at him, then looked at each other. It made him mad. He rocked back on his haunches and grabbed the arm of a little urchin of some eight years.

"You saw it, kid," he snapped. "Tell me about it!"

The youngster squirmed, rolled his eyes and, when he saw he could not escape, opened his mouth to speak. A sudden wild shriek from the hysterical woman froze the words in his tiny throat. Barnaby turned his head and met Duane's eyes.

"Take her inside!" he commanded.

As Duane dragged the woman away, the cop on the beat panted up; a moment later the police driver joined them. They drove back the sickened audience and Barnaby once more turned his attention to his child witness.

"Now tell me what happened, kid," he urged quietly.

Sweating and trembling the little chap stuttered out a vivid word-picture of the tragedy. Barnaby absorbed it in dribbles, disconnected fragments that years of bitter experience had taught him to assemble. . . .

A group of children had been playing in the street, happy to be free of school. They hadn't heard the big car until it was almost on them. Then, laughing, they had darted for the sidewalks. Nipper was the dead baby's name. There had been a man walking along the sidewalk in front of little Nipper; it was apparent that he was the object of gunfire. But he had vanished between two buildings just before the hail of lead came to chatter little Nipper's life away. The car hadn't stopped; nobody had taken the number. It had all taken place so quickly. . . .

Captain Barnaby released his grip and the little boy shot from his hand like a freed arrow to vanish into the black maw of a tenement. Barnaby rose, removed his battered fedora and combed his unruly hair with gnarled fingers. His lips moved in a bitter curse that was half prayer. Then the ambulance swerved around a nearby corner, so he left the broken baby and tramped into the house where he had seen Duane take the mother.

He had no trouble locating the room on the third floor; he simply charted his course by the compass of sound. He made his way up finally to stop at the entrance of the poverty-stricken room.

Duane stood with his back to the door, one hip resting against a square table, fists doubled, his face turned towards the sobbing woman in a chair. On one side of her stood a tall, gaunt man, his features twisted in grief as he sought to console her. Opposite was an aged woman whose snow white hair and dark skin reminded Barnaby of looking at a negative. He squared his shoulders and barged inside.

Duane turned, saw him. "It's their only kid," he jerked. "They don't know a thing about it, except that their kiddie's gone."

Barnaby swore softly, turned to the trio. "We're the police . . ." he began, but stopped at a scream from the mother.

She jerked out of her seat and faced him, wild-eyed, savage.

"Police!" she shrieked in his face. "You're just like the gangsters wat kill my baby! You know who did it, but you won't do nothin'! We're only poor people, nobody care if my baby . . ." Her voice trailed into a sob and the gaunt man pulled her back into the chair.

Barnaby swiveled and walked into the corridor. At the head of the stairs, the man overtook him.

"Captain," faltered the man, "could you just forget what my wife says? She ain't in no condition. . . . I'm workin' for the city, see, an' I can't afford to lose my position 'cause she lose her head. . . ." He stopped in anxious embarrassment.

Barnaby turned slowly and gave him a cold stare. "Your wife's opinion of the police of this particular town," he growled, "is about the same as mine." Without enlarging on the statement, he left the astonished man and clumped down the three flights to the street below. Duane caught up with him when he reached the squad car. They seated themselves in the tonneau and Barnaby waved the driver into motion.

He was silent a long time, then he said: "I wish some of the sob-sisters that romance about these damn' killers could have seen that! You know me, Sam, I'm not sentimental, but there was an awful loneliness about that poor little kid. Damn!"

Sergeant Duane passed a rough palm over his bald head. "It was probably some of Swarm's boys after one of Antecki's mob. Not that it helps us much with not a shred of evidence to go by."

Barnaby nodded stolidly. For several minutes he was lost in thought; at length he spoke.

"They didn't get the guy they came for, so they'll be back. Perhaps if we cruise around—"

Duane shrugged. "You're the doctor," he grumbled, "but I can't see what good it'll do. We don't know 'em, an' if we did we couldn't make it stick."

Barnaby called to the driver. "Hey, Murray, cruise around this district for a while. Take it easy, but be ready to roll when I bellow." He leaned back against the cushions and began to muse aloud: "We got a hell of a department, Sam! I been on it a long while; I didn't know a department could get so rotten."

"It's no worse than the other departments," Sam Duane growled. "They take their orders from the grafters just like we gotta."

Barnaby sighed, then asked: "Their only kid, you said?"

"Yeah. The father drives a garbage truck for the city—that's what he made the crack about—scared of losing his job. The old woman is the granny. Didja see how she took it?"

Barnaby nodded sourly. "I didn't like it. I hate to see people act like they *had* to take stuff like that. Poor devils! We got a hell of an outfit, Sam."

"Funny, but suppose we did run in those killers—a jury'd probably turn 'em loose."

"If they ever got to a jury," Barnaby said insinuatingly.

Duane stiffened. "You mean—? Oh, hell, Skipper, you can't pull that these days! Those lads have connections."

Barnaby growled deep in his throat, fished out his pipe and began to tamp tobacco into the bowl. He puffed it alight, then slumped back

into one corner of the seat, staring into the darkness. Duane followed his example and in a grim silence, the big squad car prowled the streets.

It was Barnaby who spotted the sedan rolling past at an intersection. He stiffened, nudged Duane and taking the briar from his teeth, pointed with the stem. Sergeant Duane slid to the edge of his seat.

"Hoods . . . !"

The Skipper gave a short brittle laugh. He jammed the pipe into a pocket, leaned over the front seat and gave the driver his instructions:

"Murray, slam that sedan into a lamp-post; I don't give a damn if you have to wreck us, don't let 'em get away."

The police chauffeur nodded without turning his head. He shifted into second, depressed the accelerator and caromed diagonally across the intersection. The siren gave one throaty snarl as he rammed the sedan over to the curb.

The other driver made no attempt to elude detention. He braked sharply to avoid a crash and thrust his head out the window.

"Hey, what's the idea . . . ?" he began, stopping when he saw Barnaby swing out of the police car, gun in hand.

Duane followed and threw a beam from his flash into the closed car. There were two men in the rear seat.

Barnaby yanked open the rear door. "File out," he ordered curtly, gesturing with his gun.

The pair in the back seat hesitated, then the larger of the two, a big blond man, grinned insolently, tilted his hat to a rakish angle and climbed to the street. His companion, a stocky fellow, followed scowling.

"You, too," Barnaby growled at the driver, and that worthy grudgingly complied.

The big man yawned. "What is this, Cap, a pinch?"

Barnaby caught him by the shoulder and spun him around. "Keep your mouth shut, Ritter," he barked. "We'll start off with a frisk." He ran practiced hands over the man's body and found a snub-nosed .38 in a shoulder harness.

"I gotta license to pack that rod," Ritter

offered, by way of explanation. "Don't get ideas, copper."

Duane searched the other pair. "Clean!" he reported disappointedly.

Barnaby inclined his head towards the tonneau. "Frisk the heap," he growled, keeping his eyes on the big man. "An' who are these muggs?" he demanded of the latter, indicating the two other hoods.

Ritter grinned. "I suppose you got a warrant to search our car, Cap?" He ignored the question.

Barnaby's eyes glowed. "I don't need a warrant to frisk a load of rats."

Ritter shrugged. "*No?* Then maybe they changed the Constitution since lunch time. My mouthpiece told me then. . . ."

Duane came running around the back of the sedan. He had a sawed-off shot-gun in his hands.

"The car was clean," he snapped, "but I found this in the gutter. They must have heaved it out when we stopped 'em."

Ritter smiled maliciously. "You'll have a hell of a time proving. . . ."

Barnaby hit him alongside the jaw, knocking him over the left-front fender. "You damned . . . !"

Duane caught his arm. "Easy, Cap, easy!" Lowering his voice, he added, "We ain't got a thing on 'em!"

The man came up massaging his jaw. "That'll cost you your job, flatfoot!"

Barnaby shook his arm free of Duane and started another swing, but Ritter stumbled hastily out of range. The captain flexed his fingers and backed up a stride. "All right," he rasped. "Pile in!" He waved them into the squad car with his gun.

The trio climbed into the rear seat. Barnaby ordered the police chauffeur to drive the sedan while Duane piloted the official car. Then he took his place in the front, sitting sidewise so he could cover the cargo of hoods in the rear.

Ritter made one more prophecy. "You can't lock us up in this town, flatfoot!"

He was right. They had barely reached Central Station when a criminal lawyer named Hymie Croker magically appeared armed with writs of *habeas corpus.* The three guns swaggered from the station, free, and from the shadow of the sergeant's desk, Captain Barnaby and Sergeant Duane watched in sullen silence.

When they had gone, Duane commented: "It's sure a swell system, Skipper. Not much like it was twenty years ago, when my old man was chief."

"Mike Duane was a man," Barnaby snarled through clenched teeth. "He'd have fired us if we'd brought those hoods in without first beatin' 'em so they couldn't walk. We haven't got a chief no more, we got a puppet. To hell with it, I'm goin' to bed!" He turned, slapped open the swinging doors and barged out into the night.

A court appearance in the morning and a lengthy conference with a deputy prosecutor after that kept Captain Barnaby away from Headquarters until late the following afternoon. When he finally strode into the station, the desk sergeant flagged him.

"Chief Grogan wants to see you, Captain. He left orders to shoot you right up the moment you came in."

Barnaby bobbed his rugged head, turned and tramped up the stairs to Grogan's office on the second floor. He was admitted at once.

Chief of Police Grogan squatted behind a desk, his broad back to the windows. His full, moon-shaped face was an apoplectic purple and his heavy jowls welled over the tight collar band of his tunic as though it strangled him. He had a small, querulous mouth that was permanently puckered as though he was just about to whistle. What hair he had left was gray and he wore it plastered sidewise across his pate in a vain attempt at deception. His thick hands toyed with an onyx lighter.

"You wanted to see me?" Barnaby asked.

Grogan nodded sourly. "Sit down," he commanded; and as Barnaby complied, he rose to his feet and began to pace the stuffy office. He made two complete circuits, then jerked to a stop and glared down at the Captain.

"What in hell kind of a cop are you?" he roared. "I understand you stopped a carload of citizens last night without a damn' bit of evidence, beat up one of the men for no good reason and then didn't have enough facts even to lock them up!"

Barnaby's eyes narrowed.

"You understand wrong," he retorted dryly. "I stopped a sedan of professional hoods for a frisk. A rat named Ritter, an ace gunman of Coxy Swarm's, got tough, so I slapped him. Ritter had a gun. . . ."

". . . for which he has a permit," cut in Grogan. "By what authority did you search that machine?"

What little warmth remained in Barnaby's eyes faded abruptly. "By what right, you ask? D'you know what happened down there last evenin'? A child was cut down by a mob of killers! They was tryin' to knock off another hood an' this kid of three took it instead."

Grogan made a disgusted motion with his big hand. "A *wop* kid!"

"He lived an' breathed," Barnaby said slowly. "He died because we coppers tolerate a lot of rats in this town."

The Chief's mouth shrank. "Captain Barnaby," he rasped, "you're relieved of your command immediately. You are suspended for ten days, after which you will report in uniform to night patrol duty in a suburban precinct."

Barnaby ran his tongue around the inside of his cheek. "I see. I rate this demotion because . . ."

"Because of conduct unbecoming an officer of the law; because you violated the laws you are sworn to uphold; because you have a vicious temper and beat up citizens; because . . ."

Barnaby stood up, lifted a restraining hand. There was fire glowing in the caverns under his shaggy brows.

"Grogan, you're a blustering *dummy*. You mouth a lot of words but you're tryin' this act because Coxy Swarm ordered to you to get rid of me. Ritter told me this was comin'."

The Chief swelled his chest. "Wait a minute, Captain Barn . . ."

The older copper interrupted him. "Shut up! You can take your crooked graft-eaten force an' go straight to hell with it." With an explosive oath, he swiveled and stalked out of the room.

He went down to the street and began to walk. Sweat stood out on his corrugated forehead; sweat of rage. Then as time passed and his temper cooled, he began to realize the cold truth.

He had *quit!*

Quit! That meant he wasn't a copper anymore! Or did it? Twenty years—no, it was longer than that; it was twenty-six years next June that he came to the Department. Hell, he'd headed the Homicide Squad for nearly a decade. He spread his big hands before him—with battered knuckles, calloused palms. His quizzical eyes stole to his heavy feet. Not a copper . . . ? That was a laugh!

He had *quit!*

What was wrong? It hadn't been like that in the old days! Sure, there was graft—you can't change human nature entirely—but small stuff that meant little, not this wholesale business. But murder was murder and the old laws of war or peace always offered safety to women and babies. Was it the laws, the tricks the crooks' shysters were skilled in under the guise of legality? Was it the way they were enforced, or the present administration?

Grogan had accused him of unbecoming conduct. What in hell had he done to rate that? Slap a baby killer? Was *that* unbecoming of an officer? The Old Man had called him a law violator! Huh! What was he paid a salary for?

Unable to find the answers to his muttered queries, Barnaby shrugged and raised his chin. Darkness had settled over the city; street lights sputtered into being. He glanced at a corner post and found himself in the district where Sam Duane lived. . . .

Cold sweat dampened his collar. Had Sam got it, too? Sam had a wife and family . . . ! Barnaby fished out a handkerchief and daubed his face. He'd better have a talk with Sam. It was one thing for Barnaby to throw up his job, he had no one to worry about. Somehow he'd just never found the time to get married. It wasn't that he hadn't wanted to—he had. He wanted a real home, loved kids, but a copper doesn't get much time for courting women—not the kind he'd want to mother his kids.

It took him ten minutes to reach the shabby little duplex that Sam Duane called home. A woman admitted him. Her wan features were wrinkled and worn, her body shapeless, and her head wore a crown of pale silver, but to Barnaby, Molly Duane was still the golden-locked colleen she had been the day she married Sam. One look at her patient face warned him.

She smiled and inclined her head to a curtained opening.

"Sam's in the parlor. Go right in, Clyde."

Barnaby squared his shoulders, swung on his heel and pushed into the room.

Sam Duane was sitting in a decrepit rocker, his stockinged feet on the windowsill, his chin resting on his chest, clamping his briar between his teeth. He spoke without turning his head.

"H'lo, Skipper. I hoped you'd drop in."

Barnaby pulled up a chair without invitation and straddled it. He probed through his pockets for his own pipe, found it and rapped it against the heel of his palm.

"Grogan haul you up?" he asked with studied casualness.

Duane bobbed his bald head. "Yep. Back to the *goats* with a *log* of wood." Which is a copper's descriptive phrase to explain that he was transferred to the suburbs to swing a club as he patrolled a foot beat.

"You quit, eh?" Duane added.

Barnaby thumbed tobacco into his pipe. "Yeah, I . . ." He stopped as the front door-bell whirred. He heard Molly pad down the corridor, heard the door creak open, then the booming voice of Dennis Hallahan flooded the small home.

Sam lifted his chin. "Come on in, Denny," he invited. Simultaneously the curtains were brushed aside and Hallahan and another dick named Louis Forsythe came in. The parlor seemed crowded.

Hallahan and Forsythe belonged to the same breed as Duane and Barnaby; born coppers, disillusioned, bitter, but patriotic to a losing cause—*justice*. To describe them would be to describe any typical old harness bull. Big men, with wide hunched shoulders, powerful biceps and cold, neutral eyes. They hold their heads a certain way after some twenty years of forced aggressiveness, a sort of cross between a Seville bull and an English bull dog. Their mouths grow straight and thin from cynicism, faces furrow and seam from the sight of constant tragedy. They grow to look alike, to think alike, to act alike. . . . A grand breed—a vanishing race.

That was Barnaby, that was Duane, and Hallahan, and Forsythe!

"You gave Grogan some good advice, Clyde," Hallahan commented. Hallahan had retired a year ago; Forsythe was due to take his pension in another eight months.

Barnaby nodded. "I couldn't help myself," he explained slowly. "The sight of him sittin' there, a beefy, blusterin' figurehead . . . well, somethin' snapped inside of me and . . . I quit!"

Hallahan sighed. "It's too damn' bad you threw away your pension. This town needs men like you! The city's in a hell of a shape; the criminal element are in power. What this town needs is a new department. Why a half-dozen old timers could clean this rat's nest up in forty-eight hours! Why, I remember when Old Mike Duane was chief we . . ."

He droned on, but ex-Captain Barnaby was not listening.

"*. . . old timers could clean this rat's nest up in forty-eight hours!*"

Old timers? He raised smoldering eyes and looked into the dim-lit faces around him. *Forty-eight hours?* Two days! And why not?

Forsythe was talking when Barnaby held up a commanding hand for silence. Forsythe paused. . . .

Barnaby's voice knifed the sudden hush. "Dennis, could *you* an' *me* raise a few old timers for a clean-up?"

No one spoke for nearly five minutes. These were not impulsive youngsters; these were veterans. They knew the seriousness of the suggestive question; knew the potential dynamite packed into the simple phrase.

Hallahan spoke first, almost defensively, for he remembered it was his own words that prompted the query.

"You mean, Clyde, to gun out these hoods?"

Barnaby leaned forward and his voice took on a saw-edge. "I mean to form a real department, to investigate, to convict, to execute." The idea assumed shape as he spoke. "To clean up; to deal out, not shyster's law, but justice. Every one of you boys knows the problem—it isn't enough to find out who commits crime, it's to make a jury believe it. *We* know the guilty ones, the thieves, the killers, and the grafters, but we can't do anything about it. Hallahan, you're a widower, independent—what do you think?"

Hallahan leaned back in his chair, his eyes watching the blue spiral of smoke that eddied ceilingward from his corncob.

"To deal out justice, not law," he mused absently. Then a laugh rang from his throat and he sat very straight.

"Think?" he roared. "I think it's a hell of a good idea! You an' me. . . ."

"Count me in," Forsythe interrupted.

Hallahan shook his head. "No, Louis, not you. There's your pension to think about. You'd lose that. An' of course Sam is out, too. We can't use married men with families that might suffer."

Barnaby nodded in accord. "That's right," he growled. "We'll get no thanks if we succeed. If we fail. . . ." He made an eloquent gesture with his big hands.

Duane never moved his head, but his voice roared out.

"*Molly . . . !*"

Steps sounded in the hallway and a moment later, Molly Duane's head appeared in the opening.

"Yes, Sam?"

Sam turned his face towards her. "Molly," he said quietly, "the boys are going to form an unofficial police department. They're goin' to clean up this town, gun out baby killers an' the like.

They may get themselves killed, Molly. What do you think about it?"

She hesitated just an instant, then: "And you want to go with them, Sam?" she whispered.

Barnaby cut in. "That's out! Sam ain't gonna do no such a damn' fool thing. Why it's practically suicide an' . . ."

In the wan light, they saw her smile. "If Sam wants to go, he can," she told them firmly. "Our babies are all grown and have families of their own; they don't need us now. It sounds like a mighty good thing. I've confidence in Sam and I can go to the children if anything should . . . well, *happen*."

"Thanks, Molly," Duane said huskily.

She went away.

"Four of us should be enough," Sam Duane went on quietly. "An' since we'll need a Chief, I suggest Clyde."

Hallahan stared for a minute at the drapes, still swaying from Molly Duane's passing. Then a deep sigh escaped him. "What a woman," he whispered, then added with a deeper growl: "I think that's another damn' swell idea. What do you say, Louis?"

Forsythe got up and walked over to the telephone. "Just a minute," he begged. "I got just one job to do before I take orders from our new Chief." He dialed a number, waited until the receiver made a metallic noise, then began:

"Hello, Grogan? This is Lieutenant Forsythe. Well, get this straight the first time, you thick-headed —— ——"

Hallahan's explosive laughter drowned Forsythe's words.

"Louis," Hallahan boomed, "is resigning!"

At exactly eleven thirty, "Big Dutch" Ritter was comfortably ensconced at a ring-side table in *La Parisienne Café* in company with his swart bodyprotector, Whisper Rieg, affectionately known as "The Scourge," and a pair of blonde entertainers. The redoubtable Ritter paused in the middle of a humorous tale when his alert eyes glimpsed the bulky figure of Barnaby and Duane bearing across the polished dance-floor towards his table. He had just time to remark out of the corner of his mouth that, "this ought to be good," when Barnaby reached his side.

"All right, Ritter, you're comin' with us!"

"The Scourge" slid to his feet, but made no overt move when he caught the imperceptible shake of his boss' head. Ritter grinned, tilted back in his chair and eyed the two veterans.

"Don't clown, Cap. Sit down an' have a drink. I heard you got canned."

One of the girls tittered nervously; perhaps she thought Skipper Barnaby didn't look like a man to fool with. She started up from her chair.

Barnaby glanced sidewise at Duane; their eyes met. "Okey, Sam!" he rasped; and made a dive for Ritter.

Rieg tried to earn his salary; he went for his gun. But big Sam Duane's persuader thudded behind his left ear and he immediately lost all interest in the encounter. Before he hit the polished floor, Duane caught him, slung him over his shoulder.

But "The Scourge" didn't know anything about it.

Barnaby's dive carried the now startled Ritter to the floor. He made a vague motion in the general direction of his arm-pit but all it earned him was a stunning blow on the jaw from one of the copper's massive fists. The "ace" mobster stole a hasty glance at his assailant towering above him . . . and surrendered.

He was rudely yanked erect, a steel bracelet bit into his right wrist and by it, he was unceremoniously dragged out of the café in the wake of the well-burdened Duane. And no one interfered with their going. Ritter balked outside when he saw that the car awaiting him was not an official machine—Ritter had learned that a ride in a regular police car invariably terminated at Police Headquarters where one of the mob's shysters would be waiting to spring him.

But his obstinacy was short-lived. Barnaby mouthed an expressive oath, then half-threw, half-kicked him into the rear seat where he was at once handcuffed to the unconscious "Scourge."

The car swung into motion.

Duane drove, eyes glued on the road ahead, mouth tightened. Barnaby sat sidewise on the seat beside him, his left elbow resting on the back seat, his bitter gaze riveted on the pair in the rear. In his right hand, he cradled a long nightstick; it swayed suggestively in his restless grip.

Ritter saw the stick, remembered the car, and stark terror gripped him. Some of the angry color seeped from his avaricious features, leaving them the shade of stale dough.

"Wait a minute, Barnaby," he jerked. "You can't do this!"

Barnaby's mocking laughter hit him like a blow. There was no mirth in the sound, rather a menace. . . .

"But this ain't official!" protested Ritter.

The doughty veteran sneered. "Sure it's official, you rat. You got me canned from one police force, but I got on another. You're arrested, Ritter; you'll get a trial all legal-like. But you won't have no crooked lawyers, Ritter."

The gunman's eyes protruded. "Another police force?" he gasped. "What city hired you? Where are you takin' us . . . ?"

"To a city where you belong, Ritter—*The City of Hell!*"

Duane toured around several blocks, crossing his own trail to make sure they had no tail, then satisfied at last there was no one following, he cut rapidly across the city to the warehouse district. He came to an abandoned loft building, circled it twice, finally to stop in a pool of black shadow. As he stepped out one side of the car, Barnaby went out the opposite side.

"All right, Ritter," Barnaby growled, opening the rear door. "Pile out." Duane turned the beam of his flash in the tonneau.

Rieg had regained part of his sense. He sat blinking at the light. Ritter shrank back into the seat, but when Barnaby hit him across the shins with the night-stick, he bounced to the edge of the seat and filed out, dragging the still dazed Rieg with him.

Ritter said: "On the level, Cap, ain't there some way we can square this beef? I'll see you get your old job back an' . . ."

Barnaby stiffened, his thin smile widened into a wolfish grin.

"So you can get me my old job back, eh?" he whispered softly. His voice changed abruptly to a savage growl. "Why you lousy . . . !"

Smack! It was only an open-handed slap, but it floored the astonished Ritter and he, in turn, pulled "The Scourge" down with him.

It was Duane who prodded them erect. He motioned them to follow the big form of Barnaby, who was striding through the darkness. The reflected light of his flash painted him in eery shadow; he loomed there like some fabled giant.

"I wouldn't irritate him," Duane suggested mildly. "He's in good humor now, but he might get peevish."

Ritter shuddered and hurried in Barnaby's wake.

Barnaby's course led him through long-deserted rooms, down a dusty stairway to a basement. He explored the filth-laden floor for a few minutes until he found a heavy iron plate set flush with the cement. He scuffed dirt away from an iron ring, hooked his fingers through it and lifted the lid, disclosing a black hole that vanished into the bowels of the earth.

He leaned forward and rapped briskly on the rim of the hole with a night-stick. The noise echoed out of the blackness to be followed by a ponderous silence. . . .

Abruptly, as from a great distance, the sound of a tapping came to them; an echo, as it were, of Barnaby's own raps.

Barnaby prodded Ritter with the club. Duane unlocked the cuffs.

"Get down, muggs," he ordered; and when he saw them hesitate, added, "get, or I'll heave you down!"

They went . . . down a rusty ladder, into the arms of Hallahan and Forsythe.

Barnaby came down last, pulling the iron cover in place after him. When he reached the bottom, he grinned.

"Ritter, meet the new police department; coppers of *The City of Hell!*"

Duane swung his light so it illuminated the others. "Any luck?" he asked.

"Plenty!" chortled Hallahan. "Come on."

He led the way down a great brick tube about twelve feet in diameter. The concave floor was slimy and a thin trickle of filthy water crawled along the middle. The wan glow of the flashlights showed dripping walls and on several occasions, huge bats swept squealing at the heads of the grim paraders.

Suddenly Rieg shrieked in terror.

"Something stabbed my ankle!" he wailed.

Barnaby grunted. "Rats! Big sewer rats. Better stick close; they'll attack a single man."

Rieg huddled closer.

The tunnel branched abruptly. Hallahan, leading, swung off. A hundred yards farther along, he turned the beam of his light on an opening several feet above the floor of the main tube. He nodded to the others and climbed the iron rungs to disappear into the cave-like hole.

At a prod from Barnaby's night-stick, Ritter and his trembling companion followed.

They found themselves in a square, windowless room. It was like the dungeon of some medieval castle. In the center was a crude table, rotten with age. Along two of the walls were winches. A candle was stuck in a whiskey bottle. Hallahan lighted it and extinguished the flash. Hidden drafts made the single flame flicker and ghostly shadows danced on the brick walls.

Hallahan seated himself at the table. He took a small note-book from his pocket, fingered the stub of a pencil and looked at Barnaby.

"Have you told him, Chief?"

Barnaby shook his head. "You're the *judge*," he remarked.

Hallahan nodded soberly and turned to the gaping prisoners. He surveyed them for a while, then began to speak in a slow, judicial tone.

"You're in the court of a new order, boys," he told them. "Chief Barnaby called it *The City of Hell.* Up above, you crooks run things; your boss makes and breaks judges, coppers, politicians. You and your lawyers rule the courts, the city government, the law. Well, we've started a new city down here. This old sewer is a monument to the system; it was built years ago by a bunch of crooked grafters and had to be abandoned because it wouldn't work. For nearly three decades it's been a breeding place for rats so we figgered this was a good place to bring you birds. Now you're under arrest and you'll get a fair trial. First we want you to take the stand an' tell us . . ."

"Aw, cut out this baloney!" Ritter sneered. "What the hell do you think you're settin' yourself up to be? We'll stand trial whenever we have to, in a court of law—what's this farce anyway? You guys gone goofy?"

Hallahan sighed patiently. "The Constitution guarantees every citizen the right of trial by jury, but the Constitution was made before your breed came into existence; it was intended to protect decent citizens from oppression. Since you're not a decent citizen, Ritter, you an' 'The Scourge' can't expect that sort of protection. We want you to tell us the truth about that baby killin' last night."

Ritter stiffened. "I'll be damned if I will! Come on with your rough stuff. I can take it!"

Hallahan nodded. "That's been the trouble up above. The cops beat up you guys but it didn't work because the human body can only absorb just so much punishment an' after that you don't feel it. We got a better stunt." He swung his gaze on Forsythe. "Lieutenant, lock up the prisoners!"

Forsythe strode willingly out of the shadows and clamped a big hand on each of the two crooks.

"Gladly, *Your Honor.*" He jerked them around and started for the door, then paused in front of Duane. "Sam, would you take that club an' beat off the rats until I chain these muggs to the floor?"

Duane hefted a club. "Sure," he agreed.

"The Scourge" leapt sidewise. "Rats! Good God! You can't do that! We'd be eaten alive!"

Forsythe jerked him towards the opening. "That's your funeral; you heard the Judge's orders."

Rieg continued to struggle. "No, no, I tell you!"

Barnaby strode over and caught "The Scourge" by the neck. He hustled him through the opening into a smaller tunnel. As the flash sent an explorative beam ahead, large gray shapes scurried into the deeper shadows where twin eyes glowed in the darkness at the human intruders.

Ritter snarled through his teeth. "Shut up, Rieg! It's a bluff!"

Barnaby snorted but made no reply. He threw the squirming gunman to the slimy floor, snapped a cuff on his wrist and hooked the other end to an iron ring sunk in the floor. "The Scourge" sobbed brokenly, but Ritter kept his nerve up.

"Swarm will take care of you finks!" he prophesied grimly.

Barnaby wiped his hands together. "An' these wharf rats will take care of you. That makes it even." He started to leave the cavern, but Rieg's cry stopped him.

"You're murderin' me!" he shrieked.

Barnaby wagged his gray head. "No Whisper, you're commitin' suicide. If you talk, you got a fightin' chance. For instance, if you was to tell us who ordered you killers out. . . ."

"I can't!" screamed "The Scourge."

Barnaby shrugged and passed through the opening. He heard Ritter's husky tones pleading, cajoling Rieg to keep up his nerve. Then a rat must have bitten "The Scourge" for he uttered one long wail of terror.

"Listen to reason, in God's name!" he howled.

Barnaby paused, winked to Forsythe, then called back. "Give us names, Whisper, not an argument."

"Swarm. . . ."

Coxy Swarm leaned forward, his elbows propped on the arms of his chair, and his cold fish-eyes focused on the slender little man striding up and down the room.

"If Rieg and Ritter had been snatched by some of the other boys it would be my job, Hymie," he growled. "But you're paid a damn' good salary to act as the mouthpiece for this outfit, and when the cops grab two of my best boys, it's *your* job to see they get sprung. I'm waiting for service." The cold cigar on one side of his thin-lipped mouth crawled up at an aggressive angle.

The little lawyer stopped, combed his black tousled hair with nervous fingers, then made a futile gesture with his hands.

"But I tell you, Coxy," he shouted, after the manner of a man who has been repeating the same explanation over and over, "these two men, Barnaby and Duane, are not with the police department! I did what you asked and had them demoted, but they got tough and quit. But in spite of that, I have assistants staked out at every precinct station within fifty miles of here. So far, these ex-cops haven't taken Ritter and Rieg to a jail. If they do, I'll spring 'em; I can get any man I want released from any jail in this county. But, Coxy, be reasonable! I can't get a man out of jail when he hasn't been put in!"

A tall, gangling hood sitting near the door spoke. "You don't suppose these cops took the boys for a ride, do you?"

Lawyer Croker stiffened to his full five feet four inches. "They wouldn't dare!" he shouted. "I'd have them broke!"

Swarm jerked the cigar out of his mouth, glanced at the cold ash and hurled it from him with an oath. He reached a big hand into a niche in the wall beside him and grabbed a telephone. Then he called an unlisted number.

"Judge Tweedie? Listen, Tweedie, this is Swarm. Two dumb cops named Barnaby and Duane snatched a pair of my best boys, see. I want those flat-feet nailed to the cross! Get in touch with the foreman of your Grand Jury and have 'em bring in an indictment first thing in the morning. No, don't wait until morning to call the foreman, do it right now. I don't give a damn if it is nearly midnight! Maybe we can smoke that pair out in the open with an indictment, but if my boys find 'em in the meantime, you won't need to bother with the Grand Jury. Goodbye!" He waited for no answer, but hung up.

He let his eyes wander over the assembled group. Besides Croker the lawyer, five of his ablest lieutenants sat quietly in a semi-circle,

awaiting his orders. Despite his rage, he felt a suffusion of pride creep over him. These were not the beetle-browed gorillas of fiction; these men were well educated—with the exception of Gebardi, an importation from Sicily—and versed in modern business administration. They could organize a union, break a strike, control a voting precinct, or examine a company's account books with equal facility. And what was even more important, they could and would carry out his orders without question.

"Miller," he said finally, to the lanky hood by the door, "take Gebardi and find out if either Duane or Barnaby's got a wife. If so, grab her and take her up to the farm. Gebardi'll know how to make her talk. But don't actually kill her because we might need her to write a note to her husband."

Croker wiped sudden sweat from his face. "I can save you time," he wheezed. "This guy Barnaby is not married, but Duane is. He lives on Becker Street, the third duplex from the corner of Hansard Avenue. His wife's name is Molly. Duane's nuts about her."

Miller stood up, motioned to Gebardi and adjusted his fedora. "That'll help, Hymie. If she knows where her old man is we'll make her tell us. If she don't," he shrugged grimly, "it'll be tough on her." With Gebardi at his heels, he went out.

Lawyer Hymie Croker's mouth opened and closed in a quick, nervous smile. He wiped the moist handkerchief over his face and sought to conceal the involuntary shudder that shook his slender frame. Croker belonged to that peculiar breed of jackal who could cheerfully frame an innocent man into the penitentiary, or even to the gallows, and feel no pang of conscience. He could advise his assorted clients on the slickest manner of evading the laws; even assist them in their work under the cloak of his profession. But when he stood in the presence of violence, the yellow stripe that lined his back widened until he trembled.

Swarm took a fresh cigar from his vest pocket, ripped off the end with his teeth and set it on the table before him. "I can't exactly figure this out," he mused, scowling. "There's just a chance that these two cops took the boys for a buggy ride. But it don't look that way; they took too much of a chance in snatching them out of *La Parisienne*. At least a hundred people saw them do it."

"Perhaps they wanted to make 'em talk," suggested a mobster named Haight.

Croker answered that one. "Talk? What for? Grogan takes his orders from me and Judge Tweedie has the Grand Jury in tow. Tweedie'll have the Grand Jury return an indictment as Coxy told him to do and Barnaby and Duane will be in jail. I can promise you service along that line." He used the handkerchief again.

"Anyway," drawled a big man, "they couldn't make Ritter talk. He can take it."

Swarm shrugged. "Hymie's right. There's nobody for them to tell anything to. You're right about Ritter, Slade, but I got my doubts if Rieg could keep his mouth shut under pressure. 'The Scourge' is mean as hell with a gun in his hand, but . . ." He shrugged and pulled his chair closer to the table. "Well, sit down, Hymie, and we'll have a round of stud."

Croker prodded a chair into position with his foot. "I'll sit in until Miller and Gebardi call back. We ought to hear from them within half an hour."

About forty minutes later, Haight quit the game and walked to the door of the office. He mumbled something about a drink and went out, only to reappear about a minute later with his face the color of damp cement.

Swarm frowned, slowly put down his cards, started to push back his chair. "Well, what in hell's the matter with you?"

Haight made a vague motion with his head towards the darkness behind.

"Gebardi . . . !"

The way he said it brought them to their feet in unison, but Swarm was the first man to reach the crumpled body of his ace executioner.

Gebardi was quite dead. He lay across the curb, his bloody knees in the gutter, his torso sprawled across the sidewalk. A nearby street lamp loaned ghastly shadows to the scene. The corpse looked like a great black spider which had been stepped on.

Swarm cursed, shot a quick glance up and down the street. It was practically deserted; the body could have lain there but a few minutes.

"Come on," he snarled. "Carry it inside."

Three of the men grabbed their erstwhile companion and whisked him inside the office. From a closet, Swarm took out a large rubber sheet and spread it on the floor. They dumped the battered remains of Gebardi on to this. It was then that Swarm glimpsed the folded piece of paper pinned to the dead man's chest.

He retrieved it and moved closer to the light. Examination disclosed the obvious fact that the paper had been clipped from an advertisement in a newspaper. It simply stated in large black type:

SURE CURE FOR RODENTS!

That was all.

"And Miller . . . ?" gasped Croker. "They've grabbed Miller!"

Swarm crushed the clipping in the palm of his fist. "Every one of you birds get out and see what you can find. Get your boys moving. I want these two crazy cops dead by daylight." As the men started for their haunts, he swung on Croker.

"Have you got your car with you, Hymie?"

The lawyer nodded. "I told my driver to wait around the corner."

Swarm nodded impatiently. "Okey. Now you beat it to Grogan. Tell him to find Barnaby and Duane before morning, or there'll be another Chief of Police in this damn' town!" He made a gesture of dismissal and the lawyer waited no longer. He scooped up his hat and cane and fled the office. And the last thing he saw as he went out was the bloody corpse of the late Antonio Gebardi spread-eagled on the rubber sheet.

Although the night air was cold, Attorney Croker was sweating when he rounded the corner and headed for the shelter of his own limousine. He rapped his cane sharply against the running-board to awaken the driver who sat slumped over the steering wheel, opened the door himself and climbed into the tonneau. Then he picked up the speaking tube and issued his orders.

"Central Police Station, Gunner; and step on it!"

As the big machine got into motion, he relaxed against the soft cushions and lighted a cigarette. He shuddered involuntarily as he recalled the finding of Gebardi; he couldn't stand blood or physical torture. He felt his stomach knotting and knew he was in for another attack of indigestion. He inhaled deeply, letting the smoke dribble through his nostrils. . . .

And then he suddenly became aware that the limousine had drawn up in front of a small, darkened drug-store!

Disdaining to use the speaking tube, he jumped forward to the edge of his seat, jerked open the glass window that separated the tonneau from the driver's compartment and shouted:

"What's the meaning of this, Gunner? Didn't I tell you to hurry! I . . ." The words froze in his throat.

For the driver turned abruptly. Instead of the battered, familiar features of his own chauffeur, Gunner McSpadden, he found himself staring at the rugged, leathery face of old Dennis Hallahan.

Hallahan shoved back the chauffeur's cap so that the visor would not shield his features. He was grinning, but somehow, Croker could read no mirth in the expression.

The dapper little lawyer carried a gun by way of ornamentation. Now, as he suddenly recalled the picture of Gebardi, half-chewed with slugs, fear gripped him and he made a vague pass for his own weapon. But he didn't complete the movement. The door jerked open and the enormous bulk of Lieutenant Forsythe crowded into the tonneau beside him.

"Hello, Hymie," Forsythe said, and the tinge of his voice matched Hallahan's smile. "We want to have a nice long chat with you." He picked up the speaking tube and gave his orders. "Home, James, and don't spare the nags."

Lawyer Croker knew the meaning of the word *fear.* Sheer panic gripped him; sweat dampened his clothing in one awful rush; he went sick.

"Where are you taking me?" he screamed, struggling forward in his seat.

Forsythe grabbed him by the collar and jerked him back so hard his spine quivered.

"To your home town, Hymie; *The City of Hell!*"

He laughed, but Hymie Croker didn't hear him. Hymie Croker had fainted. . . .

Judge Alexander Z. Tweedie looked like a judge even arrayed in his pajamas. His leonine head was crowned with a silver mane which he brushed straight back. His eyes were hidden in shadowed caves, guarded by bushy brows and out front, a pair of nose glasses acted as a barricade. His skin was rugged, seamed, and he had the kind of a jaw that is popularly supposed to denote great strength of character—but which does nothing of the kind. In his younger days, Alexander Tweedie had wanted to be an actor; his father wanted him to be a lawyer. Now he was both. He made a successful politician because he was a good actor, looked the part he chose to play, and knew how to obey orders. He was an impressive judicial fraud.

At twelve-thirty at night, he sat closeted in his study with William Greeves, foreman of the Grand Jury. Greeves was a slight figure, nearly bald, who wore thick lensed glasses and suffered from an inferiority complex. His appointment to the Grand Jury had been one of the greatest surprises in his life; now he spent most of his time attempting to convince himself, as well as a rather cynical wife, that it came as a reward for his business sagacity and his civic loyalty. What made him of value to the powers-that-be was the fact that he honestly believed in himself. He was still dizzy from his sudden exaltation and was pathetically grateful to Judge Tweedie, whom he knew was responsible for the appointment.

Tweedie ran his long fingers through his showy mane and peered over his glasses into the anxious features of his guest.

"Greeves," he boomed, "I called you here so

that we could be ready to act first thing in the morning. This is . . . well . . . almost a crisis in our city. These two ex-policemen have run amuck. I know them both; hard, calloused brutes who hesitate not at all to kill."

"Just what have they done?" William Greeves wanted to know.

"Done!" Judge Tweedie looked sad. He took off his nose-glasses and rapped on the desk between them. "They have murdered a young Italian, they have kidnaped at least three other young men and now . . ." he paused to let the full import of his words soak in, ". . . they have apparently kidnaped one of the cleverest and finest members of our bar."

"Why?" asked Greeves.

"Retaliation! These two policemen were demoted. None of us is safe as long as they are free. It will hasten the end of this reign of terror if we act in unison." A happy thought came to him so he added: "You or I may be next, Greeves! Think of that!"

William Greeves thought and didn't like the image his mind conjured. "I'll attend to it first thing in the morning," he assured his mentor. "We'll put through an indictment at once." He scooped up his hat, carefully placed it on his head and offered his hand.

"Good night, Your Honor."

Tweedie unlimbered from his chair, rose with studied dignity, and grasping the proffered hand with one of his own, he put the other hand on Greeves' shoulder.

"It is only by putting our shoulders to the wheel together, Greeves, will we succeed in our efforts to make our city the fairest in the land."

The foreman of the county Grand Jury nodded; he was visibly impressed. Tweedie held onto his hand and steered him to the front door.

"Good night, Greeves," he said, and closed the door.

He smiled then and turning, started for the stairs. He was tired and anxious to return to the bed he had so recently deserted. But halfway down the hall, he heard a hesitant knock on the door. He frowned impulsively, about faced and

walked back. Greeves had probably forgotten something, he decided, and by the time he folded his hand around the knob, his face was set in a benign smile.

He opened the door . . . and the smile died.

Captain Clyde Barnaby's massive bulk filled the opening. Without pausing for an invitation, he pushed the jurist back into the house, entered and heeled the door shut.

"You're invited to a party, Judge," Barnaby leered. "You don't need to dress, but let's go back to your study so's we can get some papers. We want to play some games."

Tweedie struck an attitude. "This is an outrage, sir! I'll have you arrested and . . ."

Barnaby tapped him on his inflated chest with a stubby forefinger. "Now, listen to me, you old fraud. You do as I say an' you won't get hurt, but one peep out of you an' I'll knock you colder than Little America." He caught Tweedie by the arm, spun him around and gave him a hard push in the general direction of the study.

He turned when they got into the study. Barnaby softly closed the door, leaned against it.

"Now, Judge," he suggested slyly, "fill up a brief-case with a lot of printed forms, writs, warrants, complaints, search-warrants, forthwith subpoenas and whatever else you have. Also don't forget your seals, pen, and other apparatus."

"Why this is ridiculous!" protested Tweedie, giving an excellent imitation of outraged dignity.

Barnaby sighed, fished a blackjack from the recesses of his baggy side-pocket and dangled it from his right thumb. Some of the apoplectic color went out of Tweedie's face. He tightened the cord of his bathrobe, grabbed a brief-case from a nearby desk and began to jam it with papers. His fingers trembled so that he had trouble securing the straps.

"Now," said Barnaby, "you'll come with me . . . quietly."

Tweedie hesitated. "And if I refuse . . . ?"

The captain shrugged indifferently. "You go in either case; it's merely a choice of whether you come with your eyes open or . . . closed."

"May I have the opportunity to clothe myself?"

"You don't need no more clothes," Barnaby assured him dryly, opening the hall door. "You look funny enough the way you are."

Something akin to a sob escaped the jurist's lips, but he took the lead without further protest and stalked down the corridor. At a nod from the copper he opened the front door and stepped out into the night. Barnaby fell in step beside him and together they strode to the sidewalk, where a car awaited them.

Tweedie recognized Duane behind the wheel. He muttered something and stumbled into the tonneau. Half-in, he suddenly saw the slender figure huddled in a corner of the seat.

It was William Greeves.

The bitter night wind whipped Judge Tweedie's flimsy garments, but the judge was not cold . . .

He was scared.

It was the strangest court proceedings ever held in the long annals of legal history! Perhaps the most amazing feature of it all was that the idea was born, not in the cunning brain of a criminal lawyer, but in the honest heads of four old harness bulls. The courtroom was in the bowels of the earth, an abandoned sewer, and the city was directly overhead. Barnaby sat in the middle of a long, improvised table. At one end sat his Honor, Judge Alexander Z. Tweedie, garbed in striped pajamas and a dark blue bathrobe; at the other end, William Greeves shivered on a small soap-box chair.

The room was more like a dungeon than a courtroom, and the crude lighting fixtures—beer-bottles and candles—sent jumpy little shadows carousing around the bat-infested ceiling. There was only one door—a sort of arch—and on either side of this stood Hallahan and Duane. Forsythe was down with the prisoners.

Then Captain Clyde Barnaby began to speak.

"Greeves," he addressed himself to the little man, "we believe you are merely a fool, not dishonest. Like a lot of business men, you think you can dabble in politics with no experience whatever, trusting to your limited judgement of men to carry you through. We brought you here for two reasons, first, to use you for the ends of justice and because we believe you really would do the thing we are going to do if you had the knowledge and the strength. You keep your eyes and ears open and you'll learn more about politics in the next thirty minutes than you ever dreamed of knowing. If you play smart, you can have the glory of this clean-up and perhaps get to be governor of the State on the strength of it; who knows? However, you have little choice; if you interfere, we'll . . ." He paused significantly, fixed his steely eyes on the slack-jawed Greeves.

"I won't interfere!" promised Foreman Greeves.

Barnaby swung towards the jurist. "An' you, you graftin' old scoundrel, we ought to send you to the Federal pen. We got enough evidence already to do just that, but we feel we can use you more profitably. That's your luck just so long as you obey orders. When we're finished, you, like Greeves, will be regarded as a civic benefactor."

"What," shivered Tweedie, and not from the cold, "do you want?"

"In the first place," Barnaby went on, "we want you to declare this a real court of law."

"But . . . but *jurisdiction* . . ." protested Tweedie.

Barnaby nodded. "We got the answer to that one. This place is within the city limits; a city goes *down* as well as up. You declare this a legal court and hear testimony and admit evidence. The first thing we want are some nine or ten subpoenas and a dozen or so blank warrants of arrests. That will erase any possible charges cropping up later."

"You . . . you damned blackguards!" choked Tweedie. "I refuse!"

Barnaby sighed. He glanced at Duane. "Sergeant, will you take the judge into the next chamber and . . . well . . . *talk* to him privately!"

Duane grinned pleasantly, unlimbered a short length of rubber-hose from under his coat and strode forward. Tweedie gulped, shrank back against his chair.

It was Greeves who made him pause.

The little foreman sat on the edge of his chair, eyes bulging. "Just . . . just a minute!" he begged with a courage that must have surprised even himself; it would assuredly have amazed his wife. "Just what are you men trying to do?"

Barnaby frowned, squinted with one eye. He stopped Duane's advance with a motion of one hand, then he studied William Greeves for a full three minutes of absolute silence. At length he spoke:

"All right, Greeves, that's a fair question. This city up above has been slowly worked into the hands of grafters, hoodlums, mobsters and professional killers: in a word, the machine has it by the throat. Chief of Police Grogan—we have him a prisoner, by the way—takes his orders from Coxy Swarm, our local Al Capone. Tweedie here, heads the Grand Jury, tells you fellows what he wants done, but he gets his orders from much the same source. The whole mess is so rotten it stinks, yet the way it's tangled, there's no way of unraveling it except by cleaning it out wholesale. Since it would be impossible to do that by any known regular means, we've improvised our own system. We've got the key man of every crooked outfit in the city, got 'em here under chains and handcuffs. We've got Hymie Croker, the mouthpiece of Swarm and the other mobs; we got Grogan, head of the police department; we got Tweedie, senior judge of the bench and head of the local bar association."

"What good will that do you?" Greeves asked in a strangely awed tone.

"Plenty. When Tweedie declares this a legal court of law, we'll issue search-warrants, go through the homes, the offices and the safe deposit vaults of these grafters. We'll find enough evidence so that the courts up above will have to act to save their own faces; if they refuse, we'll step into a Federal court and indict the whole outfit with a Federal Grand Jury."

Greeves was very white of face. "Is . . . is that the true state of affairs?" He looked from one grim face to the other and his shoulders came back.

"I see it is," he declared harshly. "I've been a fool, a . . . a . . . damn' fool! You show me some proof of your statements, something *I* can act on, and you won't need to go before any Federal Grand Jury!"

Barnaby grinned. "We'll show you," he promised.

Greeves looked sternly at Tweedie. "Judge, as Foreman of the Grand Jury, I demand that you sift the evidence these officers produce!"

Tweedie's skin was yellow. "These men are renegades," he stormed. "They are no longer officers of the law!"

Barnaby snorted. "Dennis," he commanded, "bring Grogan in, will you?"

Hallahan vanished, to reappear a few minutes later with Chief Grogan in tow. Grogan was indignant, to say the least, and tough.

Barnaby looked at him. "Grogan, take your choice; you either reinstate the four of us to our commands, or we'll produce the contents of your safe deposit box to the Federal District Attorney."

Grogan tensed himself. "What do you know about my safe deposit box?"

Barnaby grinned. "Which'll it be?"

Grogan glanced furtively at Greeves, winced and looked at Tweedie. What he saw there failed to reassure him.

"Okey," he agreed reluctantly, "you're back."

Hallahan shoved him over to the table. "Put that in writing, Grogan." As Grogan reached for a pen, Barnaby suggested:

"You might add that we are conducting a special investigation into municipal graft at the instigation of the Grand Jury and Judge Alexander Tweedie." He turned to the two men at the table. "How about that, Greeves? And you, Judge?"

"Excellent!" snapped Greeves, wiping his face. "If you can only prove . . ." His voice trailed, died.

Tweedie swallowed, combed his white mane,

and nodded. "You may use my name, Captain Barnaby," he agreed with a sigh.

Grogan glanced from one strained face to the other. Then he bent over the paper and wrote rapidly. When he finished, Barnaby picked up the document, read it with a growing smile, and nodded to Hallahan.

"Take the Chief out, Dennis, and bring up the shyster."

As Hallahan went out with Grogan, Barnaby said to the others:

"You'll listen to the conversation to come. If you feel we have a case, you can act; if you don't, you are at liberty to refuse. This may not be strictly admissible testimony, but I wager you'll feel justified in voting for an indictment and in giving us warrants to proceed with our investigations."

Hallahan appeared at the doorway and thrust Croker into the center of the room. The little lawyer stumbled, caught his balance and glared at Barnaby. He opened his mouth to speak, then, apparently for the first time, saw Tweedie and Greeves. His jaw sagged, his eyes bulged and he looked sick. Before he could recover his surprise, Barnaby took over the command.

"Croker, you're in a court of law. You know these gentleman at the table with me, so I can skip the introductions and get down to business. You are not only a criminal lawyer, you are a lawyer-criminal! The present charge against you is conspiracy to commit murder."

"You're crazy!" screamed the attorney. "What kind of a frame-up is this?"

"This is no frame," Barnaby went on smoothly. "The day before yesterday, Swarm sent three of his boys out to gun a rat from the Antecki mob. You were in on that plot and advised the men to drop the machine-gun into the river at the completion of the crime. Instead of the hood, however, a little kid was murdered, an innocent bystander. You've got that crime on your hands, as well as others, Croker. What have you to say?"

"I say you're nuts!" shouted Croker, waving his arms. "You can't prove a damn' thing!" He

swung on the white-haired jurist. "You can't get away with this, Tweedie! I'll have . . ."

The Honorable Tweedie was caught between two fires, but he scented the direction of the wind and proved his diplomacy.

"Are those things true, Counselor?" he demanded heavily.

Croker gasped. "You can't get away with this!" he reiterated, but his tone was beginning to lack conviction.

Greeves asked: "Can you prove . . . ?"

Barnaby grunted. "One of the guns—a hood named Rieg—confessed to the whole thing. He told us Swarm ordered them out after a conference with Croker."

"You tortured Rieg!" Croker interrupted hysterically. "You can't use that kind of testimony . . ."

"He talked," Barnaby went on grimly. "After they killed the baby, they threw the machine-gun over the West bridge so that it couldn't be traced and then went back with a sawed-off riot-gun to complete the job. Well, we fished the machine-gun out of the river. We can now definitely tie up that job to Swarm and Ritter with the help of a ballistician—the guy that can tell which gun fired which bullet.

"Now that dead baby stands over this whole proceedings. Rieg's testimony isn't enough to circumvent a lot of legal red-tape, but he did tell me where to find evidence. Croker's got a safe deposit box in the First National Bank under the name of Peter Hoople. I want a search warrant, or better still, a forthwith subpoena and have the contents of that box brought before you men. That will supply us with priceless data to continue our work. What do you say?"

Croker became shrieking. "You can't do this!" he wailed. "It isn't legal! I'll bring charges against you that will . . ."

Barnaby made an imperceptible motion with his hand. Hallahan stepped up and drove his fist against Croker's jaw. The lawyer folded like a carpenter's rule.

Tweedie daubed his face. "This is irregular . . ." he began helplessly.

Greeves' features were tense. "I demand that you issue the subpoena as Captain Barnaby requests, Judge Tweedie! And have you any more witnesses, Captain?"

Barnaby nodded. "Plenty," he promised; then to Hallahan. "Take Croker away and bring on another."

Tweedie gulped. "Where is this going to end, Captain?"

"It's going to end, Judge, when I get enough evidence to smear over every court in this county; when you and the rest of the judicial trained-seals *have* to act to save your own hides; when I have the necessary evidence to get a warrant and go legally gunning for Coxy Swarm and Dave Antecki. Not that I care for your flimsy warrants; I just don't want those rats to die martyrs. It'll soon be daylight, Judge, and when the banks open, I want my boys there with warrants and subpoenas signed by *you*."

Skipper Barnaby had his wish. In a variable night of hell, a scared jurist and a dumfounded juror listened to the whines and sobs, the lies and ratting of gunmen and thieves. And later, when Forsythe, Hallahan and Duane began to bring back the evidence they claimed by search warrants, the work began in deadly earnest. In the case of Croker's safe deposit box, claimed by a forthwith subpoena, a representative of the bank came with the evidence. He was amazed and terrified when Hallahan steered him into the subterranean courtroom, but after a talk with Greeves, he fell into the spirit of the thing. Barnaby commandeered him to examine accounts.

It was late afternoon when the work was finally completed. Gaunt, haggard, weary, but very game, Greeves pushed aside the papers before him and looked at Barnaby.

"This is incredible! It will shake the city to its very foundations! At least a score of the biggest names in local politics will go to the penitentiary!"

Barnaby nodded heavily. "And now for the real job." He turned to Hallahan. "Bring in 'The Scourge.'"

Rieg was brought in to stand in fear before the grim board. All his bravado was gone, leaving a spineless, trembling rat.

Barnaby glared at him for a full minute before speaking. Then he began:

"Rieg, I'm turning you loose!"

Greeves burst out: "But he'll warn the gang . . ."

"That's just what I want him to do," Barnaby stopped him, and continued speaking to the startled gunman, "I want you to tell Coxy Swarm that Clyde Barnaby, Dennis Hallahan, Sam Duane and Louis Forsythe are coming to get him. Tell him we have warrants for not only his own person, but for every man in his gang. You can assure him from me that if he submits peaceably to arrest, we will take him alive . . . and hang him later. Now get out!"

Rieg bolted, uninterrupted. He left behind him a void of startled silence. Greeves broke in:

"You deliberately warned Swarm! You've provoked a fight!"

Barnaby pushed himself erect. "I hope I did," he growled savagely. "I can still see that little kid!"

Dave Antecki was a mobster of the old school. He was built close to the ground, with a flat face to match his figure. He was called Dave the Ape, but never in his presence; he had a blow-torch personality.

Dave the Ape made no pretension as to his headquarters. Where Swarm picked the quiet seclusion of the city's finest residential quarter, Antecki preferred the section that spawned him. As a thin front, he ran a small beer-parlor. It was a tough joint, with a tough clientele; the music was discordant, but it was loud; the food came in quantity rather than quality.

Antecki was seated at his favorite table, in the lee of the trap-drummer, eating a raviola dinner in company with a flousy blonde. She was as loud as the music and as coarse as the food, but she was young and big-chested and that was all that interested Dave the Ape. He had unbuttoned his vest in anticipation of some heavy eating, when one of his trusted henchmen came up to the table.

"Dave, Coxy is on his way over here!"

Antecki gagged, belched and sat very stiff. "*Him* . . . ? Comin' *here?*" Assured that his man was in earnest, he shouted, "He wants trouble, eh? All okey. Call in the boys. . . ."

The informer shook his head. "He don't want no trouble, Dave. He's in a jam . . . we all are. Somebody's snatched Chief Grogan . . ."

"*Grogan?*" Antecki gasped.

"An' Judge Tweedie an' Hymie Croker, an' Ritter an' . . ."

Dave the Ape stopped him. "Somebody's crazy!" he growled, "but if this is a frame, we'll be ready. Get Tony an' Perez to get behind them palms on either side of the dance-floor with the choppers. I'll meet Swarm right here."

The blonde with the big chest and the willing way started to get up. "Well, thanks for the salad, Dave, an' so long. I just remembered I got to see a man about a dog some place."

"What's the matter, Amy, scared?"

"Uh-huh," demurred the charmer, "just my stomach. I can't stand the taste of hot lead." She tossed him a kiss and moved away. Antecki might have stopped her, but at that moment, a stir near the entrance attracted his attention.

Swarm stepped into the big room, followed closely by five men. Their hands were all in plain sight, obviously so. Swarm took his bearings, glanced around the place and saw Antecki standing beside his table. He raised his right hand like an Indian and walked quickly across the room. As his men fell in behind him, a half dozen of Antecki's boys converged from various parts of the room.

Swarm paid no attention to them, nor did he offer to shake hands with Dave the Ape. He said:

"Hello, Dave. Can we talk some place?"

Antecki's eyes strayed casually in the direction of his machine-gunners, and nodded.

"Sure, sit down; we're as good here as any place. These are all my boys."

Swarm dropped into a chair and motioned his men to do likewise. They all sat down and carefully placed their hands on the tables.

Swarm spoke again.

"Do you know Captain Barnaby and Sergeant Duane?"

Antecki nodded. "Sure. Cops. I heard you got 'em fired."

"They quit," Swarm corrected him. "Well, they've snatched about five of my best boys and killed at least one."

"You want me to take my hair down an' have a good cry, perhaps?"

"The only reason I came to you, Dave," Swarm snapped pointedly, "is because we're in a spot. It ain't only my boys, but Croker, Tweedie, every key man in the machine is snatched. Maybe the Federals are behind this, but we got to find that out."

"*We* . . . ?"

"Yes, *we!* Maybe it'll interest you to know that Grogan's gone, too. That leaves *you* in a hole, Dave."

Antecki made no admissions. He massaged his heavy jowl thoughtfully, a little stupidly. He had paid well for protection and it never occurred to him that any force on earth could disrupt the *whole* machine. His own lawyer had advised him he was safe from prosecution as long as he paid his tribute.

Rieg came stumbling into the place at that moment.

Swarm swore. "Rieg . . . ?" and the others just stared.

Rieg picked up a glass of red wine that still stood in front of Antecki's plate, emptied it down his throat and stared wild-eyed at the group.

"Barnaby is comin' for you, Coxy!" he choked.

Swarm smiled grimly. "Where you been?"

In halting, broken phrases, "The Scourge" mouthed out the story of what had happened to him from the moment big Clyde Barnaby had snatched him from the table in *La Parisienne* until his release. He told them about Tweedie, about Greeves and about Hymie Croker. He choked out the story of the warrants, of the bank secrets and of the work of the bank's representative.

"It ain't legal!" shouted Dave the Ape.

Rieg gave him a sour glance. "He's got enough to send us all to the gallows!"

Swarm reached over and caught "The Scourge" by the throat. "You ratted, Rieg! You must have . . . !"

Rieg's protestations of innocence did him no good. At a sign from Swarm, two men rose and grabbed Rieg by the arms.

Swarm nodded his head towards the door. "He ratted, boys," was all he said, but that was sufficient. The pair started out, dragging the snivelling gun-man between them.

At that moment, a man appeared at the door.

"A coupla cops!" he shouted. "A guy named Barnaby says he's comin' in after Swarm an' you, Dave!"

Antecki stood up. "There ain't no damn' cop alive what can take me outa my own place! You can beat it out the back way, Swarm. I got two tommy-guns in this room. . . ."

Swarm smiled a little thinly. "Just two dumb flatfeet and no witnesses. We'll see this out right now, Dave." He gestured for his boys to spread out.

In a great semi-circle they lined the end of the big room facing the double entrance-doors. Antecki took out his gun and held it under a napkin atop the table. Swarm slid his automatic into a side pocket and kept his hand glued to the butt.

In silence they waited.

And abruptly the silence was broken by the voice of Captain Barnaby. He was calling from beyond the doors.

"I got warrants for you muggs," came the unseen voice. "Come out with your hands in the air."

Antecki and Swarm exchanged glances. Swarm answered for them both.

"Come in and take us, flatfoot!"

As though operated by unseen hands, the wide, double-doors swung outward. The waiting audience tensed themselves for sudden action . . . then stared unbelievingly at the apparition that met their slitted eyes.

About fourteen men came through the door

in one thick mass; not fourteen coppers, but men they knew well, all handcuffed together in a giant ring, backs to the middle. Ritter, Miller, Hymie Croker, Grogan . . . and about eight more ace-mobsters. Like children playing ring-around-the-rosy, their hands were joined in a protecting band, a human barricade. . . .

And in the middle of this trembling stockade, stood Captain Barnaby and Dennis Hallahan with riot-guns in their hands.

"Drop those guns, Coxy, an' you too, Dave!" commanded Barnaby coldly.

Croker cried like a burnt child. "Don't shoot, Coxy! We'll all be killed!"

Barnaby and Hallahan advanced with terrible finality, prodding the human fence ahead.

"Come an' get in the game, boys," Barnaby jeered. "We'll have a good dance."

Antecki glanced around the room. "Stop where you are!" he yelled. "I got machine-guns on you!"

Barnaby mocked him. "Don't shoot, Dave! You'll cheat the State out of a hangin'! Put down your guns an' come out with your hands in the air. Do what I tell you! We're comin' for you!" He advanced slowly, grimly.

The mobsters stood, uncertain. Swarm was backed up against the slight rise of the orchestra dais; Antecki waited in front of the bass drum. At the first indication of trouble, the colored musicians had vanished.

Swarm tried guile. "You can't take us, Barnaby. We won't be bluffed!"

The circle drew closer, Barnaby hurled a taunting laugh. "I could kill you from here, Coxy, but I want you alive. I want to see you sweat in death row, I want to see you dance on the gallows and watch them open you up in the morgue. I want . . ."

It was Antecki that gave way first. He screamed a foreign oath, threw aside the concealing napkin and shouted to his gunners:

"Tony, Perez! Let 'em have it!" Then he fired point blank into the approaching mass. . . .

All hell broke loose! With the deafening chatter of the twin machine-guns came the screams of stricken men. And then it seemed that the stuttering crash of the Tommies was double in volume. Barnaby and Hallahan dropped in unison. Croker, his head almost torn away by the stream of lead, fell across Barnaby. But Hallahan had time to send Antecki into eternity before the corpse of Miller pinned him down.

The chaos of sound ceased as abruptly as it had started. No gun thunder now, only gurgling sobs and low, throaty curses. And then Sam Duane's voice filled the hall.

"Are you all right, Skipper?"

Barnaby pushed the body of the lawyer off him and lifted his head. The place was in shambles. He glanced back at the doorway. Duane and Forsythe loomed in the opening, each with a smoking sub-machine-gun in their hands. He rose, looked down at Hallahan.

Hallahan sat up, pulled himself erect.

Duane and Forsythe, white of features, came over. "It went off on schedule," Sam Duane said through clenched teeth. "I never want another experience like that, though."

Barnaby shrugged. "It saved the State a lot of money an' the taxpayers have earned a little con-

sideration. That's literally gettin' two birds with one stone."

Forsythe put his gun on the table and wiped his face. "We didn't have much to do," he told Barnaby. "Those two gunmen of Antecki's went crazy. They cleaned the decks of everything that was standing and then we finished them."

Barnaby walked over to the dais. Antecki had fallen backwards and was sitting in the middle of the giant bass drum.

Duane said: "Look, Skipper, seems like Swarm was tryin' to run away."

Barnaby turned. Coxy Swarm lay across the edge of the dais, feet and knees on the dancefloor, tuxedoed torso flattened on the dais itself. There were three welling holes across his back and blood seeped over the polished floor.

Skipper Barnaby sighed. "It took a guidin' hand to put a finish like that," he growled, a touch of reverence in his tone. "Destiny, I reckon some 'ud call it."

"Hows that?" Hallahan wanted to know.

"That's just the way that little kid got it," Barnaby grunted, and turned away.

Red Wind

Raymond Chandler

ONE COULD EASILY make the argument that Raymond Chandler (1888–1959) was the greatest writer who ever sold a story to a pulp magazine, and I would further make the case that he was one of the half-dozen great American writers of the twentieth century.

An oil company executive until the Great Depression caused the industry to collapse, he sold his first short story in 1933 at the age of 45. Less popular than either Carroll John Daly or Dashiell Hammett, he did not achieve fame until the publication of his first novel, *The Big Sleep,* in 1939 after having produced twenty novellas for *Black Mask* and other pulps.

Few authors in any genre matched Chandler's prose, which employed the use of metaphor and simile in a masterly way. The poet W. H. Auden described his books as "works of art" rather than escape literature. Among his most important contributions to detective fiction may be his definition of what a private eye should be, as he wrote in "The Simple Art of Murder" for *The Atlantic Monthly* in December 1944. He compared him to a modern knight.

"Down these mean streets a man must go who is not himself mean, who is neither tarnished nor afraid. The detective in this kind of story must be such a man. He is the hero, he is everything. He must be a complete man and a common man, and yet an unusual man. He must be, to use a rather weathered phrase, a man of honor."

"Red Wind" was first published in *Dime Detective* in January 1938.

Red Wind

Raymond Chandler

ONE

THERE WAS A DESERT WIND blowing that night. It was one of those hot dry Santa Anas that come down through the mountain passes and curl your hair and make your nerves jump and your skin itch. On nights like that every booze party ends in a fight. Meek little wives feel the edge of the carving knife and study their husbands' necks. Anything can happen. You can even get a full glass of beer at a cocktail lounge.

I was getting one in a flossy new place across the street from the apartment house where I lived. It had been open about a week and it wasn't doing any business. The kid behind the bar was in his early twenties and looked as if he had never had a drink in his life.

There was only one other customer, a souse on a bar stool with his back to the door. He had a pile of dimes stacked neatly in front of him, about two dollars' worth. He was drinking straight rye in small glasses and he was all by himself in a world of his own.

I sat farther along the bar and got my glass of beer and said: "You sure cut the clouds off them, buddy. I will say that for you."

"We just opened up," the kid said. "We got to build up trade. Been in before, haven't you, mister?"

"Uh-huh."

"Live around here?"

"In the Berglund Apartments across the street," I said. "And the name is Philip Marlowe."

"Thanks, mister. Mine's Lew Petrolle." He leaned close to me across the polished dark bar. "Know that guy?"

"No."

"He ought to go home, kind of. I ought to call a taxi and send him home. He's doing his next week's drinking too soon."

"A night like this," I said. "Let him alone."

"It's not good for him," the kid said, scowling at me.

"Rye!" the drunk croaked, without looking up. He snapped his fingers so as not to disturb his piles of dimes by banging on the bar.

The kid looked at me and shrugged. "Should I?"

"Whose stomach is it? Not mine."

The kid poured him another straight rye and I think he doctored it with water down behind the bar because when he came up with it he looked as guilty as if he'd kicked his grandmother. The drunk paid no attention. He lifted coins off his pile with the exact care of a crack surgeon operating on a brain tumor.

The kid came back and put more beer in my glass. Outside the wind howled. Every once in a while it blew the stained-glass door open a few inches. It was a heavy door.

The kid said: "I don't like drunks in the first place and in the second place I don't like them getting drunk in here, and in the third place I don't like them in the first place."

"Warner Brothers could use that," I said.

"They did."

Just then we had another customer. A car

squeaked to a stop outside and the swinging door came open. A fellow came in who looked a little in a hurry. He held the door and ranged the place quickly with flat, shiny, dark eyes. He was well set up, dark, good-looking in a narrow-faced, tight-lipped way. His clothes were dark and a white handkerchief peeped coyly from his pocket and he looked cool as well as under a tension of some sort. I guessed it was the hot wind. I felt a bit the same myself only not cool.

He looked at the drunk's back. The drunk was playing checkers with his empty glasses. The new customer looked at me, then he looked along the line of half-booths at the other side of the place. They were all empty. He came on in—down past where the drunk sat swaying and muttering to himself—and spoke to the bar kid.

"Seen a lady in here, buddy? Tall, pretty, brown hair, in a print bolero jacket over a blue crêpe silk dress. Wearing a wide-brimmed straw hat with a velvet band." He had a tight voice I didn't like.

"No, sir. Nobody like that's been in," the bar kid said.

"Thanks. Straight Scotch. Make it fast, will you?"

The kid gave it to him and the fellow paid and put the drink down in a gulp and started to go out. He took three or four steps and stopped, facing the drunk. The drunk was grinning. He swept a gun from somewhere so fast that it was just a blur coming out. He held it steady and he didn't look any drunker than I was. The tall dark guy stood quite still and then his head jerked back a little and then he was still again.

A car tore by outside. The drunk's gun was a .22 target automatic, with a large front sight. It made a couple of hard snaps and a little smoke curled—very little.

"So long, Waldo," the drunk said.

Then he put the gun on the barman and me.

The dark guy took a week to fall down. He stumbled, caught himself, waved one arm, stumbled again. His hat fell off, and then he hit the floor with his face. After he hit it he might have been poured concrete for all the fuss he made.

The drunk slid down off the stool and scooped his dimes into a pocket and slid towards the door. He turned sideways, holding the gun across his body. I didn't have a gun. I hadn't thought I needed one to buy a glass of beer. The kid behind the bar didn't move or make the slightest sound.

The drunk felt the door lightly with his shoulder, keeping his eyes on us, then pushed through it backwards. When it was wide a hard gust of air slammed in and lifted the hair of the man on the floor. The drunk said: "Poor Waldo. I bet I made his nose bleed."

The door swung shut. I started to rush it—from long practice in doing the wrong thing. In this case it didn't matter. The car outside let out a roar and when I got onto the sidewalk it was flicking a red smear of taillight around the nearby corner. I got its license number the way I got my first million.

There were people and cars up and down the block as usual. Nobody acted as if a gun had gone off. The wind was making enough noise to make the hard quick rap of .22 ammunition sound like a slammed door, even if anyone heard it. I went back into the cocktail bar.

The kid hadn't moved, even yet. He just stood with his hands flat on the bar, leaning over a little and looking down at the dark guy's back. The dark guy hadn't moved either. I bent down and felt his neck artery. He wouldn't move—ever.

The kid's face had as much expression as a cut of round steak and was about the same color. His eyes were more angry than shocked.

I lit a cigarette and blew smoke at the ceiling and said shortly: "Get on the phone."

"Maybe he's not dead," the kid said.

"When they use a twenty-two that means they don't make mistakes. Where's the phone?"

"I don't have one. I got enough expenses without that. Boy, can I kick eight hundred bucks in the face!"

"You own this place?"

"I did till this happened."

He pulled his white coat off and his apron and came around the inner end of the bar. "I'm locking this door," he said, taking keys out.

He went out, swung the door to and jiggled the lock from the outside until the bolt clicked into place. I bent down and rolled Waldo over. At first I couldn't even see where the shots went in. Then I could. A couple of tiny holes in his coat, over his heart. There was a little blood on his shirt.

The drunk was everything you could ask—as a killer.

The prowl-car boys came in about eight minutes. The kid, Lew Petrolle, was back behind the bar by then. He had his white coat on again and he was counting his money in the register and putting it in his pocket and making notes in a little book.

I sat at the edge of one of the half-booths and smoked cigarettes and watched Waldo's face get deader and deader. I wondered who the girl in the print coat was, why Waldo had left the engine of his car running outside, why he was in a hurry, whether the drunk had been waiting for him or just happened to be there.

The prowl-car boys came in perspiring. They were the usual large size and one of them had a flower stuck under his cap and his cap on a bit crooked. When he saw the dead man he got rid of the flower and leaned down to feel Waldo's pulse.

"Seems to be dead," he said, and rolled him around a little more. "Oh yeah, I see where they went in. Nice clean work. You two see him get it?"

I said yes. The kid behind the bar said nothing. I told them about it, that the killer seemed to have left in Waldo's car.

The cop yanked Waldo's wallet out, went through it rapidly and whistled. "Plenty jack and no driver's license." He put the wallet away. "O.K., we didn't touch him, see? Just a chance we could find did he have a car and put it on the air."

"The hell you didn't touch him," Lew Patrolle said.

The cop gave him one of those looks. "O.K., pal," he said softly. "We touched him."

The kid picked up a clean highball glass and began to polish it. He polished it all the rest of the time we were there.

In another minute a homicide fast-wagon sirened up and screeched to a stop outside the door and four men came in, two dicks, a photographer and a laboratory man. I didn't know either of the dicks. You can be in the detecting business a long time and not know all the men on a big city force.

One of them was a short, smooth, dark, quiet, smiling man, with curly black hair and soft intelligent eyes. The other was big, raw-boned, long-jawed, with a veined nose and glassy eyes. He looked like a heavy drinker. He looked tough, but he looked as if he thought he was a little tougher than he was. He shooed me into the last booth against the wall and his partner got the kid up front and the bluecoats went out. The fingerprint man and photographer set about their work.

A medical examiner came, stayed just long enough to get sore because there was no phone for him to call the morgue wagon.

The short dick emptied Waldo's pockets and then emptied his wallet and dumped everything into a large handkerchief on a booth table. I saw a lot of currency, keys, cigarettes, another handkerchief, very little else.

The big dick pushed me back into the end of the half-booth. "Give," he said. "I'm Copernik, Detective Lieutenant."

I put my wallet in front of him. He looked at it, went through it, tossed it back, made a note in a book.

"Philip Marlowe, huh? A shamus. You here on business?"

"Drinking business," I said. "I live just across the street in the Berglund."

"Know this kid up front?"

"I've been in here once since he opened up."

"See anything funny about him now?"

"No."

"Takes it too light for a young fellow, don't he? Never mind answering. Just tell the story."

I told it—three times. Once for him to get the outline, once for him to get the details and once for him to see if I had it too pat. At the end he said: "This dame interests me. And the killer called the guy Waldo, yet didn't seem to be anyways sure he would be in. I mean, if Waldo wasn't sure the dame would be here, nobody could be sure Waldo would be here."

"That's pretty deep," I said.

He studied me. I wasn't smiling. "Sounds like a grudge job, don't it? Don't sound planned. No getaway except by accident. A guy don't leave his car unlocked much in this town. And the killer works in front of two good witnesses. I don't like that."

"I don't like being a witness," I said. "The pay's too low."

He grinned. His teeth had a freckled look. "Was the killer drunk really?"

"With that shooting? No."

"Me too. Well, it's a simple job. The guy will have a record and he's left plenty prints. Even if we don't have his mug here we'll make him in hours. He had something on Waldo, but he wasn't meeting Waldo tonight. Waldo just dropped in to ask about a dame he had a date with and had missed connections on. It's a hot night and this wind would kill a girl's face. She'd be apt to drop in somewhere to wait. So the killer feeds Waldo two in the right place and scrams and don't worry about you boys at all. It's that simple."

"Yeah," I said.

"It's so simple it stinks," Copernik said.

He took his felt hat off and tousled up his ratty blond hair and leaned his head on his hands. He had a long mean horse face. He got a handkerchief out and mopped it, and the back of his neck and the back of his hands. He got a comb out and combed his hair—he looked worse with it combed—and put his hat back on.

"I was just thinking." I said.

"Yeah? What?"

"This Waldo knew just how the girl was dressed. So he must already have been with her tonight."

"So, what? Maybe he had to go to the can. And when he came back she's gone. Maybe she changed her mind about him."

"That's right," I said.

But that wasn't what I was thinking at all. I was thinking that Waldo had described the girl's clothes in a way the ordinary man wouldn't know how to describe them. Printed bolero jacket over blue crêpe silk dress. I didn't even know what a bolero jacket was. And I might have said blue dress or even blue silk dress, but never blue crêpe silk dress.

After a while two men came with a basket. Lew Petrolle was still polishing his glass and talking to the short dark dick.

We all went down to Headquarters.

Lew Petrolle was all right when they checked on him. His father had a grape ranch near Antioch in Contra Costa County. He had given Lew a thousand dollars to go into business and Lew had opened the cocktail bar, neon sign and all, on eight hundred flat.

They let him go and told him to keep the bar closed until they were sure they didn't want to do any more printing. He shook hands all around and grinned and said he guessed the killing would be good for business after all, because nobody believed a newspaper account of anything and people would come to him for the story and buy drinks while he was telling it.

"There's a guy won't ever do any worrying," Copernik said, when he was gone. "Over anybody else."

"Poor Waldo," I said. "The prints any good?"

"Kind of smudged," Copernik said sourly. "But we'll get a classification and teletype it to Washington some time tonight. If it don't click, you'll be in for a day on the steel picture racks downstairs."

I shook hands with him and his partner, whose name was Ybarra, and left. They didn't know who Waldo was yet either. Nothing in his pockets told.

TWO

I got back to my street about 9 p.m. I looked up and down the block before I went into the

Berglund. The cocktail bar was farther down on the other side, dark, with a nose or two against the glass, but no real crowd. People had seen the law and the morgue wagon, but they didn't know what happened. Except the boys playing pinball games in the drugstore on the corner. They know everything, except how to hold a job.

The wind was still blowing, oven-hot, swirling dust and torn paper up against the walls.

I went into the lobby of the apartment house and rode the automatic elevator up to the fourth floor. I unwound the doors and stepped out and there was a tall girl standing there waiting for the car.

She had brown wavy hair under a wide-brimmed straw hat with a velvet band and loose bow. She had wide blue eyes and eyelashes that didn't quite reach her chin. She wore a blue dress that might have been crêpe silk, simple in lines but not missing any curves. Over it she wore what might have been a print bolero jacket.

I said: "Is that a bolero jacket?"

She gave me a distant glance and made a motion as if to brush a cobweb out of the way.

"Yes. Would you mind—I'm rather in a hurry. I'd like—"

I didn't move. I blocked her off from the elevator. We stared at each other and she flushed very slowly.

"Better not go out on the street in those clothes," I said.

"Why, how dare you—"

The elevator clanked and started down again. I didn't know what she was going to say. Her voice lacked the edgy twang of a beer-parlor frill. It had a soft light sound, like spring rain.

"It's not a make," I said. "You're in trouble. If they come to this floor in the elevator, you have just that much time to get off the hall. First take off the hat and jacket—and snap it up!"

She didn't move. Her face seemed to whiten a little behind the not-too-heavy make-up.

"Cops," I said, "are looking for you. In those clothes. Give me the chance and I'll tell you why."

She turned her head swiftly and looked back along the corridor. With her looks I didn't blame her for trying one more bluff.

"You're impertinent, whoever you are. I'm Mrs. Leroy in Apartment Thirty-one. I can assure—"

"That you're on the wrong floor," I said. "This is the fourth." The elevator had stopped down below. The sound of doors being wrenched open came up the shaft.

"Off!" I rapped. "Now!"

She switched her hat off and slipped out of the bolero jacket, fast. I grabbed them and wadded them into a mess under my arm. I took her elbow and turned her and we were going down the hall.

"I live in Forty-two. The front one across from yours, just a floor up. Take your choice. Once again—I'm not on the make."

She smoothed her hair with that quick gesture, like a bird preening itself. Ten thousand years of practice behind it.

"Mine," she said, and tucked her bag under her arm and strode down the hall fast. The elevator stopped at the floor below. She stopped when it stopped. She turned and faced me.

"The stairs are back by the elevator shaft," I said gently.

"I don't have an apartment," she said.

"I didn't think you had."

"Are they searching for me?"

"Yes, but they won't start gouging the block stone by stone before tomorrow. And then only if they don't make Waldo."

She stared at me. "Waldo?"

"Oh, you don't know Waldo," I said.

She shook her head slowly. The elevator started down in the shaft again. Panic flicked in her blue eyes like a ripple on water.

"No," she said breathlessly, "but take me out of this hall."

We were almost at my door. I jammed the key in and shook the lock around and heaved the door inward. I reached in far enough to switch lights on. She went in past me like a wave. Sandalwood floated on the air, very faint.

I shut the door, threw my hat into a chair and watched her stroll over to a card table on which I had a chess problem set out that I couldn't solve. Once inside, with the door locked, her panic had left her.

"So you're a chess player," she said, in that guarded tone, as if she had come to look at my etchings. I wished she had.

We both stood still then and listened to the distant clang of elevator doors and then steps— going the other way.

I grinned, but with strain, not pleasure, went out into the kitchenette and started to fumble with a couple of glasses and then realized I still had her hat and bolero jacket under my arm. I went into the dressing room behind the wall bed and stuffed them into a drawer, went back out to the kitchenette, dug out some extra-fine Scotch and made a couple of highballs.

When I went in with the drinks she had a gun in her hand. It was a small automatic with a pearl grip. It jumped up at me and her eyes were full of horror.

I stopped, with a glass in each hand, and said: "Maybe this hot wind has got you crazy too. I'm a private detective. I'll prove it if you let me."

She nodded slightly and her face was white. I went over slowly and put a glass down beside her, and went back and set mine down and got a card out that had no bent corners. She was sitting down, smoothing one blue knee with her left hand, and holding the gun on the other. I put the card down beside her drink and sat with mine.

"Never let a guy get that close to you," I said. "Not if you mean business. And your safety catch is on."

She flashed her eyes down, shivered, and put the gun back in her bag. She drank half the drink without stopping, put the glass down hard and picked the card up.

"I don't give many people that liquor," I said. "I can't afford to."

Her lips curled. "I supposed you would want money."

"Huh?"

She didn't say anything. Her hand was close to her bag again.

"Don't forget the safety catch," I said. Her hand stopped. I went on: "This fellow I called Waldo is quite tall, say five-eleven, slim, dark, brown eyes with a lot of glitter. Nose and mouth too thin. Dark suit, white handkerchief showing, and in a hurry to find you. Am I getting anywhere?"

She took her glass again. "So that's Waldo," she said. "Well, what about him?" Her voice seemed to have a slight liquor edge now.

"Well, a funny thing. There's a cocktail bar across the street . . . Say, where have you been all evening?"

"Sitting in my car," she said coldly, "most of the time."

"Didn't you see a fuss across the street up the block?"

Her eyes tried to say no and missed. Her lips said: "I knew there was some kind of disturbance. I saw policemen and red searchlights. I supposed someone had been hurt."

"Someone was. And this Waldo was looking for you before that. In the cocktail bar. He described you and your clothes."

Her eyes were set like rivets now and had the same amount of expression. Her mouth began to tremble and kept on trembling.

"I was in there," I said, "talking to the kid that runs it. There was nobody in there but a drunk on a stool and the kid and myself. The drunk wasn't paying any attention to anything. Then Waldo came in and asked about you and we said no, we hadn't seen you and he started to leave."

I sipped my drink. I like an effect as well as the next fellow. Her eyes ate me.

"Just started to leave. Then this drunk that wasn't paying any attention to anyone called him Waldo and took a gun out. He shot him twice"— I snapped my fingers twice—"like that. Dead."

She fooled me. She laughed in my face. "So my husband hired you to spy on me," she said. "I might have known the whole thing was an act. You and your Waldo."

I gawked at her.

"I never thought of him as jealous," she snapped. "Not of a man who had been our chauffeur anyhow. A little about Stan, of course—that's natural. But Joseph Coates—"

I made motions in the air. "Lady, one of us has this book open at the wrong page," I grunted. "I don't know anybody named Stan or Joseph Coates. So help me, I didn't even know you had a chauffeur. People around here don't run to them. As for husbands—yeah, we do have a husband once in a while. Not often enough."

She shook her head slowly and her hand stayed near her bag and her blue eyes had glitters in them.

"Not good enough, Mr. Marlowe. No, not nearly good enough. I know you private detectives. You're all rotten. You tricked me into your apartment, if it is your apartment. More likely it's the apartment of some horrible man who will swear anything for a few dollars. Now you're trying to scare me. So you can blackmail me—as well as get money from my husband. All right," she said breathlessly, "how much do I have to pay?"

I put my empty glass aside and leaned back. "Pardon me if I light a cigarette," I said. "My nerves are frayed."

I lit it while she watched me without enough fear for any real guilt to be under it. "So Joseph Coates is his name," I said. "The guy that killed him in the cocktail bar called him Waldo."

She smiled a bit disgustedly, but almost tolerantly. "Don't stall. How much?"

"Why were you trying to meet this Joseph Coates?"

"I was going to buy something he stole from me, of course. Something that's valuable in the ordinary way too. Almost fifteen thousand dollars. The man I loved gave it to me. He's dead. There! He's dead! He died in a burning plane. Now, go back and tell my husband that, you slimy little rat!"

"I'm not little and I'm not a rat," I said.

"You're still slimy. And don't bother about telling my husband. I'll tell him myself. He probably knows anyway."

I grinned. "That's smart. Just what was I supposed to find out?"

She grabbed her glass and finished what was left of her drink. "So he thinks I'm meeting Joseph. Well, perhaps I was. But not to make love. Not with a chauffeur. Not with a bum I picked off the front step and gave a job to. I don't have to dig down that far, if I want to play around."

"Lady," I said, "you don't indeed."

"Now, I'm going," she said. "You just try and stop me." She snatched the pearl-handled gun out of her bag. I didn't move.

"Why, you nasty little string of nothing," she stormed. "How do I know you're a private detective at all? You might be a crook. This card you gave me doesn't mean anything. Anybody can have cards printed."

"Sure," I said. "And I suppose I'm smart enough to live here two years because you were going to move in today so I could blackmail you for not meeting a man named Joseph Coates who was bumped off across the street under the name of Waldo. Have you got the money to buy this something that cost fifteen grand?"

"Oh! You think you'll hold me up, I suppose!"

"Oh!" I mimicked her, "I'm a stick-up artist now, am I? Lady, will you please either put that gun away or take the safety catch off? It hurts my professional feelings to see a nice gun made a monkey of that way."

"You're a full portion of what I don't like," she said. "Get out of my way."

I didn't move. She didn't move. We were both sitting down—and not even close to each other.

"Let me in on one secret before you go," I pleaded. "What in hell did you take the apartment down on the floor below for? Just to meet a guy down on the street?"

"Stop being silly," she snapped. "I didn't. I lied. It's his apartment."

"Joseph Coates'?"

She nodded sharply.

"Does my description of Waldo sound like Joseph Coates?"

She nodded sharply again.

"All right. That's one fact learned at last. Don't you realize Waldo described your clothes before he was shot—when he was looking for you—that the description was passed on to the police—that the police don't know who Waldo is—and are looking for somebody in those clothes to help tell them? Don't you get that much?"

The gun suddenly started to shake in her hand. She looked down at it, sort of vacantly, and slowly put it back in her bag.

"I'm a fool," she whispered, "to be even talking to you." She stared at me for a long time, then pulled in a deep breath. "He told me where he was staying. He didn't seem afraid. I guess blackmailers are like that. He was to meet me on the street, but I was late. It was full of police when I got here. So I went back and sat in my car for a while. Then I came up to Joseph's apartment and knocked. Then I went back to my car and waited again. I came up here three times in all. The last time I walked up a flight to take the elevator. I had already been seen twice on the third floor. I met you. That's all."

"You said something about a husband," I grunted. "Where is he?"

"He's at a meeting."

"Oh, a meeting," I said, nastily.

"My husband's a very important man. He has lots of meetings. He's a hydroelectric engineer. He's been all over the world. I'd have you know—"

"Skip it," I said. "I'll take him to lunch some day and have him tell me himself. Whatever Joseph had on you is dead stock now. Like Joseph."

"He's really dead?" she whispered. "Really?"

"He's dead," I said. "Dead, dead, dead. Lady, he's dead."

She believed it at last. I hadn't thought she ever would somehow. In the silence, the elevator stopped at my floor.

I heard steps coming down the hall. We all have hunches. I put my finger to my lips. She didn't move now. Her face had a frozen look. Her big blue eyes were as black as the shadows below them. The hot wind boomed against the shut windows. Windows have to be shut when a Santa Ana blows, heat or no heat.

The steps that came down the hall were the casual ordinary steps of one man. But they stopped outside my door, and somebody knocked.

I pointed to the dressing room behind the wall bed. She stood up without a sound, her bag clenched against her side. I pointed again, to her glass. She lifted it swiftly, slid across the carpet, through the door, drew the door quietly shut after her.

I didn't know just what I was going to all this trouble for.

The knocking sounded again. The backs of my hands were wet. I creaked my chair and stood up and made a loud yawning sound. Then I went over and opened the door—without a gun. That was a mistake.

THREE

I didn't know him at first. Perhaps for the opposite reason Waldo hadn't seemed to know him. He'd had a hat on all the time over at the cocktail bar and he didn't have one on now. His hair ended completely and exactly where his hat would start. Above that line was hard white sweatless skin almost as glaring as scar tissue. He wasn't just twenty years older. He was a different man.

But I knew the gun he was holding, the .22 target automatic with the big front sight. And I knew his eyes. Bright, brittle, shallow eyes like the eyes of a lizard.

He was alone. He put the gun against my face very lightly and said between his teeth: "Yeah, me. Let's go on in."

I backed in just far enough and stopped. Just the way he would want me to, so he could shut the door without moving much. I knew from his eyes that he would want me to do just that.

I wasn't scared. I was paralyzed.

When he had the door shut he backed me some more, slowly, until there was something against the back of my legs. His eyes looked into mine.

"That's a card table," he said. "Some goon here plays chess. You?"

I swallowed. "I don't exactly play it. I just fool around."

"That means two," he said with a kind of hoarse softness, as if some cop had hit him across the windpipe with a blackjack once, in a third-degree session.

"It's a problem," I said. "Not a game. Look at the pieces."

"I wouldn't know."

"Well, I'm alone," I said, and my voice shook just enough.

"It don't make any difference," he said. "I'm washed up anyway. Some nose puts the bulls on me tomorrow, next week, what the hell? I just didn't like your map, pal. And that smug-faced pansy in the bar coat that played left tackle for Fordham or something. To hell with guys like you guys."

I didn't speak or move. The big front sight raked my cheek lightly almost caressingly. The man smiled.

"It's kind of good business too," he said. "Just in case. An old con like me don't make good prints, all I got against me is two witnesses. The hell with it."

"What did Waldo do to you?" I tried to make it sound as if I wanted to know, instead of just not wanting to shake too hard.

"Stooled on a bank job in Michigan and got me four years. Got himself a nolle prosse. Four years in Michigan ain't no summer cruise. They make you be good in them lifer states."

"How'd you know he'd come in there?" I croaked.

"I didn't. Oh yeah, I was lookin' for him. I was wanting to see him all right. I got a flash of him on the street night before last but I lost him.

Up to then I wasn't lookin' for him. Then I was. A cute guy, Waldo. How is he?"

"Dead," I said.

"I'm still good," he chuckled. "Drunk or sober. Well, that don't make no doughnuts for me now. They make me downtown yet?"

I didn't answer him quick enough. He jabbed the gun into my throat and I choked and almost grabbed for it by instinct.

"Naw," he cautioned me softly. "Naw. You ain't that dumb."

I put my hands back, down at my sides, open, the palms towards him. He would want them that way. He hadn't touched me, except with the gun. He didn't seem to care whether I might have one too. He wouldn't—if he just meant the one thing.

He didn't seem to care very much about anything, coming back on that block. Perhaps the hot wind did something to him. It was booming against my shut windows like the surf under a pier.

"They got prints," I said. "I don't know how good."

"They'll be good enough—but not for teletype work. Take 'em airmail time to Washington and back to check 'em right. Tell me why I came here, pal."

"You heard the kid and me talking in the bar. I told him my name, where I lived."

"That's how, pal. I said why." He smiled at me. It was a lousy smile to be the last one you might see.

"Skip it," I said. "The hangman won't ask you to guess why he's there."

"Say, you're tough at that. After you, I visit that kid. I tailed him home from Headquarters, but I figure you're the guy to put the bee on first. I tail him home from the city hall, in the rent car Waldo had. From Headquarters, pal. Them funny dicks. You can sit in their laps and they don't know you. Start runnin' for a streetcar and they open up with machine guns and bump two pedestrians, a hacker asleep in his cab, and an old scrubwoman on the second floor workin' a mop. And they miss the guy they're after. Them funny lousy dicks."

He twisted the gun muzzle in my neck. His eyes looked madder than before.

"I got time," he said. "Waldo's rent car don't get a report right away. And they don't make Waldo very soon. I know Waldo. Smart he was. A smooth boy, Waldo."

"I'm going to vomit," I said, "if you don't take that gun out of my throat."

He smiled and moved the gun down to my heart. "This about right? Say when."

I must have spoken louder than I meant to. The door of the dressing-room by the wall bed showed a crack of darkness. Then an inch. Then four inches. I saw eyes, but didn't look at them. I stared hard into the baldheaded man's eyes. Very hard. I didn't want him to take his eyes off mine.

"Scared?" he asked softly.

I leaned against his gun and began to shake. I thought he would enjoy seeing me shake. The girl came out through the door. She had her gun in her hand again. I was sorry as hell for her. She'd try to make the door—or scream. Either way it would be curtains—for both of us.

"Well, don't take all night about it," I bleated. My voice sounded far away, like a voice on a radio on the other side of a street.

"I like this, pal," he smiled. "I'm like that."

The girl floated in the air, somewhere behind him. Nothing was ever more soundless than the way she moved. It wouldn't do any good though. He wouldn't fool around with her at all. I had known him all my life but I had been looking into his eyes for only five minutes.

"Suppose I yell," I said.

"Yeah, suppose you yell. Go ahead and yell," he said with his killer's smile.

She didn't go near the door. She was right behind him.

"Well—here's where I yell," I said.

As if that was the cue, she jabbed the little gun hard into his short ribs, without a single sound.

He had to react. It was like a knee reflex. His mouth snapped open and both his arms jumped out from his sides and he arched his back just a little. The gun was pointing at my right eye.

I sank and kneed him with all my strength, in the groin.

His chin came down and I hit it. I hit it as if I was driving the last spike on the first transcontinental railroad. I can still feel it when I flex my knuckles.

His gun raked the side of my face but it didn't go off. He was already limp. He writhed down gasping, his left side against the floor. I kicked his right shoulder—hard. The gun jumped away from him, skidded on the carpet, under a chair. I heard the chessmen tinkling on the floor behind me somewhere.

The girl stood over him, looking down. Then her wide dark horrified eyes came up and fastened on mine.

"That buys me," I said. "Anything I have is yours—now and forever."

She didn't hear me. Her eyes were strained open so hard that the whites showed under the vivid blue iris. She backed quickly to the door with her little gun up, felt behind her for the knob and twisted it. She pulled the door open and slipped out.

The door shut.

She was bareheaded and without her bolero jacket.

She had only the gun, and the safety catch on that was still set so that she couldn't fire it.

It was silent in the room then, in spite of the wind. Then I heard him gasping on the floor. His face had a greenish pallor. I moved behind him and pawed him for more guns, and didn't find any. I got a pair of store cuffs out of my desk and pulled his arms in front of him and snapped them on his wrists. They would hold if he didn't shake them too hard.

His eyes measured me for a coffin, in spite of their suffering. He lay in the middle of the floor, still on his left side, a twisted, wizened, baldheaded little guy with drawn-back lips and teeth spotted with cheap silver fillings. His mouth looked like a black pit and his breath came in little waves, choked, stopped, came on again, limping.

I went into the dressing room and opened the

drawer of the chest. Her hat and jacket lay there on my shirts. I put them underneath, at the back, and smoothed the shirts over them. Then I went out to the kitchenette and poured a stiff jolt of whiskey and put it down and stood a moment listening to the hot wind howl against the window glass. A garage door banged, and a power-line wire with too much play between the insulators thumped the side of the building with a sound like somebody beating a carpet.

The drink worked on me. I went back into the living room and opened a window. The guy on the floor hadn't smelled her sandalwood, but somebody else might.

I shut the window again, wiped the palms of my hands and used the phone to dial Headquarters.

Copernik was still there. His smart-aleck voice said: "Yeah? Marlowe? Don't tell me. I bet you got an idea."

"Make that killer yet?"

"We're not saying, Marlowe. Sorry as all hell and so on. You know how it is."

"O.K., I don't care who he is. Just come and get him off the floor of my apartment.

"Holy Christ!" Then his voice hushed and went down low. "Wait a minute, now. Wait a minute." A long way off I seemed to hear a door shut. Then his voice again. "Shoot," he said softly.

"Handcuffed," I said. "All yours. I had to knee him, but he'll be all right. He came here to eliminate a witness."

Another pause. The voice was fully of honey. "Now listen, boy, who else is in this with you?"

"Who else? Nobody. Just me."

"Keep it that way, boy. All quiet. O.K.?"

"Think I want all the bums in the neighborhood in here sightseeing?"

"Take it easy, boy. Easy. Just sit tight and sit still. I'm practically there. No touch nothing. Get me?"

"Yeah." I gave him the address and apartment number again to save him time.

I could see his big bony face glisten. I got the .22 target gun from under the chair and sat holding it until feet hit the hallway outside my door and knuckles did a quiet tattoo on the door panel.

Copernik was alone. He filled the doorway quickly, pushed me back into the room with a tight grin and shut the door. He stood with his back to it, his hand under the left side of his coat. A big hard bony man with flat cruel eyes.

He lowered them slowly and looked at the man on the floor. The man's neck was twitching a little. His eyes moved in short stabs—sick eyes.

"Sure it's the guy?" Copernick's voice was hoarse.

"Positive. Where's Ybarra?"

"Oh, he was busy." He didn't look at me when he said that. "Those your cuffs?"

"Yeah."

"Key."

I tossed it to him. He went down swiftly on one knee beside the killer and took my cuffs off his wrists, tossed them to one side. He got his own off his hip, twisted the bald man's hands behind him and snapped the cuffs on.

"All right, you bastard," the killer said tonelessly.

Copernik grinned and balled his fist and hit the handcuffed man in the mouth a terrific blow. His head snapped back almost enough to break his neck. Blood dribbled from the lower corner of his mouth.

"Get a towel," Copernik ordered.

I got a hand towel and gave it to him. He stuffed it between the handcuffed man's teeth, viciously, stood up and rubbed his bony fingers through his ratty blond hair.

"All right. Tell it."

I told it—leaving the girl out completely. It sounded a little funny. Copernik watched me, said nothing. He rubbed the side of his veined nose. Then he got his comb out and worked on his hair just as he had done earlier in the evening, in the cocktail bar.

I went over and gave him the gun. He looked at it casually, dropped it into his side pocket. His eyes had something in them and his face moved in a hard bright grin.

I bent down and began picking up my chessmen and dropping them into the box. I put the box on the mantel, straightened out a leg of the card table, played around for a while. All the time Copernik watched me. I wanted him to think something out.

At last he came out with it. "This guy uses a twenty-two," he said. "He uses it because he's good enough to get by with that much gun. That means he's good. He knocks at your door, pokes that gat in your belly, walks you back into the room, says he's here to close your mouth for keeps—and yet you take him. You not having any gun. You take him alone. You're kind of good yourself, pal."

"Listen," I said, and looked at the floor. I picked up another chessman and twisted it between my fingers. "I was doing a chess problem," I said "Trying to forget things."

"You got something on your mind, pal," Copernik said softly. "You wouldn't try to fool an old copper, would you, boy?"

"It's a swell pinch and I'm giving it to you," I said. "What the hell more do you want?"

The man on the floor made a vague sound behind the towel. His bald head glistened with sweat.

"What's the matter, pal? You been up to something?" Copernick almost whispered.

I looked at him quickly, looked away again. "All right," I said. "You know damn well I couldn't take him alone. He had the gun on me and he shoots where he looks."

Copernik closed one eye and squinted at me amiably with the other. "Go on, pal. I kind of thought of that too."

I shuffled around a little more, to make it look good. I said, slowly: "There was a kid here who pulled a job over in Boyle Heights, a heist job. It didn't take. A two-bit service station stick-up. I know his family. He's not really bad. He was here trying to beg train money off me. When the knock came he sneaked in—there."

I pointed at the wall bed and the door beside. Copernik's head swiveled slowly, swiveled back. His eyes winked again. "And this kid had a gun," he said.

I nodded. "And he got behind him. That takes guts, Copernik. You've got to give the kid a break. You've got to let him stay out of it."

"Tag out for this kid?" Copernik asked softly.

"Not yet, he says. He's scared there will be."

Copernik smiled. "I'm a homicide man," he said. "I wouldn't know—or care."

I pointed down at the gagged and handcuffed man on the floor. "You took him, didn't you?" I said gently.

Copernik kept on smiling. A big whitish tongue came out and massaged his thick lower lip. "How'd I do it?" he whispered.

"Get the slugs out of Waldo?"

"Sure. Long twenty-two's. One smashed a rib, one good."

"You're a careful guy. You don't miss any angles. You know anything about me? You dropped in on me to see what guns I had."

Copernik got up and went down on one knee again beside the killer. "Can you hear me, guy?" he asked with his face close to the face of the man on the floor.

The man made some vague sound. Copernik stood up and yawned. "Who the hell cares what he says? Go on, pal."

"You wouldn't expect to find I had anything, but you wanted to look around my place. And while you were mousing around in there"—I pointed to the dressing room— "and me not saying anything, being a little sore, maybe, a knock came on the door. So he came in. So after a while you sneaked out and took him."

"Ah," Copernik grinned widely, with as many teeth as a horse. "You're on, pal. I socked him and I kneed him and I took him. You didn't have no gun and the guy swiveled on me pretty sharp and I left-hooked him down the backstairs. O.K.?"

"O.K.," I said.

"You'll tell it like that downtown?"

"Yeah," I said.

"I'll protect you, pal. Treat me right and I'll always play ball. Forget about that kid. Let me know if he needs a break."

He came over and held out his hand. I shook

it. It was as clammy as a dead fish. Clammy hands and the people who own them make me sick.

"There's just one thing," I said. "This partner of yours—Ybarra. Won't he be a bit sore you didn't bring him along on this?"

Copernik tousled his hair and wiped his hatband with a large yellowish silk handkerchief.

"That guinea?" he sneered. "To hell with him!" He came close to me and breathed in my face. "No mistakes, pal—about that story of ours."

His breath was bad. It would be.

FOUR

There were just five of us in the chief-of-detective's office when Copernik laid it before them. A stenographer, the chief, Copernik, myself, Ybarra. Ybarra sat on a chair tilted against the side wall. His hat was down over his eyes but their softness loomed underneath, and the small still smile hung at the corners of the clean-cut Latin lips. He didn't look directly at Copernik. Copernik didn't look at him at all.

Outside in the corridor there had been photos of Copernik shaking hands with me, Copernik with his hat on straight and his gun in his hand and a stern, purposeful look on his face.

They said they knew who Waldo was, but they wouldn't tell me. I didn't believe they knew, because the chief-of-detectives had a morgue photo of Waldo on his desk. A beautiful job, his hair combed, his tie straight, the light hitting his eyes just right to make them glisten. Nobody would have known it was a photo of a dead man with two bullet holes in his heart. He looked like a dance-hall sheik making up his mind whether to take the blonde or the redhead.

It was about midnight when I got home. The apartment door was locked and while I was fumbling for my keys a low voice spoke to me out of the darkness.

All it said was: "Please!" but I knew it. I turned and looked at a dark Cadillac coupe parked just off the loading zone. It had no lights. Light from the street touched the brightness of a woman's eyes.

I went over there. "You're a darn fool," I said. She said: "Get in."

I climbed in and she started the car and drove it a block and a half along Franklin and turned down Kingsley Drive. The hot wind still burned and blustered. A radio lilted from an open, sheltered side window of an apartment house. There were a lot of parked cars but she found a vacant space behind a small brand-new Packard cabriolet that had the dealer's sticker on the windshield glass. After she'd jockeyed us up to the curb she leaned back in the corner with her gloved hands on the wheel.

She was all in black now, or dark brown, with a small foolish hat. I smelled the sandalwood in her perfume.

"I wasn't very nice to you, was I?" she said.

"All you did was save my life."

"What happened?"

"I called the law and fed a few lies to a cop I don't like and gave him all the credit for the pinch and that was that. That guy you took away from me was the man who killed Waldo."

"You mean—you didn't tell them about me?"

"Lady," I said again, "all you did was save my life. What else do you want done? I'm ready, willing, and I'll try to be able."

She didn't say anything, or move.

"Nobody learned who you are from me," I said. "Incidentally, I don't know myself."

"I'm Mrs. Frank C. Barsaly, Two-twelve Fremont Place, Olympia Two-four-five-nine-six. Is that what you wanted?"

"Thanks," I mumbled, and rolled a dry unlit cigarette around in my fingers. "Why did you come back?" Then I snapped the fingers of my left hand. "The hat and jacket," I said. "I'll go up and get them."

"It's more than that," she said. "I want my pearls." I might have jumped a little. It seemed as if there had been enough without pearls.

A car tore by down the street going twice as fast as it should. A thin bitter cloud of dust lifted in the street lights and whirled and vanished. The girl ran the window up quickly against it.

"All right," I said. "Tell me about the pearls. We have had a murder and a mystery woman and a mad killer and a heroic rescue and a police detective framed into making a false report. Now we will have pearls. All right—feed it to me."

"I was to buy them for five thousand dollars. From the man you call Waldo and I call Joseph Coates. He should have had them."

"No pearls," I said. "I saw what came out of his pockets. A lot of money, but no pearls."

"Could they be hidden in his apartment?"

"Yes," I said. "So far as I know he could have had them hidden anywhere in California except in his pockets. How's Mr. Barsaly this hot night?"

"He's still downtown at his meeting. Otherwise I couldn't have come."

"Well, you could have brought him," I said. "He could have sat in the rumble seat."

"Oh, I don't know," she said. "Frank weighs two hundred pounds and he's pretty solid. I don't think he would like to sit in the rumble seat, Mr. Marlowe."

"What the hell are we talking about anyway?"

She didn't answer. Her gloved hands tapped lightly, provokingly on the rim of the slender wheel. I threw the unlit cigarette out the window, turned a little and took hold of her.

When I let go of her, she pulled as far away from me as she could against the side of the car and rubbed the back of her glove against her mouth. I sat quite still.

We didn't speak for some time. Then she said very slowly: "I meant you to do that. But I wasn't always that way. It's only been since Stan Phillips was killed in his plane. If it hadn't been for that, I'd be Mrs. Phillips now. Stan gave me the pearls. They cost fifteen thousand dollars, he said once. White pearls, forty-one of them, the largest about a third of an inch across. I don't know how many grains. I never had them appraised or showed them to a jeweler, so I don't know those things. But I loved them on Stan's

account. I loved Stan. The way you do just the one time. Can you understand?"

"What's your first name?" I asked.

"Lola."

"Go on talking, Lola." I got another dry cigarette out of my pocket and fumbled it between my fingers just to give them something to do.

"They had a simple silver clasp in the shape of a two-bladed propeller. There was one small diamond where the boss would be. I told Frank they were store pearls I had bought myself. He didn't know the difference. It's not so easy to tell, I dare say. You see—Frank is pretty jealous."

In the darkness she came closer to me and her side touched my side. But I didn't move this time. The wind howled and the trees shook. I kept on rolling the cigarette around in my fingers.

"I suppose you've read that story," she said. "About the wife and the real pearls and her telling her husband they were false?"

"I've read it," I said, "Maugham."

"I hired Joseph. My husband was in Argentina at the time. I was pretty lonely."

"*You* should be lonely," I said.

"Joseph and I went driving a good deal. Sometimes we had a drink or two together. But that's all. I don't go around—"

"You told him about the pearls," I said. "And when your two hundred pounds of beef came back from Argentina and kicked him out—he took the pearls, because he knew they were real. And then offered them back to you for five grand."

"Yes," she said simply. "Of course I didn't want to go to the police. And of course in the circumstances Joseph wasn't afraid of my knowing where he lived."

"Poor Waldo," I said. "I feel kind of sorry for him. It was a hell of a time to run into an old friend that had a down on you."

I struck a match on my shoe sole and lit the cigarette. The tobacco was so dry from the hot wind that it burned like grass. The girl sat quietly beside me, her hands on the wheel again.

"Hell with women—these fliers," I said. "And you're still in love with him, or think you are. Where did you keep the pearls?"

"In a Russian malachite jewelry box on my dressing table. With some other costume jewelry. I had to, if I ever wanted to wear them."

"And they were worth fifteen grand. And you think Joseph might have hidden them in his apartment. Thirty-one, wasn't it?"

"Yes," she said. "I guess it's a lot to ask."

I opened the door and got out of the car. "I've been paid," I said. "I'll go look. The doors in my apartment are not very obstinate. The cops will find out where Waldo lived when they publish his photo, but not tonight, I guess."

"It's awfully sweet of you," she said. "Shall I wait here?"

I stood with a foot on the running board, leaning in, looking at her. I didn't answer her question. I just stood there looking in at the shine of her eyes. Then I shut the car door and walked up the street towards Franklin.

Even with the wind shriveling my face I could still smell the sandalwood in her hair. And feel her lips.

I unlocked the Berglund door, walked through the silent lobby to the elevator, and rode up to Three. Then I soft-footed along the silent corridor and peered down at the sill of Apartment 31. No light. I rapped—the old light, confidential tattoo of the bootlegger with the big smile and the extra-deep hip pockets. No answer. I took the piece of thick hard celluloid that pretended to be a window over the driver's license in my wallet, and eased it between the lock and the jamb, leaning hard on the knob, pushing it toward the hinges. The edge of the celluloid caught the slope of the spring lock and snapped it back with a small brittle sound, like an icicle breaking. The door yielded and I went into near darkness. Street light filtered in and touched a high spot here and there.

I shut the door and snapped the light on and just stood. There was a queer smell in the air. I made it in a moment—the smell of dark-cured tobacco. I prowled over to a smoking stand by the window and looked down at four brown butts—Mexican or South American cigarettes.

Upstairs, on my floor, feet hit the carpet and somebody went into a bathroom. I heard the toilet flush. I went into the bathroom of Apartment 31. A little rubbish, nothing, no place to hide anything. The kitchenette was a longer job, but I only half searched. I knew there were no pearls in that apartment. I knew Waldo had been on his way out and that he was in a hurry and that something was riding him when he turned and took two bullets from an old friend.

I went back to the living room and swung the wall bed and looked past its mirror side into the dressing room for signs of still current occupancy. Swinging the bed farther I was no longer looking for pearls. I was looking at a man.

He was small, middle-aged, iron-gray at the temples, with a very dark skin, dressed in a fawn-colored suit with a wine-colored tie. His neat little brown hands hung slimply by his sides. His small feet, in pointed polished shoes, pointed almost at the floor.

He was hanging by a belt around his neck from the metal top of the bed. His tongue stuck out farther than I thought it possible for a tongue to stick out.

He swung a little and I didn't like that, so I pulled the bed shut and he nestled quietly between the two clamped pillows. I didn't touch him yet. I didn't have to touch him to know that he would be cold as ice.

I went around him into the dressing room and used my handkerchief on drawer knobs. The place was stripped clean except for the light litter of a man living alone.

I came out of there and began on the man. No wallet. Waldo would have taken that and ditched it. A flat box of cigarettes, half full, stamped in gold: "Louis Tapia y Cia, Calle de Paysandú, 19, Montevideo." Matches from the Spezia Club. An under-arm holster of dark-grained leather and in it a 9-millimeter Mauser.

The Mauser made him a professional, so I didn't feel so badly. But not a very good professional, or bare hands would not have finished him, with the Mauser—a gun you can blast through a wall with—undrawn in his shoulder holster.

I made a little sense of it, not much. Four of the brown cigarettes had been smoked, so there had been either waiting or discussion. Somewhere along the line Waldo had got the little man by the throat and held him in just the right way to make him pass out in a matter of seconds. The Mauser had been less useful to him than a toothpick. Then Waldo had hung him up by the strap, probably dead already. That would account for haste, cleaning out the apartment, for Waldo's anxiety about the girl. It would account for the car left unlocked outside the cocktail bar.

That is, it would account for these things if Waldo had killed him, if this was really Waldo's apartment—if I wasn't just being kidded.

I examined some more pockets. In the left trouser one I found a gold penknife, some silver. In the left hip pocket a handkerchief, folded, scented. On the right hip another, unfolded but clean. In the right leg pocket four or five tissue handkerchiefs. A clean little guy. He didn't like to blow his nose on his handkerchief. Under these there was a small new keytainer holding four new keys—car keys. Stamped in gold on the keytainer was: Compliments of R.K. Vogelsang, Inc. "The Packard House."

I put everything as I had found it, swung the bed back, used my handkerchief on knobs and other projections, and flat surfaces, killed the light and poked my nose out the door. The hall was empty. I went down to the street and around the corner to Kingsley Drive. The Cadillac hadn't moved.

I opened the car door and leaned on it. She didn't seem to have moved, either. It was hard to see any expression on her face. Hard to see anything but her eyes and chin, but not hard to smell the sandalwood.

"That perfume," I said, "would drive a deacon nuts . . . no pearls."

"Well, thanks for trying," she said in a low, soft vibrant voice. "I guess I can stand it. Shall I . . . Do we . . . Or . . . ?"

"You go on home now," I said. "And whatever happens you never saw me before. Whatever happens. Just as you may never see me again."

"I'd hate that."

"Good luck, Lola." I shut the car door and stepped back.

The lights blazed on, the motor turned over. Against the wind at the corner the big coupe made a slow contemptuous turn and was gone. I stood there by the vacant space at the curb where it had been.

It was quite dark there now. Windows, had become blanks in the apartment where the radio sounded. I stood looking at the back of a Packard cabriolet which seemed to be brand new. I had seen it before—before I went upstairs, in the same place, in front of Lola's car. Parked, dark, silent, with a blue sticker pasted to the right-hand corner of the shiny windshield.

And in my mind I was looking at stomething else, a set of brand-new car keys in a keytainer stamped: "The Packard House," upstairs, in a dead man's pocket.

I went up to the front of the cabriolet and put a small pocket flash on the blue slip. It was the same dealer all right. Written in ink below his name and slogan was a name and address— Eu´genie Kolchenko. 5315 Arvieda Street, West Los Angeles.

It was crazy. I went back up to Apartment 31, jimmied the door as I had done before, stepped in behind the wall bed and took the keytainer from the trousers pocket of the neat brown dangling corpse. I was back down on the street beside the cabriolet in five minutes. The keys fitted.

FIVE

It was a small house, near a canyon rim out beyond Sawtelle, with a circle of writhing eucalyptus trees in front of it. Beyond that, on the other side of the street, one of those parties was going on where they come out and smash bottles on the sidewalk with a whoop like Yale making a touchdown against Princeton.

There was a wire fence at my number and some rose trees, and a flagged walk and a garage that was wide open and had no car in it. There was no car in front of the house either. I rang the bell. There was a long wait, then the door opened rather suddenly.

I wasn't the man she had been expecting. I could see it in her glittering kohl-rimmed eyes. Then I couldn't see anything in them. She just stood and looked at me, a long, lean, hungry brunette, with rouged cheekbones, thick black hair parted in the middle, a mouth made for three-decker sandwiches, coral-and-gold pajamas, sandals—and gilded toenails. Under her ear lobes a couple of miniature temple bells gonged lightly in the breeze. She made a slow disdainful motion with a cigarette in a holder as long as a baseball bat.

"We-el, what ees it, little man? You want sometheeng? You are lost from the bee-ootiful party across the street, hein?"

"Ha-ha," I said. "Quite a party, isn't it? No, I just brought your car home. Lost it, didn't you?"

Across the street somebody had delirium tremens in the front yard and a mixed quartet tore what was left of the night into small strips and did what they could to make the strips miserable. While this was going on the exotic brunette didn't move more than one eyelash.

She wasn't beautiful, she wasn't even pretty, but she looked as if things would happen where she was.

"You have said what?" she got out, at last, in a voice as silky as a burnt crust of toast.

"Your car." I pointed over my shoulder and kept my eyes on her. She was the type that uses a knife.

The long cigarette holder dropped very slowly to her side and the cigarette fell out of it. I stamped it out, and that put me in the hall. She backed away from me and I shut the door.

The hall was like the long hall of a railroad flat. Lamps glowed pinkly in iron brackets.

There was a bead curtain at the end, a tiger skin on the floor. The place went with her.

"You're Miss Kolchenko?" I asked, not getting any more action.

"Ye-es. I am Mees Kolchenko. What the 'ell you want?"

She was looking at me now as if I had come to wash the windows, but at an inconvenient time.

I got a card out with my left hand, held it out to her. She read it in my hand, moving her head just enough. "A detective?" she breathed.

"Yeah."

She said something in a spitting language. Then in English: "Come in! Thees damn wind dry up my skeen like so much teesue paper."

"We're in," I said. "I just shut the door. Snap out of it, Nazimova. Who was he? The little guy?"

Beyond the bead curtain a man coughed. She jumped as if she had been stuck with an oyster fork. Then she tried to smile. It wasn't very successful.

"A reward," she said softly. "You weel wait 'ere? Ten dollars it is fair to pay, no?"

"No," I said.

I reached a finger towards her slowly and added: "He's dead."

She jumped about three feet and let out a yell.

A chair creaked harshly. Feet pounded beyond the bead curtain, a large hand plunged into view and snatched it aside, and a big hard-looking blond man was with us. He had a purple robe over his pajamas, his right hand held something in his robe pocket. He stood quite still as soon as he was through the curtain, his feet planted solidly, his jaw out, his colorless eyes like gray ice. He looked like a man who would be hard to take out on an off-tackle play.

"What's the matter, honey?" He had a solid, burring voice, with just the right sappy tone to belong to a guy who would go for a woman with gilded toenails.

"I came about Miss Kolchenko's car," I said.

"Well, you could take your hat off," he said. "Just for a light workout."

I took it off and apologized.

"O.K.," he said, and kept his right hand shoved down hard in the purple pocket. "So you came about Miss Kolchenko's car. Take it from there."

I pushed past the woman and went closer to him. She shrank back against the wall and flattened her palms against it. Camille in a high-school play. The long holder lay empty at her toes.

When I was six feet from the big man he said easily: "I can hear you from there. Just take it easy. I've got a gun in this pocket and I've had to learn to use one. Now about the car?"

"The man who borrowed it couldn't bring it," I said, and pushed the card I was still holding towards his face. He barely glanced at it. He looked back at me.

"So what?" he said.

"Are you always this tough?" I asked. "Or only when you have your pajamas on?"

"So why couldn't he bring it himself?" he asked. "And skip the mushy talk."

The dark woman made a stuffed sound at my elbow.

"It's all right, honeybunch," the man said. "I'll handle this. Go on."

She slid past both of us and flicked through the bead curtain.

I waited a little while. The big man didn't move a muscle. He didn't look any more bothered than a toad in the sun.

"He couldn't bring it because somebody bumped him off," I said. "Let's see you handle that."

"Yeah?" he said. "Did you bring him with you to prove it?"

"No," I said. "But if you put your tie and crush hat on, I'll take you down and show you."

"Who the hell did you say you were, now?"

"I didn't say. I thought maybe you could read." I held the card at him some more.

"Oh, that's right," he said. "Philip Marlowe, Private Investigator. Well, well. So I should go with you to look at who, why?"

"Maybe he stole the car," I said.

The big man nodded. "That's a thought. Maybe he did. Who?"

"The little brown guy who had the keys to it in his pocket, and had it parked around the corner from the Berglund Apartments."

He thought that over, without any apparent embarrassment. "You've got something there," he said. "Not much. But a little. I guess this must be the night of the Police Smoker. So you're doing all their work for them."

"Huh?"

"The card says private detective to me," he said. "Have you got some cops outside that were too shy to come in?"

"No, I'm alone."

He grinned. The grin showed white ridges in his tanned skin. "So you find somebody dead and take some keys and find a car and come riding out here—all alone. No cops. Am I right?"

"Correct."

He sighed. "Let's go inside," he said. He yanked the bead curtain aside and made an opening for me to go through. "It might be you have an idea I ought to hear."

I went past him and he turned, keeping his heavy pocket towards me. I hadn't noticed until I got quite close that there were beads of sweat on his face. It might have been the hot wind but I didn't think so.

We were in the living room of the house.

We sat down and looked at each other across a dark floor, on which a few Navajo rugs and a few dark Turkish rugs made a decorating combination with some well-used overstuffed furniture. There was a fireplace, a small baby grand, a Chinese screen, a tall Chinese lantern on a teakwood pedestal, and gold net curtains against lattice windows. The windows to the south were open. A fruit tree with a whitewashed trunk whipped about outside the screen, adding its bit to the noise from across the street.

The big man eased back into a brocaded chair and put his slippered feet on a footstool. He kept his right hand where it had been since I met him—on his gun.

The brunette hung around in the shadows

and a bottle gurgled and her temple bells gonged in her ears.

"It's all right, honeybunch," the man said. "It's all under control. Somebody bumped somebody off and this lad thinks we're interested. Just sit down and relax."

The girl tilted her head and poured half a tumbler of whiskey down her throat. She sighed, said, "Goddam," in a casual voice, and curled up on a davenport. It took all of the davenport. She had plenty of legs. Her gilded toenails winked at me from the shadowy corner where she kept herself quiet from then on.

I got a cigarette out without being shot at, lit it and went into my story. It wasn't all true, but some of it was. I told them about the Berglund Apartments and that I had lived there and that Waldo was living there in Apartment 31 on the floor below mine and that I had been keeping an eye on him for business reasons.

"Waldo what?" the blond man put in. "And what business reasons?"

"Mister," I said, "have you no secrets?" He reddened slightly.

I told him about the cocktail lounge across the street from the Berglund and what had happened there. I didn't tell him about the printed bolero jacket or the girl who had worn it. I left her out of the story altogether.

"It was an undercover job—from my angle," I said. "If you know what I mean." He reddened again, bit his teeth. I went on: "I got back from the city hall without telling anybody I knew Waldo. In due time, when I decided they couldn't find out where he lived that night, I took the liberty of examining his apartment."

"Looking for what?" the big man said thickly.

"For some letters. I might mention in passing there was nothing there at all—except a dead man. Strangled and hanging by a belt to the top of the wall bed—well out of sight. A small man, about forty-five, Mexican or South American, well-dressed in a fawn-colored—"

"That's enough," the big man said. "I'll bite, Marlowe. Was it a blackmail job you were on?"

"Yeah. The funny part was this little brown man had plenty of gun under his arm."

"He wouldn't have five hundred bucks in twenties in his pocket, of course? Or are you saying?"

"He wouldn't. But Waldo had over seven hundred in currency when he was killed in the cocktail bar."

"Looks like I underrated this Waldo," the big man said calmly. "He took my guy and his pay-off money, gun and all. Waldo have a gun?"

"Not on him."

"Get us a drink, honeybunch," the big man said. "Yes, I certainly did sell this Waldo person shorter than a bargain-counter shirt."

The brunette unwound her legs and made two drinks with soda and ice. She took herself another gill without trimmings, wound herself back on the davenport. Her big glittering black eyes watched me solemnly.

"Well, here's how," the big man said, lifting his glass in salute. "I haven't murdered anybody, but I've got a divorce suit on my hands from now on. You haven't murdered anybody, the way you tell it, but you laid an egg down at police Headquarters. What the hell! Life's a lot of trouble, anyway you look at it. I've still got honeybunch here. She's a white Russian I met in Shanghai. She's safe as a vault and she looks as if she could cut your throat for a nickel. That's what I like about her. You get the glamor without the risk."

"You talk damn foolish," the girl spat at him.

"You look O.K. to me," the big man went on ignoring her. "That is, for a keyhole peeper. Is there an out?"

"Yeah. But it will cost a little money."

"I expected that. How much?"

"Say another five hundred."

"Goddam, thees hot wind make me dry like the ashes of love," the Russian girl said bitterly.

"Five hundred might do," the blond man said. "What do I get for it?"

"If I swing it—you get left out of the story. If I don't—you don't pay."

He thought it over. His face looked lined and tired now. The small beads of sweat twinkled in his short blond hair.

"This murder will make you talk," he grumbled. "The second one, I mean. And I don't have what I was going to buy. And if it's a hush, I'd rather buy it direct."

"Who was the little brown man?" I asked.

"Name's Leon Valesanos, a Uruguayan. Another of my importations. I'm in a business that takes me a lot of places. He was working in the Spezzia Club in Chiseltown—you know, the strip of Sunset next to Beverly Hills. Working on roulette, I think. I gave him the five hundred to go down to this—this Waldo—and buy back some bills for stuff Miss Kolchenko had charged to my account and delivered here. That wasn't bright, was it? I had them in my briefcase and this Waldo got a chance to steal them. What's your hunch about what happened?"

I sipped my drink and looked at him down my nose. "Your Uruguayan pal probably talked curt and Waldo didn't listen good. Then the little guy thought maybe that Mauser might help his argument—and Waldo was too quick for him. I wouldn't say Waldo was a killer—not by intention. A blackmailer seldom is. Maybe he lost his temper and maybe he just held on to the little guy's neck too long. Then he had to take it on the lam. But he had another date, with more money coming up. And he worked the neighborhood looking for the party. And accidentally he ran into a pal who was hostile enough and drunk enough to blow him down."

"There's a hell of a lot of coincidence in all this business," the big man said.

"It's the hot wind," I grinned. "Everybody's screwy tonight."

"For the five hundred you guarantee nothing? If I don't get my coverup, you don't get your dough. Is that it?"

"That's it," I said, smiling at him.

"Screwy is right," he said, and drained his highball. "I'm taking you up on it."

"There are just two things," I said softly, leaning forward in my chair. "Waldo had a getaway car parked outside the cocktail bar where he was killed, unlocked with the motor running. The killer took it. There's always the chance of a kickback from that direction. You see, all Waldo's stuff must have been in that car."

"Including my bills, and your letters."

"Yeah. But the police are reasonable about things like that—unless you're good for a lot of publicity. If you're not, I think I can eat some stale dog downtown and get by. If you are—that's the second thing. What did you say your name was?"

The answer was a long time coming. When it came I didn't get as much kick out of it as I thought I would. All at once it was too logical.

"Frank C. Barsaly," he said.

After a while the Russian girl called me a taxi. When I left, the party across the street was doing all that a party could do. I noticed the walls of the house were still standing. That seemed a pity.

SIX

When I unlocked the glass entrance door of the Berglund I smelled policeman. I looked at my wrist watch. It was nearly 3 a.m. In the dark corner of the lobby a man dozed in a chair with a newspaper over his face. Large feet stretched out before him. A corner of the paper lifted an inch, dropped again. The man made no other movement.

I went on along the hall to the elevator and rode up to my floor. I soft-footed along the hallway, unlocked my door, pushed it wide and reached in for the light switch.

A chain switch tinkled and light glared from a standing lamp by the easy chair, beyond the card table on which my chessmen were still scattered.

Copernik sat there with a stiff unpleasant grin on his face. The short dark man, Ybarra, sat across the room from him, on my left, silent, half smiling as usual.

Copernik showed more of his big yellow horse teeth and said: "Hi. Long time no see. Been out with the girls?"

I shut the door and took my hat off and wiped the back of my neck slowly, over and over again. Copernik went on grinning. Ybarra looked at nothing with his soft dark eyes.

"Take a seat, pal," Copernik drawled. "Make yourself to home. We got pow-wow to make.

Boy, do I hate this night sleuthing. Did you know you were low on hooch?"

"I could have guessed it," I said. I leaned against the wall.

Copernik kept on grinning. "I always did hate private dicks," he said, "but I never had a chance to twist one like I got tonight."

He reached down lazily beside his chair and picked up a printed bolero jacket, tossed it on the card table. He reached down again and put a wide-brimmed hat beside it.

"I bet you look cuter than all hell with these on," he said.

I took hold of a straight chair, twisted it around and straddled it, leaned my folded arms on the chair and looked at Copernik.

He got up very slowly—with an elaborate slowness, walked across the room and stood in front of me smoothing his coat down. Then he lifted his open right hand and hit me across the face with it—hard. It stung but I didn't move.

Ybarra looked at the wall, looked at the floor, looked at nothing.

"Shame on you, pal," Copernik said lazily. "The way you was taking care of this nice exclusive merchandise. Wadded down behind your old shirts. You punk peepers always did make me sick."

He stood there over me for a moment. I didn't move or speak. I looked into his glazed drinker's eyes. He doubled a fist at his side, then shrugged and turned and went back to the chair.

"O.K.," he said. "The rest will keep. Where did you get these things?"

"They belong to a lady."

"Do tell. They belong to a lady. Ain't you the lighthearted bastard! I'll tell you what lady they belong to. They belong to the lady a guy named Waldo asked about in a bar across the street— about two minutes before he got shot kind of dead. Or would that have slipped your mind?"

I didn't say anything.

"You was curious about her yourself," Copernik sneered on. "But you were smart, pal. You fooled me."

"That wouldn't make me smart," I said.

His face twisted suddenly and he started to get up. Ybarra laughed, suddenly and softly, almost under his breath. Copernik's eyes swung on him, hung there. Then he faced me again, bland-eyed.

"The guinea likes you," he said. "He thinks you're good."

The smile left Ybarra's face, but no expression took its place. No expression at all.

Copernik said: "You knew who the dame was all the time. You knew who Waldo was and where he lived. Right across the hall a floor below you. You knew this Waldo person had bumped a guy off and started to lam, only this broad came into his plans somewhere and he was anxious to meet up with her before he went away. Only he never got the chance. A heist guy from back East named Al Tessilore took care of that by taking care of Waldo. So you met the gal and hid her clothes and sent her on her way and kept your trap glued. That's the way guys like you make your beans. Am I right?"

"Yeah," I said. "Except that I only knew these things very recently. Who was Waldo?"

Copernik bared his teeth at me. Red spots burned high on his sallow cheeks. Ybarra, looking down at the floor, said very softly: "Waldo Ratigan. We got him from Washington by Teletype. He was a two-bit porch climber with a few small terms on him. He drove a car in a bank stick-up job in Detroit. He turned the gang in later and got a nolle prosse. One of the gang was this Al Tessilore. He hasn't talked a word, but we think the meeting across the street was purely accidental."

Ybarra spoke in the soft quiet modulated voice of a man for whom sounds have a meaning. I said: "Thanks, Ybarra. Can I smoke—or would Copernik kick it out of my mouth?"

Ybarra smiled suddenly. "You may smoke, sure," he said.

"The guinea likes you all right," Copernik jeered. "You never know what a guinea will like, do you?"

I lit a cigarette. Ybarra looked at Copernik and said very softly: "The word guinea—you overwork it. I don't like it so well applied to me."

"The hell with what you like, guinea."

Ybarra smiled a little more. "You are making a mistake," he said. He took a pocket nail file out and began to use it, looking down.

Copernik blared: "I smelled something rotten on you from the start, Marlowe. So when we make these two mugs, Ybarra and me think we'll drift over and dabble a few more words with you. I bring one of Waldo's morgue photos—nice work, the light just right in his eyes, his tie all straight and a white handkerchief showing just right in his pocket. Nice work. So on the way up, just as a matter of routine, we rout out the manager here and let him lamp it. And he knows the guy. He's here as A. B. Hummel, Apartment Thirty-one. So we go in there and find a stiff. Then we go round and round with that. Nobody knows him yet, but he's got some swell finger bruises under that strap and I hear they fit Waldo's fingers very nicely."

"That's something," I said. "I thought maybe I murdered him."

Copernik stared at me a long time. His face had stopped grinning and was just a hard brutal face now. "Yeah. We got something else even," he said. "We got Waldo's getaway car—and what Waldo had in it to take with him."

I blew cigarette smoke jerkily. The wind pounded the shut windows. The air in the room was foul.

"Oh, we're bright boys," Copernik sneered. "We never figured you with that much guts. Take a look at this."

He plunged his bony hand into his coat pocket and drew something up slowly over the edge of the card table, drew it along the green top and left it there stretched out, gleaming. A string of white pearls with a clasp like a two-bladed propeller. They shimmered softly in the thick smoky air.

Lola Barsaly's pearls. The pearls the flier had given her. The guy who was dead, the guy she still loved.

I stared at them, but I didn't move. After a long moment Copernik said almost gravely: "Nice, ain't they? Would you feel like telling us a story about now, Mis-ter Marlow?"

I stood up and pushed the chair from under me, walked slowly across the room and stood looking down at the pearls. The largest was perhaps a third of an inch across. They were pure white, iridescent, with a mellow softness. I lifted them slowly off the card table from beside her clothes. They felt heavy, smooth, fine.

"Nice," I said. "A lot of the trouble was about these. Yeah, I'll talk now. They must be worth a lot of moey."

Ybarra laughed behind me. It was a very gentle laugh. "About a hundred dollars," he said. "They're good phonies—but they're phony."

I lifted the pearls again. Copernik's glassy eyes gloated at me. "How do you tell?" I asked.

"I know pearls," Ybarra said. "These are good stuff, the kind women very often have made on purpose, as a kind of insurance. But they are slick like glass. Real pearls are gritty between the edges of the teeth. Try."

I put two or three of them between my teeth and moved my teeth back and forth, then sideways. Not quite biting them. The beads were hard and slick.

"Yes. They are very good," Ybarra said. "Several even have little waves and flat spots, as real pearls might have."

"Would they cost fifteen grand—if they were real?" I asked.

"Sí. Probably. That's hard to say. It depends on a lot of things."

"This Waldo wasn't so bad," I said.

Copernik stood up quickly, but I didn't see him swing. I was still looking down at the pearls. His fist caught me on the side of the face, against the molars. I tasted blood at once. I staggered back and made it look like a worse blow than it was.

"Sit down and talk, you bastard!" Copernik almost whispered.

I sat down and used a handkerchief to pat my cheek. I licked at the cut inside my mouth. Then I got up again and went over and picked up the cigarette he had knocked out of my mouth. I crushed it out in a tray and sat down again.

Ybarra filed at his nails and held one up against the lamp. There were beads of sweat on Copernik's eyebrows, at the inner ends.

"You found the beads in Waldo's car," I said, looking at Ybarra. "Find any papers?"

He shook his head without looking up.

"I'd believe you," I said. "Here it is. I never saw Waldo until he stepped into the cocktail bar tonight and asked about the girl. I knew nothing I didn't tell. When I got home and stepped out of the elevator this girl, in the printed bolero jacket and the wide hat and the blue silk crêpe dress—all as he had described them—was waiting for the elevator, here on my floor. And she looked like a nice girl."

Copernik laughed jeeringly. It didn't make any difference to me. I had him cold. All he had to do was know that. He was going to know it now, very soon.

"I knew what she was up against as a police witness," I said. "And I suspected there was something else to it. But I didn't suspect for a minute that there was anything wrong with her. She was just a nice girl in a jam—and she didn't even know she was in a jam. I got her in here. She pulled a gun on me. But she didn't mean to use it."

Copernik sat up very suddenly and he began to lick his lips. His face had a stony look now. A look like wet gray stone. He didn't make a sound.

"Waldo had been her chauffeur," I went on. "His name was then Joseph Coates. Her name is Mrs. Frank C. Barsaly. Her husband is a big hydroelectric engineer. Some guy gave her the pearls once and she told her husband they were just store pearls. Waldo got wise somehow there was a romance behind them and when Barsaly came home from South America and fired him, because he was too good-looking, he lifted the pearls."

Ybarra lifted his head suddenly and his teeth flashed. "You mean he didn't know they were phony?"

"I thought he fenced the real ones and had imitations fixed up," I said.

Ybarra nodded. "It's possible."

"He lifted something else," I said. "Some stuff from Barsaly's briefcase that showed he was keeping a woman—out in Brentwood. He was blackmailing wife and husband both, without either knowing about the other. Get it so far?"

"I get it," Copernik said harshly, between his tight lips. His face was still wet gray stone. "Get the hell on with it."

"Waldo wasn't afraid of them," I said. "He didn't conceal where he lived. That was foolish, but it saved a lot of finagling, if he was willing to risk it. The girl came down here tonight with five grand to buy back her pearls. She didn't find Waldo. She came here to look for him and walked up a floor before she went back down. A woman's idea of being cagey. So I met her. So I brought her in here. So she was in that dressing room when Al Tessilore visited me to rub out a witness." I pointed to the dressing-room door. "So she came out with her little gun and stuck it in his back and saved my life," I said.

Copernik didn't move. There was something horrible in his face now. Ybarra slipped his nail file into a small leather case and slowly tucked it into his pocket.

"Is that all?" he said gently.

I nodded. "Except that she told me where Waldo's apartment was and I went in there and looked for the pearls. I found the dead man. In his pocket I found new car keys in a case from a Packard agency. And down on the street I found the Packard and took it to where it came from. Barsaly's kept woman. Barsaly had sent a friend from the Spezzia Club down to buy something and he had tried to buy it with his gun instead of the money Barsaly gave him. And Waldo beat him to the punch."

"Is that all?" Ybarra said softly.

"That's all," I said licking the torn place on the inside of my cheek.

Ybarra said slowly: "What do you want?"

Copernik's face convulsed and he slapped his long hard thigh. "This guy's good," he jeered.

"He falls for a stray broad and breaks every law in the book and you ask him what does he want? I'll give him what he wants, guinea!"

Ybarra turned his head slowly and looked at him. "I don't think you will," he said. "I think you'll give him a clean bill of health and anything else he wants. He's giving you a lesson in police work."

Copernik didn't move or make a sound for a long minute. None of us moved. Then Copernik leaned forward and his coat fell open. The butt of his service gun looked out of his underarm holster.

"So what do you want?" he asked me.

"What's on the card table there. The jacket and hat and the phony pearls. And some names kept away from the papers. Is that too much?"

"Yeah—it's too much," Copernik said almost gently. He swayed sideways and his gun jumped neatly into his hand. He rested his forearm on his thigh and pointed the gun at my stomach.

"I like better that you get a slug in the guts resisting arrest," he said. "I like that better, because of a report I made out on Al Tessilore's arrest and how I made the pinch. Because of some photos of me that are in the morning sheets going out about now. I like it better that you don't live long enough to laugh about that baby."

My mouth felt suddenly hot and dry. Far off I heard the wind booming. It seemed like the sound of guns.

Ybarra moved his feet on the floor and said coldly: "You've got a couple of cases all solved, policeman. All you do for it is leave some junk here and keep some names from the papers. Which means from the D.A. If he gets them anyway, too bad for you."

Copernik said: "I like the other way." The blue gun in his hand was like a rock. "And God help you, if you don't back me up on it."

Ybarra said: "If the woman is brought out into the open, you'll be a liar on a police report and a chisler on your own partner. In a week they won't even speak your name at Headquarters. The taste of it would make them sick."

The hammer clicked back on Copernik's gun

and I watched his big finger slide in farther around the trigger.

Ybarra stood up. The gun jumped at him. He said: "We'll see how yellow a guinea is. I'm telling you to put that gun up, Sam."

He started to move. He moved four even steps. Copernik was a man without a breath of movement, a stone man.

Ybarra took one more step and quite suddenly the gun began to shake.

Ybarra spoke evenly: "Put it up, Sam. If you keep your head everything lies the way it is. If you don't—you're gone."

He took one more step. Copernik's mouth opened wide and made a gasping sound and then he sagged in the chair as if he had been hit on the head. His eyelids dropped.

Ybarra jerked the gun out of his hand with a movement so quick it was no movement at all. He stepped back quickly, held the gun low at his side.

"It's the hot wind, Sam. Let's forget it," he said in the same even, almost dainty voice.

Copernik's shoulders sagged lower and he put his face in his hands. "O.K.," he said between his fingers.

Ybarra went softly across the room and opened the door. He looked at me with lazy, half-closed eyes. "I'd do a lot for a woman who saved my life, too," he said. "I'm eating this dish, but as a cop you can't expect me to like it."

I said: "The little man in the bed is called Leon Valesanos. He was a croupier at the Spezzia Club."

"Thanks," Ybarra said. "Let's go, Sam."

Copernik got up heavily and walked across the room and out of the open door and out of my sight. Ybarra stepped through the door after him and started to close it.

I said: "Wait a minute."

He turned his head slowly, his left hand on the door, the blue gun hanging down close to his right side.

"I'm not in this for money," I said. "The Barsalys live at Two-twelve Fremont Place. You can take the pearls to her. If Barsaly's name stays

RAYMOND CHANDLER

out the paper, I get five C's. It goes to the Police Fund. I'm not so damn smart as you think. It just happened that way—and you had a heel for a partner."

Ybarra looked across the room at the pearls on the card table. His eyes glistened. "You take them," he said. "The five hundred's O.K. I think the fund has it coming."

He shut the door quietly and in a moment I heard the elevator doors clang.

SEVEN

I opened a window and stuck my head out into the wind and watched the squad car tool off down the block. The wind blew in hard and I let it blow. A picture fell off the wall and two chessmen rolled off the card table. The material of Lola Barsaly's bolero jacket lifted and shook.

I went out to the kitchenette and drank some Scotch and went back into the living room and called her—late as it was.

She answered the phone herself, very quickly, with no sleep in her voice.

"Marlowe," I said. "O.K. your end?"

"Yes . . . yes," she said. "I'm alone."

"I found something," I said. "Or rather the police did. But your dark boy gypped you. I have a string of pearls. They're not real. He sold the real ones, I guess, and made you up a string of ringers, with your clasp."

She was silent for a long time. Then, a little faintly: "The police found them?"

"In Waldo's car. But they're not telling. We have a deal. Look at the papers in the morning and you'll be able to figure out why."

"There doesn't seem to be anything more to say," she said. "Can I have the clasp?"

"Yes. Can you meet me tomorrow at four in the Club Esquire bar?"

"You're really rather sweet," she said in a dragged out voice. "I can. Frank is still at his meeting."

"Those meetings—they take it out of a guy," I said. We said goodbye.

I called a West Los Angeles number. He was still there, with the Russian girl.

"You can send me a check for five hundred in the morning," I told him. "Made out to the Police Relief Fund, if you want to. Because that's where it's going."

Copernik made the third page of the morning papers with two photos and a nice half-column. The little brown man in Apartment 31 didn't make the paper at all. The Apartment House Association has a good lobby too.

I went out after breakfast and the wind was all gone. It was soft, cool, a little foggy. The sky was close and comfortable and gray. I rode down to the boulevard and picked out the best jewelry store on it and laid a string of pearls on a black velvet mat under a daylight-blue lamp. A man in a wing collar and striped trousers looked down at them languidly.

"How good?" I asked.

"I'm sorry, sir. We don't make appraisals. I can give you the name of an appraiser."

"Don't kid me," I said. "They're Dutch."

He focused the light a little and leaned down and toyed with a few inches of the string.

"I want a string just like them, fitted to that clasp, and in a hurry," I added.

"How, like them?" He didn't look up. "And they're not Dutch. They're Bohemian."

"O.K., can you duplicate them?"

He shook his head and pushed the velvet pad away as if it soiled him. "In three months, perhaps. We don't blow glass like that in this country. If you wanted them matched—three months at least. And this house would not do that sort of thing at all."

"It must be swell to be that snooty," I said. I put a card under his black sleeve. "Give me a name that will—and not in three months—and maybe not exactly like them."

He shrugged, went away with the card, came back in five minutes and handed it back to me. There was something written on the back.

The old Levantine had a shop on Melrose, a junk shop with everything in the window from a folding baby carriage to a French horn, from a

· 158 ·

mother-of-pearl lorgnette in a faded plush case to one of those .44 Special Single Action six-shooters they still make for Western peace officers whose grandfathers were tough.

The old Levantine wore a skull cap and two pairs of glasses and a full beard. He studied my pearls, shook his head sadly, and said: "For twenty dollars, almost so good. Not so good, you understand. Not so good glass."

"How alike will they look?"

He spread his firm strong hands. "I am telling you the truth," he said. "They would not fool a baby."

"Make them up," I said. "With this clasp. And I want the others back, too, of course."

"Yah. Two o'clock," he said.

Leon Valesanos, the little brown man from Uruguay, made the afternoon papers. He had been found hanging in an un-named apartment. The police were investigating.

At four o'clock I walked into the long cool bar of the Club Esquire and prowled along the row of booths until I found one where a woman sat alone. She wore a hat like a shallow soup plate with a very wide edge, a brown tailor-made suit with a severe mannish shirt and tie.

I sat down beside her and slipped a parcel along the seat.

"You don't open that," I said. "In fact you can slip it into the incinerator as is, if you want to."

She looked at me with dark tired eyes. Her fingers twisted a thin glass that smelled of peppermint. "Thanks." Her face was very pale.

I ordered a highball and the waiter went away. "Read the papers?"

"Yes."

"You understand now about this fellow Copernik who stole your act? That's why they won't change the story or bring you into it."

"It doesn't matter now," she said. "Thank you, all the same. Please—please show them to me."

I pulled the string of pearls out of the loosely wrapped tissue paper in my pocket and slid them across to her. The silver propeller clasp winked in the light of the wall bracket. The little diamond winked. The pearls were as dull as white soap. They didn't even match in size.

"You were right," she said tonelessly. "They are not my pearls."

The waiter came with my drink and she put her bag on them deftly. When he was gone she fingered them slowly once more, dropped them into the bag and gave me a dry mirthless smile.

I stood there a moment with a hand hard on the table.

"As you said—I'll keep the clasp."

I said slowly: "You don't know anything about me. You saved my life last night and we had a moment, but it was just a moment. You still don't know anything about me. There's a detective downtown named Ybarra, a Mexican of the nice sort, who was on the job when the pearls were found in Waldo's suitcase. That is in case you would like to make sure—"

She said: "Don't be silly. It's all finished. It was a memory. I'm too young to nurse memories. It may be for the best. I loved Stan Phillips—but he's gone—long gone."

I stared at her, didn't say anything.

She added quietly: "This morning my husband told me something I hadn't known. We are to separate. So I have very little to laugh about today."

"I'm sorry," I said lamely. "There's nothing to say. I may see you sometime. Maybe not. I don't move much in your circle. Good luck."

I stood up. We looked at each other for a moment. "You haven't touched your drink," she said.

"You drink it. That peppermint stuff will just make you sick."

I stood there a moment with a hand on the table.

"If anybody ever bothers you," I said, "let me know."

I went out of the bar without looking back at her, got into my car and drove west on Sunset and down all the way to the Coast Highway. Everywhere along the way gardens were full of withered and blackened leaves and flowers which the hot wind had burned.

But the ocean looked cool and languid and just the same as ever. I drove on almost to Malibu and then parked and went and sat on a big rock that was inside somebody's wire fence. It was about half-tide and coming in. The air smelled of kelp. I watched the water for a while and then I pulled a string of Bohemian glass imitation pearls out of my pocket and cut the knot at one end and slipped the pearls off one by one.

When I had them all loose in my left hand I held them like that for a while and thought. There wasn't really anything to think about. I was sure.

"To the memory of Mr. Stan Phillips," I said aloud. "Just another four-flusher."

I flipped her pearls out into the water one by one at the floating seagulls.

They made little splashes and the seagulls rose off the water and swooped at the splashes.

Wise Guy

Frederick Nebel

FEW PULP WRITERS WERE as prolific as Frederick Nebel (1903–1967), who wrote several long-running series, mainly in *Black Mask* and its closest rival, *Dime Detective*, in a career that essentially ended after a single decade (1927–1937). His crimefighting heroes are tough and frequently violent, but they bring a strong moral code to their jobs, and a level of realism achieved by few other pulp writers.

Homicide Captain Steve MacBride, who is as tough as they come, and his ever-present sidekick, *Free Press* reporter Kennedy, who provides comic relief in most of the thirty-seven stories in which they appear, was a *Black Mask* fixture for nearly a decade.

Donny "Tough Dick" Donahue of the Interstate Agency, with twenty-one adventures, all in *Black Mask*, ran from 1930 to 1935; a half-dozen of the best were collected in *Six Deadly Dames* (1950).

The stories featuring Cardigan, an operative for the Cosmos Detective Agency, nearly fifty in all, ran from 1931 to 1937 in the pages of *Dime Detective;* the best of them were published in *The Adventures of Cardigan* (1988).

Both of Nebel's novels were filmed: *Sleepers East* (1933) in 1934 and *Fifty Roads to Town* (1936) in 1937.

"Wise Guy," a MacBride and Kennedy story, was first published in *Black Mask* in April 1930.

*An Alderman who does not want to play
Gangland's racket calls for the help of
Capt. Steve MacBride*

Wise Guy

Frederick Nebel

I

LDERMAN TONY MAR-
atelli walked up and down
the living-room of his
house in Riddle Street.
Riddle was the name of
a one-time tax commis-
sioner. Maratelli was a fat
man, with fat dark eyes and two generous chins.
His fingers were fat, too, and the fingers of one
hand were splayed around a glass of Chianti,
from which at frequent intervals he took quick,
sibilant draughts. Now an Italian does not drink
Chianti that way. But Maratelli looked worried.
He was.

The winter night wind keened in the street
outside and shook the windows in a sort of
brusque, sharp fury. Riddle Street is a dark
street. Also a windy one. That is because one end
of it disembogues into River Road, where the
piers are. One upon a time Riddle Street was
aristocratic. Then it became smugly middle-
class and grudgingly democratic. Then proletariat. Other streets around it went in for
stores and warehouses and shipping offices. But
Riddle Street clung to its brownstone fronts
and its three-step stoops. It was rated a decent
street.

Maratelli stopped short as his five-year-old
daughter bowled into the room wearing a variety
of night attire known as teddy bears.

"'Night, poppa."

Maratelli put down the glass of Chianti, picked up the baby and bounced her playfully up and down on the palms of his fat hands.

"Good-night, angel," he said.

His wife, who was taller than he, and heavier, came in and smiled and held out her arms.

"Give her to me, Tony," she said.

"Yes, mama," said Maratelli. "Put her to bed and then close that door. Captain MacBride will be here maybe any minute."

"You want to be alone, Tony, don't you?"

"Yes, mama."

She looked at him. "It's about . . ."

"Yes, mama. Please take angel to bed and then you, too, leave me alone."

"All right, Tony." She looked a little sad.

He laughed, and his ragtag mustache fanned over his mouth. He pinched the baby's cheeks, then his wife's, then marched with her to the inner door. They went out, and he closed the door and sighed.

He went over to the table, picked up the glass of Chianti and marched up and down the room. His broad, heavy shoes thumped on the carpet. He wore a henna-colored shirt, a green tie, red suspenders and tobacco-brown pants. His shoes creaked.

When the bell rang, he fairly leaped into the hallway. He snapped back the lock and opened the door.

"Ah, Cap! Good you come!"

MacBride strolled in. He wore a neat gray Cheviot overcoat, a flap-brimmed hat of lighter gray. His hands were in his pockets and he smoked a cigar.

"Slow at Headquarters, so I thought I'd come down."

"Yes—yes—yes."

Maratelli closed the hall door. The lock snapped automatically. He bustled into the living-room, eyed a Morris chair, then took a couple of pillows from the lounge, placed them in the Morris chair and patted hollows into them. He spread his hands towards the chair.

"Have a nice seat, Cap."

"Thanks."

"Give me the overcoat and the hat."

"That's all right, Tony."

MacBride merely unbuttoned his coat, sat down and laid his hat on the table. He was freshly shaven, neatly combed, and his long, lean face had the hard, ruddy glint of a face that knows the weather. He leaned back comfortably, crossing one leg over the other. The pants had a fine crease, the shoes were well polished, and the laces neatly tied.

"Chianti, Cap?"

"A shot of Scotch'd go better."

"Yes—yes—yes!"

Maratelli brought a bottle from the sideboard, along with a bottle of Canada Dry.

"Straight," said MacBride.

Maratelli took one with him, said, "Here's how," and they drank.

MacBride looked at the end of his cigar.

"Well, Tony, what's the trouble?"

The wind kept clutching at the windows. Maratelli went over and tightened a latch. Then he pulled up a rocker to face MacBride, sat down on the edge of it, lit a twisted cheroot and took a couple of quick, nervous puffs. He stared vacantly at MacBride's polished shoe.

Finally—"About my boy Dominick."

"H'm."

"You know?"

"Go on, Tony."

"Yes—yes. Look, Cap, I'm a good guy. I'm a good wop. I got a wife and kids and business and I been elected alderman and—well, I'm a pretty good guy. I don't want to be on no racket, and I don't want any kind of help from any rough guys in the neighborhood. I been pestered a lot, Cap, but I ain't gonna give in. I got a wife and kids and a good reputation and I want to keep the slate what you call pretty damn clean. Cap, I ask you to come along here tonight after I been thinking a lotta things over in my head. I need help, Cap. What's a wop gonna do when he needs help? I dunno. But I ask you, and maybe you be my friend."

"Sure," said MacBride. "Get it off your chest."

"This wop—uh—Chibbarro, you know him?"

"Sam Chibbarro?"

"Yes—yes—yes."

"Uhuh."

"Him."

"What about him?"

Maratelli took a long breath. It was coming hard, and he wiped his face with his fat hand. He cleared his throat, took a drink of Chianti and cleared his throat again.

"Him. It's about him. Him and my boy Dominick. You know my boy Dominick is only twenty-one. And—and—"

"Going around with Chibby?"

"Yes—yes. Look. This is it, and Holy Mother, if Chibby knows I talk to you—" He exhaled a vast breath and shook his head. "Look. I have lotsa trucks, Cap, being what I am a contractor. I have ten trucks, some big, some not that big. Chibby—uh—Chibby he wants my trucks for to run booze at night!"

MacBride uncrossed his legs and put both heels on the floor. He leaned forward and, putting the elbow of one arm on his knee, jack-knifed the other arm against his side. His eyes, which had a windy blue look, stared point-blank at Maratelli.

"And you?"

"Well—" Maratelli sat back and spread his hands palmwise and opened his eyes wide—"me, I say no!"

"How long has this been going on?"

"Maybe a month."

"And Dominick. Where does he come in?"

Maratelli fell back in his chair like a deflated balloon. "That is what you call it, Cap. He is very good friends. He thinks Chibby is a great guy. He says I am the old fool."

MacBride looked at the floor, and his eyelids came down thoughtfully; the ghost of a curl came to his wide mouth, slightly sardonic.

Maratelli was hurrying on—"Look, Cap. My Dominick is a good boy, but if he keeps friends with that dirty wop Chibbarro it is gonna be no good. I can't stand for it, Cap. And what can I do

with Dominick? He laughs at me. Puts the grease on his hair and wears the Tuxedo and goes around with Chibby like a millionaire. Dominick has done nothing bad yet, but if this Chibby—Look, Cap, whatcha think I'm gonna do?"

MacBride sat back. "Hell, Tony, I've had a lot of tough jobs in my day, but you hand me a lulu. It's too bad. You've got my sympathy, and that's no bologney. I'll think it over. I'll do the best I can."

"Please, Cap, please. Every night Dominick goes out with Chibby. Dominick ain't got the money, so Chibby he pays the bills. And where do they go? Ah—the *Club Naples*, and places like that, and women—Holy Mother, it ain't good, Cap! My wife and my baby—I ask you, Cap, for my sake."

"Sure, Tony."

MacBride stood up.

Maratelli stood up, his breath whistling in his throat. "But if Chibby knows I speak to you—"

"He won't," clipped MacBride.

He buttoned his coat, put on his hat and shoved his hands into his pockets. "I'll be going."

"Have another drink."

"Thanks—no."

Maratelli let him out into the street and hung in the doorway.

"Night, Cap."

"Night, Tony."

MacBride was already swinging away, his cigar a red eye in the wind.

II

Jockey Street was never a good street. It was the wayward offspring of a wayward neighborhood. Six blocks of it made a bee line from the white-lights district to the no-lights district, and then petered off into the river.

The way was dark after the third block, except for a solitary electric sign that winked seductively in the middle of the fourth. It projected over the sidewalk, and the winking, beckoning letters were painted green:

L U
C   B
N A P L E S

MacBride did not come down from the bright lights. He came up from River Road, up from the bleak, unlovely waterfront. He still walked with his hands in his pockets, and the wind blew from behind, flapping his coat around his knees.

A man in a faded red uniform with tarnished gold braid stood in front of the double doors. As MacBride drew near, the man reached back and laid his hand on the knob. He opened the door as MacBride came up, and MacBride went inside.

The ante-room was quite dim, and the sound of a jazz band was muffled. To the right was a cloak-room, and the girl came over to take MacBride's coat. But MacBride paid no attention to her. A man came forward out of the dim-lit gloom, peering hard. He wore a Tux, and he had white, doughy jowls and thin hair plastered back, and he was not so young.

"Your eyesight bad, Al?" chuckled MacBride.

"Oh . . . that you, Cap?"

"Yeah."

"Cripes, I'm glad to see you, Cap!"

He grabbed MacBride's hand and wrung it. MacBride stood still, slightly smiling, his face in shadow, and Al laughed showing a lot of uncouth teeth.

This was Al Vassilakos, a Greek who went over big with the wops and who was on speaking terms with the police. Mike Dabraccio really started the joint, a couple of years ago, but Mike talked out of turn to the old Sciarvi gang, and Sciarvi told Mike to go places. Al was instated by Sciarvi himself, and when Sciarvi got himself balled up—and subsequently shot—in a city-wide gang feud, Al carried on with the club. He'd kept clean since then, but Sam Chibbarro,

called Chibby, was back, and MacBride had his doubts.

It looked as if Al was a little put out at MacBride's imperturbable calm.

"You—you looking for some guy, Cap?"

"No. Just wandering around, Al. How's business?"

"Pretty good."

"Mind if I sit inside?"

"Glad to have you, Cap."

MacBride took off his overcoat and his hat and gave them to the girl. Al walked with him across the ante-room and opened a door. A flood of light and a thunder of jazz rushed out as MacBride and Al went in. Al closed the door and MacBride drifted over to a small table beside the wall and sat down. Al signaled to a waiter and motioned to MacBride.

"Snap on it, Joe. That's Captain MacBride from Headquarters. Don't give him none of that cheap alky."

"Okey, boss."

Al went over and put his hands palm-down on the table and asked, "How about a good cigar, Cap? And I've got some good Golden Wedding."

"All right, Al—on both."

"Hey, Joe! A box of Coronas and that bottle of Golden Wedding. Bring the bottle out, Joe."

"Okey, boss."

"Anything you want, Cap, ask me. I'll be outside. I gotta be outside, you know."

"Sure, Al."

Vassilakos went out to the ante-room, but he still looked a bit worried.

It didn't take long for MacBride to spot Sam Chibbarro. Chibby was at a big table near the dance-floor. Dominick was there, too. And MacBride picked out Kid Barjo, a big bruiser swelling all out of his Tux. There were some women—three of them. One had red hair and looked rather tall. Another had hair black as jet pulled back over the ears. The third was a little doll-faced blonde and she was necking Dominick. MacBride recognized her. She was Bunny Dahl, who used to hoof with a cheap burlesque troupe and was for a while mama to Jazz Millio before Jazz died by the gun. The whole party looked tight. A lot of people were there, and many of them looked uptownish.

This Club Naples was no haven for a piker. A drink was two dollars a throw, and the *couvert* four. If a hostess sat down with you, your drink or hers was three dollars a throw, and her own drinks were doctored with nine parts Canada Dry. A sucker joint.

Joe brought the bottle of Golden Wedding and a fresh box of cigars. MacBride took one of the cigars, bit off the end, and Joe held a match. MacBride puffed up and Joe went away, leaving the Golden Wedding on the table. MacBride poured himself a drink and watched Chibby and his crowd making whoopee.

Presently Kid Barjo got up, wandered around the table and then flung his arms around Bunny Dahl. Dominick didn't like that, and he took a crack at Barjo, and Chibby stood up and jumped between them. Bunny thought it was a great joke, and laughed. Chibby dragged Barjo to the other side of the table and made him sit down. Barjo was cursing and looking daggers at Dominick.

The jazz band struck up, and Chibby took the red-haired girl and pulled her out to the dance-floor. Barjo sulked and Dominick seemed to be bawling out Bunny. Then Bunny got up in a huff and hurried through a door at the other end of the cabaret. Barjo jumped up and followed her. Dominick took a drink and lit a cigarette and turned his back on the door. But he kept throwing looks over his shoulder. Finally he got up and went through the door, too, not so steady on his feet.

MacBride took another drink and sat back. When the dance was over Chibby and the red-haired girl came back to the table, and Chibby looked around and asked some questions. He shot a look towards the door, cursed and went through it.

MacBride leaned forward on his elbows and watched the door. The jazz band cut loose, and the saxophone warbled. The two girls at Chibby's table were both talking at the same

time, and both of them looked peeved. The small dance-floor was jammed.

Joe came over and said, "Everything okey, Cap?"

"Yeah," said MacBride, watching the door.

"Maybe you'd like a nice sandwich? Al told me to ask you."

"No, Joe."

"Okey, Cap."

"Okey."

Joe turned, swooped down on a table that had been temporarily abandoned by two couples. He swept up four glasses that were only half empty, swept out, and came back with four full ones. He marked it all down on his pad. A gyp-joint waiter has no conscience.

The drummer was singing out of the side of his mouth, "*Through the black o' night, I gotta go where you go.*"

Chibby came out of the door. He was frowning. He walked swiftly to his table, clipped a few words to the girls. They started to get up. He snapped them down. Then he turned and headed towards the ante-room.

"Hello, Chibby," said MacBride.

Chibbarro jerked his head around.

"Jeeze . . . well, hello, MacBride! Where'd you come from?"

"I've been here—for a while—Chibby."

"Yeah?"

"Yeah."

"Hell . . . ain't that funny!"

"Funny?"

"Yeah, I mean funny I didn't see you."

"That is funny, Chibby."

"Yeah, it sure is. See you in a minute, Cap."

Chibby hurried out to the ante-room. MacBride turned his head and looked after him. Chibby looked over his shoulder as he pushed open the door. MacBride squinted one eye. His lips flattened perceptibly against his teeth, and one corner of his mouth bent downward. A curse grunted in his throat, behind his tight mouth. He looked back towards the door at the other end of the dance-floor.

The two girls who had been sitting at

Chibby's table were now walking towards the ante-room. MacBride watched them go out. A frown grew on his forehead, then died. Joe came in from the ante-room and stood with his back to the door. He was looking at MacBride. His face was a little pale. He backed out again.

MacBride turned in time to see the door swing shut, but he did not see Joe. He stood up and took a fresh grip on his cigar. He walked towards the door and shoved it open. He stood with the light streaming down over his shoulders.

"Goin', Cap?" asked Al Vassilakos.

MacBride let the door shut behind him. "Where's Chibby?"

Al was standing in the shadows, his face a pale blur. "I guess he went, Cap."

"Where're those two women were with him?"

"They . . . all went, Cap."

The red end of MacBride's cigar brightened and then dimmed.

"Al, what the hell's wrong?"

"Wrong? Well, hell, I don't know. They just went out."

MacBride turned and pushed open the door leading into the cabaret. He strode swiftly among the tables, crossed the dance-floor and went through the door at the farther end. This led him into a broad corridor. He stopped and looked around, one eye a-squint. He pushed open a door at his left. It was dark beyond. He reached for and found a switch; snapped on the lights. The room was well-furnished—but empty.

When he backed into the corridor, Al was there.

"What the hell, Cap?"

"Don't be dumb!"

MacBride went to the next door on the right, opened it and switched on the lights. It, too, was empty. He came back into the corridor and bent a hard eye on Al. Then he pivoted and went on to the next door on the left. He opened it and turned on the lights. He looked around. It was empty. There was an adjoining room, with the door partly open.

"Jeeze, Cap, what's the matter?"

"Pipe down!"

MacBride crossed the room and pulled the door wide open. He felt a draught of cold night air. He reached around and switched on the lights in the next room.

A table was overturned.

Kid Barjo lay on the floor with a bloody throat.

"H'm," muttered MacBride, and turned to look at Al.

The Greek's jowls were shaking.

MacBride took a couple of steps and bent down over Kid Barjo. He stood up and turned and looked at the Greek.

"Dead, Al. Some baby carved his throat open."

"My God Almighty!" choked Al.

MacBride spun and dived across the room to the open window. He looked out. An alley ran behind. He jumped out and ran along, followed a sharp turn to the right. He saw that the alley led to the street. He ran down it and into Jockey Street. There was no one in sight.

He entered the Club Naples through the front door and returned to the room where the Greek was still standing. He looked at a telephone on the wall.

"Listen, Al. Did Chibby make a call in the lobby?"

"I—I—"

"Come on, Al, if you know what's good for you."

"I think he did."

"Okey. He called whoever was in here when he knew I was outside and they breezed through this window. And you've been stalling, you two-faced bum!"

"So help me, Cap—"

"Can it! There's one of three people killed this guy."

"Jeeze!"

The Greek fell into a chair, stunned.

MacBride called Headquarters.

Outside in the cabaret the drummer was singing, "*That's what you get for making whoope-e-e-e! . . .*"

Out in the street the green sign blinked seductively:

C L U B
N A P L E S

III

Sergeant Otto Bettdecken was eating a frankfurter and roll when MacBride barged into Headquarters followed by Moriarity and Cohen, and Kennedy of the *Free Press*.

MacBride said, "Otto, that guy's full name was Salvatore Barjo; age, twenty-six; address, the Atlantic Hotel. Stabbed twice in the front of the neck."

Bettdecken filled out a blue card and his moon face clouded. "Crime of passion, Cap?"

"Ha!" chirruped Kennedy.

"We don't know yet," said MacBride. "The morgue bus picked the stiff up and I closed the joint for the night."

"How about the Greek?"

MacBride shrugged. "He's free. I want to give him some rope first. He ain't tough enough to worry about. He came across with the names of the three broads. Mary Dahl—the one they call Bunny; there was a red-head named Flossy Roote, and the other broad, the one that was originally with Barjo—she's Freda Hoegh. Flossy's this guy Chibbarro's woman, and I understand Freda's a friend of Bunny's. Chibby lived with Flossy in a flat at number 40 Brick Street. We went down there, but of course they weren't there. I parked Corson on the job. Freda and Bunny have a flat at number 28 Turner Street, but they haven't shown up either. I put De Groot on that job. No doubt they're hiding out, along with Dominick Maratelli."

Bettdecken shook his head. "This'll drive Tony crazy."

"Yeah," said MacBride, and headed for his office.

Moriarity and Cohen and Kennedy trailed after him, and MacBride got out of his overcoat and hung it up. He started a fresh cigar and took a turn up and down the room.

Kennedy leaned against the wall and tongued a cigarette from one side of his mouth to the other.

"That guy Barjo always was a bum welter anyhow."

MacBride snapped, "Which is no reason why he should be knifed in the throat! And this young Dominick—"

"A wise guy," drawled Kennedy. "A young wop just out of his diapers and trying to be a man about town. I know his kind. In fact, I know Dom. Flash. Jazz. He's not the only slob this jazz racket has taken for a buggy ride. And take it from me, old tomato, he's not going to get out of this with a slap on the wrist."

Moriarity said, "The thing is, after all your gas, Kennedy, who—who *did* poke Barjo in the throat?"

"Well, first the broad—this Bunny Dahl— goes in," said Kennedy. "Then Barjo. Then Dominick. Well—I'd say Dominick."

"Nix," popped Ike Cohen, swinging around from the window.

"No?"

"The broad," said Cohen. "The other guys were just covering her. Cripes, from what Cap says, they were all pretty tight. And the broad, having not much brains, would be the first to pull a dumb stunt like that. What do you say, Cap?"

"Not a hell of a lot," growled MacBride. "I'll leave the theory to you bright boys. I'm just waiting till we nail one of those babies. But as for the broad rating no brains, I don't know. And I don't see where Dominick rates big in brains, either."

Moriarity sat on the desk, dangling his feet. He said, "Anyhow, I'm inclined kind of to think it was the broad. It looks like a dizzy blonde's work."

Kennedy laughed wearily. "Well, if it was, Mory, we'll have a nice time in Richmond City. All the sob-sisters will sharpen up their pencils.

Bunny will put a crack in her voice and try to look like a virgin that this guy Barjo tried to ruin. "I did it to save my honor!" Like that. As if she ever had any honor. Listen, I saw that little trollop in a burlesque show one night, down near the river and—"

"All right, all right," horned in MacBride. "We can imagine."

"Anyhow," said Kennedy, "I'll bet it wasn't the broad."

The papers had it next morning. Dominick Maratelli's name was prominent—"wayward son of Alderman Antonio Maratelli."

MacBride, who had gone home at two, was back on the job at noon. There were reports on his desk, but nothing of importance. Chibbaro and Dominick and the three girls were still missing, and none of them had been to their flats following the murder.

The city was being combed thoroughly by no less than a dozen detectives, and every cop was on the lookout too. The fade-away had probably been maneuvered by Chibby. MacBride thought so, anyway, and it struck him as a pretty dumb move on Chibbaro's part. For why should Chibby entangle himself in a murder with which, apparently, he was not vitally concerned?

Tony Maratelli blundered into Headquarters a little past noon. He was shaking all over. He was hard hit.

"Cap, for the love o' God, what am I gonna do?"

"You can't do a thing, Tony."

"Yes, yes. I mean—but I mean, can't I do something?"

"No. Calm yourself, that's all. Dominick's in Dutch, and that's that. I can't save him, Tony."

"But, Holy Mother, the disgrace, Cap! And my wife, you should see her!"

"I know, I know, Tony. I'm sorry as hell for you and the wife, but the kid pulled a bone, and what can we do?"

Tony walked around the office and then he sat down and put his head in his hands and groaned. MacBride creaked in his chair and looked at Tony and felt sorry for him. Here was a wop who had kept his hands clean and tried to attach some dignity to his minor office. His record was a good one. He was a good husband, a square shooter and a conscientious alderman. But what mattered all that to the public when his son ran with a bum like Chibbarro and got mixed up in a drunken brawl that terminated in the killing of Kid Barjo the popular welter?

"You go home, Tony," said MacBride. "There's nothing to do but hope for the best."

Tony went home. He dragged his feet out of Headquarters, and he looked dazed. This was tragedy, no less. It was the tragedy of a good man tainted by the blood of his kin. And it is the warp and woof of life; you can't choose your heritage, nor can you choose your offspring. A man in public office is a specimen eternally held beneath the magnifying glass of public opinion, and public opinion can metamorphose a saint into a devil.

The police net which MacBride had caused to be flung out, seemed not very effective. Three days and three nights passed. No one was apprehended. Kid Barjo was buried, and Moriarity and Cohen attended the funeral—not from any feeling of sorrow or respect for the newly dead. But—sometimes—killers turn up when the dead go down. That was one of the times they didn't.

At the end of a week the *News-Examiner* printed a neatly barbed editorial relative to the inability of certain police officials to cope with existing crime conditions. The innuendo was thrown obliquely at MacBride, who took it with a curse. The editorial made much of the fact that a representative of the law had been in the Club Naples at the time of the killing. . . .

"Of course I was there," MacBride told Kennedy. "But I had no reason to suppose that a murder was in the wind. Drunks will be drunks, and I give any guy a decent break."

"Some folks think you're getting soft, Cap," smiled Kennedy.

"Yeah?"

"Yeah."

MacBride creaked in his chair and wagged a

finger at Kennedy. "You tell those—folks, Kennedy, that I'm just as tough today as I was twenty years ago."

"Have you seen any more of Tony Maratelli?"

"No—not since the day after the killing. I told him to go home and calm down."

There was a knock on the door, but before MacBride could reply, it burst open and Sergeant Bettdecken stood there, a banana in one hand and his face all flushed.

"God, Cap, I just got a call from Scofield! There's hell in Riddle Street. Uh—the front of Tony Maratelli's house been blown off!"

"Ain't that funny?" said Kennedy. "We were just talking about him."

MacBride bounced out of his chair and reached for his hat and coat.

IV

There was a crowd in Riddle Street.

The night was dark, but the red glow of the burning house lit up part of the street. Fire engines were there, and hose lay like great black serpents in the lurid glow, and the black rubber coats and helmets of firemen gleamed as they shot water into the flames.

The water fell back into the street and froze and glazed the pavements. Behind the fire lines stood men pointing and talking; and there were women with shawls around their heads and with coats flung hastily over night-dresses. There were a few women with children in arms.

A sleek red touring car with a brass bell on the cowl drove up and the fire chief, white-haired beneath his gold-braided cap, got out and looked up at the flames and had a few words with a lieutenant.

Part of the house wall caved in with a muffled roar, and dust and smoke billowed, and some of the onlookers cried out. A couple of patrolmen kept walking up and down and pushing back those who tried to edge in beyond the lines.

MacBride arrived in a police flivver driven by Hogan. Kennedy was in the back seat with him.

MacBride got out and shoved his hands into the pockets of his neat gray cheviot and looked around and then spotted Patrolman Scofield. Scofield came over and saluted and MacBride asked:

"Where's Tony?"

"In that house across the street—number 55."

"Anybody hurt?"

"Tony got a bash on the head, that's all. His wife wasn't hit, but she's pretty hysterical."

"Where were you when this place was blown?"

"Three blocks up River Road. I heard it and came on the run."

"I'll take a look at Tony."

He went into number 55. The hall-door was open, and there were some people in the hall. The sitting-room was off to the right, and MacBride saw a white-coated ambulance doctor sitting on a chair and listlessly smoking a cigarette. Tony was sitting on another chair wrapped in a heavy bathrobe and staring into space. His wife was sitting on a cot, holding her baby in her arms and moaning and rocking from side to side. Several women were grouped around her, trying to comfort her, and one held a glass of water.

MacBride drifted into the room, looked everybody over with quick scrutiny, and then went over and stood before Tony. After a moment Tony became aware of his presence and looked up and tried to say something, but he could only shake his head in dumb horror. MacBride took one hand out of his pocket and laid it on Tony's shoulder and pressed the shoulder with brief but sincere reassurance.

"Snap out of it, Tony."

"Holy Mother. . . . Holy Mother. . . ."

"I know, I know. But snap out of it. You're alive. Your wife and baby're alive."

"Like—like the end of the world. . . ."

MacBride caught his toe in the rung of a chair and slewed it nearer. He sat down and took a puff on his cigar and then took the cigar from his mouth and braced the hand that held it on his knee.

"You've got to snap out of it, Tony. . . ."

Tony winced. "Out of bed I was throwed . . . out of bed . . . like—" He groaned and put his hands to his head.

MacBride looked at the cigar in the hand on his knee and then looked up at Tony. "Were you asleep when it happened?"

"Yes . . . I was asleep. The wall fell in. . . ."

"Did you get any warning before-hand? I mean, was there any threatening letter?"

"No—no."

"Well, try to snap out of it, Tony. I'll see you again."

MacBride got up and put the cigar back in his mouth and his hands back in his pockets. He looked around the room, his windy blue eyes thoughtful. Then he went out into the hallway and so on out into the street. He stood at the top of the three stone steps and watched the firemen pouring water into the demolished house. The flames had died, but the water was still hissing on hot beams.

Kennedy came out of the crowd, his face in shadow but the red end of a cigarette marking out his mouth. From the bottom of the steps he said:

"Now why do you suppose they chucked a bomb at Tony's house, Cap?"

"Who chucked a bomb?" said MacBride.

"Are we thinking about the same guys?"

MacBride went down the steps. "Yeah, I guess so. But I don't know why."

"Let's go back to Headquarters and get a drink."

"I'm hanging around a while," said Mac-Bride.

Half an hour later water stopped pouring into the ruins. The firemen began to draw in the hose. The front of the building had disappeared. You could look into the lower and upper stories and see the debris.

MacBride went over and had a few words with the chief. He borrowed a flashlight from one of the firemen and went up the blackened stone steps. He climbed over the broken door and swung his flash around. He stepped from one broken beam to another and finally reached the living-room. The floor was slushy with black ashes that had been soaked by the water. The smell was acrid. He looked at the chair wherein he had sat one night and talked with Tony. It was burnt and broken.

He proceeded over fallen plaster that was gummy beneath his feet and reached a stairway. He climbed this and came to the floor above. The white beam of his flash probed the tattered darkness. Overturned chairs, beds soaked with water and blackened with soot. Tony's home in ruin. . . . He sighed.

There were three bedrooms, and he went from one to another, and looked around and meditated over several things, and then he went down by the cluttered stairway and worked his way back to the street.

He returned the flashlight to the fireman and said, "Thanks."

He stood on the curb, his chin on his chest and his hands in his pockets. Presently he was aware of Kennedy standing beside him.

"Where've you been, Cap?"

"Places," said MacBride.

"What did you see?"

"Things."

V

Tony Maratelli stood by the window of number 55 Riddle Street and looked across at the epitaph of his home.

It was not a pleasant sight, in the sharp clear light of a winter morning. He could see the broad bed wherein he and his wife were used to sleeping; the smaller bed in another room wherein his daughter had narrowly escaped death; the other room and the other bed that were Dominick's. . . .

Tony looked sad and haggard, and when a fat man looks haggard it is in a way pathetic. A couple of men were already at work removing the debris from the sidewalk, and a policeman walked back and forth, guarding what remained of Tony's possessions.

Of course, mused Tony, he would have a nice house again, somewhere. He had plenty of money. But—that house was an old one, and he had lived there for fifteen years—first as tenant, then as owner. It had been one of the milestones of his success as a building contractor. Wherefore its ruin made him feel sad. He pulled his heavy bathrobe tighter about his short, adipose body and sniffed.

He saw MacBride come down the opposite side of the street, pause to have a talk with the patrolman on duty, then run his eyes over the ruined house. Tony's eyes steadied. He licked his lips. MacBride was his friend, but. . . .

The captain turned abruptly and crossed the street. Tony waited for the sound of the doorbell. It came. Mrs. Reckhow, who had been good enough to give him and his family shelter overnight, appeared from another room.

But Tony said, "It's for me, Mrs. Reckhow, thanks."

"All right, Mr. Maratelli," she said, and disappeared.

Tony went out into the hall and opened the door and MacBride said, "Morning, Tony," and walked in.

They came back into the living-room and MacBride took off his hat, looked at it, creased the crown and then laid the hat on a table.

"How you feeling, Tony?"

"Not so good. I feel rotten, Cap. Yeah, I feel rotten."

His black hair was tousled about the ears and he needed a shave and his jowls seemed to hang forlornly towards his shoulders.

MacBride, who had had only six hours sleep, looked fresh and vigorous. He went over by the window and looked at the men working on the sidewalk and then he turned around and looked at Tony.

"Tony," he said, and looked at the floor, pursing his lips.

"Uh?" came Tony's voice from somewhere in the roof of his mouth.

"Tony . . . about Dominick."

Tony wiped a hand in front of his face as though he were brushing away a spider-web. "Uh . . . you found him?"

"No."

"Oh . . . I thought you found him."

"No, I didn't find him."

"Oh." His voice was weary, coming out like weary footsteps.

MacBride brought his eyes up from the floor and fastened them on Tony's eyes and seemed to screw down the bolts of his gaze with slow but sure precision.

"We'd better talk plain, Tony."

Tony's eyes glazed and seemed to stare as though at something beyond MacBride's shoulder.

"Plain," said MacBride, his voice going down.

"Well. . . ." Tony shrugged and looked around the room as if there was something there he wanted.

MacBride clipped, "How long was Dominick in your house before they blew the front off?"

Tony muttered, "Holy Mother!" and sat down heavily in a chair.

"How long, Tony?"

"Look, Cap! Could I go and give my boy up when he come to me for protection, crying like a baby? Could I? Didn't my wife she plead with me, too? But she did not have to plead, no. Dominick is my son, my flesh and blood, and if his father will not give him protection, who will? He is only the boy, Cap! He—"

"Now, wait a minute, Tony," broke in MacBride. "I can guess all that. What I want to know is, how long was he there?"

"Three days—just three days. But—I couldn't go tell you, Cap! The boy he ask me to protect him. He is sorry. He is sorry he got mixed up with that Chibby. He didn't do nothing, Cap. He didn't kill that box-fighter—"

"Who did?"

"I don't know."

"Tony. . . ."

"Please to God, I don't know!"

A muscle jerked alongside MacBride's mouth. "Dominick knew! He told you!"

"No—no!"

"Tony"—MacBride's voice was like a keen wind far off—"Tony, I've given you every break I could. I know you're a good guy—the best wop I've ever known. But—you've got to come clean. Listen to me: I'm being razzed for that killing. You know why—because I happened to be in Al's joint when these bums got soused and Barjo got knifed. But aside from that—even if I wasn't razzed—I'd want the killer just the same—"

"But Dominick he didn't kill—"

"Don't go over that. He must have told something. What did he tell you?"

Tony spread his arms and looked as if he were going to cry. "Nothing, Cap." And he kept wagging his head from side to side. "Didn't I keep asking him? Sure. Didn't I beg him to tell me? But he don't tell. He just say he didn't kill Barjo—and he swear by the cross and kiss it. Cap, please to God, that is the truth!"

MacBride took one hand out of his pocket and rubbed his jaw and put the hand back into his pocket again. A flush of color was in his lean hard cheeks, and there was a cool subdued fury lurking in his wide direct eyes. His voice became almost laconic:

"All right, then. He was in your house. When did he get away?"

"It must have been when the fire started. I heard him yell from the other room, and then he was gone when I got there. He must have run right out. And now—now, where is he?"

"That's what I'm trying to find out. I knew he'd been there when I poked around after the fire. He must have left in a hurry. His dress shirt and his studs were on the dresser, and his Tux was hanging on the wall. That's why I knew he'd been home."

"Yes, he didn't go out once. He was . . . afraid."

"Sure."

"And now—"

His life," put in MacBride, "won't be worth two cents if Chibby and his crowd find him. That's why I want to know where he is. He must have run out on the crowd and come home.

They're afraid he'll spring something. That's why they crashed your house."

Tony rocked back and forth. "And if I knowed where he is, Cap, sure I'd tell you. I don't want my boy murdered. God, if I only knowed where he is!"

"Listen," said MacBride, "where are you going from here?"

"I think we'll go to a hotel. The Maxim, yes."

"Okey. But remember—if Dominick gets in touch with you, tell me right away. The only safe place for him is in the jail."

"Jail!"

"Now calm yourself. Jail—yes. Let me know when you get in The Maxim."

"Yes." He got up, wobbling about. "Cap, you're my friend, ain't you?"

"Yeah, sure, Tony."

"Thanks, Cap—thanks!" His breath wheezed. "My poor wife, she is all bust up."

"Well, you're not helping her any by slopping all over the place. Buck up. Get a shave. Don't crack up like a damn' hop-head. For crying out loud!"

He laughed bluntly and slapped Tony on the back and went out.

VI

Moriarity and Cohen were trying to get a kick out of playing two-handed Michigan when Mac-Bride breezed into the office. They looked up once and then went on playing while MacBride got out of his overcoat. He came over and sat down and said:

"Deal me a hand."

Cohen said, "Well, how'd you make out?"

"Yes and no. Tony doesn't know a damned thing. But Dominick did come back to his house. He breezed when the place was blown."

"And didn't the kid tell his old man anything?" asked Cohen.

"No."

Moriarity said, "What makes you think Tony was playing ball?"

"I just know it."

Moriarity laughed. "Maybe you are getting soft, Cap."

"Lay off," said MacBride. "Tony's a square wop."

"Then why the cripes didn't he tell you his kid was home?"

MacBride looked at his cards. "You haven't got a kid, have you?"

"Not that I know of."

Cohen laughed. "There's a wisecrack for you, Cap!"

MacBride put four chips on the queen. "Then you wouldn't know, Mory, why the old wop didn't tell me. But he's square."

"Oh, yeah," sighed Moriarity.

"Go ahead," said MacBride, "razz me. I can stand it. If I took you guys and the newspapers seriously I'd jump in the river as a total loss. But you're all just a bad smell to me."

Moriarity laughed. "Poor old Cap!"

"Can that, too! And listen, you gumshoes. We want Dominick. He's lone-wolfing it somewhere. Even you, Mory, would realize that after he left Chibby's crowd and went back home, he wouldn't dare show his mug again with the crowd. You'd realize that, Mory—any dumb-bell would."

Cohen said, "Chew on that, Mory."

"And," said MacBride, "we want Dominick before Chibby or one of his guns nails him. They're after him; you can bet your shirt on that. He knows something, and they're after him."

"At least," said Moriarity, "it crimps Kennedy's idea that Dominick killed Barjo. I still say it was the broad."

Cohen snapped, "Hey, you, it was me first had the idea it was the broad."

"All right, grab the gold ring, guy—grab it."

"My idea may be crimped," said Kennedy, a new voice in the doorway. "But if it was the broad, why the hell should Chibbarro be going to such great pains to keep Dominick and the three girls and himself out of sight?"

"Now you've asked something, Kennedy!" chopped off MacBride.

Kennedy strolled in and said, "All right, Mory. I was wrong, let's say, on picking Dominick as the killer. I was wrong. Now, you bright young child, *why* is Chibbarro playing hide-and-seek?"

Mory put on a long face. "Well, if the broad was his friend—"

"Bologney!" chuckled Kennedy. "She was just a broad. Chibby wouldn't waste a sneeze on her if there wasn't a reason. If she killed Barjo, and there wasn't a good reason for his trying to hide her, that bum would have come right out and told Cap what she'd done. But he *had* to save her—*for a reason.* That's how much you know, Mory."

MacBride had to chuckle, and he looked at his right-hand men. "Boys, you're both good cops. In a fight, you're the berries. But take my advice and don't try to figure things out too closely. Not when this wiseacre Kennedy is roaming about."

"I'll put your name in the paper twice for that tomorrow," said Kennedy. "But get Dominick, and make him talk. I'm not saying the broad killed Barjo. I'm saying that *if* she killed him, then there's something bigger behind this job than just a ham welter getting a knife in his gizzard."

"Kennedy," said MacBride, "sometimes you're a pain in the neck, but today you're an inspiration."

"Three times in the paper tomorrow, Cap. Two more cracks like that and I'll see about getting you a headline."

"And another crack like that, Kennedy, and I'll plant my foot in your slats."

"Ah, well," grinned Kennedy, "boys will be boys. How about a drink?"

MacBride dragged out a bottle of Dewar's.

VII

In a way of speaking, Dominick Maratelli was between the devil and the deep sea. That is reckoning, of course, on the conjecture of MacBride that Dominick had dropped the mob and that the mob was seeking him. The mob . . . and the law.

Moriarity and Cohen worked overtime on the hunt. Precinct plainclothes men worked too. And uniformed cops.

It was believed that when Dominick took hasty flight from the bombed house, he was broke. A man must eat. He must sleep somewhere. It was winter, and streets and alleys do not make comfortable lodgings.

Nor was MacBride idle. He too, roamed the streets and made inquiries at lunch-rooms, speakeasies; and most of his roaming was done during the dark hours. He went alone, looking into the twenty-five-cent-a-night flophouses, conning the bread-lines in North Street.

There was no clue yet as to the whereabouts of Chibby and the three girls. And MacBride was eternally aware of the fact that Dominick's life depended on who found him first. Tony kept calling constantly . . . but there was no news.

And in the middle of the next week there was an article in the papers relative to the fact that Antonio Maratelli had resigned as alderman. Of course, the political powers that be had asked him to resign—a request that was by way of being a threat. Tony made no kick. He was more interested in saving his son.

Kennedy said, "If you ask me, Cap, that young wise guy Dominick deserves to be bumped off. There his old man got a nice political job, and was kind of proud of it, and then this young pup pulls a song and dance that the old man has to pay for. The reward of virtue is most certainly a kick in the pants."

MacBride tightened his jaw a little harder and continued to roam the streets. . . .

There was a black cold night when he wandered into a dark windy street and saw a familiar green sign blinking seductively:

**CLUB
NAPLES**

As he drew nearer, he could hear the uniformed doorman beating cold feet on the cold pavement.

MacBride came up in the shadow of the houses and the doorman reached back for the doorknob. He did not recognize MacBride until the captain's foot was on the step, and then he seemed to hesitate in perplexed indecision.

MacBride looked at him and said, "Well?"

"Oh . . . hello, Cap. Didn't recognize you." He opened the door.

MacBride walked into the dim, stuffy anteroom and stood just inside the door and looked around. The coat-room girl came over but MacBride shook his head and she recognized him and bit her lip and retreated back into the gloom. A stiff white shirt-front came out of another corner of the gloom, and a voice said:

"Well, buddy?"

"I'm MacBride."

"Oh . . . yeah."

"Where's Al?"

"I'm Patsy. It's all right. What can I do for you?"

"Get me Al."

"Well, he ain't here right now."

"Where is he?"

"I dunno. He went out about an hour ago. If you want to wait for him—there's a little room off here."

"I don't want to wait for him."

"Well, I'm sorry, Cap."

Muffled was the racket of the jazz band.

MacBride turned and pulled open the door and stepped out and looked up and down the street.

The doorman was gone.

MacBride's hands were in his pocket, and the hand in his right pocket closed over the butt of his gun. He moved towards the narrow alley that flanked one side of the building and led to the courtyard in the rear. He looked down it and he flexed his lips and then he entered the alley and walked lightly but rapidly.

He reached the courtyard in the rear. He saw a door and a lighted window, but the shade was drawn down. He moved towards the door and grasped the knob and turned it and the door gave and opened on a crack. He pushed it wide and stepped into a corridor that was dimly lighted by shaded wall lights. He had been in this corridor once before. He closed the door behind him.

From the door farthest away on the right he saw Dominick step out, and behind him the doorman and Al Vasilakos. He started to rap out a command, but Dominick, who was on the point of making for the rear door, saw him and spun and ran in the opposite direction.

"Hey, you!" shouted MacBride.

He barged down the corridor past Al and the doorman. Through the door at the end he burst into the noisy cabaret. The jazz band was hooting and people were dancing. Dominick was running alongside the tables and making for the front. MacBride sailed after him, and the jazz band petered off and the dancers stopped and stared with amazement. MacBride bowled over a drunk that teetered into his path and reached the door to the ante-room six jumps behind Dominick. The door banged in his face, and as he flung it open he saw the front door slam shut.

He streaked through the ante-room and cannoned out in the cold dark street. He heard running footsteps and saw Dominick heading for River Road. MacBride took up the chase and pulled his gun out of his pocket.

"Hey, you, Dominick!" he shouted.

But Dominick kept running.

They were nearing River Road when MacBride raised his gun and fired a high warning shot. He saw Dominick duck and run closer to the shadows of the houses. He fired another shot, bringing it closer but still reluctant to kill.

Suddenly beneath the arc-light that stood on the corner of Jockey Street and River Road, he saw a uniformed policeman appear. At the same time Dominick cut across to the opposite side of the street. The policeman crossed too, to head him off, and then Dominick swerved back into the center of the street and turned around, ran this way and that, and finally stopped and crouched.

MacBride reached him first and clipped, "Now put your hands up, kid!"

I—I'll—"

"You'll shut up! Is that you, Zeloff? Frisk him. I don't think he's got anything, but frisk him."

Patrolman Zeloff went through Dominick quickly and deftly. "Naw, not a thing, Cap."

MacBride took out manacles and locked Dominick's hands behind his back. Then he shoved his gun back into his pocket. Dominick was shivering with the cold. He wore no overcoat.

MacBride said, "Zeloff, go back to the Club Naples and pinch Al and bring him to Headquarters. I'll take this bird along in a cab."

"Okey, Cap."

"And close the joint."

"Sure."

MacBride grabbed Dominick's arm and walked with him towards River Road.

"For cripes sake, Cap, listen. Al hasn't done a thing—"

"Shut up. *Hey, taxi!*"

VIII

The light with the green shade hung over the shiny flat-topped desk and the light umbrellaed outward over the desk and included in its radiance Dominick and MacBride, who sat and faced each other across the desk.

Dominick was thin and a black stubble was on his face and black circles were beneath his eyes, but there was also black mutiny in his eyes. He had on a shirt beneath his thin coat, but no collar, and his black hair was rumpled but still a bit shiny from the last application of hair oil.

"You," said MacBride, "you caused all this."

"Well, why the hell bring it up?"

"I intend bringing it up and up. You're just a wise guy who tried to run with big, bad boys. You worried hell out of your father and mother. Because of you your father's house was blown up. Because of you your father lost his aldermanic job. Now what the hell kind of a break do you suppose you deserve?"

"Did I ask for a break? Did I?"

"Of course not. But you're expecting one. What I want to know is, who killed Barjo?"

"I don't know."

"You mean you don't feel like telling me."

"About that."

MacBride leaned forward and put his elbows on the table and drew his brows close down until they almost met at the top of his nose. "Dom, my boy, you're going to spring what you know."

"Like hell I am."

"Like hell you arc."

"Listen, you. I didn't kill Barjo. You've got nothing on me—not a thing! I didn't kill him."

"Why did you drop out of sight?"

"That's my business."

"Why did you sneak home and hide away?"

"That's my business too."

MacBride put his voice down low. "We know of course that Chibby is after you."

"You don't know anything."

MacBride snapped, "Listen to me, you little two-tongued dago! I'm giving your old man a break. I'm trying to give you a break—not because I like you—but because I like your old man! As for you, I think you're a lousy pup! But get this—get it!—I want Chibby or one of the broads was on that party the night Barjo got knifed. I don't care what the hell one I get, I want one of them! And you—you're going to play ball with me or, by cripes, I'll whale hell out of you!"

"I'm not playing ball!" rasped Dominick. "I was on that party, I know that. But I didn't do a thing to anybody. And I ain't going to squeal!"

"You poor dumb slob!" MacBride half rose out of his chair and planted his palms on the desk. "Don't you realize that Chibby wants to blow your head off? Don't you realize that we're the only guys can save you?"

Dominick was biting his lip and his black eyes were jerking back and forth across the desk. He shook his head. "I—I ain't going to say a thing."

The door opened and Patrolman Zeloff shoved in Al Vassilakos. "There he is, Cap."

"Okey, Zeloff. Hello, Al. What the hell are you looking all hot and bothered about?"

"This—this is a dirty trick, Cap!"

"Is it? Listen to me, Al. I've given you all the breaks you're going to get. You were harboring a fugitive from the law."

"I wasn't!" choked the Greek. "So help me, I wasn't. This guy came to me and asked me to give him some jack so he could blow the town. He didn't have no jack. I gave him hell for coming around."

Dominick cut in, "He didn't do anything, Cap. I went there and asked him for some jack, just like he said."

"Sure," said Al, waving his hand. "See?"

"All right, all right," said MacBride. "I see. But you've always tried to kid me, Al, and you'll warm your pants here a while. I don't like your joint. You're two-faced as hell. And I don't like you. Zeloff, put this guy in the cooler for a while."

"Okey, Cap."

"Aw, say, Cap," said Al, "give me a break."

"Break? I'm through giving guys breaks."

"Aw—"

"Come on, you!" snapped Zeloff, and pulled Al out into the hall.

MacBride swung around in his chair, sitting bolt upright, and threw his gaze across the desk like two penetrating beams of blue fire.

"You see the kind of a palooka you went to looking for help! The first yap out of him is to save his own face!"

"Well, d' you see me yapping?"

"Dominick . . ." MacBride said the word with deadly softness as he leaned back. "Dominick, I warn you, you're in for a beating if you don't come across. I don't care if you are Tony's son. I'm trying to give you a break, but maybe I'll have to break you first. You can be nice . . . or I can be—nasty. Do you get me?"

Dominick drew his face up tightly and pinched his brows down over his midnight eyes. "You can't lay a hand on me!"

"I don't—personally. I've got men who do it for me."

"Yah, you're just the bull-dozing cop I heard you were! Just a big flat-foot! Just a big, loud-mouthed tough guy!"

"Just," said MacBride, "that."

Dominick jumped up, a lean shaft of vibrating dark fire. "You won't beat me! You won't! By God Almighty . . . you *won't*."

"Unless you play ball."

The telephone bell rang. MacBride picked up the instrument.

"Captain MacBride talking," he said. "Yeah, Mory . . . What? . . . No, no; go ahead. . . ." He listened, his eyes narrowing "What's that address? . . . Yeah; 22 Rumford Street. Okey. I'll shoot right down."

He slammed the telephone back to the desk and went to the door and yelled down the corridor. A reserve came on the run.

"Shove this guy in a cell, Mike. I got a date with a good break."

He piled into his overcoat, grabbed his hat and went out into the central room. He called Hogan, and Hogan ran out to get the police flivver. MacBride was waiting for him on the sidewalk.

IX

Rumford Street is on the northern frontier of the city. It is a hilly street, climbing up from Marble Road. A drab street, walled in by three- and four-story rooming-houses. Ordinarily a peaceful neighborhood.

The police flivver swung off Marble Road and labored up the grade. When it was half way up MacBride saw an ambulance and a small group of people.

"That's it, Hogan."

"Yeah."

The flivver drove up behind the ambulance, and MacBride got out and saw a patrolman and the patrolman saw him and saluted.

"Second floor, Cap."

"Right."

MacBride entered the hall door and climbed the dusty narrow staircase. On the second landing he saw light streaming out through a door, and a policeman was standing in the door. He saw MacBride and stepped aside, and MacBride went into a small living-room.

Kennedy was sitting on a chair with his feet on a table and his hands clasped behind his back. Cohen was walking back and forth taking quick drags on a cigarette.

"Hello, Cap," he said, and jerked his head towards the next room.

But MacBride had caught sight of a doctor and a couple of uniformed patrolmen and Moriarity standing beside a bed, and there was a pulmotor working. He caught sight, too, of a girl's legs protruding from a nightgown, and then Moriarity turned around and saw him and shrugged and came out.

"It's Bunny Dahl," he said.

"What happened?"

"Gas."

"What—suicide?"

"Dunno. Ike and me stopped in a speakeasy just around on Marble Road. Kennedy was there, and we were just about to start a card game when Patrolman Cronkheiser came busting in looking for a telephone. It seems he was walking his beat down Rumford Street when a woman ran out hollering for help. She lives next door. She'd smelt gas and got up and went out in the hall, and then when she knocked on this door and got no answer she ran out and hollered and Cronkheiser came up and busted in. Bunny was laying on the floor, by one of them gas heaters—there it is."

"How is she?"

"Pretty rotten. They want to try the pulmotor because they think she may pass out before they reach the hospital."

MacBride went in and looked at her and then came back into the other room.

"Queer," he said.

"Yeah," said Kennedy. "Looks as if she got cold feet."

MacBride said nothing for a minute, and then he said, "I got Dominick."

Kennedy's feet fell down from the table. "Things come in bunches, like bananas, don't they? Where'd you get him?"

"Club Naples. He was feeling Al for some jack when I wandered in. I got Al, too. I don't like that two-faced Greek. I'm going to get something on him yet."

"Did he say anything?" asked Moriarity.

"No. The kid's got spirit. He won't squeal. But—he'll have to. Even if we have to beat him."

MacBride turned and looked into the other room and then he rubbed his hand slowly across his jaw. The doctor looked over his shoulder and beckoned, and MacBride came in and stood beside the bed.

"She's trying to say something, Captain."

"What's she trying to say?"

"About a chap named Chibby."

"Oh . . . Chibby."

MacBride sat down on the edge of the bed and took out a pencil and an old envelope. "Bunny," he said. "What's it all about, Bunny?"

"Chibby . . . did it . . ."

"How?"

"He got me drunk . . . then he tied a rag around my mouth . . . so I couldn't yell . . . then he held my head down by the gas stove . . ."

"H'm." One side of MacBride's mouth drew down hard. He leaned closer. "Bunny, where is he?"

"I don't know. . . . Al knows."

"Why did he do this to you, Bunny?"

"Because I knew he . . ." Her voice trailed off.

The doctor said, "We'd better try getting her to the hospital. She hasn't got much of a chance."

"Okey." MacBride stood up. He went back into the other room and said, "Ike, I want you to go to the hospital with Bunny and hang around and see if she says anything more. Mory, you come with me to Headquarters. Al is in for hell."

He went out into the hall and down the narrow dusty stairs. Moriarity followed him, and Kennedy trailed along behind. They all climbed into the flivver, and Hogan started the motor and they drove off.

X

MacBride had removed his hat, but his overcoat was still on and his hands were in his pockets. His face was gray and hard like granite, and his eyes were like blue cold ice, and he stood with his feet spread apart and his square jaw down close to his chest.

Kennedy sat on the desk with his feet on a chair and his elbows on his knees and his hands loosely clasped. Moriarity stood with his back to the radiator and a dead cigarette hanging from one side of his mouth.

Al Vassilakos sat in the swivel-chair with the light streaming brightly into his white puffed face. It was a face that seemed to have been crudely molded out of dough. His knees were pressed together and his toes were turned in and pressed hard against the floor, and his pudgy hands gripped the arms of the swivel-chair.

MacBride said, "You know where Chibby is, Al."

"So help me, Cap—"

"Shut up! You know where he is. I want to know where he is."

"Uh—honest, Cap—"

"Shut up! There's no time for stalling. You've been playing me for the fool and I'm sick of it. I want to know where Chibby is. I'll give you one minute to come across."

He took his left hand out of his pocket and crooked his arm and stared down at the watch on his wrist.

Al gripped the arms of the chair harder with his pudgy hands. His toes screwed against the floor. His white stiff shirt-front moved up and down jerkily. His lower lip, which had been caught under his teeth, flopped out and gleamed wet, and his nose wrinkled and his eyes bulged wildly. His breath was beginning to grate in his throat. His body was straining in the chair, and the chair creaked, and he was stretching his throat in his tight stiff collar, as if fighting for breath. Sweat burst out on his forehead and gleamed like globules of grease, and his whole face, that had been dead like dough, began to twitch and convulse as agitated nerve muscles raced around beneath his skin.

MacBride looked dispassionately at the watch on his wrist. Kennedy seemed interested in his hands. Morarity's eyes were hidden behind shuttered lids, but he was staring at Al.

MacBride shoved his hand back into his pocket. "Minute's up, Al."

Kennedy looked up from his hands.

Al strained harder in his chair, his white face ghastly in the light that poured down upon it.

"Well, Al? . . ." MacBride drew his lips flat back against his teeth.

Al choked. "No-no!"

MacBride walked to the door and opened it and called, "Hey, Mike!"

He came back into the room and after a while a patrolman came in buttoning his coat.

"Mike," said MacBride, "take this guy upstairs and put him over the hurdles. You, too, Mory."

The policeman and Moriarity heaved Al out of the chair and dragged him out of the room. Al was blubbering and breaking at the knees.

MacBride closed the door and sat down in the swivel-chair. Kennedy lit a cigarette and shot smoke through his nostrils.

"Bunny sure got hell, didn't she, Cap?"

"Yeah. It's like that song about what you get for making whoopee."

"I wonder what's behind this. I wonder why Chibby tried to bump off the broad. Maybe *he* killed Barjo."

"Maybe."

They didn't talk much. MacBride started a cigar and sat back in his chair, and after a while Kennedy got down from the desk and wandered about the room.

Half an hour later the door opened and Moriarity stood there. He carried his coat under his arm.

"Okey, Cap."

"Yeah?"

"Yeah. Chibby's hiding out at 95 Hector Street with about six other guns."

"All right, Mory. Put your coat on."

XI

It was a big, powerful touring car that left Headquarters and droned through the dark streets. Hogan was at the wheel. Beside him sat Moriarity and MacBride. In the rear were five policemen and Kennedy. It was half-past two in the morning. The dark streets were empty, and the big car plunged from one into another, and the men in the back swayed from side to side as the car bent sharply around corners.

"This is Hector," said Hogan.

"What's the number?" asked MacBride.

"The numbers begin here," said Kennedy. "That 95 should be about three blocks down."

MacBride said, "Pull up about a block this side, Hogan."

"Okey."

The car slowed down and rolled along leisurely, and presently Hogan swung into the curb and applied the brake.

MacBride got out first and looked up and down the street. The policemen got out and stood around him, and their badges, fastened to the breasts of their heavy blue overcoats, flashed intermittently.

"It must be on the other side of the street," said MacBride. "Come on."

They crossed the street and walked along close to the houses. The houses were set back from the sidewalk and fronted by iron fences, and just behind the fences were depressions and short flights of stone steps that led down to the basement floors. The street lights were few and far between, and the windows of the houses were darkened.

MacBride was saying, "We'll try to get in through the cellar."

They reached number 95 and went in through the gate and crowded noiselessly down the stone steps until their heads were level with the sidewalk. There were two windows, without shades, and the windows were dirty.

"They're supposed to be on the top story," whispered Moriarity.

"And it's four stories," muttered MacBride. "Let's try the windows."

They tried them, but the windows were locked. MacBride stood for a moment thinking. Then—"There's no fire-escapes in front. They must be in the rear. Let's find a way to the rear. The next block."

They came back to the sidewalk and walked on, took the next left turn and then turned left again into the street that paralleled Hector. MacBride counted the houses.

"You might have noticed," said Kennedy, "that 95 was the only four-storied house. The others were three."

"It should be about here," said MacBride.

He mounted the steps and rang the bell. After a few minutes the door opened and an old woman wearing a nightcap looked out.

"Madam," said MacBride, "we're from Police Headquarters. We'd like to pass through your house so that we can get to the one behind it in Hector Street."

"What's the trouble?"

"We're looking for someone."

"Well—well—all right. But waking an old woman up on these cold nights . . ."

"I'm very sorry, madam."

She led them through the hall and opened a door in the rear that led into a small yard. Beyond the yard was a low board fence. Beyond the fence was the back of the four-storied house.

"Thank you, madam," said MacBride.

"It's all right, but with my sciatica . . ."

MacBride and the cops and Kennedy passed out into the yard. MacBride scaled the fence and dropped down into the other yard, and the others were close behind.

"There's the fire-escape," he said, and walked towards it.

He was the first to go up. Whatever may be said of him, good or bad, he never hung back in the face of impending danger. If he planned a dangerous maneuver, he likewise led the way, remarking, with ironic humor, that he carried heavy insurance.

He climbed quite noiselessly, and the men were like an endless chain behind him, a dark chain of life moving up the metal ladders. The windows they moved past were black as black slabs of slate. The skirts of their long blue coats swung about their knees as the knees rose and fell with each upward step.

MacBride went slower as he neared the top landing. He stopped and looked back down over the line of men, and right behind him was Patrolman Haviland, and behind Haviland was Patrolman Kreischer, who was getting on in years. And looking at them, MacBride felt a little proud of them.

He looked upward and climbed slowly, and Haviland came up to crowd on one side of him and Kreischer came up to crowd on the other side. They all had their guns out. MacBride had his out, too, but he reached over and took Haviland's nightstick.

He looked at the window, and then he raised the heavy stick and smashed the glass. He struck four times, and then plunged in through the yawning aperture.

Somewhere in the darkness there was a shout. A split-second later a gun boomed and a flash of fire stabbed the darkness and a bullet slammed into the window frame. MacBride fired around the room and lunged across the floor. He heard a man scream. If he could find a door, then he could find a light-switch, he reasoned.

Someone cannoned into him, and MacBride crashed against the wall. A gun exploded so close to his face that the smoke made him choke. He ducked and sprang away and banged into another twisting body, and ducked away again. He brought up suddenly against a door and then he groped around for the light-switch. He could not find it. A body hurtled against him with such force that the captain went down.

Somebody pulled the door open, and the dim light from the hall filtered in. Two or three forms dived out through the door. MacBride leaped up and lunged towards the door and collided with another man who was trying to get out. Both went down under a rush of four policeman who had not time to recognize MacBride. MacBride disentangled himself in a hurry and heaved up as Haviland was on the point of swinging his nightstick.

"Hey!" shouted MacBride.

"Oh . . . you, Cap!"

Another man came barging out of the door behind a flaming gun, and one of the bullets put a hole through MacBride's new hat but did not budge it the fraction of an inch. Kreischer fired three times, and the man threw up his hands and screamed, and the momentum of his dive carried him over the banister and crashing down to the hall below.

And in the hall below the cops who had run down were fighting with the men who had opened the door and sought to escape. Somebody in the room had found the light-switch—it turned out to be Kennedy—and the light revealed two gangsters lying dead on the floor and Kennedy mildly scratching his nose, as though he were trying to figure out why the men did not get up.

MacBride ran to the head of the stairs and saw the spurts of gunfire below. He forked the banister backward and slid down with lightning-like speed. He flew off the end and did a backward somersault, and as he was getting up Patrolman Mendelwitz toppled over him groaning and then slid to the floor like a bag of wet meal.

The fighting moved down the next stairway, and MacBride went after it, and Kreischer and Haviland came pounding down behind him. MacBride, going down the staircase, stumbled over a body, but caught hold of the banister and steadied himself. It was the body of a gangster.

MacBride looked over the banister and saw three gangsters backing towards the next landing below. He climbed over the banister, hung out a bit and then dropped. It was a fall of about fifteen feet, and MacBride landed on somebody's shoulders and created a new panic. He saw one of the other gangsters swing towards him, and he recognized Sam Chibbarro, and Chibarro recognized him. The gunman swung his rod towards MacBride's head, but another body sailed down from above and crashed Chibbarro to the floor. It was Kennedy, unarmed, but effective, nevertheless. The third gangster turned and ran for the head of the next staircase, and Haviland fired along the banister and got him in the side and the

gangster fell against the wall and then slid down to the floor.

Chibbarro flung off Kennedy and bolted, but MacBride, having knocked his own man out, dived for Chibbarro and caught him by the tail of the coat. Chibbarro cursed and tried to get out of his coat, and then he pivoted and his gun swung close. MacBride let go of the coat-tail and caught Chibbarro's gun hand as the gun went off. The shot walloped the floor, and then MacBride swung Chibbarro's arm up and backward and clouted him over the head with the barrel of his own gun. Chibbarro went down like a felled tree.

Kreischer came up on the run, big-footed, and then stopped and watched Chibbarro fall. Then he looked at MacBride and grinned with his beet-red face.

"*Himmel!*" he said.

"I guess that's that, Fritz," said MacBride. "Hey, Haviland, how is Mandelwitz?"

"He's laying back here and cursing like hell."

"Okey. Then he's all right. Harrigan, find a telephone and call the hospital and then call the wagon. Hey, Sokalov, for God's sake, don't keep pointing that gun this way! It's all over. Put it away."

"All right. . . . I forgot, Cap."

MacBride looked around and saw Kennedy leaning against the wall and lighting a cigarette. Kennedy's hat was twisted sidewise on his head, and two buttons were gone from his coat, and his face was dirty. He looked comical. MacBride chuckled bluntly.

"How come you're alive, Kennedy?"

"There is a Providence," said Kennedy with mock gravity, "that watches over fools, drunks and bum reporters."

"I always said you were a bum reporter," put in Moriarity.

Kennedy spun away his match. "Imagine a guy like that!"

XII

Dawn was breaking, but the light in the office still streamed down over the flat, shiny desk.

Chibbarro sat in a chair within the radius of the light, his hair plastered down over his ears and forehead and a streak of dried blood on his cheek. His brows were bent, and he scowled at the top of the flat shiny desk.

Moriarity stood with his back to the radiator, and Kennedy had reversed a chair and now straddled it with his arms crossed on the back and his chin on his crossed arms.

MacBride sat in the swivel-chair and looked at Chibbarro.

"You did wrong, Chibby," he said, "to come to Richmond City. It's a tough town."

"Tough hell!"

"Tougher than you are, Chibby. I always wondered why you came here. I'm wondering now why you tried to kill Bunny Dahl."

"She was a chicken-hearted broad!"

"Bad . . . doing what you did, Chibby."

Chibbarro took out his handkerchief and blew his nose. "I been framed all around. That boy scout Dominick—"

"Didn't spring a thing."

"Bah!"

"It was Al."

"The lousy pup!"

MacBride leaned back and put his hands behind his head. "So you didn't kill Barjo."

"No, of course I didn't kill him! D' you think I'm a fool, to put a knife in a guy at a souse party?"

"I didn't think you were so much of a fool. But why did you try to put Bunny out of the way?"

Chibbarro turned his back on MacBride. "You can ask my lawyer all them things."

"That's all right by me, Chibby. But it won't help your case."

The door opened and Ike Cohen walked in. "Hello, Cap—Mory—Kennedy." He looked at Chibbarro. "Hello, Chibby, you small-time greaseball!"

"Go to hell!" said Chibbarro.

"Funny, you are!"

MacBride said, "What news, Ike?"

"The frail just died."

Chibbarro looked up with a start, and his dark eyes widened and horror bulged from the pupils. Then he pulled his face together and crouched sullenly in the chair.

Cohen drew a folded piece of paper from his pocket and handed it to MacBride.

"She regained consciousness long enough to spring this, Cap. It's signed by her and witnessed by the doctor and me."

MacBride unfolded the paper and spread it on the desk. He read it over carefully, then settled back in his chair holding it in one hand.

"Listen to this, gang," he said, and read aloud:

" 'I killed Salvatore Barjo. He was drunk. He followed me into a room in the Club Naples and tried to attack me. I picked up a paper cutter that was laying on the table and stabbed him. Then Dominick came in. Then Chibby came in. Chibby cursed hell out of me, and Dominick yelled at him and said I had to be got out of the jam. Chibby said like hell. Then I said he'd get me out of it or I'd tell what I knew about him. That's why he got me out of it. So we hid out. Then Dominick and Chibby got in a fight and Dominick skinned out. He was a good guy, Dominick. He didn't know what Chibby had up his sleeve. He thought Chibby was just a bootlegger.

" 'Then Chibby got his gang together and they hunted for Dominick to bump him off before the cops got him. Chibby thought Dominick knew more than he did. Chibby came here from Chicago. He was one of the Rizzio gang, and he came here to work up a white slave trade. He got me to work with him, and in the month here I helped him get twelve girls for houses in Dayton and Columbus. That was his real racket, but he wanted to try booze on the side, and he wanted to be friends with Dominick because his old man was alderman, and that might help.

" 'When we heard the cops had Dominick I wanted to go to Headquarters and get him out. I was sick of the whole rotten business. Chibby swore he'd kill me, and I dared him. I said I was going, and that I'd say nothing about him. But he didn't believe me. He got me tight and then he shoved my head down by the gas-heater. I guess he always was a bum.' "

"Hell's bells!" said Kennedy.

MacBride dropped the letter to the desk and got up and walked around the room.

"So that was it, Chibby," he said. "White slaving, eh?"

Chibbarro stared darkly at the shiny top of the desk.

MacBride said, "And you only protected the girl because you knew it was the only way of protecting yourself. God, but you're a louse!"

"Imagine this guy wanting a lawyer!" said Moriarity.

"Yeah," said Cohen. "Ain't he the optimistic slob?"

MacBride picked up the telephone and called a number. After a moment he said, "Hello, Tony. This is MacBride. . . . Now hold your horses. We've got the kid here. . . . Yeah, yeah, he's all right, and he'll get out after a while. . . . What's that? . . . No, I'm not going to comfort

him. I'll leave that to you. If he was my kid I'd fan him. . . . All right, come around when you feel like it."

He put down the telephone and sighed and stared at it for a long moment.

Kennedy pulled a photograph out of his pocket and stared at it.

"She wasn't such a bad-looking frail."

MacBride looked at him. "Where'd you get that?"

"In her bedroom. We'll smear it on the front page of the noon editions."

MacBride went to the window and looked out and saw the red sun coming up over the rooftops. And it occurred to him, without any blur of sentimentality, that Chibby and Dominick and Al were small-timers, and that the girl—this Bunny Dahl—had been stronger than all of them put together.

Kennedy was saying, "It's tough the way sometimes a broad has to die to get her picture in the paper."

Murder Picture

George Harmon Coxe

IT CAN BE NO surprise that George Harmon Coxe (1901–1984) began his career as a newspaperman, since his two major literary creations, Jack "Flashgun" Casey (mostly known as "Flash" Casey) and Kent Murdock were both photo-journalists.

Casey came first, created for *Black Mask* in 1934. A secondary character here to young reporter Tom Wade, he quickly moves to the fore, accompanied by his young sidekick on a regular basis. There were more than twenty "Flash" Casey stories and five novels.

Murdock, very much like Casey but not as tough or violent, made his debut the following year in the novel *Murder with Pictures* (1935). Although Casey is the better-known character, Murdock appeared in many more novels (twenty-one in all), the first of which was filmed in 1936 with Lew Ayres playing the hero.

One unusual aspect of both series is that most of the adventures feature private detectives but, unlike virtually all other fiction in *Black Mask* and the other pulps, they are bad guys, frequently hired by villains to protect their evil interests.

While the earliest stories are much in the Carroll John Daly school of "shoot first, ask questions later," they soon became more cerebral, especially the Murdock tales, as murders and their solutions tended to involve technological devices rather than merely a bullet in the skull.

"Murder Picture" was first published in *Black Mask* in the issue of January 1935.

Murder Picture

George Harmon Coxe

It was a picture that spelled dynamite for Flash Casey, with the fuse all set and burning

1

ASEY, ace photographer of the *Globe*, Flash Casey, as everyone from the copy boy to Captain Judson of the Homicide Squad called him, stood scowling down at a photographic enlargement spread on the table before him.

Big shoulders hunched above his lean waist, reddish hair ruffled, eyes narrowed and frowning, he cursed in a steady monotone of disgust.

The little man at the corner desk, busy making records of his prints, stopped work long enough to glance over at the big cameraman and grin.

"Whatsa bellyache, Flash?"

"Plenty," Casey growled. He rapped a big, bony fist on the barely dried photo. "Here I get an inside tip on that racetrack layout raid and me and Wade crash in just as they are pulling it. I shoot one—this one." The fist rapped again. "Then Haley and his pals throw us out. I knew there must be something more we missed, so I duck in a back way and shoot another through the washroom door, and this time the cops steal the plate off me before they put me out again."

"Well, ain't that one you got any good?"

"A pip, but that other one musta—"

"Hell," the little man said, fretfully, "Blaine don't *have* to know there was another one, does he?"

A slow grin drove the scowl from Casey's homely, strong features.

"You're saying something, Tim. He don't *have* to—unless he asks me. Guess I better get it in to him."

He gathered up the print and started towards the door.

"And tell him how good it is," the little man jeered. "Aw, you guys make me—"

The jangling telephone bell cut him off.

Casey, passing it, took up the receiver.

"Yeah—Casey."

The voice of Lieutenant Logan of the Homicide Squad answered him.

"Listen, Flash. I just talked with Haley. He tells me you sneaked into the washroom of that race-track dive."

"What about it?"

"Did you come across the airshaft—from the Blue Grass Products office?"

"Yeah, but—"

"I'm down there now. I want to see you."

"When? I'm busy and—"

"I don't care a damn whether you're busy or not. Get out here right away or I'll send somebody after you."

Casey said: "Aw—" and pronged the receiver.

His eyes were thoughtful as he walked into the city room, but lighted up as he approached the city editor.

Casey said: "Boy, this is a honey," and laid the eight by ten photographic enlargement on Blaine's desk.

The city editor pushed up in his chair, slid his forearms across the desk top and glanced at the print. It was an exceptionally clear reproduction of the interior of a race-track layout, taken a few

seconds after the police had staged a raid an hour previous.

The camera had caught the major part of the room, with its blackboards, loud speaker, cashier's cage; most of the milling crowd of forty or fifty people, half of them women. Casey, a look of satisfaction on his thick face, leaned down and pointed to specific features of the picture, as though he was afraid Blaine would miss them.

"There's Captain Judson," he said, "and Haley, the louse." He moved his forefinger to a stocky man with a white, fatty face who was just coming out of a door on which the word, *Men*, was barely legible. "And get a load of Mike Handy."

Casey's forefinger moved to a smartly dressed and obviously frightened lady who had thrown one arm around the neck of a plump young man with a tiny mustache: Lee Fessendon, son of the new owner of the *Globe*, brother of the managing editor. A fellow who, though married, continued to retain his reputation of man-about-town.

"Young Fessendon." Casey's voice was humorously disgusted. "Takin' an afternoon off." He straightened up, grunted. "Made a hell of a fuss about it, wanted the plate."

Blaine leaned back in his chair and his clasped hands made a cradle for the nape of his neck.

"This all you took?" he said finally.

"It ain't all I took." Casey's mouth dipped at the corners and his brows knotted in a scowl as he thought of the second picture he had taken, of the trouble he had surmounted to get it.

"But it's all I got," he growled. "Haley and a couple of his dicks took the other one away from me."

His brows flattened out. "But what's the matter with that one? It's exclusive—and it's good, ain't it?"

"Very good," said Blaine sardonically. "Very good indeed; only we can't use it."

"Can't use it?" Casey exploded. "Who says we can't?"

Blaine would have been poor copy for the

movies. He did not look the part. He was too well dressed, and he had no eyeshade. Slender, distinguished looking with his prematurely gray hair, he had a lean, hawklike face and small gray eyes that met Casey's in a cold, contemptuous stare.

"I do," he said, and his voice was thin, abrupt.

"Oh." Casey's eyes narrowed. "So that's how it is?" He thrust his hands deep in his trousers pockets, brought his chin down on his chest and surveyed Blaine from under bushy brows. "If anybody'd told me this an hour ago, I'd called him a liar."

"Told you what?" said Blaine irritably.

Casey made no direct answer. Leaning stiff armed on the desk, he made a bulky figure with a thick, upward-arching chest, and tousled hair that was peppered with gray at the temples and too long at the back. A squarish face, set, thin-lipped now, held dark eyes that were narrowed and smoldering.

"The only thing I ever liked about you," he said flatly, "was that you played ball. You protected confidential channels, but you never squashed a story or picture because it was about a friend of somebody's Aunt Emma. But Fessendon's got your number, huh? When he cracks the whip—"

"You interest me," sneered Blaine.

Casey pointed at the picture on the desk. "Lee Fessendon got caught out of school with one of his women. He's scared to take a bawling out from his wife, huh?"

He made noises in his throat and shook his head. "He tried to talk me out of the plate down there in the hall. But you—you have to humor the boss' brother, huh?"

"Finished?" purred Blaine. And when Casey remained silent, "Satisfied now, are you?"

He leaned forward in his chair, smiled a smile that held no mirth, spoke in a voice that was brittle.

"I don't have to make explanations to a camera. But sometimes I like to humor you, Flash. And I'm going to tell you the answer to this one;

because you amuse me, and because it helps illustrate my original and permanent contention—that you are a thick-headed sap."

Blaine reached for one of the telephones on the desk, spoke a few words. When he looked back at Casey, he said:

"You sneaked this picture over on Captain Judson. And the reason we are killing it, sweetheart, is because Judson called Fessendon and told him if we printed it he'd close us out at Headquarters for a month."

"Judson called—" Casey broke off and a slow flush crept into his lean cheeks. His widened eyes looked chagrined, incredulous.

In another moment, J. H. Fessendon, brother of Lee, son of the new owner, and managing editor of the *Globe*, swung through the doorway of a corridor behind the desk. He accepted the photograph from Blaine with a manicured hand, studied it.

Casey's flushed face knotted in a scowl as he watched Fessendon. He did not like him or his pseudo go-getter methods. A plump, baldish man of forty-five: pink skin that looked as if a massage was part of his daily ritual; expensive tweeds, tailored with a tight vest and waistband, as though to control and mold the paunch.

"Yes—yes." Fessendon said crisply. "This must be the one. Too bad we can't use it. Where's the plate?" He glanced at Blaine, who eyed him narrowly, then at Casey. "Get the plate, Casey."

Casey fastened contemptuous eyes on Blaine, wheeled and left the desk. In the photographic department, he asked Tom Wade if he had made an extra print. Wade said he had, and Casey growled:

"Swell. I'll paste it in my diary." At the doorway, he turned. "Put it in my desk."

Fessendon was pacing back and forth beside Blaine's desk, followed by surreptitious glances from the crew in the "slot," the half dozen rewrite men scattered about the city room. Casey handed Fessendon the plate, and he held it up to the light. Grunting in approval, he struck the glass against the corner of the desk. The plate shattered in a dozen pieces. Then Fessendon tore up the print.

"Got to make sure," he said easily, picking up the pieces and dropping them in a wastebasket, "got to make sure, you know."

Blaine turned in his chair and watched Fessendon through the doorway, as did every other eye in the room. When he turned back, he met Casey's humid, searching gaze for a moment, and his face flushed. Then he busied himself with some copy, said:

"Don't stand there gawking. If you got legitimate shots we'd have something to print."

Casey opened his mouth and rage kept it open. But he did not speak. He could not think of the right thing to say.

2

Tom Wade was talking on the telephone when Casey returned to the anteroom of the photographic department and slid into the chair behind his desk. He lit a cigarette, puffed once, then let it hang from his half opened lips.

The hot anger which streaked through his brain when Fessendon smashed the plate was a smoldering, cancerous growth now. A heaviness that was a mixture of dejection and disappointment weighed upon him. It was not so much the loss of the plate; that had happened before; it was the way Blaine had let him down—and Fessendon's gesture, as though he could trust neither Casey nor the city editor.

Wade talked for nearly five minutes longer, and when he hung up Casey told him what had happened.

"It's like I told you before," he finished. "The sheet's goin' to seed since Fessendon bought it. And I still think Lee is the guy that gyped us out of the shot. He probably called Blaine and Blaine gave me the song about Judson—"

"That don't sound like Blaine to me," Wade said slowly.

"And Fessendon," Casey rasped. "Bustin' the plate like we was crooks or something." He

began to curse, and after a moment said: "Who the hell were you talkin' with so long?"

"Alma Henderson."

"That tramp that was—"

"Wait a minute!" Wade's voice was unnaturally harsh. A blond, round-faced youth with a guileless manner and a happy-go-lucky philosophy, Wade's ordinarily good-natured face was now flushed, his blue eyes snapping.

"Oh," said Casey and his brows came up. "So that's the way it is."

"No," Wade said doggedly, flushing at his burst of temper, "but she's no tramp. She's a good kid and—"

Casey's mind flashed back to the raid. To get the second picture, the one Haley had taken, he and Wade had crashed into the office of the Blue Grass Products, which was separated from the race-track room by an airshaft. Casey had been in the building before, knew there was an airshaft and had crossed this to get to the men's room of the gambling hall.

Alma Henderson was apparently in charge of the Blue Grass office. It had surprised Casey that Wade knew her, because heretofore the youth had but little time for women. But Casey, intent on getting another picture, dismissed his curiosity and had left Wade arguing with the girl while he crossed the airshaft with his camera.

He said: "She's a good kid, huh? Okey. But she works for the Blue Grass outfit, and Moe Nyberg runs it. A cheap tout, a first-class thug. Why, the heel; everything he touches stinks. He's probably hooked up with that race-track dive, now that I think of it. And he plays with Mike Handy who runs the biggest gyp stable in the East. So what does that make this Henderson dame?"

"What the hell?" Wade flung out. "A girl's got to eat."

"All right, all right. I don't care. I got troubles of my own."

Casey lit another cigarette, puffed at it until his head was shrouded in blue. But it wasn't all right. Wade was impulsive, and he had a lot to learn. To get mixed up with any woman connected with Nyberg might put him on the skids.

He said: "What did she want?"

"She wants me to come over to her place."

"What for? She knows you're workin', don't she?"

"She's got a story." Wade said jerkily. "She wouldn't tell me over the phone, but she says it's a job for the cops."

"Hah!" rasped Casey. "Then why don't she go down to Headquarters and spill it?"

"Here's why." Wade took a newspaper from his desk, opened it, pointed to a single column head on page 12.

Casey read:

GIRL PRISONER FLEES DOCTOR

Brought to the State Hospital in East Concord Street for a physical examination, Miss Mary Merkle, 21, serving a sentence at the Reformatory for Women until 1937, escaped today from the office of Doctor . . .

Casey looked up. "I told you she was a tramp."

Wade flushed. "You're wrong, Flash. She gave me part of the story over the phone. She came down from Vermont three years ago. She got mixed up in a bad crowd, there was a raid, she had no near relatives—"

Wade went on with his story and Casey looked at the date line of the paper. May 17th.

"When she escaped," Wade went on, "she had no place to go, so she looked up one of the guys she used to know and he got her a job with Moe Nyberg. If she goes to the cops with her story, bingo. Back to the Reformatory."

"That's probably where she belongs," growled Casey, and was half ashamed of his words when he saw the hurt look in Wade's eyes.

"She's scared, Flash. And"—Wade hesitated, caught his lower lip between his teeth—"I think she wants me to help her out of town."

"You're nuts," Casey said. He looked at the youth, read correctly the stubborn set of the jaw. He spread his hand wearily, said:

"Listen. I gotta go back to Roxbury and see Logan. Something's up. You can go with me. And after that I'll go and see this Henderson dame with you."

Wade shook his head. "She told me to hurry."

"But—" snorted Casey.

"Wait." Wade backed towards the door and his voice was a bit thick. "She's depending on me, says I'm the only one in town she can trust. I told her I'd come and I'm not letting her down—not even for you."

Casey blew out his breath. Guileless as hell. And just as stubborn. Sold on the girl—or her story. He said:

"What's her address?"

"Seven sixty-three Pratt Street."

Casey smiled then and the smile was genuine, tinged with a certain admiration for the youth's earnest loyalty. He said: "Okey, give it a whirl. Only watch your step and remember she works for Moe Nyberg."

When Wade went out, Casey shrugged and picked up his camera and platecase. "I'd better take 'em," he said half aloud. "Logan sounded tough."

Fifteen minutes later, Casey set his camera and case on the floor in front of a door whose upper panel of frosted glass bore the inscription: *Blue Grass Products,* and scowled.

The transverse corridor on the third floor of the ancient and deserted looking office building was empty, ominously quiet, lighted by a single bulb at the far end. A half dozen doors, with upper panels of glass, gave on the hall, and in each case they were dark. The one in front of him was dark, and this he could not understand.

Where the hell was Logan?

Casey sucked at his upper lip, pushed his hat forward and scratched his shaggy nape. He swept the tails of his topcoat aside as he jammed his fists on his hips; then he yanked the hat brim down, said: "Nerts," and banged his fist on the doorframe.

He waited a moment, banged again. Then, although he heard no sound, he happened to glance at the doorknob. It was turning slowly.

Doubt, chilled and gripping, reared up in his brain. He reached quickly for the platecase, but as he straightened up, prepared to retreat, the door came open a three-inch crack.

Casey froze there, an open-mouthed, wide-eyed statue. Surprise, momentary panic, riveted his gaze on that vertical strip of blackness, on the muzzle of a gun which had been thrust forward in the opening so that the dim light of the hall caught the round barrel, burnished it.

For a second or two there was no sound but the sharp suck of Casey's breath as it caught in his lungs. Then the door swung open and a low, matter-of-fact voice said:

"Okey, Flash. Come on in."

Casey exhaled noisily and stepped forward with sweat breaking out on his forehead. The lights of the room went on. Logan moved out of the doorway and Casey cursed, said: "Why you louse!"

He stopped in front of Logan, glared at him, and the lights of the room glistened on the thin film of moisture on his forehead.

"You louse! You scared hell out of me."

"Couldn't be helped," said Logan flatly, making no apology.

"Ah—" Casey brushed his forehead, pushed back his hat. "You knew I was comin'. You called me up, didn't you? What the hell do—"

"I knew you were coming," said Logan holstering his gun, "but I'm hopin' we might get some other callers."

Something in Logan's cold abrupt tone caught and held Casey's interest. It was no gag, that gun business. Logan was in dead earnest. And when he got that way—

Casey glanced around. From where he stood, the office was as he remembered it; long, well furnished with a flat-topped desk, a typewriter desk, leather upholstered chairs. The doorway on the right, apparently leading to a connecting office, had been closed this afternoon. It was open now and two detectives stood in the doorway.

Casey recognized the short, stocky fellow with the red face and the heavy chain draped across his bulging vest as Sergeant Manahan. The other fellow was from Headquarters, too, but he did not know his name. He said:

"Well, what's the act for?"

Logan took him by the arm, walked him out of the entryway so that he could get a full view of the room. Then Casey saw the man on the floor.

Between the little entryway and the cubby-hole, with its washstand and window giving on the airshaft, was a closet. The door of this was open, and the body of a man, lying on his stomach, his face cocked to one side, was half in, half out of the closet, as though he had fallen out when the door was opened.

He was well dressed, his oxford gray topcoat looked new and his shoes were polished. From what Casey could see, the fellow appeared to be about thirty-five, dark-haired, average height. Now there was a definite stiffness about the still form, and in the back a reddish blotch fused with the gray fabric of the coat.

Casey looked at Logan. "Who is he?"

"Grady. A private dick from New York."

"Shot in the back?"

"Twice—from close range."

"Where do I come in?" asked Casey, frowning.

"That's what I want to know," said Logan. "I want to know all about the horseplay you staged here this afternoon. I may be wrong. But I think this guy was in that closet—dead—when you were in this room."

Casey's eyes widened. He stared at Logan, said: "——!" Then he thought about the Henderson woman, and Wade, and some of the color oozed from his face.

"Then she saw it!" he wheezed huskily. "She must've seen it. And it was a plant. That's why she wanted Wade."

"Keep your pants on," Logan said bruskly, "and start at the beginning."

3

Lieutenant Logan, sitting on the massive, flat-topped desk at the end of the room, his arms angling out beside him, propping him up, was a well built fellow with black hair and eyes. About Casey's age, he had a flair for clothes. His linen was immaculate, so was his police record. Right now he wore spats—and nobody said anything about them either.

"Wait a minute," he said when Casey told him about the girl—and the telephone call which had summoned Wade. "At the beginning. How'd you get here, what'd you do—everything. I want it all."

Casey glared at Logan for a moment, then spoke in thick jerky tones.

"I got the tip from Gerry at Headquarters. When Wade and I got downstairs Judson and Haley and their gang were just gettin' ready to start. We went up the stairs and when they broke down the door I went in behind the cops. I got one picture, then Judson threw me out."

Casey cursed at the thought, continued rapidly.

"I knew there was an airshaft some place around so Wade and I cut down this other hall. I figured it oughtta be about there, so we crashed in here; didn't know what it was but took a chance.

"The Henderson dame was alone here. She gave us an argument, looked scared as hell, but Wade talked to her and—"

"The closet was closed," Logan said.

"Yeah," chafed Casey, "so was this other door—to the next office. And anyway I opened the window"—he pointed to the frosted glass pane in the wall of the cubbyhole—"and saw that the window across the shaft was partway open."

He stepped towards a wide shelf which lay on iron brackets on one wall of the cubbyhole. "The dame was arguing all the time, but I found out this shelf was loose, I shoved it across the shaft and it just reached. So I took the camera and slid across. It was the men's room."

"Anybody in it?" asked Logan.

"No. And I went through to the hall, got one picture. But Haley saw me, caught me before I could reach the door. He and a couple of those thugs you call detectives took the plate away from me."

"Did you come back here?"

"Yeah, but"—Casey's thick face cracked in a scowl—"the place was closed."

"Hah!" snapped Logan. "Then what?"

"I couldn't figure it," Casey went on, still scowling, "but I finally found Wade downstairs. He said that the girl was afraid Nyberg might get sore, and it was time to close up anyway, so she chased him out of the office and locked up."

Casey shook his head. Logan waited silently.

"It sounded screwy at the time, but I had other things on my mind. Anyway she wanted Wade to take her downstairs—said she was afraid the cops might think she had been in the gambling place. So Wade took her downstairs. He was out on the street when I found him—the crazy fool. He said a car with a couple tough-looking eggs came along and the dame got in and left him standing there."

"That's all, huh?" Logan asked.

"That's all that happened to me, yeah."

"All right." Logan pushed back his gray felt, pursed his lips, finally said: "It begins to add up. Now I'll tell you my side.

"You're about the only button pusher I know that's satisfied to take pictures and leave the police work for the cops. And that's important this time—because there's no pictures—no story—tonight. We're gambling that the killers might come back for the body *if they think the kill is covered.*"

Logan watched Casey drop into a chair, then continued.

"Grady was working for three or four race-tracks—the stewards or something. Remember that stink about the horse doping ring a couple years or so ago?" Casey nodded and Logan said: "The Feds were in on that. This is something new.

"Grady was about ready to crack this ring

until Dopey Donlan got knocked off a couple days ago."

"He was in it?" Casey asked.

"Yeah. And that's why he was killed. Because the big shots were afraid he'd squawk under pressure. He's a hophead and he probably would.

"But Grady had some dope on that kill. I didn't know a thing about it till last night. Grady worked under cover until he came down to Headquarters and told me what he had. He said he thought he'd be ready for the showdown today. But you know these private dicks. Afraid we'd steal his stuff. Wouldn't spill a thing till he was ready."

Logan shrugged. "Well, he was ready this afternoon. He was the guy that tipped us off to this joint. He had the man he wanted. When he pulled the raid, Judson was to pinch the killer—or the big hot, or somebody."

Logan slid off the desk and walked over to the body.

"What an idea. He's cleaned. Nothing on him but his clothes. If he hadn't come to see me last night, we'd have a hell of a time identifying him at all."

"How'd you get wise he was here," said Casey, taking out a cigarette and trying to get his mind off Wade.

"Haley found some blood in that washroom across the way. He found some—just a spot or two—on the window sill. He remembered you being there, looked around, tumbled to this office. But it was locked. I came down. We found him in the closet."

Casey stood up, began to pace the floor. "Then somebody got him into the washroom from the race-track dive, or followed him in, put the slug on him and"—he stopped, turned to glance at the wide shelf he had used—"and slid his body across here."

"Yeah," said Logan. "And you and Wade busted in. The killers might've been in this next office. The girl had to get Wade out. That's why she got him to go downstairs with her." Logan's voice got thin, thready.

"That's why we're waiting. If they aren't wise they'll come back for the body—I hope. That must've been their original plan—to leave it here till tonight. No word got out of this. Judson, Haley, the examiner and us are the only ones that know about it.

"We've got a guy that tried to get in that washroom about three or four minutes before the raid. He says the door was locked, that he watched it from then on till the raid. Nobody came out. So that must've been the time that Grady got it. Somebody got wise to him—but they couldn't know about the raid. It just happened to break right after they'd killed him and—"

Logan broke off in surprise as Casey spun towards him with a thick, throaty curse.

"The picture!" Casey's eyes got bright and glaring. "The one I took first. That's it. I caught Handy with the camera, *caught him coming out of the washroom a couple seconds after the raid.* He must've been in there when the door was locked, and—"

"Wait a minute!" rapped Logan, and grabbed Casey. "What picture—what the hell you talking about?"

Casey told him then. Described the picture he had taken in short, clipped sentences. But he could not keep still when he talked. He had to walk, keep moving, because of the thought that festered in his brain and gave him no peace.

"It's gotta be that way. And the girl knew Grady was dead—in that closet. She musta told Nyberg and—"

"We got word out to pick Moe up," Logan interrupted. "We had Handy—and let him go."

"They must've made that Henderson tramp get Wade out to her place," Casey rushed on, "so they could put the pressure on him. Maybe force him to get that place. Only—"

Casey broke off and went slack-jawed.

"Only what?" rapped Logan.

"Only there ain't any plate. Blaine—Fessendon, the ——!" Casey explained what had happened. "Those hoods won't believe the kid when he tells 'em it's smashed."

Logan jerked Casey around. "Take it easy.

You got too much imagination. That girl might be on the level. And Wade. Hell, with his kind of dumb luck—"

He broke off as Casey jerked loose and started for the door. He leaped after the big photographer, caught him again.

"Where you goin'?"

"I'm goin' to that girl's place and—"

"No you're not." Logan's chin jutted out and his brows drew down. "You're goin' down to the *Globe* with me and get that picture first. After that we'll go."

Casey put balled fists on his hips and leaned forward so that his chin was three inches from Logan's nose.

"I am, huh?" he grunted.

"It's a murder picture," said Logan. "With that and this other guy's testimony about the washroom, and the M.E.'s verdict to the time of death—"

"And Judson callin' in, sayin' we can't print it," flared Casey.

"I don't know about Judson, but—" Logan began.

"And Blaine," grated Casey. "If he'd had his way there wouldn't be any picture. But there is; I held out on him. And you oughtta be —— damn' glad I did. You can have it. But I'm not gonna waste time goin' to the office now; and you're not gonna take me down till I find that girl."

Anger flooded Logan's face and he started to speak. For just a moment he met Casey's burning stare; then he backed a step and threw up his hands.

Those black eyes of Logan's could see beneath many surfaces; and when Casey spoke like that you believed him. Logan believed him now. And strangely enough, his lips twitched in a flicker of a smile.

"If that's the way it is," he said caustically, "I guess I'd better go with you." Turning to Manahan he added: "Call Judson. Get a couple more men up here. You may get action yet. But if word of this gets out I'm gonna beat the hell out of you, personally."

He grabbed Casey, who had already shouldered his platecase, said: "The kid'll be okey as long as the kill is covered. But that girl. We can use her."

Pratt Street is a narrow offshoot of Massachusetts Avenue. The sidewalks are narrow and made to look more so because the apartments, seedy looking three and four-story brick structures, jammed close together, are all set right out to the edge of the legal building line.

Seven sixty-three, in the middle of the block, had but two characteristics to distinguish it from its adjoining neighbors and those across the street: its number, and the name *Edgemere*, painted in gilt across its single door.

The tunnel-like entryway was so dark Logan had to strike a match to inspect the name cards above the mailboxes along the right wall. "This is the place, all right," he said. "Alma Henderson—3-C."

The inner door was unlocked and the air here seemed hot and stuffy after the chilled sweep of the night outside. They climbed silently, Logan in the lead, and the soft pounding of a steam radiator on the second floor paced their steps up the last flight of stairs.

Three-C was on the right, rear. Logan knocked once, turned the knob. The door was not locked and as he opened it, Casey grunted impatiently and pushed him into the lighted room. Logan took two steps and stopped short and stiff, so that Casey ran into him and heard him breathe a curse.

Casey looked over his shoulder and saw why. Alma Henderson was on the floor by a wide-open window. A crumpled heap of arms and legs and orange dress.

Casey closed the door softly, and automatically. Logan started across the room. Casey remained where he was, glanced about and became vaguely aware of a cheaply furnished living-room that tried hard to be smart.

Then, because a new indefinable sense of fear reached at his nerve ends with icy fingers, he called: "Wade!" and was instantly aware of the hollowness of his voice, and the absurdity of the act. Wade was not here. Because if he were here—

"Shot her in the back, too," Logan said bitterly.

Casey lurched across the room. He looked down at the lifeless figure of a girl who was tall, and young, and slender—too slender, and had nice hands. Even in death her face held a youthful prettiness that makeup could not hide.

His gaze held by the discolored spot in the left side of that orange dress, Casey continued to stare at Alma Henderson. But after a moment he was not conscious of what he saw. It was a mental picture that sickened him and he put his thoughts into words.

"She saw Grady killed. She had to go, but before that they got her to spot Wade."

"That puts the weight on your picture," Logan said slowly. "It's not as good as the girl, but she can't testify."

"Suppose Wade saw her get it?" Casey spoke as though talking to himself. "You know how that sets him up."

"If he's not here, he's still alive."

"You look around then," Casey muttered. "I'll stay here."

"Sure," said Logan, moving away. "It's gonna be a pleasure to meet up with these guys. In the back. And it looks like she might've been trying to open that window." He cursed softly. "It's kinda screwy. It don't look like a planned kill."

Casey backed away a step, lifted his head and looked out the window. City lights from beyond suffused the drab sky and made a dirty blue background for the rear rooflines of houses in the next block, for spindly antennae, and a pot-bellied water-tower. A sound of movement behind him flicked his eyes away from the somber picture and he turned.

A man stood beside the doorway to the inner hall. A stocky man with a twisted grin on his broad, sallow face. He had a small automatic in his right hand.

Then Logan came into the room. He had his hands raised shoulder high, and he walked slowly. Behind him came a thin, hollow-chested, ratty-looking youth who held the muzzle of his gun stiffly against Logan's back.

"Just be nice," the stocky man said. "Both of you."

4

The tableau held motionless a second or two; then the thin man's glance slid sidewise to Casey and he jabbed with his gun, spoke to Logan.

"So it's gonna be a pleasure to meet up with us, huh?" He chuckled but his lips were sneering. "Well, the pleasure's all yours. How do you like it?"

Casey felt a thickness in his throat and he cleared it with a grunt, said: "Where's Wade?" ominously.

"Who's Wade?" asked the stocky man and cocked one eyebrow in an expression of mock concern.

"You know who," said Casey huskily and slid one foot forward across the rug.

"Hold it!" clipped the stocky man. "We know how we stand, and if you think you can crowd us, you're nuts."

Casey stopped with his left foot advanced. He was a good eight feet from Logan, ten feet or more from the stocky man. He'd never get that far, and he knew it. He had no weapon, and there was nothing he could get his hands on—except the vase on the gateleg table, and that was back by the wall.

The stocky man pocketed his gun, moved towards the telephone stand near the doorway to the inner hall, said: "Get him away from that phone. I'd better find out what we do with these punks."

The thin man marched Logan forward three steps, and as they stopped Casey watched the lieutenant. The handsome face was set now, and there was a tight, pinched smile on his lips. The smooth skin at his cheekbones was stretched like a banjo head, but it was the eyes that held Casey's gaze.

There was an intense gleam in their dark depths, and, as Casey watched, he saw one lid pull down in a slow, deliberate wink. The lid remained narrowed.

Casey knew then that Logan was going to fight for it. He weighed their chances and then forgot about that angle. He would be ready when Logan moved. He waited.

The stocky man had dialed a number and was talking in low, jerky tones.

"One of 'em's that picture-taker; the other acts like a cop. . . . Yeah. . . . Yeah. Because we couldn't get out. We didn't lock the door, and these muggs bust in with only one knock. We couldn't make the back door, so we ducked in the bedroom. Sure. But what do we do with 'em?"

He was silent for a moment after that: then he said: "Okey. Yeah."

Casey did not see the fellow hang up, because his eyes were still on Logan. But he heard the click of the receiver. And at that instant, Logan acted.

His movement was a peculiar, spinning maneuver that should have been awkward, but wasn't. The spin was catlike in its quickness, compact, and to the right.

As he moved his right fist swung down from the shoulder height, smashed on the thin man's gun wrist. The automatic spun from the fellow's grasp, skidded towards Casey. Then Logan completed the spin as his left came up and around in a looping hook.

Casey went into action as he heard the smack of fist on jawbone. One step brought him over the fallen automatic. As he stooped, a slanting, corner-of-the-eye picture presented the stocky man straightening from the telephone table, clawing at his pocket.

The automatic was cool in Casey's hot fingers. As he snatched it up he went to one knee and swung his arm over. He saw the sweep of the stocky man's gun, caught sight of the muzzle. Then the roar in his ears, the slap of recoil in his wrist told him the shot was his own.

The gun barrel that threatened him wavered, dipped. The automatic began to slide from limp fingers. Then Casey raised his eyes. The man's mouth was open, quivering. There was a bluish hole over the one eye. He put one hand on the telephone table. The hand slipped off and he went over, crashing down with the table and the instrument under him.

Logan blew out his breath and let go of the unconscious gunman he had been holding for a shield. The fellow thudded down on his haunches, toppled over on his side. Logan pulled the telephone out from under the stocky man's body and slipped the receiver into place before he spoke.

"I coulda smacked this egg before," he said grimly. "Only I thought maybe we could learn something from the phone call."

Casey had straightened up. Logan stepped over, took the gun away from him. He turned it over in his hands thoughtfully, and looked at Casey's with eyes that were speculative.

"You're handy with that thing. How'd you learn to put 'em where you want 'em?"

"In France," said Casey absently. "I was a sergeant, and a .45 was the only gun I had. I did some practicing."

He went across to the davenport and sat down, his mind relieved of the necessity of action, returning once more to Wade. Then the thin man stirred on the floor. Casey watched him until he sat up. He stepped towards the fellow, jerked him to his feet and jammed him back against the wall.

"What'd you do with Wade?"

The thin man's eyes showed fear, but his lips tightened. Casey grunted, hauled off and threw a looping right that landed flat-handed against the side of the man's head and knocked him down.

Casey pulled the fellow up again. He repeated the question and when he got no answer, repeated the dose. The fellow began to curse in a whining, yet vicious voice. Logan said: "Lay off."

Casey knocked the man down again. The side

of the face was beet-red now, but he was otherwise unmarked. "Where's Wade?" He shook the fellow. "What'd you do with him?"

This time the answer blurted in his face.

"They took him out. Buck'n me stuck around to search the place, to see if there was anything around that might—"

"Who took him out?"

The man seemed to flinch, but his teeth bared and clenched.

"Where'd they take him? Where is he now?"

"Go to hell! I won't—"

Casey lost his temper then. The right came over again, but this time the hand was a fist and it landed on the side of the jaw. The fellow stiffened and he was still stiff when he hit the floor. Casey started after him again, then Logan yanked him back, spun him around.

"I told you to lay off."

"We gotta find Wade," rasped Casey.

"Yeah. Sure. But you mark that guy all up and I'll get blamed for it, and we won't get a chance to work him over. It takes more than a wallop to make some guys talk."

"Well?" Casey's eyes got bright and glaring and his voice was thick. "What do we do, sit here and wait for something to happen?"

"You get down to the *Globe* and camp on the picture. I'll be down after it inside of ten minutes—just as soon as I can get somebody to take over here."

He picked up the telephone, barked a number. Casey, scowling, hesitant, watched Logan until the lieutenant said: "Go on get the hell out of here."

Casey's eyes slid to the girl in the orange dress, with the stain on the back. Then he turned quickly and left the room.

It was not until Casey reached the *Globe* that he remembered his camera in the rumble seat of the roadster, remembered that he had it with him all the time, and that he had taken no pictures in Alma Henderson's apartment.

Ordinarily this would have rankled; his pride in his work would have taunted him. To have a chance like that and get no pictures. This time he

did not seem to care. And it was not entirely that the affair was to be kept quiet for a while. The answer, he told himself, was that he did not give a damn whether he got exclusive pictures or not. What the hell good did it do to break your neck for pictures for a lug like Fessendon? And Blaine. In a mind that was already harassed with thoughts of Wade, there was room for further doubt and uncertainty. It wasn't like Blaine to let even the managing editor pull a stunt like breaking that plate.

To Casey, Blaine had always been the sort of fellow who would quit a job, rather than compromise with his duty or his scruples. And quitting would entail no hardship. He was the best desk man in the city—could get a job in any office.

Casey took the photograph from his desk, studied it. Then, cursing softly, he went down to the photo-engraving room, spoke to a sturdy looking man in blue jumpers and shirt sleeves.

"This is the only print Mac. I've gotta turn it over to the police, so make me a cut of it, will you, just in case this gets lost?"

Mac said sure, and Casey waited while the fellow set up the print and made his negative. As he returned the picture he said:

"What size you want it?"

"Same size, I guess."

"What'll I do with the cut?"

"Oh—" Casey hesitated, not caring particularly what was done with it. All he wanted was to have something to fall back on, some margin of safety in case something happened to the print. Blaine or no Blaine, he was going to hang on to it, until Handy and Nyberg were rounded up, until he found Wade. "Just pull a proof and keep it on hand for me," he finished.

5

Casey was slouched down behind his desk when Logan came in five minutes later. The lieutenant took the print, scanned it eagerly.

"It's gonna help," he said. "And it's about all

we got, because I couldn't find anyone in that gambling take that remembered seeing anyone come out of that washroom."

"What're you gonna do?" Casey asked morosely.

"I've got that skinny guy outside. I'm takin' him down to work over."

"Well damn you, Logan, put on the pressure! He knows where Wade is—make him talk and hurry it up!"

"I'll crack him," Logan said resentfully. "Hang on till you hear from me."

When the lieutenant left an office boy stuck his head in the doorway. "Hey, Flash. There's a guy here wants to see you."

"Tell him I'm busy," grunted Casey.

The boy went out. But he came back a few minutes later, said: "That guy won't go," apologetically. "He says Wade told him to come and see you, that Wade owes him for the trip an—"

"Jeeze!" Casey's eyes widened in sudden hope and amazement. "Get him up here!"

The taxi-driver, a beetle-browed husky, came in a moment later and immediately took the offensive.

"Somebody owes me some dough," he barked. "I want it."

"Maybe you'll get it," said Casey. "Where's Wade?"

"I drove him to Pratt Street. He told me to wait, but he acted kinda nervous about something. He started in the house, then came back and said that if he didn't come out in half an hour I was to come to you and tell you, that you'd pay."

"Nervous, huh?" wheezed Casey. "Boy, am I glad I threw a little scare into him before he left."

The driver blinked, said: "What?" and Casey snapped:

"Never mind—never mind."

"Well," the driver shrugged, "anyway, he came out about twenty minutes later—with a couple guys I'd seen go in before. But he didn't come near my cab. They got in another bus. Well, it shaped up kinda screwy to me so I fol-lowed that other car. Then I came back here. I been waiting for—"

Casey blew out his breath and a tight smile pressed his lips against his teeth. "Where'd they go?"

The driver gave an address on Alson Street, and Casey said:

"Did you see 'em go in the place?"

"No. I didn't want to stop. But I saw 'em get out of the car before I turned the next corner. Now how about my dough? It's two-forty, waitin' time and all."

Casey took out a five-dollar bill, and as he passed it to the driver his brain focused on one thought. He knew where Wade had been taken. He might have been moved since; he might not be there now. But it was a red hot lead.

The driver said: "I can't change that."

"Who said anything about change?" snapped Casey. Then, before the driver could do more than grin, the telephone rang. Casey answered it and a harsh baritone said:

"Casey?"

"Yeah."

"You got a picture of that raid this afternoon. The kid buddy of yours says it hadn't been developed when he left the office. Is it still that way?"

Casey was not long in making up his mind. Wade, knowing no one would believe him if he said the plate was smashed—that would be too much like a stall—had sold somebody on the idea that the plate had not been developed.

"Sure." Casey hunched forward, then, seeing the taxi-driver edging towards the door, he motioned him to wait. "What about it?"

"I want it, that's all."

"Who's talking?" Casey, grasping for some idea, tried to stall.

"Don't give me that," rasped the voice. "You got the plate. I want it. And if I get it, the kid'll be okey."

"What's all the fuss about?" Casey made his voice bored, indulgent. "You can have the plate if that's the way it is. We weren't gonna use it anyway. I'll bring it out myself if you say so."

"You'll do as I say if you know what's good for the kid."

"Sure," said Casey.

"Then shut up and listen. You say the plate hasn't been developed. Okey I'll believe you because if you cross me, it's your tough luck, not mine. I'll have somebody pick up that plate. Don't try to tip off the cops, don't worry about havin' this call traced because it's a pay-station. If we get the plate and things are on the level, we'll have it developed. If it's the right one, the kid'll be okey.

"We'll hold him for a few days—to make sure you don't shoot off your mouth about this—and let him go. But try anything screwy—give me the wrong plate—and do you know what'll happen to this guy Wade?"

"I can guess," said Casey bitterly.

"And with your experience you oughtta be pretty close."

Casey glanced up at the taxi-driver and the germ of an idea caught in the recesses of his brain, expanded. He pulled a pad of paper across the desk, began to write hurriedly—a note to Potter, a leg man, telling him to take Casey's roadster and go to the Alson Street address the taxi-driver had given him, and wait outside.

He could take no chances on that angle. That address had to be watched—until he could get in touch with Logan—and Potter could do that much anyway.

"What's to prevent me from callin' the cops and have 'em here waiting for your hoods when they come for the plate?" he said into the phone as he wrote.

"Just this. If my plan is okey—and I don't miss many—my men are outside your door waiting for you right now.

"I'm timin' it close. You've got thirty seconds to go out, get them—without an argument—and let one of them speak to me. I'll hold the phone for that thirty seconds. Don't hang up, because if you do; if I don't hear from my men; if they don't come back—I know I've got to run for it, and I won't be takin' the kid. Now make up your mind, and step on it. I'm startin' to count."

Casey put the receiver on the desk and jumped to his feet. The sweat was creeping out on his forehead now, because he knew the man on the telephone was speaking the truth. The idea was thought out in detail. It was wild, but that voice made it convincing.

In the interval that he stepped towards the taxi-driver, he thought of many things. He had—Wade had—from now until a fake plate was developed. Blaine—Fessendon, damn them, had ruined forever any possibility of bargaining with the real plate.

Logan had the picture. It might convict Handy. But that would be damn' small satisfaction to Wade. It was too late for Grady, the private dick; for Alma Henderson. But Wade—

Casey grabbed the driver's arm, spoke in a hoarse whisper. "Take this note out to the city room. Find Potter. I don't know where he is, but find him. Give him this note. Then go out and wait for me. I'm gonna need you."

He gave the driver a shove, waited until he disappeared down the corridor; then he walked quickly along the same path, stepped into the noisy, light-flooded city room.

Two men stepped close to him. One was tall, foppishly dressed, handsome in a thin, swarthy way. He had a mustache and he smiled as he spoke, and showed large, even teeth.

"You got a phone call for us?"

Casey glanced at the other man, saw that he was a long-armed, puffy-eared fellow with a bullet head and no neck; then he said:

"Yeah. Step on it, will you?"

"After you," the swarthy man said.

Casey led the way. The men had apparently been warned to try no rough tactics. That alone showed how surely the layout had been planned. If they carried guns, they did not show them.

They hurried down the corridor to the deserted anteroom, and the idea in Casey's head, in full bloom now, put a grim smile on his lips, hope in his heart. Potter could go to Alson Street. Wade had been taken there from the Henderson woman's place; he was not necessarily there now. But if Potter covered that address, if he, Casey, could follow these hoods. . . .

He grunted softly. He had pulled a stunt like that once, gone through a window to an adjoining two-story roof. And that taxi guy should be outside. He'd had some such half-baked idea when he told him to wait. The hoods would take the plate to the boss. If they went to Alson Street, he'd be sure; if not, he'd at least have two chances—and this time he could overlook neither.

The swarthy man said: "Watch him Russo," and bent down to lift the receiver.

"Hello. Yeah—this is Jaeger. Yeah, looks okey to me. Sure, I know what to do."

He hung up, smiled at Casey, and there was something hard, merciless in the smile.

"Let's have the plate."

Casey went to his platecase, took out a plate-holder which held one unexposed plate.

Jaeger took it, slipped it into his pocket. "Okey. I like the way you're behavin'. See if you can keep it up." He turned to Russo. "Get goin'. Out in the hall and see that she's clear."

Russo went out, and Jaeger said, "I'll lock the door from the outside. Don't make too much noise—too soon." He stepped to the telephone and a vicious yank ripped the cord from the box at the baseboard. He did the same with the instrument across the room. Then he took the key from the door and went out.

Casey waited until the key clicked in the lock. Then he yanked open the drawer of his desk. Reaching far back, he drew out his .38 automatic, slipped it into his pocket. Then he crossed the anteroom to a green-shaded window and threw it open.

He'd hoped they'd forget the telephones. Then he could have called Logan, tipped him off. Well, Logan could get in on it later. Right now, and for the first time, he had something he could sink his teeth into, something tangible to work on. He had played his hand the only way he knew how, and the time left him depended on how soon that plate was developed. He did not think any more about Wade, because nothing

but action could save him now, and Casey knew it.

He went through the window, and the staggered line of the downtown city looked as if it had been cut out of stiff black cloth and hung there against the muddy blue of the sullen sky.

Casey clung to the window sill a moment with his fingertips, to steady himself, let go. He hit the gravel roof one story below, hit on his heels and went over backward. The fall shook him, but that was all, and he rolled to his knees, ran towards the fire-escape at the rear of the building.

Less than a minute later he was back on the street, huddled in the darkened doorway of a music shop, watching the *Globe* entrance. Jaeger came out first with Russo at his heels. They crossed the street to a small sedan.

Casey sidled down along the building front. He had already located his taxi. And as soon as the sedan pulled out from the curb, he was on the running-board, pounding the dozing driver, who shook himself, scowled at Casey, said:

"What the hell's the—"

"Follow that sedan," barked Casey, swinging open the rear door.

"Oh," growled the driver. "It's you, huh?" He stepped on the starter, craned his neck to get a look at the sedan as he shifted into low. "What's all this screwy followin' about?"

"About five bucks for you." Then, crisply, "Find Potter?"

The cab roared into the street and the driver said: "Yeah," and cramped the wheel for a U turn. The clock above Park Street said 11:55. There was enough traffic to screen them, but not enough to confuse their quarry with any other car.

The sedan had turned right at Boylston; the lights changed as the cab approached them, but they got a green arrow and made the turn. The theater front on the left was dark; beyond the high spiked fence on the right, the Common looked even darker. Casey leaned forward, knocked on the glass and the driver slid back the partition.

"Not too close, but if they give you the slip—"

"Give who the slip?" The driver snorted contemptuously. "Don't be crazy."

Casey grunted, took the gun out of his pocket and inspected the clip. He slipped off the safety, fondled the cold bulk of the automatic, let it rest gently in his palm. When he looked out the window again the railroad yards were slipping by on the left, and the sedan was a block and a half ahead.

They crossed the avenue, and Casey's brain fought with questions and answers. When he looked up again it was because the cab had started to slow. He saw then that the sedan was slanting in towards the curb, still a block and a half ahead. Then he saw his roadster—at least he thought it was a roadster. Yeah. They were on Alson Street.

The cab slowed still more and Casey said: "Keep going, you mugg. Right on by 'em! Don't slow down!"

He slouched on the seat as soon as he saw the two men leave the sedan and cross the sidewalk. When the cab passed the apartment house he called to the driver.

"Take another street, turn right, go around the block." He slid up on the seat, got out at the corner beyond the sedan a minute or so later. He gave the driver the promised five dollars, added: "I'll remember you. You got what it takes."

Casey spun about before the driver could thank him. As he turned into Alson Street he moved warily, and his eyes sought the shadowed niches and areaways.

Alson Street was not much different from Pratt Street. It was a little wider, and on one side, the opposite side from Casey and the parked sedan, there were some remodeled brownstone fronts. The apartments on the near side of the street were a little taller, a little more flossy and pretentious than that of Alma Henderson's; but the reputations were about the same.

The roadster was parked nearly to the next corner, but Potter stepped from the shadows directly across the street from the sedan. Casey crossed to him and pulled him back into the areaway which had concealed him.

Potter said: "What's up?" He was a stringy, long-necked fellow who wore glasses and a perpetually tired look. "I parked the roadster down the street a ways, because I wasn't sure just what you wanted me here for."

"It's just as well," said Casey and took out the automatic.

"Hey!" wheezed Potter.

"Wade's in that apartment," Casey muttered, and went on with a brief story of what had happened. "I got you to help because I wanted to check on this address, and because no matter what happens, there's gonna be a sweet story for some guy."

"But why don't you get Logan—"

"That's your job," clipped Casey. "For all I know they might try to develop that plate inside—might be developing it now. So find a phone. There's a drug-store two blocks down. Tell Logan the set-up. He oughtta get out here pretty damn' fast."

"But what—" stammered Potter. "You ain't goin' up there and try to shoot it out with those hoods alone?"

"I hope not," Casey said grimly. "I'm gonna try and stall, throw a bluff—till Logan gets here. He'll know how to handle it; only if the shooting starts, I'm not gonna be empty handed."

Casey had left the *Globe* without his topcoat. Now he took the .38, reached around and stuck it down inside his pants, right in the small of his back. The pressure of his belt held the gun securely; the coat, draped from the shoulders, showed no suspicious bulge. He started across the street.

6

The foyer of the apartment house was U shaped and the single, self-operated elevator door was directly opposite the entrance. Casey stopped in front of it, realizing that he did not know where Jaeger and Russo had gone.

He muttered, "No one's been in or out of here since they came. They mustta left the elevator where they got off," and started up the stairs.

There was no elevator at the second floor; none at the third. He found it waiting on the fourth. He thought: "It's after twelve. I'll try every place with a light in it."

Eight doors opened from the wide, deserted hall. Casey started at the front, dropping to his knees at each door and peering at the bottom crack. The first three were dark. At the fourth—the second door on the right—a hairline of yellow met his gaze.

Casey put his ear close to the keyhole. A subdued murmur of voices reached him, unexcited. He straightened a little, drew a long, silent breath, glanced, unconsciously, back over his shoulder, then bent to the keyhole again.

He felt that he could wait a few minutes, give Logan that much time. Not too long, for if the plate could not be developed here, they wouldn't waste much time in taking it where it could be, and Casey had to stall them here if he was to count on Logan's help. The slow minutes dragged. Casey tried to estimate their number; tried once to reach his watch, but gave it up in preference to keeping his ear glued to the keyhole. Finally he straightened, took a deep breath and knocked.

After a moment a voice said: "Who is it?"

Casey grunted and his lips pressed into a weird, tight smile. The palms of his hands were damp, but he wiped them on the sides of his coat.

He said: "Santy Claus."

The knob turned slowly, but the door opened in a jerk that flung it wide. Jaeger and Russo stood to one side, their automatics leveled at Casey's stomach. Beyond, Moe Nyberg stood behind Wade, held him by the coat collar and pressed a gun in his back. Over by the windows stood Mike Handy.

Casey felt no fear now. No surprise. Rather a tense grim satisfaction gripped his brain. But after that first glimpse of the occupants of that room, he went into his act. Surprise flooded his face, choked his voice.

"Hey," he wheezed. "What the hell?"

"Get in here!" clipped Jaeger.

Casey stepped across the threshold and Russo shut the door.

"How'd you get here?" jerked Nyberg.

"He followed us," said Jaeger. "He must've—"

"Followed you?" croaked Casey, licking his lips. "No. Honest to gawd. I didn't know—"

"It's a plant!" growled Handy, starting forward. "Look in the hall." He turned and looked out the windows at the street below.

Russo opened the door, peered out, said: "Naw. It's clear."

Handy said: "Clear outside too," and relaxed.

Nyberg purred: "You'd better spill it, Flash. And you'd better make it good. How did you find us?"

Casey was stuck here, and he knew it. To tell the truth about either Wade's taxi-driver, or his following the two gunmen would probably scare Handy into moving them out of the apartment—before Logan could get there.

So he let his imagination go, and made up his story as he went along. How logical it sounded did not particularly bother him; he wanted to make it interesting—and take plenty of time.

"A taxi guy told me," he said nervously. "Wade said he took the Henderson woman downstairs after the raid, and a couple tough looking muggs picked her up. Well, he was stuck on the girl; see? And he thought something might be up. But he couldn't run out on me, so he got a taxi-driver to follow this other car and find out where these two guys went.

"When the cabby came back to the office, Wade was out. He got worried about his pay so he looked me up. I took care of the fare and he gave me this address—just before you two came to the *Globe*." He nodded at Russo and Jaeger. "Maybe you saw him go out and—"

"Go on!" pressed Nyberg ominously.

"Well," Casey shrugged. "I wasn't sure of the set-up so I thought I'd do some checking."

"Oh," grunted Nyberg. He looked relieved and loosed his hold on Wade.

Casey, apparently still bewildered, glanced around. Jaeger brushed his mustache with an index finger and smiled again. Nyberg pushed Wade down on the divan. He was a sturdily built fellow, Nyberg. Bald, greasy-looking, with a heavy red nose and a thick-lipped mouth. His dress was slovenly, his fingernails dirty. Casey met his shrewd stare for a moment, then glanced at Handy.

Mike Handy looked worried. There was a film of moisture on his fatty face, and his eyes, which were black and seemed all iris, shifted nervously from the door to the windows beside him. The fingers of his other hand, which hung loosely at his side, moved spasmodically.

Wade said: "You were wrong about her, Flash."

Casey did not answer, or look at Wade. He gave no sign that he had heard, because he did not want to let on what he knew—not yet.

Then Handy said: "Let's get out of here. I don't like it. If we get caught in here—" He moved to a chair and picked up his black topcoat.

Nyberg nodded and stepped towards Wade. And Casey felt his nerves grow taut. They couldn't leave. Logan would never find them. He decided to tell what he knew—all of it. Gambling that his revelations would hold attention, postpone the present plan.

"How was I wrong about her?" he growled, and turned on Wade. "She got you to her place so these guys could take you, didn't she? She put you on the spot and—"

"So—" breathed Nyberg, "this surprise business was an act? You know about that, huh?"

"Sure," said Casey and made his voice confident, aggressive. "I oughtta. I was there when we trapped your other two hoods—in fact, I shot the stocky guy right over the eye. He's in the morgue now."

"She didn't spot me," Wade said, and Handy's gasp was a background for his words.

Casey felt the sudden tenseness in the room, but he watched the young photographer. Wade was sitting on the divan with his elbows on his knees and his head down. His voice was listless; so was his attitude. He acted as though he did not care what happened, and Casey knew, in such condition, he could get little help from Wade in a showdown.

"She was on the level," Wade went on. "You know why she chased me out of the office this afternoon? Because these guys—all but Handy—were in the next room. She was scared—for me, and for herself. She got me out and hoped to run for it.

"But these two guys"—he nodded at Jaeger and Russo—"ran down the back way and picked her up. She told 'em I didn't know a thing. Then, when she called me at the *Globe*"—Wade hesitated, continued wearily—"that was okey. Only—"

"To hell with all this crap," barked Nyberg. "What else do you know, smart guy?"

"Plenty," said Casey and grinned deliberately. "I know about Dopey Donlan, and the private dick, and the dope ring you were promoting at the tracks, and how you hooked that up with that track gambling outfit that got raided."

"You spoke your piece, smart guy," Nyberg said and his thick lips twisted in a mirthless smile, "and now you're in it up to your neck. You're gonna find out just how it feels."

Handy put on his coat. "Let's get out of here. There's something screwy about this. I don't like it."

The sweat was on his forehead again and his lip trembled. "You, Russo, put the gun on the kid. Nyberg, Jaeger, watch Casey. Better search him first." He waited while Jaeger patted Casey's pockets, and Casey held his breath and stuck out his stomach, stuck it out and leaned so that his back arched slightly and the unbuttoned coat hung out and away from the gun.

"We'll take 'em out," Handy went on. "If this plate is okey, I'm set."

"You're set?" sneered Nyberg. "How about me—the rest of us."

"Well," flared Handy. "I was in that raid this afternoon. Lucky they let me go after I paid the fine. If anybody'd seen me come out of that washroom—"

"Nerts!" said Nyberg. "I'm gettin' sick of your angles. Why all the panic? Why don't we knock these guys off right here and now?"

"No—no," said Handy, and his voice was shrill. "Take them out. I pay you plenty. I want a chance to get this plate developed, get an alibi."

"You're with us," snapped Nyberg contemptuously, "and here's once you stay with us. I'm beginnin' to hate guys like you—all mouth and no guts." He stepped to Wade, yanked him to his feet. "Come on, Kid."

Casey waited there by the door. He was glad now that he had put on the bluff. It had worked longer than he expected. But was it long enough? He couldn't tell. It was hard to judge time in this kind of a spot. And you could say things awfully quick. How much time had he killed? Five—six minutes. More, he hoped.

Russo had stepped over behind Wade. Handy opened the door and looked into the hall. Nyberg and Jaeger came alongside of Casey and he felt the guns in his side.

Casey made one more attempt to stall. "Say." He let the fear come into his voice. "What're you gonna do. You can't—"

"Who can't," sneered Nyberg. "You know what we're gonna do—so quit stallin'. You can take it, can't you? Or is all these things I've heard about you just a lot of hot air."

He dug his gun into Casey's ribs, and they went out into the hall. Handy, and Wade and the bull-necked Russo; then Casey and Nyberg and the grimly smiling Jaeger.

7

The elevator was still waiting in the hall. On the silent downward trip, Casey tried to map out some logical course of action. Logan had not arrived. Otherwise he would have been waiting in the hall.

The elevator door slid open and they started across the narrow, dimly lighted foyer. Casey

felt the reassuring pressure of his gun in his back. He thought he could get to it. But there were three other guns—and there was Wade.

The kid did not know about Casey's gun. He would have no tip-off to a plan, even if Casey had one. And if the heat went on—

Handy paused after they went through the inner doors. There, in the imitation marble entryway, he said:

"It's too risky—six of us piling in that little sedan. Besides, we've used it twice today—we might get picked up. We'll just walk down the street easy-like. I've got a car in a garage around the corner."

He hesitated and the dim light from the foyer, sifting through the glass doors, made his fatty face jaundiced and shiny with moisture. He made one more plea.

"I'll make it a grand more apiece if you'll let me—"

This time it was Jaeger who voiced his contemptuous opinion. "I'll string with Nyberg. It'll be worth my grand to see you play ball."

Handy opened the outer door without answering. Nyberg said: "Keep your hands down and walk nice, guys."

Handy kept well in the lead, but the rest of them fanned out on the wide sidewalk. Casey cast a quick glance up and down the street and a blanket of dejection settled down upon him. His roadster was parked in the same spot, but the street was deserted. Logan had not—

Then he saw Potter.

At first there was but a blacker blotch in the shadows of that entryway across the street. Then the blotch took shape. It was Potter all right, his stringy height identified him. He was on the sidewalk now, and he was starting across the street.

Casey sucked in his breath and held it. His glance slid sidewise. Wade was about an arm's length away, on his left, the curb side; beside, and slightly behind, walked Russo. Holding the same position—beside and a pace behind— Nyberg and Jaeger flanked Casey.

Casey had wanted to wait as long as he could

in the hope that Logan might come. And if he did not come, that gun was the last resort.

He and Wade? Well, they were in it: they had to take a chance, accept the risk. But Potter, the crazy fool: it was no affair of his. And he was married and—

"Moe!" Jaeger's voice was soft, jerky. "There's a guy comin' across the street."

"Let him come," said Nyberg hoarsely. "If he horns in we might just as well shoot the works and—"

Then Potter, now halfway across the street, said: "Hey!"

It was absurd, that word. And Potter's act, although he may not have known it, was suicidal. Casey inwardly cursed it as such. Yet that soft call undoubtedly gave him a second to get set, because every man but himself glanced at Potter as he spoke.

Casey leaned to the left and made a vicious backhand swipe with the flat of his hand. He caught Wade alongside the face and the force of the blow knocked him off his feet, so that he fell over against Russo, carrying him to his knees. At the same instant, Casey's right hand reached for the gun in his back.

He forgot Wade as he spun about and his fingers found the butt of the automatic, but he was aware that somebody was fighting in the gutter. Then he had the gun free, up, and squeezed the trigger, twice, rapidly.

Nyberg's body jerked. Beside him and two feet away a flash of orange exploded and Casey felt something slice between his ribs and his left arm.

The slug, the flash of flame, came from Jaeger's gun. And as he fired, the fellow stepped behind Nyberg's sagging body, intent on using it as a shield.

Casey's finger already tensed for a third shot when he saw what he faced. He had but little time to act, and he did as impulse commanded. He ducked his head and half dived forward so that his shoulder crashed into Nyberg's stomach.

They went down, all three of them. And

Jaeger was underneath. He was cursing now and so was Casey, although he did not know it. For a moment or so the three men were a tangle of arms and legs, and as they scrambled there, Casey thought he heard the shrill scream of a siren.

Then Jaeger rolled clear, rolled clear and came to his knees. Casey's right hand was partly pinioned by the now limp weight of Nyberg's body. He yanked at the wrist, felt the gun come free. But his eyes had never left Jaeger, and he knew he was too late.

The fellow's teeth flashed in some reflected ray of the street light, and the gun leveled as Casey tried to swing up his hand in time. A hundredth part of a second maybe; no longer than that. But Casey looked down the muzzle of that gun and his muscles tensed for the shock.

Somebody said: "You ——!"

The crash of the gun wiped out the phrase, pounded at Casey's right ear, half deafened him. And he could not understand it because he had seen no flash from that gun muzzle.

A car roared past. Jaeger, still on his knees, began to tip over, half on his face, half on his side. When his shoulders hit the sidewalk Casey looked around. Potter was standing three feet away. His right hand was still stiffly extended— and there was a gun in it.

Casey blew out his pent-up breath and spun about on his knees. Handy was fifty yards away, racing madly for the corner, his coat-tails flying. A touring car swung into the curb beside him.

There was a shouted command, another. Handy raced on, swerving towards an entryway. The car kept pace. Then flame streaked through the night and two sharp cracks slapped down the street, reverberating from the brick walls. Handy took three more steps at breakneck speed. He stumbled; he slid forward on his face like Rabbit Maranville stealing home.

8

Captain Judson put his fists on his hips and said: "You get in the damnedest messes."

"It took you long enough to get here," Casey said grimly.

Logan was looking down at Nyberg. Wade sat on the curb. Potter still held the gun. He lifted his arm, stared at the automatic, dropped the arm again. He kept doing it, as though he could not believe he had used it. And all the time he was saying: "Jeeze—jeeze," in thick, hushed tones.

There were two police cars in the street now, and overhead windows were up, and heads and shoulders in whitish nightclothes hung on the sills.

Logan said: "Looks like the only guy left is Russo." He stared at the bullet-headed fellow who stood flanked by two plain-clothesmen. "How did we miss him?"

Casey had told what had taken place in the apartment, finished with: "Don't ask me. I only knocked Wade into him. After that—"

"You damn' near knocked me out," Wade said. "I thought he was gonna let me have it. He could have easy enough. But I guess Potter—" he broke off.

Potter coughed, spoke apologetically. "They were both on the ground, but I saw this guy start to swing his gun around, so I kicked him in the head and took it away from him." He hesitated, looked at Casey. "Then when I saw how you were fixed—well, I had to let him have it."

"You had to do it, huh?" Casey said, and grinned wryly. "I guess it's a break for me you felt that way about it."

"I never shot anyone before," Potter said. "I was afraid I'd miss. I got as close as I could."

Logan said: "You newspaper guys do pretty well for amateurs."

Casey looked down at Nyberg, cursed once, said: "I'm glad I got that ——anyway."

An ambulance pulled into the curb. Then Casey realized that he was shivering, that he had no coat. And his side was smarting; he thought his undershirt was wet. He told Logan about it and one of the internes started to take him into the apartment house foyer.

Casey turned to Wade. "Come on, snap into it. My camera's down in my roadster. Get busy."

Judson watched the interne strap up Casey's side. The wound was superficial, grazing the ribs and cutting a shallow, two-inch furrow in the flesh.

Casey glanced up at Judson and let his voice get disgusted. "What a help you turned out to be."

Judson scowled. "What's the matter with you?"

"Was that picture I got this afternoon a break for you?"

"Sure it was a break. That tipped the business. We'd got Handy eventually—on that alone."

"Yeah," fumed Casey. "But if you'd had your way there wouldn't been any picture. I just happened to hold out that print." He snorted disdainfully. "Callin' up the office and tellin' 'em we can't print it."

"Who called up?"

"You did."

Judson's eyes widened, then narrowed. His voice had a humorous undertone.

"Maybe a scratch on the ribs makes you slug-nutty or something. You talk that way. Hell"—he grunted, pulled at his nose—"Whenever you steal a picture on me I don't want printed I won't call the office. I'll take it away from you myself—like Haley did with your second one."

Casey scowled for a moment; then his eyes got sultry and he said: "Oh," softly.

Wade took six pictures. Casey had the three plateholders in his pocket when they went into the *Globe* city room. Blaine was at the desk.

Casey who had been talking to Wade all the way in, pulled him to a stop before they crossed the room. "Listen, Kid. Shake it off. I know how you feel. And if it helps any, you were right, and I was wrong, like most wise guys are.

"She wasn't a tramp—she just ran with tramps. She had two strikes on her, just working for a guy like Nyberg. That's not your fault."

"But if I could have helped her or—"

"Sure, I know." Casey pulled Wade across the room. "We did the best we could. After all, she sorta put you on the spot by even callin' you to her place. But she was level with you and she did what she could with what she had to do with."

"I guess you're right," Wade said and seemed to shrug off some of his dejection. "Only I sorta liked her."

Blaine leaned back in his chair and his eyes were cold and unsmiling.

Casey said: "Did Potter phone in the story?"

"Yes."

"Well, I got a story you're gonna hear and—"

"And I've got one for you," snapped Blaine. "You're fired!"

Casey's jaw dropped, and Wade stiffened and froze there.

"Fired?" Casey swallowed, and amazement gave ground slowly before his anger.

He choked on a curse and had a hard time getting his words out. Not because he was fired. That had happened before. What threw him off stride was that Blaine had stolen his thunder, had taken the offensive right out of his hands.

"All right," he clipped. "I'm fired. One of your ideas huh?"

"It was Fessendon's idea," said Blaine. He lifted some copy paper from a halftone cut. Beside the metal plate was a proof. The proof was of the picture Casey had given Logan. "I think this cut came up from the engraving room by mistake, but Fessendon saw the proof. You held out on him, huh?"

"And a damn' good thing I did," flung out Casey. He put both hands on the desk top and leaned on them. He held that position while he told Blaine the whole story about that picture, what it meant to the police, how it had been used to bargain with and the reason he had had a halftone made.

There was a peculiar gleam in Blaine's eyes now. Casey saw it, but he could not fathom it. It was hard, intent, yet there seemed to be some-

thing in the background. It couldn't be humor—a grim sort of humor—

Casey flung aside the thought, and with this mental effort some of his rage evaporated. That first hot burst at Blaine's announcement came from impulsive reaction; but as the true character of the situation, as the underlying significance of the city editor's attitude dawned upon him, a new kind of anger fastened itself upon him. Anger that was logical and mixed with weariness, disillusionment, resentment.

This feeling was strange to Casey, strange but not hard to understand. He had been going at top speed since four-thirty that afternoon. The past five hours had been crammed with action, and death, and a nerve-wracking tension that centered around the safety of Tom Wade.

Perhaps it was this strain that brought about that hollow feeling of discouragement; it might have been that he was tired, that his head ached, or that the wound in his side had left him weakened. More probably it was because Blaine had let him down. Blaine, the sharp-tongued, unsympathetic driver—who always backed up his men.

"All right," Casey said finally. "I'll be glad to go." His voice was husky, a bit scornful now, his smoldering anger and resentment tinging each word.

"I only stuck here because you had something on the ball, and because I always thought you were on the level. I had you figured for the one newspaperman in town who would print the news as he saw it and not let some fat-headed guy with a lot of money call you.

"But if Fessendon's got you, if you can't take it, if you're gonna do what he says and like it"—Casey breathed deeply, tightened his lips—"why, that's okey with me. I knew damn' well I had the right dope when you pulled that Judson gag. But I never thought you were a liar."

"Who's a liar? What about Judson?" said Blaine, and his voice got thin.

"Just like I said. He didn't call here and tell you or Fessendon to kill that picture. I asked him."

"He didn't—" Blaine got up slowly, menacingly and leaned across the desk.

"It was that skirt-crazy Lee Fessendon that—"

Blaine spun about and started through the doorway behind his desk. Casey followed him, still talking. And Wade, goggle-eyed and with nothing else to do, tagged behind. Blaine moved to Fessendon's office with stiff-kneed strides, threw open the door.

Fessendon looked up from his desk, started to smile. The smile faded when Blaine spoke.

"You said Judson told you we had to kill Casey's picture."

"He—he did," said Fessendon, avoiding Blaine's stare.

"Casey says Judson said no such thing."

"Well," Fessendon stood up and his pink face got red and scowling. "Are you going to take his word against mine?"

"Any time," rapped Blaine, "and anywhere. I told you when I stayed on here I'd run this sheet my way or not at all. You framed up the Judson gag because neither you—nor your kid brother had guts enough to stand up and—"

"You can't talk that way to me," stormed Fessendon.

"You hear me, don't you?"

Fessendon took a menacing step forward. "I'm running this paper. Suppose Lee did call me up and tell me about that picture? I don't take orders from you, Blaine, and—"

"You said it." Blaine's lip curled. "Maybe you take them from that jelly-kneed brother who was afraid to face a bawling out from his wife."

"You're fired," shouted Fessendon.

"That makes two of us," said Blaine.

"Three," piped up Wade.

"And I have one thing more to toss in the pot," Blaine rapped. "Plenty of fellows think I'm a slave driver; I don't doubt they hate my guts. But I've had one sort of a reputation. I played the game and I played it square. Casey's the first man that ever said I wasn't on the level: the first guy that ever called me a liar—and I can't blame him.

"I hate a liar, too, Fessendon. I hate a double-crosser. And that's what you are, a lousy, lying, double-crossing——!"

Fessendon hit Blaine then. Hit him back of the ear and Blaine went down. Casey cursed and stepped forward, but Blaine sat up, said: "You stay out of this."

He got to his feet and deliberately repeated his opinion. Fessendon, his face a livid mask, swung his right. This time Blaine was ready. He said: "I thought so," as he moved inside that right and jabbed his left to Fessendon's stomach.

Fessendon gasped and he seemed to gag as he crumpled. Then Blaine crossed his right. It landed flush and it straightened Fessendon before it dropped him.

Blaine backed away, turned at the door. Casey and Wade followed him out. Blaine went to his desk, opened the bottom drawer, took out a brief case and systematically packed it with his personal belongings. He closed all the drawers, stepped over to the clothes-tree and got his hat and coat. As he stepped past the grinning Casey and the open-mouthed Wade, he turned, spoke irritably:

"Well, come on, you big ox. Don't stand their gawking."

In the hall Casey said: "Did Fessendon tell you to fire me?"

"Sure," said Blaine, punching the elevator button. "If I hadn't he would have."

"But you knew I had some redhot plates of that—"

"I didn't *know* you had 'em," said Blaine. But you generally pull something out of the hat, and I wanted to fire you before you showed them to me. Then you could take them down the street to the *Express* or *Mirror*—not that you need anything to bargain with."

Blaine muttered a soft curse. "You got a dirty deal from Fessendon, but you ought to be glad you're out. I was all washed up with him anyway, after he broke that plate—as if we were a bunch of blackmailers. But he just came in his office about ten minutes ago, and I was going to be nice about it and give him two weeks' notice."

Casey's broad face was cracked in a wide grin that would not come off. He was no longer tired. It was good to be free of Fessendon, to know that Blaine was level, that Wade was okey. He released a sigh of satisfaction and relief, said:

"Well, where we goin' now?"

"I'm gonna call up Gilman at the *Express* and see if he wants a city editor and a couple of cheap cameras. But first"—the elevator door opened and Blaine stepped in—"we'll stop at Steve's and have a couple to celebrate on."

Casey said: "You think of things."

Wade grunted sardonically, said: "The idea is okey so long as I don't get stuck with short beers."

The Price of a Dime
Norbert Davis

WHEN RAYMOND CHANDLER, not a young man, decided to try to write for the pulps, one of the stories that most impressed him was "Red Goose" by Norbert Davis. Years later, he reread it and wrote, in a letter, that it was not as good as he remembered it, but still very good, and that he had never forgotten it.

Davis (1909–1949) was one of the few writers who attempted to blend fast-moving violence and whimsy in his stories, the humor being an element that so displeased the great *Black Mask* editor, Joseph T. Shaw, that he published only five stories by the prolific author.

With his fiction selling easily to most of the major pulps, Davis graduated with a law degree from Stanford but never bothered to take the bar exam. His work also made it onto the pages of the higher-paying "slick" magazines (so-called because of their shiny paper) like *The Saturday Evening Post*, and into book form. Two of his novels, both featuring Doan (a private eye whose first name is never mentioned) and Carstairs (a gigantic Great Dane who is his constant companion), *The Mouse In the Mountain* (1943) and *Sally's In the Alley* (1943), are hilarious adventures that nonetheless have their share of violence, mostly presented as harmless fun.

"The Price of a Dime" is the second story about Ben Shaley and was initially published in *Black Mask* in April 1934.

The Price of a Dime
Norbert Davis

*It was an old trick
but this time it
started fireworks*

HALEY WAS SITTING behind the big desk in his private office. He had his hat on, pushed down over his forehead, so that the wide brim shaded his hard, narrowed eyes, his thin, straight nose. He had an opened penknife in his hand, and he was stabbing the soft wood of a drawer of the desk in an irritated way.

There was a sudden shrill scream from the outer office.

Shaley started. He scowled at the door.

In the outer office a chair tipped over with a crash. There was another scream, louder than the first one.

Shaley tossed his penknife on the desk and got up.

"She'll drive me crazy one of these days," he muttered, heading for the door in long-legged strides.

He banged the door open, looked through into the outer office.

Sadie, his secretary, was scuffling with a fattish blonde woman. Sadie had the woman by the shoulders, trying to push her through the door into the corridor. The blonde woman's face was puffy, tear-stained. She had a desperately hopeless expression. She was the one who was doing the screaming.

Sadie had her sleek, dark head down, pushing determinedly, but the blonde woman's weight was too much for her.

Shaley said: "Well?" in an explosively angry voice.

Both women turned on him. Sadie got started first.

"You told me you didn't want to see anybody this morning, and she wanted to see you, and I told her you couldn't see her, and she wouldn't go away, and so I tried to put her out, and she started to scream." Sadie said this all in one breath.

The blonde woman sniffed a little. "I've got to see you. I've got to see you, Mr. Shaley. It's about Bennie. I've got to see you."

"All right, all right," Shaley said helplessly. "All *right!* Come on in here."

"But you told me—" Sadie protested.

"Will you kindly sit down and get to work?" Shaley asked in an elaborately courteous voice.

Sadie blinked. "Yes, Mr. Shaley," she said meekly.

Shaley jerked his head at the blonde woman. "Come in." He shut the door of the private office again, pointed to a chair. "Sit down." He walked around his desk, sat down in his chair, and dropped his hat on the floor beside him. He frowned at the blonde woman. "Now what is it?"

She was dabbing at her puffy eyes with a handkerchief that was a moist, wadded ball. "I'm sorry I screamed and acted that way, Mr. Shaley, but I had to see you. Bennie told me to see you, and he's in bad trouble, and so I *had* to see you."

"Who's Bennie?"

The blonde woman looked surprised. "He's my brother."

"That makes it all clear," said Shaley. "Does he have a last name?"

"Oh, sure. Bennie Petersen." The blonde woman looked like she was going to start to cry again. "He told me you knew him. He told me you'd help him. He's a bellboy at the *Grover Hotel.*"

"Oh," said Shaley understandingly. "Bennie Peterson, huh? That little chiseler—" He coughed. "That is to say, yes. I remember him. What's he done now?"

"The blonde woman sniffed. "It wasn't his fault, Mr. Shaley."

"No," said Shaley. "Of course not. It never is his fault. What did he do?"

"He just lost a dime, Mr. Shaley. And now Mr. Van Bilbo is going to have him arrested."

Shaley sat up straight with a jerk. "Van Bilbo, the movie director?"

She nodded. "Yes."

"Van Bilbo is going to have Bennie arrested because Bennie lost a dime?"

"Yes."

"Hmm," Shaley said, scowling. "Now let's get this straight. Start at the beginning and tell me just what happened—or what Bennie told you happened."

"Well, Bennie took some ginger ale up to a party on the seventh floor of the hotel. This party tipped him a dime. Bennie was coming back down the hall to the elevator. He had the dime in his hand, and he was flipping it up in the air like George Raft does in the movies. But Bennie dropped the dime on the floor. He was just leaning over to pick it up when Mr. Van Bilbo came out of one of the rooms and saw him, and now he's going to have Bennie arrested."

Shaley leaned back in his chair. "So," he said quietly. "The old dropped dime gag. Bennie dropped a dime in front of a keyhole, and he was looking through the keyhole for the dime, when Van Bilbo caught him at it, huh?"

She shook her head. "Oh, no! Bennie wouldn't look through a keyhole. He wouldn't do a thing like that, Mr. Shaley. Bennie's a good boy. Our folks died when we were young, and I raised him, and I know."

Shaley studied her calculatingly. She really believed what she was saying. She really believed that Bennie was a good boy.

"All right," Shaley said gently, smiling at her. "Forget what I said. Of course Bennie wouldn't peek through a keyhole. What did he tell you to say to me?"

"He told me to tell you to go to Mr. Van Bilbo and tell him that it was all right. That Bennie was Mr. Van Bilbo's friend, and that they could get together on this matter and fix it all up. Bennie said you'd understand."

Shaley nodded slowly. "Oh, yes," he said meaningly. "I understand all right. Where is Bennie now?"

"He's hiding so the police won't find him. He told me not to tell anybody where he was."

Shaley smiled at her. "I can't help him unless I know where he is."

"Well . . ." Her voice broke a little. "You *are* his friend, aren't you, Mr. Shaley? You *will* help him, won't you? Just this time, Mr. Shaley, please. He promised me he'd never get into trouble again." She stared at him anxiously.

"I'll help him," Shaley said.

She sighed, relieved. "He's hiding in a boarding-house. I don't know the street address, but you can easily find it. It's a big white house with a hedge around it, and it's right in back of the Imperial Theater in Hollywood. He's going by the name of Bennie Smith."

"I'll find him," said Shaley. "Where can I get hold of you?"

"I work in *Zeke's Tamale Shop*. On Cahuenga, north of Sunset."

"I know the place," said Shaley, standing up. He went over and opened the door. "Don't worry about it any more. I'll fix things up for you."

She fumbled with the worn bag she was carrying. "I drew my money out of the bank this morning, Mr. Shaley. I can pay you. I'll pay you right now."

"Forget it," Shaley said, uncomfortably. "I'll send you a bill. And don't give Bennie any of that money. I'll take care of him."

He stood in the doorway and watched her go through the outer office and out the door into the corridor.

Sadie looked over one slim shoulder at him, with a slight hurt expression.

"I heard what you said to her," she stated, nodding her sleek head. "And you told me just this morning that you weren't going to take any more customers unless they paid you in advance."

"Phooey!" said Shaley. He slammed the door shut and went back and sat down behind his desk.

He picked up the penknife and stared at it thoughtfully.

"I'll fix him up, all right," he said sourly to himself. "I'll wring the little cuss' neck. Picking me to be the stooge in a blackmailing squeeze."

He began to stab the drawer again with the penknife, scowling.

Suddenly the penknife stopped in mid air. Shaley sat still for several seconds, his eyes slowly widening.

He said: "My gawd!" in a thoughtfully awed voice. He sat there for a while longer and then yelled: "Sadie!"

Sadie opened the door and looked in. "What?"

"Listen, there was a murder in some hotel around here about a week back—some woman got herself killed. What hotel was it?"

"The *Grover*," said Sadie.

Shaley leaned back in his chair. He smiled— a hard, tight smile that put deep lines around his mouth. He said: "So," in a quietly triumphant voice.

"I read all about it in the paper," said Sadie. "The woman's name was 'Big Cee.' She was mixed up with some gangsters or something in Cleveland, and the police thought she came out here to hide, and that some of the gangsters found her. The papers said there were no clues to the murderer's identity. Mr. Van Bilbo, the movie director, read about her death, and he felt sorry for her, and he paid for her funeral. I think that was very nice of him, don't you, Mr. Shaley? A woman he didn't know at all, that way."

"Yes," said Shaley. "It was very nice of Mr. Van Bilbo. Go away now. I want to think."

Sadie slammed the door. Shaley picked his hat up off the floor and put it on, tipping it down over his eyes. He slid down in his chair and folded his hands across his chest.

After about ten minutes, he reached out and

took up the telephone on his desk and dialed a number.

A feminine voice said liltingly: "This is the *Grover*—the largest and finest hotel west of the Mississippi."

Shaley said: "Is McFane there?"

"Yes, sir. Just a moment, sir, and I'll connect you with Mr. McFane."

Shaley waited, tapping his fingers on the desk top.

"Hello." It was a smoothly cordial voice.

Shaley said: "McFane? This is Ben Shaley."

"Hello there, Ben. How's the private detecting?"

"Just fair. Listen, McFane, have you got a bellhop around there by the name of Bennie Petersen?"

"We did have. The little chiseler quit us last week without any notice at all. Just didn't show up for work. He in trouble?"

Shaley said: "No. Uh-huh. I was just wondering. He quit right after that murder you had, didn't he?"

"Yes, come to think—" McFane stopped short. "Hey! Are you digging on that?"

"No, no," Shaley said quickly. "I was just wondering, that's all."

"Listen, Ben," McFane said in a worried tone. "Lay off, will you? We spent a thousand dollars' worth of advertising killing that in the papers. It gives the hotel a bad name."

"You got it all wrong," Shaley said soothingly. "I'm not interested at all. I was just wondering. So long, McFane, and thanks."

"Wait, Ben. Listen, I'll make it worth your while—I'll retain—"

Shaley hung up the receiver. He walked quickly out of the private office.

"If a guy by the name of McFane calls," he said to Sadie, "tell him I just left for Europe. I'll call you in an hour."

"From Europe?" Sadie asked innocently.

Shaley went out and slammed the door.

The high board fence had once been painted a very bright shade of yellow, but now the paint was old and faded and streaked. It was peeling off in big patches that showed bare, brown board underneath.

Shaley parked his battered Chrysler roadster around the corner and walked back along the fence. There was a group of Indians standing in a silent, motionless circle in front of the big iron gate. They all had their arms folded across their chests. They all wore very gaudy shirts, and two of the older ones had strips of buckskin with beads sewn on them tied around their heads.

They didn't look at Shaley, didn't pay any attention to him.

Shaley walked up to the iron gate and peered through the thick, rusted bars. There was a car—a yellow Rolls-Royce—parked in the graveled roadway. The hood was pushed up, and two men were listening to the engine.

"If that's what you call a piston slap," one said, "you should be chauffeuring a wheelbarrow."

Shaley said: "Hey, Mandy."

The man straightened, turned around. He was short, dumpy. He was wearing golf knickers and a checked sweater and checked golf hose and a checked cap. He had a round, reddish face sprinkled with brown spots. He was chewing on the stub of a cigar, and tobacco juice had left a brown trail from the corner of his mouth down his chin. He stared at Shaley without any sign of recognition.

"Let me in, Mandy," Shaley requested.

Mandy strolled up to the gate, looked at Shaley through it.

"I don't suppose you'd have a pass, would you?"

Shaley said: "Come on, Mandy. Let me in. I want to talk to you."

"Huh!" said Mandy. He opened the gate grudgingly.

Shaley slipped inside, and Mandy slammed the gate with a clang.

"Go ahead and talk," he invited. "It won't do you any good. I won't buy anything."

Shaley looked at the other man meaningly. This one wore a plum-colored military uniform with silver trimmings. He looked as a motion picture director's chauffeur should look. He was thin and tall with a swarthily dark face and a small black mustache. He had his military cap tipped at a jaunty angle.

He stared from Mandy to Shaley, then shrugged his thin shoulders.

"Excuse me," he said. He slammed the hood down and got into the front seat of the Rolls and backed it up the road.

"Pretty fancy," Shaley said, jerking his head to indicate the chauffeur and the car.

"He gripes me," Mandy said sourly. "I liked old Munn better."

"Why all the war-whoops outside?" Shaley asked.

"Extras. Waitin' to be put on. We ain't gonna shoot any exteriors today. We're shootin' a saloon scene. I told 'em that six times, but you can't argue with them guys. They just grunt at you."

"How's Van Bilbo coming since he's been producing independent?"

Mandy shrugged. "Just fair, I think we got a good one this time—forty-niner stuff."

They were silent, watching each other warily.

Shaley said suddenly: "Who was Big Cee, Mandy?"

"Huh?" Mandy said vacantly.

Shaley didn't say anything. He squatted down on his heels and began to draw patterns in the dust with his forefinger.

After a while, Mandy said bitterly: "I mighta known you'd get on to that. You find out everything, damn you."

There was another silence. Shaley kept on drawing his patterns in the dust.

"Her name was Rosa Lee once," Mandy said sullenly. "She worked with the old man on some serials way back in '09 or '10."

Shaley drew in a long breath. "So," he said quietly. He stood up. "Thanks, Mandy."

"Don't you try any of your sharp-shooting on the old man!" Mandy warned ferociously. "Damn you, Shaley, I'll kill you if you do!"

Shaley grinned. "So long, Mandy." He opened the gate and slipped outside.

Mandy put his head through the bars. "I mean it now, Shaley. You try anything funny on Van Bilbo, and I'll kill you deader than hell!"

Shaley went into a drug-store on Sunset and called his office.

"Anybody call me?" he asked, when Sadie answered the telephone.

She said: "Yes, Mr. Shaley. That man McFane called three times. He seems to be mad at you. He swore something terrible when I told him you'd gone to Europe. And that woman called—that woman that was here this morning and didn't pay you any money."

"What'd she want?"

"She wanted to thank you for getting Bennie that job in Phoenix."

"For what?" Shaley barked.

"For getting Bennie that job in Phoenix."

"Tell me just what she said," Shaley ordered tensely.

"She called just a little while ago. She said she wanted to thank you. She said the man you had talked to had called her up and told her that he would give Bennie a job in a hotel in Phoenix, and that she had told the man where Bennie was so the man could go and see him about the job."

Shaley stood there stiffly, staring at the telephone box.

"Hello?" said Sadie inquiringly.

Shaley slowly hung up the receiver, scowling in a puzzled way.

"Good gawd!" he said to himself suddenly in a tight whisper.

He banged open the door of the telephone booth and ran headlong out of the drug-store.

Shaley parked the Chrysler with a screech of rubber on cement. He got out and walked hurriedly along the sidewalk, along a high green hedge, to a sagging gate. He strode up an uneven brick wall, up steps into a high, old-fashioned porch.

A fat man in a pink shirt was sitting in an old rocker on the porch with his feet up on the railing.

"Where's Bennie Smith's room?" Shaley asked him abruptly.

"Who?"

"Bennie Smith?"

"What's his name?" the fat man inquired innocently.

Shaley hooked the toe of his right foot under the fat man's legs and heaved up. The fat man gave a frightened squawk and went over backwards, chair and all. He rolled over and got up on his hands and knees, gaping blankly at Shaley.

Shaley leaned over him. "Where's Bennie Smith's room?"

"Upstairs," the fat man blurted quickly. "Clear back. Last door on the left." He wiped his nose with the back of his hand. "Gee, guy, no need to get so hard about it. I'd 'a' told you. I was only fooling. No need to get so rough with a fellow."

Shaley was running across the porch. He went in the front door into a dim, moist-smelling hall with a worn green rug on the floor. He went up a flight of dark, carpeted stairs, along a hall.

The last few steps he ran on his toes, silently. He had his hand inside his coat on the butt of the big .45 automatic in his shoulder-holster.

He stopped in front of the last door on the left, listening. He pulled out the automatic and held it in his hand. He knocked softly on the door with his other hand.

There was no answer.

Shaley said: "Bennie," and knocked on the door again.

He turned the knob. The door was locked.

Working silently, Shaley took a ring of skeleton keys out of his left-hand coat pocket. The lock was old and loose. The first key turned it.

Shaley pushed the door open cautiously, standing to one side.

He drew in his breath with a hissing sound.

Bennie was lying on the bed. He looked very small and thin and young. In death his face had lost some of its sharpness, its wise-guy cynicism.

He had been stabbed several times in his thin chest. The bed was messy.

Shaley shut the door very quietly.

Shaley turned off of Sunset and drove up Cahuenga. He parked the Chrysler and walked slowly across a vacant lot towards a long, shack-like building that had a big red Neon sign on top of it that said: *Zeke's.*

Shaley walked around to the back and knocked on the door.

An angry voice from inside said: "How many times must I tell you bums that I can't give you no hand-outs until after the rush—" The man opened the door and saw Shaley. He said: "Oh! Hello, Mr. Shaley." He was a short, fat man with a round face that was shiny with perspiration. He wore a white chef's cap.

Shaley craned his neck, peering in the door. He could see into the interior of the dining-car. Bennie's sister was standing at the cash register, joking with a policeman and a man in a bus driver's uniform.

"What's the matter, Mr. Shaley?" the short man asked.

Shaley nodded his head to indicate the blonde woman. "Her brother has just been murdered."

The short man said: "Bennie?"

"Yes."

"Oh, ———!" said the short man. "And she thought he was the grandest thing that ever lived."

"You'll have to tell her," Shaley said.

"Me? Oh, ——— no! No. I don't want to. You tell her, Mr. Shaley."

Shaley said: "I can't."

The short man stared at him. "I got to tell her. And she thought he was so swell. She gave him most of her wages." He rubbed his hand across his mouth. "Oh, ———! That poor kid."

Shaley turned around and walked away. He was swallowing hard.

When Shaley came up and peered through the big iron gate, Mandy and the chauffeur were looking into the engine of the Rolls-Royce much in the same attitude as before.

"It's a wrist-pin," Mandy said. "I'm telling you it's a wrist-pin."

Shaley said: "Mandy."

Mandy came over and opened the gate. "You're like a depression," he told Shaley sourly.

"Always popping up when people don't expect you. What do you want now?"

"I want to see Van Bilbo."

"He's in his office. They're just gettin' ready for some re-takes on that saloon scene. What's the matter with you, anyway?"

Shaley said: "I just saw a kid that was murdered. He was a little rat and a chiseler and a liar, but he had a swell sister. She trusted me, and I let her down. I'm going to talk to Van Bilbo and then I'm going to start something. Stick around."

He walked along the road, his feet crunching in the gravel.

The chauffeur looked at Mandy. "Screwy?" he inquired.

Mandy was squinting at Shaley back. He shook his head slowly.

"No. He gets that way when he's mad. And when he's mad, he's a great big dose of bad medicine for somebody."

Shaley turned around the corner of a barn-like building and was in a short dusty street with false-fronted sets on each side. There were board sidewalks and a couple of big tents that had saloon signs in front of them.

There were saddled horses tied to a long hitching-rack. There were men in fringed buck-skin suits with coonskin caps and long rifles, and men in big sombreros wearing jingling spurs on their boots and big six-shooters in holsters at their waists, and men clad in black with high stovepipe hats. There were girls in low-necked dresses, and girls in calico and sun-bonnets.

A man up on a wooden tower that held an arc lamp was yelling angrily at a man on the ground, who was yelling back at him just as angrily. Two carpenters were having a loud argument in front of a saloon door. Another man had a long list in his hand and was running around checking up on the costumes of the extras. At the side of the street three men had a camera apart, examining its interior gravely.

Shaley walked along the middle of the street, went into a small wooden office building at the far end. He walked down a dusty corridor, knocked on a door that had a frosted glass panel with a crack in it running diagonally from corner to corner.

A voice said: "Come in."

Shaley opened the door and went into a small, cubby-hole of an office.

Van Bilbo was sitting behind the desk. Van Bilbo was a small, thin man. He was bald, and he wore big horn-rimmed glasses that gave him an owlish look. He always reminded Shaley of a small boy making believe he was grown up.

"Hello," he said shyly, peering over his glasses at Shaley.

"Do you remember me?" Shaley asked.

Van Bilbo shook his head, embarrassed. "I'm sorry. I meet so many people . . . I don't remember. . . ."

Shaley shut the door and sat down in a chair. "I'll tell you a story—a true one. One time there was a man who was a racetrack driver. He cracked up badly, and his nerves went haywire. He couldn't drive any more. He came out to Hollywood, hoping to find something to do. He didn't. He went broke. One day he was standing outside a studio. He'd pawned everything he owned but the clothes he wore. He was hungry and sick and pretty much down. While he was standing there a director came along. The director gave that man a ten-dollar bill and told him to go get something to eat. He gave the man a work-slip and let him work as an extra for a month, until he got on his feet again. I was that man, and you were the director. I don't forget things like that."

Van Bilbo made flustered little gestures. "It—it was nothing . . . I don't even remember. . . ."

"No," said Shaley. "Of course you don't. You've helped out plenty that were down and out and plenty that were in trouble—like Big Cee."

Van Bilbo repeated: "Big Cee," in a scared voice.

Shaley nodded. "That wasn't very hard to figure out, knowing you. She used to work for you a long time ago. She was in a jam. She called on you to help her out, and you did. She was running a joint in Cleveland. She got in wrong with some politicos, and they closed up her place. She was sore. She got hold of some affidavits that would look mighty bad in a court record. She skipped out here, intending to hide here and shake the boys back in Cleveland down for plenty. But they didn't want to play that way. They sent a guy after her, and he biffed her."

Part of this Shaley knew, and part he was guessing; but he didn't have to guess very much; with what he knew, the rest was fairly obvious.

Van Bilbo was staring at the door with widened eyes. Shaley turned to look.

A shadow showed through the frosted glass—a hunched, listening shadow.

Shaley slid the .45 out of his shoulder-holster and held it on his lap, watching the shadow. He went on talking to Van Bilbo:

"That was what happened and everything would have been closed up now and over with, only you and a bellhop, by the name of Bennie, put your fingers in the pie. Big Cee got scared somebody might be after her, and she called you in and gave you the affidavits to keep for her. Bennie saw you leaving her room, and, being a chiseler by trade, he got the idea that he might shake you down a little. He was curious about Big Cee, and he kept on watching the room. He saw the murderer go in and out. Then when he found out Big Cee had been knocked off, Bennie thought he was on easy street for fair."

Shaley paused, watching the shadow. The shadow was motionless.

"Bennie planned to put the squeeze on both you and the murderer. He made a bad mistake as far as the murderer was concerned. This murderer wasn't the kind of a boy to pay hush money. He's a dopey and a killer. Bennie found that out and went undercover while he tried to get in touch with you through me. The murderer was looking for Bennie. In the first place, Bennie knew too much, and in the second place the murderer didn't want Bennie putting the squeeze on you for fear you'd get scared and turn those affidavits over to the police."

The shadow was moving very slowly, getting closer to the door.

Shaley went on quickly: "The murderer was trailing Bennie's sister, trying to locate Bennie. He trailed the sister to me. He used my name to get the sister to give him Bennie's address. He killed Bennie. But he hasn't got those affidavits yet, and he wants them. He paid your chauffeur to quit, so he could get his job and be close to you without anybody getting suspicious. Come on in, baby!"

The glass panel of the door suddenly smashed in. An arm in a plum-colored uniform came through the opening. A thin hand pointed a stubby-barreled revolver at the two men inside.

Shaley kicked his chair over backwards just as the revolver cracked out.

Shaley's big automatic boomed loudly in the small room.

There was the pound of feet going quickly down the hall.

Shaley bounced up, kicked his chair aside, jerked the door open.

The thin form in the plum-colored uniform was just sliding around the corner at the end of the hall. Shaley put his head down and sprinted.

He tore out through the door into the street in time to see the plum-colored uniform whisk through the swinging doors of the saloon.

Extras stared open-mouthed. A man with two heavy six-guns and a fierce-looking mustache was trying to crawl under the board sidewalk. One of the dance-hall girls screamed loudly.

Shaley started across the street. There was a little jet of orange flame from the dimness behind the swinging doors. The crack of the revolver sounded slightly muffled.

The horses tied to the hitching-rack reared and kicked, squealing frantically.

Shaley trotted across the dusty street. He had one hand up to shield his eyes from the glare of the sun. He had his automatic balanced, ready, in the other hand.

He got to the swinging doors, pushed them back.

The place was fixed up as a dance-hall and saloon. There was a long bar and a cleared space for dancing with a raised platform for the fiddler at the far end.

Shaley ducked suddenly, and a bullet from the back window smashed into the wall over his head.

He ran across the room and dived headlong through the window. He saw that he had made a mistake while he was still in mid-air. The man in the plum-colored uniform hadn't run this time. He had decided to make a fight of it. He was crouched under the window.

Shaley tried to turn himself around in the air. He hit the ground on one shoulder and rolled frantically. And as he rolled, he caught a glimpse of a thin, swarthy face staring at him over the barrel of a stubby revolver.

There was a shot from the corner of the building. The man in the plum-colored uniform whirled away from Shaley, snarling.

Mandy was standing there, dumpily short, cigar still clenched in his teeth. He had a big, long-barreled revolver in his hand. As the man in the plum-colored uniform turned, Mandy pointed the revolver and fired again.

The man in the plum-colored uniform shot twice at him, and then Shaley's heavy automatic boomed once.

The man in the plum-colored uniform gave a little gulping cry. He started to run. He ran in a circle and suddenly flopped down full-length. The plum-colored uniform was a huddled, wrinkled heap on the dusty ground.

Shaley got up slowly, wiping dust from his face. Heads began to poke cautiously out of windows, and excited voices shouted questions.

Van Bilbo came running—a small, frantic figure with the horn-rimmed glasses hanging from one ear. He ran up to Mandy, pawed at him. "Are you hurt? Are you hurt, Mandy?"

Mandy said: "Aw, shut up. You're like an old hen with the pip. Of course I ain't hurt. That guy couldn't shoot worth a damn." He pushed Van Bilbo away.

Shaley said to the people who came crowding around: "This man is a dope fiend. He went crazy and suddenly attacked Mr. Van Bilbo. You can all testify that I shot in self-defense."

Mandy was pushing away through the crowd. Shaley followed him.

"Mandy," Shaley said.

Mandy turned around.

"Give me that gun," Shaley demanded and jerked the revolver out of Mandy's hand.

It was a single-action six-shooter. Shaley opened the loading gate, spun the cylinder. He punched out one of the loaded cartridges and looked at it.

The cartridge had no bullet in it. It was a blank.

"I thought so," said Shaley. "You grabbed this one off one of the extras. You damn' fool, you stood out there in the open with a gun full of blank cartridges and let that monkey shoot at you, just to give me a chance at him. That's guts, Mandy."

"Aw, nerts," said Mandy uncomfortably. "I just didn't think about it, that's all. He got old Munn's job and I didn't like him anyway."

Shaley glanced over where the whiskered man with the two big six-guns was just appearing from under the board sidewalk.

"There's a guy that thought, all right."

Mandy scowled—

"Oh, them!" He spat disgustedly. "Them heroes of the screen ain't takin' no chances gettin' hurt. It'd spoil their act."

Chicago Confetti
William Rollins, Jr.

WILLIAM ROLLINS, JR. (1897–1950) may at first glance appear to be just another standard pulp writer, working for a penny a word, as hard-boiled writers so often did in the 1920s and '30s. But there are more than a few points of unusual interest about him.

Although born in Massachusetts, he fought for the French in World War I, and his best-known novel, *The Ring and the Lamp* (1947), is set shortly after World War II—in Paris.

His first novel, *Midnight Treasure* (1929), featured a boy, much in the tradition of Huckleberry Finn, who helps solve a mystery in an adult novel. Rollins also wrote three stories for *Black Mask* in the 1920s featuring Jack Darrow, a 16-year-old crime-solving hero, when it was all but engraved in marble that children had no place in the hard-boiled fiction of the pulp magazines.

He also received acclaim for his novels that would be sure to make most readers take notice, including from the *Saturday Review of Literature* (stating that "*Treasure Island*'s best moments are rather pastoral" compared to the tension of *Midnight Treasure*); from the *Boston Transcript* (which claims that *The Obelisk* "often equals the best of Joyce"); and from Lillian Hellman (who hailed *The Shadow Before* as "the finest and most stimulating book of this generation").

"Chicago Confetti" first appeared in the March 1932 issue of *Black Mask*.

Chicago Confetti
William Rollins, Jr.

Machine-gun bullets are so much Chicago confetti to Percy Warren, private dick

"ENRY FULLER murdered? Sure, I know it!"

I looked at him over my cigar. I don't like cigars, but all dicks, public and private, are supposed to wear them; and far be it from me not to have the right office furnishings when a prospective client comes in.

"Sure, I know it!" I said again, taking the weed out of my mouth for a bit of fresh air. "Don't you suppose I take the *Times* and read the tabloids?"

"Well," he said, "you see I'm his nephew." He said it quiet, like he'd been used to being the old man's nephew all his life; which I suppose he was. But to me it was like the lad's telling me he was Santa Claus.

I stood up quick, and gave Santa a cigar from the other box. Then I sat him down in a deep seat that's hard to get out of, and looked him over.

Considering he'd basked in the light of twenty million all his life, he didn't have such a healthy tan. One of the studious kind, with goggles that made him look nearer forty than the thirty which I suppose he was. Thin light hair, thin body, thin-colored blue eyes . . . and yet, looking them over as he started talking, I got the feeling that, if necessary, he could lay down his

"Iliad," or whatever it was that guy Joyce wrote, and get to business. He was talking business now as he leaned over my desk—business that I like to hear.

"You see, Mr. Warren," he explained in a slow voice, "the police are doing the best they can—"

"The police," I muttered, waving them aside. That's part of my business.

"Exactly. The police. But the family decided we wanted to leave no stones unturned to discover the—the—"

"_____" I helped him.

"Exactly. The _____ that—that—"

"Bumped him off," I finished.

"Exac—" He hesitated, frowning. "Well, not exactly "bumped." There were no bruises on the body. He was shot with a revolver."

"I know. In his own apartment. Monday evening about eight o'clock. Nobody present. You see," I explained, "crime news is this biddie's society page. And you want—?" I raised my eyebrows questioningly.

"Your help, if we can have it."

"Hmm." I picked up a note book and studied its blank pages. Having just started in on my own, this was my first prospect. I nodded thoughtfully; shut the book and looked up. "Good," I told him. "And now as to terms."

Coleman Fuller (that's what his card said; but it hadn't meant anything to me when I first read it) stood up.

"If you can drive around with me to Mr. Bond's—that's our family lawyer—we can fix that satisfactorily, I think," he said.

I glanced at the clock.

"How's half an hour?" I asked; then, when he nodded: "I got a little business to transact. That's Harley Bond, in the United Trust Building?"

"The same." He bowed and crossed to the door. I stopped him as he opened it.

"By the way, Mr. Fuller," I said; "how'd you happen to come to me? Satisfied customer, I suppose?"

He smiled, a little self-consciously.

"Well—not exactly," he murmured; "you see—well, my cousin George and I looked through the book, under detective agencies, and we flipped a coin—that was George's idea—to see whether we'd start at the top or bottom. The Z's won, and yours was the first." He laughed, sort of embarrassed, bowed again and went out.

I gave him time to get to the street and then jumped up, clamped on my hat and went out to the corner quick lunch, where I transacted my business. I was eating light those days. Fifteen minutes later I was in my snappy second-hand bus (I'm not telling what make; but it will rattle up to sixty) and in another ten minutes I was walking through the Gothic lobby of our latest Cathedral of Business. And there I meet young Professor Fuller himself again, standing at the foot of the elevators and talking to the dizziest blonde that never glorified the American girl.

He looked sort of flustered.

"On time, I see, Mr. Warren," he murmured; and he said something to the girl that I didn't hear, lifted his lid, and stepped into the elevator. I nearly lost the car looking after her as she went out. She wasn't hiding much, and I didn't blame her.

"Charming girl," said Mr. Student as we shot up; "just an—er—acquaintance."

"Well," I shot back, stepping out at the thirteenth; "she may be an acquaintance to you, but if I had your luck in knowing her, she'd either be a friend or an enemy." We walked down the corridor, and in a couple of minutes I was standing before Harley Bond, Attorney-At-Law, and one of the stiffest priced ones in our town.

I'd seen him before, of course, in and out of court—a small terrier sort of man of about forty-five. This was the first time I'd seen him so near to, though; and as he looked at me, across his desk as big as a banquet table, I noticed the little bags under the eyes I'd missed before, and I figured Mr. Bond liked his liquor, and liked it long. He had a pleasant smile, though.

"Glad to know you, Mr. Warren," he said in that easy drawl of his that made such a hit in court. He stretched out his hand. "I've got to admit that if the family here had consulted me," he added as we shook, "I would have recommended a better known agency, but—"

"We've never had a failure yet," I broke in. His eyes twinkled at that.

"I figured as much," he said. Harley Bond was nobody's fool. "However," he sat upright, becoming serious, "now you're hired, let's get down to business. First—"

"—the terms," I finished for him.

His lips formed in a silent whistle at that.

"I see a successful future ahead of you, Mr. Warren," he murmured. "The terms, however, have already been fixed by Mr. Carl Fuller, Mr. Henry's eldest brother. Ten thousand dollars to whomever finds and successfully proves the guilt of the murderer. To be paid on the sentencing."

I nodded shortly and mentally waved the lunchroom goodbye. Then I turned to minor details.

There was little known about the murder, it seems, other than what the papers had stated. Henry Fuller had gone to his apartment, 38 Bradford Street, at seven-thirty Monday evening, to dress for dinner. At eight-thirty his valet, who had been on an errand for him (he had a dozen alibi witnesses) returned, to find him dead, shot through the heart. A doctor was called, who put the time of death at eight o'clock. Henry Fuller was unmarried. So far as was known he had no enemies.

"And the will?"

Mr. Bond coughed.

"The will divided the property equally among his two sisters and two of his three brothers," he replied. "The third—John—had not been on the best of terms with him. Mr. John is—er—" Again the lawyer coughed, "the father of Mr. Coleman here."

I turned to our young student, who so far had said nothing. He nodded solemnly.

"Exactly," he murmured. "But I, myself, have been on the best of terms with Uncle Henry for over a year now. I think, if he had lived a little longer, he would have—well, er—"

"I see," I delicately finished for him. "But he didn't, so you're out of luck." I stood up. "And

now, Mr. Bond, I'll take a look around. You might give me the names and addresses of a few bereaved friends and relatives before I go," I added.

I looked them up that afternoon, all the unfortunate kinfolk who were going to divide twenty million among them following the unhappy death of old Fuller. I didn't expect to find anything, and that's what I found. It wasn't till early the next afternoon that I got around to the valet.

Jobson was his name. He was still sticking around the old man's apartment, with the consent of the relatives, squeezing the last hour out of free lodgings until the advanced rent was used up and he'd have to move into cheaper quarters.

The building itself was a dingy affair, the kind only a millionaire can afford to live in, long, four storied, on an old aristocratic street. I had a job routing out the elevator-boy-of-all-work from where he was sleeping in an alcove by the switchboard, but at last I found him, and after a ten-minute ride up three flights, I stumbled along the dark corridor, discovered the right door, and finally was standing in the presence of the formidable Mr. Jobson himself.

He sat me down very politely when he found what I wanted; sat my one hundred and seventy pounds on the flimsiest gilded chair in all that gilded drawing-room, so he had the drop on me from the start.

"Anything I can do to help solve this horrible affair, sir, I'll be delighted to do," he rumbled, standing over me. "But, unfortunately, I am completely in the dark—"

"It seems to have been a dark night all around," I interrupted him.

He bridled at that.

"I have alibis, sir!" he declared; "at least a dozen people—"

I flapped my paw.

"Save your alibis until you're accused of something," I said. "I just dropped in for a pleasant little chat."

Well, we talked about art and literature and one thing and another, but I wasn't getting any news that I'd come for, and I was just about to let up on him and lift anchor—when I settled back again.

I'd caught him looking at the clock.

Now there are ways of looking at a clock, and then there are ways.

Well, I kept him there for another twenty minutes, and at the end of that time he was as nervous as a débuting opera singer with the hiccoughs. At last he couldn't stand it any longer.

"I'm sorry, Mr. Warren," he said, "but I must put off this pleasant conversation till another time. You see, I—I've an engagement with a—" he leered; "you understand, sir, don't you!"

I jumped up.

"I sure do," I answered. "You should have told me before. I have those engagements myself sometimes." And I gave him leer for leer. In another minute I had shaken hands with him and watched the door shut tight; and the moment the latch clicked, I was sliding across the hall to the elevator, where I rang the bell and kept my finger on it till I heard the bang of the metal door below. Even then I wasn't comfortable.

"Anybody on the switchboard downstairs?" I asked the boy as he opened the door for me.

"Nobody, sir. Just me," he replied.

I nodded. I was safe there, anyhow. And if Jobson went out or anybody came in to keep an appointment, I could spot them from that little alcove.

"Listen, son," I said, as we gently parachuted down to bottom, "they seem to give you a lot of jobs to tend to around here."

"They do that, all right," the boy grumbled. He opened the door. I passed out and waited for him.

"I guess an extra ten spot wouldn't look bad to you, hah?" I said as he settled down by the board.

He eyed me funny.

"Well . . ." he murmured. I patted him on the shoulder.

"Don't worry; nothing like that, buddy. I just want to take your switchboard job off your hands

a few minutes." I pulled my hat over one eye and set my jaw in the proper fashion, and the kid got it right away.

"You're a dick!" he whispered, all eyes. Then his glance dropped to the roll that was coming out of my pocket, and he slipped off his seat and gave me the switchboard. I pulled on the earphones and waited. I know how to run a board; a good dick has to know a lot of things. Even being an expert window-washer comes in handy because—but you've read all about that.

Then came the first call. Mrs. Winslow's maid wanted those lamb chops right away, and wanted them in a loud voice; and then in a lower voice she added: "bring them around yourself, Tony dear, if you can." Then came the second call on the heels of that one, and Hattie Somebody and I learned all about what the doctor thought of Jessie's kidneys. He didn't think they were so hot, Jessie was glad to tell us; and I was beginning to be afraid I'd pulled a boner—that either Jobson was going out or somebody was coming calling (in which case I'd hear the ring for the elevator) when a third call was put in.

"Duval 8390." That was Jobson's deep voice; there was no mistaking it.

I plugged in, passed on the call, and waited. Not long. I heard a receiver come off. Then:

"Hello." A woman's voice.

"Is this Miss Kelly?"

"Yes."

"This is Jobson. You know—Jobson."

"Yes." Short, noncommittal.

"I wanted to know is—is you know—there?"

"No, he isn't."

"Well, get ahold of him right away. Right away, you understand?"

"Yes."

"And tell him not to come around here. It's dangerous. You understand?"

"Yes."

"Tell him to meet me at the hotel there. At that room—what's the number?"

"311."

"311. In about an hour. You understand?"

"Yes. I'll tell him." Her receiver went down,

and his after it. I pulled out the plugs, and plugged in central.

"Listen, operator," I said when she answered. "Give me the address of Duval 8390, like a good girl, will you? I know it's a hotel."

"Sorry, sir," came the mechanical answer, "but we're not allowed—"

"I know, I know, honey," I cut in; "but be big hearted just for once, will you? You see, I just got a tip that my wife and another chap—"

I heard her giggle. A moment's wait. Then:

"Duvaal, a-it—thrrree—noine—O, is the *Stopover Inn,* sir, on the Eastern Highway."

I let out a noiseless whistle. I don't think I even thanked her. I was thinking just one thing. I was thinking that I was going to earn that ten grand—if I ever got it.

For the *Stopover Inn,* on the Eastern Highway, was the hangout of the Lewis gang!

I canned the whistle, hopped up, and patted the boy on the head.

"Nice boy," I said; "you'll be a millionaire some day," and passed him the ten. Then I went back to my room, packed my bag with things I didn't need and was on my way.

The *Stopover Inn* is about ten miles out, and when I swung around the last corner, a flivver was just drawing up and I saw Jobson get out. I tore on past, interested in the scenery across the road, drove on for another mile, and then turned back.

I parked my car near Jobson's, got out, dragged out my suitcase, and walked into the small dirty lobby. There was just a dumb-looking, pimpled-face boy behind the desk, and I was glad of that.

"Room," I snapped. "Top floor, where I won't get the traffic so much. I've got a lot of heavy sleeping to do." One glance had already told me there were only three floors to the place; ten rooms to a floor, five front, five back.

The boy stared at me stupidly.

"You got to wait for Miss Kelly to get back," he drawled without moving his lips; why use your lips when your nose will do? "She's upstairs."

But Miss Kelly was just whom I didn't want to see, she or anybody else who might ask questions, aloud or to themselves. I wanted to hold that off as long as I could. I glanced at the keyboard at my side. 311's key was missing from its hook; but most of the other keys were there.

"Baloney," says I, like I meant it. "I'm not waiting for Miss Kelly or anybody else. I just come in from five hundred miles." Luckily my car was turned the right way if they investigated. I glared at him. "I don't want Miss Kelly, I want sleep! You understand? Here!" I made a dive for the key of 313, which was near me. "Show me a room!"

But the boy's hand was on the rack nearly as soon as mine.

"That room's taken," he said, mighty quick for him. "I'll show you a room." He took the key of 317 and came out from behind the desk. He almost fell over my suitcase as he shambled towards the stairs. I picked up the valise and followed his shuffling steps.

The two flights of stairs were narrow, dark and dirty, and so was the corridor at the head of the second flight. But both stairs and corridors were carpeted so thick you couldn't hear your own footfalls; which had its uses and had its drawbacks. The boy showed me my room, a narrow back room with one window, and started off again. He was so dumb he didn't even fool with the shades till I came across with a tip.

"Here," I said, as I slipped him a quarter; "and I don't want to be disturbed. I'm sleeping through twenty-four hours." I slammed the door and noisily locked it, and gave him two minutes before I softly turned the key again, opened the door and stepped outside.

It was always night in that windowless corridor, but it wasn't any Gay White Way. One gas-jet burned in the middle, and even that looked pretty discouraged. I locked my door from the outside, and walked down the hall—I didn't have to tiptoe on that thick carpet—to the last back corner room, number 311.

There were two voices inside, a woman's and a man's; but I didn't stop to listen. I moved back to the room beside it, number 313. I listened there a second; then I pulled out a pass key.

Yes, it was unoccupied. A regular cheap hotel room, that was mostly bed. The bed used to be brass. You could tell that by the bits that glittered here and there over the rough rusty iron. There was one window that faced a large but mangy orchard in back, and one stiff-backed chair. I noiselessly pulled the chair over to the door that connected with 311, but which was locked with its keyhole stuffed. Then I sat down and waited.

I heard the woman speak. She must have been standing near the outer door, talking to somebody back in the room.

"Well, when he comes, I'll send him right up," she was saying. She had a nice, musical voice. I figured it must be Miss Kelly. "I called him right after you phoned. He ought to be here any minute."

There was a grunt right beside me. Jobson must be lying on the bed. The door opened and closed. I couldn't hear her feet as she walked away, past my door, down the hall.

A half an hour passed, with nothing more exciting than an occasional creak of the springs as Jobson twisted on the bed. I made myself as comfortable as I could on that lousy chair and waited; I think I even dozed once or twice. Then, all at once, I was sitting upright, ears cocked I heard the click of the outer doorknob in the next room.

Jobson sat up on the bed; I could hear the springs creak.

"Well," he grunted, "you took long enough getting here."

There wasn't an answer until the door was shut and the key creaked in the lock. Then a low voice mumbled something I couldn't hear.

"Uh-huh," Jobson answered; "well, that's all right. Now let's get down to business." And with that he moved off the bed and I heard him thump across the room, probably to a chair near the other bird. I pulled my own chair even closer to the door and stuck my ear against it. Then I got down on my knees and tried my ear at the key

hole. I even took a chance at pulling out the wadding, but that wouldn't work. And all I got for my pains was a thick mumbling conversation.

True, now and then I caught bits of conversation, and they were interesting listening, though it was always Jobson's voice, never the other guy's.

"How much?" he said, once. "Well, give me ten grand and little Freddie Jobson will be just a memory to you from then on."

I pulled one of my silent whistles at that. "Trying to blackmail the Lewis gang?" I thought: "I can think of safer things than that— like sleeping on railroad ties." Another time he said something about poor, dead Mr. Fuller, and his tone of voice brought to mind the bereaved relatives. And then came the fast one.

I heard him jump up, like he was sore.

"Listen, brother," he says, forgetting discretion; "don't pull that line on me. I might not have been there when you bumped him off, but I was listening in when you was there that same afternoon. And I heard him speak about the hundred grand the gang was trying to hold him up for. And I heard you say: "Listen," I heard you say; "I think I can show them the light if you give me fifty thousand—personally." And then: "I'll be around to get your decision shortly before eight." I wonder he didn't take a shot at you then, instead of waiting till you got back to try it, like you said. How would that story sound before a jury, brother? Hah? *And how would it sound if the gang heard about it?*"

So! I smiled to myself. *That* was why Jobson dared try blackmail! It wasn't the gang he had to face, but somebody connected with it who had tried to double-cross them! And right then there's the little buzz of a telephone in their room.

I glanced around the room here while I heard one of them thump across the floor. There wasn't any phone here; probably 311 was used for business conferences only, and the only connecting phone was in that room. I heard Jobson's voice muttering something into the mouthpiece. Then he slammed down the receiver with a vicious jerk.

"Listen!" he said in a hoarse whisper, and I could almost see him whirl around to his companion. "She says to tell you the cops are on their way upstairs! I must have been shadowed, and—and—for ——— sake, I can't be found talking to you! *Hide, man! Hide!*"

And then, for the first time, I heard the other guy's voice; just a half dozen low words:

"Just a second. I want to tell you. . . ." His voice became a mumble; then a whisper; then I couldn't hear it at all, and I figured he must be hiding. And he only had a minute to do it before I heard the thump of two or three men's feet coming along the hall. Oh, yes, I could hear it. It takes more than a thick carpet to deaden the step of a good bull.

They passed my door, went on to the next, and rapped, short and sharp. I heard steps cross the room, heard the key turn in the lock and the door open. And then I got a jolt.

A deep voice spoke, and I recognized it right away for Police Sergeant Rooney's.

"Well," he says; "so here's our little bird! You was right after all, Mr. Bond!"

And I heard Bond say in that slow drawl of his:
"Oh, I knew we'd find him, all right, Sergeant!" And I sat back and scratched my head.

So Bond was doing a little detective work on the quiet, was he! Taking a crack at that ten grand reward himself! I set my lips tight. I didn't know how he'd trailed Jobson here—unless by the bull stationed outside the apartments on Bradford Street—and I didn't give a damn; but when they brought that other bird—the guy what had done the shooting—before the Captain, little Percy Warren (Yeah, that's the name!) would be tripping alongside them, ready to put in part claim for the bonus! There are ethics in every trade, and Harley Bond was going to stick to lawyering, or I'd know the reason why! But I wasn't feeling so cheerful while I sat there listening to Jobson's pulling his sob stuff.

"Why, I wasn't doing nothing, Mr. Bond! I just came around here because—" And Bond cuts in:

"Nobody's accusing you of doing anything,

Jobson," he says; "I just wanted to have a little talk with you to see if you knew anything more about this affair; and I asked the sergeant to come along and—"

And just then a truck went rumbling by; and though it was on the other side of the inn, it shut off all connections with the next room. Before the air cleared and I could tune in again it was all over.

"Well, come along!" Rooney snaps.

I stood up, ready to join the party and do a little arguing; and then I stopped short. Had they found the other guy—the bird that did the dirty work? They'd had time, maybe, to dig him out from wherever he was hiding; but how did I know they knew he was there in the first place? I crossed the room softly, slipped my key in the lock, turned it, and waited. If they had the killer with them, that was my tough luck; if they didn't, it was Bond's. I'd produce him in my own good time, when the lawyer wasn't around to split the bonus.

I listened while they piled out the door and locked it behind them; waited while they tramped past my door. Then I opened up a crack and peeked.

There were four of them going down the hall. I could just make them out as they passed under the gasjet: the sergeant, another cop, Bond, and Jobson—and nobody else! I chuckled to myself, apologized to Lady Luck, and shut the door quick; for just then I spotted a girl down the hall ahead of them. Miss Kelly, probably.

I locked the door, pulled the key out, and slipped across to the window. With that girl out there, the hall wasn't safe. I pulled the window way up, gentle, and stuck my head out.

It wasn't easy going. I planked my toes on a little ledge, pressing them tight against the side of the house; and I edged along, quiet as I could until I had my hand on the window-sill of 311.

In a split-second I had my gun out, pointing up. I was a pretty target if the killer had heard me or came wandering my way, but I figured I'd get the first crack, if he stuck his head out.

He didn't, though; so I eased up above the

water-line, leveled my gun on the sill. Then I shifted my grip from my hand to my elbow, jerked back the curtain and looked, my finger quivering on the trigger.

There wasn't anybody in the room; at least in sight. In another second I was over the sill and inside.

It was a bigger room than the others, several chairs, a table, a bed—I slid across to the bed and pulled a quick old maid; but nobody was hiding there. I crossed to the door. Then I swung around and went over to the window on the side of the building and looked out.

There was a maple there, reaching to the roof. One branch stuck out, almost to the window. It wasn't a hefty branch; I'd hate to shinny down it, and I'd just put on an act myself that wasn't so bad. But I figured a slim active guy could manage it, if it was that or the chair.

He *could* have done it; but— I stood a minute, staring out the window. There was something wrong, somewhere; something that didn't fit into the picture. I turned back, stared at the floor, thinking. I stooped to look under the bed again, just to satisfy myself.

"Well? Lose something?"

I whirled around. A girl was standing in the doorway. That had been a fast one! I sauntered towards her.

"Just a hairpin. It doesn't matter."

She forced a little grin at that—nice lips, they were; but her eyes watched me pretty hard through a pair of horn-rimmed glasses. And now her smile got a little curl to it as she walked in to meet me.

"What did you want it for? Clean a pipe, or just pick a lock?" She halted behind a chair, rested her elbows easily on the back of it, and looked me up and down. "I suppose you know you made a mistake and got in the wrong room?" she said.

I sat down on the bed, took out my cigarettes and lit one, pretty slow, giving her look for look. I was stalling for time. I wanted to size her up, get what there was to get from her; and at the same time I was trying to put together a little puzzle that was working in my mind. She wasn't hard to look at, for all the glasses and her hair twisted in a knot at the back of her head like a biddy's on Monday morning. Somehow she looked familiar, but I shoved that off; I can only work on one thing at a time.

I said:

"You're half right on your supposition, Miss Kelly."

Her eyebrows rose at that.

"Miss Kelly, eh? Pleased to meet you, Mr.—"

"Burns. William J."

She had to laugh.

"You don't go in for false whiskers like most of them, do you?" she said. Then, going back: "So I'm half right, am I? And as this is the wrong room, I take it you didn't make a mistake in getting into it."

"Good for Vassar!" I applauded; then I got serious. "How long have you been working here, Miss Kelly?" I asked. Not that I wanted an answer. I was busy thinking.

"Let's see your tin medal before you start the third degree," she answers, coolly. "And while you're about it," she drawled, when I didn't make a move, "you might tell me how you happened to get in this locked room. It'd make interesting reading."

I looked up at her quick. I'd got hold of something.

"Do you know Jobson?" I demanded.

"Let's see the medal." She flicked a fly carelessly off her cheek.

"Do you know Jobson?" I repeated it in a monotone.

She was tapping her toe, easy, looking bored-like at the ceiling.

"Let's see the medal."

And then, in the same monotone:

"Do you know a murderer was in this room with him?"

She forgets the ceiling at that. Her eyes shot down to mine, big and startled behind her glasses. I could see the color draw out of her cheeks.

"*You saw—a murderer—here?*" she almost whispered.

"I'm not saying what I saw." I leaned forward, studying her a moment. She wasn't faking that horror; that was easily seen. But I wasn't worrying about that right now. I had a theory, and I was taking a long shot at it.

"Miss Kelly," I said, slowly and distinctly; "you were in the hall after the cops left with Jobson and another chap—Mr. Bond, the lawyer?"

She hesitated a moment. She swallowed hard; then she nodded, without speaking.

"Now!" I snapped; "answer me this, and answer me *right!* Did you see another man sneak out of here after they left?"

Again she gave me a long hard stare, like she was doing a lot of thinking. Then, finally, she nodded.

"Yes, I did," she said, low. "I thought he was one of the party, so—"

I waved explanations away.

"Never mind that," I said; but I felt a quick thrill. It looked like my guessing was coming out right. "What did he look like?" I asked.

"A medium, thin fellow; white face, big nose; sort of mean little eyes—"

That was a description of Spike Lewis himself. I jumped up.

She drew in her breath. Then she went on. "Listen. I've tended to my own business so far. But I can learn a lot of interesting news if I want to, and in quick time." She thought a moment. "Where are you going to be at eight o'clock?" she asked at last.

"Who knows? Maybe in the morgue with the unidentified bodies."

She tossed off a polite smile, and then was all serious.

"Listen. Take this number." I pulled out my note book. "Ashley 2836. That's a long way from here. I wouldn't dare give you this number. Phone that number at eight, sharp. If I'm not there, I haven't any news for you. If I have, I'll be there." She stuck out her hand, pal fashion, looking me in the eye. "And I think I'll be there," she finished.

We shook.

"Good enough for you, Miriam!" I says, starting down the hall. "I'll give you a ring."

I was half way down the next flight when I heard her call. I looked up, and saw her grinning over the banister.

"Believe it or not," she calls, softly, "it's Desdemona!" Two minutes later I was in my car and bowling towards town.

I was pretty well pleased with myself as I tore along. I was damned certain who the killer was now; all I had to do was catch him, and catch him with the goods. That may sound hard, and I knew it wasn't going to be any cinch. But Percy Warren wasn't being paid easy money for an easy job. When I reached town, I turned off the highway and slowed her up a bit. Then I sat up with a bang.

"Why, you ham sleuth you!" I muttered to myself.

Here I'd been handing myself orchids for snappy thinking. And if I was right, it meant that Jobson, instead of being safe in jail, held as material witness, suspicious character, or whatever the temperamental captain decided on, it meant he'd probably been freed to get himself murdered! I was only about ten blocks from the Bradford Street apartments, but I swung up to the curb by a drug-store, vaulted out, and ran inside to a phone booth.

Jobson answered after a minute's ringing. I breathed a sigh of relief when I heard his voice.

"Listen, Jobson," I said when I'd told him who I was, "are you alone there?"

He hesitated long enough so that I knew the answer.

"Yes, I am," he growled.

"All right," I snapped; "have it your way. But answer me this: did your little playmate come up the elevator with you, or did he sneak in some other way?"

I heard him suck in his breath. Then he turned and whispered something to somebody. I climbed inside the mouthpiece. There wasn't any time for fooling.

"Jobson!" I called. "*Jobson!*"

He came back at that.

"What is it?" he says, sulkily.

"Listen, Jobson," I says, sharp and quick. "You're playing with dynamite! You get out of that apartment *right away, you understand?* That guy's going to—" I stopped.

There was a curious dull *plop!* in my ear.

"Jobson!" I called.

Silence. Then a far-away sounding thud. *"Jobson!"*

A second I stood listening to nothing. Oh, I knew the truth, all right, but I just hung on, listening. And then, all at once, I *wasn't* listening to nothing.

I was listening to somebody breathing, close to the phone, somebody who was listening back at me. I slammed down the receiver, ran out to the car, and started her with a jerk, and in two or three minutes I was in the lobby of the Bradford Street apartments.

The overworked elevator boy was sitting on a stool in the elevator.

"Listen, kid," I says, shaking him to wake him up. "Shoot me up to the third, as fast as this hearse can go!" And then, after he'd got it running: "And give me a pass key to the Fuller apartment!" I was afraid maybe mine wouldn't work. "Snappy!"

I left him staring after me as I loped around the corner of the corridor. Another minute and I'd opened the apartment door and locked it behind me. Then I took a few steps into the front room, and stopped.

He was dead all right. His big hulk of a body lay sprawling on the floor below the telephone, where that gun with its silencer had dropped him. I noticed the receiver was back on the hook, though. And Jobson hadn't done that.

I knelt down and took a quick look at him. But before I did, I knew Mr. Jobson had gone where all good blackmailers go, and in a second I was on my feet again. I hadn't hoped to be able to help him, and I didn't expect to find the killer around. But I did hope, if I scared him away soon enough, to find some sign of the bird's job, so as to be able to nail it on him. I gave the telephone receiver the once-over.

Right away I could see it was wiped clean as a Wall Street sucker. I gave the room a quick look. I didn't expect to find a special brand of cigarette butts tucked away in dark corners; if there was anything at all, it would be right under my eyes. And it wasn't there. I moved down the carpeted corridor, off which were the rooms.

The first three were bedrooms. I hardly gave them a look. Then the bathroom; then the dining-room. I opened the door at the end of the corridor.

Here was the kitchen. There was a door open across, and a dark stairway, leading down, probably, to the tradesmen's entrance. I figured that's how the killer got in. There weren't any doormen at that entrance. I looked around, and gave one of those Percy Warren whistles.

There were two empty glasses on the table, and a beer bottle beside them. They'd been talking it over here before I called. Here was how I would nail my friend—good ole finger prints!

I crossed the kitchen floor and reached for the glasses, planning to lift them by sticking my fingers inside.

"All right. Stick them up—*and don't turn around!*"

I stuck them up. That deep hoarse voice meant business. I heard him take a step back.

"All right. Turn and look. Then turn front again."

I gave a look around.

There wasn't anybody in sight. But there was the muzzle of a gun sticking out the end of the corridor. That was all I could see, and that was all he meant for me to see. Just to show he wasn't playing.

"Are you looking front now?" the voice snapped.

"Yep."

I heard him cross the kitchen, catlike, till he was at the opposite wall.

"Now turn and walk down the corridor—*slow!*"

I turned and crossed to the corridor. I heard him come after me as I started down it. I reached the bathroom.

"Stop!"

I stopped.

"Right hand down—*slow!* Reach around for the key. Got it? Now put it in this side the door."

I followed instructions. He was close behind me now.

"Get in there. Cross to the window, hands up!"

I crossed to the window. The door slammed and the key clicked.

I didn't even bother to turn. I threw open the window, looked out, and gave a laugh. What a mistake that baby had made! In another second I was outside and running down the fire-escape.

There was an alley leading from the foot of the stairs to the street. It was surrounded on three sides by the apartment, and the only trouble was the tradesmen's stairway led to another block. But I tore on down the stairs and down the alley, and almost ran into the dick that was keeping an eagle eye on the apartment.

He was leaning against the side of the building at the head of the alley, and I reckon the sound of my feet woke him up. He stepped out to block my way.

"What's the big rush, buddy?" he says.

"Want to be on time for church," I snarled; "out of my way, flatfoot!"

But he grabbed me by both arms.

"Now listen, Major," he said, soft-like, "you don't want to run like that, it's bad for the heart. And besides, I'd love it a lot if you'd just stick around a bit, so's we can get acquainted," and a lot of soft soap like that that the old-time dick pulls before he slaps you down; and I had to argue with him and show him everything but my baby pictures before he let up on me.

And by that time my killer probably was home and had his two beer glasses tucked safe in bed. I made a couple of observations on the bull's ancestors and walked around to Bradford Street; and just as I was passing the front of the apartment, a car drew up. I turned and looked.

Coleman Fuller was climbing out. He gave me a salute.

"Coming or going, Mr. Warren?" he asked. "I was just going up to see Jobson."

I looked him over quick.

"He's something to see," I said, "if you like them dead."

His mouth and eyes opened wide at that.

"Dead?" he whispered. "You don't mean—"

"Don't I, though! Go up and take a look at him. And while you're about it, you might phone headquarters. I've kept it a little secret so far because I haven't time to go down and fill out questionnaires, like they'd want me to. I've got a job on my hands."

But he grabbed my arm as I was starting off.

"Was it the same man that killed my uncle?" he asked, all breathless.

"Same and identical."

"And—and do you know yet who it was? Have you any idea?"

I tipped him a wink.

"There's a little birdie been flitting around my ear the last couple of hours," I said. I started to go on, but he was keen for more dope. "Listen," I said, "if things go right, I'll know more about it tonight. Maybe I'll even have a little surprise package to bring you afterwards."

"Tonight?" He stared at me. Then: "Where are you staying?" he suddenly said.

I thought quick, then decided it wouldn't do any harm.

"*Stopover Inn,* on the Eastern Highway."

"*Stopover Inn?*" he gasped. "But isn't that—"

"Yep," I cut in. "The hangout of the wild and wicked Lewis gang."

He thought that over. Then he looked at me funny and said: "Are you going there—all alone?"

"What do you want to know that for?" I asked.

He looked away.

"I just—it's rather dangerous going there alone, isn't it?" he murmured.

I started off.

"Don't you worry about that," I told him. "That's your Uncle Dudley's business. Just you have that ten grand ready, or else a first class undertaker." I left him there, hopped into Lizzie, and started off. I wanted to be alone to think something over, for I'd just seen a bright light. Seeing Nephew Coleman had done that.

Desdemona. Take off those glasses, fluff up that knotted hair, throw a few glad rags on her in place of that starched dress, and what have you? You have a lady I'd seen just once before, and then only for a second.

And what did that prove?

I took that thought into a restaurant and chewed on it along with an extra tough steak. It might not prove so much, and then again it might prove a hell of a lot. The more I thought of it, the more I leaned towards the latter idea. It was just short of eight o'clock, and jumping up, I paid my check, went out to the nearest drugstore, and put in a call.

Desdemona herself answered the phone.

"Listen, Mr. Warren." She spoke in a whisper, her lips close to the mouthpiece. "I've learned something. I know who did it and I know where to find him. Have you got a car?"

"She's champing right outside here."

"Well, listen. Can you drive out now and get me? I'm on Milton Boulevard in a drug-store. Number 1038."

I whistled.

"That's a hell of a long ways out, Juliette," I said.

"Well," she answered, "if you're interested in landing this fish—"

"Right you are!" I cut in. "I'll motor right along. But listen, lady!" I added quick. "You park yourself there, understand? Maybe I'll put in a call or two for you on the way!" And I hung up, went out and whipped up the steed.

While I bowled along at a good pace, I kept my eyes peeled, watching particularly the traffic coming the other way. It must have been two miles out that I realized I was nobody's fool.

The car—a high-powered bus—was coming slow. Over the headlights I could just make out a half dozen men's heads, all turned to peer at the traffic going my way. Then they came alongside me.

I just had time to see six pair of eyes staring at me, to see one thin white face with a long nose—the face of Spike Lewis that decorates the front page of our papers so often—to hear a quick exclamation from all of them. Then they were way behind me, and I was working Elizabeth up to sixty. I gave a quick glance around.

The big car was swinging around. I turned front and tended to business.

The traffic was medium thick about now. For a couple of miles there weren't any side streets, so the cars were buzzing right along, with nothing to hinder them. But I got Elizabeth going full steam and left the most of them pretty much standing still. After a minute or two I gave another look behind me.

Boy, was that bus eating up the road! In that quick eyeful I could see it charging down on me, a powerful looking baby, with a half dozen heads peering forward. I had the same chance of pulling away from her as if I was on foot with the gout. But I tore on for a bit longer.

Then I eased up, as much as I dared. Fifty. Forty-five. Forty. I can hear those lads now, roaring behind me. I saw one long chance, and I took it.

The road was clear all around me, except for a car ahead. I eased her some more, until I could near feel the hot breath of that bus, so to speak, on the back of my neck. Then, all at once, I clamped down on clutch and brake.

It all happened in a flash. There was a *zipp!* as that juggernaut went shooting past; six tense faces turned towards me; the loud *crrrackrackrack!* of a machine-gun and a *plop!* as the tail end of the burst hit my fender. I went shooting in a crazy wide arc across to the left hand side of the road, up on the sidewalk, passing the lamppost on the wrong side; but not before, from the corner of my eye, I saw the poor innocent bozo in the car that was ahead of mine, suddenly slump in his seat.

I came down off the sidewalk—lucky it was low here—without stopping, and gave a look around. The car with the dead man had crashed into another, and the crowds were already pulling up to see the fun. Nobody noticed me; if they did, I suppose they figured I was getting out of the way and that it was the dead man they wanted. The juggernaut was probably a mile away by now, and I figured it would keep right on going. I glanced at a house number.

1104. I'd come a bit beyond where I was heading for. In another minute I was drawing up at the drug-store number 1038 and climbed out.

Desdemona Kelly met me at the door, pale and fidgety.

"You got here all right, I see," she said in a low voice.

I hauled up the eyebrows in the right fashion. "Why shouldn't I?" I asked.

"Why—I just thought—it seemed like I heard some shooting up the line," she answered, weaklike.

"Oh that." I shrugged. "Just some Chicago confetti. It seems they were after a guy in the car ahead of me—and got him. Got his wife and baby too," I added, to make the story good.

Desdemona turned all white at that.

"The wife and baby?" she whispered.

I led her out to the car.

"Why not?" I murmured. "The baby might shake a rattle at them. Brave lads like that can't take chances." I steered her in, climbed inside myself, and we started off for town. I passed her a fag and we both lit up.

"Mr. Warren," she said, slow and low, "I suppose you think I'm as good as a—as a murderer."

"Depends on how good the murderer is," I answered, easy, snapping my butt into the street.

"You think," she went on, "I worked this racket."

"Do I?" I murmured. "Tell us some more, Portia."

"What you going to do?" she asked, after about a mile.

"Eat, dance, then back to the *Stopover Inn* a day or two—"

She sucked in her breath quick.

"Ain't you—ain't you—" she commenced; and then she stopped.

"Afraid of meeting some of the boys?" I fin-

ished. "That's just what I'm hoping for. You see, Jessica, it just happens that I've got information that Lewis—or whoever the hell did the killing—was trying to double-cross the gang. That's why he bumped old Fuller off!"

She stared at me hard at that. Somehow it seemed that her face—under the drug-store blush—went white again. She didn't say a word. Just looked and looked at me.

We got back to the *Stopover* and found the place all dark. Desdemona slipped out the car first to get the lay of the land, claiming she didn't want to be seen in my company. Then she came back to the door, wig-wagged me an "all's well," and I climbed down and went in after her. There was one green-shaded lamp lighted in the lobby, over the desk, and the pimpled-faced lad was sprawled under it, fast asleep.

Desdemona turned with her finger to her lips.

"Good night," she whispered; blew me a kiss, and disappeared in a back room. I waded up the dark stairs, two flights, turned down the corridor to room 317. I shut and locked the door, and then pulled it open without bothering to turn the key back.

The bolt had been taken out of the lock.

"Oh, ho!" thought I; "there've been villains at work!" And I shut the door and shoved the flimsy washstand in front of it, just in case. I pulled out my little toy, gave it a quick loving once-over, and stuck it back in my pocket. Then I stood before the window, stripped to the waist, slipped on my pajama jacket, turned out the light, and got dressed again. After which I went over to the open window and looked out.

It was mighty dark outside, but not so dark that I couldn't make out something I'd noticed this afternoon—a little roof, about two feet wide (probably over a bay window below) running from just beneath my window to the window of 319. It was a flat roof, I found when I stepped outside; it was mighty simple to slip over to the next room. I pulled open that window, soft and wary. I stood a second, out of gun range, ears cocked. Then I climbed inside.

I slipped over to the bed, ran my hand lightly over it. It was empty. I'd been pretty sure the room wasn't taken. According to the keys on the board downstairs, I seemed to be about the only guest in the hotel. I crossed to the door, settled myself and waited.

I must have waited half an hour. I know I heard a clock somewhere outdoors strike two, and I must have waited ten minutes after that. Then, mighty faint, I heard something. I put my ear to the floor and listened.

It made all the difference in the world when I did that. I could feel the vibrations, and it sounded like three or four people must be sneaking up the corridor, along that thick carpet. I waited there a minute, ready to shoot into action. Then, all at once, I got puzzled.

I was hearing those sneaky steps, coming nearer. But I was hearing something else, too— or feeling its vibrations. It was a tiny vibration, coming right from the long board where my ear was.

I was sitting up like a flash, gun ready, pointed back into the room. Somebody was stealing across the floor towards me.

I got up to a crouch; edged along farther into the room, all set to jump to one side if the door opened. I must have made about a yard. Then a hand reached out and touched me softly on the face.

I don't know why I didn't fire. I reckon instinctive knowledge came with the feel of that soft hand. But that trigger was as near in action as I'd ever like to have it in somebody else's hand.

I heard her suck in her breath.

"Mr. Warren," she whispered.

"Present. Ready for all comers."

"I was hoping you'd go back to your room before they came. Get back in the corner, for —— sake!"

"I'm pretty well set, thanks."

But now her voice was terrified, and no acting. I could tell that, even in the dark.

"*Please!*" she breathed; "in the corner; for my sake!"

"Well . . . anything for a lady, Orphelia." I slunk back.

"*And don't show yourself!*" I heard her hand softly turn the knob, just as there was a little grating sound in the next room—my washstand being pushed back. The door of this room opened, and a faint path of gaslight shot inside. She stepped to the doorway, blocking it.

"Well! What the hell are you birds doing around here?" Her voice was low, but cutting.

I heard a deep voice mutter something.

"Yeah?" she answered. "Well, you guessed wrong. Yes, I know"—she broke in quick on the guy—"but, you damned fool, don't you know he's got half a dozen playmates hanging round outside?"

That seemed to get them. There was a bit more mumbling; then I heard them slink away. She closed the door and stood there a second, looking my way, I guess. I stepped out.

"Rosalind," I said, "my family thanks you. To tell the truth, we never trusted you much before; but—"

"Yeah?" she said, kind of rough. "Stow that. And go back bye-bye quick."

"First, though, the reward," I said; and I caught her and kissed her, a real two bits kiss.

She didn't push me away. She stood there a bit, after I was through, and I could hear her breathing heavy.

"You're a nice boy," she said at last, way low. "Why don't you quit this dick racket, and get out of this hotel—*now!*"

"Lady," I whispered, "the charm of your company—"

But I could hear her turning away.

"All right," she cut in, nonchalantly. "Do your window climbing act and get under the sheets." She opened the door and shut it after her; and in another minute I was in and out the windows, and had settled myself for the night.

I figured afterwards it must have been four o'clock when I snapped awake. I sat upright (I'd been sitting on the floor, against the wall) and listened. He was coming now—the guy I'd been laying for.

I watched where I knew the door was when I dozed off.

There was a little wait. Then it came again—the faint *squeak* of the rollers under the washstand as it was being moved. And now I could see a tiny slit of light showing where the opening door was. I got to my knees, crawled over to a point of vantage, and waited.

The slit grew wider. The light from the hall seemed almost bright, after the dead darkness. The stand squeaked, stopped; squeaked, stopped.

I waited till the door was open six inches. Then I stood up.

Plop!

The slug from the silenced gun dug into the wall back of me. With one gesture I swung around to the window, fired, and dropped.

The room rang with the shot for a while, and when it died away everything was still. The door and the stand didn't move any more; it didn't have to. Whoever had been shoving there had done his job.

Like a damned fool, I'd kept my eyes peeled on that door, just like they planned. And meanwhile the bozo himself had fired from the window; and now he was inside with me.

I softly drew myself up, ready, and then didn't move. He didn't move, either. We were both waiting. All at once there was a little clatter by the opposite wall.

Even while I pulled the trigger, I knew I was pulling my second boner. I know when somebody tosses a pencil across the room. It was just instinct, I guess, that made me fire. Right away something bit my shoulder, burning it. I rolled under the bed while the report was still whooping around. I figured he must be somewhere at the other end of it. I lay there, listening. My arm stung a little. Not much.

I guess I must have Indian blood in me. A gravestone is a noisy, nervous animal, compared to what I was. I did a little necessary breathing—not much—and that was all. The second hand went tearing round and round somebody's clock. It was his move first.

Probably he thought at last he must have got me. Anyhow, he moved a bit. Not three feet from me.

I let him have it.

By the time the noise died away, I heard them running up the stairs and along the corridor. I rolled from under, and when I got to my feet they were tumbling in the room—a whole army, it sounded like. When they lighted the light, though, I saw there were only four. Sergeant Rooney and three bobbies. Yes, and Coleman Fuller, standing there, white as a sheet.

I said:

"Have you got the girl?"

It seems they met her coming down on their way up. She stepped in, under escort, when I spoke.

"You nearly pulled a fast one, Desdy," I said, "when you got my eyes on that door you were pushing open. But then, you deserved that break, after the help you gave me."

She gave me a gum-chewing look. I wasn't a nice boy now.

"What do you mean, help you?" she said.

"Why, by keeping the gang out of talking—and shooting—distance from me when I told you I might spread the news your boy friend double-crossed them. If they could pop me at a bowing distance—like in a passing car—well and good; but it was better to leave the near-at-hand job to the boy friend himself, and keep the others away, wasn't it!"

She started to speak; stops; looks sidewise at Fuller; then back at me.

"What makes you think he's my boy friend?" she asked sullenly.

"Just clever deduction," I answered, modestly. "It took me a while to recognize you, with your glasses and fancy get-up, as the dame I'd seen talking with young Mr. Fuller here in the United Trust lobby—" (I heard Fuller mutter: "my ———!")—but then, when you were so quick to remember seeing somebody—Spike Lewis, or anybody else—steal down this hall, after Sergeant Rooney here and Bond and Jobson left, it was easy to see you were protecting one special guy. I was already pretty sure who the killer was, though," I finished. "Let's give credit where credit is due."

Rooney let out a strong Anglo-Saxon word at that.

"What's this?" he said, staring at me. "The killer was hiding in that room when we was there?"

I shook my head.

"Only half right, Sergeant," I answered. "He was in the room with you. But he wasn't hiding."

"He wasn't hid—? He was in the—?" Rooney gawked at me like one of us is nuts. "Well, who the—" he stuttered; "where—?"

"All answered with one dramatic gesture, Sergeant," I cut in. And I gave the bed a pull, rolling it a couple of feet towards the door.

Harley Bond was curled up behind the head. He wasn't dead. But he was sleeping peacefully, and wasn't apt to wake up for some little time.

I got my blood money when the jury's foreman said the harsh words. Police Captain Starr was there when they handed it to me, and he gave me a pat on the head.

"It was easy enough, Captain," I answered; downcast eyes go well at headquarters, particularly if you're a private dick. "I was stumped for a while, because I figured Bond came into the room along with the police. A bunch of trucks came by just then, so I couldn't hear much. But then I figured that what I *did* hear didn't prove he wasn't there right along, talking with Jobson."

The captain shook his head slowly.

"He was a wise baby, that lad," he muttered. "Strange how a man of his capabilities could get into a jam like this. But that's the way of it, I suppose," he said, turning philosopher. "Got doing business for a gang, saw how easy money could be pulled by playing between the gang and their sucker and was caught with the goods.

"Might have gone panicky; might have thought he was ruined unless he could stop the sucker talking. Anyway he pulled it. Then there was Jobson.

"He knew Jobson was being shadowed, so he phoned us he was meeting him to learn what he could, and for us to call around in half an hour and he'd tell us what he learned. Had himself protected coming and going." The captain stood up. "A wise baby," he said, half to himself; "about as wise as they make them."

I folded my check carefully.

"*Pretty* wise, Captain," I agreed. I looked lovingly at the piece of paper in my hand. "But not the wisest, Captain," I cooed softly, "not the wisest."

I turned to Coleman Fuller as we went out of the station. "As for you, Mr. Fuller," I said, "I suppose when you learned I was going out to the *Inn* alone your motherly instinct made you sneak out the police force to protect me."

"Exactly," he said nodding solemnly.

"And I suppose," I went on, "if the sergeant had appeared too soon and copped the prize himself, you know what would have happened to you?"

He nodded again, just as solemn. I looked him over, wondering if he was human.

"And I suppose," I said, "you know what a low-brow like me wants to do when he's come into a juicy bit of money?"

"Exactly," he murmured. He reached in his pocket and pulled out a full pint flask, and after I took a good pull at it, he finished it off himself. "That," he said, "is just about enough to last us till we reach the nearest speak."

I looked him over again; and I liked his looks.

"Exactly," I said.

Two Murders, One Crime
Cornell Woolrich

ONLY EDGAR ALLAN POE ranks with Cornell Woolrich (1903–1968) as a creator of heart-stopping suspense, and Poe produced relatively little compared with the prolific poet of darkness.

A sad and lonely figure (he dedicated books to his hotel room and to his typewriter), Woolrich is the greatest noir writer who ever lived, in spite of stylistic failings that include so much purple prose that, in the hands of a lesser writer, would make one wince. His use of coincidence, too, made believable or unnoticed because of the break-neck thrill ride of his stories, is unmatched by any author with the exception of the unreadable Harry Stephen Keeler.

In addition to hundreds of stories, mainly written for the pulps, Woolrich produced such classic novels of suspense as *The Bride Wore Black* (1940), filmed in 1968 by Francois Truffaut, and *Black Alibi* (1942), filmed the following year by Jacques Tourneur as *The Leopard Man*. The most famous film made from his work is Alfred Hitchcock's *Rear Window* (1954), based on a short story written under the pseudonym William Irish. Among numerous other Irish works to be filmed are the noir classic *Phantom Lady*, filmed by Robert Siodmak in 1944, two years after book publication, and *Deadline at Dawn*, directed by Harold Clurman in 1946, also two years after book publication.

"Two Murders, One Crime" was first published in the July 1942 issue of *Black Mask* under the title "Three Kills for One."

Two Murders, One Crime

Cornell Woolrich

THAT NIGHT, JUST like on all the other nights before it, around a quarter to twelve Gary Severn took his hat off the hook nearest the door, turned and said to his pretty, docile little wife in the room behind him: "Guess I'll go down to the corner a minute, bring in the midnight edition."

"All right, dear," she nodded, just like on all the other nights before this.

He opened the door, but then he stood there undecidedly on the threshold. "I feel kind of tired," he yawned, backing a hand to his mouth. "Maybe I ought to skip it. It wouldn't kill me to do without it one night. I usually fall asleep before I can turn to page two, anyway."

"Then don't bother getting it, dear, let it go if you feel that way," she acquiesced. "Why put yourself out? After all, it's not that important."

"No it isn't, is it?" he admitted. For a moment he seemed about to step inside again and close the door after him. Then he shrugged. "Oh well," he said, "I may as well go now that I've got my hat on. I'll be back in a couple of minutes." He closed the door from the outside.

Who knows what is important, what isn't important? Who is to recognize the turning-point that turns out to be a trifle, the trifle that turns out to be a turning-point?

A pause at the door, a yawn, a two-cent midnight paper that he wouldn't have remained awake long enough to finish anyway.

He came out on the street. Just a man on his way to the corner for a newspaper, and then back again. It was the 181st day of the year, and on 180 other nights before this one he had come out at this same hour, for this same thing. No, one night there'd been a blizzard and he hadn't. 179 nights, then.

He walked down to the corner, and turned it, and went one block over the long way, to where the concession was located. It was just a wooden trestle set up on the sidewalk, with the papers stacked on it. The tabs were always the first ones out, and they were on it already. But his was a standard size, and it came out the last of all of them, possibly due to complexities of make-up.

The man who kept the stand knew him by his paper, although he didn't know his name or anything else about him. "Not up yet," he greeted him. "Any minute now."

Why is it, when a man has read one particular paper for any length of time, he will refuse to buy another in place of it, even though the same news is in both? Another trifle?

Gary Severn said, "I'll take a turn around the block. It'll probably be here by the time I get back."

The delivery trucks left the plant downtown at 11:30, but the paper never hit the stands this far up much before twelve, due to a number of variables such as traffic-lights and weather which were never the same twice. It had often been a little delayed, just as it was tonight.

He went up the next street, the one behind his own, rounded the upper corner of that, then over, and back into his own again. He swung one hand, kept his other pocketed. He whistled a few inaccurate bars of *Elmer's Tune*. Then a few even more inaccurate bars of *Rose O'Day*. Then he quit whistling. It had just been an expression of the untroubled vacancy of his mind, anyway. His thoughts went something like this: "Swell night. Wonder what star that is up there, that one just hitting the roof? Never did know much about them. That Colonna sure was funny on the air tonight." With a grin of reminiscent appreciation. "Gee I'm sleepy. Wish I hadn't come out just now." Things like that.

He'd arrived back at his own doorway from the opposite direction by now. He slackened a little, hesitated, on the point of going in and letting the paper go hang. Then he went on anyway. "I'm out now. It'll just take a minute longer. There and back." Trifle.

The delivery truck had just arrived. He saw the bale being pitched off the back to the asphalt; for the dealer to pick up, as he rounded the corner once more. By the time he'd arrived at the stand the dealer had hauled it onto the sidewalk, cut the binding, and stacked the papers for sale on his board. A handful of other customers who had been waiting around closed in. The dealer was kept busy handing them out and making change.

Gary Severn wormed his way in through the little cluster of customers, reached for a copy from the pile, and found that somebody else had taken hold of it at the same time. The slight tug from two different directions brought their eyes around toward one another. Probably neither would have seen the other, that is to look at squarely, if it hadn't been for that. Trifle.

It was nothing. Gary Severn said pleasantly, "Go ahead, help yourself," and relinquished that particular copy for the next one below it.

"Must think he knows me," passed through his inattentive mind. The other's glance had come back a second time, whereas his own hadn't. He paid no further heed. He handed the dealer his nickel, got back two cents, turned and went off, reading the headlines as he went by the aid of the fairly adequate shop-lights there were along there.

He was dimly aware, as he did so, of numbers of other footsteps coming along the same way he was. People who had just now bought their papers as he had, and had this same direction to follow. He turned the corner and diverged up into his own street. All but one pair of footsteps went on off the long way, along the avenue, died out. One pair turned off and came up this way, as he had, but he took no notice.

He couldn't read en route any more, because he'd left the lights behind. The paper turned blue and blurred. He folded it and postponed the rest until he should get inside.

The other tread was still coming along, a few yards back. He didn't look around. Why should he? The streets were free to everyone. Others lived along this street as well as he. Footsteps behind him had no connection with him. He didn't have that kind of a mind, he hadn't led that kind of a life.

He reached his own doorway. As he turned aside he started to drag up his key. The other footsteps would go on past now, naturally. Not that his mind was occupied with them. Simply the membranes of his ears. He'd pulled out the building street-door, had one foot already through to the other side. The footsteps had come abreast—

A hand came down on his shoulder.

"Just a minute."

He turned. The man who had been buying a paper; the one who had reached for the same one he had. Was he going to pick a quarrel about such a petty—?

"Identify yourself."

"Why?"

"I said identify yourself." He did something with his free hand, almost too quick for Gary Severn to take in its significance. Some sort of a high-sign backed with metal.

"What's that for?"

"That's so you'll identify yourself."

"I'm Gary Severn. I live in here."

"All right. You'd better come with me." The hand on his shoulder had shifted further down his arm now, tightened.

Severn answered with a sort of peaceable doggedness, "Oh no, I won't go with you unless you tell me what you want with me. You can't come up to me like this outside my house and—"

"You're not resisting arrest, are you?" the other man suggested. "I wouldn't."

"Arrest?" Severn said blankly. "Is this arrest? Arrest for what?"

A note of laughter sounded from the other, without his grim lips curving in accompaniment to it. "I don't have to tell you that, do I? Arrest for murder. For the worst kind of murder there is. Murder of a police-officer. In the course of an attempted robbery. On Farragut Street." He spaced each clipped phrase. "Now do you remember?"

Arrest for murder.

He said it over to himself. It didn't even frighten him. It had no meaning. It was like being mistaken for Dutch Schultz or—some sort of a freak mix-up. The thing was, he wouldn't get to bed until all hours now probably, and that might make him late in the morning. And just when he was so tired too.

All he could find to say was a very foolish little thing. "Can't I go inside first and leave my paper? My wife's waiting in there, and I'd like to let her know I may be gone for half an hour or so—"

The man nodded permission, said: "Sure, I'll go inside with you a minute, while you tell your wife and leave your paper."

A life ends, and the note it ends on is: "Can I go inside first and leave my paper?"

On the wall was a typical optician's sight-chart, beginning with a big beetling jumbo capital at the top and tapering down to a line of fingernail-size type at the bottom. The detectives had been occupied in trying themselves out on it while they were waiting. Most, from a distance of across the room, had had to stop at the fourth line below the bottom. Normal eyesight. One man had been able to get down as far as the third, but he'd missed two of the ten letters in that one. No one had been able to get down below that.

The door on the opposite side opened and the Novak woman was brought in. She'd brought her knitting.

"Sit down there. We'd like to try you out on this chart, first."

Mrs. Novak tipped her shoulders. "Glasses you're giving out?"

"How far down can you read?"

"All the way."

"Can you read the bottom line?"

Again Mrs. Novak tipped her shoulders. "Who couldn't?"

"Nine out of ten people couldn't," one of the detectives murmured to the man next to him.

She rattled it off like someone reading a scare-head. "p, t, b, k, j, h, i, y, q, a."

Somebody whistled. "Far-sighted."

She dropped her eyes complacently to her needles again. "This I don't know about. I only hope you gentlemen are going to be through soon. While you got me coming in and out of here, my business ain't getting my whole attention."

The door opened and Gary Severn had come in. Flanked. His whole life was flanked now.

The rest of it went quick. The way death does.

She looked up. She held it. She nodded. "That's him. That's the man I saw running away right after the shots."

Gary Severn didn't say anything.

One of the detectives present, his name was Eric Rogers, he didn't say anything either. He was just there, a witness to it.

The other chief witness' name was Storm. He was a certified accountant, he dealt in figures. He was, as witnesses go, a man of good will. He made the second line from the bottom on the chart, better than any of the detectives had, even if not as good as Mrs. Novak. But then he was wearing glasses. But then—once more—he'd also been wearing them at the time the fleeing murderer had bowled him over on the sidewalk, only a few doors away from the actual crime, and snapped a shot at him which miraculously missed. He'd promptly lain inert and feigned death, to avoid a possible second and better-aimed shot.

"You realize how important this is?"

"I realize. That's why I'm holding back. That's why I don't like to say I'm 100% sure. I'd say I'm 75% sure it's him. I got 25% doubts."

"What you'd *like* to say," he was cautioned, "has nothing to do with it. Either you are sure or you aren't. Sureness has no percentages. Either it's one hundred or it's zero. Keep emotion out of this. Forget that it's a man. You're an accountant. It's a column of figures to you. There's only one right answer. Give us that answer. Now we're going to try you again."

Gary Severn came in again.

Storm moved his figures up. "90% sure," he said privately to the lieutenant standing behind him. "I still got 10% doubt left."

"*Yes* or *no?*"

"I can't say no, when I got 90% on the yes-side and only—"

"YES or NO!"

It came slow, but it came. It came low, but it came. "Yes."

Gary Severn didn't make a sound. He'd stopped saying anything long ago. Just the sound of one's own voice, unheard, unanswered, what good is that?

The detective named Rogers, he was there in the background again. He just took it in like the rest. There was nothing he felt called on to say.

The news-dealer, his name was Mike Mosconi, set in jackknife position in the chair and moved his hat uneasily around in his hands while he told them: "No, I don't know his name and I'm not even sure which house he lives in, but I know him by sight as good as you can know anybody, and he's telling the truth about that. He hasn't missed buying a paper off me, I don't think more than once or twice in the whole year."

"But he did stay away once or twice," the lieutenant said. "And what about this twenty-second of June, is that one of those once or twices he stayed away?"

The news-dealer said unhappily, "I'm out there on the street every night in the year, gents. It's hard for me to pick out a certain night by the date and say for sure that that was the one out of all of 'em— But if you get me the weather for that night, I can do better for you."

"Get him the weather for that night," the lieutenant consented.

The weather came back. "It was clear and bright on the twenty-second of June."

"Then he bought his paper from me that night," Mike Mosconi said inflexibly. "It's the God's honest truth; I'm sure of it and you can be too. The only one or two times he didn't show up was when—"

"How long did it take him to buy his paper each time?" the lieutenant continued remorselessly.

Mike Mosconi looked down reluctantly. "How long does it take to buy a paper? You drop three cents, you pick it up, you walk away—"

"But there's something else you haven't told us. At what time each night did he do this quick little buying of the paper? Was it the same time always, or did it vary, or what time was it?"

Mike Mosconi looked up in innocent surprise. "It was the same time always. It never varied. How could it? He always gets the midnight edition of the *Herald-Times*, it never hits my stand until quarter to twelve, he never came out until then. He knew it wouldn't be there if he did—"

"The twenty-second of June—?

"Any night, I don't care which it was. If he came at all, he came between quarter of and twelve o'clock."

"You can go, Mosconi."

Mosconi went. The lieutenant turned to Severn.

"The murder was at ten o'clock. What kind of an alibi was that?"

Severn said in quiet resignation, "The only one I had."

Gates didn't look like a criminal. But then there is no typical criminal look, the public at large only thinks there is. He was a big husky black-haired man, who gave a misleading impression of slow-moving genial good-nature totally unwarranted by the known facts of his career. He also had an air of calm self-assurance, that most likely came more from a lack of imagination than anything else.

He said, "So what do you expect me to say? If I say no, this ain't the guy, that means *I* was there but with someone else. If I say yes, it is him, that means the same thing. Don't worry, Mr. Strassburger, my counsel, wised me up about the kind of trick questions you guys like to ask. Like when they want to know 'Have you quit beating your wife?' "

He looked them over self-possessedly. "All I'm saying is I wasn't there myself. So if I wasn't there myself, how can there be a right guy or a wrong guy that was there with me? *I'm* the wrong guy, more than anybody else." He tapped himself on the breast-bone with emphatic conviction. "Get the right guy in my place first, and then he'll give you the right second guy."

He smiled a little at them. Very little. "All I'm saying, now and at any other time, is I never saw this guy before in my life. If you want it that way, you can have it."

The lieutenant smiled back at him. Also very little. "And you weren't on Farragut Street that night? And you didn't take part in the murder of Sergeant O'Neill?"

"That," said Gates with steely confidence, "goes with it."

Gates got up, but not fast or jerkily, with the same slowness that had always characterized him. He wiped the sweat off his palms by running them lightly down his sides. As though he were going to shake hands with somebody.

He was. He was going to shake hands with death.

He wasn't particularly frightened. Not that he was particularly brave. It was just that he didn't have very much imagination. Rationalizing, he knew that he wasn't going to be alive any more ten minutes from now. Yet he wasn't used to casting his imagination ten minutes ahead of him, he'd always kept it by him in the present. So he couldn't visualize it. So he wasn't as unnerved by it as the average man would have been.

Yet he was troubled by something else. The ridges in his forehead showed that.

"Are you ready, my son?"

"I'm ready."

"Lean on me."

"I don't have to, Father. My legs'll hold up. It ain't far." It was made as a simple statement of fact, without sarcasm or rebuke intended.

They left the death cell.

"Listen, that Severn kid," Gates said in a quiet voice, looking straight ahead. "He's following me in in five minutes. I admit I did it. I held out until now, to see if I'd get a reprieve or not. I didn't get the reprieve, so it don't matter now any more. All right, I killed O'Neill, I admit it. But the other guy, the guy with me that helped me kill him, it wasn't Severn. Are you listening? Can you hear me? It was a guy named Donny Blake. I never saw Severn before in my life until they arrested him. For ———'s sake, tell them that, Father! All right, I'm sorry for swearing at such a time. But tell them that, Father! You've got to tell them that! There's only five minutes left."

"Why did you wait so long, my son?"

"I told you, the reprieve—I been telling the warden since last night. I think he believes me, but I don't think he can get them to do anything about it, the others, over him—Listen, *you* tell him, Father! You believe me, don't you? The dead don't lie!"

His voice rose, echoed hollowly in the short passage. "Tell them not to touch that kid! He's not the guy that was with me—"

And he said probably the strangest thing that was ever said by a condemned man on the way to execution. "Father, don't walk any further with me! Leave me now, don't waste time. Go to the warden, tell him—!"

"Pray, my son. Pray for yourself. You are my charge—"

"But I don't need you, Father. Can't you take this off my mind? Don't let them bring that kid in here after me—!"

Something cold touched the crown of his head. The priest's arm slowly drew away, receded into life.

"Don't forget what you promised me, Father. Don't let—"

The hood, falling over his face, cut the rest of it short.

The current waned, then waxed, then waned again—

He said in a tired voice, "Helen, I love you. I—"

The hood, falling over his face, cut the rest of it short.

The current waned, then waxed, then waned again—

They didn't have the chart on the wall any more. It had done them poor service. The door opened and Mrs. Novak was ushered in. She had her knitting with her again. Only she was making a different article, of a different color, this time. She nodded restrainedly to several of them, as one does to distant acquaintances encountered before.

She sat down, bent her head, the needles began to flicker busily.

Somebody came in, or went out. She didn't bother looking.

The toecaps of a pair of shoes came to a halt just within the radius of vision of her downcast eyes. They remained motionless there on the floor, as though silently importuning her attention. There wasn't a sound in the room.

Mrs. Novak became aware of the shoes at last. She raised her eyes indifferently, dropped them. Then they shot up again. The knitting sidled from her lap as the lap itself dissolved into a straight line. The ball of yarn rolled across the floor unnoticed. She was clutching at her own throat with both hands.

There wasn't a sound in the room.

She pointed with one trembling finger. It was a question, a plea that she be mistaken, but more than anything else a terrified statement of fact.

"It's him—the man that ran past by my store—from where the police-officer—!"

"But the last time you said—"

She rolled her eyes, struck her own forehead. "I know," she said brokenly. "He looked *like* him. But only he looked *like* him, you understand? This one, it *is* him!" Her voice railed out

at them accusingly. "Why you haf to bring me here that other time? If you don't, I don't make such a mistake!"

"There were others made the same mistake," the lieutenant tried to soothe her. "You were only one of five or six witnesses. Every one of them—"

She wouldn't listen. Her face crinkled into an ugly mask. Suddenly, with no further ado, tears were working their way down its seams. Somebody took her by the arm to help her out. One of the detectives had to pick up the fallen knitting, hand it back to her, otherwise she would have left without it. And anything that could make her do that—

"I killed him," she mourned.

"It wasn't you alone," the lieutenant acknowledged bitterly as she was led from the room. "We all did."

They seated Donny Blake in a chair, after she had gone, and one of them stood directly behind it like a mentor. They handed this man a newspaper and he opened it and held it spread out before Blake's face, as though he were holding it up for him to read.

The door opened and closed, and Storm, the chartered accountant, was sitting there across the room, in the exact place the Novak woman had been just now.

He looked around at them questioningly, still unsure of just why he had been summoned here. All he saw was a group of detectives, one of them buried behind a newspaper.

"Keep looking where that newspaper is," the lieutenant instructed quietly.

Storm looked puzzled, but he did.

The detective behind the chair slowly began to raise it, like a curtain. Blake's chin peered below first. Then his mouth. Then nose, eyes, forehead. At last his whole face was revealed.

Storm's own face whitened. His reaction was quieter than the woman's had been, but just as dramatic. He began to tremble right as he sat there in the chair; they could see it by his hands mostly. "Oh my God," he mouthed in a sickened undertone.

"Have you anything to say?" the lieutenant urged. "Don't be afraid to say it."

He stroked his mouth as though the words tasted rotten even before they'd come out. "That's—that's the face of the man I collided with—on Farragut Street."

"You're sure?"

His figures came back to him, but you could tell they gave him no comfort any longer. "One hundred percent!" he said dismally, leaning way over his own lap as though he had a cramp.

"They're not altogether to blame," the lieutenant commented to a couple of his men after the room had been cleared. "It's very hard, when a guy looks a good deal like another, not to bridge the remaining gap with your own imagination and supply the rest. Another thing, the mere fact that we were already holding Severn in custody would unconsciously influence them in identifying him. We thought he was the guy, and we ought to know, so if we thought he was, he probably was. I don't mean they consciously thought of it in that way, but without their realizing it, that would be the effect it would have on their minds."

A cop looked in, said: "They've got Blake ready for you, lieutenant."

"And I'm ready for him," the lieutenant answered grimly, turning and leading the way out.

The doctor came forward, tipped up one of Blake's eyelids. Sightless white showed. He took out a stethoscope and applied it to the region of the heart.

In the silence their panting breaths reverberated hollowly against the basement walls.

The doctor straightened up, removed the stethoscope. "Not very much more," he warned in a guarded undertone. "Still okay, but he's wearing down. This is just a faint. You want him back?"

"Yeah," one of the men said. "We wouldn't mind."

The doctor extracted a small vial from his kit, extended it toward the outsize, discolored mass that was Blake's nose. He passed it back and forth in a straight line a couple of times.

Blake's eyelids flickered up. Then he twitched his head away uncomfortably.

There was a concerted forward shift on the part of all of them, like a pack of dogs closing in on a bone.

"Wait'll the doc gets out of the room," the lieutenant checked them. "This is our own business."

Donny Blake began to weep. "No, I can't stand any more. Doc," he called out frantically, "Doc! Don't leave me in here with 'em! They're killing me—!"

The doctor had scant sympathy for him. "Then why don't you tell 'em what they want to know?" he grunted. "Why waste everyone's time?" He closed the door after him.

Maybe because the suggestion came from an outsider, at least someone distinct from his tormentors. Or maybe because this was the time for it anyway.

Suddenly he said, "Yeah, it was me. I did. I was with Gates and the two of us killed this guy O'Neill. He horned in on us in the middle of this uncut diamond job we were pulling. He didn't see me. I came up behind him while he was holding Gates at the point of his gun. I pinned him to the wall there in the entrance and we took his gun away from him. Then Gates said, "He's seen us now," and he'd shot him down before I could stop him. I said, "He's still alive, he'll tell anyway," and I finished him off with one into the head."

He covered his face with palsied hands. "Now I've given it to you. Don't hurt me any more. Lemme alone."

"See who that is," the lieutenant said.

A cop was on the other side of the door when it had been opened. "The D.A.'s Office is on the phone for you, lieutenant. Upstairs in your own office."

"Get the stenographer," the lieutenant said, "I'll be right back."

He was gone a considerable time, but he must have used up most of it on the slow, lifeless way he came back. Dawdling along. He came in with a funny look on his face, as though he didn't see any of them any more. Or rather, did, but hated to have to look at them.

"Take him out," he said curtly.

No one said anything until the prisoner was gone. Then they all looked at the lieutenant curiously, waiting for him to speak. He didn't.

"Aren't you going to have it taken down, lieutenant, while it's still flowing free and easy?"

"No," the lieutenant said, tight-lipped.

"But he'll seal up again, if we give him time to rest—"

"We're not going to have a chance to use it, so there's no need getting it out of him." He sank deflatedly onto the chair the prisoner had just been propped in. "He's not going to be brought to trail. Those are the orders I just got. The D.A.'s Office says to turn him loose."

He let the commotion eddy unheard above his head for a while.

Finally someone asked bitterly, "What is it, politics?"

"No. Not altogether, anyway. It's true it's an election year, and they may play a part, but there's a lot more involved than just that. Here's how they lined it up to me. Severn has been executed for that crime. There's no way of bringing him back again. The mistake's been made, and it's irretrievable. To bring this guy to trial now will unleash a scandal that will affect not only the D.A.'s Office, but the whole Police Department. It's not only their own skins, or ours, they're thinking of. It's the confidence of the public. It'll get a shock that it won't recover from for years to come. I guess they feel they would rather have one guilty criminal walk out scot-free than bring about a condition where, for the next few years, every time the law tries to execute a criminal in this State, there'll be a hue and cry raised that it's another miscarriage of justice like the Severn case. They won't be able to get any convictions in our courts. All a smart defense lawyer will have to do is mention the name of Severn, and the jury will automatically acquit the defendant, rather than take a chance. It's a case of letting one criminal go now, or losing dozens of others in the future." He got up with a sigh. "I've got to go up now and get him to sign a waiver."

The handful of men stood around for a minute or two longer. Each one reacted to it according to his own individual temperament. One, of a practical turn of mind, shrugged it off, said: "Well, it's not up to us—Only I wish they'd told us before we put in all that hard work on him. Coming, Joe?"

Another, of a legalistic turn of mind, began to point out just why the D.A.'s Office had all the wrong dope. Another, of a clannish turn of mind, admitted openly: "I wouldn't have felt so sore, if only it hadn't happened to be a police sergeant."

One by one they drifted out. Until there was just one left behind. The detective named Rogers. He stayed on down there alone after all the rest had gone. Hands cupped in pockets, staring down at the floor, while he stood motionless.

His turn of mind? That of a zealot who has just seen his cause betrayed. That of a true believer who has just seen his scripture made a mockery of.

They met in the main corridor at Headquarters a few hours later, the detective and the murderer who was already a free man, immune, on his way back to the outer world.

Rogers just stood there against the wall as he went by. His head slowly turned, pacing the other's passage as their paths crossed. Not a word was exchanged between them. Blake had a strip of plaster along-side his nose, another dab of it under his lip. But Gary Severn was dead in the ground. And so was Police Sergeant O'Neill.

And the little things about him hurt even worse. The untrammelled swing of his arms. The fastidious pinch he was giving his necktie-knot. He was back in life again, full-blast, and the knot of his necktie mattered again.

He met the detective's eyes arrogantly, turning his own head to maintain the stare between them unbroken. Then he gave a derisive chuckle deep in his throat. It was more eloquent, more insulting than any number of words could have been. "Hagh!" It meant "The police—hagh! Their laws and regulations—hagh! Murder—hagh!"

It was like a blow in the face. It smarted. It stang. It hurt Rogers where his beliefs lay. His sense of right and wrong. His sense of justice. All those things that people—some of them any-way—have, and don't let on they have.

Roger's face got white. Not all over. Just around the mouth and chin. The other man went on. Along the short remainder of the corridor, and out through the glass doors, and down the steps out of sight. Rogers stood there without moving, and his eyes followed him to the bitter end, until he was gone, there wasn't anything left to look at any more.

He'd never be back here again. He'd never be brought back to answer for that one particular crime.

Rogers turned and went swiftly down the other way. He came to a door, his lieutenant's door, and he pushed it open without knocking and went in. He put his hand down flat on the desk, then he took it away again.

The lieutenant looked down at the badge left lying there, then up at him.

"My written resignation will follow later. I'm quitting the force." He turned and went back to the door again.

"Rogers, come back here. Now wait a minute—You must be crazy."

"Maybe I am a little, at that," Rogers admitted.

"Come back here, will you? Where you going?"

"Wherever Blake is, that's where I'll be from now on. Wherever he goes, that's where you'll find me." The door ebbed closed, and he was gone.

"Which way'd he go?" he said to a cop out on the front steps.

"He walked down a ways, and then he got in a cab, down there by the corner. There it is, you can still see it up ahead there, waiting for that light to change—"

Rogers hoisted his arm to bring over another, and got in.

"Where to, cap?"

"See that cab, crossing the intersection up there ahead? Just go which ever way that goes, from now on."

Blake left the blonde at the desk and came slowly and purposefully across the lobby toward the over-stuffed chair into which Rogers had just sunk down. He stopped squarely in front of him, legs slightly astraddle. "Why don't you get wise to yourself? Was the show good? Was the rest'runt good? Maybe you think I don't know your face from that rat-incubator downtown. Maybe you think I haven't seen you all night long, everyplace where I was."

Rogers answered quietly, looking up at him. "What makes you think I've been trying for you not to see me?"

Blake was at a loss for a minute. He opened his mouth, closed it again, swallowed. "You can't get me on that O'Neill thing. You guys wouldn't have let me go in the first place, if you could have held me on it, and you know it! It's finished, water under the bridge."

Rogers said as quietly, as readily as ever, "I know I can't. I agree with you there. What makes you think I'm trying to?"

Again Blake opened and closed his mouth abortively. The best answer he could find was, "I don't know what you're up to, but you won't get anywhere."

"What makes you think I'm trying to get any-where?"

Blake blinked and looked at a loss. After an awkward moment, having been balked of the opposition he'd expected to meet, he turned on his heel and went back to the desk.

He conferred with the blonde for a few min-utes. She began to draw away from him. Finally she shrugged off the importuning hand he tried to lay on her arm. Her voice rose. "Not if you're being shadowed—count me out! I ain't going to get mixed up with you. You should have told me sooner. You better find somebody else to go around with!" She turned around and flounced indignantly out.

Blake gave Rogers the venomous look of a beady-eyed cobra. Then he strode ragingly off in the opposite direction, entered the waiting elevator.

Rogers motioned languidly to the operator to wait for him, straightened up from his chair, ambled leisurely over, and stepped in in turn. The car started up with the two of them in it. Blake's face was livid with rage. A pulse at his temple kept beating a tattoo.

"Keep it up," he said in a strangled undertone behind the operator's back.

"Keep what up?" answered Rogers impassively.

The car stopped at the sixth and Blake flung himself off. The door closed behind him. He made a turn of the carpeted corridor, stopped, put his key into a door. Then he whirled savagely as a second padded tread came down the corridor in the wake of his own.

"What d'ye think you're going to do," he shrilled exasperatedly, "come right inside my room with me?"

"No," Rogers said evenly, putting a key to the door directly opposite, "I'm going into my own room."

The two doors closed one after the other.

That was at midnight, on the sixth floor of the Congress Hotel. When Blake opened the door of his room at ten the next morning, all freshly combed and shaven, to go down to breakfast, it was on the tenth floor of the Hotel Colton. He'd changed abodes in the middle of the night. As he came out he was smiling to himself behind the hand he traced lightly over the lower part of his face to test the efficacy of his recent shave.

He closed the door and moved down the corridor toward the elevator.

The second door down from his own, on the same side, opened a moment or two after he'd gone by, before he'd quite reached the turn of the hall. Something made him glance back. Some lack of completion, maybe the fact that it

hadn't immediately closed again on the occupant's departure as it should have.

Rogers was standing sidewise in it, back to door-frame, looking out after him while he unhurriedly completed hitching on his coat.

"Hold the car for me a sec, will you?" he said matter-of-factly. "I'm on my way down to breakfast myself."

On the third try he managed to bring the cup up to its highest level yet, within an inch of his lips, but he still couldn't seem to manage that remaining inch. The cup started to vibrate with the uncontrollable vibration of the wrist that supported it, slosh over at the sides. Finally it sank heavily down again, with a crack that nearly broke the saucer under it, as though it were too heavy for him to hold. Its contents splashed up.

Rogers, sitting facing him from a distance of two tables away, but in a straight line, went ahead enjoyably and calmly mangling a large dish of bacon and eggs. He grinned through a full mouth, while his jaws continued inexorably to rotate with a sort of traction movement.

Blake's wrists continued to tremble, even without the cup to support. "I can't stand it," he muttered, shading his eyes for a minute. "Does that man have to—?" Then he checked the remark.

The waiter, mopping up the place before him, let his eye travel around the room without understanding. "Is there something in here that bothers you, sir?"

"Yes," Blake said in a choked voice, "there is."

"Would you care to sit this way, sir?"

Blake got up and moved around to the opposite side of the table, with his back to Rogers. The waiter refilled his cup.

He started to lift it again, using both hands this time to make sure of keeping it steady.

The peculiar crackling, grating sound caused by a person chomping on dry toast reached him from the direction in which he had last seen Rogers. It continued incessantly after that, without a pause, as though the consumer had no sooner completed one mouthful of the highly audible stuff than he filled up another and went to work on that.

The cup sank down heavily, as if it weighed too much to support even in his double grasp. This time it overturned, a tan puddle overspread the table. Blake leaped to his feet, flung his napkin down, elbowed the solicitous waiter aside.

"Lemme out of here," he panted. "I can still feel him, every move I make, watching me, watching me from behind—!"

The waiter looked around, perplexed. To his eyes there was no one in sight but a quiet, inoffensive man a couple of tables off, minding his own business, strictly attending to what was on the plate before him, not doing anything to disturb anyone.

"Gee, you better see a doctor, mister," he suggested worriedly. "You haven't been able to sit through a meal in days now."

Blake floundered out of the dining room, across the lobby, and into the drugstore on the opposite side. He drew up short at the fountain, leaned helplessly against it with a haggard look on his face.

"Gimme an aspirin!" His voice frayed. "Two of them, three of them!"

"Century Limited, 'Ca-a-awgo, Track Twenty-five!" boomed dismally through the vaulted rotunda. It filtered in, thinned a little through the crack in the telephone-booth panel that Blake was holding fractionally ajar, both for purposes of ventilation and to be able to hear the despatch when it came.

Even now that he had come, he stayed in the booth and the phone stayed on the hook. He'd picked the booth for its strategic location. It not only commanded the clock out there, more important still it commanded the wicket leading down to that particular track that he was to use, and above all, the prospective passengers who filed through it.

He was going to be the last one on that train. The last possible one; and he was going to know just who had preceded him aboard, before he committed himself to it himself.

It was impossible, with all the precautions he had taken, that that devil in human form should sense the distance he was about to put between them once and for all, come after him this time. If he did, then he was a mind-reader, pure and simple; there would be no other way to explain it.

It had been troublesome and expensive, but if it succeeded, it would be worth it. The several unsuccessful attempts he had made to change hotels had shown him the futility of that type of disappearance. This time he hadn't made the mistake of asking for his final bill, packing his belongings, or anything like that. His clothes, such as they were, were still in the closet; his baggage was still empty. He'd paid his bill for a week in advance, and this was only the second day of that week. He'd given no notice of departure. Then he'd strolled casually forth as on any other day, sauntered into a movie, left immediately by another entrance, come over here, picked up the reservation they'd been holding for him under another name, and closed himself up in this phone-booth. He'd been in it for the past three-quarters of an hour now.

And his nemesis, meanwhile, was either loitering around outside that theatre waiting for him to come out again, or sitting back there at the hotel waiting for him to return.

He scanned them as they filed through in driblets; now one, now two or three at once, now one more again, now a brief let-up.

The minute-hand was beginning to hit train-time. The guard was getting ready to close the gate again. Nobody else was passing through any more now.

He opened the booth-flap, took a tight tug on his hat-brim, and poised himself for a sudden dash across the marble floor.

He waited until the latticed gate was stretched all the way across, ready to be latched onto the opposite side of the gateway. Then he flashed from the booth and streaked over toward it. "Hold it!" he barked, and the guard widened it again just enough for him to squeeze through sidewise.

He showed him his ticket on the inside, after it was already made fast. He looked watchfully out and around through it, in the minute or two this took, and there was no sign of anyone starting up from any hidden position around the waiting rooms or any place near-by and starting after him.

He wasn't here; he'd lost him, given him the slip.

"Better make it fast, mister," the guard suggested.

He didn't have to tell him that; the train didn't exist that could get away from him now, even if he had to run halfway through the tunnel after it.

He went tearing down the ramp, wig-wagging a line of returning redcaps out of his way.

He got on only by virtue of a conductor's outstretched arm, a door left aslant to receive him, and a last-minute flourish of tricky footwork. He got on, and that was all that mattered.

"That's it," he heaved gratifiedly. "Now close it up and throw the key away! There's nobody else, after me."

"They'd have to be homing pigeons riding a tail-wind, if there was," the conductor admitted.

He'd taken a compartment, to make sure of remaining unseen during the trip. It was two cars up, and after he'd reached it and checked it with the conductor, he locked himself in and pulled down the shade to the bottom, even though they were still in the tunnel under the city.

Then he sank back on the upholstered seat with a long sigh. Finally! A complete break at last. "He'll never catch up with me again now as long as I live," he murmured bitterly. "I'll see to that."

Time and trackage ticked off.

They stopped for a minute at the uptown station. There was very little hazard attached to that, he felt. If he'd guessed his intentions at all, he would have been right at his heels down at the main station, he wouldn't take the risk of boarding the train later up here. There wouldn't be time enough to investigate thoroughly, and he might get on the wrong train and be carried all the way to the Mid-West without his quarry.

Still, there was nothing like being sure, so after they were well under way again, he rang for the conductor, opened the door a half-inch, and asked him through it: "I'm expecting to meet somebody. Did anyone get on just now, uptown?"

"Just a lady and a little boy, that who—?"

"No," said Blake, smiling serenely, "that wasn't who." And he locked the door again. All set now.

Sure, he'd come out there after him maybe, but all he, Blake, needed was this momentary head-start; he'd never be able to close in on him again, he'd keep it between them from now on, stay always a step ahead.

They stopped again at Harmon to change to a coal-powered engine. That didn't bother him, that wasn't a passenger-stop.

There was a knock on the compartment-door, opposite West Point, and dread came back again for a moment. He leaped over and put his ear to it, and when it came again, called out tensely, making a shell of his two hands to alter his voice: "Who is it?"

A stewardess' voice came back, "Care for a pillow, sir?"

He opened it narrowly, let her hand it in to him more to get rid of her than because he wanted one. Then he locked up again, relaxed.

He wasn't disturbed any more after that. At Albany they turned west. Somewhere in Pennsylvania, or maybe it was already Ohio, he rang for a tray and had it put down outside the locked door. Then he took it in himself and locked up again. When he was through he put it down outside again, and locked up once more. That was so he wouldn't have to go out to the buffet-car. But these were just fancy trimmings, little extra added precautions, that he himself knew to be no longer necessary. The train was obviously sterile of danger. It had been from the moment of departure.

Toward midnight, way out in Indiana, he had to let the porter in to make up the two seats into a bed for him. He couldn't do that for himself.

"I guess you the las' one up on the whole train," the man said cheerfully.

"They all turned in?"

"Hours ago. Ain't nobody stirring no mo', from front to back."

That decided him. He figured he may as well step outside for a minute and stretch his legs, while the man was busy in there. There wasn't room enough in it for two of them at once. He made his way back through sleeping aisles of green berth-hangings. Even the observation-car was empty and unlighted now, with just one small dim lamp standing guard in the corner.

The whole living cargo of humanity was fast asleep.

He opened the door and went out on the observation platform to get a breath of air. He stretched himself there by the rail and drank it in. "Gee," he thought, "it feels good to be free!" It was the first real taste of freedom he'd had since he'd walked out of Head—

A voice in one of the gloom-obscured basket-shaped chairs off-side to him said mildly, "That you, Blake? Been wondering when you'd show up. How can you stand it, cooped up for hours in that stuffy two-by-four?" And a cigar-butt that was all that could be seen of the speaker glowed red with comfortable tranquillity.

Blake had to hang onto the rail as he swirled, to keep from going over. "When did you get on?" he groaned against the wind.

"I was the first one on," Rogers' voice said from the dark. "I got myself admitted before the gates were even opened, while they were still making the train up." He chuckled appreciatively. "I thought sure *you* were going to miss it."

He knew what this was that was coming next. It had been bound to come sooner or later, and this was about time for it now. Any number of things were there to tell him; minor variations in the pattern of the adversary's behavior. Not for nothing had he been a detective for years. He knew

human nature. He was already familiar with his adversary's pattern of behavior. The danger-signals studding it tonight were, to his practised eye, as plainly to be read as lighted buoys flashing out above dark, treacherous waters.

Blake hadn't sought one of his usual tinselled, boisterous resorts tonight. He'd found his way instead to a dingy out-of-the-way rat-hole over on the South Side, where the very atmosphere had a furtive cast to it. The detective could scent "trap" a mile away as he pushed inside after him. Blake was sitting alone, not expansively lording it over a cluster of girls as was his wont. He even discouraged the one or two that attempted to attach themselves to him. And finally, the very way in which he drank told the detective there was something coming up. He wasn't drinking to get happy, or to forget. He was drinking to get nerve. The detective could read what was on his mind by the very hoists of his arm; they were too jerky and unevenly spaced, they vibrated with nervous tension.

He himself sat there across the room, fooling around with a beer, not taking any chances on letting it past his gums, in case it had been drugged. He had a gun on him, but that was only because he always carried one; he had absolutely no intention of using it, not even in self-defense. Because what was coming up now was a test, and it had to be met, to keep the dominance of the situation on his side. If he flinched from it, the dominance of the situation shifted over to Blake's side. And mastery didn't lie in any use of a gun, either, because that was a mastery that lasted only as long as your finger rested on the trigger. What he was after was a long-term mastery.

Blake was primed now. The liquor had done all it could for him; embalmed his nerves like novocaine. Rogers saw him get up slowly from the table. He braced himself at it a moment, then started on his way out. The very way he walked, the stiff-legged, interlocking gait, showed that this was the come-on, that if he followed him now, there was death at the end of it.

And he knew by the silence that hung over the place, the sudden lull that descended, in which no one moved, no one spoke, yet no one looked at either of the two principals, that everyone there was in on it to a greater or a lesser extent.

He kept himself relaxed. That was important, that was half the battle; otherwise it wouldn't work. He let him get as far as the door, and then he slowly got to his feet in turn. In his technique there was no attempt to dissimulate, to give the impression he was *not* following Blake, patterning his movements on the other's. He threw down money for his beer and he put out his cigar with painstaking thoroughness.

The door had closed behind the other. Now he moved toward it in turn. No one in the place was looking at him, and yet he knew that in the becalmed silence everyone was listening to his slow, measured tread across the floor. From busboy to tawdry hostess, from waiter to dubious patron, no one stirred. The place was bewitched with the approach of murder. And they were all on Donny Blake's side.

The man at the piano sat with his fingers resting lightly on the keyboard, careful not to bear down yet, ready for the signal to begin the death-music. The man at the percussion-instrument held his drumstick poised, the trumpeter had his lips to the mouth-piece of his instrument, waiting like the Angel Gabriel. It was going to happen right outside somewhere, close by.

He came out, and Blake had remained in sight, to continue the come-on. As soon as he saw Rogers, and above all was sure Rogers had marked him, he drifted down an alley there at that end of the building that led back to the garage. That was where it was going to happen. And then into a sack, and into one of the cars, and into Lake Mich.

Rogers turned without a moment's hesitation and went down that way and turned the corner.

Blake had lit the garage up, to show him the way. They'd gotten rid of the attendant for him. He went deeper inside, but he remained visible down the lane of cars. He stopped there, near the back wall, and turned to face him, and stood and waited.

Rogers came on down the alley, toward the garage-entrance. If he was going to get him from a distance, then Rogers knew he would probably have to die. But if he let him come in close—

He made no move, so he wasn't going to try to get him from a distance. Probably afraid of missing him.

The time-limit that must have been arranged expired as he crossed the threshold into the garage. There was suddenly a blare of the three-piece band, from within the main building, so loud it seemed to split the seams of the place. That was the cover-up.

Rogers pulled the corrugated tin slide-door across after him, closing the two of them up. "That how you want it, Blake?" he said. Then he came away from the entrance, still deeper into the garage, to where Blake was standing waiting for him.

Blake had the gun out by now. Above it was a face that could only have been worn by a man who has been hounded unendurably for weeks on end. It was past hatred. It was maniacal.

Rogers came on until he was three or four yards from him. Then he stopped, empty-handed. "Well?" he said. He rested one hand on the fender of a car pointed toward him.

A flux of uncertainty wavered over Blake, was gone again.

All Rogers said, after that, was one thing more: "Go ahead, you fool. This is as good a way as any other, as far as we're concerned. As long as it hands you over to us, I'm willing. This is just what we've been looking for all along, what's the difference if it's me or somebody else?"

"You won't know about it," Blake said hoarsely. "They'll never find you."

"They don't have to. All they've got to do is find you without me." He heeled his palms toward him. "Well, what're you waiting for, I'm empty-handed."

The flux of uncertainty came back again, it rinsed all the starch out of him, softened him all up. It bent the gun down uselessly floorward in his very grasp. He backed and filled helplessly. "So you're a plant—so they want me to do this to you—I mighta known you was too open about it—"

For a moment or two he was in awful shape. He backed his hand to his forehead and stood there bandy-legged against the wall, his mind fuming like a seydlitz-powder.

He'd found out long ago he couldn't escape from his tormentor. And now he was finding out he couldn't even kill his tormentor. He had to live with him.

Rogers rested his elbow in his other hand and stroked the lower part of his face, contemplating him thoughtfully. He'd met the test and licked it. Dominance still rested with him.

The door swung back, and one of the gorillas from the club came in. "How about it, Donny, is it over? Want me to give you a hand—"

Rogers turned and glanced at him with detached curiosity.

The newcomer took in the situation at a glance. "What're ya, afraid?" he shrilled. "All right, I'll do it for you!" He drew a gun of his own.

Blake gave a whinny of unadulterated terror, as though he himself were the target. He jumped between them, protecting Rogers with his own body. "Don't you jerk! They *want* me to pull something like that, they're *waiting* for it, that's how they're trying to get me! It didn't dawn on me until just now, in the nick of time! Don't you see how he's not afraid at all? Don't you notice how he keeps his hands empty?" He closed in on the other, started to push him bodily back out of the garage, as though it were his own life he was protecting. It was, in a way. "Get out of here, get out of here! If you plug him it's me you kill, not him!"

The gun went off abortively into the garage-roof, deflected by Blake's grip on his wrist. Blake forced him back over the threshold, stood there blocking his way. The gorilla had a moment or two of uncertainty of his own. Blake's panic was catching. And he wasn't used to missing on the first shot, because he was used to shooting down his victims without warning.

"I've drawn on him now, they can get me for

that myself!" he muttered. "I'm gonna get out of here—!" He suddenly turned and went scurrying up the alley whence he'd come.

The two men were left alone there together, the hunter and the hunted. Blake was breathing hard, all unmanned by two close shaves within a minute and a half. Rogers was as calm as though nothing had happened. He stood there without moving.

"Let him go," he said stonily. "I don't want him, I just want you."

Rogers sat there on the edge of his bed, in the dark, in his room. He was in trousers, undershirt, and with his shoes off. He was sitting the night through like that, keeping the death-watch. This was the same night as the spiked show-down in the garage, or what there was left of it. It was still dark, but it wouldn't be much longer.

He'd left his room door open two inches, and he was sitting in a line with it, patiently watching and waiting. The pattern of human behavior, immutable, told him what to be on the look-out for next.

The door-opening let a slender bar of yellow in from the hall. First it lay flat across the floor, then it climbed up the bed he was on, then it slanted off across his upper arm, just like a chevron. He felt he was entitled to a chevron by now.

He sat there, looking patiently out through the door-slit, waiting. For the inevitable next step, the step that was bound to come. He'd been sitting there like that watching ever since he'd first come in. He was willing to sit up all night, he was so sure it was coming.

He'd seen the bellboy go in the first time, with the first pint and the cracked ice, stay a minute or two, come out again tossing up a quarter.

Now suddenly here he was back again, with a second pint and more cracked ice. The green of his uniform showed in the door-slit. He stood there with his back to Rogers and knocked lightly on the door across the way.

Two pints, about, would do it. Rogers didn't move, though.

The door opened and the boy went in. He came out again in a moment, closed it after him.

Then Rogers did move. He left the bed in his stocking feet, widened his own door, went "Psst!," and the boy turned and came over to him.

"How much did he give you this time?"

The boy's eyes shone. "The whole change that was left! He cleaned himself out!"

Rogers nodded, as if in confirmation of something or other to himself. "How drunk is he?"

"He's having a hard time getting there, but he's getting there."

Rogers nodded again, for his own private benefit. "Lemme have your passkey," he said.

The boy hesitated.

"It's all right, I have the house-dick's authorization. You can check on it with him, if you want. Only, hand it over, I'm going to need it, and there won't be much time."

The boy tendered it to him; then showed an inclination to hang around and watch.

"You don't need to wait, I'll take care of everything."

He didn't go back into his own room again. He stayed there outside that other door, just as he was, in undershirt and stocking feet, in a position of half-crouched intentness, passkey ready at hand.

The transom was imperfectly closed, and he could hear him moving around in there, occasionally striking against some piece of furniture. He could hear it every time the bottle told off against the rim of the glass. Almost he was able to detect the constantly-ascending angle at which it was tilted, as its contents became less.

Pretty soon now. And in between, footsteps faltering back and forth, weaving aimlessly around, like those of someone trying to find his way out of a trap.

Suddenly the bottle hit the carpet with a discarded thud. No more in it.

Any minute now.

A rambling, disconnected phrase or two became audible, as the tempo of the trapped footsteps accelerated, this way and that, and all around, in blundering search of a way out. "I'll

fool him! I'll show him! There's one place he can't—come after me—"

There was the sound of a window going up. Now!

Rogers plunged the passkey in, swept the door aside, and dove across the room.

He had both feet up on the windowsill already, ready to go out and over and down. All the way down to the bottom. The only thing still keeping him there was he had to lower his head and shoulders first, to get them clear of the upper pane. That gave Rogers time enough to get across to him.

His arms scissored open for him, closed again, like a pair of pliers. He caught him around the waist, pulled him back, and the two of them fell to the floor together in a mingled heap.

He extricated himself and regained his feet before the other had. He went over, closed and securely latched-down the window, drew the shade. Then he went back to where the other still lay soddenly inert, stood over him.

"Get up!" he ordered roughly.

Blake had his downward-turned face buried in the crook of one arm. Rogers gave him a nudge with his foot that was just short of a kick.

Blake drew himself slowly together, crawled back to his feet by ascending stages, using the seat of a chair, then the top of a table next to it, until finally he was erect.

They faced one another.

"You won't let me live, and you won't even let me die!" Blake's voice rose almost to a full-pitched scream. "Then whaddya *after*? Whaddya *want*?"

"Nothing." Rogers' low-keyed response was almost inaudible coming after the other's strident hysteria. "I told you that many times, didn't I? Is there any harm in going around where you go, being around where you are? There's plenty of room for two, isn't there?" He pushed him back on the bed, and Blake lay there sprawled full-length, without attempting to rise again. Rogers took a towel and drenched it in cold water, then wound it around itself into a rope. He laced it across his face a couple of times, with a heavy, sluggish swing of the arm, trailing a fine curtain of spray through the air after it. Then he flung it down.

When he spoke again his voice had slowed still further, to a sluggard drawl. "Take it easy. What's there to get all steamed-up about? Here, look this over."

He reached into his rear trouser-pocket, took out a billfold, extracted a worn letter and spread it open, holding it reversed for the other to see. It was old, he'd been carrying it around with him for months. It was an acknowledgment, on a Police Department letterhead, of his resignation. He held it a long time, to let it sink in. Then he finally put it away again.

Blake quit snivelling after awhile, and was carried off on the tide of alcohol in him into oblivion.

Rogers made no move to leave the room. He gave the latched window a glance. Then he scuffed over a chair and sat down beside the bed. He lit a cigarette, and just sat there watching him. Like a male nurse on duty at the bedside of a patient.

He wanted him alive and he wanted him in his right mind.

Hatred cannot remain at white heat indefinitely. Neither can fear. The human system would not be able to support them at that pitch, without burning itself out. But nature is great at providing safety-valves. What happens next is one of two things: either the conditions creating that hatred or fear are removed, thus doing away with them automatically. Or else custom, familiarity, creeps in, by unnoticeable degrees, tempering them, blurring them. Pretty soon the hatred is just a dull red glow. Then it is gone entirely. The subject has become *used* to the object that once aroused hatred or fear; it can't do so any more. You can lock a man up in a room even with such a thing as a king cobra, and, always provided he isn't struck dead in the meantime, at the end of a week he would probably he moving about unhampered, with just the elementary precaution of watching where he puts his feet.

Only the lower-voltage, slower-burning ele-

ments, like perseverance, patience, dedication to a cause, can be maintained unchanged for months and years.

One night, at the same Chicago hotel, there was a knock at the door of Rogers' room around six o'clock. He opened it and Blake was standing there. He was in trousers, suspenders, and collarless shirt, and smelling strongly of shaving tonic. His own door, across the way, stood open behind him.

"Hey," he said, "you got a collar-button to spare, in here with you? I lost the only one I had just now. I got a dinner-date with a scorchy blonde and I don't want to keep her waiting. By the time I send down for one—"

"Yeah," Rogers said matter-of-factly, "I've got one."

He brought it back, dropped it in Blake's cupped hand.

"Much obliged."

They stood looking at one another a minute. A tentative grin flickered around the edges of Blake's mouth. Rogers answered it in kind.

That was all. Blake turned away. Rogers closed his door. With its closing his grin sliced off as at the cut of a knife.

A knock at the door. A collar-button. A trifle? A turning-point? The beginning of acceptance, of habit. The beginning of the end.

"This guy's a dick," Blake confided jovially to the redhead on his left. "Or at least he used to be at one time. I never told you that, did I?" He said it loud enough for Rogers to hear it, and at the same time dropped an eyelid at him over her shoulder, to show him there was no offense intended, it was all in fun.

"A dick?" she squealed with mock alarm. "Then what's he doing around you? Aren't you scared?"

Blake threw back his head and laughed with hearty enjoyment at the quaintness of such a notion. "I used to be in the beginning. I'd have a hard time working up a scare about him now, I'm so used to him. I'd probably catch cold without him being around me these days."

Rogers swivelled his hand deprecatingly at the girl. "Don't let him kid you. I resigned long ago. He's talking about two years back, ancient history."

"What made you resign?" the other girl, the brunette, began. Then she checked herself. Blake must have stepped warningly on her toe under the table. "Let it lie," he cautioned in an undertone, this time not meant for Rogers to hear. "He don't like to talk about it. Probably—" And he made the secretive gesture that has always stood for graft; swinging his thumb in and out over his palm. "Good guy, though," he concluded. Rogers was looking off the other way. He smiled to himself at something out on the dance-floor just then. Or maybe it wasn't out on the dance-floor.

"Let's break it up," Blake suggested, as one co-host to another. "This place is going stale."

The waiter came up with the check, and Blake cased his own billfold, down low at his side. "I'm short again," he admitted ruefully.

"Let's have it, I'll pay it for you," Rogers, who had once been a detective, said to the man he considered a murderer. "We can straighten it out between us some other time."

Rogers, paring a corn with a razor-blade, looked up as the familiar knock came on his door. "That you, Donny?" he called out.

"Yeah. You doing anything, Rodge?"

They were Donny and Rodge to each other now.

"No, come on in," Rogers answered, giving the razor-blade a final deft fillip that did the trick.

The door opened and Blake leaned in at an angle, from the waist up. "Fellow I used to know, guy named Bill Harkness, just dropped in to the room. Haven't seen him in years. We been chewing the rag and now we're fresh out of gab. Thought maybe you'd like to come on over and join us in a little three-handed game, what d'ya say?"

"Only for half-an-hour or so," Rogers answered, shuffling on the sock he had discarded. "I'm turning in early tonight."

Blake withdrew, leaving the door ajar to speed Rogers on his way in to them. He left his own that way too, opposite it.

Rogers put out his light and got ready to go over to them. Then he stopped there on the threshold, half in, half out, yawned undecidedly, like someone else once had, one night a long time ago, on his way out to get a midnight edition of the paper.

He didn't have to be right at his elbow every night, did he? He could let it ride for one night, couldn't he, out of so many hundreds of them? He'd be right across the hall from them, he could leave his door slightly ajar—He was tired, and that bed looked awfully good. He was a human being, not a machine. He had his moments of let-down, and this was one of them. Nothing was ever going to happen. All he'd managed to accomplish was play the parole-officer to Blake, keep him straight. And that wasn't what he'd been after.

He was about to change his mind, go back inside again.

But they'd seen him from where they were, and Blake waved him on. "Coming, Rodge? What're you standing there thinking about?"

That swung the balance. He closed his own door, crossed over, and went in there with them.

They were sitting there at the table waiting for him to join them. This Harkness struck him as being engaged in some shady line of business. But then that was an easy guess, anyone on Blake's acquaintance-list was bound to be from the other side of the fence anyway.

"Pleased to meet you."

"Likewise."

He shook hands with him without demur. That was a thing he'd learned to do since he'd been around Blake, shake hands with all manner of crooks.

Blake, to put them at their ease together, trotted out that same worn theme he was so fond of harping on. "Harkness don't wanna believe you used to be a dick. Tell him yourself." He told it to everyone he knew, at every opportunity. He seemed to take a perverse pride in it, as though it reflected a sort of distinction on him. A detective had once been after him, and he'd tamed him into harmlessness.

"Don't you ever get tired of that?" was all Rogers grunted, disgustedly. He took up his cards, shot a covert glance at Blake's friend. "No folding money, only nickels and dimes."

Blake took it in good part. "Ain't that some guy for you?"

The game wore on desultorily. The night wore on desultorily along with it. Just three people at a table, killing time.

Harkness seemed to have a fidgety habit of continually worrying at the cuff of his coat-sleeve.

"I thought they quit hiding them up there years ago," Blake finally remarked with a grin. "We're not playing for stakes, anyway."

"No, you don't get it, there's a busted button on my sleeve, and it keeps hooking onto everything every time I reach my arm out."

Only half of it was left, adhering to the thread, sharp-pointed and annoying as only such trivial things are apt to be. He tried to wrench it off bodily and it defeated him because there wasn't enough of it left to get a good grip on. All he succeeded in doing was lacerating the edges of his fingers. He swore softly and licked at them.

"Why don't you take the blame coat off altogether? You don't need it," Blake suggested, without evincing any real interest.

Harkness did, and draped it over the back of his chair.

The game wore on again. The night wore on. Rogers' original half-hour was gone long ago. It had quadrupled itself by now. Finally the game wore out, seemed to quit of its own momentum.

They sat there, half-comatose, around the table a moment or two longer. Rogers' head was actually beginning to nod. Harkness was the first one to speak. "Look at it, one o'clock. Guess I'll shove off." He stood up and got back into his coat. Then he felt at the mangled thatch the game had left in its wake. "Got a comb I can borry before I go."

Blake, mechanically continuing to shuffle cards without dealing them any more, said: "In that top drawer over there," without looking around. "And wipe it off after you use it, I'm particular."

The drawer slid out. There was a moment of silence, then they heard Harkness remark, "Old Faithful."

Rogers opened his heavy-lidded eyes and Blake turned his head. He'd found Blake's gun in the drawer, had taken it out and was looking it over. "Ain't you afraid of him knowing you've got this?" he grinned at Blake.

"Aw, he's known I've had it for years. He knows I'm licensed for it, too." Then he added sharply, "Quit monkeying around with it, put it back where it belongs."

"Okay, okay," Harkness consented urbanely. He laid it down on the bureau-scarf, reached for the comb instead.

Blake turned back again to his repetitious card-shuffling. Rogers, who was facing that way, suddenly split his eyes back to full-size at something he saw. The blurred sleepiness left his voice. "Hey, that busted button of yours is tangled in the fringe of the scarf, I can see it from here, and the gun's right on the edge. Move it over, you're going to—"

The warning had precisely a reverse effect. It brought on what he'd been trying to avoid instead of averting it. Harkness jerked up his forearm, to look and see for himself; anyone's instinctive reflex in the same situation. The scarf gave a hitch along its entire length, and the gun slid off into space.

Harkness made a quick stabbing dive for it, to try to catch it before it hit the floor. He made it. His mind was quick enough, and so was his muscular coordination. He got it on the drop, in mid-air, in the relatively short distance between bureau-top and floor. But he got it the wrong way, caught at it in the wrong place.

A spark jumped out of his hand and there was a heavy-throated boom.

Then for a minute more nothing happened. None of them moved, not even he. He remained bent over like that, frozen just as he'd grabbed for it. Rogers remained seated at the table, staring across it. Blake continued to clutch the cards he'd been shuffling, while his head slowly came around. Rogers, at least, had been a witness to what had happened; Blake had even missed seeing that much.

Harkness was moving again. He folded slowly over, until his face was resting on the floor, while he remained arched upward in the middle like a croquet-wicket. Then he flattened out along there too, and made just a straight line, and lay quiet, as though he was tired.

Rogers jumped up and over to him, got down by him, turned him over. "Help me carry him over onto the bed," he said, "It musta hit him—" Then he stopped again.

Blake was still stupidly clutching the deck of cards.

"He's gone," Rogers said, in an oddly-blank voice. "It musta got him instantly." He straightened up, still puzzled by the suddenness with which the thing had occurred. "I never saw such a freaky—" Then he saw the gun. He stooped for it. "What did you leave it lying around like that for?" he demanded irritably. "Here, take it!" He thrust it at its owner, and the latter's hand closed around it almost unconsciously.

Blake was finally starting to get it. "A fine mess!" he lamented. He went over to the door, listened. Then he even opened it cautiously, looked out into the hall. The shot apparently hadn't been heard through the thick walls and doors of the venerable place they were in. He closed it, came back again. He was starting to perspire profusely. Then, as another thought struck him belatedly, he took out a handkerchief and began to mop at himself with something akin to relief. "Hey, it's a good thing you were right in here with the two of us, saw it for yourself. Otherwise you might have thought—"

Rogers kept staring down at the still figure, he couldn't seem to come out of his preoccupation.

Blake came over and touched him in anxious supplication on the arm, to attract his attention. "Hey, Rodge, maybe you better be the one to

report it. It'll look better coming from you, you used to be on the force yourself—"

"All right, I'll handle it," Rogers said with sudden new-found incisiveness. "Let's have the gun." He lined his hand with a folded handkerchief before closing it on it.

Blake relinquished it only too willingly, went ahead mopping his face, like someone who has just had the narrowest of narrow escapes.

Rogers had asked for his old precinct number. "Give me Lieutenant Colton." There was a moment's wait. He balanced the instrument on one shoulder, delved into his pockets, rid himself of all the paper currency he had on him. He discarded this by flinging it at the table, for some reason best known to himself.

In the moment's wait, Blake said again, mostly for his own benefit: "Boy, it's the luckiest thing I ever did to ask you in here with us to—"

Rogers straightened slightly. Three years rolled off him. "Eric Rogers reporting back, lieutenant, after an extended leave of absence without pay. I'm in room Seven-ten at the Hotel Lancaster, here in the city. I've just been a witness to a murder. Donny Blake has shot to death, with his own gun, a man named William Harkness. Under my own eyes, that's right. Orders, lieutenant? Very well, I'll hold him until you get here, sir." He hung up.

Blake's face was a white bubble. It swelled and swelled with dismay, until it had exploded into all the abysmal fright there is in the world. "I wasn't near him! I wasn't touching it! I wasn't even *looking!* I was turned the other way, with my back to— You know that! Rogers, you know it!"

Rogers kept holding his own gun on him, with the handkerchief around it. "Sure, I know it," he agreed readily. "I know it and you know it, we both know it. You hear me say it to you now, freely, for the last time, while we're still alone here together. And after this once, neither God nor man will ever hear me say it again. I've waited three years, seven months, and eighteen days for this, and now it's here. You found a loophole once. Now I've found a loophole this time. Your loophole was to get out. My loophole is to get you back in again.

"Listen to me so you'll understand what I'm doing, Blake. You're going to be arrested in a few more minutes for murder. You're going to be tried for murder. You're going to be—if there's any virtue left in the laws of this State—executed for murder. They're going to call that murder by the name of this man, Harkness.

That's the only name that'll be mentioned throughout the proceedings. But the murder you're really about to be arrested, tried, and electrocuted for will be that of a man whose name won't appear in it once, from first to last, from beginning to end—Police Sergeant O'Neill. *That's* the murder you're going to die for now!

"We couldn't get you for the one you did commit. So we'll try you for another you didn't commit and get you for that instead."

The Third Murderer
Carroll John Daly

IT DOESN'T TAKE a genius to recognize that there are better airplanes than the ones flown by the Wright Brothers, but they were there first, assuring themselves an important place in history.

The same holds true for Carroll John Daly (1889–1958). There have been many practitioners of the hard-boiled private eye story who are far superior to Daly, but he was the first, inventing the form nearly three-quarters of a century ago with a story titled "Three Gun Terry" featuring private investigator Terry Mack. The story appeared in *Black Mask* in the issue of May 15, 1923, and served as the prototype for all the tough, wise-cracking private dicks who followed.

The first story featuring Race Williams, his most famous character, soon followed with the publication of "Knights of the Open Palm" in *Black Mask* on June 1, 1923. When he followed with another Race Williams story, "Three Thousand to the Good," in the July 15, 1923, issue, Daly had created the first hard-boiled private eye series in fiction.

While in no way a distinguished literary performer, the relentless narrative drive of Daly's fiction made him one of the highest paid pulp writers for a quarter of a century, so popular that it was widely reported that his name on the cover automatically increased sales of the issue by 15%. *The Third Murderer* was originally serialized in *Black Mask* (June–August 1931) as *"The Flame" and Race Williams.*

The Third Murderer
Carroll John Daly

CHAPTER I

A THREAT TO KILL

DIDN'T LIKE his face and I told him so.

He was handsome enough in a conceited, sinister sort of way. And the curve to the corner of his mouth was natural too—but more pronounced now by the involuntary twitching of his upper lip; a warning that a lad is carrying too much liquor and is getting to the stage where he'll slop over. Which is his own business, of course, and not mine—except when that lad decides to slop over on me.

"You don't like my face, eh?" Pale blue eyes narrowed: The skin on his forehead contracted and formed little ridges up close to the heavy blackness of his hair. The quivering lips turned into a sneer. Maybe you couldn't call that leering, threatening face natural—but you couldn't exactly call it acting either. Perhaps it would be best to say that it had started with acting years back and was more a habit now than either a natural contortion or a voluntary set-up. Something that came with long practice.

I looked at the clock above the bar. It lacked ten minutes to the half hour and five minutes past the hour I was to meet Rudolph Myer, criminal lawyer and the best mouthpiece in the city of New York—that is, for my purpose. "Criminal lawyer" is right. Just "criminal" might fit him. But then, if he is most times only a half block ahead of the District Attorney's office, he holds that lead—and on three different occasions had made monkeys out of the bar associations when he was brought up on charges of "unethical practice." Which any one has to admit is hardly a malicious way of classing jury fixing, wholesale perjury, and even extortion.

But I could use Myer at times, when some overzealous gunman got the idea that he could draw a little quicker than I, and later his relatives or friends found out that he couldn't. After such bits of shooting Rudolph Myer was the best man in the world to get me out of stir on a Habeas Corpus writ, and the best man also to keep me out. But back to the lad leaning against the bar in the Golden Dog Night Club, who was playing the game of "Who can Make the Funniest Faces?" and winning in a gallop.

Now, the time—and Myer's promise that he would put something interesting in my way—sort of toned down my childish impulse to play "ugly looks" with the youth who had missed his forte in life and should have been an impersonator instead of a racketeer.

So I moved down the bar, pretended that I didn't see him lift his glass and follow me, and also ignored the bartender's pantomime, which was to indicate to the youthful wise-cracker that he was holding a roman candle in his hand, with the wrong end up. Which was sound advice—even if I didn't fancy the bartender butting into my affairs.

"You're a smart guy, ain't ya?" His elbow crooked on the bar and his cheek went into his open palm. "Race Williams—Private Investigator. Just a dirty dick, that's all you are. And you don't like my face. Well—a lot of people don't like to see it when they've got cause to fear it." He paused a moment, licked at his lips, smiled sort of pleasantly to himself—then opened his eyes a bit and fairly glared at me like an animal, his lips slipping back.

"You read the papers. Be careful you don't look a Gorgon in the face—and die."

"Well—it's ugly enough," I told him. "Why don't you take it down to Headquarters and use it to frighten policemen?"

"Yeah—yeah?" He wasn't the sort of a guy who went in for light banter—not him. He took himself very seriously. "Yeah?" he said again, and then, "Well—it's been down to Headquarters many times—see? And no dick dared to lay a fist on it. They didn't 'third degree' me, buddy—not me, a Gorgon."

"Been stealing milk cans?" I raised my voice, for his was fairly loud now and others were listening. Maybe I'm not so hot at the repartee, but talking around this lad was like talking around a clothing store dummy. I knew him, of course. Eddie Gorgon, who had more than once beaten the rap for murder.

"Milk cans!" he said. "Not me." And when some one laughed he lost his head slightly and cut loose. "The yellow dick, Williams," he raised his head for the few others to get the remark, "let's his moll hide out in a dirty dump. When she was making the grade and turning over the big shots he lived off her and—" My hand shot up and fastened on the lapels of his coat. I jerked him straight and gave him the office.

"If you don't want that face of yours mussed up for a change, why—" and as too many others were taking an interest I tried hard and got a smile over, though I was boiling. "Since I never trail with a woman I guess you've got your dates mixed or you're thinking of yourself," I finished. There was a chance for him to pull back, but he didn't take it.

"Face mussed up!" he repeated, in what he considered great sarcasm. He rather liked his twisted map, I guess. "Don't trail with women! You? No—not with women who can't pay their way—and your way. No women! Why, all the boys on the Avenue know about The Fla— Take your dirty hands off 'a me." He jerked free, and throwing open his coat let me see the gun beneath his armpit. "You'd like a name for her? You'd like to muss the face of Eddie Gorgon? You'd like to chuck the front that you have the guts to cross me—Joe Gorgon's brother?" A slight pause as he shoved his face out. "Well—the little moll was called The Flame—Florence Drummond. The Girl with the Criminal Mind. The—"

And I pasted him. Maybe I lost my head. Maybe I didn't. Certainly though, there was nothing definite in my mind when I let him have it. Maybe I should have provoked him into drawing a gun. Maybe it would have saved a lot of later unpleasantness. But it's not what you should have done that counts in life. It's what you do. And truth is truth. I had nothing in my mind but his glaring eyes and protruding chin and quivering lips. If I had any desire at all, it was to shut his lying, foul mouth—and perhaps that's even stretching the truth a little. The desire, after all, was just to sock him.

Now I won't say that he was "out" before he hit the floor, though I like to think that he was. No, he wasn't dead—just out. To put it simply: I landed flush on his protruding button and—and he hit the floor like a thousand tons of brick. Maybe, if he hadn't landed on his thick head he would have been badly hurt. As it was, he stretched himself out on his back and listened to the birdies chirp.

But one birdie chirped a final message to Eddie Gorgon as he opened his eyes and looked dazedly around. That birdie was yours truly—Race Williams. I simply bent over him.

"All right, Eddie," I told him pleasantly. "You've made your next to last crack about The Flame, in this life. Remember that. The next one is your last."

"I'll kill you for this. I'll kill you for this," he said over and over again, in a dazed sort of way. But though I lingered by his side for a moment he made no effort to reach for his gun.

People were gathering now. The manager had run in from the main dining room, two burly waiters behind him. I didn't expect trouble—but then I'm always ready for it, so I sort of got my back to the wall and stood smiling at the manager.

The manager looked from me to the still prostrate Gorgon. It wasn't a memory that would linger pleasantly in his mind. Eddie Gorgon was a big shot, with his brothers behind him. But then, I was something of a big shot, with nothing but myself behind me—or maybe a gun or two, though they're generally before me.

I think the manager would have decided in my favor, for I was on my feet and the more immediate danger. But he didn't have to decide. The crowd sort of fell back. A giant of a man had entered the doorway. There was something of resemblance between him and the man on the floor. Eddie Gorgon was sort of a replica of the big man in the doorway, though the face of the reclining gunman was younger and less lined. It was also less controlled. Yep, I knew the big bozo. Joe Gorgon, the active member of the feared and fawned upon Gorgon brothers. Joe Gorgon, New York's most deadly racketeer, most politically prominent—and reputed to be one of the fastest-drawing gunmen in the country's greatest city—or out of it, for that matter.

Well—maybe he was. I stood, so, with my back against the wall. If he was sure that he was faster than I, here was his chance to prove it. I don't give way to any man when it comes to pulling rods. That's my living. If it's going to be my death—well—I folded my arms and waited.

I think that he saw me but I can't be sure. At least, he never looked straight at me. I stood my ground while he went over and knelt beside his brother. There was nothing to read in his hard cruel face, with the small nervous little eyes. But he didn't have to worry if his brother was alive or dead. Already Eddie Gorgon was sitting up, and the curses died on his lips as he looked into the hard, unsympathetic face of his elder brother, Joe.

And that was all of that picture. Fingers fell upon my arm.

"Come, come—" said a soft, persuasive voice. "Don't be mixing yourself up in some common brawl that don't concern you. We don't want to be overconspicuous here tonight. At least, not yet."

I shrugged my shoulders and followed Rudolph Myer through the narrow hall, out into the cloak room, and so to the main dining room. It was a cinch he hadn't seen the little byplay. And it was a cinch I wasn't going to mention it to him. He might be of a nervous temperament, and consider it not altogether conducive to a long life and the pursuit of happiness.

CHAPTER II

AT THE GOLDEN DOG

"Mussy bit of a row inside," Rudolph Myer jerked his thumb back toward the bar when we had taken seats in the almost deserted dining room. "Looked like big Joe Gorgon crossing the—. But, there—I've got a job for you."

"Never mind that yet, Myer." I dismissed that topic for the time being. "What's new of The Flame? Still going straight?"

"Still—an hour ago, anyway. But she don't fancy the 'honesty is the best policy' racket, I guess. I don't think it's the money, Race; the drudgery of the work; the law stepping in and tipping her boss off that she's got a record, every time she lands a job. The girl's got the stuff in her. I think it's the excitement; the lure of danger; the control of men, she misses. Imagine her keen, active, if criminal, mind now solving the length of a bolt of silk! Though—damn it—the cheapness of her rooms, after being used to every luxury in life, should be enough to throw her. It's like me, Race. Maybe I wouldn't be honest if—. What are you grinning at?" He broke off suddenly.

I didn't tell him. Rudolph Myer was a queer duck and the crookedest lawyer in the city. Which is some record, no matter how you look on lawyers. But I dismissed the "honest," knowing how touchy he was on that subject. After all, honest lawyers are useless lawyers—at least, in the underworld. And Rudolph Myer was anything but useless. So I took the talk back to The Flame again.

"How about her estate—her mother's end of it, after her stepfather, Lu Roper, died?"

"Look here!" Rudolph Myer let the fingers of both his hands meet at the tips as he placed his elbows on the table. "I've done a bit of legal work for you, Race. We've been friends, and—listen. What do you really know about The Flame—Florence Drummond? Oh, I only did what you've asked me to do—helped her get jobs so that she could live honest—but as a lawyer of course I learned things. I had to, in trying to get her a bit of Mrs. Drummond's money in Philadelphia. But Mrs. Drummond wasn't her mother, Race. Mrs. Drummond simply adopted The Flame a great many years ago from an orphanage outside of Harrisburg. Things were sort of sloppy in those days. The legal papers for adoption never went through properly. Besides which, Lu Roper, her guardian, used what he could get his hands on. But he was a gangster and a killer, and got shot before they could roast him. No, there was little money for The Flame—besides which, she didn't even fancy my taking an interest in her. At least, lately." He looked toward the ceiling.

"Well—" I stroked my chin and feigned an indifference concerning The Flame I did not feel, "she's a good kid, Myer. She did me a good turn. Get her another job—good pay. Make it look natural. I'll foot the bills."

"Yeah—" His shrewd, sharp eyes danced. "You should know her best, Race. Yet you seem to be the only man who ever knew her who thinks she's feeble minded. I warned you it wouldn't work."

"What? She knows that I—"

"Maybe." He shrugged. "Read that." He shoved a note across to me. It was not sealed. I took out the single folded sheet. It read simply enough.

Race:—
    You must see me tonight. This is not a plea. Perhaps you owe me that much. I'll expect you at one o'clock exactly. Climb four flights—second door left—rear. Apt. 5-C.
    I am halfway between the girl and the woman you knew.

THE FLAME.

"I am halfway between the girl and the woman you knew."

That final line was perfectly clear to me. I thought back to my first meeting with Florence Drummond. The wistful, child-like girl who might have been just out of boarding school. And then the times when she was the hard, cruel woman of the world, taking on ten years— her mind shrewd, her every action alert, her face stony and cold—a leader and organizer of criminals. The death of Lu Roper in the Pennsylvania station, back in the Tags of Death affair! The steady hand as she killed the man to save my life; her fight in the underworld, against the distorted brain of the man known as The Angel of the Underworld, in his mad, fantastic, yet almost real grasping for a single Power. Of the night she destroyed that collection of evidence that would set the streets of the lower city aflow with blood; of her disappearance into the maelstrom of a great city; her fight now to go straight.

I looked up at Rudolph Myer, and in my mind was the question: When The Flame wrote that note to me, did she love me—or did she hate me? And I—. Well—The Flame was her name. Given to her because men were attracted to her as the moth to a flame. And again my knowledge that to love The Flame—for a man to hold The Flame in his arms—was to die. Call it superstition if you like. But those who had held her had died. As well to call it a superstition to believe

that if you look down the loaded end of a six-gun and press the trigger you're apt to be amazed at the results.

"You read this?" I asked, for Rudolph Myer was watching me closely.

"Why not?" he said. "It was open. A confidence between lawyer and client. And if you seek legal advice, it is—Don't go."

"Why?"

"Because," he said very slowly, as he lit a cigar, "The Flame is a very remarkable woman. You will either hold her in your arms and die, or—" He shrugged his shoulders. "But after all that might be the way. A lovely woman! I am sometimes glad that the lure of the flesh does not appeal to me."

"And how does she stand toward me now?" I wasn't paying much attention to Rudolph's chatter. Greed, I believed, was his single passion.

"I think—as she writes. Halfway between love and hate, with your presence there tonight to decide. But I've got something more important for you—or at least, something that may be important. Look here!" He placed his hand in his pocket, drew forth a long thick envelope and handed it across the table to me.

This time I had to break the seal. And inside the envelope were five one hundred dollar bills.

"From a client," said Rudolph Myer. "The fee for keeping a closed mouth and escorting an individual from—from one destination to another."

"And the client?" I fingered the bills. They were new and fresh.

"Proposes to remain incognito." The shoulders hunched again. "But if you recognize his features—I can not prevent that. I might add," he winked broadly at me, "that I knew him at once. And to miss this opportunity might be the mistake of your life."

"Might?"

"Yes—might. The thing might go no further, of course. There is that possibility. Your name is in his head. His task is a tremendous one. But there are times when even a man whose pen is weighty enough finds the gun a much surer weapon. At least, tonight he needs the service of a bodyguard."

I fingered through the bills a moment, tucked them carefully into the envelope again and handed it back to Rudolph Myer.

"It's not enough," I told him. "I'll want a thousand for the job."

No, I wasn't greedy, but I knew Rudolph Myer. I thought this client, who had consulted him, had paid more than that—told him to offer me more than that. Rudolph would certainly subtract a good commission for himself.

He saw my reasoning too, for he nodded his understanding as he waved away the proffered envelope.

"It's a small job, Race. I told him five hundred wasn't enough to interest you, but he wouldn't pay more. 'I'm not thinking of the five hundred,' he said, 'and if Race Williams is the kind of a man I think he is and some have described him, neither will he. It's small work—half an hour by a man's side, with the chances a hundred to one that nothing will happen. I don't believe Williams is a grafter, like other private detectives in the city. But he may get out of this the biggest thing in his career. Myer, I could hire a half dozen strong armed men tonight—trusted men—for less than half that sum. Don't tell Williams this, but I'm paying five hundred dollars for the opportunity to look him straight in the eyes and read what's behind them—and judge.' "

"Yeah?" Somehow I believed that Myer hadn't got much out of it for himself after all. "What do you think?"

Myer hesitated a moment.

"I think this man could offer you certainly the biggest case of your career—and certainly too, if not the most hopeless one, the most dangerous. If I were you I'd cop off the five hundred, tip my hat to the gentleman in question and leave him flat. I'll be waiting here until you come back."

"Here? Why?"

"Well—" said Myer, "I'm acting for—shall I say 'our' client, and expect to be paid my regular fee. I've engaged this table for the evening. There will be interesting people at the adjoining table—or so I understand. I think you'll be asked to deliver a message to one of them, and I shall report his reactions to that message."

"Then what?" I was growing interested. Mysteries are all right in books, but you don't meet so many in real life. Besides, I like guys who give you straight talk. And when Myer didn't say anything, I said:

"I'm going to meet The Flame by one o'clock, you know."

Rudolph Myer snapped out his watch.

"It's twenty minutes to eleven. You're to meet—er—our client at eleven. He promises to keep you only half an hour. You'll be back here before twelve, and on your way as soon after as you wish."

I nodded at that. "But—how come this man picks you to pick me? Why don't he come straight to me?"

"I'll tell you this much. More, I'd consider betraying the interest of a client; and at present it's to my best interest not to. This client came to me, spoke of my familiarity with the underworld, and asked me to deliver a message to a certain party."

"And the party was—?"

"That you will probably learn later."

"And the message?"

"That I didn't find out. The name of the party who was to be the recipient of that message was quite sufficient for me. Even though I didn't learn the contents of that message, my—or rather—our client was honest enough to tell me that the delivery of that message would gain the animosity of the greatest menace in the city of New York. I like money. But I like life better. I turned him down flat." Rudolph Myer grinned across at me. "But I did tell him there was only one man fool enough to take the chance. Of course, Race, I named you."

"And then?"

"He walked about a bit and said, 'I have thought of him. I have often thought of Williams.' And half to himself, 'But if it had to come out, I wonder how the papers and the people—and even the officials—might take it.' "

"Tell me some more."

"That is all. Name yourself a good price if you go on with the thing. But make no promises until you are sure of the circumstances. And get yourself a job chasing pickpockets before you decide to cross the man our client names."

Now, if Rudolph Myer had not wanted me to mix myself up in this thing he couldn't have gone about it in a worse way. I may be fussy about the cases I take and don't take, and where the lack of money won't always keep me out of a job—the lack of danger might. When I get mixed up in a case I like things to happen.

When there was no more to come out of Myer I grabbed up my hat, was rather amazed at the place I was to meet my unknown client—which was in front of a drug store—and with a final sentence to Rudolph Myer, left the table.

"See you some more," was all I said.

At the main street door of the dining room I met the head waiter, and parted company with a yellow boy that brought a smile to his face. And when you can buy a smile out of Russett, the head waiter at the Golden Dog, you've spent some real money.

"Who'll be the party at the next table to Mr. Myer tonight?" I asked him. I don't invest money in smiles alone. I like talk.

"Tonight!" Russett looked down at the bill in his hand before he spoke. "Tonight—and most every Monday night—who else but Mr. Gorgon—Mr. Joseph Gorgon."

"Ah—yes," was all I said. But I must have liked it, for I repeated that bit of eloquence, "ah—yes" to myself again as I sought the street.

The Gorgons, for some time prominent in the city of New York, were suddenly shoving themselves into my life—or perhaps, to be more exact—I was shoving myself into their lives. But, any way you take it—things looked promising. That is, if you look on sudden and violent death as promising.

CHAPTER III

THE MAN OF VENGEANCE

I bought a paper as I rode down town in the subway. Things certainly were breaking wide open in our peaceful city. One more city magistrate had been forced to resign from office. The Grand Jury had indicted two others, and the name of a Supreme Court judge was featured pretty conspicuously in the latest investigation—featured with an indifference to a libel suit that bespoke great confidence on the part of the *Morning Globe*.

And once again on the first page was the picture of Joe Gorgon, with the caption below it.

TWENTY YEARS AGO HE SOLD PEANUTS. TODAY DOES HE SELL JUDGESHIPS?

And through the story was a rehash of the several examinations of Joe Gorgon: The rise of the Gorgon brothers to fortune, if not exactly fame; how Joe Gorgon, back in the days when his name was Gorgonette, had pushed himself up to the leadership of the old Gorilla Bridge Gang, when his younger brother, Eddie, was running barefoot in the streets of New York.

The article went on more or less sarcastically about the unfortunate "breaks that young Eddie Gorgon was getting in life" according to his brother Joe. Twice Eddie had actually been indicted for murder, and to the knowledge of the newspapers Eddie was questioned on half a dozen crimes of extreme violence. But how many times the hand of the law, hampered by criminal magistrates, crooked politics and the brotherly love of Joe Gorgon, had been stayed, was beyond the record of that newspaper.

"Investigations may come and magistrates may go, but the rule of Joe Gorgon in the city of New York is still with us. But where his brother, Eddie, is constantly in trouble, the breath of scandal has not blown upon Joe Gorgon—at least, not hard enough to blow him into a prison cell, where he undoubtedly belongs."

That was headline stuff. I skipped to the column heads. One, at least, was good for a grin and reminded me of Eddie Gorgon's last laugh, about looking a Gorgon in the face and dying.

LATEST EAST SIDE GUN-MURDER RECALLS COLUMNIST'S STORY OF THREE GORGON BROTHERS.

And the reporter here had played upon his imagination a bit, but made a rather plausible story for the public at that. He dished up first the article written by a well known columnist comparing the Gorgons to the old myth, and Hawthorne's immortal tale of how Perseus was sent out by the wicked king to bring back to him the head of one of the Gorgons, three winged monsters with claws of bronze and serpents for hair. In this article the writer had nicely called the Gorgon brothers monsters with claws of gold, whose many hairs were the gangsters, crooked public servants and racketeers whom they controlled. But the old Greek myth said that to look a Gorgon in the face meant that the one who looked would turn to stone—or die.

And, continued the story, Eddie Gorgon had certainly stared long enough at Butch Fitzgerald, in an East Side dive, to fulfill the old myth. It is sufficient to say that Butch Fitzgerald had died—been shot to death on Delancey Street. Though Eddie Gorgon presented indisputable evidence that at the time he was visiting friends in New Bedford, Massachusetts, there are many who would bet their last nickel that Eddie Gorgon had a face, if not a hand, in the murder.

But the article, in conclusion, said that the enterprising columnist, not forgetting that the old myth and Hawthorne's tale consisted of three Gorgons, had gone out and not only hunted himself up another Gorgon brother, but had interviewed that brother, Professor Michelle Gorgon, a quiet man surrounded by his books. "An artist and a scholar, whose collection of first prints is the envy and admiration of both amateur and professional collectors. If Michelle Gorgon feels the notoriety which his brothers have given his name, he keeps it well buried inside him. But it is rather well known that neither Joe nor Eddie often visit their brother's apartment atop one of Park Avenue's most pretentious dwellings.

"It would be a queer trick of fate if this educated and quiet, soft spoken Michelle Gorgon after all turned out to be the fine Italian hand that has guided his brothers up the ladder of doubtful fame. For, after all, to talk with Joe Gorgon leaves one with the impression that despite his rather forced smoothness of surface, his Gorilla days are not far behind him."

Of course I had heard that story before. Just the fanaticism of a columnist, but maybe very real to Eddie Gorgon or his brother, Joe. After all, I've often said that crooks are like children at play. Anything that stimulates or satisfies their vanity is quickly grabbed at. Yep, I could very easily see them coddle to that Gorgon myth, rather than resent it. And certainly Eddie Gorgon had glared me down. But then, if I remem-

ber Hawthorne's tale of the GORGON'S HEAD, Perseus had used a sword, and I—well—I go in heavy for guns, and I'm still alive to tell you that a forty-four in the hands of a man who knows how and has the will to use it takes a lot of glaring down—even from a Gorgon. But I shrugged my shoulders, folded up my paper, and stepping out on the subway platform climbed to the street above.

I met my man—or rather, he met me. I was hardly out of the subway station before he walked straight up to me.

"Race Williams." He eyed me closely from under his gray felt hat. Keen, sharp, hard eyes. But I gave him look for look. And I didn't know him. That is, I did and didn't. His face was familiar. But we'll simply say that he was about forty-five; clear, weather beaten skin; piercing, cold, but honest eyes—and the chin of a fighter. Not pugnacious, you understand more, determined, ambitious. A go-getter, and what I liked mostly—not a guy to be sidetracked from his purpose.

He had a way of talking straight talk.

"You will not, of course, presume on my identity. If you discover it, forget it. I shan't go into details about your qualifications. I believe in laying my hand on men personally. If I'm fooled, I want to fool myself. I don't want to blame any one but myself. You have been paid for this job tonight. If it is my pleasure, afterwards, I want you to forget this—this incident. That's agreeable, of course."

"Suits me." I was trying to place him, but couldn't. This much I felt. I had spotted that map in a daily paper—and not so long since either. But I shrugged my shoulders. If he wanted it strictly business he could have it his way.

He led me to a car, threw open the door and watched me climb in.

"I shall drive," he said. "You shall watch that we are not followed. I am putting a great confidence in you."

"Okay!" was the best I gave him as he slid behind the wheel.

"You are not a very talkative man."

"It's your racket." I shrugged.

"Yes—my racket." And he seemed to think aloud, as Rudolph Myer had described it. "Entirely my racket." And then, with a half turn of his head toward me, "I am placing in your hands tonight the life of a man. Maybe, the life and honor of a great many men. What do you say to that?" He fairly snapped the last words at me. I didn't like it. I didn't like his attitude. He was treating me like an ordinary gunman—the gunman the papers sometimes painted me.

"You're trying to buy a lot of silence in New York for five hundred dollars," was what I said to that.

He sort of jumped the car around the corner.

"If a man's honor is for sale, I could never raise a sufficient sum to bid for his silence against—" He hesitated, and then, "I am not buying your silence, Mr. Williams. It is my understanding that it is not for sale. I'm paying you for your time—and your courage, which I understand is for sale. I back my judgment of character rather than my bank balance." I think that he smiled. "Perhaps it's less altruistic and laudable when I confess that my bank balance, compared with my judgment, is negligible. I must confess that I picked you first from—well—if not exactly hearsay, from the opinion of another."

"Rudolph Myer." I smiled a bit.

He smiled too. A hard sort of smile.

"You believe that?" he asked.

"Well—Myer told me so."

"Quite so. I told him that." He nodded, pulled the car up by the iron fence of St.—well—I'll just say, a well known city hospital, and leaving it there in the dark walked by my side to a small gate.

We passed slowly into the hospital, down the dimly lit corridor, ignored the elevator and climbed to the second floor. There another long corridor, a turn to the left, through a curtain into a dark alcove at the end—and a man who had been sitting beside a partly open door jumped to his feet, and with a hand to his hip swung and faced us.

I got a jolt out of that. The man, in plain clothes, was Detective Sergeant O'Rourke, of the New York City police.

"A police case." I guess the words were jarred out of me, and probably not in an enthusiastic voice. The police don't often want me in with them—and I don't want them in with me. Fair is fair! Now, was it simply to identify a man that I was there? I turned to my guide and client. Let the police fight their own battles! They do everything to hamper mine. Five hundred dollars to identify a suspect that the police couldn't lay a finger to! Well—I'd tell this lad where he got off. But I didn't tell him. He was talking.

"Detective Sergeant O'Rourke," he said very slowly, "is off duty tonight. That is, off regular police duty."

O'Rourke was all right. It wasn't working with him I objected to. In fact, I'd go a long way for O'Rourke any time—and had. And O'Rourke would go a long way for me—and maybe, after all, he had. But, as I said, I swallowed my hasty words. I would see what broke.

A white clad nurse opened a door for us, stepped quickly aside, sniffed once—then bowed and left the room. Another nurse, who was sitting by the side of the single bed, rose as we passed behind the screen and I looked at the man on the bed.

He was very old, I thought. His hair was gray. But it was the corrugated skin of his sunken cheeks, the deep lines that set off vividly the hollows that were his eyes. Emaciated parchment covered the single hand upon the white sheet; thick, purple ridges ran from his fingers to his wrist, to lose themselves in the sleeve of the snowy white hospital night shirt.

"You don't know that man?" my client asked me. And there was nothing of anxiety or hope in his voice. It was simply a question; an ordinary question he might ask any one. So he hadn't brought me there for the purpose of identification, for he hardly looked at me when I shook my head.

The old eyes opened. Burning, colorless orbs, except that they shone like two coals of fire. My unknown client stepped to the bed and took him by the hand. The old man clutched the hand frantically, dragging his other with a great effort from beneath the clothes. Eyes alight with both fear and fever burnt from those hollows as his fingers clutched that single strong hand in a grip of terror.

My client spoke.

"It is all right, my friend. I have come back as I promised. I have come to take you away from here. Take you where you'll be comfortable." And as the eyes still burned steadily—terror and horror in their flaming depths, but no recognition—my client leaned down and barely whispered, "Take you to a place where you will find safety—safety and vengeance."

"Vengeance! That is it. That is it. That is what you promise me." There was a decided foreign accent to the old man's words, that was not hidden by the thickness of his voice as he pulled himself up in the bed and kissed that hand he held over and over. "Vengeance!" he said again. "The soul of Rose Marie cries out for vengeance. It is years ago—many. They feared me then. I am not so young now. The Devil. Yes, that was it. They called me The Devil. And now—" And he fell back on the bed, muttering to himself "prison" and "sickness" and "silence." That was all I could understand.

It was at that moment that the nurse who had left the room came back with a doctor. An elderly gentleman who, from his dignity and bearing, was evidently the big medical shot at the hospital.

"I have waited for your return." The doctor snapped out his watch as he spoke. "Not simply to advise you, but to warn you. The patient will get better here, with proper care, the right nourishment, and—and less disturbances. If you move him there is the possibility—I'll say more—the gravest probability that he will die." And at the request of my unknown client he dismissed the nurses.

"I understand and appreciate your interest." My boss had some dignity of his own when he wished to use it. "Let me assure you, Doctor, that you have done all that your professional ethics demand—even as your deepness of human feeling dictates. Let me assure you again that for this man to remain here means almost certain death. No." He raised his hand. "I have said more than I should, now."

"But an ambulance, surely?"

My client hesitated a moment, and then:

"I am afraid not. Too many would know—and to drive it myself would create hospital talk. No." And suddenly and abruptly, "You will kindly ask the nurses to return and make the patient ready to travel."

"But my dear sir, it is a question of human life, and—"

"You are not going to dispute my authority." A hand went into his pocket and came out with a folded sheet of paper.

"No—no." The doctor turned slightly sulky. "I took the trouble to check you up more fully on that this evening from the district attorney's office."

"From the district attorney, himself—personally?"

"No. From the district attorney's office."

"You've been a fool." My client exploded slightly for the first time, and then calmer, "or perhaps I have. But let me assure you that the importance of the man being moved is now even graver. You will call the nurses—at once. Any delay on your part is hampering the cause of justice."

"It's kidnaping," the doctor mumbled. Looked again at the document which my client held in his hand before him, and finally went to the door.

"Kidnaping, certainly—but official kidnaping." And as the nurses came into the room, "You will do me the kindness, Doctor, to tell me just how long ago you telephoned to the—" with a glance at the nurses, "officials."

"Shortly. Perhaps an hour ago. The thing worried me. I—. Can't you wait a minute, sir? The whole thing is unseemly—inhuman—and without precedent in the hospital."

"So—they suggested that you hold the man. Not by force, Doctor—not by official authority—but, let us say, by diplomacy."

And he had the doctor. He squirmed beneath those eyes—the accusation in the man's face. But years and breeding will tell. Dignity won out and the doctor gave him eye for eye.

"And what if they did, sir? It was most natural. You are not hinting that the district attorney's office of New York City would enter into a conspiracy with me to hamper, as you put it, the cause of justice—or that they are not acting in this situation in good faith! I believe, sir, were it as you have hinted, the word would be 'crooked.' "

"Not 'crooked,' Doctor. Let us say 'a hurt pride'—'a false ambition'—or perhaps just the word 'politics.' A word with you in private?"

And I was out of it. But the doctor was a more friendly man when, ten minutes later, we descended to the basement of the hospital in the slowly moving elevator, while Detective Sergeant O'Rourke held the limp, unconscious body of a little old man in his strong arms.

As we passed that main floor I breathed easier. Not in fear or even excitement, you understand. Perhaps in relief. For, after all, the game as I play it is always in the interest of my client. And the man who moved so quickly by the open steel work of the old elevator shaft door was John H. Holloway, an assistant district attorney of the city of New York.

CHAPTER IV

NOT BAD SHOOTING

Now, one thing seemed certain. My client was quite a lad, any way you look at it. If he put something over on the hospital and walked out with a patient he was a high class criminal, which I didn't for an instant believe—even if the presence of O'Rourke didn't eliminate such a possibility. Detective Sergeant O'Rourke was known in the city as "The Honest Cop." Which being an honest cop was the reason for his still being a sergeant, despite his recognized courage and ability that should have entitled him to an Inspector's shield.

But whoever my client was, he was a big shot in his own field. Big enough evidently to keep the district attorney's office from crossing him— at least, in an official capacity. I was getting a bit interested, also I was taking an interest in this lad's map again. It was familiar all right—but not from life, I thought again, but from the newspapers. The newspapers! I liked the taste of that and spun it around on my tongue. It would be worth recalling later.

There we were, out in the hospital grounds. My client leading, O'Rourke following, with the unconscious burden, and I bringing up the rear. Nothing exciting? Maybe not. Yet to me there was a feeling of tension in the air—pending disaster. This client of mine walked with such a steady, almost grim step of determination. If ever a lad had set himself one tough task to bring to a conclusion, this was the bozo.

Tall buildings all around us, the dull lights of the hospital behind us. The outline of the white coated doctor, who stood in the doorway rubbing his chin and moving his lips as if he talked. Nothing but the quiet, somber, and somewhat iodoformed air of a summer night in an orderly city hospital. Yet, for all that, I swung a gun from under a shoulder holster beneath my right arm and stuck it in my jacket pocket.

We made a little gate and came out on the street, perhaps half a block from where our car was, for we had entered by a different gate.

Right behind the car was another, a closed car—parked. We had to pass it to reach our own. It didn't have such a sinister appearance. My client plodded straight on, but O'Rourke slowed up a minute and spoke to me.

"Don't be too free and easy with them guns of yours now, Race. Tonight, it looks like diplomacy. That boat there behind our car is from the district attorney's office. I'd hate to be recognized on this job, but the city's rotten with racketeering graft, or—" And he jostled the human burden in his great arms as he pulled his slouch hat down over his eyes.

Did instinct warn me of danger as we turned on that sidewalk and started toward the car parked so close behind ours? No, I guess it wasn't just instinct. I'm always ready for danger, and there was something wrong about that car. I could see behind the wheel. No well trained police chauffeur sat straight and stiff, ready and waiting. No uniformed man leaned against the car or paced the sidewalk behind it.

One thing I did know. My client wasn't anxious to have the district attorney's office in on his little adventure tonight. And the district attorney's office would like very much to be in on it—that is, without seeming to force their presence. It would be simple then for a man to crouch low in the rear of that apparently deserted car, and then follow us. And my boss got the same idea, for he paused suddenly—waved O'Rourke to stand back, and turned toward that car.

A strange thing happened. The red rear light on that car went off—the brake light. You'd hardly have noticed it but for the fact that a moment before I had been looking aimlessly at the make of the car, wondering if it came to a dash through the city streets, if we'd be able to lose it.

The tiny rear light remained. The red brake light, just below it, had gone out. That meant one thing only. Some one crouched in the front of that car had released his foot or his hand from the brake pedal. Why?

An auto horn screeched suddenly, down the block behind us. A motor raced as a car started in second speed far down the street. O'Rourke turned quickly, facing the sudden screech of the siren. Of course my client reacted in the same manner as did O'Rourke. Just as he stretched out his hand and grasped the open window edge of the car, he straightened, turned his head and looked down the street.

But not me. Gangsters don't announce themselves in that style—at least, if they're making an attack. And if it were the police, the job to assure them of our respectability must come from my client or O'Rourke. As for me—I kept my eyes trained straight on that parked car; the front window. The siren and the racing motor would not distract my attention, if that was its purpose—and it was.

It happened. I won't say it was expected, or even what I was looking for. But then, I won't say it was unexpected. Not unexpected, because in plain words—I don't allow the unexpected to happen, if I can prevent it.

A face bobbed up in that car window. A dark coated arm shot above the half open glass, and the heavy bore of a nickel plated six-gun was smacked right against the side of my client's head. I saw the flashing eyes, the set chin, the thick sensuous lips of the gunman, and knew that the rod he held was, at that distance, heavy enough to blow my client's head to pieces. I knew too that the hand that held that gun was steady, and that the thick lips were cruel. My client turned his head suddenly and looked straight into the weapon which in the fraction of a second would carry death. And—. But why go into it?

I simply raised my right hand slightly, closed my finger upon the trigger and shot the gunman smack through the side of his head. Hard? Cold blooded? Little respect for life? Maybe. But after all, it didn't seem to me to be the time to argue the point with the would-be killer. Remember—I was some twenty feet from him—and shooting at an angle.

The gun crashed to the step of the car. The gunman jumped back. And as I ran around the rear of that car he tumbled to the street and lay still. It was a cinch that he had the door open behind him. It was a cinch too that the car which shot up the street was neither a police car nor that of attacking gangsters. It was simply the getaway car for the man who had attempted the life of my client—for it half slowed, swerved to avoid the body in the street, and as its headlight played upon the dead white face, shot away up the block.

I didn't run out and take pot shots at the fleeing car, but made sure that the gunman had been alone. I jerked out my pocket flash, and with that in one hand and my gun in the other, looked the car over. The gunman had been there alone—that is, as far as life was concerned. But in the back of the car lay the body of the chauffeur. The job was a quiet one. Some one had stuck a knife in his heart and twisted it around. There was a welt on his forehead, too, from a blackjack, the butt of a gun, or some other blunt instrument. He had been knocked out, then, before he was killed.

A brutal bit of work certainly. But maybe

necessary from the gangster's point of view. You can't tell how long a guy will stay "out" from a smack on the head. And the waiting killer couldn't know how long it would take for my client to appear on the street.

O'Rourke had laid his human burden against the stone wall surrounding the hospital and was taking a look-see into the car with me.

"It's Conway," he said, and his voice shook slightly. "A good boy. Only taken off his beat three weeks ago and assigned to the district attorney's office. Been married two months, on the strength of the promised promotion. It's a tough break for a guy—a tough break for a cop. And the lad you—you gave it to. Just another gangster. A lad that Joe Gorgon's gotten out more than once."

"Joe Gorgon's some guy." I put the flash back in my pocket. "But I'd like to see him get his friend out of this mess." And in what I think was justifiable pride, "It wasn't a bad shot, O'Rourke."

"No—" said O'Rourke, "it wasn't. I turned just in time to see you give it to him. He had it coming."

"You'll make a good witness when—" I straightened suddenly as a police whistle came from down the block. "Do I have to explain this, and—"

"You won't have to worry this time, Race. Colonel—" he stopped suddenly. "Our man's a big shot. He—. But it looks like all hell's going to break loose in the city. Like—"

"Our last case together. The Angel of the Underworld—and Power." I helped him out.

"No." O'Rourke shook his head. "For that

was a man who looked for power—who grasped it, too, in rather a fantastic way. But here is Power already established. Nothing fantastic. A reality of money and greed, tearing into the bowels of a great city. Influence—justice—"

"You're talking like a book," I told him. "Let's think of this present mess, and—"

But my client, who O'Rourke called Colonel had already broken into life. He came around from the off side of the car, where he no doubt had been examining the stiff and getting a justifiable and personal kick out of it. Anyway, he had snapped back into life. I saw him talking to O'Rourke just before the harness bull came up the street.

"Just a coincidence that you were here," I heard him say, as he turned quickly from O'Rourke and picked up the unconscious old man from the grass beside the wall. "And if that doesn't go over—" a moment's pause, and very slowly, "But mine is an authority that will carry far." And this time in determination, and nothing slow about it, "To the Mayor of the city itself, if it must be—though notoriety is the last thing we wish. Foul murder has been—. Come!" He turned to me, and half staggered down the street with the sick man in his arms.

"I'll take the boy friend." I nudged his arm. He seemed very shaky—his face very white. The old man was a load for him.

"No—no." He half wiped at his forehead, jarring the man, who muttered something unintelligible. "It's better so—much better so." A pause as I opened the door of his car for him. "I didn't think they'd go as far as that with me—with me."

CHAPTER V

LET THE DEAD REST

O'Rourke was talking to the harness bull down the block when the Colonel took the wheel and despite my efforts to get him to let me handle the car, we pulled from the curb.

"It was horrible," he said. "He died—his face not a foot from mine. I saw the light go out of his eyes."

"Pretty bit of shooting, eh?" I leaned back in the rear seat and braced the sick man's head against my shoulder. Personally, I didn't see anything to grumble about. Things had broken good—for him.

"It was awful—terrible."

"Yeah?" This lad riled me. "Let me tell you something, friend. You got the finest bit of shooting you'll ever get—at any price. And when I think of a job like that for five hundred smackers I could burst out crying."

Maybe I was a bit sore. But then, wouldn't you be? I pride myself on doing my work well. And though there was nothing really remarkable about the shooting itself—the circumstances sort of being in my favor—it had taken quick thinking. The real artistic end of it was not in the bullet beside the gunman's ear, but in the fact that I was in a position to put that bullet there. Another lad—especially the sort of talent the Colonel would get from a private detective agency—would have needed a search warrant to find his gun at the right moment.

"It isn't you," the Colonel said. "But that he should die like that, my eyes on his eyes and—"

"Next time keep your eyes closed then," I snapped at him.

"I'm not blaming you—" he started.

And that was enough. The old boy had let his head sink down so that it rested on my knees, which gave me a chance to lean forward and spill my stuff close to my client's ear.

"Let me tell you this. A split second's delay in that bit of gun-play, and—bing! there'd be some one to say 'Doesn't the Colonel look natural?' You got me into it. You brought me along. If you were aiming on committing suicide, so that the insurance companies would call it homicide, you should have told me so." And waxing just a bit sarcastic now, "You misrepresented the job—or at least Myer did for you. You got your life saved and a lad knocked over for five hundred dollars."

"I never expected it. Never thought they'd dare. It couldn't have been the old man, Giovoni, they wanted to kill. They couldn't have known. It must have been me. But—I'll pay you more. What you wish—what you charge for—"

"A flat rate for a corpse, eh? Well—I took the five hundred and I'll call it a day, unless unpleasant complications arise. It was your party—your fun—and you've got to foot the bills."

"I shouldn't mind." He was nodding his head now, as he narrowly missed a cruising taxi. "I've been through it all—in the war. But here, in the city streets—sudden and violent death!"

"Then don't stick your face into the business end of strange guns," I told him. I was a bit hot under the collar as I ducked another look back over my shoulder to be sure we weren't tailed.

You've got to admit I had a right to feel sore. Here I was, due for a pat on the back—or several pats for that matter, and this lad was crabbing and throwing the "human life" stuff into my face. What did he want me to do? Break down and run to the district attorney's office with a confession? If ever a lad needed one good killing, that gunman was the lad. I started to rake it into the Colonel again—and stopped dead. It took his mind off his driving—at least I thought it did, for he dashed toward the curb and a pole— and finally stopped before a large house on an up-town side street. There was a name that stretched across between the entrances of two houses. I didn't get the lettering then.

The occupants of those two combined houses were more or less expecting us, for the Colonel had hardly climbed the stone steps and pressed the bell when two men in white coats came down the steps, bearing a stretcher. They made quick work of the old guy, Giovoni, in the back of the car. He was muttering now, and breathing sort of heavy. It didn't take a minute to place him on that stretcher and carry him inside.

I climbed out of the car and walked up and down a bit, as the Colonel followed them inside. There was a round shouldered, mustached gent who stood by the door as the stretcher bearers passed. You didn't need three guesses to tell you that he was a doctor—The Doctor.

From the sidewalk it was easy to lamp the name across the two buildings. ELROD'S PRIVATE SANITARIUM it read. But I didn't need that bit of information to wise me up that it was a Quack House.

I spent my time killing butts and looking the street over, but it was a cinch we hadn't been followed. Twenty minutes passed, and one of the white coated stretcher bearers came down the steps and asked me to go inside. I did that little thing. Entered the hall, turned left and stepped into a large waiting room, where the Colonel and the lad I had spotted for the boss sawbones were chewing the fat over a bottle which stood on a table. The white coated stretcher bearer closed the door, leaving himself on the outside.

"Mr. Williams—Doctor Elrod." The Colonel smiled as the Doctor and I shook hands. Doctor Elrod was a harmless, slightly bent, calm little man, with the professional grin of confidence perpetually stamped on his good natured face. I passed him up and listened to the Colonel.

"I have told Doctor Elrod a little—just a little of our experience and strain of this evening. The Doctor was in the war with me." The Colonel emptied his glass, lifted the bottle, poured himself out another hooker, shoved the bottle toward me and indicated a glass with his free hand.

"What's this for?" I looked at the liquor. It said "Genuine Bourbon" on the outside of the bottle.

"It's been a trying evening," said the Colonel, "and I've been a little severe with you." He shoved a glass across the table now. "You'll need something to steady your nerves. I think I have—have further work for you."

I shoved the bottle back across the table to him. He was the army man again, I thought. Severe—kindly—patronizing. I didn't like it. And I'm not a guy to nurse a thing. I gave him what was on my chest.

"You couldn't be severe with me," I told him, and meant it. "You're not big enough." And letting him down on that, "Nor is any one else. And I haven't any nerves. Some day maybe I'll drink with you. But liquor comes under the head of pleasure with me—not business. It's not that the stuff would bother me any," I threw in, for I didn't like the way he nodded his head. "It's the psychological effect. I like to feel that when a guy," and I looked at the Doctor and toned my line down a bit, "falls down, he didn't collapse through the neck of a bottle I'd been handling."

"The Doctor's as right as they make them." The Colonel nodded. "We've discussed you together, Mr. Williams. Now—well—I wonder about those nerves. I'm sure the Doctor would like to—. Rather—in a professional way, it would be interesting to study your reactions to sudden—sudden danger."

And Doctor Elrod had quickly and perhaps nervously stepped forward and clutched at my wrist. I could see the watch in his hand.

I jerked myself free and stepped back a bit. I didn't like it. I spoke my piece.

"The Doctor," I said sarcastically, "can experiment with rabbits and guinea pigs. I'm not playing either tonight. Science, Colonel, can not play a part in a man's—well—a man's guts. The Doctor wasn't there tonight to hold my hand or feel my pulse." And suddenly, "If you must have a demonstration—" I snatched up the bottle of liquor, poured the small glass full to the very brim, and sticking it on the back of my outstretched hand, held it so. Never a drop of the "perfect stuff" fell to the floor to eat a hole in the rug.

"You can laugh that off," I told him, "if you're bent on some low scientific relief."

And he did. I liked the look in the Colonel's eyes then. Maybe not admiration exactly—rather, call it good sportsmanship. But he only nodded, winked once at the Doctor, knocked off his drink, and taking me by the arm walked to the outer door.

"You will guard the patient well, Doc," he threw over his shoulder. "Your medical skill is not half as important as the secrecy of the man's whereabouts. I—" and turning suddenly to me, "Good God! Williams—I never thought to tell you—to ask you. We might have been followed."

"We were not followed," I told him flat. "You can kiss the book on that."

"Ah—yes, yes." And as we went down the steps and climbed into the car, "I was upset, Williams. Very much upset. You could not have acted differently, of course. Indeed, if you had, I—"

"Would have been as stiff as a mackerel." I finished for him. There was no use to let him minimize the part I had played.

"Yes—exactly." He was thoughtful now. "I have a family back in Washington; a responsibility which makes me think that perhaps—" and straightening as he climbed in behind the wheel and I shoved in along side of him, "But I'll see the thing through to the end—and I apologize for my rudeness. My—. There!" He stretched out a hand and gripped mine. "You saved my life tonight, and there are no two ways about that."

"Okay—" I told him. "Forget it. Let the dead rest. You paid for it. It was part of the job." Funny. When you get credit you don't want it, and when you don't get it you're sore as a boil.

We drove for several blocks without a word. Then:

"I think I'll drive you home with me. I have a job that it's almost suicide to give a man."

I smiled at him, and chirped:

"The suicide clause has run out on all my insurance policies. Besides which, I'm considered a bad risk, anyway, now. So—"

"Williams," he said very slowly, "in some respects you are a very remarkable man."

Well—he wasn't the first one who had given me that line. But somehow I liked it. He didn't strike me as a guy who went in much for the old oil.

CHAPTER VI

A THOUSAND DOLLAR MESSAGE

His house proved the regulation brown stone front—just a copy of the private hospital affair, a shade closer to the center of things in the city.

He let us in with a key, carefully closed the heavy front door and pushed me quickly before him up the stairs to the floor above.

"I have taken this house for my stay in the city," he said, as we climbed to the first landing. "Just a man and his wife to look after me. An elderly, not over bright couple, who are long since in bed."

A pause as we passed along a narrow hall, and he stood with his hand upon a door knob—a key turning the lock with his other hand.

"I think I shall take you quite a bit into my confidence, Williams. Yes—quite a bit. But come in."

He threw open the door and we entered a comfortable living room facing on the street.

"You'll excuse me just a moment." He walked to a door in the rear of that room, inserted a key in the lock and went on talking before unlocking it. "Make yourself quite comfortable there. I have a—. Well—a man is waiting for me behind this door. One who might grow alarmed—greatly alarmed—if he heard us talking here. I must ease his mind."

He spun the key, pushed the door open just far enough to admit his body, and slid himself through the narrow aperture, disappeared and—.

The door opened wide this time, and the Colonel was back in the living room again looking quickly around. He opened a closet, the key of which was in the lock; then without a word ducked quickly back into the bedroom again. For it was a bedroom. I could see the bed plainly now—an open window, too, across the room from it.

"What's the matter?" I spoke close to the door, my gun half drawn. Even the most particular movie director would have been satisfied with the perplexed, excited emotion his face was registering.

"Nothing—nothing. It's just my nerves, I guess." The Colonel blocked my way for a moment, then with a jerk to his shoulders stood aside and pointed into the bedroom. "He's gone," he said. "I've searched the room. There's—. And he used the lamp cord—the wiring—to lower himself to the alley." He pointed excitedly to the length of wire that was twisted around the bed post and hung over the window-sill.

"Yes." I saw that. The house was old—there was only one electric floor plug and that was across the room, so there was a generous length of wire needed to reach the lamp. The wire was made of heavy rubber. I leaned out the window and pulled it in. Offhand, I'd say that it reached within—well—ten feet of the ground. Not much of a drop for a man of average height. But my flash, cutting a ray of light into the blackness below, disclosed the fact that whoever had left that room was certainly not lying on the flagging below. I ran the light along the alley a bit, and found it as empty as a country constable's helmet.

"It's your show." I turned to the Colonel. "It wasn't much of a place to lock a guy up in anyway, unless he was hog tied—which—"

"There was no man a prisoner in this room." He had a way of pushing his chin forward and his neck back when he hit his dignity. "That is, an involuntary prisoner." He amended his last statement slightly. "Poor—poor, unfortunate creature."

"I don't want to stick my nose into your affairs," I said, "But I don't go in for riddles either. Wise me up or drop the subject. I don't care which."

"The man in this room," the Colonel broke in, "was the man who brought me the information about Giovoni—the old man in the hospital. It was worth his life if certain parties discovered it."

"Oh. A squealer—a rat. A—"

"No." The Colonel shook his head. "Not in that sense, for I paid him nothing. I would trust you with his name, but that would be breaking a confidence. I promised him secrecy. He came here of his own accord, a withered, sickly, drug addict. He had no money, no friends, and he would not tell me who sent him. At one time he was useful to a certain—a certain trio of criminals. And then the drug. Once a relief from the nightmare of his life; now, to still the craving of his body—and the fear of his mind. He had been useful before; now he feared that he was to be killed. Not because he had ever betrayed these murderers, but because he knew something. Something that he was afraid they might read in his eyes, or that he might let slip in a drug-crazed moment. Yes, he feared death—murder."

"Sure. Some one was going to put him on the spot." I nodded. It may have been a rather new and unique procedure to the Colonel, but to me it was an old racket—a natural one. A member of a gang no longer able to hold up his end. Body and mind weakened, and the gang afraid that if he was dragged over the coals at police headquarters—denied his drug—he would talk.

But the Colonel was talking again.

"Yes—on the spot. That's why he told me what he did. He wanted protection; protection I could have given him. Tomorrow I would have put him where they could not find him. In fear that they would get him, he came to me. Now—in fear that he was not safe here, he has lost himself in a great city."

"It all depends on who THEY are," I suggested. This running up and down an alley after another guy's hat was beginning to lose its interest.

"Ah!" The Colonel stroked his chin, pushed me into the living room, indicated a chair and sat down across from me. I took the cigar he offered me, shoved it into my pocket, and lit a cigarette.

"Mr. Williams," the Colonel said very slowly, as he drummed on the arm of his chair, "would you like to see the city purged of vice and crime—racketeers, and most of all, corrupt officials—crooked magistrates. Yes, and even members of the higher courts perhaps? For the hand of graft can find its way into the pockets of the mighty. It is bad indeed when greed and ambition enter the same brain."

He was so serious that I tried not to smile as he went on.

"You are a good citizen—a staunch citizen. Wouldn't you like to feel that you played an important part in cleansing New York's cesspool—wouldn't you?"

"At the right price?" I looked straight at him.

His dignity hit him again. The outward chin—the backward neck. I killed his words.

"Before you go on with your altruistic oration, let me spill a bit of chatter." I leaned forward and gave him what was on my chest. "I daresay there isn't a big shoe manufacturer who wouldn't want to see every child in the country wear a pair of his shoes—but he don't give them away. Henry Ford would like to see every man, woman and child sporting a Ford coupe—but he don't give them away. It's business with them. When these men are called upon to give to charity, they make out a check. You never saw John D. Rockefeller alleviate the suffering of the unemployed by giving each one of them ten gallons of gas. But he has given away more money for charitable purposes than any man in the country.

"Now—if you want a man hunter, I'm open for such work. And I expect to get paid for it. If a contractor builds a small house he gets a small sum. If he builds an apartment—. Well—that's me. I'll take small pay for a small job and big pay for a big job. If you're raising a fund to help clean up the city and want me, as a good citizen, to contribute to it—all right. I'll give you a check, and expect to see ninety per cent of the money go back into that cesspool you were speaking so elegantly about.

"I'm no amateur detective. I'm a hard working, private investigator. I won't take a job that isn't straight and don't interest me. I may be just a common gunman in your estimation, but I'm a big shot in my own—my own line. At least, others think enough of me to pay me well. I don't know your racket, but I know mine. There. That's a chestful for me, but it's gospel. At least I've made myself clear—that I'm not doubling for a Saint Patrick and driving the snakes out of New York."

"Yes," he said slowly, "you've made yourself clear. But I expect to pay you. You're a very conceited man, Race Williams." And more slowly even, "Undoubtedly a very courageous one also. The man I will want you to face—the man I will want you to deliver a message to is a man who has crushed every one who has stood in his way, politically or financially—and though I can not prove it, I believe that behind him is the greatest villain—the greatest murderer—the—. Here!" He took a folded bit of paper and threw it into my lap.

"Just what price does a big shot like you want, to deliver that message to Joe Gorgon? Stop!" His hand went up as I read the single line on the paper. "The message means nothing to you. But, as God is my judge, I believe that Joe Gorgon would murder, without a moment's hesitation, the man who delivered that message to him—if he believed, as he must believe, that that man was familiar with its significance."

"Just hand this to Joe Gorgon—nothing more?"

"No. Repeat the message to him tonight. Say it as if you were giving him some information. Say it loud enough for his friends to hear. Oh—they won't understand it. Then report to me his reactions to the message."

"Don't you think I'll be blasted right then and there?" I couldn't help but be sarcastic.

"No, not then and there. Not you—after what I saw tonight." And his face paled slightly, in memory of the dead gunman, I thought.

"And that's all you want me to do? When is the message to be delivered?"

"At once—at the Golden Dog. Mr. Myer is keeping the table for your return."

I looked down at the message again. It seemed simple enough. Cryptic, perhaps. I was thinking of my knocking Eddie Gorgon about, just for amusement. Now—well—this little bit of by-play would only accentuate the animosity of the Gorgons. Besides which, I'd be paid for a hatred that I had already acquired under the head of pleasure.

"And that ends my job?" I asked.

"I hope not. If things are as I believe, I will be able to employ you in the biggest case of your career. The anger of the Gorgons won't matter to you then. It will already be established after you deliver—. But here. It is not fair—it is not right. You are a man whose business brings him into queer places; the blackness of dismal, deserted city streets in the late hours. Come! Give me back the message. I forget that you saved my life tonight."

But I closed my fist about that bit of paper as I came to my feet.

"Friend," I told him, "I'll hurl this message into the teeth of the devil himself for one thousand dollars."

"Yes, yes—I believe that you would." And suddenly, "Done! For after all it is a great step toward a glorious accomplishment. Here." He took my hand, pressed it a moment and then dragged open a drawer.

I counted the money and pushed it into my pocket. He went on.

"There will be five hundred more if you do it knowingly! As if the message means as much to you as I hope it will to Joe Gorgon—or the man behind Joe Gorgon. The Third Gorgon. Doctor Michelle Gorgon."

"And that's the whole show?" I asked him, as we left the room and descended the stairs together.

"No. I would like, if possible, to know where Joe Gorgon goes after you deliver that message."

"I can arrange that." I was thinking of my assistant, Jerry. A product of the underworld—a boy I could always count on.

"Good!" said the Colonel. "Telephone me here, then." And he gave me his phone number. "And, Mr. Williams—would you be willing to," and he smiled, "at a price, of course, work for me? Work for the overthrow of the Gorgon brothers? Work silently and secretly, to get evidence against them—rid the city of their presence? A big job, a hard job, and a job that must be accomplished before the opposing political forces appeal to the governor for another investigation of the racketeering. One man is responsible for it all—you know that."

"You mean Joe Gorgon?" I nodded. Yes, I thought I knew that.

"No—" he said. "I mean Doctor Michelle Gorgon. Neither Joe Gorgon nor his racketeers take a step that is an important step without its having been ordered by his brother, Doctor Michelle Gorgon. And Doctor Michelle Gorgon buys judgeships, has crooked officials appointed, and fixes juries. Yes, he is the brains that directs the hands of murderers."

"I've heard that too. But I don't know if I fully believe it."

"Well—fully believe it now. For if you don't, you too may be caught in—. But, there—I can count on you."

"Yes." I tossed my cigarette out in the street, for we stood on the steps of the house now. "But just how do you fit?"

"That—. Well—it might break a confidence. But be sure that I hold the interests of the people, the honest public officials; the citizens who would wish to see their own forces—their own elected officials, their own law and order clean out the menace before outsiders are brought in."

"Why not come down to cases?" I looked at him under the brim of the slouch hat I jerked onto my head.

"Yes, yes." He seemed to think a moment. And then suddenly gripping my hand, "Deliver this message. Then I'll see if you still feel—feel that I have a right to ask you to work with me, since they will suspect—yes, know—that you have taken sides with the enemy."

I grinned at that one. But I saw his point, even if it did sound silly.

"All right," I said simply. "You want to see if I still have the stomach for it. You've been reading your Hawthorne again. THE GORGON'S HEAD. To look a Gorgon in the face is to die! And it would be useless for you to come to terms with a man who is about to do that. Yep—you can't make a deal with a dead man."

And before he could find an answer to that one I was down the steps, after flinging my final line.

"Joe Gorgon will get your message—and it's the easiest thousand dollars I ever earned."

And I was gone. Swinging down the street—breathing deeply of the cool summer air.

When I finally found a taxi I looked again at the message I still held in my hand, stamping the words into my mind.

"THE DEVIL IS UNCHAINED," read the message. And I wondered. Was the devil the little sick old man, Giovoni, we had left at Elrod's Private Sanitarium? And if so, would he throw fear into the heart of a Gorgon—the city's biggest racketeer? Joe Gorgon. Absurd? Maybe. But I remembered once, when the accusing words of a ten year old child sent a shrewd, intelligent man to the chair for murder. "Out of the mouths of babes and old men come—" And though it don't seem to be quoted just right, it might make a deal of sense at that.

CHAPTER VII

A BIT OF MURDER

But I didn't drive straight to the Golden Dog, for I had plenty of time to put on my act for Joe Gorgon and still meet The Flame. I went smack to the Morning Globe office. I knew the man who'd be on the desk at that hour and I'd done a bit of thinking.

They work fast in newspaper offices. They have to. I was turned loose in the morgue, with a man who knew his pictures. Ten minutes later I was staring into the face of the man known as the Colonel. That set chin and those determined eyes stood out in that photo. There was quite a bit to read about him. His war record; his marriage; and his wonderful accomplishments in the army intelligence department.

His full name was Charles Halsey McBride, and he had graduated from college with a deputy Police Commissioner of the city of New York. A commissioner who was taking his job seriously and raising hell all up and down the line, for he was a wealthy man who had the money to do it with and even the backing of the Commissioner—at least, that was the rumor.

"Sure," said the newsman, chewing what he must have thought was a cigarette. "McBride's done some good work, though he blew up in the Chicago investigation. Too much notoriety, I guess, though he never made a squawk. There was talk of the government sending him into New York, but on account of his friendship with the Deputy Commissioner it might make hard feelings. At present, I think he's got a leave of absence, though there's a rumor he's working secretly for Washington on the Power Trust. It's unconfirmed though, and we don't know where he is. But city rackets are out of his line. Trusts—big business—mergers—and oil investigations are his meat. He's got a brain in his head, but you can't sit down in a courtroom behind locked doors and hang murders on lads who have witnesses kidnaped or killed—intimidate witness, who won't dare talk—and hire others to do their killing; others, who don't know for sure who really paid them to do—" The phone rang. "But McBride isn't the lad for that kind of job. It doesn't call for sharp questions from behind a desk."

"No," I said, "it doesn't." But I was rather thoughtful at that, as I left the chap to his phone and departed.

Colonel McBride! Here was a lad who didn't intend to sit behind his desk and listen to big guys explain their positions through the mouths of clever and high paid lawyers. This lad had guts—and sense, I thought, when he took me on. But it was a cinch he hadn't come on orders from Washington. If he had, it would have been in the papers. Then, who was behind him? Certainly he wasn't doing this on his own initiative—besides, Detective Sergeant O'Rourke was taking orders from him—and what's more, Colonel McBride had authority. But—he had said that he wished to clean up the city—the Gorgon brothers—before outside authority stepped in. It might be possible that he was working for the Commissioner himself—privately and secretly, until the time to strike came—building up an evidence that would stand the gaff of a jury trial.

And I didn't feel that I had broken a confidence by looking him up. He knew who he was hiring. I had a right to know for whom I was working. A lad in my position can't tell what might be put over on him. I wouldn't even put it past certain officials to try and frame me. But— I had other things to think of. Jerry, the boy who worked for me, would have to be reached and be outside the Golden Dog to tail Joe Gorgon.

After giving Jerry a jingle at my apartment, I drove up town and entered the Golden Dog at exactly seven minutes after twelve o'clock.

Rudolph Myer had something under the table that wasn't ginger ale. He was pounding nervously on the table, but bobbed up straight as I entered the room.

And at the next table was Joe Gorgon with four other men. His great bulk was shoved far back in the chair, his knees crossed, his thumbs stuck in the armholes of his vest, and a cigar protruding from the corner of his mouth. The other four men I knew. One was a ward leader, called Jamison, and beside him my little playmate, Eddie Gorgon. The other two guys' faces were familiar. One, a fairly well known lawyer—and the other, well—just a face. I couldn't place the name of either.

Joe Gorgon didn't see me. His mind was suddenly occupied by the entrance of Billy Riley, one of the three biggest political leaders in the city.

I heard Gorgon call to Riley as he passed the table, and what's more, Riley was nearer to Gorgon than to me. It was a cinch that Riley heard him. It was a cinch too that Riley didn't want to hear him. Like most of us, Riley liked to claim the acquaintance of well-known men—influential men. But Joe Gorgon was getting himself just a bit too well known. Yet Riley didn't have the stomach to turn him down flat. Money flowed from Joe Gorgon's pocket like from the United States mint—and Riley had a fondness for money.

Jamison, the ward leader, looked up quickly—questioningly, from Joe Gorgon to Billy Riley. I

read, just as well as Joe Gorgon did, what was in his mind. Perhaps Jamison didn't word it as the book of etiquette might, but in his own way Jamison sensed that Joe Gorgon was getting "the cut" direct.

"Riley! Riley!" And Joe Gorgon was on his feet with a rapidity that was astounding in one of his size. Two steps he took, and clutched Riley by the arm. Riley turned, and his smile of greeting was nervous—strained.

"Join us for a few minutes." Joe Gorgon made no effort to keep the conversation private. But there was nothing in his voice but hearty good fellowship.

"Can't, Joe." And Riley nearly choked over the name. A moment's hesitation, and when Joe Gorgon still held his arm but said nothing, Riley stammered, "Got a party waiting—" and then something low.

"Nonsense. Everybody's got time for Joe Gorgon." And Joe clapped a great hand down on Riley's shoulder. "Friends of mine always have time to join me." A moment's pause, and again, "Always—while they're friends." And the last just reached me as I passed to the next table and flopped down beside Rudolph Myer. But I did see that Billy Riley wasn't so big but that he took the chair Joe Gorgon pushed out for him.

Eddie Gorgon looked around and saw me. His sullen eyes flashed into life—his left hand gripped the table cloth—his right hand slipped beneath his armpit. There was a cut on the side of his mouth. I liked that. I smiled over at him. The hot blood went to his head. He came suddenly to his feet and stood so.

An outside influence had come between Eddie Gorgon and me. The head waiter called out. A heavy-set waiter laid down a tray and hurried to the table of Joe Gorgon. But the running, shabby little form was there before him. An emaciated, wild-eyed man, twitching, gripping fingers that stretched quickly out as he fell to his knees and clutched Joe Gorgon by the coat. Joe Gorgon looked from the crouching figure to his brother, Eddie. Eddie nodded, turned quickly and disappeared toward the bar.

The kneeling man cried out.

"Don't let them kill me! Don't let them kill me! Don't have me——"

And Joe Gorgon was on his feet. His two hands stretched out and gripped the kneeling man by the collar. Seemingly without effort he jerked him to his feet, held him so—tightly, and stared into that drawn, unshaven face.

I knew the lad. A harmless, half crazy little snowbird in the underworld. Just "Toney" they called him. If he had any other name I hadn't heard it. But he spoke no more. Whether the grip on his collar was so tight as to cut off his speech, or whether the glaring, staring narrow eyes of Joe Gorgon cowed him I couldn't judge. It was all over in a matter of seconds. Joe Gorgon thrust the man roughly into the hands of two waiters, with the single statement:

"Some bum, I guess. I don't know him." But his eyes followed the whining, crouching, helpless body as the two waiters half carried, half dragged him from the room. And, somehow I wondered if the fantastic newspaper story of the Gorgon myth had—had—. But Joe Gorgon was seated now, and Rudolph Myer was talking—saying the thing that was on my mind.

"Did you see him stare at that man? Did you see the glare in his eyes? A superstitious lot, these warm-blooded people. I tell you, Race, Joe Gorgon was marking that poor unfortunate for death. Not consciously, perhaps—just that he half believes in his own power. Did you hear what the man said? His final words? 'Don't have me—killed' was what he would have said. I saw it in his eyes, before fear kept the words from his lips. And Joe Gorgon. He's a man, Race—a brute without pity—without fear—without nerves. See him now. No emotion of any kind."

"Well——" I came to my feet, grinning at Myer. "We'll see if we can't knock a bit of emotion into him."

"You're not—not now!" Myer half leaned forward to clutch at my coat, thought better of it and watched me cross to the other table. I made a hit too as I approached. Billy Riley smiled

uncertainly. Jamison gulped his drink. Joe Gorgon turned and looked lazily up at me.

"You—Gorgon!" I flipped a finger against Joe's chest. "I want a word with you."

"And you are—?" He pretended not to know me.

"Williams—Race Williams." I fell into his humor. I didn't intend to cross him or rile him. I wanted him in an open, happy mood. I wanted the emotions, if any, that came from my message to start from scratch.

"Williams?" He seemed to think, then grinned at the others. "Not the boy detective?"

"Exactly. It's nice, Mr. Gorgon, to think that you remember me. I'm flattered indeed." And I grinned like a school boy who has gulped his cake in one swallow and not burst before the horrified gaze of the principal.

Joe Gorgon frowned slightly. I wasn't one to take anybody's lip, and Joe Gorgon knew it. Or if he didn't know it, Eddie must have told him. Then I guess his own conceit got the better of him, and he figured out that he and Eddie were two different people and that I'd think twice before I tried that game on him. For his frown disappeared and he smiled, his huge head bobbing up and down.

"Well——" he looked around to see that the others appreciated his high class humor, "let us hear what you have to say. Surely I shouldn't mind. Already one of your breed—at least, one who sells his information to the highest bidder—has——. But, come—don't stand there grinning like an ape."

"I've got a message for you." And I leaned down suddenly, twisted my lips slightly, and shot the words at him like any gangster, with deep secret meaning behind them.

"Joe Gorgon," I said. "The Devil is Unchained."

Now, there didn't seem to me much sense in the words, or much for a man to get gaga over. But they paid a grand to deliver and therefore must carry some weight. And they did. If ever a lad got a thousand dollars' worth out of a message, that lad was my client. Those words wiped the smile off Joe Gorgon's face like you'd run a vacuum cleaner over it. There was a sudden quick flash of bright red to his heavy jowls, that gave place almost at once to a dull white. His right hand stretched out and gripped at the table. He half came to his feet, and sank back again—reached for his untasted cup of coffee, slopped it over his vest, set it down again, and gave the sickest smile that ever a gangster pulled off.

"All right, Mr. Joe Gorgon." I guess there was elation in my voice. "Laugh that one off—or play the look of death, and—" I stopped dead and jerked erect. From outside on the street came a shot; another—half a dozen in quick succession, with the rapidity of machine gun action. People jumped to their feet. I stepped back from the table. Billy Riley had taken Joe Gorgon by the arm. People were going toward the door. The head waiter was trying to tell the customers in a high pitched voice that a tire had exploded, and urging them to keep their seats or they'd give the place a bad name. A bad name for the Golden Dog! Not bad comedy, that.

Some one pushed the head waiter in the stomach and walked out the door. Others hesitated. The music broke into life, and I stepped out on the street. A few buildings down the block a tiny crowd had gathered. They were standing around something on the sidewalk. A harness bull was ordering them back. Another was running up the street, and a man in his shirt sleeves stood in a doorway, wildly blowing a police whistle.

From the small private entrance to the Golden Dog came two men. Joe Gorgon walked by himself, though the man beside him—Billy Riley—held his arm. I saw Gorgon wave him aside as he climbed into a taxi, but I saw something else with a grin of satisfaction. Another taxi pulled suddenly from the curb down the street. Through the back window a hand waved to me. Like his namesake in the papers, my boy—Jerry—was also on the job.

I moved toward the ever thickening crowd, pushed my way by a couple of people, grunted as the back of a man half blocked my vision, ran smack into a policeman, and got a look at the dead man on the sidewalk.

It was Toney, the little sleigh rider who had sought Joe Gorgon's protection a short fifteen minutes before. And now—well—he had more holes in him than a sieve. He must have had his back to the gun, and spun when he fell. For plainly in the bright light from the jeweler's window his face stood out. There was no doubt of his identity.

CHAPTER VIII

FOOTSTEPS ON THE STAIRS

Well—that was that. A man had looked a Gorgon in the face and died—or a Gorgon had looked a man in the face and the man had died. Take it any way you wish. Not much loss to the community certainly. Toney had been a shrewd, clever little gangster. A sure shot to gay-cat a job or listen to conversations, or get his nose in wastepaper baskets before the city wagons carted them away. Now—I shrugged my shoulders. It was a cinch that Toney had outlived his usefulness to Joe Gorgon, and his weakening mind and body had become a danger. Anyway, it don't take much reasoning to say that he was dead. No one would deny that.

I pushed back through the crowd, walked up the street, paused before a United Cigar store and snapped my fingers. What had Joe Gorgon said to me there in the Golden Dog? Words that hadn't seemed to make sense at the time. He had said, "Let us hear what you have to say. Surely I shouldn't mind. Already one of your breed, at least one who sells his information to the highest bidder, has—" And then he broke off. What did he mean? Toney—Toney was selling information to some one—and Eddie Gorgon had left the restaurant to—. Well—Toney had died within a very few minutes. Toney, who had begged Joe Gorgon not to kill him. Toney, a drug addict who—

I shrugged my shoulders. There are times when I don't need a brick building to fall on my head to wise me up to things. And if my thought wasn't true, there was no harm in it. But—I went straight into the cigar store, stepped into a pay telephone booth, and parting with a nickel called the number Colonel McBride had given me.

He answered almost at once. I told him how well his money was spent, and of the tumble Joe Gorgon had taken out of his message.

"By the way," I said casually, "the man—the one that dropped out of your bedroom window tonight. He didn't happen to be a shabby little Italian, not too young, a worn blue suit, yellow brown shoes, a gray flannel shirt none too clean, no tie—and answering to the name 'Toney?' "

"I—why do you ask?" But the answer to my question was in the tone of his voice.

"Because," I said, "you were right about his fearing death. He was killed tonight. Less than five minutes ago, half a block from the Golden Dog." And I told him about Toney coming to the table.

"He was mad—drug crazed—to go to Joe Gorgon. You think—"

"You can't get a jury to convict on a thought," I told him. "But Eddie Gorgon left his brother's table a few minutes before the murder occurred."

"Good God! that is terrible—terrible."

"This old man—Giovoni. How important is he to you?"

"He means, perhaps everything—at least, at present. I have a man in Italy investigating the—" and he bit that off. "But Giovoni is safe. Let me know as soon as you can where Joe Gorgon went when he received that message."

"Yeah. Want me to keep an eye on Giovoni?"

"No, no—that would be the worst thing you could do. Don't go near El—that place. The man is perfectly safe now."

Silence on both sides—then he said:

"That's all!"

And we both hung up.

It lacked a half hour before I was to meet The Flame—but then, perhaps the hour had been suggested by Rudolph Myer because of my other engagement, which he had planned. But I was anxious to get back to my apartment and hear Jerry's report as to where Joe Gorgon went in such a hurry.

I won't say I reasoned things out as I rode down town in the taxi. Not me. Reason only too often confuses, especially when you've got little to reason on—not reason with. But thoughts would flash through my mind, and I let them swing along.

The message I had delivered to Joe Gorgon was a knock-out, certainly. No one would deny that. The biggest racketeer in the city had come very close to taking a nose dive. A few words had brought fear to the man who "feared nothing." Perhaps it was that he feared nothing physically, but the mental reaction to my few words was—

I tapped on the window. We were perhaps a block and a half from The Flame's address. The taxi pulled to the curb. I stepped out and paid the lad off. One thing in my mind. Was The Flame with me or against me when she sent that note? Anyway, I'd look the block over before meeting her. Not very trusting? Maybe not. Oh—I'll admit it's nice, noble, and high minded to have a trust in your fellow man—or fellow woman for that matter. But it's not exactly healthy in my line of work.

The main street was more or less deserted—just one car. But it stood out in such a neighborhood. A high priced, high powered boat, with a uniformed chauffeur at the wheel. Still, a guy gets used to seeing stranger things than that on the city streets. I passed it up, turned the corner and entered the side street, where

according to the number The Flame should live.

Perhaps I got a gulp when I walked past her number. It was a shabby, dreary looking apartment house. Rather hard to connect The Flame up with it. You sort of seemed to think of her with all that was beautiful and, maybe, expensive.

So far I spotted nothing that looked like a trap. I peered into doorways, paced down past half a dozen houses, turned quickly, walked straight to The Flame's apartment house, found the door unlocked—so ignoring the bells, slid into the dimly lit lower hall and started up those stairs.

Started up—and stopped dead. And just when I stopped, or just after I stopped—feet a floor above stopped. Not imagination, that. Not—

I went on. Slowly mounting the stairs. Good sense of hearing—instinct? Call it what you will, but something told me that feet preceded me up those stairs—feet that kept a flight ahead of me. Feet that had been coming down when mine started up, and now stepped carefully back up those stairs—in tune with my own footfalls.

I didn't stop to listen any more. I listened without stopping. Some of my steps I made heavy, some I made light. Sometimes I increased my speed, and it threw the other lad—whoever he was—off his stride. He couldn't keep step with me, and two or three times I heard him plainly on the flight above. He was still steadily increasing his speed as I advanced, and I don't believe I gained a step on him.

Then I tried a light whistle—started an air—broke off in the middle of it and heard his running feet stop, and again try to step with mine.

All right. While he retreated there was no danger. He didn't intend to attack me, then. So I started up the third flight, ever watching above for glaring eyes or a threatening form. But none came. Distinctly I heard old boards creak down that hall. A dull sound as if a foot struck against wood, and a door closed as I reached the landing, turned on the fourth floor and mounted the final flight.

In the dim light I made out apartment 5-C. Listened just a moment, before I knocked on the door. I shrugged my shoulders. After all, it wasn't an inviting neighborhood. There was no reason to connect up the slinking, retreating figure with my visit to The Flame. No reason at all. Yet—I did.

The door opened and I saw her again. There was a hesitancy in her manner which was new to The Flame.

"You—Race. You're early. Just a minute." She closed the door quickly as I entered, left me—so—in the small hall, slipped quickly down the narrow passage and disappeared from view.

I followed her of course—quickly—silently. She slipped through worn, old curtains, and almost ran across the room. But I reached the curtains in time to see her sweep a bundle of bank notes from the table into a drawer—and something else. Something that glittered, and clinked in the drawer before it snapped shut.

"Now—" She turned, stopped dead when she saw that I was already in the room, half glanced toward the table, shrugged her shoulders and smiled.

"Same old trust in The Flame, eh, Race? Well—what do you think of my diggings—my outfit—the reward of honesty?" And in a mock sort of sincerity, "Honesty—the one thing that the rich leave for the poor to fatten on."

I didn't like her mood, so I waited and looked the room over. Things were old and worn, but the place was spotless. The skirt and jacket she wore might have passed for a fashion picture until she got near the light. Then the cheapness of the material forced itself on you in spite of the aristocratic carriage. And as I looked at her I thought of her final sentence in that note. Certainly she was halfway between the girl and the woman.

CHAPTER IX

THE GIRL WITH THE CRIMINAL MIND

When The Flame didn't speak, I tried:

"You didn't bring me here to fill me up on Communism?"

And she laughed.

"No—hardly. That wouldn't be fitting in me. Communism is a hatred of the poor for the rich—not simply an envy. But—" She stepped quickly forward and laid both her hands on my shoulders. "I had to see you again," she said, and those brown eyes sparkled as she looked up at my face. "Sometimes I wonder if it's just my pride that you're the only man I wanted, that I couldn't have—and then I hate myself. Other times I wonder if it's that thing we read about in best sellers, and laugh secretly at. Simply love. Funny. You're the only man who ever—"

"Let's not go into that, Florence." I took her hands off my shoulders. "Let me tell you it's far harder not to love you than it would be to love you. There's your life and mine. I wouldn't have the right to ask any woman to share mine and—"

"Stop!" and the youth went out of her face and the woman crept in. "I made an agreement with you. Anyway, I made it with myself. I'd go straight. And I did. I went straight, though every cop in New York was trying his damnedest to drag me back into the life again. The joke of it, Race! They pulled me out of twenty dollar a week jobs, where the chance to rob the cash till might bring me a few dollars. Me. The Flame! Whose advice—or even suggestion—was bid for

in the thousands. And what right had they? I've never done a stretch—never even seen the inside of stir. And they rode me, Race. Didn't want to let me take twenty dollars for ten to twelve hours work a day."

She laughed now, and I didn't like her laugh.

"They even had me tossed out of jobs where the boss was paid to take me on. A bought position in a sixth grade store. Even the slimy employment agents, who send you to a job or hire you for one, take it out of a girl's pocketbook or her body. Yes, I found the same graft in the East Side sweat shops. All my life the law has taken things from me—even to that real love in the orphanage, when I was a child. A memory. The one decent thing in my life. But why try to make you understand? Honesty? Why, honesty is simply avoiding or evading the law. You can buy a job in the city today—from the position of the meanest worker on the city dump, to a judgeship of even the higher courts. Well—I'm through."

"Easy does it, Florence." I knew what a woman she was when she worked herself up into one of these fits.

"Easy does it! That's what you tell me. But through the months you let me sit night after night in this lonely room. I loved you then. Maybe I love you now. I don't know. But I hate myself for it. I had you come tonight because I thought—well—just pride. I looked at myself in the glass. I'm still The Flame. I've still got the same active—and, yes—maybe criminal mind;

still the same beautiful body. You can't deny that. Now—what do you want me to do with it. Sit here and rot it out in this dirty dive? Sit here—for what? So that you can come in to me during my old age, and tell me that you've bought me a bid to the poorhouse? The poorhouse! Why, you've even got to have money or influence to get into it."

I'd seen The Flame bad before, but never quite like this. Rudolph Myer was right. I shouldn't have come. But still, if I had known the truth—known exactly how I was going to find her—I'd have come anyway, I suppose. But I simply said:

"I didn't think you wanted me, Florence."

"That's a lie," she said, very calmly. More dangerous for that calm I thought. "That's a lie, Race. You knew I wanted you—and I wanted you tonight. I wanted to look at you again. I've been living in a dream, but Myer let me know the truth. You bought and paid for half the rotten jobs I worked on. He didn't tell me in so many words. He didn't have to. And, Myer—" she stopped, flashed those bright, keen eyes on me now. "Well?"

And that "Well?" was a stickler, you got to admit.

"Florence—" I tried the "soft words turneth away wrath" business. "Why don't you be a good sport? You and I have played the game together—faced death together. Just a couple of good pals. I've got some money. Let me give you a stake, until—"

"Just chums!" And her laugh was like finger nails along a wall. "I suppose you'd want me to show you a good behavior card every month; report in person to Rudolph Myer once a week; hit the sawdust trail and shake a tambourine down in the Bowery! And all this while you go around with a gun in your hand and the peculiar idea of personal ethics which allow you to knock over some gunman and trust to the city to give him a decent burial. No—I don't want your money. When I take something I give something in return for it, and—"

"Such as this." My hand had fallen upon the table and rested on a small object that dug into my palm. I picked that thing up now and held it out to The Flame. I'm no jeweller, you understand, but the thing I held was a ring—and the diamond in it was large and real.

"Yes." The Flame cocked up her chin. "Such as this." She snatched it from me, looked at it a moment and shoved it onto a finger. "Such as this. You want to know why I brought you here tonight? Well—I wanted to tell you this. I wanted to look at you again and know. Now—I'm through. The city doesn't want honest citizens. There are dicks right on the Force today who opened car doors for me and touched their hats when they knew I was riding high in the rackets, who have insulted me when I was straight. Politicians—public office holders—and perhaps even a big criminal lawyer, who you—" She stopped dead, pulled open the drawer of her desk and tossed a roll of bills out to me. "That evens it up. There's every penny, as nearly as I can figure it out, that you spent to keep my brain straight and my body—" She shrugged her shoulders, stepped back and looked at me. "You don't like that line, do you?"

"No—" I said, "I don't. It's cheap stuff. And by 'a criminal lawyer' you don't by any chance refer to Rudolph Myer?"

She laughed. But she ignored my question.

"I've tasted the virtue of poverty and didn't find it palatable. Now—I'm through. I've a chance. I'm going to take it." She looked straight up into my eyes, and those brown glims of hers were brilliant. "And I'm not starting over. I'm not building up something. I'm to meet a mind that is like mine—brilliant, quick, active. I'm starting in again. Starting in at the top of the ladder."

"Yeah?" I pulled a butt, stuck a match to the end of it and took a chestful of smoke. "I'm sure glad, Florence, that you're not overmodest about your own abilities." And as she just looked at me, "Well—you didn't bring me here to walk up and down my vest and dig your heels in at each button, did you?" And when she still played the looking game—the brilliance fading from her eyes and a shrewd, speculative cunning creeping in, I forgot the "you catch more flies with molasses than with vinegar" and opened up like a valedictorian.

"Kid," I told her, "you've got guts or you haven't got guts. There are no two ways about that. You can't play the game if you can't stand the gaff. I—" And suddenly, seeing the woman of the night—the Girl with the Criminal Mind—creep into her face, I lost my nerve or made a stab at bringing to the surface the good that I knew—or maybe felt—or maybe only thought—was in The Flame. "Look here, Florence—I'll play along with you. We'll meet occasionally. We'll have dinner together. We'll come up here afterwards and—"

"And you'll explain to me the virtues of honest living." She snapped in on me, and the eyes blazed again. "I've told you I'm through. I am giving you a break. After tonight—The Flame lives again. The Girl with the Criminal Mind takes her place on Broadway. And the police and the rotten officials, who thought my reign was over through lack of guts—not being able to stand the gaff—will bow and scrape again."

I reached out and placed my hands upon her shoulders. She swung slightly, raised those small delicate hands with the quick, living fingers toward me—swayed once, I thought—and maybe only thought—then with a quick jerk she tore my hands from her shoulders.

A simple movement mine—a quick movement hers. But—well—we all have our moments. Weak or strong, I won't try to lay a name to that one. I'll simply say that The Flame was a very beautiful woman. I'll simply say that experience had taught me that to love The Flame was to die, and for a split second I didn't care. Maybe she lost her chance; maybe I'm wrong, and I simply lost mine. Maybe, again, I stood on the brink of disaster and was saved. Anyway, she spoke her piece. I'll give her credit for saying what was on her mind, so that there was no misunderstanding it.

"Race," she said, "you can't help me and you can't hurt me. But I can hurt you. I want one favor from you—one last thing I'll ask. You've often said you owe me something."

"Yes," I told her very seriously, "I do. If ever you need me I'll come to you." I stood watching her now as I finished very slowly. "Even knowing that I may be walking to—into—. Well—I'll come. That much you can count on. I'll come."

"And come armed." There was a sneer in her voice.

"Yes—and come armed," I told her. A guy may be willing to be a fool, but draws the line at being a damned fool.

"Well—" she said, "I'm willing to cry quits. You owe me nothing. I owe you nothing. Just one promise I want. That—for two—" and stopping and looking at my face, "that for two weeks you'll enter into no case—no matter what the inducement—no matter what the incentive."

I thought a moment, and then:

"I'm crossing your plans—your crooked plans?"

"Yes," she said very slowly, "you're crossing my plans—my crooked plans."

Another moment of thought. A straight look into those brown, hard eyes, and I gave her a direct answer.

"I won't do it." That was flat. My ethics may be warped, my ideas twisted, but there's no guy who can say I don't like my own game, and don't play that game as I see it.

"All right!" she snapped suddenly. "You've had your warning—or rather, should I say—your notice." And with the slightest twist to those thin, delicate lips, "I suppose you still think—or still say—you'll come to me when I need you—if I need you."

I looked her smack in the eyes.

"I still say I'll come to you if you need me—if you send for me." And very slowly, "And I still say that I'll come armed."

"That's a threat." She jerked up her chin.

"You can take it as you please. I'll pay my debt. For no man can tell when The Flame will be a good citizen—a fine woman. But no man can tell either when—"

"She'd lead Race Williams to—to his death, eh? That's what you want to say, isn't it?"

"Maybe." I guess my smile was sort of dead. I won't say that I loved The Flame. But I will say that I admired her. Certainly, if she was built to do great wrong, she might just as well be built to do great good. You see, the dual personality doesn't fit in with my practical nature. I always sort of look on it as synonymous with "two faced." That is, that it's an outward change, and doesn't really take place in the individual—but only in the mind of some one who knows the individual. In plain words, there were times when I thought The Flame was all bad, and the good—that youthful, innocent sparkle—was put on to fool others. But fair is fair. There were times also when I felt that The Flame was really all good, and the hard, cruel face—that went with the woman of the night—was put on to hide the real good in her.

There we were, facing each other in that small, sparsely furnished room. The Flame with her back to the curtain by the window, and me with my back against a bare wall, my right hand thrust indifferently into a jacket pocket.

The Flame bit her lip, and emotions you couldn't lay a finger to ran over her beautiful face. I didn't bite my lip. I waited. A long minute passed—feet seemed to creak on the worn stairs outside—steal along the hall and stop by the door of apartment 5-C. Just seemed to, you understand. That don't mean it was nerves on my part. I haven't any. But I have got a keen pair of ears. Ears that weren't sure that the sounds—the faint, almost imperceptible sounds they caught—weren't from the natural, but eerie creakings of an old structure. Let us just say that I liked my back against the wall.

The Flame seemed to be listening too. After a bit, she spoke quickly and hurriedly.

"I've played the game as I've seen the game. I've given you your chance. Now—" she spread out her hands, and her voice was raised—at least, it was shriller, "you stand in my way, Race Williams, and I'll—I'll—by God! I'll crush you."

There was a curve to the corner of her mouth, a narrowness to those brown eyes from which the sparkle of youth was entirely missing. There was almost a sneer in her words—but certainly there was a threat to them.

"All right," I told her. "We've played the game together and we've played it as opponents. I haven't squawked yet, and I won't squawk now. I—"

And I broke off suddenly. A knock, not too loud and not too low, upon the outside apartment door.

I swung quickly, half stepped toward that door—and stopped.

"Don't!" The Flame clutched me by the arm. "I—It's better not to have it known you came here. Please! The fire-escape. It's the top floor—a single flight to the roof. Please, Race. It means more than you think, to me."

"Then it's not war yet." I smiled at her now, took a few steps forward, threw back the tiny curtain, flipped the window open higher, and took a last glance over my shoulder at The Flame, who stood there uncertain—at least, seemingly uncertain—for it's hard to believe that The Flame could be uncertain about anything. So I'll just say that she stood there in the center of the room.

With half an eye on that small, aristocratic right hand of hers with the long tapering fingers, I threw up a leg and placed a foot on the window sill—and stepped back into the room again. I was looking straight into the sneering eyes and twisted lips of the gangster, Eddie Gorgon—but, much worse, I was also looking straight into the mean, snubbed nose of a forty-five automatic.

As I stepped back, Eddie Gorgon quickly slipped through the window I had so accommodatingly raised for him, and stood with a look of triumphant hatred on his face.

CHAPTER X

THE TRAP IS SPRUNG

THERE WAS NO excuse for it. I wasn't proud of myself at that moment. Certainly I didn't trust The Flame, but at the same time I didn't expect—even if she did decide to hate me—that she'd shove me on the spot so quickly. Truth is truth. I didn't trust The Flame. Hadn't trusted her when I came. But a mind like The Flame's doesn't lead a man to a trap in her own apartment. And the reason why isn't "good ethics" or even "good sportsmanship." It's just common sense. Even in a city where gang murders have ceased to be front page news it's not quite safe to decorate your own room with a corpse.

Now, as I say, the thing was surprising—but not unexpected. And maybe "unexpected" is not the correct word there. Maybe it might be a better choice of words to say that I was simply not unprepared for such an emergency. If I happened to be looking down the nose of Eddie Gorgon's gun, my gun was drawing a bead some place along about the center of Eddie Gorgon's stomach. And my finger too was tightening upon the trigger as I raised my jacket pocket slightly and picked out the spot where any ordinary man, according to Gray's Anatomy, would wear his heart.

I won't mince words. And I won't say that there aren't heroes in the pictures, and in real life too, for that matter, who can knock a gun out of a man's hand even when shooting from a jacket pocket. I can do it myself—probably could have done it right then. But "probably" isn't enough. And where a bullet through Eddie's arm or leg would have been noble and high minded, it wouldn't have interfered with the quick pressure of his finger upon the trigger of his automatic.

No. I know gangsters. I knew Eddie Gorgon. There was death in those bloodshot eyes. Bum hooch in them too, but I didn't get that then— and his twisted lips were cut and raw, where I'd leaned on him a few hours before.

But truth is truth. I was going to kill Eddie Gorgon—kill him before he killed me. Nothing saved him now but his tongue, which licked at his lips—and his eyes, that gloated before he talked. He was a lad who liked to shoot a little bull before he shot an enemy—especially when he had that enemy covered.

I wasn't worried. A single roar, a prayer for the dead, and the stiff on the slab in the morgue would be labeled EDDIE GORGON. Eddie Gorgon, the racketeer who had beaten his last rap. I like to see a lad go out with a gun in his hand—a gun gripped tightly in a dead hand. It has a soothing effect on a jury.

Eddie didn't say, "Throw up your hands." He was lucky there. Those simple words would have been the same as the medical examiner's signature on his death certificate, though he didn't know that.

"So," and there was a sort of snap to Eddie's lips when he spoke, "I was right about the dame and you. She's to step out again—so you're back. And I was right about myself too. Me—Eddie Gorgon. There ain't a guy living who's mussed up Eddie Gorgon and lived to tell about it. The boys will know who done you in. The boys'll know why. They'll say it took a Gorgon to step in and smack a gun against Race Williams's chest and blow hell out of him." The grin went, the gun came forward more menacingly. His face shot closer to mine, and his whisky sodden breath made halitosis seem like a rare perfume from the Orient.

"Don't move!" Eddie almost spat the words as I half drew my face back. "I want you to know the truth before you go out. I've not only taken your life but I've taken your dame. The Flame won't be sorry for the message she sent me that you were coming here. She'll be Big Time now. No one will bother Eddie Gorgon's woman." And with a sneer or a leer—or just a twisted pan, call it what you will, Eddie sputtered on. "She's a neat piece of goods, Race—but they don't come too good for Eddie Gorgon. A guy's life and a guy's woman! Well—it ain't so bad for a bust in the mouth when I wasn't looking. I guess, Race—"

My finger tightened upon the trigger, hesitated a moment, and I shot the words through the side of my mouth at The Flame.

"Is what this rat says true? I don't mind the trap so much." I half shrugged my shoulders and glued my eyes on his finger that held the trigger of the automatic. "But I do think you might have grabbed yourself off a pickpocket, or even a stool-pigeon. Besides which—"

"All right—now," Eddie Gorgon horned in. I had seen the sign in his face while I talked. Just the lust to kill, that so many gangsters work up with dope, or hatred, or passion—but which Eddie Gorgon didn't need to work much in order to bring it to the surface. He was an alley rat; a great guy to hide behind an ash can and shoot a lad in the back. A great guy to—

But no more words. He was a killer. And my finger started to close upon the trigger of my gun. Just a sudden tightening, and—

I held back, my finger half closed, my eyes glued on Eddie's gun. The Flame spoke.

"He lies, of course. Eddie, drop that gun!" There was the single movement of The Flame's right hand, a flash of nickel and ivory, and the girl had jammed a gun against the racketeer's ribs. There was nothing of fear or desperation or hysteria in her action or her words. Just that single movement—and the slightest grunt from Eddie. He didn't have to look down to know. And what's more, he didn't look down.

The sudden impulse to raise my left hand and twist the gun from his died without a movement.

I'll give Eddie credit for that much. He wasn't the movie villain, who, at the first disturbance or even suggestion to look up, lets his gun be taken from him. It takes time, you know, to raise your hand and grab a gun—a second or two. And a second or two may not be much time in life, but it is an eternity in death. Even a novice can close his finger upon a gun trigger in a second. But as I said, Eddie knew his stuff. He saw the danger—from me more than The Flame, and cried out his warning.

"Don't you make a move, Race, or I'll plug ya. The girl ain't got the guts to put a Gorgon on the spot. She ain't—"

"Drop your gun, Eddie." The Flame's voice was hard and cold. "The Flame fears neither man nor devil, and that last, I guess, throws in a Gorgon. I'd rub you out like a dirty mark. Where do you get that stuff about me? Where—"

"You! What did you bring me here for? Why did you send for me?" His gun dropped from close to my head to my chest, and flattened there. "Why, I was smack on the fire-escape." And half incredulous—half pleading, "What's eatin' ya, kid? Didn't I set you up handsome? Didn't I get you rocks and—"

"You! You talk too much. You bought my mind, not—" She laughed. "The Flame your woman! Drop that gun."

"Not me." Eddie Gorgon jabbed the gun harder against my chest. "You ain't still got a yen for this yellow dick, eh? I drop my gun, get knocked over, and you send me a wreath!"

"Talk sense, Eddie." The Flame seemed to try to reason now. "Suppose I did send for you. I didn't expect you to come up here to my rooms; to have the police drag me over the coals just when I'm ready to step out again. And, you—"

"Me!" said Eddie. "They can't do nothing to me. I'm a Gorgon. Why, kid, I have an alibi that—"

"Would roast me," she cut in, and her voice was hard again. "I tell you, Eddie, if you press that trigger—"

A soft voice broke in from the little hallway.

"Race Williams will shoot suddenly from his right jacket pocket, and be a very much honored newspaper hero." And as my finger half closed, the mellow voice went on, "No, no—Williams. I am sure things should be done more amicably. The gun, Eddie—on the floor—at once!" And in a sudden change of tone that was as metallic as a cheap phonograph, "Drop that gun—Edward!"

Eddie's gun smacked to the floor, like you'd knocked it from his hand with a crowbar. Mine came from my pocket and pounded against the chest of Eddie Gorgon. For the time I had forgotten that knock upon the door. Now—I didn't turn. I didn't need to. Some one stood in the doorway, and that some one undoubtedly had me covered.

CHAPTER XI

THE THIRD GORGON

The voice behind me went on—soft, persuasive, almost like a woman's, but with a sinister meaning to it that belied the words themselves.

"That's a good boy—a fine boy. You are impetuous, Eddie—and I am afraid you have been drinking. You will stand back—so—close to the wall." Eddie moved as if a hand directed him. "And you, Florence, will lay your gun there upon the table. Mr. Williams, of course, will keep his. It is his trade. I am afraid he is not so susceptible to suggestion. But I am sure he is not so religiously fanatical as to object if I paraphrase even so great a book as the Bible. 'Those that live by the sword shall perish by the sword.' Which, I suppose, if we had a more modern version would go for guns too."

Feet moved now—slow moving feet. Both Eddie Gorgon and The Flame were unarmed. Eddie Gorgon was leaning against the wall, breathing heavily, but not watching me. Rather, the slow moving feet—and I could just see the shadow cast upon the floor.

I swung quickly and faced the man. Maybe I knew—and maybe I didn't. Here was the man who hobnobbed with greatness. Here was the man whom a few felt, and fewer mentioned, as the secret power of Joe Gorgon. The man who called judges by their first names, and political leaders by their last. One who had written books on civil and criminal law, though he had never practiced law. But I'll give you the eyeful as I caught it.

In the first place, he was not armed. There was a thin, Malacca cane over his left arm, a gray glove upon his right hand, and its mate clutched in the fingers of that hand. His muffler, slightly open at the neck, disclosed the whiteness of a boiled shirt. And his braided trouser legs added assurance to the impression that he was in evening dress. But his face got you, and the eyes in that face held you—held you in spite of the shadow thrown on them by his black felt hat.

His face was as white as marble, and his eyes such a deep dark blue that at first glance you'd almost think they were black. There was not a single bit of color in his face and his nose was sharp and straight, his lips a single, thin red line. His eyes didn't blink when they looked at me. They just regarded me fixedly; too alive to be compared to glass. Watched me from between heavy lashes that didn't flicker. The whole outline of his face and perfection of his features couldn't be compared to a portrait because of the unnatural whiteness of his skin—and the living fire of his eyes.

I hadn't seen him often—few saw him often. And his picture never graced the papers. But somehow I knew that I was looking into the granitelike countenance of the Third Gorgon, Doctor Michelle Gorgon.

None of us spoke for a moment. Eddie leaned against the wall and stared at the man who, through some freak of Nature, was his brother. The Flame looked at him too, studied him, I think. Maybe I was wrong, but I did get the impression that she had never seen him before—despite the fact that he had called her Florence.

And the Third Gorgon spoke.

"I am not sure," he said very slowly, "but I feel that at least one of you, and perhaps all of you, owe me a debt of gratitude. But we'll skip that. It savors too much of our criminal courts. Plenty of knowledge but not enough evidence." He paused a moment, sniffed at the air, let those flickerless eyes rest on his brother, and half bowed to me.

"We must bow to you, Williams, as the physical dominance in this room—perhaps, thanks to me. Fine wines warm a man's blood and make more active his brain. Poor liquor, even when taken by another, nauseates me. I know you, of course—have read about you and seen your picture in the papers. I understand you do not go in for murder." A moment's pause, and his head cocked sideways as he put those eyes on me. "That—that is true?"

"It depends on what you call murder." Somehow I couldn't feel exactly at ease with this guy.

He shook his head.

"Ah, no. No—not at all. My ideas of murder are not entirely expounded in my books. They are private thoughts and opinions which must be withheld for the public good. And I will not say murder in the legal sense, for if I've followed your exploits correctly you have not obtained your ethics from the criminal code."

"Well—get to the point. What's on your chest?"

His thin lips dropped slightly, and just for the fraction of a second those eyelids flickered before he spoke.

"You disappoint me, Williams. You really disappoint me." And with a sudden snap, "I am speaking of the putrid condition of the air, caused by the presence of my brother. Will you stand in the way of his departure? In plain words—he is unarmed. Are you bent on murdering him?"

"There's the police." Maybe I was sparring for time. "He attempted my life, you know."

"Come—come, my dear Williams." Doctor Gorgon seemed annoyed, and then he smiled—only his lips moving. "But you joke." He turned and looked at The Flame. He stepped close to her. For a minute he stood so—then his hand went beneath his coat, and despite the fact that he was sideways to me I half raised my gun. But when he withdrew his hand it held nothing more dangerous than a pair of nose glasses attached to a very thin black ribbon.

He placed the glasses upon his nose, leaned forward and stooped—for he was close to a head above The Flame. Then he raised his hand and removed his hat.

If The Flame resented his attitude she did not show it. I saw her little head bob up—those brown eyes, hard and cold, stare back into his. Then he turned to Eddie Gorgon, half impatiently.

"You may go, Eddie." And with a raise of his hand as Eddie started to say something sulkily, "Tut—tut, boy. He shan't kill you, you know. And if he intended to, he would hardly do it in my presence." And when Eddie still held his ground, "That will be all, Edward. Not by the window, you scamp." He crossed the room quickly this time, patted Eddie on the back as he half pushed him toward the door. "I am sure that Williams realizes there is a lady present and will not object to your leaving us."

I didn't object. Maybe I realized there would have been nothing to do. That is, nothing to do but lay a chunk of lead in Eddie's carcass or call the police. But one thing I did get, and that was that Eddie Gorgon feared that affected "Edward" of his brother's more than even my gun.

"Affected." Well—I'll withdraw that word. No— Damn it. One thing that Doctor Gorgon got over to me, even if I don't get it over to others, was his sincerity—or perhaps, just his own belief in himself. He sure was the white haired boy, though now that his hat was off, there was just the glimmer of gray in the jet blackness of his hair. The first few strands of it, which hung near his forehead.

The Flame looked quickly up at me as Doctor Gorgon followed his brother to the hall. I smiled back at her. Not a pleasant smile, maybe—but one of confidence. There was a peculiar look in her eyes. A questioning, uncertain look.

"Well—" she said at length—while the hollow, whispered, inaudible tones of conversation came from the little hall, "why don't you say something? Don't stand there looking accusingly at me. I—. What right have you? Why—. Well—say something!"

And I did.

"He travels farthest who travels alone." I did a bit of quoting myself, like the Doctor. "And that probably goes for traveling fastest too. Your friend, the Doctor, noticed the gun in my pocket, which covered his brother." And after a pause, "I wonder if you did, and if you were protecting Eddie or me."

"You think I brought you here to—to your death? Well—why don't you say so?"

"Should I?" I shrugged my shoulders. "Is it necessary? Rudolph Myer said I was the only one who took you for being weak minded. At least, Eddie was here—said you sent for him, and you didn't deny it. That he muffed the works by acting too soon, and—perhaps—talking too much, isn't your fault. But you certainly picked yourself a fine little playmate, when you did decide to—"

"Race," she said very slowly, "you and I can't fool ourselves any longer. At least, I can't fool myself. I've never posed as being good. Quite the contrary. To hear you talk you'd think I had suddenly changed. Just one thing. You don't believe I led you into a trap tonight?"

I sort of laughed.

"What else could I—"

"The same old song." She came close to me, put those glims on me. "Always accusing—never believing. Come—" I let her get close to me, let her place her hands on my shoulders—even let her slip them back about my neck and onto the back of my head.

"Come—" she said again, "you don't believe it. Yes or no."

"Yes—" I said, "I do believe it. You can't come the 'kid act' on me any longer. You can't—"

"You fool," she whispered hoarsely, looking toward the door. "I never ate my heart out because I couldn't get you—have you. I could have had you whenever I wanted you—you or any other man. But I wanted you to want me, too. Don't you see? I didn't want you like the others. I could always have made you—can make you love me. Because—well—look here."

That little body of hers was close to me. Warm breath was on my cheeks, hands pressed the back of my head. I just grinned down at her, lifted my hands slowly to take hers from about my neck—and she did it. One quick movement; one quick jerk—lips that touched mine; a breath that seemed to go deep into my body; a burning in my forehead; a quick, dizzy rush of blood—and her eyes, flaming and soft, and—. Oh, hell—it happened. Just for a second—maybe a split second—I crushed The Flame to me, held her so—then thrust her from me, flinging her half across the room. A chair turned, spun a moment, and toppled to the floor.

CHAPTER XII

QUEER TALK

Had I lost my head? I don't know. Why lie about such things? Yet—. Maybe I hadn't been carried away by her presence—. But The Flame was beautiful; The Flame was—. Why shouldn't a man hold a beautiful woman?

I leaned against the wall and looked at her. She was smiling at me. What was in her mind? Here was a wonderful woman. No—something else struck me then. The line I had just pulled on her. "He travels farthest who travels alone." And she was coming across the room to me.

The woman! No—the woman was gone now. It was the girl, Florence Drummond. The sparkle of youth in her eyes—a softness—a realness that made me rub my hand across my glims and blink.

"You're right, Race. Maybe, after all—" She stopped dead, and straightened. The hall door closed. Soft, slow feet—and Doctor Michelle Gorgon was in the room.

He ignored my presence completely—went straight to Florence, lifted both her hands in his and stared at her without a word. And The Flame looked back at him. Nothing of anger, just a straight look from clear deep eyes. No color came into her cheeks; no embarrassment to those great brown orbs.

"So you are The Flame. The Girl with the Criminal Mind. Do you know that you are a very fortunate young lady? Very fortunate indeed. I think that I could like you a great deal. I—"

"Doctor Gorgon," I crossed the room, "Miss Drummond has had a very trying evening as it is. I think perhaps we will call it a night."

He was very tall. He turned his head slowly and looked back over his shoulder at me. For some time he regarded me fixedly with those unblinking blue eyes.

There was nothing of anger in them—nothing even of hostility. More annoying for lack of either, I guess. He looked like a scientist studying some bug. And, damn it all—what's more, he looked natural. Not as if he was affecting it, but as if he really meant it. As if he were trying to be—well—not polite—say, tolerant—and hide from me the fact that he regarded himself very much my superior.

"I wonder," he said at length, "if you know exactly who I am."

"Yes—" I said, "I do. And it don't mean a thing to me. And I wonder if you know exactly who I am and—"

"And that it will mean quite a bit to me?" I think that he smiled—at least, his lips parted. "I am afraid, Race Williams, that you mean very little to me. To my brothers—yes. Their blood is hot, and the brute strength of the beast is dominant in them. But I am very sure that in you I would find little to worry about. I am afraid I have little interest in the physical. I abhor, as I said, firearms—shrink most appallingly from violence, and physical exertion of any kind incapacitates me for days. You don't go in for murder, you see—and where I must bow most humbly to your physical superiority, it wouldn't really interest me personally. No—you can not mean anything to me. You—" he paused a moment, and I saw his eyes rest upon the overturned chair, move quickly from The Flame to me, and then he said, "Well—perhaps you may mean something to me, but not in the sense you believe."

He certainly could talk. There were no two ways about that. And what's more, he could read what was on my mind—or, maybe, written upon my face. Anyway, I did have it in my mind to show him something of the physical that would surprise him. He looked big and strong enough not to be playing the woman.

"Really, Williams, I am sure you do not intend to use physical violence—at least, in the presence of a lady. You—"

"Doctor," I told him, "you may be hot stuff with Eddie and a few other bar flies. And you may stand in with certain big men—and it may even be true what's hinted; that you—well—that you're the Third Gorgon that I'd always looked on as sort of an underworld myth until you stared Eddie down. But if you are the big guy behind the political racket, the judgeship scandal racket, and even the murder racket—well—drop Miss Drummond's hands, or I'll throw you down the stairs."

He didn't get mad—which made me just a bit madder.

"I wonder if you would," he said slowly. "It might be interesting and—" He shook his head. "No—no, we anticipate things." But he dropped The Flame's hands.

"I think you had better go, Race," The Flame said.

"Not me," I told her. "I'll wait until the Doctor decides to make an 'out'—which will be soon, I'm sure."

"Don't be a fool." But there was more of interest in The Flame's face than anger. "I—I won't need you."

"Good God!" I didn't like that "I kissed you and got you" look in her eyes and I let her know it. "I wasn't thinking of you—but myself," I told her. Which was true. And I looked at Michelle Gorgon when I got off that last crack—and wondered. Yep, here was a lad I didn't understand, and what I don't understand I don't like.

"But Doctor Gorgon has something to say to me. Something that I'd like very much to hear." And she didn't put those glims of hers on him like she did when she wanted to swing a lad her way. She looked him straight in the eyes—clear, interested—more than interested. Deeply anxious.

"In his way Williams is right." Doctor Gorgon nodded condescendingly. "We must see life—or even death—through the brain that is given us. I do not think, dear lady, that I need say more than I have already said to you. I will not say that you have been foolish, for I do not know the thoughts that that mind of yours might carry. Certainly, not what others might read there. But let us say that if you are not correcting an error, you are making a change of plans." He walked to the table where the money The Flame had tossed there for me still laid. He ran his fingers through the bills, looked at The Flame, jerked open the drawer, and without hesitation lifted out some bills and some jewelry—held them out, so, to The Flame.

"This is all?" he asked.

"No—" The Flame pointed to the ring on her finger.

"I see," he said. "I will take it. No—just throw it there on the table. You understand, even though it all comes from the same treasury, it is better that it is returned to the—the sender. For it was his thought, you see—and I am afraid, not exactly a business one."

"The money on the table," The Flame spoke very slowly, "belongs to Mr. Williams."

"Seven hundred dollars." This time Michelle Gorgon's eyebrows moved slightly. "Well—comparisons might be odious. This is yours, Mr. Williams?" He held the bills out to me.

I was just about to knock them from his hand when The Flame spoke.

"Surely, Race," she said. "If later events prove unpleasant to you, you're not planning on throwing that in my face."

I took the money and shoved it into my pocket. I didn't like the present racket. I felt stupid standing there with the gun in my hand, but I was still standing there—and stupid or not stupid, I shoved that gun into my jacket pocket and still kept my hand on it.

Very methodically Michelle Gorgon searched through the drawer of that table, found an envelope, studied its size a moment, then put the money and the jewelry into it, added something from his own wallet and carefully sealed it. Then he crossed again to The Flame and started in with his line as he looked steadily at her and ignored me.

"You are a very beautiful woman—that is, to any man. To me, now—if your limbs were twisted things; your face a hideous death mask, you would still be a very beautiful woman—if those eyes remained untouched. The eyes, my dear, are the peepholes to the inner beauty of the mind. I wonder if you understand me. Understand why I verbally maim your beautiful body."

"I think I do," said The Flame. "I think—I do."

"And you do not mind?"

"No—" she said. "I do not mind."

"I am not playing at the magician, then. The mystery of whose tricks are known only to himself."

"No—" she said. "I understand you fully."

I had stood enough of being made monkeys out of, and I let them know it.

"Well—I don't understand," I said. "And now, Doctor, you and I are on our way. If you don't believe in the physical, here's your chance."

He turned, thrust the envelope toward me and said:

"I wonder if you would care to return this envelope to its rightful owner."

"No—" said The Flame. "He'd—he'd kill him, or be killed."

"I think not," said Michelle Gorgon. "But even so," he shrugged his shoulders, "the one is a cross which I am beginning unwillingly to bear—and the other—" he looked at me hard now—and I glared back at him, "a threatening menace on the horizon. Maybe an imaginary menace," and turning from me to The Flame—and back to me again, "perhaps a real one whom—" A pause, and suddenly, before I could get a word in, "Will you, or will you not return these—this envelope to its sender."

I took the envelope and shoved it carelessly into my pocket.

"Yes—" I said, "I will. Who is the man?"

"Eddie Gorgon." There was a slight chuckle. The arm that I had half raised, to bring down on his shoulder was caught, and I was walking from the room with Doctor Michelle Gorgon.

I didn't break away. I didn't twist my arm free and hurl him across the room. Somehow I felt silly enough. Somehow, kid like and foolish like, I wanted to carry the thing off as well as he did. Here was a lad who talked and talked, and said nothing. Or did he say a lot, and I didn't have the wits to get it? But he never threatened—never raised his voice in anger. Treated me in rather good natured contempt—and, to myself, I wondered if we'd been alone would it have been the same. Wouldn't I have just hauled off and cracked him one, or—? But there's not much pride in that thought.

And The Flame. Damn The Flame. I wondered if she knew how I felt. That was what hurt the most—that was what cut. Yep, The Flame was laughing at me. Not out loud. Not in a way you could notice even. Maybe she wasn't even laughing at me. But that will give you an idea of the way I felt. These two seemed to have reached an understanding which I did not get, though I heard every word.

This Third Gorgon—this wop with the white skin and the steady, unblinking eyes, the soft voice and—. Damn it, he didn't seem like a wop—didn't seem like anything but what he represented himself to be—a—. But that's what I was representing him to be. Certainly he had done something to The Flame—reached some understanding with her.

Mind you, a guy can feel stupid, silly, and what have you, and still not walk up in front of a machine gun and wait for the gunman to turn the crank.

I let Doctor Gorgon hold his elbow crooked beneath my arm. One reason was because of The Flame. The other because he had taken my left elbow and my right hand still held the gun. Why hadn't he grabbed at that right arm? Then I'd have some excuse to hit him one.

CHAPTER XIII

JUST ANOTHER WOP

Now, in the outer hall I jerked my arm free, twisted Michelle Gorgon slightly and none too gently, and slapped my gun against his side. Maybe he wasn't any gangster—maybe he didn't tote a gun. But the lower city just reeked with the rumor that, if the truth were told, Doctor Michelle Gorgon had put more men on the spot, big guys, racketeers, than any gang leader that ever putrified our city. It was even rumoured that a noted jurist had dined with Michelle Gorgon at his home the night of his disappearance.

But back to facts as I knew them and concerned me personally. Eddie Gorgon had gone out in that hall a short while before. The hall was dimly lit, but enough to see plainly our two figures walking down those stairs, and distinguish one from the other. Besides which, I hadn't and wouldn't search Michelle Gorgon. Oh—not that I believed all that talk about his not carting a gun—though certainly he hadn't produced one when he entered The Flame's apartment. But—I just couldn't search him. That superior air of his! I'd show him I didn't care if he carried a gun or not. If he did, and wanted to use it on me, that was his privilege.

No, it wasn't because of him personally, that I shoved a gun against his side. It was because of the gang he represented, ruled, through his brothers—or maybe just his brother, Joe—for Eddie could only be counted on to shoot a guy through the back at three paces.

"You know, Williams, you are not a very trusting soul," Michelle Gorgon said to me as we went down those stairs. "A gun in my side, now. I abhor the melodramatic—sudden death by violence except of course in the abstract."

I didn't exactly get that one, so I let it ride. Later, I got the impression that by "abstract" he meant he killed his enemies without being present in person—just his mind controlling and directing the hand of the one he selected to do his murdering for him.

My gun clamped against his side, though, was paying a few dividends. For, late as the hour was, Doctor Gorgon hummed softly as he descended the stairs, and once a lump of blackness which might have been a shadow or the lurking body of a gunman, seemed to fade back into the darkness. Of course, shadows don't make boards creak, as they fade away. But, again, the house was old, and I wasn't in a particularly good humor.

When we stepped out on the pavement a Rolls Royce stood before the building. A man wrapped in a great coat swung open the car door as I caught the initials in gold stamped upon it. Another, at the wheel, brought the engine into life—though that part I guessed at, for you hardly heard it purr.

"I'll take you home, of course," he told me, as I hid the gun partly under my coat as we neared the car door. "Not just courtesy, my dear Williams—not just because you were about to suggest any such procedure—but because your life is very dear to me tonight. I wouldn't have anything happen to you while with me, or just after leaving me. You see, the police—or at least one imaginative policeman has taken quite an interest in me. It is a help, of course. It is convenient to know that, when anything unpleasant happens that might be laid to the interests of my brother, Joe, through the watchfulness of our great police system suspicion can not direct its unpleasant breath upon me."

I was willing to go with him, all right. And as I got into the car and sat down beside him, he said—and there was little of humor in his voice—rather, he seemed to think he was stating a great universal truth.

"Yours is rather a silly position tonight—now. Like the man who held the lion by the tail and was both afraid to hang on and afraid to let go." He raised the speaking tube. "Park Avenue, and home," he said.

Michelle Gorgon dropped the tube.

"Do you know, Williams, that doesn't seem quite courteous; that you should see me home instead of my seeing you? But a strange fancy struck me. I would like you to pay me a visit—like to talk with you. You wouldn't consider it venturesome to visit me—now—at this late hour? I think that maybe I can interest you." And as he rambled on I began to like it better—feel better toward him. I just leaned back and listened. Sometimes these lads who talk, no matter how clever they are, say something—say something they shouldn't. Yet, never for a moment did I forget that Michelle Gorgon was a big man. Not one seeking power, but one who had obtained it. And even in the underworld, even in crooked politics, you don't talk yourself to the top—or, at least, if you do—you talk yourself out again. Now—why was he dragging me along? Why did he take such an interest in me?

And once he cut in quickly in his ramblings.

"Are you listening to me?"

"Who could help it?" I answered, for there had been an irritable note in his voice, and I rather liked it. So, I thought, there is a way to get under that skin of his. And with that thought I felt better. Funny. I encouraged him to talk now.

"Why do you want me to visit you—and why should I?"

"Because I will interest you. As to your safety. If you were my most feared enemy, my home would be the safest spot for you in the whole city of New York. The police watch it occasionally. One policeman in particular. And I think, while I'm on the subject, I'll tell you his name. It amuses me and helps establish my reputation, this interest in me. My life is an open book. The police see me come and go. But my mind is closed to all but myself. Silly, this following me about, watching my home. And how long do you think it would take me to stop it—have this busy-body removed from the Force? Just long enough to lift a phone and put a word in the ear of the right party. You might tell my shadow that. I believe you know him. His name is Detective Sergeant O'Rourke, an efficient officer. I should hate to see him removed from duty. You might tell him that, any day, I may grow tired of his attentions. And when that day comes, it will be too late for Sergeant O'Rourke. You see, it will be greatly to his advantage to grow tired of me before I grow tired of him."

"Yeah. I'll tell him when I see him, Doctor. This is your place?"

I was just a bit surprised. We had drawn up before one of the finest apartment houses on Park Avenue. No rendezvous of gangsters, this.

"You hardly expect hidden passageways here, and secret methods of disposing of bodies." He smiled. "As to sub-cellars—well—my quarters are thirty-three stories above the street. There are thirty-two to the building.

"You are on the roof?" I asked.

"On the roof. One might fall off, of course. But even one with your love of violence can see the danger to me in that. Really, it is possible—but a man would have to be most desperate, and greatly in fear of—of you. No, no—" this as we walked into the spacious hall and entered an elevator. "Death must have its part in life, even in my life, Williams. But it must be smoothed over, and distant—seen, as I said, in the abstract. In plain words. If one annoys, it is better to have him removed through, shall I say—suggestion?"

We sped quickly to the roof, walked down a corridor. Gorgon stopped before a heavy door, waited several seconds, then placed a key in the lock and swung the door open. And as we walked across the wind-swept roof, beneath the brightness of the stars, toward that California bungalow, he chatted on.

"You see, Williams, why I might go a long way not to give all this up. The Italian emigrant has gone far in your city—risen perhaps by the customs your laws so agreeably set out for him. In your city—my city—a man first must banish conscience. Second, create a mind without a body, without emotions."

We had crossed the roof now, passed under a canopy by the small trees between giant plants. There was real grass, clipped as smooth as a putting green, a tiny fountain, and the ripple of falling water against the slight night wind.

There were three steps of fancy brick and we were on the small porch. A single twist of the door knob—no waiting this time—and I followed Doctor Gorgon into a large, square hall.

He tossed his coat and stick onto a high backed chair, placed his hat upon them, and motioned me to do the same with my hat. But the night was not cold. I wasn't sporting a top coat. My felt hat had cost me twelve bucks—I'd keep it with me. It wouldn't be at all surprising if I had to leave the house of Michelle Gorgon in a hurry.

But he was persistent, and I wasn't going to be small about it. I let him take the hat from me and place it on the chair.

"A social call, Williams—and let us hope, a friendly call. A hat upon your knee would break the illusion and savor distinctly of the law, the police, at least, as we know the police detective in books and plays. Come, I never keep the servants up. I have always felt rather mentally above the teeming millions of the city. This home of mine is perhaps the realization in a material way of my mental attitude. In here—we will be quite alone."

He walked across the generous hall to a smaller

hall, and across that narrow stretch through curtains, and stood aside for me to precede him, as he held a door open.

I didn't like it but I couldn't see any harm in it. My hand was still in my jacket pocket; the Doctor's body so close to mine that I pushed against it as I passed, and just stepped far enough into that room to—. And I drew a surprise.

It was a library. Expensively bound volumes, deep, soft chairs, heavily curtained recesses before windows. But I saw none of that then. I was looking at the figure of a woman in a large chair, the rug hiding her limbs and body to well above the waist. The neck was long and slender, but there were discolorations upon it—heavy, purplish-yellow stretches, which covered the face as well. Patches of skin that seemed to have long since healed, after a burn.

And the woman's hand. I saw her left hand stretched out upon the rug. Twisted, sort of inhuman fingers, thin, emaciated, crippled arm. And Doctor Gorgon had stepped into the room beside me. He too saw the woman.

Yep—you could knock him. He was no superman at that moment. Chalk white, his face may have been before—perhaps it couldn't get any whiter—but at least it took on a new hue. A yellowish white of milk, with blotches in the perfect skin. Blotches like the curdling of milk, just as it turns sour. One hand went under his collar and pulled at it as his mouth hung open. For nearly a minute he looked at the woman. And so did I.

And I was onto Doctor Michelle Gorgon. I thought, too, as I watched his face that perhaps I was the only one in the whole city who was onto him. For that minute, maybe less, he was just what I had placed him for—Eddie for—Joe Gorgon for. Doctor Michelle Gorgon was just a wop, just a human, physical, rotten bit of the life he controlled and stood above. A racketeer, a gangster, a slimy underworld rat. Believe me, for that best part of sixty seconds he did more tricks with his pan than our greatest actor ever pulled off in a Doctor Jekyll and Mr. Hyde performance.

His mouth opened, his lower lip hung down.

Little bubbles of saliva gathered as he tucked his lip in and pulled at it with his upper teeth. He didn't speak. Not quite. One read, though, all the foul words he would have said if he could have spoken when he desired. But in a moment of mental strain and physical reaction he got hold of himself. Yet, his voice trembled when he finally spoke to the woman.

"What are you doing here? How dare you come, and—" He swung suddenly on me. "Outside," he said. "In the hall. Outside, Williams!"

Outside it was. It wasn't my party. The heavy door leading to that little hall nearly took my arm off as he closed it and clicked the key. One thing I had seen before that door got me. That was the woman's eyes. Deep brown they were. Mysterious, living, beautiful eyes, like—. And I took a gasp. Like The Flame's. Like—. And the words of Doctor Gorgon popped into my head, chased one another around and formed a picture. A

woman with a maimed, twisted body. Nothing but her eyes; nothing—

And from behind that locked door the woman cried out— Shrill, piercing. A scream of terror, even horror.

"No—God! No. He must never see me like this. I won't come again. I swear I won't. I wanted a glass—a mirror." A sound like an open palm against a face and the cry of the woman. "Help—he's going to kill me." And this time the voice died, as if a hand stilled it. Not a hand across the mouth—but a sudden gurgling sound to the stilled voice, as if fingers had clutched at her throat—followed by the sound as if bodies struggled, or one body moved heavily.

I lifted my hand and knocked upon the door. A moment of silence followed my knock. Then I struck the door again. And when I say "struck" I mean just that. Heavy as the door was, it rattled like thin slats when I pounded my fist against it.

CHAPTER XIV

I GO IN FOR ACTION

That second knock was a wow, and no mistake.

It brought response from inside. There was a jolt, the slipping of a chair, a whispered voice—another, I thought, which sounded like a man's. Feet crossed to the door, and Michelle Gorgon spoke. His voice was soft again, but there was still a tremor in it.

"There, there, Mr. Williams. A little difficulty—family difficulty, that you would not understand. And please don't pound like that again. I'll be with you in a minute. I—"

Feet moved across the floor. Feet that didn't belong to Michelle Gorgon, by the door. Feet that were too heavy for that delicate, crippled woman in the big chair.

I know I was silly. It wasn't any of my business. If I had any sense I'd have lifted my hat and left the place. Yet, I'm the sort of a guy who does silly things, and likes to do them. Why think it out and reason it? Reason's a damn poor excuse, most times, for not having guts. I didn't reason then—and I didn't think it out. I obeyed the impulse. And the impulse was to—well—here was a chance to talk to Doctor Gorgon. And in a way, at least, I understood—and he would understand in a minute. Damn it, he didn't expect me to keep pounding on that door, like an hysterical woman.

"Open that door—and keep the lady there," I said. "No talking like a book now, Doctor. You'll have to talk like a man for once. Open the door now, or, by God! I'll put a bullet through the lock."

He answered.

"If you do that you will wake the house. Men who might not understand." Feet were moving quickly inside—heavy feet, that were weighted under a burden, I thought. The woman was being taken from the room by another door.

"No more wind, Doc." I was giving him the truth now. "Open the door, or get out of the way while a bullet goes through the lock."

"Williams, I—"

And that was that. Doctor Gorgon might speak just to hear himself talk, but I didn't. There was a single roar of my gun, the splintering of wood—and a shattered lock. My hand on the knob, my shoulders hunched, with a thrust of my body I had that door open and was in the room. The time for talk was over. When I want an "in" I generally get an "in." And when I take a shot at a lock, that ends that lock. Forty-four is the caliber of my guns. Maybe old fashioned and not much in use today—but a forty-four can certainly do a surprising lot of damage.

This was my field, my game. I didn't more than step through that door when I slammed it behind me and took one quick slant at Doctor Gorgon. His eyes were staring now, but for a different reason than his usual attitude—the "nothing can excite me" stuff. Well—I won't say staring—rather, bulging. The deep blue pools were hitting high tide, and sort of flooding their banks.

But both his hands were empty, and a curtain on the far side of the library was swinging slightly as I caught a glimpse of the trouser leg of a man.

I brought up my gun, leveled it on that waving curtain and the disappearing leg, and gave the boy who owned the blue trousered limb a chance to live.

"You behind the curtain. Stop—or I'll—"

"Stop!" Doctor Gorgon's voice rang out. "There has been a grave misunderstanding. You may return Madame to the room at once."

And Madame was returned. Michelle Gorgon may have known a lot more words than I did, but, believe me, the few words I have serve my purpose at times. This was one of those times.

Two men carried the woman. She shrieked as they brought her back, in a kind of a swing chair, between them. Personally, they were rather stupid looking fellows but they knew what a gun was and the purpose of it, and the havoc it might raise, for they kept their eyes riveted on mine.

And Madame bellowed when they brought her in. She was not a pretty sight now, worse even than before. Her hair streamed over her forehead and her mouth was twisting spasmodically.

She sort of gasped out her words.

"Michelle—please—good God! not like this. That any man could see me like this—my hair—" She was trying to fix her hair with that twisted hand, and making a mess out of it.

Well, I was into it now, and I stepped across the room and stood before her.

Doctor Gorgon crossed quickly to her too, smoothed back her hair and patted her hand. He was leaning down and looking at her. I pulled at his shoulder and straightened him.

"Madame," I said, "you called for help. What—"

"She is not well." Michelle Gorgon horned in quickly—rather too quickly, I thought, though I don't know why I thought it. "She has had a sudden illusion that she would see some one again—some one very dear to her. And unless she is more careful, that illusion will come true—much more careful." And as I turned sharply on

him, "I mean her health, of course. As you see, it is not—"

"Can the chatter." And turning to the woman, "What's the trouble, lady?"

Her eyes were suddenly alive.

"Trouble—trouble. I dreamed it. I do not know. Take me away, Michelle. That a man should see me like this, when I was once so beautiful. A young man too. Take me away. But tell him, Michelle. Let me hear you tell the gentleman how very beautiful I was before. Tell him." There was almost a child-like anxiety in her voice, a sudden quick flash to her eyes, that died in the making, a simper in her voice, a coquettish tilt to her head that was either disgusting or tragic, I wasn't sure which.

"Yes, she was a very beautiful woman, Mr. Williams. Very beautiful indeed." Michelle Gorgon leaned close to her again and looked into her eyes. "Indeed—" he said very slowly, "she was once—once very beautiful."

The woman screamed, threw herself back in the chair and lay quite still. I was very close to her—very close to Michelle Gorgon. He had said nothing to her that I hadn't heard. Certainly he had not touched her, or even pulled "a face on her."

"Take Madame to Mrs. O'Connor." Gorgon spoke to the men who held the chair—then to me, "With your permission, of course." And there was a bit of a sneer to his voice.

"Sure. It's all right by me," I said easily. But, damn it, I didn't feel entirely at ease. Not that I was sorry I shot through that lock. Maybe it was a mistake, maybe it wasn't. But we all make lots of mistakes. None, more than I. I'm not a lad who won't admit a thing is wrong, just because he did it. Not me. But—well if it was wrong it was just too damn bad. Nothing could change it now. Nothing I could do then would take a forty-four bullet and shove it back into my gun again. Why cry over it?

"Explain the—the explosion," Michelle Gorgon said to one of the men. And when the man he spoke to looked at me rather blankly, "You might say to the servants that Madame has caused a disturbance. That is all." He watched them carry the woman from the room, even walked to the curtains and pulled the rug that covered her legs slightly closer about her feet, and held the curtains open as they passed from view. Then he turned to me.

"You might have killed me with that shot," he said. "Absurd, of course—but I could swear I felt or heard the bullet pass very close to me. The newspapers evidently do not exaggerate your— your idiosyncrasies. You do not know it, Williams, but you took quite an advantage of me. I allow nothing untoward to happen in my house."

He was talking more, I think to pull himself together. And one thing struck me. I hadn't noticed it before. Maybe it was because he was disturbed, but when he threw a big word into his conversation he seemed to grope for it—feel for it, as if he tried it out first in his own mind before he spoke it. He walked up and down a bit as he talked, finally paused, looked at me a moment, and walking to the wall pressed a button.

The man who came to the door I had rather demolished was old, bent, and every inch the trained servant. Michelle Gorgon looked at him a moment, hesitated, then spoke.

"The No. 1 Sherry, Carleton—Carleton." He repeated the name "Carleton" very slowly, as if he liked the sound of it and hoped that I would. Then to the man again, "Madame has had a spell. We are very fond of her, Carleton—very fond of her indeed. We must put up with a great deal."

"Very good, sir. The No. 1 Sherry." And the man left the room.

Michelle Gorgon had exaggerated, to say the least, when he told me the servants had retired.

"There, there, Williams." Michelle Gorgon paced the room slowly as he talked. "You have made it a trying evening. I do not believe, though, that the shot was heard outside, or below. It was unfortunate, and I forgive you. I was angry of course, to see—to see Madame so." He shrugged his shoulders and half extended his arms. "It is my burden, my cross, and I am afraid there are times when I do not bear it like a man. I hope you will need no further explanation. You are my

guest. May I simply say that the lady is my wife and that she met with a very serious accident, which maimed her body and affected her mind. She has never seen her face since the accident. The shock might kill her. We watch her rather closely. As you see, there are no mirrors in this room. But the reflection in the glass of a picture, the highly polished surface of a cigarette case, and such objects, have given her more than a suspicion. But she does not know the whole truth. Only a mirror could tell her that.

"I have been advised to send her away—a private hospital. But she does not wish to go." He looked dreamily at the ceiling, as if in reminiscent thought. "It would be better for her, of course, far better. But we cling to sentiment, Williams, almost childishly hang onto the subconscious allurements of the past. Indeed, she was a very beautiful, and a very accomplished woman. Like—" He paused, the door opened, and the servant entered with a tray.

"Like The Flame." I helped him out. I don't know why that was on my mind, but it was.

"Like The Flame—yes," he said very slowly. He reached for a glass, lifted the bottle and poured me out a drink, and taking one himself, motioned Carleton to place the tray and bottle on the table.

"You, if you are a judge, will appreciate this wine," he held the amber glass, with its long stem, before the lamp. "I have a friend who puts a seal upon it before it leaves France. It comes from the very cellars of the Marguery, in Paris. My own seal is placed upon each bottle before it is even moved from the shelf. It is very rare and—"

Michelle Gorgon paused and looked at a white card which lay upon the tray. He half bowed to me, stayed Carleton with a raised hand and said:

"You'll excuse me, Williams." And he turned over the card, read it through carefully, moved his eyebrows a bit, but did not permit his eyes to blink.

"I told him, sir—" Carleton started.

"Apologies are unnecessary, Carleton. He would not have come unless— You may tell him to come in." A moment's hesitation, and just before Carleton passed out the door, "A bottle of whisky. We must not be inhospitable." And to me, "It is my brother, Joe. You do not object, I am sure."

Maybe I did object. At least unconsciously, for I half came to my feet. Then I shrugged my shoulders but said nothing. Joe Gorgon had pushed himself to the top as a racketeer because of his speed with a gun. Yet, I don't believe there's a lad living today, or dead either for that matter, who can pull on me. But then, a lad with a gun hand like that wouldn't be dead, which gave me the thought that Joe Gorgon was still alive.

"You will excuse me again, Williams." Doctor Gorgon picked up a bit of paper beside the telephone on the table, studied it a moment, turned it face down and glanced at the clock on the mantel. It was eighteen minutes past two.

"It is almost like a play," he went on. "Each scene set to intrigue the audience. Each scene—. But this will be my brother, Joe. An impetuous man, dynamic, invigorating. But let me know what you think of the Sherry."

I watched him sip his and heard him say, as he tipped the glass.

"Here's to crime—your business, and mine."

And, damn it, the "mine" was gotten off in a way that made the wine stick in my throat before going down. Sinister, crafty, evil. There was no expression on his face, but for a moment I thought that I saw the real man. The man I had seen a part of that minute when Madame—or whatever fancy name you'd hang on her—was discovered in the room. A stern face, an intelligent face. Nothing of the sensual or animal in it. Yet, again, for a fraction of a second I saw, or felt that I saw, the real Michelle Gorgon, and it gave me a certain satisfaction.

CHAPTER XV

DEATH STRIKES AGAIN

Joe Gorgon walked into the room. His eyes flashed and his lips twitched as he saw me. He had known I was there, all right. There were no two ways about that. He hardly noticed the quick steps of Carleton, but he did spot the bottle of whisky the servant placed on the table, poured himself a quick and generous drink and threw it into him before he spoke a word. Somehow I felt that Joe was the kind of a lad for me, the kind of a lad to do business with. His first words were classic, as I understand the classic. He looked at his brother and jerked a thumb toward me.

"What's he here for?" And then quickly, "Williams and me had words tonight. I have a message for you, alone. God in—"

He stopped, poured himself another drink, knocked it off, stared at his brother, Michelle Gorgon, a moment, half raised a hand as if to slap it down upon the table, changed his mind and threw himself into a chair, crossing his legs in a position of ease. Just a position, mind you. Joe Gorgon was a worried man.

"What's he here for!" Michelle Gorgon repeated his brother's words. "I might ask you the same question about yourself, Joe. I invited Mr. Williams up to pay me a visit. That's more than you—but no matter. My home is chaos. My—" And suddenly, "Why am I indebted to you for this visit?"

"I want to see you alone," said Joe. And leaning forward, "I've got to see you alone."

I liked the byplay between the brothers. The one, Joe, the best known character on Broadway. The other, well, no man could lay a finger to Doctor Michelle Gorgon.

"Got to!" Michelle Gorgon leaned slightly forward. "Got to—Joseph. Really, I'm afraid you forget—" and a smile, at least a smile with his lips—or anyway, a twist to his lips, "You forget the duty of a host to his guest."

"Cripes!" Joe Gorgon came to his feet. "Williams is here. He knows something. He—. Damn it, Mike—he's not going out of here a—"

I fingered my gun, of course, raised my pocket slightly too. Even thought of pulling the rod out and laying it on my knees, in a sociable way. But I didn't. I took another sip of the wine and understood why Joe drank whisky. Not that the wine wasn't good. It was probably great stuff, great stuff for a garden party. But you'd have to go at it wholesale to get a kick out of it.

"When thieves fall out honest men get their due," was going strong with me—of course, fully realizing that the honest man must have his hand on a rod and a finger caressing a trigger—or he'd get a "due" that would be surprising to him.

Joe Gorgon stopped talking. Michelle's eyelids never flickered. The good natured twist to his mouth, that might be better described as tolerance rather than a smile, never changed. But the pupils of his eyes seemed to contract, as if you looked too long at a thing in a bright light, and found it getting smaller and smaller, yet sharper, as it got smaller. His right hand went below the table, and he lifted a book and tossed it across the polished surface so that it spun slightly before it struck Joe's outstretched hand and lay still.

Joe's hand fell upon the book. His mean little eyes grew large as his brother's contracted. He sort of clutched at his side when he spoke.

"For me?" he said. "Good God! you're not giving that book to me!" And his face cleared slightly as he glanced at me. "For Williams."

"Maybe. I hope not." Michelle Gorgon turned his eyes on me, and I looked down at the expensively bound volume. I saw the title stamped in gold upon the cover.

"*The Tanglewood Tales,*" I read, "*by Nathaniel Hawthorne.*"

I took another sip of the wine, leaned out, and with my free left hand flipped back the pages. It was a de luxe edition, and the volume opened at once to THE GORGON'S HEAD. I grinned up at Michelle.

"For me?" I said, fingering the book.

"I hope not," said Michelle Gorgon again. "Indeed, I hope not. But it's not all fancy, Race, that mythical tale of Hawthorne's. History repeats itself."

"I want to speak to you alone." Joe Gorgon threw off another drink, and his brother glanced disparagingly at the bottle and sipped his wine.

"Anything you have to say, Joe, can be said in front of Williams, here."

"No, it can't," said Joe. And the liquor was doing him some good, for he glared back at his brother now. "This talking around corners may be good stuff with your crowd, not mine. Williams, here, is one of my kind. He wants straight talk. At least, he gives straight talk. You're—. Yes, damn it, I'll get it in. You're sitting on the edge of a volcano and—. I have a message to deliver to you, alone."

And that was my cue. I thought I knew why Joe Gorgon had visited his brother. I thought I knew the message he had to deliver. I had seen that message of mine throw Joe higher than a kite. Why not work it for a double header? Why

not find what effect it would have on the Third Gorgon, the brains of the three brothers? Why not deliver that message myself? And I decided to try it. I said:

"Why argue the point out? I delivered a little message to Joe, here. He wants to pass it on to you. I'll save you trouble and give it to you myself, Doctor." And before Joe could horn in I shot it out, with all my flair for the dramatic, and with the memory of Joe's contorted map when he heard it.

"Michelle Gorgon," I said. "The Devil is Unchained."

It worked twice on Joe. He stretched out a hand quickly and grabbed his brother's arm. His face twisted, and his lips parted at the corners. And he watched carefully the features of his brother, Michelle; watched, I thought, for Michelle to give a single shriek, lie down and roll over.

But Michelle Gorgon still smiled with his lips. He said simply:

"How droll. What a droll message!"

"Don't you understand?" Joe Gorgon shook his brother by the arm. "Have these years so dulled your—"

"Stop!" Michelle Gorgon shot the words through his teeth. There was an animal-like viciousness in the way his head shot forward, as he glared at his brother. "You're trying to push a peanut wagon across this living room, just as you pushed it on Canal street twenty-three years ago. You had your stand then, Joe. You protected that stand. You enticed rival vendors up an alley and put the fear of Joe Gorgon into their hearts, and went your way and protected your corner, and sold two bags of peanuts where you had sold one before. And now, in your heart you're still running the same peanut racket, still entertaining the same fears, still drinking the same poison. Now—" Michelle Gorgon paused. The phone rang sharply on the table beside him.

"You'll pardon me, gentlemen." He half bowed to me, very seriously, and to his brother with a touch of sarcasm. "I think that I am to have a message that will be of much interest to each one of us, more so than Williams' rather em—epigrammatic reference to the devil."

He picked up the phone and said:

"Doctor Gorgon speaking. Yes, I understand. I have not been at home. Oh, I see. No, I was not asleep. I am interested in all that affects the life, the tranquil life, of our city." A long pause, and then, "Thank you very much. I shall read of it at breakfast, in the morning."

He placed the receiver on the hook. Carefully filled up his wine glass, lit a cigarette and settled back comfortably in the chair. He eyed us now.

Those same unblinking globes, his elbows on the arm of his chair, the tips of his fingers on either hand coming slowly together. It was some time before he spoke, and then only in way of forestalling the sudden words that started from Joe Gorgon.

"It's a funny world," said Michelle Gorgon slowly. "A very funny world indeed. It will hardly interest either of you. But I just received a message that an Italian gentleman, lately landed in this country, was stabbed to death at Doctor Elrod's Sanitarium. Ah—most distressing. Most distressing."

CHAPTER XVI

ON THE SPOT

Of course I understood what Michelle Gorgon meant. Giovoni, whom Colonel McBride and I had gone to so much trouble to protect—Colonel McBride very nearly losing his life when we moved the Italian gentleman from the city hospital to Doctor Elrod's Sanitarium—was dead. Murdered within a few hours. I knew it. I believed it. But—.

"No—" I cried out as I jumped to my feet. "What time—and where were you, Doctor Michelle Gorgon?" I stopped and sat down again. But this time when I stretched out my hand, it reached for Joe Gorgon's bottle of whisky and not the No. 1 Sherry.

"Really," said Michelle Gorgon, "your emotions, Williams, do you proud. A poor Italian gentleman. How distressing. But you were saying something about—. Was it—er—that an evil spirit had broken his chains?" And leaning forward slightly, "Or was it that the devil was chained again, chained this time forever, in death."

Confused? Yes, I was confused, and mad. Was this the reason that Michelle Gorgon had brought me to his home? So that I would be with him? So that he would know I could not be interfering with this murder he had planned? For that he had planned it I had little doubt. As to Joe, it seemed a cinch that he wasn't in it. His eyes just bulged.

Michelle Gorgon walked slowly around the table and laid a hand upon his brother's shoulder.

"Like our good friend, Williams, here,

Joseph, you are a man of action. And I daresay it serves our purpose and is necessary in our every day life. But we must not forget that the physical is only an impulse, directed by the mental. When it is not so, we are told that it is reactionary, impulsive, instinctive, maybe—which is simply the polite way of placing us on the level with animals. When the brain ceases to function and leaves the body, it becomes a useless thing, no matter, Joe, if that brain is not a part of that particular body." A pause. "I see I confuse you there. But try and remember that a brain is necessary to the body, to your body, whether it be your brain or my brain, Joe. One brain, then, may control many bodies—but many bodies can not control one brain. It—" Michelle Gorgon stopped and looked at the bewildered face of his brother. "But no matter," he said quickly. "You understand that I am always ready to help and advise you. Ready and anxious, even, but never compelled to. In plain words, your visit here tonight was unnecessary and inopportune. You have seen that."

"Yes—" said Joe, "I have seen that. And, the visit of Williams?"

Michelle Gorgon smiled at me.

"A weakness of mine, Joe. A petty vanity, which all great minds are subject to. For the present you have nothing to worry you. You may sleep and play and—" He looked at the bottle and shrugged his shoulders. "Mr. Race Williams has been taken care of for tonight." He put his hand before his mouth, stifled a yawn or an affected yawn. "The hour is late. You will excuse me, Williams, I know. The interview is over."

I hadn't had my say; hadn't had half a chance to open up, and now, damn it, he didn't give me the opportunity. Joe Gorgon had moved toward the hall door. Of course I moved with him. Maybe I should have held my ground and believed in the Sanctity of the Home stuff. But I didn't. And it was too late now. Like a woman, Michelle Gorgon had had the last word. He turned, sought the little door that his wife had gone through before, and left us flat.

There was nothing for me to do but leave—leave with Joe Gorgon, presumably New York's biggest and most feared racketeer.

We passed out the front door, across the roof under the covered canopy, and through the thick, steel door which let us into the upper hall of the apartment house.

"He's a great guy, isn't he, Race?" Joe pushed out his chest and looked me over.

The elevator door clanged open, a sleepy eyed operator banged the door closed, and we descended to the street.

Silently Joe and I made our way through the spacious hall with its great pillars and towering plants—out onto Park Avenue.

"Williams," Joe Gorgon didn't threaten. He spoke his stuff like a man. "You know me and I know you. Judgeships have been bought and sold before your time and before my time—and will be long after it. Things haven't changed any in the city. It's simply newspaper competition. My world—our world—is a rather small one, after all. I've never laid a sucker on the spot. Men want money—you and me and them. You're a persistent bird and no mistake. You rile a guy—rile him bad. But you can't change life. I daresay there ain't a lad in the city today better informed than you. Yet, you can't do anything to me—nor Mike." He half looked back up the apartment as he chucked in the "Mike." "Well—Michelle may talk in circles, but when he strikes he strikes straight and hard."

"Well," I said, "come to the point."

"Yeah." He bit at a match and spat a piece of it in the gutter. "It's a bad time for too much excitement. How much do you want to chuck the game and take up golf?"

"I don't play golf," I told him.

"Oh—I mean—" He paused, scratched the other end of the match on the box and stuck it to a black cigar. "All right. You and me have made our names stand out a bit. We've both seen plenty of trouble. Now, you're asking for it. That's it, isn't it?"

"I guess so, Joe," I said.

"Okay!" He looked at me a moment and grinned. "The look of a Gorgon." But his smile was pleasant. "It's a silly racket. But it's paid dividends in the right places. You'd be surprised if you knew the sales increase in Hawthorne's bit of work. But—take care of yourself. S'long."

Joe Gorgon turned, and was gone. There were no two ways about what he meant. In the language of the underworld, Race Williams was on the spot.

I went home. Any way you look at it, it had been a busy night. On the spot. Well, it wasn't the first time I was put on the spot and wouldn't be the last, I hoped. If I took a little trip for my health every time I was threatened I'd have been around the world a hundred or more times, and still traveling. No, sir, there would be nothing for yours truly, Race Williams, to do for a living unless it was conducting world tours.

That doesn't mean I didn't take the threat of the Gorgons seriously. Besides which, it rather pleased and flattered me. In the first place, they had something to fear from me. A dope fiend might be knocked over on the public street. An unknown Italian might be stabbed to death in a hospital. But the doing in of Race Williams is a different thing, again. Besides, which, some of the best racketeers in the city have been after me, and missed. But they didn't stay after me very long.

I'm not a lad who runs when the bullets fly—at least, if I do run, I run forward and not backward. And if Joe Gorgon wouldn't have any touch of conscience about putting a bullet in me,

I wouldn't have any either about putting one in him. An even break, that.

Jerry was waiting up for me.

"There's a lad been calling you on the phone. Sputtered, he did—and seemed to think you spent your time with the receiver clamped to your ear. Trying to make a telephone operator out of me too, and—"

"Did he hang a tag on himself, Jerry?" I asked.

"No. He said you'd know. And for you not to go out again until he got you. He'd ring every fifteen minutes. But, Gawd! He's been buzzing up the bell every five, I think. There you are. Seven minutes, by the clock." Jerry pushed his hands out as the phone rang.

It was my client, Colonel McBride. His mouth was full of words, his words full of sputters. He sounded like a bunch of Japanese fire-crackers.

But I got enough.

"The man, Giovoni—dead—murdered—stabbed to death in the hospital."

"I know," I said. Giovoni, of course, was our little friend that I had carted about.

"How—how do you know?" he demanded breathlessly.

"Does it matter?" I asked him. "The question is, how did they know where he was? But here's a surprise for you. I spent the evening, or the last hour, with Doctor Michelle Gorgon. Some one was kind enough to ring him up and tell him of the murder. How important was Giovoni? I mean, to you, not himself."

"Important!" He fairly gasped the words. "Giovoni was Michelle Gorgon's father-in-law. He was everything. The man who could return Doctor Gorgon to Italy for a brutal murder—clear him out of the country—straighten—"

When he stopped for breath I encouraged.

"His father-in-law?" I didn't get that. The woman called Madame had not looked like a wop.

The fire-crackers went on.

"Yes, at least, I think so. I was told that. Oh—damn it—I have nothing to go on, now. Giovoni never talked much, never gave me much information. He wanted to confront Michelle Gorgon and denounce him. Pay him back for—Michelle Gorgon killed Giovoni's daughter years back, in Italy. It was a brutal murder. Damn it, man, he saw his daughter murdered, watched it, helpless and—"

So he, Giovoni, was not the father of Madame.

"He told you this? He—"

"No, he didn't tell me. He was an old man. He lived his life, spent his days, in an Italian prison. It was vengeance to him. Toney, who you said was killed, told me, the little drug addict. I brought Giovoni from Italy. Now he's dead. How did they know where he was?"

"You must have talked to some one."

"No one, not a soul. I learned enough from Giovoni and Toney. I have sent an agent to Naples to investigate the story that Michelle Gorgon killed his wife there, over twenty years ago. She was Giovoni's daughter, and her name was Rose Marie. The story is that Michelle Gorgon was convicted of the crime, and escaped. It may be another week before I learn the truth from Italy. In that week of waiting we will leave Michelle Gorgon alone—make him feel that he is safe from the crimes of the past, that he actually committed himself—at least, if the whole thing is not a fabric of lies or the hallucinations of a drug crazed mind. It is possible that Toney may have misled both Giovoni and me.

"Would you be willing, Mr. Williams? I need your services against the Gorgons if this proves true or false, and I will mail you a check in the morning as a retainer. But don't come to see me. Don't ring me up. I want Michelle Gorgon to think that I have dropped you, perhaps even dropped him. I will get in touch with you when I hear from Italy, or from one who knows much, but will not talk yet. It may be only a few days. It may be a week. What do you say? Will you risk it? The pay will be good."

"Don't forget to mail the check in the morning," was my answer.

CHAPTER XVII
INFLUENCE VERSUS GUN-PLAY

As a matter of fact it was ten days before I again heard from my client, Colonel Charles Halsey McBride. But the check had come, and where it wasn't a fortune, it was for ten thousand dollars. Which is plenty of jack, as real money goes today.

But I kept to the letter of Colonel McBride's instruction. I didn't frequent any place where I might meet the Gorgons. That was a little tough. It might look to the Gorgons as if I were afraid of that "on the spot" threat. Also, I still had the envelope containing the currency and jewelry which Michelle Gorgon had asked me to return to his brother, Eddie. Yep, the temptation was strong to look Eddie up and slip it in his hand. For the money and jewelry were given to The Flame by Eddie—as an inducement, I guess, to bring her into the Gorgon outfit. But Doctor Michelle Gorgon had looked at The Flame and seen bigger things for her. So it was that he suggested rather sarcastically that I return the money and jewelry to Eddie Gorgon.

Anyway, since the killing of Toney, the little drug addict, not far from the Golden Dog night club, Eddie had sort of disappeared from his usual haunts in the city. That is, for several days. The last couple of days he was back again. But I understood that the police were not looking for him. Such was the power of Michelle Gorgon—or the so-called cleverness of the police in giving Eddie a free run. Take your choice.

But, as I said, it was ten days before I heard from Colonel McBride. Then, on Thursday evening, at exactly eleven-fifteen, he called me on the phone.

"I should have called you before." He got down to business. "Giovoni, Toney, it all seemed so strange. Yet Toney came over on the boat with the Gorgon brothers, over twenty years ago. They were called Gorgonette them. Michelle was twenty-seven then, but looked younger, Joe no more than in his twenties, and Eddie just a small boy. Williams, we may have to start over, try to prove something here in New York. You see, I thought we could pin this crime of years back on Michelle Gorgon. No excitement in the city; no involving others; no influence, no bribery, no jury fixing to fight against. Just the turning of Michelle Gorgon over to the Italian authorities for the murder of his wife years back. Now the Italian investigation seems to have proved a—well—entirely false."

"There must be something in it. Giovoni was murdered. Toney was murdered. And certainly by the Gorgons. Why kill them if they didn't fear what they could say?"

"Yes. But, Williams, we should have a long talk. My life was attempted yesterday. Some one else has told me that Michelle Gorgon did kill his wife in Italy. But on top of that I have indisputable evidence from my agent in Naples that Michelle Gorgon, or Michelle Gorgonette was never married in Italy. But, enough talk on the phone. I am wondering if I should come to see you or have you come and—"

"I'll come and see you," I cut in quickly. "The Gorgons have killed two men, who for all they know may have told you something. There was an attempt on your life, you say. If the Gorgons think you know too much, then you are a menace to them. And get this straight, Colonel. The Gorgons have a direct and efficient way of dealing with menaces. I've been looking up the Gorgon record during the past week. And I guess I can name as many murders that they committed as any dick on the Force, including your friend, Sergeant O'Rourke. But naming them and presenting them as evidence to a jury are two different stories, which the Gorgons know as well as I do.

"It's well known in the underworld that Joe Gorgon shot down Lieutenant Carlsley over four years ago. Yet, they couldn't even get the grand jury to indict Joe. Then there's Eddie Gorgon's brutal murder of the laundry owner who defied the laundry racket and paid for it with his life. At least four people saw that murder. No graft there. The jury was composed of honest citizens. That was straight out and out terror. One witness was drowned; another had disappeared; and two others changed their stories right on the witness stand, giving a description of a murderer that would better fit any man in the city of New York than it would Eddie Gorgon. Friends gave Eddie a dinner and presented him with a loving cup the night he was freed.

"And what's more, you're right about Michelle Gorgon. He's the brains of the whole show. Directs the killing, covers himself, and never has a hand in it. 'Murder in the abstract' is what he calls it. He—" I paused, strained my ear against the receiver. Not a sound. "Are you listening?" I asked, just in a natural voice. No one likes to shoot his trap off just to hear himself talk. At least, I don't.

"Are you listening?" I tried again, his time louder. Perhaps an anxious note came into my voice as I strained my ears to catch the faintest breath. And I thought that I heard something. A distant voice, or a buzzer, or, damn it, maybe just the odd sounds that the telephone wires put on as an added attraction to the subscriber.

I jiggled the receiver hook, spoke quickly—maybe louder—maybe fearfully. Just instinct. Just those nerves I talk about in others and deny having myself. But somehow I felt that tragedy had suddenly stepped into that distant room, that something had happened to—. And then, when I was sure, and about to jerk the receiver back on the hook and dash from the room, his voice came, low, soft—and maybe it was caution in it instead of fear, maybe an anxiety instead of dread, maybe—. But he whispered, for I barely caught the words.

"Come down then. I've got a visitor. I think maybe I'll learn the truth."

The voice died. The receiver clicked across the wire, and silence. But had there been a roar—the beginning of a roar, just before that receiver dropped back upon the hook, or had there—? Hell, these Gorgon boys could stir up fancies. Fancies? I thought of the dead snowbird before the night club, the little Italian with the knife in his chest, the—.

"Jerry," I grabbed up my hat and stepped to the apartment door, "I'm going out again. And put your hat on. I'm taking you bye-bye."

Jerry's eyes shone, his lips parted and his big, uneven teeth jumped into the sudden gap. But he didn't say anything. He didn't have to get ready. Though I seldom took Jerry with me on any such errand he always hoped that I would, and was always ready. Besides which, Jerry knew his underworld by being kicked around it, not from books or the papers. And he was the best shadow since Mary's little lamb fell foul of some mint sauce.

It didn't take Jerry long to turn the corner, dash to the garage and rush my car out. And we were on our way.

"Big thing you're going on, isn't it, Boss?" Jerry just bubbled with enthusiasm.

"Big enough, Jerry," I told him, as I skipped over to Fifth Avenue. I like action, none better. Maybe I got a thrill now. I daresay I was the only man in the city of New York, or out of it, that the

Gorgons had put on the spot, and still lived. And what's more, still intended to remain alive.

Jerry tried again.

"Them Gorgons ain't it?" And when I looked at him, "When I followed Big Joe I knew who lived in the swell dump he went to. His brother, the Doctor. It's gospel in the right places that Joe never makes a big move but the Doctor advises it. He never pushed no cart on the Avenue, did the Doctor. He never played any gat in Joe's rise. Most of the big timers don't even know the Doctor to speak to. But they know what Joe means when he says, "I'll think it over," or "I'll tell ya tomorrow." I remember once O'Hara, the big bootlegger, the wise money, hearing him say to Joe Gorgon, a year or two before O'Hara got bumped off, and I came with you—"

"All right, Jerry," I helped him out. This lingering over a story was Jerry's way of finding out if I were interested, "what did Mr. O'Hara pull on Mr. Joseph Gorgon?"

"It was a liquor deal, I think, a big one, for control of the entire Bronx. When Joe told him what was what, O'Hara says, 'Are you speaking through your own mouth, Joe, or through the mouth of the Third Gorgon?' And, Bing! Like that, when Joe gave him the office that he was simply an echo, O'Hara smacked right in on the deal—like nothing at all. I hear as how the Doctor makes judges now, and sells justice at so much a head. They say as how he can pull a murderer right out of the Tombs for the right price. That's how he gets his money, and—. But if it was me, I'd say this Eddie Gorgon is the worst of the lot. Shoot you in the back like THAT." He snapped his fingers.

"In the back, eh Jerry?"

"Yeah. That's his way, unless it's a snowbird. Do you think he got little Toney that night?"

"Maybe." I was listening though. "But I think, Jerry, if I had to fear any man, I'd pick the influence to fear. It comes natural and sometimes easy to pop at a guy who's standing behind a rod he didn't aim right, or pull the trigger quick enough. But influence, you see, hasn't any body."

Jerry scratched his head.

"It don't sound right." He seemed to think aloud. "But I think I get what you mean. This Third Gorgon don't sport no firearms. That may be hot stuff for the police, or you, with your finicky ideas. But there's a hundred or more guys in the city who'd find it much easier to give a guy the works who's unarmed than—"

"But those guys won't. Maybe there's no reason for them to do it. And maybe a good reason why they shouldn't. You wouldn't want to be the guy who knocked over Joe Gorgon's brother, would you?"

"No," said Jerry, "I wouldn't. But Joe Gorgon only kills for business, for necessity, while Eddie—. Well—he's got the killer instinct, Boss. You might duck in and out, and hide from influence—but you can't do nothing with a gun against your back."

"And that's the point," I told him. "It's influence, Jerry, that puts that gun against your back, whether it's Eddie's gun or Joe's gun, or a hundred or more other guns. If you kill a rat, another takes its place. If you kill a dozen rats, a dozen take their place. But if you kill influence, you kill where the rats breed. How the devil can you walk in and shoot down an unarmed man," and, very slowly, "and get away with it?"

"Well, they all get it sooner or later," Jerry said, philosophically. "But if Eddie Gorgon was after me, like I hear as how he's after you, I'd forget influence and shoot the guts out of Eddie Gorgon."

Not elegant? Maybe not. But practical just the same. I simply said:

"Eddie Gorgon is only a common murderer, and as such not to be worried about. You see, it's influence again, Jerry. If it wasn't for his brother, he'd have been taken for a ride or roasted at Sing Sing long ago. Now, get this training into your head. A common murderer is only as good as the gun he draws, if you can forget what's behind him. But—. Here's where we lay up. My business is just around the corner."

CHAPTER XVIII

ON THE LONELY STREET

We parked the car and I took Jerry as far as the corner with me. Colonel McBride's hangout was Number 137.

"No. 137," I told Jerry, as I tried to point out the house down the street. "It's possible—" and I stepped back from the corner. Of course I couldn't be sure, that is, as to the identity of the man who moved restlessly in the shadows across from 137, but one thing was certain. He was conspicuous enough to be a flat-foot; defiant enough to give the office to any marauder that No. 137 was protected by the law and not a safe place to bother. I often wonder why the police go in so much to prevent crime, that is, temporarily, by a display of law, when a little cagy work might capture the criminal and prevent the crime permanently.

"Stick around," I told Jerry. "If you see any one you fancy, follow him and give me a report later." And as Jerry grinned up at me, I gave him the orders he liked so well. "On your own, Jerry," I said, "Scout around the block behind, if you like."

"Right'o, Boss." Jerry half raised a hand in salute. And I turned the corner and walked toward 137. Nearly half a short block, it was, and I'm telling you that, for some reason, no one ever found a block so enmeshed with danger, maybe imaginary danger. But you've got to admit that since I was in this case every trick had been taken by the Gorgons. And now the fear, well, I won't admit the word fear, maybe, but anyway, the apprehension that the Gorgons were about to

take another trick—yep, in spite of the fact that a bulky shadow, without an attempt at concealment, was crossing the street before I got halfway down the block. And that bulky shadow had all the earmarks of a headquarters detective.

So things were safe enough from that position. I spun on my heel and turned quickly back, slipping close to the shadows of the old houses. Once I looked over my shoulder. The man was hurrying toward me. I increased my pace, reached the corner again and turned it quickly, paused by the building and stuck my eye back down the street.

The man was on my side of the street now, on the house No. 137's side. He had his hat in his hand and was scratching his head. Twice he stepped toward the corner and twice he drew back again. I couldn't even see his face, yet I thought that I could read his mind. He was told to watch that house, to watch who came to it. It wasn't up to him to think for himself.

Finally he hurried back down the street, paused for a moment before 137, and then quickly crossed the street and hurried up the steps of the house opposite. I smiled at that. It struck me that I was to gather the impression that he was an ordinary householder, going home, while he watched me from the darkness of the doorway.

I shrugged my shoulders. There are front doors as well as back doors. After all, I might be wrong about this watcher. But anyway, I wanted my visit to be private.

My car was still parked in the middle of the

block, but Jerry was gone. I knew Jerry's way. He'd walk clean around that block. I skipped down to the next side street. It wouldn't be so hard to measure off the distance, slip down an alley, straddle a fence and drop into the rear yard of 137.

But I didn't do that little thing. Just about where I guessed the house behind 137 should be two figures emerged and crossed quickly to a big sedan parked by the curb. You could clearly make the figures out, though to recognize them was not so easy. There was not enough light. But one was big enough to be Colonel Charles Halsey McBride.

As that black sedan door opened, the smaller one of the two men paused, drew back a bit and quickly shoved off the arm of the other, that clutched at his. I jerked out a gun and ran down the street.

One of those two men, the one I thought my client, the Colonel, had thrown up his hands and cried out. A figure had suddenly jumped from the closed car and clutched him. Two other shadows bounded down the steps from a dark vestibule and were on him from behind. Almost in the time it takes to tell it, that one man was bundled into the car and the other man had escaped and was running down the street, away from me.

There was no chance to overtake that car. It had jumped ahead in second gear and was dashing down the block. I saw it swing into Broadway under a light, sway perilously as it turned left, and disappeared from view. But I thought too that I saw a slim, boyish form come from an areaway and start in pursuit of the man who had fled. And with a little gulp of satisfaction I thought that I recognized that slim pursuing figure as my assistant, Jerry.

Now, I could have gotten the man who ran down the block in the same direction the fleeing car had taken. He wasn't very fast, and slightly bent, and rather uncertain.

But just as I took out after him came more trouble from behind me. I heard the tires skid as a car turned the corner from the same direction I had come. I jumped quickly for the first retreat.

A two foot drop into a basement entrance. Turning, I leveled my gun as the car screeched to a stop at the curb. The occupants of that car had seen me all right, for two men hopped to the street.

I put my gun in my pocket and called out to the broad shouldered man who was slipping along with his back close to the building, toward my hiding place. I had gotten a good look at his map.

"Glory be to God, Race Williams," said Sergeant O'Rourke. "Surely it's not you that's making all this disturbance! You'll be the bloke that started down the street a few minutes ago, just before the light flashed."

"What light?" I asked him.

"The—well—the Colonel's. If he needed help he had only to flash his light on and off in the front room, where he sleeps. And he did just that."

"When?" I asked.

"Less than three minutes ago."

I counted up quickly. The time to leave his room, go down the stairs, pass through the lower floor into the back yard, climb the high fence that must be there and pass through the alley to the street. And he hadn't left that alley in a hurry. Just a slow walk, and—.

"He couldn't have flashed a light in his front room," I told O'Rourke, "less than three minutes ago."

"But he did." O'Rourke nodded emphatically as he grinned. "I had me own eyes on it. I thought maybe the—some one might try and pay him a visit, so I left the way open for an 'in,' you understand. Not an 'out.' And it'll be about three minutes, now, since the light flashed. The boys will be playing the front door, while we take the back. Come on, Race. The Colonel will be safe as a fiddle, with his door locked and his gun in his hand and the police busting in. Make it snappy. I've got a few boys across from the front of the house who'll be in by now. I took no chances."

I grabbed O'Rourke's arm as I followed him into the alley, two other dicks closing in behind us.

And I told him what I had seen, watched his feet hesitate, watched his hands that were gripping the high fence let go their hold, as the full significance of what I said caught him.

"You don't think one of those men was the Colonel?" O'Rourke asked anxiously; then shaking me, "You do?"

"I do." I gave him the truth.

"Did the other man have a gun in his ribs and—? But he couldn't. The Colonel's door was heavy. Two windows facing on the street with a man below them and one in the house across the way, watching. No, he wouldn't open that door for any one. That, he promised me. But come on. Maybe it was—"

"Two other fellows," I started sarcastically, and stopped. What was the good of riding O'Rourke now? If damage was done, it was done. And, another thing. It struck me suddenly. O'Rourke, or no one else, could have prevented the man leaving that house. Certainly, if it was the Colonel, he went of his own free will. Maybe, under some threat, maybe, under some promise, maybe, with some one he trusted. Maybe—. But the light! If he had flashed the light as the pre-prepared signal to O'Rourke, then he had gone in fear. But that light! He wouldn't have had time. And I gave it up. We were over the fence, in the yard, at the foot of the steps leading to the back door.

O'Rourke gave his orders in a low voice. Placing men carefully to watch the cellar windows, and then growling roughly for me to come on, he climbed the steps to the rear kitchen door—found it open and entered the house.

Lights were blazing now. Flatties pounded through the rooms. Some of them I knew, some I didn't. Some were the best detectives on the city Force. A tall, straight figure with iron gray hair spoke to O'Rourke.

"The front room is empty. The bed has not been slept in. Evidently he wasn't expecting to retire at—at the time whatever it was happened. But the Colonel's gone."

"Yes," said O'Rourke. "No sign of any one. Search the house."

"Men going through it now," said the gray haired dick. And as a lad holding an axe came into the room, black and disheveled, "About the cellar, Tim?"

"Even stirred up the coal." A round Irish face grinned. "Not a chance for a mouse to hide away."

"You got the axe, I see. Give it to me." The old dick addressed Tim.

"Er, what for?" demanded O'Rourke.

"There's a closet door that's locked, and a key missing, in his nib's bedroom." The dick jerked a thumb upward. "It may mean nothing, but we'll have a look."

"Give me that axe." O'Rourke took the axe, pounded up the stairs, with me at his heels. He nodded to the cop who stood in the outer room, and walked to the closet door in the bedroom. He pulled at the knob and said:

"Hi, Colonel." Listened a moment, half lifted the axe and put it down again, and turned to the cop. "Don't want anything disturbed here. Papers and the likes of that. A strong man should jerk that door smack off its hinges." He grabbed at the door. A quick jerk, and O'Rourke cursed. The door held fast. Then he spotted the lamp cord knotted to the end of the bed, and it took his mind off the door. But it was curled on the floor and no longer hung over the sill, as it did when I first visited that house.

"A lad might have come up by that, slipped through the bedroom, and, damn it, I forgot about this window. But how the devil could he throw it down to himself? Certainly he didn't leave by it and—"

"I don't think that fits this racket." And I told O'Rourke about Toney, the little snow-bird who had left the house where he had sought protection.

"The lad who was killed last week." O'Rourke nodded. "That's what comes of being so secretive. This Colonel has more information coming to him than you'd find in the World Almanac. He tells you this and he tells you that, and shuts up like a clam when you want to know the how of it. Passes his word to stoolies, his word of honor as a gentleman, he tells me. Now, see what comes of it? Two men dead, and me not even knowing where the Italian, Giovoni, was till I looked at his dead body at Elrod's Sanitarium. I'm to take orders, Race." He looked at me suddenly, "I think we'll keep quiet on this—this disappearance 'till we hear something. It will be the biggest and worst thing in the world if the Colonel turns up dead. You know who he is, of course."

"Of course," I said. "Colonel Charles Halsey McBride, friend of the deputy police commissioner, and no doubt working secretly for him."

"Well, it sounds good, in theory. And one can't blame the Commissioner for showing the district attorney's office, and maybe state officials, that he can take care of his own department. If Michelle Gorgon rides, it bursts up the biggest racket the city has ever known. Just now, I'd lay you a hundred to one that I can name twenty-five murders in New York that Michelle Gorgon is responsible for, directly responsible for. Yet, I'd lay you another hundred to one that I couldn't prove a one of them in a court of law. I—" He threw up his head. Some one called him.

"Coming!" said O'Rourke, in answer to a shout from down stairs. "I'll leave you here, Race to keep an eye on that locked closet door. I wouldn't keep a thing from you. But men are men, and you couldn't expect them to coddle to an outsider. Come on!" he said to the cop by the door, and following that cop out into the hall he closed the door behind him.

What a break for an amateur detective! To go over the room alone, find those hundreds of little clews that the regular police officer misses. You know what I mean. The man is found dead in his palatial library. The police search the place. And then the amateur detective discovers in one corner of the room a cord of wood, or under the bed an Austin car, that the hard boiled Inspector of police had overlooked. Oh, I daresay there are clews, if guys are willing to leave them. But a burnt cigar ash only tells me that some one has smoked a cigar, and nothing more. Real clews, to me, are letters, letters that any guy able to read can understand.

I jerked around from the desk I was pawing over. A key had clicked in a lock, the lock of the closet door.

I stepped a little to one side, drew a bead about the center of that door, saw the knob turn, but heard no click as the latch was slowly slipped back again when the door gave an inch. Then that closet door opened very slowly. Wider—wider—and I saw the figure.

The face was very pale and slightly dirty beneath the long peaked hat. The blue shirt was rather a bad fit, at least, baggy, and little hands were shoved in jacket pockets. A man's clothes and a boy's figure it may have been. But I knew her at once, of course. It was The Flame, alias Florence Drummond. The Girl with the Criminal Mind.

CHAPTER XIX

THE FLAME FIGHTS FOR FREEDOM

Well—" The Flame sort of gasped, as if breathing had suddenly become a luxury, after the closet. "I'm in a mess, I guess."

"You guess right," I said, when I got my own breath back, but I didn't lower my gun.

She smiled a wan little smile as she looked at my gun, and lifted both her hands from her jacket pockets, empty.

"There isn't time for a plea, Race, even an explanation, if I had any. What are you going to do—about me?"

"What do you think?" Maybe I sneered slightly. "You picked the Gorgons as little playmates. There have been two murders already, and may be another, now. You," and with a smile of my own, "you even have put me, or are in with those who have put me on the spot."

"God in heaven!" she half threw up her hands. "Don't preach. And there have been as many spots picked out for you, in your day, as for a leopard."

"You're in bad, Florence." I came a little closer to her. She looked very tired; there were rings under her eyes. "There's no reason I should protect you. If you'll sell out the Gorgons, I'll—"

"A stool-pigeon! You want to make a stoolie out of The Flame. You—. I might tell you that letting me go may mean a man's life. I might tell you—. But just one question. Will you let me go? Yes or no."

"Florence," I ignored her question, "if I get you out of this. If—. What will you promise me. What will—"

"Don't play the heavy dick. I'll never squeal, for a price, if I could squeal." She glanced quickly down at the watch upon her wrist. "Well, shout out, or stand aside."

She pushed by me suddenly and made for the door, just as if she didn't know the whole house was thick with police.

I clutched her by the arm and swung her back. She spun, and looked at me. There was hatred, or anger, or defiance, in her eyes. Then she read the truth in mine, I guess, because her eyes went sort of fearful, like a frightened animal, before I spoke.

"The Flame," I said, as I gripped her arm tighter, "has swung with her mind and her eyes the honor of many men. You know something, and, by God! you're going to talk. You've made monkeys out of me long enough. Yes, you're right." I looked straight into her eyes. "I'm going to turn you in to the cops."

And she wilted. Was in my arms, her little head upon my shoulder, her arms about my neck. She was sobbing softly. I leaned down and forced up her head. The tears in her eyes were real, the quiver to her lips seemed hardly possible of acting. It was the girl again, but this time without the sparkle of youth in her eyes, the laughter on her lips, and—.

"Race," she said. "Race, Race, give me a break. Give me a—. You can't hold me like this and turn me in to the police. You don't know what it may mean. Why, why—let me go. Let me go."

Maybe I held her tighter. Maybe I bit my lip. Maybe I even brushed back her hair. I looked straight down at her a moment, and spoke words that my lips formed but my brain never directed. The truth too, perhaps, though who is to tell it.

"Florence," I said, "I love you."

She raised herself on her toes, the sparkle blazed through the mist in her eyes, and—oh, damn it—she kissed me, held me so a moment, then jerking herself free smiled up at me.

"That's what I wanted, Race, that's what I needed to make me—. Goodbye." She thrust the key of the closet door into my hand, turned again toward the hall door, as my hand shot out and gripped her by the arm.

"You're—you're not going to let me go?" I guess just bewilderment raced over her face at that moment.

"No," I said very slowly, "I'm not going to let you go."

"But you must, now—after—after—"

"I've got to keep you," I interrupted. "I've got to turn you in. It isn't you I'm going to live with. It isn't your eyes I'm going to look into the rest of my life. It's myself I've got to live with. It's myself I've got to face in the glass each morning. Maybe I'm hard, cruel. Maybe, as more than one paper has said, I'm a natural killer. Maybe— But, by God! I've never sold out a client, and I won't now. I—"

And I stopped. Feet beat down stairs, along the hall outside the door, seemed to hesitate, then go slowly on, to fall heavily upon other stairs.

"All right," The Flame said slowly and with an effort, I thought. But she had a way of pulling herself together, and a way of putting something into her eyes that cut like a lash. "You let me go and I'll give back to you the life of your client."

I thought that one out.

"Your word, your honor?"

"The honor of The Flame." She laughed, like a shovel being scraped over a cellar floor. "I'll give you back the life of your client. That's the whole ticket. Take it or leave it." And she folded her arms defiantly.

"When?"

"I'll meet you in," again her eyes went to her watch, "In thirty minutes, at Maria's Cafe."

"Maria's been closed by the police, two days ago," I said.

"Not for you or for me. I told Rudolph Myer to tell you to meet me there anyway. I had something to—. You got the message?"

"No," I said, "I didn't."

"No? Well, perhaps not. What do you say?"

"But how to get you out of here." I scratched my head. What about O'Rourke? Would I take him into my confidence? Would he let The Flame go, or—? No. I thought I knew how a cop would feel about that. And I thought of the window, the lamp cord. But there would be a cop in the alley. I might call him off. I might—. I turned to The Flame.

She was at the door, had it partly open, was peering into the hall.

"You can't—the police—droves of them," I whispered hurriedly. "The window, maybe, if—"

She shook her head and put her finger on her lips. It was in my mind to detain her now. Not because of any duty to a client, though. Because, well, I didn't believe a rabbit could slip through that cordon of police.

I shrugged my shoulders. After all, had I made a right decision? Was it because of my client that I let The Flame go? Or was I just anxious for an excuse not to be the one that turned her in? If the Colonel were dead, they might even hold her for murder.

"At Maria's Cafe, then," she whispered. And as my hand stretched toward her arm, "I have an 'out,'" and she was gone, closing the door silently behind her.

Perhaps it was the best way out. I wouldn't be responsible if she were caught now. And I found myself listening for her feet in the hall, listening vainly. Not a sound. But they wouldn't shoot a woman. They wouldn't—. And I remembered suddenly that The Flame was dressed as a man, also, with a little pang, that The Flame, for all I knew, might be armed and that—. Damn it, which had I let free in that house? The woman of evil or the girl of good?

I threw open the door and listened. Voices

from below, just murmurs. Heavy feet on the floor above. Feet that turned and came down the stairs. Loud feet. A dick nodded to me in the dim light, his hand clutching at the banister.

"I don't know what the racket is," he said, "but except for them two servants, the man and his wife upstairs, frightened silly, and who never heard a sound, the house is empty."

"Yeah." I tried to listen. Would there be a shout as they caught The Flame, or would there be a shot as The Flame was spotted, lurking in some dark corner? Or, and I waited as the cop looked over my shoulder into the room, and then went on his way.

Maybe there were visions of a crumpled little body at the foot of a flight of stairs, a white, childish face, eyes that had no sparkle—and—.

A minutes, two, three, perhaps five passed. Then feet coming up the stairs; Sergeant O'Rourke's gruff voice; his hand upon my shoulder, pushing me into the room. And he spoke.

"Hello!" He stood, looking at the open closet door. Then he turned to me, looked at my hand, and the key I held stupidly in it. "You found the key, eh?"

"Sure," I said. "On the desk, under the blotter, near the phone." But I still stood by the door, listening.

"Empty, of course." O'Rourke was in and out of the closet. "Well, Race, it's a big racket, a big responsibility." A moment of silence. "Guess I'll shift the burden, though the orders were to act alone." He ran fingers through his mottled hair, "I guess I'll give the Commissioner a buzz." He reached for the telephone. "It may turn out a mess if we keep it from the press too long, what with the district attorney's office wondering about it and the entire blame falling on the shoulders of the Commissioner if—. Colonel McBride is quite a lad, you know."

"Wait." I held O'Rourke's hand. "It's just possible I—"

"I—what?" demanded O'Rourke, his hand gripping the phone.

"I may stir up something. Wait."

"Wait?" gulped O'Rourke. "Well, I'll pass the 'wait' along to the Commissioner. It's his show. I don't want to be an official goat, after all these years."

We both straightened. The phone rang.

"Now what the hell?" said O'Rourke eagerly, and as he jerked off the receiver, "Yeah, what do you want?"

A moment's pause, and then from O'Rourke:

"Who wants to know? Who are you? Why, unless I know you, you can't. All right, he's here." O'Rourke pushed the phone to me, his hand over the mouthpiece.

"Guy wants you. Don't sound like the Colonel. Don't sound like any one. A mouth full of marbles. Better take it."

"Race," said a disguised, mechanical voice, that I couldn't recognize.

"Right," I said. "Race Williams."

"Talk a bit, so I can be sure."

And I did, pressing the receiver close to my ear and pushing O'Rourke off with my shoulder. O'Rourke had a curious turn of mind.

"Now you talk," I finished.

"It's Rudolph Myer," came the faint message. "Tried to get you at your apartment. The Flame must see you at the Cafe Maria. It means a lot, so she says. Suit yourself about going. Some one may be listening. Why she can't put over her own message, I don't know. But she said to come alone, unseen."

"How did you know I was—"

And I turned to O'Rourke. The click over the wire told me that Myer had cut me off. There's no percentage in talking to yourself.

"Who was that?" asked O'Rourke.

"It was—a lad about another case. I told him to call me here."

"Mighty liberal with your client's phone." O'Rourke bit off the end of a cigar, spat it across the room, and added, more sarcastically, "And forgot you told him you'd be here."

"Well—" I said. "Then it's business, this business. I've got to leave you."

"Sure!" nodded O'Rourke. "I'll give you an 'out' down stairs. The boys wouldn't pass the district attorney through this house tonight without my orders. Remember that."

"Okay. And sit tight for a bit, O'Rourke. I'll give you a jingle later."

O'Rourke looked at me before he spoke. Then he said very seriously:

"God! Race—it would be a great thing if your yen for gun-play developed in the right direction, if a certain party, a certain Gorgon got a little round hole in his forehead."

"Yes," was the best I could answer. Damn it all, was I getting nerves? Was I still listening for the sharp report that would tell me The Flame was— But I pulled myself together and looked hard at O'Rourke.

"Don't put a tail on me tonight," I said.

"No." He seemed to think, and then, "No, I won't. But remember what I said about the district attorney himself not getting out of here tonight without my Okay." And raising his voice as he walked with me to the stairs, "Brophey, see Williams to the corner and let him ride—alone."

I chewed over O'Rourke's last crack about the district attorney not getting out. I didn't get it then, unless—unless—. But certainly, after the cards O'Rourke and I had dealt each other over the years, he couldn't distrust me. As to holding out on him, he couldn't resent that. It had been our way of playing the game, always. If you don't talk to any one, you can't suspect any one of giving your plans away. When things go wrong, then, you can lay your finger smack on your own chest and nail the guy who's to blame. That much is gospel.

CHAPTER XX

AT MARIA'S CAFE

I had a little time to kill and entered an all night drug store, called up my apartment. Not actually expecting that Jerry would be back, you understand, but just not bent on missing any tricks. Jerry had not returned yet. I hoped he had spotted and, maybe, followed the man who had run when Colonel McBride was grabbed.

Then I drove around the town a bit, just getting the air. And I didn't exactly do any thinking, that is, constructive thinking. But, mostly, I never do. The Flame had certainly pulled a Houdini on the police and Sergeant O'Rourke. Was she still hidden in that house, or had she walked smack through the police net unseen, or had she bought her way out?

There's nothing fantastic about bribery. It's a matter of how much, and the type of man the receiver of the bribe is. You don't have to know him first. It works, from a ten spot to a strange speed cop, to a grand for a police captain, who has found the stock market a sucker's game, but hasn't recognized himself as that sucker yet.

The Flame was clever. There are no two ways about that. She had gotten into the house, maybe, even arranged that bit of kidnaping. Doctor Michelle Gorgon had picked himself some rare talent when he picked The Flame and—my hand went to my breast pocket. Damn it, I was still carrying around that envelope containing that bit of change and the jewelry which I had been requested to turn over to Eddie Gorgon.

Maybe The Flame would answer some questions at the Cafe Maria. The Flame had already

intended to meet me there, before she popped out of that closet. And you know—. Well, we're all a bit of a fool, I guess. Somehow I wasn't worried so much about The Flame any more. A guy gets cocky at times. I had held her, told her I loved her. And—she loved me. There were no two ways about that. Any lad who had held The Flame as I did—. But the time was drawing near, so I sped over to Maria's Cafe.

According to my custom I left my car around the corner, walked leisurely down the block, spotted the darkness of the entrance, and went to the little side door down a few steps and knocked.

The door opened almost at once. I nodded as I recognized the bartender.

"Hello, Race." He opened the door far enough for me to slip into the dimness of the hall, but spotted almost at once the bulge in my right jacket pocket.

"Gawd!" he sort of laughed. "And me thinking it was just an affair of the heart."

"There's a lady waiting to see me, Fred?" It was half a question, half a statement.

"Yeah." He nodded. "The little room back of the bar."

"Any one in the bar?"

"No. The Federal officers have closed us up."

"You're a nice boy, Fred." I followed him into the bar. "I wouldn't like to see anything happen to you." No threat. Just a warning in my words.

"Cripes!" He slowed, and looked at me. "You

ain't got nothing up your sleeve, I don't know about?"

"Nothing up my sleeve. Be sure there's nothing up yours." I followed him to the door in the rear, down another hall and to another small door.

"You weren't dragged in here." Fred gave me the words over his shoulder. "And the door 'out' ain't barred and locked now." He put a hand on the knob. "What do you say? Got a change of mind? Want to beat it?"

"Do your stuff," was my say.

"Right!" He spun the knob, shoved open the door and chirped, "The gent to see you." He turned quickly, pushed by me and closed the door after him. I heard his feet slipping over the uncarpeted floor of the outer hall.

The room was like any other back room of a speak-easy. A single dome light hung from the ceiling, giving a sharp light. There were eight or ten tables, plain wooden armchairs drawn close to them. Not piled up on top, for they wouldn't be doing any cleaning for a bit. The room still reeked of bum hooch. The open window on the alley didn't help much. There was an old fashioned mantel to one side, above a fireplace that had been bricked up, and a battered but shining silver loving cup supposedly in the center of that mantel.

And, alone in that room, was The Flame. No dirty masculine get-up now. Silk stockings, black skirt, and a tight fitting, worsted sweater coat affair. To crown that off she had a beret cocked on the side of her head, and a cigarette perched jauntily between her lips.

"You did turn up," she said. "But then, you would. You always were a fool for courage. Sit down."

I walked to the window, closed it, and pulled down the heavy shade. I'd rather chance slow death by poison air than a bullet in the back. There was another exit, with a key in the door. I spun the key and turned the knob. It locked all right. An alcove recess, with dirty curtains, proved to be a blind. Just a closet with shelves. Across from that was the door I had entered by.

There was no key in the lock. I kicked a chair in front of the door, stuffed a cigarette into my mouth, saw that The Flame was close to the mantel, so dragged up a chair and sat beside her. I could see the window and the door with the chair against it, and had the alcove on the right.

The Flame started. It was the old racket all over again.

"Race, I'll make you a proposition. I'll chuck the Gorgon outfit if you do. I'll chuck the city. We'll cross the pond, hop down to the Riviera, and—"

"Same old hoey," I cut in. "Florence, you've given that to any guy you wanted to make— make for the time being—make and then break."

"Yes." She nodded very seriously. "I have. Because I've always thought of it. Thought of it with you, Race." A hand crept across the table and rested on one of mine. "We could meet every day, spend long evenings together, understand each other—and bust up the show or stick together for life. There's something big between us, something I never understood. There's been times when I wished you were dead. Times—"

"Florence," I cut in, "I'm here for one purpose only. Your promise. I want to know where—"

"Yes, that's so." She seemed to be listening. "It's not a good place to talk names here. But, somehow, I wanted you to know." She leaned forward now, and barely whispered the words. "I don't know about you, sometimes you simply blunder through things. I've hashed up my life; maybe I wouldn't go if you wished it, maybe I'm hell bent for destruction. But you're looking at a woman now, not a girl. A woman that's going straight to her death, who's got to go through with it."

I didn't like that talk. Somehow I believed it though. Somehow—. And I stiffened. There, slightly to my left, the knob of a door was turning—the door I had pushed the chair against. I didn't say anything to The Flame. I simply laid both my elbows on the smeared table, my hands up close to my chin, one hand also close to the shoulder holster beneath my left armpit.

The door moved slightly too, very slightly, not enough to even push the chair—that is, the chair by the door. But it moved my chair—or, at least I moved my chair enough to bring me directly facing that turning knob which put my back to the alcove closet, and left me just about on the opposite side of the table from The Flame.

The Flame looked up as I moved. The color seemed to suddenly drain out of her face. Her fingers half reached for her handbag upon the table, hesitated, and she stretched her hand to the mantel and lifted down the loving cup, looking it over. Then she read aloud the inscription on it.

"To Eddie Gorgon," she read, very slowly. "On the occasion of his return to the Maria Club—August 27th—1929." She read it in such a low voice, such a forced, almost ominous voice, that it startled me. But I remembered that dinner too. It was the day Eddie Gorgon was released from the Tombs, when the jury failed to convict him for the murder of an East Side laundry man, who had courageously fought against the then notorious Laundry racketeers.

The door knob quit turning. The door gave a sudden jerk and a voice spoke behind me, by those curtains, from the little alcove closet that I thought had no "out." Yep, I had let that door take my attention.

"Don't move," said the voice of Eddie Gorgon. "This time, Race, we'll be satisfied with the bullet in your back, where the bullet in any rat should be found. That a girl, Florence. Read him again what's on the cup."

Trapped? Certainly. Trapped like a child. I could hear Eddie Gorgon cross the floor; knew that he stood a few feet behind me. And there I was, with my right hand under my left armpit, the fingers clasping a gun that I—I could never use. Why hadn't I made sure of that closet? Certainly, those shelves in it hid another door. Was it my stupidity, or my conceit, or my belief in The Flame, or—.

I looked at Florence. I wanted to see how she took it. I wanted to see if at the last minute she

would regret my death. I wanted—. And her face was deathly white. She had betrayed me into the hands of the enemy and was paying a price for it. But a hell of a lot of good that would do me now.

"Show him the cup. Read him again what's on the cup." Eddie mouthed the words. "Just once more, then I'll let him have it."

The girl moved the cup. Her eyes sought mine, mine hers, until the cup blocked them both. Yes, the cup blocked them both. And I saw something else. I saw the sinister, rat-like eyes, the twisted lips, and the gun too, the gun held in a steady hand but a thin hand. For Eddie Gorgon seemed long and gaunt—some sixteen or more feet tall, and his arm was as thin as a match stick. And I knew. I was looking at Eddie's reflection in the polished surface of the oval cup.

It was in my mind to draw, swing and fire. All that, of course, while Eddie Gorgon pressed the trigger of his gun. It couldn't save my life. He was too close to miss, too close not to have a chance to fire several times. Just the one chance that I might take him over the hurdles with me.

There was no use to make excuses to myself. Eddie Gorgon had entered that closet while some lad attracted my attention at the moving door. No, I wasn't proud of that moment. There might be one excuse for it, and the worst kind of an excuse. My own vanity. Perhaps subconsciously I had thought that once I had told The Flame I loved her I was safe. That the ambition of her life was realized, that if she could have me she would never think of—. And then just one thought. He travels farthest who travels alone. But The Flame was talking.

"Easy does it, Eddie," she said. "Race might talk. You know what he might tell, what your brother wants to know. What—"

"This is my show," Eddie snarled in on her. "Look the rat in the eyes, kid. Watch 'em dim. Not a move, Race. Keep them elbows so I can see them. Just a single jerk of your shoulders, and out you go."

And what was I doing? Just sitting there waiting for death to strike through the mouth of a blazing gun held in the hand of an underworld rat, a common murderer, I had told Jerry.

No. Plainly in that cup I could see the long, gawky form of Eddie Gorgon. My elbows never moved their position on that table. But my hand moved—my fingers moved. Already my right hand had pulled my gun from the shoulder holster, eased it out and shoved it up toward my shoulder. And The Flame still held the cup in her hands—very steady.

Would I try one quick jerk and a shot over my shoulder at Eddie? Maybe I'd have to. The reflection in that cup was clear enough, the features of Eddie, the skinny appearing extended arm, the snub-nosed automatic, the barrel of which appeared long enough, as reflected in that cup, to be a rifle barrel. And—.

"Don't shoot yet, Eddie," The Flame said. "I got him here for you, didn't I? I want him to answer a question."

And my gun crept slowly higher up my left shoulder, my arm never moving, my elbows steady upon the table—just my wrist curling upward and my head moving slightly sideways, slowly sideways. I hoped Eddie was far enough behind me not to see my gun—at least, until it had crept up and over my shoulder.

"Yeah," snarled Eddie Gorgon. "But what about me? You made a deal with me. You let me horn you in with us Gorgons, played me for a sucker until Michelle came along, and then what, then what? I got a mind to snuff you, too."

"It's all the same." The Flame seemed to half appeal. "It's the same business, the same racket. I have to listen to Michelle just as you have to listen to him. Whether you brought me in or he brought me in, I'd be working for him just the same. I—"

"That may be Michelle's idea, but not mine," said Eddie quickly. "He could have your mind, but not me. I was staking your body, not your mind. Besides which, I still think you've got a yen for this dick. I've played the game, taken orders, done Michelle's dirty work. But no man can take my woman. No, by God! not even Michelle. And Michelle would never know but it was an accident if I knocked you over."

My gun was higher, right on my shoulder now. Not over enough to show, Just—. The face of Eddie looked so long and lean in that cup, the eyes were so close together.

"Eddie," and The Flame's voice was soft and low, "don't talk like that. I saw in Michelle only your interest. I saw only—"

"I seen your face and I seen Michelle's there in your apartment, when you stuck me up. His talk of 'in the abstract!' Well, the abstract wasn't in his eyes then. He was just a man who wanted a woman, my woman, and you were just a woman who wanted a man, a bigger man than Eddie Gorgon. You knew what Michelle might mean to you, and you dropped me. Michelle didn't want no mind, he wanted a body. You sold yourself to me, I paid you cash. And, tonight, after the dick, Williams, crashes out I'll—. But he'll take it first."

And my gun was up. I won't say that I read the will to fire suddenly in Eddie's reflection in the cup. I won't say that I recognized it in his voice, though I think I did. I won't even say that The Flame's sudden shrill cry did the trick.

But she did call out.

"Now, Race!"

Zip! Like that. My finger closed upon the trigger—and I threw myself forward on the table.

CHAPTER XXI
THE MAN IN THE WINDOW

There were two roars, a clang like a bell in a shooting gallery—and I was on my feet. If the cup didn't betray me I had placed a hunk of lead smack between Eddie Gorgon's eyes.

And Eddie Gorgon stood there, his mouth hanging open in surprise. I jerked up my gun to fire again, but I didn't fire. Eddie's gun hung by his side, then his fingers opened and he dropped it to the floor. Not a mark of a bullet on him. No hole in the center of his forehead. And I saw his eyes just before he folded himself up like a jack-knife and sank to the floor. Eddie Gorgon had died on his feet, and only a missing tooth or two in the mouth that hung open, and the tiny bubbles forming on his lips—red bubbles—told me where the bullet had gone. Not exactly a perfect shot, maybe, but a serviceable one just the same. I'm no miracle man.

After all, Eddie Gorgon had meant to kill me, and he was dead. I shrugged my shoulders. The thing I had pressed that trigger to do had been accomplished.

The Flame was on her feet too—and clutching the cup to her. She was very white and very shaky, and I noticed that she turned her head from the body. I saw too that the cup had a hole in it—that the first two letters of the word EDDIE were missing. That was the bell-like ring then, as Eddie's bullet hit the cup.

"Did you—? He didn't hit you, Florence?" I was close to her now, supporting her trembling body and placing the cup on the table.

"No, no. It was the cup—saved me. His cup—saved me—and you too."

"You saved my life, Florence. I—. And after trapping me here."

"Fool, fool," she cried out, beating me away as I would have held her. "I've taken on too much and can't think it out. You, you won't think. It seems impossible and too grotesque to believe, but we must believe it, must. I've never trapped you." And suddenly pushing me from her and backing away:

"You have nothing to thank me for, Race. He had to go. He had to die. Brains—brains—brains. And it took the animal in Eddie to nearly ruin everything. I can't die yet. I mustn't die yet. I'll die with him, as she died with him, for she died. Damn his soul, what a living death she died!"

Which was all confusing to me, you've got to admit.

The Flame didn't raise a hand this time to stop me as I went toward her. She didn't need to. It was her face, the distorted hatred of it, or was it fear, that I took for hate, or perhaps it was horror. Anyway, I held my ground and simply looked at her, turned, and picking up the cup wiped it clean of finger-prints and placed it back on the mantel.

"We better get out of here, Florence. The shot, the man by the door. The bartender, Fred, and—"

"You can be sure that there is not a soul in this house tonight, right now. If the shot was heard, it was heard outside." She clutched at her throat and half glanced at the body.

"He's lying there," she said. "After all, he was

human. Made by the same hand that made you and me and Michelle, and even good people we read about. I must lie like that some day. Soon—very soon—and I know it—and go on toward it. But he's lying there, Race, a human, like you and me. Is he dead?"

I took another look at Eddie, lifted his hand and let it fall back again. I didn't need any medical certificate of death to tell me the truth. It had to be Eddie or me, and—well—if I wasn't exactly glad it was Eddie, I was glad it wasn't me.

"He's dead," I told The Flame, felt the long envelope in my pocket bend as I knelt so—the envelope which Michelle Gorgon had asked me to deliver to his brother, Eddie. I drew it out. To leave it with Eddie now, there on his chest, would be a gruesome sort of humor, maybe. But it wasn't that which made me stick it back in my pocket. Some one beside the Gorgon crowd might first find Eddie. No need to advertise this bit of killing yet. At least there was no need to implicate The Flame, if others knew about that money and jewelry in the envelope.

No one but Fred, the bartender, had seen me come into the Maria Cafe, and Fred was off for the night. Wise men of the underworld don't speak of the events which precede violent death, at least, to the police, they don't. And certainly it wouldn't take a lot of brain work on the part of either of the Gorgon brothers to guess who sent Eddie bye-bye.

"Come!" The Flame went to the window and threw it open, and let in the cool night air. It felt good. I turned, looked the room over once for any sign of my visit, was satisfied with the inspection and reached the window in time to take the girl by the arm.

"You forget, Florence, what I came here for. I want to know where Colonel McBride is. Is he alive?"

"Yes, he must be. Let us get away from here first. Surely," she looked at me as I still held her arm, "we can talk as well in the alley."

"Yeah, with every ash can concealing a gunman, for all I know? You trapped me twice. You—. Oh, I give you credit for saving my life, Florence. But you change so quickly that I can't

chance it. This may be one of your weak, or perhaps, from your point of view, one of your strong moments. Anyway, to love The Flame is to die," and somewhat bitterly maybe, "and I put myself on that sucker list tonight, in the house of Colonel McBride when you popped out of the closet. Oh, I'm not blaming you, Florence. I'm beginning to think that label you've won is not just a moniker of the night. The Girl with the Criminal Mind."

She swung suddenly on me, her hands gripping my arms above the elbows, her eyes looking into mine. Anxious, fearful, haunted eyes. Different than I had ever seen her before. But then, The Flame was always different. Of course women are supposed to faint at violent death, but then, The Flame never ran true to biological or physiological, or what have you, form. Still the death of Eddie had knocked her, it seemed. Yep, The Flame was out of character, or maybe, in character. No one knew the real Flame, I guess, least of all me.

"One question, Race, just one question now. Do you, do you love me?"

"I don't know." I guess that was the truth.

"Did you mean what you said, there in Colonel McBride's house, when you thought I must be caught or killed? You, you said you loved me, you know. Did you mean it?"

"Yes, I meant it then," I told her, almost viciously. "And maybe I mean it now. It's a queer thing though, Florence. No one can lay a finger to it. But love you or not, I don't trust you. I don't think you even trust yourself. I—"

She half glanced at the body again, and shivered slightly. And I let her slip over the sill and drop into the alley. Yes, I let her. But I very nearly stepped on her heels, I dropped so quickly after her.

"You better put out the light," she told me. "I imagine that's the way Eddie would have done it, if it were you lying in there. You see, the place is closed. They expect, or Eddie expected, to let the crime ride. Maybe it would be days before they were supposed to find you."

"Then you did trap me," I cut in.

"Ah," she swung on me suddenly, "then you didn't believe I trapped you. You tried to believe it, but couldn't. That's it, isn't it?" She shook me by the shoulders. "You couldn't believe it. Try as you might, you could not believe it."

"Couldn't!" And maybe my laugh was queer. Maybe I didn't want to believe it, but that I didn't was a different thing, again. Inside of me, maybe, I denied it to myself. But I'm a reasoning man, and certainly I believed it.

"You mean to tell me that you didn't know Eddie was there!" I demanded.

"No, I didn't know. I don't expect you to believe me. But I didn't know until I heard him, saw him."

"But who told Eddie? Fred, the bartender?"

"Fred didn't know whom I was to meet, until you came. He didn't know I was to meet any one until five minutes before you came. That he got in touch with Eddie, or that Eddie just happened to come here, would be impossible."

"And you didn't have Eddie come to the apartment, your apartment, that night he jumped me from the window?" There certainly was disbelief in my voice.

"No," she said slowly, "I didn't."

"Quite a coincidence, quite a coincidence. And I don't believe in coincidences."

"Nor do I." She snapped that back at me as she slipped down the alley and we reached the street. "But I do believe in using your brains, just once in a while, Race. You can't plug on always like you do." And with what might have been a smile, "There won't always be a woman, a woman with a criminal mind, to lift loving cups for you and—"

"Florence," I said, "what of Colonel McBride? You promised if I let you go—"

"Oh, I may have lied to you, to get away. It might have been a promise I can never keep. But I'll try, I'll try. Michelle Gorgon knows where he is, and I—. Michelle Gorgon is friendly toward me."

"Yes," I said, "he is." And with an effort I stuck to my client. "What about Colonel McBride?"

"Well." She blazed up. "Michelle Gorgon wants information from him. He wants to know who is behind McBride, where McBride learns things, and—. Race, go to Michelle, tell him you'll quit the case."

"Quit for that mountebank!" I sniffed. "I should say not. A client hired me, and—. But I'll go to Michelle Gorgon all right."

"If you stay on the case, nothing can save your life now, now that Eddie is dead. Don't you see? Michelle Gorgon loves me. And superstition or not, to love The Flame is to die." Her lips curled, and her smile was more sad than sinister.

"Death for me too, then." I half laughed. I could feel her fingers bite into my arm, but she did not speak.

"Florence," I said. "You love this man, this Michelle Gorgon. You have been swept off your feet by his influence, his money, his air of superiority, and his admiration for—"

She turned on me viciously. Then, after a moment, she said, almost softly:

"But, yes, he attracts me greatly. To have him love me, want me. It is the ambition of my life."

She tried to go. I held her arm. But I couldn't say anything. She looked straight at me and spoke again.

"Race, use your head. When the day comes that you believe in me, absolutely trust me, take pencil and paper and go over this, all of this, from the beginning—from the very second that you stepped into the case. Think who is the best informed one you know, of you and me, and—" Then suddenly, "O'Rourke brought you into this, didn't he?"

"No, he didn't."

"No—No—But he must have. He must have. It couldn't have been—"

"It was—" And I stopped. I couldn't trust her.

"Rudolph Myer, maybe." She thought aloud. Then, "No. That wouldn't be logical. That wouldn't—. But of course it was Rudolph Myer."

She turned suddenly, flung both arms about my neck, and kissed me. And she left me. Walked smack out of the alley just as a harness bull turned the corner and sauntered leisurely down the street, half a block away.

As for me. I went back down that alley, hopped in the window again and turned out the light. I'd pay a little visit to Michelle Gorgon before Eddie's body was cold.

But I wasn't to pay my little visit to Michelle Gorgon just then. Feet sounded in the alley outside, feet that hit heavily for a moment against stone, then moved cautiously toward that window. It was a cinch that those feet belonged to a heavy body that had dropped from the fence dividing the houses.

It wasn't the harness bull from outside then. My first impulse was to beat it by the front way. My second, to stick it out. It might be one of the Gorgon outfit, come to see if Eddie had disposed of me. There was only one way to find out, that was to wait and see what broke. Nothing dangerous in my position now. There I was, close to one side of the window, my back pushed against the wall, my gun in my hand. No, there was nothing to be alarmed about.

A form blotted out the faint semblance of light from the window. Not light enough there to recognize a man, or anywhere near it. But light enough to barely make out the bulkiness of huge shoulders, and the whiteness of a face. For a moment I got a thrill. To myself I said, "The Second Gorgon, Joe Gorgon." My finger squeezed a gun trigger slightly. I was beginning to dislike the Gorgons.

A white hand crept over the sill. A split second later a pencil of light bit into the darkness, crept along the floor, picked out a lifeless foot, ran quickly up the body of Eddie Gorgon and smacked on the side of his face. I rather liked that. The dead gangster lay so that you could not recognize him. My friend at the window would have to come into the room if he wanted to identify the thing that had been Eddie Gorgon, feared racketeer.

He did just that little thing. And what's more, he didn't like it overmuch. Not from any lack of moral courage, I guess, but from the physical effort. For although he started in the window without a moment's hesitation, he didn't like the bodily exertion, for I heard him grunt plainly.

CHAPTER XXII

O'ROURKE HAS A HUNCH

He was in the room now, across to the body, leaning over and turning the dead face into the light of the flash. He whistled softly, muttered something to himself that didn't seem like a curse, and I was smack behind him, my gun in his back.

"Don't move, brother," I said, "unless you want to lie down beside your little playmate. Now—that flash. Good." And the man laughed, and the light struck his face.

Maybe I laughed too, but not with quite as much mirth. The hard, grizzled map I looked into was that of the "honest cop," Detective Sergeant O'Rourke.

"Well," I said, "what are you going to do?" And I didn't drop my gun. The first thing I thought of then was Rudolph Myer, a habeas corpus writ, and the amount of bail. Not that I didn't trust O'Rourke, but he might be the efficient cop now, not the loyal friend. Through and through O'Rourke was a cop.

"What am I going to do?" He ignored my gun, walked to the window, closed it, pulled down the shade and pressed the electric button. "It's what are you going to do, and what did you do?"

"I took your advice," I told him, "and laid a bullet in one of the Gorgons. It was self-defense, and more. I was, was trapped here. And you put a tail on me, after you promised you wouldn't."

"Well," he said, "it don't look like you were trapped. Let's talk it out, Race. You and me are in the same racket and under the same boss, but working at odds. And I ain't above telling you

now, that I got you into the Gorgon mess. But that's confidential."

"*You* got me in. I thought—"

"You thought it was Rudolph Myer, and so it was. That was my little plan. I didn't want you to know. But no matter, now. Working the same game or not, here's a lad been croaked. We can't just pretend it never happened, you know. We'll run it through as a matter of form. There's big people behind you. McBride, if he's alive."

"He's alive," I told O'Rourke. "Don't charge me with this shooting. Let me put it in a form of a complaint. I went to the Maria Cafe, was attacked, and shot a man in self-defense—and I call on the authorities to investigate the attack on me. Then it's the district attorney's move against me. I'll be ready with bail, and—"

"Good stuff, and does credit to your honest nature." O'Rourke grinned. "But Eddie isn't going to be missed that bad. At least, by the police department. You may not know it exactly, but you're just as much a part of the city's police system, with their rights," and with a little grimace, "and without their restrictions, as I am. I've got a lot of authority, and a big lad to take the blame, if things go wrong. We'll let it stand as a gang killing for a little bit, at least, to outsiders."

"O'Rourke." I cut in with a sudden idea. "Could you keep this quiet, just for a few hours, maybe, until—" And I went into the thing. "I want to see Michelle Gorgon. I want a good talk with him. I—. But if he knows I got his brother, well, it won't give me a chance to work on this thing. Every—"

· 335 ·

"I know," said O'Rourke, rubbing his chin. "How long do you want?"

"A couple of hours."

"It's after twelve," said O'Rourke, snapping out his watch. "I'll give you until morning, five o'clock, or if you can make it earlier, better still. But you can't go to Michelle Gorgon now—not quite yet." And very slowly, "His wife was moved last night to a private hospital down town. Do you know what that means, Race?"

"No," I said, "I don't."

"But I think I do." O'Rourke nodded vigorously. "Nothing can happen in Doctor Gorgon's home. He's through with her. She's going to die."

"But she couldn't. He wouldn't dare murder his own wife. That would be the end. The—"

"He murdered his wife years ago. But who the wife was—?" he scratched his head. "The best detective in the city has been to Italy, Race, and if that little Giovoni spoke the truth, there's no evidence to show that Michelle Gorgon was ever married before, in Italy or any place else. I tell you, I've been working on Michelle Gorgon for over a year, and it wasn't until this judgeship business came up and Colonel McBride was secretly called in by his buddy, the Deputy Commissioner, that I carried authority in it. The Commissioner himself is behind McBride. I tell you, this judgeship business is nothing to Michelle Gorgon's murder racket. He has many enemies, of course. But when an enemy becomes big enough for him to notice—that enemy dies.

"But if I couldn't find out anything about Michelle Gorgon's former wife, whose, at least claimed to be, father-in-law got rubbed out the other night—I have found out plenty about his present wife. More than any man in the world knows; more than Michelle Gorgon himself knows; more than the wife herself knows. Laugh that off." There was a ring of pride in his voice.

"And Gorgon's wife—. What do you intend to do?"

"I intend to talk to her. I understand she's slightly loose in the upper story. And I know that she had a terrible accident, airplane accident, in which Michelle Gorgon didn't get hurt, and I understand that she had a gentleman friend, for she was a very beautiful woman. There's a story that Michelle Gorgon maimed her purposely, but like his other activities it can't be proved. Anyway, she didn't jump from the plane, but crashed with it. I want to talk to her before anything happens to her. That's that. If that isn't playing the game with you, Race, nothing is."

"But you promised not to put a tail on me, and—"

"So that rankles. Well, forget it. I didn't. No more questions about that, now. Let it drop. But the phone in Colonel McBride's house leaked as soon as it rang. Anyway, we'll forget who you came here to meet. But come on. We'll have to chance the discovery of the body. You'd have chanced that anyway."

"Isn't it a little late for a hospital interview?" I asked.

"Sure," said O'Rourke. "But if it were four in the morning I'd go anyway. It isn't something, I think, that can be delayed overlong.

"You know, Race," O'Rourke told me, when we were safely out of the Maria Cafe and speeding to the private hospital in my car, "you're a man of your word and I'm a man of mine. Remember that. We've got to work fast on this, before something else happens. I work for the city. I work against time. I use stool-pigeons. Play on crooks who have been, or think they have been, double crossed. Even ignore some small crime if the individual will give information concerning a bigger one. I thought I'd go any length to reach my ends, and I have—I did. I've stirred up thoughts of passion, hatred, and vengeance. Now and here's a terrible thing for a lad who's been an honest cop over twenty years to say. If you were to put a bullet between them cute eyes of Michelle Gorgon, I'd, well, I don't ask you to do it and I don't say I'd thank you for doing it, but I'd sleep easier at night and, and, by God! I might even go on the witness stand and perjure myself that I saw Doctor Gorgon draw a rod and heard him threaten to kill you."

"You've got a little hatred for this bird yourself, O'Rourke."

"Yes," he said, "I have. But it isn't so much hatred of Michelle Gorgon, but fear, fear of what I've done, fear of the uncontrollable fires I lit. But maybe the day will come, Race, when you'll be wanting to put a little lead bullet between these same two eyes of mine."

I laughed and said:

"It wouldn't be a hard mark to hit."

"No," said O'Rourke, very seriously, "it wouldn't. But this'll be the place. And it's as respectable as it looks." I stopped the car before the building, as O'Rourke talked on. "Ritzy too, and high priced. There's a doctor's name behind this institution that's gospel to the medical profession; a lad to run it who hasn't had ten minutes to himself to hobnob in the underworld since he graduated from medical school. It looks just like the sort of a place to faze the lowly Mick, known as Detective Sergeant O'Rourke. So, under those conditions, we'll go through with it. In we go."

And in we went.

Somehow O'Rourke seemed different to me. He talked more. Was it nerves? But surely, after his years as the most active detective on the police force, he wouldn't get finicky over a few murders more or less. I guess, maybe, he was just the man hunter on the hunt. The eagerness gets under your skin, you know. Still, he seemed different. But then, every one seemed different. Maybe we were all feeling that sinister air of superiority of the Third Gorgon. And I grinned to myself—of the Second Gorgon now. After all, Eddie was one of them. Eddie was protected by his association and relationship. And you couldn't get away from the fact that all Eddie needed now was a shovel and some loose dirt.

The nurse who let us in was not so much surprised, but the lad in the white coat, who came out of the little room behind her, was more than surprised. He was shocked, and let us know it.

"Mrs. Gorgon—really. You can't see her, of course. And at this hour, under no circumstances."

"I know it's irregular." O'Rourke scratched his head.

"Irregular!" Doctor Importance, in the white coat, elevated his nose to avoid the stench of our presence. "It's impossible."

"Police business." O'Rourke produced his shield. "And damned important police business. We'll see the lady at once."

The nose came down and had to breathe the same air with us.

"May I—? You have authority, of course." But there wasn't much confidence in the young doctor's voice. He was simply repeating something he had read some place.

"You see the ticket of admission to the show." O'Rourke shoved the badge up higher. "I'll see Mrs. Gorgon now, just us two. Or if you want to stand on ceremony, I'll bring in the boys and make a party of it."

"I—I may notify Doctor Revel?" he half stammered. "It's—We couldn't disturb the other patients. Surely you wouldn't—Good God! It's not a raid. Not a raid, here."

"Never mind Doctor Revel. Come on, shake a leg." And we were all three leaving the room.

There was no doubt that O'Rourke had bulldozed the young doctor into taking us to Mrs. Gorgon's, or Madame's room.

"She has a weak heart, a very weak heart. You'll—"

"Tut, tut, young feller, me lad." O'Rourke was patronizing. "We're here to protect her." And as we left the elevator and entered the little white room, O'Rourke said, "Doctor Revel will be glad we came. You can notify him now." With that he pushed the young doctor into the hall, hesitated a moment, saw the nurse that came down the long corridor toward us, and holding the door open, said:

"We're police officers, Miss. We've got to question Mrs. Gorgon. Better come along with us." And to me, "I'm taking a chance, Race, but I think it's justified—but we better have this young lady with us."

O'Rourke switched on the light, closed the young doctor out in the hall, motioned the nurse toward the bed, and finding no key in the lock, dragged a chair against the door. The nurse was bright but slightly nervous. However, if she resented our presence, or even found it distasteful, she didn't let us know it. She obeyed O'Rourke to the letter.

We stood back while she approached the bed and spoke to the restless form upon it. The brown eyes opened now and blinked in the light— searching—fearful—dead, haunted eyes. Perhaps as the eyes of The Flame had been, for a moment.

"Two gentlemen to see you, Madame. Two gentlemen," the nurse repeated, softly. "They want to talk to you. They—"

And Madame saw us. A withered hand went to the scraggy hair; a sheet was jerked quickly up to hide the discoloration on her neck, and almost as quickly the twisted hand went back under the clothes again. She spoke, her teeth getting in the way of her words.

"They mustn't see me, Miss Agnes—not like this. I'm not ready to receive callers. Two gentlemen, Miss Agnes? One a young man, a handsome young man, like—. No—no." And off she went under the covers.

But I won't go into the tricks of Madame. Both O'Rourke and I were glad we had the nurse, Miss Agnes, with us.

She looked at us once, more questioning than disdainfully. But O'Rourke held his ground.

"I must talk to her," he told the nurse, and at her suggestion we parked ourselves behind the bed screen while Madame was made what she called "respectable."

She talked too. Clearly enough sometimes, incoherently at others.

She sort of wandered on.

"No mirror, Miss Agnes. But then, I never have a mirror. What do you think the gentlemen wish, Miss Agnes? The young man, now—he came to see me once before. My skin does not feel so soft and beautiful—but then, my hand has lost its sense of touch. A little more powder, my dear. I'm sure, a little powder. It's my vanity, Miss Agnes." She lowered her voice to a hoarse whisper. "My husband was always so jealous," and she

giggled. It was a girlish giggle. It was eerie. "Now, why can't I see myself, just once. He was a musician, so young, so handsome. He adored me, played to me, wrote a song just for me. And this accident. No, he mustn't see my twisted body. But my face, it is still beautiful, my eyes, at least. Michelle always said so, until last week. There— put my hand beneath the coverlet, and—"

We stepped out and saw the woman. What a hideous sight she was! Far worse now for the powder and rouge and nightcap on her head. But most of all it was the glint in her eyes—the simper to cracked lips that were now a vivid red. The yellow skin, great patches of it raw flesh, that were more horrible for the thickness of the rouge and the great daubs of powder.

"Madame is ready," said the nurse, Miss Agnes, looked at us. Partly in warning, maybe, for the woman was indeed terrible to look at.

O'Rourke jerked erect, went to the bed and sat down upon it.

"Mrs. Gorgon," he said. "We—I'm a friend. I heard you had some trouble. You wanted to talk about it with me."

"Trouble, to talk with you? I thought—. But then, maybe it is not true—and it is my face also. It was a very beautiful face. Who are you?"

"I am a police officer. I—"

The door knob turned, the chair slipped, and O'Rourke swung his head and spoke to me.

"Keep him in the hall," he said.

And I did. I pushed through the door and backed the gray haired man into the hall before me. He was wearing a dark dressing gown, and plenty of dignity.

"I am Doctor Revel," he said. "What is the meaning of this intrusion?"

And you had to admire the doctor. He didn't fuss and fume, and I didn't give him any heavy line.

"Police duty." I let it go at that, but I blocked the doorway.

The doctor looked at his wrist watch.

"Let me see your warrant," he said.

"Everything's Okay," I told him. "You have no cause for alarm. It—"

"If things were strictly as they should be, you would have seen me first."

"You can take the matter up with Headquarters in the morning, if you're not satisfied with the proceedings." I pretended an indifference.

"That has already been attended to." The doctor nodded. "At least, the police precinct nearest the hospital has been called. To me, the matter is very serious indeed. I can not of course create a disturbance in the hospital; there are some very sick people here. The disturbance, my dear friend, will be created tomorrow, make very sure of that." The doctor had a mean sort of calm about him.

The woman inside screamed. The nurse spoke quickly. I think O'Rourke cursed, but I'm not sure. But the doctor stiffened, and I stuck my head back in the door and said:

"The head doctor's here and he's not friendly and he's telephoned the precinct."

And the doctor stepped by me and into the room. Of course I could have stopped him, but I didn't. I wasn't fooling with any medical student now, and I knew it. This guy cut some ice.

He ignored O'Rourke and went straight to the woman on the bed, bent over her a moment, pulled out the twisted hand, pressed his other hand across her forehead, spoke quickly to the nurse, and I saw the bottle from which she measured the drops. It was digitalis. A strong heart stimulant.

O'Rourke and I stood around like a couple of saps. At length the doctor turned on O'Rourke and backed us toward the door.

"Well—" he said, when he had us in the hall, "have you an explanation?"

O'Rourke stiffened, and the bulldog chin shot out. The cop was ever dominant. He wouldn't take water even then. He was a tough old bird, and no mistake.

"Yes, I have," he said. "You read about the murder in Elrod's Sanitarium last week. Do you want to see that poor woman there snuffed out the same way? Don't high hat me, Doctor. I've been on the Force too long. And don't look so hurt. You read your papers. If you don't, some

one must have told you. You know who that woman is. You know who brought her here. And you know what the name Gorgon stands for—unless you simply think, like a lot of others, that it stands for money only."

It was good stuff. The doctor didn't seem so cocky. Oh, his dignity was still there, but it had dents all over it. Finally he won out, and said:

"Are you hinting that my cupidity made me, made me take in this unfortunate woman?"

"I'm hinting at nothing," said O'Rourke. "Doctor Gorgon buys what he wants. That woman's life is in grave danger, and not from what's ailing her. I came in, didn't I? And he came in, didn't he?" O'Rourke jerked a thumb at me. "Now, what's to prevent some one else coming in, who hasn't got the woman's interest at heart, like us? And you can't throw hard looks and pompous words down the muzzle of a murderer's gun. Nor will they wait while you notify the nearest precinct."

Doctor Revel had a mental picture of the stabbing at Elrod's, I guess. A mental picture that for the first time he permitted himself to think might happen in his tony establishment. His placid map and dignity of bearing were playing him false.

"I never guessed. I didn't know." He wiped the beads of sweat from his forehead. O'Rourke wasn't a bad talker, a bad cop. "Why didn't you tell me? Why—"

"Because I thought maybe you'd do just what you did do. Start the phone working. Get the newspapers into it, and—"

"The papers? The newspapers? The woman must go, of course. She's strong enough to move. We can't keep her here. She must go." The doctor was getting panicky. The word "murder" had thrown him.

"I thought—" O'Rourke started—clamped his mouth shut again and looked down the hall.

The slow old fashioned elevator had come to a stop. The door opened almost silently and a figure stepped into the light. It was Doctor Michelle Gorgon. Malacca cane, gray suède gloves, black ribbon dangling from his glasses, and all.

CHAPTER XXIII

DOCTOR MICHELLE GORGON

"Really," Michelle Gorgon said when he reached us. "Doctor Revel, Mr. Williams, and our dear friend, Sergeant O'Rourke. Surely something must have happened. Not, Madame, not a bad turn. Not—"

"You'll have to move your wife, Doctor Gorgon." Doctor Revel got that off first crack. "We can't have a scandal here. We—"

"Scandal! You will explain yourself, Doctor." And Michelle Gorgon's voice was just the right pitch, just the right touch of doubtful indignation.

O'Rourke didn't try to stop Revel. I guess it would have been useless just then.

"Sergeant O'Rourke tells me that your wife—that she may be murdered here, and—"

"Good Lord! an attempt on her life." Michelle Gorgon clutched at his heart—and, damn it! looked as if he meant it.

"No—no. But there will be—there is to be—. Sergeant O'Rourke—"

And O'Rourke horned in.

"It's like this," he said easily. "I was tipped off that there would be, or might be, an attempt on her life. I came here to see that everything was right, just right. No objections to that, eh, Doctor Gorgon?"

"Most certainly not. Most commendable." Michelle Gorgon nodded approval. "But, really, it seems absurd. Why should any one wish to harm her? Poor thing, she has not long for this world, I'm afraid."

"Vengeance on you, Doctor," said O'Rourke. "That might be it."

"On me, on me. But surely. Ah! yes, I see. This imaginary hue and cry in the yellow sheets. Connecting me up with my brother's activities. We make enemies in life, of course. We—" He put both hands to his head. Not tragically, not dramatically even—rather, a natural movement—which, if acting, was superb. "My wife, Madame. I shall see her. I shall comfort her." This, as Madame called out.

And he did comfort her. At least he quieted her in the few minutes he was alone in the room with his wife, while we stood in the hall, Doctor Revel still insisting that the woman be moved, and O'Rourke just as insistent that she stay at the hospital.

"You can't throw her out tonight. The papers would get hold of you and razz you. To move her would work right into their hands if—" And O'Rourke, seeing that that wasn't a good line, killed it with a sudden snap to his lips. Doctor Revel was interested in human life, of course. But naturally he was interested in the reputation of his establishment. Certainly, any one will admit that a murder in his hospital wouldn't help business any.

"I'll tell you," said O'Rourke. "I could put a couple of men in the house for you, or better still, one inside and one outside."

"Wouldn't that be conspicuous?" But Doctor Revel was coddling to the idea now.

"They'll be in plain clothes. You might even tack a white coat on the inside one. He can stay by the woman's door. That'll protect your hospital, my reputation, and the woman's life. But here's Doctor Gorgon." And O'Rourke turned and told Michelle Gorgon what was on his mind.

Michelle Gorgon seemed enthusiastic.

"Excellent, Sergeant. Madame won't have to know, and won't have to be unprotected. That is settled then, though I think and hope that Sergeant O'Rourke's information about that unfortunate woman is—is erroneous. But you disturbed her, Sergeant. Oh, unintentionally, I know. What you said to her I could not discover, of course, from her. Her mind does not function coherently on the same thought for five minutes. Does it, Doctor?" He smiled encouragingly at Doctor Revel.

"She is lucid at times," said Revel. "She talks often of some imaginary poet or musician whom she loves. She would rather die before he could see her as she is, and—and—. Huh—huh—" The doctor cleared his throat as Michelle Gorgon frowned slightly. "Nothing odd in that hallucination, sir. To the contrary, rather to be expected."

"No," O'Rourke whispered to me. "Nothing wrong in that, Race, because it happens to be the truth."

Then the front doorbell rang, and a cop was at the door, and some explanations were in order in the little reception room below.

Michelle Gorgon insisted that Doctor Revel see the patient, Madame, once more before he left.

"It will ease my mind, Doctor," Gorgon said. "It is some time since I was interested actively in medicine. I have brought her a few books, rather trashy, Doctor. Love stories, the old ten and fifteen cent variety. But she seems to be able to read them, or get snatches from them, for they ease her mind. Kindly let her have the light on until she becomes calmer. I do not wish to interfere, of course, with the regulations of the hospital, but she has been in the habit of awakening and reading until one-thirty, or playing at reading. She likes, too, to be alone when she reads. Miss Agnes can wait outside her door, or—as you see fit."

Doctor Revel left us. Five minutes later he returned. Not a word had been spoken between us as we waited.

"Mrs. Gorgon is rather restless and disturbed, but didn't wish to talk to me," Doctor Revel told Michelle Gorgon.

"There is no danger!" Michelle Gorgon came to his feet. "Nothing—"

"If you mean that she may take a bad turn in the night. Certainly not. Not more than any other night. But I expect that she will have a restless night, a most unsatisfactory night."

And he looked around at the three of us, seemingly to place the blame equally between us.

"May I drive you gentlemen home?" There was perhaps the slightest twist to Michelle Gorgon's lips as he spoke.

"I'll stay here for a bit," said O'Rourke. And when Doctor Revel frowned, "Just till I get a man over. And I won't disturb your patient further tonight."

Michelle Gorgon looked at me.

"And you, my dear Williams, will you favor me with your company?"

"I don't know if I'll favor you—but I'll go along with you. I'd like a talk with you."

"Talk, talk seriously?" He stopped and looked down at me as we descended the steps of the private hospital.

"Seriously." I nodded, and meant it.

"Then you will come home with me, to my sanctuary, to my library. You're not afraid, of course?"

"Hardly." I shrugged my shoulders. "Are you?"

"Really, you joke. Really, Williams, I would fear you more dead than living. For the memory of the dead always so far outshines and even magnifies the petty significance of the living."

"I don't get that," I told him. And what's more, I wasn't sure that he got it. Somehow I had the idea that Doctor Gorgon's pretty vanities with words were simply the wish being father to the thought, and in his case, perhaps, farther from the thought. In plain words, I mean he'd like to be considered one of the literati, and was far from it.

"No, perhaps you don't understand it. But

tonight I shall not be epigrammatic. You will get in?" We had reached his car.

"No. I've got my own boat, and may need it later. I'll follow you home."

Michelle Gorgon shook his head.

"Do not follow me." And when I showed some surprise, "Precede me. To follow is dangerous. It might be misunderstood. Your life may become very precious to me. I am glad you have not run across my brother, Eddie. You see, he understands that your sudden evaporation from our every day existence would not be entirely displeasing to me. You are very fortunate, Williams. For the time being, I have taken you off what we so vulgarly hear expressed as 'the spot.'"

"Why?" I stopped as I moved toward my car, behind his.

"Why?" He hesitated a moment, and then, "Because I have suddenly decided to go out in society. Because I have decided to marry again. I would rather, for a bit, at least until after this marriage, be compared with the living rather than the dead."

"But you are married." The thing just blurted out.

"So I am, so I am." He playfully tapped me on the chest with a long, delicate finger. "But I have a feeling that it will not be for long. There are times when I really believe I have psychic power. This is one of those times."

"But who are you to—"

"Tut, tut, Williams. A man does not announce a bride while he has a wife living. But take care of yourself. My car will follow yours closely. Do not fail to visit me. I shall make you a most enticing offer of money, and introduce you to my future wife."

"But a man does not announce a bride while he has a wife living." I repeated his crack half sarcastically.

"Quite so, quite so," he told me. "And I repeat—I shall introduce you to my future bride."

With that he was gone, stepping into the huge Rolls Royce, the door of which a man held open for him.

CHAPTER XXIV
HIGH-PRICED INFORMATION

I started toward my car, hesitated and stood in the middle of the sidewalk. Had that last crack of his been a threat against his wife's life? Should I go and tell O'Rourke? Should I—. But the Rolls still stood at the curb and O'Rourke surely expected more than I did that the woman's life might be attempted. Also O'Rourke and another cop were already in that private hospital. One thing was sure. O'Rourke was a thorough police officer. Only the best men would watch over Madame's life, and—

"The night air grows chilly," Michelle Gorgon was calling from the window of his car. "If you would rather postpone our little talk, and chat with the genial Sergeant O'Rourke, it is perfectly agreeable to me."

"Be right with you," I said confidentially, hopped into my car, stepped on the starter, shoved the old girl in second gear, and was away, shooting down the street before the big Rolls Royce could even get moving.

No, sir, I didn't believe that business of taking me off the spot, or if I did believe it, I wasn't going to test out the accuracy of my instinct in such matters. It might be easy for Michelle Gorgon to pass the word along to certain racketeers, "Empty your machine gun into the car I'm following."

I burnt up the city streets, lost track of the Rolls entirely, and had my car parked around the corner and was waiting in the pretentious lobby of the Park Avenue apartment when Michelle Gorgon came in.

"An astounding man, Williams, most astound-ing." He shook my shoulders playfully. "You do everything with such enthusiasm. Now, when I wish speed," he went on, as we rode up in the elevator, "I take the airplane. I'm a great believer in the future of air travel, perhaps, even the present. I have more than one plane of my own."

"Yes," I said, "I've heard about your plane. Your wife likes it too, I suppose." And the sneer would not keep out of my voice.

Michelle Gorgon looked at the elevator operator, but said nothing until we had alighted at the top floor and the elevator door closed behind us. Then he said:

"That was untactful, and if not unkind, at least thoughtless. I am a man, Williams, who is no longer young. It has only been given me in life to love two women."

"Then you were married twice." I wasn't trying to be tactful.

"Not yet," he told me, let himself in the heavy steel door, and we walked across the roof, up the steps of the porch and into the bungalow. Once again I found myself in the library. Once again the old servant brought the No. 1 Sherry and left us alone.

I got up, walked about the room, spotted the door behind the curtain, that Madame had left by on a previous occasion and found it locked. Michelle Gorgon watched me without objection, but with a little twist to his thin lips, and perhaps a narrowness to his eyes, though they never blinked. Just regarded me steadily, like the unblinking orbs of a young baby.

One thing I made certain of. That was—that no one was hiding in that room, or behind those curtained windows. Now, I'd fix my chair, back against real solid plaster and keep it there. I wouldn't be trapped again. Not twice in one night, by a Gorgon, anyway.

"You are perfectly safe here," Michelle Gorgon told me. "Besides, Sergeant O'Rourke knows you came with me." And he added, rather suggestively I thought, "Sergeant O'Rourke also knows that I came here with you, as does my servant."

I looked up.

"What do you mean?"

"That Sergeant O'Rourke probably knows why you came here."

"Do you know why?" My hand was on my gun now; I was leaning slightly forward. "Do you know why I took a chance like this, coming here alone with you, to your home, again?"

"Yes," he said, "I do know. To threaten me with physical violence unless I disclose certain information to you. That would be your way."

That startled me. In fact, that was almost exactly what was on my mind, but not altogether.

"You're partly right," I told him. "But not to threaten you, Michelle Gorgon, to act. You know my ways. You took your chance when you brought me here. Colonel McBride has paid me, trusted me. He has disappeared."

"Not an affair of the heart, I hope." Michelle Gorgon looked up at me from his easy chair.

And that was that. Not heroic, nor moving picture stuff. Not the sort of blood that runs through the body of a hero, maybe. But I was alone in that room, with probably the greatest murderer who ever cheated the hot seat. I took two steps forward, and had him by the throat. And I was talking.

"Now, where's McBride? You don't believe in the physical, Doctor Gorgon, except in the abstract. Well, you'll believe in it now. Where—" My fingers started to tighten upon that throat, but stopped. Those eyes held me, still staring, still unblinking, and yet there was nothing of alarm in them. Perhaps, just a touch

of the curious. He spoke very slowly as he watched me.

"You are acting rather childishly, Race Williams. Just a moment—" he cut that in quickly, as my fingers started to tighten and I started to talk. "Let me assure you," he went on, "that all arrangements are made for such a contingency as this. I believe, if I wished, I could go through physical violence, even torture, with a silent tongue, but," and he actually smiled, "I will not put myself to the test. I am just as determined a man as Colonel McBride. I imagine he has resisted pressure. But the point is—if you so much as close those fingers on my throat, the place will be alive with servants, not gunmen, maybe, but servants. I assure you that my system of protection here is unassailable."

He didn't speak like a man who was bluffing. He didn't—I let go of his throat and stepped back. I had something else up my sleeve.

"You may be right," I told him. "You may have a system that will protect you from physical violence. But what would prevent me placing a bullet smack between those cute eyes of yours?" Somehow, O'Rourke's words crept in then.

"Well," he smiled with his lips, and actually sipped the sherry, "you and I would call it, shall I say, ethics. My brothers would call it 'lack of guts.' And do you know, Williams, I think that my brothers would be right."

Maybe he was right. Maybe he wasn't. I was fingering my gun speculatively. Oh, it's a weakness. I guess he was right, after all. It's the "woman" in all of us. I just couldn't bring myself to press that trigger and snuff him out. Couldn't? And I wondered. The men he had murdered, the man, Colonel McBride, whom he now spoke of as being under "pressure," which probably meant "torture." And, I let the trigger of my gun slip back and forth slowly. Who was the woman he was going to marry? Was it The Flame? I half raised my gun.

Did he read what was in my face, or was there anything in my face? I don't know, and so he couldn't. But I have always had an idea that at that moment Doctor Gorgon was nearer to death than he ever was before. And so did he, for he cut in quickly, and his eyes blinked now.

"Also," he said slowly, "it would be most disastrous for the Colonel, most disastrous."

"What you're telling me practically amounts to a confession." I tried police work.

"Hardly." And his smile came back as my gun went down on my knees. "Let us not be children at play. You knew that I knew where Colonel McBride was before you came here. O'Rourke knows that I know. At Albany they know that it is my hand that guides the destiny of our courts. The rookies on the police force know that, when a man dies who has displeased the right people, that it is the hand of a Gorgon who directs that death. But what does it avail them? Nothing. Absolutely nothing! Protection is money. I have that. Protection is influence. I have that. Protection is fear. I have established that. Big men have sought my influence because it gratifies their ambition. They have taken my money because it gratifies their greed. And they've taken my orders because they recognize fear. And I can gratify that emotion to the last degree."

He was leaning forward now. And suddenly he unclosed his hand and hurled a bit of paper across the table at me. I unfolded it with my left hand as I watched him.

"The soul of Rose Marie cries out for vengeance," was all that was now written on that paper. But a word, two words or perhaps three, following the word "vengeance" had been carefully erased.

And the face that I had seen once before in that room was looking at me now. The face I had seen that first night, when Michelle Gorgon found his wife in the library. The contorted, evil features that Michelle Gorgon couldn't control. What a rotten soul the beast must have. The distorted mouth, the eyes now protruding, the lips quivering like an animal's. Yep, Michelle Gorgon was just what Joe was, what Eddie had been. Just an underworld rat. And this time his face stayed coarse and evil when he spoke.

"I'll give you one hundred thousand dollars for the name of the person who wrote that message, who for the past week has been sending those messages. Who—"

"What do you mean?"

"What do I mean!" He fairly cried out the words. "Who is it that rings the phone at night? Who is it that speaks that same message in the cracked voice of a man who tries to imitate a woman? Yet, it is a woman's trick. But there can be no woman, no man either, no living man, now. Don't you see? Don't you understand? No one in the world but myself knows who that— who Rose Marie is."

"Your first wife, in Italy." I tried to throw him. He only laughed.

"McBride thinks of a first wife, in Italy. The shrewdest Italian detective on the Force has visited my home town in Italy, traced me until I left for America, traced every move I made since leaving the boat in New York, twenty-three years ago. But they know nothing. Giovoni told them nothing. Williams, I offer you one hundred thousand dollars for the name of the person behind McBride, behind O'Rourke. The person who tells them so much, but no more. The person who seeks a personal vengeance against me. The only thing in life I have feared. And I don't know, don't know who it is, nor why it is."

"Rose Marie, eh?" I was looking at the name.

"Yes, Rose Marie. Let that help you. But, one hundred thousand dollars for the name of the person. It's a lot of money." He was calmer now. "I have the cash here, ready to pay. Crisp, new bills."

"But suppose I don't know who wrote it?" I wouldn't admit I didn't know, yet. Which, from his next words, was an unnecessary precaution on my part.

"Of course you don't know. If you knew what this person—" he spread his arms far apart. "Colonel McBride don't know, or he would have acted. But Colonel McBride knows who the person is, for that person gave him such information as he has. That person suddenly decided to work it alone. Yes, McBride knows who it is, and McBride won't tell. Won't tell yet." A drawer in the table came open.

"One hundred thousand dollars. I have it here. It is yours if you will tell me the name of every one, and what's taken place, to the least detail, since you entered this attempt to eliminate the Gorgons, last week."

I shrugged my shoulders.

"You'd be wasting your money," I said, but I was trying to think. Was some one onto Michelle Gorgon? Did some one know what that little Italian, Giovoni, had known, and was that some one waiting to get a good price for that information from Colonel McBride? But that couldn't be. If it was simply a question of money they'd blackmail Michelle Gorgon. So I tried that question on him while he seemed ready to talk.

"Has any one tried to shake you down?"

"No, no. There is something deeper than that, far deeper. I can not understand it. But this person who knows, keeps it, keeps the knowledge from all but me. Why? Why?"

"Why do you tell me, why put anything into my hands?"

"Put anything into your hands!" His voice was scornful. "McBride was told, and O'Rourke was told, that I murdered my wife back in Italy. They—. But no matter. You have been told it too. But like every other accusation against me, it fell through, when—"

"Giovoni died," I tried.

Michelle Gorgon ignored that. He said:

"I tell you because, because it may be that such—certain information may come to you—and I assure you, Williams, that it will be to your best interests to sell that information to me. But some one told McBride of Giovoni, some one told McBride of—but no matter. The subject is dropped. You will remember it only when you wish money. If I could, could—" He took his head in his hands and pressed the temples at the sides.

Then he changed suddenly.

"And now, Williams, for my little treat. I wish to take you below with me. Just a few floors. It is perfectly safe. Really, you're not alarmed? I promise you that I shall interest you."

CHAPTER XXV
APARTMENT 12-D

But I was alarmed. Not afraid, you understand. There's a deal of difference between the two, at least, in my way of thinking, there is. And you've got to admit that I've got to live or die on my way of thinking, and not some one else's.

"Maybe I am like you in some things, Williams. If I have made my plans I go through with them no matter what may threaten." This, as we left the bungalow and entered the upper hall of the apartment. "Yes, go through with them even if they lead to destruction. For, like Aristotle, I must follow my star."

"Like Napoleon, you mean." For once I knew something that he didn't and had to get my oar in like a kid.

"Napoleon. Yes, I said Napoleon." He fairly snapped the words, and for the first time I saw color in his cheeks. He did have his weak side then, and, damn it! it was brought out by a reflection on his—well—I suppose the word is culture, which is rather a laugh there.

"I meant Napoleon," he said as we entered the elevator, "if perhaps I didn't say it. You can see, then, how disturbed I am tonight." And in a louder voice, directed to the elevator operator, "Very much disturbed. Madame is very ill, John. I'm quite worried about her. The twelfth floor, please."

"I'm sorry, sir. I hope it's nothing serious." The operator didn't appear overinterested, but Michelle went on.

"Not serious from a medical point of view; not serious physically, John. But then, they have

not watched over Madame as I have. It's her mental condition. There have been times when I was afraid she'd do herself a harm. She's threatened it. I spoke of it tonight, didn't I, Williams?"

"No, you didn't." I looked at him strangely. He was a talker, there was no doubt about that. But I had not expected that he'd hold forth with the elevator operator on his domestic affairs, at least the mental afflictions of his wife.

"But I should have mentioned it to you, Williams. It worries me greatly." This, as we stepped out on the twelfth floor and I followed him down the wide hall to a mahogany door, labeled 12-D.

A moment's wait while a bell buzzed far back behind that door.

"It's all right, Williams. I am going to introduce you to my future bride," and as a maid opened the door, "I am expected, of course, Lillian."

"Of course, sir," said the colored maid, and held the door open for us to enter.

"A little surprise, Lillian. Don't mention that I've brought a friend. Not a word, now." And something passed from Michelle Gorgon's hand to the maid's hand as we entered a beautifully furnished living room.

Was I a fool to come? I didn't know. But I'd have come anyway, and bride or no bride my hand still rested on the gun in my jacket pocket. I remembered that I wasn't in the "sanctuary" of Michelle Gorgon now, and though I remembered also that the elevator man, John, had seen us get off at the twelfth floor and that O'Rourke knew I was in the building—Well, I'm noble minded and all that, but I wasn't a good enough citizen to be willing to play the part of the corpse that finally roasted this inhuman murderer, Michelle Gorgon.

And that was that. There was a sound of laughter and running feet, and a girl was across the room. Two arms were around Michelle's neck.

"It was nice, nice of you to come, and I stayed up. Who—" She dropped to the floor and looked at me. "What is he doing here?" And the girlish sparkle went out of those eyes; the youthful softness went from her face. It was the woman now. The woman of the night. As I had expected, but never let myself believe, it was The Flame, Florence Drummond. The Girl with the Criminal Mind. And perhaps half a hundred other aliases in her innocent young life.

Bitter? Yes, I was bitter. Only a short while ago she had told me that she loved me. Maybe Michelle Gorgon's presence had some strange power over her. I had half thought that from her previous actions. But, she had not felt his presence when she ran from that room to greet him.

"You see, I'm disturbing the lady." I half turned toward the door.

"Ah! Yes, yes." Michelle Gorgon seemed to be enjoying himself. "We just stopped in, Florence. I have an engagement, and I wanted to tell you that I couldn't visit you tonight."

"If it's a test—" The girl looked sharply at him.

"If it is, it's not for you, my dear." Michelle sort of plucked at her arm. "My confidence in myself, the beautiful things I can shower on you, in the wonderful places I can take you. In—" And turning to me, "Just a minute, Williams. For the last time, you are looking on The Flame, The Girl with the Criminal Mind. Now, that mind will be occupied with nothing more criminal than making a man happy by, by—." He went very close to her but still watched me. "By allowing him to adore her," he finished.

And The Flame laughed.

"You're somewhat of a dumb bunny, Michelle." Her voice was that of the young girl again, but her eyes and face weren't. She looked at me defiantly as she stretched both hands upon his shoulders. "You too listen to the gossip of the street, Michelle." She put her head close to him and whispered something softly. I didn't get it, but somehow it riled me just the same. I said, purely vindictively, and perhaps without point, but anyway what was on my chest.

"High class house, this. No references needed to get an apartment here, I guess."

Michelle Gorgon shook his head.

"On the contrary, the clientele is picked most carefully. Miss Drummond's references were of the best. From the owner of the apartment himself." And with a smile, "You see, the deeds to this property happen to be in my name."

While I tried to laugh that one off Michelle Gorgon raised an arm and placed it about The Flame's shoulder. What did it all mean? Was Florence tired of poverty, and taking riches? Was she tired of being ruled, and wanted to rule? Was—? And Michelle drew her close to him, his eyes ever on me, steady, staring things. Watching me, not in alarm or fear; more, a curious glint, as if he had brought me there for this very purpose. To watch how I took it.

Maybe I didn't take it well. My left hand clenched at my side, my right caressed the butt of a heavy caliber six-gun in my jacket pocket.

The temptation was strong to slap him down. Maybe I would have acted upon that temptation. Maybe I wouldn't have. But the thought came then. Was The Flame, after all, the one lured by wealth, by the strange influence of this man? Or was Michelle Gorgon the one lured? Lured, as so many other men had been, by the fascination of this strange girl? Was Michelle Gorgon now the moth attracted by the flame?

Any way you put it, I turned my head, hesitated a moment, then walked toward the exit door. I heard The Flame say:

"And these strange messages, this shadow that bothers you, Michelle. Can't I—"

"Uh-huh." At least Michelle Gorgon made a funny noise in his throat that sounded like that before he said, "At a time like this, Florence, why bring that up?" He was annoyed, and showed it.

But Michelle Gorgon reached the apartment door almost the same time I did. We passed out into the wide hall together. He hadn't gotten my goat, and I'd show him he hadn't. I said:

"I thought a man doesn't introduce his future bride with a wife still living."

"No, not with a wife still living. I have a presentiment that—" He paused and looked at his watch, and smiled with his lips. "But the offer I made you, Race, the money I will pay for the name of the one behind McBride, behind O'Rourke. Tut, tut, don't answer yet. The shadow that overhangs my—yes, my life—will be wiped out, as all other shadows have been wiped out that threatened a Gorgon, The Gorgon.

"Since you've entered this, shall we call it a case, what has happened? Who has taken every trick? Toney, the little Italian drug addict. He died before he spoke out the whole truth to McBride. Giovoni. He died before he spoke out the whole truth to McBride. Every one who has stood in my way has died."

"Every one but your wife." I was thinking of his talk of marrying The Flame.

"I have told you that I am psychic. I have a feeling now, a strong feeling now, that the wife you speak of, God rest her soul—is dead."

He pressed the two elevator buttons. The one for an up car and the other for a down, and we waited. Almost at once the machinery broke into life. There was the hum of a motor far below. But it was the down car that came first. Just before the elevator reached our floor, Michelle Gorgon said:

"No. A man never introduces his future bride while his wife is living." And, damn it! he rubbed

his hands together, as if he gloated over something, something which I could not believe. "You have been with me all the evening, Race, no one is to deny that. What a nice alibi for a husband who might be suspected of murder. The abstract, Williams. The abstract is—"

The door of the car clanked open and I stepped within.

"Every trick." Michelle Gorgon stood by the door a minute. "And not a single one for you."

"No. No." Maybe it was foolish, maybe it wasn't. But I was mad—damn good and mad. Anyway, I did it. I shoved my hand quickly into my pocket and drew out that envelope. The envelope Michelle had asked me so sarcastically to deliver to his brother, Eddie.

"I won't get a chance to deliver this message, Doctor." I tried to keep the vindictiveness and the gloating out of my own voice, but I guess they crept in. After all I'm only human. "So, since you'll see Eddie before I do, I'll ask you to deliver this."

He just eyed me, steadily, unblinkingly, as his hand stretched out for the envelope. But I didn't give it to him then.

"I'll just put Eddie's address on the envelope for you," I told him, jerked out my pencil and scribbled quickly upon the white surface. Then I shoved it into his hand, pushed him back from the door, slammed it shut and said:

"Down, John. Make it snappy."

Maybe I'd made a mistake, but I didn't care. I'd have done it again any time, under the same circumstances. I'll bet that grin was wiped off his lips, and the unblinking baby-like stare out of his eyes. For I had written on that envelope:

Eddie Gorgon, Esq.,
Slab One,
The City Morgue.

CHAPTER XXVI

MURDER IN THE ABSTRACT

As I left the building and hurried to my car, yes, hurried, I thought to myself: There, let Michelle Gorgon count up the tricks in the game, and laugh that one off.

There was nothing to do now, of course, but tip O'Rourke off that Eddie Gorgon's body could be picked up and carted away, for Michelle Gorgon to deliver the envelope to.

Michelle Gorgon was some boy. He had a way of getting at you, a convincing way. I thought of Colonel McBride, and more than half wished that I had gone through with the thing and sunk fingers into that white, delicate skin of Michelle Gorgon, until he told me where Colonel McBride was. And then, there was The Flame. I didn't try to think overmuch on that. I didn't want to think about that.

There was also the guy who had something on Michelle Gorgon, knew who his first wife was, if there was a first wife. At least, knew enough to put fear into Michelle Gorgon. It looked as if, for once in his younger days, Michelle Gorgon had gone in for a bit of murder that wasn't in the abstract, after all. But enough of that.

One other dominant thought. Michelle Gorgon's crack about "a bride and a living wife," and his crack about having psychic power. I entered a subway station and found a telephone booth, decided to pass up the hospital as a call at that hour, but buzzed O'Rourke at home. His wife answered my jingle. She was not reassuring.

"The Sergeant," Mrs. O'Rourke always called him that, "hasn't been home. But he called a little while ago, saying he wouldn't be home tonight at all. And him only a Sergeant, with the worries of an Inspector." And after a few more natural complaints, she told me, "He said, if you called him, Mr. Williams, for you to come straight to—to some hospital. I don't mind the name of it, but—.

And I hung up on the good lady, dashed from the station, sprang into my car and made monkeys out of the few traffic lights which were still operating.

O'Rourke was the first lad I saw when the cop by the door of the hospital stood aside for me to enter. O'Rourke didn't wait, or couldn't wait. Anyway, he led me smack into a little room and chirped it out.

"She's dead, Race. Yes, I know, with a cop in the alley and me at the door—in the hall, mind you."

"Shot?" I said.

"No." His laugh wasn't pleasant. "I'm not as bad a cop as that." He clasped his hands together. "Poisoned. Murdered by her husband, just the same as if he stuck a knife in her chest and turned the blade. But you won't get a verdict on it, not a chance. There ain't a jury in the country, nor the medical examiner for that matter, but will call it suicide."

"What sort of poison?"

"There was no label on the bottle, but the smell of burnt almonds was strong. Prussic acid. I guess we all agree on that."

"And how— Who do you think gave it to her?"

"She gave it to herself, you fool. I tell you I was at the door, Donnelly under the window. Michelle Gorgon left it for her. I can swear to that. But who's to believe it? Not the doctors. Not the medical examiner. And certainly no twelve men in a jury box. There's enough evidence to disprove that Michelle Gorgon brought it here. Listen!" And O'Rourke gave me the whole show.

"Most of the time I heard Madame moving in the bed. Then she sort of cried out. Miss Agnes, who was writing right across from me, on the other side of the door, went in to her. I went as far as the door, and looked in. Madame waved us out. She spoke too, said she was all right. She was holding a book very tightly closed in her hand, but she didn't want anything, wouldn't take anything. And Miss Agnes came out and closed the door. Madame asked that the door be closed, when we left it open a crack.

"She was restless, Race, very restless. And I couldn't swear that she didn't get out of that bed and crawl across the room. But I would swear to that if it would roast Michelle Gorgon.

"The whole thing seemed silly, my sitting there like that, when I ought to be out on the McBride hunt, and I was just about to call it a night and put another lad on the door, when— well—it's almost funny. I didn't hear anything, unless you can hear a sudden quiet. But Madame wasn't restless any more, hadn't been for some time—hadn't—. And I called to Miss Agnes. Not because I was alarmed at the quiet, but because I just wanted to have a last look at Madame before I left.

"And," O'Rourke's hand went under his collar, "she was dead, Race, and in one hand was the empty bottle that had held the poison, and in the other withered hand— Well, make a guess."

"The book of love stories," I tried.

"Wrong," said O'Rourke. "In the other hand she held a tiny mirror. For the first time, she looked at her face in a mirror—and took her life. That'll be the verdict, and don't you forget it."

I put my oar in.

"But who gave her the mirror? Who left her the mirror and poison? Michelle Gorgon, of course. He had the opportunity when we were out of the room, and—"

"Yes, he did. If that was all there was to it we might pin it on him, at least as manslaughter. But there is more to it. The devilish cunning of the man, or—. But listen to this. Beneath her bed was an open bag, the small, over-night bag she brought with her to the hospital. And that bag had an inside flap, a sort of secret pocket, that was now open. No—" he saw the question on my lips, "Miss Agnes had put the bag in the small closet. She hadn't noticed the flap when she unpacked the bag—it was well hidden. And she hadn't noticed since early evening if the bag was still in the closet or under the bed. But in the pocket beneath the flap that now hung open was another tiny bottle of the same poison. Pointing out nicely to a jury where Madame hid her poison, maybe for weeks.

"Brophey sums it up like any dick, any lawyer for the defense would, and any jury would believe. Madame had secreted that poison there for the moment she could bear her terrible affliction no longer. And the mirror too—for the day she got the nerve to look at herself. For the mirror was a pocket affair, and could be hidden in a case. The case was on the bed beside her."

"And you sum it up, O'Rourke?"

"Like you," he said harshly. "Michelle Gorgon planned this for a long time. He came here tonight, gave her the mirror and the poison. Maybe he threatened her, maybe he didn't. Maybe she had been pleading for the chance to end her life. But he did it. Defiantly, while I was there. Just laughed at me."

"Murder in the abstract." I thought aloud.

"Abstract or no abstract, the woman's dead. God!" O'Rourke threw up both his hands, "if I only had the guts to lay a hand on him and drag him in for it."

"No, O'Rourke, you can't do that. With what Michelle Gorgon told me, for he knew his wife was going to die, and what you suspect—well—

the jury would just think it a police frame-up. We couldn't hang the crime on him."

"No, we couldn't," O'Rourke admitted grudgingly. "Doctor Revel says it's quite possible that Madame crawled to the closet and got the bag. But he'd like it a straight suicide, with no investigation, of course."

"Of course." I agreed. "Did you—did some one notify Doctor Michelle Gorgon?"

"Yes. He should have been here by this. Word was left with his servant. Gorgon had stepped out of his apartment for the moment."

"Yes." I thought aloud. "He was with me."

And now what? I suddenly realized that I had entirely forgotten, in the rapid happenings, that I had had no word of my boy, Jerry, whom I had left waiting for me when I went to visit Colonel McBride. Jerry, who had disappeared when I decided to make my appearance at the Colonel's house from the rear instead of the front. Jerry, whom I thought I had seen leave an areaway far down the street and follow the person—the man who had left McBride's house with Colonel McBride. Jerry, who might be able to tell me who—. But no more thought. I had forgotten Jerry. I'd give my home a buzz now and see if he had returned.

But first I told O'Rourke about my message to Michelle Gorgon, but not of the envelope, for I didn't want to bring The Flame into it—at least, yet. Just that I had wised Michelle Gorgon up as to where they could find his brother, Eddie's, body. At the City Morgue.

"Good!" O'Rourke snapped up the phone on the little table. "I'll have the boys pick up the stiff, just say I was tipped off to a bump in Maria's Cafe. Let the surprise and joy be theirs." And he grinned at me, but his grin had lost much of its spontaneous good nature.

As for me. I grabbed myself another phone and buzzed my number. And this time I got results. I'm telling you I breathed easier when Jerry's voice came over the wire.

"Never mind me, Jerry," I cut short his interest. "Did you recognize the lad who left the block in such a hurry?"

And Jerry did. And Jerry told me so. And the name of the man brought back to me the words of The Flame. "Use your brains. Go over this thing from the beginning."

And I did go over it—did think. And the thoughts I got were amazing, astounding, but not unbelievable. When I came to, O'Rourke was standing beside me.

"O'Rourke," I said, "now that that bit of shooting is out, I think I'll go down and talk to Rudolph Myer."

"But I'll cover you. The Commissioner will cover you, if we don't find the Colonel. Hell! Race," he cut in on himself, "you said to sit tight on that, you might know something."

"Might," I said. "I will know something soon. But just for safety's sake I'll get over to Rudolph Myer. You can't tell who might step over your head."

"The Commissioner's head too?"

"Who is Rose Marie?" The question just came to me.

"God!" said O'Rourke. "If we knew that we'd know everything. Toney said it was Michelle Gorgon's wife. Giovoni spoke of Rose Marie as Michelle Gorgon's wife. And—oh, some one else said it was Michelle Gorgon's wife. But we've gone back over the years and Michelle Gorgon was never married in Italy."

"Couldn't Michelle have been married under another name?"

"He could have, but he wasn't."

"But if Giovoni was his father-in-law, then—then who was Giovoni's daughter, and who was her husband?"

"Giovoni's daughter's name was Rose Marie, all right. We've established that as a fact. And she was brutally murdered, too, by her husband. We've established that too, even if it was many years ago. But Michelle Gorgon's name in Italy was Gorgonette, and Rose Marie's husband's name was Nicholas Tremporia and he was a Greek. He escaped after the murder, and was picked up on the railroad tracks on a dock near Naples. Fairly ruined by the train, he was. We only found that out since Giovoni was murdered. So you see, if Giovoni had lived and talked his head off, it wouldn't have hurt Michelle Gorgon any. Giovoni was a little bugs, I guess."

"Then why have him killed?"

"I don't know," O'Rourke said despairingly. "Something else, maybe. But certainly Michelle Gorgon was not Giovoni's son-in-law. That much is established beyond a doubt."

"Yes?" I chewed that one over, but I didn't like it. There didn't seem any sense, then, in the kicking over of Giovoni. The phone rang and O'Rourke answered it. I had already started for the door.

O'Rourke held up his hand. I waited until the call was over. Then O'Rourke said, and though his voice was calm, it was a false calm:

"You needn't bother about Rudolph Myer. The body of Eddie Gorgon has—disappeared."

"Disappeared!"

"Well, it isn't there in the Maria Cafe," snapped O'Rourke. "Choose your own word for it. But if there's no corpse there's no criminal lawyer necessary. That much is a cinch."

"Nevertheless," I told him, as I passed through the hall to the front door, "I'm a boy scout and believe in preparedness. I'm going to see Rudolph Myer. Wait here. I think something is going to break."

And smack at the front door I bumped into Doctor Michelle Gorgon.

"Ah! Race Williams," he said, and though he looked at me unblinkingly I read hatred in his eyes, "I have another presentiment, quite contrary to former thoughts of you. It is that you are about to die; to be found with—" He broke off as O'Rourke followed me to the door. Then he said, "I have just heard of Madame's sad end. How distressing. Most distressing, Detective Sergeant O'Rourke."

CHAPTER XXVII
THE KILLER INSTINCT

But I was gone, hurrying to my car, speeding down the street. Something big was about to break. Any possible doubt that Colonel McBride was held prisoner by the Gorgon outfit was dissipated by my conversation with Michelle Gorgon, and that the man was being tortured for information—information that seemed imperative to the liberty, if not actually the life, of Michelle Gorgon seemed also sure. I shuddered slightly. Michelle Gorgon possessed, in his best moments, not the least touch of human compassion. Now, with his very life in the balance, he'd do anything to get that information from Colonel McBride.

Another thing was certain. McBride would have to be rescued very quickly. There wasn't one chance in a hundred that he would be let free, even if he talked, and I remembered that set jaw of his, the determined eyes. Oh, it may have knocked him to see another killed, shot down before his eyes, as I had shot down the lad the night we were moving Giovoni to the private sanitarium—and it may have unnerved him to think that Toney and Giovoni, whom he wished to protect, met their death, but I didn't think he'd talk, and I knew what that would mean for him.

With this important thing on my mind I was going to consult my lawyer, Rudolph Myer? That's right. That's exactly what I was going to do. As I drove down town and through Greenwich Village to Rudolph Myer's house, I thought upon, and even enlarged upon, if that could be done, the sufferings that Colonel McBride was to be put through, was now going through, or had been put through. Not nice thoughts? No, decidedly not. Nevertheless, I had them, and I held them, for they stirred a hate and a passion, and perhaps even a lust to kill. Bad business? Maybe. But my business tonight was bad business.

There was no guard at Rudolph Myer's house, and I'm not sure if there was a light, though I think one shone beneath the second story window shade, that overlooked the side alley. Side alley? That's right. For I was looking the place over. Rudolph Myer and I were good friends. Had been so for a good many years. He was my lawyer in many instances, and a mighty good one, if a high priced one. But I never begrudged him a cent I paid him.

Now, I guessed that I knew Rudolph well enough to play a practical joke on him. Sort of slip in and surprise him. And surprise him I certainly would. He was alone in that house. The only servant he had left each night. There was nothing for him to fear. He was the friend of the unfortunate, the criminal. The finest fixer in the city of New York.

I went to the back, crossed the stone court, carefully up-ended an ash can, stood upon it and rapped myself a little hole in the window pane. No feeling for electric burglar alarm wires. No need of that. I had been in that room too often not to know. Rudolph Myer knew crooks. He was a firm believer in that saying that any crook who wanted "in" got "in"—if he wanted "in" bad enough.

Well, I'm no crook, but I wanted "in" bad

enough. I just stuck my fingers through the hole, snapped back the window lock, lifted it carefully, slowly, silently, and stepped into the room. My rubber soled shoes made no noise across the linoleum of the kitchen and even less noise as I crossed the thick rug of the dining room, through to the hall and onto the wooden stairs. I picked the front stairs because, well, they were less likely to make noise—had no door bottom and top— and besides which, they would bring me up to the hall and close to that door, the door of the room from which I thought that tiny light had peeped.

All stairs are creaky, of course, no exception to this old outfit. But I had luck, in a way. Some one was moving around up stairs—some one was moving quickly, furtively, quietly back and forth, back and forth across the floor.

I made the upper hall, took a couple of quick steps down it, guided by a light from a partly open door, and stopped dead before that door as the quickly moving feet inside ceased, and some one seemed to listen.

Then it wasn't "seemed" any more. Some one was listening. For the person in that room had held his breath, and then let it go again in a sort of whistling sound.

Finally the feet crossed to the door, paused, fingers reached to the side of the door and pushed it open wider, and I stepped through the opening and faced Rudolph Myer.

Certainly he was surprised. Maybe even shocked. He rubbed his hands across his eyes as if he wasn't sure, then half straightened his bent shoulders and tried playing at the corners of his mouth with the thumb and index finger of his right hand. He was fully dressed, and a hat and top coat lay over the end of the bed.

"Surprise!" I said, closed the door behind me and spun the key in the lock. Then I looked around the room as he backed away from me. One suitcase already packed stood shut by the bed. It had heavy straps around it. The other was a big affair and needed another shirt or a couple of socks before locking. There was little doubt that Rudolph intended to go bye-bye. Five minutes later and—. But I hadn't been five minutes later. Why dwell on that?

And Rudolph Myer spoke first.

"Race, Race Williams. How did you get in? And why?"

"And the answer is—Who cares? I won't waste time, Myer." I backed him across the room, my eyes on him. "You two-timing skunk! After all these years you sell me out. You left the house of Colonel McBride tonight with McBride. You trapped him into the hands of the Gorgons. You two-timed him as you did me."

"I didn't," he cried out. "It's a lie. Before God I swear I didn't."

And I had him by the throat, forced him to his knees.

"Don't try to lie out of it. My boy, Jerry, was down the block and saw you. They're torturing McBride," I told him, and my voice shook. "You know me, Myer. I don't have to threaten you. You've kidded me about my shooting, for I've paid you well. Now, you double-crossed me and I'm going to kill you, kill you." I squeezed his throat tighter, saw his eyes bulge, watched his tongue protrude, then I thrust him from me. Disgusted? Maybe. Through with him? Not me.

Rudolph Myer stretched a hand, let it slip into his open suitcase and half pulled out an automatic. I liked that. He couldn't possibly believe he had a chance against me with a gun, yet he tried to get one. Why? Because he was afraid. He read the truth in my blazing eyes.

I didn't fire. I simply leaned over and rapped his knuckles with the nose of my forty-four. Then I kicked his gun under the bed and told him what was on my chest.

"Listen, Myer." And I didn't have to do any acting to get my part over. "Understand this. I've come here tonight for the purpose of killing you."

"That would be—murder." He half lay, half knelt on the floor.

"You can't murder a rat," I told him. "Anyway, what difference does the name it goes by matter to you, or to me either? No one saw me come here. No one will see me go. And don't be thinking up wise cracks. Let me tell you what I know.

"You got me into this Gorgon case, because the Gorgons knew I was coming in anyway. You found out that McBride was coming on, to help the Commissioner. You knew that O'Rourke had been after the Gorgons for years. Michelle Gorgon probably told you. He has a way of hearing things, through crooked officials, and crooked, shyster lawyers, like you.

"You knew where McBride planned to take Giovoni, to Elrod's Sanitarium. You told Gorgon and he had him murdered. And it was you who told me The Flame wanted to see me at her rooms, and you, alone, who knew I was going to meet The Flame there. Then you told the Gorgons, or at least, Eddie Gorgon, and you let Eddie think that The Flame sent the message. I don't know why, I don't care why, but you did it again at Maria's Café, and Eddie Gorgon died. You somehow got McBride out of his house tonight and into the Gorgon trap. I don't know how you did it, why you did it, though I guess you were paid for it."

"No, no. Not then, Race. It was The Flame. I wanted her. I loved her. I thought—"

"The Flame? You!" I had to laugh.

"Why not?" And Rudolph Myer's beady eyes snapped back to life. "Many have, others have. Am I any different? I'm not so young, but neither is Michelle Gorgon. I'm not so, not—. Don't you see, Race? What she did to others she did to me. And, Race, she led me on. I swear she did. I've done business for Michelle Gorgon. She got it out of me, all out of me. She sucked me dry of every bit of information, then laughed in my face and—"

He read it in my eyes. He clutched at my coat now, kneeling there at my feet.

"Don't kill me, don't. I know you can get away with it. I know the man-made laws can't touch you. But you've never done that. Never gone in for murder, Race. Never—. You've lived clean. There's other laws beside those of man. There's God's."

"There's the laws of God and the laws of man, Myer. And there's the law of death, for the rat, for the stoolie, for the two-timer. You sent Giovoni to his death. You sent Colonel McBride to worse than death. You tried to send me to

death, and—By God! you've got to pay the price." I half raised my gun.

Was I going to kill him then? I don't know, so you don't know. But certainly Rudolph Myer thought he knew. He screamed out as he clutched at my knees and begged for life.

"I'll tell you where McBride is if you let me go. Don't you see? It was The Flame, The Girl with the Criminal Mind. Am I made of different stuff than other men? Isn't there blood in my body too? And she laughed at me and told me she loved you, and you only. And, and—. God! Race, I was mad, mad. I wanted you dead. I thought, if you were—if you—. Don't, don't kill me. It'll be death for McBride. Death for The Flame."

Was it to save McBride that my finger didn't close on that trigger, or was it because of The Flame? What Rudolph Myer said might easily be true, for I guess most any man would fall a victim to The Flame. Most any would, and many had. Or was it simply that I couldn't get up the guts to press that trigger and snap out Myer's life? Or—? But I did say:

"You, you wouldn't know where McBride is."

"Yes, I do. I do! Promise, give me your word that you won't—won't kill me if I tell you."

"If I save McBride, you can go free," I told him. "But I'll know if you lie about him. I know more than you think. To begin with, I know that you fled down that street, stopped in a telephone booth in a drug store and made two telephone calls. One to me, the other to—"

"To Michelle Gorgon," he told me, and I believed him. Then he gave me his story.

"Michelle Gorgon found out that Colonel McBride was coming to the city by the request of the Police Commissioner, through the Deputy Commissioner. He had me worm my way into McBride's confidence by telling him things about the Gorgons—things that O'Rourke had already unearthed, but were not evidence. McBride told me about this Giovoni, but no more than his name and that he had arrived in New York, and was taken sick. He didn't tell me where he was, nor where he was going to take him. That was the night before I met you. I watched McBride's house and saw him go to Doctor Elrod's Sanitarium the following morning. So I knew that would be where he'd take Giovoni. I was working, alone, for Michelle Gorgon. Joe or Eddie knew nothing about my connection with Michelle. Michelle Gorgon liked to play without his brothers once in a while. It strengthened his hold over them."

"Did Michelle have you notify Eddie when The Flame had you date me up for her, both those times?"

"No. I did it myself. I let Eddie think it came from The Flame. I wanted you—. I, I loved The Flame."

That was a funny one, maybe—but easy to believe.

CHAPTER XXVIII

THE POLICE HORN IN

I looked at my watch. The "whys" the "wherefores" of the thing were not as important as knowing where McBride was. I told Myer to talk, and quickly. He did. He said:

"I went to see Colonel McBride. He expected me and left the kitchen door open, as he didn't want the police to know I was there. He was telephoning, up stairs. I whistled up to him from the kitchen door. I was nervous. I thought I heard some one in one of the front rooms, so I kept in the dark. I thought it might be the police. Colonel McBride came down to me. I pretended excitement. I told him I had some one in a car on the street behind, who would tell him all about Rose Marie, and how she was murdered. I told him the person wouldn't come in, for him to come out. He said he was expecting you, Race, but he came with me when I said it would only take a minute. He—" Myer had the good grace to gulp, anyway, "He trusted me. Joe Gorgon was out in the car, with some others and—. I didn't know they intended to torture him. That's the truth."

"And they told you where they were going to take him?"

"No," he said, "they didn't. But I had a—a colleague around the corner with a car to follow them. I—well—I like to have information of my own if things go wrong, like now." He looked at my gun and tried to smile.

I nodded at that. It would be like Myer. Slippery—never trusting any one. Always with a card up his sleeve. Yes—I believed him.

Then he gave me the address where Joe Gorgon and his racketeers had taken Colonel McBride. Ricorro's garage. A notorious, all night garage, where the front doors never closed. I had a hunch Myer was speaking the truth. Somehow, at such times you KNOW.

One more question I couldn't help. I had always looked on Myer as a straight shooter to the one who paid him, if crooked every other way, and certainly not in the cesspool of the city's rackets.

"What made you double-cross McBride, Myer?" I asked. "Did Michelle Gorgon hold something over your head?"

"Not in the sense of blackmail, if you mean that." Rudolph Myer had recovered quickly and was on his feet now, lighting a cigarette with a shaky hand. "I don't think any one could ever get anything on me again. No, Michelle Gorgon's methods are much simpler and much more direct. He came to me, Race, and pounded a long finger against my chest. 'I need you, Myer,' he said. 'Come come, we won't quibble. I'll pay you well to act for me. I always do. It's not for you to decide, but for me to decide. You're in with me now, till I'm through with you—or you're dead by morning.' That was all he said, Race. That was all he needed to say. I know my city. I know my law, and know too what little protection it could offer me. I'd have felt safer hearing my sentence of death passed by a judge in court. For law or no law, I knew as well, or even better than any man, that Michelle Gorgon is above the law. And—and I wanted very much to live."

And the worst of it was, it was true.

But I didn't kill any more time. And I didn't

listen to Rudolph Myer's protestations when I took those straps from the bag and a couple of bathrobe cords from the closet and trussed him up.

"I daresay you can work yourself free of those straps, but not these," I said, as I jerked out my irons and fastened them about his ankles. "I'll come back and release you as soon as Colonel McBride is free. Now, anything else to tell me? For your life depends on my success."

He could take that any way he liked—but he talked. He said:

"Joe Gorgon'll be there tonight, not Michelle though. How many Joe will have with him I don't know, but he won't trust many in this— this, I don't think."

And I gagged him. But his eyes bothered me. They were watching that bag, the closed bag. I wondered why, tried to open the bag and found it locked, started to take the gag out of Myer's mouth, saw the excitement in his eyes and tried his vest pocket—and there was the key, attached to the generous watch chain.

I snapped open that bag and got a jar. No wonder Myer was interested in that bag. He was afraid to tell me about it, and was afraid not to. The bag was full of money. Crisp, new bills of large denominations. Rudolph Myer, then, had been leaving the city for an extended visit. I didn't have to count it. But I closed the bag, carried it to the closet and chucked it behind a lot of clothes.

"I don't blame you, worrying," I told him. "That's a lot of jack. But it'll be safe there until I return."

There were many things I wanted to ask him. Each one perhaps more important than the other. But there wasn't time. Not long now before dawn, and the life of Colonel McBride at stake. Who was Rose Marie? Why did she cry out for vengeance? Did Myer know whose voice on the phone so upset Michelle Gorgon? I didn't wait for that information. I only stopped long enough down stairs to put through a call to O'Rourke.

"Hop a subway," I told him, "and I'll pick you up at The Bridge. Don't argue. I've got a line on McBride. The time for chin-chin is passed. Snap into it."

Well, I had used my brains for once, as The Flame had suggested, but I hadn't used them until Jerry told me that Rudolph Myer was the man who escaped down the street after the attack and abduction of Colonel McBride. Then, maybe it wasn't much thinking. I just got a kaleidoscope picture of past events and knew that Rudolph Myer was my meat.

I met O'Rourke and I told him what was on my chest.

"They'll kill McBride if we come in force, yet we can't chance an attack alone. Just one man may be guarding that garage and maybe ten. Here's the ticket. I know Ricorro's. It's an all-night garage. The big front doors are always open. It would look bad if they closed them now. I'm for betting they'll be open."

"Ricorro's Garage!" O'Rourke stroked his chin. "Well, it's got a bad enough name, though we've never really pinned a thing on Ricorro. And you don't know if McBride is in the basement below or on the floor above."

"I don't know even if he's there at all. But dying men are supposed to speak the truth. And I'm telling you, O'Rourke, Rudolph Myer was as near death as any man who ever peeped a final message. But I'm strong for the basement. Here's the lay. There may be a way out that we don't know of. You get a raiding squad and cover the block, but not till I'm inside."

"You and me inside," O'Rourke horned in.

"No. Just me. This is my racket. If I'm discovered, they may think I'm alone, and not kill McBride. I work alone. If you're with me—but you have a wife and kid."

O'Rourke laughed.

"I've been reported killed so many times, and given up by the ambulance surgeon so many times, that the old lady wouldn't even get a bad turn. Besides which, what has the old lady got to do with police business? As for my kid, well, he's going to be a copper, Race—a real copper." And suddenly bursting out on me, "Where do you get the stuff that you're the only living man in New York with any guts, any eye—and any gun hand? I'll be a—"

I switched that talk and turned to McBride's

interest. Finally O'Rourke saw it enough my way to let me flop into the garage first. Once the surprise was over, he'd follow. That seemed fair enough. What I was mostly afraid of were spies. Watchers on the outside, who'd give the alarm as soon as the cops got anywhere near the garage.

O'Rourke put through a call for the boys to meet us. He had a picked crew waiting and ready, and told me it wouldn't take five minutes to fill that garage with flatties. I didn't like waiting for the coppers there in the dark street some six blocks from Ricorro's Garage. I get restless just before a bit of action, not nervous, you understand, sort of rarin' to go, and the longer I wait the worse I get. So I spent my time telling O'Rourke all that had taken place in my talk with Michelle Gorgon, and his offer of a hundred thousand dollars for the name of the party behind McBride, the party who rang up Michelle Gorgon. Of the note, "Rose Marie cries out for Vengeance—" with a couple of words erased at the end of it.

"Yeah, Michelle Gorgon would like to know." O'Rourke chewed an unlighted cigar. "McBride could tell him, but won't. I could tell him, but won't. I—.

"O'Rourke," I cut in, "I've laid my cards on the table. What about yours? Who is the one who knows so much, and why can't you get the information from that party?"

"Because I can't," snapped O'Rourke. "And I have passed my—. Well—I can't tell you who it is—that's flat." And suddenly changing the subject, "Who'd think it of Rudolph Myer? Imagine it! The police have been trying to get something on Myer for years and always failed, and finally he mixes himself up with a bit of murder, kidnaping, maybe torture, and what have you, all at once. There's no understanding human nature, Race. But it'll just show you what a lad we're dealing with in Michelle Gorgon. Certainly he must have put the stony, Gorgon look on Myer. And you say Myer was ready to jump the city, bags packed and all. But why? He never guessed you were onto him. He couldn't know that Jerry

saw and recognized him. Maybe he was just leaving for a day or so, on business, business for the Gorgons, Michelle Gorgon."

"Not Myer." I nodded confidently. And I told O'Rourke of the suitcase full of money. "Did that look like a short trip?" I asked.

"Yeah?" And O'Rourke let his mouth hang open a minute. "One hundred thousand dollars for the name of the one behind McBride," he said thoughtfully. "For the one who strikes fear in Michelle Gorgon's stomach, for he hasn't any heart. One hundred thousand dollars for even a hint of who it might be. One hundred thousand dollars for—" And O'Rourke suddenly clutched me by the arm. "You don't think—think that bag contained exactly one hundred thousand dollars?"

"It might. Why? You don't think—?"

"But I do think, exactly what you think now. That Rudolph Myer knew, or guessed, and sold the information to Michelle Gorgon. It—. Wait." And O'Rourke climbed suddenly from the car, went back into that all-night drug store, and following him to the corner I saw him step into the telephone booth.

"Phew—" he rubbed his forehead when he came out. "At least, no harm has been done yet."

"O'Rourke—" I started, and stopped. The riot squad was on the job. Two big cars were coming down the street.

Now, I didn't have things my own way. O'Rourke did agree with me that the police cars stay five blocks from Ricorro's. But O'Rourke trailed along with me to within a couple of blocks of the garage—then I let him out of my boat.

"I don't know what you told the cops, O'Rourke," was my final message to him, "but I'm certain that a police parade will kill the show."

"Nothing to worry about," O'Rourke told me. "They've got orders to wait, then surround the block. I'll sort of keep an eye on you."

"Too much interest, and McBride dies." I took the hand that O'Rourke held out to me. And I grinned as I put the police whistle into my pocket. Why argue over that?

"You've sure got guts, Race," he said simply, and I drove off.

CHAPTER XXIX

JOE GORGON DOES HIS STUFF

THERE ARE TIMES when I feel that I earn my money. This was one of them. I had an idea that one man, working alone, might get to McBride. One man, driving alone into that garage, would probably not send a signal of warning to Joe Gorgon. One man might—. But I swung the corner, dashed down the main street, spotted the wide open doors of Ricorro's Garage and drove smack in. I want to tell you it was a big moment.

Certainly I got service—service one doesn't expect in a garage.

A lad sitting on the running board of a truck jumped to his feet and came quickly toward me. He carried a wrench in his hand. Though he was dolled up like a car washer I recognized him as I stepped from the car, and what's more, he recognized me. He was more or less of a well known gangster. And I had the advantage of him. Where he didn't expect me I expected him, or one of his kind.

We faced each other a split second only, as I stepped from the running board. My car protected us from being seen from the little lighted room that would be an office.

He never spoke, never more than half raised that wrench, when I let him have it. Just a single up-swing of my right hand, and the barrel of my gun crashed home. Yes, I know. If I were real high minded I'd have hit him with my fist. But I'm not high minded, and besides, my knuckles bruise easily and I have yet to see the head that will dent my rod.

His eyes did a "Charlie Chaplin" as his knees gave. Then he laid down on the floor. So much for that. I don't waste time on these birds, and I didn't waste time now.

Not a soul in that dimly lit garage as I crossed the smeared cement floor to that little office. Boy, what a break! As I pushed open the door, Ricorro's fat little form was coming toward me. He stopped dead in the center of that office and gaped at me. Then he turned quickly to the roll-top desk.

"Don't be a fool, Ricorro," I told him. "It's Race Williams. I'm killing tonight."

Melodramatic? Sure. Who's to deny that? But then, in the new underworld of our great city, melodrama is real life—and death too. Anyway, it was the kind of talk Ricorro understood. He stopped dead, chucked up both his hands and stood so. He knew his stuff, did Ricorro; knew my reputation also. Life in the underworld had taught him that the man with the gun talks, and the man without a gun listens.

A sudden noise behind me and I half swung aside, so as to face both Ricorro and the office door. Then I shrugged my shoulders and let it go at that. O'Rourke was there, slightly out of breath, slightly red of face, but with a gun in his hand. He must have run the two blocks.

"I'm sorry, Race. I had to—. Look out!"

A revolver cracked. A figure, or rather, the shadow of a figure fled down the little hall back of the office, where he had been hiding. With a warning to O'Rourke, I dashed into that little hallway. There wasn't much to fear from a lad who couldn't shoot better than to miss both of us.

"Watch that bird, Ricorro, O'Rourke," was all I said as I got under way.

I saw the running figure through the glass of the door which led into the garage again. Just another door where Ricorro could go in and out, and miss people he didn't want to see in the front.

Now, had this scurrying rat spoiled the party? If Joe Gorgon was in the basement, did he hear the shot? Somehow, I thought not. The motor of my car was still running. The floor was of thick cement. And as I dashed into the dimness of the garage I called out my warning to the fleeing, ducking figure ahead.

I could have shot him, but I didn't. I thought I knew his kind, his breed. I thought he'd drop his gun and cry out for mercy at the first warning. But he didn't. He ducked quickly behind a car, fired once from the darkness, where I couldn't see him, and I cursed out my big heart, or my assurance that he'd stop when I warned him.

Now the going was not so good. This lad was bent on warning the others or making his escape. But while he was loose in that garage he was a real menace—both to my plans and my life. And I saw him again—far in the rear now, a dim figure between two cars. He was kneeling on the floor, pulling at something. I covered him and again called out. You have to admit I was giving him a break.

And this time he had to have it. He raised his gun and it spouted flame. And that was enough of that. I only fired once, saw him sort of straighten, clutch at his chest and go down. I don't go in to miss. It's not good business.

I was on him before he could fire again, that is, if he was alive, to fire again. And he was alive, but not in condition to cause trouble. Besides which, he had shown me the entrance to the basement. A great slab of heavy timber in the cement floor, with an iron ring in it.

I grabbed his gun, took a grip on that iron ring, lifted the trap door and started down wooden steps. Things were as quiet as the grave below. The grave! I wondered. But faint heart never filled a spade flush, or rescued a McBride, and I believe in going after things with a bit in my teeth.

I didn't find blackness below. As soon as I spotted enough light I jumped those steps two at a time and made the bottom. A quickly moving figure is much harder to hit than a slowly moving one. That makes sense, though a lot of people think you must creep up on an enemy to be effective.

If Joe Gorgon had heard those shots, he wasn't in the open, waiting. The basement was musty and damp. Perhaps half a dozen cars stood out weirdly in the dim yellowish light. There were barrels, that looked as if they might contain oil; a part of a car here and another part there. Loose lumber, old tires, and great hunks of tin, or what looked like great hunks of tin.

There were no little side rooms, no locked doors. No doors at all, except two big ones which, I thought, opened into the car elevator, for I had spotted doors like them directly above.

But you couldn't tell. The doors might be a blind. I stepped over to them, and stepped back from them again. Low, but distinct, just the same, was the hum of an elevator. Was it going up or down? I thought down, then KNEW down. For, as I raised my gun, those doors opened and—Colonel McBride stood smack before me, right in the center of that elevator. Despite the fact that I was looking from the light into the semi-darkness of the unlighted elevator, I recognized him. His face was white, bruised, and cut too. But he was standing on his feet. Standing alone. And I saw the bulky shadow behind him just as that bulky shadow saw me. It was Joe Gorgon.

From behind McBride Joe Gorgon fired. No word of warning. Just a spit of orange blue flame, and a sudden icy coldness across my cheek, as if some one had pulled a red hot iron over it. Yes— I mean that. It was a coldness that burnt.

Joe Gorgon had half turned his great bulk sideways, so that he was completely protected from my fire by Colonel McBride. Joe wasn't like his brother, Eddie. He didn't gloat over his kill. And what's more, he wasn't going to talk himself out of his kill. He was drawing a bead now over McBride's shoulder—his head low, his eye down close to McBride's arm—just a fraction of a sight from under that arm. Joe didn't hurry, but he didn't lag either. Maybe a second. Maybe two. Maybe less, even.

I had to do it. I wasn't fifteen feet from the standing, staring, sort of lifeless McBride, and the hidden crouching bulk of Joe Gorgon. It was my death, McBride's death, or—.

And I did it. I jumped forward and fired, to be closer even when my heavy forty-four found its mark. I fired smack at the right arm of Colonel McBride.

Just the roar and the flash of my gun echoing upon the roar and the flash of Joe Gorgon's single shot. It worked. McBride crumpled to the floor. Joe Gorgon jumped sort of in the air, half spun, fired wildly, and I laid my next bullet smack between his eyes. Just a little round hole, ever growing larger. Joe Gorgon waved his hands once. His right foot came slowly up, like a lad in the slow motion pictures. Then he pitched forward on his face.

Yep, a forty-four is a mighty handy weapon, even if old fashioned. My bullet had gone through the fleshy part of McBride's arm as if it were papier-mâché, and landing in Joe's shoulder had knocked him back, just as if you'd hit him with a battering ram.

But it was McBride I was thinking of. He was so white and silent. The blood was pouring from his arm just above the elbow. An awkward place to tackle, but I did the best I could to make a tourniquet with my handkerchief and pencil as I blew frantically upon the police whistle. Police whistle! Imagine it! I never thought I'd have use for one of those things. But now, I was glad O'Rourke had forced it on me. The thing was over! McBride was safe, and Joe Gorgon—. Already his body was cold enough for little devils to be skating on his chest.

They came. Half a dozen plainclothesmen, a police surgeon, and O'Rourke leading them.

"I had a doctor in the car," O'Rourke said, "though I should have brought an undertaker. Joe's dead of course. And he got McBride first!"

"He did not!" I told O'Rourke emphatically.

Then I explained the necessity of plugging McBride, felt O'Rourke dabbing at my neck with a handkerchief, and for the first time realized that the warm stream running under my collar was not perspiration, but blood, and that the bullet had been closer to doing me in than I thought, for the wound was along the side of my neck and not my cheek. Queer, that? Maybe. But queer or not, it was the truth just the same. I guess it's much easier to see where you plug another guy than to know where you're hit your-self. But why bother? After the police surgeon had fixed up McBride I let him play around my neck. And he did. With a gallon or two of iodine, and a lot of conversation as to what might have happened if the bullet had been a fraction of an inch to the right.

CHAPTER XXX

A LETTER FROM THE DEAD

McBride came around in that little office up stairs and talked a bit. I listened but didn't get it at all.

"I never told him," Colonel McBride said over and over, until he seemed to get his bearings better. "Joe Gorgon threatened me and struck me with his gun while my hands and feet were bound. And then he decided to go after me in earnest. A hot iron that he heated in the little stove up stairs. It was the shot that saved me, for he stopped and listened. Then untied my feet, and with a gun pressed against my back led me to the elevator."

"Yes, we know all that," I cut in. That wasn't very important now. "How did they get you here—Rudolph Myer, wasn't it?"

"Yes, though he may be an innocent party to it. He came to me and said that the girl had decided to talk. That she would tell me everything. That she was waiting in the car on the street behind. That seemed right. She had promised to come to my house. Promised to, at least—"

"What girl?" I asked quickly.

"The Flame, of course. She—"

But O'Rourke was at him—shutting him up—speaking hurriedly.

I turned on O'Rourke.

"The Flame? She knows! The voice on the wire that so worried Michelle Gorgon; the cracked voice of a man trying to imitate a woman. The Flame? Why, she's going to marry Michelle Gorgon. She's—. Come, O'Rourke, out with it."

"Now, now, Race." And as two white coated lads came in with a stretcher for Colonel McBride, O'Rourke finished, "I guess it's time you knew everything, but it's not for me to tell you. I passed my word to The Flame. Come, we'll go up to her apartment and see her. Tut, tut, don't look at me like that, Race. She'll be expecting us."

And up to her apartment we did go. And maybe I did look at him "like that." Like what? Oh, like anything O'Rourke thought I looked like.

Think! The Flame had said, "Think." And the one thing I couldn't do as we made that trip up Park Avenue was—think.

This time we drove straight to the door of the flashy apartment. The dawn was breaking in the sky. Brophey, the detective who had been at McBride's house after his disappearance, stepped from the shadows and saluted O'Rourke. O'Rourke explained the dick's presence before the apartment to me.

"When I left you in the car by the drug store," he said, "I made a couple of calls. One, was to cover this apartment and drag in Michelle Gorgon."

"On what charge?"

"The murder of his wife," said O'Rourke. "I couldn't think of any better charge, and even if I couldn't hold him it wouldn't look so bad. Prussic acid is hard to buy—especially by a crippled, half witted woman who has never been on the street alone since her—her accident."

"I think that was a mistake," I told O'Rourke, and meant it.

"I had another reason. I had to do it to protect The Flame. Any luck, Brophey?" he asked the dick.

"Doctor Michelle Gorgon has not come in," Brophey said, "And The Fla— Miss Drummond has not gone out—at least, since I've been here."

"Good!" said O'Rourke as we passed into the apartment house. "We'll see The Flame." And as I started to question him again, "Just a jaunt to the twelfth floor, Race, then it's up to her."

The night man didn't like the hour we sought The Flame. O'Rourke didn't argue. He showed his badge, pushed the elevator man, John, back and said, "Twelfth floor, and no lip."

Another plainclothesman, who was sitting on the cold stairs beside the elevator, came to his feet when we reached the twelfth floor. O'Rourke was thorough, anyway. But certainly Michelle Gorgon would get wind of the police display and not return. I said as much to O'Rourke.

"I didn't want him to return," said O'Rourke. "I didn't want to make the pinch unless he came here for The Flame. I'd of had to pinch him to save her. Anything stirring, Cohen?"

"Not a thing," said Cohen. "No one in or out of 12-D since I've been here."

It took time to get into that apartment. At last the colored maid, Lillian, opened the door.

"Miss Drummond?" said O'Rourke. "Miss—" And the girl didn't have to tell us. We both read it in her face. But when she came out with it, it startled me just the same. Florence, The Flame, had received a telephone call and left the house, perhaps a half hour earlier.

"Just before the boys got here," said O'Rourke, the mental figuring showing on his face.

"Miss Florence left a letter for a Mr. Williams—" the maid started, but O'Rourke had shoved by her and was into the living room, snatching an envelope quickly from the table. He held it a moment in his hand, then tore it open. When I followed him and grabbed at his arm, he said:

"All right, it's for you." He chucked the envelope in the basket and handed me several sheets of paper. Then he turned to the maid. She was frightened. She was talking.

"You're the police, ain't you, Mister?" she said to O'Rourke. "Well, Miss Florence acted funny. There were two telephone calls. The first woke me up. I didn't hear what she said."

"That would be my call." O'Rourke thought aloud.

"The second call came right after it," the maid went on. "I didn't try to listen but I couldn't help it." Which meant she had her ear to the keyhole, I thought, but said nothing. "Of course I didn't hear what came over that wire, but I heard Miss Florence say, 'All right—the airport.'"

"What airport—My God! What airport?" And O'Rourke was shaking her by the shoulders and saying over and over, "Good God! he's going to do it again." And suddenly, to me, when there was nothing more to get from the now thoroughly frightened maid:

"Read that, Race. Read all The Flame wrote."

He picked up the phone, and I heard him say, "Roosevelt Field airstation. Damn the number! This is police headquarters."

But I was reading the closely and hastily written letter The Flame had left for me. It started bluntly enough—but here it is.

"I love you, Race.

"What a beginning for the last will and testament of The Flame. At least, the last if you should read this.

"I am going back a great many years. I never knew my real father or mother. I was brought up in an orphanage outside of Harrisburg, Pennsylvania. But in that orphanage I had a mother's love. It was my sister who stood between me and the heartaches, and even the brutality of the institutions of those days. She gave up opportunities of adoption, suffered undeserved punishments, to give herself a bad name so that she would

not be taken from me. For she was not the incorrigible girl the orphanage authorities painted her. She was good and kind and beautiful, and the criminal instinct in my mind was not in hers.

"She was older than I—much older. Then one day a lady took me away. That was Mrs. Drummond. A kind, wealthy, and somewhat foolish widow. She believed those stories about my sister—that she was bad, and never let me see her or speak of her.

"Then Mrs. Drummond married Lu Roper, and later she died—an unhappy woman, I called him my stepfather. If Lu Roper did not actually plant the seed of crime in my childish mind, at least he developed it to its present perfection. But he is dead now. Criminal! Murderer! Gang leader! You remember him.

"I learned later that my sister escaped from the orphanage—ran away when she was held illegally after coming of age. She never knew what became of me. I never knew what became of her—except, that it was charged that she took money with her from that orphanage, which charge I never did believe. I never tried to find her. I never wished to find her. It would have broken her heart to know that I wear—and deservedly wear—the name: The Girl with the Criminal Mind.

"Things were done rather shabbily back when I was adopted. And that's why I did not inherit the money from Mrs. Drummond that I should have received. But other things were brought up in that fight for Mrs. Drummond's wealth.

"One man, Race—a fair and honest man—in his pursuit of Doctor Michelle Gorgon, came as far as that court when Mrs. Drummond's money was being kept from me. He was a clever, determined man. I joined forces, to a certain extent, with this man— but why hide his name? He will tell you now. He was Detective Sergeant O'Rourke. And this is what he discovered:

"The wife of Michelle Gorgon was my sister. And Michelle Gorgon had taken her in an airplane, and—. But you know that terrible story. Michelle Gorgon didn't expect my sister would live. But she did live, maimed and twisted in body; wracked and dead of mind. He did this because she was going to leave him—for another man—some one she loved only in her heart and soul, and would love only so—until she was free of her husband, Michelle Gorgon.

"So I went in with O'Rourke and Colonel McBride. Such is my mind. I wanted—not justice, Race—but vengeance, I guess.

"And I learned who Michelle Gorgon really was. I learned who Giovoni was. He was an Italian criminal, known as 'The Devil' years ago. I gave Giovoni into the hands of Colonel McBride, but I didn't tell him all I knew. I couldn't. I wouldn't. Until I was sure that the so-called Michelle Gorgon had purposely planned my sister's terrible 'accident.' Rudolph Myer helped me, but until tonight I didn't suspect how much he really understood.

"Toney, the little drug addict, came over on the boat from Italy with the Gorgon brothers twenty-three years ago. He knew the truth. There was no Michelle Gorgon. Michelle Gorgon met his death in Naples, beneath a train, twenty-three years before. And it was the escaped murderer of Giovoni's daughter, Rose Marie—Nicholas Temporia—who took his place. He came to America as Michelle Gorgon—or Gorgonette—as the Gorgon brothers were then called.

"The immigration laws were not so strict in those days. Michelle Gorgon's body was mangled beyond recognition by the train, and it was wearing Nicholas Temporia's clothes and carrying Nicholas Temporia's papers and little possessions—which gives the idea that, perhaps, after all, the death of Michelle Gorgon was not an accident—but that he was laid, drugged, upon the tracks by Joe Gorgon and Nicholas Temporia, as Eddie was but a *child then. For Michelle Gorgon had money; had a good reputation in his home town. And, again, what points to his murder is the fact that Joe Gorgon was as much upset by the coming of Giovoni as was his supposed brother, Michelle. Let us still, for clearness, call him Michelle.*

"So much for that. I did not tell what I knew to Colonel McBride. Toney did not tell what he knew to Colonel McBride. We left it in the hands of Giovoni to identify the murderer of his daughter.

"After Giovoni died and Michelle Gorgon thought himself safe, I began to hound him—with telephone calls—little notes, which, if another found them, would mean his end. Each night I'd send him a note, that read:

"THE SOUL OF ROSE MARIE CRIES OUT FOR VENGEANCE
    —MR. NICHOLAS TREMPORIA.

I paused a moment in reading the letter. I recalled the note Michelle Gorgon had shown me—the words that were erased at the end of it, and knew they were the three words he feared so much. MR. NICHOLAS TREMPORIA.

O'Rourke was still telephoning. I heard him calling the airport at Newark. I went on reading.

"I know now that my sister is dead. I know now that Rudolph Myer sold me out. I know that—because Sergeant O'Rourke telephoned me that Michelle knew it was I who held his secret. But I am not certain that it can be proven, now, that Michelle Gorgon is really Nicholas Tremporia.

"I know too, Race, that if ever you read this it is Goodbye. For I have just received word from Michelle Gorgon to meet him at the airport. He knows, now, that I was the voice on the wire—that I sent him those notes—and no doubt knows, too, that his wife was my sister. But he doesn't know that I know he knows. Yes—I am going with him. If he plans my death, he will perhaps tell me the truth first—that he purposely maimed his wife—my sister. He may gloat over his vengeance on me. But it will be worth death to—.

"I love you, Race. Since you are reading this note; since you have kept your word with me. Since your honor would forbid you opening this letter after reading what was on the envelope—until now. Goodbye. Look for my body in Northern Westchester. But let me hope it will not lie there alone.

        "To the End,
        "The Girl with the
            Criminal Mind,
        "FLORENCE."

CHAPTER XXXI

DEATH FROM THE SKY

I laid down the letter and looked at O'Rourke. He was still telephoning, madly.

"Newark airport, yeah. Michelle Gorgon—no. Not at all. I—" And down went the receiver.

It wasn't the time yet to have things out with O'Rourke. The Flame was dead. She had more than hinted as much. But she couldn't be if she had only left the apartment a short while before. Another thing in that letter struck me. "Since your honor would forbid you opening this letter after reading what was on the envelope."

O'Rourke was buzzing the phone again. I said to him in a cracked voice:

"Is there an airport in Westchester—northern Westchester?"

And he didn't answer me. The receiver clicked up and down. O'Rourke was an almanac of information. I heard him calling an airport some eight or ten miles above White Plains.

As for me. I'm not a dumb ox altogether. I was fishing into that waste basket for the envelope that O'Rourke had tossed there. And I found it, spread it out, and read what was written on it.

"Race—I trust to your honor not to read this note until twelve o'clock, noon." I looked at my watch. It was now exactly twenty minutes to five. I guess my eyes got a little harder as they looked at O'Rourke. He had made sure I wouldn't see what was on that envelope. But I didn't say anything. He was talking on the phone.

"Never heard of Michelle Gorgon! Well, it's damn near time you bought a New York newspaper. No order for a plane to go up—none gone up—and wait—just a minute. Any plane there owned by a Miss Drummond? A—. That's it. That's it. Her pilot dropped in with it early in the week? Listen. Get in touch with the police and see that—that that plane—. Listen—Damn it!" He pounded the hook up and down. "The fool's cut off. Central— Damn it, give me that number I—" O'Rourke dropped the receiver. "Some one cut the wires, I'll bet. Come on, Race. There's a chance yet."

"Yes, a chance yet." I faced him as he stood up. "So you're the light haired boy who got The Flame into his—. Who let her take this trip tonight. Who—. And you once suggested a bullet between your own eyes, O'Rourke, once—" Maybe my hand touched my gun. "Why didn't you warn her?"

"But I did," said O'Rourke. "As soon as you told me about that pile of jack in Rudolph Myer's bag I rang her up and warned her not to open the door to any one, that my men would be there shortly. For her not to see Michelle Gorgon, and—"

"Maybe you did." I thought of the letter. "She knew and she went anyway. God! O'Rourke. How could you do it? How—"

"If we've got to differ, Race, let it be later. Maybe, in a different way, I think as much of The Flame as you do. I'll talk now. She's talked in that letter. But let's be friends now, Race, at least allies. It looks like The Flame went, purposely, to her death. Come on. To the airport in Westchester. There's a chance."

"There's no chance," I told him, as we hurried from the apartment. "He's taking her as he took his wife. The Flame crossed him. She was out to ruin him, and he knows it."

The sky was brightening as we dashed through the city streets. I wasn't quite my own man. I let Brophey drive the police car, and I sat in the back with O'Rourke. That car carried the police insignia. There would be less delays.

"Look here." O'Rourke leaned close to me and spoke. "I saw a chance to get the Gorgons through The Flame. And I was right. She found out more in a month than I had found out in a year. But she wouldn't tell me, wouldn't tell McBride. At least, not until she was sure, beyond any doubt, that Michelle Gorgon had maimed her sister. She was afraid I told her that simply to get her in with me."

"Then she was working for you all along."

"Yes and no," said O'Rourke. "In a way she was working with me, but really working for herself. But I thought, once she was convinced of the truth, she would turn Michelle Gorgon in. It was she who found out that Toney came over on the ship with the Gorgons, though what that information was worth I never did know. It was she who discovered, through Toney, about Giovoni. But Giovoni wouldn't talk out until he could confront Michelle Gorgon. Besides, he was taken desperately ill, aboard ship. But we got enough from him to know that he was called 'The Devil' years back. And you never suspected The Flame?"

"No." And suddenly, "You knew she was at McBride's house that night, in the locked closet?"

"Sure," said O'Rourke. "I thought as much as soon as I found that closet door locked, and remembered that I had told The Flame about McBride signalling me with the light, for help—when she warned me that he should never be unprotected. She had come in the back way, through the door that was left open for Rudolph Myer. She knew, or felt, that McBride was in

great danger and came to warn him. She hid in one of the front rooms when McBride came down stairs to meet Rudolph Myer. She thought it was the police though, and never suspected McBride was leaving by the back door with some one. So she didn't see with whom he left. But the moment she knew he was gone she suspected some trap of the Gorgons, ran up those stairs and flashed the danger signal with the light.

"Yes, I suspected she was there in the closet, but I didn't know for sure until I met her in the hall and gave her safe passage from the house. That's what I meant when I said to you that the district attorney himself couldn't leave that house without my Okay. You must have thought me an awful hick cop. But she didn't want you to know too much, Race. She was afraid you would give the show away trying to protect her, but in her heart I think she wanted you out of the case, because she thought you'd—well—get yourself a hole in the ground."

"I never thought of her working in with the police."

"And she wasn't," snapped O'Rourke. "It was vengeance, or retribution, or a great love—or a great hate. But each day I thought she would get the proof from Michelle Gorgon himself that he had maimed his wife, her sister. And then, I thought, she'd blow it all to me. Now, she's gone with him, knowing that he's onto her. Why?"

"Do you think—maybe she don't—didn't understand you?"

"Hell! I told her flat, that Rudolph Myer had sold her out to Michelle Gorgon. Then I gave her the office to sit tight. The Flame's no child, you know."

"No." Death—destruction. All that The Flame had told me came up before me now. "O'Rourke," I said slowly, "I don't know. But if The Flame's dead, get away from me—get—. Good God! I—. We've been almost pals. I—. Why didn't you tell me The Flame was in it—with—with us?"

"I couldn't. I passed my word. She wouldn't help me unless I did. And I also passed my word not to ask you into the case. In a way, I broke that promise. I had McBride bring you in—through Myer."

"And the note, with what was written on the envelope. She trusted to my honor, and—"

"That's it," said O'Rourke. "There's too much honor, been too damned much honor. If you hadn't read that note we wouldn't be on our way to save her now. I'm a stickler about my own honor, Race, yet not a guardian of yours. It's best you read it, and—"

"Yes," I said, "it's best that I read it."

"Good!" He stuck out his hand, but I didn't see it. Finally he put it back in his pocket. "We must all go our way according to our light," he said.

"Yeah. I thought you were a friend, a real friend. And you're just, just a cop," was the best I could give him.

"But an honest cop," said O'Rourke. "An honest cop."

Brophey could drive. And the police siren screeched but little in the city streets. No talk, now, between us. Up Broadway to Van Cortland Park, through the park to Central Avenue. Sometimes sixty, sometimes sixty-five. It was then that I wished I had my own car. Out on that long stretch of concrete road I could have pushed it to eighty, and perhaps ninety on that down grade just before you reach that slight upswing to the Tuckahoe Road. But, be fair about it. That down grade is quite some curve and maybe, maybe—. But this is not an automobile tour I'm writing about—nor a real estate ad for "Buy in Westchester"—nor even a treatise on the merits of certain automobile motors. It was a race against death. At least, I hoped it was. But maybe, after all, it was just a race with death, to find death.

It was perhaps five miles out of White Plains that I saw O'Rourke stick his head out of the window, then lean forward and tap the driver, Brophey, on the shoulder. The brakes ground; the car came to a stop just at a cross road. And that was the first time I came to life, and heard plainly the roar of a motor—an airplane motor.

Looking up I saw the plane. A biplane, pretty

high. But even at that distance one could see that the motor was sputtering, and that the plane was circling. Then it suddenly dived, hesitated a moment, seemed to gain altitude and shoot toward the west and on a beeline with the road to our right.

And we were after it. A pitiful, hopeless little trio, in that modern invention known as the automobile, as helpless and as prehistoric as if we ran on foot, armed with huge clubs cut from the trees. Still, we sped down that road in the wake of the slowly diminishing plane.

Sixty! Sixty-five! A curve in the road, our wheels in the roadbed, a sudden jerk and we were straightened out again, with great empty fields behind the trees to our left. And again O'Rourke had tapped our driver, Brophey, on the shoulder. Again the brakes. This time we stopped beneath the shadows of a cluster of huge trees.

"Drive her off, in the grass there, out of the way," said O'Rourke.

"Good God!" I said to O'Rourke, as we climbed from the car, "I know it's no use and all that, but it seems like doing something to keep going. At least trying to save her life."

O'Rourke spoke.

"Here, keep in the protection of those trees. I haven't trailed Michelle Gorgon all these weeks without knowing his car when I see it. And that Rolls of his was parked in the field back there. Look!"

And I looked through the foliage. Yep, there was the outline of a car all right. But it wasn't the car I looked at. It was the figure that stood so still beside a tree. A figure that seemed like part of the landscape, or a scarecrow. Then it moved, and I knew that it was human. The figure watched that plane, the plane which had turned now and was coming back over the field. And then I saw the flash. Not for certain, not for sure.

But O'Rourke cried out.

"The plane's on fire, and some one is jumping."

A far distant figure, with a great hump on its back, balanced, swayed, seemed to clutch at a wing—then pitched out, swung slowly and came hurtling toward the earth. I waited, breathless, for a sudden jerk of that body and the great silk of a parachute to check the flight, and send the form drifting gently to earth. But no parachute opened. The body began to turn rapidly now; hands gripped frantically at the air; even legs seemed to be attempting to entwine space.

"Good God!" said O'Rourke, "he's thrown her from the plane, and—"

The falling body struck in some trees, went crashing through them, and I sunk my head in my arms. So, destruction and death! That was the end of The Flame—that was—.

"And he ain't having such an easy time of it." O'Rourke gripped me by the shoulder. "The plane's on fire. Something's gone wrong. Look! It's out of control, entirely."

And it was. Fascinated, I watched that plane. Twisting, turning, diving, ever falling—ever nearer to the ground—ever—. And it swerved suddenly, about a hundred feet from the ground—seemed to straighten, then shoot upward, dip again, and dash straight toward a clump of trees not a hundred yards away from us.

"You can't do anything for—for her." And the words choked in O'Rourke's throat. "But him, the dirty, lousy murderer! We've got him red handed this time. In death The Flame gave him to us."

And we were running across that field. I'm not sure just what happened. But I think the plane paused in its drop, turned its nose up so suddenly that you could hear struts hum—snap, even—and with a crash it dove smack into a tree, twisted slightly, seemed to fall, and hung there. You could see it blazing now.

"Quick!" shouted O'Rourke, dashing by me. "The damn thing may blow up in a minute. We—"

"Let him burn to death," I cried out, and the next instant thought better of it. I hurled O'Rourke from me as we reached the now blazing wreck, jumped and caught a branch, and swung myself into the tree beside the plane.

I saw it all, and didn't care. I saw the jury filing from the room. I knew my story in that second's flash. I'd say I thought that Michelle Gorgon had a gun in his hand—and I shot him in self-defense. For I was going to kill him—put a bullet right through his head before ever O'Rourke could stop me. Catch Michelle Gorgon for the murder of The Flame? Hang murder on such a notorious racketeer—who could influence judges, keep witnesses silent, intimidate jurors? No—he was going before a jury now that he couldn't buy, couldn't intimidate, a Judge he couldn't fix.

And I saw him crouched there in the cock-pit. He'd know too. The flames flashed back suddenly, whipped by a touch of wind.

"All right, Doctor Michelle Gorgon," I cried out, almost mad with rage and hate, and something else, something that made me half sob out the words before I killed him. But I wanted him to know. He must know. And he would know. For his body stirred, his head low on his chest beneath the helmet, tried to rise.

My right hand gripped my gun. My left hand stretched in, clutched at the face that was turned from me. I jerked that head around, and—and looked straight into the wide, questioning, frightened eyes of The Flame—Florence Drummond.

CHAPTER XXXII

THE END OF THE RACKET

I don't know how I got The Flame out of that cock-pit. Maybe O'Rourke and Brophey did most of it. Maybe they didn't. But, anyway, she was on the grass beside us.

O'Rourke was hollering something about water. Brophey was yapping about a flask in the car, and I held The Flame close in my arms.

"It wasn't murder, Race," she said over and over. "It wasn't that. I ripped the parachute pack on his back with my knife when we got into the plane. But I told him, I did tell him before he jumped. I couldn't help it. I—but he was gone—on the edge—and he left me there to burn with it—crash with it—for my parachute was useless. He had seen to that."

"Ssh." I warned her. "O'Rourke will hear." Maybe he did hear, and maybe he didn't. But, anyway, he was running across the fields, running to where the body of Michelle Gorgon had dropped through the trees. I could barely make out the unshapely mass on the ground.

And The Flame talked.

"I had to know about my sister. I had to know if he really planned it so that she was crippled like that. That's why I went to meet him when he telephoned me. You see, the plane was in my name. Michelle brought it to the airport only a few days ago. He registered it at the field under my name because he was afraid, then, that the truth could come out about Rose Marie. He was afraid—deadly afraid—of that voice on the wire, and was ready for a get-away. He told me everything, once we were in the air. Gloated over the way he had broken my sister. Told me, too, that he had killed her—made her kill herself.

"It was a horrible crime, that murder of my sister. He played upon both her mental and physical weakness. Told her that in the secret flap of her bag was a bottle of poison, and a mirror. And told her that if she were alive in two hours' time he would bring to see her the man she loved—the man who had loved her."

She stopped a minute and rubbed at her dry eyes. The Flame didn't know how to cry, I guess. Then she went on.

"I couldn't protect myself, Race. I had not expected him to act so quickly. Before we were off the ground he had taken my gun—and the mechanic who turned our propeller struck me a blow on the head. I was stunned, didn't fully recover until we were up in the air, high up.

"He was clever, Race. The mechanic was one of his men. That mechanic would swear that I had gone up alone. Michelle was to set fire to the plane, leap with a parachute, be picked up by a man waiting with his car and driven back to the city.

" 'This was to be our bridal chariot,' he said. 'Now—it's your coffin, Florence. Like your sister, you crossed me. I loved you; I could have made you very happy. But you proved yourself a rat and a stool-pigeon. I give you death. I fight my own battles, I do not need the police.' "

" 'And I too can fight my own battles,' I cried out, as he tossed something on the hot engine and did something to the controls. 'Don't jump,

Michelle Gorgon! You've planned for me to be burnt to death in this blazing plane. I—' as I saw him on the edge of the cock-pit, his gun covering me, his index finger cocked through the loop of his parachute chord, 'I ripped the pack on your back with a knife as soon as you climbed into the plane. I cut your parachute. You'll—you'll have to burn with me.'

"He seemed to hesitate for a moment—then he smiled and stretched his hand back over his shoulder. The plane lurched. He cried out once, slipped, tottered—and fell. It seemed like hours that I heard his terrible screech of horror. Then the earth coming up, the trees and the crash—and you. But I swear I warned him that I cut—"

I put my hand across her mouth. O'Rourke was coming back.

"I'll telephone at the first town and have them pick up that Rolls and that mechanic at the field—and then have a look at Rudolph Myer," O'Rourke said, as we climbed into the police car. "And to ease your mind, Race. That lad was as dead as old King Tut, and it was our mutual friend, Michelle Gorgon."

"Yes, and anything The Flame had to do with it was self-defense, and—"

"You talk too much." O'Rourke looked at me as he lit a big black cigar, and I gathered The Flame close to me in the back of the machine. "You know, the body of Gorgon still hung in the trees when I reached it." And when I looked at him, surprised—for I had seen plainly that the body was on the ground, "I say it still hung in the trees. Get that! I know it, for I had to cut that parachute pack to ribbons with my knife to get him loose. Cut it to ribbons, understand!" And after a pause, while he glared at me, "It's funny it didn't open right, but then, they very often don't, and there's no explaining—no explaining it."

After all, O'Rourke wasn't a bad scout. But Michelle Gorgon was dead, and Michelle Gorgon had held The Flame in his arms. And—oh, I wasn't superstitious or anything like that. That thought had nothing to do with my moving over in a corner of the back seat and sticking a cigarette in my mouth. I—I just needed a smoke, I guess.

Any more to it? Well—hardly. The body of Eddie Gorgon turned up in the river three days later. We could only guess that Michelle Gorgon had some of his crowd put it there. Why? Well—maybe because he didn't want it discovered in the underworld, just then, that some one—particularly a lad known as Race Williams—had the guts to shoot his brother, Eddie—or the lad every one thought was his brother, Eddie.

INTRODUCTION BY HARLAN ELLISON

I, FELON

NOT THAT IT'S any of your damned business, but the first time I went to jail was in 1945. I was eleven years old. In 1958 I wrote a story about it. The title was "Free With This Box!" I was twenty-four. Now shuddup and leave me alone.

There are three sections in this group of homages to the pulp writers of a dear and departed era in popular literature. One of them, I'm told, is *The Crimefighters*, the third will be *The Dames*, and this one, dealing with the villains. As I am not a woman, it is manifest why I was not solicited by the *éminence grise* of this project, the esteemed editor Mr. Otto (we calls him "Slow Hand Poppa") Penzler, to pen the introductory exegesis for the book about the broads; and as you will understand in mere moments, selecting me to front a book extolling the virtues of cops, pseudo-cops, hemi/semi/demi cops, and P.I. cops is about as apropos as a piñata at a paraplegics' picnic.

I was importuned by Penzler to write a foreword for a book of stories about *crooks*. We're talkin' here thieves, thugs, knaves, poltroons, bilkers, milkers, murderers, arsonists, liars, blackmailers, footpads, cat burglars, shakedown artists, pigeon-drop and 3-card monte swindlers, bloodthirsters, and backstabbers . . . in short, criminals.

Now, you may ask, what is this delicate flower of advanced age, this pinnacle of society, this world-famous and multiple-award-winning credit to his species, getting at? Is he, heaven forfend, suggesting that it is right and proper, even condign that this Penzler fellah thinks Ellison is *as one with* this fictional cadre of creeps and culprits, similar in spirit or outlook or past experience? Is that what we are to believe?

What is it witchu? Didn't I tell you to shuddup and leave me alone?

First of all, I grew up *reading* the pulps. I was born in '34 and, unlike most of the Jessica Simpson–admiring twerps of contemporary upbringing, for whom nostalgia is what they had for breakfast, I actually *remember* what a hoot it was to plonk myself into the Ouroboros root-nest of the ancient oak tree in the front yard of our little house at 89 Harmon Drive, Painesville, Ohio, with the latest issue of *Black Book Detective Magazine* or *The Shadow*. Ah me, those wood-chip-scented, cream-colored pulp pages dropping their dandruff onto the lap of my knickers . . .

(Those were corduroy boys' pants, here in America. In England, as I later discovered to my priapic delight, the same word is used to designate female panties—ah yes, in the aphorism of G. B. Shaw: "The United States and England are two countries divided by a common language.")

. . . and while Jack Wheeldon and his cronies yelled "kike" as they rode their Schwinns past my eyrie, I went away from that place and that time with the adventures of masked riders, square-jawed crimefighters, mightily-thewed barbarian warriors, spacemen accompanied by gorgeous women in brass brassieres, and culprits too smooth and sagacious to be nobbled by some cigar-masticating flatfoot from the Central Office. There was something called "escapism" in the pop lit of those days. It's too bad that word has fallen on such hard times. Escapism now, I'm told, is Not A Good Thing. Yet in its place we have "entertainment" that deifies the idle, the infamous, the egregious, and the shallow. In place of Raffles and Flambeau and Jimmy Valentine we have rapper thugs for whom human speech is not their natural tongue, a morbid fascination with those missing and presumed buried or drowned in the Bahamas, the need for a daily fix of tabloid ink infusion anent the presumed grotesqueries of child molesters, serial killers, televangelist alarmists, racists and ratfinks and raucous riffraff. We have been led down the societal garden path to a place where an honest crook who carries no firearm and would not stoop to such ignominious behavior as a carjacking or ballbatting of an ATM is no-price, and we are surfeited with "entertainment" that cheapens us, distances us, turns us into an unworthy people who accept no responsibility for our bad actions, and fills us with a sense of American Idol entitlement that has no substance in reality.

If I seem to be extolling the chimerical "virtues" of felons and crooks, one might assume in much the same way as the naive and gullible praised Dillinger, Capone, Ma Barker and her boys, back in the day, well, I live in the real world and I do truly *really* understand that Billy the Kid and Murder, Inc. and even Bonnie & Clyde were way less than icons to hold up to one's children . . . *but* . . . nonetheless . . .

I would rather spend time reading about Boston Blackie and Fantomas and Harry Lime than have to put up with one more pelvic twitch of Christina Aguilera or pelvic piercing of Pink. What used to be a necessary and even enriching, innervating, if not ennobling retreat to the made-up worlds of high crimes and low misdemeanors in the pulps, has been relentlessly, ceaselessly, tirelessly bastardized by corporate and advertising thugs (far worse than the Bad Guys you'll find in this volume), into a pounding, remorseless assault of empty trivial crap that fills the air, saturates our perceptions of the received world, and turns us away from ourselves and our true values and our important pursuits. Distractions that make the tomfoolery and toughtalk of the pulps seem as rich and golden as the Analects of Confucius or a paraphrasing of Lao Tzu. In the stories in this book, taken from the heart and core of that popular entertainment engine of the '20s, '30s, and '40s, you will experience an escapism that steals nothing from you, reduces you not one scintilla, pleasures and distracts you the way a tall champagne flute of good, tart lemonade does on a blistering August afternoon.

The fictions may creak a bit in the joints, some of the writing may be too prolix for modern tastes (don't forget, they were writing for ½¢ to a penny-a-word in those halcyon days of post-Depression America), and we have been exposed to an electronically-linked world for so long now, that some of the attitudes and expressions in these fables may seem giggle-worthy, but this is a muscular writing that sustained us through some very tough times, and their preserved quality of sheer entertainment value is considerable. So be kind.

As for me, well, I come to this book with credentials that are not trumpeted in the "official biographies" or in a *Who's Who* or the *Encyclopedia of American Authors*. But mine is exactly the proper vita for a book'a'crooks.

As I said, I grew up *in situ* with the pulp detective magazines. And in my earliest days as a professional I *wrote* for the metamorphosed hard-boiled pulps in digest-size (which stick-in-the-mud Penzler has trouble perceiving as equally valid cred for "pulp" as the larger-sized magazines). I wrote for *Manhunt, Mantrap, Mayhem, Guilty, Sure-Fire Detective, Trapped, The Saint Mystery Magazine* (both U.S. and U.K. editions), *Mike Shayne's, Tightrope, Crime and Justice Detective Story*, and *Terror Detective Story Magazine*, just to glaze your eyes and bore yo ass with a select few of the rags for which I toiled. So that's a *second* good reason for me being the one who stands here at the prow of the ship, urging you aboard.

But the cred that stands, the one that beats the bulldog, is that I *was* a felon. I mentioned my first incarceration at age eleven, a spree of petty theft involving comic character pinback buttons concealed in boxes of Wheaties; but that was just the first. Age thirteen, ran off and wound up in a huge free-standing cell in the old (now-razed) Kansas City slam, all alone save for a carny geek who went nuts without his bottle of gin a day, and impressed me forever with the stench of rotgut sweated out via armpits. Booted out of Ohio State University in 1954, in part, for shoplifting. Saw the inside of the Columbus jail on that one.

U.S. Army brigs of various venues, 1957–59, mostly for insubordination. 1960: I'm in New York, living down in the Village, guy I had a beef with phones in bullshit charges of "possession of firearms" to the cops, they bust me, toss me in The Tombs (see my book *Memos from Purgatory*), and finally the Grand Jury looks at it, the D.A. knows it's bullshit so he urges them to return No True Bill, and that was that.

Civil Rights days. I was in jails in Mississippi, Georgia, Alabama with Martin, and on and on. In Louisiana, a couple of redneck cops grabbed me on a back road in Plaquemine Parish, hauled me in, stripped me to the waist, cuffed me behind my back, lifted me up between them, hung the cuffs over a meat hook turned into the top-half of a Dutch door, and took turns walloping me across the belly with a plastic kiddie ballbat, careful to leave barely a mark on the outside. Did that till the Boss of Plaquemine, the infamous Leander Peres showed up, thumbed through my wallet full of I.D. and credit cards, discovered I was from Hollywood, knew there'd be a *geshry* (as we say in Yiddish) if I vanished, had his boys take me down, and redeposited me: in a ditch somewhere out on a dark back road, with this admonition, which I recall with telephonic accuracy more than four decades later: "Nex' tahm you show yo ass in Plack-uh-mun, jew-boy, we gonna jus' kill you."

Is it appropriate that Otto picked me for the introductory remarks about crooks and felons? You better believe it, dawg. Now go thee hence, inside farther, and enjoy yourself.

Tell 'em Harlan sent you. And now, just shuddup and leave me alone. A tired old felon slumped and maundering about his days on the other side of the law.

The Cat-Woman
Erle Stanley Gardner

OF THE MANY pulp creations of Erle Stanley Gardner (1889–1970), one of his personal favorites was Ed Jenkins, known as the Phantom Thief, his first significant series character (after Bob Larkin, who lasted only two adventures), who appeared in seventy-four novellas, more than any other protagonist.

Much of Gardner's career is important and inspiring because of the sheer numbers. In the decade before the first novel about Perry Mason, *The Case of the Velvet Claws* (1933), he averaged approximately 1,200,000 published words a year—the equivalent of one 10,000-word novella every three days, for 365 days. And he had a day job as a lawyer.

He dictated cases to his secretary and, in 1932, it finally occurred to him that he could dictate fiction, too, which greatly speeded up the writing process, enabling him to produce novels for the first time. *Velvet Claws* famously took three and a half days, though Gardner mostly said it was really four days, since he needed a half day to think up the plot.

Jenkins made his debut with "Beyond the Law" in the January 1925 issue of *Black Mask* and was one of the most popular series detectives in the history of the magazine. When Gardner decided to write no more about him, readers caused such an uproar that he was forced to continue producing his capers. "The Cat-Woman" was first published in the February 1927 issue of *Black Mask*.

The Cat-Woman

Erle Stanley Gardner

BIG BILL RYAN slid his huge bulk into the vacant chair opposite my own and began toying with the heavy watch chain which stretched across the broad expanse of his vest.

"Well," I asked, showing only mild annoyance, for Big Ryan had the reputation of never wasting time, his own or anyone else's.

"Ed, I hear you've gone broke. I've got a job for you."

He spoke in his habitual, thin, reedy voice. In spite of his bulk his mouth was narrow and his tone shrill. However, I fancied I could detect a quiver of excitement underlying his words, and I became cold. News travels fast in the underworld. He knew of my financial setback as soon as I did, almost. My brokers had learned my identity—that I was a crook, and they had merely appropriated my funds. They were reputable business men. I was a crook. If I made complaint the courts would laugh at me. I've had similar experiences before. No matter how honest a man may appear he'll always steal from a crook—not from any ethical reasons, but because he feels he can get away with it.

"What's on your mind?" I asked Ryan, not affirming or denying the rumor concerning my financial affairs.

It was a matter of seconds . . .
I heard running steps on the walk . . .

His pudgy fingers seemed to be fairly alive as he twisted and untwisted the massive gold chain.

"It's just a message," he said, at length, and handed me a folded slip of paper.

I looked it over. It was a high class of stationery, delicately perfumed, bearing a few words in feminine handwriting which was as perfect and characterless as copper plate.

Two hours after you get this message meet me at Apartment 624, Reedar Arms Apartments. The door will be open.

H. M. H.

I scowled over at Ryan and shook my head. "I've walked into all the traps I intend to, Ryan."

His little, pig eyes blinked rapidly and his fingers jammed his watch chain into a hard knot.

"The message is on the square, Ed. I can vouch for that. What the job will be that opens up I can't tell. You'll have to take the responsibility of that; but there won't be any police trap in that apartment."

I looked at the note again. The ink was dark. Evidently the words had been written some little time ago. The message did not purport to be to anyone in particular. Big Ryan was a notorious fence, a go-between of crooks. Apparently he had been given the note with the understanding that he was to pick out the one to whom it was to be delivered. The note would clear his skirts, yet he must be in on the game. He'd have to get in touch with the writer after he made a delivery of the note so that the time of the appointment would be known.

I reached a decision on impulse, and determined to put Ryan to the test. "All right, I'll be there."

I could see a look of intense relief come over his fat face. He couldn't keep back the words. "Bully for you, Ed Jenkins!" he shrilled. "After I heard you were broke I thought I might get you. You're the one man who could do it. Remember, two hours from now," and, with the words, he pulled out his turnip watch and carefully checked the time. Then he heaved up from the

chair and waddled toward the back of the restaurant.

I smiled to myself. He was going to telephone "H. M. H." and I filed that fact away for future reference.

Two hours later I stepped from the elevator on the sixth floor of the Reedar Arms Apartments, took my bearings and walked directly to the door of 624. I didn't pause to knock but threw the door open. However, I didn't walk right in, but stepped back into the hallway.

"Come in, Mr. Jenkins," said a woman's voice.

The odor of incense swirled out into the hall, and I could see the apartment was in half-light, a pink light which came through a rose-colored shade. Ordinarily I trust the word of no man, but I was in desperate need of cash, and Big Bill Ryan had a reputation of being one who could be trusted. I took a deep breath and walked into the apartment, closing the door after me.

She was sitting back in an armchair beneath a rose-shaded reading lamp, her bare arm stretched out with the elbow resting on a dark table, the delicate, tapering fingers holding a long, ivory cigarette holder in which burned a half-consumed cigarette. Her slippered feet were placed on a stool and the light glinted from a well-proportioned stretch of silk stocking. It was an artistic job, and the effect was pleasing. I have an eye for such things, and I stood there for a moment taking in the scene, appreciating it. And then I caught the gaze of her eyes.

Cat eyes she had; eyes that seemed to dilate and contract, green eyes that were almost luminous there in the half-light.

I glanced around the apartment, those luminous, green eyes studying me as I studied the surroundings. There was nothing at all in the apartment to suggest the personality of such a woman. Everything about the place was suggestive merely of an average furnished apartment. At the end of the room, near the door of a closet, I saw a suitcase. It merely confirmed my previous suspicion. The woman had only been in that apartment for a few minutes. She rented the place merely as a meeting ground for the crook she had selected to do her bidding. When Big Bill Ryan had picked a man for her, he had telephoned her and she had packed her negligee in the suitcase and rushed to the apartment.

She gave a little start and followed my gaze, then her skin crinkled as her lips smiled. That smile told me much. The skin seemed hard as parchment. She was no spring chicken, as I had suspected from the first.

The cat-woman shrugged her shoulders, reached in a little handbag and took out a blue-steel automatic which she placed on the table. Then she hesitated, took another great drag at the cigarette and narrowed her eyes at me.

"It is no matter, Mr. Jenkins. I assure you that my desire to conceal my identity, to make it appear that this was my real address, was to protect myself only in case I did not come to terms with the man Ryan sent. We had hardly expected to be able to interest a man of your ability in the affair, and, now that you are here, I shan't let you go, so there won't be any further need of the deception. I will even tell you who I am and where I really live—in a moment."

I said nothing, but watched the automatic. Was it possible she knew so little about me that she fancied I could be forced to do something at the point of a pistol?

As though she again read my mind, she reached into the handbag and began taking out crisp bank notes. They were of five-hundred-dollar denomination, and there were twenty of them. These she placed on the table beside the gun.

"The gun is merely to safeguard the money," she explained with another crinkling smile. "I wouldn't want you to take the cash without accepting my proposition."

I nodded. As far as possible I would let her do the talking.

"Mr. Jenkins, or Ed, as I shall call you now that we're acquainted, you have the reputation of being the smoothest worker in the criminal game. You are known to the police as The Phantom Crook, and they hate, respect and fear you.

Ordinarily you are a lone wolf, but because you are pressed for ready cash, I think I can interest you in something I have in mind."

She paused and sized me up with her cat-green eyes. If she could read anything on my face she could have read the thoughts of a wooden Indian.

"There are ten thousand dollars," she said, and there was a subtle, purring something about her voice. "That money will be yours when you leave this room if you agree to do something for me. Because I can trust you, I will pay you in advance."

Again she stopped, and again I sat in immobile silence.

"I want you to break into a house—my own house—and steal a very valuable necklace. Will you do it?"

She waited for a reply.

"That is all you wish?" I asked, killing time, waiting.

She wrinkled her cheeks again.

"Oh yes, now that you speak of it, there is one other thing. I want you to kidnap my niece. I would prefer that you handle the entire matter in your own way, but I will give you certain suggestions, some few instructions."

She paused waiting for a reply, and I let my eyes wander to the cash piled on the table. Very evidently she had intended that the actual cash should be a strong point in her argument and it would disappoint her if I didn't look hungrily at it.

"How long shall I hold your niece captive?"

She watched me narrowly, her eyes suddenly grown hard.

"Ed Jenkins, once you have my niece you can do anything with her or about her that you want. You must keep her for two days. After that you may let her go or you may keep her."

"That is all?" I asked.

"That is all," she said, and I knew she lied, as she spoke.

I arose. "I am not interested, but it has been a pleasure to have met you. I appreciate artistry."

Her face darkened, and the corners of her

upper lip drew back, the feline snarl of a cat about to spring. I fancied her hand drifted toward the automatic.

"Wait," she spat, "you don't know all."

I turned at that, and, by an effort, she controlled herself. Once more the purring note came into her voice.

"The necklace you will steal is my own. I am the legal guardian of my niece and I will give you my permission to kidnap her. What is more, I will allow you to see her first, to get her own permission. You will not be guilty of any crime whatever."

I came back and sat down in the chair.

"I have the necklace and it is insured for fifty thousand dollars," she said in a burst of candor. "I must have the money, simply must. To sell the necklace would be to cause comment of a nature I cannot explain. If I secrete the necklace I will be detected by the insurance company. If the notorious Ed Jenkins breaks into my house, steals my necklace, kidnaps my niece, the insurance company will never question but what the theft was genuine. You will, of course, not actually take the necklace. You will take a paste copy. The insurance company will pay me fifty thousand dollars, and, when occasion warrants, I can again produce the necklace."

I nodded. "You intend then that I shall be identified as the thief, that the police shall set up a hue and cry for me?"

She smiled brightly. "Certainly. That's why I want you to kidnap my niece. However, that should mean nothing to you. You have a reputation of being able to slip through the fingers of the police any time you wish."

I sighed. I had enjoyed immunity from arrest in California because of a legal technicality; but I was broke and in need of cash. All honest channels of employment were closed to me, and, after all, the woman was right. I had been able to laugh at the police.

I reached forward and took the money, folded the crisp bills and put them in my pocket.

"All right. I will accept. Remember one thing, however, if you attempt to double-cross me, to

play me false in any way, I will keep the money and also get revenge. Whatever your game is you must keep all the cards on the table as far as my own connection with it is concerned. Otherwise . . . ?"

I paused significantly.

"Otherwise?" she echoed, and there was a taunt in her voice.

I shrugged my shoulders. "Otherwise you will be sorry. Others have thought they could use Ed Jenkins for a cat's-paw, could double-cross him. They never got away with it."

She smiled brightly. "I would hardly give you ten thousand dollars in cash unless I trusted you, Ed. Now that we've got the preliminaries over with we may as well get to work and remove the stage setting."

With that she arose, stretched with one of those toe stretching extensions of muscles which reminded me of a cat arising from a warm sofa, slipped out of the negligee and approached the suitcase. From the suitcase she took a tailored suit and slipped into it in the twinkling of an eye. She threw the negligee into the suitcase, took a hat from the closet, reached up and switched out the light.

"All right, Ed. We're ready to go."

She had her own machine in a nearby garage, a long, low roadster of the type which is purchased by those who demand performance and care nothing for expense of operation. I slipped into the seat and watched her dart through the traffic. She had skill, this cat-woman, but there was a ruthlessness about her driving. Twice, pedestrians barely managed to elude the nickeled bumpers. On neither occasion did she so much as glance backward to make sure she had not given them a glancing blow in passing.

At length we slowed up before an impressive house in the exclusive residential district west of Lakeside. With a quick wriggle she slipped out from behind the steering wheel, vaulted lightly to the pavement and extended her long, tapering fingers to me. "Come on, Ed. Here's where we get out."

I grinned as she held the door open. Whatever her age she was in perfect condition, splendidly formed, quick as a flash of light, and she almost gave the impression of assisting me from the car.

I was shown into a drawing-room and told to wait.

While the cat-woman was gone I looked about me, got the lay of the land, and noticed the unique furnishings of the room. Everywhere were evidences of the striking personality of the woman. A tiger rug was on the floor, a leopard skin on the davenport. A huge painted picture hung over the fireplace, a picture of a cat's head, the eyes seeming to have just a touch of luminous paint in them. In the semi-darkness of the nook the cat's eyes blazed forth and dominated the entire room. It was impossible to keep the eyes away from that weird picture; those steady, staring eyes drew my gaze time after time.

At length there was the rustle of skirts and I rose.

The cat-woman stood in the doorway. On her arm was a blonde girl attired in flapper style, painted and powdered, and, seemingly, a trifle dazed.

"My niece, Jean Ellery, Ed. Jean, may I present Mr. Ed Jenkins. You folks are destined to see a good deal of each other so you'd better get acquainted."

I bowed and advanced. The girl extended her hand, a limp, moist morsel of flesh. I took it and darted a glance at the cat-woman. She was standing tense, poised, her lips slightly parted, her eyes fixed upon the girl, watching her every move.

"Hullo, Ed. Mr. Jenkins. I understand you're goin' to kidnap me. Are you a cave-man or do you kidnap 'em gently?"

There was a singsong expression about her voice, the tone a child uses in reciting a piece of poetry the import of which has never penetrated to the brain.

"So you want to be kidnapped, do you, Jean?"

"Uh, huh."

"Aren't you afraid you may never get back?"

"I don't care if I never come back. Life here is

the bunk. I want to get out where there's somethin' doin', some place where I can see life. Action, that's what I'm lookin' for."

With the words she turned her head and let her vacant, blue eyes wander to the cat-woman. Having spoken her little piece, she wanted to see what mark the teacher gave her. The cat-woman flashed a glance of approval, and the doll-faced blonde smiled up at me.

"All right, Jean," she said. "You run along. Mr. Jenkins and I have some things to discuss."

The blonde turned and walked from the room, flashing me what was meant to be a roguish glance from over her shoulder. The cat-woman curled up in a chair, rested her head on her cupped hands, and looked at me. There in the half-light her eyes seemed as luminous as those of the cat in the painting over the fireplace.

"Tomorrow at ten will be about right, Ed. Now, here are some of the things you must know. This house really belongs to Arthur C. Holton, the big oil man, you know. I have been with him for several years as private secretary and general house manager. Tomorrow night our engagement is to be announced and he is going to present me with the famous tear-drop necklace as an engagement present. I will manage everything so that the presentation takes place at about nine-thirty. Just before ten I will place the necklace on my niece to let her wear the diamonds for a few minutes, and she will leave the room for a moment, still wearing the diamonds.

"Really, I'll slip the genuine necklace in my dress and put an imitation around my niece's neck. She will leave the room and an assistant will bind and gag her and place her in a speedy roadster which I have purchased for you and is to be waiting outside. Then you must show your face. It won't look like a kidnapping and a theft unless I have some well-known crook show himself for a moment at the door.

"You can pretend that you have been doublecrossed in some business deal by Mr. Holton. You suddenly jump in the doorway and level a gun at the guests. Then you can tell them that this is merely the first move in your revenge, that you will make Mr. Holton regret the time he double-crossed you. Make a short speech and then run for the machine. I have a little cottage rented down on the seashore, and I have had Jean spend several days there already, under another name, of course, and you can go there as Jean's husband, one who has just returned from a trip East. You will be perfectly safe from detection because all the neighbors know Jean as Mrs. Compton. You will post as Mr. Compton and adopt any disguise you wish. But, remember; you must not stop and open the luggage compartment until you reach the cottage."

She spilled all that and then suddenly contracted her eyes until the pupils seemed mere slits.

"That may sound unimportant to you, Ed, but you've got to play your part letter perfect. There is a lot that depends on your following instructions to the letter. In the meantime I will give you plenty of assurance that I will shoot square with you."

I sat there, looking at this cat-woman curled up in the chair before the crackling fire, and had all I could do to keep from bursting out laughing right in her face. I've seen some wild, farfetched plots, but this had anything cheated I had ever heard of.

"Think how it will add to your reputation," she went on, the singing, purring note in her soothing tone.

I yawned. "And you can double-cross me and have me arrested ten minutes later, or tip the police off to this little cottage you have reserved for me, and I'll spend many, many years in jail while you laugh up your sleeve."

She shook her head. "What earthly reason would I have for wanting to have you arrested? No, Ed, I've anticipated that. Tomorrow we go to a notary public and I'll execute a written confession of my part in the affair. This confession will be placed in safekeeping where it will be delivered to the police in the event you are caught. *That* will show you how my interests are the same as your own, how I cannot afford to

have you captured. This paper will contain my signed statement that I have authorized you to steal the jewels, and my niece will also execute a document stating the kidnapping is with her consent. Think it over, Ed. You will be protected, but I must have that insurance money, and have it in such a way that no one will suspect me."

I sat with bowed head, thinking over the plan. I had already digested everything she had told me. What I was worrying about was what she hadn't told me.

I arose and bowed.

"I'll see you tomorrow then?"

She nodded, her green eyes never leaving my face.

"Meet me at the office of Harry Atmore, the lawyer, at eleven and ask for Hattie M. Hare. He will see that you are protected in every way. I guarantee that you won't have any cause for alarm about my double-crossing you."

Apparently there was nothing more to be gained by talking with this woman and I left her.

I had ten thousand dollars in my pocket, a cold suspicion in my mind and a determination to find out just what the real game was. I didn't know just how deep Big Ryan was mixed in this affair—not yet I didn't, but I proposed to find out. In the meantime I wasn't taking any chances, and I slipped into my apartment without any brass band to announce my presence.

At first I thought everything was in proper order, and then I noticed something was missing. It was a jade handled, Chinese dagger, one that I had purchased at a curio store not more than a month ago. What was more, the Chinaman who sold it to me had known who I was. That dagger could be identified by the police as readily as my signature or my fingerprints.

I sat down by the window in my easy chair and thought over the events of the evening. I couldn't see the solution, not entirely, but I was willing to bet the cat-woman wouldn't have slept easily if she had known how much I was able to put together. Right then I could have dropped the whole thing and been ten thousand dollars ahead; but there was big money in this game that was being played. I couldn't forget how Big Bill Ryan had twisted and fumbled at his watch chain when he had delivered that note to me. He was a smooth fence, was Big Ryan, and he wouldn't have let his fat fingers get so excited over a mere thirty or forty thousand dollar job. There was a million in this thing or I missed my guess.

At last I figured I'd checked things out as far as I could with the information I had, and rolled in.

At eleven on the dot I presented myself at the office of Harry Atmore. Atmore was a shyster criminal lawyer who charged big fees, knew when and where to bribe, and got results for his clients. I gave the stenographer my name, told her that I had an appointment, and was shown into the private office of Henry Atmore, attorney-at-law.

Atmore sat at a desk, and his face was a study. He was trying to control his expression, but his face simply would twitch in spite of himself. He held forth a flabby hand, and I noticed that his palm was moist and that his hand trembled. To one side of the table sat the cat-woman and the blonde. Both of them smiled sweetly as I bowed.

Atmore got down to business at once. He passed over two documents for my inspection. One was a simple statement from Hattie M. Hare to the effect that I had been employed by her to steal the Holton, "tear-drop" necklace, and that we were jointly guilty of an attempt to defraud the insurance company. The other was a statement signed by Jean Ellery to the effect that I had arranged with her to kidnap her, but that she gave her consent to the kidnapping, and that it was being done at her request.

I noticed that the Hare statement said nothing about the kidnapping, and the other said nothing about the necklace. I filed those facts away for future reference.

"Now here's what we'll do, Jenkins," Atmore said, his moist hand playing with the corners of some papers which lay on his desk, "we'll have both of these statements placed in an envelope and deposited with a trust company to be held indefinitely, not to be opened, and not to be withdrawn. That will prevent any of the parties from withdrawing them, but if you should ever

be arrested the district attorney, or the grand jury could, of course, subpoena the manager of the trust company and see what is in the envelope. The idea of these statements is not to give you immunity from prosecution, but to show you that Miss Hare is as deep in the mud as you are in the mire. She can't afford to have you arrested or to even let you get caught. Of course, if you *should* get arrested on some other matter we're relying on you to play the game. You've never been a squealer, and I feel my clients can trust you."

I nodded casually. It was plain he was merely speaking a part. His plan had already been worked out.

"I have one suggestion," I said.

He inclined his head. "Name it."

"That you call in a notary public and have them acknowledge the confessions."

The lawyer looked at his client. He was a beady-eyed, sallow-faced rat of a man. His great nose seemed to have drawn his entire face to a point, and his mouth and eyes were pinched accordingly. Also his lip had a tendency to draw back and show discolored, long teeth, protruding in front. He was like a rat, a hungry, cunning rat.

The cat-woman placed her ivory cigarette holder to her vivid lips, inhaled a great drag and then expelled two streams of white smoke from her dilated nostrils. She nodded at the lawyer, and, as she nodded, there was a hard gleam about her eyes.

"Very well," was all she said, but the purring note had gone from her voice.

Atmore wiped the back of his hand across his perspiring forehead, called in a notary, and, on the strength of his introduction, had the two documents acknowledged. Then he slipped them in one of the envelopes, wrote "Perpetual Escrow" on the back, signed it, daubed sealing wax all over the flap and motioned to me.

"You can come with me, Jenkins, and see that I put this in the Trust Company downstairs."

I arose, accompanied the lawyer to the elevator and was whisked down to the office of the Trust

Company. We said not a word on the trip. The lawyer walked to the desk of the vice-president, handed him the envelope, and told him what he wanted.

"Keep this envelope as a perpetual escrow. It can be opened by no living party except with an order of court. After ten years you may destroy it. Give this gentleman and myself a duplicate receipt."

The vice-president looked dubiously at the envelope, weighed it in his hand, sighed, and placed his signature on the envelope, gave it a number with a numbering machine, dictated a duplicate receipt, which he also signed, and took the envelope to the vaults.

"That should satisfy you," said Atmore, his beady eyes darting over me, the perspiration breaking out on his forehead. "That is all fair and above board."

I nodded and started toward the door. I could see the relief peeping in the rat-like eyes of the lawyer.

At the door I stopped, turned, and clutched the lawyer by the arm. "Atmore, do you know what happens to people who try to double-cross me?"

He was seized with a fit of trembling, and he impatiently tried to break away.

"You have a reputation for being a square shooter, Jenkins, and for always getting the man who tries to double-cross you."

I nodded.

There in the marble lobby of that trust company, with people all around us, with a special officer walking slowly back and forth, I handed it to this little shyster.

"All right. You've just tried to double-cross me. If you value your life hand me that envelope."

He shivered again.

"W-w-w-what envelope?"

I gave him no answer, just kept my eyes boring into his, kept his trembling arm in my iron clutch, and kept my face thrust close to his.

He weakened fast. I could see his sallow skin whiten.

"Jenkins, I'm sorry. I told her we couldn't get away with it. It was her idea, not mine."

I still said nothing, but kept my eyes on his.

He reached in his pocket and took out the other envelope. My guess had been right. I knew his type. The rat-like cunning of the idea had unquestionably been his, but he didn't have the necessary nerve to bluff it through. He had prepared two envelopes. One of them had been signed and sealed before my eyes, but in signing and sealing it he had followed the mental pattern of another envelope which had already been signed and sealed and left in his pocket, an envelope which contained nothing but blank sheets of paper. When he put the envelope with the signed confession into his coat pocket he had placed it back of the dummy envelope. The dummy envelope he had withdrawn and deposited in his "perpetual escrow."

I took the envelope from him, broke the seals, and examined the documents. They were intact, the signed, acknowledged confessions.

I turned back to the shyster.

"Listen, Atmore. There is a big fee in this for you, a fee from the woman, perhaps from someone else. Go back and tell them that you have blundered, that I have obtained possession of the papers and they will expose you, fire you for a blunderer, make you the laughing stock of every criminal rendezvous in the city. If you keep quiet about this no one will ever know the difference. Speak and you ruin your reputation."

I could see a look of relief flood his face, and I knew he would lie to the cat-woman about those papers.

"Tell Miss Hare I'll be at the house at nine forty-five on the dot," I said. "There's no need of my seeing her again until then."

With that I climbed into my roadster, drove to the beach and looked over the house the cat-woman had selected for me. She had given me the address as well as the key at our evening interview, just before I said good night. Of course, she expected me to look the place over.

It was a small bungalow, the garage opening on to the sidewalk beneath the first floor. I didn't go in. Inquiry at a gasoline station showed that the neighbors believed Compton was a traveling salesman, away on a trip, but due to return. The blonde had established herself in the community. So much I found out, and so much the cat-woman had expected me to find out.

Then I started on a line she hadn't anticipated.

First I rented a furnished apartment, taking the precaution first to slip on a disguise which had always worked well with me, a disguise which made me appear twenty years older.

Second, I went to the county clerk's office, looked over the register of actions, and found a dozen in which the oil magnate had been a party. There were damage suits, quiet title actions, actions on oil leases, and on options. In all of these actions he had been represented by Morton, Huntley & Morton. I got the address of the lawyers from the records, put up a good stall with their telephone girl, and found myself closeted with old H. F. Morton, senior member of the firm.

He was a shabby, grizzled, gray-eyed old campaigner and he had a habit of drumming his fingers on the desk in front of him.

"What was it you wanted, Mr. Jenkins?"

I'd removed my disguise and given him my right name. He may or may not have known my original record. He didn't mention it.

I shot it to him right between the eyes.

"If I were the lawyer representing Arthur C. Holton I wouldn't let him marry Miss Hattie Hare."

He never batted an eyelash. His face was as calm as a baby's. His eyes didn't even narrow, but there came a change in the tempo of his drumming on the desk.

"Why?" he asked.

His tone was mild, casual, but his fingers were going rummy-tum-tum; rummy-tum-tum; rummy-tum-tummy-tum tummy-tum tum.

I shook my head. "I can't tell you all of it, but she's in touch with a shyster lawyer planning to cause trouble of some kind."

"Ah, yes. Mr.-er-Jenkins. You are a friend of Mr. Holton?"

I nodded. "He doesn't know it though."

"Ah, yes," rummy-tum-tum; rummy-tum-tum; "what is it I can do for you in the matter?"

"Help me prevent the marriage."

Rummy-tum-tum; rummy-tum-tum.

"How?"

"Give me a little information as a starter. Mr. Holton has a great deal of property?"

At this his eyes did narrow. The drumming stopped.

"This is a law office. Not an information bureau."

I shrugged my shoulders. "Miss Hare will have her own personal attorney. If the marriage should go through and anything should happen to Mr. Holton another attorney would be in charge of the estate."

He squirmed at that, and then recommenced his drumming.

"Nevertheless, I cannot divulge the confidential affairs of my client. This much is common knowledge. It is street talk, information available to anyone who will take the trouble to look for it. Mr. Holton is a man of great wealth. He owns much property, controls oil producing fields, business property, stocks, bonds. He was married and lost his wife when his child was born. The child was a boy and lived but a few minutes. Mr. Holton created a trust for that child, a trust which terminated with the premature death of the infant. Miss Hare has been connected with him as his secretary and general household executive for several years. Mr. Holton is a man of many enemies, strong character and few friends. He is hated by the working class, and is hated unjustly, yet he cares nothing for public opinion. He is noted as a collector of jewels and paintings. Of late he has been influenced in many respects by Miss Hare, and has grown very fond of her.

"How do you propose to prevent his marriage, and what do you know of Miss Hare?"

I shook my head.

"I won't tell you a thing unless you promise to give me all the information I want, and keep me posted."

His face darkened. "Such a proposition is

unthinkable. It is an insult to a reputable attorney."

I knew it, but I made the stall to keep him from finding out that I had all the information I wanted. I only wanted a general slant on Holton's affairs, and, most of all, I wanted a chance to size up his attorney, to get acquainted with him so he would know me later.

"Stick an ad in the personal columns of the morning papers if you want to see me about anything," I said as I made for the door.

He watched me meditatively. Until I had left the long, book-lined corridor, and emerged from the expensive suite of offices, I could still hear his fingers on the desk.

Rummy-tum-tum; rummy-tum-tum; rummy-tum-tummy-tum-tummy-tum-tum.

I went to a hotel, got a room and went to sleep. I was finished with my regular apartment. That was for the police.

At nine-forty-five I sneaked into the back door of Holton's house, found one of the extra servants waiting for me, and was shown into a closet near the room where the banquet was taking place. The servant was a crook, but one I couldn't place. I filed his map away for future reference, and he filed mine.

Ten minutes passed. I heard something that might or might not have been a muffled scream, shuffling footsteps going down the hall. Silence, the ringing of a bell.

I stepped to the door of the banquet room, and flung it wide. Standing there on the threshold I took in the scene of hectic gaiety. Holton and the cat-woman sat at the head of the table. Couples in various stages of intoxication were sprinkled about. Servants stood here and there, obsequious, attentive. A man sat slightly apart, a man who had his eyes riveted on the door of an ante-room. He was the detective from the insurance company.

For a minute I stood there, undiscovered.

The room was a clatter of conversation. The detective half arose, his eyes on the door of the ante-room. Holton saw me, stopped in the middle of a sentence, and looked me over.

"Who are you, and what do you want?"

I handed it out in bunches. "I'm Ed Jenkins, the phantom crook. I've got a part of what I want. I'll come back later for the rest."

The detective reached for his hip, and I slammed the door and raced down the corridor. Taking the front steps in a flying leap I jumped into the seat of the powerful speedster, noticed the roomy luggage compartment, the running engine, the low, speedy lines, slammed in the gear, slipped in the clutch, and skidded out of the drive as the detective started firing from the window.

I didn't go direct to the beach house.

On a dark side-road I stopped the car, went back and opened up the luggage compartment and pulled out the bound and gagged girl. She was one I had never seen before, and she was mad. And she was the real Jean Ellery or else I was dumb.

I packed her around, parked her on the running board, took a seat beside her, left on the gag and the cords, and began to talk. Patiently, step by step, I went over the history of the whole case, telling her everything. When I had finished I cut the cords and removed the gag.

"Now either beat it, go ahead and scream, or ask questions, whichever you want," I told her.

She gave a deep breath, licked her lips, wiped her face with a corner of her party gown, woefully inspected a runner in the expensive stockings, looked at the marks on her wrists where the ropes had bitten, smoothed out her garments and turned to me.

"I think you're a liar," she remarked casually.

I grinned.

That's the way I like 'em. Here this jane had been grabbed, kidnapped, manhandled, jolted, forced to sit on the running board of a car and listen to her kidnapper talk a lot of stuff she naturally wouldn't believe, and then was given her freedom. Most girls would have fainted. Nearly all of 'em would have screamed and ran when they got loose. Here was a jane who was as cool as a cucumber, who looked over the damage to her clothes, and then called me a liar.

She was a thin slip of a thing, twenty or so, big, hazel eyes, chestnut hair, slender figure, rosebud mouth, bobbed hair and as unattainable as a girl on a magazine cover.

"Read this," I said, and slipped her the confession of the cat-woman.

She read it in the light of the dash lamp, puckered her forehead a bit, and then handed it back.

"So you are Ed Jenkins— Why should auntie have wanted me kidnapped?"

I shrugged my shoulders. "That's what I want to know. It's the one point in the case that isn't clear. Want to stick around while I find out?"

She thought things over for a minute.

"Am I free to go?"

I nodded.

"Guess I'll stick around then," she said as she climbed back into the car, snuggling down next to the driver's seat. "Let's go."

I got in, started the engine, and we went.

A block from the beach house I slowed up.

"The house is ahead. Slip out as we go by this palm tree, hide in the shadows and watch what happens. I have an idea you'll see some action."

I slowed down and turned my face toward her, prepared to argue the thing out, but there was no need for argument. She was gathering her skirts about her. As I slowed down she jumped. I drove on to the house, swung the car so it faced the door of the garage and got out.

I had to walk in front of the headlights to fit the key to the door of the garage, and I was a bit nervous. There was an angle of this thing I couldn't get, and it worried me. I thought something was due to happen. If there hadn't been so much money involved I'd have skipped out. As it was, I was playing my cards trying to find out what was in the hand of the cat-woman.

I found out.

As though the swinging of the garage door had been a signal, two men jumped out from behind a rosebush and began firing at the luggage compartment of the car.

They had shotguns, repeaters, and they were shooting chilled buckshot at deadly range through the back of that car. Five times they shot, and then they vanished, running like mad.

Windows began to gleam with lights, a woman screamed, a man stuck his head out into the night. Around the corner there came the whine of a starting motor, the purr of an automobile engine, the staccato barks of an exhaust and an automobile whined off into the night.

I backed the speedster, turned it and went back down the street. At the palm tree where I'd left the flapper I slowed down, doubtfully, hardly expecting to see her again.

There was a flutter of white, a flash of slim legs, and there she was sitting on the seat beside me, her eyes wide, lips parted. "Did you get hurt?"

I shook my head and jerked my thumb back in the direction of the luggage compartment.

"Remember, I wasn't to stop or open that compartment until I got to the beach house," I said.

She looked back. The metal was riddled with holes, parts of the body had even been ripped into great, jagged tears.

"Your beloved auntie didn't want you kidnapped. She wanted you murdered. Right now she figures that you're dead, that I am gazing in shocked surprise at the dead body of a girl I've kidnapped, the police on my trail, the neighborhood aroused. Naturally she thinks I'll have my hands full for a while, and that she won't be bothered with me any more, either with me or with you."

The girl nodded.

"I didn't say so before, but I've been afraid of Aunt Hattie for a long time. It's an awful thing to say about one's own aunt, but she's absolutely selfish, selfish and unscrupulous."

I drove along in silence for a while.

"What are you going to do?" asked the kid.

"Ditch this car, get off the street, hide out for a few days, and find out what it's all about. Your aunt tried to double-cross me on a deal where there's something or other at stake. I intend to find out what. She and I will have our accounting later."

She nodded, her chin on her fist, thinking.

"What are *you* going to do?"

She shrugged her shoulders. "Heaven knows.

If I go back I'll probably be killed. Having gone this far, Aunt Hattie can't afford to fail. She'll have me killed if I show up. I guess I'll have to hide out, too."

"Hotel?" I asked.

I could feel her eyes on my face, sizing me up, watching me like a hawk.

"I can't get a room in a hotel at this hour of the night in a party dress."

I nodded.

"Ed Jenkins, are you a gentleman?"

I shook my head. "Hell's fire, no. I'm a crook."

She looked at me and grinned. I could feel my mouth soften a bit.

"Ed, this is no time to stand on formalities. You know as well as I do that I'm in danger. My aunt believes me dead. If I can keep under cover, leaving her under that impression, I'll stand a chance. I can't hide out by myself. Either my aunt or the police would locate me in no time. You're an experienced crook, you know all the dodges, and I think I can trust you. I'm coming with you."

I turned the wheel of the car.

"All right," I said. "It's your best move, but I wanted you to suggest it. Take off those paste diamonds and leave 'em in the car. I've got to get rid of this car first, and then we'll go to my hide-out."

An hour later I showed her into the apartment. I had run the car off the end of a pier. The watchman was asleep and the car had gurgled down into deep water as neatly as a duck. The watchman had heard the splash, but that's all the good it did him.

The girl looked around the place.

"Neat and cozy," she said. "I'm trusting you, Ed Jenkins. Good night."

I grinned.

"Good night," I said.

I slept late the next morning. I was tired. It was the girl who called me.

"Breakfast's ready," she said.

I sat up in bed and rubbed my eyes.

"Breakfast?"

She grinned.

"Yep. I slipped down to the store, bought some fruit and things, and brought you the morning papers."

I laughed outright. Here I had kidnapped a girl and now she was cooking me breakfast. She laughed, too.

"You see, I'm about broke, and I can't go around in a party dress. I've got to touch you for enough money to buy some clothes, and it's always easier to get money out of a man when he's well-fed. Aunt Hattie told me that."

"You've got to be careful about showing yourself, too," I warned her. "Some one is likely to recognize you."

She nodded and handed me the morning paper.

All over the front page were smeared our pictures, hers and mine. Holton had offered a reward of twenty thousand dollars for my arrest. The insurance company had added another five.

Without that, I knew the police would be hot on the trail. Their reputation was at stake. They'd leave no stone unturned. Having the girl with me was my best bet. They'd be looking for me alone, or with a girl who was being held a prisoner. They'd hardly expect to find me in a downtown apartment with a girl cooking me breakfast.

I handed Jean a five-hundred-dollar bill.

"Go get yourself some clothes. Get quiet ones, but ones that are in style. I'm disguising myself as your father. You look young and chic, wear 'em short, and paint up a bit. Don't wait, but get started as soon as we eat."

She dropped a curtsey.

"You're so good to me, Ed," she said, but there was a wistful note in her voice, and she blinked her eyes rapidly. "Don't think I don't appreciate it, either," she added. "You don't have to put up with me, and you're being a real gentleman. . . ."

That was that.

I was a little nervous until the girl got back from her shopping. I was afraid some one would spot her. She bought a suit and changed into that right at the jump, then got the rest of her things. She put in the day with needle and thread, and I did some thinking, also I coached the girl as to her part. By late afternoon we were able to buy an automobile without having anything suggest that I was other than an elderly, fond parent and the girl a helter-skelter flapper.

"Tonight you get educated as a crook," I told her.

"Jake with me, Ed," she replied, flashing me a smile. Whatever her thoughts may have been she seemed to have determined to be a good sport, a regular pal, and never let me see her as other than cheerful.

We slid our new car around where we could watch Big Bill Ryan's place. He ran a little cafe where crooks frequently hung out, and he couldn't take a chance on my having a spotter in the place. One thing was certain. If he was really behind the play he intended to have me caught and executed for murder. He knew me too well to think he could play button, button, who's got the button with me and get away with it.

We waited until eleven, parked in the car I'd purchased, watching the door of the cafe and Big Ryan's car. It was crude but effective. Ryan and the cat-woman both thought I had been left with the murdered body of Jean Ellery in my car, a car which had to be got rid of, a body which had to be concealed, and with all the police in the state on my track. They hardly expected I'd put in the evening watching Big Ryan with the kid leaning on my shoulder.

At eleven Ryan started out, and his face was all smiles. He tried to avoid being followed, but the car I'd purchased had all sorts of speed, and I had no trouble in the traffic. After that I turned out the lights and tailed him into West Forty-ninth Street. I got the number of the house as he stopped, flashed past once to size it up and then kept moving.

"Here's where you get a real thrill," I told the girl as I headed the car back toward town. "I've a hunch Harry Atmore's mixed up in this thing as a sort of cat's-paw all around, and I want to see what's in his office."

We stopped a block away from Atmore's office building. I was a fatherly-looking old bird with mutton chop whiskers and a cane.

"Ever done any burglarizing?" I asked as I clumped my way along the sidewalk.

She shook her head.

"Here's where you begin," I said, piloted her into the office building, avoided the elevator, and began the long, tedious climb.

Atmore's lock was simple, any door lock is, for that matter. I had expected I'd have to go take a look through the files. It wasn't necessary. From the odor of cigar smoke in the office there'd been a late conference there. I almost fancied I could smell the incense-like perfume of the cat-woman and the aroma of her cigarettes. Tobacco smoke is peculiar. I can tell just about how fresh it is when I smell a room that's strong with it. This was a fresh odor. On the desk was a proof of loss of the necklace, and a memo to call a certain number. I looked up the number in the telephone book. It was the number of the insurance company. That's how I found it, simply looked up the insurance companies in the classified list and ran down the numbers.

The insurance money would be paid in the morning.

That house on West Forty-ninth Street was mixed up in the thing somehow. It was a new lead, and I drove the kid back to the apartment and turned in. The situation wasn't ripe as yet.

Next morning I heard her stirring around, getting breakfast. Of course it simplified matters to eat in the apartment; but if the girl was going to work on the case with me she shouldn't do all the housework. I started to tell her so, rolled over, and grabbed another sleep. It was delicious lying there, stretching out in the warm bed, and hearing the cheery rattle of plates, knives and forks, cups and spoons. I had been a lone wolf so long, an outcast of society, that I thrilled with a delicious sense of intimacy at the idea of having Jean Ellery puttering around in my kitchen. Almost I felt like the father I posed as.

I got up, bathed, shaved, put on my disguise and walked out into the kitchen. The girl was gone. My breakfast was on the table, fruit, cream, toast in the toaster, coffee in the percolator, all ready to press a button and eat. The morning paper was even propped up by my plate.

I switched on the electricity; and wondered about the girl. Anxiously I listened for her step in the apartment. She was company, and I liked her. The kid didn't say much, but she had a sense of humor, a ready dimple, a twinkle in her eyes, and was mighty easy to look at.

She came in as I was finishing my coffee.

"Hello, Ed. I'm the early bird this morning, and I've caught the worm. That house out on Forty-ninth Street is occupied by old Doctor Drake. He's an old fellow who used to be in San Francisco, had a breakdown, retired, came here, lost his money, was poor as could be until three months ago, and then he suddenly blossomed out with ready money. He's retiring, crabbed, irascible, keeps to himself, has no practice and few visitors."

I looked her over, a little five-foot-three flapper, slim, active, graceful, but looking as though she had nothing under her chic hat except a hair bob.

"How did you know I wanted to find out about that bird; and how did you get the information?"

She ignored the first question, just passed it off with a wave of the hand.

"The information was easy. I grabbed some packages of face powder, went out in the neighborhood and posed as a demonstrator representing the factory, giving away free samples, and lecturing on the care of the complexion. I even know the neighborhood gossip, all the scandals, and the love affairs of everyone in the block. Give me some of that coffee, Ed. It smells good."

I grinned proudly at her. The kid was there. It would have been a hard job for me to get that information. She used her noodle. A doctor, eh? Big Ryan had gone to see him when he knew he would have the insurance money. The aunt wanted the girl killed. The engagement had been announced. Then there was the matter of my jade-handled dagger. Those things all began to mill around in my mind. They didn't fit together

exactly, but they all pointed in one direction, and that direction made my eyes open a bit wider and my forehead pucker. The game was drawing to the point where I would get into action and see what could be done along the line of checkmating the cat-woman.

A thought flashed through my mind. "Say, Jean, it's going to be a bit tough on you when it comes time to go back. What'll you tell people, that you were kidnapped and held in a cave or some place? And they'll have the police checking up on your story, you know?"

She laughed a bit and then her mouth tightened. "If you had been one of the soft-boiled kind that figured you should have married me or some such nonsense I wouldn't have stayed. It was only because you took me in on terms of equality that I remained. You take care of your problems and I'll take care of mine; and we'll both have plenty."

"That being the case, Jean," I told her, "I'm going to stage a robbery and a burglary tonight. Are you coming?"

She grinned at me.

"Miss Jean Ellery announces that it gives her pleasure to accept the invitation of Ed Jenkins to a holdup and burglary. When do we start?"

I shrugged my shoulders. "Some time after eight or nine. It depends. In the meantime we get some sleep. It's going to be a big night."

With that I devoted my attention to the paper. After all, the kid was right. I could mind my own business and she could mind hers. She knew what she was doing. Hang it, though, it felt nice to have a little home to settle back in, one where I could read the papers while the girl cleaned off the table, humming a little song the while. All the company I'd ever had before had been a dog, and he was in the hospital recovering from the effects of our last adventure. I was getting old, getting to the point where I wanted company, someone to talk to, to be with.

I shrugged my shoulders and got interested in what I was reading. The police were being panned right. My reputation of being a phantom crook was being rubbed in. Apparently I could disappear, taking an attractive girl and a valuable necklace with me, and the police were absolutely powerless.

Along about dark I parked my car out near Forty-ninth Street. I hadn't much that was definite to go on, but I was playing a pretty good hunch. I knew Big Ryan's car, and I knew the route he took in going to the house of Dr. Drake. I figured he'd got the insurance money some time during the day. Also I doped it out that the trips to the house of Dr. Drake were made after dark. It was pretty slim evidence to work out a plan of campaign on, but, on the other hand, I had nothing to lose.

We waited there two hours before we got action, and then it came, right according to schedule. Big Bill Ryan's car came under the street light, slowed for a bad break that was in the gutter at that point, and then Big Ryan bent forward to shift gears as he pulled out of the hole. It was a bad spot in the road and Bill knew it was there. He'd driven over it just the same way the night I'd followed him.

When he straightened up from the gearshift he was looking down the business end of a wicked pistol. I don't ordinarily carry 'em, preferring to use my wits instead, but this job I wanted to look like the job of somebody else anyway, and the pistol came in handy.

Of course, I was wearing a mask.

There wasn't any need for argument. The gun was there. Big Bill Ryan's fat face was there, and there wasn't three inches between 'em. Big Bill kicked out the clutch and jammed on the brake.

There was a puzzled look on his face as he peered at me. The big fence knew every crook in the game, and he probably wondered who had the nerve to pull the job. It just occurred to me that he looked too much interested and not enough scared, when I saw what I'd walked into. Big Bill had the car stopped dead before he sprung his trap. That was so I couldn't drop off into the darkness. He wanted me.

The back of the car, which had been in shadow, seemed to move, to become alive. From beneath a robe which had been thrown over the seat and floor there appeared a couple of arms,

the glint of the street light on metal arrested my eye; and it was too late to do anything, even if I could have gotten away with it.

There were two gunmen concealed in the back of that car. Big Bill Ryan ostensibly was driving alone. As a matter of fact he had a choice of body-guard. Those two guns were the best shots in crookdom, and they obeyed orders.

Big Bill spoke pleasantly.

"I hadn't exactly expected this, Jenkins, but I was prepared for it. You see I credit you with a lot of brains. How you found out about the case, and how you learned enough to intercept me on this little trip is more than I know. However, I've always figured you were the most dangerous man in the world, and I didn't take any chances.

"You're a smart man, Jenkins; but you're running up against a stone wall. I'm glad this happened when there was a reward out for you in California. It'll be very pleasant to surrender you to the police, thereby cementing my pleasant relations and also getting a cut out of the reward money. Come, come, get in and sit down. Grab his arms, boys."

Revolvers were thrust under my nose. Grinning faces leered at me. Grimy hands stretched forth and grabbed my shoulders. The car lurched forward and sped away into the night, headed toward the police station. In such manner had Ed Jenkins been captured by a small-time crook and a couple of guns. I could feel myself blush with shame. What was more, there didn't seem to be any way out of it. The guns were awaiting orders, holding fast to me, pulling me over the door. Ryan was speeding up. If I could break away I'd be shot before I could get off of the car, dead before my feet hit ground. If I stayed where I was I'd be in the police station in ten minutes, in a cell in eleven, and five minutes later the reporters would be interviewing me, and the papers would be grinding out extras.

It's the simple things that are hard to beat. This thing was so blamed simple, so childish almost, and yet, there I was.

We flashed past an intersection, swung to avoid the lights of another car that skidded around the corner with screeching tires, and then we seemed to be rocking back and forth, whizzing through the air. It was as pretty a piece of driving as I have ever seen. Jean Ellery had come around the paved corner at full speed, skidding, slipping, right on the tail of the other machine, had swung in sideways, hit the rear bumper and forced Ryan's car around and over, into the curb, and then she had sped on her way, uninjured. Ryan's car had crumpled a front wheel against the curb, and we were all sailing through the air.

Personally, I lit on my feet and kept going. I don't think anyone was hurt much, although Ryan seemed to make a nosedive through the windshield, and the two guns slammed forward against the back of the front seat and then pitched out. Being on the running board, I had just taken a little loop-the-loop through the atmosphere, gone into a tail spin, and pancaked to the earth.

The kid was there a million. If she had come up behind on a straight stretch there would have been lots of action. Ryan would have spotted her, and the guns would have gone into action. She'd either have been captured with me, or we'd both have been shot. By slamming into us from around a corner, however, she'd played her cards perfectly. It had been damned clever driving. What was more it had been clever headwork. She'd seen what had happened when I stuck the gun into Ryan's face, had started my car, doubled around the block, figured our speed to a nicety, and slammed down the cross street in the nick of time.

These things I thought over as I sprinted around a house, through a backyard, into an alley, and into another backyard. The kid had gone sailing off down the street, and I had a pretty strong hunch she had headed for the apartment. She'd done her stuff, and the rest was up to me.

Hang it! My disguise was in my car, and here I was, out in the night, my face covered by a mask, a gun in my pocket, and a reward out for me, with every cop in town scanning every face that passed him on the street. Oh well, it was all in a lifetime and I had work to do. I'd

liked to have handled Bill Ryan; seeing I couldn't get him, I had to play the next best bet, Dr. Drake.

His house wasn't far, and I made it in quick time. I was working against time.

I took off my mask, walked boldly up the front steps and rang the doorbell.

There was the sound of shuffling feet, and then a seamed, sallow face peered out at me. The door opened a bit, and two glittering, beady eyes bored into mine.

"What d'yuh want?"

I figured him for Doctor Drake. He was pretty well along in years, and his eyes and forehead showed some indications of education. There was a glittering cupidity about the face, a cunning selfishness that seemed to be the keynote of his character.

"I'm bringing the money."

His head thrust a trifle farther forward and his eyes bored into mine.

"What money?"

"From Bill Ryan."

"But Mr. Ryan said he would be here himself."

I shrugged my shoulders.

I had made my play and the more I kept silent the better it would be. I knew virtually nothing about this end of the game. He knew everything. It would be better for me to let him convince himself than to rush in and ruin it trying to talk too much of detail.

At length the door came cautiously open.

"Come in."

He led the way into a sort of office. The furniture was apparently left over from some office or other, and it was good stuff, massive mahogany, dark with years; old-fashioned bookcases; chairs that were almost antiques; obsolete text books, all of the what-nots that were the odds and ends of an old physician's office.

Over all lay a coating of gritty dust.

"Be seated," said the old man, shuffling across to the swivel chair before the desk. I could see that he was breaking fast, this old man. His forehead and eyes retained much of strength, indicated some vitality. His mouth was sagging, weak. Below his neck he seemed to have decayed, the loose, flabby muscles seemed incapable of functioning. His feet could hardly be lifted from the floor. His shoulders lurched forward, and his spine curved into a great hump. Dandruff sprinkled over his coat, an affair that had once been blue serge and which was now spotted with egg, grease, syrup and stains.

"Where is the money?"

I smiled wisely, reached into an inner pocket, half pulled out a wallet, then leered at him after the fashion of a cheap crook, one of the smart-aleck, cunning kind.

"Let's see the stuff first."

He hesitated, then heaved out of his chair and approached a bookcase. Before the door he suddenly stiffened with suspicion. He turned, his feverish eyes glittering wildly in the feeble light of the small incandescent with which the room was redly illuminated.

"Spread out the money on the table."

I laughed.

"Say, bo, the coin's here, all right; but if you want to see the long green you gotta produce."

He hesitated a bit, and then the telephone rang, a jangling, imperative clamor. He shuffled back to the desk, picked up the receiver in a gnarled, knotty hand, swept back the unkempt hair which hung over his ear, and listened.

As he listened I could see the back straighten, the shoulders straighten. A hand came stealing up the inside of the coat.

Because I knew what to expect I wasn't surprised. He bent forward, muttered something, hung up the receiver, spun about and thrust forward an ugly pistol, straight at the chair in which I had been sitting. If ever there was desperation and murder stamped on a criminal face it was on his.

The only thing that was wrong with his plans was that I had silently shifted my position. When he swung that gun around he pointed it where I had been, but wasn't. The next minute I had his neck in a stranglehold, had the gun, and had him all laid out for trussing. Linen bandage was available, and it always makes a nice rope for tying people up with. I gagged him on general

principles and then I began to go through that bookcase.

In a book on interior medicine that was written when appendicitis was classified as fatal inflammation of the intestines, I found a document, yellow with age. It was dated in 1904 but it had evidently been in the sunlight some, and had seen much had usage. The ink was slightly faded, and there were marks of old folds, dog-eared corners, little tears. Apparently the paper had batted around in a drawer for a while, had perhaps been rescued at one time or another from a wastebasket, and, on the whole, it was genuine as far as date was concerned. It couldn't have had all that hard usage in less than twenty-two years.

There was no time then to stop and look at it. I took out my wallet, dropped it in there, and then went back to the bookcase, turning the books upside down, shaking them, fluttering the leaves, wondering if there was something else.

I was working against time and knew it. Big Bill Ryan wouldn't dare notify the police. He wouldn't want to have me arrested at the home of Doctor Drake; but he would lose no time in getting the house surrounded by a bunch of gunmen of his own choosing, of capturing me as I sought to escape the house, and then taking me to police headquarters.

It was a matter of seconds. I could read that paper any time; but I could only go through that bookcase when I was there, and it looked as though I wouldn't be in that house again, not for some time. At that I didn't have time to complete the search. I hadn't covered more than half of the books when I heard running steps on the walk, and feet came pounding up the steps.

As a crook my cue was to make for the back door, to plunge out into the night, intent on escape. That would run me into the guns of a picked reception committee that was waiting in the rear. I knew Big Ryan, knew that the hurrying impatience of those steps on the front porch was merely a trap. I was in a house that was surrounded. The automobile with engine running out in front was all a part of the stall. Ryan had probably stopped his machine half a block away, let out his men, given them a chance to surround the house, and then he had driven up, stopped the car with the engine running and dashed up the steps. If Dr. Drake had me covered all right; if I had managed to overpower the old man, I would break and run for the rear.

All of these things flashed through my mind in an instant. I was in my element again. Standing there before the rifled bookcase, in imminent danger, I was as cool as a cake of ice, and I didn't waste a second.

The door of the bookcase I slammed shut. The books were in order on the shelves. As for myself, I did the unexpected. It is the only safe rule.

Instead of sneaking out the back door, I reached the front door in one jump, threw it open and plunged my fist in the bruised, bleeding countenance of Big Bill Ryan. That automobile windshield hadn't used him too kindly, and he was badly shaken. My maneuver took him by surprise. For a split fraction of a second I saw him standing like a statue. The next instant my fist had crashed home.

From the side of the house a revolver spat. There was a shout, a running of dark figures, and I was off. Leaping into the driver's seat of the empty automobile, I had slammed in the gears, shot the clutch, stepped on the throttle and was away.

I chuckled as I heard the chorus of excited shouts behind, the futile rattle of pistol shots. There would be some explaining for Big Bill Ryan to do. In the meantime I was headed for the apartment. I was going to decorate Jean Ellery with a medal, a medal for being the best assistant a crook ever had.

I left the car a couple of blocks from the apartment and walked rapidly down the street. I didn't want the police to locate the stolen car too near my apartment, and yet I didn't dare to go too far without my disguise. The walk of two blocks to my apartment was risky.

My own machine, the one in which Jean had made the rescue, was parked outside. I looked it over with a grin. She was some driver. The front bumper and license plate had been torn off, and the paint on the radiator was scratched a bit, but that was all.

I worried a bit about that license number. I'd bought that car as the old man with the flapper daughter, and I had it registered in the name I had taken, the address as the apartment where Jean and I lived. Losing that license number was something to worry about.

I made record time getting to the door of the apartment, fitting the latchkey and stepping inside. The place was dark, and I pressed the light switch, then jumped back, ready for anything. The room was empty. On the floor was a torn article of clothing. A shoe was laying on its side over near the other door. A rug was rumpled, a chair overturned. In the other room there was confusion. A waist had been ripped to ribbons and was lying by another shoe. The waist was one that Jean had been wearing. The shoes were hers.

I took a quick glance around, making sure the apartment was empty, and then I got into action. Foot by foot I covered that floor looking for something that would be a clue, some little thing that would tell me of the persons who had done the job. Big Bill had acted mighty quick if he had been the one. If it had been the police, why the struggle? If it was a trap, why didn't they spring it?

There was no clue. Whoever it was had been careful to leave nothing behind. I had only a limited amount of time, and I knew it. Once more I was working against time, beset by adverse circumstances, fighting overwhelming odds.

I made a run for the elevator, got to the ground floor, rushed across the street, into the little car Jean had driven, and, as I stepped on the starter and switched on the lights, there came the wail of a siren, the bark of an exhaust, and a police car came skidding around the corner and slid to a stop before the apartment house.

As for me, I was on my way.

Mentally I ran over the characters in the drama that had been played about me, and I picked on Harry Atmore. The little, weak, clever attorney with his cunning dodges, his rat-like mind, his cowering spirit was my meat. He was the weak point in the defense, the weak link in the chain.

I stopped at a telephone booth in a drug store. A plastered-haired sheik was at the telephone fixing up a couple of heavy dates for a wild night. I had to wait while he handed out what was meant to be a wicked line. Finally he hung up the receiver and sauntered toward his car, smirking his self-satisfaction. I grabbed the instrument and placed the warm receiver to my ear.

Atmore wasn't at home. His wife said I'd find him at the office. I didn't call the office. It would suit me better to walk in unannounced if I could get him by himself. I climbed into my machine and was on my way.

I tried the door of Atmore's office and found it was open. There was a light in the reception room. Turning, I pulled the catch on the spring lock, slammed the door and turned out the light. Then I walked into the private office.

There must have been that on my face which showed that I was on a mission which boded no good to the crooked shyster, an intentness of purpose which was apparent. He gave me one look, and then shrivelled down in his chair, cowering, his rat-like nose twitching, his yellow teeth showing.

I folded my arms and glared at him.

"Where's the girl?"

He lowered his gaze and shrugged his shoulders.

I advanced. Right then I was in no mood to put up with evasions. Something seemed to tell me that the girl was in danger, that every second counted, and I had no time to waste on polite formalities. That girl had grown to mean something to me. She had fitted in, uncomplaining, happy, willing, and she had saved me when I had walked into a trap there with Big Bill Ryan. As long as I was able to help that girl she could count on me. There had never been very much said, but we understood each other, Jean Ellery and I. She had played the game with me, and I would play it with her.

"Atmore," I said, pausing impressively between the words, "I want to know where that girl is, and I mean to find out."

He ducked his hand, and I sprang, wrenched his shoulder, pulled him backward, crashed a chair to the floor, struck the gun up, kicked his wrist, smashed my fist in his face and sprawled him on the floor. He didn't get up. I was standing over him, and he crawled and cringed like a whipped cur.

"Miss Hare has her. Bill Ryan got her located through the number on a machine, and Hattie Hare went after her. She is a devil, that woman. She has the girl back at the Holton house."

I looked at his writhing face for a moment trying to determine if he was lying. I thought not. Big Ryan had undoubtedly traced that license number. That was but the work of a few minutes on the telephone with the proper party. He couldn't have gone after the girl himself because he had been at Dr. Drake's too soon afterward. On the other hand, he had gone to a public telephone because he had undoubtedly telephoned Dr. Drake and told him of his accident, probably warned him against me. From what the doctor had said, Ryan knew I was there, and he had dropped everything to come after me. What more natural than that he should have telephoned the cat-woman to go and get the girl.

I turned and strode toward the door.

"Listen, you rat," I snapped. "If you have lied to me, you'll die!"

His eyes rolled a bit, his mouth twitched, but he said nothing. I ran into the dark outer office, threw open the door, snapped the lock back on the entrance door, banged it and raced to the elevator. Then I turned and softly retraced my steps, slipped into the dark outer office, and tiptoed to the door of the private office. By opening it a crack I could see the lawyer huddled at his desk, frantically clicking the hook on the telephone.

In a minute he got central, snapped a number, waited and then gave his message in five words. "He's on his way out," he said, and hung up.

I only needed one guess. He was talking to the

cat-woman. They had prepared a trap, had baited it with the girl, and were waiting for me to walk into it.

I went back into the hall, slipped down the elevator, went to my car and stepped on the starter. As I went I thought. Time was precious. Long years of being on my own resources had taught me to speed up my thinking processes. For years I had been a lone wolf, had earned the name of being the phantom crook, one who could slip through the fingers of the police. Then there had been a welcome vacation while I enjoyed immunity in California, but now all that was past. I was my own man, back in the thick of things. I had accomplished everything I had done previously by thinking fast, reaching quick decisions, and putting those decisions into instant execution. This night I made up my mind I would walk into the trap and steal the bait; whether I could walk out again depended upon my abilities. I would be matching my wits against those of the cat-woman, and she was no mean antagonist. Witness the manner in which she had learned that the girl had not been murdered, that I had convinced the girl of the woman's duplicity, had taken her in as a partner, the manner in which the cat-woman had known she could reach me through the girl, that I would pick on Atmore as being the weak link in the chain.

I stopped at a drug store long enough to read the paper I had taken from the book at Dr. Drake's house, and to telephone. I wanted to know all the cards I held in my hand before I called for a showdown.

The document was a strange one. It was nothing more nor less than a consent that the doctor should take an unborn baby and do with it as he wished. It was signed by the expectant mother. Apparently it was merely one of thousands of such documents which find their way into the hands of doctors. Yet I was certain it represented an important link in a strong chain. Upon the back of the document were three signatures. One of them was the signature of Hattie M. Hare. There were addresses, too, also telephone numbers. Beneath the three signatures were the words "nurses and witnesses."

I consulted the directory, got the number of H. F. Morton, and got him out of bed.

"This is Mr. Holton," I husked into the telephone. "Come to my house at once."

With the words I banged the receiver against the telephone a couple of times and hung up. Then I sprinted into the street, climbed into the machine and was off.

I had no time to waste, and yet I was afraid the trap would be sprung before I could get the bait. It was late and a ring at the doorbell would have been a telltale sign. I parked the machine a block away, hit the backyards and approached the gloomy mass of shadows which marked the home of Arthur C. Holton, the oil magnate. I was in danger and knew it, knew also that the danger was becoming more imminent every minute.

I picked a pantry window. Some of the others looked more inviting, but I picked one which I would hardly have been expected to have chosen. There had already been a few minutes' delay. Seconds were precious. I knew the house well enough to take it almost at a run. When I have once been inside a place I can generally dope out the plan of the floors, and I always remember those plans.

In the front room there was just the flicker of a fire in the big fireplace. Above the tiles there glowed two spots of fire. I had been right in my surmise about the painting of the cat's head. The eyes had been tinted with luminous paint.

In the darkness there came a faint, dull, "click." It was a sound such as is made by a telephone bell when it gives merely the jump of an electrical contact, a sound which comes when a receiver has been removed from an extension line. With the sound I had out my flashlight and was searching for the telephone. If anyone was using an extension telephone in another part of the house I wanted to hear what was being said.

It took me a few seconds to locate the instrument, and then I slipped over to it and eased the receiver from the hook. It was the cat-woman who was talking:

"Yes, Arthur C. Holton's residence, and come right away. You know he threatened to return.

Yes, I know it's Ed Jenkins. I tell you I saw his face. Yes, the phantom crook. Send two cars and come at once."

There was a muttered assent from the cop at the other end of the line, and then the click of two receivers. Mine made a third.

So that was the game, was it? In some way she had known when I entered the place. I fully credited those luminous, cat-eyes of hers with being able to see in the dark. She had laid a trap for me, baited it with the girl, and now she had summoned the police. Oh well, I had been in worse difficulties before.

I took the carpeted stairway on the balls of my feet, taking the stairs two at a time. There was a long corridor above from which there opened numerous bedrooms. I saw a flutter of pink at one end of the hall, a mere flash of woman's draperies. I made for that point, and I went at top speed. If my surmise was correct I had no time to spare, not so much as the tick of a watch.

The door was closed and I flung it open, standing not upon ceremony or formalities. I was racing with death.

Within the room was a dull light, a reflected, diffused light which came from the corridor, around a corner, against the half-open door, and into the room. There was a bed and a white figure was stretched upon the bed, a figure which was struggling in the first panic of a sudden awakening. When I had flung the door open it had crashed against the wall, rebounded so that it was half closed, and then remained shivering on its hinges, catching and reflecting the light from the hall.

In that semi-darkness the cat-woman showed as a flutter of flowing silk. She moved with the darting quickness of a cat springing on its prey. She had turned her head as I crashed into the room, and her eyes, catching the light from the hall, glowed a pale, baleful green, a green of hate, of tigerish intensity of rage.

Quick as she was, I was quicker. As the light caught the flicker of cold steel I flung her to one side, slammed her against the wall. She was thin, lithe, supple, but the warm flesh of her which met my hands through the thin veil of sheer silk was

as hard as wire springs. She recoiled from the wall, poised lightly on her feet, gave me a flicker of the light from those cat-eyes once more, and then fluttered from the room, her silks flapping in the breeze of her progress. Two hands shot from the bed and grasped me by the shoulders, great, hairy hands with clutching fingers.

"Jenkins! Ed Jenkins!" exclaimed a voice.

I shook him off and raced for the door. From the street below came the sound of sliding tires, the noise of feet hurrying on cement, pounding on gravel. Someone dashed up the front steps and pounded on the door, rang frantically at the bell. The police had arrived, excited police who bungled the job of surrounding the house.

There was yet time. I had been in tighter pinches. I could take the back stairs, shoot from the back door and try the alley. There would probably be the flash of firearms, the whine of lead through the night air, but there would also be the element of surprise, the stupidity of the police, the flat-footed slowness of getting into action. I had experienced it all before.

In one leap I made the back stairs and started to rush down. The front door flew open and there came the shrill note of a police whistle. I gathered my muscles for the next flying leap, and then stopped, caught almost in midair.

I had thought of the girl!

Everything that had happened had fitted in with my theory of the case, and in that split fraction of a second I knew I was right. Some flash of inner intuition, some telepathic insight converted a working hypothesis, a bare theory, into an absolute certainty. In that instant I knew the motive of the cat-woman, knew the reason she had rushed from that other room. Jean Ellery had been used by her to bait the trap for Ed Jenkins, but she had had another use, had served another purpose. She was diabolically clever, that cat-woman, and Jean Ellery was to die.

I thought of the girl, of her charm, her ready acceptance of life as the working partner of a crook, and I paused in mid flight, turned a rapid flip almost in the air and was running madly down the corridor, toward the police.

There are times when the mind speeds up

and thoughts become flashes of instantaneous conceptions, when one lives ages in the space of seconds. All of the thoughts which had pieced together the real solution of the mystery, the explanation of the actions of the cat-woman had come to me while I was poised, balanced for a leap on the stairs. My decision to return had been automatic, instantaneous. I could not leave Jean Ellery in danger.

The door into which the cat-woman had plunged was slightly ajar. Through it could be seen the gleam of light, a flicker of motion. I was almost too late as I hurtled through that door, my outstretched arm sweeping the descending hand of the cat-woman to one side.

Upon the bed, bound, gagged, her helpless eyes staring into the infuriated face of the cat-woman, facing death with calm courage, watching the descent of the knife itself, was the form of Jean Ellery. My hand had caught the downthrust of the knife just in time.

The cat-woman staggered back, spitting vile oaths, lips curling, eyes flashing, her words sounding like the explosive spats of an angry cat. The knife had clattered to the floor and lay at my very feet. The green-handled dagger, the jade-hilted knife which had been taken from my apartment. At that instant a shadow blotted the light from the hallway and a voice shouted:

"Hands up, Ed Jenkins!"

The cat-woman gave an exclamation of relief.

"Thank God, officer, you came in the nick of time!"

There was the shuffling of many feet: peering faces, gleaming shields, glinting pistols, and I found myself grabbed by many hands, handcuffs snapped about my wrists, cold steel revolvers thrust against my neck. I was pushed, jostled, slammed, pulled, dragged down the stairs and into the library.

The cat-woman followed, cajoling the officers, commenting on their bravery, their efficiency, spitting epithets at me.

And then H. F. Morton walked into the open door, took in the situation with one glance of his steely eyes, deposited his hat and gloves on a chair, walked to the great table, took a seat behind it and peered over the tops of his glasses at the officers, at the cat-woman, at myself.

The policeman jostled me toward the open front door.

The lawyer held up a restraining hand.

"Just a minute," he said, and there was that in the booming authority of the voice which held the men, stopped them in mid-action.

"What is this?" he asked, and, with the words, dropped his hands to the table and began to drum regularly, rhythmically, "rummpy-tum-tum; rummpy-tum-tum; rummpy-tum-tumpty-tum-tumpty-tum-tum."

"Aw g'wan," muttered one of the officers as he pulled me forward.

"Shut up, you fool. He's the mayor's personal attorney!" whispered another, his hands dragging me back, holding me against those who would have taken me from the house.

The word ran through the group like wildfire. There were the hoarse sibilants of many whispers, and then attentive silence.

"'Tis Ed Jenkins, sor," remarked one of the policemen, one who seemed to be in charge of the squad. "The Phantom Crook, sor, caught in this house from which he kidnapped the girl an' stole the necklace, an' 'twas murder he was after tryin' to commit this time."

The lawyer's gray eyes rested on my face.

"If you want to talk, Jenkins, talk now."

I nodded.

"The girl, Jean Ellery. She is the daughter of Arthur C. Holton."

The fingers stopped their drumming and gripped the table.

"What?"

I nodded. "It was supposed that his child was a boy, a boy who died shortly after birth. As a matter of fact, the child was a girl, a girl who lived, who is known as Jean Ellery. A crooked doctor stood for the substitution, being paid a cash fee. A nurse originated the scheme, Miss Hattie M. Hare. The boy could never be traced. His future was placed in the doctor's hands before birth and when coincidence played into the hands of this nurse she used all her unscrupulous knowledge, all her cunning. The girl was to be brought up to look upon the nurse as her aunt, her only living relative. At the proper time the whole thing was to be exposed, but the doctor was to be the one who was to take the blame. Hattie M. Hare was to have her connection with the scheme kept secret.

"But the doctor found out the scheme to make him the goat. He had in his possession a paper signed by the nurse, a paper which would have foiled the whole plan. He used this paper as a basis for regular blackmail.

"It was intended to get this paper, to bring out the girl as the real heir, to have her participate in a trust fund which had been declared for the child of Arthur C. Holton, to have her inherit all the vast fortune of the oil magnate;— and to remember her aunt Hattie M. Hare as one of her close and dear relatives, to have her pay handsomely for the so-called detectives and lawyers who were to 'unearth' the fraud, to restore her to her place, to her estate.

"And then there came another development, Arthur C. Holton became infatuated with the arch-conspirator, Hattie M. Hare. He proposed marriage, allowing himself to be prevailed upon to make a will in her favor, to make a policy of life insurance to her.

"The girl ceased to be an asset, but became a menace. She must be removed. Also Arthur C. Holton must die that Miss Hattie M. Hare might succeed in his estate without delay. But there was a stumbling block, the paper which was signed by Hattie M. Hare, the paper which might be connected with the substitution of children, which would brand her a criminal, which would be fatal if used in connection with the testimony of the doctor.

"Doctor Drake demanded money for his silence and for that paper. He demanded his money in cash, in a large sum. The woman, working with fiendish cunning, decided to use me as a cat's-paw to raise the money and to also eliminate the girl from her path as well as to apparently murder the man who stood between her and his wealth. I was to be enveigled into apparently stealing a necklace worth much money, a necklace which was to be insured, and the insurance payable to Miss Hare; I was to be tricked into kidnapping a girl who would be murdered; I was to be persuaded to make threats against Mr. Holton, and then I was to become the apparent murderer of the oil magnate. My dagger was to be found sticking in his breast. In such manner would Miss Hare bring about the death of the man who had made her the beneficiary under his will, buy the silence of the doctor who knew her for a criminal, remove the only heir of the blood, and make me stand all the blame, finally delivering me into the hands of the law.

"There is proof. I have the signed statement in my pocket. Doctor Drake will talk. Harry Atmore will confess. . . . There she goes. Stop her!"

The cat-woman had seen that her play was ended. She had realized that she was at the end of her rope, that I held the evidence in my possession, that the bound and gagged girl upstairs would testify against her. She had dashed from the room while the stupefied police had held me and stared at her with goggle eyes.

Openmouthed they watched her flight, no one making any attempt to take after her, eight or ten holding me in their clumsy hands while the cat-woman, the arch criminal of them all, dashed out into the night.

H. F. Morton looked at me and smiled.

"Police efficiency, Jenkins," he said.

Then he faced the officers. "Turn him loose."

The officers shifted uneasily. The man in charge drew himself up stiffly and saluted. "He is a noted criminal with a price on his head, the very devil of a crook, sor."

Morton drummed steadily on the desk.

"What charge have you against him?"

The officer grunted.

"Stealin' Mr. Holton's necklace, an' breakin' into his house, sor."

"Those charges are withdrawn," came from the rear of the room in deep, firm tones.

I turned to see Arthur C. Holton. He had dressed and joined the group. I did not even know when he had entered the room, how much he had heard. By his side, her eyes starry, stood Jean Ellery, and there were gleaming gems of moisture on her cheeks.

The policeman grunted.

"For kidnappin' the young lady an' holdin' her. If she stayed against her will 'twas abductin', an' she wouldn't have stayed with a crook of her own accord, not without communicatin' with her folks."

That was a poser. I could hear Jean suck in her breath to speak the words that would have freed me but would have damned her in society forever; but she had not the chance.

Before I could even beat her to it, before my confession would have spared her name and sent me to the penitentiary, H. F. Morton's shrewd mind had grasped all the angles of the situation, and he beat us all to it.

"You are wrong. The girl was not kidnapped. Jenkins never saw her before."

The policeman grinned broadly.

"Then would yez mind tellin' me where she was while all this hue an' cry was bein' raised, while everyone was searchin' for her?"

Morton smiled politely, urbanely.

"Not at all, officer. She was at my house, as the guest of my wife. Feeling that her interests were being jeopardized and that her life was in danger, I had her stay incognito in my own home."

There was tense, thick silence.

The girl gasped. The clock ticked. There was the thick, heavy breathing of the big-bodied policemen.

"Rummy-tum-tum; rummy-tum-tum; rum-iddy, tumptidy, tumpy tum-tum," drummed the lawyer. "Officer, turn that man loose. Take off those handcuffs. Take . . . off . . . those . . . handcuffs . . . I . . . say. You haven't a thing against him in California."

As one in a daze, the officer fitted his key to the handcuffs, the police fell back, and I stood a free man.

"Good night," said the lawyer pointedly, his steely eyes glittering into those of the officers.

Shamefacedly, the officers trooped from the room.

Jean threw herself into my arms.

"Ed, you came back because of me! You risked your life to save mine, to see that a wrong was righted, to see that I was restored to my father! Ed, dear, you are a man in a million."

I patted her shoulder.

"You were a good pal, Jean, and I saw you through," I said. "Now you must forget about it. The daughter of a prominent millionaire has no business knowing a crook."

Arthur Holton advanced, hand outstretched.

"I was hypnotized, fooled, taken in by an adventuress and worse. I can hardly think clearly, the events of the past few minutes have been so swift, but this much I do know. I can never repay you for what you have done, Ed Jenkins. I will see that your name is cleared of every charge against you in every state, that you are a free man, that you are restored to citizenship, and that you have the right to live," and here he glanced at Jean: "You will stay with us as my guest?"

I shook my head. It was all right for them to feel grateful, to get a bit sloppy now that the grandstand play had been made, but they'd probably feel different about it by morning.

"I think I'll be on my way," I said, and started for the door.

"Ed!" It was the girl's cry, a cry which was as sharp, as stabbing as a quick pain at the heart. *"Ed, you're not leaving!"*

By way of answer I stumbled forward. Hell, was it possible that the difficulty with that threshold was that there was a mist in my eyes? Was Ed Jenkins, the phantom crook, known and feared by the police of a dozen states, becoming an old woman?

Two soft arms flashed about my neck, a swift kiss planted itself on my cheek, warm lips whispered in my ear.

I shook myself free, and stumbled out into the darkness. She was nothing but a kid, the daughter of a millionaire oil magnate. I was a crook. Nothing but hurt to her could come to any further acquaintance. It had gone too far already.

I jumped to one side, doubled around the house, away from the street lights, hugging the shadow which lay near the wall. From within the room, through the half-open window there came a steady, throbbing, thrumming sound: "Rummy-tum-tum; rummy-tum-tum; rummy-tum-tummy; tum-tummy-tum-tum."

H. F. Morton was thinking.

The Dilemma of the Dead Lady
Cornell Woolrich

THE MASTER OF NOIR fiction, Cornell Woolrich (1903–1968) wrote literally hundreds of stories, of which fewer than you might think have happy endings.

It was difficult to find the right story for this section because so many of his characters are shades of gray. People with whom we empathize choose to murder someone, or are put in positions where there seems to be no choice. Policemen, the upholders of the law, are frequently fascistic thugs who enjoy torturing suspects. Pretty girls with faces of angels turn out to be liars and cheats, and often worse. His situations ended unjustly when other authors would have resolved them neatly, and a Woolrich character often still faces a future barren of love, joy, or hope at the end of a story.

"The Dilemma of the Dead Lady" has had a varied life. Inspired by a cruise he took with his mother in 1931, he twists the memories into one of his most horrifying suspense stories. Although it was common for Woolrich to visit great terrors on ordinary, decent people, in this tale the central character is such a lowlife that we almost feel he deserves whatever befalls him.

After its original publication in the July 4, 1936, issue of *Detective Fiction Weekly*, it was retitled "Wardrobe Trunk" for its book publication in *The Blue Ribbon* (1946) by William Irish, Woolrich's pseudonym. Oddly, Woolrich rewrote it as a radio play titled "Working Is for Fools," which was never produced but did appear in the March 1964 issue of *Ellery Queen's Mystery Magazine*.

The Dilemma of the Dead Lady

Cornell Woolrich

1

It was already getting light out, but the peculiar milky-white Paris street lights were still on outside Babe Sherman's hotel window. He had the room light on, too, such as it was, and was busy packing at a mile-a-minute rate. The boat ticket was in the envelope on the bureau. All the bureau drawers were hanging out, and his big wardrobe trunk was yawning wide open in the middle of the room. He kept moving back and forth between it and the bureau with a sort of catlike tread, transferring things.

He was a good-looking devil, if you cared for his type of good looks—and women usually did. Then later on, they always found out how wrong they'd been. They were only a sideline with him, anyway; they were apt to get tangled around a guy's feet, trip him up when he least expected it. Like this little—what was her name now? He actually couldn't remember it for a minute, and didn't try to; he wouldn't be using it any more now, anyway. She'd come in handy, though—or rather her life's savings had—right after he'd been cleaned at the Longchamps track. And then holding down a good job like she did with one of the biggest jewelry firms on the Rue de la Paix had been damned convenient for his purposes. He smiled when he thought of the long, slow build-up it had taken—calling for her there twice a day, taking her out to meals, playing Sir Galahad. Boy, he'd had to work hard for his loot this time, but it was worth it! He unwrapped the little tissue-paper package in his breastpocket, held the string of pearls up to the light, and looked at them. Matched, every one of them—and with a diamond clasp. They'd bring plenty in New York! He knew just the right fence, too.

The guff he'd had to hand her, though, when she first got around to pointing out new articles in the display cases, each time one was added to the stock! "I'd rather look at you, honey." Not seeming to take any interest, not even glancing down. Until finally, when things were ripe enough to suit him: "Nice pearls, those. Hold 'em up to your neck a minute, let's see how they look on you."

"Oh, I'm not allow' to take them out! I am only suppose' to handle the briquets, gold cigarette cases—" But she would have done anything he asked her by that time. With a quick glance at the back of M'sieu Proprietor, who was right in the room with them, she was holding them at her throat for a stolen moment.

"I'll fasten the catch for you—turn around, look at the glass."

"No, no, please—" They fell to the floor, somehow. He picked them up and handed them back to her; they were standing at the end of the long case, he on his side, she on her side. And when they went back onto the velvet tray inside the case, the switch had already been made. As easy as that!

He was all dressed, even had his hat on the back of his skull, but he'd left his shoes off, had been going around in his stocking feet, hence the catlike tread. Nor was this because he intended beating this cheesy side-street hotel out of his bill, although that wouldn't have been anything new to his experience either. He could possibly have gotten away with it at that—there was only what they called a "concierge" on duty below until seven, and at that he was always asleep. But for once in his life he'd paid up. He wasn't taking any chances of getting stopped at the station. He wanted to get clear of this damn burg and clear of this damn country without a hitch. He had a good reason, $75,000-worth of pearls. When they said it in francs it sounded like a telephone number. Besides, he didn't like the looks of their jails here; you could smell them blocks away. One more thing: you didn't just step on the boat like in New York. It took five hours on the boat train getting to it, and a wire to Cherbourg to hold you and send you back could make it in twenty minutes. So it was better to part friends with everyone. Not that the management of a third-class joint like this would send a wire to Cherbourg, but they would go to the police, and if the switch of the pearls happened to come to light at about the same time. . . .

He sat down on the edge of the bed and picked up his right shoe. He put the pearls down for a minute, draped across his thigh, fumbled under the mattress and took out a tiny screwdriver. He went to work on the three little screws that fastened his heel. A minute later it was loose in his hand. It was hollow, had a steel rim on the end of it to keep it from wearing down. He coiled the pearls up, packed them in. There was no customs inspection at this end, and before he tackled the Feds at the other side, he'd think up something better. This would do for now.

It was just when he had the heel fitted in place again, but not screwed on, that the knock on the door came. He got white as a sheet for a minute, sat there without breathing. Then he remembered that he'd left word downstairs last night that he was making the boat train; it was probably the porter for his wardrobe trunk. He got his windpipe going again, called out in his half-baked French, "Too soon, gimme another ten minutes!"

The knocking hadn't quit from the time it began, without getting louder it kept getting faster and faster all the time. The answer froze him when it came through the door: "Let me in, let me in, Bébé, it's me!"

He knew who "me" was, all right! He began to swear viciously but soundlessly. He'd already answered like a fool, she knew he was there! If he'd only kept his trap shut, she might have gone away. But if he didn't let her in now, she'd probably rouse the whole hotel! He didn't want any publicity if he could help it. She could make it tough for him, even without knowing about the pearls. After all, she had turned over her savings to him. Her knocking was a frantic machine-gun tattoo by now, and getting louder all the time. Maybe he could stall her off for an hour or two, get rid of her long enough to make the station, feed her some taffy or other. . . .

He hid the screwdriver again, stuck his feet into his shoes without lacing them, shuffled over to the door and unlocked it. Then he tried to stand in the opening so that she couldn't see past him into the room.

She seemed half-hysterical, there were tears standing in her eyes. "Bébé, I waited for you there last night, what happen'? Why you do these to me, what I have done?"

"What d'ya mean by coming here at this hour?" he hissed viciously at her. "Didn't I tell you never to come here!"

"Nobody see me, the concierge was asleep, I walk all the way up the stairs—" She broke off suddenly. "You are all dress', at these hour? You, who never get up ontil late! The hat even—"

"I just got in," he tried to bluff her, looking up and down the passageway. The motion was his undoing; in that instant she had peered inside, across his shoulder, possibly on the lookout for some other girl. She saw the trunk standing there open in the middle of the room.

He clapped his hand to her mouth in the nick of time, stifling her scream. Then pulled her roughly in after him and locked the door.

He let go of her then. "Now, there's nothing to get excited about," he said soothingly. "I'm just going on a little business trip to, er—" He snapped his fingers helplessly, couldn't think of any French names. "I'll be back day after tomorrow—"

But she wasn't listening, was at the bureau before he could stop her, pawing the boat ticket. He snatched it from her, but the damage had already been done. "But you are going to New York! This ticket is for one! You said never a word—" Anyone but a heel like Babe Sherman would have been wrung by the misery in her voice. "I thought that you and I, we—"

He was getting sick of this. "What a crust!" he snarled. "Get hep to yourself! I should marry you! Why, we don't even talk the same lingo!"

She reeled as though an invisible blow had struck her, pulled herself together again. She had changed now. Her eyes were blazing. "My money!" she cried hoarsely. "Every sou I had in the world I turned over to you! My *dot*, my marriage dowry, that was suppose' to be! No, no, you are not going to do these to me! You do not leave here ontil you have give it back—" She darted at the locked door. "I tell my story to the gendarmes—"

He reared after her, stumbled over the rug but caught her in time, flung her backward away from the door. The key came out of the keyhole, dropped to the floor, he kicked it sideways out of her reach. "No, you don't!" he panted.

Something was holding her rigid, though his hands were no longer on her. He followed the direction of her dilated eyes, down toward the floor. His loosened heel had come off just now. She was staring, not at that, but at the lustrous string of pearls that spilled out of it like a tiny snake, their diamond catch twinkling like an eye.

Again she pounced, and again he forestalled her, whipped them up out of her reach. But as he did so, they straightened out and she got a better look at them than she would have had they stayed coiled in a mass. "It is number twenty-nine, from the store!" she gasped. "The one I showed you! Oh, *mon Dieu,* when they find out, they will blame me! They will send me to St. Lazare—"

He had never yet killed anyone, didn't intend to even now. But death was already in the room

with the two of them. She could have still saved herself, probably, by using her head, subsiding, pretending to fall in with his plans for the time being. That way she might have gotten out of there alive. But it would have been superhuman; no one in her position would have had the self-control to do it. She was only a very frightened French girl after all. They were both at a white-heat of fear and self-preservation; she lost her head completely, did the one thing that was calculated to doom her. She flung herself for the last time at the door, panic-stricken, with a hoarse cry for help. And he, equally panic-stricken, and more concerned about silencing her before she roused the house than even about keeping her in the room with him, took the shortest way of muffling her voice. The inaccurate way, the deadly way. He flung the long loop of pearls over her head from behind like a lasso, foreshortened them into a choking noose, dragged her stumbling backward. They were strung on fine platinum wire, almost unbreakable. She turned and turned, three times over, like a dislodged tenpin, whipping the thing inextricably around her throat, came up against him, coughing, clawing at herself, eyes rolling. Too late he let go, there wasn't any slack left, the pearls were like gleaming white nail heads driven into her flesh.

He clawed now, too, trying to free her as he saw her face begin to mottle. There wasn't room for a finger hold; to pluck at one loop only tightened the other two under it. Suddenly she dropped vertically, like a plummet, between his fumbling hands, twitched spasmodically for an instant at his feet, then lay there still, face black now, eyes horrible protuberances. Dead. Strangled by a thing of beauty, a thing meant to give pleasure.

2

Babe Sherman was a realist, also known as a heel. He saw from where he was that she was gone, without even bending over her. No face could turn that color and ever be alive again. No eyes could swell in their sockets like that and ever see again. He didn't even bend down over her, to feel for her heart; didn't say a word, didn't make a sound. The thought in his mind was: "Now I've done it. Added murder to all the rest. It was about the only thing missing!"

His first move was to the door. He stood there listening. Their scuffle hadn't taken long; these old Paris dumps had thick stone walls. Her last cry at the door, before he'd corralled her, had been a hoarse, low-pitched one, not a shrill, woman's scream. There wasn't a sound outside. Then he went to the window, peered through the mangy curtains, first from one side, then the other. He was low enough—third story—and the light had been on, but the shutters were all tightly closed on the third floor of the building across the way, every last one of them. He carefully fitted his own together; in France they come inside the vertical windows.

He went back to her, and he walked all around her. This time the thought was, appropriately enough: "How is it I've never done it before now? Lucky, I guess." He wasn't as cool as he looked, by any means, but he wasn't as frightened as a decent man would have been, either; there'd been too many things in his life before this, the edge had been taken off long ago. He had no conscience.

He stopped over her for the first time, but only to fumble some more with the necklace. He saw that it would have to stay; opening the catch was no good, only a wire clipper could have severed it, and he had none. He spoke aloud for the first time since he'd been "alone" in the room. "Y' wanted 'em back," he said gruffly, "well, y' got 'em!" A defense mechanism, to show himself how unfrightened he was. And then, supreme irony, her given name came back to him at last, for the first time since she'd put in an appearance, "Manon," he added grudgingly. The final insult!

He straightened up, flew at the door like an arrow almost before the second knocking had begun, to make sure that it was still locked. This time it *was* the porter, sealing him up in there, trapping him! "M'sieu, the baggages."

"Wait! One little minute! Go downstairs again, then come back—"

But he wouldn't go away. "M'sieu hasn't much time. The boat train leaves in fifteen minutes. They didn't tell me until just now. It takes nearly that long to the sta—"

"Go back, go back I tell you!"

"Then m'sieu not want to make his train—"

But he had to, it meant the guillotine if he stayed here even another twenty-four hours! He couldn't keep her in the damned place with him forever; he couldn't smuggle her out, he couldn't even blow and leave her behind! In ten minutes after he was gone they'd find her in the room, and a wire could get to Cherbourg four and a half hours before his train!

He broke for just a minute. He groaned, went around in circles in there, like a trapped beast. Then he snapped right out of it again. The answer was so obvious! His only safety lay in taking her with him, dead or not! The concierge had been asleep, hadn't seen her come in. Let her employer or her landlord turn her name over to the Missing Persons Bureau—or whatever they called it here—a week or ten days from now. She'd be at the bottom of the deep Atlantic long before that. The phony pearls in the showcase would give them their explanation. And she had no close relatives here in Paris. She'd already told him that. The trunk, of course, had been staring him in the face the whole time.

He put his ear to the keyhole, could hear the guy breathing there on the other side of the door, waiting! He went at the trunk, pitched out all the things he'd been stuffing in it when she interrupted him. Like all wardrobes, one side was entirely open, for suits to be hung in; the other was a network of small compartments and drawers, for shoes, shirts, etc. It wasn't a particularly well-made trunk; he'd bought it secondhand. He cleared the drawers out, ripped the thin lath partitions out of the way bodily. The hell with the noise, it was no crime partly to destroy your own trunk. Both sides were open now, four-square; just the metal shell remained.

He dragged her over, sat her up in the middle of it, folded her legs up against her out of the way, and pushed the two upright halves closed over her. She vanished, there was no resistance, no impediment, plenty of room. Too much, maybe. He opened it again, packed all his shirts and suits tightly around her, and the splintered partitions and the flattened-out drawers. There wasn't a thing left out, not a thing left behind, not a nail even. Strangest of biers, for a little fool that hadn't known her man well enough!

Then he closed it a second time, locked it, tilted it this way and that. You couldn't tell. He scanned his boat ticket, copied the stateroom number onto the baggage label the steamship company had given him: 42–A. And the label read: NEEDED IN STATE-ROOM. It couldn't go into the hold, of course. Discovery would be inevitable in a day or two at the most. He moistened it, slapped it against the side of the trunk.

He gave a last look around. There wasn't a drop of blood, nothing to give him away. The last thing he saw before he let the porter in was the hollow heel that had betrayed him to her, lying there. He picked it up and slipped it in his pocket, flat.

He opened the door and jerked his thumb. The blue-bloused porter straightened up boredly. "*Allons!*" Babe said. "This goes right in the taxi with me, understand?"

The man tested it, spit on his hands, grabbed it. "He'll soak you an extra half-fare."

"I'm paying," Babe answered. He sat down on the edge of the bed and finished lacing his shoes. The porter bounced the trunk on its edges out of the room and down the passageway.

Babe caught up with him at the end of it. He wasn't going to stay very far away from it, from now on. He was sweating a little under his hat band; otherwise he was okay. She hadn't meant anything to him anyway, and he'd done so many lousy things before now. . . .

He'd never trusted that birdcage French elevator from the beginning, and when he saw Jacques getting ready to tilt the trunk onto it, he had a bad half-minute. The stairs wouldn't be any too good for it, either; it was a case of six of one, half a dozen of the other. "Will it hold?" he asked.

"Sure, if we don't get on with it." It wobbled like jelly, though, under it. Babe wiped his forehead with one finger. "Never dropped yet," the porter added.

"It only has to once," thought Babe. He deliberately crossed his middle and index fingers and kept them that way, slowly spiraling around the lethargic apparatus down the stair well.

Jacques closed the nutty-looking little wicket gate, reached over it to punch the bottom button, and then came after him. They'd gone half a flight before anything happened. Then there was a sort of groan, a shudder, and the thing belatedly started down after them.

It seemed to Babe as if they'd already been waiting half an hour, when it finally showed up down below. He'd been in and out and had a taxi sputtering at the door. The concierge was hanging around, and by looking at him, Babe could tell Manon had spoken the truth. He had been asleep until now, hadn't seen her go up.

The porter lurched the trunk ahead of him down the hall, out onto the Rue l'Ecluse, and then a big row started right in. One of those big French rows that had always amused Sherman until now. It wasn't funny this time.

The driver didn't mind taking it, but he wanted it tied on in back, on top, or even at the side, with ropes. The porter, speaking for Babe, insisted that it go inside the body of the cab. It couldn't go in front because it would have blocked his gears.

Sherman swore like a maniac. "Two fares!" he hollered. "Damn it, I'll never make the North Station—" A baker and a scissors-grinder had joined in, taking opposite sides, and a gendarme was slouching up from the corner to find out what it was about. Before they got through, they were liable to, at that. . . .

He finally got it in for two and a half fares; it just about made the side door, taking the paint off it plentifully. The gendarme changed his mind and turned back to his post at the crossing. Sherman got in with it, squeezed around it onto the seat, and banged the door. He slipped the porter a five-franc note. "Bon voyage!" the concierge yelled after him.

"Right back at ya!" he gritted. He took a deep breath that seemed to come up from his shoes, almost. "Hurdle number one," he thought. "Another at the station, another at Cherbourg—and I'm in the clear!"

The one at the Gare du Nord was worse than the one before. This time it was a case of baggage car versus the compartment he was to occupy. It wasn't that he was afraid to trust it to the baggage car, so much—five hours wouldn't be very dangerous—it was that he was afraid if he let it go now, it would go right into the hold of the ship without his being able to stop it, and that was where the risk lay. He couldn't get rid of her at sea once they put her in the hold.

The time element made his second hurdle bad, too; it had narrowed down to within a minute or two of train time. He couldn't buy the whole compartment, as he had the extra taxi fare, because there was already somebody else in it, one of the bulldog-type Yanks who believed in standing up for his rights. The driver had made the Gare as only a Paris driver can make a destination, on two wheels, and "All aboard!" had already been shouted up and down the long platform. The station-master had one eye on his watch and one on his whistle. Once he tooted that, the thing would be off like a shot—the boat trains are the fastest things in Europe—and Sherman would be left there stranded, without further funds to get him out and with a death penalty crime and a "hot" pearly necklace on his hands. . . .

3

He kept running back and forth between his compartment and the stalled baggage hand-truck up front, sweating like a mule, waving his arms—the conductor on one side of him, the baggage-master on the other.

"Put it in the car aisle, outside my door," he pleaded. "Stand it up in the vestibule for me, can't you do that?"

"Against the regulations." And then ominously, "Why is this trunk any different from all the others? Why does m'sieu insist on keeping it with him?"

"Because I lost one once that way," was all Babe could think of.

The whistle piped shrilly, doors slammed, the thing started to move. The baggage-master dropped out. "Too late! It will have to be sent after you now!" He turned and ran back to his post.

Sherman took out his wallet, almost emptied it of napkin-size banknotes—what was left of Manon's savings—about forty dollars in our money. His luck was he'd left that much unchanged yesterday, at the Express. "Don't do this to me, Jacques! Don't make it tough for me! It'll miss my boat if I don't get it on this train with me!" His voice was hoarse, cracked by now. The wheels were slowly gathering speed, his own car was coming up toward them. They'd been up nearer the baggage car.

The conductor took a quick look up and down the platform. The money vanished. He jerked his head at the waiting truck-man; the man came up alongside the track, started to run parallel to the train, loaded truck and all. Babe caught at the next vestibule hand-rail as it came abreast, swung himself in, the conductor after him. "Hold on to me!" the latter warned. Babe clasped him around the waist from behind. The conductor, leaning out, got a grip on the trunk from above. The truckman hoisted it from below, shoved it in on them. It went aboard as easily as a valise.

They got it up off the steps and parked it over in the farther corner of the vestibule. The conductor banged the car door shut. "I'll lose my job if they get wise to this!"

"You don't know anything about it," Babe assured him. "I'll get it off myself at Cherbourg. Just remember to look the other way."

He saw the fellow counting over the palm-oil, so he handed him the last remaining banknote left in his wallet—just kept some silver for the dockhand at Cherbourg. "You're a good guy, Jacques," he told him wearily, slapped him on the back, and went down the car to his compartment. Hurdle number two! Only one more to go. But all this fuss and feathers wasn't any too good, he realized somberly. It made him and trunk too conspicuous, too easily remembered later on. Well, the hell with it, as long as they couldn't prove anything!

His compartment mate looked up, not particularly friendly. Babe tried to figure him, and he tried to figure Babe. Or maybe he had already.

"Howja find it?" he said finally. Just that. Meaning he knew Babe had been working Paris in one way or another. Babe got it.

"I don't have to talk to you!" he snarled. "Whaddya think y'are, an income tax blank?"

"Tell you what I am, a clairvoyant; read the future. First night out you'll be drumming up a friendly little game—with your own deck of cards. Nickels and dimes, just to make it interesting." He made a noise with his lips that was the height of vulgarity. "Lone wolf, I notice, though. Matter, Sûreté get your shill?"

Babe balled a fist, held it back by sheer will power. "Read your own future." He slapped himself on the shoulder with his other hand. "Find out about the roundhouse waiting for you up in here."

The other guy went back to his Paris *Herald* contemptuously. He must have known he'd hit it right the first time, or Babe wouldn't have taken it from him. "You know where to find me," he muttered. "Now or after we're aboard. I'll be in 42-A."

The label on that wardrobe trunk of his outside flashed before Babe's mind. He took a deep breath, that was almost a curse in itself, and closed his eyes. He shut up, didn't say another word. When he opened his eyes again a minute later, they were focused for a second down at the feet of the guy opposite him. Very flat, that pair of shoes looked, big—and very flat.

The motion of the train seemed to sicken him for a moment. But this guy was going back alone. A muffed assignment? Or just a vacation? They didn't take 3,000-mile jaunts for vacations. They didn't take vacations at all! Maybe the assignment hadn't had a human quarry—just data or evidence from one of the European police files?

The irises of the other man's eyes weren't on him at all, were boring into the paper between his fists—which probably meant he could have read the laundry mark on the inside of Babe's collar at the moment, if he'd been called on to do so. Federal or city? Babe couldn't figure. Didn't look government, though. The dick showed too plainly all over him—the gentleman with the whiskers didn't use types that gave themselves away to their quarry that easy.

"So I not only ride the waves with a corpse in my cabin with me, but with a dick in the next bunk! Oh, lovely tie-up!" He got up and went outside to take a look at his trunk. Looked back through the glass after he'd shut the door; the guy's eyes hadn't budged from his paper. There's such a thing as underdoing a thing; there's also such a thing as overdoing it, Babe told himself knowingly. The average human glances up when someone leaves the room he's in. "You're good," he cursed him, "but so am I!"

The trunk was okay. He hung around it for a while, smoking a cigarette. The train rushed northwestward through France, with dead Manon and her killer not a foot away from one another, and the ashes of a cigarette were the only obsequies she was getting. They were probably missing her by now at the jewelry shop on the Rue de la Paix, phoning to her place to find out why she hadn't showed. Maybe a customer would come in today and want to be shown that pearly necklace, number twenty-nine; maybe no one would ask to see it for a week or a month.

He went back in again, cleaned his nails with a pocket-knife. Got up and went out to look, in another half-hour. Came back in again. Gee, Cherbourg was far away! At the third inspection, after another half-hour, he got a bad jolt. A fresh little flapper was sitting perched up on top of it, legs crossed, munching a sandwich! The train motion gave him a little qualm again. He slouched up to her. She gave him a smile, but he didn't give her one back. She was just a kid, harmless, but he couldn't bear the sight.

"Get off it, Susie," he said in a muffled voice, and swept his hand at her vaguely. "Get crumbs all over it, it ain't a counter."

She landed on her heels. "Oh, purrdon me!" she said freshly. "We've got the President with us!" Then she took a second look at his face. He could tell she was going mushy on him in another minute, so he went back in again. The flatfoot—if he was one—was preferable to that, the way he felt right now.

Cherbourg showed about one, and he'd already been out there in the vestibule with it ten minutes before they started slowing up. The train ran right out onto the new double-decker pier the French had put up, broadside to the boat; all you had to do was step up the companionway.

His friend the conductor brushed by, gave him the office, accomplished the stupendous feat of not seeing the huge trunk there, and went ahead to the next vestibule. The thing stopped. Babe stuck his head out. Then he found out he wouldn't even need a French middleman, the ship's stewards were lined up in a row on the platform to take on the hand-luggage for the passengers. One of them came jumping over. "Stand by," Babe said. The passengers had right of way first, of course. They all cleared out—but *not* the wise guy. Maybe he'd taken the door at the other end of the coach, though.

Then the third hurdle reared—sky-high. "In the stateroom?" the steward gasped respectfully. "That's out of the question, sir—a thing that size! That has to go in the hold!"

About seven minutes of this, two more stewards and one of the ship's officers—and he wasn't getting anywhere. "Tell you what," he said finally, groggy with what he was going through, "just lemme have it with me the first day, till I can get it emptied a little and sorted out. Then you can take it down the hold." He was lighting one cigarette from another and throwing them away half-smoked, his eyebrows were beaded with sweat, the quay was just a blur in front of him. . . .

"We can't do that, man!" the officer snapped. "The hold's loaded through the lower hatches. We can't transfer things from above down there, once we're out at sea!"

Behind Babe a voice said gruffly: "Lissen, I'm in there with him and I got something to say—or haven't I? Your objection is that it'll take up too much room in there, cramp the party sharing the cabin with him, right? Well, cut out this belly-aching, the lot of you, and put it where the guy wants it to go! It's all right with me, I waive my rights—"

4

Babe didn't turn around. He knew what had just happened behind him though, knew by the way their opposition flattened out. Not another word was said. He knew as well as if he'd seen it with his own eyes: the guy had palmed his badge at them behind his back!

He would have given anything to have it go into the hold now, instead, but it was too late! He swallowed chokedly, still didn't turn, didn't say thanks. He felt like someone who has just had a rattlesnake dropped down the back of his neck while he's tied hand and foot.

He got down from the car, and they hopped in to get it. He didn't give it another look. He headed slowly toward the companionway he'd been directed to, to show his ticket, and was aware of the other man strolling along at his elbow. "What's your game?" he said, out of the corner of his mouth, eyes straight ahead.

There was mockery in the slurring answer. "Just big-hearted. Might even help you make out your customs' declaration on what y'got in it—"

Babe stumbled over something on the ground before him that wasn't there at all, stiff-armed himself against a post, went trudging on. He didn't have anything in his shoulder for this guy before. He had something in his heart for him now—death.

He looked up at the triple row of decks above

him while an officer was checking his ticket and passport at the foot of the companionway. It was called the *American Statesman*. "You're going to be one short when you make the Narrows seven days from now!" he told it silently. "This copper's never going to leave you alive."

They maneuvered the trunk down the narrow ship's corridor and into the stateroom by the skin of its teeth. It was a tight squeeze. It couldn't, of course, go under either one of the bunks. One remaining wall was taken up by the door, the other by the folding washstand, which opened like a desk. The middle of the room was the only answer, and that promptly turned the cabin into nothing more than a narrow perimeter around the massive object. That his fellow passenger, who wasn't any sylph, should put up with this was the deadest give-away ever, to Babe's way of thinking, that he was on to something. Some of these punks had a sixth sense, almost, when it came to scenting crime in the air around them. He wouldn't need more than one, though, in about a day more, if Babe didn't do something in a hurry! It was July, and there were going to be two of them in there with it.

He tried half-heartedly to have it shunted down to the hold after all—although that would have been just jumping from a very quick frying pan to a slower but just as deadly fire—but they balked. It would have to be taken out again onto the quay and then shipped aboard from there, they pointed out. There was no longer time enough. And he'd cooked up a steam of unpopularity for himself as it was that wouldn't clear away for days.

The dick didn't show right up, but a pair of his valises came in, and Sherman lamped the tags. "E. M. Fowler, New York." He looked out, and he saw where he'd made still another mistake. He'd bought a cabin on the A-deck, the middle of the three, just under the promenade deck; a C-cabin would have been the right one, below deck level. This one had no porthole opening directly above the water, but a window flush with the deck outside. But then he hadn't known he was going to travel with a corpse, and

her money had made it easy to buy the best. Now he'd have to smuggle her outside with him, all the way along the passageway, down the stairs, and out across the lowest deck—when the time came.

He beat it out in a hurry, grinding his hands together. Should have thought of it sooner, before he'd let them haul it in there! He'd ask to be changed, that was all. Get the kind he wanted, away from that bloodhound and by himself. Sure they could switch him, they must have some last-minute cancellations! Always did.

The purser spread out a chart for him when he put it to him in his office, seemed about to do what he wanted; Sherman felt better than he had at any time since five that morning. Then suddenly he looked up at him as though he'd just remembered something. "You Mr. Sherman, 42-A?" Babe nodded. "Sorry, we're booked solid; you'll have to stay in there." He put the chart away.

Arguing was no use. He knew what had happened; Fowler and his badge again. He'd foreseen this move, beat him to it, blocked it! "You weren't bragging, brother, when you called yourself a clairvoyant!" he thought bitterly. But the guy couldn't actually *know* what was in the trunk, what was making him act like this? Just a hunch? Just the fact that he'd sized Babe up as off-color, and noticed the frantic way Babe had tried to keep the trunk with him when he boarded the train? Just the way any dick baited anyone on the other side of the fence, not sure but always hoping for the worst? Well, he was asking for it and he was going to get it—and not the way he expected, either. He'd foreclosed his own life by nailing Babe down in the cabin with him!

Just the same, he felt the need of a good stiff pick-up. They were already under way when he found his way into the bar, the jurisdiction of the French Republic was slipping behind them, it was just that pot-bellied old gent now with the brass buttons, the captain. The straight brandy put him in shape; the hell with both sides of the pond! Once he got rid of her there wouldn't be any evidence left, he could beat any extradition rap they tried to slap on him. Water scotches a trail in more ways than one.

He spent the afternoon between the bar and 42, to make sure Fowler didn't try to tackle the trunk with a chisel or pick the lock while his back was turned. But the dick didn't go near the cabin, stayed out of sight the whole time. The sun, even going down, was still plenty hot; Sherman opened the window as wide as it would go and turned on the electric fan above the door. It would have to be tonight, for plenty of good reasons! One of the least was that he couldn't keep checking on the thing like this every five minutes without going bughouse.

A steward went all over the ship pounding a portable dinner gong, and Sherman went back to the cabin, more to keep his eye on Fowler than to freshen up. He wouldn't have put on one of his other suits now even if he could have gotten at it.

Fowler came in, went around on his side of the trunk, and stripped to his undershirt. Sherman heard a rustle and a click, and he'd turned off the fan and pulled down the shade. Almost instantaneously the place got stuffy.

Babe said, "What's the idea? You ain't that chilly in July!"

Fowler gave him a long, searching look across the top of the trunk. "You seem to want ventilation pretty badly," he said, very low.

It hit Sherman, like everything the guy seemed to say, and he forgot what he was doing for a minute, splashed water on his hair from force of habit. When it was all ganged up in front of his eyes, he remembered his comb was in there, too, he didn't have a thing out. He tried combing with his fingers and it wouldn't work. He stalled around while the dick slicked his own, waiting for him to get out and leave it behind.

The dick did some stalling of his own. It started to turn itself an endurance, the second dinner gong went banging by outside the window. Sherman, nerves tight as elastic bands, thought: "What the hell is he up to?" His own shirt was hanging on a hook by the door, he saw Fowler glance at it just once, but didn't get the idea in time. Fowler parked a little bottle of liq-

uid shoe-blackening on the extreme edge of the trunk, stopper out, right opposite the shirt. Then he brushed past between the two, elbows slightly out. He had no right to come around on that side; it was Sherman's side of the place. The shirt slipped off the hook and the shoe-polish toppled and dumped itself on top of it on the floor. The shirt came up black and white, mostly black, in his hand.

"Oops, sorry!" he apologized smoothly. "Now I've done it—have it laundered for you—"

Sherman got the idea too late, he'd maneuvered him into opening the trunk in his presence and getting a clean one out, or else giving up his evening meal; he couldn't go in there wearing that piebald thing!

He jerked the thing away from the detective, gave him a push that sent him staggering backward, and went after him arm poised to sock him. "I saw you! Y'did that purposely!" he snarled. He realized that he was giving himself away, lowered his arm. "Hand over one of yours," he ordered grimly.

Fowler shook his head, couldn't keep the upward tilt from showing at the corners of his mouth though. "One thing I never do, let anybody else wear my things." He fished out a couple of singles. "I'll pay you for it, or I'll have it laundered for you—" Then very smoothly, "Matter, mean to say you haven't got another one in that young bungalow of yours?"

Sherman got a grip on himself; this wasn't the time or the place. After all, he still held the trump in his own hands—and that was whether the trunk was to be opened or to stay closed. He punched the bell for the steward and sat down on the edge of his berth, pale but leering.

"Bring me my meal in here, I can't make the dining saloon."

Fowler shrugged on his coat and went out, not looking quite so pleased with himself as he had a minute ago. Sherman knew, just the same, that his own actions had only cinched the suspicions lurking in the other's mind about the trunk. The first round had been the detective's after all.

That thought, and having to eat with his dinner tray parked on top the trunk—there was no other place for it—squelched the little appetite he'd had to begin with. He couldn't swallow, had to beat it around the other side and stick his head out the window, breathing in fresh air, to get rid of the mental images that had begun popping into his dome.

"Going soft, am I?" he gritted. After a while he pulled his head in again. There were a few minor things he could do right now, while the dick was in the dining room, even if the main job had to wait for tonight. Tonight Fowler would be right in here on top of him, it would have to be done with lightning-like rapidity. He'd better get started now, paving the way.

5

He closed the window and fastened it, so the shade wouldn't blow in on him. He set the untouched tray of food down outside the door, then locked it. The boat was a pre-war model reconditioned, one of the indications of this was the footwide grilled vent that pierced the three inside partitions just below the ceiling line—a continuous slitted band that encircled the place except on the deck side. It was the best they could do in 1914 to get a little circulation into the air. He couldn't do anything about that, but it was well over anyone's head.

He got out his keys and turned the trunk so that it opened *away* from the door. He squatted down, took a deep breath, touched the key to the lock, swung back the bolts, and parted the trunk. He didn't look up, picked up a handkerchief, unfolded it, and spread it over her face. He got out a couple of the shirts that had been farthest away, protected by other things, and his comb, and then he took a file that was in there and went to work on the pearls.

It was hard even to force any two of them far enough apart to get at the platinum wire underneath without damaging them in the filing, but he managed to force a split in their ranks right

alongside the clasp, which stood out a little because of its setting. The wire itself was no great obstacle, it was just getting the file in at it. In five minutes the place he had tackled wore out under the friction, and it shattered to invisibility. Three pearls dropped off before he could catch them and rolled some place on the floor. He let them go for a minute, poised the file to change hands with it and unwind the gnarled necklace—and heard Fowler saying quietly: "What's the idea of the lock-out? Do I get in, or what?"

His face was peering in and down at Sherman through that damnable slotted ventilator, high up but on a line with the middle of the door, smiling—but not a smile of friendliness or good omen.

Sherman died a little then inside himself, as he would never die again, not even if a day came when he would be kneeling under the high knife at Vincennes or sitting in the electric chair at Ossining. Something inside him curled up, but because there was no blade or voltage to follow the shock, he went ahead breathing and thinking.

His eyes traveled downward from Fowler's outlined face to the top of the trunk in a straight line. Her handkerchief-masked-head was well below it on his side, her legs stayed flat up against her as he'd first folded them, from long confinement and now rigor. He thought: "He doesn't see her from where he is. He can't or he wouldn't be smiling like that!"

But the opening ran all around, on the side of him and in back of him. He must be up on a stool out there; all he'd have to do would be jump down, shift it farther around to where he could see, and spring up on it again. If he did that in time, he could do it much quicker than Babe could get the trunk closed. "He hasn't thought of it yet!" Babe told himself frantically. "Oh, Joseph and Mary, keep it from occurring to him! If I can hold him up there just a split minute, keep talking to him, not give him time to think of it—"

His eyes bored into Fowler's trying to hold him by that slight ocular magnetism any two people looking at each other have. He said very slowly: "I'll tell you why I locked the door like that; just a minute before you showed up—"

Whang! The two halves of the trunk came together between his outstretched arms. The rest of it was just reflex action, snapping the bolts home, twisting the key in the lock. He went down lower on his haunches and panted like a fish out of water.

He went over to the door and opened it, still weak on his pins. Fowler got down off the folding stool he'd dragged up. If he was disappointed, he didn't show it.

"I didn't hear you knock," Sherman said. There was no use throwing himself at him right now, absolutely none, it would be a fatal mistake. "I'll get him tonight—late," he said to himself.

Fowler answered insolently. "Why knock, when you know ahead of time the door's going to be locked? You never get to see things that way."

"More of that mind-reading stuff." Sherman tried to keep the thing as matter-of-fact as possible between them, for his own sake, not let it get out of bounds and go haywire before he was ready. "I don't mind telling you you're getting on my nerves, buddy."

He spotted one of the pearls, picked it up before Fowler saw what it was, put it in his pocket. "First you gum up a good shirt on me. Then you pull a Peeping Tom act—" He kept walking aimlessly around, eyes to the floor. He saw the second one and pocketed that, too, with a swift snake of the arm. His voice rose to a querulous protest. "What are you, some kind of a stool pigeon? Am I marked lousy, or what?" Trying to make it sound like no more than the natural beef of an unjustly persecuted person.

Fowler said from his side of the trunk: "Couple little things like that shouldn't get on your nerves—" pause—"unless you've got something else on them already."

Sherman didn't answer that one, there didn't seem to be a satisfactory one for it. He couldn't locate the third pearl either—if there had been one. He wasn't sure any more whether two or three had rolled off her neck.

He flung himself down on his bunk, lay there on his back sending up rings of cigarette smoke at the ceiling. Fowler, hidden on his side of the trunk, belched once or twice, moved around a little, finally began rattling the pages of a magazine. The ship steamed westward, out into the open Atlantic. They both lay there, waiting, waiting. . . .

The human noises around them grew less after an hour or so; suddenly the deck lights outside the window went out without warning. It was midnight. A minute later, Sherman heard the door open and close, and Fowler had gone out of the cabin. He sat up and looked across the trunk. He'd left his coat and vest and tie on his berth—gone to the washroom. He listened, heard his footsteps die away down the oilcloth-covered passageway outside. That was exactly what Babe Sherman was waiting for.

He swung his legs down and made a beeline across the cabin, didn't bother locking the door this time, it was quiet enough now to hear him coming back anyway. He went through that coat and vest with a series of deft scoops, one to a pocket, that showed how good he must have once been at the dip racket. The badge was almost the first thing he hit, settling his doubts on that score once and for all—if he'd still had any left. New York badge, city dick. Sherman had no gun with him, didn't work that way as a rule. He thought, "He almost certainly has. If I could only locate it before he comes back—" He didn't intend to use it in any case—too much noise—but unless he got his hands on it ahead of time, it was going to be very risky business!

The fool had left one of his two valises open under the bunk, ready to haul out his pajamas! Sherman went all through it in no time flat, without messing it too much either. Not in it. It was either in the second one, or he carried it in a hip-holster, but probably the former was the case. Then one of those hunches that at times visit the deserving and the undeserving alike, smote him from nowhere; he tipped the upper end of the mattress back and put his hand on it!

A minute later it was broken and the cartridges were spilling out into his palm. He jammed it closed, put it back, and heaved himself back onto his own bunk just as the slap-slap of Fowler's footsteps started back along the passageway. "Now, buddy!" he thought grimly.

Fowler finished undressing and got under the covers. "Gosh, the air's stale in here!" he muttered, more to himself than Sherman. "Seems to get ranker by the minute!"

"Whaddya want me to do, hand yuh a bunch of violets?" Babe snarled viciously. He got up and went out, for appearance's sake, then stayed just outside the door, head bent, listening. Fowler didn't make a move, at least not to or at the trunk. Sherman took good aim out through the open window that gave onto the little cubicle between their cabin and the next, let fly with the handful of bullets. They cleared the deck beautifully, every last one of them.

He went back in again, saw that Fowler already had his eyes closed, faking it probably. He took off his coat and shoes, put out the light, lay down like he was. The motion of the boat, and the black and orange frieze of the ventilator high up near the ceiling—the corridor lights stayed on all night—were all that remained. And the breathing of two mortal enemies, the stalker and the stalked. . . .

Sherman, who had cursed the ventilator to hell and back after it had nearly betrayed him that time, now suddenly found that it was going to come in handy after all. It let in just enough light, once your eyes got used to the change, so that it wouldn't be necessary to turn on the cabin light again when the time came to get her out. He couldn't have risked that under any circumstances, even if it took him half the night to find the keyhole of the trunk with the key. This way it wouldn't.

The guy was right at that, though, it *was* getting noticeable in here.

He planned it step by step first, without moving his shoulders from the berth. Get rid of her first and then attend to the dick later was the best way. She couldn't wait, the dick could. They had

six days to go yet, and the dick couldn't just drop from sight without it backfiring in some way. Down here wasn't the right spot either. They might run into heavy weather in a day or two, and if he watched his opportunity he might be able to catch the dick alone on the upper deck after the lights went out. Even raise a "Man overboard!" after he went in, if it seemed advisable. Or if not, be the first to report his disappearance the day after.

So now for her. He knew the set-up on these boats. There was always a steward on night duty at the far end of the corridor, to answer any possible calls. He'd have to be gotten out of the way to begin with, sent all the way down to the pantry for something, if possible. Yet he mustn't rap on the door here in answer to the call and wake up the flatfoot. And he mustn't come back too quickly and catch Babe out of the cabin—although that was the lesser danger of the two and could always be explained away by the washroom. Now for it; nothing like knowing every step in advance, couldn't be caught off-base that way.

6

There is an art in being able to tell by a person's breathing if he is asleep or just pretending to be; it was one of Sherman's many little accomplishments. But there is another art, too, that goes with it—that of being able to breathe so you fool the person doing the listening. This, possibly, may have been the other man's accomplishment. His breathing deepened, got scratchier—but very slowly. It got into its stride, and little occasional burblings welled up in it, very artistically. Not snores by any means, just catches in the larynx. Sherman, up on his elbow, thought: "He's off. He couldn't breathe that way for very long if he wasn't—be too much of a strain."

He got up off the bunk and put on his coat, so the white of his undershirt wouldn't show. He picked up the shirt that Fowler had ruined and balled it up tightly into fist-size, or not much bigger. He got out the trunk key and put it down on the floor right in front of the trunk, between his bent legs. He spit muffedly into his free hand, soaked the hollow of it. Then he gave that a half-turn up against the lock and each of the clamps. The lock opened quietly enough, but the clamps had a snap to them that the saliva alone wouldn't take care of. He smothered them under the ganged-up shirt as he pressed each one back. He got it down to a tiny click. Then he took a long, hard look over at Fowler through the gloom. That suction was still working in his throat.

The trunk split apart fairly noiselessly, with just one or two minor squeaks, and he had to turn his head for a minute—for a different reason this time. The way it had opened, though, was all to the good, one side of it shielded him from Fowler's bunk.

He had to go carefully on the next step, couldn't just remove her. There were too many loose things in there, all the busted partitions and drawers would clack together and racket. He got them out first, piece by piece. She came last, and wasn't very heavy.

Now here was where the steward came into it. He had a choice of risks: not to bother with the steward at all, to try sneaking down the passageway in the opposite direction with her. That was out entirely. All the steward would have to do was stick his head out of the little room where the call-board was and spot him. Or, to leave her out, but in here, in the dark, and tackle the steward outside. He didn't like that one either. Fowler might open his eyes from one moment to the next and let out a yell. So he had to get her out of here, and yet keep the steward from coming near her outside. The inset between the cabins, outside the door, was the answer—but the steward must *not* turn the corner and come all the way! It was all a question of accurate timing.

He was as far as the cabin door now, but that was a problem in itself. He was holding her up against him like a ventriloquist's dummy, legs still folded up flat while she hung down straight. He got the door open without any creaking, but a sunburst of orange seemed to explode around him and his burden. It didn't reach all the way to

Fowler's berth, but it could very well tickle his eyelids open if it was left on too long.

He stepped across the raised threshold with her, holding on to the door so it wouldn't swing with the ship's motion. Then without letting go of it he managed to let her down to the floor out there. He turned and went in again alone, to ring for the steward; as he did so an optical illusion nearly floored him for a second. It was that Fowler had suddenly stiffened to immobility in the midst of movement. But he was in the same position that he had been before—or seemed to be—and his lids were down and the clucking was still going on in his throat. There was no time to worry about it, either he was awake or he wasn't—and he wasn't, must have just stirred in his sleep.

The steward's bell, Sherman knew, didn't make any sound in the cabin itself, only way out at the call-board. He punched it, got back to the door before it had time to swing too far shut or open, and then eased it closed. She was right beside him on the floor out there, but he didn't look at her, listened carefully. In a minute he heard the put-put of shoeleather coming down from the other end of the passageway. Now!

He drifted negligently around the corner, started up toward the steward to head him off; the man was still two of those lateral insets away. They came together between his, Babe's and the next.

"Did you ring, sir?"

Sherman put his head on the steward's arm appealingly. "I feel rotten," he said in a low voice. "Get me some black coffee, will you? Too many brandies all afternoon and evening." He looked the part, from what he'd just gone through—if nothing else.

"Yes, sir, right away," the steward said briskly. And then instead of turning back, he took a step to get around Sherman and continue on down the passageway, toward where the body was!

"What're you going that way for?" Sherman managed to say, gray now.

"The main pantry's closed, sir, at this hour. We have a little one for sandwiches and things in back of the smoking room, I'll heat you some up there—"

"Here I go!" was all Sherman had time to think. The whole boat went spinning around him dizzily for a minute, but his reflexes kept working for him. Without even knowing what he was doing, he got abreast of the steward—on the side where she was—and accompanied him back, partly turned toward him. The steward was a shorter man, only Sherman's outthrust shoulder kept him from seeing what lay sprawled there as the inset opened out to one side of them. He pulled the same stunt he had on Fowler when he was getting the trunk closed under his nose, kept jabbering away with his eyes glued on the steward's, holding them steady on his own face.

The steward stepped past, and the opening closed behind him again. Sherman dropped back, but still guarding it with his body. His jaws were yammering automatically: "—never could stand the coffee in Paris, like drinking mud. All right, you know where to find me—"

The steward went on and disappeared at the upper end. Sherman, in the inset, crumpled to his hands and knees for a minute, like an animal, stomach heaving in and out. This last tension had been too much for him, coming on top of everything else. "All to keep from dying twenty years too soon!" he thought miserably, fighting his wretchedness.

He got himself in shape again in a hurry, had to, and a minute later was groping up the corridor in the opposite direction, lopsidedly, borne down by her dimensions if not her weight on one side, his other arm out to steady himself against the wall.

There was no one out at the stairlanding now that the steward was out of the way, and only a single overhead light was burning. He decided to chuck the stairs and do it right from this A-deck. One deck higher or lower couldn't make any difference if he went far enough back to the stern. And there might be other stewards on night duty on the other deck levels.

He put her down for a minute on a wicker set-tee out there, unhooked the double doors to the deck, and looked out. Deserted and pitch dark. A minute later she was out there with him, and the end of his long, harrowing purgatory was in sight. Babe couldn't keep his hands from trembling.

He didn't go right to the rail with her. There was still the necklace, for one thing, and then the nearer the stern the better to make a clean-cut job of it. You couldn't see your hand in front of your face beyond the rail, but the deck wall on the other side of him showed up faintly white in the gloom, broken by black squares that were the cabin windows.

Near the end of the superstructure there was a sharp indentation, an angle where it jutted farther out, and in this were stacked sheaves of deck chairs, folded up flat and held in place by a rope. There were, however, three that had been left unfolded side by side, perhaps made use of by some late strollers and that the deck steward had missed putting away, and one of them even had a steamer rug left bunched across it.

He let her down on one of them and bent over her to finish freeing the necklace. The handkerchief had remained in place all this time, for some reason. But it was one of his own and huge, touched her shoulders. He had to discard it to be able to see what he was doing. Loosened, the breeze promptly snatched it down the deck and it vanished. His hands reached for the loose end of the necklace, where he had already filed it through close to the clasp—and then stayed that way, poised, fingers pointing inward in a gesture that was like a symbol of avarice defeated.

The platinum strand was there, but invisible now in the dark, naked of pearls! Not two or three but the whole top row had dropped off, one by one, somehow, somewhere along the way! The motion of carrying her, of picking her up and setting her down so repeatedly, must have loosened them one at a time, jogged them off through that break in the wire he himself had caused. And since it obviously hadn't happened while she was still in the trunk, what it amounted to was: he had left a trail of pearls behind him, every step of the way he had come with her from the cabin out here—like that game kids play with chalk marks called Hare-and-hounds—but with death for its quarry. An overwhelming sense of futility and disaster assailed him.

They wouldn't stay in one place, they'd roll around, but they were there behind him just the same, pointing the way. It was only the top row that had been stripped clean, the other two had been tourniqueted in too tight for any to fall off. . . .

He had no more than made the discovery, with his fingertips and not his eyes, than a figure loomed toward him out of the deck gloom, slowly, very slowly, and Fowler's voice drawled suavely:

"I'll take the rest of 'em now, that go with the ones I been pickin' up on the way."

Sherman automatically gave the blanket beside him a fillip that partly covered her, then stood up and went out toward him, knees already crouched for the spring that was to come. The gloom made Fowler seem taller than he was. Sherman could sense the gun he was holding leveled at him by the rigid foreshortening of his one arm. The thing was, was it still empty or had he reloaded it since?

7

He started circling, with Fowler for an axis, trying to maneuver him closer to the rail. That brought the chair more clearly into Fowler's line of vision, but the position of his head never changed, slowly turned in line with Sherman. Suddenly it dawned on Sherman that the dick didn't know the whole story even yet; hadn't tumbled yet to what was on that chair! Must have taken it for just a bunched-up steamer rug in the dark. Sure! Otherwise he'd be hollering blue murder by this time, but all he'd spoken about was the pearls. Hadn't seen Sherman carry her out after all, then; thought he was just on the trail of a jewel smuggler.

"But in a minute more he'll see her; he's bound to!" he told himself. "Dark or not, his eyes'll be deflected over that way. And that's when—"

While his feet kept carrying him slowly sidewise across the deck, from the chair toward the rail, he muttered: "*You* will? Who says so?"

Fowler palmed his badge at him with his left hand. "This says so. Now come on, why make it tough for yourself? I've got you dead to rights and you know it! They're so hot they're smoking. Fork 'em over and don't keep me waiting out here all night, or I'll—"

Sherman came up against the rail. Had he reloaded that persuader or hadn't he? "I can only be wrong once about it," he figured grimly. He jerked his head at the chair. "The tin always wins. Help yourself!" His knees buckled a notch lower.

He saw the pupils of Fowler's eyes follow the direction his head had taken, start back again, then stop dead—completely off him. "Oh, so you *are* working with a shill after all! What's she showing her teeth, grinning so about? D'ye think I'm a kid—?"

He never finished it. Sherman's stunning blow—the one he'd promised him in the train—his whole body following it, landed in an arc up from where he'd been standing. His fist caught Fowler on the side of the neck, nearly paralyzing his nerve centers for a minute, and the impact of Sherman's body coming right after it sent him down to the deck with Sherman on top of him. The gun clicked four times into the pit of Sherman's stomach before they'd even landed, and the impact with which the back of the dick's head hit the deck told why it didn't click the two remaining times. He was stunned for a minute, lay there unresisting. Less than a minute—much less—but far too long!

Sherman got up off him, pulled him up after him, bent him like a jackknife over the rail, then caught at his legs with a vicious dip. The gun, which was still in the dick's hand, fell overboard as he opened it to claw at the empty night. His legs cleared the rail at Sherman's heave like those of a pole vaulter topping a bar, but his faculties had cleared just in time for his finish. His left hand closed despairingly around a slim, vertical deck-support as the rest of his body went over. The wrench nearly pulled it out of its socket, turned him completely around in mid-air so that he was facing Sherman's way for a brief instant. His face was a piteous blur against the night that would have wrung tears from the Evil One himself.

But a human being was sending him to his death, and they can be more remorseless than the very devils of hell. "I don't want to die!" the blurred face shrieked out. The flat of Sherman's foot, shooting out between the lower deck-rails like a battering-ram, obliterated it for a minute. The gripping hand flew off the upright support into nothingness. When Sherman's foot came back through the rails again, the face was gone. The badge was all that was left lying there on the deck.

The last thing Sherman did was pick that up and shie it out after him. "Take that with you, Cop, you'll need it for your next pinch!"

Carrying out his original purpose, after what had just happened, was almost like an anticlimax; he was hardly aware of doing so at all, just a roundtrip to the rail and back. He leaned up against the deck wall for a minute, panting with exertion. The partly denuded necklace, freed at last from its human ballast, in the palm of his hand. "You've cost me plenty!" he muttered to it. He dumped it into his pocket.

Suddenly the deck lights had flashed on all around him, as if lightning had struck the ship. He cringed and turned this way and that. They were standing out there, bunched by the exit through which he himself had come a little while ago, stewards and ship's officers, all staring ominously down toward him. He knew enough not to try to turn and slink away; he was in full sight of them, and a second group had showed up behind him, meanwhile, at the lower end of the deck, cutting him off in that direction. That last scream Fowler ripped out from the other side of the rail, probably; the wind must have carried it like an amplifier all over the ship at once.

"But they didn't see me do it!" he kept repeating to himself vengefully, as they came down the deck toward him from both directions, treading warily, spread out fanwise to block his escape. "They didn't see me do it! They gave it the lights out here just a minute too late!"

The chief officer had a gun out in his hand, and a look on his face to match it. They meant business. One by one the cabin windows facing the deck lighted up; the whole ship was rousing. This wasn't just another hurdle any more; this was a dead end—the last stop, and he knew it.

Suddenly he came to a decision. The net was closing in on him and in a minute more his freedom of action would be gone forever. He didn't waste it, but used it while he still had it to cut himself free from the first crime even while the second was tangling around him tighter every instant.

He found the rail with the backs of his elbows, leaned there negligently, waiting for them. Right as they came up, his elbows slipped off the rail again, his hands found his trouser pockets in a gesture that looked simply like cocky bravado. Then he withdrew them again, gave one a slight unnoticeable backhand-flip through the rails. The motion, screened by his body, remained unobserved; their eyes were on his face. The necklace had gone back to Manon, the job had blown up—but it couldn't be helped, he had his own skin to think of now.

The chief officer's eyes were as hard as the metal that pointed out of his fist at Sherman's middle. "What'd you do with that man Fowler?" he clipped.

Sherman grinned savagely back around his ear. "What'd *I* do with him? I left him pounding his ear in 42-A. We're not Siamese twins. Is there a regulation against coming out here to stretch my legs—?"

The night steward cut in with: "I didn't like how he acted when he ordered the cawfee a while ago, sir. That's why I reported to you. When I took it in to him they were both gone, and the insides of this man's trunk were all busted up and lying around, like they had a fierce fight—"

A woman leaning out of one of the cabin windows shrilled almost hysterically: "Officer! Officer! I heard somebody fall to the deck right outside my window here, the sound woke me up, and then somebody screamed: 'I don't want to die!' And when I jumped up to look out—" Her voice broke uncontrollably for a minute.

The officer was listening intently, but without turning his head away from Sherman or deflecting the gun.

"—he was kicking at a *face* through the rails! I saw it go down—! I—I fainted away for a minute, after that!" She vanished from the window, someone's arm around her, sobbing loudly in a state of collapse.

The net was closing around him, tighter, every minute. "We all heard the scream," the officer said grimly, "but that tells us what it meant—"

The bulky captain showed up, one of his shirttails hanging out under his hurriedly donned uniform-jacket. He conferred briefly with the chief officer, who retreated a pace or two without taking his gun off Sherman. The latter stood there, at bay against the rail, a husky deckhand gripping him by each shoulder now.

The gun was lowered, only to be replaced by a pair of hand-cuffs. The captain stepped forward. "I arrest you for murder! Hold out your hands! Mr. Moulton, put those on him!"

The deckhands jerked his forearms out into position, his cuffs shot back. The red welt across his knuckles where he'd bruised them against Fowler's jawbone revealed itself to every eye there.

He flinched as the cold steel locked around him. "I didn't do it—he fell overboard!" he tried to say. "It's her word against mine—!" But the net was too tight around him, there was no room left to struggle, even verbally.

The captain's voice was like a roll of drums ushering in an execution—the first of the hundreds, the thousands of questions that were going to torment him like gadflies, drive him out

of his mind, until the execution that was even now rushing toward him remorselessly from the far side of the ocean would seem like a relief in comparison. "What was your motive in doing away with this man, sending him to his death?"

He didn't answer. The malevolent gods of his warped destiny did it for him, sending another of the stewards hurrying up from the deck below, the answer in both his outstretched hands, a thin flat badge, a gnarled string of pearls, half-gone.

"I found this and this, sir, on the B-deck just now! I thought I heard a scream out there a while back and I went out to look. Just as I turned to come in again this, this shield landed at my feet, came sailing in from nowhere on the wind like a boomerang. I put on the lights thinking someone had had an accident down on that deck, and a little while afterward I caught sight of this necklace down at the very end. The wind had whipped it around one of the deck-supports like a paper streamer—"

Sherman just looked at the two objects, white and still. The night had thrown back the evidence he had tried to get rid of, right into his very teeth! There were two executions waiting for him now, the tall knife at Vincennes, the electric chair at one of the Federal penitentiaries—and though he could only die once, what consolation was it that only by one death could he cheat the other?

The captain said: "He's as good as dead already! Take him down below and keep him under double guard until we can turn him over to the Federal authorities when we reach Quarantine."

Sherman stumbled off in the middle of all of them, unresisting. But he did crack up completely when the captain—just as they were taking him inside—folded a yellow wireless message and showed it to the chief officer. "Funny part of it is," he heard him say, "this came in not fifteen minutes ago, from the New York City police authorities, asking us to hold this man Fowler for them, for blackmail, for preying on people on ships and trains, impersonating a detective abroad. The badge is phony, of course. If our friend here had kept his hands off him for just a quarter of an hour more—"

Sherman didn't hear the rest of it. There was a rush of blood to his ears that drowned it out, and the laughter of the Furies seemed to shriek around him while they prodded him with white-hot irons. All he knew was that he was going to die for a murder that could have been avoided, in order to cover up one that otherwise would quite probably never have been revealed!

The House of Kaa
Richard Sale

A PROLIFIC WRITER for the pulps, Richard Sale (1911–1993) also wrote such successful novels as *Lazarus #7* (1942), *Passing Strange* (1942), *Not Too Narrow—Not Too Deep* (1936), which was filmed in 1940 as *Strange Cargo,* and *For the President's Eyes Only* (1971). He devoted most of his writing energy to writing and directing movies, including *Mr. Belvedere Goes to College* (1949), the Frank Sinatra vehicle *Suddenly* (1954), and *Gentlemen Marry Brunettes* (1955).

Among his pulp fiction, he is most remembered for the reporter/detective series about Daffy Dill, written for *Detective Fiction Weekly,* and his adventure-packed tales written for *Ten Detective Aces* about The Cobra, one of the early examples of what is generally known among pulp aficionados as a "Weird Menace" or "Avenger" story. Such characters as The Shadow, The Avenger, The Spider, Operator 5, and The Phantom Detective were among the most popular figures in the pulps. They mainly dressed in costumes, usually with masks, sometimes with capes, as they wreaked justice without bothering about the police, judges, or juries.

In "The House of Kaa," first published in the February 1934 issue of *Ten Detective Aces,* villains abound and The Cobra kills them with impunity. No masked avenger is worth his salt unless confronted by larger-than-life crooks, and those in the following story meet the standard.

The House of Kaa

Richard Sale

Scotland Yard thought it strange that the firm of Gorgan & Wilkins imported only regal pythons. But no law was being broken. And they thought it very strange when the Cobra, a lone avenger from India, suddenly appeared in London. But the Cobra had once helped them, so there was no investigation. And the greatest surprise of all was the appearance of Deen Bradley of the British Intelligence—who had an amazing plan to offer.

The python mauled the corpse

JACK KIRK, whose profession had never been anything but sordid murder, paused before the dreary brownstone house on Rokor Street. He glanced all about him in a wary and frightened sort of way.

He could have sworn that some one was following him. If not some one—*something!* A black, misshapen, baroque giant. A flitting spectre.

Kirk had seen a shadow—only for an instant.

Then the shadow had disintegrated like the whispering dissipation of a gliding ghost.

Kirk shook his shoulders and blamed it on his imagination. He went slowly up the short flight of stairs in the front of the house and glanced at the sign over the door. It read:

GORGAN & WILKINS—REPTILE IMPORTERS

Quickly, Kirk pulled a key from his pocket, inserted it in the lock, and opened the door. He entered with alacrity, slamming it after him.

The main hall was dark as pitch. But Kirk knew where he was going. He ascended the long, creaking staircase to the second floor of the dreary place. A solitary light on the second floor led him to a door marked "Office."

He rapped sharply four times and entered.

Three men were in the room. He recognized them as Maxie Gorgan, John Wilkins, and the man from India, Wentworth Lane. They had been talking but now they looked up at him.

"Sit down, Jack," Gorgan smirked. "Lane here is reporting on our—ah—Indian importations." He grinned knowingly.

Kirk smiled and sat down. Lane bit his lip angrily.

"You can be as sarcastic as you like, Maxie," he snapped, "but I tell you it's so. I don't know about this end, but I do know that the police are close to catching us in Bombay. There was an American operative on my trail for several days before I left for London. You know, the one we checked on."

"What do they suspect you of?" Gorgan leered. "Maybe they think you're maltreating snakes!" He laughed harshly. "Listen, Lane, you're an agent for a company. You're an importer of reptiles from India."

"But the trouble is—the only reptiles I ever import to you are regal pythons. It's damned suspicious."

"If you're afraid—" Gorgan began coldly.

Lane leaped to his feet, his eyes blazing.

"You want me to deny I am. Well, I'm not lying for any one. And you can't make me! I *am* afraid! And I'm going to get out!"

Gorgan eyed Wilkins surreptitiously and nodded. Kirk, watching the proceedings, was mildly amused. He failed to see what had gotten Lane's wind up so. Lane had been a good reliable man on the Bombay end.

"Just a second, Lane," Wilkins purred softly. "Maybe you're right. Maybe we've misjudged you. We don't want you to quit."

"No," Gorgan added with a trace of acerbity, "you can't quit."

"Well, I'm going to nevertheless," Lane declared stridently. His voice lowered as he leaned forward. "Did you ever hear of the Cobra?" he whispered.

Gorgan and Wilkins looked dumb. They shook their heads.

"Did you, Kirk?"

Jack Kirk smiled amusedly.

"Yeah," he replied. "Sure, I've heard of him. Some sort of a guy who thinks he's a public avenger. Goes around alone."

Lane nodded. "That's he—the Cobra."

"But he's supposed to be in India." Kirk was enjoying this baiting Lane. "You know how those yarns get around the underworld. The last thing they had on that guy was when he put down the Persian uprising in Bombay. Last month, I think."

Lane said, "Yes, last month. And we started this business last month. It was all right when we got away with those emeralds and that Mahar diamond. I thought the whole layout was foolproof. But I haven't felt right since I shipped the Kubij opal to you. That's a damned unlucky stone. It belonged to Sarankh, a rajah of the Hindustan country. I hired three dacoits to steal it, paid them well, and sent the stone through the customs with our regular snake freight.

"Right after that, this American detective came around and asked a lot of queer questions. But we have a good front with this reptile-importing set-up and I got around him.

"Then the Cobra stepped in—and I was so upset over the affair that I took the first and fastest boat here to see you. I tell you, a child could guess the answer from the fact that the only snakes we ship are pythons!"

Wilkins laughed. "Don't be an ass!"

Jack Kirk leaned forward. "What's this about the Cobra, Lane?" he asked frowning. "What happened?"

"The three dacoits I hired," Lane explained soberly, "were found dead the day before I left for London—*dead from cobra venom!* And there were tiny darts in their throats!"

"Darts?" Kirk echoed, feeling his own throat in dread.

Lane smiled mirthlessly. "Yes, darts. The mark of the Cobra. A dart in the throat covered with noxious cobra venom. That's how the devil gets his name."

"Listen," Gorgan snarled, "don't let him hypnotize you, Jack. This Cobra stuff is crazy! I've

THE HOUSE OF KAA

had enough of this cock-and-bull yarn, Lane. You're welching and you're taking the easiest way out. There's nothing wrong. The Kubij opal will arrive tomorrow with our python shipment."

"I tell you, I'm afraid!" Lane cried. "I'm quitting, Maxie. I'm getting out. I don't want any money from the jewels. I want my life. You can split my share among the three of you."

Maxie Gorgan rose steadily to his feet. His voice was icy and sinister. His hand stole stealthily inside of his coat.

"You can't quit this game, Lane," he warned.

Lane looked at him coolly, evenly.

"You heard me, Maxie," he replied fearlessly. "When the Cobra steps in—I step out. And that's final."

The three shots from Gorgan's pistol sounded like one. Three hot slugs buried themselves in Lane's chest like lightning. Lane stared at Gorgan's tense face in stupefaction. His lips moved soundlessly. He struggled bravely to speak. Blood poured from his mouth. His legs sagged and he fell forward on his face, crashing to the floor with an ominous thump. He did not move after he hit.

Kirk wet his lips and put out the cigarette he had been smoking.

"God, Max!" Wilkins exclaimed in horror. "You shouldn't have done it!"

Gorgan shrugged and put his gun back.

"It's his own funeral. I told him. We can't afford to have a welcher, Wilky. There's too much money involved. Besides, there's only a split of three now, and dead men tell no tales. Kirk—get rid of this stiff. Use the car outside. Dump him out at Yorkshire."

Kirk sighed.

"Okay, chief," he said.

Jack Kirk did not notice the black sedan which followed him and his macabre burden through Surrey. Kirk was intent upon the operation of his vehicle, since even the slightest accident would incur the intervention of police. And with a dead man to be explained, Kirk was taking no chances.

The black car tailed him tenaciously out past Surrey into the suburbs of London.

Nor could Kirk see the figure at the wheel of the mystery car—a dark incongruous figure, covered by a black cloak, its face concealed by the dark shadows of the turbid night.

To a prowling cat, whose green eyes might have pierced the darkness, the hawklike features of Deen Bradley would have been discernible. Deen was an operative of the Bombay Department of Justice. High-foreheaded, dark-skinned, he had black eyes which glittered coldly like ebony diamonds, hard, unemotional. He had no mustache. His face was thin and sharp. His lips, narrow and straight-lined.

He handled the car with natural dexterity, never shifting his cobra eyes from the red taillight of the cadaver-car before him.

At Yorkshire, Kirk left the main highway and swerved to the right. Deen followed quickly, stepping down on the gas.

The American suddenly saw the brake-light of the other machine flare into being. Kirk slowed momentarily and, as he did so, a limp bundle tumbled lifelessly from the rolling car.

Then, Kirk sped away with amazing alacrity, his engine roaring sonorously into the night.

The fog drifting across the open countryside swallowed the lights of his car.

Deen slammed his brakes to the floor of the sedan, and the automobile skidded perilously to a halt. Beside it, in a ditch, lay the bundle which had been thrown from Kirk's car.

Deen leaped from the sedan and ran forward. He found a man, bleeding profusely and unconscious. He bent down and lifted up the fellow on his right arm.

The face of Wentworth Lane stared at him, eyes sightless and horrible.

"Zah!" Deen muttered in repugnance. "So it is murder, too!"

He grasped the wrist of the unconscious Lane and felt for a possible flicker of life.

Instantly he jumped to his feet and dashed for the sedan, carrying Lane in his arms. His strength was astonishing. He carried Lane, who was heavy-set, as though the latter was a child. Carefully he laid the wounded man on the cushions. Then he hopped agilely into the front seat and pressed the accelerator to the floor.

Twenty minutes later, Lane was on a white-enameled operating table in the Yorkshire hospital while two doctors bent over him, working furiously to save his life. Deen stood by, anxiously waiting.

Presently one of the doctors looked up and shook his head.

"He's dying."

Deen frowned. He asked, "There is no chance?"

"None. I don't see how he keeps alive. Two bullets through his right lung. A third against his spine. It's miraculous!"

The dying man gasped paroxysmally.

"Can he be made to talk?" asked Deen.

The doctor shrugged dubiously. He turned to a nurse.

"Adrenalin," he snapped.

He leaned over the naked chest of Lane and drove a hypodermic syringe into the flesh directly over the heart. Then he emptied the contents.

Momentarily, there was no visible result.

Then Lane's staring eyes gained the power of sight and recognition. They glanced around furtively. Finally they rested on Deen's dark face.

"You—"

"Yes. It is I. From India. I followed you. Quick, you must speak. You are dying."

Lane coughed rackingly.

"Gorgan," he muttered whisperingly. "Pythons—code word is—House of Kaa—"

His lips had hardly stopped moving when he sighed. His body relaxed.

The doctors made preparations to transfer the corpse into the mortuary for identification and signing of the death certificate. With the American to establish identity—

But when they glanced around for him, Deen was gone.

That night, the police found the cadaver of Jack Kirk in Rokor Street, London. Kirk was sprawled crazily in the gutter—dead. Protruding from his throat was a small dart, about a half an inch long.

The chief medical examiner found that Kirk

had died as the result of the violent neurotoxic destruction of cobra venom.

And throughout the underworld of London, a dire, foreboding wail echoed—a wail that spelled the nemesis of criminals.

The Cobra had come to England!

"Well, what are we going to do?" Commissioner Marshall asked sharply.

Inspector Ryder shrugged. The two men were sitting in the commissioner's office at the C. I. D. headquarters in Scotland Yard. In Marshall's hand was the coroner's report on the Jack Kirk murder the night preceding.

"I'd suggest nothing," the inspector said with a flip of his hand. "The department has been after Kirk for two years. He was a killer. One of the few English bandits who carried and used a gun. He was working for that Gorgan-Wilkins reptile firm over on Rokor Street. There's something damned queer going on over there, too. As far as I'm concerned, chief, I'd let it go."

"You mean—drop the case entirely?"

"Yes, sir." Ryder leaned forward. "We've had excellent reports about this Cobra from Bombay headquarters. It was he who brought those Persian renegades to justice after they murdered Kilgore, one of the C. I. D.'s best men."

"I remember that," Marshall nodded.

Ryder grimaced. "We owe him a good turn. Commissioner—I don't know who or what the Cobra is. But I *do* know that he gets results because he goes outside of the law. He saved me a lot of trouble getting Kirk. And there must be a reason. I wager that important business has brought the Cobra to London."

"Very well," the commissioner sighed. "Drop investigation."

At that moment, there was a knock on the door. An attendant looked in. "Mr. Bradley to see you, sir."

"Send him in."

The door opened, and the dark-skinned, hawk-faced Deen Bradley walked in.

"Happy to know you, Bradley," Marshall exclaimed, rising and shaking hands with sincere enthusiasm. "Meet Inspector Ryder. Bradley is one of the best in Bombay, Ryder."

"I know," the inspector said. "Thanks for helping us out on that Kilgore case down there."

"I did very little," Deen replied softly. "In reality, you should thank him who calls himself the Cobra."

"That's a coincidence!" Marshall cried. "Your Bombayan avenger happens to be in London. Did you read it? The Kirk affair."

"The commissioner's called off an investigation," Ryder remarked, eyeing the American keenly.

Deen nodded without a trace of emotion, said: "Very wise."

"But what brings you here?" Marshall queried. "Bombay cabled me to watch for you and give you any aid you asked."

Deen sat down and pulled a peculiar greenish cigarette holder from his pocket. Slowly, he inserted a cigarette in it and lighted it.

"For the last month," he began, "there have been strange robberies in India along the eastern coast. Emeralds and diamonds of priceless value have been purloined by hired dacoits. Most notorious was the recent theft of the Kubij opal of the Rajah Sarankh."

"We heard of that," put in Ryder.

"All these jewels are being exported from India," Deen continued. "Somehow they are being smuggled out—past the customs officials. More paradoxical—they are being smuggled *into* England past the watchful scrutiny of your revenue officers here.

"I resolved to investigate. It was no general sneak-thief job, I knew. It appeared to be an international imbroglio, carefully planned and executed. A jewel ring. I tracked a Wentworth Lane to London to lead me to the lost jewels. Last night, he too was murdered—by his own cohorts."

"But how can these jewels get into England past the customs?" the inspector demanded. "They are very rigid, you know."

"True, they are rigid," Deen murmured. "But do the customs men cut open the bellies of regal pythons to look for stolen jewels?"

Ryder stared at the American, dumbfounded.

"Good Gad!" he cried sharply. "Smuggling by snakes! You mean, then, that Gorgan-Wilkins reptile outfit is the center of the ring! They import nothing but pythons. And they hardly ever sell any of the snakes. The reptiles just disappear. I checked that when I first became suspicious of that company."

"You see," Deen explained, "it is very simple. The jewels are stolen in India by hired dacoits. Then, securely wrapped, they are placed in food which is swallowed by the pythons immediately prior to shipment. Since a big snake takes ten to eighteen days to assimilate and digest its food before throwing off waste, the seven-day sea trip to London is completed within that time. When the snakes arrive, they are killed and the jewels recovered from the stomach!"

"Amazing!" breathed the commissioner. "We'll arrest them at once!"

"No." Deen's voice was clear and firm. "You must not arrest them yet. You must help me. We will need evidence—the Kubij opal, perhaps. And I have a simple plan."

Maxie Gorgan eyed John Wilkins thoughtfully as the latter paced the floor of the House of Kaa in Rokor Street. Wilkins was highly excited and nervous. He had been smoking incessantly.

"You're acting like a kid," Gorgan muttered.

"I can't help it, Maxie," Wilkins said. "This thing's getting my goat. First you knock off Lane—"

"Keep your mouth shut!"

"Aw, no one can hear us. Anyway, Lane dies first. Then Kirk, after dumping him, is found dead right outside with one of those damned poisoned darts in his throat. I wouldn't give a hang, Maxie, if it weren't for that Cobra story that Lane told us before you rubbed him out."

"You're getting scared over nothing," Gorgan said. "Suppose this guy who calls himself the Cobra *is* on to us. What of it? He's outside the law, isn't he? And he's a lone wolf, isn't he? And above all, remember, he's a man—a single man. And he'll have to come to us. He can't go to the police. One man. I can handle him, Wilky."

Wilkins shook his head.

"I'm leery. Suppose they're on to the shipment we got today. The pythons. They're here, aren't they?"

"Yeah," Gorgan growled. "And when you lose those jitters, we'll go down and get the Kubij opal."

"I don't like it, Maxie," Wilkins protested. "The whole organization is shot. With Kirk gone, who's going to fence the jewels after we melt them down? With Lane gone—who's going to take over the Bombay end of the business?"

The doorbell at the front of the house jingled stridently.

A deep pall of silence covered the office. Gorgan's hand crept inside his coat and brought out an ugly automatic. He waved Wilkins away and went to the window.

A solitary man was standing before them. A tall, gaunt man with piercing black eyes. No one else was in sight.

"Let him in," Gorgan said curtly. "Keep him covered all the time. Lock the door after you. Hurry!"

Wilkins complied nervously and went downstairs.

He presently reappeared behind Deen Bradley who entered the office smoking a cigarette, that same peculiar green holder held tightly between his teeth. He bowed to Gorgan.

"Sit down," Maxie said, nodding to a chair.

Deen seated himself and smiled mirthlessly. "You may remove that finger from the trigger of your gun," he purred. "I am unarmed."

Gorgan flushed guiltily and his eyes narrowed. He lifted the pistol from his pocket and laid it on the desk in front of him, his right hand still curled around it.

"Frisk him, Wilky," he said.

"I did before," Wilkins replied. "No gun, Maxie."

Gorgan nodded. He said, "Okay, then. What do you want?"

Deen shifted the cigarette holder to the corner of his mouth. "I know you killed Lane," he said quietly.

Instantly Maxie Gorgan hurled himself to his feet and glowered at the American, the heavy Luger held tensely in his hand and aimed point-blank at Deen's skull.

"No need to fire," Deen said jocosely. "I could never prove it."

Gorgan hesitated, eyeing Deen warily. He sat down and fingered the trigger of the gun longingly.

"Who in hell are you?" he spat, "and what do you want? You'd better get down to business, mister. You're due for a slug."

"My name is Sam Trent," Deen replied. "I want to cut in."

"Cut in?"

"I know that Lane and Kirk were cogs in your jewel-smuggling organization," Deen said. "Since they are defunct, the necessity of engaging a capable man to assume charge of the Bombay headquarters is imminent. I learned all this from Lane. I saw, in India, that his courage was dissipating, that he would attempt to withdraw, so I followed him to London. Zah! There you have it. You need a man. I am he."

"You know a helluva lot for a stranger," Gorgan exclaimed belligerently, both disturbed and interested. "Maybe—since you're so smart— you also know the code word?"

Gorgan expected to catch Deen there. He paused triumphantly and his gun rose to a level with Deen's chest.

"But, of course," Deen said mildly. "House of Kaa."

Wilkins leaped to his feet like a shot. He cried, "Kaa! He knows it, Maxie. He must be straight. Lane would never have trusted him. How else could he have gotten hold of that? Kirk didn't even know. It was between Lane and you and me. For telegraphic correspondence to assure identification."

"So Lane told you, eh?" Gorgan mused.

"Yes."

"You know about the—business, too?"

"You refer to the shipping of the jewels in the pythons—"

"Okay." Maxie held up his hand. "You know

all right." He turned to Wilkins. "This may be a cross. I don't see how, but it may be. Better check him."

Deen smiled. "And how do you 'check' me?"

Gorgan regarded him coldly. "Lane told us more than once about a Yankee dick at the Bombay office who was always asking questions. We anticipated the guy might try something. His name is Deen Bradley. Maybe you're on the level. Maybe you're not. Wilkins—check those fingerprints he just left on the chair."

Deen frowned as Wilkins hurried forward and sprinkled a quantity of grayish powder on the spot where his hand had rested.

"You see," Gorgan said, grinning evilly, "Lane sent me a copy of that Yank dick's prints from India. We were taking no chances."

Deen's lips were a thin, bloodless line. The green cigarette holder stiffened between his teeth. Wilkins opened a file drawer and brought out two photographs. Carefully he compared them with the marks on the arm of the chair.

"The same, Maxie!"

Gorgan sighed, relieved. "I thought so. I thought if I prattled on a little, he'd leave his prints somewhere. So you're Deen Bradley, the famous Bombay operative, eh?" His voice snapped into a vicious snarl. "Well, you're on your last case! You're through. What do you think we are—pulling a raw stunt like this?"

Wilkins was trembling with excitement.

"What are we going to do, Maxie?" he demanded.

Gorgan smiled without humor.

"We'll take him down into the snake room. We'll put him in the pit and let him make friends with the big boy. The thirty-foot constrictor. The one we haven't fed for three weeks. Let's see how a rat can fight a python. And then we'll get the Kubij opal from the new shipment and take it on the lam. This business is all washed up, Wilky. We've made enough out of it."

Gorgan rose, his pistol ominously steady in his hand. "Okay, Deen," he growled. "Keep ahead of me. If you make any funny moves, this lead bites you instead of the snake."

Deen rose silently, his immobile face void of expression. He left the office, Gorgan's automatic prodding painfully into his back. They descended the stairs.

The descent took them into the cellar of the house, which, Deen noted, was not damp at all, the floors being amazingly desiccated. Before a huge metal door, the two men stopped him. Wilkins accepted the proffered pistol while Maxie unlocked the door. It swung open. Gorgan snapped on the lights. They entered, leaving the metal door unlocked behind them.

Deen stared in astonishment at the room. It was enormous, the entire breadth of the house above. In the center of the room was a pit, about twenty feet deep. It was lined with opaque glass and was empty. An iron railing surrounded it. Near the railing, on the far side, was a large packing case.

"A pretty showroom, isn't it?" Gorgan leered. "Watch!"

Deen gazed into the bottom of the pit, fascinated. Gorgan went to the wall and pulled down a short lever. The glass partition on one side began to rise. Instantly there was a sickening slithery scrape. The macabre head of a huge serpent slid out of the compartment in the wall to wind a path across the bottom of the pit, shaking the kinks and curls out of its great length. It was orange-brown and repugnantly thick. It raised its terrible snout, hungrily searching.

"He wants living food," Gorgan growled alarmingly.

He moved threateningly on Deen while Wilkins still held the pistol in Deen's back.

With a lightning blow, Deen twisted around and cracked Wilkins on the side of the jaw with fearful strength. The punch clipped the man cleanly, eliciting a resounding crack. Wilkins fell like an ox. The pistol dropped from his nerveless hand as a red welt flamed on his chin.

Deen dived for the gun, conscious of Gorgan behind him.

He felt a ringing blow on his head, as Gorgan slashed down his clenched fists like a lunatic. It stunned him momentarily. He fell dazedly on his side and struggled courageously for the pistol.

Maxie Gorgan reached it first. He lifted it and fired.

The slug ripped through Deen's coat and buried itself in the opaque glass of the snake pit behind the detective.

Painfully, Deen strove to raise himself, hanging precariously to the iron railing at his back.

Gorgan raised the gun quickly for a second shot.

"Wait!" Deen called breathlessly.

Gorgan hesitated, then relaxed his trigger finger still holding the heavy automatic at Deen's head. "What do you want? Talk fast!"

Deen nodded dejectedly.

"I admit defeat," he said in a low voice. "I have failed and therefore deserve to die. But before you kill me, I have one last request to make."

"What is it?" Gorgan snapped.

"I would like to smoke a last cigarette," Deen replied. "Surely you can not deny a doomed man that courtesy?"

A crafty look narrowed Gorgan's eyes as he threw a surreptitious glance at the glass pit and the huge python. He lowered the gun and nodded.

"Okay," he said. "Go ahead."

Deen rapidly felt in his pockets for his odd greenish cigarette holder. He found it and placed it between his teeth. Then he found a cigarette and started to make a pretense of lighting it.

Simultaneously, Gorgan sprang forward when Deen's head was slightly turned, and with almost preternatural strength, shoved the detective through the railing, hurling him cruelly into the glass pit.

Deen turned a complete somersault and landed thuddingly on his feet at the bottom. He turned. The regal serpent was not three feet away from him, its elliptical eyes regarding him with sinister austerity.

Meanwhile, Gorgan, certain that the detective was safely in the python pit, turned savagely to John Wilkins who had recovered from Deen's furious blow and was struggling to regain his feet.

"Your ace is in!" Gorgan snarled at him.

"You're through, Wilky. This is just the chance I've wanted. Lane dead. Kirk dead. The dick with the python. And now—*you!* There'll be no split on the jewels. They're all mine, mine!"

Crackling like a madman, he aimed the deadly Luger.

Wilkins gaped at him in horror and shrilly screamed.

Crack! Crack!

Jagged blue holes appeared in Wilkins' forehead as red blood poured copiously down his neck where the two bullets ripped his skull to pieces on the way out.

His legs collapsed suddenly, even while his eyes rolled sightlessly at Gorgan's smoking gun. He fell—right into the glass pit and on top of the python's back!

The great reptile reared up in pain and shock. Its terrible head slashed around in a razorlike strike and knocked Wilkins' dead body clear across the bottom of the pit from the force of the blow. The curved rows of fangs bit into Wilkins' clothes. They were not venomous but chewed into the cadaver viciously.

The two crushing loops of the serpentine phantasmagoria fell over the dead man, encircled him, and began to contract, the muscles rippling comberlike beneath the scaly skin.

It was a horrid spectacle—a python crushing a dead man.

Deen stood by, unhurt, watching the gruesome scene in lethargic fascination.

Suddenly, above him, he heard a harsh, bitter cry. Gorgan had watched his plans go awry. Wilkins' corpse had diverted the snake from the detective. The snake would try and swallow the cadaver but would get no further than the head, since it is impossible for any living constrictor to gulp down a man because of the width of the shoulders. He would have to kill Deen himself.

Bestially, Gorgan flung up the pistol.

Deen was taken almost unawares. He saw the ugly black nozzle of the automatic draw a bead on his eyes. With the alacrity of a bullet, he hurled himself to the floor of the pit. Simultaneously, the gun spat flame and death.

The slug tore Deen's coat and crashed against

the glass of the pit, crumbling the glass and leaving irregular footing against the side of the wall.

Deen had lifted himself on his hands, half-kneeling. The peculiar green cigarette holder was between his teeth again. It was held taut, stiff against his gleaming white teeth.

Gorgan was pulling the trigger of the pistol frantically but the lead was going wild, breaking down the glass of the pit.

There was a piercing, whistling *hiss* like that of an angry, hooded hamadryad.

Gorgan was suddenly transfixed. His eyes bulged maniacally. A purplish cyanotic color pervaded his flesh. His lips moved jabberingly but uttered no sound. A thin trickle of blood coursed slowly down from his throat, from a minute hole directly above his jugular vein. A tiny black hole—a dart-hole.

Gruesomely, Maxie Gorgan fought against the powerful nerve-destroying cobra venom which was seeping through his blood stream and tearing the vortex of his vasomotor system and lungs to shreds. His breath came in agonizing, sobbing gulps and each one was filled with inhuman pain. His face slowly grew black as the toxin destruction grew greater.

For a second, his voice gained audibility.

"You—" he rasped, a death rattle sounding in his throat—"the Cobra. . . ."

He fell forward into the pit, smashing down on his face and rolling over on his back, dead.

Deen climbed out of the pit where the python had swallowed the head of Wilkins and was fighting to engulf the man's shoulders, an impossibility. He stepped on the scant indentations of broken glass which the bullets had created.

The sound of axes tearing wood floated down to the cellar. He glanced at his watch. True to the hour, the police—as he had outlined in his plan with Ryder and Marshall—were raiding the gloomy House of Kaa.

Inspector Ryder burst into the pit-room, almost at the same instant, service revolver in hand. He surveyed the wreckage of the pit and whistled in horror. Quickly he put a hot bullet through the skull of the regal python. He gazed down and saw the noxious dart imbedded in the upturned throat of Maxie Gorgan.

"The Cobra!" Ryder exclaimed.

"Yes," Deen said. "The Cobra saved my life. Quick, may I have your revolver?"

Ryder regarded Deen keenly. The green cigarette holder in Deen's hand caught his eye. For the time being, he said nothing. He handed his gun over.

Deen went around the pit to the packing case which stood next to the railing. He found a hammer and ripped the top unceremoniously off the base. There were three more pythons within, all small specimens, from six to ten feet in length.

One had a small white piece of adhesive tape on the back of its head.

Fearlessly, Deen reached in and yanked the snake out with both his hands. Holding one hand behind the neck, he laid the snake on the floor, placed the gun against its brain and pulled the trigger. The snake thrashed slightly and was still.

Then, opening a knife, the detective slit open the belly, cut away the fatty tissues and lacerated the stomach.

When Deen stood up, a gleaming, dazzling flash of red fire struck Inspector Ryder in the eyes.

"The Kubij Opal!" he cried.

"Exactly," Deen murmured. "The case is over."

Ryder eyed the green cigarette holder in the detective's other hand.

"But what of the Cobra?" he asked.

Deen hastily pocketed the holder. His eyes twinkled.

"The Cobra disappeared just before you came in."

The Invisible Millionaire
Leslie Charteris

IT IS ALMOST impossible to measure the success of Leslie Charteris's famous creation, Simon Templar, better known as the Saint.

The Saint is anything but. He is an adventurer, a romantic hero who works outside the law and has grand fun doing it. Like so many crooks in literature, he is imbued with the spirit of Robin Hood, which suggests that it is perfectly all right to steal, so long as it is from someone with wealth. Most of the more than forty books about the Saint are collections of short stories or novellas, and in the majority of tales he also functions as a detective. Unconstricted by being an official policeman, he steps outside the law to retrieve money or treasure that may not have been procured in an honorable fashion, either to restore it to its proper owner or to enrich himself.

"Maybe I am a crook," Templar once says, "but in between times I'm something more. In my simple way I am a kind of justice."

In addition to the many books about the Saint, there were ten films about him, mainly starring George Sanders or Louis Hayward; a comic strip; a radio series that ran for much of the 1940s; and a television series starring Roger Moore, an international success with 118 episodes.

Leslie Charteris (1907–1993), born in Singapore, became an American citizen in 1946.

"The Invisible Millionaire" was first published in the June 1938 issue of *Black Mask*.

The Invisible Millionaire

Leslie Charteris

I

The girl's eyes caught Simon Templar as he entered the room, ducking his head instinctively to pass under the low lintel of the door; and they followed him steadily across to the bar. They were blue eyes with long lashes, and the face to which they belonged was pretty without any distinctive feature, crowned with curly yellow hair. And besides anything else, the eyes held an indefinable hint of strain.

Simon knew all this without looking directly at her. But he had singled her out at once from the double handful of riverside week-enders who crowded the small barroom as the most probable writer of the letter which he still carried in his pocket—the letter which had brought him out to the Bell that Sunday evening on what anyone with a less incorrigibly optimistic flair for adventure would have branded from the start as a fool's errand. She was the only girl in the place who seemed to be unattached: there was no positive reason why the writer of that letter should have been unattached, but it seemed likely that she would be. Also she was the best looker in a by no means repulsive crowd; and that was simply no clue at all except to Simon Templar's own unshakable faith in his guardian angel, who had never thrown any other kind of damsel in distress into his buccaneering path.

But she was still looking at him. And even though he couldn't help knowing that women often looked at him with more than ordinary interest, it was not usually done quite so fixedly. His hopes rose a notch, tentatively; but it was her turn to make the next move. He had done all that had been asked of him when he walked in there punctually on the stroke of eight.

He leaned on the counter, with his wide shoulders seeming to take up half the length of the bar, and ordered a pint of beer for himself and a bottle of Vat 69 for Hoppy Uniatz, who trailed up thirstily at his heels. With the tankard in his hands, he waited for one of those inevitable moments when all the customers had paused for breath at the same time.

"Anyone leave a message for me?" he asked.

His voice was quiet and casual, but just clear enough for everyone in the room to hear. Whoever had sent for him, unless it was merely some pointless practical joker, should need no more confirmation than that. He hoped it would be the girl with the blue troubled eyes. He had a weakness for girls with eyes of that shade, the same color as his own.

The barman shook his head.

"No, sir. I haven't had any messages."

Simon went on gazing at him reflectively, and the barman misinterpreted his expression. His mouth broadened and said: "That's all right, sir. I'd know if there was anything for you."

Simon's fine brows lifted a little puzzledly.

"I haven't seen you before," he said.

"I've seen your picture often enough, sir. I suppose you could call me one of your fans. You're the Saint, aren't you?"

The Saint smiled slowly.

"You don't look frightened."

"I never had the chance to be a rich racketeer, like the people you're always getting after. Gosh, though, I've had a kick out of some of the things you've done to 'em! And the way you're always putting it over on the police—I'll bet they'd give anything for an excuse to lock you up. . . ."

Simon was aware that the general buzz of conversation, after starting to pick up again, had died a second time and was staying dead. His spine itched with the feel of stares fastening on his back. And at the same time the barman became feverishly conscious of the audience which had been captured by his runaway enthusiasm. He began to stammer, turned red and plunged confusedly away to obliterate himself in some unnecessary fussing over the shelves of bottles behind him.

The Saint grinned with his eyes only, and turned tranquilly round to lean his back against the bar and face the room.

The collected stares hastily unpinned themselves and the voices got going again; but Simon was as oblivious of those events as he would have been if the rubber-necking had continued. At that moment his mind was capable of absorbing only one fearful and calamitous realisation. He had turned to see whether the girl with the fair curly hair and the blue eyes had also been listening, and whether she needed any more encouragement to announce herself. And the girl was gone.

She must have got up and gone out even in the short time that the barman had been talking. The Saint's glance swept on to identify the other faces in the room—faces that he had noted and automatically catalogued as he came in. They were all the same, but her face was not one of them. There was an empty glass beside her chair, and the chair itself was already being taken by a dark slender girl who had just entered.

Interest lighted the Saint's eyes again as he saw her, awakened instantly as he appreciated the subtle perfection of the sculptured cascade of her brown hair, crystallised as he approved the contours of her slim yet mature figure revealed by a simple flowered cotton dress. Then he saw her face for the first time, and held his tankard a shade tighter. Here, indeed, was something to call beautiful, something on which the word could be used without hesitation even under his most dispassionate scrutiny. She was like— "Peaches in autumn," he said to himself, seeing the fresh bloom of her cheeks against the russet shades of her hair. She raised her head with a smile, and his blood sang carillons. Perhaps after all. . . .

And then he saw that she was smiling and speaking to an ordinarily good-looking young man in a striped blazer who stood possessively over her; and inward laughter overtook him before he could feel the sourness of disappointment.

He loosened one elbow from the bar to run a hand through his dark hair, and his eyes twinkled at Mr. Uniatz.

"Oh well, Hoppy," he said. "It looks as if we can still be taken for a ride, even at our age."

Mr. Uniatz blinked at him. Even in isolation, the face that nature had planted on top of Mr. Uniatz' bull neck could never have been mistaken for that of a matinee idol with an inclination toward intellectual pursuits and the cultivation of the soul; but when viewed in exaggerating contrast with the tanned piratical chiselling of the Saint's features it had a grotesqueness that was sometimes completely shattering to those who beheld it for the first time. To compare it with the face of a gorilla which had been in violent contact with a variety of blunt instruments during its formative years would be risking the justifiable resentment of any gorilla which had been in violent contact with a variety of blunt instruments during its formative years. The best that can be said of it is that it contained in mauled and primitive form all the usual organs of sight, smell, hearing and ingestion, and prayerfully let it go at that. And yet it must also be said that Simon Templar had come to regard it with a fondness which even its mother could scarcely have shared. He watched it with good-humoured patience, waiting for it to answer.

"I dunno, boss," said Mr. Uniatz.

He had not thought over the point very deeply. Simon knew this, because when Mr. Uniatz was thinking his face screwed itself into even more frightful contortions than were stamped on it in repose. Thinking of any kind was an activity which caused Mr. Uniatz excruciating pain. On this occasion he had clearly escaped much suffering because his mind—if such a word can be used without blasphemy in connection with any of Mr. Uniatz' cerebral processes—had been elsewhere.

"Something is bothering you, Hoppy," said the Saint. "Don't keep it to yourself, or your head will start aching."

"Boss," said Mr. Uniatz gratefully, "do I have to drink dis wit' de paper on?"

He held up the parcel he was nursing.

Simon looked at him blankly for a moment, and then felt weak in the middle.

"Of course not," he said. "They only wrapped it up because they thought we were going to take it home. They haven't got to know you yet, that's all."

An expression of sublime relief spread over Mr. Uniatz' homely countenance as he pawed off the wrapping paper from the bottle of Vat 69. He pulled out the cork, placed the neck of the bottle in his mouth and tilted his head back. The soothing fluid flowed in a cooling stream down his asbestos gullet. All his anxieties were at rest.

For the Saint, consolation was not quite so easy. He finished his tankard and pushed it across the bar for a refill. While he was waiting for it to come back, he pulled out of his pocket and read over again the note that had brought him there. It was on a plain sheet of good note paper, with no address.

DEAR SAINT,

I'm not going to write a long letter, because if you aren't going to believe me it won't make any difference how many pages I write.

I'm only writing to you at all because I'm utterly desperate. How can I put it in the baldest possible way? I'm being forced into making myself an accomplice in one of the most gigantic frauds that can ever have been attempted, *and I can't go to the police for the same reason that I'm being forced to help.*

There you are. It's no use writing any more. If you can be at the Bell at Hurley at eight o'clock on Sunday evening I'll see you and tell you everything. If I can only talk to you for half an hour, I know I can make you believe me.

Please, for God's sake, at least let me talk to you.

My name is

NORA PRESCOTT

Nothing there to encourage too many hopes in the imagination of anyone whose mail was as regularly cluttered with crank letters as the Saint's; and yet the handwriting looked neat and sensible, and the brief blunt phrasing had somehow carried more conviction than a ream of protestations. All the rest had been hunch—that supernatural affinity for the dark trails of ungodliness which had pitchforked him into the middle of more brews of mischief than any four other freebooters of his day.

And for once the hunch had been wrong. If only it hadn't been for that humdrumly handsome excrescence in the striped blazer. . . .

Simon looked up again for another tantalizing eyeful of the dark slender girl.

He was just in time to get a parting glimpse of her back as she made her way to the door, with the striped blazer hovering over her like a motherly hen. Then she was gone; and everyone else in the bar suddenly looked nondescript and obnoxious.

The Saint sighed.

He took a deep draught of his beer and turned back to Hoppy Uniatz. The neck of the bottle was still firmly clamped in Hoppy's mouth, and there was no evidence to show that it had ever been detached therefrom since it was first inserted. His Adam's apple throbbed up and down with the regularity of a slow pulse. The angle of the bottle indicated that at least a pint of its contents had already reached his interior.

Simon gazed at him with reverence.

"You know, Hoppy," he remarked, "when

you die we shan't even have to embalm you. We'll just put you straight into a glass case, and you'll keep for years."

The other customers had finally returned to their own business, except for a few who were innocently watching for Mr. Uniatz to stiffen and fall backwards; and the talkative young barman edged up again with a show of wiping off the bar.

"Nothing much here to interest you tonight, sir, is there?" he began chattily.

"There was," said the Saint ruefully, "but she went home."

"You mean the dark young lady, sir?"

"Who else?"

The man nodded knowingly.

"You ought to come here more often, sir. I've often seen her in here alone. Miss Rosemary Chase, that is. Her father's Mr. Marvin Chase, the millionaire. He just took the New Manor for the season. Had a nasty motor accident only a week ago. . . ."

Simon let him go on talking, without paying much attention. The dark girl's name wasn't Nora Prescott, anyhow. That seemed to be the only important item of information—and with it went the last of his hopes. The clock over the bar crept on to twenty minutes past eight. If the girl who had written to him had been as desperate as she said, she wouldn't come as late as that—she'd have been waiting there when he arrived. The girl with the strained blue eyes had probably been suffering from nothing worse than biliousness or thwarted love. Rosemary Chase had happened merely by accident. The real writer of the letter was almost certainly some fat and frowsy female among those he had passed over without a second thought, who was doubtless still gloating over him from some obscure corner, gorging herself with the spectacle of her inhibition's hero in the flesh.

A hand grasped his elbow, turning him round, and a lightly accented voice said: "Why, Mr. Templar, what are you looking so sad about?"

The Saint's smile kindled as he turned.

"Giulio," he said, "if I could be sure that keeping a pub would make anyone as cheerful as you, I'd go right out and buy a pub."

Giulio Trapani beamed at him teasingly.

"Why should you need anything to make you cheerful? You are young, strong, handsome, rich—and famous. Or perhaps you are only waiting for a new romance?"

"Giulio," said the Saint, "that's a very sore point, at the moment."

"Ah! Perhaps you are waiting for a love letter which has not arrived?"

The Saint straightened up with a jerk. All at once he laughed. Half-incredulous sunshine smashed through his despondency, lighted up his face. He extended his palm.

"You old son of a gun! Give!"

The landlord brought his left hand from behind his back, holding an envelope. Simon grabbed it and ripped it open. He recognized the handwriting at a glance. The note was on a sheet of hotel paper.

Thank God you came. But I daren't be seen speaking to you after the barman recognised you.

Go down to the lock and walk up the towpath. Not very far along on the left there's a boathouse with green doors. I'll wait for you there. Hurry.

The Saint raised his eyes, and sapphires danced in them.

"Who gave you this, Giulio?"

"Nobody. It was lying on the floor outside when I came through. You saw the envelope— 'Deliver at once to Mr. Templar in the bar.' So that's what I do. Is it what you were waiting for?"

Simon stuffed the note into his pocket, and nodded. He drained his tankard.

"This is the romance you were talking about—maybe," he said. "I'll tell you about it later. Save some dinner for me. I'll be back." He clapped Trapani on the shoulder and swung round, newly awakened, joyously alive again. Perhaps, in spite of everything, there was still adventure to come. . . . "Let's go, Hoppy!"

He took hold of Mr. Uniatz' bottle and pulled it down. Hoppy came upright after it with a plaintive gasp.

"Chees, boss—"

"Have you no soul?" demanded the Saint sternly as he herded him out of the door. "We have a date with a damsel in distress. The moon will be mirrored in her beautiful eyes, and she will pant out a story while we fan the gnats away from her snowy brow. Sinister eggs are being hatched behind the scenes. There will be villains and mayhem and perhaps even moider. . . ."

He went on talking lyrical nonsense as he set a brisk pace down the lane toward the river; but when they reached the towpath even he had dried up. Mr. Uniatz was an unresponsive audience, and Simon found that some of the things he was saying in jest were oddly close to the truth that he believed. After all, such fantastic things had happened to him before.

He didn't fully understand the change in himself as he turned off along the riverbank beside the dark shimmering sleekness of the water. The ingrained flippancy was still with him—he could feel it like a translucent film over his mind—but underneath it he was all open and expectant, a receptive void in which anything might take shape. And something was beginning to take shape there—something still so nebulous and formless that it eluded any conscious survey, and yet something as inescapably real as a promise of thunder in the air. It was as if the hunch that had brought him out to the Bell in the first place had leapt up from a whisper to a great shout; and yet everything was silent. Far away, to his sensitive ears, there was the ghostly hum of cars on the Maidenhead road; close by, the sibilant lap of the river, the lisp of leaves, the stertorous breathing and elephantine footfalls of Mr. Uniatz; but those things were only phases of the stillness that was everywhere. Everything in the world was quiet, even his own nerves, and they were almost too quiet. And ahead of him, presently, loomed the shape of a building like a boathouse. His pencil flashlight stabbed out for a second and caught the front of it. It had green doors.

Quietly he said: "Nora."

There was no answer, no hint of movement anywhere. And he didn't know why, but in the same quiet way his right hand slid up to his shoulder rig and loosened the automatic in the spring clip under his arm.

He covered the last two yards in absolute silence, put his hand to the handle of the door and drew it back quickly as his fingers slid on a sticky dampness. It was queer, he thought even then, even as his left hand angled the flashlight down, that it should have happened just like that, when everything in him was tuned and waiting for it, without knowing what it was waiting for. Blood—on the door.

II

Simon stood for a moment, and his nerves seemed to grow even calmer and colder under an edge of sharp bitterness.

Then he grasped the door handle again, turned it and went in. The inside of the building was pitch dark. His torch needled the blackness with a thin jet of light that splashed dim reflections from the glossy varnish on a couple of punts and an electric canoe. Somehow he was quite sure what he would find, so sure that the certainty chilled off any rise of emotion. He knew what it must be; the only question was, who? Perhaps even that was not such a question. He was never quite sure about that. A hunch that had almost missed its mark had become stark reality with a suddenness that disjointed the normal co-ordinates of time and space: it was as if, instead of discovering things, he was trying to remember things he had known before and had forgotten. But he saw her at last, almost tucked under the shadow of the electric canoe, lying on her side as if she were asleep.

He stepped over and bent his light steadily on her face, and knew then that he had been right. It was the girl with the troubled blue eyes. Her eyes were open now, only they were not troubled any more. The Saint stood and looked down at her. He had been almost sure when he saw the curly yellow hair. But she had been wearing a white blouse when he saw her last, and now there was a splotchy crimson pattern on the front of it. The pattern glistened as he looked at it.

Beside him, there was a noise like an asthmatic foghorn loosening up for a burst of song.

"Boss," began Mr. Uniatz.

"Shut up."

The Saint's voice was hardly more than a whisper, but it cut like a razor blade. It cut Hoppy's introduction cleanly off from whatever he had been going to say; and at the same moment as he spoke Simon switched off his torch, so that it was as if the same tenuous whisper had sliced off even the ray of light, leaving nothing around them but blackness and silence.

Motionless in the dark, the Saint quested for any betraying breath or sound. To his tautened eardrums, sensitive as a wild animal's, the hushed murmurs of the night outside were still an audible background against which the slightest stealthy movement even at a considerable distance would have stood out like a bugle call. But he heard nothing then, though he waited for several seconds in uncanny stillness.

He switched on the torch again.

"Okay, Hoppy," he said. "Sorry to interrupt you, but that blood was so fresh that I wondered if someone mightn't still be around."

"Boss," said Mr. Uniatz aggrievedly, "I was doin' fine when ya stopped me."

"Never mind," said the Saint consolingly. "You can go ahead now. Take a deep breath and start again."

He was still partly listening for something else, wondering if even then the murderer might still be within range.

"It ain't no use now," said Mr. Uniatz dolefully.

"Are you going to get temperamental on me?" Simon demanded sufferingly. "Because if so—"

Mr. Uniatz shook his head.

"It ain't dat, boss. But you gotta start wit' a full bottle."

Simon focused him through a kind of fog. In an obscure and apparently irrelevant sort of way, he became aware that Hoppy was still clinging to the bottle of Vat 69 with which he had been irrigating his tonsils at the Bell, and that he was holding it up against the beam of the flashlight as though brooding over the level of the liquid left in it. The Saint clutched at the buttresses of his mind.

"What in the name of Adam's grandfather," he said, "are you talking about?"

"Well, boss, dis is an idea I get out of a book. De guys walks in a saloon, he buys a bottle of scotch, he pulls de cork, an' he drinks de whole bottle straight down wit'out stopping. So I was tryin' de same t'ing back in de pub, an' was doin' fine when ya stopped me. Lookit, I ain't left more 'n two-t'ree swallows. But it ain't no use goin' on now," explained Mr. Uniatz, working back to the core of his grievance. "You gotta start wit' a full bottle."

Nothing but years of training and self-discipline gave Simon Templar the strength to recover his sanity.

"Next time you'd better take the bottle away somewhere and lock yourself up with it," he said with terrific moderation. "Just for the moment, since we haven't got another bottle, is there any danger of your noticing that someone has been murdered around here?"

"Yeah," said Mr. Uniatz brightly. "De wren."

Having contributed his share of illumination, he relapsed into benevolent silence. This, his expectant self-effacement appeared to suggest, was not his affair. It appeared to be something which required thinking about; and Thinking was a job for which the Saint possessed an obviously supernatural aptitude which Mr. Uniatz had come to lean upon with a childlike faith that was very much akin to worship.

The Saint was thinking. He was thinking with a level and passionless detachment that surprised even himself. The girl was dead. He had seen plenty of men killed before, sometimes horribly; but only one other woman. Yet that must not make any difference. Nora Prescott had never meant anything to him: he would never even have recognized her voice. Other women of whom he knew just as little were dying everywhere, in one way or another, every time he breathed; and he could think about it without the slightest feeling. Nora Prescott was just another name in the world's long roll of undistinguished dead.

But she was someone who had asked him for help, who had perhaps died because of what she had wanted to tell him. She hadn't been just another twittering fluffhead going into hysterics over a mouse. She really had known something—something that was dangerous enough for someone else to commit murder rather than have it revealed.

". . . one of the most gigantic frauds that can ever have been attempted."

The only phrase out of her letter which gave any information at all came into his head again, not as a merely provocative combination of words, but with some of the clean-cut clarity of a sober statement of fact. And yet the more he considered it, the closer it came to clarifying precisely nothing.

And he was still half listening for a noise that it seemed as if he ought to have heard. The expectation was a subtle nagging at the back of his mind, the fidget for attention of a thought that still hadn't found conscious shape.

His torch panned once more round the interior of the building. It was a plain wooden structure, hardly more than three walls and a pair of double doors which formed the fourth, just comfortably roomy for the three boats which it contained. There was a small window on each side, so neglected as to be almost opaque. Overhead, his light went straight up to the bare rafters which supported the shingle roof. There was no place in it for anybody to hide except under one of the boats; and his light probed along the floor and eliminated that possibility.

The knife lay on the floor near the girl's knees—an ordinary cheap kitchen knife, but pointed and sharp enough for what it had had to do. There was a smear of blood on the handle; and some of it must have gone on the killer's hand, or more probably on his glove, and in that way been left on the doorknob. From the stains and rents on the front of the girl's dress, the murderer must have struck two or three times; but if he was strong he could have held her throat while he did it, and there need have been no noise.

"Efficient enough," the Saint summed it up aloud, "for a rush job."

He was thinking: "It must have been a rush job, because he couldn't have known she was going to meet me here until after she'd written that note at the Bell. Probably she didn't even know it herself until then. Did he see the note? Doesn't seem possible. He could have followed her. Then he must have had the knife on him already. Not an ordinary sort of knife to carry about with you. Then he must have known he was going to use it before he started out. Unless it was here in the boathouse and he just grabbed it up. No reason why a knife like that should be lying about in a place like this. Bit too convenient. Well, so he knew she'd got in touch with me, and he'd made up his mind to kill her. Then why not kill her before she even got to the Bell? She might have talked to me there, and he couldn't have stopped her—could he? Was he betting that she wouldn't risk talking to me in public? He could have been. Good psychology, but the hell of a nerve to bet on it. Did he find out she'd written to me? Then I'd probably still have the letter. If I found her murdered, he'd expect me to go to the police with it. Dangerous. And he knew I'd find her. Then why—"

The Saint felt something like an inward explosion as he realised what his thoughts were leading to. He knew then why half of his brain had never ceased to listen—searching for what intuition had scented faster than reason.

Goose pimples crawled up his spine onto the back of his neck.

And at that same moment he heard the sound.

It was nothing that any other man might have heard at all. Only the gritting of a few tiny specks of gravel between a stealthy shoe sole and the board stage outside. But it was what every nerve in his body had unwittingly been keyed for ever since he had seen the dead girl at his feet. It was what he inevitably had to hear, after everything else that had happened. It spun him round like a jerk on the string wound round a top.

He was in the act of turning when the gun spoke.

Its bark was curt and flat and left an impression of having been curiously thin, though his ears rang with it afterwards. The bullet zipped past his ear like a hungry mosquito; and from the hard fierce note that it hummed he knew that if he had not been starting to turn at the very instant when it was fired it would have struck him squarely in the head. Pieces of shattered glass rattled on the floor.

Lights smashed into his eyes as he whirled at the door, and a clear clipped voice snapped at him: "Drop that gun! You haven't got a chance!"

The light beat on him with blinding intensity from the lens of a pocket searchlight that completely swallowed up the slim ray of his own torch. He knew that he hadn't a chance. He could have thrown bullets by guesswork; but to the man behind the glare he was a target on which patterns could be punched out.

Slowly his fingers opened off the big Luger, and it plonked on the boards at his feet.

His hand swept across and bent down the barrel of the automatic which Mr. Uniatz had whipped out like lightning when the first shot crashed between them.

"You too, Hoppy," he said resignedly. "All that scotch will run away if they make a hole in you now."

"Back away," came the next order.

Simon obeyed.

The voice said: "Go on, Rosemary—pick up the guns. I'll keep 'em covered."

A girl came forward into the light. It was the dark slender girl whose quiet loveliness had unsteadied Simon's breath at the Bell.

III

She bent over and collected the two guns by the butts, holding them aimed at Simon and Hoppy, not timidly, but with a certain stiffness which told the Saint's expert eye that the feel of them

was unfamiliar. She moved backwards and disappeared again behind the light.

"Do you mind," asked the Saint ceremoniously, "if I smoke?"

"I don't care." The clipped voice, he realised now, could only have belonged to the young man in the striped blazer. "But don't try to start anything, or I'll let you have it. Go on back in there."

The Saint didn't move at once. He took out his cigarette case first, opened it and selected a cigarette. The case came from his breast pocket, but he put it back in the pocket at his hip, slowly and deliberately and holding it lightly, so that his hand was never completely out of sight and a nervous man would have no cause to be alarmed at the movement. He had another gun in that pocket, a light but beautifully balanced Walther; but for the time being he left it there, sliding the cigarette case in behind it and bringing his hand back empty to get out his lighter.

"I'm afraid we weren't expecting to be held up in a place like this," he remarked apologetically. "So we left the family jools at home. If you'd only let us know—"

"Don't be funny. If you don't want to be turned over to the police, you'd better let *me* know what you're doing here."

The Saint's brows shifted a fraction of an inch.

"I don't see what difference it makes to you, brother," he said slowly. "But if you're really interested, we were just taking a stroll in the moonlight to work up an appetite for dinner, and we happened to see the door of this place open—"

"So that's why you both had to pull out guns when you heard us."

"My dear bloke," Simon argued reasonably, "what do you expect anyone to do when you creep up behind them and start sending bullets whistling round their heads?"

There was a moment's silence.

The girl gasped.

The man spluttered: "Good God, you've got a nerve! After you blazed away at us like that—why, you might have killed one of us!"

The Saint's eyes strained uselessly to pierce

beyond the light. There was an odd hollow feeling inside him, making his frown unnaturally rigid. Something was going wrong. Something was going as immortally cockeyed as it was possible to go. It was taking him a perceptible space of time to grope for a bearing in the reeling void. Somewhere the scenario had gone as paralysingly off the rails as if a Wagnerian soprano had bounced into a hotcha dance routine in the middle of *Tristan*.

"Look," he said. "Let's be quite clear about this. Is your story going to be that you thought I took a shot at you?"

"I don't have to think," retorted the other. "I heard the bullet whizz past my head. Go on—get back in that boathouse."

Simon dawdled back.

His brain felt as if it was steaming. The voice behind the light, now that he was analysing its undertones, had a tense unsophistication that didn't belong in the script at all. And the answers it gave were all wrong. Simon had had it all figured out one ghostly instant before it began to happen. The murderer hadn't just killed Nora Prescott and faded away, of course. He had killed her and waited outside, knowing that Simon Templar must find her in a few minutes, knowing that that would be his best chance to kill the Saint as well and silence whatever the Saint knew already and recover the letter. That much was so obvious that he must have been asleep not to have seen it from the moment when his eyes fell on the dead girl. Well, he had seen it now. And yet it wasn't clicking. The dialogue was all there, and yet every syllable was striking a false note.

And he was back inside the boathouse, as far as he could go, with the square bow of a punt against his calves and Hoppy beside him.

The man's voice said: "Turn a light on, Rosemary."

The girl came round and found a switch. Light broke out from a naked bulb that hung by a length of flex from one of the rafters, and the young man in the striped blazer flicked off his torch.

"Now," he started to say, "we'll—"

"*Jim!*"

The girl didn't quite scream, but her voice tightened and rose to within a semitone of it. She backed against the wall, one hand to her mouth, with her face white and her eyes dilated with horror. The man began to turn toward her, and then followed her wide and frozen stare. The muzzle of the gun he was holding swung slack from its aim on the Saint's chest as he did so—it was an error that in some situations would have cost him his life, but Simon let him live. The Saint's head was whirling with too many questions, just then, to have any interest in the opportunity. He was looking at the gun which the girl was still holding, and recognizing it as the property of Mr. Uniatz.

"It's Nora," she gasped. "She's—"

He saw her gather herself with an effort, force herself to go forward and kneel beside the body. Then he stopped watching her. His eyes went to the gun that was still wavering in the young man's hand.

"Jim," said the girl brokenly, "she's dead!"

The man took a half step toward the Saint.

"You swine!" he grunted. "You killed her—"

"Go on," said the Saint gently. "And then I took a pot at you. So you fired back in self-defence, and just happened to kill us. It'll make a swell story even if it isn't a very new one, and you'll find yourself quite a hero. But why all the play acting for our benefit? We know the gag."

There was complete blankness behind the anger in the other's eyes. And all at once the Saint's somersaulting cosmos stabilized itself with a jolt—upside down, but solid.

He was looking at the gun which was pointing at his chest, and realising that it was his own Luger.

And the girl had got Hoppy's gun. And there was no other artillery in sight.

The arithmetic of it smacked him between the eyes and made him dizzy. Of course there was an excuse for him, in the shape of the first shot and the bullet that had gone snarling past his ear. But even with all that, for him out of all people in the world, at his time of life . . .

"Run up to the house and call the police, Rosemary," said the striped blazer in a brittle bark.

"Wait a minute," said the Saint.

His brain was not fogged any longer. It was turning over as swiftly and smoothly as a hair-balanced flywheel, registering every item with the mechanical infallibility of an adding machine. His nerves were tingling.

His glance whipped from side to side. He was standing again approximately where he had been when the shot cracked out, but facing the opposite way. On his right quarter was the window that had been broken, with the shards of glass scattered on the floor below it—he ought to have understood everything when he heard them hit the floor. Turning the other way, he saw that the line from the window to himself continued on through the open door.

He look a long drag on his cigarette.

"It kind of spoils the scene," he said quietly, "but I'm afraid we've both been making the same mistake. You thought I fired at you—"

"I don't have—"

"All right, you don't have to think. You heard the bullet whizz past your head. You said that before. You're certain I shot at you. Okay. Well, I was just as certain that you shot at me. But I know now I was wrong. You never had a gun until you got mine. It was that shot that let you bluff me. I'd heard the bullet go past *my* head, and so it never even occurred to me that you were bluffing. But we were both wrong. The shot came through that window—it just missed me, went on out through the door and just missed you. And somebody else fired it!"

The other's face was stupid with stubborn incredulity.

"Who fired it?"

"The murderer."

"That means you," retorted the young man flatly. "Hell, I don't want to listen to you. You see if you can make the police believe you. Go on and call them, Rosemary. I can take care of these two."

The girl hesitated.

"But, Jim—"

"Don't worry about me, darling. I'll be all right. If either of these two washouts tries to get funny, I'll give him plenty to think about."

The Saint's eyes were narrowing.

"You lace-pantie'd bladder of hot air," he said in a cold even voice that seared like vitriol. "It isn't your fault if God didn't give you a brain, but he did give you eyes. Why don't you use them? I say the shot was fired from outside, and you can see for yourself where the broken windowpane fell. Look at it. It's all on the floor in here. If you can tell me how I could shoot at you in the doorway and break a window behind me, and make the broken glass fall inwards, I'll pay for your next marcel wave. Look at it, nitwit."

The young man looked.

He had been working closer to the Saint, with his free fist clenched and his face flushed with wrath, since the Saint's first sizzling insult smoked under his skin. But he looked. Somehow, he had to do that. He was less than five feet away when his eyes shifted. And it was then that Simon jumped him.

The Saint's lean body seemed to lengthen and swoop across the intervening space. His left hand grabbed the Luger, bent the wrist behind it agonisingly inwards, while the heel of his open right hand settled under the other's chin. The gun came free; and the Saint's right arm straightened jarringly and sent the young man staggering back.

Simon reversed the automatic with a deft flip and held it on him. Even while he was making his spring, out of the corner of his eye he had seen Hoppy Uniatz flash away from him with an electrifying acceleration that would have stunned anyone who had misguidedly judged Mr. Uniatz on the speed of his mental reactions; now he glanced briefly aside and saw that Hoppy was holding his gun again and keeping the girl pinioned with one arm.

"Okay, Hoppy," he said. "Keep your Betsy and let her go. She's going to call the police for us."

Hoppy released her, but the girl did not move. She stood against the wall, rubbing slim wrists that had been bruised by Mr. Uniatz' untempered energy, looking from Simon to the striped blazer with scared, desperate eyes.

"Go ahead," said the Saint impatiently. "I

won't damage little Jimmy unless he makes trouble. If this was one of my murdering evenings, you don't think I'd bump him and let you get away, do you? Go on and fetch your policeman—and we'll see whether the boy friend can make them believe *his* story!"

IV

They had to wait for some time. . . .

After a minute Simon turned the prisoner over to Hoppy and put his Luger away under his coat. He reached for his cigarette case again and thoughtfully helped himself to a smoke. With the cigarette curling blue drifts past his eyes, he traced again the course of the bullet that had so nearly stamped the finale on all his adventures. There was no question that it had been fired from outside the window—and that also explained the peculiarly flat sound of the shot which had faintly puzzled him. The cleavage lines on the few scraps of glass remaining in the frame supplied the last detail of incontrovertible proof. He devoutly hoped that the shining lights of the local constabulary would have enough scientific knowledge to appreciate it.

Mr. Uniatz, having brilliantly performed his share of physical activity, appeared to have been snared again in the unfathomable quagmires of the Mind. The tortured grimace that had cramped itself into his countenance indicated that some frightful eruption was taking place in the small core of grey matter which formed a sort of glutinous marrow inside his skull. He cleared his throat, producing a noise like a piece of sheet iron getting between the blades of a lawn mower, and gave the fruit of his travail to the world.

"Boss," he said, "I dunno how dese mugs t'ink dey can get away wit' it."

"How which mugs think they can get away with what?" asked the Saint somewhat vacantly.

"Dese mugs," said Mr. Uniatz, "who are tryin' to take us for a ride, like ya tell me in de pub."

Simon had to stretch his memory backwards almost to breaking point to hook up again with Mr. Uniatz' train of thought; and when he had

finally done so he decided that it was wisest not to start any argument.

"Others have made the same mistake," he said casually and hoped that would be the end of it.

Mr. Uniatz nodded sagely.

"Well, dey all get what's comin' to dem," he said with philosophic complacency. "When do I give dis punk de woiks?"

"When do you— What?"

"Dis punk," said Mr. Uniatz, waving his Betsy at the prisoner. "De mug who takes a shot at us."

"You don't," said the Saint shortly.

The equivalent of what on anybody else's face would have been a slight frown carved its fearsome corrugations into Hoppy's brow.

"Ya don't mean he gets away wit' it after all?"

"We'll see about that."

"Dijja hear what he calls us?"

"What was that?"

"He calls us washouts."

"That's too bad."

"Yeah, dat's too bad." Mr. Uniatz glowered disparagingly at the captive. "Maybe I better go over him wit' a paddle foist. Just to make sure he don't go to sleep."

"Leave him alone," said the Saint soothingly. "He's young, but he'll grow up."

He was watching the striped blazer with more attention than a chance onlooker would have realised. The young man stood glaring at them defiantly—not without fear, but that was easy to explain if one wanted to. His knuckles tensed up involuntarily from time to time; but a perfectly understandable anger would account for that. Once or twice he glanced at the strangely unreal shape of the dead girl half hidden in the shadows, and it was at those moments that Simon was studying him most intently. He saw the almost conventionalised horror of death that takes the place of practical thinking with those who have seen little of it, and a bitter disgust that might have had an equally conventional basis. Beyond that, the sullen scowl which disfigured the other's face steadily refused him the betraying evidence that might have made everything so much simpler. Simon blew placid and meditative smoke rings to pass the time; but there was an irking bafflement behind the cool patience of his eyes.

It took fifteen minutes by his watch for the police to come, which was less than he had expected.

They arrived in the persons of a man with a waxed moustache in plain clothes, and two constables in uniform. After them, breathless when she saw the striped blazer still inhabited by an apparently undamaged owner, came Rosemary Chase. In the background hovered a man who even without his costume could never have been mistaken for anything but a butler.

Simon turned with a smile.

"Glad to see you, Inspector," he said easily.

"Just 'Sergeant,' " answered the plain-clothes man in a voice that sounded as if it should have been "sergeant major."

He saw the automatic that Mr. Uniatz was still holding, and stepped forward with a rather hollow but courageous belligerence.

"Give me that gun!" he said loudly.

Hoppy ignored him and looked inquiringly at the only man whom he took orders from; but Simon nodded. He politely offered his own Luger as well. The sergeant took the two guns, squinted at them sapiently and stuffed them into his side pockets. He looked relieved, and rather clever.

"I suppose you've got licences for these firearms," he said temptingly.

"Of course," said the Saint in a voice of saccharine virtue.

He produced certificate and permit to carry from his pocket. Hoppy did the same. The sergeant pored over the documents with surly suspicion for some time before he handed them to one of the constables to note down the particulars. He looked so much less clever that Simon had difficulty in keeping a straight face. It was as if the Official Mind, jumping firmly to a foregone conclusion, had spent the journey there developing an elegantly graduated approach to the obvious climax, and therefore found the entire structure staggering when the first step caved in under its feet.

A certain awkwardness crowded itself into the scene.

With a businesslike briskness that was only a trifle too elaborate, the sergeant went over to the body and brooded over it with portentous solemnity. He went down on his hands and knees to peer at the knife, without touching it. He borrowed a flashlight from one of the constables to examine the floor around it. He roamed about the boathouse and frowned into dark corners. At intervals he cogitated. When he could think of nothing else to do, he came back and faced his audience with dogged valour.

"Well," he said less aggressively, "while we're waiting for the doctor I'd better take your statements." He turned. "You're Mr. Forrest, sir?"

The young man in the striped blazer nodded. "Yes."

"I've already heard the young lady's story, but I'd like to hear your version."

Forrest glanced quickly at the girl and almost hesitated. He said: "I was taking Miss Chase home, and we saw a light moving in here. We crept up to find out what it was, and one of these men fired a shot at us. I turned my torch on them and pretended I had a gun too, and they surrendered. We took their guns away; and then this man started arguing and trying to make out that somebody else had fired the shot, and he managed to distract my attention and get his gun back."

"Did you hear any noise as you were walking along? The sort of noise this—er—deceased might have made as she was being attacked?"

"No."

"I—did—not—hear—the—noise—of—the —deceased—being—attacked," repeated one of the constables with a notebook and pencil, laboriously writing it down.

The sergeant waited for him to finish and turned to the Saint.

"Now, Mr. Templar," he said ominously. "Do you wish to make a statement? It is my duty to warn you—"

"Why?" asked the Saint blandly.

The sergeant did not seem to know the answer to that.

He said gruffly: "What statement do you wish to make?"

"Just what I told Comrade Forrest when we were arguing. Mr. Uniatz and I were ambling around to work up a thirst, and we saw this door open. Being rather inquisitive and not having anything better to do, we just nosed in, and we saw the body. We were just taking it in when somebody fired at us; and then Comrade Forrest turned on the spotlight and yelled 'Hands up!' or words to that effect, so to be on the safe side we handed up, thinking he'd fired the first shot. Still, he looked kind of nervous when he had hold of my gun, so I took it away from him in case it went off. Then I told Miss Chase to go ahead and fetch you. Incidentally, as I tried to tell Comrade Forrest, I've discovered that we were both wrong about that shooting. Somebody else did it from outside the window. You can see for yourself if you take a look at the glass."

The Saint's voice and manner were masterpieces of matter-of-fact veracity. It is often easy to tell the plain truth, and be disbelieved; but Simon's pleasant imperturbability left the sergeant visibly nonplused. He went and inspected the broken glass at some length, and then he came back and scratched his head.

"Well," he admitted grudgingly, "there doesn't seem to be much doubt about that."

"If you want any more proof," said the Saint nonchalantly, "you can take our guns apart. Comrade Forrest will tell you that we haven't done anything to them. You'll find the magazines full and the barrels clean."

The sergeant adopted the suggestion with morbid eagerness, but he shrugged resignedly over the result.

"That seems to be right," he said with stoic finality. "It looks as if both you gentlemen were mistaken." He went on scrutinising the Saint grimly. "But it still doesn't explain why you were in here with the deceased."

"Because I found her," answered the Saint reasonably. "Somebody had to."

The sergeant took another glum look around. He did not audibly acknowledge that all his castles in the air had settled soggily back to earth, but the morose admission was implicit in the majestic stolidity with which he tried to keep anything that might have been interpreted as a confession out of his face. He took refuge in an air of busy inscrutability, as if he had just a little more up his sleeve than he was prepared to share with anyone else for the time being; but there was at least one member of his audience who was not deceived, and who breathed a sigh of relief at the lifting of what might have been a dangerous suspicion.

"Better take down some more details," he said gruffly to the constable with the notebook, and turned to Rosemary Chase. "The deceased's name is Nora Prescott—is that right, miss?"

"Yes."

"You knew her quite well?"

"Of course. She was one of my father's personal secretaries," said the dark girl; and the Saint suddenly felt as if the last knot in the tangle had been untied.

V

He listened with tingling detachment while Rosemary Chase talked and answered questions. The dead girl's father was a man who had known and helped Marvin Chase when they were both young, but who had long ago been left far behind by Marvin Chase's sensational rise in the financial world. When Prescott's own business was failing, Chase had willingly lent him large sums of money, but the failure had still not been averted. Illness had finally brought Prescott's misfortunes to the point where he was not even able to meet the interest on the loan, and when he refused further charity Chase had sent him to Switzerland to act as an entirely superfluous "representative" in Zurich and had given Nora Prescott a job himself. She had lived more as one of the family than as an employee. No, she had given no hint of having any private troubles or being afraid of anyone. Only she had not seemed to be quite herself since Marvin Chase's motor accident. . . .

The bare supplementary facts clicked into place in the framework that was already there as if into accurately fitted sockets, filling in sections of the outline without making much of it more recognizable. They filed themselves away in the Saint's memory with mechanical precision; and yet the closeness which he felt to the mystery that hid behind them was more intuitive than methodical, a weird sensitivity that sent electric shivers coursing up his spine.

A grey-haired ruddy-cheeked doctor arrived and made his matter-of-fact examination and report.

"Three stab wounds in the chest—I'll be able to tell you more about them after I've made the post-mortem, but I should think any one of them might have been fatal. Slight contusions on the throat. She hasn't been dead much more than an hour."

He stood glancing curiously over the other faces.

"Where's the ambulance?" said the sergeant grumpily.

"They've probably gone to the house," said the girl. "I'll send them down if I see them—you don't want us getting in your way any more, do you?"

"No, miss. This isn't very pleasant for you, I suppose. If I want any more information I'll come up and see you in the morning. Will Mr. Forrest be there if we want to see him?"

Forrest took a half step forward.

"Wait a minute," he blurted. "You haven't—"

"They aren't suspicious of you, Jim," said the girl with a quiet firmness. "They might just want to ask some more questions."

"But you haven't said anything about Templar's—"

"Of course." The girl's interruption was even firmer. Her voice was still quiet and natural, but the undercurrent of determined warning in it was as plain as a siren to the Saint's ears. "I know we owe Mr. Templar an apology, but we don't have to waste Sergeant Jesser's time with it. Perhaps he'd like to come up to the house with us and have a drink—that is, if you don't need him any more, Sergeant."

Her glance only released the young man's eye after it had pinned him to perplexed and scowling silence. And once again Simon felt that premonitory crisping of his nerves.

"All this excitement certainly does dry out the tonsils," he remarked easily. "But if Sergeant Jesser wants me to stay. . . ."

"No sir." The reply was calm and ponderous. "I've made a note of your address, and I don't think you could run away. Are you going home tonight?"

"You might try the Bell first, in case we decide to stop over."

Simon buttoned his coat and strolled toward the door with the others; but as they reached it he stopped and turned back.

"By the way," he said blandly, "do you mind if we take our lawful artillery?"

The sergeant gazed at him and dug the guns slowly out of his pocket. Simon handed one of them to Mr. Uniatz and leisurely fitted his own automatic back into the spring holster under his arm. His smile was very slight.

"Since there still seems to be a murderer at large in the neighborhood," he said, "I'd like to be ready for him."

As he followed Rosemary Chase and Jim Forrest up a narrow footpath away from the river, with Hoppy Uniatz beside him and the butler bringing up the rear, he grinned inwardly over that delicately pointed line and wondered whether it had gone home where he intended it to go. Since his back had been turned to the real audience, he had been unable to observe their reaction; and now their backs were turned to him in an equally uninformative reversal. Neither of them said a word on the way, and Simon placidly left the silence to get tired of itself. But his thoughts were very busy as he sauntered after them along the winding path and saw the lighted windows of a house looming up through the thinning trees that had hidden it from the riverbank. This, he realised with a jolt, must be the New Manor, and therefore the boathouse where Nora Prescott had been murdered was presumably a part of Marvin Chase's property. It made no difference to the facts, but the web of riddles seemed to draw tighter around him. . . .

They crossed a lawn and mounted some steps to a flagged terrace. Rosemary Chase led them through open french windows into an inoffensively furnished drawing room, and the butler closed the windows behind him as he followed. Forrest threw himself sulkily into an armchair, but the girl had regained a composure that was just a fraction too detailed to be natural.

"What kind of drinks would you like?" she asked.

"Beer for me," said the Saint with the same studied urbanity. "Scotch for Hoppy. I'm afraid I should have warned you about him—he likes to have his own bottle. We're trying to wean him, but it isn't going very well."

The butler bowed and oozed out.

The girl took a cigarette from an antique lacquer box, and Simon stepped forward politely with his lighter. He had an absurd feeling of unreality about this new atmosphere that made it a little difficult to hide his sense of humour, but all his senses were vigilant. She was even lovelier than he had thought at first sight, he admitted to himself as he watched her face over the flame—it was hard to believe that she might be an accomplice to wilful and messy and apparently mercenary murder. But she and Forrest had certainly chosen a very dramatic moment to arrive. . . .

"It's nice of you to have us here," he murmured, "after the way we've behaved."

"My father told me to bring you up," she said. "He seems to be quite an admirer of yours, and he was sure you couldn't have had anything to do with—with the murder."

"I noticed—down in the boathouse—you knew my name," said the Saint thoughtfully.

"Yes—the sergeant used it."

Simon looked at the ceiling.

"Bright lads, these policemen, aren't they? I wonder how *he* knew?"

"From—your gun licence, I suppose."

Simon nodded.

"Oh yes. But before that. I mean, I suppose he must have told your father who I was. Nobody else could have done it, could they?"

The girl reddened and lost her voice; but

Forrest found his. He jerked himself angrily out of his chair.

"What's the use of all this beating about the bush, Rosemary?" he demanded impatiently. "Why don't you tell him we know all about that letter that Nora wrote him?"

The door opened, and the butler came back with a tray of bottles and glasses and toured the room with them. There was a strained silence until he had gone again. Hoppy Uniatz stared at the newly opened bottle of whiskey which had been put down in front of him, with a rapt and menacing expression which indicated that his grey matter was in the throes of another paroxysm of Thought.

Simon raised his glass and gazed appreciatively at the sparkling brown clearness within it.

"All right," he said. "If you want it that way. So you knew Nora Prescott had written to me. You came to the Bell to see what happened. Probably you watched through the windows first; then when she went out, you came in to watch me. You followed one of us to the boathouse—"

"And we ought to have told the police—"

"Of course." The Saint's voice was mild and friendly. "You ought to have told them about the letter. I'm sure you could have quoted what was in it. Something about how she was being forced to help in putting over a gigantic fraud, and how she wanted me to help her. Sergeant Jesser would have been wild with excitement about that. Naturally he'd've seen at once that that provided an obvious motive for me to murder her, and none at all for the guy whose fraud was going to be given away. It really was pretty noble of you both to take so much trouble to keep me out of suspicion, and I appreciate it a lot. And now that we're all pals together, and there aren't any policemen in the audience, why don't you save me a lot of headaches and tell me what the swindle is?"

The girl stared at him.

"Do you know what you're saying?"

"I usually have a rough idea," said the Saint coolly and deliberately. "I'll make it even plainer, if that's too subtle for you. Your father's a millionaire, they tell me. And when there are any gigantic frauds in the wind, I never expect to find the Big Shot sitting in a garret toasting kippers over a candle."

Forrest started toward him.

"Look here, Templar, we've stood about enough from you—"

"And I've stood plenty from you," said the Saint without moving. "Let's call it quits. We were both misunderstanding each other at the beginning, but we don't have to go on doing it. I can't do anything for you if you don't put your cards on the table. Let's straighten it out now. Which of you two cooled off Nora Prescott?"

He didn't seem to change his voice, but the question came with a sharp stinging clarity like the flick of a whip. Rosemary Chase and the young man gaped at him frozenly, and he waited for an answer without a shift of his lazily negligent eyes. But he didn't get it.

The rattle of the door handle made everyone turn, almost in relief at the interruption. A tall cadaverous man, severely dressed in a dark suit and high old-fashioned collar, his chin bordered with a rim of black beard, pince-nez on a loop of black ribbon in his hand, came into the room and paused hesitantly.

Rosemary Chase came slowly out of her trance.

"Oh, Doctor Quintus," she said in a quiet forced voice. "This is Mr. Templar and . . . er. . . ."

"Hoppy Uniatz," Simon supplied.

Dr. Quintus bowed; and his black sunken eyes clung for a moment to the Saint's face.

"Delighted," he said in a deep burring bass; and turned back to the girl. "Miss Chase, I'm afraid the shock has upset your father a little. Nothing at all serious, I assure you, but I think it would be unwise for him to have any more excitement just yet. However, he asked me to invite Mr. Templar to stay for dinner. Perhaps later . . ."

Simon took another sip at his beer, and his glance swung idly over to the girl with the first glint of a frosty sparkle in its depths.

"We'd be delighted," he said deprecatingly. "If Miss Chase doesn't object. . . ."

"Why, of course not." Her voice was only the

minutest shred of a decibel out of key. "We'd love to have you stay."

The Saint smiled his courteous acceptance, ignoring the wrathful half movement that made Forrest's attitude rudely obvious. He would have stayed anyway, whoever had objected. It was just dawning on him that out of the whole fishy setup, Marvin Chase was the one man he had still to meet.

VI

"Boss," said Mr. Uniatz, rising to his feet with an air of firm decision, "should I go to de terlet?"

It was not possible for Simon to pretend that he didn't know him; nor could he take refuge in temporary deafness. Mr. Uniatz' penetrating accents were too peremptory for that to have been convincing. Simon swallowed, and took hold of himself with the strength of despair.

"I don't know, Hoppy," he said bravely. "How do you feel?"

"I feel fine, boss. I just t'ought it might be a good place."

"It might be," Simon conceded feverishly.

"Dat was a swell idea of yours, boss," said Mr. Uniatz, hitching up his bottle.

Simon took hold of the back of a chair for support.

"Oh, not at all," he said faintly. "It's nothing to do with me."

Hoppy looked puzzled.

"Sure, you t'ought of it foist, boss," he insisted generously. "Ya said to me, de nex time I should take de bottle away someplace an' lock myself up wit' it. So I t'ought I might take dis one in de terlet. I just t'ought it might be a good place," said Mr. Uniatz, rounding off the résumé of his train of thought.

"Sit down!" said the Saint with paralysing ferocity.

Mr. Uniatz lowered himself back onto his hams with an expression of pained mystification, and Simon turned to the others.

"Excuse us, won't you?" he said brightly.

"Hoppy's made a sort of bet with himself about something, and he has a rather one-track mind."

Forrest glared at him coldly. Rosemary half put on a gracious smile, and took it off again. Dr. Quintus almost bowed, with his mouth open. There was a lot of silence, in which Simon could feel the air prickling with pardonable speculations on his sanity. Every other reaction that he had been deliberately building up to provoke had had time to disperse itself under cover of the two consecutive interruptions. The spell was shattered, and he was back again where he began. He knew it, and resignedly slid into small talk that might yet lead to another opening.

"I heard that your father had a nasty motor accident, Miss Chase," he said.

"Yes."

The brief monosyllable offered nothing but the baldest affirmation; but her eyes were fixed on him with an expression that he tried unavailingly to read.

"I hope he wasn't badly hurt."

"Quite badly burned," rumbled the doctor. "The car caught fire, you know. But fortunately his life isn't in danger. In fact, he would probably have escaped with nothing worse than a few bruises if he hadn't made such heroic efforts to save his secretary, who was trapped in the wreckage."

"I read something about it," lied the Saint. "He was burned to death, wasn't he? What was his name, now?"

"Bertrand Tamblin."

"Oh yes. Of course."

Simon took a cigarette from his case and lighted it. He looked at the girl. His brain was still working at fighting pitch; but his manner was quite casual and disarming now—the unruffled conversational manner of an accepted friend discussing a minor matter of mutual interest.

"I just remembered something you said to the sergeant a little while ago, Miss Chase—about your having noticed that Nora Prescott seemed to be rather under a strain since Tamblin was killed."

She looked back at him steadily, neither denying it nor encouraging him.

He said in the same sensible and persuasive way: "I was wondering whether you'd noticed them being particularly friendly before the accident—as if there was any kind of attachment between them."

He saw that the eyes of both Forrest and Dr. Quintus turned toward the girl, as if they both had an unexpectedly intense interest in her answer. But she looked at neither of them.

"I can't be sure," she answered, as though choosing her words carefully. "Their work brought them together all the time, of course. Mr. Tamblin was really Father's private secretary and almost his other self, and when Nora came to us she worked for Mr. Tamblin nearly as much as Father. I thought sometimes that Mr. Tamblin was—well, quite keen on her—but I don't know whether she responded. Of course I didn't ask her."

"You don't happen to have a picture of Tamblin, do you?"

"I think there's a snapshot somewhere. . . ."

She stood up and went over to an inlaid writing table and rummaged in the drawer. It might have seemed fantastic that she should do that, obeying the Saint's suggestion as if he had hypnotized her; but Simon knew just how deftly he had gathered up the threads of his broken dominance and woven them into a new pattern. If the scene had to be played in that key, it suited him as well as any other. And with that key established, such an ordinary and natural request as he had made could not be refused. But he noticed that Dr. Quintus followed her with his hollow black eyes all the way across the room.

"Here."

She gave Simon a commonplace Kodak print that showed two men standing on the steps of a house. One of them was apparently of medium height, a little flabby, grey-haired in the small areas of his head where he was not bald. The other was a trifle shorter and leaner, with thick smooth black hair and metal-rimmed glasses.

The Saint touched his forefinger on the picture of the older man.

"Your father?"

"Yes."

It was a face without any outstanding features, creased in a tolerant if somewhat calculating smile. But Simon knew how deceptive a face could be, particularly in that kind of reproduction.

And the first thought that was thrusting itself forward in his mind was that there were two people dead, not only one—two people who had held similar and closely associated jobs, who from the very nature of their employment must have shared a good deal of Marvin Chase's confidence and known practically everything about his affairs, two people who must have known more about the intricate details of his business life than anyone else around him. One question clanged in the Saint's head like a deep jarring bell: Was Nora Prescott's killing the first murder to which that unknown swindle had led, or the second?

All through dinner his brain echoed the complex repercussions of that explosive idea, under the screen of superficial conversation which lasted through the meal. It gave that part of the evening a macabre spookiness. Hoppy Uniatz, hurt and frustrated, toyed halfheartedly with his food, which is to say that he did not ask for more than two helpings of any one dish. From time to time he washed down a mouthful with a gulp from the bottle which he had brought in with him, and put it down again to leer at it malevolently, as if it had personally welshed on him; Simon watched him anxiously when he seemed to lean perilously close to the candles which lighted the table, thinking that it would not take much to cause his breath to ignite and burn with a blue flame. Forrest had given up his efforts to protest at the whole procedure. He ate most of the time in sulky silence, and when he spoke at all he made a point of turning as much of his back to the Saint as his place at the table allowed: plainly he had made up his mind that Simon Templar was a cad on whom good manners would be wasted. Rosemary Chase talked very little, but she spoke to the Saint when she spoke at all, and she was watching him all the time with enigmatic intentness. Dr. Quintus was the only one who helped to shoulder the burden of maintaining an exchange of urbane trivialities. His reverberant basso bumbled obligingly into every

conversational opening, and said nothing that was worth remembering. His eyes were like pools of basalt at the bottom of dry caverns, never altering their expression, and yet always moving, slowly, in a way that seemed to keep everyone under ceaseless surveillance.

Simon chatted genially and emptily, with faintly mocking calm. He had shown his claws once, and now it was up to the other side to take up the challenge in their own way. The one thing they could not possibly do was ignore it, and he was ready to wait with timeless patience for their lead. Under his pose of idle carelessness he was like an arrow on a drawn bow with ghostly fingers balancing the string.

Forrest excused himself as they left the dining room. Quintus came as far as the drawing room but didn't sit down. He pulled out a large gold watch and consulted it with impressive deliberation.

"I'd better have another look at the patient," he said. "He may have settled down again by now."

The door closed behind him.

Simon leaned himself against the mantelpiece. Except for the presence of Mr. Uniatz, who in those circumstances was no more obtrusive than a piece of primitive furniture, he was alone with Rosemary Chase for the first time since so many things had begun to happen. And he knew that she was also aware of it.

She kept her face averted from his tranquil gaze, taking out a cigarette and lighting it for herself with impersonal unapproachability, while he waited. And then suddenly she turned on him as if her own restraint had defeated itself.

"Well?" she said with self-consciously harsh defiance. "What are you thinking, after all this time?"

The Saint looked her in the eyes. His own voice was contrastingly even and unaggressive.

"Thinking," he said, "that you're either a very dangerous crook or just a plain damn fool. But hoping you're just the plain damn fool. And hoping that if that's the answer, it won't be much longer before your brain starts working again."

"You hate crooks, don't you?"

"Yes."

"I've heard about you," she said. "You don't care what you do to anyone you think is a crook. You've even—killed them."

"I've killed rats," he said. "And I'll probably do it again. It's the only treatment that's any good for what they've got."

"Always?"

Simon shrugged.

"Listen," he said, not unkindly. "If you want to talk theories we can have a lot of fun, but we shan't get very far. If you want me to admit that there are exceptions to my idea of justice, you can take it as admitted; but we can't go on from there without getting down to cases. I can tell you this, though. I've heard that there's something crooked being put over here, and from what's happened since, it seems to be true. I'm going to find out what the swindle is and break it up if it takes fifty years. Only it won't take me nearly as long as that. Now if you know something that you're afraid to tell me because of what it might make me do to you or somebody else who matters to you, all I can say is that it'll probably be a lot worse if I have to dig it out for myself. Is that any use?"

She moved closer toward him, her brown eyes searching his face.

"I wish—"

It was all she had time to say. The rush of sounds that cut her off hit both of them at the same time, muffled by distance and the closed door of the room, and yet horribly distinct, stiffening them both together as though they had been clutched by invisible clammy tentacles. A shrill incoherent yell, hysterical with terror but unmistakably masculine. A heavy thud. A wild shout of "*Help!*" in the doctor's deep thundery voice. And then a ghastly inhuman wailing gurgle that choked off into deathly silence.

VII

Balanced on a knife edge of uncanny self-control, the Saint stood motionless, watching the girl's expression for a full long second before she turned

away with a gasp and rushed at the door. Hoppy Uniatz flung himself after her like a wild bull awakened from slumber: he could have remained comatose through eons of verbal fencing, but this was a call to action, clear and unsullied, and such simple clarions had never found him unresponsive. Simon started the thin edge of an instant later than either of them; but it was his hand that reached the doorknob first.

He threw the door wide and stepped out with a smooth combination of movements that brought him through the opening with a gun in his hand and his eyes streaking over the entire scene outside in one whirling survey. But the hall was empty. At the left and across from him, the front door was closed; at the opposite end a door which obviously communicated with the service wing of the house was thrown open to disclose the portly emerging figure of the butler with the white frightened faces of other servants peering from behind him.

The Saint's glance swept on upwards. The noises that had brought him out had come from upstairs, he was certain: that was also the most likely place for them to have come from, and it was only habitual caution that had made him pause to scan the hall as he reached it. He caught the girl's arm as she came by him.

"Let me go up first," he said. He blocked Hoppy's path on his other side, and shot a question across at the butler without raising his voice. "Are there any other stairs, Jeeves?"

"Y—yes sir—"

"All right. You stay here with Miss Chase. Hoppy, you find these back stairs and cover them."

He raced on up the main stairway.

As he took the treads three at a time, on his toes, he was trying to find a niche for one fact of remarkable interest. Unless Rosemary Chase was the greatest natural actress that a generation of talent scouts had overlooked, or unless his own judgment had gone completely cockeyed, the interruption had hit her with the same chilling shock as it had given him. It was to learn that that he had stayed to study her face before he moved: he was sure that he would have caught any shadow of deception, and yet if there had really been no shadow there to catch it meant that something had happened for which she was totally unprepared. And that in its turn might mean that all his suspicions of her were without foundation. It gave a jolt to the theories he had begun to put together that threw them into new and fascinating outlines, and he reached the top of the stairs with a glint of purely speculative delight shifting from the grim alertness of his eyes.

From the head of the staircase the landing opened off in the shape of a squat long-armed T. All the doors that he saw at first were closed; he strode lightly to the junction of the two arms, and heard a faint movement down the left-hand corridor. Simon took a breath and jumped out on a quick slant that would have been highly disconcerting to any marksman who might have been waiting for him round the corner. But there was no marksman.

The figures of two men were piled together on the floor, in the middle of a sickening mess; and only one of them moved.

The one who moved was Dr. Quintus, who was groggily trying to scramble up to his feet as the Saint reached him. The one who lay still was Jim Forrest; and Simon did not need to look at him twice to see that his stillness was permanent. The mess was blood—pools and gouts and splashes of blood, in hideous quantity, puddling on the floor, dripping down the walls, soddening the striped blazer and mottling the doctor's clothes. The gaping slash that split Forrest's throat from ear to ear had almost decapitated him.

The Saint's stomach turned over once. Then he was grasping the doctor's arm and helping him up. There was so much blood on him that Simon couldn't tell what his injuries might be.

"Where are you hurt?" he snapped.

The other shook his head muzzily. His weight was leaden on Simon's supporting grip.

"Not me," he mumbled hoarsely. "All right. Only hit me—on the head. Forrest—"

"Who did it?"

"Dunno. Probably same as—Nora. Heard Forrest . . . yell. . . ."

"Where did he go?"

Quintus seemed to be in a daze through which outside promptings only reached him in the same form as outside noises reach the brain of a sleepwalker. He seemed to be making a tremendous effort to retain some sort of consciousness, but his eyes were half closed and his words were thick and rambling, as if he were dead drunk.

"Suppose Forrest was—going to his room—for something. . . . Caught murderer—sneaking about. . . . Murderer—stabbed him. . . . I heard him yell. . . . Rushed out. . . . Got hit with—something. . . . Be all right—soon. Catch him—"

"Well, where did he go?"

Simon shook him, roughly slapped up the sagging head. The doctor's chest heaved as though it were taking part in his terrific struggle to achieve coherence. He got his eyes wide open.

"Don't worry about me," he whispered with painful clarity. "Look after—Mr. Chase."

His eyelids fluttered again.

Simon let him go against the wall, and he slid down almost to a sitting position, clasping his head in his hands.

The Saint balanced his Luger in his hand, and his eyes were narrowed to chips of sapphire hardness. He glanced up and down the corridor. From where he stood he could see the length of both passages which formed the arms of the T-plan of the landing. The arm on his right finished with a glimpse of the banisters of a staircase leading down—obviously the back stairs whose existence the butler had admitted, at the foot of which Hoppy Uniatz must already have taken up his post. But there had been no sound of disturbance from that direction. Nor had there been any sound from the front hall where he had left Rosemary Chase with the butler. And there was no other normal way out for anyone who was upstairs. The left-hand corridor, where he stood, ended in a blank wall; and only one door along it was open.

Simon stepped past the doctor and over Forrest's body, and went silently to the open door.

He came to it without any of the precautions

that he had taken before exposing himself a few moments before. He had a presentiment amounting to conviction that they were unnecessary now. He remembered with curious distinctness that the drawing-room curtains had not been drawn since he entered the house. Therefore anyone who wanted to could have shot at him from outside long ago. No one had shot at him. Therefore. . . .

He was looking into a large white-painted airy bedroom. The big double bed was empty, but the covers were thrown open and rumpled. The table beside it was loaded with medicine bottles. He opened the doors in the two side walls. One belonged to a spacious built-in cupboard filled with clothing; the other was a bathroom. The wall opposite the entrance door was broken by long casement windows, most of them wide open. He crossed over to one of them and looked out. Directly beneath him was the flat roof of a porch.

The Saint put his gun back in its holster and felt an unearthly cold dry calm sinking through him. Then he climbed out over the sill onto the porch roof below, which almost formed a kind of blind balcony under the window. He stood there recklessly, knowing that he was silhouetted against the light behind, and lighted a cigarette with leisured, tremorless hands. He sent a cloud of blue vapor drifting toward the stars; and then with the same leisured passivity he sauntered to the edge of the balustrade, sat on it and swung his legs over. From there it was an easy drop onto the parapet which bordered the terrace along the front of the house, and an even easier drop from the top of the parapet to the ground. To an active man the return journey would not present much more difficulty.

He paused long enough to draw another lungful of night air and tobacco smoke, and then strolled on along the terrace. It was an eerie experience, to know that he was an easy target every time he passed a lighted window, to remember that the killer might be watching him from a few yards away, and still to hold his steps down to the same steady pace; but the Saint's nerves were hardened to an icy quietness, and all his senses were working together in taut-strung vigilance.

He walked three quarters of the way round the building and arrived at the back door. It was unlocked when he tried it; and he pushed it open and looked down the barrel of Mr. Uniatz' Betsy.

"I bet you'll shoot somebody one of these days, Hoppy," he remarked; and Mr. Uniatz lowered the gun with a faint tinge of disappointment.

"What ya find, boss?"

"Quite a few jolly and interesting things." The Saint was only smiling with his lips. "Hold the fort a bit longer, and I'll tell you."

He found his way through the kitchen, where the other servants were clustered together in dumb and terrified silence, back to the front hall where Rosemary Chase and the butler were standing together at the foot of the stairs. They jumped as if a gun had been fired when they heard his footsteps; and then the girl ran toward him and caught him by the lapels of his coat.

"What is it?" she pleaded frantically. "What happened?"

"I'm sorry," he said as gently as he could.

She stared at him. He meant her to read his face for everything except the fact that he was still watching her like a spectator on the dark side of the footlights.

"Where's Jim?"

He didn't answer.

She caught her breath suddenly with a kind of sob, and turned toward the stairs. He grabbed her elbows and turned her back and held her.

"I wouldn't go up," he said evenly. "It wouldn't do any good."

"Tell me, then. For God's sake, tell me! Is he"—she choked on the word—"dead?"

"Jim, yes."

Her face was whiter than chalk, but she kept her feet. Her eyes dragged at his knowledge through a brightness of unheeded tears.

"Why do you say it like that? What else is there?"

"Your father seems to have disappeared," he said, and held her as she went limp in his arms.

VIII

Simon carried her into the drawing room and laid her down on a sofa. He stood gazing at her introspectively for a moment; then he bent over her again quickly and stabbed her in the solar plexus with a stiff forefinger. She didn't stir a muscle.

The monotonous *cheep-cheep* of a telephone bell ringing somewhere outside reached his ears, and he saw the butler starting to move mechanically toward the door. Simon passed him and saw the instrument half hidden by a curtain on the other side of the hall. He took the receiver off the hook and said: "Hullo."

"May I speak to Mr. Templar, please?"

The Saint put a hand on the wall to save himself from falling over.

"Who wants him?"

"Mr. Trapani."

"Giulio!" Simon exclaimed. The voice was familiar now, but its complete unexpectedness had prevented him from recognizing it before. "It seems to be about sixteen years since I saw you—and I never came back for dinner."

"That's quite all right, Mr. Templar. I didn't expect you, when I knew what had happened. I only called up now because it's getting late and I didn't know if you would want a room for tonight."

The Saint's brows drew together.

"What the hell is this?" he demanded slowly. "Have you taken up crystal gazing or something?"

Giulio Trapani chuckled.

"No, I am not any good at that. The police sergeant stopped here on his way back, and he told me. He said you had got mixed up with a murder, and Miss Chase had taken you home with her. So of course I knew you would be very busy. Has she asked you to stay?"

"Let me call you back in a few minutes, Giulio," said the Saint. "Things have been happening, and I've got to get hold of the police again." He paused,

and a thought struck him. "Look, is Sergeant Jesser still there, by any chance?"

There was no answer.

Simon barked: "Hullo."

Silence. He jiggled the hook. The movements produced no corresponding clicks in his ear. He waited a moment longer, while he realized that the stillness of the receiver was not the stillness of a broken connection, but a complete inanimate muteness that stood for something less easily remedied than that.

He hung the receiver up and traced the course of the wiring with his eyes. It ran along the edge of the wainscoting to the frame of the front door and disappeared into a hole bored at the edge of the wood. Simon turned right round with another abrupt realization. He was alone in the hall—the butler was no longer in sight.

He slipped his pencil flashlight out of his breast pocket with his left hand and let himself out of the front door. The telephone wires ran up outside along the margin of the door frame and continued up over the exterior wall. The beam of his torch followed them up, past a lighted window over the porch from which he had climbed down a few minutes ago, to where they were attached to a pair of porcelain insulators under the eaves. Where the wires leading on from the insulators might once have gone was difficult to decide: they dangled slackly downwards now, straddling the balcony and trailing away into the darkness of the drive.

The Saint switched off his light and stood motionless. Then he flitted across the terrace, crossed the drive and merged himself into the shadow of a big clump of laurels on the edge of the lawn. Again he froze into breathless immobility. The blackness ahead of him was stygian, impenetrable, even to his noctambulant eyes, but hearing would serve his temporary purpose almost as well as sight. The night had fallen so still that he could even hear the rustle of the distant river; and he waited for minutes that seemed like hours to him, and must have seemed like weeks to a guilty prowler who could not have travelled very far after the wires were broken. And while he waited, he was trying to decide at exactly what point in his last speech the break had occurred. It could easily have happened at a place where Trapani would think he had finished and rung off. . . . But he heard nothing while he stood there—not a snap of a twig or the rustle of a leaf.

He went back to the drawing room and found the butler standing there, wringing his hands in a helpless sort of way.

"Where have you been?" he inquired coldly.

The man's loose bloodhound jowls wobbled.

"I went to fetch my wife, sir." He indicated the stout red-faced woman who was kneeling beside the couch, chafing the girl's nerveless wrists. "To see if she could help Miss Chase."

Simon's glance flickered over the room like a rapier blade and settled pricklingly on an open french window.

"Did you have to fetch her in from the garden?" he asked sympathetically.

"I—I don't understand, sir."

"Don't you? Neither do I. But that window was closed when I saw it last."

"I opened it just now, sir, to give Miss Chase some fresh air."

The Saint held his eyes ruthlessly, but the butler did not try to look away.

"All right," he said at length. "We'll check up on that presently. Just for the moment, you can both go back to the kitchen."

The stout woman got to her feet with the laboured motions of a rheumatic camel.

" 'Oo do you think you are," she demanded indignantly, "to be bossing everybody about in his 'ouse?"

"I am the Grand Gugnune of Waziristan," answered the Saint pleasantly. "And I said—get back to the kitchen."

He followed them back himself and went on through to find Hoppy Uniatz. The other door of the kitchen conveniently opened into the small rear hall into which the back stairs came down and from which the back door also opened. Simon locked and bolted the back door and drew Hoppy into the kitchen doorway and propped him up against the jamb.

"If you stand here," he said, "you'll be able to cover the back stairs and this gang in the kitchen at the same time. And that's what I want you to do. None of them is to move out of your sight— not even to get somebody else some fresh air."

"Okay, boss," said Mr. Uniatz dimly. "If I only had a drink—"

"Tell Jeeves to buy you one."

The Saint was on his way out again when the butler stopped him.

"Please, sir, I'm sure I could be of some use—"

"You are being useful," said the Saint and closed the door on him.

Rosemary Chase was sitting up when he returned to the drawing room.

"I'm sorry," she said weakly. "I'm afraid I fainted."

"I'm afraid you did," said the Saint. "I poked you in the tummy to make sure it was real, and it was. It looks as if I've been wrong about you all the evening. I've got a lot of apologies to make, and you'll have to imagine most of them. Would you like a drink?"

She nodded; and he turned to the table and operated with a bottle and siphon. While he was doing it, he said with matter-of-fact naturalness: "How many servants do you keep here?"

"The butler and his wife, a housemaid and a parlourmaid."

"Then they're all rounded up and accounted for. How long have you known them?"

"Only about three weeks—since we've been here."

"So that means nothing. I should have had them corralled before, but I didn't think fast enough." He brought the drink over and gave it to her. "Anyway, they're corralled now, under Hoppy's thirsty eye, so if anything else happens we'll know they didn't have anything to do with it. If that's any help. . . . Which leaves only us— and Quintus."

"What happened to him?"

"He said he got whacked on the head by our roving bogeyman."

"Hadn't you better look after him?"

"Sure. In a minute."

Simon crossed the room and closed the open window and drew the curtains. He came back and stood by the table to light a cigarette. There had been so much essential activity during the past few minutes that he had had no time to do any constructive thinking; but now he had to get every possible blank filled in before the next move was made. He put his lighter away and studied her with cool and friendly encouragement, as if they had a couple of years to spare in which to straighten out misunderstandings.

She sipped her drink and looked up at him with dark stricken eyes from which, he knew, all pretence and concealment had now been wiped away. They were eyes that he would have liked to see without the grief in them; and the pallor of her face made him remember its loveliness as he had first seen it. Her red lips formed bitter words without flinching.

"I'm the one who ought to have been killed. If I hadn't been such a fool this might never have happened. I ought to be thrown in the river with a weight round my neck. Why don't you say so?"

"That wouldn't be any use now," he said. "I'd rather you made up for it. Give me the story."

She brushed the hair off her forehead with a weary gesture.

"The trouble is—I can't. There isn't any story that's worth telling. Just that I was—trying to be clever. It all began when I read a letter that I hadn't any right to read. It was in this room. I'd been out. I came in through the french windows, and I sat down at the desk because I'd just remembered something I had to make a note of. The letter was on the blotter in front of me—the letter you got. Nora must have just finished it, and then left the room for a moment, just before I came in, not thinking anyone else would be around. I saw your name on it. I'd heard of you, of course. It startled me so much that I was reading on before I knew what I was doing. And then I couldn't stop. I read it all. Then I heard Nora coming back. I lost my head and slipped out through the window again without her seeing me."

"And you never spoke to her about it?"

"I couldn't—later. After all that, I couldn't sort of come out and confess that I'd read it. Oh, I know I was a damn fool. But I was scared. It seemed as if she must know something dreadful that my father was involved in. I didn't know anything about his affairs. But I loved him. If he was doing something crooked, whatever it was, I'd have been hurt to death; but still I wanted to try and protect him. I couldn't talk about it to anybody but Jim. We decided the only thing was to find out what it was all about. That's why we followed Nora to the Bell, and then followed you to the boathouse."

"Why didn't you tell me this before?"

She shrugged hopelessly.

"Because I was afraid to. You remember I asked you about how much you hated crooks? I was afraid that if my father was mixed up in—anything wrong—you'd be even more merciless than the police. I wanted to save him. But I didn't think—all this would happen. It was hard enough not to say anything when we found Nora dead. Now that Jim's been killed, I can't go on with it any more."

The Saint was silent for a moment, weighing her with his eyes; and then he said: "What do you know about this guy Quintus?"

IX

"Hardly anything," she said. "He happened to be living close to where the accident happened, and Father was taken to his house. Father took such a fancy to him that when they brought him home he insisted on bringing Doctor Quintus along to look after him—at least, that's what I was told. I know what you're thinking." She looked at him steadily. "You think there's something funny about him."

" 'Phony' is the way I pronounce it," answered the Saint bluntly.

She nodded.

"I wondered about him too—after I read that letter. But how could I say anything?"

"Can you think of anything that might have given him a hold over your father?"

She moved her hands desperately.

"How could I know? Father never talked business at home. I never heard anything—discreditable about him. But how could I know?"

"You've seen your father since he was brought home?"

"Of course. Lots of times."

"Did he seem to have anything on his mind?"

"I can't tell—"

"Did he seem to be worried or frightened?"

"It's so *hard*," she said. "I don't know what I really saw and what I'm making myself imagine. He was badly hurt, you know, and he was still trying to keep some of his business affairs going, so that took a lot out of him, and Doctor Quintus never let me stay with him very long at a time. And then he didn't feel like talking much. Of course he seemed shaky, and not a bit like himself; but after an accident like that you wouldn't expect anything else. . . . I don't know what to think about anything. I thought he always liked Jim, and now— Oh, God, what a mess I've made!"

The Saint smoothed the end of his cigarette in an ash tray, and there was an odd kind of final contentment in his eyes. All the threads were in his hands now, all the questions answered—except for the one answer that would cover all the others. Being as he was, he could understand Rosemary Chase's story, forgetting the way it had ended. Others might have found it harder to forgive; but to him it was just the old tale of amateur adventuring leading to tragic disaster. And even though his own amateur adventures had never led there, they were still close enough for him to realise the hairbreadth margin by which they had escaped it. . . . And the story she told him gathered up many loose ends.

He sat down beside her and put his hand on her arm.

"Don't blame yourself too much about Jim," he said steadyingly. "He made some of the mess himself. If he hadn't thrown me off the track by the way he behaved, things might have been a lot different. Why the hell did he have to do that?"

"He'd made up his mind that you'd only come into this for what you could get out of it— that if you found out what Nora knew, you'd use it to blackmail Father, or something like that. He wasn't terribly clever. I suppose he thought you'd killed her to keep the information to yourself—"

The Saint shrugged wryly.

"And I thought one of you had killed her to keep her mouth shut. None of us has been very clever—yet."

"What are we going to do?" she said.

Simon thought. And he may have been about to answer when his ears caught a sound that stopped him. His fingers tightened on the girl's wrist for an instant, while his eyes rested on her like bright steel; and then he got up.

"Give me another chance," he said in a soft voice that could not even have been heard across the room.

And then he was walking across to greet the doctor as the footsteps that had stopped him arrived at the door and Quintus came in.

"Doctor Quintus!" The Saint's air was sympathetic, his face full of concern. He took the doctor's arm. "You shouldn't have come down alone. I was just coming back for you, but there've been so many other things—"

"I know. And they were probably more valuable than anything you could have done for me."

The blurry resonance of the other's voice was nearly normal again. He moved firmly over to the table on which the tray of drinks stood.

"I'm going to prescribe myself a whiskey and soda," he said.

Simon fixed it for him. Quintus took the glass and sat down gratefully on the edge of a chair. He rubbed a hand over his dishevelled head as though trying to clear away the lingering remnants of fog. He had washed his face and hands, but the darkening patches of red stain on his clothing were still gruesome reminders of the man who had not come down.

"I'm sorry I was so useless, Mr. Templar," he said heavily. "Did you find anything?"

"Not a thing." The Saint's straightforwardness sounded completely ingenuous. "Mr. Chase must have been taken out of the window—I climbed down from there myself, and it was quite easy. I walked most of the way round the house, and nothing happened. I didn't hear a sound, and it was too dark to see anything."

Quintus looked across at the girl.

"There isn't anything I can say, Miss Chase. I can only tell you that I would have given my own right hand to prevent this."

"But *why?*" she said brokenly. "Why are all these things happening? What is it all about? First Nora, and then—Jim. . . . And now my father. What's happened to him? What have they done with him?"

The doctor's lips tightened.

"Kidnapped, I suppose," he said wretchedly. "I suppose everything has been leading up to that. You father's a rich man. They'd expect him to be worth a large ransom—large enough to run any risks for. Jim's death was—well, just a tragic accident. He happened to run into one of them in the corridor, so he was murdered. If that hadn't confused them, they'd probably have murdered me."

"They?" interposed the Saint quickly. "You saw them, then."

"Only one man, the one who hit me. He was rather small, and he had a handkerchief tied over his face. I didn't have a chance to notice much. I'm saying 'they' because I don't see how one man alone could have organized and done all this. . . . It must be kidnapping. Possibly they were trying to force or bribe Nora to help them from the inside, and she was murdered because she threatened to give them away."

"And they tried to kill me in case she had told me about the plot."

"Exactly."

Simon put down the stub of his cigarette and searched for a fresh one.

"Why do you think they should think she might have told me anything?" he inquired.

Quintus hesitated expressionlessly. He drank slowly from his glass and brought his cavernous black eyes back to the Saint's face.

"With your reputation—if you will forgive me—finding you on the scene . . . I'm only theorising, of course—"

Simon nodded good-humouredly.

"Don't apologize," he murmured. "My repu-

tation is a great asset. It's made plenty of clever crooks lose their heads before this."

"It *must* be kidnapping," Quintus repeated, turning to the girl. "If they'd wanted to harm your father, they could easily have done it in his bedroom when they had him at their mercy. They wouldn't have needed to take him away. You must be brave and think about that. The very fact that they took him away proves that they must want him alive."

The Saint finished chain-lighting the fresh cigarette and strolled over to the fireplace to flick away the butt of the old one. He stood there for a moment, and then turned thoughtfully back to the room.

"Talking of this taking away," he said, "I did notice something screwy about it. I didn't waste much time getting upstairs after I heard the commotion. And starting from the same commotion, our kidnapping guy or guys had to dash into the bedroom, grab Mr. Chase, shove him out of the window and lower him to the ground. All of which must have taken a certain amount of time." He looked at the doctor. "Well, I wasted a certain amount of time myself in the corridor, finding out whether you were hurt, and so forth. So those times begin to cancel out. Then, when I got in the bedroom, I saw at once that the bed was empty. I looked in the cupboard and the bathroom, just making sure the old boy was really gone; but that can't have taken more than a few seconds. Then I went straight to the window. And then, almost immediately, I climbed out of it and climbed down to the ground to see if I could see anything, because I knew Marvin Chase could only have gone out that way. Now you remember what I told you? *I didn't hear a sound.* Not so much as the dropping of a pin."

"What do you mean?" asked the girl.

"I mean this," said the Saint. "Figure out our timetable for yourselves—the kidnappers' and mine. They can't have been more than a few seconds ahead of me. And from below the window they had to get your father to a car, shove him in and take him away—*if they took him away*. But I told you! I walked all round the house, slowly, listening, and I didn't hear anything. When did they start making those completely noiseless cars?"

Quintus half rose from his chair.

"You mean—they might still be in the grounds? Then we're sure to catch them! As soon as the police get here—you've sent for them, of course?"

Simon shook his head.

"Not yet. And that's something else that makes me think I'm right. I haven't called the police yet because I can't. I can't call them because the telephone wires have been cut. And they were cut *after* all this had happened—after I'd walked round the house and come back in and told Rosemary what had happened!"

The girl's lips were parted, her wide eyes fastened on him with a mixture of fear and eagerness. She began to say: "But they might—"

The crash stopped her.

Her eyes switched to the left, and Simon saw blank horror leap into her face as he whirled toward the sound. It had come from one of the windows, and it sounded like smashing glass. . . . It was the glass. He saw the stir of the curtains and the gloved hand that came between them under a shining gun barrel, and flung himself fiercely backwards.

X

He catapulted himself at the main electric-light switches beside the door—without conscious decision, but knowing that his instinct must be right. More slowly, while he was moving, his mind reasoned it out: the unknown man who had broken the window had already beaten him to the draw, and in an open gun battle with the lights on the unknown had a three-to-one edge in choice of targets. . . . Then the Saint's shoulder hit the wall, and his hand sliced up over the switches just as the invader's revolver spoke once, deafeningly.

Blam!

Simon heard the spang of the bullet some distance from him, and more glass shattered. Quintus gasped deeply. The Saint's ears sang with the concussion, but through the buzzing

he was trying to determine whether the gunman had come in.

He moved sideways, noiselessly, crouching, his Luger out in his hand. Nothing else seemed to move. His brain was working again in a cold fever of precision. Unless the pot-shot artist had hoped to settle everything with the first bullet, he would expect the Saint to rush the window. Therefore the Saint would not rush the window. . . . The utter silence in the room was battering his brain with warnings.

His fingers touched the knob of the door, closed on it and turned it without a rattle until the latch disengaged. Gathering his muscles, he whipped it suddenly open, leapt through it out into the hall and slammed it behind him. In the one red-hot instant when he was clearly outlined against the lights of the hall, a second shot blasted out of the dark behind him and splintered the woodwork close to his shoulder; but his exposure was too swift and unexpected for the sniper's marksmanship. Without even looking back, Simon dived across the hall and let himself out the front door.

He raced around the side of the house and dropped to a crouch again as he reached the corner that would bring him in sight of the terrace outside the drawing-room windows. He slid an eye round the corner, prepared to yank it back on an instant's notice, and then left it there with the brow over it lowering in a frown.

It was dark on the terrace, but not too dark for him to see that there was no one standing there.

He scanned the darkness on his right, away from the house; but he could find nothing in it that resembled a lurking human shadow. And over the whole garden brooded the same eerie stillness, the same incredible absence of any hint of movement, that had sent feathery fingers creeping up his spine when he was out there before. . . .

The Saint eased himself along the terrace, flat against the wall of the house, his forefinger tight on the trigger and his eyes probing the blackness of the grounds. No more shots came at him. He reached the french windows with the broken pane, and stretched out a hand to test the handle.

They wouldn't open. They were still fastened on the inside—as he had fastened them.

He spoke close to the broken pane.

"All clear, souls. Don't put the lights on yet, but let me in."

Presently the window swung back. There were shutters outside, and he folded them across the opening and bolted them as he stepped in. Their hinges were stiff from long disuse. He did the same at the other window before he groped his way back to the door and relit the lights.

"We'll have this place looking like a fortress before we're through," he remarked cheerfully; and then the girl ran to him and caught his sleeve.

"Didn't you see anyone?"

He shook his head.

"Not a soul. The guy didn't even open the window—just stuck his gun through the broken glass and sighted from outside. I have an idea he was expecting me to charge through the window after him, and then he'd 've had me cold. But I fooled him. I guess he heard me coming round the house, and took his feet off the ground." He smiled at her reassuringly. "Excuse me a minute while I peep at Hoppy—he might be worried."

He should have known better than to succumb to that delusion. In the kitchen a trio of white-faced women and one man who was not much more sanguine jumped round with panicky squeals and goggling eyes as he entered; but Mr. Uniatz removed the bottle which he was holding to his lips with dawdling reluctance.

"Hi, boss," said Mr. Uniatz with as much phlegmatic cordiality as could be expected of a man who had been interrupted in the middle of some important business; and the Saint regarded him with new respect.

"Doesn't anything ever worry you, Hoppy?" he inquired mildly.

Mr. Uniatz waved his bottle with liberal nonchalance.

"Sure, boss, I hear de firewoiks," he said. "But I figure if anyone is gettin' hoit it's some udder guy. How are t'ings?"

"T'ings will be swell, so long as I know you're on the job," said the Saint reverently, and withdrew again.

He went back to the drawing room with his hands in his pockets, not hurrying; and in spite of what had happened he felt more composed than he had been all the evening. It was as if he sensed that the crescendo was coming to a climax beyond which it could go no further, while all the time his own unravellings were simplifying the tangled undercurrents toward one final resolving chord that would bind them all together. And the two must coincide and blend. All he wanted was a few more minutes, a few more answers. . . . His smile was almost indecently carefree when he faced the girl again.

"All is well," he reported, "and I'm afraid Hoppy is ruining your cellar."

She came up to him, her eyes searching him anxiously.

"That shot when you ran out," she said. "You aren't hurt?"

"Not a bit. But it's depressing to feel so unpopular."

"What makes you think you're the only one who's unpopular?" asked the doctor dryly.

He was still sitting in the chair where Simon had left him, and Simon followed his glance as he screwed his neck round indicatively. Just over his left shoulder a picture on the wall had a dark-edged hole drilled in it, and the few scraps of glass that still clung to the frame formed a jagged circle around it.

The Saint gazed at the bullet scar, and for a number of seconds he said nothing. He had heard the impact, of course, and heard the tinkle of glass; but since the shot had missed him he hadn't given it another thought. Now that its direction was pointed out to him, the whole sequence of riddles seemed to fall into focus.

The chain of alibis was complete.

Anyone might have murdered Nora Prescott—even Rosemary Chase and Forrest. Rosemary Chase herself could have fired the shot at the boathouse, an instant before Forrest switched on his torch, and then rejoined him. But Forrest wasn't likely to have cut his own

THE INVISIBLE MILLIONAIRE

throat; and even if he had done that, he couldn't have abducted Marvin Chase afterwards. And when Forrest was killed, the Saint himself was Rosemary Chase's alibi. The butler might have done all these things; but after that he had been shut in the kitchen with Hoppy Uniatz to watch over him, so that the Saint's own precaution acquitted him of having fired those last two shots a few minutes ago. Dr. Quintus might have done everything else, might never have been hit on the head upstairs at all; but he certainly couldn't have fired those two shots either—and one of them had actually been aimed at him. Simon went back to his original position by the fireplace to make sure of it. The result didn't permit the faintest shadow of doubt. Even allowing for his dash to the doorway, if the first shot had been aimed at the Saint and had just missed Quintus instead, it must have been fired by someone who couldn't get within ten feet of the bull's-eye at ten yards range—an explanation that wasn't even worth considering.

And that left only one person who had never had an alibi—who had never been asked for one because he had never seemed to need one. The man around whom all the commotion was centred—and yet the one member of the cast, so far as the Saint was concerned, who had never yet appeared on the scene. Someone who, for all obvious purposes, might just as well have been nonexistent.

But if Marvin Chase himself had done all the wild things that had been done that night, it would mean that the story of his injuries must be entirely fictitious. And it was hardly plausible that any man would fabricate and elaborate such a story at a time when there was no conceivable advantage to be gained from it.

Simon thought about that, and everything in him seemed to be standing still.

The girl was saying: "These people wouldn't be doing all this if they just wanted to kidnap my father. Unless they were maniacs. They can't get any ransom if they kill off everyone who's ever had anything to do with him, and that's what they seem to be trying to do—"

"Except you," said the Saint, almost inattentively. "You haven't been hurt yet."

He was thinking: "The accident happened a week ago—days before Nora Prescott wrote to me, before there was ever any reason to expect me on the scene. But all these things that a criminal might want an alibi for have happened *since* I came into the picture, and probably on my account. Marvin Chase might have been a swindler, and he might have rubbed out his secretary in a phony motor accident because he knew too much; but for all he could have known that would have been the end of it. He didn't need to pretend to be injured himself, and take the extra risk of ringing in a phony doctor to build up the atmosphere. Therefore he didn't invent his injuries. Therefore his alibi is as good as anyone else's. Therefore we're right back where we started."

Or did it mean that he was at the very end of the hunt? In a kind of trance he walked over to the broken window and examined the edges of the smashed pane. On the point of one of the jags of glass clung a couple of kinky white threads—such as might have been ripped out of a gauze bandage. Coming into the train of thought that his mind was following, the realization of what they meant gave him hardly any sense of shock. He already knew that he was never going to meet Marvin Chase.

Dr. Quintus was getting to his feet.

"I'm feeling better now," he said. "I'll go for the police."

"Just a minute," said the Saint quietly. "I think I can have someone ready for them to arrest when they get here."

XI

He turned to the girl and took her shoulders in his hands.

"I'm sorry, Rosemary," he said. "You're going to be hurt now."

Then, without stopping to face the bewildered fear that came into her eyes, he went to the door and raised his voice.

"Send the butler along, Hoppy. See that the curtains are drawn where you are, and keep an eye on the windows. If anyone tries to rush you from any direction, give 'em the heat first and ask questions afterwards."

"Okay, boss," replied Mr. Uniatz obediently.

The butler came down the hall as if he were walking on eggs. His impressively fleshy face was pallid and apprehensive, but he stood before the Saint with a certain ineradicable dignity.

"Yes sir?"

Simon beckoned him to the front door; and this time the Saint was very careful. He turned out all the hall lights before he opened the door, and then drew the butler quickly outside without fully closing it behind them. They stood where the shadow of the porch covered them in solid blackness.

"Jeeves," he said, and in contrast with all that circumspection his voice was extraordinarily clear and carrying, "I want you to go to the nearest house and use their phone to call the police station. Ask for Sergeant Jesser. I want you to give him a special message."

"Me, sir?"

Simon couldn't see the other's face, but he could imagine the expression on it from the tremulous tone of the reply. He smiled to himself, but his eyes were busy on the dark void of the garden.

"Yes, you. Are you scared?"

"N-no sir. But—"

"I know what you mean. It's creepy, isn't it? I'd feel the same way myself. But don't let it get you down. Have you ever handled a gun?"

"I had a little experience during the war, sir."

"Swell. Then here's a present for you." Simon felt for the butler's flabby hand and pressed his own Luger into it. "It's all loaded and ready to talk. If anything tries to happen, use it. And this is something else. I'll be with you. You won't hear me and you won't see me, but I'll be close by. If anyone tries to stop you or do anything to you, he'll get a nasty surprise. So don't worry. You're going to get through."

He could hear the butler swallow.

"Very good, sir. What was the message you wished me to take?"

"It's for Sergeant Jesser," Simon repeated with the same careful clarity. "Tell him about the murder of Mr. Forrest and the other things that have happened. Tell him I sent you. And tell him I've solved the mystery, so he needn't bother to bring back his gang of coroners and photographers and fingerprint experts and what not. Tell him I'm getting a confession now, and I'll have it all written out and signed for him by the time he gets here. Can you remember that?"

"Yes sir."

"Okay, Jeeves. On your way."

He slipped his other automatic out of his hip pocket and stood there while the butler crossed the drive and melted into the inky shadows beyond. He could hear the man's softened footsteps even when he was out of sight, but they kept regularly on until they faded in the distance, and there was no disturbance. When he felt as sure as he could hope to be that the butler was beyond the danger zone, he put the Walther away again and stepped soundlessly back into the darkened hall.

Rosemary Chase and the doctor stared blankly at him as he re-entered the drawing room; and he smiled blandly at their mystification.

"I know," he said. "You heard me tell Jeeves that I was going to follow him."

Quintus said: "But why—"

"For the benefit of the guy outside," answered the Saint calmly. "If there is a guy outside. The guy who's been giving us so much trouble. If he's hung around as long as this, he's still around. He hasn't finished his job yet. He missed the balloon pretty badly on the last try, and he daren't pull out and leave it missed. He's staying right on the spot, wondering like hell what kind of a fast play he can work to save his bacon. So he heard what I told the butler. I meant him to. And I think it worked. I scared him away from trying to head off Jeeves with another carving-knife performance. Instead of that, he decided to stay here and try to clean up before the police arrive. And that's also what I meant him to do."

The doctor's deep-set eyes blinked slowly.

"Then the message you sent was only another bluff?"

"Partly. I may have exaggerated a little. But I meant to tickle our friend's curiosity. I wanted to make sure that he'd be frantic to find out more about it. So he had to know what's going on in this room. I'll bet money that he's listening to every word I'm saying now."

The girl glanced at the broken window, beyond which the venetian shutters hid them from outside but would not silence their voices, and then glanced at the door; and she shivered. She said: "But then he knows you didn't go with the butler—"

"But he knows it's too late to catch him up. Besides, this is much more interesting now. He wants to find out how much I've really got up my sleeve. And I want to tell him."

"But you said you were only bluffing," she protested huskily. "You don't really know anything."

The Saint shook his head.

"I only said I was exaggerating a little. I haven't got a confession yet, but I'm hoping to get one. The rest of it is true. I know everything that's behind tonight's fun and games. I know why everything has been done, and who did it."

They didn't try to prompt him, but their wide-open eyes clung to him almost as if they had been hypnotized. It was as if an unreasoned fear of what he might be going to say made them shrink from pressing him, while at the same time they were spellbound by a fascination beyond their power to break.

The Saint made the most of his moment. He made them wait while he sauntered to a chair, and settled himself there, and lighted a cigarette, as if they were only enjoying an ordinary casual conversation. The theatrical pause was deliberate, aimed at the nerves of the one person whom he had to drive into self-betrayal.

"It's all so easy, really, when you sort it out," he said at length. "Our criminal is a clever guy, and he'd figured out a swindle that was so simple and audacious that it was practically foolproof— barring accidents. And to make up for the thousandth fraction of risk, it was bound to put millions into his hands. Only the accident happened; and one accident led to another."

He took smoke from his cigarette and returned it through musingly half-smiling lips.

"The accident was when Nora Prescott wrote to me. She had to be in on the swindle, of course; but he thought he could keep her quiet with the threat that if she exposed him her father would lose the sinecure that was practically keeping him alive. It wasn't a very good threat, if she'd been a little more sensible, but it scared her enough to keep her away from the police. It didn't scare her out of thinking that a guy like me might be able to wreck the scheme somehow and still save something out of it for her. So she wrote to me. Our villain found out about that but wasn't able to stop the letter. So he followed her to the Bell tonight, planning to kill me as well, because he figured that once I'd received that letter I'd keep on prying until I found something. When Nora led off to the boathouse, it looked to be in the bag. He followed her, killed her and waited to add me to the collection. Only on account of another accident that happened then, he lost his nerve and quit."

Again the Saint paused.

"Still our villain knew he had to hang on to me until I could be disposed of," he went on with the same leisured confidence. "He arranged to bring me up here to be got rid of as soon as he knew how. He stalled along until after dinner, when he'd got a plan worked out. He'd just finished talking it over with his accomplice—"

"Accomplice?" repeated the doctor.

"Yes," said the Saint flatly. "And just to make sure we understand each other, I'm referring to a phony medico who goes under the name of Quintus."

The doctor's face went white, and his hands whitened on the arms of his chair; but the Saint didn't stir.

"I wouldn't try it," he said. "I wouldn't try anything, brother, if I were you. Because if you do, I shall smash you into soup meat."

Rosemary Chase stared from one to the other.

"But—you don't mean—"

"I mean that that motor accident of your

father's was a lie from beginning to end." Simon's voice was gentle. "He needed a phony doctor to back up the story of those injuries. He couldn't have kept it up with an honest one, and that would have wrecked everything. It took me a long time to see it, but that's because we're all ready to take too much for granted. You told me you'd seen your father since it happened, so I didn't ask any more questions. Naturally you didn't feel you had to tell me that when you saw him he was smothered in bandages like a mummy, and his voice was only a hoarse croak; but he needed Quintus to keep him that way."

"You must be out of your mind!" Quintus roared hollowly.

The Saint smiled.

"No. But you're out of a job. And it was an easy one. I said we all take too much for granted. You're introduced as a doctor, and so everybody believes it. Now you're going to have another easy job—signing the confession I promised Sergeant Jesser. You'll do it to save your own skin. You'll tell how Forrest wasn't quite such a fool as he seemed; how he listened outside Marvin Chase's room and heard you and your pal cooking up a scheme to have your pal bust this window here and take a shot at you, just for effect, and then kill me and Hoppy when we came dashing into the fight; how Forrest got caught there, and how he was murdered so he couldn't spill the beans—"

"And what else?" said a new voice.

Simon turned his eyes toward the doorway and the man who stood there—a man incongruously clad in dark wine-colored silk pajamas and bedroom slippers, whose head was swathed in bandages so that only his eyes were visible, whose gloved right hand held a revolver aimed at the Saint's chest. The Saint heard Rosemary come to her feet with a stifled cry, and answered to her rather than to anyone else.

"I told you you were going to be hurt, Rosemary," he said. "Your father was killed a week ago. But you'll remember his secretary. This is Mr. Bertrand Tamblin."

XII

"You're clever, aren't you?" Tamblin said viciously.

"Not very," said the Saint regretfully. "I ought to have tumbled to it long ago. But as I was saying, we all take too much for granted. Everyone spoke of you as Marvin Chase, and so I assumed that was who you were. I got thrown off the scent a bit further when Rosemary and Forrest crashed into the boathouse at an awkward moment, when you got up the wind and scrammed. I didn't get anywhere near the mark until I began to think of you as the invisible millionaire—the guy that all the fuss was about and yet who couldn't be seen. Then it all straightened out. You killed Marvin Chase, burnt his body in a fake auto crash and had yourself brought home by Quintus in his place. Nobody argued about it; you had Quintus to keep you covered; you knew enough about his affairs to keep your end up in any conversation—you could even fool his daughter on short interviews, with your face bandaged and talking in the sort of faint unrecognizable voice that a guy who'd been badly injured might talk in. And you were all set to get your hands on as much of Marvin Chase's dough as you could squeeze out of banks and bonds before anyone got suspicious."

"Yes?"

"Oh yes. . . . It was a grand idea until the accidents began to happen. Forrest was another accident. You got some of his blood on you—it's on you now—and you were afraid to jump back into bed when you heard me coming up the stairs. You lost your head again and plunged into a phony kidnapping. I don't believe that you skipped out of your window at all just then—you simply hopped into another room and hid there till the coast was clear. I wondered about that when I didn't hear any car driving off, and nobody took a shot at me when I walked round the house."

"Go on."

"Then you realized that someone would send for the police, and you had to delay that until you'd carried out your original plan of strengthening

Quintus' alibi and killing Hoppy and me. You cut the phone wires. That was another error: an outside gang would have done that first and taken no chances, not run the risk of hanging around to do it after the job was pulled. Again you didn't shoot at me when I went out of doors the second time, because you wanted to make it look as if Quintus was also being shot at first. Then when you chose your moment, I was lucky enough to be too fast for you. When you heard me chasing round the outside of the house, you pushed off into the night for another think. I'd 've had the hell of a time catching you out there in the dark, so I let you hear me talking to the butler because I knew it would fetch you in."

Tamblin nodded.

"You only made two mistakes," he said. "Forrest would have been killed anyway, only I should have chosen a better time for it. I heard Rosemary talking to him one night outside the front door, directly under my window, when he was leaving—that is how I found out that Nora had written to you and where she was going to meet you."

"And the other mistake?" Simon asked coolly.

"Was when you let your own cleverness run away with you. When you arranged your clever scheme to get me to walk in here to provide the climax for your dramatic revelations, and even left the front door ajar to make it easy for me. You conceited fool! You've got your confession; but did you think I'd let it do you any good? Your bluff only bothered me for a moment when I was afraid Quintus had ratted. As soon as I found he hadn't, I was laughing at you. The only difference you've made is that now I shall have to kill Rosemary as well. Quintus had ideas about her, and we could have used her to build up the story—"

"Bertrand," said the Saint gravely, "I'm afraid you are beginning to drivel."

The revolver that was aimed on him did not waver.

"Tell me why," Tamblin said interestedly.

Simon trickled smoke languidly through his nostrils. He was still leaning back in his chair, imperturbably relaxed, in the attitude in which he had stayed even when Tamblin entered the room.

"Because it's your turn to be taking too much for granted. You thought my cleverness had run away with me, and so you stopped thinking. It doesn't seem to have occurred to you that since I expected you to come in, I may have expected just how sociable your ideas would be when you got here. You heard me give Jeeves a gun, and so you've jumped to the conclusion that I'm unarmed. Now will you take a look at my left hand? You notice that it's in my coat pocket. I've got you covered with another gun, Bertrand, and I'm ready to bet I can shoot faster than you. If you don't believe me, just start squeezing that trigger."

Tamblin stood gazing motionlessly at him for a moment; and then his head tilted back and a cackle of hideous laughter came through the slit in the bandages over his mouth.

"Oh no, Mr. Templar," he crowed. "You're the one who took too much for granted. You decided that Quintus was a phony doctor, and so you didn't stop to think that he might be a genuine pickpocket. When he was holding on to you in the corridor upstairs—you remember?—he took the magazines out of both your guns. You've got one shot in the chamber of the gun you've got left, and Quintus has got you covered as well now. You can't get both of us with one bullet. You've been too clever for the last time."

It was no bluff. Simon knew it with a gambler's instinct, and knew that Tamblin had the last laugh.

"Take your hand out of your pocket," Tamblin snarled. "Quintus is going to aim at Rosemary. If you use that gun, you're killing her as surely as if—"

The Saint saw Tamblin's forefinger twitch on the trigger, and waited for the sharp bite of death.

The crisp thunder of cordite splintered the unearthly stillness; but the Saint felt no shock, no pain. Staring incredulously, he saw Tamblin stagger as if a battering-ram had hit him in the back; saw him sway weakly, his right arm drooping until the revolver slipped through his fingers; saw his knees fold and his body pivot slantingly over them like a falling tree. . . . And saw the cubist figure and pithecanthropoid visage of Hoppy Uniatz coming through the door with a smoking Betsy in its hairy hand.

He heard another thud on his right, and looked round. The thud was caused by Quintus' gun hitting the carpet. Quintus' hands waved wildly in the air as Hoppy turned toward him.

"Don't shoot!" he screamed. "I'll give you a confession. I haven't killed anyone. Tamblin did it all. Don't shoot me—"

"He doesn't want to be shot, Hoppy," said the Saint. "I think we'll let the police have him—just for a change. It may help to convince them of our virtue."

"Boss," said Mr. Uniatz, lowering his gun, "I done it."

The Saint nodded. He got up out of his chair. It felt rather strange to be alive and untouched.

"I know," he said. "Another half a second, and he'd 've been the most famous gunman on earth."

Mr. Uniatz glanced cloudily at the body on the floor.

"Oh, him," he said vaguely. "Yeah. . . . But listen, boss—I done it!"

"You don't have to worry about it," said the Saint. "You've done it before. And Comrade Quintus' squeal will let you out."

Rosemary Chase was coming toward him, pale but steady. It seemed to Simon Templar that a long time had been wasted in which he had been too busy to remember how beautiful she was and how warm and red her lips were. She put out a hand to him; and because he was still the Saint and always would be, his arm went round her.

"I know it's tough," he said. "But we can't change it."

"It doesn't seem so bad now, somehow," she said. "To know that at least my father wasn't doing all this. . . . I wish I knew how to thank you."

"Hoppy's the guy to thank," said the Saint, and looked at him. "I never suspected you of being a thought reader, Hoppy, but I'd give a lot to know what made you come out of the kitchen in the nick of time."

Mr. Uniatz blinked at him.

"Dat's what I mean, boss, when I say I done it," he explained, his brow furrowed with the effort of amplifying a statement which seemed to him to be already obvious enough. "When you call out de butler, he is just opening me anudder bottle of scotch. An' dis time I make de grade. I drink it down to de last drop wit'out stopping. So I come right out to tell ya." A broad beam of ineffable pride opened up a gold mine in the centre of Mr. Uniatz' face. "I done it, boss! Ain't dat sump'n?"

You'll Always Remember Me
Steve Fisher

IT WAS THE GOAL, the dream, of the penny-a-word writers for the pulps to break out, to get into the higher-paying slick magazines, to have books published, or to get a break in Hollywood. Of the handful who made it, few enjoyed more success than Steve Fisher (1912–1980), the extraordinarily prolific pulp writer (almost two hundred stories between 1935 and 1938) who became a sought-after screenwriter.

Of the twenty novels written under his own name and as Stephen Gould and Grant Lane, the most famous is *I Wake Up Screaming*, the basis for the classic film noir starring Victor Mature.

Among the many notable motion pictures on which he received screen credit are such war films as *To the Shores of Tripoli, Destination Tokyo,* and *Berlin Correspondent.* Crime films include *Lady in the Lake* and *Song of the Thin Man.* He also wrote more than two hundred television scripts for such popular shows as *Starsky & Hutch, McMillan & Wife,* and *Barnaby Jones.*

"You'll Always Remember Me" is not a subtle story, as expected of a tale written for a pulp magazine, but its theme still resonates more than a half-century after it was written. What should society do with juvenile killers who cannot be tried as adults? William March explored this successfully in his play *The Bad Seed,* which later became a controversial movie.

This story, with its chilling last paragraph, was originally published in the March 1938 issue of *Black Mask.*

*This kid is smart—
so smart he'll die of it!*

You'll Always Remember Me

Steve Fisher

COULD TELL IT was Pushton blowing the bugle and I got out of bed tearing half of the bed clothes with me. I ran to the door and yelled, "Drown it! Drown it! Drown it!" and then I slammed the door and went along the row of beds and pulled the covers off the rest of the guys and said:

"Come on, get up. Get up! Don't you hear Pushton out there blowing his stinky lungs out?"

I hate bugles anyway, but the way this guy Pushton all but murders reveille kills me. I hadn't slept very well, thinking of the news I was going to hear this morning, one way or the other,

and then to be jarred out of what sleep I could get by Pushton climaxed everything.

I went back to my bed and grabbed my shoes and puttees and slammed them on the floor in front of me, then I began unbuttoning my pajamas. I knew it wouldn't do any good to ask the guys in this wing. They wouldn't know anything. When they did see a paper all they read was the funnies. That's the trouble with Clark's. I know it's one of the best military academies in the West and that it costs my old man plenty of dough to keep me here, but they sure have some dopy ideas on how to handle kids. Like dividing the dormitories according to ages. Anybody with any sense knows that it should be according to grades because just take for instance this wing. I swear there isn't a fourteen-year-old-punk in it that I could talk to without wanting to push in his face. And I have to live with the little pukes.

So I kept my mouth shut and got dressed, then I beat it out into the company street before the battalion got lined up for the flag raising. That's a silly thing, isn't it? Making us stand around with empty stomachs, shivering goose pimples while they pull up the flag and Pushton blows the bugle again. But at that I guess I'd have been in a worse place than Clark's Military Academy if my pop hadn't had a lot of influence and plenty of dollars. I'd be in a big school where they knock you around and don't ask you whether you like it or not. I know. I was there a month. So I guess the best thing for me to do was to let the academy have their Simple Simon flag-waving fun and not kick about it.

I was running around among the older guys now, collaring each one and asking the same question: "Were you on home-going yesterday? Did you see a paper last night? What about Tommy Smith?" That was what I wanted to know. What about Tommy Smith.

"He didn't get it," a senior told me.

"You mean the governor turned him down?"

"Yeah. He hangs Friday."

That hit me like a sledge on the back of my head and I felt words rushing to the tip of my tongue and then sliding back down my throat. I felt weak, like my stomach was all tied up in a knot. I'd thought sure Tommy Smith would have had his sentence changed to life. I didn't think they really had enough evidence to swing him. Not that I cared, particularly, only he had lived across the street and when they took him in for putting a knife through his old man's back—that was what they charged him with—it had left his two sisters minus both father and brother and feeling pretty badly.

Where I come in is that I got a crush on Marie, the youngest sister. She's fifteen. A year older than me. But as I explained, I'm not any little dumb dope still in grammar school. I'm what you'd call bright.

So that was it; they were going to swing Tommy after all, and Marie would be bawling on my shoulder for six months. Maybe I'd drop the little dame. I certainly wasn't going to go over and take that for the rest of my life.

I got lined up in the twelve-year-old company, at the right end because I was line sergeant. We did squads right and started marching toward the flag pole. I felt like hell. We swung to a company front and halted.

Pushton started in on the bugle. I watched him with my eyes burning. Gee, I hate buglers, and Pushton is easy to hate anyway. He's fat and wears horn-rimmed glasses. He's got a body like a bowling ball and a head like a pimple. His face looks like yesterday's oatmeal. And does he think being bugler is an important job! The little runt struts around like he was Gabriel, and he walks with his buttocks sticking out one way and his chest the other.

I watched him now, but I was thinking more about Tommy Smith. Earlier that night of the murder I had been there seeing Marie and I had heard part of Tommy's argument with his old man. Some silly thing. A girl Tommy wanted to marry and the old man couldn't see it that way. I will say he deserved killing, the old grouch. He used to chase me with his cane. Marie says he used to get up at night and wander around stomping that cane as he walked.

Tommy's defense was that the old boy lifted the cane to bean him. At least that was the defense the lawyer wanted to present. He wanted to present that, with Tommy pleading guilty, and hope for an acquittal. But Tommy stuck to straight denials on everything. Said he hadn't killed his father. The way everything shaped up the State proved he was a drunken liar and the jury saw it that way.

Tommy was a nice enough sort. He played football at his university, was a big guy with blond hair and a ruddy face, and blue eyes. He had a nice smile, white and clean like he scrubbed his teeth a lot. I guess his old man had been right about that girl, though, because when all this trouble started she dropped right out of the picture, went to New York or somewhere with her folks.

I was thinking about this when we began marching again; and I was still thinking about it when we came in for breakfast about forty minutes later, after having had our arms thrown out of joint in some more silly stuff called setting-up exercises. What they won't think of! As though we didn't get enough exercise running around all day!

Then we all trooped in to eat.

I sat at the breakfast table cracking my egg and watching the guy across from me hog six of them. I wanted to laugh. People think big private schools are the ritz and that their sons, when they go there, mix with the cream of young America. Bushwa! There are a few kids whose last names you might see across the front of a department store like Harker Bros., and there are some movie stars' sons, but most of us are a tough, outcast bunch that couldn't get along in public school and weren't wanted at home. Tutors wouldn't handle most of us for love or money. So they put us here.

Clark's will handle any kid and you can leave the love out of it so long as you lay the money on the line. Then the brat is taken care of so far as his parents are concerned, and he has the prestige of a fancy Clark uniform.

There wasn't another school in the State that would have taken me, public or private, after looking at my record. But when old man Clark had dough-ray-me clutched in his right fist he was blind to records like that. Well, that's the kind of a bunch we were.

Well, as I say, I was watching this glutton stuff eggs down his gullet which he thought was a smart thing to do even though he got a belly-ache afterward, when the guy on my right said:

"I see Tommy Smith is going to hang."

"Yeah," I said, "that's rotten, ain't it?"

"Rotten?" he replied. "It's wonderful. It's what that rat has coming to him."

"Listen," said I, "one more crack like that and I'll smack your stinking little face in."

"You and how many others?" he said.

"Just me," I said, "and if you want to come outside I'll do it right now."

The kid who was table captain yelled: "Hey, you two pipe down. What's the argument anyway?"

"They're going to hang Tommy Smith," I said, "and I think it's a dirty rotten shame. He's as innocent as a babe in the woods."

"Ha-ha," said the table captain, "you're just bothered about Marie Smith."

"Skirt crazy! Skirt crazy!" mumbled the guy stuffing down the eggs.

I threw my water in his face, then I got up, facing the table captain, and the guy on my right. "Listen," I said, "Tommy Smith is innocent. I was there an hour before the murder happened, wasn't I? What do you loud-mouthed half-wits think you know about it? All you morons know is what you read in the papers. Tommy didn't do it. I should know, shouldn't I? I was right there in the house before it happened. I've been around there plenty since. I've talked to the detectives."

I sat down, plenty mad. I sat down because I had seen a faculty officer coming into the dining-room. We all kept still until he walked on through. Then the table captain sneered and said:

"Tommy Smith is a dirty stinker. He's the one that killed his father all right. He stuck a knife right through his back!"

"A lie! A lie!" I screamed.

"How do you know it's a lie?"

"Well, I—I know, that's all," I said.

"Yeah, you know! Listen to him! You know! That's hot. I think I'll laugh!"

"Damn it," I said. "I *do* know!"

"How? How? Tell us that!"

"Well, maybe *I* did it. What do you think about that?"

"You!" shouted the table captain. "A little fourteen-year-old wart like you killing anybody! Ha!"

"Aw, go to hell," I said, "that's what you can do. Go straight to hell!"

"A little wart like you killing anybody," the table captain kept saying, and he was holding his sides and laughing.

ALL THAT Monday I felt pretty bad thinking about Tommy, what a really swell guy he had been, always laughing, always having a pat on the back for you. I knew he must be in a cell up in San Quentin now, waiting, counting the hours, maybe hearing them build his scaffold.

I imagine a guy doesn't feel so hot waiting for a thing like that, pacing in a cell, smoking up cigarettes, wondering what it's like when you're dead. I've read some about it. I read about Two Gun Crowley, I think it was, who went to the chair with his head thrown back and his chest out like he was proud of it. But there must have been something underneath, and Crowley, at least, knew that *he* had it coming to him. The real thing must be different than what you read in the papers. It must be pretty awful.

But in spite of all this I had sense enough to stay away from Marie all day. I could easily have gone to her house which was across the street from the campus, but I knew that she and her sister, Ruth, and that Duff Ryan, the young detective who had made the arrest—because, as he said, he thought it was his duty—had counted on the commutation of sentence. They figured they'd have plenty of time to clear up some angles of the case which had been plenty shaky even in court. No, sir. Sweet Marie would be in no mood for my consolation and besides I was sick of saying the same things over and over and watching her burst into tears every time I mentioned Tommy's name.

I sat in the study hall Monday evening thinking about the whole thing. Outside the window I could see the stars crystal clear; and though it was warm in the classroom I could feel the cold of the air in the smoky blue of the night, so that I shivered. When they marched us into the dormitory at eight-thirty Simmons, the mess captain, started razzing me about Tommy being innocent again, and I said:

"Listen, putrid, you wanta get hurt?"

"No," he said, then he added: "Sore head."

"You'll have one sore face," I said, "if you don't shut that big yap of yours."

There was no more said and when I went to bed and the lights went off I lay there squirming while that fat-cheeked Pushton staggered through taps with his bugle. I was glad that Myers had bugle duty tomorrow and I wouldn't have to listen to Pushton.

But long after taps I still couldn't sleep for thinking of Tommy. What a damn thing that was—robbing me of my sleep! But I tell you, I did some real fretting, and honestly, if it hadn't been for the fact that God and I parted company so long ago, I might have even been sap enough to pray for him. But I didn't. I finally went to sleep. It must have been ten o'clock.

I didn't show around Marie's Tuesday afternoon either, figuring it was best to keep away. But after chow, that is, supper, an orderly came beating it out to the study hall for me and told me I was wanted on the telephone. I chased up to the main building and got right on the wire. It was Duff Ryan, that young detective I told you about.

"You've left me with quite a load, young man," he said.

"Explain," I said. "I've no time for nonsense." I guess I must have been nervous to say a thing like that to the law, but there was something about Duff Ryan's cool gray eyes that upset me and I imagined I could see those eyes right through the telephone.

"I mean about Ruth," he said softly, "she feels pretty badly. Now I can take care of her all right, but little Marie is crying her eyes out and I can't do anything with her."

"So what?" I said.

"She's your girl, isn't she, Martin?" he asked.

"Listen," I said, "in this school guys get called by their last name. Martin sounds sissy. My name is Thorpe."

"I'm sorry I bothered you, Martin," Duff said in that same soft voice. "If you don't want to cooperate—"

"Oh, I'll cooperate," I said. "I'll get right over. That is, provided I can get permission."

"I've already arranged that," Duff told me. "You just come on across the street and don't bother mentioning anything about it to anyone."

"O.K.," I said, and hung up. I sat there for a minute. This sounded fishy to me. Of course, Duff *might* be on the level, but I doubted it. You can never tell what a guy working for the law is going to do.

I trotted out to the campus and on across to the Smith house. Their mother had died a long while ago, so with the father murdered, and Tommy in the death house, there were only the two girls left.

Duff answered the door himself. I looked up at the big bruiser and then I sucked in my breath. I wouldn't have known him! His face was almost gray. Under his eyes were the biggest black rings I had ever seen. I don't mean the kind you get fighting. I mean the other kind, the serious kind you get from worry. He had short clipped hair that was sort of reddish, and shoulders that squared off his figure, tapering it down to a nice V.

Of course, he was plenty old, around twenty-six, but at this his being a detective surprised you because ordinarily he looked so much like a college kid. He always spoke in a modulated voice and never got excited over anything. And he had a way of looking at you that I hated. A quiet sort of way that asked and answered all of its own questions.

Personally, as a detective, I thought he was a big flop. The kind of detectives that I prefer seeing are those giant fighters that blaze their way through a gangster barricade. Duff Ryan was none of this. I suppose he was tough but he never showed it. Worst of all, I'd never even seen his gun!

"Glad you came over, Martin," he said.

"The name is Thorpe," I said.

He didn't answer, just stepped aside so I could come in. I didn't see Ruth, but I spotted Marie right away. She was sitting on the divan with her legs pulled up under her, and her face hidden. She had a hankerchief pressed in her hand. She was a slim kid, but well developed for fifteen, so well developed in fact that for a while I had been razzed about this at school.

Like Tommy, she had blond hair, only hers was fluffy and came part way to her shoulders. She turned now and her face was all red from crying, but I still thought she was pretty. I'm a sucker that way. I've been a sucker for women ever since I was nine.

She had wide spaced green eyes, and soft, rosy skin, and a generous mouth. Her only trouble, if any, was that she was a prude. Wouldn't speak to anybody on the Clark campus except me. Maybe you think I didn't like that! I'd met her at Sunday school or rather coming out, since I had been hiding around waiting for it to let out, and I walked home with her four Sundays straight before she would speak to me. That is, I walked along beside her holding a one-way conversation. Finally I skipped a Sunday, then the next one she asked me where I had been, and that started the ball rolling.

"Thorpe," she said—that was another thing, *she* always called me by my last name because that was the one I had given her to start with— "Thorpe, I'm so glad you're here. Come over here and sit down beside me."

I went over and sat down and she straightened up, like she was ashamed that she had been crying, and put on a pretty good imitation of a smile. "How's everything been?" she said.

"Oh, pretty good," I said. "The freshmen are bellyaching about Latin this week, and just like algebra, I'm already so far ahead of them it's a crying shame."

"You're so smart, Thorpe," she told me.

"Too bad about Tommy," I said. "There's always the chance for a reprieve though."

"No," she said, and her eyes began to get dim again, "no, there isn't. This—this decision that went through Sunday night—that's the— Unless, of course, something comes up that we—the lawyer can—" and she began crying.

I put my arm round her which was a thing she hadn't let me do much, and I said, "Come on, kid. Straighten up. Tommy wouldn't want you to cry."

About five minutes later she did straighten up. Duff Ryan was sitting over in the corner looking out the window but it was just like we were alone.

"I'll play the piano," she said.

"Do you know anything hot yet?"

"Hot?" she said.

"Something popular, Marie," I explained. Blood was coming up into my face.

"Why, no," she replied. "I thought I would—"

"Play hymns!" I half screamed. "No! I don't want to hear any of those damned hymns!"

"Why, Thorpe!"

"I can't help it," I said. "I've told you about that enough times. Those kinds of songs just drone along in the same pitch and never get anywhere. If you can't play something decent stay away from the piano."

My fists were tight now and my fingers were going in and out. She knew better than to bring up that subject. It was the only thing we had ever argued about. Playing hymns. I wanted to go nuts every time I heard "*Lead Kindly Light*" or one of those other goofy things. I'd get so mad I couldn't see straight. Just an obsession with me, I guess.

"All right," she said, "but I wish you wouldn't swear in this house."

I said, "All right, I won't swear in this house."

"Or anywhere else," she said.

I was feeling good now. "O.K., honey, if you say so."

She seemed pleased and at least the argument had gotten her to quit thinking about Tommy for a minute. But it was then that her sister came downstairs.

Ruth was built on a smaller scale than Marie so that even though she was nineteen she wasn't any taller. She had darker hair too, and an oval face, very white now, making her brown eyes seem brighter. Brighter though more hollow. I will say she was beautiful.

She wore only a rich blue lounging robe which was figure-fitting though it came down past her heels and was clasped in a high collar around her pale throat.

"I think it's time for you to come to bed, Marie," she said. "Hello, Thorpe."

"Hello," I said.

Marie got up wordlessly and pressed my hand, and smiled again, that faint imitation, and went off. Ruth stood there in the doorway from the dining-room and as though it was a signal—which I suspect it was—Duff Ryan got up.

"I guess it's time for us to go, Martin," he said.

"You don't say," I said.

He looked at me fishily. "Yeah. I do say. We've got a job to do. Do you know what it is, Martin? We've got to kill a kitten. A poor little kitten."

I started to answer but didn't. The way he was saying that, and looking at me, put a chill up my back that made me suddenly ice cold. I began to tremble all over. He opened the door and motioned for me to go out.

THAT CAT thing was a gag of some kind, I thought, and I was wide awake for any funny stuff from detectives, but Duff Ryan actually had a little kitten hidden in a box under the front steps of the house. He picked it up now and petted it.

"Got hit by a car," he said. "It's in terrible pain and there isn't a chance for recovery. I gave it a shot of stuff that eased the pain for a while but it must be coming back. We'll have to kill the cat."

I wanted to ask him why he hadn't killed it in the first place, whenever he had picked it up from under the car, but I kept my mouth shut and we walked along, back across the street to the Clark campus. There were no lights at all here and we walked in darkness, our feet scuffing on the dirt of the football gridiron.

"About that night of the murder, Martin," Duff said. "You won't mind a few more questions, will you? We want to do something to save Tommy. I made the arrest but I've been convinced since that he's innocent. I want desperately to save him before it's too late. It's apparent that we missed on something because—well, the way things are."

I said, "Are you sure of Tommy's innocence, or are you stuck on Ruth?"

"Sure of his innocence," he said in that soft

voice. "You want to help, don't you, Martin? You don't want to see Tommy die?"

"Quit talking to me like a kid," I said. "Sure I want to help."

"All right. What were you doing over there that night?"

"I've answered that a dozen times. Once in court. I was seeing Marie."

"Mr. Smith—that is, her father—chased you out of the house though, didn't he?"

"He asked me to leave," I said.

"No, he didn't, Martin. He ordered you out and told you not to come back again."

I stopped and whirled toward him. "Who told you that?"

"Marie," he said. "She was the only one who heard him. She didn't want to say it before because she was afraid Ruth would keep her from seeing you. That little kid has a crush on you and she didn't think that had any bearing on the case."

"Well, it hasn't, has it?"

"Maybe not," snapped Duff Ryan, "but he did chase you out, didn't he? He threatened to use his cane on you?"

"I won't answer," I said.

"You don't have to," he told me. "But I wish you'd told the truth about it in the first place."

"Why?" We started walking again. "You don't think *I* killed him, do you?" I shot a quick glance in his direction and held my breath.

"No," he said, "nothing like that, only—"

"Only what?"

"Well, Martin, haven't you been kicked out of about every school in the State?"

"I wouldn't go so far as to say *every* school."

Duff said, "Quite a few though, eh?"

"Enough," I said.

"That's what I thought," he went on quietly, "I went over and had a look at your record, Martin. I wish I had thought of doing that sooner."

"Listen—"

"Oh, don't get excited," he said, "this may give us new leads, that's all. We've nothing against you. But when you were going to school at Hadden, you took the goat, which was a class

mascot, upstairs with you one night and then pushed him down the stairs so that he broke all his legs. You did that, didn't you?"

"The goat slipped," I said.

"Maybe," whispered Duff. He lit a cigarette, holding onto the crippled cat with one hand. "But you stood at the top of the stairs and watched the goat suffer until somebody came along."

"I was so scared I couldn't move."

"Another time," Duff continued, "at another school, you pushed a kid into an oil hole that he couldn't get out of and you were ducking him—maybe trying to kill him—when someone came along and stopped you."

"He was a sissy. I was just having some fun!"

"At another school you were expelled for roping a newly born calf and pulling it up on top of a barn where you stabbed it and watched it bleed to death."

"I didn't stab it! It got caught on a piece of tin from the drain while I was pulling it up. You haven't told any of this to Marie, have you?"

"No," Duff said.

"All those things are just natural things," I said. "Any kid is liable to do them. You're just nuts because you can't pin the guilt on anybody but the guy who is going to die Friday and you're trying to make me look bad!"

"Maybe," Duff answered quietly, and we came into the chapel now and stopped. He dropped his cigarette, stepped on it, then patted the cat. Moonlight shone jaggedly through the rotting pillars. I could see the cat's eyes shining. "Maybe," Duff breathed again, "but didn't you land in a reform school once?"

"Twice," I said.

"And once in an institution where you were observed by a staff of doctors? It was a State institution, I think. Sort of a rest home."

"I was there a month," I said. "Some crab sent me there, or had me sent. But my dad got me out."

"Yes," Duff replied, "the crab had you sent there because you poisoned two of his Great Dane dogs. Your dad had to bribe somebody to get you out, and right now he pays double tuition for you here at Clark's."

I knew all this but it wasn't anything sweet to hear coming from a detective. "What of it?" I said. "You had plenty of chance to find that out."

"But we weren't allowed to see your records before," Duff answered. "As a matter of fact I paid an orderly to steal them for me, and then return them."

"Why, you dirty crook!"

I could see the funny twist of his smile there in the moonlight. His face looked pale and somehow far away. He looked at the cat and petted it some more. I was still shaking. Scared, I guess.

He said, "Too bad we have to kill you, kitten, but it's better than that pain."

Then, all at once I thought he had gone mad. He swung the cat around and began batting its head against the pillar in the chapel. I could see the whole thing clearly in the moonlight, his arm swinging back and forth, the cat's head being battered off, the bright crimson blood spurting all over.

He kept on doing it and my temples began to pound. My heart went like wild fire. I wanted to reach over and help him. I wanted to take that little cat and squeeze the living guts out of it. I wanted to help him smash its brains all over the chapel. I felt dizzy. Everything was going around. I felt myself reaching for the cat.

But I'm smart. I'm no dummy. I'm at the head of my class. I'm in high school. I knew what he was doing. He was testing me. *He wanted me to help him.* The son of a —— wasn't going to trick *me* like that. Not Martin Thorpe. I put my arms behind me and grabbed my wrists and with all my might I held my arms there and looked the other way.

I heard the cat drop with a thud to the cement, then I looked up, gasping to catch my breath. Duff Ryan looked at me with cool gray eyes, then he walked off. I stood there, still trying to get my breath and watching his shadow blend with the shadows of the dark study hall. I was having one hell of a time getting my breath.

UT I slept good all night. I was mad and I didn't care about Tommy any more. Let him hang. I slept good but I woke up ten minutes before reveille remembering that it was Pushton's turn at the bugle again. He and Myers traded off duty every other day.

I felt pretty cocky and got up putting on only my slippers and went down to the eleven-year-old wing. Pushton was sitting on the edge of the bed working his arms back and forth and yawning. The fat little punk looked like an old man. He took himself that seriously. You would have thought maybe he was a general.

"What you want, Thorpe?" he said.

"I want your bugle. I'm going to break the damn thing."

"You leave my bugle alone," he said. "My folks aren't as rich as yours and I had to save all my spending money to buy it." This was true. They furnished bugles at school but they were awful and Pushton took his music so seriously that he had saved up and bought his own instrument.

"I know it," I said, "so the school won't be on my neck if I break it." I looked around. "Where is it?"

"I won't tell you!"

I looked under the bed, under his pillow, then I grabbed him by the nose. "Come on, Heinie. Where is it?"

"Leave me alone!" he wailed. "Keep your hands off me." He was talking so loud now that half the wing was waking up.

"All right, punk," I said. "Go ahead and blow that thing, and I hope you blow your tonsils out."

I went back to my bed and held my ears. Pushton blew the bugle all right, I never did find out where he had the thing hidden.

I dressed thinking well, only two more days and Tommy gets it. I'd be glad when it was over. Maybe all this tension would ease up then and Marie wouldn't cry so much because once he was dead there wouldn't be anything she could do about it. Time would go by and eventually she would forget him. One person more or less isn't so important in the world anyway, no matter how good a guy he is.

Everything went swell Wednesday right through breakfast and until after we were marching out of the chapel and into the schoolroom. Then I ran into Pushton who was trotting around with his bugle tucked under his arm. I stopped and looked him up and down.

His little black eyes didn't flicker. He just said, "Next time you bother me, Thorpe, I'm going to report you."

"Go ahead, punk," I said, "and see what happens to you."

I went on into school then, burning up at his guts, talking to *me* that way.

I was still burned up and sore at the guy when a lucky break came, for me, that is, not Pushton. It was during the afternoon right after we had been dismissed from the class room for the two-hour recreation period.

I went into the main building, which was prohibited in the day time so that I had to sneak in, to get a book I wanted to read. It was under my pillow. I slipped up the stairs, crept into my wing, got the book and started out. It was then that I heard a pounding noise.

I looked around, then saw it was coming from the eleven-year-old wing.

I walked in and there it was! You wouldn't have believed anything so beautiful could have been if you hadn't seen it with your own eyes. At least that was the way I felt about it. For, who was it, but Pushton.

The bugler on duty has the run of the main building and it was natural enough that he was here but I hadn't thought about it. There was a new radio set, a small portable, beside his bed. I saw that the wires and ear phone—which you have to use in the dormitory—were connected with the adjoining bed as well and guessed that it belonged to another cadet. But Pushton was hooking it up. He was leaning half-way out the window trying, pounding with a hammer, to make some kind of a connection on the aerial wire.

Nothing could have been better. The window was six stories from the ground with cement down below. No one knew I was in the building. I felt blood surge into my temples. My face got red, hot red, and I could feel fever throbbing in my throat. I moved forward slowly, on cat feet, my hands straight at my sides. I didn't want him to hear me. But I was getting that dizzy feeling now. My fingers were itching.

Then suddenly I lunged over, I shoved against him. He looked back once, and that was what I wanted. He looked back for an instant, his fat face green with the most unholy fear I have ever seen. Then I gave him another shove and he was gone. Before he could call out, before he could say a word, he was gone, falling through the air!

I risked jumping up on the bed so I could see him hit, and I did see him hit. Then I got down and straightened the bed and beat it out.

I ran down the stairs as fast as I could. I didn't see anybody. More important, no one saw me. But when I was on the second floor I ran down the hall to the end and lifted the window. I jumped out here, landing squarely on my feet.

I waited for a minute, then I circled the building from an opposite direction. My heart was pounding inside me. It was difficult for me to breathe. I managed to get back to the play field through an indirect route.

Funny thing, Pushton wasn't seen right away. No one but myself had seen him fall. I was on the play field at least ten minutes, plenty long enough to establish myself as being there, before the cry went up. The kids went wild. We ran in packs to the scene.

I stood there with the rest of them looking at what was left of Pushton. He wouldn't blow any more bugles. His flesh was like a sack of water that had fallen and burst full of holes. The blood was splattered out in jagged streaks all around him.

We stood around about five minutes, the rest of the kids and I, nobody saying anything. Then a faculty officer chased us away, and that was the last I saw of Pushton.

Supper was served as usual but there wasn't much talk. What there was of it seemed to establish the fact that Pushton had been a thick-witted sort and had undoubtedly leaned out too far try-ing to fix the aerial wire and had fallen.

I thought that that could have easily been the case, all right, and since I had hated the little punk I had no conscience about it. It didn't bother me nearly so much as the fact that Tommy Smith was going to die. I had liked Tommy. And I was nuts about his sister, wasn't I?

That night study hall was converted into a lit-tle inquest meeting. We were all herded into one big room and Major Clark talked to us as though we were a bunch of Boy Scouts. After ascertain-ing that no one knew any more about Pushton's death than what they had seen on the cement, he assured us that the whole thing had been unavoidable and even went so far as to suggest that we might spare our parents the worry of telling them of so unfortunate an incident. All the bloated donkey was worrying about was los-ing a few tuitions.

Toward the end of the session Duff Ryan came in and nodded at me, and then sat down. He looked around at the kids, watched Major Clark a while, and then glanced back at me. He kept doing that until we were dismissed. He made me nervous.

RIDAY morning I woke up and listened for reveille but it didn't come. I lay there, feeling comfortable in the bed clothes, and half lazy, but feeling every minute that reveille would blast me out of my place. Then I suddenly realized why the bu-gle hadn't blown. I heard the splash of rain across the window and knew that we wouldn't have to raise the flag or take our exercises this morning. On rainy days we got to sleep an extra half-hour.

I felt pretty good about this and put my hands behind my head there on the pillow and began thinking. They were pleasant, what you might call mellow thoughts. A little thing like an extra half-hour in bed will do that.

Things were working out fine and after tonight I wouldn't have anything to worry about. For Duff Ryan to prove Tommy was innocent *after* the hanging would only make him out a damn fool. I was glad it was raining. It would make it easier for me to lay low, to stay away from Marie until the final word came. . . .

That was what I thought in the morning, lying there in bed. But no. Seven-thirty that night Duff came over to the school in a slicker. He came into the study hall and got me. His eyes were wild. His face was strained.

"Ruth and I are going to see the lawyer again," he said, "you've got to stay with Marie."

"Nuts," I said.

He jerked me out of the seat, then he took his hands off me as though he were ashamed. "Come on," he said. "This is no time for smart talk."

So I went.

Ruth had on a slicker too and was waiting there on the front porch. I could see her pretty face. It was pinched, sort of terrible. Her eyes were wild too. She patted my hand, half crying, and said, "You be good to Marie, honey. She likes you, and you're the only one in the world now that can console her."

"What time does Tommy go?" I asked.

"Ten-thirty," said Duff.

I nodded. "O.K." I stood there as they crossed the sidewalk and got into Duff Ryan's car and drove away. Then I went in to see Marie. The kid looked scared, white as a ghost.

"Oh, Thorpe," she said, "they're going to kill him tonight!"

"Well, I guess there's nothing we can do," I said.

She put her arms around me and cried on my shoulder. I could feel her against me, and believe me, she was nice. She had figure, all right. I put my arms around her waist and then I kissed her neck and her ears. She looked at me, tears on her cheeks, and shook her head. "Don't."

She said that because I had never kissed her before, but now I saw her lips and I kissed her. She didn't do anything about it, but kept crying.

Finally I said, "Well, let's make fudge. Let's play a game. Let's play the radio. Let's do *some-thing*. This thing's beginning to get me."

We went to the kitchen and made fudge for a while.

But I was restless. The rain had increased. There was thunder and lightning in the sky now. Again I had that strange feeling of being cold, although the room was warm. I looked at the clock and it said ten minutes after eight. Only ten minutes after eight! And Tommy wasn't going to hang until ten-thirty!

"You'll always stay with me, won't you, Thorpe?" said Marie.

"Sure," I told her, but right then I felt like I wanted to push her face in. I had never felt that way before. I couldn't understand what was the matter with me. Everything that had been me was gone. My wit and good humor.

I kept watching the clock, watching every minute that ticked by, and thinking of Tommy up there in San Quentin in the death cell pacing back and forth. I guess maybe he was watching the minutes too. I wondered if it was raining up there and if rain made any difference in a hanging.

We wandered back into the living-room and sat down at opposite ends of the divan. Marie looking at nothing, her eyes glassy, and me watching and hating the rain, and hearing the clock.

Then suddenly Marie got up and went to the piano. She didn't ask me if she could or anything about it. She just went to the piano and sat down. I stared after her, even opened my mouth to speak. But I didn't say anything. After all, it was *her* brother who was going to die, wasn't it? I guess for one night at least she could do anything she wanted to do.

But then she began playing. First, right off, "*Lead Kindly Light,*" and then "*Onward Christian Soldiers,*" and then "*Little Church in the Wildwood.*" I sat there wringing my hands with that agony beating in my ears. Then I leapt to my feet and began to shout at her.

"Stop that! Stop it! Do you want to drive me crazy?"

But her face was frozen now. It was as though she was in a trance. I ran to her and shook her shoulder, but she pulled away from me and played on.

I backed away from her and my face felt as though it was contorted. I backed away and stared at her, her slim, arched back. I began biting my fingernails, and then my fingers. That music was killing me. Those hymns . . . those silly, inane hymns. Why didn't she stop it? The piano and the rain were seeping into my blood stream.

I walked up and down the room. I walked up and down the room faster and faster. I stopped and picked up a flower vase and dropped it, yelling: "*Stop it! For the love of heaven, stop!*"

But she kept right on. Again I began staring at her, at her back, and her throat, and the profile of her face. I felt blood surging in me. I felt those hammers in my temples. . . .

I tried to fight it off this time. I tried to go toward her to pull her away from that damn piano but I didn't have the strength to move in her direction. I stood there feeling the breath go out of me, feeling my skin tingle. And I didn't want to be like that. I looked at my hands and one minutes they were tight fists and the next my fingers were working in and out like mad.

I looked toward the kitchen, and then I moved quietly into it. She was still slamming at the piano when I opened the drawer and pulled out the knife I had used to kill her father.

At least it was a knife like it. I put it behind me and tiptoed back into the room. She wasn't aware that I had moved. I crept up on her, waited.

Her hands were flying over the piano keys. Once more I shouted, and my voice was getting hoarse: "Stop it!"

But of course she didn't. She didn't and I swore. I swore at her. She didn't hear this either. But I'd show the little slut a thing or two.

I was breathing hard, looking around the room to make sure no one was here. Then I lifted the knife and plunged down with it.

I swear I never knew where Duff Ryan came from. It must have been from behind the divan. A simple place like that and I hadn't seen him, merely because I had been convinced that he went away in the car. But he'd been in the room all the time waiting for me to do what I almost did.

It had been a trick, of course, and this time I'd been sap enough to fall into his trap. He had heard me denounce hymns, he knew I'd be nervous tonight, highly excitable, so he had set the stage and remained hidden and Marie had done the rest.

He had told Marie then, after all.

Duff Ryan grabbed my wrist just at the right moment, as he had planned on doing, and of course being fourteen I didn't have much chance against him. He wrested away the knife, then he grabbed me and shouted:

"Why did you murder Marie's father?"

"Because the old boy hated me! Because he thought Marie was too young to know boys! Because he kicked me out and hit me with his cane!" I said all this, trying to jerk away from him, but I couldn't so I went on:

"That's why I did it. Because I had a lot of fun doing it! So what? What are you going to do about it? I'm a kid, you can't hang *me!* There's a law against hanging kids. I murdered Pushton too. I shoved him out the window! How do you like that? All you can do is put me in reform school!"

As my voice faded, and it faded because I had begun to choke, I heard Ruth at the telephone. She had come back in too. She was calling long distance. San Quentin.

Marie was sitting on the divan, her face in her hands. You would have thought she was sorry for me. When I got my breath I went on:

"I came back afterward, while Tommy was in the other room. I got in the kitchen door. The old man was standing there and I just picked up the knife and let him have it. I ran before I could see much. But Pushton. Let me tell you about Pushton—"

Duff Ryan shoved me back against the piano. "Shut up," he said. "You didn't kill Pushton. You're just bragging now. But you did kill the old man and that's what we wanted to know!"

Bragging? I was enraged. But Duff Ryan clipped me and I went out cold.

So I'm in reform school now and—will you believe it?—I can't convince anyone that I murdered Pushton. Is it that grown-ups are so unbelieving because I'm pretty young? Are they so stupid that they still look upon fourteen-year-old boys as little innocents who have no minds of their own? That is the bitterness of youth. And I am sure that I won't change or see things any differently. I told the dopes that too, but everyone assures me I will.

But the only thing I'm really worried about is that no one will believe about Pushton, not even the kids here at the reform school, and that hurts. It does something to my pride.

I'm not in the least worried about anything else. Things here aren't so bad, nor so different from Clark's. Doctors come and see me now and then but they don't think anything is wrong with my mind.

They think I knifed Old Man Smith because I was in a blind rage when I did it, and looking at it that way, it would only be second-degree murder even if I were older. I'm not considered serious. There are lots worse cases here than mine. Legally, a kid isn't responsible for what he does, so I'll be out when I'm twenty-one. Maybe before, because my old man's got money. . . .

You'll always remember me, won't you? Because I'll be out when I'm older and you might be the one I'll be seeing.

Faith

Dashiell Hammett

Not only is Dashiell Hammett regarded as one of the greatest of all pulp writers, he is often recognized as one of the most important and influential, as well as popular, American writers of the twentieth century. His work has never been out of print, being reprinted again and again in many parts of the world. His stories have been anthologized more frequently than such Nobel laureates as Theodore Dreiser, Thomas Mann, Pearl S. Buck, and John Galsworthy.

How rare it is, then, to be able to offer a story that you cannot have read before. "Faith" appears in print here for the very first time anywhere.

The copy of the typescript from which the story was set has Hammett's address, 1309 Hyde Street, San Francisco, on it. It provides an unusual opportunity to see a story in the form in which it was originally mailed out—before e-mail and before agents worked as middlemen. It is clean, with a few minor corrections made in his hand, a few words crossed out.

Candidly, it is not his greatest story, a bit thin when compared with "The House on Turk Street" or "Dead Yellow Women." Still, it's more than just a literary scrap, providing a searing look at hobo life in the Great Depression. These men lived on the roughest fringes of society, stealing when they had to, drinking when there was money, brawling with each other and with railroad security guards and other elements of the law enforcement community.

Were they criminal? Was the protagonist of "Faith"? You decide.

Faith

Dashiell Hammett

SPRAWLED IN A LOOSE evening group on the river bank, the fifty-odd occupants of the slapboard barrack that was the American bunkhouse listened to Morphy damn the canning-factory, its superintendent, its equipment, and its pay. They were migratory workingmen, these listeners, simple men, and they listened with that especial gravity which the simple man—North American Indian, Zulu, or hobo—affects.

But when Morphy had finished one of them chuckled.

Without conventions any sort of group life is impossible, and no division of society is without its canons. The laws of the jungles are not the laws of the drawing-room, but they are as certainly existent, and as important to their subjects. If you are a migratory workingman you may pick your teeth wherever and with whatever tool you like, but you may not either by word or act publicly express satisfaction with your present employment; nor may you disagree with any who denounce the conditions of that employment. Like most conventions, this is not altogether without foundation in reason.

So now the fifty-odd men on the bank looked at him who had chuckled, turned upon him the stare that is the social lawbreaker's lot everywhere: their faces held antagonism suspended in expectancy of worse to come; physically a matter of raised brows over blank eyes, and teeth a little apart behind closed lips.

"What's eatin' you?" Morphy—a big bodied dark man who said "the proletariat" as one would say "the seraphim"—demanded. "You think this is a good dump?"

The chuckler wriggled, scratching his back voluptuously against a prong of uptorn stump that was his bolster, and withheld his answer until it seemed he had none. He was a newcomer to the Bush River cannery, one of the men hurried up from Baltimore that day: the tomatoes, after an unaccountable delay in ripening, had threatened to overwhelm the normal packing force.

"I've saw worse," the newcomer said at last, with the true barbarian's lack of discomfiture in the face of social disapproval. "And I expect to see worse."

"Meanin' what?"

"Oh, I ain't saying!" The words were light-flung, airy. "But I know a few things. Stick around and you'll see."

No one could make anything of that. Simple men are not ready questioners. Someone spoke of something else.

The man who had chuckled went to work in the process-room, where half a dozen Americans and as many Polacks cooked the fresh-canned tomatoes in big iron kettles. He was a small man, compactly plump, with round maroon eyes above round cheeks whose original ruddiness had been tinted by sunburn to a definite orange. His nose was small and merrily pointed, and a snuff-user's pouch in his lower lip, exaggerating the lift of his mouth at the corners, gave him a perpetual grin. He held himself erect, his chest arched out, and bobbed when he walked, rising on the ball of the propelling foot midway each step. A man of forty-five or so, who answered to the name Feach and hummed through his nose while he guided the steel-slatted baskets from truck, to kettle, to truck.

After he had gone, the men remembered that from the first there had been a queerness about Feach, but not even Morphy tried to define that queerness. "A nut," Morphy said, but that was indefinite.

What Feach had was a secret. Evidence of it was not in his words only: they were neither many nor especially noteworthy, and his silence held as much ambiguity as his speech. There was in his whole air—in the cock of his round, boy's head, in the sparkle of his red-brown eyes, in the nasal timbre of his voice, in his trick of puffing out his cheeks when he smiled—a sardonic knowingness that seemed to mock whatever business was at hand. He had for his work and for the men's interests the absent-minded, bantering sort of false-seriousness that a busy parent has for its child's affairs. His every word, gesture, attention, seemed thinly to mask preoccupation with some altogether different thing that would presently appear: a man waiting for a practical joke to blossom.

He and Morphy worked side by side. Between them the first night had put a hostility which neither tried to remove. Three days later they increased it.

It was early evening. The men, as usual, were idling between their quarters and the river, waiting for bed-time. Feach had gone indoors to get a can of snuff from his bedding. When he came out Morphy was speaking.

"Of course not," he was saying. "You don't think a God big enough to make all this would be crazy enough to do it, do you? What for? What would it get Him?"

A freckled ex-sailor, known to his fellows as Sandwich, was frowning with vast ponderance over the cigarette he was making, and when he spoke the deliberation in his voice was vast.

"Well, you can't always say for certain. Sometimes a thing looks one way, and when you come to find out, is another. It don't *look* like there's no God. I'll say *that*. But—"

Feach, tamping snuff into the considerable space between his lower teeth and lip, grinned around his fingers, and managed to get derision into the snapping of the round tin lid down on the snuff-can.

"So you're one of *them* guys?" he challenged Morphy.

"Uh-huh." The big man's voice was that of one who, confident of his position's impregnability, uses temperateness to provoke an assault. "If somebody'd *show* me there was a God, it'd be different. But I never been showed."

"I've saw wise guys like you before!" The jovial ambiguity was suddenly gone from Feach; he was earnest, and indignant. "You want what you call proof before you'll believe anything. Well, you wait—you'll get your proof *this* time, and plenty of it."

"That's what I'd like to have. You ain't got none of this proof *on* you, have you?"

Feach sputtered.

Morphy rolled over on his back and began to roar out a song to the Maryland sky, a mocking song that Wobblies sing to the tune of "When the bugle calls up yonder I'll be there."

"You will eat, by and by,
In that glorious land they call the sky—
'Way up high!
Work and pray,
Live on hay.
You'll get pie in the sky when you die."

Feach snorted and turned away, walking down the river bank. The singer's booming notes followed him until he had reached the pines beyond the two rows of frame huts that were the Polacks' quarters.

By morning the little man had recovered his poise. For two weeks he held it—going jauntily around with his cargo of doubleness and his bobbing walk, smiling with puffed cheeks when Morphy called him "Parson"—and then it began to slip away from him. For a while he still smiled, and still said one thing while patently thinking of another; but his eyes were no longer jovially occupied with those other things: they were worried.

He took on the look of one who is kept waiting at a rendezvous, and tries to convince himself that he will not be disappointed. His nights became restless; the least creaking of the clapboard barrack or the stirring of a sleeping man would bring him erect in bed.

One afternoon the boiler of a small hoisting engine exploded. A hole was blown in the storehouse wall, but no one was hurt. Feach raced the others to the spot and stood grinning across the wreckage at Morphy. Carey, the superintendent, came up.

"Every season it's got to be something!" he complained. "But thank God this ain't as bad as the rest—like last year when the roof fell in and smashed everything to hell and gone."

Feach stopped grinning and went back to work.

Two nights later a thunderstorm blew down over the canning-factory. The first distant rumble awakened Feach. He pulled on trousers, shoes, and shirt, and left the bunk-house. In the north, approaching clouds were darker than the other things of night. He walked toward them, breathing with increasing depth, until, when the clouds were a black smear overhead, his chest was rising and falling to the beat of some strong rhythm.

When the storm broke he stood still, on a little hummock that was screened all around by bush and tree. He stood very straight, with upstretched arms and upturned face. Rain—fat thunderdrops that tapped rather than pattered—drove into his round face. Jagged streaks of metal fire struck down at ground and tree, house and man. Thunder that could have been born of nothing less than the impact of an enormous something upon the earth itself, crashed, crashed, crashed, reverberations lost in succeeding crashes as they strove to keep pace with the jagged metal streaks.

Feach stood up on his hummock, a short man compactly plump, hidden from every view by tree and undergrowth; a little man with a pointed nose tilted at the center of the storm, and eyes that held fright when they were not blinking and squinting under fat rain-drops. He talked aloud, though the thunder made nothing of his words. He talked into the storm, cursing God for half an hour without pause, with words that were vilely blasphemous, in a voice that was suppliant.

The storm passed down the river. Feach went back to his bunk, to lie awake all night, shivering in his wet underwear and waiting. Nothing happened.

He began to mumble to himself as he worked. Carey, reprimanding him for over-cooking a basket of tomatoes, had to speak three times before the little man heard him. He slept little. In his bunk, he either tossed from side to side or lay tense, straining his eyes through the darkness for minute after minute. Frequently he would leave the sleeping-house to prowl among the buildings, peering expectantly into each shadow that house or shed spread in his path.

Another thunderstorm came. He went out into it and cursed God again. Nothing happened. He slept none after that, and stopped eating. While the others were at table he would pace up and down beside the river, muttering to himself. All night he wandered around in distorted circles, through the pines, between the buildings, down to the river, chewing the ends of his fingers and talking to himself. His jauntiness was gone: a shrunken man who slouched when he walked, and shivered, doing his daily work only because it required neither especial skill nor energy. His eyes were more red than brown, and dull except when they burned with sudden fevers. His fingernails ended in red arcs where the quick was exposed.

On his last night at the cannery, Feach came abruptly into the center of the group that awaited the completion of night between house and river. He shook his finger violently at Morphy.

"That's crazy!" he screeched. "Of course there's a God! There's got to be! That's crazy!"

His red-edged eyes peered through the twilight at the men's faces: consciously stolid faces once they had mastered their first surprise at this picking up of fortnight-old threads: the faces of men to whom exhibitions of astonishment were childish. Feach's eyes held fear and a plea.

"Got your proof with you tonight?" Morphy turned on his side, his head propped on one arm, to face his opponent. "Maybe you can *show* me why there's *got* to be a God?"

"Ever' reason!" Moisture polished the little man's face, and muscles writhed in it. "There's the moon, and the sun, and the stars, and flowers, and rain, and—"

"Pull in your neck!" The big man spit for emphasis. "What do you know about them things? Edison could've made 'em for all you know. Talk sense. Why has there got to be a God?"

"Why? I'll tell you why!" Feach's voice was a thin scream; he stood tiptoe, and his arms jerked in wild gestures. "I'll tell you why! I've stood up to Him, and had His hand against me. I've been cursed by Him, and cursed back. That's how I know! Listen: I had a wife and kid once, back in Ohio on a farm she got from her old man. I come home from town one night and the lightning had came down and burnt the house flat—with them in it. I got a job in a mine near Harrisburg, and the third day I'm there a cave-in gets fourteen men. I'm down with 'em, and get out without a scratch. I work in a box-factory in Pittsburgh that burns down in less'n a week. I'm sleeping in a house in Galveston when a hurricane wrecks it, killing ever'body but me and a fella that's only crippled. I shipped out of Charleston in the *Sophie,* that went down off Cape Flattery, and I'm the only one that gets ashore. That's when I began to know for sure that it was God after me. I had sort of suspected it once or twice before— just from queer things I'd noticed—but I hadn't been certain. But now I knew what was what, and I wasn't wrong either! For five years I ain't been anywhere that something didn't happen. Why was I hunting a job before I came up here? Because a boiler busts in the Deal's Island packing-house where I worked before and wiped out the place. That's why!"

Doubt was gone from the little man; in the

quarter-light he seemed to have grown larger, taller, and his voice rang.

Morphy, perhaps alone of the audience not for the moment caught in the little man's eloquence, laughed briefly.

"An' what started all this hullabaloo?" he asked.

"I done a thing," Feach said, and stopped. He cleared his throat sharply and tried again. "I done a thi—" The muscles of throat and mouth went on speaking, but no sound came out. "What difference does that make?" He no longer bulked large in the dimness, and his voice was a whine. "Ain't it enough that I've had Him hounding me year after year? Ain't it enough that everywhere I go He—"

Morphy laughed again.

"A hell of a Jonah you are!"

"All right!" Feach gave back. "You wait and see before you get off any of your cheap jokes. You can laugh, but it ain't ever' man that's stood up to God and wouldn't give in. It ain't ever' man that's had Him for a enemy."

Morphy turned to the others and laughed, and they laughed with him. The laughter lacked honesty at first, but soon became natural; and though there were some who did not laugh, they were too few to rob the laughter of apparent unanimity.

Feach shut both eyes and hurled himself down on Morphy. The big man shook him off, tried to push him away, could not, and struck him with an open hand. Sandwich picked Feach up and led him in to his bed. Feach was sobbing—dry, old-man sobs.

"They won't listen to me, Sandwich, but I know what I'm talking about. Something's coming here—you wait and see. God wouldn't forget me after all these years He's been riding me."

"Course not," the freckled ex-sailor soothed him. "Everything'll come out all right. You're right."

After Sandwich had left him Feach lay still on his bunk, chewing his fingers and staring at the rough board ceiling with eyes that were perplexed in a blank, hurt way. As he bit his fingers he muttered to himself. "It's something to have stood up to Him and not give in. . . . He wouldn't forget . . . chances are it's something new. . . . He wouldn't!"

Presently fear pushed the perplexity out of his eyes, and then fear was displaced by a look of unutterable anguish. He stopped muttering and sat up, fingers twisting his mouth into a clown's grimace, breath hissing through his nostrils. Through the open door came the noise of stirring men: they were coming in to bed.

Feach got to his feet, darted through the door, past the men who were converging upon it, and ran up along the river—a shambling, jerky running. He ran until one foot slipped into a hole and threw him headlong. He scrambled up immediately and went on. But he walked now, frequently stumbling.

To his right the river lay dark and oily under the few stars. Three times he stopped to yell at the river.

"No! No! They're wrong! There's got to be a God! There's got to!"

Half an hour was between the first time he yelled and the second, and a longer interval between the second and third; but each time there was a ritualistic sameness to word and tone. After the third time the anguish began to leave his eyes.

He stopped walking and sat on the butt of a fallen pine. The air was heavy with the night-odor of damp earth and mold, and still where he sat, though a breeze shuffled the tops of the trees. Something that might have been a rabbit padded across the pine-needle matting behind him; a suggestion of frogs' croaking was too far away to be a definite sound. Lightning-bugs moved sluggishly among the trees: yellow lights shining through moth-holes in an irregularly swaying curtain.

Feach sat on the fallen pine for a long while, only moving to slap at an occasional pinging mosquito. When he stood up and turned back toward the canning-factory he moved swiftly and without stumbling.

He passed the dark American bunk-house, went through the unused husking-shed, and came to the hole that the hoisting engine had made in the store-house wall. The boards that had been nailed over the gap were loosely nailed. He pulled two of them off, went through the opening, and came out carrying a large gasoline can.

Walking downstream, he kept within a step of the water's edge until to his right a row of small structures showed against the sky like evenly spaced black teeth in a dark mouth. He carried his can up the slope toward them, panting a little, wood-debris crackling under his feet, the gasoline sloshing softly in its can.

He set the can down at the edge of the pines that ringed the Polacks' huts, and stuffed his lower lip with snuff. No light came from the double row of buildings, and there was no sound except the rustling of tree and bush in the growing breeze from southward.

Feach left the pines for the rear of the southernmost hut. He tilted the can against the wall, and moved to the next hut. Wherever he paused the can gurgled and grew lighter. At the sixth building he emptied the can. He put it down, scratched his head, shrugged, and went back to the first hut.

He took a long match from his vest pocket and scraped it down the back of his leg. There was no flame. He felt his trousers; they were damp with dew. He threw the match away, took out another, and ignited it on the inside of his vest. Squatting, he held the match against the frayed end of a wall-board that was black with gasoline. The splintered wood took fire. He stepped back and looked at it with approval. The match in his hand was consumed to half its length; he used the rest of it starting a tiny flame on a corner of the tar-paper roofing just above his head.

He ran to the next hut, struck another match, and dropped it on a little pile of sticks and paper that leaned against the rear wall. The pile became a flame that bent in to the wall.

The first hut had become a blazing thing, flames twisting above as if it were spinning under them. The seething of the fire was silenced by a scream that became the whole audible world. When that scream died there were others. The street between the two rows of buildings filled with red-lighted figures: naked figures, underclothed figures—

men, women and children—who achieved clamor. A throaty male voice sounded above the others. It was inarticulate, but there was purpose in it.

Feach turned and ran toward the pines. Pursuing bare feet made no sound. Feach turned his head to see if he were being hunted, and stumbled. A dark athlete in red flannel drawers pulled the little man to his feet and accused him in words that had no meaning to Feach. He snarled at his captor, and was knocked down by a fist used club-wise against the top of his head.

Men from the American bunk-house appeared as Feach was being jerked to his feet again. Morphy was one of them.

"Hey, what are you doing?" he asked the athlete in red drawers.

"These one, 'e sit fire to 'ouses. I see 'im!"

Morphy gaped at Feach.

"You did that?"

The little man looked past Morphy to where two rows of huts were a monster candelabra among the pines, and as he looked his chest arched out and the old sparkling ambiguity came back to his eyes.

"Maybe I done it," he said complacently, "and maybe Something used me to do it. Anyways, if it hadn't been that it'd maybe been something worse."

Pastorale

James M. Cain

IT WOULD BE only a slight exaggeration to say that James M. Cain (1892–1977) wrote stories and novels so hard-boiled that he made the other pulp writers of his era seem like sissies. No one wrote prose that was as lean as his. No word was wasted—a style that influenced many outstanding authors who followed him, notably Albert Camus and Elmore Leonard, whose works have been as generous with words as Scrooge was with shillings.

While other tough-guy writers recognized that not all women were warm and fuzzy, Cain elevated their malevolence to heights seldom matched, then or now. Perhaps the fact that he was married four times contributed to his feelings toward the female of the species.

In such memorable masterpieces as *Double Indemnity* and *The Postman Always Rings Twice*, Cain's women are so desirable that men will, literally, kill for them. He once said that he wrote about the most terrifying thing he knew: the wish that comes true. The men in these novels and other stories are not entirely rational in their longings and it is their grave misfortune that they are successful in their quests for the wrong women.

It is cheating a little to use "Pastorale" in an omnibus of pulp fiction because it was originally published in the March 1938 issue of *The American Mercury*, which, as one of the leading intellectual journals of its time, was anything but pulpy. However, when the great tough writers of the 1930s are listed, the big three are Hammett, Chandler, and Cain, so here it is.

Pastorale

James M. Cain

1

Well, it looks like Burbie is going to get hung. And if he does; what he can lay it on is, he always figured he was so damn smart.

You see, Burbie, he left town when he was about sixteen year old. He run away with one of them travelling shows, "East Lynne" I think it was, and he stayed away about ten years. And when he come back he thought he knowed a lot. Burbie, he's got them watery blue eyes what kind of stick out from his face, and how he killed the time was to sit around and listen to the boys talk down at the poolroom or over at the barber shop or a couple other places where he hung out, and then wink at you like they was all making a fool of theirself or something and nobody didn't know it but him.

But when you come right down to what Burbie had in his head, why it wasn't much. 'Course, he generally always had a job, painting around or maybe helping out on a new house, like of that, but what he used to do was to play baseball with the high school team. And they had a big fight over it, 'cause Burbie was so old nobody wouldn't believe he went to the school, and them other teams was all the time putting up a squawk. So then he couldn't play no more. And another thing he liked to do was sing at the entertainments. I reckon he liked that most of all, 'cause he claimed that a whole lot of the time he was away he was on the stage, and I reckon maybe he was at that, 'cause he was pretty good, 'specially when he dressed hisself up like a old-time Rube and come out and spoke a piece what he knowed.

Well, when he come back to town he seen Lida and it was a natural. 'Cause Lida, she was just about the same kind of a thing for a woman as Burbie was for a man. She used to work in the store, selling dry goods to the men, and kind of making hats on the side. 'Cepting only she didn't stay on the dry goods side no more'n she had to. She was generally over where the boys was drinking Coca-Cola, and all the time carrying on about did they like it with ammonia or lemon, and could she have a swallow outen their glass. And what she had her mind on was the clothes she had on, and was she dated up for Sunday night. Them clothes was pretty snappy, and she made them herself. And I heard some of them say she wasn't hard to date up, and after you done kept your date why maybe you wasn't going to be disappointed. And why Lida married the old man I don't know, lessen she got tired working at the store and tooken a look at the big farm where he lived at, about two mile from town.

By the time Burbie got back she'd been married about a year and she was about due. So her and him commence meeting each other, out in the orchard back of the old man's house. The old man would go to bed right after supper and then she'd sneak out and meet Burbie. And nobody wasn't supposed to know nothing about it. Only everybody did, 'cause Burbie, after he'd get back to town about eleven o'clock at night, he'd kind of slide into the poolroom and set down easy like. And then somebody'd say, "Yay, Burbie, where you been?" And Burbie, he'd kind of look around, and then he'd pick out somebody and wink at him, and that was how Burbie give it some good advertising.

So the way Burbie tells it, and he tells it plenty since he done got religion down to the jailhouse, it wasn't long before him and Lida thought it would be a good idea to kill the old man. They figured he didn't have long to live nohow, so he might as well go now as wait a couple of years. And another thing, the old man had kind of got hep that something was going on, and they figured if he throwed Lida out it wouldn't be no easy job to get his money even if he died regular. And another thing, by that time the Klux was kind of talking around, so Burbie figured it would be better if him and Lida was to get married, else maybe he'd have to leave town again.

So that was how come he got Hutch in it. You see, he was afeared to kill the old man hisself and he wanted some help. And then he figured it would be pretty good if Lida wasn't nowheres around and it would look like robbery. If it would of been me, I would of left Hutch out of it. 'Cause Hutch, he was mean. He'd been away for a while too, but him going away, that wasn't the same as Burbie going away. Hutch was sent. He was sent for ripping a mail sack while he was driving the mail wagon up from the station, and before he come back he done two years down to Atlanta.

But what I mean, he wasn't only crooked, he was mean. He had a ugly look to him, like when he'd order hisself a couple of fried eggs over to the restaurant, and then set and eat them with his head humped down low and his arm curled around his plate like he thought somebody was going to steal it off him, and handle his knife with his thumb down near the tip, kind of like a nigger does a razor. Nobody didn't have much to say to Hutch, and I reckon that's why he ain't heard nothing about Burbie and Lida, and et it all up what Burbie told him about the old man having a pot of money hid in the fireplace in the back room.

So one night early in March, Burbie and Hutch went out and done the job. Burbie he'd already got Lida out of the way. She'd let on she had to go to the city to buy some things, and she went away on No. 6, so everybody knowed she was gone. Hutch, he seen her go, and come running to Burbie saying now was a good time, which was just what Burbie wanted. 'Cause her and Burbie had already put the money in the pot, so Hutch wouldn't think it was no put-up job. Well, anyway, they put $23 in the pot, all changed into pennies and nickels and dimes so it would look like a big pile, and that was all the money Burbie had. It was kind of like you might say the savings of a lifetime.

And then Burbie and Hutch got in the horse and wagon what Hutch had, 'cause Hutch was in the hauling business again, and they went out to the old man's place. Only they went around the back way, and tied the horse back of the house so nobody couldn't see it from the road, and knocked on the back door and made out like they was just coming through the place on their way back to town and had stopped by to get warmed up, 'cause it was cold as hell. So the old man let them in and give them a drink of some hard cider what he had, and they got canned up a little more. They was already pretty canned, 'cause they both of them had a pint of corn on their hip for to give them some nerve.

And then Hutch he got back of the old man and crowned him with a wrench what he had hid in his coat.

2

Well, next off Hutch gets sore as hell at Burbie 'cause there ain't no more'n $23 in the pot. He didn't do nothing. He just set there, first looking at the money, what he had piled up on a table, and then looking at Burbie.

And then Burbie commences soft-soaping him. He says hope my die he thought there was a thousand dollars anyway in the pot, on account the old man being like he was. And he says hope my die it sure was a big surprise to him how little there was there. And he says hope my die it sure does make him feel bad, on account he's the one had the idea first. And he says hope my die it's all his fault and he's going to let Hutch keep all the money, damn if he ain't. He ain't going to take none of it for hisself at all, on account of how bad he feels. And Hutch, he don't say nothing at all, only look at Burbie and look at the money.

And right in the middle of while Burbie was talking, they heard a whole lot of hollering out in front of the house and somebody blowing a automobile horn. And Hutch jumps up and scoops the money and the wrench off the table in his pockets, and hides the pot back in the fireplace. And then he grabs the old man and him and Burbie carries him out the back door, hists him in the wagon, and drives off. And how they was to drive off without them people seeing them was because they come in the back way and that was the way they went. And them people in the automobile, they was a bunch of old folks from the Methodist church what knowed Lida was away and didn't think so much of Lida nohow and come out to say hello. And when they come in and didn't see nothing, they figured the old man had went in to town and so they went back.

Well, Hutch and Burbie was in a hell of a fix all right. 'Cause there they was, driving along somewheres with the old man in the wagon and they didn't have no more idea than a bald-headed coot where they was going or what they was going to do with him. So Burbie, he commence to whimper. But Hutch kept a-setting there, driving the horse, and he don't say nothing.

So pretty soon they come to a place where they was building a piece of county road, and it was all tore up and a whole lot of toolboxes laying out on the side. So Hutch gets out and twists the lock off one of them with the wrench, and takes out a pick and a shovel and throws them in the wagon. And then he got in again and drove on for a while till he come to the Whooping Nannie woods, what some of them says has got a ghost in it on dark nights, and it's about three miles from the old man's farm. And Hutch turns in there and pretty soon he come to a kind of a

clear place and he stopped. And then, first thing he's said to Burbie, he says,

"Dig that grave!"

So Burbie dug the grave. He dug for two hours, until he got so damn tired he couldn't hardly stand up. But he ain't hardly made no hole at all. 'Cause the ground is froze and even with the pick he couldn't hardly make a dent in it scarcely. But anyhow Hutch stopped him and they throwed the old man in and covered him up. But after they got him covered up his head was sticking out. So Hutch beat the head down good as he could and piled the dirt up around it and they got in and drove off.

After they'd went a little ways, Hutch commence to cuss Burbie. Then he said Burbie'd been lying to him. But Burbie, he swears he ain't been lying. And then Hutch says he *was* lying and with that he hit Burbie. And after he knocked Burbie down in the bottom of the wagon he kicked him and then pretty soon Burbie up and told him about Lida. And when Burbie got done telling him about Lida, Hutch turned the horse around. Burbie asked then what they was going back for and Hutch says they're going back for to git a present for Lida. So they come back for to git a present for Lida. So they come back to the grave and Hutch made Burbie cut off the old man's head with the shovel. It made Burbie sick, but Hutch made him stick at it, and after a while Burbie had it off. So Hutch throwed it in the wagon and they get in and start back to town once more.

Well, they wasn't no more'n out of the woods before Hutch takes hisself a slug of corn and commence to holler. He kind of raved to hisself, all about how he was going to make Burbie put the head in a box and tie it up with a string and take it out to Lida for a present, so she'd get a nice surprise when she opened it. Soon as Lida comes back he says Burbie has got to do it, and then he's going to kill Burbie. "I'll kill you!" he says. "I'll kill you, damn you! I'll kill you!" And he says it kind of singsongy, over and over again.

And then he takes hisself another slug of corn and stands up and whoops. Then he beat on the horse with the whip and the horse commence to run. What I mean, he commence to gallop. And then Hutch hit him some more. And then he commence to screech as loud as he could. "Ride him, cowboy!" he hollers. "Going East! Here come old broadcuff down the road! Whe-e-e-e!" And sure enough, here they come down the road, the horse a-running hell to split, and Hutch a-hollering, and Burbie a-shivering, and the head a-rolling around in the bottom of the wagon, and bouncing up in the air when they hit a bump, and Burbie damn near dying every time it hit his feet.

3

After a while the horse got tired so it wouldn't run no more, and they had to let him walk and Hutch set down and commence to grunt. So Burbie, he tries to figure out what the hell he's going to do with the head. And pretty soon he remembers a creek what they got to cross, what they ain't crossed on the way out 'cause they come the back way. So he figures he'll throw the head overboard when Hutch ain't looking. So he done it. They come to the creek, and on the way down to the bridge there's a little hill, and when the wagon tilted going down the hill the head rolled up between Burbie's feet, and he held it there, and when they got in the middle of the bridge he reached down and heaved it overboard.

Next off, Hutch give a yell and drop down in the bottom of the wagon. 'Cause what it sounded like was a pistol shot. You see, Burbie done forgot that it was a cold night and the creek done froze over. Not much, just a thin skim about a inch thick, but enough that when that head hit it it cracked pretty loud in different directions. And that was what scared Hutch. So when he got up and seen the head setting out there on the ice in the moonlight, and got it straight what Burbie done, he let on he was going to kill Burbie right there. And he reached for the pick. And Burbie jumped out and run, and he didn't never stop till he got home at the place where he lived at, and locked the door, and climbed in bed and pulled the covers over his head.

Well, the next morning a fellow come running into town and says there's hell to pay down at the bridge. So we all went down there and first thing we seen was that head laying out there on the ice, kind of rolled over on one ear. And next thing we seen was Hutch's horse and wagon tied to the bridge rail, and the horse damn near froze to death. And the next thing we seen was the hole in the ice where Hutch fell through. And the next thing we seen down on the bottom next to one of the bridge pilings, was Hutch.

So the first thing we went to work and done was to get the head. And believe me a head laying out on thin ice is a pretty damn hard thing to get, and what we had to do was to lasso it. And the next thing we done was to get Hutch. And after we fished him out he had the wrench and the $23 in his pockets and the pint of corn on his hip and he was stiff as a board. And near as I can figure out, what happened to him was that after Burbie run away he climbed down on the bridge piling and tried to reach the head and fell in.

But we didn't know nothing about it then, and after we done got the head and the old man was gone and a couple of boys that afternoon found the body and not the head on it, and the pot was found, and them old people from the Methodist church done told their story and one thing and another, we figured out that Hutch done it, 'specially on account he must have been drunk and he done time in the pen and all like of that, and nobody ain't thought nothing about Burbie at all. They had the funeral and Lida cried like hell and everybody tried to figure out what Hutch wanted with the head and things went along thataway for three weeks.

Then one night down to the poolroom they was having it some more about the head, and one says one thing and one says another, and Benny Heath, what's a kind of a constable around town, he started a long bum argument about how Hutch must of figured if they couldn't find the head to the body they couldn't prove no murder. So right in the middle of it Burbie kind of looked around like he always done and then he winked. And Benny Heath, he kept on a-talking, and after he got done Burbie kind of leaned over and commence to talk to him. And in a couple of minutes you couldn't of heard a man catch his breath in that place, accounten they was all listening at Burbie.

I already told you Burbie was pretty good when it comes to giving a spiel at a entertainment. Well, this here was a kind of spiel too. Burbie act like he had it all learned by heart. His voice trimmled and ever couple of minutes he'd kind of cry and wipe his eyes and make out like he can't say no more, and then he'd go on.

And the big idea was what a whole lot of hell he done raised in his life. Burbie said it was drink and women what done ruined him. He told about all the women what he knowed, and all the saloons he's been in, and some of it was a lie 'cause if all the saloons was as swell as he said they was they'd of throwed him out. And then he told about how sorry he was about the life he done led, and how hope my die he come home to his old home town just to get out the devilment and settle down. And he told about Lida, and how she wouldn't let him cut it out. And then he told how she done led him on till he got the idea to kill the old man. And then he told about how him and Hutch done it, and all about the money and the head and all the rest of it.

And what it sounded like was a piece what he knowed called "The Face on the Floor," what

was about a bum what drawed a picture on the barroom floor of the woman what done ruined him. Only the funny part was that Burbie wasn't ashamed of hisself like he made out he was. You could see he was proud of hisself. He was proud of all them women and all the liquor he'd drunk and he was proud about Lida and he was proud about the old man and the head and being slick enough not to fall in the creek with Hutch. And after he got done he give a yelp and flopped down on the floor and I reckon maybe he thought he was going to die on the spot like the bum what drawed the face on the barroom floor, only he didn't. He kind of lain there a couple of minutes till Benny got him up and put him in the car and tooken him off to jail.

So that's where he's at now, and he's went to work and got religion down there, and all the people what comes to see him, why he sings hymns to them and then he speaks them his piece. And I hear tell he knows it pretty good by now and has got the crying down pat. And Lida, they got her down there too, only she won't say nothing 'cepting she done it same as Hutch and Burbie. So Burbie, he's going to get hung, sure as hell. And if he hadn't felt so smart, he would of been a free man yet.

Only I reckon he done been holding it all so long he just had to spill it.

The Sad Serbian

Frank Gruber

FEW PULP WRITERS were as prolific as Frank Gruber (1904–1969), who at the peak of his career produced three or four full-length novels a year, many about series characters Johnny Fletcher and his sidekick, Sam Cragg; numerous short stories, many featuring Oliver Quade, "the Human Encyclopedia"; and screenplays, including such near-classics as *The Mask of Dimitrios*, *Terror by Night*, and, with Steve Fisher, *Johnny Angel*. He also wrote two dozen Western novels.

In addition to a relentless work ethic and a fertile imagination, he developed an eleven-point formula for his novels which certainly helped speed the writing process. In his autobiography, *The Pulp Jungle*, which is also an informal history of pulp magazines and the era in which they flourished, he outlined the formula for his mystery stories.

The successful adventure, he believed, needed a colorful hero, a theme with information the reader is unlikely to know, a villain more powerful than the hero, a vivid background for the action, an unusual murder method or unexpected circumstances surrounding the crime, unusual variations on the common motives of greed and hate, a well-hidden clue, a trick or twist that will snatch victory from the jaws of defeat, constantly moving action, a protagonist who has a personal involvement, and a smashing climax. These key points, of course, may well describe all of pulp fiction—and a lot of later adventure and crime stories as well.

"The Sad Serbian" first appeared in the March 1939 issue of *Black Mask*.

The Sad Serbian

Frank Gruber

*A racket to mulct the multitudes is
plenty reason for murder*

TO LOOK AT ME reading the death notices while I'm having my breakfast in Thompson's, you'd think I was an undertaker. I'm not, but my job is just as cheerful. Take this business today. I've got a bunch of cards with names, and I'm comparing them with the names in the death notices. I do this every morning and about twice a year I find a name I'm looking for. I strike pay-dirt this morning with the name Druhar.

I finish my breakfast and go out and hunt for my jaloppy, which I've got parked a couple of blocks down the street. I climb in and head for the North Side; 598 Blackhawk Street.

These foreigners certainly bury them early in the morning. Although it's only nine-thirty,

they've already taken the crepe down from the door. There are a couple of kids hanging around and I ask them: "At what church are they having the mass for Mrs. Druhar?"

"Saint John's on Cleveland Avenue," one of the kids replies.

I miss them at the church, so the only thing I can do is go out to the cemetery, which, according to the paper, is St. Sebastian's, seven miles outside the city limits. It takes me about an hour to get out there, so when I get to the cemetery, they're breaking up; going back to the cars that have brought them out. I grab an old envelope out of my pocket and wave it around as if it's a telegram, or something.

"Mr. Tony Druhar!" I yell.

A big fellow, who is just about to climb into a green sedan, says: "Here I am."

I run over and see that the license number on the sedan checks with the number on one of my cards. So I pull out the old repossess warrant and stick it into Mr. Druhar's hand. "Sorry, Mr. Druhar," I say. "I'm taking your car, on account of you haven't done right by the Mid-West Finance Company."

This Druhar looks stupidly at the piece of paper in his hand for a minute. Then he lets out a roar you could have heard over on Grant Avenue. "Why, you lousy, grave-robbing—! Is this a time to pull something like this, when I have just buried my poor grandmother?"

"That's how I found you," I tell him. "It says in the paper: 'Mourned by her sons, so-and-so, and grandsons, Tony Druhar, and so-and-so.'"

Some people certainly get mad. This Druhar fellow jumps up and down and takes off his hat and throws it on the ground and jumps on it. Then three fellows just as big as Druhar climb out of his sedan and surround me.

"So you're a skip-tracer!" one of them says, and lets a handful of knuckles fly in my direction.

I'm lucky enough to duck them, but I can see that this isn't the safest place in the world right now for Sam Cragg. I get a lucky break, though. A motorcycle cop who's escorted the funeral out here is just a little way off, and when Druhar starts all his yelling, he comes over.

"What's the trouble?" he asks.

Druhar starts swearing again, but I grab hold of the cop's arm. "I've got a repossess warrant for this car. This Druhar has missed six payments, and the Mid-West Finance Company wants $188 or the car."

The cop gives me a funny look and takes the warrant from Tony Druhar. He looks at it and then he looks at me. "I'll bet you hate yourself, mister, when you look at your face in the mirror every morning."

"Maybe I do," I tell the cop, "but if I didn't have this job somebody else would, and I haven't got a pull, so I can't get on the WPA, and I have to eat."

"Why?" asks the cop.

I can see he's all on the other side, so I give him some law. "Officer, this is a regular warrant, good anywhere in this country. As an officer of the law, I'm calling on you to see that it's properly served. I want this car or $188."

There's some hullabaloo, but after a while Druhar and his pals get together and make me a proposition, which I am sap enough to accept. I'm a softie, and you oughtn't to be a skip-tracer if you are a softie. They've pooled up $32 and they say that Druhar will have the rest of the money for me tomorrow. I'm just cagy enough, though, to make them all give me their names and addresses and prove them by letters and stuff they've got with them.

That's where I made my big mistake and how I got mixed up with the phoney prince.

 NEXT MORNING I drive up to 736 Gardner Street. Gardner Street is a little one-block chopped up street that has been dumped in between Stanton Park and Ogden Avenue. There are only about thirty houses on the street, and every one of them should have been condemned twenty years ago. Druhar is supposed to live on the first floor of one of these dumps.

I can't ring the doorbell because there isn't a doorbell, so I bang the door with my fist. Nothing happens so I bang it again. Then I figure I have been given the runaround and I get sore, and push on the door. It goes open and I walk into the place. Druhar is at home. He's lying on the floor.

He's dead.

For a minute I look down at him and all sorts of cold shivers run up and down my back. This Druhar is a big fellow, but somebody has twisted his neck so that his face is looking over his shoulder.

There's a slip of paper sticking out of Druhar's pants pocket. I don't like corpses any better than the next fellow, but I reach down and pull out this piece of paper. And then my eyes pop out. The paper reads:

"For value received, I promise to pay to Tony Druhar, Five Thousand Dollars."

W. C. ROBERTS

A promissory note, good in any man's court, if this W. C. Roberts has got $5000.

I look at the thing and finally stick it in my pocket. After all, Tony Druhar, dead or alive, owes the Mid-West Finance Company about $156.00.

I back out of the house and I'm on the porch when I see the taxicab that is pulled up behind my jalopy. The prince is coming across the sidewalk.

Of course I don't know that he's a prince then. I find that out later. But he certainly dresses the part. He's wearing a black, single-breasted coat, which is open, showing a fawn-colored waistcoat. Under it is a pair of striped trousers and below that, believe it or not, white spats. On his head he's got a pearl-gray Homburg. He's carrying a pair of yellow pigskin gloves and a cane. So help me, he's coming up to Druhar's house.

"Good morning, sir," he says to me in a voice that drips with some foreign accent. His face is long and very sad and aristocratic. "I'm looking for Mr. Druhar."

What I want to do is jump into my jalopy and get the hell out of there, but I know how cops are, and it's just my luck that either the prince or the taxicab driver will remember the license number of my car, so I figure I may as well face the thing out.

"Mr. Druhar," I say, "is inside the house. He's dead."

The prince's mouth falls open, but only for a second. Then he reaches into his waistcoat and brings out a monocle and sticks it in his eye. He looks at me and says, "I do not understand."

"Maybe he doesn't either, but he's dead just the same."

He lets out a sigh. "That is too bad. I am Prince Peter Strogovich. This Druhar had applied to me for a position, and I was just about to employ him. It is sad."

The prince takes the monocle out of his eye and polishes it with his gloves. "You say he is inside? The police do not yet know?"

They know soon enough. Some of the neighbors have been attracted by the triple event—my jalopy, the taxicab and the prince in his fancy outfit. They have gathered and they've heard some of our talk, so there's a lot of chattering and running around.

In about five minutes, a squad car rolls up. In a few minutes more, there are ten or twelve cops around, an ambulance, and the emergency squad from the Fire Department.

There's a lot of excitement and when it all sifts down, the prince and myself are down at Headquarters, and Captain Riordan is swearing and asking a lot of questions.

Most of the swearing is at me. "I don't like your story at all," he tells me. "You were pretty sore at this Druhar. According to the neighbors, and his friends, you cut a pretty scene yesterday at the funeral of his grandmother. My idea is that you went there this morning to collect the money and you got into a fight with him."

"Wait a minute, Captain," I cut in. "Call up Oscar Berger, who's the Argus Adjustment Agency. Ask him if I've killed any of my skips before."

"There's always a time to start, you know."

The captain grunts and picks up the telephone. He calls the office and says, "Hello, Mr. Berger? This is Police Headquarters. I've got a man here by the name of Sam Cragg who says he works for you. . . . What's the charge? Why, he said he was after a fellow who owed some money and it seems that the fellow got his neck twisted. What?" He listens for a minute, then he turns to me. "He wants to know if you collected the money."

I give the captain my opinion of Oscar Berger, which the captain translates into "No." He listens a minute more and then says, "O.K.," and hangs up.

"Berger says he fired you a couple of days ago."

I really get sore then. That was about the kind of loyalty you can expect from a man who'd run that kind of a collection agency.

Prince Peter comes to my assistance.

"Captain, I do not think this man killed Mr. Druhar. I do not think he is strong enough to do it. Besides, there are no marks on him, and Mr. Druhar would not have submitted without fighting."

"I could figure that out myself," snaps the captain. "He could have come on Druhar from the back and caught him by surprise."

The prince shrugs. "At any rate, you are not going to hold me? I have important matters. . . ."

"You can go," says the captain. He scowls at me. "I still don't like your story, but I'm going to give you the benefit of the doubt. If I find out anything more, I can pick you up easily enough."

That's enough for me. I get out of Headquarters as quickly as I can. Outside, Prince Peter is just climbing into a taxicab.

I get a street car and ride back to Gardner Street where the jaloppy is still parked. It's there all right, only it hasn't got any tires or headlights now. The damn crooks in the neighborhood have stripped them off.

When I start swearing even the kids on the street duck into the houses. I've got a good mind just to leave the rest of the junk right there, but when I get to Division Street I go into a saloon and telephone a garage.

By the time I get down to the rattle-trap building on Wells Street where AAA has its lousy offices, I'm in a swell mood—for murder.

I slam into the office and Betty Marshall, who practically runs the business from the inside, gives me the ha-ha. "So you finally landed in jail!"

"And it's no thanks to our boss that I'm not still there. Is he inside?"

He's trying to lock his office door, when I push it open and knock him halfway across the room. "Listen, Berger," I says to him, "what kind of a double-crosser are you?"

He ducks behind the desk. "Now take it easy, Cragg. I was just going to call Goldfarb, my lawyer, and have him spring you."

"I'll bet you were! Every day of the week I do things for you that keep me awake nights, and that's the kind of loyalty you give me."

"Now, now, Sam," he soft-soaps me. "I got a nice bunch of easy skips for you. To make it up, I'll pay you the regular five buck rate on them, although these are so easy you oughtn't to get more than three on them. It's the new account I landed, the O. W. Sugar Jewelry Company."

"You call those easy skips? Hell, three-fourths of the people that buy jewelry on the installment plan pawn it before they finish paying for it!"

"Yeah, but they're all working people in the lower brackets. You've just got to find out where they work and threaten to garnishee their wages and they'll kick in."

I take the cards he gives me. Like I said before, I hadn't any pull and couldn't get on the WPA.

These Sugar Jewelry skips are no better or worse than others I've handled. I find the first one, a middle-age Italian woman, cracking pecans in a little dump near Oak and Milton—the Death Corner. She gets eight cents a pound for shelling the pecans and if she works hard she can shell two pounds an hour. Why a woman like that ever bought a wrist watch I don't know, but she did—and I make her promise to pay a dollar a week on the watch.

 I AM working on the second skip on Sedgwick near Division, when I get the surprise of my life. Prince Pete Strogovich, cane and white spats and all, comes out of a little confectionery store. I step into a doorway and watch him saunter across the street and go into a saloon. Then I walk into the confectionery store. It's a dump; dirty showcases, stationery, candy boxes and empty soft drink bottles standing all around. There's a magazine rack on one side.

Next to it sits the biggest woman I've ever seen in my life. She's six feet one or two inches tall and big all around. She weighs two-ninety or three hundred and none of it is flabby fat.

"What can I do for you?" she asks, her voice a hoarse bass.

I pretend not to hear her and started pawing over the magazines.

"Can I help you?" she goes on. "What magazines are you looking for?"

I make up the name of a dick mag.

"I don't carry that one, but there's plenty of detective magazines, just as good."

"They're not just as good," I retort. "That's the trouble with you storekeepers. You're always trying to sell something just as good."

She starts panting like she has the asthma and I give her a look. Her eyes are slits in her fat cheeks, but they're glittering slits. She's good and sore.

"Get the hell out of here!" she snaps at me. She starts getting up from the big reinforced chair and I beat it to the door.

When I get outside Prince Peter's coming out of the saloon, dabbing a handkerchief to his aristocratic mouth. I walk across the street and meet him on the corner.

"Hi, Pete!" I say to him.

He knows me all right. But he isn't overjoyed to meet me. "What are you doing here?" he asks.

"Nothin' much, Pete, just trying to locate a skip."

"Skip?" he asks. "What is a skip?"

"Well, suppose you buy a suit of clothes on the installment plan, or a diamond ring or a car. You try to beat the firm out of the money and move without leaving a forwarding address. A skip tracer runs you down and hands you a summons. That's me."

"Then you are a detective, no?"

"Well, I do detective work, all right, but I'm not exactly a detective."

"So!" The prince gets out his monocle and begins polishing it on his gloves. He's sizing me up. After a minute, he decides I'm O.K. "My friend, would you do a job for me? For two weeks I have been looking for a man and I can not find him. He—he owes me some money, just like your skips. You think, perhaps, you can find him?"

"Probably, but you see, I work for a collection agency and I only look for people they want."

"But I would pay you well. Here!" He whips out a leather wallet and pulls out a couple of bills. Fifties. I take them from his hand and rub them. "You're paying me a hundred dollars to find this man for you?"

"One hundred dollars now. When you find him I give you four hundred dollars more. You work for me, huh?"

I fold the bills four ways and put them into my pocket. Argus Adjustment Agency pays me five dollars for finding a skip. Sometimes I find two in one day. Sometimes I don't find two in a week.

"What's this fellow's name?"

"Roberts," the prince says, "W. C. Roberts."

I don't tumble right away, not until the prince says: "He owes me five thousand dollars. He has give me the note and promise to pay. . . ."

And then I know. W. C. Roberts is the name on Tony Druhar's note, the one I'd slipped out of his pocket and had in my own right now. I say: "What was the last address you had of this Roberts, and what does he look like?"

"I do not know what he looks like," the prince says. "But his last address is—was," he pulls a tiny notebook from his pocket, "518 Rookery Building."

I write the address down on a card.

"He isn't there any more, I take it."

"No, he have moved and not give the new address. But you find him?"

"For five hundred bucks I'd find John Wilkes Booth," I tell him.

"Booth? I do not know him."

"Never mind. And where'll I find you?"

He thinks that over before giving me the answer. "At the Gregorian Towers on Michigan Boulevard."

I write that down, too, then I ask him the question that's been bothering me for a long time. "Say, Prince, would you mind telling me what nationality you are?"

He likes that. He pulls himself up straight and sticks the monocle in his eye. "I am Serbian," he says proudly. "My cousin was the king of Serbia. King Peter Karageorgovich."

Me, I don't even know where Serbia is. The name's vaguely familiar, but that's about all. I make up my mind to look it up sometime.

I leave the prince and get on a south-bound Sedgwick Street car, but at Chicago Avenue it moves too slow and I get off and grab a cab. I have a hundred bucks and I want to see what it's like to spend money.

THE ROOKERY BUILDING is one of those old office buildings that was built right after the war—the Civil War. One of these days they're going to tear it down and use the ground as a parking lot.

I go straight to the superintendent's office. "I'm looking for a Mr. W. C. Roberts, who used to have an office in this building," I say to him.

"Is that so?" The supe comes back at me. "Some other people are looking for him, too—including the cops."

"Ha, the cops! And why're they looking for him?"

"You ain't never heard of W. C. Roberts, mister?"

"What'd he do, kill someone?"

"Uh-uh." He gives me a funny look, then reaches into his pocket and brings out a slip of paper. He hands it to me and I look at it. It has some writing on it:

"For value received I promise to pay to William Kilduff, five thousand dollars."
                                 W. C. ROBERTS.

I pull out my own note—the one made out to Tony Druhar. I show it to the superintendent. "Hello, sucker," says the superintendent. "How much you pay for yours?"

I stall. "The usual amount, I guess."

"Five bucks?"

"Ten."

"You *are* a sucker. Us Irish only paid five. I heard some Polacks and Serbians paid as high as twenty bucks."

"Oh," I say, not knowing what this was all about, "so it depends on the nationality how big a sucker you are?"

"Yeah, sure. Most of us Irish know now we got gypped. But those hunkies—I hear they're still going for it. They refuse to believe that Roberts is a crook. That phoney prince keeps them bulled."

"Prince? You mean Prince Peter Strogovich?"

"Yeah, the guy with the fancy duds," he says.

"He claims to be a Serbian prince." I laugh. "I'll bet he gives his fellow countrymen a good line. Like to hear him some time."

"Why don't you go to one of their meetings, then? I think tonight is the Serbians' night. They hold their meeting at some hall on Halsted Street, near North Avenue."

"Say, what's this Roberts guy look like?" I ask.

"That's the funny part of it. No one knows. He never came to his office here. A dame ran it for him. When the cops came in one day, she just went out and never came back."

"Cagy, huh? Well, so long, sucker!"

"So long, sucker!"

When I get out of the Rookery Building I walk over to Adams Street and go into a saloon and have two good hookers of rye. I need them. This set-up is the screwiest I've ever run across in all my life.

Promissory notes, five bucks apiece. . . . Serbians.

I have another snort, then go back to the office of AAA, on Wells near Randolph. Betty has just come from getting her hair done. I give it the once-over. "Like it?" she asked.

It's set in the new up-and-at-'em style. "You dames get screwier every day," I tell her.

"Is that so?" she says, coldly. "Well, it's a good thing I didn't get my hair done for *you*."

It's an idea I haven't thought about before, but I make a mental note of it. Inside his private office, Oscar Berger rubs his hands together. He can do it better than a Maxwell Street clothing merchant.

"Well, how many did you find?"

"One, but I got some good leads on two more."

"Only one, and such good prospects!"

"Nuts, Berger," I say to him, "they're as tough as any others and you know it. Look, tell me something, ever hear of a crook by the name of W. C. Roberts?"

"Yeah, sure. Haven't you? But maybe that case broke when you were on your vacation."

"It must have. What'd Roberts do?"

"Nothing much. Except swindle about five thousand hunkies in this man's town. He's an inventor, see, or claims to be one. He gets a bunch of these hunkies together and tells them he invented four-wheel brakes for automobiles, but Henry Ford or General Motors swiped the patent from him. He invented wireless, but Marconi gypped him out of the patent. So what? So he wants to sue Henry Ford and General Motors. But lawsuits cost money and that's what he hasn't got much of. So he gets the hunkies to finance the lawsuits. Mr. Roberts gives them notes. They lend him ten bucks now, they get five thousand when he collects from the big shots."

"How much does he collect?"

Berger screws up his mouth. "Ten or fifteen billion. Boxcar numbers."

"And the chumps fall for it?"

"They like it! According to the papers, ten or fifteen thousand hunkies kicked in from five to a hundred bucks per each."

"And Roberts skipped?"

"Wouldn't you?"

"That depends. If the suckers were milked dry, maybe. But I understand there's a lot of Bulgarians and Serbians and such still believe in Roberts."

"Oh, sure, that's the sweet part of it. Roberts warned them even before the law jumped on him, that he was expecting something like that. On account of Mr. Ford, Westinghouse and Edison owning the cops and sicking them on him. Slick guy, this Roberts."

"Yeah? What'd he look like?"

"That's the funny part of it. No one knows. He doesn't show himself. When the cops tried to get him, they discovered that no one would even admit ever having seen him."

"Not bad," I say, "not bad at all."

Oscar Berger gives me the once-over. "What's your interest in this? Roberts didn't put the bite into you, did he?"

"No. When someone offers me over four per cent interest I know he's crooked. Not that I'd ever get enough to invest at four per cent."

When I come out of Berger's office, Betty is putting lipstick on her mouth. "All right, sister," I say to her, "I'm going to give you a break tonight. Where do you live?"

"At 4898 Winthrop, but if you come up you're traveling just for the exercise."

"I like exercise," I tell her. "I'll be there at seven."

"I won't be home. . . . What'll I wear?"

Nice girl, Betty. "Nothing fancy. We'll go to some quiet spot."

 I STILL have the best part of my hundred bucks the Serbian prince had given me. I get a haircut and a shave and have a bite at Harding's Grill on Madison. Then I take a taxi to 4898 Winthrop Avenue, which is a block north of Lawrence and one east of Broadway.

The place is a second-rate apartment hotel. They won't let me upstairs without being announced and when I get Betty on the phone she says she'll be right down.

She's down in five minutes. I almost don't recognize her. She's wearing a silver evening dress that must have cost her at least a month's pay. Her hair's brushed soft and shiny.

She certainly doesn't look like the type of girl who'd work for a sleazy outfit like AAA. I say to her: "You look very interesting."

"You never noticed it before," she says.

"How could I? All the time I'm working for Triple A I've got a grouch. Skip tracing is a lousy business."

"I'm figuring on quitting myself," Betty says. "One of your chumps came into the office last week. He was a big fellow, but he bawled like a baby. You were going to garnishee his wages unless he paid ten dollars a month on a cheap piano he bought for his daughter who wanted to be a musician, but changed her mind and eloped with a greaseball."

"Nix," I say. "Let me forget skip tracing for one night. I dream about it."

"All right. Where we going?"

"A little place I discovered," I tell her. "You've never seen one like it."

I flag a taxi. Betty looks at me suspiciously when I give the driver the address, but she doesn't make any comment until we climb out on Halsted Street, down near North Avenue.

She looks around while I pay the driver. "What is this, one of your jokes?"

We're in front of a dump that has a sign on the window. "Plennert's Café. Lodge Hall for Rent."

"No. A fellow told me this place would be interesting."

The café is a cheap saloon. You have to go through the saloon to get into the lodge hall, in the rear.

Betty's game, I've got to say that for her. We go through the saloon into the lodge hall. There are rows of folding chairs set up in the hall and most of them are filled with men, women and kids. You can cut the smoke.

Almost all the men in the place are dark complected. Some of them have to shave twice a day. The women are swarthy, too, although here and there you can see a blonde, just by way of contrast.

Betty comes in for a lot of gawking. She's glad when I pull her down in a seat near the rear.

"What is this?" she whispers to me. Her face is red and I know she doesn't like it any too well.

I say, "This is a patriotic meeting of the Sons and Daughters of Serbia. Look, up there on the platform, there's something you'll never see again—a Serbian prince."

Yeah, Prince Peter. He's pouring out a glass of water on a speaker's stand and the way some of the Serbs on the platform stand around, you can tell that they think a lot of Prince Pete.

There are about eight men on the platform and one woman. The woman is as big as three of the men. Yeah, she's the amazon who keeps the confectionery store on Sedgwick Street. She's sitting on a stout wooden bench near the side of the stage, where she can watch Prince Pete. She's pretty interested in him.

The prince drinks his water and holds up his hands. The room becomes as still as a cemetery at midnight.

"My country people," the prince says in English. And then he starts jabbering in the damnedest language. He sounds off for ten minutes and I don't understand a word of it—until everyone in the place begins clapping hands and cheering and one or two of the younger fellows yell in English:

"The hell with Henry Ford! The hell with General Motors! We'll stick with Mr. Roberts!"

"Fun, isn't it?" I say to Betty, next to me.

"Is it? I suppose this is your idea of a joke."

"Not at all. You see in this room about two hundred of the choicest suckers in the city of Chicago. And do they like it? Listen to them."

About twenty or thirty of the Serbians climb up onto the platform. Prince Pete gives them some aristocratic condescension and they like it. Every one of them.

"You want to see the prince's monocle?" I ask Betty. "Wait here a minute."

I push through the crowd and climb up on the platform.

"Hello, Prince," I say to his royal highness.

Sure enough, the monocle comes out. He gets it out of his fancy vest and sticks it into his eye. Then he says: "Ah, Mister Cragg! How *do* you do?"

"Fine. And you—you're doing all right yourself, I see."

He drops his voice. "You have information for me, yes?"

"I have information, no. But I've got a clue. Another day or two—"

"Good! You let me know damn quick, yes? This," he shrugs deprecatingly, "it is part of the game. You understand?"

"Yeah, sure, I understand."

I go back to Betty. "Well, you got enough?"

"Oh, no," she replies sweetly. "I'd like to attend another patriotic meeting. How about the Bulgarians, haven't they got one tonight?"

"No, theirs is Thursday. But there's a beer stube over on North Avenue—"

She gets up quick. In the saloon, the amazon gets up from a chair and grabs my arm. "You're the man was in my store this afternoon," she says.

I try to take my arm out of her grip and can't. "That's right, I wanted to buy a detective magazine. Uh, you got it for me?"

"Don't try to kid me, young man," she snaps at me. "I'm not as dumb as I look. I saw you talking to the Prince. That's why I came out here. What's he up to?"

I take hold of her wrist and this time she lets me take it off my arm. "Sorry, madam," I tell her. "The affair between the prince and myself is confidential."

Her eyes leave me for a second and she sizes up Betty. "This your girl?"

"Uh-huh. Why?"

"You're a cop," she says. "I can always smell one. You're a private dick. And you're working for the Prince. Well, I want you to do a little job for me. And I'll pay you twice what he paid you."

"He's paying me a grand."

"That's a lie! Pete hasn't got that kind of money. I'll give you six hundred." She's wearing a tweed suit that would have made a fine tent for Mr. Ringling's biggest elephant. She digs a fist into a pocket and brings out a roll of bills. She counts out six hundred dollars, in fifties.

"Here, now tell me what the Prince hired you for?"

I struck the word ethics out of my dictionary when I became a skip tracer. But Betty is breathing down my neck. I say to the fat woman. "That's against the rules. A dick never betrays a confidence."

Her piggish eyes glint like they had that afternoon when she'd got sore at me. She says, "All right, you don't have to tell me that. I think I can guess. But I want you to work for me just the same. I think Pete's two-timing me."

"Two-timing *you?*"

She shows her teeth. They are as big as a horse's. "He's got a woman somewhere. I want you to shadow him."

"And then? After I see him with the dame?"

"You give me her name and address, that's all. I'll do the rest."

She would, too. She'd probably snatch the woman bald-headed. But that isn't my worry. Not yet. I say to the amazon: "Oke, I'll work for you."

"Start tonight. Shadow the Prince. I—I can't do it myself." She scowls. "I'm too conspicuous . . . my size."

Betty pokes me in the back with her fist, but I pretend not to notice. "All right, Miss—"

"Kelly, Mamie Kelly. You know my address. When you get results, give me a buzz on the phone."

She waddles out of the saloon and about two second later, the prince comes in. He catches up with Betty and me at the door says, "Ah, Mr. Cragg!" and looks at Betty like she was modeling lingerie. But he doesn't stop.

WHEN we get outside, he's waving his yellow cane at a taxicab. By luck there's another parked across the street. Even though it is facing the wrong way, I want it and want it bad.

I grab hold of Betty's wrist. "Come on!"

She jerks away. "What're you going to do? You louse, you can't double-cross your—your client, like that."

"Double-cross, hell!" I snort. "That's the only game the prince understands. We're following him!"

I drag her across the street and heave her into the cab. "Follow that yellow taxi!" I tell the driver. "Five bucks if you keep on his tail."

"For ten bucks, I'll run him down!" says the cabby.

He makes a beautiful U turn, just missing a street car. Then we are off, up Halsted Street.

"Some fun," Betty says to me. But she doesn't mean it.

I grin at her. "Now, kid, you got to take the good with the bad. I work like a dog all week for Oscar Berger. I do things that make me ashamed to look in a mirror and what do I get? Twenty, maybe thirty measly bucks a week. And now comes a chance to make some real dough—and you squawk!"

"It's dirty money," she says.

I reach into my pocket and pull out Tony Druhar's five thousand dollar promissory note. "Look, Betty, I almost got thrown in the can this morning, because a guy was killed. I found this on his body."

She looks at the piece of paper. "Why, it's an I.O.U. for five thousand dollars!"

"Uh-huh, and every one of these Serbians tonight has at least one chunk of paper like this. Prince Pete's one of the higher-ups in as lousy a racket I ever heard of. That's why I'm working on all these angles. I'd do it even if I wasn't getting a cent."

Well, maybe I would at that. But I know it is a lot more fun doing with a flock of fifties in my pocket, and the promise of some more.

It goes over. Betty hands the note back to me and her eyes are shining. "I didn't understand, Sam. I think—I think you're swell!"

"So're you, kid!" I say. I throw my arm about her. And then the cab stops all of a sudden and the driver yells, "Here, buddy!"

"What? Where is he?"

"He just went into The Red Mill."

I look around and see that we are on Lawrence near Broadway. I climb out of the cab and help Betty, then hand the cabby a five dollar bill.

I say to Betty, "Maybe we'll get a chance to do some of that dancing you wanted."

We go inside and the headwaiter looks at Betty's silver evening dress and gives me a big smile. "Good evening, sir. A table near the front?"

"Umm," I say, looking around as if night clubs were regular stuff with me. "Something not too public, if you know what I mean?"

"Yes, sir!"

He starts off down the side along the booths. At the fourth booth I stop. "Well, well, Prince!"

He's in the booth with as dizzy a blonde as I

ever saw. He looks up at me and the monocle almost falls from his eye. "You!" he says.

"Yeah, me. Ain't it a coincidence?"

Then he sees Betty and catches hold of himself. He comes to his feet and bows. I say: "Betty, allow me to introduce his royal highness, Prince Peter Strogovich . . . or something."

So help me, he takes her hand and kisses it. Then he says, "But won't you join us? Ah, Mitzi, this is my old friend, Mr. Cragg. And Miss—"

"Betty Marshall."

The headwaiter is disappointed. He's losing a tip. I wave him away. "We're joining our friends."

Mitzi is giving Betty the once-over. She says, bluntly: "I saw him first."

"My eyes aren't very good," Betty gives her back.

It's over the Prince's head. He gives Betty an eye-massage, his face still sad, but lecherous. "That is a beautiful dress you are wearing, Miss Marshall."

I say, "Ain't it? Look, Betty, your nose is shiny. Why don't you and Mitzi go spruce up?"

"I was just going to do that," Betty says. "Coming along, Mitzi?"

Mitzi gives me a dirty look, but she gets up. When the girls are gone, the prince says to me, "She is charming, no?"

"She's only my secretary. Her steady is a prize fighter, who's very jealous. And now that we've got that cleared away, let's talk business. You've been holding out on me, Prince. You want me to find W. C. Roberts and all the time you're working for him."

"Of course I am working for him. But I do not know Mr. Roberts. I have never seen him. Always, he sends me just letters."

"What about the dough you collect from these hunkies, these countrymen of yours."

"I send it to him, all! Then he mail me the commission, ten per cent."

"A very likely story. You collect from these people and mail it to Roberts. He trusts you?"

The prince scowls sadly. "That is the trouble.

He does not trust me. One time, just for a joke, you know, I send him not as much money as I collect. Next week I get the letter from him. He know how much I have hold out."

"Ah, he's got a spotter. Someone who goes to the meetings and checks up on you. Right?"

The prince shrugs wearily. "That is what I think. But I do not know who it is. I have try to find out and I cannot."

I make a guess. "Maybe the spotter's name was Tony Druhar!"

The prince gets sore about that. "What you mean by that, Mr. Cragg?"

"Nothing. I was just joking."

"It is not a good joke. I go to see Mr. Druhar, yesterday, because he wants sell me note for ten dollars."

"You said you were seeing him because he'd applied to you for a job of some kind."

"When I say that I do not know you. It was because of note. I buy note sometimes at bargain."

He's lying like hell. Maybe a Serbian's note is a bargain at five dollars, but it isn't to an Irishman.

I say, "You send this money to Mr. Roberts; to what address?"

"I send the letter to General Delivery. In two-three days I get back letter, with my commission."

"Where's the letter mailed, Chicago?"

"Yes, that is why I know Mr. Roberts still live here."

"Well, it's a nice racket for you, Prince. As long as you get your dough, what're you kicking about? Why do you want to see Roberts?"

He doesn't like that. He gives me a once-over through his monocle. "Mr. Cragg, I pay you five hundred dollars to find Mr. Roberts. You wish to continue working for me?"

"Why, certainly, Prince!" I tell him. "I was just trying to get a line on Mr. Roberts. . . . Ah, here're the girls."

They look like they'd chewed up the olive branch in the ladies' room. I get up and say to Betty: "Gosh, I just remembered we're supposed to be at Bill's party."

"I was about to remind you," Betty says smartly.

I say, "So long, Prince. Be seeing you in a day or two."

He grabs hold of Betty's hand and tries to kiss it. She jerks it away. "I just washed it," she tells him.

"But your telephone number? And your address? I like to send you the flowers."

"I've got hay fever," Betty says. "I can't stand flowers. And I haven't got a telephone. I never learned how to work one. So long, Prince."

"Good-by!" snaps Mitzi. "It was nice meeting you."

We exit.

Outside, Betty says, "Nice boy, that Prince. Some woman's husband is going to shoot him one of these days."

"You forget Mamie Kelly. She's got something on him."

"You going to snitch on him?"

"Not yet. Still a few things to settle with him."

"You get anything out of him?"

"Uh-huh, the reason he wants me to find this Roberts. He tried holding out one week and discovered Roberts has a checker on him. My hunch is the Prince prefers a hundred per cent to ten."

The Red Mill is only a couple of blocks from Betty's apartment hotel. I walk east on Lawrence Avenue with her. I turn her into Winthrop and we are almost to Ainslee before she's aware of it. Then she says, "You're taking me home? What a large evening!"

"Be a large one next time. Maybe tomorrow?"

"You'll probably take me to the Bulgarian or Siberian meeting."

I leave her outside her apartment hotel. She's sore when she goes inside. I can't help it. I'll see her in the morning. There's a couple of little things I still have to do and I have to get up early in the morning.

I go to a stationery store on Broadway that is still open and buy a large children's book, one with stiff covers. I have the clerk wrap it in the reddest paper he has in the store, some glossy Christmas wrapping paper.

Then I get an address label from him and a bunch of postage stamps.

It's a long ride downtown so I take the elevated. I get off at Quincy and walk over to the post office and mail the red package at the mailing window. Then I go to my cheap hotel on Jackson Street and go to bed.

 EVEN-THIRTY I get up and have breakfast at Thompson's—without the Death Notices, this time. After which I hoof over to the post office to see if my little trick works.

There are a couple of thousand lock boxes in the General Delivery room at the main Chicago post office. To watch them all during the rush hours would take eighteen pairs of eyes. That's why I mailed the book to Mr. Roberts. The postal clerk would put a card in his box, saying there was a package for him. He'd have to call at one of the windows for it.

So I fool around at a writing stand near the windows. I fill out eighteen or twenty post-office money orders for fancy amounts and tear them up or stick them in my pocket. I make one out every time someone comes from a box and goes to one of the windows to get a package.

It's nine forty-five when the red package is handed out. I'm almost caught sleeping, because I'd been expecting a man and this is a girl, a young girl probably just out of high school.

I'm right behind her when she goes out of the post office. She doesn't even suspect she's being followed. She walks north up Clark Street to Monroe, then turns east and goes into a building. I ride up in the same elevator with her to the tenth floor.

When she goes in a door I walk over and look at the inscription on it. It reads: "Harker Service Company."

I wait about five minutes, then go inside. The girl I'd followed from the post office is at a typewriter, but another, a big horsy-faced dame, is behind a desk just inside the door. Beside her, against the wall is a big cabinet with narrow pigeon-holes. There are letters in most of the pigeon-holes and another stack on the desk in front of the girl. The red package is there, too.

I say, "I understand you run a business mail service here."

"That's right," the girl replies. "We also take telephone calls, forward mail and provide you with a business address. No room number is necessary. The charge is only $2.00 per month."

"That's fine," I say. "Now, tell me, does a man named Brown get his mail here?"

She freezes up, right away. "Our service is absolutely confidential!"

"But I got a letter from Brown; he gave this address. I want to see him."

"In that case, you'd have to leave a message for him. Although," her face twists, "there's no Mr. Brown in our service."

"I must have got the address wrong then," I say.

I go out. There's a cigar stand in the lobby on the first floor, with a marble game next to it. I buy a package of cigarettes and shove a nickel in the slot of the marble game. There was a sticker on the glass: "For Amusement Only. No Prizes or Awards."

It's a bumper game; the steel marbles make electric contact with springs and light up lights and register a score. I waste three nickels, then get some change from the cigar stand. "You're playing that just for fun, you know," the cigar stand man warns me.

"Sure, I'm killing time, that's all."

I spend a dollar on the game, then loaf around for a half hour and spend another dollar. It's about eleven-thirty by then and the man at the cigar stand's getting nervous about me.

I buy a candy bar and get the change in nickels and shove them into the marble game. "That's costing you money," the fellow at the stand says.

"So's the dame I'm s'posed to meet here!" I snap at him.

He chuckles. "Boy, how you can take it. Two hours!"

I pump two of the steel marbles into the slot and slam them both out with the plunger. Lights go up, a bell rings.

"Jackpot!" the cigar stand man yelps.

"No prizes, huh?" I glare at him. There's a little knob in the front of the machine. I pushed it and a small door pops open, exposing a box almost filled with nickels. There are about five pounds of nickels. I stow them in my coat pocket while the cigar stand chap looks on, sick. He's still afraid that I'm a cop.

I quit then. It's just twelve when I go into the Gregorian Towers on North Michigan and ride up to Prince Peter's apartment.

He's just having his breakfast. He's wearing a purple dressing gown on which is embroidered a big red monogram.

"You have found him, Mr. Cragg?" he asks eagerly.

"Practically," I say. "But the expenses on this job are very heavy. If you could let me have another hundred. . . ."

He doesn't like that. "What do you mean, you have found him—practically?"

"Well, I got past the post office, anyway. A girl gets his mail at General Delivery and takes it to an address on Monroe Street."

"How do you know it is Mr. Roberts' mail?" he cuts in. "Hah! Four days I have waited at General Delivery and cannot spot this girl, his messenger."

"I can understand that. There're about five thousand boxes there. I knew I couldn't watch them all, so last night after I left you I bought a big flat book that I knew was too big to put into a post-office box. I had it wrapped in red paper and mailed it to Mr. Roberts. When the girl got this red package, I followed her."

"To what number on Monroe Street?"

"The Davis Building. Room 1023. It's a mail address outfit."

"Mail address? What is that?"

There was a loud knock on the prince's door. He says: "The waiter for these dishes. . . . Come in!"

The door opens and Mamie Kelly, all three hundred pounds of her, comes in. The prince jumps to his feet and turns about four shades whiter.

"Madame!" he exclaims.

She comes all the way into the room. She has something under her arm, a flat red package. The string's broken on the package and the paper disarranged. I can see the cover of a children's book.

I say: "Well, Prince, I must be going."

Mamie Kelly blocks the way to the door. She says, "Stick around, young fellow. Something I want to ask you."

"Yeah, sure," I say. "I'll run over to your store after a while. I've got to report at my office."

She shakes her big head. "No." She takes the book from under her arm and says, "Look, Pete!" and slams it over the prince's head. He goes down to the floor and stays there.

"Get up, you dirty rat!" Mamie Kelly yells.

The prince begins to whine. He sounds like a dog that has been whipped. Big Mamie reaches down and twists one of her meat hooks in the back of his purple dressing gown. She picks him up and tosses him into an easy chair. Man Mountain Dean couldn't have done it easier.

All of a sudden I think of something. Tony Druhar, the Serbian I'd found dead—with his face turned around to his spine. . . .

Maybe you think I don't feel funny. A three-hundred-pound woman, all muscle and bone. My skin gets hot and cold and begins to crawl. What the hell, a man—you could belt him in the jaw, butt him in the stomach or kick him where it'll do the most good. But a woman—can you do those things to a woman?

The prince is as big as me, if not bigger. Yet Mamie Kelly handles him as if he was a baby. She turns to me and says, "So you think you're smart, sending me this book?"

"Me?" I say.

"None of that, now! Della Harker's a cousin of mine. I never got a package before. When you came in there with your phoney stuff she got me on the telephone. I saw you from across the street fooling around with that damn pin game."

"Mamie!" yelps the Prince suddenly. "You—you are W. C. Roberts?"

"Of course I am. How the hell you suppose I got all the money to set you up in this swell hotel? You think I made it in that lousy store I run on Sedgwick for a blind?"

The prince is about ready to faint. I'm not far from it, myself. I'm concentrating on the door, wondering if I can get to it and out, before she can head me off.

Mamie Kelly says, "I give you all that dough, buy you the fancy clothes and what do you do in return? You spend the money on blond floozies, and try to muscle in on my racket. You think I don't know about Druhar?"

"Druhar?" the prince gasps.

"Yes, Druhar, the punk. He was starving, and I gave him a job at the store. He had to nose around, and then try to sell me out to you. Well, he got what he deserved."

"*You* killed him?"

"Like that!" she makes a motion with her two hands like wringing out a wet dishrag.

I take a deep breath and make a dash for the door.

I don't get to it. Mamie takes a quick step to one side and falls against me. She knocks me spinning and before I can get up, she swoops down on me and grabs my left arm. She twists it behind my back in a hammerlock.

I yell and heave up, trying to turn a forward somersault. A bunch of nickels fall on the floor. And then—

I yelled to high heaven. She breaks my arm. The big, fat murderess! The bones grate in my elbow and I yell bloody murder.

I guess that saves my life. After all, it's a hotel and she doesn't want a flock of cops busting in. She lets go of my arm to grab my neck. I have just enough strength left to roll away.

She comes after me again, her big face twisted in a snarl. I can't see her eyes at all, they're buried in the fat of her cheeks. I'm so scared of her that I go a little crazy. I kick a chair in her way and she knocks it aside with one punch of her fist.

I try for the door again. She heads me off. I back away and step on some of the nickels that've spilled from my pocket.

And then I know what to do. It's my only chance. Two minutes more in this room with the amazon—and I'd wind up like Tony Druhar. Only more broken bones.

My left arm is hanging limp at my side and I'm dizzy with the pain of it. But there's nothing wrong with my right arm. I rip open my coat with my right hand, shrug out of the right side of it and reach over to slide it down my left shoulder.

Mamie makes a noise like a female gorilla and starts for me. I jump back and find myself against the wall. But I've got the coat in my hand now, the coat with about five pounds of nickels in the pockets. A half-pound of them in the toe of a sock would have made a dandy black-jack.

She comes at me and I swing the coat with all that's left in me. The noise she makes when she hits the floor reminds me of the time I got drunk at a dance and fell into the bass drum.

Prince Pete thinks this is a good time to make his getaway, but I beat him to the door and swing the weighted coat in his face.

"Wait a minute, pal," I say to him. "You made a bargain with me—four hundred bucks more if I found W. C. Roberts for you. There's Roberts. Now kick in. I need the dough, on account of I figure on quitting my skip tracing job and maybe getting married!"

He pays. Then I pick up the telephone and call police headquarters.

Finger Man
Raymond Chandler

ARGUABLY THE GREATEST mystery writer of the twentieth century, Raymond Chandler (1888–1959) brought a literary sensibility to that least likely of places—pulp magazines. Pulps were very clearly and specifically designed to be fast, cheap, action-filled entertainment for the masses. No literary aspirations or pretensions were welcomed by the hard-working editors of even the best of them, notably *Black Mask* and *Dime Detective*. Still, Dashiell Hammett brought important realism to his pulp stories, and Chandler elevated the form even further.

Philip Marlowe, the hero of all seven of Chandler's novels, appears in this printing of "Finger Man," a novella filled with bad guys and corruption. When the story was first published in the October 1934 issue of *Black Mask*, the first-person narrator was unnamed. For its first book appearance, the anonymous shamus in "Finger Man" was given the Marlowe name, as Chandler had become the "hottest" mystery writer in America because of his Marlowe novels. The majority of Chandler's short fiction was collected in three paperback originals published by Avon in its "Murder Mystery Monthly" series, *5 Murderers* (1944), *Five Sinister Characters* (1945), and *Finger Man* (1946), and his detectives, whether named Carmody, Dalmas, Malvern, Mallory, or unnamed, were transformed into Marlowe. As the detectives evolved from the earliest experiments to the more complex and nuanced hero he envisioned and later compared to a modern-day knight, the adventures became classics of the American crime story.

Finger Man
Raymond Chandler

*Putting the finger on a murder
victim is rarely a safe bet*

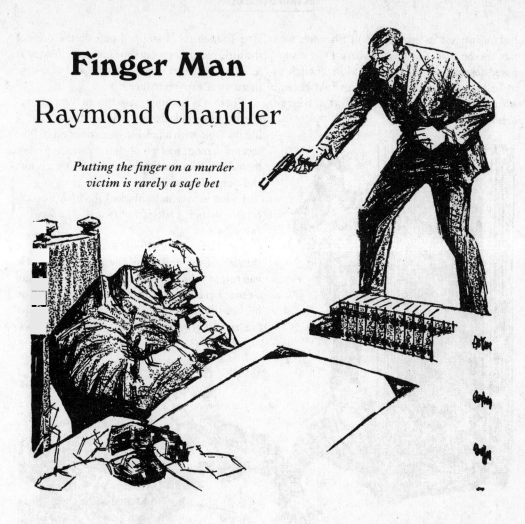

ONE

I GOT AWAY from the Grand Jury a little after four, and then sneaked up the back-stairs to Fenweather's office. Fenweather, the D.A., was a man with severe, chiseled features and the gray temples women love. He played with a pen on his desk and said: "I think they believed you. They might even indict Manny Tinnen for the Shannon kill this afternoon. If they do, then is the time you begin to watch your step."

I rolled a cigarette around in my fingers and finally put it in my mouth. "Don't put any men on me, Mr. Fenweather. I know the alleys in this town pretty well, and your men couldn't stay close enough to do me any good."

He looked towards one of the windows. "How well do you know Frank Dorr?" he asked, with his eyes away from me.

"I know he's a big politico, a fixer you have to see if you want to open a gambling hell or a bawdy house—or if you want to sell honest merchandise to the city."

"Right." Fenweather spoke sharply, and brought his head around towards me. Then he lowered his voice. "Having the goods on Tinnen was a surprise to a lot of people. If Frank Dorr had an interest in getting rid of Shannon who was the head of the Board where Dorr's supposed to get his contracts, it's close enough to make him take chances. And I'm told he and Manny Tinnen had dealings. I'd sort of keep an eye on him, if I were you."

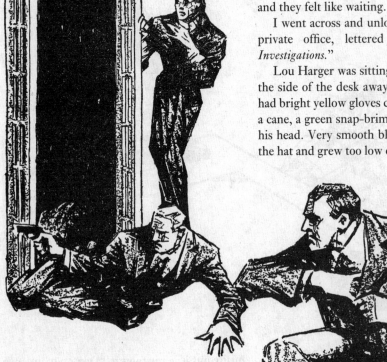

I grinned. "I'm just one guy," I said. "Frank Dorr covers a lot of territory. But I'll do what I can."

Fenweather stood up and held his hand across the desk. He said: "I'll be out of town for a couple of days, I'm leaving tonight, if this indictment comes through. Be careful—and if anything should happen to go wrong, see Bernie Ohls, my chief investigator."

I said: "Sure."

We shook hands and I went out past a tired-looking girl who gave me a tired smile and wound one of her lax curls up on the back of her neck as she looked at me. I got back to my office soon

after four-thirty. I stopped outside the door of the little reception room for a moment, looking at it. Then I opened it and went in, and of course there wasn't anybody there.

There was nothing there but an old red davenport, two odd chairs, a bit of carpet, and a library table with a few old magazines on it. The reception room was left open for visitors to come in and sit down and wait—if I had any visitors and they felt like waiting.

I went across and unlocked the door into my private office, lettered "*Philip Marlowe . . . Investigations.*"

Lou Harger was sitting on a wooden chair on the side of the desk away from the window. He had bright yellow gloves clamped on the crook of a cane, a green snap-brim hat set too far back on his head. Very smooth black hair showed under the hat and grew too low on the nape of his neck.

"Hello. I've been waiting," he said, and smiled languidly.

" 'Lo, Lou. How did you get in here?"

"The door must have been unlocked. Or maybe I had a key that fitted. Do you mind?"

I went around the desk and sat down in the

swivel chair. I put my hat down on the desk, picked up a bulldog pipe out of an ash tray and began to fill it up.

"It's all right as long as it's you," I said. "I just thought I had a better lock."

He smiled with his full red lips. He was a very good-looking boy. He said: "Are you still doing business, or will you spend the next month in a hotel room drinking liquor with a couple of Headquarters boys?"

"I'm still doing business—if there's any business for me to do."

I lit a pipe, leaned back and stared at his clear olive skin, straight, dark eyebrows.

He put his cane on top of the desk and clasped his yellow gloves on the glass. He moved his lips in and out.

"I have a little something for you. Not a hell of a lot. But there's carfare in it."

I waited.

"I'm making a little play at Las Olindas tonight," he said. "At Canales' place."

"The white smoke?"

"Uh-huh. I think I'm going to be lucky—and I'd like to have a guy with a rod."

I took a fresh pack of cigarettes out of a top drawer and slid them across the desk. Lou picked them up and began to break the pack open.

I said: "What kind of play?"

He got a cigarette halfway out and stared down at it. There was a little something in his manner I didn't like.

"I've been closed up for a month now. I wasn't makin' the kind of money it takes to stay open in this town. The Headquarters boys have been putting the pressure on since repeal. They have bad dreams when they see themselves trying to live on their pay."

I said: "It doesn't cost any more to operate here than anywhere else. And here you pay it all to one organization. That's something."

Lou Harger jabbed the cigarette in his mouth. "Yeah—Frank Dorr," he snarled. "That fat, bloodsuckin' sonofabitch!"

I didn't say anything. I was way past the age when it's fun to swear at people you can't hurt. I watched Lou light his cigarette with my desk lighter. He went on, through a puff of smoke: "It's a laugh, in a way. Canales bought a new wheel—from some grafters in the sheriff's office. I know Pina, Canales' head croupier, pretty well. The wheel is one they took away from me. It's got bugs—and I know the bugs."

"And Canales don't . . . That sounds just like Canales," I said.

Lou didn't look at me. "He gets a nice crowd down there," he said. "He has a small dance floor and a five-piece Mexican band to help the customers relax. They dance a bit and then go back for another trimming, instead of going away disgusted."

I said: "What do *you* do?"

"I guess you might call it a system," he said softly, and looked at me under his long lashes.

I looked away from him, looked around the room. It had a rust-red carpet, five green filing cases in a row under an advertising calendar, an old costumer in the corner, a few walnut chairs, net curtains over the windows. The fringe of the curtains was dirty from blowing about in the draft. There was a bar of late sunlight across my desk and it showed up the dust.

"I get it like this," I said. "You think you have that roulette wheel tamed and you expect to win enough money so that Canales will be mad at you. You'd like to have some protection along—me. I think it's screwy."

"It's not screwy at all," Lou said. "Any roulette wheel has a tendency to work in a certain rhythm. If you know the wheel very well indeed—"

I smiled and shrugged. "Okey, I wouldn't know about that. I don't know enough roulette. It sounds to me like you're being a sucker for your own racket, but I could be wrong. And that's not the point anyway."

"What is?" Lou asked thinly.

"I'm not much stuck on bodyguarding—but maybe that's not the point either. I take it I'm supposed to think this play is on the level. Suppose I don't, and walk out on you, and you get in a box? Or suppose I think everything is aces, but Canales don't agree with me and gets nasty."

"That's why I need a guy with a rod," Lou said, without moving a muscle except to speak.

I said evenly: "If I'm tough enough for the job—and I didn't know I was—that still isn't what worries me."

"Forget it," Lou said. "It breaks me up enough to know you're worried."

I smiled a little more and watched his yellow gloves moving around on top of the desk, moving too much. I said slowly: "You're the last guy in the world to be getting expense money that way just now. I'm the last guy to be standing behind you while you do it. That's all."

Lou said: "Yeah." He knocked some ash off his cigarette down on the glass top, bent his head to blow it off. He went on, as if it was a new subject: "Miss Glenn is going with me. She's a tall redhead, a swell looker. She used to model. She's nice to people in any kind of a spot and she'll keep Canales from breathing on my neck. So we'll make out. I just thought I'd tell you."

I was silent for a minute, then I said: "You know damn well I just got through telling the Grand Jury it was Manny Tinnen I saw lean out of that car and cut the ropes on Art Shannon's wrists after they pushed him on the roadway, filled with lead."

Lou smiled faintly at me. "That'll make it easier for the grafters on the big time; the fellows who take the contracts and don't appear in the business. They say Shannon was square and kept the Board in line. It was a nasty bump-off."

I shook my head. I didn't want to talk about that. I said: "Canales has a noseful of junk a lot of the time. And maybe he doesn't go for redheads."

Lou stood up slowly and lifted his cane off the desk. He stared at the tip of one yellow finger. He had an almost sleepy expression. Then he moved towards the door, swinging his cane.

"Well, I'll be seein' you some time," he drawled.

I let him get his hand on the knob before I said: "Don't go away sore, Lou. I'll drop down to Las Olindas, if you have to have me. But I don't want any money for it, and for Pete's sake don't pay any more attention to me than you have to."

He licked his lips softly and didn't quite look at me. "Thanks, keed. I'll be careful as hell."

He went out then and his yellow glove disappeared around the edge of the door.

I sat still for about five minutes and then my pipe got too hot. I put it down, looked at my strap watch, and got up to switch on a small radio in the corner beyond the end of the desk. When the A.C. hum died down the last tinkle of a chime came out of the horn, then a voice was saying: "KLI now brings you its regular early evening broadcast of local news releases. An event of importance this afternoon was the indictment returned late today against Maynard J. Tinnen by the Grand Jury. Tinnen is a well-known City Hall lobbyist and man about town. The indictment, a shock to his many friends, was based almost entirely on the testimony—"

My telephone rang sharply and a girl's cool voice said in my ear: "One moment, please. Mr. Fenweather is calling you."

He came on at once. "Indictment returned. Take care of the boy."

I said I was just getting it over the radio. We talked a short moment and then he hung up, after saying he had to leave at once to catch a plane.

I leaned back in my chair again and listened to the radio without exactly hearing it. I was thinking what a damn fool Lou Harger was and that there wasn't anything I could do to change that.

TWO

It was a good crowd for a Tuesday but nobody was dancing. Around ten o'clock the little five-piece band got tired of messing around with a rhumba that nobody was paying any attention to. The marimba player dropped his sticks and reached under his chair for a glass. The rest of the boys lit cigarettes and sat there looking bored.

I leaned sidewise against the bar, which was on the same side of the room as the orchestra stand. I was turning a small glass of tequila around on the top of the bar. All the business was at the center one of the three roulette tables.

The bartender leaned beside me, on his side of the bar.

"The flame-top gal must be pickin' them," he said.

I nodded without looking at him. "She's playing with fistfuls now," I said. "Not even counting it."

The red-haired girl was tall. I could see the burnished copper of her hair between the heads of the people behind her. I could see Lou Harger's sleek head beside hers. Everybody seemed to be playing standing up.

"You don't play?" the bartender asked me.

"Not on Tuesdays. I had some trouble on a Tuesday once."

"Yeah? Do you like that stuff straight, or could I smooth it out for you?"

"Smooth it out with what?" I said. "You got a wood rasp handy?"

He grinned. I drank a little more of the tequila and made a face.

"Did anybody invent this stuff on purpose?"

"I wouldn't know, mister."

"What's the limit over there?"

"I wouldn't know that either. How the boss feels, I guess."

The roulette tables were in a row near the far wall. A low railing of gilt metal joined their ends and the players were outside the railing.

Some kind of a confused wrangle started at the center table. Half a dozen people at the two end tables grabbed their chips up and moved across.

Then a clear, very polite voice, with a slightly foreign accent, spoke out: "If you will just be patient, madame . . . Mr. Canales will be here in a minute."

I went across, squeezed near the railing. Two croupiers stood near me with their heads together and their eyes looking sideways. One moved a rake slowly back and forth beside the idle wheel. They were staring at the red-haired girl.

She wore a high-cut black evening gown. She had fine white shoulders, was something less than beautiful and more than pretty. She was leaning on the edge of the table, in front of the wheel. Her long eyelashes were twitching.

There was a big pile of money and chips in front of her.

She spoke monotonously, as if she had said the same thing several times already.

"Get busy and spin that wheel! You take it away fast enough, but you don't like to dish it out."

The croupier in charge smiled a cold, even smile. He was tall, dark, disinterested: "The table can't cover your bet," he said with calm precision. "Mr. Canales, perhaps—" He shrugged neat shoulders.

The girl said: "It's your money, highpockets. Don't you want it back?"

Lou Harger licked his lips beside her, put a hand on her arm, stared at the pile of money with hot eyes. He said gently: "Wait for Canales. . . ."

"To hell with Canales! I'm hot—and I want to stay that way."

A door opened at the end of the tables and a very slight, very pale man came into the room. He had straight, lusterless black hair, a high bony forehead, flat, impenetrable eyes. He had a thin mustache that was trimmed in two sharp lines almost at right angles to each other. They came down below the corners of his mouth a full inch. The effect was Oriental. His skin had a thick, glistening pallor.

He slid behind the croupiers, stopped at a corner of the center table, glanced at the red-haired girl and touched the ends of his mustache with two fingers, the nails of which had a purplish tint.

He smiled suddenly, and the instant after it was as though he had never smiled in his life. He spoke in a dull, ironic voice.

"Good evening, Miss Glenn. You must let me send somebody with you when you go home. I'd hate to see any of that money get in the wrong pockets."

The red-haired girl looked at him, not very pleasantly.

"I'm not leaving—unless you're throwing me out."

Canales said: "No? What would you like to do?"

"Bet the wad—dark meat!"

The crowd noise became a deathly silence. There wasn't a whisper of any kind of sound. Harger's face slowly got ivory-white.

Canales' face was without expression. He lifted a hand, delicately, gravely, slipped a large wallet from his dinner jacket and tossed it in front of the tall croupier.

"Ten grand," he said in a voice that was a dull rustle of sound. "That's my limit—always."

The tall croupier picked the wallet up, spread it, drew out two flat packets of crisp bills, riffled them, refolded the wallet and passed it along the edge of the table to Canales.

Canales did not take it. Nobody moved, except the croupier.

The girl said: "Put it on the red."

The croupier leaned across the table and very carefully stacked her money and chips. He placed her bet for her on the red diamond. He placed his hand along the curve of the wheel.

"If no one objects," Canales said, without looking at anyone, "this is just the two of us."

Heads moved. Nobody spoke. The croupier spun the wheel and sent the ball skimming in the groove with a light flirt of his left wrist. Then he drew his hands back and placed them in full view on the edge of the table, on top of it.

The red-haired girl's eyes shone and her lips slowly parted.

The ball drifted along the groove, dipped past one of the bright metal diamonds, slid down the flank of the wheel and chattered along the tines beside the numbers. Movement went out of it suddenly, with a dry click. It fell next the double-zero, in red twenty-seven. The wheel was motionless.

The croupier took up his rake and slowly pushed the two packets of bills across, added them to the stake, pushed the whole thing off the field of play.

Canales put his wallet back in his breast pocket, turned and walked slowly back to the door, went through it.

I took my cramped fingers off the top of the railing, and a lot of people broke for the bar.

THREE

When Lou came up I was sitting at a little tile-top table in a corner, fooling with some more of the tequila. The little orchestra was playing a thin, brittle tango and one couple was maneuvering self-consciously on the dance floor.

Lou had a cream-colored overcoat on, with the collar turned up around a lot of white silk scarf. He had a fine-drawn glistening expression. He had white pigskin gloves this time and he put one of them down on the table and leaned at me.

"Over twenty-two thousand," he said softly. "Boy, what a take!"

I said: "Very nice money, Lou. What kind of car are you driving?"

"See anything wrong with it?"

"The play?" I shrugged, fiddled with my glass. "I'm not wised up on roulette, Lou . . . I saw plenty wrong with your broad's manners."

"She's not a broad," Lou said. His voice got a little worried.

"Okey. She made Canales look like a million. What kind of car?"

"Buick sedan. Nile green, with two spotlights and those little fender lights on rods." His voice was still worried.

I said: "Take it kind of slow through town. Give me a chance to get in the parade."

He moved his glove and went away. The red-haired girl was not in sight anywhere. I looked down at the watch on my wrist. When I looked up again Canales was standing across the table. His eyes looked at me lifelessly above his trick mustache.

"You don't like my place," he said.

"On the contrary."

"You don't come here to play." He was telling me, not asking me.

"Is it compulsory?" I asked dryly.

A very faint smile drifted across his face. He leaned a little down and said: "I think you are a dick. A smart dick."

"Just a shamus," I said. "And not so smart. Don't let my long upper lip fool you. It runs in the family."

Canales wrapped his fingers around the top of a chair, squeezed on it. "Don't come here again—for anything." He spoke very softly, almost dreamily. "I don't like pigeons."

I took the cigarette out of my mouth and looked it over before I looked at him. I said: "I heard you insulted a while back. You took it nicely . . . So we won't count this one."

He had a queer expression for a moment. Then he turned and slid away with a little sway of the shoulders. He put his feet down flat and turned them out a good deal as he walked. His walk, like his face, was a little negroid.

I got up and went out through the big white double doors into a dim lobby, got my hat and coat and put them on. I went out through another pair of double doors onto a wide veranda with scrollwork along the edge of its roof. There was sea fog in the air and the wind-blown Monterey cypresses in front of the house dripped with it. The grounds sloped gently into the dark for a long distance. Fog hid the ocean.

I had parked the car out on the street, on the other side of the house. I drew my hat down and walked soundlessly on the damp moss that covered the driveway, rounded a corner of the porch, and stopped rigidly.

A man just in front of me was holding a gun—but he didn't see me. He was holding the gun down at his side, pressed against the material of his overcoat, and his big hand made it look quite small. The dim light that reflected from the barrel seemed to come out of the fog, to be part of the fog. He was a big man, and he stood very still, poised on the balls of his feet.

I lifted my right hand very slowly and opened the top two buttons of my coat, reached inside and drew out a long .38 with a six-inch barrel. I eased it into my overcoat pocket.

The man in front of me moved, reached his left hand up to his face. He drew on a cigarette cupped inside his hand and the glow put brief light on a heavy chin, wide, dark nostrils, and a square, aggressive nose, the nose of a fighting man.

Then he dropped the cigarette and stepped on it and a quick, light step made faint noise behind me. I was far too late turning.

Something swished and I went out like a light.

FOUR

When I came to I was cold and wet and had a headache a yard wide. There was a soft bruise behind my right ear that wasn't bleeding. I had been put down with a sap.

I got up off my back and saw that I was a few yards from the driveway, between two trees that were wet with fog. There was some mud on the backs of my shoes. I had been dragged off the path, but not very far.

I went through my pockets. My gun was gone, of course, but that was all—that and the idea that this excursion was all fun.

I nosed around through the fog, didn't find anything or see anyone, gave up bothering about that, and went along the blank side of the house to a curving line of palm trees and an old type arc light that hissed and flickered over the entrance to a sort of lane where I had stuck the 1925 Marmon touring car I still used for transportation. I got into it after wiping the seat off with a towel, teased the motor alive, and choked

it along to a big empty street with disused car tracks in the middle.

I went from there to De Cazens Boulevard, which was the main drag of Las Olindas and was called after the man who built Canales' place long ago. After a while there was town, buildings, dead-looking stores, a service station with a night-bell, and at last a drugstore which was still open.

A dolled-up sedan was parked in front of the drugstore and I parked behind that, got out, and saw that a hatless man was sitting at the counter, talking to a clerk in a blue smock. They seemed to have the world to themselves. I started to go in, then I stopped and took another look at the dolled-up sedan.

It was a Buick and of a color that could have been Nile-green in daylight. It had two spotlights and two little egg-shaped amber lights stuck up on thin nickel rods clamped to the front fenders. The window by the driver's seat was down. I went back to the Marmon and got a flash, reached in and twisted the license holder of the Buick around, put the light on it quickly, then off again.

It was registered to Louis N. Harger.

I got rid of the flash and went into the drugstore. There was a liquor display at one side, and the clerk in the blue smock sold me a pint of Canadian Club, which I took over to the counter and opened. There were ten seats at the counter, but I sat down on the one next to the hatless man. He began to look me over, in the mirror, very carefully.

I got a cup of black coffee two-thirds full and added plenty of the rye. I drank it down and waited for a minute, to let it warm me up. Then I looked the hatless man over.

He was about twenty-eight, a little thin on top, had a healthy red face, fairly honest eyes, dirty hands and looked as if he wasn't making much money. He wore a gray whipcord jacket with metal buttons on it, pants that didn't match.

I said carelessly, in a low voice: "Your bus outside?"

He sat very still. His mouth got small and tight and he had trouble pulling his eyes away from mine, in the mirror.

"My brother's," he said, after a moment.

I said: "Care for a drink? . . . Your brother is an old friend of mine."

He nodded slowly, gulped, moved his hand slowly, but finally got the bottle and curdled his coffee with it. He drank the whole thing down. Then I watched him dig up a crumpled pack of cigarettes, spear his mouth with one, strike a match on the counter, after missing twice on his thumbnail, and inhale with a lot of very poor nonchalance that he knew wasn't going over.

I leaned close to him and said evenly: "This doesn't *have* to be trouble."

He said: "Yeah . . . Wh-what's the beef?"

The clerk sidled towards us. I asked for more coffee. When I got it I stared at the clerk until he went and stood in front of the display window with his back to me. I laced my second cup of coffee and drank some of it. I looked at the clerk's back and said: "The guy the car belongs to doesn't have a brother."

He held himself tightly, but turned towards me. "You think it's a hot car?"

"No."

"You don't think it's a hot car?"

I said: "No. I just want the story."

"You a dick?"

"Uh-huh—but it isn't a shakedown, if that's what worries you."

He drew hard on his cigarette and moved his spoon around in his empty cup.

"I can lose my job over this," he said slowly. "But I needed a hundred bucks. I'm a hack driver."

"I guessed that," I said.

He looked surprised, turned his head and stared at me. "Have another drink and let's get on with it," I said. "Car thieves don't park them on the main drag and then sit around in drugstores."

The clerk came back from the window and hovered near us, busying himself with rubbing a rag on the coffee urn. A heavy silence fell. The clerk put the rag down, went along to the back of the store, behind the partition, and began to whistle aggressively.

The man beside me took some more of the whiskey and drank it, nodding his head wisely at me. "Listen—I brought a fare out and was supposed to wait for him. A guy and a jane come up alongside me in the Buick and the guy offers me a hundred bucks to let him wear my cap and drive my hack into town. I'm to hang around here an hour, then take his heap to the Hotel Carillon on Towne Boulevard. My cab will be there for me. He gives me the hundred bucks."

"What was his story?" I asked.

"He said they'd been to a gambling joint and had some luck for a change. They're afraid of holdups on the way in. They figure there's always spotters watchin' the play."

I took one of his cigarettes and straightened it out in my fingers. "It's a story I can't hurt much," I said. "Could I see your cards?"

He gave them to me. His name was Tom Sneyd and he was a driver for the Green Top Cab Company. I corked my pint, slipped it into my side pocket, and danced a half-dollar on the counter.

The clerk came along and made change. He was almost shaking with curiosity.

"Come on, Tom," I said in front of him. "Let's go get that cab. I don't think you should wait around here any longer."

We went out, and I let the Buick lead me away from the straggling lights of Las Olindas, through a series of small beach towns with little houses built on sandlots close to the ocean, and bigger ones built on the slopes of the hills behind. A window was lit here and there. The tires sang on the moist concrete and the little amber lights on the Buick's fenders peeped back at me from the curves.

At West Cimarron we turned inland, chugged on through Canal City, and met the San Angelo Cut. It took us almost an hour to get to 5640 Towne Boulevard, which is the number of the Hotel Carillon. It is a big, rambling slate-roofed building with a basement garage and a forecourt fountain on which they play a pale green light in the evening.

Green Top Cab No. 469 was parked across the street, on the dark side. I couldn't see where anybody had been shooting into it. Tom Sneyd found his cap in the driver's compartment, climbed eagerly under the wheel.

"Does that fix me up? Can I go now?" His voice was strident with relief.

I told him it was all right with me, and gave him my card. It was twelve minutes past one as he took the corner. I climbed into the Buick and tooled it down the ramp to the garage and left it with a colored boy who was dusting cars in slow motion. I went around to the lobby.

The clerk was an ascetic-looking young man who was reading a volume of *California Appellate Decisions* under the switchboard light. He said Lou was not in and had not been in since eleven, when he came on duty. After a short argument about the lateness of the hour and the importance of my visit, he rang Lou's apartment, but there wasn't any answer.

I went out and sat in my Marmon for a few minutes, smoked a cigarette, imbibed a little from my pint of Canadian Club. Then I went back into the Carillon and shut myself in a pay booth. I dialed the *Telegram*, asked for the City Desk, got a man named Von Ballin.

He yelped at me when I told him who I was. "You still walking around? That ought to be a story. I thought Manny Tinnen's friends would have had you laid away in old lavender by this time."

I said: "Can that and listen to this. Do you know a man named Lou Harger? He's a gambler. Had a place that was raided and closed up a month ago."

Von Ballin said he didn't know Lou personally, but he knew who he was.

"Who around your rag would know him real well?"

He thought a moment. "There's a lad named Jerry Cross here," he said, "that's supposed to be an expert on night life. What did you want to know?"

"Where would he go to celebrate," I said. Then I told him some of the story, not too much. I left out the part where I got sapped and the part about the taxi. "He hasn't shown at his hotel," I ended. "I ought to get a line on him."

"Well, if you're a friend of his—"

"Of his—not of his crowd," I said sharply.

Von Ballin stopped to yell at somebody to take a call, then said to me softly, close to the phone: "Come through, boy. Come through."

"All right. But I'm talking to you, not to your sheet. I got sapped and lost my gun outside Canales' joint. Lou and his girl switched his car for a taxi they picked up. Then they dropped out of sight. I don't like it too well. Lou wasn't drunk enough to chase around town with that much dough in his pockets. And if he was, the girl wouldn't let him. She had the practical eye."

"I'll see what I can do," Von Ballin said. "But it don't sound promising. I'll give you a buzz."

I told him I lived at the Merritt Plaza, in case he had forgotten, went out and got into the Marmon again. I drove home and put hot towels on my head for fifteen minutes, then sat around in my pajamas and drank hot whiskey and lemon and called the Carillon every once in a while. At two-thirty Von Ballin called me and said no luck. Lou hadn't been pinched, he wasn't in any of the Receiving Hospitals, and he hadn't shown at any of the clubs Jerry Cross could think of.

At three I called the Carillon for the last time. Then I put my light out and went to sleep.

In the morning it was the same way. I tried to trace the red-haired girl a little. There were twenty-eight people named Glenn in the phone book, and three women among them. One didn't answer, the other two assured me they didn't have red hair. One offered to show me.

I shaved, showered, had breakfast, walked three blocks down the hill to the Condor Building.

Miss Glenn was sitting in my little reception room.

FIVE

I unlocked the other door and she went in and sat in the chair where Lou had sat the afternoon before. I opened some windows, locked the outer door of the reception room, and struck a match for the unlighted cigarette she held in her ungloved and ringless left hand.

She was dressed in a blouse and plaid skirt with a loose coat over them, and a close-fitting hat that was far enough out of style to suggest a run of bad luck. But it hid almost all of her hair. Her skin was without make-up and she looked about thirty and had the set face of exhaustion.

She held her cigarette with a hand that was almost too steady, a hand on guard. I sat down and waited for her to talk.

She stared at the wall over my head and didn't say anything. After a little while I packed my pipe and smoked for a minute. Then I got up and went across to the door that opened into the hallway and picked up a couple of letters that had been pushed through the slot.

I sat down at the desk again, looked them over, read one of them twice, as if I had been alone. While I was doing this I didn't look at her directly or speak to her, but I kept an eye on her all the same. She looked like a lady who was getting nerved for something.

Finally she moved. She opened up a big black patent-leather bag and took out a fat manila envelope, pulled a rubber band off it and sat holding the envelope between the palms of her hands, with her head tilted way back and the cigarette dribbling gray smoke from the corners of her mouth.

She said slowly: "Lou said if I ever got caught in the rain, you were the boy to see. It's raining hard where I am."

I stared at the manila envelope. "Lou is a pretty good friend of mine," I said. "I'd do anything in reason for him. Some things not in reason—like last night. That doesn't mean Lou and I always play the same games."

She dropped her cigarette into the glass bowl of the ash tray and left it to smoke. A dark flame burned suddenly in her eyes, then went out.

"Lou is dead." Her voice was quite toneless.

I reached over with a pencil and stabbed at the hot end of the cigarette until it stopped smoking.

She went on: "A couple of Canales' boys got him in my apartment—with one shot from a small gun that looked like my gun. Mine was gone when I looked for it afterwards. I spent the night there with him dead . . . I had to."

She broke quite suddenly. Her eyes turned up in her head and her head came down and hit the desk. She lay still, with the manila envelope in front of her lax hands.

I jerked a drawer open and brought up a bottle and a glass, poured a stiff one and stepped around it, heaved her up in her chair. I pushed the edge of the glass hard against her mouth— hard enough to hurt. She struggled and swallowed. Some of it ran down her chin, but life came back into her eyes.

I left the whiskey in front of her and sat down again. The flap of the envelope had come open enough for me to see currency inside, bales of currency.

She began to talk to me in a dreamy sort of voice.

"We got all big bills from the cashier, but makes quite a package at that. There's twenty-two thousand even in the envelope. I kept out a few odd hundreds.

"Lou was worried. He figured it would be pretty easy for Canales to catch up with us. You might be right behind and not be able to do very much about it."

I said: "Canales lost the money in full view of everybody there. It was good advertising—even if it hurt."

She went on exactly as though I had not spoken. "Going through the town we spotted a cab driver sitting in his parked cab and Lou had a brain wave. He offered the boy a C note to let him drive the cab into San Angelo and bring the Buick to the hotel after a while. The boy took us up and we went over on another street and made the switch. We were sorry about ditching you, but Lou said you wouldn't mind. And we might get a chance to flag you.

"Lou didn't go into his hotel. We took another cab over to my place. I live at the Hobart Arms, eight hundred block on South Minter. It's a place

where you don't have to answer questions at the desk. We went up to my apartment and put the lights on and two guys with masks came around the half-wall between the living room and the dinette. One was small and thin and the other one was a big slob with a chin that stuck out under his mask like a shelf. Lou made a wrong motion and the big one shot him just the once. The gun just made a flat crack, not very loud, and Lou fell down on the floor and never moved."

I said: "It might be the ones that made a sucker out of me. I haven't told you about that yet."

She didn't seem to hear that either. Her face was white and composed, but as expressionless as plaster. "Maybe I'd better have another finger of the hooch," she said.

I poured us a couple of drinks, and we drank them. She went on: "They went through us, but we didn't have the money. We had stopped at an all-night drugstore and had it weighed and mailed it at a branch post office. They went through the apartment, but of course we had just come in and hadn't had time to hide anything. The big one slammed me down with his fist, and when I woke up again they were gone and I was alone with Lou dead on the floor."

She pointed to a mark on the angle of her jaw. There was something there, but it didn't show much. I moved around in my chair a little and said: "They passed you on the way in. Smart boys would have looked a taxi over on that road. How did they know where to go?"

"I thought that out during the night," Miss Glenn said. "Canales knows where I live. He followed me home once and tried to get me to ask him up."

"Yeah," I said, "but why did they go to your place and how did they get in?"

"That's not hard. There's a ledge just below the windows and a man could edge along it to the fire escape. They probably had other boys covering Lou's hotel. We thought of that chance but we didn't think about my place being known to them."

"Tell me the rest of it," I said.

"The money was mailed to me," Miss Glenn

explained. "Lou was a swell boy, but a girl has to protect herself. That's why I had to stay there last night with Lou dead on the floor. Until the mail came. Then I came over here."

I got up and looked out of the window. A fat girl was pounding a typewriter across the court. I could hear the clack of it. I sat down, stared at my thumb.

"Did they plant the gun?" I asked.

"Not unless it's under him. I didn't look there."

"They let you off too easy. Maybe it wasn't Canales at all. Did Lou open his heart to you much?"

She shook her head quietly. Her eyes were slate-blue now, and thoughtful, without the blank stare.

"All right," I said. "Just what did you think of having me do about it all?"

She narrowed her eyes a little, then put a hand out and pushed the bulging envelope slowly across the desk.

"I'm no baby and I'm in a jam. But I'm not going to the cleaners just the same. Half of this money is mine, and I want it with a clean get-away. One-half net. If I'd called the law last night, there'd have been a way to chisel me out of it . . . I think Lou would like you to have his half, if you want to play with me."

I said: "It's big money to flash at a private dick, Miss Glenn," and smiled wearily. "You're a little worse off for not calling cops last night. But there's an answer to anything they might say. I think I'd better go over there and see what's broken, if anything."

She leaned forward quickly and said: "Will you take care of the money? . . . Dare you?"

"Sure. I'll pop downstairs and put it in a safe-deposit box. You can hold one of the keys—and we'll talk split later on. I think it would be a swell idea if Canales knew he had to see me, and still sweller if you hid out in a little hotel where I have a friend—at least until I nose around a bit."

She nodded. I put my hat on and put the envelope inside my belt. I went out, telling her there was a gun in the top left-hand drawer, if she felt nervous.

When I got back she didn't seem to have moved. But she said she had phoned Canales' place and left a message for him she thought he would understand.

We went by rather devious ways to the Lorraine, at Brant and Avenue C. Nobody shot at us going over, and as far as I could see we were not trailed.

I shook hands with Jim Dolan, the day clerk at the Lorraine, with a twenty folded in my hand. He put his hand in his pocket and said he would be glad to see that "Miss Thompson" was not bothered.

I left. There was nothing in the noon paper about Lou Harger of the Hobart Arms.

SIX

The Hobart Arms was just another apartment house, in a block lined with them. It was six stories high and had a buff front. A lot of cars were parked at both curbs all along the block. I drove through slowly and looked things over. The neighborhood didn't have the look of having been excited about anything in the immediate past. It was peaceful and sunny, and the parked cars had a settled look, as if they were right at home.

I circled into an alley with a high board fence on each side and a lot of flimsy garages cutting it. I parked beside one that had a For Rent sign and went between two garbage cans into the concrete yard of the Hobart Arms, along the side to the street. A man was putting golf clubs into the back of a coupe. In the lobby a Filipino was dragging a vacuum cleaner over the rug and a dark Jewess was writing at the switchboard.

I used the automatic elevator and prowled along an upper corridor to the last door on the left. I knocked, waited, knocked again, went in with Miss Glenn's key.

Nobody was dead on the floor.

I looked at myself in the mirror that was the back of a pull-down bed, went across and looked out of a window. There was a ledge below that had once been a coping. It ran along to the fire escape. A blind man could have walked in. I didn't notice anything like footmarks in the dust on it.

There was nothing in the dinette or kitchen except what belonged there. The bedroom had a cheerful carpet and painted gray walls. There was a lot of junk in the corner, around a waste-basket, and a broken comb on the dresser held a few strands of red hair. The closets were empty except for some gin bottles.

I went back to the living room, looked behind the wall bed, stood around for a minute, left the apartment.

The Filipino in the lobby had made about three yards with the vacuum cleaner. I leaned on the counter beside the switchboard.

"Miss Glenn?"

The dark Jewess said: "Five-two-four," and made a check mark on the laundry list.

"She's not in. Has she been in lately?"

She glanced up at me. "I haven't noticed. What is it—a bill?"

I said I was just a friend, thanked her and went away. That established the fact that there had been no excitement in Miss Glenn's apartment. I went back to the alley and the Marmon.

I hadn't believed it quite the way Miss Glenn told it anyhow.

I crossed Cordova, drove a block and stopped beside a forgotten drugstore that slept behind two giant pepper trees and a dusty, cluttered window. It had a single pay booth in the corner. An old man shuffled towards me wistfully, then went away when he saw what I wanted, lowered a pair of steel spectacles on the end of his nose and sat down again with his newspaper.

I dropped my nickel, dialed, and a girl's voice said: "Telegrayam!" with a tinny drawl. I asked for Von Ballin.

When I got him and he knew who it was, I could hear him clearing his throat. Then his voice came close to the phone and said very distinctly: "I've got something for you, but it's bad. I'm sorry as all hell. Your friend Harger is in the morgue. We got a flash about ten minutes ago."

I leaned against the wall of the booth and felt my eyes getting haggard. I said: "What else did you get?"

"Couple of radio cops picked him up in somebody's front yard or something, in West Cimarron. He was shot through the heart. It happened last night, but for some reason they only just put out the identification."

I said: "West Cimarron, huh? . . . Well, that takes care of that. I'll be in to see you."

I thanked him and hung up, stood for a moment looking out through the glass at a middle-aged gray-haired man who had come into the store and was pawing over the magazine rack.

Then I dropped another nickel and dialed the Lorraine, asked for the clerk.

I said: "Get your girl to put me on to the red-head, will you, Jim?"

I got a cigarette out and lit it, puffed smoke at the glass of the door. The smoke flattened out against the glass and swirled about in the close air. Then the line clicked and the operator's voice said: "Sorry, your party does not answer."

"Give me Jim again," I said. Then, when he answered, "Can you take time to run up and find out why she doesn't answer the phone? Maybe she's just being cagey."

Jim said: "You bet. I'll shoot right up with a key."

Sweat was coming out all over me. I put the receiver down on a little shelf and jerked the booth door open. The gray-haired man looked up quickly from the magazines, then scowled and looked at his watch. Smoke poured out of the booth. After a moment I kicked the door shut and picked up the receiver again.

Jim's voice seemed to come to me from a long way off. "She's not here. Maybe she went for a walk."

I said: "Yeah—or maybe it was a ride."

I pronged the receiver and pushed on out of the booth. The gray-haired stranger slammed a magazine down so hard that it fell to the floor. He stooped to pick it up as I went past him. Then he straightened up just behind me and said quietly, but very firmly: "Keep the hands down, and quiet. Walk on out to your heap. This is business."

Out of the corner of my eye I could see the old man peeking shortsightedly at us. But there wasn't anything for him to see, even if he could see that far. Something prodded my back. It might have been a finger, but I didn't think it was.

We went out of the store very peacefully.

A long gray car had stopped close behind the Marmon. Its rear door was open and a man with a square face and a crooked mouth was standing with one foot on the running board. His right hand was behind him, inside the car.

My man's voice said: "Get in your car and drive west. Take this first corner and go about twenty-five, not more."

The narrow street was sunny and quiet and the pepper trees whispered. Traffic threshed by on Cordova a short block away. I shrugged, opened the door of my car and got under the wheel. The gray-haired man got in very quickly beside me, watching my hands. He swung his right hand around, with a snub-nosed gun in it.

"Careful getting your keys out, buddy."

I was careful. As I stepped on the starter a car door slammed behind, there were rapid steps, and someone got into the back seat of the Marmon. I let in the clutch and drove around the corner. In the mirror I could see the gray car making the turn behind. Then it dropped back a little.

I drove west on a street that paralleled Cordova and when we had gone a block and a half a hand came down over my shoulder from behind and took my gun away from me. The gray-haired man rested his short revolver on his leg and felt me over carefully with his free hand. He leaned back satisfied.

"Okey. Drop over to the main drag and snap it up," he said. "But that don't mean trying to sideswipe a prowl car, if you lamp one . . . Or if you think it does, try it and see."

I made the two turns, speeded up to thirty-five and held it there. We went through some nice residential districts, and then the landscape began to thin out. When it was quite thin the gray car behind dropped back, turned towards town and disappeared.

"What's the snatch for?" I asked.

The gray-haired man laughed and rubbed his broad red chin. "Just business. The big boy wants to talk to you."

"Canales?"

"Canales—hell! I said the *big boy*."

I watched traffic, what there was of it that far out, and didn't speak for a few minutes. Then I said: "Why didn't you pull it in the apartment, or in the alley?"

"Wanted to make sure you wasn't covered."

"Who's this big boy?"

"Skip that—till we get you there. Anything else?"

"Yes. Can I smoke?"

He held the wheel while I lit up. The man in the back seat hadn't said a word at any time. After a while the gray-haired man made me pull up and move over, and he drove.

"I used to own one of these, six years ago, when I was poor," he said jovially.

I couldn't think of a really good answer to that, so I just let smoke seep down into my lungs and wondered why, if Lou had been killed in West Cimarron, the killers didn't get the money. And if he really had been killed at Miss Glenn's apartment, why somebody had taken the trouble to carry him back to West Cimarron.

SEVEN

In twenty minutes we were in the foothills. We went over a hogback, drifted down a long white concrete ribbon, crossed a bridge, went halfway up the next slope and turned off on a gravel road that disappeared around a shoulder of scrub oak and manzanita. Plumes of pampas grass flared on the side of the hill, like jets of water. The wheels crunched on the gravel and skidded on the curves.

We came to a mountain cabin with a wide porch and cemented boulder foundations. The windmill of a generator turned slowly on the crest of a spur a hundred feet behind the cabin. A mountain blue jay flashed across the road, zoomed, banked sharply, and fell out of sight like a stone.

The gray-haired man tooled the car up to the porch, beside a tan-colored Lincoln coupe, switched off the ignition and set the Marmon's long parking brake. He took the keys out, folded them carefully in their leather case, put the case away in his pocket.

The man in the back seat got out and held the door beside me open. He had a gun in his hand. I got out. The gray-haired man got out. We all went into the house.

There was a big room with walls of knotted pine, beautifully polished. We went across it walking on Indian rugs and the gray-haired man knocked carefully on a door.

A voice shouted: "What is it?"

The gray-haired man put his face against the door and said: "Beasley—and the guy you wanted to talk to."

The voice inside said to come on in. Beasley opened the door, pushed me through it and shut it behind me.

It was another big room with knotted pine walls and Indian rugs on the floor. A driftwood fire hissed and puffed on a stone hearth.

The man who sat behind a flat desk was Frank Dorr, the politico.

He was the kind of man who liked to have a desk in front of him, and shove his fat stomach against it, and fiddle with things on it, and look very wise. He had a fat, muddy face, a thin fringe of white hair that stuck up a little, small sharp eyes, small and very delicate hands.

What I could see of him was dressed in a slovenly gray suit, and there was a large black Persian cat on the desk in front of him. He was scratching the cat's head with one of his little neat hands and the cat was leaning against his hand. Its busy tail flowed over the edge of the desk and fell straight down.

He said: "Sit down," without looking away from the cat.

I sat down in a leather chair with a very low seat. Dorr said: "How do you like it up here? Kind of nice, ain't it? This is Toby, my girl friend. Only girl friend I got. Ain't you, Toby?"

I said: "I like it up here—but I don't like the way I got here."

Dorr raised his head a few inches and looked at me with his mouth slightly open. He had beautiful teeth, but they hadn't grown in his mouth. He said: "I'm a busy man, brother. It was simpler than arguing. Have a drink?"

"Sure I'll have a drink," I said.

He squeezed the cat's head gently between his two palms, then pushed it away from him and put both hands down on the arms of his chair. He shoved hard and his face got a little red and he finally got up on his feet. He waddled across to a built-in cabinet and took out a squat decanter of whiskey and two gold-veined glasses.

"No ice today," he said, waddling back to the desk. "Have to drink it straight."

He poured two drinks, gestured, and I went over and got mine. He sat down again. I sat down with my drink. Dorr lit a long brown cigar, pushed the box two inches in my direction, leaned back and stared at me with complete relaxation.

"You're the guy that fingered Manny Tinnen," he said. "It won't do."

I sipped my whiskey. It was good enough to sip.

"Life gets complicated at times," Dorr went on, in the same even, relaxed voice. "Politics—even when it's a lot of fun—is tough on the nerves. You know me. I'm tough and I get what I want. There ain't a hell of a lot I want any more, but what I want—I want bad. And ain't so damn particular how I get it."

"You have that reputation," I said politely.

Dorr's eyes twinkled. He looked around for the cat, dragged it towards him by the tail, pushed it down on its side and began to rub its stomach. The cat seemed to like it.

Dorr looked at me and said very softly: "You bumped Lou Harger."

"What makes you think so?" I asked, without any particular emphasis.

"You bumped Lou Harger. Maybe he needed the bump—but you gave it to him. He was shot once through the heart, with a thirty-eight. You wear a thirty-eight and you're known to be a fancy shot with it. You were with Harger at Las Olindas last night and saw him win a lot of money. You were supposed to be acting as body-guard for him, but you got a better idea. You caught up with him and that girl in West Cimarron, slipped Harger the dose and got the money."

I finished my whiskey, got up and poured myself some more of it.

"You made a deal with the girl," Dorr said, "but the deal didn't stick. She got a cute idea. But that don't matter, because the police got your gun along with Harger. And you got the dough."

I said: "Is there a tag out for me?"

"Not till I give the word . . . And the gun hasn't been turned in . . . I got a lot of friends, you know."

I said slowly: "I got sapped outside Canales' place. It served me right. My gun was take from me. I never caught up with Harger, never saw him again. The girl came to me this morning with the money in an envelope and a story that Harger had been killed in her apartment. That's how I have the money—for safekeeping. I wasn't sure about the girl's story, but her bringing the money carried a lot of weight. And Harger was a friend of mine. I started out to investigate."

"You should have let the cops do that," Dorr said with a grin.

"There was a chance the girl was being framed. Besides there was a possibility I might make a few dollars—legitimately. It has been done, even in San Angelo."

Dorr stuck a finger towards the cat's face and the cat bit it, with an absent expression. Then it pulled away from him, sat down on a corner of the desk and began to lick one toe.

"Twenty-two grand, and the jane passed it over to you to keep," Dorr said. "Ain't that just like a jane?

"You got the dough," Dorr said. "Harger was killed with your gun. The girl's gone—but I could bring her back. I think she'd make a good witness, if we needed one."

"Was the play at Las Olindas crooked?" I asked.

Dorr finished his drink and curled his lips around his cigar again. "Sure," he said carelessly. "The croupier—a guy named Pina—was in on it. The wheel was wired for the double-zero. The old crap. Copper button on the floor,

copper button on Pina's shoe sole, wires up his leg, batteries in his hip pockets. The old crap."

I said: "Canales didn't act as if he knew about it."

Dorr chuckled. "He knew the wheel was wired. He didn't know his head croupier was playin' on the other team."

"I'd hate to be Pina," I said.

Dorr made a negligent motion with his cigar. "He's taken care of . . . The play was careful and quiet. They didn't make any fancy long shots, just even money bets, and they didn't win all the time. They couldn't. No wired wheel is that good."

I shrugged, moved about in my chair. "You know a hell of a lot about it," I said. "Was all this just to get me set for a squeeze?"

He grinned softly: "Hell, no! Some of it just happened—the way the best plans do." He waved his cigar again, and a pale gray tendril of smoke curled past his cunning little eyes. There was a muffled sound of talk in the outside room. "I got connections I got to please—even if I don't like all their capers," he added simply.

"Like Manny Tinnen?" I said. "He was around City Hall a lot, knew too much. Okey, Mister Dorr. Just what do you figure on having me do for you? Commit suicide?"

He laughed. His fat shoulders shook carefully. He put one of his small hands out with the palm towards me. "I wouldn't think of that," he said dryly, "and the other way's better business. The way public opinion is about the Shannon kill. I ain't sure that louse of a D.A. wouldn't convict Tinnen without you—if he could sell the folks the idea you'd been knocked off to button your mouth."

I got up out of my chair, went over and leaned on the desk, leaned across it towards Dorr.

He said: "No funny business!" a little sharply and breathlessly. His hand went to a drawer and got it half open. His movements with his hands were very quick in contrast with the movements of his body.

I smiled down at the hand and he took it away from the drawer. I saw a gun just inside the drawer.

I said: "I've already talked to the Grand Jury."

Dorr leaned back and smiled at me. "Guys make mistakes," he said. "Even smart private dicks . . . You could have a change of heart—and put it in writing."

I said very softly. "No. I'd be under a perjury rap—which I couldn't beat. I'd rather be under a murder rap—which I can beat. Especially as Fenweather will *want* me to beat it. He won't want to spoil me as a witness. The Tinnen case is too important to him."

Dorr said evenly: "Then you'll have to try and beat it, brother. And after you get through beating it there'll still be enough mud on your neck so no jury'll convict Manny on your say-so alone."

I put my hand out slowly and scratched the cat's ear. "What about the twenty-two grand?"

"It *could* be all yours, if you want to play. After all, it ain't my money . . . If Manny gets clear, I might add a little something that *is* my money."

I tickled the cat under its chin. It began to purr. I picked it up and held it gently in my arms.

"Who did kill Lou Harger, Dorr?" I asked, not looking at him.

He shook his head. I looked at him, smiling. "Swell cat you have," I said.

Dorr licked his lips. "I think the little bastard likes you," he grinned. He looked pleased at the idea.

I nodded—and threw the cat in his face.

He yelped, but his hands came up to catch the cat. The cat twisted neatly in the air and landed with both front paws working. One of them split Dorr's cheek like a banana peel. He yelled very loudly.

I had the gun out of the drawer and the muzzle of it into the back of Dorr's neck when Beasley and the square-faced man dodged in.

For an instant there was a sort of tableau. Then the cat tore itself loose from Dorr's arms, shot to the floor and went under the desk. Beasley raised his snub-nosed gun, but he didn't look as if he was certain what he meant to do with it.

I shoved the muzzle of mine hard into Dorr's neck and said: "Frankie gets it first, boys . . . And that's not a gag."

Dorr grunted in front of me. "Take it easy," he growled to his hoods. He took a handkerchief from his breast pocket and began to dab at his split and bleeding cheek with it. The man with the crooked mouth began to sidle along the wall.

I said: "Don't get the idea I'm enjoying this, but I'm not fooling either. You heels stay put."

The man with the crooked mouth stopped sidling and gave me a nasty leer. He kept his hands low.

Dorr half turned his head and tried to talk over his shoulder to me. I couldn't see enough of his face to get any expression, but he didn't seem scared. He said: "This won't get you anything. I could have you knocked off easy enough, if that was what I wanted. Now where are you? You can't shoot anybody without getting in a worse jam than if you did what I asked you to. It looks like a stalemate to me."

I thought that over for a moment while Beasley looked at me quite pleasantly, as though it was all just routine to him. There was nothing pleasant about the other man. I listened hard, but the rest of the house seemed to be quite silent.

Dorr edged forward from the gun and said: "Well?"

I said: "I'm going out. I have a gun and it looks like a gun that I could hit somebody with, if I have to. I don't want to very much, and if you'll have Beasley throw my keys over and the other one turn back the gun he took from me, I'll forget about the snatch."

Dorr moved his arms in the lazy beginning of a shrug. "Then what?"

"Figure out your deal a little closer," I said. "If you get enough protection behind me, I might throw in with you . . . And if you're as tough as you think you are, a few hours won't cut any ice one way or the other."

"It's an idea," Dorr said and chuckled. Then to Beasley: "Keep your rod to yourself and give him his keys. Also his gun—the one you got today."

Beasley sighed and very carefully inserted a hand into his pants. He tossed my leather keycase across the room near the end of the desk. The man with the twisted mouth put his hand up, edged it inside his side pocket and I eased down behind Dorr's back, while he did it. He came out with my gun, let it fall to the floor and kicked it away from him.

I came out from behind Dorr's back, got my keys and the gun up from the floor, moved sidewise towards the door of the room. Dorr watched with an empty stare that meant nothing. Beasley followed me around with his body and stepped away from the door as I neared it. The other man had trouble holding himself quiet.

I got to the door and reversed a key that was in it. Dorr said dreamily: "You're just like one of those rubber balls on the end of an elastic. The farther you get away, the suddener you'll bounce back."

I said: "The elastic might be a little rotten," and went through the door, turned the key in it and braced myself for shots that didn't come. As a bluff, mine was thinner than the gold on a week-end wedding ring. It worked because Dorr let it, and that was all.

I got out of the house, got the Marmon started and wrangled it around and sent it skidding past the shoulder of the hill and so on down to the highway. There was no sound of anything coming after me.

When I reached the concrete highway bridge it was a little past two o'clock, and I drove with one hand for a while and wiped the sweat off the back of my neck.

EIGHT

The morgue was at the end of a long and bright and silent corridor that branched off from behind the main lobby of the County Building. The corridor ended in two doors and a blank wall faced with marble. One door had "Inquest Room" lettered on the glass panel behind which there was no light. The other opened into a small, cheerful office.

A man with gander-blue eyes and rust-colored hair parted in the exact center of his head was pawing over some printed forms at a table. He looked up, looked me over, and then suddenly smiled.

I said: "Hello, Landon . . . Remember the Shelby case?"

The bright blue eyes twinkled. He got up and came around the table with his hand out. "Sure. What can we do—" He broke off suddenly and snapped his fingers. "Hell! You're the guy that put the bee on that hot rod."

I tossed a butt through the open door into the corridor. "That's not why I'm here," I said. "Anyhow not this time. There's a fellow named Louis Harger . . . picked up shot last night or this morning, in West Cimarron, as I get it. Could I take a look-see?"

"They can't stop you," Landon said.

He led the way through the door on the far side of his office into a place that was all white paint and white enamel and glass and bright light. Against one wall was a double tier of large bins with glass windows in them. Through the peepholes showed bundles in white sheeting, and, further back, frosted pipes.

A body covered with a sheet lay on a table that was high at the head and sloped down to the foot. Landon pulled the sheet down casually from a man's dead, placid, yellowish face. Long black hair lay loosely on a small pillow, with the dankness of water still in it. The eyes were half open and stared incuriously at the ceiling.

I stepped close, looked at the face, Landon pulled the sheet on down and rapped his knuckles on a chest that rang hollowly, like a board. There was a bullet hole over the heart.

"Nice clean shot," he said.

I turned away quickly, got a cigarette out and rolled it around in my fingers. I stared at the floor.

"Who identified him?"

"Stuff in his pockets," Landon said. "We're checking his prints, of course. You know him?"

I said: "Yes."

Landon scratched the base of his chin softly with his thumbnail. We walked back into the office and Landon went behind his table and sat down.

He thumbed over some papers, separated one from the pile and studied it for a moment.

He said: "A sheriff's radio car found him at

twelve thirty-five a.m., on the side of the old road out of West Cimarron, a quarter of a mile from where the cutoff starts. That isn't traveled much, but the prowl car takes a slant down it now and then looking for petting parties."

I said: "Can you say how long he had been dead?"

"Not very long. He was still warm, and the nights are cool along there."

I put my unlighted cigarette in my mouth and moved it up and down with my lips. "And I bet you took a long thirty-eight out of him," I said.

"How did you know that?" Landon asked quickly.

"I just guess. It's that sort of hole."

He stared at me with bright, interested eyes. I thanked him, said I'd be seeing him, went through the door and lit my cigarette in the corridor. I walked back to the elevators and got into one, rode to the seventh floor, then went along another corridor exactly like the one below except that it didn't lead to the morgue. It led to some small, bare offices that were used by the District Attorney's investigators. Halfway along I opened a door and went into one of them.

Bernie Ohls was sitting humped loosely at a desk placed against the wall. He was the chief investigator Fenweather had told me to see, if I got into any kind of a jam. He was a medium-sized bland man with white eyebrows and an out-thrust, very deeply cleft chin. There was another desk against the other wall, a couple of hard chairs, a brass spittoon on a rubber mat and very little else.

Ohls nodded casually at me, got out of his chair and fixed the door latch. Then he got a flat tin of little cigars out of his desk, lit one of them, pushed the tin along the desk and stared at me along his nose. I sat down in one of the straight chairs and tilted it back.

Ohls said: "Well?"

"It's Lou Harger," I said. "I thought maybe it wasn't."

"The hell you did. I could have told you it was Harger."

Somebody tried the handle of the door, then knocked. Ohls paid no attention. Whoever it was went away.

I said slowly: "He was killed between eleven-thirty and twelve thirty-five. There was just time for the job to be done where he was found. There wasn't time for it to be done the way the girl said. There wasn't time for me to do it."

Ohls said: "Yeah. Maybe you could prove that. And then maybe you could prove a friend of yours didn't do it with your gun."

I said: "A friend of mine wouldn't be likely to do it with my gun—if he was a friend of mine."

Ohls grunted, smiled sourly at me sidewise. He said: "Most anyone would think that. That's why he might have done it."

I let the legs of my chair settle to the floor. I stared at him.

"Would I come and tell you about the money and the gun—everything that ties me to it?"

Ohls said expressionlessly: "You would—if you knew damn well somebody else had already told it for you."

I said: "Dorr wouldn't lose much time."

I pinched my cigarette out and flipped it towards the brass cuspidor. Then I stood up.

"Okey. There's no tag out for me yet—so I'll go over and tell my story."

Ohls said: "Sit down a minute."

I sat down. He took his little cigar out of his mouth and flung it away from him with a savage gesture. It rolled along the brown linoleum and smoked in the corner. He put his arms down on the desk and drummed with the fingers of both hands. His lower lip came forward and pressed his upper lip back against his teeth.

"Dorr probably knows you're here now," he said. "The only reason you ain't in the tank upstairs is they're not sure but it would be better to knock you off and take a chance. If Fenweather loses the election, I'll be all washed up—if I mess around with you."

I said: "If he convicts Manny Tinnen, he won't lose the election."

Ohls took another of the little cigars out of the

box and lit it. He picked his hat off the desk, fingered it a moment, put it on.

"Why'd the redhead give you that song and dance about the bump in her apartment, the stiff on the floor—all that hot comedy?"

"They wanted me to go over there. They figured I'd go to see if a gun was planted—maybe just to check up on her. That got me away from the busy part of town. They could tell better if the D.A. had any boys watching my blind side."

"That's just a guess," Ohls said sourly.

I said: "Sure."

Ohls swung his thick legs around, planted his feet hard and leaned his hands on his knees. The little cigar twitched in the corner of his mouth.

"I'd like to get to know some of these guys that let loose of twenty-two grand just to color up a fairy tale," he said nastily.

I stood up again and went past him towards the door.

Ohls said: "What's the hurry?"

I turned around and shrugged, looked at him blankly. "You don't act very interested," I said.

He climbed to his feet, said wearily: "The hack driver's most likely a dirty little crook. But it might just be Dorr's lads don't know he rates in this. Let's go get him while his memory's fresh."

NINE

The Green Top Garage was on Deviveras, three blocks east of Main. I pulled the Marmon up in front of a fireplug and got out. Ohls slumped in the seat and growled: "I'll stay here. Maybe I can spot a tail."

I went into a huge echoing garage, in the inner gloom of which a few brand new paint jobs were splashes of sudden color. There was a small, dirty, glass-walled office in the corner and a short man sat there with a derby hat on the back of his head and a red tie under his stubbled chin. He was whittling tobacco in the palm of his hand.

I said: "You the dispatcher?"

"Yeah."

"I'm looking for one of your drivers," I said. "Name of Tom Sneyd."

He put down the knife and the plug and began to grind the cut tobacco between his two palms. "What's the beef?" he asked cautiously.

"No beef. I'm a friend of his."

"More friends, huh? . . . He works nights, mister . . . So he's gone I guess. Seventeen twenty-three Renfrew. That's over by Gray Lake."

I said: "Thanks. Phone?"

"No phone."

I pulled a folded city map from an inside pocket and unfolded part of it on the table in front of his nose. He looked annoyed.

"There's a big one on the wall," he growled, and began to pack a short pipe with his tobacco.

"I'm used to this one," I said. I bent over the spread map, looking for Renfrew Street. Then I stopped and looked suddenly at the face of the man in the derby. "You remembered that address damn quick," I said.

He put his pipe in his mouth, bit hard on it, and pushed two quick fingers into the pocket of his open vest.

"Couple other mugs was askin' for it a while back."

I folded the map very quickly and shoved it back into my pocket as I went through the door. I jumped across the sidewalk, slid under the wheel and plunged at the starter.

"We're headed," I told Bernie Ohls. "Two guys got the kid's address there a while back. It might be—"

Ohls grabbed the side of the car and swore as we took the corner on squealing tires. I bent forward over the wheel and drove hard. There was a red light at Central. I swerved into a corner service station, went through the pumps, popped out on Central and jostled through some traffic to make a right turn east again.

A colored traffic cop blew a whistle at me and then stared hard as if trying to read the license number. I kept on going.

Warehouses, a produce market, a big gas tank, more warehouses, railroad tracks, and two bridges dropped behind us. I beat three traffic signals by a hair and went right through a fourth. Six blocks on I got the siren from a motorcycle cop. Ohls passed me a bronze star and I flashed it out of the car, twisting it so the sun caught it. The siren stopped. The motorcycle kept right behind us for another dozen blocks, then sheered off.

Gray Lake is an artificial reservoir in a cut between two groups of hills, on the east fringe of San Angelo. Narrow but expensively paved streets wind around in the hills, describing elaborate curves along their flanks for the benefit of a few cheap and scattered bungalows.

We plunged up into the hills, reading street signs on the run. The gray silk of the lake dropped away from us and the exhaust of the old Marmon roared between crumbling banks that shed dirt down on the unused sidewalks. Mongrel dogs quartered in the wild grass among the gopher holes.

Renfrew was almost at the top. Where it began there was a small neat bungalow in front of which a child in a diaper and nothing else fumbled around in a wire pen on a patch of lawn. Then there was a stretch without houses. Then there were two houses, then the road dropped, slipped in and out of sharp turns, went between banks high enough to put the whole street in shadow.

Then a gun roared around a bend ahead of us.

Ohls sat up sharply, said: "Oh-oh! That's no rabbit gun," slipped his service pistol out and unlatched the door on his side.

We came out of the turn and saw two more houses on the down side of the hill, with a couple of steep lots between them. A long gray car was slewed across the street in the space between the two houses. Its left front tire was flat and both its front doors were wide open, like the spread ears of an elephant.

A small, dark-faced man was kneeling on both knees in the street beside the open right-hand door. His right arm hung loose from his shoulder and there was blood on the hand that belonged to it. With his other hand he was trying to pick up an automatic from the concrete in front of him.

I skidded the Marmon to a fast stop and Ohls stumbled out.

"Drop that, you!" he yelled.

The man with the limp arm snarled, relaxed, fell back against the running boat, and a shot came from behind the car and snapped in the air not very far from my ear. I was out on the road by that time. The gray car was angled enough towards the houses so that I couldn't see any part of its left side except the open door. The shot seemed to come from about there. Ohls put two slugs into the door. I dropped, looked under the car and saw a pair of feet. I shot at them and missed.

About that time there was a thin but very sharp crack from the corner of the nearest house. Glass broke in the gray car. The gun behind it roared and plaster jumped out of the corner of the house wall, above the bushes. Then I saw the upper part of a man's body in the bushes. He was lying downhill on his stomach and he had a light rifle to his shoulder.

He was Tom Sneyd, the taxi driver.

Ohls grunted and charged the gray car. He fired twice more into the door, then dodged down behind the hood. More explosions occurred behind the car. I kicked the wounded man's gun out of his way, slid past him and sneaked a look over the gas tank. But the man behind had had too many angles to figure.

He was a big man in a brown suit and he made a clatter running hard for the lip of the hill between the two bungalows. Ohls' gun roared. The man whirled and snapped a shot without stopping. Ohls was in the open now. I saw his hat jerk off his head. I saw him stand squarely on well-spread feet, steady his pistol as if he was on the police range.

But the big man was already sagging. My bullet had drilled through his neck. Ohls fired at him very carefully and he fell and the sixth and last slug from his gun caught the man in the chest and twisted him around. The side of his head slapped the curb with a sickening crunch.

We walked towards him from opposite ends of the car. Ohls leaned down, heaved the man over on his back. His face in death had a loose, amiable expression, in spite of the blood all over his neck. Ohls began to go through his pockets.

I looked back to see what the other one was doing. He wasn't doing anything but sitting on the running board holding his right arm against his side and grimacing with pain.

Tom Sneyd scrambled up the bank and came towards us.

Ohls said: "It's a guy named Poke Andrews. I've seen him around the poolrooms." He stood up and brushed off his knee. He had some odds and ends in his left hand. "Yeah, Poke Andrews. Gun work by the day, hour or week. I guess there was a livin' in it—for a while."

"It's not the guy that sapped me," I said. "But it's the guy I was looking at when I got sapped. And if the redhead was giving out any truth at all this morning, it's likely the guy that shot Lou Harger."

Ohls nodded, went over and got his hat. There was a hole in the brim. "I wouldn't be surprised at all," he said, putting his hat on calmly.

Tom Sneyd stood in front of us with his little rifle held rigidly across his chest. He was hatless and coatless, and had sneakers on his feet. His eyes were bright and mad, and he was beginning to shake.

"I knew I'd get them babies!" he crowed. "I knew I'd fix them lousy bastards!" Then he stopped talking and his face began to change color. It got green. He leaned down slowly, dropped his rifle, put both his hands on his bent knees.

Ohls said: "You better go lay down somewhere, buddy. If I'm any judge of color, you're goin' to shoot your cookies."

TEN

Tom Sneyd was lying on his back on a day bed in the front room of his little bungalow. There was a wet towel across his forehead. A little girl with honey-colored hair was sitting beside him, holding his hand. A young woman with hair a couple of shades darker than the little girl's sat in the corner and looked at Tom Sneyd with tired ecstasy.

It was very hot when we came in. All the windows were shut and all the blinds down. Ohls opened a couple of front windows and sat down beside them, looked out towards the gray car. The dark Mexican was anchored to its steering wheel by his good wrist.

"It was what they said about my little girl," Tom Sneyd said from under the towel. "That's what sent me screwy. They said they'd come back and get her, if I didn't play with them."

Ohls said: "Okey, Tom. Let's have it from the start." He put one of his little cigars in his mouth, looked at Tom Sneyd doubtfully, and didn't light it.

I sat in a very hard Windsor chair and looked down at the cheap, new carpet.

"I was readin' a mag, waiting for time to eat and go to work," Tom Sneyd said carefully. "The little girl opened the door. They come in with guns on us, got us all in here and shut the windows. They pulled down all the blinds but one and the Mex sat by that and kept looking out. He never said a word. The big guy sat on the bed here and made me tell him all about last night—twice. Then he said I was to forget I'd met anybody or come into town with anybody. The rest was okey."

Ohls nodded and said: "What time did you first see this man here?"

"I didn't notice," Tom Sneyd said. "Say eleven-thirty, quarter of twelve. I checked in to the office at one-fifteen, right after I got my hack at the Carillon. It took us a good hour to make town from the beach. We was in the drugstore talkin' say fifteen minutes, maybe longer."

"That figures back to around midnight when you met him," Ohls said.

Tom Sneyd shook his head and the towel fell down over his face. He pushed it back up again.

"Well, no," Tom Sneyd said. "The guy in the drugstore told me he closed up at twelve. He wasn't closing up when we left."

Ohls turned his head and looked at me without expression. He looked back at Tom Sneyd. "Tell us the rest about the two gunnies," he said.

"The big guy said most likely I wouldn't have to talk to anybody about it. If I did and talked right, they'd be back with some dough. If I talked wrong, they'd be back for my little girl."

"Go on," Ohls said. "They're full of crap."

"They went away. When I saw them go on up the street I got screwy. Renfrew is just a pocket—one of them graft jobs. It goes on around the hill half a mile, then stops. There's no way to get off it. So they had to come back this way . . . I got my twenty-two, which is all the gun I have, and hid in the bushes. I got the tire with the second shot. I guess they thought it was a blowout. I missed with the next and that put 'em wise. They got guns loose. I got the Mex then, and the big guy ducked behind the car . . . That's all there was to it. Then you come along."

Ohls flexed his thick, hard fingers and smiled grimly at the girl in the corner. "Who lives in the next house, Tom?"

"A man named Grandy, a motorman on the interurban. He lives all alone. He's at work now."

"I didn't guess he was home," Ohls grinned. He got up and went over and patted the little girl on the head. "You'll have to come down and make a statement, Tom."

"Sure." Tom Sneyd's voice was tired, listless. "I guess I lose my job, too, for rentin' out the hack last night."

"I ain't so sure about that," Ohls said softly. "Not if your boss likes guys with a few guts to run his hacks."

He patted the little girl on the head again, went towards the door and opened it. I nodded at Tom Sneyd and followed Ohls out of the house. Ohls said quietly: "He don't know about the kill yet. No need to spring it in front of the kid."

We went over to the gray car. We had got some sacks out of the basement and spread them over the late Andrews, weighted them down with stones. Ohls glanced that way and said absently: "I got to get to where there's a phone pretty quick."

He leaned on the door of the car and looked in at the Mexican. The Mexican sat with his head back and his eyes half-closed and a drawn expression on his brown face. His left wrist was shackled to the spider of the wheel.

"What's your name?" Ohls snapped at him.

"Luis Cadena," the Mexican said it in a soft voice without opening his eyes any wider.

"Which one of you heels scratched the guy at West Cimarron last night?"

"No understand, señor," the Mexican said purringly.

"Don't go dumb on me, spig," Ohls said dispassionately. "It gets me sore." He leaned on the window and rolled his little cigar around in his mouth.

The Mexican looked faintly amused and at the same time very tired. The blood on his right hand had dried black.

Ohls said: "Andrews scratched the guy in a taxi at West Cimarron. There was a girl along. We got the girl. You have a lousy chance to prove you weren't in on it."

Light flickered and died behind the Mexican's half-open eyes. He smiled with a glint of small white teeth.

Ohls said: "What did he do with the gun?"

"No understand, señor."

Ohls said: "He's tough. When they get tough it scares me."

He walked away from the car and scuffed some loose dirt from the sidewalk beside the sacks that draped the dead man. His toe gradually uncovered the contractor's stencil in the cement. He read it out loud: "Dorr Paving and Construction Company, San Angelo. It's a wonder the fat louse wouldn't stay in his own racket."

I stood beside Ohls and looked down the hill between the two houses. Sudden flashes of light darted from the windshields of cars going along the boulevard that fringed Gray Lake, far below.

Ohls said: "Well?"

I said: "The killers knew about the taxi—maybe—and the girl friend reached town with the swag. So it wasn't Canales' job. Canales isn't the boy to let anybody play around with twenty-two grand of his money. The redhead was in on the kill, and it was done for a reason."

Ohls grinned. "Sure. It was done so you could be framed for it."

I said: "It's a shame how little account some folks take of human life—or twenty-two grand. Harger was knocked off so I could be framed and the dough was passed to me to make the frame tighter."

"Maybe they thought you'd highball," Ohls grunted. "That would sew you up right."

I rolled a cigarette around in my fingers. "That would have been a little too dumb, even for me. What do we do now? Wait till the moon comes up so we can sing—or go down the hill and tell some more little white lies?"

Ohls spat on one of Poke Andrews' sacks. He said gruffly: "This is county land here. I could take all this mess over to the sub-station at Solano and keep it hush-hush for a while. The hack driver would be tickled to death to keep it under the hat. And I've gone far enough so I'd like to get the Mex in the goldfish room with me personal."

"I'd like it that way too," I said. "I guess you can't hold it down there for long, but you might hold it down long enough for me to see a fat boy about a cat."

ELEVEN

It was late afternoon when I got back to the hotel. The clerk handed me a slip which read: "Please phone F. D. as soon as possible."

I went upstairs and drank some liquor that was in the bottom of a bottle. Then I phoned down for another pint, scraped my chin, changed clothes and looked up Frank Dorr's number in the book. He lived in a beautiful old house on Greenview Park Crescent.

I made myself a tall smooth one with a tinkle and sat down in an easy chair with the phone at my elbow. I got a maid first. Then I got a man who spoke Mister Dorr's name as though he thought it might blow up in his mouth. After him I got a voice with a lot of silk in it. Then I got a long silence and at the end of the silence I got Frank Dorr himself. He sounded glad to hear from me.

He said: "I've been thinking about our talk this morning, and I have a better idea. Drop out and see me . . . And you might bring that money along. You just have time to get it out of the bank."

I said: "Yeah. The safe-deposit closes at six. But it's not your money."

I heard him chuckle. "Don't be foolish. It's all marked, and I wouldn't want to have to accuse you of stealing it."

I thought that over, and didn't believe it—about the currency being marked. I took a drink out of my glass and said: "I *might* be willing to turn it over to the party I got it from—in your presence."

He said: "Well—I told you that party left town. But I'll see what I can do. No tricks, please."

I said of course no tricks, and hung up. I finished my drink, called Von Ballin of the *Telegram*. He said the sheriff's people didn't seem to have any ideas about Lou Harger—or give a damn. He was a little sore that I still wouldn't let him use my story. I could tell from the way he talked that he hadn't got the doings over near Gray Lake.

I called Ohls, couldn't reach him.

I mixed myself another drink, swallowed half of it and began to feel it too much. I put my hat on, changed my mind about the other half of my drink, went down to my car. The early evening traffic was thick with householders riding home to dinner. I wasn't sure whether two cars tailed me or just one. At any rate nobody tried to catch up and throw a pineapple in my lap.

The house was a square two-storied place of old red brick, with beautiful grounds and a red brick wall with a white stone coping around them. A shiny black limousine was parked under the porte-cochère at the side. I followed a red-flagged walk up over two terraces, and a pale wisp of a man in a cutaway coat let me into a wide, silent hall with dark old furniture and a glimpse of garden at the end. He led me along that and along another hall at right angles and ushered me softly into a paneled study that was dimly lit against the gathering dusk. He went away, leaving me alone.

The end of the room was mostly open french windows, through which a brass-colored sky showed behind a line of quiet trees. In front of the trees a sprinkler swung slowly on a patch of velvety lawn that was already dark. There were large dim oils on the walls, a huge black desk with books across one end, a lot of deep lounging chairs, a heavy soft rug that went from wall to wall. There was a faint smell of good cigars and beyond that somewhere a smell of garden flowers and moist earth. The door opened and a youngish man in nose-glasses came in, gave me a slight formal nod, looked around vaguely, and said that Mr. Dorr would be there in a moment. He went out again, and I lit a cigarette.

In a little while the door opened again and Beasley came in, walked past me with a grin and sat down just inside the windows. Then Dorr came in and behind him Miss Glenn.

Dorr had his black cat in his arms and two lovely red scratches, shiny with collodion, down his right cheek. Miss Glenn had on the same clothes I had seen her in the morning. She looked dark and drawn and spiritless, and she went past me as though she had never seen me before.

Dorr squeezed himself into the high-backed chair behind the desk and put the cat down in front of him. The cat strolled over to one corner of the desk and began to lick its chest with a long, sweeping, businesslike motion.

Dorr said: "Well, well. Here we are," and chuckled pleasantly.

The man in the cutaway came in with a tray of cocktails, passed them around, put the tray with the shaker down on a low table beside Miss Glenn. He went out again, closing the door as if he was afraid he might crack it.

We all drank and looked very solemn.

I said: "We're all here but two. I guess we have a quorum."

Dorr said: "What's that?" sharply and put his head to one side.

I said: "Lou Harger's in the morgue and Canales is dodging cops. Otherwise we're all here. All the interested parties."

Miss Glenn made an abrupt movement, then relaxed suddenly and picked at the arm of her chair.

Dorr took two swallows of his cocktail, put the glass aside and folded his small neat hands on the desk. His face looked a little sinister.

"The money," he said coldly. "I'll take charge of it now."

I said: "Not now or any other time. I didn't bring it."

Dorr stared at me and his face got a little red. I looked at Beasley. Beasley had a cigarette in his mouth and his hands in his pockets and the back of his head against the back of his chair. He looked half asleep.

Dorr said softly, meditatively: "Holding out, huh?"

"Yes," I said grimly. "While I have it I'm fairly safe. You overplayed your hand when you let me get my paws on it. I'd be a fool not to hold what advantage it gives me."

Dorr said: "Safe?" with a gentle sinister intonation.

I laughed. "Not safe from a frame," I said. "But the last one didn't click so well . . . Not safe from being gun-walked again. But that's going to be harder next time too . . . But fairly safe from being shot in the back and having you sue my estate for the dough."

Dorr stroked the cat and looked at me under his eyebrows.

"Let's get a couple of more important things straightened out," I said. "Who takes the rap for Lou Harger?"

"What makes you so sure *you* don't?" Dorr asked nastily.

"My alibi's been polished up. I didn't know how good it was until I knew how close Lou's death could be timed. I'm clear now . . . regardless of who turns in what gun with what fairy tale . . . And the lads that were sent to scotch my alibi ran into some trouble."

Dorr said: "That so?" without any apparent emotion.

"A thug named Andrews and a Mexican calling himself Luis Cadena. I daresay you've heard of them."

"I don't know such people," Dorr said sharply.

"Then it won't upset you to hear Andrews got very dead, and the law has Cadena."

"Certainly not," Dorr said. "They were from Canales. Canales had Harger killed."

I said: "So that's your new idea. I think it's lousy."

I leaned over and slipped my empty glass under my chair. Miss Glenn turned her head towards me and spoke very gravely, as if it was very important to the future of the race for me to believe what she said: "Of course—*of course* Canales had Lou killed . . . At least, the men he sent after us killed Lou."

I nodded politely. "What for? A packet of money they didn't get? They wouldn't have killed him. They'd have brought him in, brought both of you in. You arranged for that kill, and the taxi stunt was to sidetrack me, not to fool Canales' boys."

She put her hand out quickly. Her eyes were shimmering. I went ahead.

"I wasn't very bright, but I didn't figure on anything so flossy. Who the hell would? Canales had no motive to gun Lou, unless it got back the money he had been gypped out of. Supposing he could know that quick he *had* been gypped."

Dorr was licking his lips and quivering his chins and looking from one of us to the other with his small tight eyes. Miss Glenn said drearily: "Lou knew all about the play. He planned it with the croupier, Pina. Pina wanted some get-away money, wanted to move on to Havana. Of course Canales would have got wise, but not too soon, if I hadn't got noisy and tough. I got Lou killed—but not the way you mean."

I dropped an inch of ash off a cigarette I had forgotten all about. "All right," I said grimly. "Canales takes the rap . . . And I suppose you two chiselers think that's all I care about . . . Where was Lou going to be when Canales was *supposed* to find out he'd been gypped?"

"He was going to be gone," Miss Glenn said tonelessly. "A damn long way off. And I was going to be gone with him."

I said: "Nerts! You seem to forget *I* know *why* Lou was killed."

Beasley sat up in his chair and moved his right hand rather delicately towards his left shoulder. "This wise guy bother you, chief?"

Dorr said: "Not yet. Let him rant."

I moved so that I faced a little more towards Beasley. The sky had gone dark outside and the sprinkler had been turned off. A damp feeling came slowly into the room. Dorr opened a cedarwood box and put a long brown cigar in his mouth, bit the end off with a dry snap of his false teeth. There was the harsh noise of a match striking, then the slow, rather labored puffing of his breath in the cigar.

He said slowly, through a cloud of smoke: "Let's forget all this and make a deal about that money . . . Manny Tinnen hung himself in his cell this afternoon."

Miss Glenn stood up suddenly, pushing her arms straight down at her sides. Then she sank slowly down into the chair again, sat motionless. I said: "Did he have any help?" Then I made a sudden, sharp movement—and stopped.

Beasley jerked a swift glance at me, but I wasn't looking at Beasley. There was a shadow outside one of the windows—a lighter shadow than the dark lawn and darker trees. There was a hollow, bitter, coughing plop; a thin spray of whitish smoke in the window.

Beasley jerked, rose halfway to his feet, then fell on his face with one arm doubled under him.

Canales stepped through the windows, past Beasley's body, came three steps further, and stood silent, with a long, black, small-calibered gun in his hand, the larger tube of a silencer flaring from the end of it.

"Be very still," he said. "I am a fair shot—even with this elephant gun."

His face was so white that it was almost luminous. His dark eyes were all smoke-gray iris, without pupils.

"Sound carries well at night, out of open windows," he said tonelessly.

Dorr put both his hands down on the desk and began to pat it. The black cat put its body very low, drifted down over the end of the desk and went under a chair. Miss Glenn turned her head towards Canales very slowly, as if some kind of mechanism moved it.

Canales said: "Perhaps you have a buzzer on that desk. If the door of the room opens, I shoot.

It will give me a lot of pleasure to see blood come out of your fat neck."

I moved the fingers of my right hand two inches on the arm of my chair. The silenced gun swayed towards me and I stopped moving my fingers. Canales smiled very briefly under his angular mustache.

"You are a smart dick," he said. "I thought I had you right. But there are things about you I like."

I didn't say anything. Canales looked back at Dorr. He said very precisely: "I have been bled by your organization for a long time. But this is something else again. Last night I was cheated out of some money. But this is trivial too. I am wanted for the murder of this Harger. A man named Cadena has been made to confess that I hired him . . . That is just a little too much fix."

Dorr swayed gently over his desk, put his elbows down hard on it, held his face in his small hands and began to shake. His cigar was smoking on the floor.

Canales said: "I would like to get my money back, and I would like to get clear of this rap—but most of all I would like you to say something—so I can shoot you with your mouth open and see blood come out of it."

Beasley's body stirred on the carpet. His hands groped a little. Dorr's eyes were agony trying not to look at him. Canales was rapt and blind in his act by this time. I moved my fingers a little more on the arm of my chair. But I had a long way to go.

Canales said: "Pina has talked to me. I saw to that. You killed Harger. Because he was a secret witness against Manny Tinnen. The D.A. kept the secret, and the dick here kept it. But Harger could not keep it himself. He told his broad—and the broad told you . . . So the killing was arranged, in a way to throw suspicion with a motive on me. First on this dick, and if that wouldn't hold, on me."

There was silence. I wanted to say something, but I couldn't get anything out. I didn't think anybody but Canales would ever again say anything.

Canales said: "You fixed Pina to let Harger

and his girl win my money. It was not hard—because I don't play my wheels crooked."

Dorr had stopped shaking. His face lifted, stone-white, and turned towards Canales, slowly, like the face of a man about to have an epileptic fit. Beasley was up on one elbow. His eyes were almost shut but a gun was labouring upwards in his hand.

Canales leaned forward and began to smile. His trigger finger whitened at the exact moment Beasley's gun began to pulse and roar.

Canales arched his back until his body was a rigid curve. He fell stiffly forward, hit the edge of the desk and slid along it to the floor, without lifting his hands.

Beasley dropped his gun and fell down on his face again. His body got soft and his fingers moved fitfully, then were still.

I got motion into my legs, stood up and went to kick Canales' gun under the desk—senselessly. Doing this I saw that Canales had fired at least once, because Frank Dorr had no right eye.

He sat still and quiet with his chin on his chest and a nice touch of melancholy on the good side of his face.

The door of the room came open and the secretary with the nose-glasses slid in pop-eyed. He staggered back against the door, closing it again. I could hear his rapid breathing across the room.

He gasped: "Is—is anything wrong?"

I thought that very funny, even then. Then I realized that he might be short-sighted and from where he stood Frank Dorr looked natural enough. The rest of it could have been just routine to Dorr's help.

I said: "Yes—but we'll take care of it. Stay out of here."

He said: "Yes, sir," and went out again. That surprised me so much that my mouth fell open. I went down the room and bent over the gray-haired Beasley. He was unconscious, but had a fair pulse. He was bleeding from the side, slowly.

Miss Glenn was standing up and looked almost as dopy as Canales had looked. She was talking to me quickly, in a brittle, very distinct voice: "I didn't know Lou was to be killed, but I couldn't have done anything about it anyway.

They burned me with a branding iron—just for a sample of what I'd get. Look!"

I looked. She tore her dress down in front and there was a hideous burn on her chest almost between her two breasts.

I said: "Okey, sister. That's nasty medicine. But we've got to have some law here now and an ambulance for Beasley."

I pushed past her towards the telephone, shook her hand off my arm when she grabbed at me. She went on talking to my back in a thin, desperate voice.

"I thought they'd just hold Lou out of the way until after the trial. But they dragged him out of the cab and shot him without a word. Then the little one drove the taxi into town and the big one brought me up into the hills to a shack. Dorr was there. He told me how you had to be framed. He promised me the money, if I went through with it, and torture till I died, if I let them down."

It occurred to me that I was turning my back too much to people. I swung around, got the telephone in my hands, still on the hook, and put my gun down on the desk.

"Listen! Give me a break," she said wildly. "Dorr framed it all with Pina, the croupier. Pina was one of the gang that got Shannon where they could fix him. I didn't—"

I said: "Sure—that's all right. Take it easy."

The room, the whole house seemed very still, as if a lot of people were hunched outside the door, listening.

"It wasn't a bad idea," I said, as if I had all the time in the world. "Lou was just a white chip to Frank Dorr. The play he figured put us both out as witnesses. But it was too elaborate, took in too many people. That sort always blows up in your face."

"Lou was getting out of the state," she said, clutching at her dress. "He was scared. He thought the roulette trick was some kind of a pay-off to him."

I said: "Yeah," lifted the phone and asked for police headquarters.

The room door came open again then and the secretary barged in with a gun. A uniformed chauffeur was behind him with another gun.

I said very loudly into the phone: "This is Frank Dorr's house. There's been a killing . . ."

The secretary and the chauffeur dodged out again. I heard running in the hall. I clicked the phone, called the *Telegram* office and got Von Ballin. When I got through giving him the flash Miss Glenn was gone out of the window into the dark garden.

I didn't go after her. I didn't mind very much if she got away.

I tried to get Ohls, but they said he was still down at Solano. And by that time the night was full of sirens.

I had a little trouble but not too much. Fenweather pulled too much weight. Not all of the story came out, but enough so that the City Hall boys in the two-hundred-dollar suits had their left elbows in front of their faces for some time.

Pina was picked up in Salt Lake City. He broke and implicated four others of Manny Tinnen's gang. Two of them were killed resisting arrest, the other two got life without parole.

Miss Glenn made a clean getaway and was never heard of again. I think that's about all, except that I had to turn the twenty-two grand over to the Public Administrator. He allowed me two hundred dollars fee and nine dollars and twenty cents mileage. Sometimes I wonder what he did with the rest of it.

The Monkey Murder
Erle Stanley Gardner

THERE IS A RICH tradition in mystery fiction of the Robin Hood thief, the sympathetic figure who steals from the rich to give to the deserving poor. Lester Leith, the hero of more than seventy novelettes, all written for the pulps, approached his thievery from a slightly different angle. He did steal from the rich, but only those who were themselves crooks, and he gave the money to charities—after taking a 20% "recovery" fee.

Debonair, quick-witted, and wealthy, he enjoyed the perks of his fortune, checking the newspapers in the comfort of his penthouse apartment for new burglaries and robberies to solve, and from which he could reclaim the stolen treasures.

He has a valet, Beaver, nicknamed "Scuttle" by Leith, who is a secret plant of Sergeant Arthur Ackley. Leith, of course, is aware that his manservant is an undercover operative, using that knowledge to plant misinformation to frustrate the policeman again and again.

Leith is only one of a huge number of characters created by the indefatigable Erle Stanley Gardner (1889–1970), many of whom were criminals, including Ed Jenkins (the Phantom Crook), the sinister Patent Leather Kid, and Señor Arnaz de Lobo, a professional soldier of fortune and revolutionary.

"The Monkey Murder" was first published in the January 1939 issue of *Detective Story*.

The Monkey Murder

Erle Stanley Gardner

LESTER LEITH, his slender, well-knit form attired in a cool suit of Shantung pongee, sprawled indolently in the reclining wicker chair. The cool afternoon breezes filtered through the screened windows of the penthouse apartment. Leith's valet, Beaver, nicknamed "Scuttle" by Lester Leith, ponderous in his obsequious servility, siphoned soda into a Tom Collins and deferentially placed the glass on the table beside his master's chair.

If Leith had any knowledge that this man who served him, ostensibly interested only in his creature comforts, was in reality a police undercover man, planted on the job by Sergeant Arthur Ackley, he gave no indication. His slate-gray eyes, the color of darkly tarnished silver, remained utterly inscrutable as he stared thoughtfully at the bubbles which formed on the glass only to detach themselves and race upward through the cool beverage.

The valet coughed.

Leith's eyes remained fixed, staring into the distance.

The police spy squirmed uneasily, then said: "Begging your pardon, sir, was there something you wanted?"

Leith, without turning his head, said, "I think not, Scuttle."

The big undercover man shifted his weight from one foot to the other, fidgeted uneasily, then said: "Begging your pardon, sir, please don't think I'm presumptuous, but I was about to venture to suggest— Well, sir—"

"Come, come, Scuttle," Lester Leith said. "Out with it. What is it?"

"About the crime news, sir," the undercover man blurted. "It's been some time since you've taken an interest in the crime news, sir."

Leith sipped his Tom Collins. "Quite right, Scuttle," he said. "And it will probably be a much longer time before I do so."

"May I ask why, sir?"

"On account of Sergeant Ackley," Leith said. "Damn the man, Scuttle. He's like a woman convinced against her will, and of the same opinion still. Somewhere, somehow, he got it through that fat head of his that I was the mysterious hijacker who has been ferreting out the criminals who have made rich hauls, and relieving them of their ill-gotten spoils."

"Yes, sir," the spy said. "He certainly *has* been most annoying, sir."

"As a matter of fact," Leith went on, "whoever that mysterious hijacker is—and I understand the police are firmly convinced there is such an individual—he has my sincere respect and admiration. After all, Scuttle, crime *should* be punished. Crime which isn't detected isn't punished. As I understand it, the criminals who have been victimized by this hijacker are men who have flaunted their crimes in the faces of the police and got away with it. The police have been unable to spot them, let alone get enough evidence to convict them. Then along comes this mysterious hijacker, solves the crime where the police have failed, locates the criminal, and levies a hundred-per-cent fine by relieving him of his ill-gotten gains. That, Scuttle, I claim is a distinct service to society."

"Yes, sir," the spy said. "Of course, you will admit that your charities for the widows and orphans of police and firemen killed in the line of duty, your donations to the associated charities and the home for the aged have been steadily mounting."

"Well, what of it, Scuttle? What the devil has that to do with the subject under discussion?"

"Begging your pardon, sir, I think the sergeant wonders where you're getting the money, sir."

Lester Leith placed the half-empty glass back on the table, and reached for his cigarette case. "Confound the man's impudence, Scuttle. What business is it of his where I get my money?"

"Yes, sir, I understand, sir. Oh, quite, sir. But even so, sir, if you'll pardon my making the suggestion, sir, it seems that you shouldn't let such a trivial matter interfere with your enjoyment of life."

"My enjoyment of life, Scuttle?"

"Well, sir, I know that you always derived a great deal of pleasure from looking over the crime clippings. As you've so frequently remarked, you used to feel that a man could study the newspaper accounts of crime and in many cases spot the guilty party, just from the facts given in the newspapers."

"I still maintain that can be done, Scuttle."

"Yes, sir," the spy said, lowering his voice. "And has it ever occurred to you, sir, that what Sergeant Ackley doesn't know won't hurt him?"

"Won't hurt him," Lester Leith exclaimed. "It's what Sergeant Ackley doesn't know that's ruining him! If knowledge is power, Sergeant Ackley has leaky valves, loose pistons, scored cylinders, and burnt-out bearings. He's narrow-minded, egotistical, suspicious, mercenary, selfish, and pig-headed. In addition to all of which, Scuttle, I find that I don't like the man."

"Yes, sir," the spy said, "but if you'd only interest yourself in the crime clippings just once more, sir, I have several very interesting items

saved up for you. And Sergeant Ackley would never know, sir."

Leith said reprovingly, "Scuttle, you're trying to tempt me."

"I'm sorry, sir. I didn't mean to . . . that is, really, sir. Well, of course, you may depend upon my discretion, sir."

Leith half turned in his chair. "I can trust you, Scuttle?" he asked, looking at the spy with his inscrutable silver-gray eyes.

"Absolutely, sir, with your very life, sir."

Lester Leith sighed, settled back, and tapped a cigarette on a polished thumbnail. "Scuttle," he said, "perhaps it's my mood, perhaps it's the weather, perhaps it's the drink; but I've decided to indulge in my hobby *just* once more, only mind you, Scuttle, this time it will be merely an academic pursuit. We'll merely speculate on who the criminal *might* be and keep that speculation entirely to ourselves, a sacred confidence within the four walls of this room."

"Yes, sir," the spy said, quivering with eagerness as he pulled a sheaf of newspaper clippings from his pocket.

"Sit down, Scuttle," Leith invited. "Sit down and make yourself comfortable."

"Very good, sir. Thank you, sir."

Lester Leith snapped a match into flame, held it to the tip of the cigarette, and inhaled deeply, extinguishing the match with a single smoky exhalation. "Proceed, Scuttle," he said.

"Yes, sir. The affair of the Brentwood diamond seems to have been made to order for you, sir."

"Made to order for *me*, Scuttle?"

"Yes, sir," the undercover man said, forgetting himself for the moment as he perused the newspaper clipping. "The police have never found the culprit. There's a chance for you to make a good haul and—"

"Scuttle!" Lester Leith interrupted.

The valet jumped. "Oh, I *beg* your pardon, sir. I didn't mean it in that way, sir. What I meant—"

"Never mind, Scuttle. We'll pass the Brentwood diamond. What else do you have?"

"That was the main one, sir."

"Well, forget it, Scuttle."

The spy thumbed through the clippings. "There's the man who was choked and robbed of some two thousand dollars he'd won at gambling."

"Skip it, Scuttle," Lester Leith interrupted. "A man who wins two thousand dollars at gambling, and hasn't sense enough to go to a downtown hotel and stay there until daylight, deserves to lose his winnings. That's an old gambling-house trick. What else do you have?"

"There was the woman who shot her husband and claimed—"

"Tut, tut, Scuttle," Lester Leith said. "You've been reading the tabloids again. That is completely stereotyped. She shot him because he had forfeited her respect. She shot him because she couldn't demean herself to accept the status in life which he thought a wife should have. She had been married ten years, but she made the revolting discovery of his baser instincts at a time when a revolver happened to be handy. She snatched it from her purse, thinking only to bring him to his senses, and then she can't remember exactly what happened. She thinks he started for her, and everything went blank. She felt the recoil of the revolver as it roared in her hand. Then she couldn't remember anything until she found herself at the telephone notifying the police. That was right after she'd slipped out of her house dress and put on her best outfit."

"I see you've read it, sir," the undercover man said. "I didn't realize you were familiar with the case. May I ask, if you don't mind, sir, how you happened to know about it? Were they friends of yours?"

"I'm not familiar with *that* case," Leith said wearily, "but with dozens of others of the same type. Come on, Scuttle; let's have something fresh."

"Well, sir, I don't think there's— Oh, yes, sir, here's something rather unusual. The murder of a monkey, sir."

"The murder of a monkey?" Leith said, turning half around, so that he could study the spy's face. "Why the devil should anyone want to murder a monkey?"

"Well, of course, strictly speaking, sir, it isn't murder, but I've referred to it as murder because if what the police suspect is true, that's virtually what it amounted to . . . that is, sir, I trust you understand me . . . I mean—"

"I don't understand you," Lester Leith interrupted, "and I have no means of knowing what you mean except from what you say. Kindly elucidate, Scuttle."

"Yes, sir, it was a monkey belonging to Peter B. Mainwaring. Mr. Mainwaring was returning from a year spent abroad, principally in India and Africa."

"Come, come, Scuttle," Lester Leith said. "Get to the point. Why was the monkey murdered?"

"It was Mr. Mainwaring's monkey, sir."

"And who killed it, Scuttle?"

"The police don't know. It was a holdup man."

"A holdup man, Scuttle?"

"Yes, sir. According to Mr. Mainwaring's story, the bandit held up the automobile, shot the monkey through the head, and slit its body open. Mr. Mainwaring thinks the killer came from India. It's some sort of a ceremony having to do with thuggee and the monkey priests who worship the monkeys and exact a death penalty from any monkey that deserts the clan."

"I've never heard of anything like that before," Leith said.

"Yes, sir. That's the story that Mr. Mainwaring has given to the police."

"Bosh and nonsense," Lester Leith said. "Thuggee is one thing; the monkey worship of India is entirely different . . . that is, there's no possible connection which could result in a man following another from India to America just to kill a monkey and slit him open."

"Yes, sir," the spy said dubiously. "The police don't know much about it. I don't mind telling you, sir, however, that . . . well, perhaps I shouldn't mention it."

"Go ahead," Leith said. "What is it?"

"I think I mentioned at one time that one of my lady friends was quite friendly with a member of the force, not that she's encouraged him, but he persists in—"

"Yes, yes, I remember," Leith said. "A policeman, isn't it, Scuttle?"

"No, sir. He's been promoted to a detective."

"Oh, yes, Scuttle. I remember now. Where's he stationed?"

The spy said: "Begging your pardon, sir, I'd rather not talk about that. But I don't mind repeating a bit of information occasionally."

"Am I to understand," Lester Leith asked, "that this detective habitually tells this young woman police secrets, and the young woman in turn makes a practice of passing them on to you?"

The big spy smirked. "That's rather a bald statement, sir."

"Bald, nothing," Leith observed; "you are doubtless referring to its whiskers."

"Beg your pardon, sir?"

Leith said: "Nothing, Scuttle. I was merely making a comment to myself. Go on. Tell me what you were going to say about Mainwaring."

"Well, sir, the police had an idea that Mainwaring may have been in league with a gang of smugglers and that he *may* have killed the monkey himself in order to cover up the real reason of the holdup. Or, then again, the man may have been an accomplice who had been tricked, and shot at Mainwaring and hit the monkey instead.

"You may be interested in knowing that the police have reason to believe Mainwaring left India in fear of his life."

"What has all this to do with smuggling, Scuttle?"

"Well, sir, *if* the native rumors are true, sir, Mainwaring *may* have slipped two very valuable gems to some native accomplice with instructions to smuggle them into this country. The gems weren't in the car with Mainwaring, but he *may* have had them in India and intrusted this native to—"

"What gems, Scuttle?"

"The jewels of the monkey god, sir."

"The jewels of the monkey god? Come, come, Scuttle; this is beginning to sound like one of Sergeant Ackley's wild accusations."

"Yes, sir. Over in India there's the special god for monkeys, a god that's named . . . Hanne . . . Hanney—"

"Hanuman?" Lester Leith suggested.

"Yes, sir. That's it, sir. Hanuman. I remember the name now that you've helped me, sir. Thank you, sir."

"What about Hanuman, the monkey god?" Lester Leith asked.

"It seems that back in the jungles, sir, there's a huge statue of the monkey god. He's covered with gold leaf. His eyes were emeralds, and his breast nipples consist of two huge emeralds. It seems that some adventurer managed to gain access to this temple and substituted bits of green glass for the emeralds. The substitution wasn't discovered for some time."

"And what has this to do with Mainwaring's smuggling?" Lester Leith asked.

"The police, sir, have reason to believe that it was Mainwaring who made the substitution."

"Peter B. Mainwaring?" Lester Leith asked.

The valet nodded.

Leith said thoughtfully: "Now, Scuttle, you interest me. You interest me very much indeed. I think you'll agree with me, Scuttle, that if that were the truth, Mainwaring shouldn't be allowed to retain the fruits of his nefarious action."

"Yes, sir," the spy agreed, his eyes eager. "Only Mainwaring apparently doesn't have them."

"And, by the same sign," Leith said, "you will also admit that there is nothing to be gained by sending these stones back to the jungle to become part of the anatomy of a heathen idol."

"Yes, sir, I agree with you upon *that* absolutely, sir," the spy said with alacrity.

"Under the circumstances," Leith announced, "we'll consider the murder of this monkey, Scuttle. Tell me about it."

"Yes, sir. Well, you see, sir, the police had been notified. They thought that perhaps Mr. Mainwaring was bringing the emeralds in with him although Mainwaring had denied having them in his possession or knowing anything about them. He admitted that he had been in that section of the country at about the time the stones disappeared. In fact, he said it was due to this fact and only to this fact that the natives thought he was responsible for the theft."

"Yes," Leith said. "I can understand how it would happen that a white man, under such circumstances, would be considered responsible for the loss by ignorant or superstitious natives. Perhaps Mainwaring was telling the truth after all, Scuttle."

"Well, sir. You see, it was this way, sir. The police and the customs officials were watching Mainwaring closely. Mainwaring made no declaration of the gems, nor did a most thorough search of his baggage reveal them. But he must have been mixed up with Indian gangsters, the disciples of thuggee. At any rate, this stickup looks like it."

"Mainwaring was traveling alone?" Lester Leith asked.

"His nurse was with him, sir."

"His nurse, Scuttle?"

"Yes, sir. Mr. Mainwaring is suffering from an indisposition, an organic heart trouble. At times when he's seized with an attack, it is necessary that a nurse administer a hypodermic at once."

"A male nurse, Scuttle?"

"No, sir. A female nurse, and rather a good-looking nurse at that."

"*Heart* trouble, did you say, Scuttle?"

"Yes, sir."

"I can well understand it," Leith said. "And the nurse was in India with him?"

"Yes, sir. Airdree Clayton is her name. There's a photograph of both of them here if you'd like to see it, sir."

Lester Leith nodded. The big spy passed across the newspaper photograph. Leith looked at it and then read the caption.

Peter B. Mainwaring and his nurse, Airdree Clayton, who have just returned from extensive travels in India and Africa. While customs officials were going through the baggage of himself and nurse with what Mainwaring indignantly insisted was unusual thoroughness, Miss Clayton sat on a table in the inspector's office, chewed gum, and entertained Mr. Mainwaring's pet monkey. This monkey was subsequently killed in a most mysterious holdup. Mainwaring threatened to report the customs officials for rudeness, unnecessary search, and unfounded accusations. Miss Clayton, on the other hand, said the customs inspector was "delightful," and returned to his office after having been searched by a matron, to thank the inspector for his consideration.

Lester Leith said, "She chews gum, Scuttle?"

"So the newspaper article says. Apparently she chews gum vigorously."

Leith digested that information for several thoughtful seconds.

"Scuttle," he said, "I can imagine nothing more soothing to the nerves than a nurse who chews gum. There's a quieting monotony in the repetition of chewing, as sedative in its effect as rain on a roof. *I* want a nurse who chews gum. Make a note of that, Scuttle."

"A nurse who chews gum, sir!"

"Yes," Leith said, "and she should be rather good-looking. I noticed that Miss Clayton's . . . er . . . pedal extremities and the anatomical connecties are rather peculiarly adapted to photography."

"Yes, sir," the spy said. "Do I gather that you want a nurse with shapely legs, sir?"

"Not exactly that," Lester Leith replied. "I want a nurse who chews gum. If her means of locomotion are attractive to the eye, Scuttle, that'd be an added inducement."

"But there's no reason why *you* should have a nurse, is there? That is, I mean, sir, you aren't sick?"

"No," Leith said. "I feel quite all right, Scuttle. Thank you."

"Therefore," the spy said, "begging your pardon, sir, employing a nurse would seem rather . . . er . . . conspicuous, would it not?"

"Perhaps so," Lester said. "And yet, on the other hand, Scuttle, I can imagine nothing which would more readily reconcile me to Sergeant Ackley's continued existence than association with a young woman with shapely pedal extremities, who makes a habit of placidly chewing gum."

The spy blinked his small, black eyes rapidly as he strove to comprehend the significance of Leith's remark.

"Therefore," Leith went on, "since a nurse seems conspicuous, as you have termed it, I shall insist upon a gum-chewing secretary, Scuttle. Make a note to call the employment agencies asking for an adroit, expert, inveterate gum chewer, a secretary with pulchritude and bovine masticational habits, a careless parker— Here, Scuttle, take a pencil, and take this down as I dictate it."

"Yes, sir," the dazed spy said.

"A position at good salary is open," Lester Leith dictated, "for a pulchritudinous young woman with shapely means of locomotion, amiable, easygoing, good-natured, acquiescent young woman preferred, one who never becomes nervous under any circumstances, a proficient, adroit, expert, and inveterate gum chewer, preferably a careless parker, must be able to pop her gum loudly. Salary, three hundred dollars per month with all traveling expenses. . . . Have you got that, Scuttle?"

"Yes, sir," the spy said, his voice showing dazed incredulity.

"Very good," Leith observed. "Telephone the employment agencies, and now let's get back to Mainwaring."

"Mainwaring got through customs on the evening of the thirteenth, sir. The customs officials found nothing which hadn't been declared. It was then about seven o'clock and getting dark. Mainwaring's chauffeur was waiting for him. He—"

"Just a minute, Scuttle. Mainwaring didn't take his chauffeur on this tour with him, did he?"

"No, sir. The chauffeur stayed and acted as a caretaker at the house."

"I see. Go on, Scuttle."

"Well, the chauffeur loaded the hand baggage into the car, and they started for Mainwaring's house. When they were somewhere around Eighty-sixth Street, the right rear tire blew out; and when the chauffeur went to fix it, he found the jack was broken. He knew of a garage some half dozen blocks away, and Mainwaring said he and Miss Clayton would wait in the car while the chauffeur went to the garage. The chauffeur had some difficulty as the garage was closed. He thinks he was gone perhaps some thirty minutes in all. The robber held up Mainwaring only a few minutes after the chauffeur started out. In fact the chauffeur saw the bandit drive past him, noticed him particularly because of his build. He was big, fat, massive, and with a swarthy complexion. The chauffeur actually saw his features, sir. He was the only one who did. The stickup man had put on a mask by the time he had driven abreast of the Mainwaring car."

"Why did the chauffeur notice him so particularly, Scuttle?"

"Because he thought the man might stop, pick him up, and drive him to a garage, sir. The chauffeur had his livery on, and he stepped out from the curb and motioned to this man. The chauffeur's quite thin himself, sir, and he naturally noticed the other's corpulence."

"The man didn't stop, Scuttle?"

"No, sir. He seemed, according to the chauffeur, to be driving fast and with a purpose. When the chauffeur saw his swarthy complexion, he wondered if the man might not be following Mainwaring's car; but he dismissed the thought as being a bit farfetched. Yet there can be no doubt of it that it was this man who held up Mainwaring and killed the monkey."

"Killed the monkey!" Lester Leith exclaimed. "Do you mean that this was *all* the man accomplished?"

"Yes, sir. He killed the monkey. That seemed to be what he wanted to overtake the car for."

"And didn't take anything?"

"No, sir."

"That's odd," Leith said. "And the man was masked?"

"Yes, sir, he was, but the nurse feels quite certain that he was a native of Southern India. Both she and Mainwaring agree that he was very fat although he moved with catlike quickness. He was driving a car which had been stolen."

"How do they know the car was stolen?" Leith asked.

"Because the chauffeur, returning with the jack, saw this same car again. This time it was speeding away from the scene of the holdup. He noticed that the driver was wearing a mask which concealed his features, so he took occasion to notice the license number. He gave it to the police, of course, as soon as he learned of the holdup. The police found that the car had been stolen. Later on, they found the car itself parked on Ninety-third Street. It had been abandoned there."

"On Ninety-third Street," Lester Leith said, frowning. "Wait a minute, Scuttle. Isn't there a suburban railroad station there?"

"Yes, sir. I believe there is, sir. That's the station where nearly all of the incoming and outgoing trains stop to pick up passengers who prefer to avoid the congestion of the central depot."

"And the monkey was slit open, Scuttle?"

"Yes, sir."

"What was the chauffeur's name, Scuttle?"

"Deekin. Parsley B. Deekin, sir."

"Any photographs of him?"

"Yes, sir. Here's one, sir."

Leith studied the photograph of the thin hatchet face, prominent cheekbones, and large eyes. "Rather young to be a chauffeur, isn't it, Scuttle?"

"I don't think he's so young, sir. It's because he's thin that he looks young; the effect of a slender figure, you know."

"I see," Leith said, frowning thoughtfully. "And after the monkey was killed, he was slit open?"

"That's right, cut almost in two, and then tossed back into the car. Mainwaring said he's been afraid all along that an attempt would be made on

the monkey's life by some religious fanatic. He said that the monkey was a temple monkey, that his life was supposed to have been consecrated to the priests of Hanuman. He says that in India when a monkey has been so consecrated and then leaves the temple, the priests consider it a desertion just as they do when a priest has consecrated his life to the monkey god and then tries to leave the temple and take up life somewhere else."

"Sounds like a barbarous custom, Scuttle." Lester Leith said.

"Yes, sir, it is, sir. Oh, quite."

"Any other witnesses, Scuttle?"

"None who saw the man's face, sir. A young woman glimpsed a very fat, paunchy man with a mask which concealed his entire face driving a car. She couldn't even tell the make of the car, however. She thought it was a sedan. The car the man used was, in reality, a coupé. It had been stolen about six o'clock in the evening. Because the man took such pains to conceal all of his skin, the police deduce he must have been swarthy."

Leith grinned.

"Aided in that deduction, of course, Scuttle, by the chauffeur's statement."

"Yes, sir, I suppose so, sir. But Mainwaring and the nurse both thought he was a native of Southern India, you'll remember, sir."

Lester Leith held up his hand for silence. "Wait a minute, Scuttle; I want to think."

For several seconds he sat rigid in the chair, his face an expressionless mask, his eyes slitted in thought. The valet-spy, his big form perched on the edge of the chair, regarded Lester Leith thoughtfully.

Suddenly Lester Leith said: "Scuttle, let me have the telephone book, and find out what trains pull out of the Ninety-third Street Station between seven and nine thirty in the evening. Get me the information at once."

"Very good, sir," the spy said, vanishing in the direction of the soundproof closet in which the telephone was housed.

Five minutes later, he was back with the information. "A train leaving the central depot at seven twenty, sir, stops at Ninety-third Street at seven fifty, at Belting Junction at eight ten, at Robbinsdale at eight thirty, and at Beacon City at nine thirty. After that, it becomes a limited train and makes no stops until after midnight. Those other stops are merely for the purpose of taking on suburban passengers."

Leith said: "Very well, Scuttle. Plug in the telephone extension, and put the desk phones over here."

When the spy had done so, Lester Leith called the baggageman at Belting Junction, and said: "Hello, I'm trying to trace a suitcase which was checked through on the train which leaves Central Depot at seven twenty in the evening. This suitcase went forward on the evening of the thirteenth, and has not been claimed. I have reason to believe it was checked to your depot."

"Who is this talking?" the baggageman asked.

"This is the claim adjuster's office," Leith said. "Shake a leg."

"Just a minute," the baggageman said. And then after a few moments, he reported, "No, there's no such suitcase here."

"Thank you," Leith said, and hung up.

He called the station agent at Robbinsdale, made the same statement, and secured the same answer. But at Beacon City, the situation was different. The baggageman said:

"Yeah, we've got a suitcase here. It came on that train, and has never been called for. I've been charging storage on it at the rate of ten cents for every twenty-four hours, after it was uncalled for forty-eight hours. What do you want me to do with it?"

"Describe the suitcase," Leith said.

"Well, it's cheap, split-leather suitcase, tan, with straps. It's rather large."

"Any initials on it?" Leith said.

"Yes, there are the initials A.B.C. in black on both ends of the suitcase."

"Well," Leith said, "a man will probably call for it tomorrow. He won't have his claim check. Make him deposit a bond of fifty dollars and describe the contents, then give him the suitcase."

"It'll be all right to give it to him if he doesn't have the check?" the baggage agent asked.

"Yes, *if* he describes the contents, and *if* he puts up a fifty-dollar bond. The check's been lost, and this party claims the baggageman here put a wrong check on it. I don't think he did, but anyhow we've located the suitcase, and that's all that's necessary. He'll be out tomorrow. In the meantime you open the suitcase, familiarize yourself with the contents, and don't let anyone who can't describe those contents have the suitcase. That's important."

Lester Leith hung up the telephone, and nodded to the spy.

"I think, Scuttle," he said, "that the situation is now greatly clarified."

"What do you mean, sir?" the spy asked.

Leith said: "Has it ever occurred to you, Scuttle, that Mainwaring resorted to rather a clever trick? Before he landed, he opened the mouth of the monkey and forced those emeralds into the monkey's stomach, probably intending to kill the monkey himself and remove the stones when he had reached his home. However some clever holdup man, who deduced what must have happened, swooped down on him, killed the monkey, cut the animal open, and took out the stones. Mainwaring naturally isn't in a position to make a complete explanation to the police because then he'd be guilty of smuggling and subject to a fine. So he had to put the best face he could on the matter and make up this cock-and-bull story about the priests of Hanuman following the monkey and exacting his life as a sacrifice."

"Good heavens, sir! You're right!" the spy exclaimed.

"Of course I'm right," Leith said, frowning slightly. "Don't seem so surprised, Scuttle. I have shown what is, after all, only very ordinary intelligence."

"But what happened to the gems, sir?"

Lester Leith stared thoughtfully into space for several seconds. At length he said: "In order to answer that question, Scuttle, I would require two specially constructed canes, four imitation emeralds, a package of cotton, and a gum-chewing secretary."

"You've already asked me to get the secretary," the spy suggested.

"So I have," Leith said, "so I have."

"If you don't mind my asking, sir, what type of cane did you have in mind?"

"I would need two canes, identical in appearance," Lester Leith said, "two very large canes with hollow handles; that is, there must be a receptacle hollowed out in the handle of each cane. This receptacle must be capable of concealing two of the imitation emeralds; and one cane must have a telescopic metal ferrule so it can be extended and locked into position, or telescoped back and locked into position. Aside from that, both canes must be exactly alike."

The spy blinked his eyes. "I don't see what that has to do with it, sir," he said.

Leith smiled. "After all, Scuttle, the gum-chewing secretary is of prime importance. However, Scuttle, I think I've exercised my wits enough for this afternoon. I believe I have a dinner engagement?"

"Yes, sir. That's right, sir. But when do you want these canes, sir?"

"I'd require them by tomorrow morning at the very latest. I— What's that, Scuttle?"

"You were talking about the canes, sir, when you wanted them."

"Good heavens," Leith said. "*I* don't want the canes. I was merely working out an academic solution for a crime. Under no circumstances, Scuttle, are you to take me seriously."

"Yes, sir," the spy said.

"And I don't want the canes."

"No, sir."

"Nor the cotton."

"No, sir."

"But," Leith said, "you *might* get me the secretary, Scuttle. Have each agency send its most proficient gum chewer."

CHAPTER II
BEAVER REPORTS

Sergeant Ackley sat at a battered desk in police headquarters and scowled across at the undercover man who had finished making his report.

"Damn it, Beaver," he said. "The thing doesn't make sense."

The undercover man sighed resignedly. "None of his stuff ever makes sense," he said, "and yet somehow he always fits everything together into a perfect pattern and whisks the swag right out from under our noses. I'm getting tired of it."

"Of course," Sergeant Ackley went on, "this suitcase is important. You can see what happened, Beaver. The robber, whoever he was, stopped in at the depot and checked this suitcase."

"That, of course, gives us a clue to work on," the spy observed. "But Heaven knows what's in that suitcase. Leith told the baggageman to open it, familiarize himself with the contents, and not to let anyone have it who couldn't describe those contents. Now, of course, we *could* go down there with a warrant and—"

"Absolutely not," Sergeant Ackley interrupted. "That's foolish, Beaver. We've been working for months to catch this man, and now that we have a perfect trap all prepared, we'd be foolish to go down and steal the bait ourselves."

"Then you don't think the gems are in the suitcase?"

"Why the devil should they be?" Sergeant Ackley asked.

The undercover man shrugged his shoulders, and said, "Stranger things have happened."

"Well, not *that* strange," Sergeant Ackley snapped. "After all, the robber took considerable chances in order to get those gems. He undoubtedly must have followed Mainwaring from India. That much of Mainwaring's story is true; and the robber, once having secured possession of those stones, certainly made tracks for parts unknown. He's probably thousands of miles away from here by this time, traveling by airplane, but there must be something in that suitcase—something which fits into the scheme of the thing. But I don't see how it's going to do Leith any good, because he can't describe the contents of that suitcase any better than we can."

"Well," Beaver said, "I've made *my* report."

And his voice indicated that he considered himself relieved from further responsibility.

Sergeant Ackley said: "We'll plant a couple of men around the depot. The minute that suitcase leaves the place, we'll get busy and follow it to its destination. If Leith picks it up, so much the better. If he sends some messenger, we'll follow the messenger until he leads us to Leith. If it's an accomplice of the crook, we'll follow him. Of course, we've known all along that Mainwaring's account of the crime was fishy. We felt certain the stickup was over those gems. That was why I wanted you to get Leith interested in working it out. Of course that suitcase may . . . well, we'll just keep that as bait."

Beaver got to his feet.

"Well," he said, "I've told you everything I know. Now, I've got to get busy and give those girls a once-over as they come in. I suppose they'll have chewing gum stuck all over the place."

Sergeant Ackley assayed a ponderous attempt at humor. "Be careful they don't gum the works, Beaver."

The undercover man started to say something, then changed his mind, and marched to the door.

"Be sure to keep me posted, Beaver," Sergeant Ackley warned. "This case is the most important one you've handled yet. We'll catch Lester Leith redhanded. We'll get enough proof to convict Mainwaring of smuggling, and if those two gems are equal to descriptions, we'll pick up a nice reward."

The undercover man said: "You thought you had him before. If you'll take my advice, you'll figure out what he wants those two canes for and where those four counterfeit stones fit into the picture. Otherwise you'll come another cropper."

"That will do, Beaver," Sergeant Ackley roared. "*I'm* running this case. *You* get back on the job and stay there!"

"Very well, sergeant," the undercover man said with that synthetic humility which he had learned to assume until it had become almost second nature to him.

He opened the door a few inches, oozed his huge bulk out into the corridor, then quietly closed the door behind him.

Sergeant Ackley reached for the telephone.

CHAPTER III
GUM CHEWERS

The undercover man surveyed the dozen young women who had gathered in response to Lester Leith's summons. They sat grouped about the room in postures which were well calculated to show what Lester Leith's memorandum had referred as to "shapely means of locomotion." Each seemed vying with the other to attract attention to the fact that she was possessed of the necessary qualifications.

As might have been expected, however, from the nature of the request which had been sent to the employment agency, only those young women who had seen enough of life to become slightly calloused to the treatment afforded a working girl had applied. The qualification of being a blatant and inveterate gum chewer had also tended to accomplish the same purpose. Had Lester Leith deliberately sought to acquire a young woman who knew her way around, who was willing to take chance, and was unusually self-reliant, he could not have thought of any means better designed to give him exactly what he wanted.

Beaver, the undercover man, entered the room and surveyed the twelve waiting applicants, noted the rhythmic swing of the rapidly chewing jaws, heard unmistakable evidences of a proficiency in gum popping; and his black greedy eyes swept in eager appraisal the exposed lengths of sheer silk terminating in shapely, well-shod feet.

The undercover man took from his pocket twelve twenty-dollar bills, and cleared his throat.

Twelve pairs of eyes fastened on those twenty-dollar bills. The girls, with one accord and as though at some preconcerted signal, quit chewing, some of them holding their jaws poised, the wad of gum balanced precariously between upper and lower molars.

The valet said: "You young ladies are all applicants for this position. Mr. Leith has instructed me to give to each applicant a twenty-dollar bill. This will be in addition to the three hundred dollars a month salary which is to be paid to the one who gets the job. Mr. Leith has asked me to state that he appreciates your courtesy in coming here, and he wanted me to tell you that he felt quite certain that each of you had . . . 'the external qualifications' were the words he used," the spy said, letting his eyes once more slither along the row of shapely limbs. "In just a moment Mr. Leith will—"

Lester Leith interrupted him by flinging open the door of his sitting room.

"Good afternoon," he said.

Twelve pairs of eyes changed from cynical appraisal to interest.

"Good afternoon," the applicants chorused.

Leith looked them over and said: "Obviously since there is only one position, eleven of you must necessarily be disappointed. I have tried to make some small contribution which will alleviate your disappointment somewhat, and, as you are all working girls, I believe that it is only fair to all concerned to pick a person to fill the position in the quickest manner possible. I will, therefore, look you over, and interview the person I consider the most talented first. I believe you understand that I am looking for young women with symmetrical limbs, and women who are inveterate gum chewers."

"Say," one of them said, "what's the idea about the gams?"

"Just what do you mean?" Leith asked.

"Is this a *job* or ain't it?" the girl asked.

"This," Leith assured her gravely, "is a job."

"Well," the girl said, "I didn't want to have any misunderstandings, that's all."

Lester Leith surveyed the girl with interest. "What," he asked, "is your name?"

"Evelyn Rae," she said, "and I think I'm speaking for most of the others as well as myself when I say that I came up here to look the proposition over. I'm not so certain I'm making an application for the job. I don't like that crack about what you call shapely means of locomotion. I do *my* shorthand and *my* typewriting with my hands."

One or two of the others nodded.

A blond at the far end of the line shifted her gum, and said: "Speak for yourself, dearie. *I'll* do my own talking."

Lester Leith smiled at Evelyn Rae. "I think," he said, "you're the young woman I want to interview first. Come in, please."

She followed him into his private sitting room, surveying him with frankly dubious eyes.

"You may think I'm the one you want to work for you," she said, "but *I'm* not so sure you're the person *I* want to be *my* boss."

"I understand," Leith said. "I understood you the first time."

"All right," she said. "What are the duties?"

"Well," Leith told her, "you will take a train out of the city which leaves the depot at seven twenty tonight. You will arrive in Beacon City at nine thirty. From there on, the train is a limited train, making no stops until after midnight. I'll travel with you as far as Beacon City. We will have a drawing room."

"Oh, yeah?" she said. "That's what *you* think."

"At Beacon City," Leith went on heedless of the interruption, "a suitcase will be placed aboard the train. You will not open that suitcase. Under no circumstances are you even to look in it. At approximately ten p.m. you will be arrested."

"Arrested for what?" she asked.

"For being an accessory after the fact in the theft of two emeralds," Leith said.

"What'll I be guilty of?"

"Nothing."

"Then how can they arrest me?"

"It's a habit some of the more impulsive officers have," Leith pointed out.

"Well, I don't like it."

"Neither do I," Leith told her.

"What else do I do?"

"You will continue aboard the train in the custody of the officers until they make arrangements to stop and take you off and return you to the city. At that time, you will be released. The officers will apologize. You will retain counsel and threaten a suit for false arrest. The officers will be glad to compromise. I don't think you'll receive a very large sum by the way of a cash settlement, but you doubtless will wind up with sufficient pull to square any parking or speeding tickets you or your friends may get within the city limits for some time to come. There will be no other duties."

"Is this," she asked, "a line of hooey?"

Leith took three one-hundred-dollar bills from his pocket.

"I am," he said, "willing to show my good faith by paying you a month's salary in advance. You look honest to me."

"Honest but direct," she said. "What'll *you* be doing in that drawing room between Central Depot and Beacon City?"

"Reading."

"What'll you be doing *after* the train leaves Beacon City?"

Lester Leith smiled, and said, "The less you know about that the better."

Evelyn Rae looked at the three hundred-dollar bills speculatively. "That," she said, "is a lot of money."

Leith nodded.

"And not much work," she added.

Again Leith nodded.

"What else am I supposed to do?" she asked.

"Chew gum," Leith said. "Chew large quantities of gum. The gum, incidentally, will be furnished as a part of the traveling expenses. You will not have to pay for it."

She studied him for several seconds with thoughtful worldly-wise eyes, then she slowly nodded her head, and said: "I don't believe you're on the level, but what's the odds? It's a go."

Leith handed her the three one-hundred-dollar bills.

"And the first duty which you have," he said, "will be to explain to the other applicants that the position is filled."

She said: "Well, I've got to talk fast to put *that* idea across, particularly with that blonde." She moistened her fingers, slipped a wad of chewing gum from her mouth absent-mindedly, and mechanically stuck it under the arm of the chair.

Lester Leith nodded to himself, smiling his approval.

As she reached for the doorknob, Leith said:

"And you will start your duties at once. Please explain to Scuttle, my valet, that I do not wish to be disturbed for the next hour, and, in the meantime, arrange to pack your suitcase and get ready to travel. You will meet me at the Central Depot tonight, ready to board the seven-twenty train."

When the door had closed behind her, Leith opened a drawer in his desk, and took from it a piece of clear green glass which had been ground into facets, giving it the general appearance of a huge gem. Tiptoeing across to the chair where the young woman had been sitting, he took the piece of glass and pushed it up into the wad of chewing gum, held it there by a firm steady pressure of thumb and forefinger for several seconds, then gradually released it.

CHAPTER IV
PLANTED CLUE

The valet quietly opened the door of Leith's private sitting room, thrust in a cautious hand, and then eased himself through the narrow opening.

Lester Leith, watching him with eyes that were lazy-lidded in amusement, said: "Scuttle, it doesn't cost any more to open the door wide enough to walk through, instead of opening it a few inches and squeezing through sideways."

"Yes, sir. I know, sir," the spy said. "You mentioned it to me before. It's just a habit I have, sir."

Leith stared at him with wide startled eyes.

"Scuttle, what the devil are you carrying under your arm?"

"The canes, sir."

"The canes, Scuttle?"

"Yes, sir."

"Good heavens, *what* canes?"

"Don't you remember, sir, those that you ordered, the ones that have hollow handles, and one of them has an adjustable ferrule so it can be telescoped and locked in position?"

"Scuttle," Lester Leith said, "*I* didn't want those canes."

"You *didn't*, sir? I thought you told me to get them."

"Why no," Leith said, "I merely mentioned that I thought a person who had two canes such as that and an attractive secretary who was addicted to promiscuous gum chewing could solve the mystery of the murdered monkey. But I told you not to get the canes."

"I'm sorry, sir. I must have misunderstood you. I thought *you* wanted to solve it."

"No, no!" Lester Leith exclaimed. "I was merely outlining an academic solution."

"But you've hired the secretary."

"I know I have," Leith said. "That's an entirely different matter. I hired her on general principles."

"I'm sorry, sir. I'm frightfully sorry, but I thought you wanted me to get the canes. Now that I have them, sir . . . well—"

Leith said: "Oh, well, now that you have them, I may as well take a look at them. Pass them over, Scuttle."

The spy handed over the canes. Leith regarded them with pursed lips and narrowed eyes.

"It's rather a neat job," the spy said. "You see, they're canes with just a knob for a handle, and that knob unscrews. The joint is rather cleverly concealed, don't you think so?"

Leith nodded, twisted the head of one of the canes. It promptly unscrewed. Leith looked inside and gave a sudden start of surprise.

"Why, Scuttle," he said, "there are emeralds in here!"

"No, sir, not emeralds, sir. Just the imitations which you ordered."

"Ordered, Scuttle?"

"Well, you mentioned them as being things which would enable you to solve the mystery of the murdered monkey."

Leith said reprovingly: "Scuttle, I don't like this. I was outlining merely an academic solution. Why the devil would I want to solve the mystery of the murdered monkey?"

"I'm sure I don't know, sir, except that it would be a source of great gratification for you to know that your reasoning had proved correct."

Leith said irritably: "I don't need to go to all that trouble to demonstrate the correctness of my reasoning, Scuttle. It's self-evident when you consider the basic facts of the case."

The spy wet his thick lips with the tip of an anxious tongue.

"Yes, sir," he said eagerly. And then after a moment, "You were about to mention what you consider the basic facts, sir?"

Lester Leith eyed him coldly. "I was not, Scuttle."

"Oh," the spy said.

"By the way," Leith observed, "I've given Evelyn Rae a month's wages in advance."

"Yes, sir. So Miss Rae told me, sir. She said that you didn't wish to be disturbed for an hour so I waited to give you the canes. You were, perhaps, busy?"

Leith said, "Perhaps, Scuttle."

"I've just had the devil of a time, sir, if you don't mind my saying so," the spy complained.

"How come?" Leith inquired.

"Cleaning up after those young women."

"Were they untidy?" Leith asked.

"Chewing gum, sir. I don't think I ever had quite so disagreeable a job in my life. It was stuck to the underside of the chair arms, the chair buttons, under the table. It was in the most unlikely places and the most annoying places, sir. You'd drop your hand to the arm of the chair, and a wad of moist chewing gum would stick to your fingers."

Leith yawned, and stifled the yawn with four

polite fingers. "Doubtless, Scuttle," he said, "you'll remember in the call which I sent out for secretaries, I asked for gum chewers who were careless with their parking, inclined to be promiscuous with their leftovers. Doubtless, Scuttle, the young ladies were merely attempting to show that they were properly qualified for the position. After all, Scuttle, you know jobs aren't easily obtained these days, so one can hardly blame the young ladies for being anxious to secure one which pays a good salary."

The spy said: "That's one of the things I couldn't understand . . . if you don't think I'm presumptuous, sir."

"What is that, Scuttle?"

"*Why* you wanted a young woman who was such an inveterate gum chewer and what you were pleased to describe as such a promiscuous parker."

Leith nodded. "I dare say, Scuttle."

"Dare say what, sir?"

"That you couldn't understand it," Leith said.

The spy's face flushed an angry brick-red.

"And now," Leith said, "I have some preparations to make. By the way, Scuttle, did you notice in the newspaper that Mr. Mainwaring was to address the Explorers' Club tonight on 'Changes in the Psychology of Native Religions'?"

"Yes, sir," the spy said.

"Probably it will be a most interesting lecture," Leith observed.

"Did you intend to be present?" Beaver asked.

"I?" Leith inquired. "Good heavens, no, Scuttle! I'd be bored to death, but I merely commented that the lecture would probably be interesting . . . to those who have a taste for that sort of thing. By the way, Scuttle, you'd better pack my bag, and get me a drawing room on the seven-twenty train tonight."

"A drawing room, sir?"

"Yes, Scuttle."

"Very good, sir. Where to?"

"Oh, clean through," Leith said airily. "As far as the train goes. I don't believe in halfway measures, Scuttle."

The valet said, "I thought perhaps you wanted it only as far as Beacon City, sir."

"Beacon City?" Leith inquired. "Why the devil should I want to go to Beacon City?"

"I'm sure I don't know, sir," the spy said.

"And *I'm* quite sure you don't," Leith observed in a tone of finality as he terminated the interview.

After Leith had left the room, the big spy, his face twisted with rage, shook clenched fists at the door.

"Damn you," he said. "Damn your sneering, supercilious hide! One of these days I'll have the pleasure of watching you in a cell, and when I do, I'll give you something to think of! You're quite sure I don't, eh? You and your chewing gum. Bah!"

The spy sat down in the big chair, mopped his perspiring forehead, then pocketing his handkerchief, wrapped his thick fingers around the arm of the chair. With an exclamation of annoyance, he jumped up and scrubbed at his fingers with the handkerchief.

"Another wad of gum!" he exclaimed irritably. Wearily, he opened the blade of a huge pocketknife, dropped down to his knees, and prepared to scrape off the moist wad of chewing gum.

Something green caught his eye. He tapped it experimentally with the blade of his knife. Then, with sudden interest showing in his eyes, he cut off the wad of gum, and stared at the piece of green glass which had been embedded in it.

For several seconds, the spy stared with wide, startled eyes. Then, with the wad of chewing gum and the glass gem still smeared on the blade of his knife, he stretched his long legs to the limit as he dashed for the telephone to call Sergeant Ackley.

"Hello, hello, hello, sergeant," Beaver called as soon as he heard the sergeant's voice on the line. "This is Beaver talking. I've got the whole thing doped out."

"What thing?" Sergeant Ackley asked.

"That monkey murder."

"Go ahead," Sergeant Ackley ordered. "Spill it."

"The murder of the monkey was just a blind," Beaver said. "The chewing gum is the significant thing about the whole business. Remember that the nurse sat on a table and chewed gum all the time the customs officials were searching Mainwaring, and then, of course, the customs officials searched *her*."

"Well, what about it?" Sergeant Ackley asked in his most discouraging tone. "What the devil does gum chewing have to do with it?"

"Don't you see, sergeant?" Beaver said. "While she was chewing gum with a certain amount of nervousness natural to a young woman under those circumstances, she was able to feed large quantities of gum into her mouth without exciting suspicion."

"Well?" Sergeant Ackley asked in a voice well calculated to chill even the most loyal supporter.

"Well," Beaver went on, speaking slightly slower and with less assurance, "you can see what happened. While she was chewing gum, she sat there on the table, swinging her legs. She'd chew for a while, and then she'd take a wad of gum out of her mouth and stick it on the under side of the table. Then she'd start chewing more gum. Now, *she* had those emeralds with *her*. While they were searching the baggage and asking questions of Mainwaring, she stuck those emeralds in the gum on the under side of the table in the customs inspector's office right under his very nose. Then, after they'd finished searching her and her baggage and Mainwaring and his baggage, she made an excuse to run back to the office of the customs inspector. You'll remember that the newspaper said she thanked him for his courtesy. Well, while she was thanking him, she reached her hand under the table, and slipped out the emeralds and walked out with them. It was cleverly done."

There was a long pause while the undercover man waited, listening; and Sergeant Ackley remained thoughtfully silent.

"Well," Beaver asked at length, "are you there, sergeant?"

"Yes, of course I'm here," Sergeant Ackley said. "What else, Beaver?"

"What else? Isn't that enough? I've got it all doped out. That's the manner in which—"

"I think you're getting unduly excited over a very obvious matter, Beaver," Sergeant Ackley said. "*I* had figured all that out just as soon as you told me Leith insisted upon a secretary who was an inveterate gum chewer and a promiscuous parker."

"Oh," the undercover man said, and then after a moment added: "I see. You thought of it first."

"That's right," Sergeant Ackley said. "By the way, Beaver, how did *you* happen to think of it?"

"I just thought it out," the spy said wearily.

"No, no, Beaver. Now don't hang up. There must have been something which brought the idea to your mind."

"I reasoned it out," the spy said.

"But something must have given you a clue."

"What was it gave *you* your clue?" the undercover man asked.

"*I*," Sergeant Ackley said with dignity, "have risen to greater heights in my profession than you have, Beaver. It stands to reason that my mind is trained to arrive at conclusions more rapidly than yours. Also, I have more time for concentration. You were busy with your duties as valet. I feel certain that something must have given you the tipoff. Now what was it? Don't be insubordinate, Beaver."

"Oh, all right," the undercover man said wearily. "I happened to find where Leith had been rehearsing the secretary. He'd given her a wad of gum and a piece of green glass about the size of a good big emerald. She'd practiced sticking the gum on the under side of a chair arm, and then slipping the emerald up into the chewing gum. Evidently, they're rehearsing an act they're going to put on later."

"You should have told me *that*," Sergeant Ackley said reproachfully, "as soon as you had me on the line, and not tried to make a grandstand with a lot of deductive reasoning. Don't let it happen again, Beaver. Do you understand?"

"I understand," the spy said, as he dropped the receiver into its cradle.

CHAPTER V
THE RUBBER SUIT

Evelyn Rae was standing by the train gate when Lester Leith arrived. Her jaws were swinging with the rhythmic ease of a habitual gum chewer. Despite the fact that it was only two minutes before train time, she showed no nervousness whatever, but raised her eyes to Lester Leith and said casually:

"Hello, there. I was wondering if you were going to leave me at the altar."

"Hardly," Leith said, "but I've been rather busy. Here, give your bags to this redcap. Let's go."

The conductor was yelling, "All aboard," as Leith grabbed Evelyn Rae's arm and rushed her through the gates. And as soon as the porter had juggled the baggage through behind them, the gateman snapped the brass chain into position, and swung the big doors shut—the seven-twenty limited had officially departed. Actually it waited for Leith and his newly-employed secretary to get aboard before lurching into creaking motion.

Leith settled down in the drawing room, opened his bag, and took out a case of chewing gum in assorted flavors. "I want you," he said, "to try these and see which you prefer."

Back in the depot, a plain-clothes man telephoned ahead to Sergeant Ackley, who was waiting at Ninety-third Street. "O.K., sergeant," he said, "You've got thirty minutes to get things fixed up and get aboard. Your drawing room is all reserved."

"He took the train?" Sergeant Ackley asked.

"He's aboard all right. He played it pretty slick. He had his watch set right to the second, and waited to be certain he and the girl were the last people through the gates. He did that so you couldn't follow him aboard the train, but he overlooked the fact that it stopped at Ninety-third Street."

"Well, *I* haven't overlooked it," Sergeant Ackley said gloatingly. "The time will come when that crook will realize that he's fighting a master mind. It's only luck that's enabled him to slip through my fingers so many times before. When it comes to brains, I'll match mine with his any day in the week."

"Atta boy, sergeant!" the detective exclaimed approvingly, dropped the receiver into place, and then, running out his tongue, showered the transmitter with a very moist but heartfelt razzberry.

Lester Leith took off his shoes, put on bedroom slippers, hung up his coat and vest, slipped into a lounging robe, and took a book from his suitcase.

Evelyn Rae watched him with cautious, appraising eyes. As Lester Leith became engaged in his book, she slowly settled back against the cushions.

Leith rang for the porter, ordered a table, and when it was placed in position in between the seats, put the case of chewing gum on it.

Evelyn Rae moistened her thumb and forefinger, slipped out the wad of gum she had been chewing, and absent-mindedly pushed it against the under side of the table. She tore open a package of Juicy Fruit and fed two sticks into her mouth, one after the other.

"Pretty good stuff," she said, between chews. "This must be pretty fresh."

Leith said: "It's direct from the wholesalers, and they say it left the factory less than a week ago."

After she had chewed for several minutes, Leith said: "I'd like to have you try some of that Doublemint and then contrast that flavor with the pepsin."

"O.K.," she said. "Give me a few more minutes with this. I haven't got the good out of it yet."

The train rumbled along through the darkness. Evelyn Rae began to make herself at home.

"Gotta magazine or anything?" she asked.

Leith nodded, and took several magazines from his suitcase. She settled down with a motion-picture magazine to casual reading. Soon she became interested.

"Don't forget that Doublemint," Leith said.

"I won't," she told him, and pressed the chewed Juicy Fruit against the under side of the table.

At Ninety-third Street, Sergeant Ackley gave last-minute instructions to the undercover man and two detectives who were pacing the platform.

"Now listen," Ackley said. "Remember he *may* be looking out of the window, or he may get out and walk up and down the platform. We've got to get aboard without him seeing us. You two birds stand out on the platform when you hear the train coming. He doesn't know you. His reservation is Drawing Room A in Car D57. You two get aboard, go on back to that car and make sure he's in his drawing room. Then signal with your flashlight, and Beaver and I will come aboard and go directly to *our* drawing room which is in D56, the car ahead. Do you get me?"

"O.K., sergeant," the older of the two detectives said.

"Get ready," Sergeant Ackley warned. "Here she comes."

A station bell clanged a strident warning. The big yellow headlight of the thundering locomotive loomed up out of the darkness. Passengers for the limited swirled into little excited groups, exchanging last farewells as travelers picked up their baggage.

The big limited train rumbled into the station. While Sergeant Ackley and Beaver hid in the waiting room, the two detectives spotted Lester Leith's stateroom, flashed a go-ahead signal, and the officers dashed aboard. The brass-throated bells clanged their warning, and the long line of Pullmans creaked into motion.

In Drawing Room A in Car D57, Lester Leith merely glanced at his wrist watch, then took a cigarette from the hammered silver case in his pocket, tapped it on his thumbnail, and snapped a match into flame.

On the opposite seat, Evelyn Rae, her back bolstered up with pillows, her mind absorbed in the picture magazine, slid around to draw up her knees to furnish a prop for the magazine. Absent-mindedly, she slipped the gum from her mouth, pressed it against the under side of the table, and groped with her fingers until she found a fresh package. Without taking her eyes off the article she was reading, she tore off the wrappers and fed sticks of gum into her mouth.

The train, having cleared the more congested district of the city, rumbled into constantly increasing speed.

Belting Junction at eight ten and Robbinsdale at eight thirty were passed without incident. At five minutes past nine, Lester Leith said:

"I think I'll take a stroll on the platform when we get to Beacon City."

Evelyn Rae might not have heard him. She was reading an absorbing article on one of her favorite motion-picture stars. The article told of the gameness, courage, the moral stamina of the star, and Evelyn Rae occasionally blinked back tears of sympathy as she traced the star's unfortunate search for love and understanding through the tangled skein of Hollywood's romance.

Lester Leith picked up his shoes, dropped one of them, and bent over to retrieve it.

Looking up at the under side of the table, he saw wad after wad of moist gum pressed against the wood.

Slipping two of the imitation emeralds from his pocket, he pushed them up into the soft gum. Wetting the tips of his fingers, he kneaded the sticky substance over the imitation gems.

The train slowed for Beacon City, and Evelyn Rae was not even conscious that it was slowing. Busily absorbed in reading the adventures of an extra girl who came to Hollywood and attracted the romantic interest of one of the more popular stars, she barely looked up as Lester Leith slipped out of the door and into the corridor.

As the junction point, Beacon City represented an important stop in the journey of the limited. Here two passenger coaches were transferred from one line and two Pullmans added from another. The station rated a fifteen-minute stop.

Lester Leith picked up a porter and hurried to the baggage room.

"I'm on the limited," he told the man in charge of the baggage counter. "I have a suitcase I want to pick up. I haven't the check for it, but I can describe the contents. It came down on the night of the thirteenth on the limited, and was put off here to wait for me. The whole thing was a mistake. I got in touch with the claim office, and they located—"

"Yes, I know all about it," the baggageman said. "You've got to put up a bond."

"A what?"

"A cash bond."

"That's an outrage," Leith said. "I can describe the contents. There's absolutely no possibility that you can get into any trouble by delivering that suitcase to me, and what's more—"

"No bond, no suitcase," the man said. "I'm sorry, but that's orders from headquarters. They came from the claim department."

"How much bond?" Lester Leith asked.

"Fifty dollars."

The two detectives who had followed Leith into the baggage room were busy checking articles of hand baggage. Apparently, they paid no attention to the conversation which was going on.

Leith opened his wallet, took out ten five-dollar bills, and said:

"This is an outrage."

"O.K.," the baggageman said. "You can get this money back later on. You'll have to take it up with the claim department. This is just the nature of a bond to indemnify the railroad company. Now, what's in the suitcase?"

At this point the detectives seemed suddenly to become absent-minded. They lost interest in their baggage and moved surreptitiously closer.

Leith said, without hesitating. "It's part of a masquerade costume joke that was played on some friends. There's a costume in there by which a thin man can make it appear he's enormously fat."

"You win," the baggageman said. "I'd been wondering what the devil those pneumatic gadgets were for. Regular rubber clothes. I couldn't figure it. I guess you pump them up with a bicycle pump, and that's all there is to it, eh?"

"Not a bicycle pump," Leith said, smiling. "It's quicker to stand at the nozzle of a pressure hose at a service station. All right, make me out a receipt for the fifty dollars, and I'll be on my way. I have to catch this train."

He turned to the porter, handed him a dollar, and said:

"All right, redcap, rush this aboard the train, put it in Drawing Room A in Car D57. There's a young woman in there. So knock on the door and explain to her that I had the suitcase put aboard. She's my secretary."

"Yassah, yassah," the grinning boy said. "Right away, suh."

The detectives took no chances. One of them followed the suitcase aboard the train. The other waited for Leith to get his receipt.

"All aboard. All aboard for the limited," the brakeman cried.

The station bell clanged into sharp summons.

The baggageman looked up from the receipt he was writing. "You've got a minute and a half after that," he said.

"All aboard. All aboard," cried the conductor.

The baggageman scribbled a hasty receipt. The bell of the locomotive clanged into action. The baggageman thrust the receipt into Leith's hand.

"O.K.," he said, "you'd better hustle."

Leith sprinted across the platform. Porters were banging vestibule doors. The long train creaked into motion.

A porter saw Leith coming, opened the vestibule door, and hustled Leith aboard. The detective caught the next car down.

The minute the detective had vanished into the vestibule, Leith suddenly exclaimed, "Oh, I forgot my wallet!"

"You can't get off now, boss," the porter said.

"The hell I can't!" Leith told him, jerked open the vestibule door, and stepped down to the stairs. He swung out to the platform with the easy grace of a man who has reduced the hopping of trains to a fine art.

The engineer, knowing he had a straight, uninterrupted run during which he must smoothly clip off the miles, slid the throttle open, and the powerful engine, snaking the long string of Pullmans behind it, roared into rocking speed as Lester Leith, left behind on the station, saw the red lights on the rear of the train draw closer together and then vanish into the darkness.

In the stateroom of Car D56, Sergeant Ackley sat hunched over a table, his elbows spread far apart, his chin resting in his hands, chewing nervously at a soggy cigar. His eyes, glittering with excitement, stared across at Beaver, the undercover man. The two detectives made their report.

"Hell, sergeant," the man who had followed the suitcase aboard said, "the thing's all cut and dried. Leith pulled that stickup himself. He's got a bunch of rubber clothes he can put on and inflate with air, and they made him look like a big fat guy. He stuck on a cap and mask, and—"

"Wait a minute, wait a minute," Sergeant Ackley interrupted. "Leith didn't pull that stickup himself. Leith is pulling a hijack."

"Well, that's what's in the suitcase, all right," the detective said, "and Leith knew all about it."

"That's right," the second officer chimed in. "He spoke right up and described the stuff in the suitcase—a masquerade costume to make a thin guy look fat."

Sergeant Ackley twisted the cigar between trembling lips. Suddenly he jumped to his feet.

"O.K., boys," he said. "We make the pinch!"

He jerked open the door of his drawing room.

"Do I stay here?" Beaver asked.

"No," Sergeant Ackley said, "you can come with us. You can throw off your disguise, and face him in his true colors. You can get even with him for some of these taunts and insults."

The burly undercover man's fist clenched.

"The big thing I want to get even with him for," he said, "is his calling me Scuttle. He Scuttles me this, and Scuttles me that. He says that I look like a pirate, and keeps asking me if perhaps some of my ancestors weren't pirates."

"As far as I'm concerned," Sergeant Ackley said, "the sky's the limit. My eyes aren't very good, and if you say he was resisting arrest and took a swing at you, I'll be inclined to help you defend yourself."

"I don't want any help," Beaver said. "All I want is three good punches."

Sergeant Ackley turned to the other two officers. "Remember," he said, "if Beaver swears this guy made a swing at him, we're all backing Beaver's play."

Two heads nodded in unison.

"Come on," Sergeant Ackley said, putting his star on the outside of his coat, and led the procession which marched grimly down the swaying aisle of the Pullman car where the porter, struggling with mattresses and green curtains as he made up the berths, looked up to stare with wide eyes.

"Do we knock?" Beaver asked, as they swayed down the aisle of Car D57.

"Don't be silly," Ackley commented. He twisted the knob of the stateroom door, slammed it open. The car porter watched them with wide-eyed wonder. A moment later he was joined by the porter from the car ahead.

Evelyn Rae was sprawled comfortably on the seat, her left elbow propped against the table, a pillow behind her head, her right instep fitted against the curved arm of the upholstering. She looked up with casual inquiry, then suddenly lowered her knees, pulled down her skirt, and said:

"Say, what's the idea?"

"Where's Leith?" Sergeant Ackley asked.

"Why, I don't know. Who are you? Why, hello, Beaver. What is this?"

Sergeant Ackley said, "Come on! Where's Leith?"

"I haven't seen him for a while. I was reading and—"

"How did that suitcase get here?"

"A redcap brought it in. He said Leith told him to put it aboard."

"Where was that?"

"This last stop."

"What did Leith say after we pulled out of that last stop?"

"Why, I haven't seen him since the suitcase was delivered here."

Sergeant Ackley's laugh was scornful and sarcastic. "Try and get me to fall for *that* one. You must think I'm crazy. Beaver, open the door to the lavatory. Jim, dust out and cover the train."

The undercover man jerked open the lavatory door.

"No one here," he said.

The other detective dashed out into the car.

The car porter pushed his head in the door. "What yo'-all want? The gen'man what—"

Sergeant Ackley held up the lapel of his coat to emphasize the significance of his badge. "Get the hell out of here," he said.

The porter backed out, his jaw and lips moving, but no words coming.

Sergeant Ackley slammed the door shut.

"Let's take a look in that suitcase," he said.

The officers unstrapped the suitcase, opened it. Sergeant Ackley pawed through the clothes.

"O.K.," he said to the girl, "where are those two gems?"

"What two gems?"

"Don't stall. The two gems that were in there."

"You're nuts!" she said.

"I'll show you whether I'm nuts or not," Sergeant Ackley said. "You're an accomplice in this thing right now. You give me any more of your lip, and I'll arrest you as an accessory after the fact."

"After what fact?" she asked.

Sergeant Ackley's gesture was one of irritation.

"Mr. Leith thought he'd left *you* in the city," she said to Beaver.

"What Lester Leith thinks doesn't count right now," Sergeant Ackley observed. "I want those two emeralds."

"Those two emeralds?"

"Yes."

Before she could answer, the door of the drawing room burst open, and the detective who had been sent to find Leith said:

"Say, sergeant, here's a funny story from the porter of the second car back. That's the one that Leith hopped when the train pulled out. I grabbed the one behind. I went back and asked the porter what happened to the man who got aboard and—"

"Never mind all that palaver," Sergeant Ackley interrupted irritably. "Go ahead and tell me the answer. What happened?"

"He said that Lester Leith climbed aboard all right, and then jumped right back off again."

Sergeant Ackley's face darkened. "So you let him give you the slip, did you?"

The detective said indignantly: "Let him give me nothing! He got aboard the train all right, and I saw the vestibule door shut. The train damn near jerked my arms off when I got aboard the next car back. I hurried up to follow Leith to his stateroom here, but before I could get through the car, he'd had plenty of time to reach this stateroom. Remember, he was one car ahead of me. No one else could have done the thing any differently. How was I to know he was going to jump off?"

Sergeant Ackley whirled to Evelyn Rae. "I'm going to get those two stones," he said, "if I have to search every stitch you have on. So you'd better come through with them."

"I tell you I don't know what you're talking about," she said.

Beaver said significantly: "Remember that piece of glass in the chewing gum, sergeant. I'll bet they were just trying to find out whether a wad of chewing gum would hold—"

"Now," Sergeant Ackley said, "you're talking sense." He grabbed the table, swung it up on its hinges, looked at the assortment of gum gobs which studded the under side of the table. Suddenly a flash of green light caught his eye. With a whoop of triumph, he grabbed at the blob of gum. It stuck to his fingers, but pulled away enough to show the surface of a huge green object which was embedded in the sticky depths. "Hooray," Sergeant Ackley cried. "Caught at last. Snap the handcuffs on that woman."

CHAPTER VI
THE TWO TRICK CANES

There were lights in the building occupied by the Explorers' Club. From time to time could be heard bursts of laughter or spatterings of applause. The curb around the building was crowded with parked automobiles. Here and there chauffeur-driven cars showed a driver huddled over the steering wheel dozing or, perhaps, listening to the radio.

Lester Leith, swinging along the sidewalk, spotted the license number of Peter B. Mainwaring's automobile without difficulty. The chauffeur of the car was slumped over the wheel.

Leith walked around the car, and tapped him on the shoulder.

The man snapped to quick attention as he felt the touch of Lester Leith's finger. His right hand started toward his left coat lapel.

Lester Leith said easily, "You're Mainwaring's chauffeur?"

The man's thin, hatchet face was without expression as he said, from one side of his mouth, "What's it to you?" His right hand was held hovering over the left coat lapel.

"I have the cane that Mainwaring ordered," Lester Leith said. "He told me to deliver it to you, and to show you the secret compartment."

"Secret compartment?" Deekin said. "Say, I don't know what you're talking about."

Leith said: "Well, I don't give a damn whether you do or not. You don't need to be so short about it. I'm a working man, same as you are, and a damn good cane maker. I'm carrying out instructions, that's all. Now, here's the cane for Mainwaring. You tell him when he wants to get at the hidden receptacle, all he has to do is unscrew the top."

"What does he want a receptacle in a cane for?" Deekin asked, his voice more friendly.

Lester Leith smirked and said: "Probably to carry liver pills in. How the hell do I know? I have about a dozen clients who give me orders like this, and I'm paid enough to keep my mouth shut. Do you understand?"

Slow comprehension began to dawn on Deekin's face. The right hand which had been hovering near his chest moved away to rest on the steering wheel.

"What's this about unscrewing the head of the cane?" he asked.

Leith said, "Let me show you."

With deft fingers, he unscrewed the head of the cane, showed a cotton-lined receptacle on the interior. He pushed two fingers down into the cavity to show its depth. "There you are," he said. "Four and a half inches deep as ordered, and I defy anyone to look at this cane and tell that there's anything phony about it. Here it is."

"What's that other cane you've got?" Deekin asked.

"One I'm delivering to another customer," Leith told him.

"Say, what do you want me to do with this?"

"Just give it to Mr. Mainwaring, that's all," Leith said. "It's all paid for. Mainwaring will understand. He told me to be at the Explorers' Club, but not to ask for him, that his car would be waiting outside, and I was to leave the cane with his chauffeur. Don't be so damn dumb."

"I'm *not* so damn dumb," Deekin said, inspecting the cane with approval. "Say, buddy," with increasing friendliness, "that's a neat job."

"You're damn right it's a neat job," Leith said. "You ain't telling me anything. . . . Say, I wonder if Mainwaring is interested in knowing that they've caught the guy that robbed him."

"What do ya mean, robbed him?" Deekin asked.

Leith laughed scornfully. "I wasn't born yesterday," he said. "That story about the priests of Hanuman who showed up to avenge the monkey deserter from the temple is a lot of hooey that might go with some people, but you can save your breath as far as I'm concerned. They cut that monkey open to get at the smuggled gems. If your boss had had this cane with him, they wouldn't— Oh, well, never mind."

"What's this about catching the robber?" Deekin demanded.

"Well, they've just as good as caught him," Leith said. "They found out he wasn't a fat man at all. That was just a disguise. The guy stole a car just to pull the stickup, then he ran the car down to the Ninety-third Street Station, went in the men's room and took off his clothes. He had a specially constructed rubber-lined suit. All he had to do was put an air hose on it and blow it up so he looked as though he weighed about three hundred pounds. He stuck that suit in the suitcase, bought a railroad ticket to Beacon City, and checked the suitcase on the ticket. He figured no one would pay any attention to it there, and he'd have a chance to pick it up sometime later."

"Say, how about this?" Deekin interrupted. "Who did it?"

"I don't know who did it. I heard this other stuff come in over the radio just a little while ago," Leith said, "and I thought Mainwaring would probably be interested."

"How long ago?" the chauffeur asked.

"Oh, I don't know; ten or fifteen minutes ago. The police said they were working on some hot clues and expected an arrest to be made before midnight. You know how it is, the news announcers don't hand out too much information over the radio in a crime like that until the police tell them it's O.K. to release it. Well, buddy, I've got to be going. Be sure Mainwaring gets this cane. So long."

"So long," Deekin said.

Lester Leith walked down the street, swinging the other cane behind him.

The chauffeur mopped cold perspiration from his forehead. He looked apprehensively up at the Explorers' Club, then apparently seized with a sudden inspiration, jumped out of the car, pulled up the front seat, and attacked the body of the automobile with a screwdriver. A few moments later, he had lifted up a cleverly concealed plate and removed two blazing green

stones from a hidden receptacle. He unscrewed the head of the cane, dropped the two emeralds into the cotton-lined hollow, and screwed the head of the cane back on. He replaced the front seat in the automobile, jumped out, and started walking rapidly toward the corner, swinging the cane casually in his hand.

He heard running steps behind him.

"Hey," Lester Leith called. "I've made a mistake in that cane."

Deekin stopped, bracing himself ominously. His right hand once more sought the vicinity of his necktie.

Leith, drawing closer, said, "Gosh, I entirely forgot about the difference in length. The colonel is a long-legged guy, and the long cane is for him. I think I gave you the long cane, instead of the short one."

Deekin said ominously, "Well, what *you* think, don't count. *I* think this is the cane that Mainwaring wanted."

"By gosh," Leith said, with relief in his voice, "I guess you're right. That *is* the short cane after all."

Deekin clutched the cane firmly in his left hand, but appeared somewhat mollified as Leith made the announcement.

"Just a minute," Leith said; "let's measure them, just to be sure."

Still holding his cane firmly in his left hand, his right hand ready to dive under the lapel of his coat, Deekin stood perfectly still while Leith compared the canes. The one which Leith was holding was a full inch longer than the other.

Leith heaved a sigh.

"By gosh," he said, "I didn't realize that I was as long-legged as I am. You know, after I left you and started out to deliver this cane to the colonel, I swung it around a couple of times and damned if it didn't almost fit me. So then I got scared and—"

"Well, it's all right now," Deekin said.

"I'll say it is," Leith told him, twisting the ferrule of the cane in his gloved hands as though to polish it. "What were you doing, taking a walk?"

"Yes," Deekin said shortly.

"Well," Leith told him, "I'll go with you as far as the corner."

Deekin hesitated a moment, then said shortly, "All right, as far as the corner."

The two men walked side by side. Lester Leith took out his handkerchief and polished the glass surface of the cane which he held in his hand.

Deekin, after a hundred feet, surreptitiously turned to cast an apprehensive glance over his shoulder.

At that moment, Lester Leith shoved his cane down and to the left. It caught in between Deekin's legs just as the chauffeur was taking a long step forward.

The cane was wrenched free from Leith's grasp. Deekin fell heavily forward, losing the grip on his own cane. At the same time, an ugly blue-steel automatic shot from its holster under his left armpit and slid for a foot or two along the sidewalk.

Leith said: "Good heavens, man, are you hurt? I'm so sorry. I was polishing that cane and—"

Deekin grabbed for the gun. "Say," he said, "I've seen enough of you. Beat it!"

"But, my heavens!" Leith said. "It was an accident, purely and simply. Great heavens, man, what are you doing with that gun? I suppose Mainwaring makes you carry it, but—"

Deekin said: "Never mind all that talk. Just pass over that cane of mine."

"Oh, yes," Leith said, "a thousand pardons. I'm so sorry. Here, let me help you to your feet."

"You keep your distance," Deekin said, menacing him with the gun. "Give me that cane. Hold 'em out so I can see both of them. Don't try any funny stuff now. Give me that shorter one. O.K., that's it. Pass it over, and don't come close."

"But I don't understand," Leith said. "After all, this was just an accident. Perhaps the blunder was on my part, but still—"

"Go on," Deekin said. "Beat it. I've seen all of you I want to see. I crave to be alone. I don't want

to have anyone tagging around. Turn around and walk back the other way, and keep walking for ten minutes."

"But I simply can't understand," Leith said, "why you should adopt this attitude. Man, you're pointing that gun at me! You're—"

"Beat it," the chauffeur ordered.

Leith, apparently realizing all at once the menace of that gun, turned and took to his heels, the cane held under his arm.

Deekin took four or five quick steps, then paused to dust off his clothes, walked another fifteen or twenty feet, and then apprehensively twisted the head off the cane, and peered into the interior. The street light reflected in reassuring green scintillations from the interior, and Deekin, breathing easier, swung into a rapid walk.

CHAPTER VII
BEAVER'S DEDUCTIONS

Beaver, the undercover man, coughed significantly until he caught Sergeant Ackley's eye, then motioned toward the door.

They held a conference in the car vestibule.

"There's something fishy about this, sergeant," the undercover man said.

"I'll say there's plenty fishy about it," Sergeant Ackley said suspiciously. "I'm going to put that guy who let Leith give him the slip back to pounding pavements."

"He couldn't have helped it," Beaver said, "but that isn't what I wanted to talk to you about, sergeant."

"Well, what is it?"

"Those two emeralds *couldn't* have been in that suitcase."

"What do you mean, they couldn't have been?" Sergeant Ackley shouted. "Where else could they have been?"

"Right in Lester Leith's pockets," Beaver said.

"Bosh and nonsense," Sergeant Ackley snapped. "If that's all you have to offer in the way of suggestions, I'm—"

"Just a moment, sergeant," Beaver said. "You forget that Leith told the baggageman to look through the suitcase in order to familiarize himself with the contents. Now, if those emeralds had been in there, the baggageman certainly would have seen them, and then he wouldn't have let the suitcase go for any fifty-dollar deposit. He'd have got in touch with the claim department and—"

Sergeant Ackley's expression of dismay showed that he appreciated only too keenly the logic of the undercover man's words.

"So you see what that means," Beaver said. "If those gems weren't in the suitcase, then Leith must have brought them; and if Leith brought them, he'd never have stuck them to the under side of that table and then got off the train."

"Well, then the girl stuck them there," Ackley said.

"No, she didn't, sergeant. That girl is just a plant."

"What do you mean?"

"Just a réd herring to keep us occupied while Leith is actually getting the stones."

"You're crazy!" Sergeant Ackley said. "We have the stones."

"No, we haven't, sergeant. You left the chewing gum on them so they'd be evidence, but if you'll pull that chewing gum off and wash those stones in gasoline, I'll bet you'll find they're two of the imitation stones that I got for Leith. He fixed this whole thing so that we'd be carried away on the train 'way past Beacon City while he was doubling back by an airplane to shake down the guy who has those stones."

"Who?" Sergeant Ackley asked.

"The chauffeur," Beaver said. "Can't you see? The chauffeur was a thin guy. He had a board with some nails in it planted so he could puncture a tire on the car right where he wanted to. No one knows that the jack was broken. They only have his word for it. He said he was going out to get another jack. What he really did was climb in this stolen car which he'd planted before he went down to the dock to meet the

boat. He slipped this rubberized suit of clothes over his others, drove into a service station, blew himself up, put on a mask, went over to the stalled automobile, stuck them up, killed the monkey, took the stones, drove back, parked the car, deflated the suit, put it in the suitcase, checked it up, salted the emeralds somewhere, and then came back to the car. To keep suspicion from centering on him, he said that he'd seen this fat man and gave the license number of the car. He—"

Sergeant Ackley groaned. "You're right! But, by gosh, we'll get a plane, we'll telephone, we'll —" His hand shot up to the emergency air cord.

A moment later, the long string of Pullmans, rocketing through the night, suddenly started screaming to an abrupt stop, with passengers thrown about in their berths like popcorn in a corn popper. Sergeant Ackley started forward. His right shoe went stickety-stick—stickety-stick. He looked down at the wad of chewing gum stuck to the sole of his shoe. Curses poured from his quivering lips. He pawed at the wad of moist chewing gum. The motion of the stopping train pitched him forward, threw him off balance. His hat was jerked from his head. With gum-covered fingers, he retrieved the hat, clamped it back on his head, and then, feeling a lump between his hair and the hatband, realized too late that he had pressed the wad of moist gum into his hair.

CHAPTER VIII
BEAVER'S BIG MOMENT

Sergeant Ackley, Beaver, and the two detectives burst into Leith's apartment to find Lester Leith sprawled in a lounging robe, reading. He looked up with a frown as the men came charging through the door.

"Scuttle," he said, "what the devil's the meaning of this, and where have you been, Scuttle? I didn't tell you you could have the evening off— Good evening, sergeant and . . . *gentlemen.*"

"Never mind all that stuff," Sergeant Ackley yelled. "What the hell did you do with those emeralds?"

"Emeralds, sergeant?" Lester Leith asked. "Come, come, sergeant; let's get at this logically and calmly. You're all excited, sergeant. Sit down and tell me what you're talking about. And is that gum in your hair, sergeant? Tut, tut, I'm afraid you're getting careless."

"Search him," Sergeant Ackley yelled to the two detectives.

"Now, just a minute, sergeant," Lester Leith said. "This is indeed an utterly useless procedure. I certainly don't know what you're looking for, but—"

"Search him!" Sergeant Ackley repeated, his voice rising with his rage. The detectives searched the unresisting Leith.

"Come, come, sergeant," Leith said, when they had finished with their search. "I suppose you've made another one of your perfectly asinine blunders, but, after all, there's no use getting so incensed about it. Do you know, sergeant, I'm commencing to get so I'm rather attached to you, and you're going to burst a blood vessel if you don't control your temper. Tut, tut, man, your face is all purple."

Sergeant Ackley tried to talk, but his first few words were incoherent. After a moment, he managed to control himself enough to say: "We caught Mainwaring's chauffeur. He had a cane with two imitation emeralds in it."

"Did he, indeed?" Lester Leith said. "Do you know, sergeant, *I* gave him that cane."

"So I gather."

"Yes," Lester Leith said, "I gave it to him. I thought that perhaps Mr. Mainwaring might be interested in it."

"And why did you think Mainwaring might be interested in it?"

"Oh, just as a curiosity," Leith said. "I had two of them, and I really had use only for one, you know. And Mainwaring's a traveler, an explorer who—"

"Where's the other one?" Ackley interrupted.

"Over there in the corner, I believe," Leith said unconcernedly. "Would you like it, sergeant? I'll give it to you as a souvenir of your visit. I had some idea for a while that a person *might* be able to work out a solution—and, mind you, sergeant, I mean a purely academic solution—of a crime by using these canes. But I find that I was in error, sergeant. So many times one makes mistakes, or do you find that to be true in your case, sergeant?

"Tut, tut, sergeant, don't answer, because I can see it's going to embarrass you. I can realize that the professional officer doesn't make the errors that a rank amateur would, yet I see that I've embarrassed you by asking the question.

"Anyway, sergeant, I decided there was a flaw in my reasoning so I decided to get rid of the canes. I gave one to Mr. Mainwaring, thinking he might like it—that is, I left it with his chauffeur—and I'm giving you this other one."

Sergeant Ackley said: "Like hell you made a mistake. You solved that Mainwaring robbery."

"Robbery!" Lester Leith asked. "Surely sergeant, you must be mistaken. It was the killing of a monkey, wasn't it? The malicious, premeditated killing of a harmless pet. I felt very much incensed about it myself, sergeant."

"You felt incensed enough so you went out and grabbed the emeralds," Sergeant Ackley charged.

"What emeralds?"

"You know very well what emeralds—the two that were in the monkey's stomach, the two that the chauffeur stole."

"Did the chauffeur *tell* you that he stole any emeralds?" Lester Leith asked.

"Yes, he did. He made a complete confession," Sergeant Ackley snorted. "He and Mainwaring's nurse had been corresponding. She wrote him a letter mentioning the emeralds and their plan for smuggling them in by making a monkey swallow them. Of course, she denies all that, but we know Deekin's right about it. You trapped Deekin into taking two emeralds out of their place of concealment in the car he was driving, and putting them into that cane."

"Indeed, I did nothing of the sort," Lester

Leith said. "I had no idea there were any emeralds in the cane."

"Don't hand me a line like that," Sergeant Ackley told him. "You figured it all out."

"And what did the chauffeur do with the emeralds?" Leith asked.

"Put them into the hollowed-out place in the cane he was carrying."

"Then you must have *found* them in the cane, sergeant! Congratulations on an excellent piece of detective work! The newspapers will give you a big hand over this."

"Those emeralds in the cane were imitations, and you know it," Sergeant Ackley said.

"Tut, tut," Lester Leith said sympathetically. "I'm *so* sorry, sergeant. I was hoping you'd been able to solve a case which would result in a great deal of newspaper credit, perhaps a promotion. But you can't go to the newspapers with a lot of hullabaloo about getting two *imitation* emeralds. It's too much like killing a caged canary with a ten-gauge shotgun, sergeant. They'd laugh at you. It's anticlimactic. Now tell me, sergeant, in his confession, did the chauffeur state that the same two emeralds he had taken from the monkey's stomach were in that cane?"

"Yes, he did, because he *thought* those were the two, but by some sleight-of-hand hocus-pocus you must have switched canes and got the cane which had the genuine emeralds."

Lester Leith smiled. "Really, sergeant, at times you're exceedingly credulous, and opinionated, and careless with your accusations. If the chauffeur swears that the emeralds *he* took from the monkey's stomach were the ones which were concealed in that cane, then they must be the ones; and if there's anything wrong with those emeralds, any question as to their genuineness or authenticity, it must have been the monkey who made the substitution. Monkeys are quite apt to do that, sergeant. They're very mischievous.

"And, incidentally, sergeant, I'd be very, very careful, if I were you, about making an accusation against a reputable citizen based entirely upon the word of a self-confessed crook, on the

one hand, and an assumption of yours, on the other. There's really nothing to connect them up. As I see it, sergeant, you simply cannot make a case against me unless you could find those genuine emeralds in my possession. Of course, I have only a layman's knowledge of the law, but that would seem to me to be the rule. As I gather it, Mainwaring will swear he never had any emeralds. And certainly Mainwaring's word will be more acceptable than that of his chauffeur, a self-confessed crook, according to your statement, sergeant. Of course, if there never were any emeralds stolen from Mainwaring, I could hardly be convicted of taking what had never been taken. At any rate, that's the way I look at it. Larceny involves the taking of property. If you can't show that there ever was any property, you can't support a charge of larceny. That's the way it appears to me, sergeant, although I'm just an amateur.

"What do you think about it, Beaver? You know something of police matters; that is, you're friendly with a young woman who is friendly with— But perhaps I shouldn't mention that in front of the sergeant. He's so zealous, he might resent any possible leak from headquarters."

Sergeant Ackley stood in front of Leith, clenching and unclenching his hands.

"Leith," he said, "you got by this time by the skin of your eyeteeth. I *almost* had you. If it weren't for making myself appear so damned ridiculous if the facts ever became public, I'd throw you in right now and take a chance on convicting you."

Lester Leith said: "Well, sergeant, don't let your personal feelings stand between you and your duty. Personally, I think it would be an awful mistake for you to do anything like that. In the first place, you couldn't convict me; and in the second place, it *would* put you yourself in a very ridiculous light. To think that with all the facilities which the police had at their command, they couldn't solve a case so simple that a rank amateur by merely reading a newspaper clipping— No, no, sergeant, it would *never* do. They'd laugh you out of office."

Sergeant Ackley nodded to the two men. "Come on," he said; "let's go. Beaver, step this way. I want a word with you."

Sergeant Ackley led the undercover man into the soundproof closet where the telephone was kept.

"Beaver," he said, "you've got to fix up a story to square yourself."

"Great Scott, sergeant!" the undercover man exclaimed. "I can't. He's seen me working with you. He knows—"

"Now listen," Sergeant Ackley interrupted. "We've spent a lot of money getting you planted on this job. With you here, we can keep track of what he's doing. The very next time he tries anything, we'll be *certain* to get him. But without you to keep us posted, he'll laugh at us, flaunt his damned hijacking right in our faces, and get away with it. The man's too diabolically clever to be caught by any ordinary methods."

"I can't help that," the spy said doggedly. "I've shown myself in my true colors now, thanks to you."

"What do you mean, thanks to me?" Sergeant Ackley demanded.

"You insisted that I accompany you."

Sergeant Ackley's face flushed with rage. "If you want to come right down to facts, Beaver," he said, "*you're* the one who's responsible for this whole mess."

"How do you mean I'm responsible for it?"

"I had the idea all along that those emeralds were in the monkey's stomach. Then you got that brainstorm of yours that the nurse had stuck 'em in the chewing gum, and damned if I didn't let you sell me on the idea. I should have known better. You—"

"I thought that was *your* idea," Beaver charged.

"Mine?" Sergeant Ackley's eyes were round with surprise. "Why, don't you remember telephoning me, Beaver, that—"

"Yes, and you said it was your idea."

Sergeant Ackley said patronizingly: "You misunderstood me, Beaver. I told you that I'd already considered that possibility. That was all."

The undercover man sighed.

"Now then," Ackley went on, "you'll have to make up for that mistake by devising some way of getting yourself back in Leith's good graces."

The big undercover man, his black eyes suddenly glittering, said. "O.K., I have an idea!"

"What is it?" Sergeant Ackley wanted to know.

"I could claim that *I* was under arrest; that you came here and pinched me first and then kept me with you all the time you were laying for him on the train and—"

"That's fine," Ackley said. "We'll put that across."

"But," Beaver went on, "it won't explain our conversation in the closet. *You've* spilled the beans now."

"You'll have to think up some explanation," Sergeant Ackley said. "You thought up that other, now you can think up—"

"Of course," Beaver said, "I *could* say that you'd called me in here and made me a proposition to spy on him and that I resented it."

"Swell," Sergeant Ackley said. "That's exactly what we want. I knew we could think up something if we put our minds to it, Beaver."

"Oh, *we* thought of this, did we?" Beaver asked.

"Certainly," Sergeant Ackley said. "That is, I outlined to you what was required, and directed your thoughts in the proper channels. It shows you the value of supervision."

"I see," the spy said, his eyes still glittering, craftily. "But Lester Leith won't believe that story unless I tell him that I bitterly resented your attempt to bribe me."

"Well, go ahead and resent it," Sergeant Ackley said.

"But how can I resent it?"

"You can shout at me, abuse me in a loud tone of voice."

"No," Beaver said, "this closet is virtually soundproof."

"Well, think of something," Sergeant Ackley said impatiently.

"I could push you up against the wall,"

Beaver said, "and he could hear that. Then I'd have to hit you."

Sergeant Ackley seemed dubious. "I don't think we need to carry things that far, Beaver. We can scuffle around a bit and—"

"No. That will never do," Beaver said. "We have to put this thing on right, or not at all. I won't stay here unless we can do it convincingly."

"Oh, all right," Sergeant Ackley said. "Just to make it seem convincing, I'll hit you first. You hit me easy, Beaver. You're a big man. You don't know your own strength. Come on; let's get started. Now remember, Beaver, after things quiet down, I want you to get him started on the affair of the drugged guard."

"What's that?" Beaver asked. "I hadn't heard of it."

"Well, you will hear of it. We'll give you all the dope. It happened last night. Karl Bonneguard was collecting funds for a political cult movement in this country. We don't know how far it had gone. But he'd collected quite a bit of money. There was a grand jury investigation in the offing, so Bonneguard drew all the money out of the bank and—"

"I get you," Beaver said. "What happened?"

"Somebody drugged the guard, and burgled the safe. We can't find out how the guard got doped. It's a mix-up that simply doesn't make sense."

"You don't think the guard framed it and copped the dough?"

"No. The guard's O.K. He warned Bonneguard soon as he felt drowsy. I'll have to tell you about it later, Beaver. We haven't time to discuss it now. We'll go ahead with the act. We'll open the door. You'll be indignant."

"O.K.," Beaver said, "let's go."

They raised their voices in loud and angry altercation. Beaver flung open the closet door and said:

"I think it's the most contemptible thing I ever heard of."

"Go ahead and be a dumb cluck, then," Sergeant Ackley roared. "You keep playing around with this crook and you'll wind up behind the bars. You're a crook yourself!"

"Liar!" Beaver shouted.

Sergeant Ackley lunged a terrific swing at Beaver's jaw.

The undercover man, moving with the swift dexterity of a trained boxer, stepped inside of the blow. For a fraction of a second, he set himself. A look of supreme enjoyment became apparent on his face. He moved his right in a short, pivoting jab which caught Sergeant Ackley on the point of the jaw.

Ackley's head snapped back. The force of the punch lifted him from the floor, slammed him back into the arms of the two detectives.

One of the detectives reached for his blackjack. The other dragged out a gun. Beaver whirled to face them, so that his back was to Lester Leith. He gave a series of warning winks and said:

"I call on you to witness that he struck me first, after accusing me of being a crook. Do you know what he wanted? He wanted to bribe me to stay on in this job and act as spy. I told him what I thought of him. I told him Mr. Leith was the best man I ever worked for."

He took a deep breath and turned to Lester Leith. "I'm very sorry, sir," he said, "for losing my temper. But Sergeant Ackley took me into custody, very much against my will, earlier in the evening. Disregarding my demands that I be taken before a magistrate, he dragged me aboard that train and forced me to accompany him. I didn't dare disobey him. However, when he made this infamous proposal to me, I felt that I was well within my rights as a citizen in couching my refusal in no uncertain language and in defending myself against attack. I trust I haven't done wrong, sir."

The police officers stared in amazement at the spy. Lester Leith regarded the limp form of Sergeant Ackley with eyes that were half closed in thoughtful concentration. At length he said:

"No, Beaver, you've done exactly what I should have done under similar circumstances. I distinctly saw Sergeant Ackley make an unprovoked assault upon you."

Turning to the two officers, Beaver said: "And I call on you two gentlemen to be witness to what has happened. I demand that you take Sergeant Ackley out of here. I think, when he recovers consciousness, he will be the first to tell you that I have done exactly what the situation called for."

One of the detectives returned the spy's wink. "O.K., Beaver," he said, "you win. Come on, Al. Give me a hand and we'll drag the sarge out of here before there's any more trouble."

When the door had closed behind them, Beaver said to Lester Leith: "Disloyalty, sir, is one of my pet abominations. I detest one who is disloyal. I couldn't restrain myself."

"I don't blame you in the least," Lester Leith said. "I'm surprised that Sergeant Ackley had the temerity to arrest you and drag you aboard that train."

"So am I, sir," the spy said. And then, with a look of cunning in his eyes, added: "Incidentally, sir, while I was with them in the drawing room, I heard them discussing a crime which was committed no later than last night; a crime involving a drugged guard—"

Lester Leith held up his hand, palm outward. "Not now, Scuttle," he said. "I don't want to hear it."

The spy said, "Perhaps tomorrow, when you're feeling rested—"

"No, not tomorrow, Scuttle."

The spy did not press the point. "Very well, sir," he said.

"By the way, Scuttle," Leith commented, "I think I'd like a brandy, and you'd better join me. I derived a great deal of satisfaction from the way you hung that punch on Sergeant Ackley's jaw."

About Kid Deth
Raoul Whitfield

THE PULP COMMUNITY was not a huge one. The editors knew each other, and they knew the writers. The writers, too, knew each other, and their common meeting place was often a bar. While the two greatest writers for the pulps, Raymond Chandler and Dashiell Hammett, are believed to have met only once, Hammett became very close to one of the other giants of the era, Raoul Whitfield. There seems to be a good deal of evidence that Hammett became even closer to Whitfield's wife, Prudence, but that's another story.

Whitfield was prolific and quickly became one of *Black Mask*'s best and most popular writers, both under his own name and as Ramon Decolta, as whom he wrote numerous stories about the Filipino detective Jo Gar. His career was cut short when he became ill in 1935; he never fully recovered and died ten years later at the age of forty-seven.

Joey (Kid) Deth was an unusual protagonist for the pulps, whose readers didn't mind criminals as central characters just so long as they stole only from the rich. Few aristocrats read pulp magazines, so editors encouraged Robin Hood stories without fear of offending their readers. While Deth admits he's a crook, he salvages himself to some degree by swearing (and, apparently, truly) that he never shot anyone. That is left to the thugs who are chasing him.

"About Kid Deth" was first published in the February 1931 issue of *Black Mask*. This is the first time it has been published in book form.

About Kid Deth

Raoul Whitfield

A crook caught between two gangs maneuvers the guns of Blind Justice

1

he Kid passed the coupé twice, on the far side of the street, before he crossed back of it, got close to the figure slumped forward over the wheel. The driver's arms were crossed loosely over the rim of black; his hat was half off his head. His face was turned sideways—there was red color staining the lips. The eyes were opened and staring in the faint light from the instrument board. The engine of the car made faint vibration.

The street was fairly deserted—the snow had turned to slush and it was raining a little. A few squares to the northward there was a power house, along the East River. Greenish lights gleamed from high windows. The Kid turned away from the dead man and walked towards the river. He was smiling twistedly. He was small in size with round, dead-gray eyes. He wore a tight-fitting coat that was short, and a dark hat pulled low over his forehead. He smoked a cigarette and coughed sharply at intervals.

He didn't see Rands until the detective came down the few steps of the lunch-wagon that was located about fifty yards from the wooden dock used by the dump carts. When he did see him Rands was lightning a cigar and watching him approach, his eyes leveled above the flare of the match in his cupped hands.

Kid Deth changed his smile to a grin and stopped a few feet from the detective. Rands was a big man with broad shoulders that were slightly rounded. His face was red and squarish. He shook the match, tossed it into the slush. He said in a cheerful voice:

"Hello, Deth—back in town, eh?"

The Kid pulled on what was left of his cigarette and widened his dead-gray eyes.

"Haven't been away, Lou," he said in a voice that sounded strangely heavy for one of his slight build.

Rands whistled a few notes of a popular theme song and looked with faint amusement towards the tail-light of the coupé.

"No?" he said finally. "Been sick?"

Joey Deth shook his head. "Feelin' swell," he replied. "How you been, Lou?"

The detective grinned. "Nice," he replied. "I've been looking for you, Kid."

Joey Deth nodded. "Sure," he said. "A guy got dead out in Frisco, maybe?"

Rands grinned. It was a hard grin. He looked serious.

"Maybe," he agreed. "But I don't figure *you* got *that* far away from New York, Kid."

Joey Deth narrowed his eyes and shrugged. The big detective kept looking towards the tail-light of the coupé, but he didn't seem to be thinking about the car. There was something about that that struck Deth as being funny. But he didn't show it.

"My mother's sick," he said slowly. "I been sticking close to the flat."

Lou Rands nodded his head and looked sad. "The weather's been bad," he said. "She got the flu?"

The Kid nodded. A river boat whistle reached the two of them from some water spot in the distance. There was just a fine mist of rain falling. Inside the lunch-wagon old Andy was clattering dishes around. Rands said slowly:

"Guess you'd better come down to Headquarters with me, Kid. I've been looking for you."

Joey Deth frowned. "I've got a date at one," he said. "How about tomorrow?"

The detective grinned. "Stick your hands up a little," he said quietly.

The Kid swore. He raised his hands and Rands stepped close to him. He patted the pockets of the tight-fitting coat, unbuttoned it, patted other pockets. Then he stepped away from the Kid and nodded his head.

"Sorry," he said.

Joey Deth lowered his hands and swore. "Sorry—you didn't find a rod," he breathed. "Sure."

The detective shrugged his shoulders. He looked towards the rear end of the coupé again, and stopped smiling.

"Before we grab the subway to Center Street—we'll have a look at that car," he said. "Not much parking done over this way."

Kid Deth yawned, but his body shivered a little. Rands' blue eyes were on him, smiling.

"Better be careful—wandering around at night," he said. "*You* might get the flu, too."

Joey Deth shrugged. "I'm thinkin' about moving close to Headquarters," he said with sarcasm. "Make things easier for you."

Lou Rands looked towards the coupé and nodded. He didn't smile.

"One of these days you'll walk in—and you *won't* walk out, Kid," he said quietly. "You get too close to dead people. You always have."

Kid Deth swore. "It's just happened that way," he said. "You oughta know that—by this time. You oughta be sick of ridin' me downtown."

The detective chuckled. "I'm sick of a lot of things," he said. "But I keep on doing them. All right—let's move over near that car."

Joey Deth looked inside the lunch-wagon. His lips twisted a little. Lou Rands wasn't watching him, and he didn't see the hate that flared in the Kid's eyes—flared and died into a smile. They moved westward on Thirty-ninth Street, away from the East River, towards the coupé. Joey Deth tried to keep his voice steady.

"What's the pull for—*this* time?" he asked sarcastically. "I never pack a rod, you know that. You've had me downtown a half dozen times— you never kept me there."

The tone of Rands' voice got suddenly hard. He got his right hand buried in the right pocket of his brown coat.

"I'm going to keep you there—*this* time, Joey," he said.

The Kid jerked his head towards the detective. He'd never heard Rands talk like this before. The big dick was usually easy going, almost jocular. But now his voice was hard—and his eyes were hard. And his right-hand fingers were gripping a rod, Joey knew that.

He asked shakily: "What for?"

They were near the coupé now. Rands smiled with his lips, turned his big head towards the Kid's.

"You've been mixed up with killings since you were able to shove over pedlers' carts, down in Rivington Street," he said slowly. "They put an *a* in that name of yours—and you rate it, Kid. I've been on your tail a long time. And I've got you right."

The Kid widened his dead-gray eyes. He said very softly:

"Like hell you have!"

Rands nodded. He stopped smiling, stopped walking. He looked towards the wheel seat of the coupé. He backed up a step, moved around to the left of Kid Deth. His right coat pocket bulked a little.

"Jeeze," he said softly—"that guy back of the wheel looks sick, Kid!"

Joey Deth didn't look at the figure of Barney Nasser. He'd seen Barney too many times when he'd been alive. He hated Barney, dead or alive. And he was fighting down fear now. He suddenly realized that Rands was mocking him, that Rands knew Barney Nasser was slumped across the wheel of the coupé—and that the detective knew Nasser was dead.

Instinct drove words from between his lips. They were uncertain words.

"He's drunk—maybe," he said.

The detective narrowed his eyes on Kid Deth's. They held a grimly amused expression.

"Yeah?" Rands said. "You think so, Kid?"

Joey Deth forced a smile. He felt cold. It was difficult for him to keep his eyes away from the right-hand pocket of the big detective's coat. He nodded.

"He looks that way," he said thickly.

Lou Rands nodded his big head slowly. The bulk in his right coat pocket moved a little.

"Dead men look that way, too," the detective said slowly. "Move over near him, Kid."

Kid Deth moved over near the coupé. He kept his eyes on the arms of Barney Nasser. They were half closed, and he tried to make them expressionless. He was thinking of the night that Nasser had turned Charlie Gay up, almost five years ago. And he was remembering that Charlie had come down the river from the Big House, three days ago. He was thinking of four or five other humans that had hated the man slumped over the wheel.

His eyes went to the eyes of Rands. The detective was smiling down at the dead man; he reached out a hand suddenly, jerked the head up from the arms. The arms of the dead man slipped off the wheel. Lou Rands sucked in his breath sharply, let the dead man's head fall forward again. He swore.

"It's Barney Nasser," he breathed grimly. "He's—dead!"

Kid Deth stood motionless. He didn't speak. He was thinking that the big detective was a pretty good actor. He was afraid, and fighting fear. He said, after a little silence:

"Dead?"

Lou Rands reached into the coupé with his left hand, lifted an automatic from the seat beside Nasser. He swung towards Kid Deth, held out the gun.

"That got him," he said softly.

The Kid stared at the automatic. Rands took his right hand away from the pocket, caught Deth's left wrist. He was strong, and his movements were swift. Instinctively the Kid tried to twist loose. He spread his fingers—the grip of the gun struck against his palm. For a second the muzzle pointed towards the detective.

The Kid closed his fingers, felt for the trigger. Even as he squeezed he realized that the detective was framing him. He hated Rands—he had hated him for years. He had never killed—and Rands had always been trying to frame him. He squeezed hard. The trigger clicked.

Rands made a chuckling sound. He said fiercely as he pulled the Kid towards his big body.

"Got you—this time, Kid—with the goods—the gun—"

He struck out with his right hand. Joey Deth jerked his head to one side—the blow caught him high on the left temple. He went backward, releasing his grip on the gun. He stumbled, sprawled to the broken pavement. Rocking on his knees he saw Lou Rands through a blur before his eyes.

The detective had something white in his hands—a handkerchief. He was wrapping the gun in it. And the gun had the imprint of his fingers on it. And Barney Nasser was dead in the coupé.

Kid Deth said bitterly:

"You're—framin' me—you dirty, yellow—"

Rands cut in, sharply staring down at the swaying figure before him.

"You tried to squeeze me out, Kid. If the rod had been loaded—"

The big detective broke off. His body half turned away from the kneeling Kid. Two figures were in sight, just beyond the coupé. They had crossed the street under cover of the coupé—and the detective's back had been turned to them. Rands swore hoarsely—said something Joey Deth failed to catch.

The Kid got to his feet. He saw Rands' right hand move towards the right pocket of his coat. Then the bullets whined from two guns. They made sharp, echoed sound in the quiet street. Rands' body jerked; he wheeled away from the two men. He turned jerkily towards Kid Deth, his face white and twisted. His lips were bared in pain. He said hoarsely:

"You dirty—mob hiding—rat—"

The material of his right pocket jumped—the bullet ricocheted from the pavement close to the Kid's feet. Then Lou Rands' head fell forward—he dropped. He went down heavily, and Joey Deth knew he was dead, even before his body rolled over and was motionless.

Blocks away, towards Forty-second Street, a police whistle made a shrilling sound. There was the patter of feet, near First Avenue. They died away. The Kid lifted his right hand and touched the bruised spot over his left temple. He said softly, with fear in his voice:

"Jeeze—Jeeze—they got him!"

Then he came out of it. The police whistle shrilled again. A truck rolled along First Avenue, making back-fire racket. But it was a different sound than that of the guns that had crashed. And the police in the distance knew it.

Joey Deth got a soiled handkerchief from his pocket, put it over the fingers of his left hand. He twisted Rands' gun from his grip. He took the gun wrapped in the handkerchief, from the detective's pocket. He was breathing heavily—there wasn't much time. His brain was clear—the dead detective had been right about one thing—Kid Deth had been close to dead humans many times.

He moved close to the coupé, wiping the grip of the automatic carefully with the handkerchief. He wiped the barrel, too. Lou Rands had tried to frame him with this gun—that meant that a bullet or bullets from it had killed Barney Nasser. Perhaps Rands had murdered Nasser, perhaps not. But he had known that the gangster was dead—and he had tried to frame the Kid.

Joey dropped the weapon from the handkerchief to the coupé seat, beside Nasser's right hand. The handkerchief he slipped in his pocket. He turned away from the car, glanced at the body of the detective. Then he crossed the street, went down an alley that ran through to Fortieth Street. He was halfway through the alley when he looked back and saw the lights of a car shining on the slush near the spot where the coupé rested. The siren wail died to a low whine.

The Kid smiled twistedly, patted the dead dick's gun. On Fortieth Street he went towards the river, reached a small, wooden dock and tossed the gun into the water. He kept away from the few lights, found a stone and wrapped Rands' handkerchief around it. There was a splash as East River water swallowed the fabric. The Kid moved along the river's edge to Forty-second Street. He walked westward and picked up a cab at First Avenue. The driver looked sleepy and dumb—and that suited Joey Deth. He gave an address in Harlem, on the edge of the Black Belt.

The cab had traveled three blocks before the Kid remembered something. It pulled him up straight in the seat. He swore shakily. Then he sat back and swore softly and more steadily. Until this moment he had forgotten the lunch-wagon and Old Andy. Andy might have seen him with Lou Rands, might have heard them talking. Probably he had. And the police would see the lunch-wagon—they would question Andy. And Andy would talk.

Kid Deth sat on the seat of the cab and swayed with the motion of it. There were several things he didn't know—and each thing had to do with death. But there was one thing he *did* know—he was in a tough spot. That had to do with death, too. A hot spot on the electric chair. If Old Andy had seen, heard—and talked—

He sat up straight and lighted a cigarette. His left temple ached, throbbed. He looked through the rear window of the cab and saw only the lights of a big truck, far behind. He closed his little fingers tightly and showed white, even teeth in a smile.

"Like hell—they'll get me!" he breathed.

2

At one o'clock the Kid kept the date he had spoken about to Lou Rands. He sat at a small table near the piano, in the cellar speakeasy just beyond the Black Belt—and the girl came to him. She was a blonde of around twenty-five, with blue eyes and a face that had once been babyish. Kid Deth reached under the table with his right foot and kicked out a chair for her. She sat down, got her chin resting on cupped palms and leaned towards him.

"Well—" she said in a voice that wasn't too pleasant—"there's hell to pay, Kid."

Joey Deth widened his dead-gray eyes and tried to look puzzled.

"Yeah?" he replied. "What about?"

She made a clicking sound with tongue and lips. Her blue eyes narrowed; she took one hand away from her chin and tapped pointed nails against the wood of the table. She said:

"Someone got that Rands dick. I'm thirsty—how about a beer?"

Joey ordered a beer and watched a dark-skinned man at a table across the room talk to himself as he drank. He sipped his own whiskey and frowned.

"Rands, eh?" he said softly. "Well—he had it comin'."

The girl nodded. There was an expression in her eyes that Joey didn't like; he hadn't been sure of her for weeks now. Since Barney Nasser had stated that he was out to get Joey—the girl had changed. She was more cautious. She was playing safe.

The waiter brought her beer. Kid Deth smiled a little.

"Who got him, Bess?" he asked quietly.

The waiter went away and the girl drank half her beer in one try. Her fingers were shaking a little when she set the glass down on the table.

"You did, Kid," she said very slowly.

Joey Deth slitted his eyes on hers. He breathed through his nose, was silent for a short time. Then he shook his head.

"Like hell I did," he said almost pleasantly. "Who says so, Bess?"

She kept her blue eyes steady on his. She downed half of the remaining half glass of beer.

"Barney Nasser's brother," she said quietly. "I ran into him at Alma's flat. He's sore as hell."

The Kid drew a deep breath. Barney Nasser's brother—Gil Nasser. A killer who had been tried three times for murder without a conviction. A gun who hated only a week or so, and then stopped hating because there wasn't any percentage in hating a dead human.

Joey Deth said slowly: "Gil's hopped up—he's talkin' wild."

The girl shook her head. "He doesn't use the bad stuff, and you know it," she said. "He says Barney Nasser picked you up over near Times Square—you had some talk to get finished. He drove you over between First and the East River, and you didn't like what he said. You gave him the works. The Rands dick went over on a chance—to talk with a lunch-wagon owner named Andy Polson. Old Andy, he's called. He spotted you and took you to the car. He had the goods on you, and you gunned him out. Then you slipped the gun beside Barney's body and made a duck. That's the way Gil figures."

Kid Deth shook his head, smiling with his narrow lips.

"It's no good, Bess," he said. "I never killed in my life, you know that. I don't pack a gun."

She smiled grimly. "Barney Nasser did," she said. "A .38 automatic. Gil thinks there were those kind of bullets in his lungs—and a flock of them in the dick's body. He thinks you got Barney—and when Rands grabbed you—you got him."

Kid Deth stopped smiling. He ordered another whiskey and a beer. When the waiter went away he said:

"They're framing me, Bess—maybe we'd better try Chi for a look around."

The girl shook her head. "I'm putting you wise—and I'm quitting, Kid," she said. "You told Barney you'd lay out of New York—but Brooklyn's a part of the big town. Maybe you forgot that. From now on—where you are it won't be too healthy. I'm quitting."

Kid Deth shrugged. "It's quiet across the bridges," he said. "But Barney didn't want it that way. I went in there first—"

He broke off. The waiter brought the drinks. Joey said:

"Mac—let me know who comes in—before they start the walk, will you?"

The waiter nodded. "Sure, Kid," he said. "An' we ain't seen you tonight."

Joey Deth nodded. "That's it, I ain't been around," he replied.

The girl chuckled mirthlessly. "You never did have luck with the slot machines, Kid," she said. "Even at Coney—"

Kid Deth leaned across the table and bared his lips. Bess Grote's eyes got big and frightened. She didn't like to see Joey looking at her this way.

"You know too much," he said in a hard voice. "And you're pretty anxious to quit. Maybe you know that Charlie Gay has been out of stir for three days—and that it was Barney Nasser who turned him up for the stretch."

He watched the girl's lips tremble. She lifted her beer glass and drank.

"Charlie didn't do for Barney," she said, as she set the glass down again. "Charlie went—out West—right away."

Kid Deth shook his head. "Better be careful, Bess," he said in a hard tone. "I saw Charlie tonight—while I was—"

He checked himself. But the girl had a quick mind. That was one of the things he had liked about her. She was shrewd.

"While you was ridin'—with Barney," she finished.

The Kid looked at her for several seconds. He did some thinking and reached a decision. He leaned across the wet table surface.

"I'll be right with you, Bess," he said slowly and very softly. "You'd better be that way with me. Things are getting tight. I never used a rod in my life. I've been around killings—and dead guys. But I never knocked a guy out. You know that."

She wasn't afraid of him; he could see that in her eyes. And it worried him. Weeks ago she *had* been afraid of him. But she figured another way now.

"You never did for a guy—until tonight, maybe," she said slowly.

He kicked back his chair suddenly, stood up. Her eyes stayed on his; they got hard. She made a quick movement with her right hand half out of sight, and he heard the lock snap in the gray bag she always carried. He stared down at her. She said slowly:

"Sit down, Kid—and keep your hands in sight."

He pulled his chair up, sat down. He smiled at her. After a few seconds he spoke slowly.

"So you're playing for Gil Nasser?"

She shook her head. "Don't get rough, that's all. I'm not playing for anyone. But I'm quitting you. And I wouldn't start for Chi with you. You wouldn't reach the station, Kid."

Joey Deth tried not to shiver. The tone of her voice was so certain. He said very quietly:

"Barney Nasser sent word he wanted to see me. I didn't want to see him. I've been working the racket across the river—and I put the slot machines in. I didn't cut in on Barney. He was on this side—and in Jersey. But he got sore because I was takin' coin out of Brooklyn. He wanted to buy me off. He wanted to talk."

She just smiled. Kid Deth said, with his eyes on her tired blue ones:

"He picked me up in the coupé—and we drove over near the river. We talked on the way, but we didn't say much. I got the idea he was going to boost the price he was offering. Maybe I'd have taken it and cleared, Bess."

She said: "Maybe," in a doubtful tone, and lighted a cigarette. She smiled at him.

He narrowed his dead-gray eyes on hers. He said in a toneless voice:

"I needed cigarettes. We don't smoke the same brand, and there was talking to be done. I remembered a speak two squares up First Avenue. We figured it would be better not to drive. I got the cigarettes, and when I came back—Barney was dead across the wheel. I hadn't heard a shot, but there are always trucks along First Avenue, and I'm used to back-fire racket."

Bess Grote's eyes closed momentarily. When she opened them she had stopped smiling.

"You're lying, Kid," she said softly. "You're lying—and you're in—for the works!"

He stiffened a little, and her right hand went to the bag. He shrugged.

"I saw the lunch-wagon, went down to ques-

tion Old Andy. Rands came out and grabbed me. He took me back to the car, tried to frame me. He knocked me down."

Kid Deth touched the bruised spot on his left temple. The girl watched him closely.

"Two guns came around the far side of the car—and opened on him. I didn't see their faces—they didn't come in close. They were medium sized, Bess. That's—what happened."

The girl finished her beer and nodded her head. She said slowly:

"That's what *you* say, Kid. But I'm quittin' you, just the same. The others may not think the same way."

Joey Deth looked beyond the girl. A bell jangled outside. The waiter nodded to the Kid and went towards the speak-easy street door. The one who had been talking to himself was sleeping, his head pillowed in his arms. Kid Deth muttered to himself as he looked at the man—he reminded him of Barney Nasser.

"You always did—like Charlie Gay," he said softly.

The girl's mouth tightened. She shoved back her chair a little. There was rage in her blue eyes. It told the Kid a lot.

"You always did hate—Barney Nasser!" she snapped. "Only you never had the guts—"

She broke off as the waiter came into the back room. He reached Joey's side.

"It's that—tall, skinny dick!" he said. "I seen him through the peephole. The one that's tied up with that Rands dick—his partner!"

The girl shoved back her chair and got to her feet. Her movements were quick, jerky. Kid Deth looked at her and chuckled without amusement in his tone.

"Going to—tip off Charlie?" he mocked.

The girl's face was white. She swore at him. She said shakily:

"Listen—Kid—you'd better go out back— keep your rod handy—"

He shook his head. "I don't use a rod—and you know it," he cut in steadily.

Her eyes went to the waiter's. He spoke in a thick tone.

"We're all right—an' I got to let this guy inside. I got to—"

Kid Deth narrowed his eyes on the blue, wide ones of Bess Grote.

"Sure," he said. "Let him in. It's Sarlow, Rands' partner. They worked together most of the time. Let him in, Mac."

The girl looked at Kid Deth. "You damn' fool," she said. "He'll take you downtown. They'll beat hell out of you."

Joey smiled. "That'll suit Charlie Gay fine, Bess," he said. "But maybe not so well as if I went out the back way, alone."

She turned towards him—took a step in his direction. The Kid shook his head.

"Don't," he warned. "I know what I'm up against. You wanted to quit a month ago—now's the right time. If you want to give me a break, just because we went places and did—"

He stopped. She faced the waiter. Her voice was hard and certain now.

"Talk to the quiet clothes bull a little—before you let him in," she said. "I'll ease out the back way—and maybe the Kid'll go with me."

The waiter nodded. "He's not dumb," he said. "He'll go."

He went towards the speakeasy door. Bess Grote bent forward across the table. She said in a low voice:

"Gil's sure you did for Barney. I don't know what the bulls think about Rands' kill. But what Gil got from Old Andy—the police can get. A crook and a copper are dead—and you're sitting in between them, Kid."

Kid Deth nodded. "And you lied to me about Gay," he said quietly. "He didn't go West—and he did hate Barney Nasser. And his mob—"

Her eyes held anger again. She spoke in a low, bitter tone.

"You can't pull Charlie in this, Kid. I was with him until an hour ago. We went to a show. He never even—"

The voice of Sarlow reached them. It was a slow voice, almost a drawl. It was asking questions. The Kid spoke in a whisper.

"Better call—as you go out back, Bess. There might be a mistake—"

She turned away from him abruptly. But near the door she stopped. She half turned towards the wet-surfaced table.

"If you get a break—get clear, Kid," she said in a whisper. "You've been lucky—too long—"

He lifted his right hand a little, made a small gesture. Then she was out of sight—she was moving towards the alley in back. Her footfalls died.

The Kid lighted a cigarette and smiled bitterly. He touched the bruised spot on his temple, finished his drink. He moved his chair back from the table. He remembered that this partner of the dead detective had shot down Eddie Birch, less than a year ago. Sarlow was a veteran. He was hard, cold. And his partner had been killed, murdered.

Joey said slowly, half aloud: "Another guy—looking for a chance—to frame me—"

There were footfalls in the hallway beyond the room. The outside door slammed. The waiter was whistling loudly. The Kid raised his eyes and looked into the dark eyes of Sarlow. There was a half smile on the dick's face; his right hand was buried in the pocket of his coat—his left arm swung a little at his side. He leaned carelessly against a wall, ten feet from the Kid.

"Hello, Deth," he said in a casual tone. "Just drinking alone?"

Joey Deth nodded. "Just drinking alone," he replied slowly. "How're things, Sarlow?"

There was a flicker of light in the black color of the detective's eyes. But he kept smiling.

"Not so good, Kid," he said softly. "They— got Lou."

Joey Deth parted his lips and widened his eyes. He swore softly and said in a surprised tone:

"You mean—Lou Rands—your sidekick?"

Sarlow's lean body twitched. His eyes looked hurt. He lifted his left hand and took off his hat. He had gray hair; it was rumpled. A few locks were sticking damply to his forehead. His thin face was white.

"Yeah," he said slowly. "Lou Rands."

Kid Deth said: "Hell—I'm sorry. Jeeze— that's tough, Sarlow."

Sarlow half closed his eyes. "Think so?" he said in a strange tone.

Joey Deth nodded a little. "I guess Rands was all right," he said slowly. "He tagged me a lot, but I guess—"

Sarlow looked at the Kid's hands—they rested on the surface of the table. He took his right hand from the pocket, held his gun low.

"Get up, Kid," he said slowly. "I got a cab outside."

Kid Deth shrugged his shoulders. He said very softly:

"I didn't get him, Sarlow. I'm givin' it to you straight."

Sarlow straightened his lean body. "You've been giving things straight—for a long time, Kid," he said in a hard voice. "And squirming loose."

Joey Deth got up. He shook his head. "Two guns got him, Sarlow," he said. "I know how you feel—he was your side-kick. I know how you think. But it's wrong. And he tried—"

He checked himself, thinking of the gun in Sarlow's grip. No use telling the dick that his partner had tried to frame him.

"You've been lucky—for a long time, Kid." Sarlow's voice was almost toneless. "We gave you rope. Lou figured you'd get the dose from the inside. But you were getting coin, across the river. Barney Nasser didn't like that. He got careless—and you gave him the works. Then Lou grabbed you—"

Kid Deth kept his eyes on the dark ones of Sarlow. He shook his head.

"I didn't get Barney," he said. "I'm giving it to you straight—"

His words died; Sarlow's body jerked as the first shot sounded. It came from somewhere out back. There was a second's pause—then the scream reached them. It was a woman's scream—short and high pitched. Then the gun clattered. It beat a staccato song, died abruptly. There were no more screams.

Sarlow, his body tense, kept his eyes on the Kid. When the waiter came into the room he got his back to the wall and moved his gun a little.

"Get over there—by Deth!" he ordered.

McLean walked over and stood beside the Kid. His eyes were wide and he rubbed the material of his trousers with the fingers of his right hand. The man across the room muttered to himself and rolled his head. Sarlow said:

"Who—got clear, when I came in?"

The Kid got his left hand fingers on the back of the chair from which he had risen. His face was very white. There was no color in his thin lips.

Sarlow smiled. "Whoever it was—they got the long dose," he said. "Tommy gun. Sounded like a frail, Kid. Was she yours?"

Kid Deth closed his eyes and tried not to rock from side to side. One thought was beating into his brain—Bess had screamed after the first shot. And *then* the Tommy had been turned loose. It had been no mistake.

Sarlow made a chuckling sound. "Cheer up, Kid," he said. "Maybe it was a miss—maybe she got clear."

Joey drew in his breath sharply. At his side the waiter muttered to himself.

"We oughta—get out there—we oughta—"

Kid Deth tried to smile. "Like hell we oughta!" he breathed. "It's a frame—"

Sarlow stopped smiling and moved his gun hand a little.

"That yelp sounded as if someone was hurt," he said grimly. "Want to go out—and look around, Kid?"

Joey shook his head. He took his left hand away from the back of the chair. He didn't speak. Sarlow listened for several seconds. He looked at the waiter.

"A blackjack hurts," he said slowly. "Who went out of here—when I came in?"

McLean wet his lips with the tip of his tongue. He shook his head.

"The Kid—was alone," he breathed.

Sarlow swore. His eyes flickered to Joey Deth's; they held hate. He looked at the waiter again.

"You tried to stall for time," he said. "And the Kid waited for me to come in. Who went out back—and got that dose?"

The Kid said softly: "Mac ain't in this, Sarlow. He's—all right."

The lean detective swore at him. "Getting big hearted, eh?" he mocked. "But you look sick, Kid."

A door slammed beyond the room, out back. The three men who were standing stood motionless. The Kid and the waiter stared towards the darkness beyond the room. A narrow corridor ran to the rear door. Sound came from it now—the sound of a body falling, not too heavily.

Joey said fiercely: "Listen—let Mac go out there, Sarlow! He'll be all right—"

The waiter took a step forward, but the lean-faced detective moved his gun arm swiftly.

"You—stick where you are—both of you!" he gritted.

Joey Deth turned his twisted face away from Sarlow. The detective changed his position slightly—he was listening to a faint sound that reached the room. It might have been the sound of a human trying to drag along the wooden floor. It stopped. A half-sobbing voice came faintly into the room.

"Joey—"

Kid Deth swayed a little, in front of the partner of Lou Rands. His lips were twitching. Bess Grote called again. Her voice was very weak.

"Kid—Deth—"

The Kid said fiercely: "Let me—go out there, Sarlow—they got her—"

Sarlow shook his head. "And *you* got Lou," he said grimly. "And you lied—like you've always lied—"

There was no more sound from the dark corridor. McLean said in a husky voice:

"You're killing—that woman, Sarlow. You can't keep us in here—"

The detective looked at the Kid. "What did you send her out back for?" he said softly. "Maybe you—*wanted* her—to get that dose, Deth!"

Kid Deth smiled at the detective. It was a peculiar, tight-lipped smile. He nodded his head.

"Sure," he replied, and his voice was strangely calm. "Sure—anything you say, Sarlow. But I'm going out there, see? And if you squeeze lead—"

He broke off, walked towards the door. His movements were swift, steady. He read indecision in Sarlow's eyes. The gun muzzle came up a little. Then he saw the veins of the detective's right wrist stand out—he was squeezing the trigger—

The Kid sprang at Sarlow—swinging sideways and downward with his left arm. The gun crashed—the bullet seared Deth's right thigh. Sarlow went back under his weight, went off balance. McLean was on him now—the two of them battered him to the floor. The Kid twisted the gun from his grip.

"Outside, Mac—" he breathed heavily, getting to his feet. "Bring her—in here—"

Sarlow pulled himself to his knees and swore at Joey.

"And I held—back on you!" he muttered thickly. "I should have—"

Kid Deth backed against the wall. He heard the foot-falls of McLean, heard the breathing of the waiter as he moved towards the room from the corridor. The man breathed heavily, as though there was a weight in his arms.

Kid Deth watched the detective as he got to his feet. He didn't look at the body of the girl, when McLean carried her into the room. He said slowly:

"Any chance—Mac?"

There was a little silence. Then the waiter's voice reached him.

"She's finished, Kid—"

Joey Deth nodded. His eyes were expressionless. He kept them fixed on the dark ones of Sarlow.

"I'm taking the lead out of your rod," he said after a few seconds. "You go out the front way—and keep moving. When you get outside I'll toss the rod out. Be at Headquarters tomorrow at four. I'll walk in."

Sarlow wiped his lips with the back of his right hand. There was a thin streaking of red across his chin.

"Yeah," he said heavily. "Sure you will."

Kid Deth smiled. It was a bitter, twisted smile.

"I didn't get Barney Nasser. I didn't get your partner. I'm givin' it to you straight. I never squeezed a rod on a bull—"

He stopped, thinking of Lou Rands trying to frame him, jamming the gun in his hand. He had squeezed the rod then. And it had been empty.

"Tomorrow—at Headquarters. Four o'clock. I've got—something to do—"

He jerked his right hand towards the door. Sarlow said slowly:

"That's a lot of time—for a getaway."

The Kid shook his head. "I'll be in—at four," he said. "I've got something—to do."

Sarlow glanced towards the body of the girl. But the Kid didn't look in that direction. He half closed his dead-gray eyes.

"Get out, dick!" he gritted. "I need—all the time—that's left!"

3

KID DETH stopped the taxi at Forty-second Street, near Sixth Avenue, slipped from behind the wheel. His face was pale and his gray eyes were streaked with red. He was tired and something inside of him was hurt. He hadn't thought any dead woman could hurt him so much.

He went into the coffee house and sat at the counter. He drank two cups of coffee, black—and tried to eat a doughnut. The waiter stood back of the counter and read an early edition of a tabloid. It was after four, and there was a light rain falling.

After a while he finished the coffee, tossed a quarter on the counter and went outside.

He slid back of the wheel, got the cab going. He drove down Sixth Avenue, swearing softly. He didn't think he'd been recognized, but he couldn't take a chance. The papers were carrying his pictures—he knew it would be worth a lot to any copper to bring him in. And the quiet clothes boys were out, too.

The cab was Bennie Golin's—and Bennie was all right. They were about the same size—he had borrowed clothes from Bennie. It was to Bennie's flat that he had taken the battered body of Bess Grote. He'd set the man up in business—and Bennie was paying him back a little. But Golin had been afraid; the Kid had seen the expression in his eyes when he had told him what he wanted.

"If they wise up—it's my finish, Kid," Bennie had said.

And Kid Deth had smiled grimly. "If who wise up?" he had asked. "The bulls?"

Golin had shaken his head. "To hell with *them*," he had said. "You ain't worryin' about them."

Joey turned the cab eastward on Thirty-fourth Street. He drove slowly, carefully. Golin had been right. The Kid wasn't so worried about the police.

But there was something he wanted to do. Something important. He wanted to rub out the murderer of Bess Grote. He wanted to do that job, and do it right. Then he wanted to walk into the Center Street building and hand himself over. He could beat the rap. Berman was a smart mouthpiece. He would come high but he would see that he wasn't framed. And he would give himself up.

He cruised northward, hunching low back of the wheel. He had spent an hour in the cab, driving past spots where he might have seen something that would have helped. But he hadn't seen anything. It was still a toss-up. Gil Nasser—or Charlie Gay. One of the two had done for Bess Grote. One of the two had bossed the kill of Lou Rands. One of the two had finished Barney Nasser, perhaps. He wasn't so sure of *that*. Rands might have got Barney, working for a frame. It wasn't likely that Gil had drummed out his own brother.

At Thirty-ninth Street he took a chance and looked towards the river. The street was deserted, but there was a light shining from Old Andy's lunch-wagon.

He sped the cab down the street. Near the wagon he turned it around, headed it towards First Avenue. The street was a cul de sac—there was only one exit for machines.

He slipped from the wheel, leaving the engine running. For a few seconds he looked towards First Avenue. Rain made pattering sounds on the street surface. There was no clattering of dishes from the lunch-wagon.

He moved towards the few steps—opened the door. Fingers of his left hand gripped the gun in his pocket. His eyes searched the narrow aisle before the counter, as he looked in through the misted glass of the door. He saw no customer.

He opened the door, stepped inside. He was breathing quickly, and the one thought running through his head was that he was a fool to have come. But he *had* come.

There was sound at one end of the counter—Old Andy got to his feet. He was a big, round-shouldered man. His eyes blinked as he looked at Joey Deth. He had sandy colored hair and big features.

Joey said: "Yeah, Andy—it's me. How're things?"

He smiled a little. Andy's eyes went to his left pocket. The lunch-wagon owner shook his head from side to side.

"I didn't—want to tell 'em, Kid," he said. "I didn't want—"

Joey Deth kept on smiling. "That's all right," he said. "Who got Barney Nasser, Andy?"

The lunch-wagon proprietor stared at him blankly. Kid Deth stopped smiling. He spoke in a low, hard voice.

"Give me a break, Andy—the bulls are after me. Lou Rands tried to frame me—he's been trying for a long time. But not this hard. Something was up—and something went wrong. Give me a break, Andy."

The lunch-wagon owner shook his head. "You ain't usin' your head—comin' here, Kid," he breathed. "The police—they come every few hours—and ask me something they forgot—"

Kid Deth turned and looked out towards the cab. There were no lights beyond it, near First Avenue. He faced Old Andy again.

"Listen, Andy—" he said slowly—"someone got Bess Grote tonight. Got her rotten-like. I'm being framed, Andy—and the job's being done tough. I may not be able to beat it. I got to know things. What did Lou Rands say to you, just before he grabbed me?"

Old Andy shook his head. Kid Deth took the automatic from his pocket. He watched the lunch-wagon owner's eyes get wide, watched fear creep into them.

"You had a good memory—when Gil Nasser got to you," he said slowly. "And you talked to the bulls. Now—you'd better talk—to me."

Old Andy nodded his head. His eyes were on the gun. He said shakily:

"You never—used to pack a rod, Kid—"

Joey Deth smiled grimly. "And I never used—to be framed," he replied. "What happened—after I left Barney Nasser in his coupé, Andy? Better talk!"

The man back of the counter shook his head again. He tapped his right ear with a big finger. Joey Deth said softly:

"You've been working that line for years, Andy. But I know it's the bunk. You ain't deaf—not unless you want to be. You'll even hear this gun crack—before you drop. What did Rands say—to you?"

He raised the gun a little. Old Andy's lips were twitching. He stepped close to the counter.

"He'd found a man dead—Barney Nasser," he said. "He asked—about you, Kid."

Kid Deth said: "What did you tell him?"

Old Andy shook his head. "Told him I hadn't seen you—for a week or so. Said you used to come in, after theatre time. Rands was wised up—he figured some of the boys talked things over—around here."

Kid Deth said: "Yeah?"

There was a little silence. The rain made a soft patter on the glass windows of the lunch-wagon. Kid Deth looked towards the cab again. He got his face close to the door glass, looked towards the Avenue. The street was empty of everything except the cab. Joey faced the lunch-wagon owner again. He spoke in a very low voice. It was toneless.

"You're lying, Andy—and I'm sick of lies. You squealed on me—and you framed me. I've never killed a guy—not until now. You know that, Andy. But you're lying. Lou Rands shot out Barney Nasser—and you know it. And you know why. But you're still workin' with Lou—still trying to frame me. Maybe you've done enough—maybe not. Anyway—you're through. To hell with you—Andy—straight to hell—"

The finger next to his left thumb started to pull back on the trigger. Old Andy's face was ghastly—his eyes were wide with fear.

"For God's sake—wait—Kid!" he breathed hoarsely.

Joey Deth said: "Wait—for what? For more lies?"

Andy Polson shook his head. "No—I swear I'll give it to you, Kid! I didn't know—"

He broke off. The Kid eased off pressure on the trigger. He said in a hard voice:

"You didn't know—I'd pack a gun, eh? You thought I'd never hurt—right to the finish. Well—you got it wrong, Andy. I'm walking down to Headquarters at four in the afternoon, see—and before I walk in—"

He checked himself. Old Andy stood leaning against the wall, back of the counter. There was a color in his face now—red streaked the white of his skin, his eyes were protruding, he was breathing heavily.

"Barney—an' Rands—they was together, Kid," he muttered. "They was workin' the slot machines together. Then Rands—he got scared. When you went across the river Barney wanted Rands to—get you, Kid. But the dick—he was afraid. He was gettin' worried—about bein' so thick with Barney. And he was—"

Kid Deth said in a hard voice: "Wait—how do *you* figure to know so much?"

The lunch-wagon owner said in a whisper: "I passed the coin—from Barney—"

Kid Deth stood tensely, his eyes narrowed on the staring ones of Andy Polson. He cut in sharply:

"And Rands—gave Barney the dose? Because he was afraid of a break."

Old Andy shook his head. His eyes were on the gun that the Kid was holding a little lower now.

"Barney tried—to get Rands," he said thickly. "I seen you go along First Avenue. Rands came close to the car—passed it. Barney got out and followed him. The lights were out in here—something went wrong with the power. Maybe Barney didn't think I was inside. I was watchin' 'em come up."

Kid Deth said: "Don't lie, Andy—this counts big."

The lunch-wagon owner stared at the gun. He moved his head from side to side.

"I ain't lyin', Kid," he said. "I'm an old man and—"

"What happened—with Barney Nasser back of Rands?" the Kid cut in.

"He opened up," Polson muttered. "But Rands was swingin' around—maybe he heard him. He got Barney right away. I seen him pick him up. He carried him to the coupé, then he come back here. The lights went on while he was comin' back, and he was sore as hell. He swore he'd kill me if I crossed him up. He said it was a chance—to get you. Barney had wised him that you was ridin' with him. He'd been hidin' out—an' he'd seen you get clear of the car."

Kid Deth said slowly: "I didn't figure that Barney tried for *him* first," he muttered. "But I figured he got Nasser—and wanted to frame me—"

Old Andy nodded. "I swear I give it to you straight, Kid—"

Joey Deth lowered the pistol. "Who gunned out Rands?" he said slowly.

The lunch-wagon owner shook his head. "That's all I know, Kid," he said. "If I can square you—"

The Kid swore softly. "You can't—not that way," he said in a hard tone. "They'd figure it was a deal—in court."

There was silence except for the patter of rain against the lunch-wagon windows.

Old Andy said slowly, breathing with an effort:

"Maybe they was—tryin' for you, Kid—and got Rands."

Kid Deth grunted. "Like hell they were!" he breathed. "They were guns—and they didn't miss. They wanted Rands—and they got him. And they wanted—"

He smiled grimly. He knew something now—something important. Barney Nasser and Lou Rands had been working together. Nasser had tried to finish the detective—but the dick had got him. He'd tried to frame the Kid, but he'd been gunned out. Why?

The Kid thought: I'm getting closer. Either Gil Nasser or Charlie Gay got Rands. The mob of one of them, anyway. Or maybe Gil wasn't in on it, and Barney had his men close by, in case something went wrong in *our* talk. They saw Rands carry Barney to the coupé—and they got him. There was a chance of getting me framed, so they didn't turn loose on me. If Charlie Gay pulled the shoot—it was straight hate. He was wise that Rands had been working with Barney.

Old Andy said in a monotone: "Barney Nasser tried to get Rands in the back. Rands got him. And there are a lot of guys—that hate the dick. You better get clear, Kid—you better jump town. I've put you wise—"

The Kid shook his head. "Someone got Bess Grote," he said slowly. "It wasn't a mistake, Andy. They tricked her. Maybe she was supposed to send me out back. She didn't do it. When she went out—they got her. That's what I've got to do, Andy—get the one—"

He stopped. Old Andy half closed his eyes. He touched his sandy hair with shaking fingers.

"You never used a rod, Kid—" he started. His voice died abruptly.

The Kid heard the sound, too. He swung around, half opened the door of the lunch-wagon. But the car was coming down the center of the street. It had bright lights—and it skidded to one side as the driver worked the brakes. Figures spilled to the wet street pavement—they moved swiftly and without sound.

Kid Deth stepped back and shut the door. He snapped the bolt.

"Bulls!" he breathed fiercely. "Out the back of the wagon—"

He turned. Old Andy was close to the counter. His right arm was lifted. The fingers held a gun leveled low, above the wood. The gun was shaking a little. The trigger finger was moving. Kid Deth let his body slump forward and downward, dived towards the counter. The gun crashed as his hands and knees hit the floor—wood spurted from the counter.

The second shot sent a bullet through the glass of the lunch-wagon door. The Kid crawled towards the end of the counter on the left, pulled himself up from his knees. He muttered huskily:

"You—crazy Swede—"

From outside of the lunch-wagon two shots sounded. Something clattered, behind the counter. Old Andy made a heavy, grunting sound. He swore weakly. Two more shots sounded from outside.

There was a low cough from Old Andy. Then his body struck the floor back of the counter. Kid Deth crawled around behind—saw the outstretched hands, the half-opened eyes. There was red on Old Andy's lips. Coffee hissed downward from the percolator.

The Kid crawled around past the body of the man who had tried to kill him. Polson was dead; crouching low, the Kid went through the door that led to the small room back of the space where Old Andy lay. There was a narrow door on his right—he opened it, stared out into the rain. No one was in sight.

There were no steps. He dropped to the street, kept the lunch-wagon between himself and the men on the far side. He crouched low, and held the automatic in his left hand. At the end of the street there was a dock; the Kid worked his way northward of it, along the river bank. He found a narrow alley that led back from the river, traveled along it. There was no sound of voices.

He could guess what had happened. The men who had come up in the car were detectives. Either they had blundered into him, or Old Andy had been expecting them. Joey could see no way that he had tipped them off. There was no phone in the lunch-wagon; even if the proprietor had seen him before he got inside there would not have been time for him to have called.

Old Andy had tried to get him—to kill the story he had just told—and his second shot had crashed through the door of the lunch-wagon. Perhaps the bullet had hit one of the men outside. In any case, they had opened up—and Andy had dropped.

He lowered his head, moved rapidly westward across the avenue. When he had reached the far side he did not look back. He guessed that the detectives were getting inside the lunch-wagon, but doing it cautiously. He was halfway to Second Avenue when he heard the shrill of a police whistle. Almost immediately it was followed by the wail of the car siren.

4

JOEY DETH kept close to the fronts of tenements, reached Second Avenue. He went northward, and heard the siren wail again as he climbed the Elevated Station.

When the train reached One Hundred and Twenty-fifth Street the Kid got off, descended from the station. He walked westward, got a cab, gave the address of a flat less than four squares from the speakeasy in back of which Bess Grote had been gunned out.

McLean's flat was a half square from the address he gave. The cab driver was sleepy; he came close to hitting a milk wagon at an intersection, and the Kid swore at him beneath his breath.

He gave the driver a half dollar, walked past McLean's place once, then turned back and went inside. The waiter lived alone on the top floor—the Kid pressed the button four times, and the last time it was a short buzz. The lock made a ticking sound almost immediately, and the Kid went inside.

He climbed the stairs slowly—they were dimly lighted and there were many odors drifting through the hallways. A baby was crying fretfully as he started up the last flight. When he made the turn at the head of the stairs, to go along the hallway, he saw that McLean's door was opened on a narrow crack.

Instinctively he hesitated; his left hand reached towards his left coat pocket. Then the door was opened a little more—he saw the waiter's face. He moved up close, said softly:

"You—alone?"

McLean nodded his head. He opened the door most of the way, stepped to one side. The Kid walked inside the flat.

He went over to the uncomfortable divan and dropped down on it. He said grimly:

"The dicks—almost got me, Mac."

McLean stood with his back to the door and narrowed his eyes on Kid Deth.

"Where—at Bennie Golin's?"

Joey shook his head. "At Old Andy's," he replied in a low tone. "Maybe they were tipped—maybe they just drove in. I had a cab—stopped in to get Andy to wise me to what Rands had been spilling, before that dick grabbed me. Andy came through."

McLean said: "Yes?" His voice was low and husky. His eyes kept shifting around. Kid Deth looked at him and remembered that he didn't know the man well, that six months ago he hadn't known him at all. He wondered if Bennie Golin wouldn't be better for the job. Then he remembered that Bennie had a wife and a kid.

The Kid lighted a cigarette, tossed the pack towards the other man. McLean shook his head, tossed the pack back.

Joey Deth said: "I got to be sure, Mac. You sittin' in with me, or just playing safe?"

McLean smiled. It was a hard smile. "Didn't I go out—and bring Bess into the room, Kid? Ain't I taking a chance in having you in here?"

Joey nodded. "Sure," he agreed. "But that don't answer the question. I'm in the way, Mac—and a lot of guys want to get me. But they're being careful—and that means something."

McLean grunted. "What?" he asked.

Kid Deth pulled on his cigarette. He shrugged. His eyes were on the waiter.

"What you sticking so close to that door for?" he asked, his voice very soft.

McLean looked surprised. He stepped away from the door, halted suddenly. He turned his body a little, so that he half faced the door. The Kid listened too. And while he listened he got his automatic out of his pocket.

He said: "Yeah—someone's coming up, Mac."

McLean's body jerked. He faced the Kid—his breath made a sucking sound as his eyes spotted the weapon. Joey smiled.

"*Who's* coming up, Mac?" he asked coldly.

The waiter stared at him. "What are you—getting at, Kid?" he muttered. "I'm a little shaky—that's all. With you—in here—"

Kid Deth nodded. "I know," he said. "Who's

comin' to see you, Mac? It's a funny hour—for a call."

The steps on the stairs were not heavy—the creaking sound ceased now. The Kid had made a guess, and he knew now that it was a good one. He could read the answer in McLean's eyes.

"You, too," he said softly. "Jeeze—but the quitting came fast when it got started. You're all crowdin' for the kill—crowding or squealing—or quitting."

McLean said: "I don't get you, Kid. I told you to get clear—"

Joey Deth smiled. "But you didn't tell me *how*," he cut in. "Now shut up—and when you hear the tap—"

The sound of footfalls was very faint. It died away abruptly. There was a short silence—then knuckles rapped against the wood of the flat door. They knocked four times.

Kid Deth looked at McLean's white face and smiled. He slumped on the divan, held the automatic low between his knees. He got a handkerchief from his pocket and placed it over the gun. Then he nodded at McLean, made a sign with his right hand.

McLean whispered: "For God's sake, Kid—you never packed a rod before—"

Joey Deth smiled with half-closed eyes. He motioned again for the waiter to open the door. The handkerchief moved a little. McLean opened the door and stepped to one side. A voice said:

"It's Charlie, Mac—"

McLean's face was twisted. He said in a husky voice:

"Yeah, Charlie—all right."

Charlie Gay stepped inside the flat. For a second he didn't see the slumped figure of the Kid. When he did see it he muttered an exclamation, dropped his right hand towards his left coat pocket.

Kid Deth said: "Don't, Charlie!"

Gay stopped. He stood with his head shoved forward a little; his eyes on the handkerchief that was over the automatic. His breath came in short, hissing sounds. The Kid said:

"Close that door, Mac—snap the lock. Expecting anyone else?"

McLean closed the door, shook his head. He said in an uncertain tone:

"Watch what you do, Kid."

Charlie Gay said nothing. He was medium in size with a pallid face and eyes that were set back of bushy brows. His fingers moved nervously as his hands strayed at his sides.

Joey Deth chuckled a little. "*You* do the watching, Mac," he said.

He looked at Gay. He spoke in a low, easy tone.

"You got brains, Charlie—even if you did let Barney Nasser do a squeal on you. What did you mob out Lou Rands for?"

Charlie Gay shook his head. "Take that rod off me, Kid," he said. "I wasn't in on the deal, an' you know it."

His voice was thin, rasping. When he talked he showed no fear. He kept his eyes on the white handkerchief. McLean stood close to him—both men faced the Kid.

Joey Deth said: "You got brains, Charlie—use 'em now. Talk straight to me. There isn't too much time, for what I've got to do."

Charlie Gay narrowed his eyes until they were narrow slits under his brows.

"I don't get you, Kid," he said. "I've been away a long time—"

Joey Deth nodded. "It'll be a longer trip, this time," he said. "And there won't be picture shows on Saturdays, Charlie."

McLean said: "Listen, Kid—"

Joey moved the gun slightly, and the material of the handkerchief wavered. McLean kept quiet. Joey looked at Charlie Gay.

"You got yourself a sweet alibi, Charlie—and then you got afraid—"

His voice shook a little. He stopped. Charlie Gay's eyes flickered on the dead-gray ones of the Kid, beneath the bushy brows.

"Take the rod off me, Kid," he said again.

Joey Deth smiled. "Why should I?" he asked. "You didn't take the Tommy gun off Bess Grote—even when she screamed, Charlie."

Gay's body twitched. "You don't think—I ran that job, Kid?" he muttered.

Joey said: "You know about it, Charlie."

Gay's eyes flickered towards McLean. He said harshly:

"If you sucked me into this, Mac—it'll go tough with you! The Kid's all hopped—"

Joey Deth interrupted. "Mac's all right, Charlie," he said quietly. "He's just like the rest—tryin' to play in between. He didn't suck you in. Old Andy—he did the talking."

Charlie Gay widened his eyes. "Old Andy—" he started, and checked himself. "Listen, Kid—" he muttered. "Bess—she said she was—off you. I always did—like her—"

The Kid sucked in his breath. "Yeah?" he said sharply. "And you gunned her out just the same."

Charlie Gay swung on McLean. "You squealed—you dirty—"

Joey Deth said: "Shut up, Charlie! You'll wake the neighbors."

McLean showed fear in his eyes. "He got it—from Old Andy," he said shakily. "I'm tellin' you, Charlie—I didn't squeal."

Kid Deth sat up a little on the divan. He leaned forward and took the handkerchief away from the automatic. He pressed it to his lips with his right hand fingers.

"It's no good, Charlie," he said quietly. "You wanted Barney Nasser out—and you wanted to frame me. Your mob didn't get Barney, but they got Lou Rands. They got him because I was close to him—and it was a deal to finish me. Maybe it did—I'm giving myself up at four."

"They'll give you—the hot spot, if you go down there," Gay said softly.

The Kid shook his head. "I've got things they'd like to know," he said. "I've got coin, Charlie. I can get Berman."

He was mocking Charlie Gay, and he could see the rage in the other man's eyes. McLean said slowly:

"It was just—that you were there, Kid—there with Barney."

Joey Deth nodded. "I never framed a guy for the chair," he said. "I never even cut in on the other guy's territory. I've worked the rackets—but I worked them right."

There was a little silence. Charlie Gay moved the fingers of his left hand.

"How much do you want, Kid?" he asked.

Joey shook his head. "You haven't got enough to stop me, Charlie," he said. "I'm giving you the dose right in here—and maybe Mac can squirm out of it. Maybe not."

The waiter stared at him, fear widening his eyes. His voice was hoarse.

"Jeeze, Kid—you wouldn't fix it like that!"

He looked at the gun. Charlie Gay stared at it, too. His hands were restless at his side.

Joey Deth nodded. "Why not?" he said softly. "Gay and the Nassers—they tried to frame me. I never hurt them. And when they started to jump me—all of you started to quit or squeal. You were tipping Charlie off, Mac—you knew he was coming here. Old Andy—he got yellow when I made him talk. Even the dicks—Sarlow is after me. You all want to see me burn—because a burned guy don't talk. But Charlie here—he's not too anxious for me to get inside Headquarters."

Charlie Gay said slowly: "Listen, Kid—I ain't lying. I sent the guns down to get Barney. He turned me up—and Lou Rands was the dirty dick that took me in. The boys knew that—and they got him, after he'd finished Barney. That's straight."

Kid Deth was silent for several seconds. He kept his dead-gray eyes on the flickering ones of Gay.

"How about—Bess?" he asked finally.

Charlie Gay shook his head. "It wasn't my deal," he breathed. "I swear to that, Kid. I used her for an alibi. I had to have someone—"

Kid Deth said with contempt in his voice:

"Maybe if I had a gun on me—like this one's on you, *I'd* lie for my life, too."

Charlie Gay said: "I ain't lying, Kid. I heard about her getting the dose a half hour ago. I called Mac and told him I wanted to see him and was coming over. I wanted to know how she got it."

Kid Deth leaned forward, sat on the edge of the divan.

"All right, Charlie," he said. "That just means one thing—Gil Nasser got her. *One* of you did the job. I'm giving you a choice."

Gay stared at him. There was faint eagerness in his voice, but it was the eagerness of trickery.

"What do I do, Kid?" he asked.

Joey Deth sighed. "We go and find Gil," he said slowly. "It'll be light pretty quick—and that'll make it harder. We've got the coppers to beat. Know where Gil is, Charlie?"

Charlie Gay's eyes were slits beneath his bushy brows.

"He might be—at that black boy's place—drinkin'."

The Kid smiled with his eyes half closed. He looked beyond McLean, at the cuffs of steel on the table in a corner. He nodded.

"Sure," he said. "He might be there. Mac—you know where it is?"

McLean hesitated, then shook his head. The Kid chuckled. He stood up and held the automatic in front of his left thigh.

"Listen, Charlie—" he said slowly—"we don't want to make any mistakes. Get those cuffs and put Mac's arms around something. The end of that iron bed, Charlie. You still usin' it, Mac?"

McLean nodded. He was frowning. "You don't have to fix me like that, Kid," he said.

Joey Deth moved his right arm towards the steel cuffs.

"Fix him—like that, Charlie," he said slowly. His voice got hard. "It's a lot easier than being fixed—like some other guys I know."

5

ANK SARLOW sat in a corner of the speakeasy that "Blackie" Wade ran for Gil Nasser. There were a half dozen men in the room; two of them were standing at the bar. It was almost dawn, and

Sarlow sat with his rain-soaked hat pulled low over his forehead. He was drinking beer and muttering to himself. At intervals his head rocked from side to side, across his narrow shoulders. It was the first time he had been inside the place—he had come in pretending to be drunk. A card that he had taken from the clothes of the dead Rands had been offered to Blackie—and he had been admitted.

Sarlow knew none of the men present. He had been in the place almost an hour, and he was there because he remembered that Rands had once told him the Negro ran the place for Nasser. And because of the fact that Barney Nasser had been murdered—and Bess Grote had been shot out. Sarlow had been to several places; now he was waiting, swaying in the chair, and watching out of the corners of his eyes.

Hank Sarlow swore softly. A woman laughed shrilly, from one of the rooms above. A tall man with broad shoulders and reddish hair stepped around the corner of the bar. Sarlow had not noticed him before—he guessed that there was an entrance back of the bar. The man's eyes went around the room and Sarlow kept his head low and swaying a little. He saw the man beckon to the negro he had heard called Blackie, saw his lips move swiftly. Blackie left the room, and Sarlow could hear him faintly, climbing stairs.

There was another peal of laughter, and then sudden silence. The one with the reddish hair turned so that light struck his sharp features clearly.

Sarlow said in a whisper: "Gil—Nasser."

A voice called from below. "Oh, Blackie—"

There were footfalls on the stairs that led to the third floor—Blackie was descending. The speakeasy was on the second floor—a straight, narrow flight had to be climbed to reach the bar-room. The voice below called again:

"Hey—Blackie!"

The Negro came into the room and nodded towards the red-haired one. Then he went on down the stairs. There was a sudden burst of laughter from the group about the slot machine—one man wheeled away from it.

"Drinks are on me!" he announced loudly. "The big shot—turned up!"

The men moved towards the bar. Sarlow kept his eyes on the red-haired one. A short man with a growth of beard went over to him and touched him on the shoulder. He said something, and the red-haired one shook his head, made a gesture with his right hand. Then he turned away and went to a table behind the slot machine. He sat with his body half facing the entrance from the stairs.

Sarlow breathed: "Gil Nasser, all right. Feelin' pretty bad—"

He raised a dirty hand and pulled his wet hat brim lower over his face. There were footfalls on the stairs again—more than one person was coming up.

Sarlow kept his head low, but his eyes were narrowed on the entrance from the hallway. His body stiffened as the first man came into the room, moved towards the bar. It was Charlie Gay.

The detective felt his heart pound as he saw Kid Deth, close beside Charlie. The left pocket of the Kid's coat was pressing against Gay's right side—the two men walked to the bar almost as one human. Gay's face was white; there was a strained expression in his eyes.

The Kid was smiling a little. He didn't see Sarlow, but he did see Gil Nasser. The detective knew that, and he knew that Gil Nasser recognized the Kid—and the man his brother had turned up.

At the bar Charlie Gay turned his white face towards the Kid, who had the ex-convict between him and the seated brother of the dead crook. He tried a smile that looked bad. He said something that Sarlow didn't catch. The Kid spoke to the bartender, who was staring at him.

"Two—whiskey straight," he ordered.

He kept his body close to the bar, but he looked around the room. Gil Nasser was sitting low in his chair—his big shoulders hunched forward. Sarlow lowered his head and slitted his eyes.

"It's going to be—a killing!" he breathed to

himself. "The Kid has guts—he's got a rod on Charlie Gay—he went after him—"

Out of the corner of his eyes he saw that Gil Nasser was watching the Kid. Suddenly he saw the brother of the dead crook rise. He moved slowly towards the door. He was within ten feet of it when Kid Deth saw him in the mirror, swung around. The Kid got his back against the wood of the bar—his left hand shoved the material of his coat pocket out.

"All right, Nasser!" he said in a hard voice. "That's far—enough!"

Gil Nasser swung around. He smiled with his lips bared.

"Jeeze!" he muttered. "If it ain't—Kid Deth!"

There had been the sound of voices, the clinking of glasses in the room. Now all sound died. Men stood or sat motionless, watching the Kid or Gil Nasser.

Joey Deth said: "Yeah, Nasser—it's Kid Deth. How're things?"

Beside the Kid, his body crouched a little, was Charlie Gay. The muscles around his lips were twitching—his eyes were on Gil Nasser's right hand. The hand was only half in sight—the fingers were buried beneath the material of his left coat lapel.

Gil Nasser said in a voice that was very hard: "Lousy, Kid."

Joey Deth kept a smile in his dead-gray eyes. He nodded his head.

"Sure," he agreed. "Lousy is right."

Nasser's right elbow came up a little, but his hand didn't go deeper behind his coat lapel. Kid Deth said in a voice that barely filled the room.

"Charlie here—he says you gunned out Bess. You figured the bulls would grab me, so I was fixed for the hot spot or a life stretch. And Bess knew too much—so you made her quiet."

Nasser said: "Yeah? Did Charlie say that?"

Charlie Gay was breathing heavily. His nerve broke—he cried out.

"That's a—dam' lie, Nasser—he's got a gun on me. I never said that—"

His voice broke. The Kid looked at Gil and kept on smiling.

"He's going yellow, Nasser. The Rands job got him. His mob did for the dick, trying to frame me."

Gil Nasser stood motionless. He said in a grim tone:

"Yeah? Did he do that job?"

Sarlow sat up a little straighter, stared at Kid Deth. But the Kid was looking at only one human in the room—and that human was watching him in the same manner.

The Kid nodded. "After your brother tried to get Rands—and missed," he said.

Gil Nasser's eyes widened a little. He closed his lips and moved the hand inside the coat just a little. Kid Deth said:

"Don't swing that rod, Nasser. I don't have to swing mine—just a squeeze—"

Gil Nasser bared his teeth in a smile that wasn't pretty.

"You—dam' fool!" he breathed. "You'd never get out of here."

Joey Deth nodded. "I'd get out—just like you would," he said. "In the coroner's basket. And that's better—than being framed."

Gil Nasser narrowed his eyes again. He took his right hand away from his coat lapel, let it fall at his side. He shrugged.

"You got me wrong, Kid," he said. "When did you start packin' a rod?"

There was a half smile on his face. Joey Deth didn't smile.

"When you started rubbing out women!" he said steadily.

Nasser took his eyes away from Deth's and looked at the white face of Charlie Gay. He said with a hard smile:

"Tryin' to put that deal off on me, eh? Dirty rat!"

Charlie Gay said in a voice that held a half sob of fear:

"I never said—you done it. I swear to God I never said—"

His voice died away. A woman's voice from somewhere up above called:

"Blackie—come up here—"

Kid Deth smiled almost gently. His eyes were on Gil Nasser's.

"Blackie's quiet—from a butt rap," he said. "Tell her to shut up—we're talkin'."

Gil Nasser said: "Sure, Kid—anything to keep you—"

He turned his back to the Kid, took a step towards the door that led to the hallway. But Joey saw his right arm crook—the hand flash upward. As Nasser's words died he swung around. The first bullet from his gun got Charlie Gay in the stomach—the second got the wood of the bar.

Charlie Gay staggered out—and Kid Deth stepped behind him. The third bullet caught Gay in the left arm—it battered him off balance. He screamed.

"You—lyin'—"

Sarlow stood up and aimed his gun low at Nasser, squeezed the trigger steadily. The crash of his first shot and Gil Nasser's fourth sounded simultaneously. The Kid's body jerked; he swore through clenched teeth. Gil Nasser sagged downward.

Sarlow shoved his hat back and faced the men in the room from his corner.

"The riot squad's outside," he said hoarsely. "Now—you just keep still—all of you."

Charlie Gay turned towards the bar, tried to grip it with his hands, failed. He went to his knees, swayed before the Kid for a second, pitched forward. He lay on the wooden floor, less than five feet from the motionless body of Gil Nasser.

The Kid leaned against the bar and took his left hand from his coat pocket. He said to Sarlow:

"Why in hell—didn't you let him—keep shooting?"

Sarlow said: "Keep your mouth shut, you!"

The Kid grinned. He said softly: "Jeeze—lead hurts when it scrapes your ribs."

He put his right hand down to his left side and pressed the ripped portion of his coat. Sarlow said in a steadier tone:

"One of you look at those two on the floor."

A short, round-shouldered man kneeled beside Charlie Gay. He lifted a wrist, felt it. He said thickly:

"He's—out."

Kid Deth said: "I won't miss him—a dam' bit." His voice was grim.

Sarlow spoke more quietly. "Kick that gun away from Nasser," he ordered. "Call an ambulance—one of you."

Gil Nasser groaned and tried to sit up. Sarlow said to Joey Deth, keeping his back against the wall in his corner:

"Slide your rod—across to me, Kid."

Kid Deth smiled. "You're lettin' me hold it," he said grimly.

Sarlow nodded. "I gave you a break," he said. "I got Nasser. Slide it over—"

The Kid leaned down, felt pain from his left side, and slid the automatic across the floor. It stopped near the detective's feet.

Gil Nasser sat up and held his stomach. He turned dull eyes towards Sarlow, who held his gun low. He said thickly:

"A dick—got me—"

Kid Deth looked at Nasser and smiled with his dead-gray eyes.

"When you get where Barney is—tell him you heard Bess scream—and kept working the Tommy," he said in a low, hard voice. "He might have guts enough left—to hate you—for that."

Nasser stared at Joey. He wiped his lips with the back of his right hand. He swayed a little.

"She didn't send—you out—" he breathed weakly, "She put you wise—"

Kid Deth said softly, "Jeeze—you *did* get her. You did—"

Gil Nasser spoke in a whisper. "That rat—Lou Rands—takin' the slot graft from Barney—waitin' for the chance to turn him up—"

Sarlow swore softly. His eyes were on the Kid's. Joey nodded his head.

"That's one—truth," he said simply.

Gil Nasser went down on the floor and lay on his stomach. The bartender was calling a number in a high-pitched voice. The Kid shivered a little. After a few seconds Nasser's body relaxed.

Sarlow said: "We won't need that ambulance—but let it come—"

Kid Deth touched his left side. "There's me—and the black man, downstairs," he said.

The detective stepped out from the corner, with his eyes narrowed and the gun held low.

"The rest of you—stay quiet," he warned. "Come on, Kid."

Kid Deth walked out from the bar. They went downstairs and to the street. Blackie was leaning against an iron rail holding his head. Sarlow patted him for a rod, didn't find one. Blocks away there was the clang of an ambulance bell. Sarlow said:

"Was Lou workin' with Barney Nasser, Kid?"

Kid Deth shrugged. "Maybe," he replied. "I don't know. But I didn't get him, Sarlow. I've never done a job—"

Sarlow swore softly. "It's a lousy racket, Kid," he said. "You comin' down—at four?"

The Kid's eyes widened a little. "You turning me loose?" he asked.

The lean-faced detective listened to the louder clang of the ambulance gong, stared towards the entrance of the speakeasy. It was quiet inside.

"You come down—tomorrow, at four, Kid."

His voice was tired. He was thinking of a man he'd thought was white—and who hadn't been white. He was thinking of crooks who had used guns, and one who hadn't. He was thinking of the Kid's woman.

"Get going, Kid," he said softly.

When the Kid climbed out of the taxi it was clear and cold. The photographers crowded up, and the chubby-faced Berman grinned at them.

"What's all the shooting for?" he asked. "The Kid's just down for a chat."

They went inside and the Kid saw Lieutenant of Detectives Cardigan and Hank Sarlow standing side by side. Berman kept a smile on his face.

When they got inside Cardigan's office the lieutenant of detectives said slowly:

"We got a slot machine racket charge against you, Kid. The D.A. wants to push it. He thinks we've got you nice."

Berman passed the cigars. "Yeah," he said. "The D.A. always thinks that. It's what costs the taxpayers coin."

The Kid said softly: "I'm quitting the racket, Cardigan. It's lousy."

Cardigan looked at Sarlow. The lean-faced detective said:

"Straight, Kid?"

Joey Deth nodded. "Jeeze—yes," he said bitterly. "I'm through."

Sarlow said: "Some rotten ones got hurt. And some others that were just pulled in. Maybe Lou Rands was one of those—"

He checked himself. Cardigan swore. Berman pulled on his cigar and frowned.

The Kid said: "I'm through. Make a fix and I'll clear out—somewhere West—"

Sarlow and Berman looked at Cardigan. The lieutenant of detectives nodded a little.

"We might not get you on the other charges, Kid," he said. "And some tough ones are done, out of the game. You gave us a break—and you showed up—"

The Kid was thinking of Bess Grote. Things might have been different, he was thinking. And he knew that Sarlow was thinking of Lou Rands.

"It's a lousy racket—and I'm through," he said again, slowly. "That's straight."

Cardigan said: "How about Detective Williams? A bullet from that lunch-wagon where Old Andy was found dead has got him in the hospital. He'll live, but—"

Joey Deth cut in. His voice was emotionless.

"Old Andy was trying to get me. I didn't work a rod, Cardigan. I guess you know that. Two mobs hated me a lot—and they got tipped to my talk with Barney Nasser. Maybe Barney wasn't sure about Lou Rands—maybe he thought he was framing him. He tried to get him—and lost out. Rands wanted me, so he tried to frame me. Charlie Gay closed in and mobbed Rands out. I got loose. Bess was playing safe—trying to give me a chance to get in the clear. That's the way I figure it. Charlie used her for his alibi, but she was trying to make things smooth with Gil. She told me she'd seen him. She didn't send me out back—and Gil gave her the dose. That was what I wanted to know—and I figured to shove her killer out. But I guess—"

He stopped. There was a little silence. Berman said:

"The Kid's through, Cardigan. I know when they're through—you can feel it."

Joey Deth said for the third time: "It's a lousy racket."

Cardigan half closed his eyes. He sighed, nodded his head. He picked up the French phone and said in a tired voice:

"Get me the D.A.'s office, will you? Yeah—it's important. It's about—Kid Deth."

The Sinister Sphere
Frederick C. Davis

MANY WRITERS for the pulps were extremely prolific, as they needed to be with pay rates that commonly were no more than one penny a word, but none more than Frederick C. Davis (1902–1977). He wrote about numerous characters, both under his own name, as Stephen Ransome, and, most famously, as Curtis Steele for the Operator 5 thrillers.

In addition to nearly fifty full-length novels, Davis wrote more than a thousand short stories, producing more than a million words a year, but none were more popular than his series about the Moon Man—Stephen Thatcher, the policeman by day and a notorious robber by night.

The son of the police chief, Sergeant Thatcher was utterly dedicated to helping those unable to handle the trials of America's Great Depression, even if it meant breaking the law. In the tradition of Robin Hood, he stole from the wealthy to give to the poor.

To keep his true identity a secret, Thatcher donned the most peculiar disguise in all of pulp fiction—not a mask, but a dome made of highly fragile one-way glass, fitted with a breathing apparatus that filtered air. The glass, known as Argus glass, was manufactured in France and was, at the time, unknown in the United States. As the perpetrator of innumerable crimes, he was the most-hunted criminal in the city, saving lives in equally impressive numbers along the way.

There were thirty-nine adventures about the Moon Man, all published in *Ten Detective Aces* between June 1933 to November 1939. "The Sinister Sphere" is the first adventure of the character seen by Depression-era readers as a common man who became a hero.

The Sinister Sphere

Frederick C. Davis

The girl's gun was steady

Meet the Uncanny "Moon Man" —and his Money-Mad Victims

With a strange, uncanny knowledge the Moon Man selected his victims. Those victims had climbed rough-shod to power; some within the law, and others outside the pale. And the Moon Man called on them with a very definite and grim plan— for he walked in the eternal danger of a double menace.

CHAPTER I
THE MOON MAN

IT WAS ROBBERY.

The French door inched open. A figure crept through, into the dark room. It paused.

It turned from side to side, as if looking around, a head that had no eyes, no nose, no mouth! From side to side it turned its head, a head that was a perfect sphere of silver! Mottled black markings covered the shining surface of the ball, reproducing the shaded areas of the full moon whose light streamed in through the windows.

If the silent figure had any face at all, it was the face of the man in the moon!

The silver, spherical head sat low on a pair of broad shoulders from which a long, black cape hung. A pair of black-gloved hands stole through slits in the sides of the cape.

The dark room was not silent. From below came the soft strains of dance music, mingled with laughter and the rhythmic moving of feet on polished floor. It was midnight; the party was at its height. The man whose head was a globe of silver nodded as though pleased.

He glided through the darkness across the room. At an inner door he drifted to a stop. He opened it carefully. The music became louder in the ears of him who had no ears. The hallway outside was empty. The cloaked figure closed the door and turned to the wall.

He removed from its nail a mirror which hung between two doors, and disclosed the circular front of a safe. His black hand twirled the combination dial. He turned his moon head, listening alertly. He heard faint clicks. When he drew up, he turned the handle of the safe door and opened it.

Locks meant little to him.

Into the safe he thrust a black-gloved hand, and brought out a sheaf of banknotes. He drew them inside his cape. He closed the safe and twirled the combination.

Suddenly a loud snap! . . . A flood of light drenched the room.

The figure whirled.

In the doorway stood a woman, her eyes widened with fright. She was forty and fat. She was wearing a spangled gown. Her one bejewelled hand dropped limply from the light-switch. She stood transfixed, staring at the figure with the silver head, and gasped:

"Martin!"

She had no need to call. Her husband was at her back. He stared over her shoulder, as startled as she.

"The Moon Man!" he exclaimed.

The man in the silver mask whirled toward the open French door.

Martin Richmond, clubman, broker, man of position, was wiry and athletic. He leaped past his wife with one bound. He sprang toward the French windows with the intention of blocking the way of the grotesque thief. The Moon Man reached it at the same instant.

Richmond flung up his arms to grapple with the intruder. He groped through empty air. An ebony hand, clenched into a fist, cracked against the point of Richmond's chin.

Richmond staggered, making a desperate attempt to clasp the man with the spherical head. His hand clutched a black one. Another thrust tumbled him backward. Something soft remained in his fingers as he sprawled. The Moon Man darted through the door slamming it shut behind him.

The door opened on a balcony. Beneath it was twenty feet of empty space. The Moon Man leaped over the railing of the balcony, throwing himself into the void.

Martin Richmond scrambled up. From below came a quick, smooth purr. He rushed onto the balcony and looked down. He saw nothing. The Moon Man was gone.

"Call the police!" Richmond gasped as he sprang back into the room:

He jerked to a stop and looked at the thing he had in his hand. It was a black silk glove.

"We've been robbed!"

The words came ringing over the wire into the ear of Detective Lieutenant Gil McEwen. He was perched at his desk, in his tiny office in headquarters. He clamped the receiver tightly to his ear.

"Who's talking?"

"Martin Richmond, Morning Drive. The Moon Man robbed me. He got away!"

"Coming right out!" snapped McEwen.

He slammed the receiver on its hook and whirled in his chair to face a young man who was standing by the window. McEwen's face was hard and wrinkled as old leather; the young man's was smooth-skinned and clean-cut. McEwen's eyes were gray and glittering; the young man's were blue and warm. McEwen was fifty, hardened, by twenty years on the force; the young man was half his age, and had just been made a detective sergeant.

He was Stephen Thatcher, son of Peter Thatcher, the chief of police.

"Steve, it's the Moon Man again!" the veteran detective snapped. "Come on!"

"I'll be damned!" said Steve Thatcher. "Can't we do anything to stop his robberies?"

"I'll stop him!" McEwen vowed as he grabbed for the knob. "I'll stop him if it's the last thing I ever do!"

He went out the office on a run. Steve Thatcher ran after him with long legs flexing lithely. They thumped down the wooden steps. They rushed into the adjoining garage. A moment later they swerved a police-car into the street and dashed away with the speedometer flickering around sixty.

Martin Richmond's residence on Morning Drive was five miles away. Gill McEwen made it in less than five minutes. With Steve Thatcher at his side he hurried to the front door and knocked very urgently. Martin Richmond himself opened it.

The party was still going on. Couples were still dancing in the large room at the right. McEwen saw them through closed French doors, and followed Richmond into the library opposite. Richmond wasted no time.

"My wife found the Moon Man in our room. He'd just finished robbing our safe. It was almost an hour ago."

"An hour ago? Why didn't you call me sooner?" McEwen snapped. "By this time he's crawled into a hole somewhere."

"I found that our phone wires were cut. I stopped to see how much had been stolen. Then I had to find a phone. It took some time to get my neighbors to get up and let me in. I called you as soon as I could."

"Let me see the bedroom," McEwen ordered.

He trod up the stairs with Steve Thatcher at his heels. Thatcher could well understand the veteran detective's anger. The Moon Man had done this sort of thing repeatedly. He had committed robberies without number in his characteristic daring, grotesque way.

The papers had been filled with his exploits. The police department had been absolutely unable to find a single clue pointing to his identity. He appeared like magic, robbed, and vanished.

The papers and the police commissioners were howling for an arrest. The public was demanding protection against the mysterious thief. And the police were helpless. Steve Thatcher could well understand why Gill McEwen was in no amiable mood.

McEwen paced about the bedroom. He examined the safe. He looked out the balcony. He ran downstairs and inspected the ground below. He came back red-faced and puffing.

"He used a car. Driveway right below. Stopped the car under the balcony, climbed on the top of it, then swung himself up. Beat it the same way. Not a tire-mark or a footprint! Not one damn' thing to tell who—"

"Look at this!" said Martin Richmond quickly.

He thrust the black silk glove toward McEwen. McEwen took it slowly, narrowed his eyes at it, and passed it to Steve Thatcher.

"I pulled it off his hand as he was rushing out the door," Richmond explained. "He—"

"It's a right glove," McEwen interrupted. "The chances are he's right-handed. Then he had to use his bare hand to open the door and make a getaway. The means he's probably left a fingerprint on the knob!"

He examined the knob. He could see nothing. Raising, he turned sharply on Steve Thatcher.

"Beat it to a phone and get Kenton up. Tell him we've got to dust this knob right away— can't wait. Get him up here quick!"

Hours later Gil McEwen hunched over his desk in Headquarters peering at a photograph. It was a photograph of a door knob. On the knob was a clearly defined impression of a thumb. It was not the thumb-print of Martin Richmond, nor of Mrs. Richmond, nor of any one else in the burglarized house. McEwen had made sure of that.

It was the thumb-print of the Moon Man!

McEwen settled back in his chair exhaustedly, and peered into the face of Kenton, the fingerprint expert.

"You're absolutely sure that this print doesn't match any in the files?"

"Absolutely sure," Kenton answered. "The thumb that made that print has never been recorded by any police department in the United States."

"Hell!" grunted McEwen. "Then it can't tell us who the Moon Man is—yet. But when I find a guy whose thumb-print matches up with this one, I'll collar him hard!"

Kenton went out. Steve Thatcher settled into a chair.

"We know, anyway, that the Moon Man is somebody who has no criminal record."

"Yeah, but he'll soon have! The time's coming when that guy's going to make a slip. When I grab him, he's going up the river on so many counts of robbery that he'll never live to come out of prison. And I'll grab him, all right—I'll do it!"

They looked toward an older man seated beside the desk. He was portly, with a kindly face and curly white hair. He was Chief Peter Thatcher. His were the keen eyes of a born law officer. His was the straight, stern mouth of a strict disciplinarian. He was a good chief, and at present he was a very worried one.

"We've *got* to get the Moon Man, Gil," he declared. "We've got to stop at nothing to get him."

"Listen!" McEwen said sharply. "I've been on the force twenty years. I've got a reputation. No crook has ever succeeded in getting away from me once I set out on his trail. I went to Brazil to get Doak, didn't I—and I got him. I went to India to get Stephano, and I got him. I'm not going to let any smart aleck Moon Man make a fool out of me. I've sworn to get him, and I will!"

Chief Thatcher nodded slowly. "The Police Board is clamoring for that bird's hide. So are all the papers. We've got to grab the Moon Man somehow, Gil—and quick."

"Chief, you've got my promise. I'm not going to stop trying till I've grabbed him. Nothing's going to keep me from it. And when I make a promise, I live up to my word."

"I know you do," the chief said soberly. "I'm depending on you, Gil. It's your case. It's entirely in your hands."

Steve Thatcher looked solemn.

"I haven't been a detective long enough to be of much help," he said quietly. "I wish to gosh I could do more. But you know you can count on me, Gil, for—"

The door opened. A girl came in. She was twenty-two, pretty, animated. Her face resembled Gil McEwen's strongly; she was his daughter. She greeted her father cheerfully, nodded to Chief Thatcher, and went quickly to Steve. She kissed him.

On Sue McEwen's third left finger glittered a solitaire. Steve had put it there. The wedding was not far off.

"Baffled!" she exclaimed, surveying the disgruntled expressions of the three. "Aren't the papers awful? You'd think the Moon Man was the greatest criminal of the age, the way—"

"He is, as far as I'm concerned!" her father snapped. "Sue, we're trying to get at the bottom of this thing. We'll see you later."

"Why chase me out?" Sue asked with a smile. "Maybe I can help. Perhaps the thing you need is a little womanly intuition."

"Huh!" said her father. "You're too eager to mix yourself up in police matters, Sue. I don't think you can be of any help."

"Don't be so sure," Sue insisted. "I would say, for instance, that the Moon Man must be someone far above the level of an ordinary crook. He has more intelligence. He plans his moves cleverly. So far, he has always succeeded in getting what he wants, and making a clean getaway. Going through the Rogue's Gallery would be only a waste of time. The man you want is well-bred, with a fine mind, good manners, and a broad social background."

"Trying to make a hero of him—a thief?" her father asked skeptically.

"Not at all. After all, he is a thief, and stealing, besides being illegal, is revolting to anyone of sound character. The man deserves all the punishment you want to give him, Dad. I'm only suggesting the kind of a man he is—one whose character has been despoiled by the dishonorable business of robbery. There—have I helped?"

"Not much. Now—"

"How much did he steal this time?"

"Six hundred and fifty dollars."

"Only six hundred and fifty?" Sue McEwen repeated in surprise. "Why, that pushes him even lower in the scale of thieves. He's nothing but a petty pilferer!"

The parsonage of the Congregational Church of Great City was located not far from the business district. The Reverend Edward Parker lived there alone. At nine o'clock on the night following the Moon Man's latest exploit he heard a knock at his door. He opened it.

A short, squatty man stood on the step. He had a twisted nose that evidently had once been broken in a fist-fight. He had a cauliflower ear. He had scarcely any neck. He nodded, and handed through the door a sealed envelope.

"From a friend, for the needy of the parish," he said.

Immediately the Rev. Mr. Parker accepted the envelope, the pugilistic gentleman turned and walked away. The darkness swallowed him up. Dr. Parker opened the envelope. Inside it he found a bundle of banknotes. They were bound by a single band of silver paper, and they amounted to $250.

Maude Betts was a widow with no work and three children. She lived in a tenement in the warehouse district of Great City. The stove in the kitchen was cold. There was no food in or on it. Her cupboard was bare. She was about to be evicted by a landlord who declared that the four months' rent, past due, must be paid him at once. She was facing the county poor farm.

A knock sounded at her door. She dried her eyes, opened the door, and found a tough-looking young chap handing her an envelope. She took it as he said: "From a friend."

He went away. Mrs. Betts opened the envelope and gasped with joy. From it she removed a pack of banknotes held together by a band of silver paper. They totalled just $200.

Ethel Knapp, twenty and not bad to look at, stood in her furnished room and peered at the gas jet. For ten minutes she had been peering at it, trying to summon the courage necessary to turn it on—without a lighted match above it. She had no money. She had come to Great City from her home in Ohio to work. She had no work. She had no way of returning to her mother and father. But she did have a way of saving herself from further hunger and humiliation. The gas jet.

She raised her hand toward it. Startled, she paused. A faint rustling sound came into the room. Looking down, she saw an envelope creeping under the door. She took it up, bewildered, and opened it. Inside lay money—currency held together by a band of silver paper—banknotes totalling $200!

She jerked open the door. The hall was empty. She ran down the steps. She saw a few persons on the street, and paused bewildered. She had no way of knowing that the money had been left her by the squatty, combative-looking young man who was just vanishing around the corner. But that money meant life and happiness to Ethel Knapp. . . .

For the Rev. Edward Parker, $250.
For Maude Betts, $200.
For Ethel Knapp, $200.
Just $650 in all! . . .

CHAPTER II
THE MOON MAN SPEAKS

In their delight, neither Dr. Parker, nor Mrs. Betts, nor Miss Knapp noticed the oddity of the silver band which encircled the money that had so mysteriously come to them. None of them thought to associate it with the Moon Man.

Had they suspected, they might have thought the stocky chap to be the Moon Man. They would have been wrong.

Ned Dargan, ex-lightweight—he of the broken nose and cauliflower ear—walked along a dark street in a shabby section of the city. He glanced neither right nor left; he walked steadily; he knew where he was going. When he reached the black doorway of an abandoned tenement building—a structure condemned by the city but not yet demolished—he paused.

Making sure he was not observed, he entered the lightless hallway. He closed the door carefully and tightly behind him and trod up a flight of broken, uncarpeted stairs. Plaster littered them. Dust lay everywhere. The air was musty and close. Dargan walked along the upper hall to another door.

As he reached for the knob a voice called: "Come in, Angel."

Dargan went in, smiling. The room beyond was dark. A moment passed before his eyes became accustomed to the gloom. Gradually he was able to see a form standing behind a table, a figure that blended out of the blackness like a materializing ghost. The figure was swathed in a black cape. Its head was a smooth globe of silver.

"Evenin', boss," said Dargan.

A chuckle came from the silver-headed man. "You've distributed the money, Angel?"

"Yeah. Got it out right away. And it certainly was badly needed, boss."

"I know. . . . You realize why I selected Martin Richmond as a victim, Angel?"

"I've got an idea he ain't all he seems to be."

"Not quite that," answered the voice that came from the silver head. "He's quite respectable, you know. Social position, wealth, all that. But there's one thing I don't like about him, Angel. He's made millions by playing the market short, forcing prices down."

"Nothin' wrong in that, is there?" Dargan asked.

"Not according to our standards, Angel; but the fact remains that short-selling had contributed to the suffering of those we are trying to help. I've taken little enough from Richmond's kind, Angel. I must have more—later."

Dargan peered. "I don't quite get you, boss.

You're takin' an awful chance—and you don't keep any of the money for yourself."

A chuckle came from the silver globe. "I don't want the money for myself. I want it for those who are perishing for want of the barest necessities of life. What would you do if you saw a child about to be crushed under a truck? You'd snatch her away, even at the risk of your own life.

"I can't bear to see suffering, Angel. I can no more help trying to alleviate it than I can help breathing. If there were any other way of taking money from those who hoard it, and giving it to those who desperately need it—if there were any other way than stealing, I'd take that way. But there isn't."

"Don't think I'm questioning you, boss." Dargan hastened to explain. "I'm with you all the way, and you know it."

"Yes, Angel," said the Moon Man gently, "I know it. You're the only man in the world I trust. You know what it is to suffer; that's why you're with me. Well, you've been scouting today. What's the result?"

Dargan wagged his head. "Things are pretty bad, boss. The regular charities ain't reaching all the folks they should, and they're pretty slow. I don't know what some of these folks would do without your help.

"There's a steamfitter out of a job named Ernest Miller. He's got a daughter, Agnes, who's sick with consumption. The kid's goin' to die if she ain't sent to Arizona. Miller can't send her— he hasn't got any money, boss."

The Moon Man nodded his silver head. "Miller shall have money, Angel—all he needs."

"Then there's the guy named Frank Lauder, I told you about."

"Lauder will be compensated, Angel."

"Then there're two kids—Bill and Betty Anderson—a couple of sweet kids they are. Their mother just died. They ain't got nowhere to go but to their aunt and uncle, named Anderson. The Andersons are barely gettin' along as it is, and can't take the kids in. So they'll have to go to an orphanage if somethin' ain't done for 'em."

"They won't go to the orphanage, Angel.

You've done your work well. I'll have money for all of them tomorrow."

"Tomorrow?" Dargan peered again at the small moon which was the head of the man in the black cape. "Boss, ain't you takin' an awful chance, followin' up so close? Last night—and now tonight! Ain't it gettin' dangerous?"

There was a pause. "Yes, Angel, it is getting dangerous. The police now have my thumb-print."

"Your thumb-print! Holy cripes! Now if they ever catch you they'll be able to prove you—"

"I don't think it will occur to Gil McEwen to look in the right place for me, Angel!" the Moon Man interrupted with a soft laugh. "Still, as you suggest, I've got to be very careful. At any time McEwen might accidentally find a print which matches the one he found on the Richmond bedroom door knob last night—and when he does—"

"Cripes, boss!" gasped Dargan.

The Moon Man straightened. "Don't worry, Angel. Keep an eye on yourself. Report back to me to-morrow night, half an hour after midnight, here. All clear?"

"Sure, boss."

Ned Dargan turned from the room. He closed the door tightly on the Moon Man. He peered at the panel, as though trying to penetrate it with his gaze and read the secret of the man in the room—a secret even he did not know. He walked down the stairs slowly, and eased out the front door.

"I can't figure out *who* that guy is!" he told himself wonderingly. "But, cripes! I know he's the swellest guy that ever lived!"

Ned Dargan had a solid reason for feeling as he did about the man whose face he had never seen—the Moon Man. He'd gone bad in the ring. A weakened arm made further fighting impossible. He found it just as impossible to find work. He'd drifted downward and outward; he'd become a bum, sleeping in alleys, begging food. Until, mysteriously a message had come to him from the Moon Man.

Some day Ned Dargan was going to fight again. Some day he was going to get into the ring, knock some palooka for a row, and become champ. And if he ever did, he'd have the Moon Man to thank for it. . . .

The Moon Man stood in the center of the dismal room. He watched Dargan close the door. He listened, and in a moment heard a creak, then another. He knew those sounds the stairs made. The first was pitched at A Flat and the second at B in the musical scale. When B sounded before A Flat, someone was coming up. The Moon Man heard B follow A Flat and knew that Dargan was gone.

He turned away, opened a connecting door, and stepped into an adjoining room. He turned a key in the lock. The air was pitch black. The Moon Man made motions which divested himself of his cape. He pulled off his black gloves—luckily he had provided himself with more than one pair. He removed from his head that silver sphere, and he put all his secret regalia in a closet. The closet door he also locked.

Turning again, he silently opened a window, and eased out onto a rusted fire-escape. Rung by rung he let himself down into the alleyway behind. He paused, listening and looking around. Then he stepped forth. . . .

The street-light's glow fell into the face of Stephen Thatcher!

Steve Thatcher thought of things as he walked away from the house he had made the Moon Man's rendezvous. In his mind's ear he heard Gil McEwen saying: "I've sworn to get the Moon Man, and I will!" McEwen, the toughest detective on the force, who never failed to bag his man!

And he heard the voice of the girl he loved: "He's nothing but a petty pilferer!"

Steve Thatcher lowered his head as though stubbornly to butt an obstacle. A wild scheme—his! He knew it. But, also, he knew the world—cruel and relentless—and he could not stand by and do nothing to save those who were suffering. The mere thought of letting others perish, while nothing was done to save them, was unendurable.

He was a cop's son—revolt against injustice was in his blood—and not even the law could keep him from trying to right the wrongs he knew existed. Beyond the written law was a higher one to which Steve Thatcher had dedicated himself—the law of humanity.

And if he were caught? Would he find leniency at the hands of Gil McEwen and Chief Thatcher? No. He was certain of that. Even if McEwen and the chief might wish to deal kindly with him, they would be unable to. The Moon Man now was a public enemy—his fate was in the hands of the multitude. Steve Thatcher would be dealt with like any common crook—if he were caught.

He remembered Ernest Miller's daughter, who must go to Arizona or die; he remembered Frank Lauder, who must be cared for; he remembered Bill and Betty Anderson, who must have help.

"It's got to be done!" he said through closed teeth. "Damn, it's *got* to be done!"

He walked swiftly through the night.

CHAPTER III
ANOTHER VICTIM!

Detective Lieutenant Gil McEwen's phone clattered. He took it up. He glared at a photograph he was holding—a photograph of the Moon Man's fingerprint—and grunted: "Hello!"

"Detective McEwen? Listen carefully. I'm calling—"

"Speak louder!" McEwen snapped. "I can't hear you."

"My name is Kent Atwell, Mr. McEwen," the voice came more plainly. "I'm phoning you from a pay-station downtown because I don't dare phone you from my home. I've been threatened—by the Moon Man."

"What!" barked McEwen. He knew the name of Kent Atwell. Atwell was one of Great City's most prominent citizens. His home was one of the finest. His influence went far. And here he was, huddling in a booth downtown like a rabbit in a hole, using a public phone because a threat of the Moon Man had filled him with fright!

"The devil!" McEwen said.

"I've got to see you, Mr. McEwen—immediately. The Moon Man has threatened to rob me tonight. I don't dare let you come to my home, or my office. Can I meet you somewhere?"

"Where are you?"

"In a drug store at State and Main streets."

"You're close to the Palace Theatre," McEwen said briskly. "Buy a ticket and go in. Go down into the men's room—be there in ten minutes. I'm coming right along, and I'll meet you there."

"Certainly. Thank you!"

McEwen pushed the phone back and scowled. He tramped out of his office into Chief Thatcher's. He found the chief absent, but Steve Thatcher was sitting in his father's old padded chair. The young man looked up.

"You come with me, Steve!" McEwen snapped. "This thing is getting worse and worse! The Moon Man's going to stage another robbery—and this time he's saying so ahead of time!"

"I'll be damned!" said Steve Thatcher. "Listen, Gil. I've just found out—"

"Never mind! Come with me!"

McEwen went out the door. Steve Thatcher frowned; but he followed. He loped down the steps, crowded into a police-car beside McEwen, and said nothing until the car was whizzing down the street.

"Of all the damned gall!" the veteran detective blurted. "Sending a warning ahead of time! He must think he's living a charmed life—that we can never touch him. I'll show him where he's wrong—then, by damn, he'll wish he was on the moon!"

Steve Thatcher sighed. "I was about to tell you, Gil, that I think I've found out about this mask the Moon Man wears. You've wondered how he could see his way about, with a silver globe on his head. Well, evidently he can, because the thing isn't silver at all, but glass."

"Glass?" McEwen repeated. "How do you know?"

"It must be. That mask of the Moon Man's has made us all curious, and I began trying to figure out how he could manage to move about with his head completely enclosed in a metal ball. Well, he can't, of course. I browsed around the library today, and found the answer—Argus glass."

"What's Argus glass?"

Steve Thatcher smiled. "If you were a frequenter of speakeasies in New York, you'd know. Argus glass is named for the son of the mythological god, Zeus. Argus had a countless number of eyes, and some of them were always open and watching, so the legend goes. Argus glass is a mirror when you look at it from one side, and a perfectly clear piece of glass when you see it from the other."

"Didn't know there was any such thing!" McEwen snapped, sending the car swerving around a corner.

"Nor I, until I read about it. A big French jeweller's store has in it several pillars of the glass. They look like mirrors to the customers, but they're not. They're hollow, and inside them sit detectives on revolving chairs. They can see everything that goes on in the store, but no one can see them. It wasn't so long ago that speakeasy proprietors found out about the glass. They use it in their doors now instead of peep-holes. Nobody can see in, but they can see out."

"Say! Maybe we·can learn who the Moon Man is by tracing that glass globe!" McEwen exclaimed. "Who makes the glass?"

"The Saint Gobain Company of France. Argus glass is the answer, Gil. The Moon Man can see as clearly as though he wasn't masked at all, but nobody can see his face. His mask must be split down the middle so he can get his head into it, and he's evidently painted the mirror surface to look like a moon."

"By damn!" McEwen declared. "Just let me get within reach of that guy and I'll take a whack at that glass mask. It'll turn into splinters and then we'll see who the Moon Man is!"

Stephen Thatcher smiled. He had not thought of that likelihood. A sharp blow would shatter the globe that masked the face of the Moon Man! . . . His smile faded. He was almost sorry now that he had divulged the secret. He had told McEwen this only because he was supposed to be working on the case and, to safeguard himself from suspicion, had decided that he had better make some discovery about himself.

"No kidding, Gil," he said quietly. "Aren't you keeping something back? Haven't you some idea who the Moon Man is?"

"Not a damn' notion!" McEwen declared. "How about you, Steve? Who do you think he is?"

"I," said Steve Thatcher with a sigh, "couldn't say."

McEwen parked the police car a block from the Palace Theatre. He strode to the ticket-booth with Steve Thatcher; they bought tickets and went in. Immediately they turned toward the downstairs men's room. They entered it to find Kent Atwell waiting.

Atwell was thin, dapper; his eyes were dark and deep-set. And at the moment he was visibly agitated. When McEwen identified himself, he immediately launched into a frightened, indignant explanation of the Moon Man's threat.

"Here!" he exclaimed, pushing a sheet of crumpled paper toward McEwen. "Read that! The incredible presumption of it!"

The bit of paper was torn irregularly at the bottom. It was typewritten—done, McEwen could not dream, on a machine in police headquarters! Its message was terse:

DEAR MR. ATWELL:

Withdraw from your bank today the sum of five thousand dollars. Place it in a safe in your home. I intend to call for it tonight. Let me warn you that if you notify the police of my intentions, you will suffer worse punishment than death. That is my promise to you.

McEwen looked blank. "How do you know this is from the Moon Man?" he asked sharply. "Where's the rest of it—the part that is torn off?"

Atwell turned pale. "It's of no importance—

just the typewritten signature. I accidentally tore it off and lost the piece, so—"

McEwen gestured impatiently. "Mr. Atwell, I beg your pardon, but it is my business to know when men are telling the truth. You are not being frank with me. There was more of this message—and if I'm to help you, I've got to have it."

"Really, there—"

"Unless you produce it right now, Mr. Atwell, you can count on no help from me," McEwen snapped.

Atwell sighed. He fumbled in his pocket. McEwen quickly took the bit of paper he produced—the lower half of the sheet he had already read. And he scanned a second paragraph:

What do I mean by a "worse punishment than death?" I mean disgrace and humiliation, the loss of your friends and position, becoming a pariah. I know that, while you were handling the drive for money under the United Charities, you as the treasurer of the organization helped yourself to five thousand dollars of the funds. I can and will produce proof of my statement if circumstances demand it. It is that stolen five thousand I want. You will leave it for me in your safe, as I direct, and make no move to interfere with my taking it—or I will give the facts to the newspapers.

MM

McEwen peered at Kent Atwell. "Is this true?" he demanded sharply.

"Certainly not! There is not a particle of fact in what is written there. I preferred not to let you see that paragraph, because it is all so preposterous. I refuse to be mulcted out of money that is rightfully mine, and I'm asking you to do something to protect me from this maniac who calls himself the Moon Man."

"I can't do a damned thing until he shows up and tries to rob you," McEwen answered. "He says he'll come tonight. Is there some way of my getting into your house without being seen?"

"Yes. I can tell you how. But am I to deliberately wait for him to come and—"

"If I may suggest it, Mr. Atwell," Steve Thatcher spoke up quietly, "you had better follow the Moon Man's directions to the letter. Get the money from the bank and put it in your safe as he directs. If he suspects that you're laying a trap for him, he may not show up; but if you appear to be acting in good faith, we may stand a chance of grabbing him."

"Exactly. He seems to know everything and be everywhere," McEwen agreed. "If he learns, somehow, that you haven't been at your bank today to withdraw that sum, he may stay in hiding. Our only chance of getting him is to have that money in the house—as bait."

Steve Thatcher smiled.

"But what," said Kent Atwell, "but what if your precautions fail, and the money is stolen regardless and—"

"You'll have to take that chance. This is an opportunity to grab the Moon Man tonight. If we don't make the most of it, he'll get you in some other way, and you'll be helpless." Gil McEwen fixed the gentleman with a stern eye. "If you have no faith in what I'm suggesting, you shouldn't have come to the police, Mr. Atwell."

"Yes, yes—I agree!" Atwell answered. "I will go to the bank immediately. I'll take the money home and put it in the safe. And you—"

"We'll come to your house tonight, after dark. I'll have enough men with me so that there'll be no chance of the Moon Man's escaping if he comes after that money. I'll phone you beforehand, to make arrangements."

"I'll follow your instructions to the letter."

Kent Atwell fumbled with his gloves and left. McEwen and Steve Thatcher waited a few minutes, then hurried from the theatre. McEwen's face was twisted into a grimace of distaste.

"I half believe that what the Moon Man wrote about Atwell is the truth," he said. "Damn— who is that crook, anyway? How can he know so much?" He started along the street at a stiff pace. "Tonight, Steve—tonight, unless something goes very wrong—I'll grab him!"

"Where're you heading, Gil?" Steve Thatcher asked quickly.

"I'm going to send a cable to the Saint Gobain factory in France. I'm going to find out who they made that glass mask for!"

Steve Thatcher's eyes twinkled. Again—unseen by the veteran detective—he smiled.

Outside the windows of Police Chief Thatcher's office hung veils of darkness. Inside, lights burned brilliantly. Detective Lieutenant Gil McEwen stood in the center of the room, facing a group of six men who had just entered in answer to his call. Each of the six was a plainclothes man.

"I've just made arrangements with Atwell," McEwen was saying, crisply. "We're going to slip into his house so we won't be seen, in case someone is watching. We're going to be damned careful about that. You're to follow my orders strictly, and be ready to leave here as soon as I say the word."

McEwen had chosen his men well. Each of the six was an old-timer on the force. Each had demonstrated, in the headquarters target gallery, that he was a dead shot. Each possessed a record of courage and daring.

As McEwen talked to them, the door of the chief's office opened quietly. Sue McEwen sidled in, stood aside, and listened with intense interest. His eyes strayed to those of Steve Thatcher, who was standing beside his father's desk; they exchanged a smile.

"This is our chance," McEwen declared to his men. "We've got to make it good. If the Moon Man gets away from us tonight, God only knows if we'll ever grab him. Wait downstairs."

The six men turned and filed from the office. McEwen paced across the rug. Steve Thatcher looked thoughtful. The chief of police sighed and wagged his head.

"You're all set, Gil?" Chief Thatcher asked.

"Yeah. You wait right by that phone, chief, in case of an emergency. And I hope when I phone you it will be to say we've got our man."

Sue McEwen stepped toward her father eagerly. "How soon are you leaving, dad? I wouldn't miss this for anything."

McEwen stared at her. "You're not getting in on this, young lady!"

"Why not?" Sue asked. "If I go to the house with you it won't do any harm, and I may be able to help. As long as I'm a detective's daughter, I want to make the most of it."

"How many times have I got to tell you, Sue," her father sighed, "that this sort of thing is not for you? We've argued about it a thousand times. I won't let you mix yourself up in police matters."

"You forget," Sue answered, smiling, "that I gave you the tip that helped send John Hirch, the forger, to prison. And didn't I figure out where Mike Opple was hiding after he killed his woman? I don't think I'm so bad at this. If you'll give me a chance tonight—"

"Nothing doing!" Gil McEwen snapped. "You go home and go to bed!"

"Dad," said Sue indignantly, "I'm not a child. I'm perfectly able to take care of myself. This Moon Man fascinates me, and I'm going to—"

"I think your dad's right, Sue," Steve Thatcher interrupted gently. "You'd better leave this to us. There's no telling what will happen."

Sue raised her chin defiantly. "It's going to take more than an argument to stop me this time. I—"

The telephone jangled. Gil McEwen snatched the instrument off the chief's desk. A voice twanged into his ear:

"This is Preston, downstairs, McEwen. You told me to let you know if a message came for you. There's one coming in now!"

"Be right down!" McEwen answered quickly. He dropped the telephone and hurried to the door. "Answer to my cable coming in over the teletype!" he exclaimed as he hurried out.

Steve Thatcher's eyes brightened. He hastened out the door after McEwen. They jumped down the stairs side by side, paced along the brick corridor, and squeezed into a little room. Inside it was a sergeant, a battery of telephones, a short-wave radio receiving set, and a teletype machine. The teletype was clicking and spinning out its yellow ribbon.

McEwen leaned over it and read the words as they formed:

POLICE HEADQUARTERS GREAT CITY—
ARGUS GLASS SPHERE SHIPPED TO
GILBERT MCEWEN GENERAL DELIVERY
GREAT CITY—ST. GOBAIN.

"By damn!" gasped McEwen.

He tore the strip out of the machine. He glared at it. He said unprintable things.

"By damn! He ordered that mask under *my name!*"

Steve Thatcher's eyes were twinkling. He had known what this cable would say. He had planned for this exigency. And he was enjoying the veteran detective's discomfiture.

"Looks suspicious, Gil," he remarked. "*You're* not the Moon Man, are you?"

"Yah!" snarled McEwen. "He's smart, isn't he? He's clever! Pulling a stunt like that—getting his damn' glass mask made under my name! Wait'll I get my hands on that guy!"

Steve Thatcher chuckled in spite of himself.

McEwen squeezed out of the teletype room. He hurried down the corridor to a door which opened into a larger room. His six detectives were there, perched on and around a table usually devoted to pinochle.

"Come on!" he snapped. "We're going!"

The six men began trooping after McEwen. Steve Thatcher followed the veteran detective a few steps.

"You've got all your car will carry, Gil. I'd better follow you in mine. I'll be along in a minute."

McEwen nodded his agreement and pushed through a big door into the adjoining garage, with the six following him. Steve Thatcher looked up and saw Sue McEwen coming down the stairs. He turned to her.

"I want to come with you, Steve," she said.

"Darling, I'm sorry. I'll phone you as soon as there's news."

"But, Steve—"

He did not wait to listen. He did not like this insistence of Sue's. It emphasized in his mind the painful disaster that would surely follow if it were ever learned that he, Steve Thatcher, son of the chief of police, was the Moon Man. He hurried out the entrance, turned sharply, and went into a drug store on the corner.

He slipped into a phone-booth and called a number which was unlisted in the directory, unobtainable by anyone, known to none save him and one other.

Two miles away, in the maze of the city, a phone rang. A stocky, broken-nosed young man picked it up. He heard a voice say over the wire:

"Hello, Angel."

"Hello, boss."

"Listen carefully. I want you to leave the car in front of the home of Kent Atwell at exactly five minutes before midnight tonight."

"Sure, boss."

"Don't wait. Take a taxi back. Leave the car right in front of the house, and make sure nobody sees you do it. I'll meet you at the usual place thirty-five minutes later."

"Right, boss."

"Wish me luck, Angel."

Then the line went dead.

CHAPTER IV
THE TRAP IS SET

Nine o'clock. A sedan buzzed past the front of the home of Kent Atwell. It rolled on smoothly and turned at the next corner. Halfway down the block it turned again, swinging into the driveway of a dark house. It paused in front of the garage; and out of it climbed Gil McEwen and his six detectives.

Standing silent in the darkness, they waited. A moment later another car turned from the street and crept into the driveway. It braked behind the sedan. Steve Thatcher climbed out of it and walked to Gil McEwen's side.

No one spoke. Leading the way, McEwen strode past the garage and pushed his way through a high hedge. Steve Thatcher followed, and the six men. They walked silently across the rear of an adjoining estate, and paused at a gate in the hedge. They listened a moment, then eased through.

They drifted like shadows to the rear of the home of Kent Atwell. McEwen knocked softly at the door. It opened; no light came out. McEwen, Thatcher and the six men entered. Kent Atwell closed the door, turned, and led them into a spacious library.

"Okay," said McEwen without formality. "You alone, Atwell?"

"Yes," said the gentleman. "My wife is away, and I've given the servants the night off."

"Place all locked up?"

"Every door except the front, and every window. All the blinds are drawn."

"Money in the safe?"

"Yes."

Atwell crossed the room to a stack of bookshelves. From one the height of his head he removed a unit of four thick volumes. In the wall behind shone the front of a circular safe.

"Locked?" McEwen asked.

"No," Kent answered as he replaced the books.

"Good. Now." The detective turned. "We're all going to keep out of sight and wait. First thing, I want to make sure there's only one way for the Moon Man to get in—the front door. Steve, take a quick look around, will you—upstairs and down."

Steve Thatcher circled the library, and made sure every window was locked. Stepping into the rear hallway, he determined that the bolt was in place. In the other rear rooms he repeated his examination; then he climbed the steps to the second floor and entered, in turn, each of the bedrooms. McEwen, listening, heard him moving about. In a moment Steve returned.

"All set," he announced.

"Good. Where in this room can I keep out of sight, Atwell?"

Again Atwell crossed the room. He opened a door and disclosed a closet space behind it. It offered a large, comfortable hiding-place to McEwen. The detective nodded.

"Mr. Atwell, I want you to go upstairs and prepare for bed. Pretend that you are alone. I'm going to put a man in every room upstairs and down. Every window will be watched, and every door, in case the Moon Man tries something tricky. I'm going to stay here in the library and watch the safe. Understand?"

They understood.

McEwen signalled two of his men. He conducted them across the vestibule and into the two rooms on the opposite side of the house. Stationing one man in each, he closed the doors and went up the stairs with the others following. He waited until Kent Atwell went into the master bedroom, then assigned one man to each of the remaining rooms on the second floor.

Five doors opened. Five doors closed. Behind each of them a detective began to wait. Behind one of them Steve Thatcher listened.

He heard Gil McEwen go downstairs.

McEwen stepped into the library. He closed its doors. He strode to the safe, opened it, reached inside, and removed a thick pack of banknotes. He counted them—five thousand dollars. He put them back and closed the safe.

From his pocket he removed his service automatic. He examined it very intently. Crossing the room, he opened the closet door, moved a chair inside. Stepping in, he swung the door until it was within an inch of being closed. He sat, with his automatic in his hand, and waited.

The house was utterly silent.

The vigil had begun.

An hour passed.

Another.

Silently an automobile turned the corner of the street on which the Atwell mansion sat. Its lights were dimmed. It drew to the curb near the corner and its light went out. A hand reached for the ignition switch and clicked it off. The hand was that lovely one of Miss Sue McEwen.

The young lady settled down in the cushions and looked reprovingly at the Atwell residence. Its windows were dark, save for a few chinks of light shining through the draperies on one side of the lower floor. Inside, Sue McEwen knew were her father and her fiancé and six detectives and an intended victim of the Moon Man. Inside, she knew, interesting things were almost sure to happen. She said to herself in a whisper:

"I *won't* be left out!"

She opened her handbag. From it she removed a tiny automatic. It was a fancy little thing, with handle of mother-of-pearl; but it was deadly. In the hand of an expert shot it could spout death. Sue McEwen, by dint of long and arduous practice in her own back yard, under the guidance of her father, was by way of being an expert shot.

The minutes crept past.

A quarter of twelve.

The determined young lady looked and listened and waited.

Five minutes of twelve.

A soft whirr came from behind Sue McEwen's parked roadster. She did not stir, but through the corners of her eyes she saw a coupé swing into the street. Its lights were out. It rolled along without a sound. And that, thought Miss McEwen, was strange.

The lightless car eased to a stop directly in front of the Kent Atwell home. One of its doors opened. A black figure stepped out of it and began to walk toward the farther corner. When it was halfway there another sound came from behind Sue McEwen. A second car—this time with its headlamps on and making no attempt to be quiet—purred past her. It was a taxi. It spurted toward the far corner and stopped.

The squatty young man climbed into it. The cab started up again. It swung around the corner and disappeared.

"I," said Sue McEwen to herself suddenly, "am going to see what that's all about!"

She started her engine. She spurted away from the curb—her tiny automatic lying in her lap—and eased past the dark car parked in front of the Atwell home. Should she get out and look it over? No; that would take time, and she wanted to follow that taxi; it might get away from her if she stopped now. She stepped on the gas.

At the next corner she swung left. And there, two blocks ahead, she saw the red tail-light of the taxi gleaming.

She followed it. It drove straight on. It was going toward the central business district of Great City. Just this side of the main thoroughfare it turned. When she reached that corner Sue McEwen also turned. For a moment the taxi was out of sight, but she picked it up again immediately. She was keeping well behind it. She was taking no chances.

"Something," she thought, "is up."

The taxi went on. Sue McEwen went on. The two cars, separated by two blocks, turned into a route that took them around the nocturnally popular section of the city. Presently the taxi was rolling into a region that gave Sue McEwen some uneasiness. It was dark, lonely, dangerous; and, after all, she was alone.

But she kept following that taxi. And suddenly she saw it stop.

It paused just past an intersection. The young chunky fare got out and paid the driver. Sue McEwen could not see his face. A moment later the taxi spurted off and, at the next corner, swung out of sight. The young man walked along the black street, turned and entered a "dog cart" in the middle of the block.

From the tower of the City Hall came the reverberations of a striking gong. The town clock was striking. It tolled twelve.

What, Sue McEwen wondered, was happening back in the Kent Atwell house? She could not guess. She wanted to keep an eye on that strange young man.

She drew to the curb, cut the ignition, and blinked off her dimmers. She waited. For twenty minutes she waited. And at the end of that time her quarry came out of the lunch cart and began walking away.

She started after him, cautiously. She saw him turn the corner. As she rounded the corner, she saw the young man make a quick move and disappear.

She saw that he had gone into the black doorway of an empty tenement.

She stopped. She got out of the car and, keeping in the deep darkness which flanked the buildings, slowly worked her way toward that doorway. It was empty now. The young man had gone inside. She listened and heard nothing. With the utmost care she eased the door open an inch and peered through. She saw nothing.

Then, taking a tight grip on her little automatic, she crept in.

The house was a black tomb—silent. She stood still until her eyes became accustomed to the darkness. Gradually she saw the details of a staircase leading to the second floor. She moved toward it. She went up the steps, one after another. And suddenly she stopped.

A board creaked under her foot.

Ned Dargan stood stock still in the darkness of the room which was the rendezvous of the Moon Man. He had heard that creak. A second later he heard another. His hand slipped into his coat pocket and came out grasping a gun. He turned slowly.

Stealing toward the closed door which communicated with the hallway, he listened. He heard no sound now. He wondered if the creaks had been caused by the loose boards warping back into place after being strained by his own weight. He decided he had better make sure. He opened the door stealthily, and stepped into the hallway.

Every nerve alert, he walked to the head of the stairs. He went down them slowly. The boards creaked again as he crossed them. He went on.

Again those sounds served as a signal. Sue McEwen heard them. She was hidden behind the door of a room directly across from that which Ned Dargan had just left. Realizing that the creaking of the board under her feet might have been heard, she had hastened along the hallway and slipped into the front room just as Dargan had opened the rear one. Now, seeing the way clear, she crept back into the hall.

She crossed it. She opened the door of the room which Dargan had left—the hidden headquarters of the Moon Man. She slipped inside and looked around. It was bare. It was musty. It looked unpromising; but Sue McEwen was tantalized by the mystery of what was happening.

She gasped. From the hallway again came creaks. The man she had seen enter the house was returning to the upper hallway. Even as she turned, Sue McEwen heard his step toward the door she had just entered.

She turned quickly away from that door. She hurried across to another, which apparently communicated with a room beyond; but it balked her. It was locked. She whirled again. In a corner she saw a closet. She jerked open its door. It was empty. She sidled inside and closed the door upon herself.

At that instant she heard a step in the room. The man had come back. He was standing within a few yards of her now—unaware of her presence. She stood straight, her tiny automatic leveled. She was determined to wait—and listen—and learn.

Now she was going to see what connection all this had with the Moon Man. Now, perhaps, she might even learn who the Moon Man was.

CHAPTER V
IN DEAD OF NIGHT

Faintly the sound of a tolling gong came into the library of Kent Atwell. Twelve slow strikes—midnight.

Gil McEwen, hidden in the closet, heard the trembling beats. Steve Thatcher, in a room directly above, listened to them and smiled.

He silently opened the door of the bedroom which had been assigned to him. He stepped into the hallway and closed the door behind him. Along each wall of the hall was a row of such doors, all closed. Behind one of them was Kent Atwell himself. Behind the others were detectives.

Steve Thatcher crept to the nearest door. Beneath its knob the handle of a key protruded—outward. Very slowly he turned it—without a sound. And he smiled. While making the rounds of the house he had carefully removed the keys from the inside of the bedroom doors and placed them on the outside. He passed up and down the hallway silently as a ghost. At each door he turned a key.

Now one millionaire and four detectives were securely locked in their rooms—and did not know it!

Steve Thatcher crept down the front stairs into the vestibule. Again he locked a door and imprisoned another detective. He crept to the rear hallway and made a captive of another sleuth. So far he had contrived to imprison every man save Gil McEwen.

Steve Thatcher drew the bolt of the rear entrance, slipped outside, and hurried toward the street. At the car left by Gargan, he stopped. He unlocked the rumble compartment and from it removed a black bundle. Then, quickly, he returned to the rear door of the house.

Pausing, he drew on his long, black cloak and pulled on his black silk gloves. He placed on his head the glass mask modeled as a moon. It was padded inside so that it sat firmly on his head. A deflecting plate, which came into position over his nose and mouth, sent his breath downward and out, so that it would not fog the glass and blind him. He was ready.

He stealthily opened the rear door and let himself in. Through the glass he could see as clearly as though there was nothing on his head. He trod up the rear stairs, along the hallway, then down the front flight into the vestibule. Outside the unlocked door of the library he paused.

Gil McEwen, he knew, was inside—waiting. The Moon Man laid his black hand on the knob of the library door. He twisted it. He eased the door open and peered through the narrow crack. Within six feet of him, though unseen, sat Gil McEwen.

McEwen's closet door was partly open, but he could see only the wall opposite, the wall in which the safe was set. He could not see the door opening slowly under pressure of the Moon Man's hand. He heard not the slightest sound. The Moon Man drifted into the room.

The black-cloaked figure flattened itself against the wall. It moved toward the closet door with one arm outstretched. The other arm also moved—toward a light chair. The Moon Man picked it up. His body tensed.

Suddenly he sprang. He struck the closet door and slammed it shut. Instantly he braced the chair under the knob. A startled cry came from behind the door. The knob rattled. From inside McEwen pushed—hard. The door would not open. The tilted chair wedged it firmly in place.

"By damn!" rang through the panels.

The Moon Man turned away quickly as the door shook. McEwen was throwing himself against it. From the black space within came another muffled cry:

"Get him! Carter! Landon! Winninger! Carpen! Go after him!"

The sound of McEwen's furious voice carried through the walls. Quick movements sounded upstairs. Knobs rattled. Across the lower hallway two more knobs rattled. Upstairs and down six imprisoned detectives and one imprisoned millionaire cursed.

And the Moon Man chuckled.

Suddenly the report of a gun blasted with a hollow sound. Splinters flew from a panel of McEwen's closet. A bullet hissed across the room and shattered a window pane on the opposite side. The shattered glass fell very close to the position of the wall-safe.

"No use, McEwen!" the man in the silver mask exclaimed. "I've already got it!"

McEwen snarled; and he did not fire again.

He flung himself against the door. It literally bulged under the impact of his body. The Moon Man heard the wood of the chair crack. He hurried to the wall-safe.

He grasped the four books and flung them away. He snapped open the door of the safe. He snatched out the sheaf of banknotes. They disappeared through a slit in the side of his cape.

The closet door thumped again. This time it gave a little more. Upstairs men were pounding and cursing. Bedlam filled the house. And once more McEwen crashed against the inside of the closet door.

The Moon Man hurried into the vestibule. He jerked open the front door and sped along the walk to the street. He ducked behind the car and with quick movements divested himself of his costume. Cloak, gloves and glass mask went into the rumble compartment. The next instant Steve Thatcher's hands went to the wheel.

A shot rang sharply near the house. A bullet whizzed through the air. Steve Thatcher jerked a glance backward to see one of the lower windows opening, and a plain-clothes man leaping through—after him. Steve's motor roared. He slammed into gear and spurted away.

Another shot. Another. Then Steve Thatcher sent the coupé swerving around the corner—and he was out of range.

In the library a splintering crash sounded. A panel of the closet door cracked out under the terrible impact of Gil McEwen's hard shoulder. He reached through the opening, snatched the chair away, slammed out.

He heard the shots outside the house. He went out the front door at almost a single leap. The plainclothes man with the smoking gun saw him and shouted:

"He's getting away in that car!"

McEwen whirled like a top. He sped toward the edge of the Atwell grounds and crashed through the hedge with a flying leap. As fast as his legs could swing he ran toward the driveway in which the police cars had been left. There he stopped short and cursed.

The sedan was farthest back in the driveway.

Steve Thatcher's roadster was behind it, blocking the way out! McEwen hurried to it—and saw that the ignition was locked! He spun back furiously, slipped behind the wheel of the sedan, and started the motor. With an utter disregard for law and garden, he spurted off around the opposite side of the house, jounced off the curb, twisted the wheel madly, and pressed the gas pedal against the floorboards.

The tires whined as he wrenched the car around the corner. Far away he saw a gleam of red—the tail-light of another car traveling at high speed. McEwen's eyes narrowed shrewdly. At the next corner he turned again; at the next, again. Running then along a street parallel with the fleeing coupé, he let the motor out.

He did not slow for intersections. He slowed for nothing. With the car traveling at its fastest, he plunged along the street. McEwen knew the fleeing coupé could not long keep up its breakneck speed. It must surely slow down to pass through the streets near the business center, or suffer the shots of a traffic policeman. Moreover, the city narrowed like a bottle's neck toward the river. If the fugitive coupé went on, it must soon reach the bridge.

McEwen had the advantage. No traffic officer would try to stop or shoot at his police car. Deliberately he sent the sedan catapulting through the very center of Great City, its horn blaring. Lights flashed past. Other cars scurried for the curb. Pedestrians fled to the sidewalks. In a matter of seconds McEwen had put the congested district behind him and was racing toward the bridge.

Within a block of it, where two streets intersected in a V, he turned back. He knew that he was ahead of the coupé now. He shot to the next intersection and looked up and down the cross street. The same at the next, and the next. There was no place the coupé could escape him now if it stayed in the open. Sooner or later he was sure to see it.

Soon he did!

Glancing along a dark street lined by warehouses and shabby tenements, he saw a pair of headlights blink out. Instantly McEwen shut off his own, and stopped. He saw a coupé, two blocks ahead. He saw a dark figure climb out of it, turn, and hurry back along the street. He watched with eyes as keen as an eagle's—and saw the dark figure slip into an alleyway.

McEwen got out of his car. He gripped his automatic tightly and began running through the shadows toward the alleyway. When he reached it he paused.

One second before Gil McEwen glanced down the dark alleyway, Steve Thatcher lowered the rear window on the second floor of the abandoned tenement. A quick climb up the rusty fire escape had brought him to it. In the darkness of the bare room he turned, lowering a dark bundle to the floor.

A moment later Steve Thatcher had vanished; the Moon Man had appeared.

He stepped to the closet and opened it. By the glow of a flashlight he worked quickly. He separated the sheaf of banknotes into three parcels. Each he fastened together with a band of silver paper. He snapped off the flash and turned to the connecting door.

He unlocked it. Slowly he went into the room. Ned Dargan turned at his approach. The Moon Man moved toward the table. From his one black-gloved hand dropped the four packets of currency.

"There you are, Angel."

Dargan silently took up the money. He blinked; he thrust it into his pocket.

"Boss," he said, "I'm worried."

"Why?"

"Just after I came into this place a little while ago, somebody followed me."

"Who?"

"I don't know. I heard the stairs creak. I went down to look around, but I didn't find anybody. Cripes, boss, I don't like it!"

"Nor I, Angel. I've an idea that in future we must be more careful. You had better stop delivering the money personally—send it by messenger. And we'd better change our headquarters. I'll phone you, Angel—about a new place."

The muffled voice broke off. The silver-masked head came up. Ned Dargan's breath went sibilantly into his lungs.

From the hallway came a creak!

Then another!

"Somebody's comin' up!" gasped Dargan.

The Moon Man moved. He rounded the table, crossed to the door. With a quick motion he shot a bolt in place.

"Out the rear window, Angel—quick!"

Ned Dargan hesitated. "Say, listen! I ain't goin' to skip and leave you to face the music alone! I'm in this as much as you are, boss!"

"Angel, yours is a true heart. But get out that window right now! I'll take care of myself."

The Moon Man's voice rang commandingly. Dargan did not hesitate again. He hurried into the adjoining room. He slid up the window and ducked through.

"Make it snappy, Angel! Take the car. And if you don't hear from me again—bless you."

"Boss—"

"Snappy, I said!"

Dargan moved. He disappeared downward in the blackness.

The closet door opened silently. Sue McEwen slipped into the room without a sound. She hesitated, peering through the open communicating door. In there, beyond the threshold, was a vague black figure.

It was turning—turning to close the connecting door.

Sue McEwen raised her tiny automatic.

"Please," she said sharply, "throw up your hands!"

The Moon Man stood frozen. Through the glass that masked his face he could see the girl, standing in the glow of the moonlight that was shafting through a window. He could see the glittering gun in her hand—aimed squarely at him.

If she learned—

"Take off your mask!" she commanded.

The Moon Man could not move.

Then a sound—the rattle of a door knob. The door connecting with the hallway opened. The girl glanced toward it, catching her breath. Then, in a sob—a sob of relief—she exclaimed:

"Dad!"

Gil McEwen came through the door. He stared at his daughter. He turned and stared into the adjoining room, at the black-cloaked figure standing there—the thing with the silver head.

"By damn!" he said.

He sprang toward the Moon Man.

Instantly Steve Thatcher leaped forward. With one movement he slammed the door shut and twisted the key. He leaped back as a gun roared, as a bullet crashed through the wood. He whirled toward the window. He ducked out—cloak and mask and all—and began dropping down the fire escape.

Gil McEwen raised his gun to fire again through the door. But he did not fire. He spun on his heel, sprang into the hallway, leaped down the stairs. He burst out the front door, and whirled into the alley.

He peered at the window above. It was open. He peered at the fire escape. It was empty. He peered down the black alley. The Moon Man was not in sight.

McEwen sped through the shadows behind the buildings, but soon he paused. Useless to hunt here! As he came back his eyes turned to a row of wooden boxes, each fitted with wooden lids, which sat at the base of the tenement rear wall. They were coal-bins; each of them was large enough to hold a man. With gun leveled he moved toward them.

McEwen paused, grumbling with disappointment. On each bin-cover was a rusty hasp, and on each hasp was a closed padlock, corroded and useless, untouched for perhaps years. He turned away.

McEwen hurried toward the police-car with his daughter following close. A moment later the quiet of that dismal district was broken by the snarling of a motor and the whining of tires as the car spurted away.

After that, for a long time, the alley behind the deserted tenement was silent.

Then, at last, a faint movement. The cover of one of the coal-bins shifted. One edge of it raised—not the front edge, which was fastened by the padlock, but the rear edge, from which the hinges had been removed. Like a Jack-in-the-box, a man came out of it.

"I'll get him! Don't worry—the day's comin' when I'm going to grab that crook!"

So said Gil McEwen as he paced back and forth across the office of Chief of Police Thatcher while bright sunlight streamed into the room—the sunlight of the morning after.

Chief Thatcher sighed and looked worried. His son looked at Gil McEwen solemnly.

"He's got us all buffaloed, that's all. A swell detective I am! The way I climbed out of Atwell's bedroom window, then went chasing an innocent man for blocks, thinking he might be the Moon Man!" In this way Steve Thatcher had explained his absence from the Atwell home immediately following the Moon Man's escape. "Gil, I guess if he's ever caught, you'll have to do it."

"I will do it," said McEwen. "That's my promise. I'm never going to stop until I grab that guy!"

And McEwen, Steve Thatcher knew, meant exactly that.

The chief's son looked at his watch. Inside its cover was a photograph. It was a portrait of Sue McEwen.

"If you only knew what you almost did!" he addressed the picture in silent thought. "If you only knew!"

Pigeon Blood

Paul Cain

THERE WERE A LOT of very bad writers who worked for the pulps. For a penny, or sometimes a half-penny, what could you expect? But there were some good ones, too, and even a few great ones. It is possible that Paul Cain (1902–1966) was one of the latter. Sadly, his output was too modest to make a positive judgment.

He wrote about a dozen short stories, seven of which were collected in *Seven Slayers* (1946), and one novel, *Fast One* (1933), which Raymond Chandler lavishly praised. The novel was really a collection of five closely connected novellas which ran in *Black Mask* magazine in 1932, then revised for its hardcover edition. Doubleday must have had meager enthusiasm for it, since it must have had a small print run because it is today one of the rarest and most valuable first editions in the collectors' market. Perhaps his publisher was right, as it was almost universally blasted by critics as too tough, too violent. Still, sophisticated readers loved it and it remains one of the high spots of the hard-boiled crime genre.

He was just a kid of sixteen when he showed up in Hollywood to write screenplays, at which he had fairly early success as Peter Ruric, a nom de plume for George Sims. When the movies failed to provide enough work (and income), he turned to the pulps and used the name Paul Cain. Nothing new was published during the last thirty years of his life. "Pigeon Blood" was first published in the November 1933 issue of *Black Mask;* it was collected in *Seven Slayers.*

Pigeon Blood

Paul Cain

THE WOMAN WAS BENT far forward over the steering-wheel of the open roadster. Her eyes, narrowed to long black-fringed slits, moved regularly down and up, from the glistening road ahead, to the small rearview mirror above the windshield. The two circles of white light in the mirror grew steadily larger. She pressed the throttle slowly, steadily downward; there was no sound but the roar of the wind and the deep purr of the powerful engine.

There was a sudden sharp crack; a little frosted circle appeared on the windshield. The woman pressed the throttle to the floor. She was pale; her eyes were suddenly large and dark and afraid, her lips were pressed tightly together. The tires screeched on the wet pavement as the car roared around a long, shallow curve. The headlights of the pursuing car grew larger.

The second and third shots were wild, or buried themselves harmlessly in the body of the car; the fourth struck the left rear tire and the car swerved crazily, skidded halfway across the road. Very suddenly there was bright yellow light right ahead, at the side of the road. The woman jammed on the brakes, jerked the wheel hard over; the tires slid, screamed raggedly over the gravel in front of the gas station, the car stopped. The other car went by at seventy-five miles an hour. One last shot thudded into the back of the seat beside the woman and then the other car had disappeared into the darkness.

Two men ran out of the gas station. Another man stood in the doorway. The woman was lean-ing back straight in the seat and her eyes were very wide; she was breathing hard, unevenly.

One of the men put his hand on her shoulder, asked: "Are you all right, lady?"

She nodded.

The other man asked: "Hold-ups?" He was a short, middle-aged man and his eyes were bright, interested.

The woman opened her bag and took out a cigarette. She said shakily: "I guess so." She pulled out the dashboard lighter, waited until it glowed red and held it to her cigarette.

The younger man was inspecting the back of the car. He said: "They punctured the tank. It's a good thing you stopped—you couldn't have gone much father."

"Yes—I guess it's a very good thing I stopped," she said, mechanically. She took a deep drag of her cigarette.

The other man said: "That's the third hold-up out here this week."

The woman spoke to the younger man. "Can you get me a cab?"

He said: "Sure." Then he knelt beside the blown-out tire, said: "Look, Ed—they almost cut it in two."

The man in the doorway called to her: "You want a cab, lady?"

She smiled, nodded, and the man disappeared into the gas station; he came back to the doorway in a minute, over to the car. "There'll be a cab here in a little while, lady," he said.

She thanked him.

"This is one of the worst stretches of road on Long Island—for highwaymen." He leaned on the door of the car. "Did they try to nudge you off the road—or did they just start shooting?"

"They just started shooting."

He said: "We got a repair service here—do you want us to fix up your car?"

She nodded. "How long will it take?"

"Couple days. We'll have to get a new windshield from the branch factory in Queens—an' take off that tank. . . ."

She took a card out of her bag and gave it to him, said: "Call me up when it's finished."

After a little while, a cab came out of the darkness of a side street, turned into the station. The woman got out of the car and went over to the cab, spoke to the driver: "Do you know any short-cuts into Manhattan? Somebody tried to hold me up on the main road a little while ago, and maybe they're still laying for me. I don't want any more of it—I want to go home." She was very emphatic.

The driver was a big red-faced Irishman. He grinned, said: "Lady—I know a million of 'em. You'll be as safe with me as you'd be in your own home."

She raised her hand in a gesture of farewell to the three men around her car and got into the cab. After the cab had disappeared around the street, the man to whom she had given the card took it out of his pocket and squinted at it, read aloud: "Mrs. Dale Hanan—Five-eighty Park Avenue."

The short, middle-aged man bobbed his head knowingly. "Sure," he said—"I knew she was class. She's Hanan's wife—the millionaire. Made his dough in oil—Oklahoma. His chauffeur told me how he got his start—didn't have a shoestring or a place to put it, so he shot off his big toe and collected ten grand on an accident policy—grubstake on his first well. Bright boy. He's got a big estate down at Roslyn."

The man with the card nodded. He said: "That's swell. We can soak him plenty." He put the card back into his pocket.

When the cab stopped near the corner of Sixty-third and Park Avenue the woman got out, paid the driver and hurried into the apartment house. In her apartment, she put in a long-distance call to Roslyn, Long Island; when the connection had been made, she said: "Dale—it's in the open, now. I was followed, driving back to town—shot at—the car was nearly wrecked. . . . I don't know what to do. Even if I call Crandall, now, and tell him I won't go through with it— won't go to the police—he'll probably have me killed, just to make sure. . . . Yes, I'm going to stay in—I'm scared. . . . All right, dear. 'Bye."

She hung up, went to a wide center table and poured whiskey into a tall glass, sat down and stared vacantly at the glass—her hand was shaking a little. She smiled suddenly, crookedly, lifted the glass to her mouth and drained it. Then she put the glass on the floor and leaned back and glanced at the tiny watch at her wrist. It was ten minutes after nine.

At a few minutes after ten a black Packard town-car stopped in front of a narrow building of gray stone on East Fifty-fourth Street; a tall man got out, crossed the sidewalk and rang the bell. The car went on. When the door swung open, the tall man went into a long, brightly lighted hallway, gave his hat and stick to the checkroom attendant, went swiftly up two flights of narrow stairs to the third floor. He glanced around the big, crowded room, then crossed to one corner near a window on the Fifty-fourth Street side and sat down at a small table, smiled wanly at the man across from him, said: "Mister Druse, I believe."

The other man was about fifty, well set up, well-groomed in the way of good living. His thick gray hair was combed sharply, evenly back. He lowered his folded newspaper to the table, stared thoughtfully at the tall man.

He said: "Mister Hanan," and his voice was very deep, metallic.

The tall man nodded shortly, leaned back and folded his arms across his narrow chest. He was ageless, perhaps thirty-five, forty-five; his thin, colorless hair was close-clipped, his long, bony face deeply tanned, a sharp and angular setting for large seal-brown eyes. His mouth was curved, mobile.

He asked: "Do you know Jeffrey Crandall?"

Druse regarded him evenly, expressionlessly for a moment, raised his head and beckoned a waiter. Hanan ordered a whiskey sour.

Druse said: "I know Mister Crandall casually. Why?"

"A little more than an hour ago Crandall, or Crandall's men, tried to murder Mrs. Hanan, as she was driving back from my place at Roslyn." Hanan leaned forward: his eyes were wide, worried.

The waiter served Hanan's whiskey sour, set a small bottle of Perrier and a small glass on the table in front of Druse.

Druse poured the water into the glass slowly. "So what?"

Hanan tasted his drink. He said: "This is not a matter for the police, Mister Druse. I understand that you interest yourself in things of this nature, so I took the liberty of calling you and making this appointment. Is that right?" He was nervous, obviously ill at ease.

Druse shrugged. "*What* nature? I don't know what you're talking about."

"I'm sorry—I guess I'm a little upset." Hanan smiled. "What I mean is that I can rely on your discretion?"

Druse frowned. "I think so," he said slowly. He drank half of the Perrier, squinted down at the glass as if it had tasted very badly.

Hanan smiled vacantly. "You do not know Mrs. Hanan?"

Druse shook his head slowly, turned his glass around and around on the table.

"We have been living apart for several years," Hanan went on. "We are still very fond of one another, we are very good friends, but we do not get along—together. Do you understand?"

Druse nodded.

Hanan sipped his drink, went on swiftly: "Catherine has—has always had—a decided weakness for gambling. She went through most of her own inheritance—a considerable inheritance—before we were married. Since our sepa-

ration she has lost somewhere in the neighborhood of a hundred and fifteen thousand dollars. I have, of course, taken care of her debts." Hanan coughed slightly. "Early this evening she called me at Roslyn, said she had to see me immediately—that it was very important. I offered to come into town but she said she'd rather come out. She came out about seven."

Hanan paused, closed his eyes and rubbed two fingers of one hand slowly up and down his forehead. "She's in a very bad jam with Crandall." He opened his eyes and put his hand down on the table.

Druse finished his Perrier, put down the glass and regarded Hanan attentively.

"About three weeks ago," Hanan went on, "Catherine's debt to Crandall amounted to sixty-eight thousand dollars—she had been playing very heavily under the usual gambler's delusion of getting even. She was afraid to come to me—she knew I'd taken several bad beatings on the market—she kept putting it off and trying to make good her losses, until Crandall demanded the money. She told him she couldn't pay—together, they hatched out a scheme to get it. Catherine had a set of rubies—pigeon blood—been in her family five or six generations. They're worth, perhaps, a hundred and seventy-five thousand—her father insured them for a hundred and thirty-five, forty years ago and the insurance premiums have always been paid. . . ." Hanan finished his whiskey sour, leaned back in his chair.

Druse said: "I assume the idea was that the rubies disappear; that Mrs. Hanan claim the insurance, pay off Crandall, have sixty-seven thousand left and live happily forever after."

Hanan coughed; his face was faintly flushed. "Exactly."

"I assume further," Druse went on, "that the insurance company did not question the integrity of the claim; that they paid, and that Mrs. Hanan, in turn, paid Crandall."

Hanan nodded. He took a tortoise-shell case out of his pocket, offered Druse a cigarette.

Druse shook his head, asked: "Are the insurance company detectives warm—are they making Crandall or whoever he had to do the actual job, uncomfortable?"

"No. The theft was well engineered. I don't think Crandall is worrying about that." Hanan lighted a cigarette. "But Catherine wanted her rubies back—as had, of course, been agreed upon." He leaned forward, put his elbows on the table. "Crandall returned paste imitations to her—she only discovered they weren't genuine a few days ago."

Druse smiled, said slowly: "In that case, I should think it was Crandall who was in a jam with Mrs. Hanan, instead of Mrs. Hanan who was in a jam with Crandall."

Hanan wagged his long chin back and forth. "This is New York. Men like Crandall do as they please. Catherine went to him and he laughed at her; said the rubies he had returned were the rubies that had been stolen. She had no recourse, other than to admit her complicity in defrauding the insurance company. That's the trouble—she threatened to do exactly that."

Druse widened his eyes, stared at Hanan.

"Catherine is a very impulsive woman," Hanan went on. "She was so angry at losing the rubies and being made so completely a fool, that she threatened Crandall. She told him that if the rubies were not returned within three days she would tell what he had done; that he had stolen the rubies—take her chances on her part in it coming out. Of course she wouldn't do it, but she was desperate and she thought that was her only chance of scaring Crandall into returning the rubies—and she made him believe it. Since she talked to him, Wednesday, she had been followed. Tomorrow is Saturday, the third day. Tonight, driving back to town, she was followed, shot at—almost killed."

"Has she tried to get in touch with Crandall again?"

Hanan shook his head. "She's been stubbornly waiting for him to give the rubies back—until this business tonight. Now she's frightened—says it wouldn't do any good for her to talk to Crandall now because he wouldn't believe her—and it's too easy for him to put her out of the way."

Druse beckoned the waiter, asked him to bring the check. "Where is she now?"

"At her apartment—Sixty-third and Park."

"What do you intend doing about it?"

Hanan shrugged. "That's what I came to you for. I don't know what to do. I've heard of you and your work from friends. . . ."

Druse hesitated, said slowly: "I must make my position clear."

Hanan nodded, lighted a fresh cigarette.

"I am one of the few people left," Druse went on, "who actually believes that honesty is the best policy. Honesty is my business—I am primarily a business man—I've made it pay."

Hanan smiled broadly.

Druse leaned forward. "I am not a fixer," he said. "My acquaintance is wide and varied—I am fortunate in being able to wield certain influences. But above all I seek to further justice—I mean real justice as opposed to *book* justice—I was on the Bench for many years and I realize the distinction keenly." His big face wrinkled to an expansive grin. "And I get paid for it—*well* paid."

Hanan said: "Does my case interest you?"

"It does."

"Will five thousand dollars be satisfactory—as a retaining fee?"

Druse moved his broad shoulders in something like a shrug. "You value the rubies at a hundred and seventy-five thousand," he said. "I am undertaking to get the rubies back, and protect Mrs. Hanan's life." He stared at Hanan intently. "What value do you put on Mrs. Hanan's life?"

Hanan frowned self-consciously, twisted his mouth down at the corners. "That is, of course, impossible to—"

"Say another hundred and seventy-five." Druse smiled easily. "That makes three hundred and fifty thousand. I work on a ten per cent basis—thirty-five thousand—one-third in advance." He leaned back, still smiling easily. "Ten thousand will be sufficient as a retainer."

Hanan was still frowning self-consciously. He said: "Done," took a checkbook and fountain pen out of his pocket.

Druse went on: "If I fail in either purpose, I shall, of course, return your check."

Hanan bobbed his head, made out the check in a minute, illegible scrawl and handed it across the table. Druse paid for the drinks, jotted down Hanan's telephone number and the address of Mrs. Hanan's apartment. They got up and went downstairs and out of the place; Druse told Hanan he would call him within an hour, got into a cab. Hanan watched the cab disappear in east-bound traffic, lighted a cigarette nervously and walked toward Madison Avenue.

Druse said: "Tell her I've come from Mister Hanan."

The telephone operator spoke into the transmitter, turned to Druse. "You may go up—Apartment Three D."

When, in answer to a drawled, "Come in," he pushed open the door and went into the apartment, Catherine Hanan was standing near the center table, with one hand on the table to steady herself, the other in the pocket of her long blue robe. She was beautiful in the mature way that women who have lived too hard, too swiftly, are sometimes beautiful. She was very dark; her eyes were large, liquid, black and dominated her rather small, sharply sculptured face. Her mouth was large, deeply red, not particularly strong.

Druse bowed slightly, said: "How do you do?"

She smiled, and her eyes were heavy, nearly closed. "Swell—and you?"

He came slowly into the room, put his hat on the table, asked: "May we sit down?"

"Sure." She jerked her head towards a chair, stayed where she was.

Druse said: "You're drunk."

"Right."

He smiled, sighed gently. "A commendable condition. I regret exceedingly that my stomach does not permit it." He glanced casually about the room. In the comparative darkness of a corner, near a heavily draped window, there was a man lying on his back on the floor. His arms were stretched out and back, and his legs were bent under him in a curious way, and there was blood on his face.

Druse raised his thick white eyebrows, spoke without looking at Mrs. Hanan: "Is *he* drunk, too?"

She laughed shortly. "Uh-huh—in a different way." She nodded towards a golf-stick on the floor near the man. "He had a little too much niblick."

"Friend of yours?"

She said: "I rather doubt it. He came in from the fire-escape with a gun in his hand. I happened to see him before he saw me."

"Where's the gun?"

"I've got it." She drew a small black automatic half out of the pocket of her robe.

Druse went over and knelt beside the man, picked up one of his hands. He said slowly: "This man is decidedly dead."

Mrs. Hanan stood, staring silently at the man on the floor for perhaps thirty seconds. Her face was white, blank. Then she walked unsteadily to a desk against one wall and picked up a whiskey bottle, poured a stiff drink. She said: "I know it." Her voice was choked, almost a whisper. She drank the whiskey, turned and leaned against the desk, stared at Druse with wide unseeing eyes. "So what?"

"So pull yourself together, and forget about it—we've got more important things to think about for a little while." Druse stood up. "How long ago? . . ."

She shuddered. "About a half-hour—I didn't know what to do. . . ."

"Have you tried to reach Crandall? I mean before this happened—right after you came in tonight?"

"Yes—I couldn't get him."

Druse went to a chair and sat down. He said: "Mister Hanan has turned this case over to me. Won't you sit down, and answer a few questions? . . ."

She sank into a low chair near the desk. "Are

you a detective?" Her voice was still very low, strained.

Druse smiled. "I'm an attorney—a sort of extra-legal attorney." He regarded her thoughtfully. "If we can get your rubies back and assure your safety, and"—he coughed slightly—"induce Mister Hanan to reimburse the insurance company, you will be entirely satisfied, will you not?"

She nodded, started to speak.

Druse interrupted her: "Are the rubies themselves—I mean intrinsically, as stones—awfully important to you? Or was this grandstand play of yours—this business of threatening Crandall—motivated by rather less tangible factors such as self-respect, things like that?"

She smiled faintly, nodded. "God knows how I happen to have any self-respect left—I've been an awful ass—but I have. It was the idea of being made such a fool—after I've lost over a hundred thousand dollars to Crandall—that made me do it."

Druse smiled. "The rubies themselves," he said—"I mean the rubies as stones—entirely apart from any extraneous consideration such as self-respect—would more seriously concern Mister Hanan, would they not?"

She said: "Sure. He's always been crazy about stones."

Druse scratched the tip of his long nose pensively. His eyes were wide and vacant, his thick lips compressed to a long downward curved line. "You are sure you were followed when you left Crandall's Wednesday?"

"As sure as one can be without actually knowing—it was more of a followed feeling than anything else. After the idea was planted I could have sworn I saw a dozen men, of course."

He said: "Have you ever had that feeling before—I mean before you threatened Crandall?"

"No."

"It may have been simply imagination, because you expected to be followed—there was reason for you to be followed?"

She nodded. "But it's a cinch it wasn't imagination this evening."

Druse was leaning forward, his elbows on his knees. He looked intently at her, said very seriously: "I'm going to get your rubies back, and I can assure you of your safety—and I think I can promise that the matter of reimbursement to the insurance company will be taken care of. I didn't speak to Mister Hanan about that, but I'm sure he'll see the justice of it."

She smiled faintly.

Druse went on: "I promise you these things—and in return I want you to do exactly as I tell you until tomorrow morning."

Her smile melted to a quick, rather drunken, laugh. "Do I have to poison any babies?" She stood up, poured a drink.

Druse said: "*That's* one of the things I *don't* want you to do."

She picked up the glass, frowned at him with mock seriousness. "You're a moralist," she said. "That's one of the things I *will* do."

He shrugged slightly. "I shall have some very important, very delicate work for you a little later in the evening. I thought it might be best."

She looked at him, half smiling, a little while, and then she laughed and put down the glass and went into the bedroom. He leaned back comfortably in the chair and stared at the ceiling; his hands were on the arms of the chair and he ran imaginary scales with his big blunt fingers.

She came back into the room in a little while, dressed, drawing on gloves. She gestured with her head towards the man on the floor, and for a moment her more or less alcoholic poise forsook her—she shuddered again—her face was white, twisted.

Druse stood up, said: "He'll have to stay where he is for a little while." He went to the heavily draped window, to the fire-escape, moved the drape aside and locked the window. "How many doors are there to the apartment?"

"Two." She was standing near the table. She took the black automatic from a pocket of her suit, took up a gray suede bag from the table and put the automatic into it.

He watched her without expression. "How many keys?"

"Two." She smiled, took two keys out of the bag and held them up. "The only other key is the pass-key—the manager's."

He said: "That's fine," went to the table and picked up his hat and put it on. They went out into the hall and closed and locked the door. "Is there a side entrance to the building?"

She nodded.

"Let's go out that way."

She led the way down the corridor, down three flights of stairs to a door leading to Sixty-third Street. They went out and walked over Sixty-third to Lexington and got into a cab; he told the driver to take them to the corner of Fortieth and Madison, leaned back and looked out the window. "How long have you and Mister Hanan been divorced?"

She was quick to answer. "Did he say we were divorced?"

"No." Druse turned to her slowly, smiled slowly.

"Then what makes you think we are?"

"I don't. I just wanted to be sure."

"We are *not*." She was very emphatic.

He waited, without speaking.

She glanced at him sidewise and saw that he expected her to go on. She laughed softly. "He wants a divorce. He asked me to divorce him several months ago." She sighed, moved her hands nervously on her lap. "That's another of the things I'm not very proud of—I wouldn't do it. I don't know why—we were never in love—we haven't been married, really, for a long time—but I've waited, hoping we might be able to make something out of it. . . ."

Druse said quietly: "I think I understand—I'm sorry I had to ask you about that."

She did not answer.

In a little while the cab stopped; they got out and Druse paid the driver and they cut diagonally across the street, entered an office building halfway down the block. Druse spoke familiarly to the Negro elevator boy; they got off at the forty-fifth floor and went up two flights of narrow stairs, through a heavy steel fire-door to a narrow bridge and across it to a rambling two-story penthouse that covered all one side of the roof. Druse rang the bell and a thin-faced Filipino boy let them in.

Druse led the way into a very big high-ceilinged room that ran the length and almost the width of the house. It was beautifully and brightly furnished, opened on one side onto a wide terrace. They went through to the terrace; there were steamer-chairs there and canvas swings and low round tables, a great many potted plants and small trees. The tiled floor was partially covered with strips of coco-matting. There was a very wide, vividly striped awning stretched across all one side. At the far side, where the light from the living room faded into darkness, the floor came to an abrupt end—there was no railing or parapet—the nearest building of the same height was several blocks away.

Mrs. Hanan sat down and stared at the twinkling distant lights of Upper Manhattan. The roar of the city came up to them faintly, like surf very far away. She said: "It is very beautiful."

"I am glad you find it so." Druse went to the edge, glanced down. "I have never put a railing here," he said, "because I am interested in Death. Whenever I'm depressed I look at my jumping-off place, only a few feet away, and am reminded that life is very sweet." He stared at the edge, stroked the side of his jaw with his fingers. "Nothing to climb over, no windows to raise—just walk."

She smiled wryly. "A moralist—and morbid. Did you bring me here to suggest a suicide pact?"

"I brought you here to sit still and be decorative."

"And you?"

"I'm going hunting." Druse went over and stood frowning down at her. "I'll try not to be long. The boy will bring you anything you want—even *good* whiskey, if you can't get along without it. The view will grow on you—you'll find one of the finest collections of books on satanism, demonology, witchcraft, in the world inside." He gestured with his head and eyes.

"Don't telephone anyone—and, above all, *stay* here, even if I'm late."

She nodded vaguely.

He went to the wide doors that led into the living room, turned, said: "One thing more—who are Mister Hanan's attorneys?"

She looked at him curiously. "Mahlon and Stiles."

He raised one hand in salute. "So long."

She smiled, said: "So long—good hunting."

He went into the living room and talked to the Filipino boy a minute, went out.

In the drug store across the street from the entrance to the building, he went into a telephone booth, called the number Hanan had given him. When Hanan answered, he said: "I have very bad news. We were too late. When I reached Mrs. Hanan's apartment, she did not answer the phone—I bribed my way in and found her—found her dead. . . . I'm terribly sorry, old man—you've got to take it standing up. . . . Yes—strangled."

Druse smiled grimly to himself. "No, I haven't informed the police—I want things left as they are for the present—I'm going to see Crandall and I have a way of working it so he won't have a single out. I'm going to pin it on him so that it will stay pinned—and I'm going to get the rubies back too. . . . I know they don't mean much to you now, but the least I can do is get them back—and see that Crandall is stuck so he can't wriggle out of it." He said the last very emphatically, was silent a little while, except for an occasionally interjected "Yes" or "No."

Finally he asked: "Can you be in around three-thirty or four? . . . I'll want to get in touch with you then. . . . Right. Good-bye." He hung up and went out into Fortieth Street.

Jeffrey Crandall was a medium-sized man with a close-cropped mustache, wide-set greenish gray eyes. He was conservatively dressed, looked very much like a prosperous real-estate man, or broker.

He said: "Long time no see."

Druse nodded abstractedly. He was sitting in a deep red leather chair in Crandall's very modern office, adjoining the large room in a midtown apartment building that was Crandall's "Place" for the moment. He raised his head and looked attentively at the pictures on the walls, one after the other.

"Anything special?" Crandall lighted a short stub of green cigar.

Druse said: "Very special," over his shoulder. He came to the last picture, a very ordinary Degas pastel, shook his head slightly, disapprovingly, and turned back to Crandall. He took a short-barreled derringer out of his inside coat-pocket, held it on the arm of his chair, the muzzle focused steadily on Crandall's chest.

Crandall's eyes widened slowly; his mouth hung a little open. He put one hand up very slowly and took the stub of cigar out of his mouth.

Druse repeated: "Very special." His full lips were curved to a thin, cold smile.

Crandall stared at the gun. He spoke as if making a tremendous effort to frame his words casually, calmly: "What's it all about?"

"It's all about Mrs. Hanan." Druse tipped his hat to the back of his head. "It's all about you gypping her out of her rubies—and her threatening to take it to the police—and you having her murdered at about a quarter after ten tonight, because you were afraid she'd go through with it."

Crandall's tense face relaxed slowly; he tried very hard to smile. He said: "You're crazy," and there was fear in his eyes, fear in the harsh, hollow sound of his voice.

Druse did not speak. He waited, his cold eyes boring into Crandall's.

Crandall cleared his throat, moved a little forward in his chair and put his elbows on the wide desk.

"Don't ring." Druse glanced at the little row of ivory push-buttons on the desk, shook his head.

Crandall laughed soundlessly as if the thought of ringing had never entered his mind. "In the first place," he said, "I gave her back the stones that were stolen. In the second place, I never believed her gag about telling about it." He leaned back slowly, spoke very slowly and distinctly as confidence came back to him. "In the third place, I wouldn't be chump enough to bump her off with that kind of a case against me."

Druse said: "Your third place is the one that interests me. The switched rubies, her threat to tell the story—it all makes a pip of a case against you, doesn't it?"

Crandall nodded slowly.

"That's the reason," Druse went on, "that if I shoot you through the heart right now, I'll get a vote of thanks for avenging the lady you made a sucker of, and finally murdered because you thought she was going to squawk."

All the fear came back into Crandall's face suddenly. He started to speak.

Druse interrupted him, went on: "I'm going to let you have it when you reach for your gun, of course—that'll take care of any technicalities about taking the law into my own hands—anything like that."

Crandall's face was white, drained. He said: "How come I'm elected? What the hell have you got against me?"

Druse shrugged. "You shouldn't jockey ladies into trying to nick insurance companies. . . ."

"It was her idea."

"Then you should have been on the level about the rubies."

Crandall said: "So help me God! I gave her back the stuff I took!" He said it very vehemently, very earnestly.

"How do you know? How do you know the man you had do the actual job didn't make the switch?"

Crandall leaned forward. "Because I took them. She gave me her key and I went in the side way, while she was out, and took them myself. They were never out of my hands." He took up a lighter from the desk and relighted the stump of cigar with shaking hands. "That's the reason I didn't take her threat seriously. I thought it was some kind of extortion gag she'd doped out to

get some of her dough back. She got back the stones I took—and if they weren't genuine they were switched before I took them, or after I gave them back."

Druse stared at him silently for perhaps a minute, finally smiled, said: "Before."

Crandall sucked noisily at his cigar. "Then, if you believe me"—he glanced at the derringer— "What's the point?"

"The point is that if I didn't believe you, you'd be in an awfully bad spot."

Crandall nodded, grinned weakly.

"The point," Druse went on, "is that you're still in an awfully bad spot because no one else will believe you."

Crandall nodded again. He leaned back and took a handkerchief out of his breast pocket and dabbed at his face.

"I know a way out of it." Druse moved his hand, let the derringer hang by the trigger-guard from his forefinger. "Not because I like you particularly, nor because I think you particularly deserve it—but because it's right. I can turn up the man who really murdered her—if we can get back the rubies—the real rubies. And I think I know where they are."

Crandall was leaning far forward, his face very alive and interested.

"I want you to locate the best peterman we can get." Druse spoke in a very low voice, watched Crandall intently. "We've got to open a safe—I think it'll be a safe—out on Long Island. Nothing very difficult—there'll probably be servants to handle but nothing more serious than that."

Crandall said: "Why can't I do it?" He smiled a little. "I used to be in the box business, you know—before I straightened up and got myself a joint. That's the reason I took the fake rubies myself—not to let anyone else in on it."

Druse said: "That'll be fine."

"When?" Crandall stood up.

Druse put the derringer back in his pocket. "Right now—where's your car?"

Crandall jerked his head towards the street. They went out through the crowded gambling room, downstairs, got into Crandall's car. Crossing Queensborough Bridge Druse glanced at his watch. It was twenty minutes past twelve.

At three thirty-five Druse pushed the bell of the penthouse, after searching, vainly as usual, for his key. The Filipino boy opened the door, said: "It's a very hot night, sir."

Druse threw his hat on a chair, smiled sadly at Mrs. Hanan, who had come into the little entrance-hall. "I've been trying to teach him English for three months," he said, "and all he can say is 'Yes, sir,' and 'No, sir,' and tell me about the heat." He turned to the broadly grinning boy. "Yes, Tony, it is a very hot night."

They went through the living room, out onto the terrace. It was cool there, and dim; a little light came out through the wide doors, from the living room.

Mrs. Hanan said: "I'd about given you up."

Druse sat down, sighed wearily. "I've had a very strenuous evening—sorry I'm so late." He looked up at her. "Hungry?"

"Starved."

"Why didn't you have Tony fix you something?"

"I wanted to wait." She had taken off her suit-coat, hat; in her smartly cut tweed skirt, white mannish shirt, she looked very beautiful.

Druse said: "Supper, or breakfast, or something will be ready in a few minutes—I ordered it for four." He stood up. "Which reminds me—we're having a guest. I must telephone."

He went through the living room, up four broad, shallow steps to the little corner room that he used as an office. He sat down at the broad desk, drew the telephone towards him, dialed a number.

Hanan answered the phone. Druse said: "I want you to come to my place, on top of the Pell Building, at once. It is very important. Ring the bell downstairs—I've told the elevator boy I'm expecting you. . . . I can't tell you over the phone—please come alone, and right away." He hung up and sat staring vacantly at his hands a little while, and then got up and went back to the terrace, sat down.

"What did you do with yourself?"

Mrs. Hanan was lying in one of the low chairs. She laughed nervously. "The radio—tried to improve my Spanish and Tony's English—chewed my fingernails—almost frightened myself to death with one of your damned demon books." She lighted a cigarette. "And you?"

He smiled in the darkness. "I earned thirty-five thousand dollars."

She sat up, said eagerly: "Did you get the rubies?"

He nodded.

"Did Crandall raise much hell?"

"Enough."

She laughed exultantly. "Where are they?"

Druse tapped his pocket, watched her face in the pale orange glow of her cigarette.

She got up, held out her hand. "May I see them?"

Druse said: "Certainly." He took a long flat jewel-case of black velvet out of his inside coat-pocket and handed it to her.

She opened the case and went to the door to the living room, looked at its contents by the light there, said: "They are awfully beautiful, aren't they?"

"They are."

She snapped the case closed, came back and sat down.

Druse said: "I think I'd better take care of them a little while longer."

She leaned forward and put the case on his lap; he took it up and put it back in his pocket. They sat silently, watching the lights in buildings over towards the East River. After a while the Filipino boy came out and said that they were served.

"Out guest is late." Druse stood up. "I make a rule of never waiting breakfast—anything but breakfast."

They went together through the living room, into the simply furnished dining room. There were three places set at the glittering white and silver table. They sat down and the Filipino boy brought in tall and spindly cocktail glasses of iced fruit; they were just beginning when the doorbell rang. The Filipino boy glanced at Druse, Druse nodded, said: "Ask the gentleman to come in here." The Filipino boy went out and there were voices in the entrance-hall, and then Hanan came into the doorway.

Druse stood up. He said: "You must forgive us for beginning—you are a little late." He raised one hand and gestured towards the empty chair.

Hanan was standing in the doorway with his feet wide apart, his arms stiff at his sides, as if he had been suddenly frozen in that position. He stared at Mrs. Hanan and his eyes were wide, blank—his thin mouth was compressed to a hard, straight line. Very suddenly his right hand went towards his left armpit.

Druse said sharply: "Please sit down." Though he seemed scarcely to have moved, the blunt derringer glittered in his hand.

Mrs. Hanan half rose. She was very pale; her hands were clenched convulsively on the white tablecloth.

Hanan dropped his hand very slowly. He stared at the derringer and twisted his mouth into a terribly forced smile, came slowly forward to the empty chair and sat down.

Druse raised his eyes to the Filipino boy who had followed Hanan into the doorway, said: "Take the gentleman's gun, Tony—and serve his cocktail." He sat down, held the derringer rigidly on the table in front of him.

The Filipino boy went to Hanan, felt gingerly under his coat, drew out a small black automatic and took it to Druse. Then he went out through the swinging-door to the kitchen. Druse put the automatic in his pocket. He turned his eyes to Mrs. Hanan, said: "I'm going to tell you a story. After I've finished, you can both talk all you like—but please don't interrupt."

He smiled with his mouth—the rest of his face remained stonily impassive. His eyes were fixed and expressionless, on Hanan. He said: "Your husband has wanted a divorce for some time. His principal reason is a lady—her name doesn't matter—who wants to marry him—and

whom he wants to marry. He hasn't told you about her because he has felt, perhaps justifiably, that you knowing about her would retard, rather than hasten, an agreement. . . ."

The Filipino boy came in from the kitchen with a cocktail, set it before Hanan. Hanan did not move, or look up. He stared intently at the flowers in the center of the table. The Filipino boy smiled self-consciously at Druse and Mrs. Hanan, disappeared into the kitchen.

Druse relaxed a little, leaned back; the derringer was still focused unwaveringly on Hanan.

"In the hope of uncovering some adequate grounds for bringing suit," Druse went on, "he has had you followed for a month or more—unsuccessfully, need I add? After you threatened Crandall, you discovered suddenly that you were being followed and, of course, ascribed it to Crandall."

He paused. It was entirely silent for a moment, except for the faint, faraway buzz of the city and the sharp, measured sound of Hanan's breathing.

Druse turned his head towards Mrs. Hanan. "After you left Mister Hanan at Roslyn, last night, it suddenly occurred to him that this was his golden opportunity to dispose of you, without any danger to himself. You wouldn't give him a divorce—and it didn't look as if he'd be able to force it by discovering some dereliction on your part. And now, you had threatened Crandall—Crandall would be logically suspected if anything happened to you. Mister Hanan sent his men—the men who had been following you—after you when you left the place at Roslyn. They weren't very lucky."

Druse was smiling slightly. Mrs. Hanan had put her elbows on the table, her chin in her hands; she regarded Hanan steadily.

"He couldn't go to the police," Druse went on—"they would arrest Crandall, or watch him, and that would ruin the whole plan. And the business about the rubies would come out. That was the last thing he wanted"—Druse widened his smile—"because he switched the rubies himself—some time ago."

Mrs. Hanan turned to look at Druse; very slowly she matched his smile.

"You never discovered that your rubies were fake," he said, "because that possibility didn't occur to you. It was only after they'd been given back by Crandall that you became suspicious and found out they weren't genuine." He glanced at Hanan and the smile went from his face, leaving it hard and expressionless again. "Mister Hanan is *indeed* 'crazy about stones.'"

Hanan's thin mouth twitched slightly; he stared steadily at the flowers.

Druse sighed. "And so—we find Mister Hanan, last night, with several reasons for wishing your—shall we say, disappearance? We find him with the circumstance of being able to direct suspicion at Crandall, ready to his hand. His own serious problem lay in finding a third, responsible, party before whom to lay the whole thing—or enough of it to serve his purpose."

Mrs. Hanan had turned to face Hanan. Her eyes were half closed and her smile was very hard, very strange.

Druse stood up slowly, went on: "He had the happy thought of calling me—or perhaps the suggestion. I was an ideal instrument, functioning as I do, midway between the law and the underworld. He made an appointment, and arranged for one of his men to call on you by way of the fire-escape, while we were discussing the matter. The logical implication was that I would come to you when I left him, find you murdered, and act immediately on the information he had given me about Crandall. My influence and testimony would have speedily convicted Crandall. Mister Hanan would have better than a divorce. He'd have the rubies, without any danger of his having switched them ever being discovered—and he'd have"—Druse grinned sourly—"the check he had given me as an advance. Failing in the two things I had contracted to do, I would of course return it to him."

Hanan laughed suddenly; a terribly forced, high-pitched laugh.

"It is very funny," Druse said. "It would all have worked very beautifully if you"—he moved his eyes to Mrs. Hanan—"hadn't happened to see the man who came up the fire-escape to call on you, before he saw you. The man whose return Mister Hanan has been impatiently waiting. The man"—he dropped one eyelid in a swift wink—"who confessed to the whole thing a little less than an hour ago."

Druse put his hand into his inside pocket and took out the black velvet jewel-case, snapped it open and put it on the table. "I found them in the safe at your place at Roslyn," he said. "Your servants there objected very strenuously—so strenuously that I was forced to tie them up and lock them in the wine cellar. They must be awfully uncomfortable by now—I shall have to attend to that."

He lowered his voice to a discreet drone. "And your lady was there, too. She, too, objected very strenuously, until I had had a long talk with her and convinced her of the error of her—shall we say, affection, for a gentleman of your instincts. She seemed very frightened at the idea of becoming involved in this case—I'm afraid she will be rather hard to find."

Druse sighed, lowered his eyes slowly to the rubies, touched the largest of them delicately with one finger. "And so," he said, "to end this vicious and regrettable business—I give you your rubies"—he lifted his hand and made a sweeping gesture towards Mrs. Hanan—"and your wife—and now I would like your check for twenty-five thousand dollars."

Hanan moved very swiftly. He tipped the edge of the table upward, lunged up and forward in the same movement; there was a sharp, shattering crash of chinaware and silver. The derringer roared, but the bullet thudded into the table. Hanan bent over suddenly—his eyes were dull, and his upper lip was drawn back over his teeth—then he straightened and whirled and ran out through the door to the living-room.

Mrs. Hanan was standing against the big buffet; her hands were at her mouth, and her eyes were very wide. She made no sound.

Druse went after Hanan, stopped suddenly at the door. Hanan was crouched in the middle of the living room. The Filipino boy stood beyond him, framed against the darkness of the entrance-hall; a curved knife glittering in his hand and his thin yellow face was hard, menacing. Hanan ran out on the terrace, and Druse went swiftly after him. By the dim light from the living room he saw Hanan dart to the left, encounter the wall there, zigzag crazily towards the darkness of the outer terrace, the edge.

Druse yelled: "Look out!" ran forward. Hanan was silhouetted a moment against the mauve glow of the sky; then with a hoarse, cracked scream he fell outward, down.

Druse stood a moment, staring blindly down. He took out a handkerchief and mopped his forehead, then turned and went into the living room and tossed the derringer down on the big center table. The Filipino boy was still standing in the doorway. Druse nodded at him and he turned and went through the dark entrance-hall into the kitchen. Druse went to the door to the dining-room; Mrs. Hanan was still standing with her back to the buffet, her hands still at her mouth, her eyes wide, unseeing. He turned and went swiftly up the broad steps to the office, took up the telephone and dialed a number. When the connection had been made, he asked for MacCrae.

In a minute or so MacCrae answered; Druse said: "You'll find a stiff in Mrs. Dale Hanan's apartment on the corner of Sixty-third and Park, Mac. She killed him—self-defense. You might find his partner downstairs at my place—waiting for his boss to come out. . . . Yeah, his boss was Hanan—he just went down—the other way. . . . I'll file charges of attempted murder against Hanan, and straight it all out when you get over here. . . . Yeah—hurry."

He hung up and went down to the dining room. He tipped the table back on its legs and picked up the rubies, put them back into the case. He said: "I called up a friend of mine who works for Mahlon and Stiles. As you probably know, Mister Hanan has never made a will." He smiled. "He so hated the thought of death that the idea of a will was extremely repugnant to him."

He picked up her chair and she came slowly across and sank into it.

"As soon as the estate is settled," he went on, "I shall expect your check for a hundred and thirty-five thousand dollars, made out to the insurance company."

She nodded abstractedly.

"I think these"—he indicated the jewel-case—"will be safer with me, until then."

She nodded again.

He smiled, "I shall also look forward with a great deal of pleasure to receiving your check for twenty-five thousand—the balance on the figure I quoted for my services."

She turned her head slowly, looked up at him. "A moralist," she said—"morbid—and mercenary."

"Mercenary as hell!" he bobbed his big head up and down violently.

She looked at the tiny watch at her wrist, said: "It isn't morning yet, strictly speaking—but I'd rather have a drink than anything I can think of."

Druse laughed. He went to the buffet and took out a squat bottle, glasses, poured two big drinks. He took one to her, raised the other and squinted through it at the light. "Here's to crime."

They drank.

The Perfect Crime
C. S. Montanye

CARLTON STEVENS MONTANYE (1892–1948), an active writer in the early years of pulpwood magazines, appears to have had an exceptional fondness for criminals as protagonists.

Although he wrote for many different periodicals, he achieved the peak of any pulp writer's career by selling numerous stories to *Black Mask*, beginning with the May 1920 issue and continuing through the issue of October 1939. Most were about various crooks, including the Countess d'Yls, who steals a pearl necklace in "A Shock for the Countess," Monahan, a yegg, and Rider Lott, inventor of the perfect crime.

His most famous character is the international jewel thief, Captain Valentine, who made his *Black Mask* debut on September 1, 1923, with "The Suite on the Seventh Floor," and appeared nine more times in two years, concluding with "The Dice of Destiny" in the July 1925 issue. The gentleman rogue also was the protagonist of the novel *Moons in Gold*, published in 1936, in which the debonair Valentine, accompanied by his amazingly ingenious Chinese servant Tim, is in Paris, where he has his eye on the world's most magnificent collection of opals.

Montanye also was one of the writers of the Phantom Detective series under the house name Robert Wallace.

"The Perfect Crime" first appeared in the July 1920 issue of *Black Mask*.

The Perfect Crime

C. S. Montanye

I

Two men sat at a table in a waterfront saloon. One was tall, dark and thin. He had the crafty, malevolent face of a gangster or crook. His eyes were beady and set close to a hawk-beak nose. His mouth was loose and weak but his chin was square. The other man was also tall. He was blond and broad shouldered. He was healthy in appearance and youthful looking. He resembled a stevedore or a freight handler from the docks. The two men had never seen each other until ten minutes past.

The dark man absently reached into a pocket and drew out a small, round pasteboard box. He opened it and dipped a thumb and forefinger into it and pinched out some white stuff. This he placed well into a nostril and sniffed it up his nose.

He looked across at the blond, who regarded him curiously.

"Walk in a snow storm, brother?"

"It's dope, isn't it?" the other asked.

The dark man's eyes began to sparkle.

"Happy dust. Have some? No. So much more for me, then. What's your name, brother?"

The blond youth set down his beaker of near-beer.

"My name is Klug—Martin Klug."

The dark man nodded.

"Martin Klug, you say? I knew a Klug once. He was a gay-cat, which means a blaster or a safe-blower, if you don't happen to know. He was doing a stretch in a band-house in Joplin for a job in Chi. He was old and had big ears. Was he your father?"

"No!" the other replied curtly. "He wasn't my father. My father was an honest man."

"Which implies his son isn't, eh? Now, let me see if I can guess what *you* are."

He cocked his head on one side and looked the youth over.

"You're too big and clumsy for a dip or a leather snatcher. You haven't got enough imagination to be a flash-thief or a con. Your hands are too large for peterman's work and you're too slow to swing on a derrick. What are you? I see your shoes are full of rust and stained with salt water. I'll put you down as a river rat, a rattler grab, which means you're a freight car crook. Am I right?"

The blond youth smiled a little.

"More or less. And you—what are you? *Who* are you?"

The dark man twisted his lips into a grin.

"Me? Brother, I'm Lott—Rider Lott. I'm an inventor. I'm also an author. I'm the inventor of the Perfect Crime. That is to say I've discovered how a job can be turned without any danger of a prison sentence. I'm the author of a little book I hope to publish some day. It's called a Primer of Progressive Crime. I hope you understand me."

"I don't," said Klug.

Lott raised a hand.

"Listen. Crime doctors and criminologists say it is impossible to commit a crime without leaving behind a clue. The law of Chance swings an even balance. No matter what is accomplished, so *they* declare, something tangible is always left behind. It might be a finger-print, a drop of blood, a lock of hair, a footprint, a bit of cloth—*something*. Do you get me now?"

Klug nodded.

"And you don't agree with them?"

Lott picked at his right cheek.

"No, I don't agree with them. The Perfect Criminal doesn't have to leave a clue behind. I said the law of Chance swings an even balance. He's not *compelled* to furnish the cops with clues, is he? All he has to do is—"

At this minute a girl came out of the shadows and sat down at the table. She was coarse, voluptuous but possessed of a flashy beauty. She was dressed in tawdry finery and reeked of patchouli. Under a large, dusty picture hat, Klug observed quantities of red-bronze hair. She had cow-like brown eyes, a milk white skin, a vermil mouth. She carried a black satin handbag and a pair of dirty white kid gloves.

"Well, well," Lott said, as the girl sat down, "we now have with us Beatrice the Beautiful Brakeman's Daughter. Where have you been keeping yourself, Beatrice? I haven't seen you in six weeks."

Klug watched the girl curve her painted lips in a smile.

"My name isn't Beatrice," she said, "and I never saw you before."

Lott chuckled.

"Your fault—not mine, then. Beatrice, meet my friend Mr. Martin Klug. He seems to be a nice boy in spite of his name. But he is wasting his youth and ambition robbing freight cars. Stupid occupation, isn't it? Now, if some day he should walk into a bank at twelve o'clock—when the bank cops go and get something to eat—and stick a gun through the wicket of the paying-teller's cage and dip a hand in after it and pick up a package of bills—"

The girl looked at Klug.

"I've got ten cents," she said. "Will they back me up a wash of phoney suds for that much?"

"Not while I'm around with a quarter!" Lott said quickly.

He lifted a finger for a lantern-jawed waiter's attention, gave the order and looked at the girl.

"Ten cents is your capital, you say? Beatrice, you surprise me. A swell looker like you and only a thin dime! What's the matter with you? Did you ever happen to fall out of a chair when you were a child? You should be riding around in your limousine. Ten cents! Are you laughing, Martin Klug?"

"I don't see anything funny in that," Klug growled.

"I was the upstairs maid in a private house," the girl said moodily. "Mrs. Cabbler was the madame. She's an old woman with warts on her face. She's about seventy years old, I guess."

Lott chuckled.

"Seventy, eh? Their necks crack easy when they're that age!"

"I worked there three weeks up to yesterday," the girl went on. "I only wanted to get some money together to buy a pair of long white gloves—the kind that come up to your elbows. I'll never be happy until I get long white gloves that come up to my elbows. Look at these dirty things I own. They've been cleaned twelve times—"

"Never mind about the gloves," Lott said. "Tell my young friend and myself what happened. You haven't the gloves you yearn for and therefore it stands to reason you weren't paid. You worked three weeks and weren't paid. Why not? What was the trouble? There was trouble of some kind, wasn't there?"

"Yes. Mrs. Cabbler left a ten dollar bill on the bureau in her bedroom. Someone hooked it. She called me in. She said I took it. She discharged me. She wouldn't give me my wages."

Rider Lott looked hard at the blond youth.

"You hear that, Martin Klug? Mrs. Cabbler said Beatrice took ten dollars from the bureau in her bedroom and discharged her without paying her wages. Clearly an unlawful act."

"A dirty trick!" The youth said thickly.

"No," Lott disagreed pleasantly, "a perfectly

proper course to take. Beatrice took the money. But she was forced to give it back. Then her madame took her revenge by discharging her without pay. Only natural, isn't it?"

"She's a devil, that Mrs. Cabbler!" the girl said viciously. "She looked me in the eyes and seemed to know everything. I gave her back the ten dollars. I didn't know what I was doing, hardly. Now I'll never get those long white gloves that come up to the elbows."

"I'll buy them for you," Martin Klug said, "when I get some money."

Lott picked at his left cheek.

"You'll never get any if you stick to robbing freight cars. No money in that, my friend."

The girl pushed aside her glass.

"I wish I hadn't given Mrs. Cabbler back that ten spot. She's got more now than she knows what to do with. Once I was passing along the hall and her bedroom door was ajar. She was counting her money. The whole top of the bed was covered with bills. She keeps it in a trunk under the bed. It is a small black trunk."

Rider Lott looked across the table again.

"You hear that, Martin Klug? Mrs. Cabbler is seventy years old. She has a trunk full of money. Money isn't much use to a person seventy years old, is it? Young people should have money. You're young—so am I, for that matter."

He turned his beady eyes on the girl.

"I don't suppose you have the front door key, the back door key, the side door key or any other key, have you, Beatrice? I mean to Mrs. Cabbler's house."

The girl moved restlessly.

"My name isn't Beatrice. But I have the key to the basement door. Just for spite I wouldn't give it back to her. She doesn't know I have it."

Rider Lott stretched out a thin, pale hand.

"Give me the key you have."

The girl opened her satin handbag, fumbled in the depths and drew out a key. She gave it to Lott. He dropped it in a pocket and looked at Martin Klug.

"If a person who is an enemy to society works alone," he stated, "it is excellent. If two people work together it is less excellent and yet it is not altogether foolhardy. But if three people go out on a job it is flirting with disaster. We are Three. Do you understand what I mean?"

Klug shook his blond head.

"No, I don't."

"Neither do I," said the girl.

Lott made an impatient gesture.

"I see why you, Martin Klug, are a river rat. And I see why you, Beatrice, Jewel of my Turban, have never risen above the level of a maid servant. You are both handicapped by the lack of intelligence and imagination. Both of you together don't own the intellect of a common, garden-variety spider. You disgust me."

Klug scowled.

"Well, what the hell do you mean?"

"Do you mean we should rob Mrs. Cabbler?" the girl asked, breathlessly.

"Ah, a gleam of intelligence!" Lott said mockingly. "Certainly we shall rob Mrs. Cabbler. Seventy years of age and a trunk full of money! She is made to rob. We have our own particular desires. Beatrice wants a pair of those long white gloves that come to the elbow, to replace the dirty ones she carries—"

"And I," put in Martin Klug, brightening up, "need a new pair of shoes. These are all in."

Lott smiled.

"While I am desirous of placing my books on the newsstands of the underworld. A thousand dollars will float my Primer. It will be of wonderful assistance to young, ambitious crustfloppers, grifters and heavymen. It will make me famous."

The girl grew animated.

"I should love to rob that skinny witch. And, oh, those gloves—"

Lott picked at his chin with his nervous fingers.

"We shall rob Mrs. Cabbler, the skinny witch. But two of us only must go. Beatrice must be one. She must guide one of us to the bedroom and the trunk with the money. She knows the house. Who will go with her? Martin Klug or myself? We shall draw straws and see."

He picked up a discarded newspaper, lying beside his chair, and tore two strips of unequal length from it. These he placed in his pale, thin hand and extended the hand toward the blond youth.

"Take one, Martin Klug. If you draw the long strip of paper you go with Beautiful Beatrice and rob Mrs. Cabbler. If you draw the short one I go."

Klug hesitated a minute and then drew one of the strips of paper from the hand before him. It proved to be the longest piece.

"So be it," Lott said. "Go with Beatrice and rob the skinny witch. And remember these things: Use no violence of any kind. Take no chances, leave no clues. Take great pains to cover every step and don't be in a hurry. After you have the money, if you will go back and check over every move you have made, in quest of suspicious or incriminating clues left behind, and then remove them, you will have accomplished the Perfect Crime. I hope you know and understand my meaning."

Klug inclined his head.

"I do."

Lott looked at a battered nickel watch.

"Twelve after one." He considered the two with a roving glance. "We'll spring this job on a share and share alike basis. We'll divide Mrs. Cabbler's money into three equal portions. But we must decide now on a place where we can cut the swag. It's bad business dividing in a public place. Where can we go?"

The girl stood up.

"I know the very place. I live with my sister. She has a flat up on Tenth Avenue. She's away now. You can both go there. You can stay there as long as you want."

Lott attained his feet.

"Fine. Let's start for Mrs. Cabbler's now. A woman of seventy sleeps as heavily at twelve o'clock as at three."

Martin Klug stood up.

"Are you coming, too?" he inquired, as if surprised.

Lott turned up his coat collar.

"Certainly. I shall wait outside for you both."

II

Two men and a girl sat at a table in the living-room of a cheap Tenth Avenue flat. It was the night following. A gas jet flickered garishly. An empty whisky bottle was on the table. The odor of booze mingled with that of cigarettes.

"Are you sure," Lott said, "you left no tell-tale marks behind you, incriminating evidence? Did you follow my instructions to the letter? Did you make it a Perfect Crime?"

Martin Klug shifted about in his rickety chair.

"I'm sure. I remembered what you told me. I went over the ground carefully. I even picked up the burnt matches."

"Robbery," said Lott, "means anywhere from five to twenty years. But murder means the chair. You made a mistake, Martin Klug. You shouldn't have killed the old woman."

The girl laughed.

"What else could he do? Just when we pulled out the trunk the old witch opened her eyes. She began to squawk."

Lott shook his head soberly.

"You could have tied her up. You could have gagged her. You didn't *have* to kill her!"

Martin Klug drew a breath.

"I was excited," he confessed. "I'm used to freight cars, not bedrooms. I pulled out the trunk. Then I looked up and saw the old woman's eyes looking at me. They were eyes like a fish's, cold and dead looking. Then she began to squawk. So I took her skinny throat between my hands."

"Bad business," said Lott. "Well, there's no use of shedding tears about it. It's over and done with. Get the coin, Beatrice. We'll split it up."

The girl went to the corner of the room. She pulled aside a couch and drew out a package wrapped in newspaper. She brought this to the table and laid it before Lott. He opened it and drew out three packages of money.

"Nine thousand dollars," he said. "Divide it by three and it equals three thousand dollars apiece."

"I don't see where you come off to get any of it," Martin Klug grumbled. "What did *you* do?"

Lott twisted his lips into a grim smile.

"I suppose you want my share because you croaked the old lady? What did *I* do? Nothing, not a thing, except plan the robbery. This three thousand is my royalty on the idea. Get me? What do *you* say, Beatrice?"

"My name isn't Beatrice," the girl replied. "And I don't say anything at all. Take the dough—it's yours!"

"You're a droll humorist, my young murderer, if you know what that is," Lott said to the blond young man.

"Here, take your share of the stuff and keep your mouth shut. Beatrice, Pearl of Price, put your mitts on your three thousand. Take it, my dear. Heaven is witness you earned it!"

The girl grabbed up her package of money and hugged it to her full breast.

"Mine! All mine!" she exulted. "And that's not all either! No, that's not all! Wait—look! I want to show you something!"

She jumped up, went to her wrap and dug something out of a pocket—something long and supple as a white snake. She held the objects up before Lott's eyes.

"Do you see 'em? *Gloves*—long white gloves that come up to my elbows!"

Martin Klug chuckled.

"She saw them on the dresser in the old woman's room. She made a dive for them. She seemed to want them more than the coin. Women are funny."

The girl pressed the gloves to her face.

"They're just the kind I dreamed about! It's a joke. I worked there three weeks to get the money to buy them and all the time the old hag had just the gloves I wanted. Well, they're no use to her now. Won't they look swell with that big

hat of mine? I'm terribly lucky. When Martin Klug lit the match they were the first things I saw!"

Lott picked at his chin.

"You should have heard the old dame squawk," Martin Klug said suddenly, with a laugh. "Then you should have heard her gurgle when I got hold of her windpipe. It sounded like water running out of a sink!"

He sighed.

"We've divided up the stuff, Lott. Let's get down to brass tacks. Let's divide up the girl. You want her. I want her. Who gets her? That's what I want to know."

The dark man took a deliberate sniff of snow and stretched his long arms.

"I'm in a drift. But don't dig me out! Who gets the girl? Who gets Beatrice the Beaut? Ask her? Who does get you, sweetheart?"

The girl ceased admiring the long, new white kid gloves in her hands.

"They are just my size. It was good to shake the old ones. Now these—"

"Answer the question!" Lott said briskly. "Who gets you?"

She looked slowly from one to the other.

"Well," she murmured, "you're both nice. I like you both."

"Make a choice," Lott said brusquely. "Don't beat around the bush. We both can't have you. That's polygamy; against the law. It wouldn't do to run afoul of the law—that way. So—which?"

The girl let a scowl creep across her beautiful face.

"I think," she said, after an interval, "if you would stop calling me Beatrice, I'd like *you* the best!"

Lott picked at his lips.

"Good. Then *I* get you, eh? Is that it?"

Martin Klug lurched heavily to his feet.

"Like hell you get her!"

He made a swift lunge at Lott. But the dark man was too quick for him.

Lott jumped to his feet and threw back his head with a quick, feline motion. The blow glided harmlessly over his shoulder. He seized the whisky bottle by the neck as the blond youth sprang at him like a tiger. He sidestepped and brought the bottle down with all his force on the skull of the other.

Klug stopped short, moaned faintly, groaned, and sank in an odd, limp heap on the table.

Then he rolled off it and sprawled, stirless, on the dirty uncarpeted floor.

Lott laughed a little.

"Poor fool! Now we have three thousand more than we had two minutes ago. I guess I've killed him. A tap on the façade is always like that if you use force. Maybe it's just as well. He was only a river rat. Get on your hat and coat, Beatrice. Put the cash in a bag. We've got to get out of here now in a hurry."

While the girl hastened to obey his orders, Lott took another sniff of dope and prodded Klug's body with his foot.

"No imagination," he said under his breath. "It's just as well—"

The girl loomed up before him. She had a satchel in her hand and wore the large, dusty picture hat.

"Wait until I put on these new gloves. They're soft. I love them. I always wanted them."

She began to flex her hands into them while Lott pushed Klug's body under the table.

"What did you do with the other gloves—the dirty ones?" he asked.

The girl held out a rounded arm and inspected the new glove.

"What did I do with 'em? What do you think? I just naturally chucked them away. What do I want with rotten old gloves like those, that have been cleaned twelve times?"

Lott drew his brows together and glanced at his nickel watch.

"Where did you throw them?"

She began donning the second glove.

"Oh, in the trash basket in the old witch's room. What difference does it make?"

Lott grasped her arm. His face had changed.

Color had crept into it. His eyes burned queerly.

"*In the trash basket!* You threw your old gloves in the trash basket in *that room!*"

The girl sought to wrench her arm from the tight grip he put upon it.

"What's eating you!" she said sibilantly. "You've got too much snow on board—"

Lott drew his lips over his teeth.

"*You fool!*" he cried. "*You little fool!* You've—"

He stopped and dropped her arm. The lids fell over his gleaming eyes. He moved his head to one side as if listening. Something in his attitude caused the girl to listen, too. For a long, tense minute she heard nothing. Then, on her strained ears sounded a footfall on the stairs outside . . . another.

She heard Lott draw a quick breath.

At the same instant the door burst open and two men stepped in, drawn revolvers glinting in the gaslight. Both wore derby hats and an air of authority. One motioned her to fall back against the wall; the other man jammed his gun in Lott's face.

"I'm Davis of Headquarters!" this second man snapped. "You and the moll are wanted. Case of murder—croaking old Mrs. Cabbler the rich widow! Out with your dukes and let me jewel you!"

Lott, against the table, hands trembling over his head, looked at the cowering figure of the girl.

"*In the trash basket,*" he whispered. "Oh, God—"

The detective, adjusting steel handcuffs, grunted.

"In the trash basket is right! It was a careful job and neatly turned. Not even a burnt match or a fingerprint. But no crime is perfect. We fished the dirty gloves out of the trash basket. They were full of numbers and those ink marks the cleaners put in them. We spent the day getting a line on the numbers in them. An hour ago we found the establishment that had cleaned them—"

You'll Die Laughing
Norbert Davis

THERE ARE HAPPY stories about the lives of the hard-working, hard-drinking writers for the pulps, those wildly creative typing machines who produced a hundred thousand words a year and up. Walter B. Gibson, who wrote most of The Shadow novels, famously produced more than a million words a year for more than twenty straight years. Some went into other kinds of writing: for Hollywood, slick magazines, books, radio, and, later, television.

And there are unhappy stories. One of the bright young talents who sold his first story to *Black Mask* while still a law student at Stanford, Norbert Davis (1909–1949), had so much writing success so quickly that he didn't bother to take the bar exam. As quickly as he could produce a new story, it sold—first to the pulps, then to the higher-paying slicks like *The Saturday Evening Post*. Combining the excitement of a fast-moving mystery with humor, there seemed to be no limit to his potential.

Several marriages went bad, his agent died unexpectedly, and the slicks started to reject some of his work. Having turned his back on the pulps where he got his start, he felt it would condemn him as a failure to return to those pages. At the age of forty, he closed his garage door, started his car engine, and died of carbon monoxide poisoning.

"You'll Die Laughing" was first published in the November 1940 issue of *Black Mask*. This is its first book appearance.

You'll Die Laughing

Norbert Davis

She kept the door almost closed.
"And who do you think you are, sonny boy?"

A soft-hearted loan-shark's legman learns—the hard way—never to buy a strange blonde a hamburger or complain if the neighbor's radio blasts too long and loud

CHAPTER ONE
BLOOD FROM TURNIPS

E WAS A short pudgy man, and he looked faintly benign even now with his eyes almost closed and his lips twisted awry with the effort of his breathing. He had silver-white hair that curled in smooth exact waves. It was almost dawn and it was bitter cold.

The outer door of the apartment lobby was open, and the wind made a sharp hurrying sound in the dark empty canyon of the street outside.

The pudgy man was sitting on the tiled floor of the lobby with his back against the wall, resting there, his stubby legs outspread in front of him. After a long time he began to move again, pushing his body away from the wall, turning very slowly and laboriously. His breath sounded short and sharp with the effort, but he made it and rested at last on his hands and knees.

He began to crawl toward the door and there was something inexorable about his slow stubborn progress. He opened the door wider, fumbling blindly ahead of him, and crawled out into the street.

The wind whooped down and slapped the folds of his long blue overcoat tight around his legs, pushed with impatient hands as if to hurry him. But he crawled down the steps very slowly, one by one, and reached the sidewalk and turned and made his inching patient way down the hill toward the wan glow of the street light on the corner.

Behind him, the apartment lobby was empty and cold, with the wind pushing at the half-open door and making the hinges complain in fitful little squeaks. On the wall at the spot where the pudgy man had leaned his back there was an irregular smear of blood, bright red and glistening with a sinister light all of its own.

Dave Bly had hurried as much as he could, but it was after six o'clock in the evening when he came in from the street and trotted up the long dingy flight of stairs to the second story of the office building.

Janet was still waiting for him and he could hear the *tap-tap-tap* of her typewriter. He whistled once and heard the typewriter stop with a faint *ping,* saw her slim shadow through the frosted glass as she got up from her desk and started to put on her hat.

Bly ran on up a second flight of stairs to the third floor, hurrying now, with the thought of the interview ahead making something shrink inside him. He went down the third-floor corridor toward the lighted door at the end. The letters on its glass panel were squat and fat and dignified, and they made the legend—

J. S. CROZIER
PERSONAL LOANS

Bly opened the door and went into the narrow outer office. The door into the private office was open and J. S. Crozier's harsh voice came through it.

"Bly, is that you?"

"Yes, sir."

A swivel chair squeaked and then J. S. Crozier came to the door and said: "Well, you're late enough."

"I had to do quite a lot of running around."

"Let's see what you got."

Bly handed him a neat sheaf of checks and bills and the typewritten list of delinquent debtors. J. S. Crozier thumbed through the bills and checks, and the light overhead made dark shadowed trenches of the lines in his face. He had a thick solid body that he carried stiffly erect. He wore rimless glasses that magnified his eyes into colorless blobs and a toupee that was a bulging mat of black hair so artificial it was grotesque.

"Forty-three dollars!" he said, throwing the sheaf of bills on Bly's desk. "And half these checks will bounce. That's not much to show for a day's work, Bly."

"No, sir."

J. S. Crozier flicked his finger at the typewritten list. "And what's the matter with this Mrs. Tremaine? She's been delinquent for six weeks. Did you see her?"

"She's had a serious operation. She's in the hospital."

"Well, why didn't you try there?"

"I did," said Bly. He hadn't, but he knew better than to try to explain why. "They wouldn't let me see her."

"Oh, they wouldn't! When will they?"

"Next week."

"Huh! Well, you get in there to see her as soon as you can, and you tell her that if she doesn't pay up her loan—plus the back compound interest and the delinquent collection fee—she might just as well stay in the hospital because she won't have any furniture to come home to."

"All right."

J. S. Crozier grinned at him. "Haven't got your heart in this, have you, Bly? A little on the squeamish side, eh?"

Bly didn't say anything. J. S. Crozier kept grinning at him and he let his colorless eyes move slowly from Bly's shoes, which were beginning to crack through the polish across the toes, up along the shabby topcoat to Bly's face, pale and a little drawn with pinched lines of strain around his mouth.

"I can't afford to be squeamish, Bly. Maybe you can."

Bly didn't answer, and J. S. Crozier said reflectively: "I'm disappointed in your work, Bly. Perhaps you aren't suited to such a menial task. Are you contemplating a change soon?"

"No," said Bly.

"Perhaps you'd better think about it. Although I understand jobs are very hard to find these days . . . Very hard, Bly."

Bly was quivering with a feeling of sick hopeless anger. He tried to hide it, tried so hard that the muscles of his face seemed wooden, but he knew he wasn't succeeding. J. S. Crozier chuckled knowingly. He kept Bly standing there for a full minute, and then he said with the undertone of the chuckle still in his voice: "That's all, Bly. Good-night."

"Good-night," Bly said thickly.

J. S. Crozier let him get almost to the door. "Oh, Bly."

Bly turned. "Yes?"

"This janitor at your place. This Gus Findley. He's been delinquent for three weeks now. Get something out of him tonight."

"I'll try."

"No," J. S. Crozier said gently. "Don't try, Bly. Do it. I feel that you have a responsibility there. He mentioned your name when he applied for the loan, so naturally I had confidence in his

ability to pay. Get some money from him tonight."

Bly went out and closed the door. Janet was waiting there, a slim small girl with her face white and anxious for him under the dark brim of her hat. She took his arm, and Bly leaned heavily against her, his throat so thick with the choking anger that gripped him that he couldn't breathe. He pulled himself upright in a second and started walking because he knew J. S. Crozier would be listening for his footsteps and grinning. Janet walked close beside him. They went down the steps, and Bly's anger loosened and became a sick despair.

"He knew you were there waiting, Janet. That's why he talked so loud. So you could hear him bawl me out."

"I know, dear. Never mind."

"Every day he does something like that. He knows I wouldn't do his dirty work for half a minute if I could find something else. I wouldn't anyway—I'd starve first—if it weren't for you and Bill and—and hoping. . . ."

They were in the street now and she was standing small and straight beside him, looking up into his face. "We'll go on hoping, Dave."

"For how long?" Bly demanded bitterly. "How long?"

"Forever, if we have to," said Janet quietly.

Bly stared down at her. "Thank you," he said in a whisper. "Thank you for you, my dear." He grinned wryly. "Well, I'm through crying in my beer for the moment. Shall we go squander our money on Dirty Dan's thirty-five cent de luxe dinner?"

CHAPTER TWO
THE BLONDE IN 107

 T WAS after ten when Bly got to the apartment building where he lived, and he had to use his key to open the entrance door. The air was thick and sluggish inside the small lobby, full

of a wrangling jangle of sound made by a radio being played overly loud in one of the apartments upstairs.

Bly went on a diagonal across the lobby, rapped lightly on a door beside the staircase. He could hear limping steps inside coming across a bare floor, and then Gus Findley opened the door and peered nearsightedly at him.

"Hello, Mr. Bly. You come in?"

Bly shook his head. "No thanks, Gus. I hate to ask you, but how about the money you owe on that loan you got from Crozier?"

Gus Findley had a tired resigned smile. "No, Mr. Bly. I'm sorry. I ain't got it."

Bly nodded slowly. "All right, Gus."

"I honest ain't got it."

"I know. Gus, why did you borrow money from him?"

"I thought you worked for him, Mr. Bly. I thought he's all right if you work for him."

Bly said: "He's a shark, Gus. That contract you signed carries over a hundred percent interest. It doesn't show on the contract as interest, but there it is."

"It don't make no difference, Mr. Bly. You shouldn't feel bad. I couldn't read very well anyway, that fine print, with my eyes not so good. I had to have the money for the hospital. My sister's boy got an operation."

"Why didn't he go to the clinic—on charity?"

"No," Gus said gently. "No. I couldn't have him do that. Not my sister's boy. You know how it is."

"Sure," said Bly.

Gus moved his thin, stooped shoulders. "Now he's got to have cod liver's oil and special milk and tonics. It costs so much I ain't got none left for Mr. Crozier. I ain't tryin' to cheat him, Mr. Bly. I'll pay as soon as I can."

"Sure, Gus," said Bly wearily, knowing that as soon as Gus could wouldn't be soon enough for J. S. Crozier. It would be the same bitter story again—garnishment of the major part of Gus's meager salary, attachment of what few sticks of furniture he owned. And more humiliation for Bly. J. S. Crozier would never miss

the chance of making Bly serve the papers on Gus.

The lobby seemed colder and darker. The muffled wrangle of the radio went on unceasingly and a woman's laughter sounded through it, thin and hysterical.

"Someone having a party?" Bly asked.

Gus nodded gloomily. "Yeah. That one below you—that Patricia Fitzgerald. She is no good. Six or eight complaints about the noise I got already. I called her up a couple of times and it don't do no good. I got the misery in my back and I don't like to climb them stairs. Would you maybe stop and ask her to keep quiet, Mr. Bly?"

"Sure," said Bly. "Sorry about your back, Gus."

Gus shrugged fatalistically. "Sometimes it's worse than others. How is your brother, Mr. Bly? The one that's in college."

Bly grinned suddenly. "Bill? Just swell. He's a smart kid. Going to graduate this year, and already they've offered him a job teaching in the college."

"Good," said Gus, pleased. "That's good. Then maybe, when you don't have to send him money, you can marry that nice little lady I seen you with."

"I hope so," Bly said. "But first I've got to get Bill through college. That's why I'm hanging on to this lousy job with Crozier so hard. I can't lose it now, just when Bill's all set to graduate. After he does, then I can take a chance on looking for another—something decent."

"Sure, sure," said Gus. "And you'll find it, too."

"If there is one, I will," Bly said grimly. "Well, I'll run up and see if I can tune that party down. So long, Gus."

He went up the grimy shadowed stairs and down the long hall above. The noise of the radio was much louder here, packing itself deafeningly in between the narrow walls until it was one continued formless blare. Bly stopped before the door through which it was coming and hammered emphatically on the panels.

The woman's shrill thin laughter came faintly

to him. Bly waited for a while and then began to kick the bottom of the door in a regular thumping cadence. He kept it up for almost two minutes before the door opened.

Patricia Fitzgerald, if that was her real name, was a tall thin blonde. She must have been pretty once, but she looked haggard now and wearily defiant, and there was a reckless twist to her full-lipped mouth. She was drunk enough to be slightly unsteady on her feet. Her bright hair was mussed untidily and she was wearing what looked like a black fur mitten on her right hand.

"Well?" she said over the blast of the radio.

Bly said: "Do you have to play it that loud?"

She kept the door almost closed. "And who do you think you are, sonny boy?"

"I'm just the poor dope that lives above you. Will you turn that radio down a little, please?"

She considered it, swaying slightly, watching Bly with eyes that were owlishly serious. "If I turn it down will you do a favor for me, huh?"

"What?" Bly asked.

"You wait." She closed the door.

The sound of the radio suddenly went down to a thin sweet trickle of music and the hall seemed empty without its unbearable noise.

Patricia Fitzgerald opened the door again. She no longer wore the black mitten. She was jingling some change in her right hand.

"You know where Doc's Hamburger Shack is—over two blocks on Third?"

Bly nodded. "Yes."

"You be a nice guy and run over there and get me a couple of hamburgers. If you do I won't make any more noise."

"O.K.," Bly agreed.

She gave him the change. "You tell Doc these hamburgers are for me. He knows me and he knows how I like 'em. You tell him my name and tell him they're for me. Will you?"

"All right."

"Be sure and tell him they're for me."

"Sure, sure," said Bly. "Just keep the radio turned down like it is and everything will be dandy."

"Hurry up, fella," said Patricia Fitzgerald,

and neither her eyes nor her voice were blurred now.

Bly nodded patiently. He went back down the hall, down the stairs and across the lobby. The last thing he heard as he opened the front door was Patricia Fitzgerald's laughter, sounding high and hysterical without the radio to muffle it.

Doc's Hamburger Shack was a white squat building on the corner of a weed-grown lot. Its moisture-steamed windows beamed out cheerily at the night, and when Bly opened the door the odor of frying meat and coffee swirled about his head tantalizingly.

Doc was leaning against the cash register. He was gaunt and tall and he had a bald perspiring head and a limply bedraggled mustache.

There was only one other customer. He was sitting at the far end of the counter. He was a short pudgy man and he looked pleasantly benign, sitting there relaxed with a cup of coffee on the counter in front of him. He had silver-white hair that curled in smooth exact waves. He watched Bly, sitting perfectly still, not moving anything but his round blandly innocent eyes.

"Hello, Doc," Bly said, sitting down at the counter and reaching for the crumpled evening paper on it. "I want a couple of hamburgers to go. They're not for me. They're for a blonde by the name of Patricia Fitzgerald who lives over in my apartment house. She said you'd know just how she wanted them fixed."

Doc put his hand up and tugged at one draggled end of his mustache. "Patricia Fitzgerald? Lives at the Marton Arms? Apartment 107?"

Bly nodded, engrossed in the sports page. "Yeah."

"She send you over?"

"Sure," said Bly.

"She tell you to give her name?"

Bly looked up. "Well, certainly."

"O.K.," said Doc. "O.K." He plopped two pats of meat on the grill and then sauntered casually down the counter and leaned across it in front of the pudgy man.

Bly went on reading his favorite sports column. The hamburger sizzled busily. Doc came sauntering back to the grill and began to prepare a couple of buns.

Bly had finished his sports column and was hunting through the paper for the comics when a siren began to growl somewhere near. After a while it died down and then another started up from a different direction.

"Must be a fire around here," Bly observed.

"Naw," said Doc. "Them's police sirens. Fire sirens have a higher tone." He put a paper sack on the counter. "Here's your 'burgers, all wrapped up. Be careful of 'em. She don't like 'em mussed up at all."

"O.K.," Bly said. He paid Doc with the change Patricia Fitzgerald had given him and went to the door.

The pudgy man was sipping at his coffee, but he was watching Bly calculatingly over the rim of his cup.

T HERE were several cars parked in front of the apartment building and one of them was a blue sedan with a long glittering radio antenna strung across its sloping top. Bly no more than half noticed it, and its identity didn't register on him until he unlocked the front door of the apartment house and very nearly bumped into a policeman who was standing just inside the entryway.

"What—" Bly said, startled.

"You live here?" the policeman asked. He was standing, spread-legged, as immovable as a rock, his thumbs hooked into his broad leather gun belt.

"Yes," Bly answered blankly.

"You been in here before this evening?"

"Yes. I went out to get these hamburgers for the girl who lives below me in 107."

The policeman's expression was so elaborately disinterested that it was a dead give-away. "Dame by the name of Fitzgerald?"

"Yes. She asked me—"

The policeman came one smooth sliding step closer, suddenly caught Bly's right arm by wrist and elbow.

Bly struggled unavailingly. "Here! What— what—"

"March," said the policeman. "Right up those stairs. Get tough and I'll slap you down."

He steered Bly across the lobby and up the stairs. He went down the hall with Bly stumbling along beside him willy-nilly like a clumsy partner in some weird dance.

The door of Patricia Fitzgerald's apartment was partially open and the policeman thrust Bly roughly through it and followed him inside.

"This is the bird," he said importantly. "I nabbed him downstairs in the lobby."

Bly heard the words through a thick haze that seemed to enclose his brain. He was staring unbelievably at Patricia Fitzgerald. She was lying half twisted on her back at the end of the couch. There was a bright thin line across the strained white of her throat and blood had bubbled out of it and soaked into the carpet in a pool that was still spreading sluggishly. Her eyes were wide open, and the light above her glinted in the brightness of her hair.

There were two men in the room. One was sitting on the couch. He was thick and enormously wide across the shoulders. He sat with his hands on his knees, patient and unmoving, as though he were waiting for something he didn't expect to happen very soon. His eyes were blankly empty and he wheezed a little when he breathed.

The other man was standing in the center of the room with his hands folded behind him. He was small and shabby-looking, but he had an air of queer dusty brightness about him, and his eyes were like black slick beads. He had a limp brown-paper cigarette pasted in one corner of his lower lip.

"Name?" he asked, and then more loudly, "You! What's your name?"

"Dave Bly," Bly said. "Is—is she—"

"Claims he lives upstairs," said the policeman. "Says he went out to get some hamburgers for the dame, here. I figure they was havin' a party and he gave her the business and then run and got them hamburgers and came back all innocent, tryin' to fake himself an alibi so—"

"Outside," said the shabby little man.

The policeman stared. "Huh?"

"Scram."

"Well sure, Lieutenant," the policeman said in an injured tone. He went out and shut the door.

"I'm Vargas," the shabby man said. "Lieutenant of detectives. This is my partner, Farnham. What do you know about this business here?"

Bly fought to speak coherently. "Nothing. Nothing at all. She was playing her radio too loud and I asked her to stop, and she said she would if I'd go get her a couple of hamburgers. . . ."

The big man, Farnham, got off the couch slowly and ominously. He came close to Bly, caught him by the front of the coat. Effortlessly he pulled Bly forward and then slammed him back hard against the wall. His voice was thick and sluggishly indifferent.

"You lie. She was drunk and you got in a beef with her and slapped her with a knife."

Bly felt a sinking sense of nightmare panic. "No! I didn't even know her! I wasn't here—"

"You lie," Farnham droned, slamming Bly against the wall again. "You're a dirty woman-killer. She got sassy with you and you picked up that knife and stuck it in her throat."

Bly's voice cracked. "I did not! Let go—"

The policeman who had brought Bly in was having some trouble in the hall, and they could hear him say indignantly: "Here now, lady! You can't go in there! Get away from that door! Lieutenant Vargas don't want nobody— Lady! Quit it, now! There's a corpse in there—all blood . . ."

A thin querulous voice answered snappily: "A corpse! Phooey! My dear departed husband was an undertaker, young man, and I've seen a lot more corpses than you ever will, and they

don't scare me a bit. You want me to jab you right in the eye with this knitting needle?"

Evidently the policeman didn't, because the door opened and a little old lady in a rusty black dressing-gown pushed her way into the room. She had a wad of gray hair perched up on top of her head like some modernistic hat, and she wore rimless spectacles on the end of a long and inquisitive nose.

"Hah!" she said. "I thought so. Bullying people, eh? My husband—dear Mr. Tibbet, the mortician—knew a lot of policemen when he was alive, and he always said they were extremely low-class people—rude and stupid and uncouth."

Farnham sighed. He let go of Bly and went back and sat down on the couch again. The springs creaked under his weight, and he relaxed into his position of patient ominous waiting.

"Who're you?" Vargas asked.

"Tibbet. Mrs. Jonathan Q. Tibbet—Q. for Quinlan—and you'd better listen when I talk, young man."

"I'm listening," said Vargas.

"Hah!" said Mrs. Tibbet. "Insolent, eh? And your clothes aren't pressed, either, and what's more, I'll bet you drink. Go ahead and bully me! Go ahead! I dare you! My dear dead husband was a personal friend of the mayor, and I'll call up and have you put in your place if you so much as lay a finger on me or this nice young man."

"Lady," said Vargas in a resigned tone, "I wouldn't touch you for ten dollars cash, but this lad is a suspect in a murder case and—"

"Suspect!" Mrs. Tibbet repeated contemptuously. "Bah! Did you hear me? I said *bah!*"

"I heard you," said Vargas.

Mrs. Tibbet jabbed a steel knitting needle in his direction like a rapier. "And why isn't he a suspect? Because he has an alibi, that's why! And I'm it. I was listening to this hussy carrying on in here. I saw this young man come and request her very courteously to stop playing her radio so loudly. I was watching right through my keyhole across the hall. He didn't even go inside the room. And when he left I heard her laughing in here. There was another man in here all the time, and if you and your low-class companion on the couch weren't so stupid and lazy you'd start finding out who it was."

"Did you see this other gent?" Vergas asked patiently.

"Oh! So you're insinuating I'd snoop and spy on my neighbors, are you? I'll speak to the mayor about this. Mr. Tibbet laid out his first two wives, and they were very friendly all Mr. Tibbet's life, and if I tell him that his drunken policemen are insulting and bullying me, he'll—"

"Yes, yes," said Vargas. "Sure. Absolutely. Did you see the other guy that was in here?"

"I did not."

"Did you hear his voice?"

"Yes. It was a very low-class voice—like yours."

"Yeah," said Vargas. He raised his voice. "O'Shay!"

The policeman peered in the door. "What, Lieutenant?"

"Escort Mrs. Tibbet back to her room."

The policeman looked doubtful. "Take it easy with that needle, lady. Come on, now. The lieutenant is very busy."

Mrs. Tibbet allowed herself to be guided gingerly to the door, and then turned to fire a parting shot. "And let me tell you that I won't hear of you bullying this nice young man any more. He's a very courteous and quiet and honest and hard-working and respectful young man, and he could no more commit a murder than I could, and if you had any sense you'd know it, but if you had any sense you wouldn't be a policeman, so I'm telling you."

"That's right," said Vargas, "you are. Goodbye."

Mrs. Tibbet went out with her escort and slammed the door violently and triumphantly. Farnham, sitting stolidly on the couch, wheezed once and then said: "Back door."

Vargas glanced at him with his beadily cruel eyes, then stared at Bly. "Maybe. Yeah, maybe. What about it, sonny?"

"About what?" Bly demanded, bewildered.

Vargas said: "Farnham thinks maybe you went around and came in the back after you left the front door."

"I didn't!" Bly denied angrily. "You can check up at the stand where I got these hamburgers."

"Yeah. You said you didn't know the dame. Then why did you get her those hamburgers?"

Bly's face was flushed with anger. "I could have told you in the first place if you'd given me a chance!"

"You got a chance now. Do it."

"Gus, the janitor, asked me to stop here on the way up and ask her to be more quiet. She was tight and she said she would if I'd run over and get some hamburgers for her. I didn't want to argue with her and I didn't have anything in particular to do, so I went. She gave me the money for them."

"What hamburger stand?"

"Doc's place—over on Third. He'll remember." Bly had a sudden thought. "I was in there when I heard your sirens. I was waiting then. Do—do you know when she was killed?"

"And how," said Vargas. "She let out a screech like a steam engine when she got it. We got three calls from three different tenants. Did you see the guy that was in here with her?"

"No," said Bly. "I thought there was someone, but I didn't see him. She didn't open the door wide."

Vargas nodded. "O.K. Beat it. Stick around inside the building. I'll maybe want to talk to you again."

Bly stood his ground. "Well, you listen here. You have no right to grab me and push me around and accuse me—"

"Sure, sure," Vargas agreed lazily. "Your constitutional rights have been violated. Write a letter to the governor, but don't do it here. We're going to be busy. Scram, now."

CHAPTER THREE
FALL-GUY

LY went out into the hall. He was so blindly indignant at the manhandling he had received that it wasn't until he had reached his own room that the reaction began to take effect. When he fumbled for his key, he found that he was still carrying the paper sack with the two hamburgers inside.

The odor of them and the feel of their warmness seeping through the wrappings against his palm suddenly sickened him. He went very quickly through his apartment and dropped them, still wrapped, into the garbage pail on the enclosed back porch. He sat down then in the living-room and drew several deep steadying breaths. He noticed that his forehead was wet with nervous perspiration.

Bly had never before run into violent and criminal death, and coming as it had without the slightest warning made it seem like a hazily horrible nightmare. Even now he could see Patricia Fitzgerald as plainly as if she were in the same room with him—lying so queerly crumpled on the floor, with the bright red thread across her throat and the light glinting in the metallic yellow of her hair.

Back of him the door into the kitchen swung shut with a sudden creaking swish. Bly's breath caught in his throat. He came up out of the chair and swung around, every muscle in his body achingly tense.

There was no other sound that he could hear, no other movement. He approached the door in long stealthy strides, pushed it back open again.

The kitchen was as empty as it had been when he had gone through it just the moment before, but now, standing in the doorway, he could feel a distinct draft blowing against the back of his neck.

Puzzled, he turned around. The door into his bedroom was open. There was no other place from which the draft could be coming. Bly went across the living-room and turned on the light in the bedroom.

One of the two windows on the other side of his bed was open. Bly started at it, frowning. He remembered very distinctly that he had closed and locked both of the windows before he had left for work in the morning because it had looked like it might rain.

He stepped closer, and then he saw that the glass in the upper pane of the window had been broken at a spot which, had the window been closed, would have been just above the lock. Fragments of glass glinted on the floor below the window, and there was a long gouge in the white paint of the sill.

Bly turned and walked quickly out of the apartment and down the stairs to the first-floor hall. The policeman was still on guard in front of Patricia Fitzgerald's apartment, and he surveyed Bly with evident displeasure.

"So it's you again. What do you want now?"

Bly said: "I want to see Vargas."

"It's Lieutenant Vargas to you," said the policeman. "And what do you want to see him about?"

"I'll tell that to him."

"O.K., smarty. He'll throw you right out of there on your can, I hope." The policeman opened the apartment door and announced: "Here's that dope from upstairs again."

Vargas and Farnham had changed places now. Vargas was sitting on the couch. He had his hat pulled down over his eyes and he looked like he was dozing. Farnham was standing in the center of the room staring gloomily at the rumpled contents of an ornamental desk he had hauled out into the middle of the floor.

"There ain't nothing like that in here," he said to Vargas.

"Look out in the kitchen," Vargas ordered. "Sometimes dames stick stuff away in the coffee cups or the sugar bowl. Don't paw around too much until the fingerprint guy gets here." He pushed his hat-brim back and stared at Bly. "Well?"

Bly said: "There's something upstairs—in my apartment—I think you ought to look at."

"There's plenty of things I ought to look at around here, if I could find them," Vargas said. "O.K. Come on."

The policeman said: "You want I should go along with you, Lieutenant? This guy is a suspect and—"

"If I wanted you to go along, I'd say so," Vargas informed him. "You get out in that hall and keep your big feet and your big mouth out of this apartment."

"Yes, sir," said the policeman glumly.

Vargas jerked his head at Bly. "Come along."

They went back upstairs to Bly's apartment, and Bly took Vargas into the bedroom and showed him the broken window.

"So what?" Vargas asked.

"I locked both those windows when I left this morning," Bly told him. "This apartment is directly above Patricia Fitzgerald's, and the fire-escape goes past her windows and mine. I think the man who killed her came up the fire-escape from her bedroom, broke in this window, and then went through my apartment and out into the hall."

"You're quite a thinker," Vargas said sourly. "Just why should he clown around like that when he could just as well go out the back door of Fitzgerald's apartment?"

"Because of the lay-out of the apartment building," Bly explained. "If he went out her rear door, he couldn't get away without going past the front of the building because there is a blind alley on this side that doesn't go through the block. But if he came through here, he could go along the second-floor hall, down the back steps, and out through the garage underneath and at the rear of the building. He probably didn't want to come out the front door of Patricia Fitzgerald's apartment because someone might be watching it after she screamed."

Vargas grunted. Hands in his pockets, he strolled closer to the window and examined it and the glass on the floor carefully. "Look and see if you're missing anything," he said over his shoulder.

Bly looked in his closet and the drawers of his bureau. "No. Nothing. There's nothing around here anyone could take except a few old clothes."

Farnham came quietly in the bedroom and nodded at Vargas. "I couldn't find it, but I found out why I couldn't."

"Why?" Vargas asked.

"She didn't pay none."

Vargas swung around. "What? You mean to say they let a tramp like her in here without payin' any rent in advance?"

"Yeah," Farnham said. "They had a reason for it. It seems another tenant—a party who's lived here for over a year and paid his rent on the dot every month—recommended her and said that she was a good risk."

Vargas' eyes looked beadily bright. "And who was this accommodating party?"

Farnham nodded at Bly.

"So?" said Vargas very softly.

He and Farnham stood there motionless, both of them watching Bly with the coldly detached interest of scientific observers, and Bly had the same sense of helpless bewilderment he had had when they were questioning him in the apartment below.

"What *is* this?" he demanded nervously. "What are you two talking about?"

"Sonny," said Vargas, "it seems like every time we turn around in this case, we fall over you. We're beginning to get tired of it. When you interrupted us downstairs, we were looking for Fitzgerald's rent receipt, just because we didn't have anything better to look for. We didn't find it, because she didn't have one, because she hadn't paid any rent yet. The reason she hadn't paid any is because *you* told the guys who own this building that she was O.K. and a good risk."

Bly swallowed hard. "You said that—that I recommended—"

"Yeah," said Vargas. "You. It seems mighty funny. You don't know this Patricia Fitzgerald at all, as you say, but you run errands for her and you recommend her as a good credit risk. You'd better come up with some answers about now."

"I never recommended her for anything to anyone!" Bly denied indignantly.

FARNHAM took a long step closer. "Don't pull that stuff. I called up the bank that owns the place, and I talked to Bingham, the vice-president in charge of all their rental property. He looked it up, and said you did."

"But I didn't!" Bly said. "I don't know—"

Farnham took another step. "Maybe you lost your memory. Maybe if you fell downstairs, you'd find it again."

"I heard you," said Mrs. Tibbet. She was standing in the doorway of the bedroom, nodding her head up and down meaningfully. "Oh, I heard you, all right. I'm a witness. Falling downstairs, eh? I know what that means. Third degree. Dear Mr. Tibbet told me all about it. I'm going to report you to the mayor."

The policeman's anxious face appeared over her shoulder. "Lieutenant, I couldn't help it. She sneaked up the stairs when she seen Farnham come up—"

"Scram," said Vargas curtly. "You too, lady. I got no time for fooling now. I'm busy. Get out of here."

Mrs. Tibbet still had her knitting needle, and she held it up now and sighted down its thin shining length. "Make me. Go ahead. I dare you. You're not going to beat up this poor boy, and I'm going to stay right here and see that you don't. You can't bully me. I'm not afraid of you. Not one bit. Dear Mr. Tibbet always said that policemen were bums and that he could prove it by figures."

Vargas took a deep breath. "Look, lady. We just found out now that this guy Bly, here, is the bird that recommended the Fitzgerald dame when she came in here."

"That's a lie," said Mrs. Tibbet.

Farnham wheezed indignantly. "It ain't nei-

ther! I telephoned to Bingham, the vice-president—"

"I know him," said Mrs. Tibbet. "Horace Bingham. He's fat. Not as fat as you are, nor quite as sloppy, but almost. And he's even dumber than you are—if that's possible. If either one of you had asked me I could have told you who was responsible for the Fitzgerald creature's presence here, but no, you wouldn't think of a simple thing like that. You're too busy going around shouting and threatening innocent people. Mr. Tibbet always said that no detective could count above five without using his fingers and what's more—"

"That's enough for this time," Vargas told her. "You said you knew who was responsible for the Fitzgerald girl being here. Who is it?"

"If you had any sense you'd know by this time and wouldn't have to go around asking. It is Gus Findley, of course. The janitor."

"Are you sure about that?" Vargas asked.

"I'll have you know," said Mrs. Tibbet, "that I don't go around lying to people, not even to policemen, although that would hardly count because they aren't really people. Mr. Tibbet always said that all you needed to do was furnish a policeman with a tail and he'd be at home in any tree. Gus Findley was in and out of that Fitzgerald hussy's apartment on the average of ten times a day, and in my opinion it's a scandalous affair and has been from the very first."

Vargas jerked his head at the policeman, who was still waiting nervously in the doorway. "Get Findley."

Farnham said doubtfully: "Seems like this Findley is a pretty old boy to go in for—"

"Hah!" said Mrs. Tibbet. "Men! I could tell you a thing or two—"

"Don't bother," Vargas advised wearily.

They waited and in five minutes the policeman came back and thrust Gus Findley roughly into the bedroom. "Here he is, Lieutenant."

Gus Findley blinked at them fearfully. He looked old and sick and shaken, and in the strong light his face had a leaden pallor. "What—what is it, please?"

Vargas strolled over to him. "Now look here, you. We know that you're responsible for Patricia Fitzgerald coming to this joint, and we know you've been hanging around in her apartment all the time. We want some facts, and we want 'em right now. Start talking."

Gus Findley's face twisted painfully. "She—she was my niece, sir." He turned to Bly. "Mr. Bly, I'm so sorry. Please don't be mad with me. She come here, and she didn't have no money, and I didn't have none I could give her on account of my sister's boy having the operation. So I—I said she could live here, and I—I told Mr. Bingham that you had recommended—"

"That's all right, Gus," Bly said uncomfortably. "If you had asked me, I probably would have recommended her anyway. Don't worry about it. It's O.K."

"It's not O.K. with me," said Vargas. "Just tell us a little more about this matter."

"She was no good," Gus said miserably. "She was never no good. Her name ain't Patricia Fitzgerald. It's Paula Findley. Her folks died, and I tried to raise her up right, but she wouldn't never do nothing I said, and then she run away with some fella and—and he didn't even marry her I don't think."

"What fella?" Vargas asked sharply.

Gus shook his head wearily. "I dunno. I never seen him. She said, when she come back, that he'd left her a long time ago. She said she was lookin' for the fella and that when she found him she was gonna get even with him and make herself a lotta money doin' it."

"What was his name?" Vargas inquired.

"I dunno, sir. Seems like he had a lot of names, from what she said. Seems like he wasn't no good, either."

"That's the boy we want," said Farnham.

Vargas nodded absently. "Yeah. Now listen, Findley—"

"You listen," Mrs. Tibbet invited. "Mr. Findley is an old man, and he's sick, and he's had a great shock. You're not going to ask him any more questions now. Not one more question, do you understand that? I'm going to take him right down to my apartment and give him a nice hot cup of tea, and I don't want to see any drunken, dirty, foul-mouthed detectives blundering round there while I'm doing it. You hear me, you two?"

"Oh yes, indeed," said Vargas.

CHAPTER FOUR
GARBAGE COLLECTION

BLY was ten minutes late to work the next morning, and J. S. Crozier was waiting for him, standing in the open door of his private office with his sallow face set in gleefully vindictive lines.

"Well, Bly, I'm glad to know that you feel you are so necessary here that you can afford to disregard the rules I've been at some pains to impress on your mind."

"I'm sorry," Bly said tightly. "I was delayed. . . ."

The bulging mat of black hair that made up J. S. Crozier's toupee had slipped askew over one ear, and he poked at it impatiently. "Yes, yes. I noticed, however, that you entered the building some fifteen minutes ago. I suppose your delay, as you so nicely term it, had something to do with the little lady who works as a typist in the office downstairs."

"I spoke to her on my way up," Bly admitted.

"No doubt, no doubt. I notice that you spend quite a little time speaking to her lately. Are you contemplating matrimony, Bly?"

"I think that's my affair—and hers," said Bly.

J. S. Crozier raised his eyebrows elaborately. "And mine, Bly, if you are talking to her when you are presumably working for me. Or *are* you?"

"Yes," said Bly.

"Thank you for telling me. I was wondering. If I may presume to advise you, Bly, I would say that it would be best for you to secure a position of a little more permanence before you take any rash steps. I'm not at all satisfied with your work, Bly. You're inclined to dawdle and find any excuse to keep from working. Aren't you, Bly?"

"I try to do my best," Bly answered.

"Yes," said J. S. Crozier. "Try. A good word. It is misfits and idlers like you who fill our relief rolls and burden the taxpayers. You haven't got any get-up-and-go about you, Bly. You'll never amount to anything. I feel sorry for your pretty friend downstairs if she marries you. I suppose you were so engrossed in her last night that you forgot all about the slight matter of the money Gus Findley owes me?"

Bly had to swallow and then swallow again before he could steady his voice. "I didn't really have a chance to talk to him about it. There was a murder at my apartment house last night and—"

"A murder!" said J. S. Crozier. "Now what kind of a fantastic fairy tale is this? I suppose you're going to try to tell me that someone murdered Gus Findley!"

"I didn't say so," Bly said, keeping a tight grip on his temper. "But the police were questioning him about the murdered girl and the other tenants—"

"I see," said J. S. Crozier. "Very interesting. Do you suppose you might possibly, by the exercise of some great ingenuity, get to see him tonight? I'm growing impatient with you and your excuses, Bly."

"I'll see him tonight."

"You'd better," said J. S. Crozier grimly. "Now I have a call for you to make, Bly. The party's name is Perkins. He lives in the Marigold Apartments on Halley. Judging from that hovel that you live in, you wouldn't know, but the Marigold is an expensive residence. This party called and wants to borrow five hundred dollars with his furniture as security. The furniture should be worth three or four times that. You go over and check up on it. Tell Perkins, if you find things satisfactory, that he can take a taxi and come back here with you, and I'll have the money for him."

"All right," said Bly.

J. S. Crozier pointed a blunt forefinger. "Don't make any mistake about the value of that furniture, Bly. And check up on the title. Do you understand? Have I made it perfectly clear to your limited intelligence, or do you want me to write it down?"

"I understand," said Bly thickly.

"All right. And don't you take a taxi, getting there. You take a street-car. I've noticed these delusions of grandeur in you. You seem to think you're too fine and sensitive a person to hold such a menial position as this, but just remember that if you had any brains you'd have a better one. Get out, Bly. And don't stall around with your lady friend on the second floor as you go, either."

T HE Marigold Apartments was an immense terraced graystone building that filled a whole block. Even without J. S. Crozier's word for it, Bly would have been immediately aware that it was an expensive residence. The doorman, after one look at Bly, was superciliously insolent and the glittering chrome-and-black-marble expanse of the lobby made Bly painfully aware of his own shabby clothes and cracked shoes.

Mr. Perkins, it seemed, lived on the fifth floor in a triplex de luxe apartment. The desk clerk—as supercilious as the doorman, but even more expertly insolent—made very sure Bly was expected before he would allow him to go up.

The elevator boy acted as though Bly's appearance was a personal affront to him. He deliberately stopped the elevator a foot below the floor and let Bly step up, and he stayed there ostentatiously watching until he made sure Bly was going to the apartment where he was expected.

The doorbell of Mr. Perkins' apartment was a black marble knob. Bly tried pushing it without effect, finally pulled it and heard chimes ring inside on a soft rising scale. The door opened instantly and a voice said: "Won't you come in, please, Mr. Bly?"

Bly stepped into a long low room with a far wall that was one solid expanse of windows, facing out on a private flagged terrace that looked bright and clean in the sunlight.

"Shut the door, if you please, Mr. Bly."

Bly pushed the door shut behind him, trying to place the man who was speaking to him. He was a short, pudgy man with an air that was benignly pleasant. He had silver-white hair that curled in smooth exact waves. Suddenly Bly realized he was the same man he had seen in Doc's Hamburger Shack the night before when he had gone in to order the hamburgers for Patricia Fitzgerald. He realized that and, in the same second, without quite knowing why, he felt a little cold tingle along the back of his neck.

The pudgy man had small pink hands. He put the right one in his coat pocket now and brought it out holding a flat automatic. He was still smiling.

"Sit down in that chair. The one beside the telephone, if you please."

Bly went sideways one cautious step after another, sank numbly in the chair beside the stand that held a chrome-and-gold telephone set.

"If this is a hold-up," he said huskily, "you—you're wasting your time. I didn't bring the money you wanted to borrow with me. There's no way you can get it without appearing at the office yourself."

"No hold-up," said the pudgy man in his softly amiable voice. "My name is not Perkins. It is Johanssen—two s's, if you please. You have heard it, perhaps?"

"No," said Bly numbly.

"You recognize me, though?"

Bly nodded stiffly. "Yes. You were in Doc's Hamburger Shack last night when I came in."

"Just so." Johanssen stood staring at him for a second, his bland eyes speculatively wide. "You do not look like a thief, but then one can never tell in these matters. I would like to tell you a story, Mr. Bly. You do not mind? I will not bore you?"

"No," said Bly.

Johanssen smiled. "Good. Since you do not know my name I will tell you I am a pawnbroker. But not the ordinary kind. You believe me, Mr. Bly? Not ordinary."

"Yes," said Bly.

"Good," Johanssen repeated. "My business is under my hat. I have no office. I go to my customers. They are all rich people, Mr. Bly. But sometimes they need cash—lots of cash—very quickly and very badly. They do not want people to know this. So they call Johanssen. I come to them with the cash. You see?"

"Yes," Bly admitted.

"One year ago, Mr. Bly, a person called me and gave me the name of a very prominent person with whom I had done business many many times. This person wanted ten thousand dollars at once. He is good for much more, so I say I will bring it to him. But, he says, he is not at home. He is at the apartment of a friend. Will I bring it to him there?

"So I bring the money where he says. But it is not my customer that has called me. It is a thief. You are listening carefully, Mr. Bly?"

"Yes," said Bly.

"Good. This thief, he is waiting for me on the darkness of the stairs of the apartment house. He gives me no chance, Mr. Bly. He stabs me in the back with a knife and takes my money and runs away. He thinks I am dead. But no. I crawl down the stairs and through the lobby and to the street. I crawl two blocks away before someone sees me and calls an ambulance. It was very hard, that crawling. I remember that, Mr. Bly."

Bly swallowed. "Why—why didn't you wake someone in the apartment house?"

"No," said Johanssen gently. "That would bring the police. This is not a business for police. This is Johanssen's business. You see?"

"Oh," said Bly blankly.

"You do not understand," Johanssen said. "It is known everywhere that Johanssen carries large sums of money with him. It must be known, also, that it is not safe to rob Johanssen. Not because the police will come after you, but because Johanssen will come after you—and find you. Now do you understand?"

Bly had the same sense of nightmare panic he had felt the night before when he had been accused of murdering Patricia Fitzgerald.

"You're not saying—saying that I—"

"No, no. May I go on with my story? I found out who stabbed me. It took much money and time and then I did not find the man. Only some of the names he had used. I found out that he had done many crimes—not bad ones like this, only cheating and swindling. This time he is very afraid. He runs and hides, and hides so well that I cannot locate him. But I do locate his woman. He leaves her when he runs with my money. You can guess who his woman was, Mr. Bly?"

"Patricia Fitzgerald," Bly said automatically.

"Yes. She is very angry because he left her. When I offer her five thousand dollars to point this man out to me she says she will do it if she can find him. She did. Last night he was in her apartment. He murdered her. Do you know who that man was, Mr. Bly?"

"No!" Bly exclaimed.

"I am willing to pay *you* five thousand dollars if you will tell me who it was."

"But I don't know!" Bly said. "I didn't see him."

"Then," said Johanssen gently, "then you will give me back my five thousand dollars, please."

"You—your what?"

"My five thousand dollars."

"But I haven't got—I never saw—"

"Yes. It was in an envelope in the paper sack that contained the hamburgers."

Bly's mouth opened slackly. "Envelope— hamburgers. . . ."

"Yes. You see, this Patricia Fitzgerald did not trust me. First, before she points out the man who stabs me, she must see the money. We arrange it. I will wait in the hamburger stand. She will send someone who will mention her name. I will put the money with the hamburgers.

Then she will lead this man to this apartment. I will be waiting for them. The five thousand dollars is a reward I have offered, Mr. Bly. I have even put it in the papers that I will pay that much to anyone who shows me the man who stabbed me. But you have not done so. Give me the five thousand dollars back, please, at once."

Bly shook his head dizzily. "But I didn't know—"

Johanssen moved the automatic slightly. "I am not joking, Mr. Bly. Give me my five thousand dollars."

"Listen," Bly said desperately. "I didn't even open the sack. I threw the whole business, just as Doc gave it to me, in the garbage."

"Garbage?" Johanssen repeated gently. "This is not the time to be funny, Mr. Bly. You had better realize that."

Bly leaned forward. "But it's true. I did just that. Wait! Gus Findley! The janitor at my apartment house! He's got a lame back and I hardly ever cook in my apartment. . . ."

"Yes?" Johanssen said very softly.

"Maybe he hasn't emptied the garbage! Let me call him up. It's a chance—"

"A chance that you are taking," Johanssen said. There was an icy little flicker deep back in his eyes. "You may call him up. I will listen. Be very careful what you say."

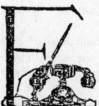

FUMBLINGLY, with cold and stiff fingers, Bly dialed the number of the apartment house. He could hear the buzz of the telephone ringing, going on and on interminably while the icy little flame in Johanssen's eyes grew steadier and brighter.

And then the line clicked suddenly and Gus Findley's voice said irritably: "Yes? What you want, please?"

Bly drew in a gulping breath of relief. "Gus! This is Dave Bly."

"Ah! Hello, Mr. Bly. How are you? I ain't got that money to pay Mr. Crozier yet, Mr. Bly. I'm sorry, but—"

"Never mind that. Listen to me, Gus. Have you emptied the garbage in my apartment this morning?"

"No, I ain't. I'm sorry, Mr. Bly, but my back has been sore like anything and them damned police has been botherin'—"

"Gus!" said Bly. "I want you to do a favor for me. Go up to my apartment. Go on the back porch and look in the garbage pail. There's a small paper sack right on top. It's closed. Bring the sack down with you. I'll hold the line."

"Well, sure. . . ."

"Hurry, Gus! It's very important!"

"You ain't sick, are you, Mr. Bly? You sound—"

"Gus!" Bly exploded. "Hurry up!"

"O.K. Sure. Hold the wire."

Bly heard the receiver bump as Gus put it down, and then there was nothing but the empty hum of the open circuit. He waited, feeling the sweat gather in cold beads on his forehead. Johanssen had come quietly closer, and Bly could catch the black slick glint of the automatic, leveled a foot from his head.

After centuries of time the receiver bumped again and Gus said cheerfully: "Sure, I got it. What you want I should do with it?"

Bly leaned back in his chair, sighing, and nodded once at Johanssen. "All right. What now?"

Johanssen's eyes had lost their frosty glint. "This Gus—he is an honest man?"

Bly nodded weakly. "Yes."

"Tell him to open the sack and the envelope."

"Gus," Bly said into the telephone, "inside the sack you'll find an envelope. Take it out and open it."

"Sure, Mr. Bly. Wait." Paper crackled distantly and then Gus's voice suddenly yammered frantically. "Mr. Bly! It's money! It's thousands—millions! Mr. Bly! Mr. Bly!"

"Take it easy, Gus," Bly said. "It was put in there by mistake. I'm going to let you talk to the man who owns the money. He'll tell you what to do."

"I don't want so much money here! I'm gonna call a cop! I'm afraid—"

"Here's Mr. Johanssen. Talk to him."

Johanssen took the telephone. Gus was still shouting at the other end of the line, and Johanssen nodded several times, beginning to smile a little more broadly, finally managed to get a word in.

"Yes, Gus. Yes, yes. It is my money. No. Don't call a policeman. Just keep it for me." The receiver fairly crackled at that last and Johanssen held it away from his ear, wincing. "No, no. No one will rob you. All right. Lock yourself in. Yes, I will knock three times and then twice. Yes, I will bring a writing from Mr. Bly. All right. Yes. Just be calm."

He hung up the receiver and nodded at Bly. "That is a good man." The flat automatic had disappeared.

Bly wiped his forehead with his handkerchief. "Yes. Gus is a swell old gent. He has a tough time."

"And you have had a tough time," said Johanssen. "Yes. I am very sorry, Mr. Bly. I beg your pardon. Can I do something for you to show I am sorry, please?"

"No," Bly said. "No. It's all right."

Johanssen watched him. "Mr. Bly, I am very anxious to find the man who was in that apartment. You may still have the reward if you will tell me anything that will lead me to him."

Bly shook his head wearily. "I don't know anything."

"Think," Johanssen urged. "Something small, perhaps. Some little thing you may have noticed. Some impression."

"No," said Bly woodenly.

Johanssen shrugged. "So it will be, then. But please let me do something to show I am sorry for this today."

"No," said Bly in an absent tone. "If you want to do something for somebody, give Gus a couple of hundred out of the five thousand so he can get free of that shark I work for."

"I will do that. Surely."

"I've got to go," Bly said. "I'm—in a hurry."

"Surely," said Johanssen, opening the door. "I am so sorry, Mr. Bly. Please forgive me."

CHAPTER FIVE
THE BLACK MITTEN

BLY took a taxi back to the office. All the way there he leaned forward on the seat, pushing forward unconsciously trying to hurry the taxi's progress. When it stopped at the curb in front of the office building he was out of it before the driver had time to open the door. He flung a crumpled bill over his shoulder and raced up the steep stairs, past the second floor and Janet's office, up to the third floor and down the corridor.

The hammer of his feet must have warned J. S. Crozier, because he was just coming out of his private office when Bly burst through the front door. Bly closed the door behind him and leaned against it, panting.

"Well," said J. S. Crozier, "you're back in a hurry, Bly. And I don't see any customer. Have you some more excuses to offer this time?"

Bly was smiling. He could feel the smile tugging at the corners of his lips, but it was like a separate thing, no part of him or what he was thinking.

J. S. Crozier noticed the smile. "Bly, what on earth is the matter with you? You've got the queerest expression—"

"I feel fine," Bly said. "Oh, very fine. Because I've been waiting for this for a long time."

"Bly! What do you mean? What are you talking—"

Bly stepped away from the door. "You've had a lot of fun with me, haven't you? You've bullied and insulted and humiliated me every chance you got. You knew I had to take it. You knew I had a brother in college who was dependent on me and my job. You knew I wanted to get ahead, but that I couldn't unless I had more training. You knew when I came here that I was taking courses in a night school, and you deliberately gave me work that kept me late so I couldn't finish those courses."

"Bly," said J. S. Crozier, "are you mad? You can't—"

"Oh, yes I can. I can tell you now. You've had your fun, and now you're going to pay for it. You're going to pay pretty heavily and you're going to know I'm the one who made you pay."

"You're being insulting," J. S. Crozier snapped. "You're fired, Bly. If you don't leave at once I'll call the police."

"Oh, no," said Bly. "You won't call the police, because that's what I'm going to do. How does it feel to be a murderer, Mr. Crozier?"

"Eh?" said J. S. Crozier. The color washed out of his cheeks and left the lines on them looking like faint indelible pencil marks. "Wh-what did you say?"

"Murderer."

"You—you're crazy! Raving—"

"Murderer," said Bly. "You murdered Patricia Fitzgerald."

"Bly! You're a maniac! You're drunk! I won't have you—"

"You murdered Patricia Fitzgerald and I'm the one who knows you did it. I'm the one who will get up on the stand and swear you did it. I'm the one—Bly, the poor devil it was so much fun for you to bully because you knew I couldn't strike back at you. Was the fun worth it, Mr. Crozier?"

J. S. Crozier's mouth opened, fish-like, and closed again before he could find words. "Bly! Bly! Now you can't make mad accusations like that. You're insane, Bly! You—you're sick."

"No. I happened to remember a couple of small things. When I came to Patricia Fitzgerald's door last night and she opened it, she was wearing what I thought was a black fur mitten. It wasn't. It was that wig of yours—your toupee. She had it wrapped around her right hand. She had been laughing at how you looked without it, or perhaps she had been trying it on herself."

"You lie!" J. S. Crozier shouted, putting his hand up over the bulging toupee protectively. "You lie!"

"No. I saw it. I'll swear I saw it. And another thing. Just a little while ago, when you were speaking about the Marigold Apartments and how luxurious they were, you said, 'Judging from that hovel you live in. . . .' You knew where I lived, but you'd never been in my apartment—until last night. You were then. You broke in the window after you murdered Patricia Fitzgerald."

Under the toupee the veins on J. S. Crozier's forehead stood out like purple cords. "You're a liar and a fool!" He laughed chokingly. "You think that evidence is enough to base a charge of murder on? Bah! Get out! Go to the police! They'll laugh at you! I'm laughing at you!" His whole body shook with insane raging mirth.

The door opened quietly and Johanssen stepped inside the office. "May I laugh, too, please?" he asked softly.

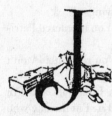 S. CROZIER'S breath hissed through his teeth. He seemed to shrink inside his clothes. The toupee had slipped down over his forehead and it fell now and lay on the floor like an immense hairy spider. J. S. Crozier's own hair was a blond, close-clipped stubble.

Johanssen smiled and nodded at Bly. "You should never play poker, Mr. Bly. Your face gives you away. I knew you had remembered something, so I followed you here. It is nice to meet you again, Mr.—ah—Crozier."

"Bly," J. S. Crozier said in a shaky whisper. "Run for help. Quick. He'll kill me."

"Mr. Bly will not move," said Johanssen gently. "No."

Bly literally couldn't have moved if he had wanted to. He was staring, fascinated, from Johanssen to J. S. Crozier. Johanssen had his right hand in his coat pocket, but he apparently wasn't at all excited or in any hurry.

"I have been looking for you for a long time," he said. "It is so very, very nice to see you at last."

J. S. Crozier began to shake. His whole body shuddered. "Johanssen," he begged hoarsely. "Wait. Wait, now. Don't shoot me. Listen to me.

It was an accident. I didn't mean—Johanssen! You can't just shoot me in cold blood! I'll pay back the money I stole from you! I—I've made a lot! I'll give it all to you! Johanssen, please—"

The door opened in back of Johanssen, pushing him forward. He stepped aside quickly and alertly, and Vargas came into the office. His eyes were bright and beadily malicious.

"Police," he said casually to Crozier. "Hello, Bly. I've been following you around today. Checking up."

J. S. Crozier caught his breath. "Officer!" he shouted hoarsely. "Arrest this man! He's going to kill me!"

"Which man?" Vargas asked. "You mean Johanssen? Why, he's a respectable businessman. Are you thinking of killing anyone, Johanssen?"

"No, Mr. Vargas," said Johanssen.

"See?" said Vargas to Crozier. "You must be mistaken. Well, I've got to run along. Behave yourself, Bly."

"No!" J. S. Crozier pleaded. "No, no! You can't! Take me with you!"

"What for?" Vargas inquired reasonably. "I couldn't take you with me unless I arrested you for something. And what would I arrest you for—unless it was maybe for murdering Patricia Fitzgerald last night?"

J. S. Crozier swayed. "That—that's absurd!"

Vargas nodded. "Sure. That's what I thought. Well, so long."

J. S. Crozier held on to a desk to keep upright. "No! You can't go and leave me to this—this . . . Wait! Johanssen thinks I stabbed him and robbed him! You've got to arrest me for that! You've got to lock me up!"

Vargas looked at Johanssen in surprise. "Did he stab you, Johanssen?"

"I have not said so."

"So long," said Vargas.

J. S. Crozier's face was horribly contorted. "No, no! You can't leave me alone with—with—"

Vargas stood in the doorway. "Well? Well, Crozier?"

"Yes," Crozier whispered hoarsely. "I did it. I killed her. I knew—the way she looked and acted after Bly went for the sandwiches. I twisted her arm and—and she told me . . ." His voice rose to a scream. "Take me out of here! Get me away from Johanssen!"

Vargas' voice was quick and sharp now. "You heard it, both of you. You're witnesses. Farnham, come on in."

Farnham came stolidly into the office. "Come on baby," he said in his heavy indifferent voice. J. S. Crozier's legs wouldn't hold his weight, and Farnham had to half carry him out the door.

"Could have nailed him anyway on that toupee business," Vargas said, casual again. "But this way made it more certain. Johanssen, you stick around where I can find you."

"I will be very glad to testify. I will also wish to witness the execution, if you please."

"I'll arrange it," Vargas promised. "Kid, that was clever work—that business about the toupee."

"It just—came to me," Bly said shakily. "It seemed all clear at once—after Mr. Johanssen told me about the arrangement for him to wait in the hamburger stand. I knew then that Patricia Fitzgerald was playing her radio loud on purpose. She thought Gus, the janitor, would come up and then she would have sent him for the sandwiches. And then I remembered the black mitten. . . ."

High heels made a quick *tap-tap-tap* along the corridor and Janet ran into the office. "Dave! Are you all right? I saw Mr. Crozier going downstairs with another man. He—he was crying. . . ."

Bly said: "It's all right now, dear. Mr. Crozier was the man who murdered that girl in my apartment house. I'll tell you about it later."

"I'll be going," said Vargas. "Bly, you stick around where I can find you."

"That will be easy," Bly said bitterly. "Just look on the handiest park bench. I was so clever I thought myself right out of a job."

"I will go also," said Johanssen, "but first there is this." He took a black thick wallet from his pocket. Carefully he counted out five one-thousand-dollar bills.

"The reward, which I have offered legally and which I have advertised in the papers. Mr. Vargas is a witness that you earned it and that I paid it."

"It's yours," Vargas said. "He made a public offer of it. If he didn't pay you, you could sue him."

"Yes," said Johanssen. "And then there is this." He took a folded sheet of blue legal paper from his pocket. "This is a lease for my apartment at the Marigold, paid a year in advance. It is too big for me. For two people it would be good. You will take it, please, Mr. Bly."

"No!" Bly said. "I couldn't. . . ."

"Bly," said Vargas conversationally, "I've been standing around here wondering when you were going to kiss this girl of yours. Don't you think it's about time you did?"

The Crimes of Richmond City
Frederick Nebel

WRITING IN THE MIDST of the Great Depression, Frederick Nebel (1903–1967) wrote prolifically for *Black Mask, Dime Detective,* and other pulps, producing scores of relatively realistic hard-boiled stories about such fixtures of their era as Cardigan, the hard-as-nails Irish operative working for the Cosmos Agency in St. Louis; tough dick Donny Donahue of the Interstate Agency; and, most important, the long-running stories about Captain Steve MacBride and the ever-present local reporter, Kennedy, who frequently takes over a story and does as much crime solving as the official member of the police department.

Nebel had two mystery novels published during his lifetime, *Sleepers East* (1934) and *Fifty Roads to Town* (1936). *The Crimes of Richmond City*, a powerful depiction of violence and corruption, has never before appeared in book form. It was published as five separate episodes in *Black Mask* in the issues of September 1928 through May 1929.

Publishing novels in serial form was common for *Black Mask* in this era, as it was responsible for such important works as Dashiell Hammett's first four novels, *Red Harvest, The Dain Curse, The Maltese Falcon,* and *The Glass Key*, as well as Paul Cain's *Fast One* and many of Carroll John Daly's books.

Raw Law

Frederick Nebel

A city of graft and crime; a man's buddy, a victim;
then the deadly game of vengeance—and justice

I

APTAIN STEVE MacBRIDE was a tall square-shouldered man of forty more or less hard-bitten years. He had a long, rough-chiseled face, steady eyes, a beak of a nose, and a wide, firm mouth that years of fighting his own and others' wills had hardened. His face shone ruddily, cleanly, as if it were used to frequent and vigorous contact with soap and water. For eighteen years he had been connected, in one capacity or another, with Richmond City's police department, and

Richmond City today is a somewhat hectic community of almost a hundred-thousand population.

MacBride sat in his office at Police Headquarters. He sat at his shining oak desk, in a swivel chair, smoking a blackened briar pipe, with the latest copy of the Richmond City *Free Press* spread before him. In one corner a steam radiator clanked and hissed intermittently. There were a half dozen chairs lined against the wall behind him. The floor was of cement, the ceiling was high and, like the walls, a light, impersonal tan. About the room there was something hollow and clean and efficient. About the borders of the two windows at MacBride's left there were irregular frames of snow left by a recent blizzard. But the room was warm and, except for the clanking of the radiator, quite silent.

Reading on, MacBride sometimes moved in his chair or took his pipe from his mouth to purse his lips, it seemed a little grimly and ironically. Once he muttered something behind clenched teeth, way down in the cavern of his throat. Presently he let the paper drop and sat back, drawing silently on his pipe and letting his eyes wander back and forth over the collection of photographs tacked on the bulletin board on the wall before him—photographs of men wanted for robbery, murder, and homicide. One of the telephones on his desk rang. He took off the receiver, listened, said, "Send him in." Then he leaned back again and swung his chair to face the door.

It opened presently, and a man neatly dressed in a blue overcoat and a gray fedora strolled in. A cigarette was drooping from one corner of his mouth. He had a young-old face, a vague smile, and the whimsical eyes of the wicked and wise.

"Hello, Cap." He kicked the door shut with his heel and leaned against it, indolently, as if he were a little weary—not in his bones, but with life.

"Hello, Kennedy," nodded MacBride. "Sit down."

"Thanks."

Kennedy dropped into a chair, unbuttoned his overcoat, but did not remove it.

MacBride creaked in his chair, looked at the newspaper on his desk and said, with a brittle chuckle, "Thanks for the editorial."

"Don't thank me, Mac."

"Your sheet's trying to ride us, eh?"

"Our business is to ride everybody we can."

"M-m-m. I know."

Kennedy knocked the ash from his cigarette. "Of course, it's tough on you." He smiled, shrugged. "I know your hands are tied."

"Eh?" MacBride's eyes steadied.

"You heard me, Mac. This little boy knows a lot. Y' know, *you* don't run the Department."

MacBride's lips tightened over his pipe.

"*You*," went on Kennedy, "would like to put the clamps on this dirty greaseball, Cavallo. Now wouldn't you?"

MacBride's eyes narrowed, and he took his pipe from his mouth. "Would I?" His hand knotted over the hot bowl of the pipe.

"Sure you would. But—" Kennedy shrugged—"you can't."

"Listen, Kennedy. What did you come here for, to razz me?"

"I don't know why I came here. It was cold out, and I know you keep it warm here. And—well, I just thought I'd drop in for a chat."

"You thought you'd get some inside dope. Go ahead, come out with it. Well, Kennedy, I've got nothing to say. News is as tight here as a drum-head. What a bunch of wise-cracking eggs you've got down in your dump. Gink Cavallo'll laugh himself into a bellyache when he reads it. The lousy bum!"

"Something's got to break, Mac. When a bootlegging greaseball starts to run a town, starts to run the Department, something's got to break."

"He's not running *me!*" barked MacBride.

"The hell he isn't! Don't tell me. I'm no greenhorn, Mac. Maybe not you personally. But your hands are tied. He's running somebody else, and somebody else is running somebody else, and the last somebody else is running you."

"You're talking through your hat, Kennedy."

"Oh, am I? No, I can't lay my hands on it all, but I can use my head. I know a few things. I know that Gink Cavallo is one of the wisest wops that ever packed a rod. He's a brother-in-law to Tony Diorio, and Diorio is president of the Hard Club, and the Hard Club swings two thousand sure votes and a thousand possible votes. And, you know, Mac, that these wops stick together. Most of the bohunks in the mills are wops, and they've sworn by the Hard Club, and—get this, Mac—it was the Hard Club that put Pozzo in for alderman and Mulroy for state's attorney. And it's the state's attorney's office that's running the Department—the rottenest administration in the history of Richmond City. It's just putting two and two together.

"You can't move, Mac. You've got your orders—hands off. What can you do? You're a captain. You've been with the Department for eighteen years. You've got a wife and a kid, and if you were kicked out of the Department you'd be on the rocks. I know you hate Cavallo like poison, and I know you're just aching to take a crack at him. It sure is a tough break for you, Mac."

MacBride had not batted an eye-lash, had not shone by the slightest flicker of eyes or expression, how he took Kennedy's speech. He drew on his pipe meditatively, looking down along his beak of a nose. It was in the heart of MacBride that seas of anger were crashing and tumbling. Because Kennedy was right; he had hit the nail on the head with every charge. But MacBride was not the man to whimper or to go back on the Department. Loyalty had been ground into him long years ago—loyalty to his badge.

His voice was casual, "Finished, Kennedy? Then run along. I'm busy."

"I know, Mac. Kind of touched you on the quick, eh? It's all right, old-timer. Your jaw's sealed, too. You'd be one hell of a fool to tell Steve Kennedy how right he is. Well." Kennedy got up and lit a fresh butt. "It's all right by me, Cap. But when the big noise breaks, don't forget yours truly. It can't go on, Mac. Somebody'll slip. Some guy'll yap for more than his share. I've seen these rotten conditions before—'Frisco, Chicago, New Orleans. I'm hard-boiled as hell, Mac, and there's no one pulling any wool over my eyes. I'm just standing by and laughing up my sleeve." He took a pull on his cigarette. "There's one wild Mick in your outfit who's very liable to spill the beans, get himself shoved out to the sticks and maybe poked in the ribs with a bullet, besides."

"You mean—?"

"Sure. Jack Cardigan. S' long, Mac."

"Good bye, Kennedy."

When the door closed, MacBride let go of himself. He heaved to his feet, spread-legged, his fists clenched, his eyes narrowed and burning intensely.

"God, Kennedy, if you only *knew* how right you are!" he muttered. "If I was only single—if I hadn't Anna and Judith. I'm tied all around, dammit! Home—and *here!*" He sank back into his chair, his head drooping, age creeping upon him visibly.

II

He was sitting there, in precisely the same position, fifteen minutes later. And fifteen minutes later the door swung open swiftly, silently, and Jack Cardigan came in. A tall, lean, dark-eyed man, this Cardigan, rounding thirty years. Men said he was reckless, case-hardened, and a flash with the gun. He was.

"You look down at the mouth, Steve," he said, offhand.

"I am, Jack. Kennedy—"

"Oh, that guy!"

"Kennedy dropped in to pay me a call. Sharp, that bird. Pulls ideas out of the air, and every idea hits you like a sock on the jaw."

"Been razzing you?"

"Has he! Jack, he's got the whole thing worked out to a T. He'd just need my O.K. to spill the whole beans to the public, and likely Police Headquarters 'd be mobbed. He's right. He's got the right slant on the whole dirty business. Jack, if I was ten years younger, I'd tell the Big Boss to go to hell and take my chances. That lousy wop is sitting on top of the world, and his gang's got Richmond City tied by the heels."

Cardigan sat down on the edge of a chair. There was something on his mind. You could see that much. He tapped with his fingers on the desk, his lips were a little set, the muscle lumps at either side of his jaw quivered, his dark eyes were close-lidded, active, flashing back and forth across MacBride's face.

"Brace up, Steve," he clipped. "I've got some news that might knock you for a row of pins."

"Eh?" MacBride straightened in his chair.

Cardigan's lips curled. "I came up alone. The sergeant said Kennedy'd gone up to see you. Didn't notice if he'd left. So I came up beforehand—to see."

"Kennedy left fifteen minutes ago. What's up?"

"Enough!" Cardigan took a vicious crack at the desk with his doubled fist. "The dirty pups got Hanley!"

"What!" MacBride's chair creaked violently. He leaned forward, laid his hand on Cardigan's knee, his breath sucked in and held.

"Two shots—through the lung and the heart! Somebody's going to pay for this, Steve! Joe Hanley was my partner—my sister's husband! There's nobody'll stop me—nobody! I'll—"

"Just a minute, Jack," cut in MacBride gently. "How'd it happen?"

Cardigan got a grip on his temper, bit his lip. "I was out at Joe's place for dinner tonight, on Webster Road. Marion was a little upset. Kid had a bad cold, and she had a streak of worrying on, just like her. I mind five years ago, how she used to say she'd never marry a cop. She used to worry about me all the time. Not that a cop wasn't good enough—hell no. But she used to say if she married a cop she'd be laying awake all night worrying. So, like a woman, she married Joe, and Joe's been a buddy of mine since we were kids. Well, you know that. Then she had two to worry over—Joe and me.

"And she was worrying tonight. Joe laughed. So did I. She got me alone in the hall and told me to watch out for Joe. She'd always been doing this. I kidded her. She said she meant it, and that she felt something was going to happen. I remember how she hung on to him when we breezed. God!"

"Steady, Jack!"

"I know. Well, Joe and I hoofed it to the park, to get a bus into the city. There was none in sight, so we began hiking down Webster Road till one 'd come. Pretty lonesome there. A car came weaving down behind us, and we heard a girl scream. We turned around and held up our hands for it to stop. The driver swerved to one side, intending to duck us. He slid into a ditch, roared his motor trying to get out. The girl was yelling hysterically. We saw her pitch out of the car. Then it heaved out of the ditch and was getting under way when Joe hopped it, pulling his rod. Two shots slammed out, and Joe keeled. I had my hands full with the girl. The car skidded and crashed into the bushes.

"I had my rod out then and ran up. Two guys in the back had jumped out and ducked into the bushes. I nailed the chauffeur. He wasn't heeled, but he was trying to get away, too. He started giving me a line and I socked him on the head so he'd stay put till I looked after Joe. Well, there wasn't much to look after. Joe was dead. The girl—she was only a flapper—was bawling and shaking in the knees. She'd been pretty well mauled. A machine came along and I stopped it."

"Wait. You say you got the chauffeur?"

"Sure. He says his name's Clark, and he's downstairs, barking for a lawyer."

"Who's the girl?"

"Pearl Carr's her name. Just a wise little flapper who thought she was smart by taking a ride. She was waiting for a bus—she told me this—when this big touring car stopped and one of the guys offered her a lift. Sure, she got in, the little fool, and these guys started playing around."

"Know the guys?"

Cardigan growled. "Two of Cavallo's guns or I don't know anything. Her description of one tallies with Bert Geer, that walking fashion-plate. You remember two years ago they nabbed Geer on suspicion for that girl out in St. Louis they found strangled near Grand Gardens. But he got out of it. The other guy sounds like that rat 'Monkey' Burns. I took the number of the touring car. I looked up the records downstairs and found the plates had been stolen from a sedan two weeks ago. If they're Geer and Burns, it means that Cavallo's in the pot, too, because they're the wop's right-hand guns. If we make them take the rap, they'll draw in Cavallo, and just as sure as you're born Diorio and Pozzo and our estimable State's Attorney Mulroy'll get in the tangle, and there'll be hell to pay all around. But I'm going through with this, Steve, and the state's attorney's office be damned! Joe was my buddy, closer to me than a brother—my sister's husband! God—can you picture Marion!"

MacBride was tight-lipped, a little pale, terribly grim. The ultimate had come. Would they tie the Department's hands now?

"Did you let Clark get a lawyer?" he asked.

"No—cripes, no!"

"Then get him up here. Where's the girl?"

"Downstairs, still bawling. I sent a cop out to get her a dress or something. I phoned her old man and he's driving in to get her."

"All right. Leave her there. But get Clark."

Cardigan went out and MacBride settled back, heaved a vast sigh, crammed fresh tobacco into his pipe. When, a few moments later, the door opened, he was puffing serenely, though deep in his heart there was a great numbness.

Clark came in, aided by a shove in the rear from Cardigan. The detective closed the door, grabbed Clark by the shoulder and slammed him not too gently into a chair.

"Say, go easy there, guy!" whined Clark, a charred clinker of a runt, with a face of seeming innocence, like a mongrel dog.

"Close your jaw!" snapped Cardigan.

Clark spread his hands toward MacBride. "Tell this guy to leave me alone, Captain. He's been treatin' me hard. First off he beans me with his gat and since then he's been chuckin' me around like I was a rag. I got my rights. I'm a citizen. You can't go cloutin' citizens. I got my—"

"Soft pedal," said MacBride heavily. "So your name's Clark, eh? How'd you come to be driving that car?"

"I was drivin' it, that's all. I'm all right. I

don't know nothin'. I was just drivin' it. You can't make a slop-rag outta me."

"Shut up," cut in MacBride.

"All right, I'll shut up. That's what I'm gonna do. You gotta let me get a lawyer. I got rights. Them's a citizen's rights."

"Listen to the bum!" chuckled Cardigan.

"There, see!" chirped Clark. "He's still insultin' me. He's just a big wise guy, he is. I got my rights. I'll see you get yours, fella. I was drivin' a car. All right, I was drivin' it. I know you guys. I ain't gotta talk."

"You're going to talk, Clark," said MacBride ominously. "And none of this cheap chatter, either. Talk that counts—see?"

"I ain't. No, I ain't. I want a lawyer. Gimme that phone."

He scrambled out of the chair, clawed for the telephone. Cardigan grabbed him by the nape of the neck, hurled him back so hard that Clark hit the chair aslant and, knocking it over, sprawled with it to the floor. He crouched, cringing, blubbering.

"You leave me alone, you! What the hell you think you're doin'? You leave me—"

"Get up—get up," gritted Cardigan. "That's only a smell compared with what's coming if you don't come clean. Get up, you dirty little rat!" He reached down, caught Clark, heaved him up and banged him down into another chair.

Clark's teeth chattered. His hands fidgeted, one with the other. His mouth worked, gasping for breath. His eyes almost popped from his head.

"Now," came MacBride's low voice, "who were the two guys that got away?"

"You can't make me talk now. You can't!" Clark gripped the sides of his chair, the stringy cords on his neck bulged. "I ain't talkin'—not me. I want a lawyer—that's what. Them's my rights, gettin' a lawyer. There!" He stuck out his chin defiantly.

MacBride turned in his chair and looked at Cardigan. Cardigan nodded, his fingers opening and closing.

"Take him into the sweat room, Jack," said MacBride. "Sweat him."

Clark stiffened in his chair, and sucked in his nether lip with a sharp intake of breath. He writhed.

"You can't do that, you can't!" he screamed. "I got my rights. You can't beat up a citizen."

"Citizen, are you?" chuckled Cardigan. "You're a bum, Clark. You were driving a car with somebody else's plates. You tried to get away with the other two birds but you weren't fast enough. My buddy was killed, see? Now you'll talk. I'll sweat it out of you, Clark, so help me!"

"You won't! I ain't gonna talk. Gawd almighty, I want a lawyer! You can't stop me from gettin' one!"

"You're stopped, Clark," bit off Cardigan. "Get up and come on along with me."

Cardigan reached for him. Clark squirmed in his chair, lashed out with his feet. One foot caught Cardigan in the stomach and he doubled momentarily, grimacing but silent. MacBride was out of his seat in a flash, and Clark was jerked to his feet so fast that he lost his breath. He was wild-eyed, straining at the arms that held him, his lips quivering, groans and grunts issuing from his throat.

"You ain't gonna beat me—you ain't! You'll see! I won't talk! I got my rights. I—I—"

"I'll take him, Steve," said Cardigan.

MacBride stepped back and Clark struggled frantically in Cardigan's grasp as the latter worked him toward the door.

The telephone bell jangled.

"Wait," said MacBride.

Cardigan paused at the door.

MacBride picked up the phone, muttered something, listened. Then, "What's that?" His hands knotted around the instrument, his eyes narrowed, his mouth hardened. "Are you sure of that?" He groaned deep in his throat, rocked on his feet. Then, bitterly, "All right!"

He slammed the receiver into the hook and banged the instrument down upon the desk violently. He turned to face Cardigan.

"It's no use, Jack. A runner for that lousy firm of Cohen, Fraser and Cohen, is downstairs, which means this bum slides out of our hands."

Cardigan's face darkened. "How'd they know we had this bird so soon?"

"That's their business. They work on a big retainer from the head of the gang Clark belongs to."

There was a knock at the door, and a sergeant and a patrolman came in. The sergeant showed MacBride a writ, and the patrolman marched Clark out of the office. Then the sergeant left, and MacBride and Cardigan were alone.

"Wires being pulled again," muttered Cardigan. "This guy will never come to trial."

"Of course not," nodded MacBride grimly.

"What a fine state of affairs! We nab a guy, and have every chance to make him come across, and then he's taken out of our hands. What's the use of a Police Department, anyhow?"

"Clark is one of Cavallo's boys. No doubt about it. And we can't do a thing—just sit and curse the whole thing. It's tough to be on the Force eighteen years—and have to stand for it."

"I know, Steve, you can't move. Your wife and kid to think of. But there's one way to get back at these wops, and the only way. They killed Joe, and they've got to pay for it! I'm going to make 'em pay—pound for pound! By God, I am, and the Department and the State's Attorney and everybody else be damned!"

"Jack, you can't—alone. You're a dick and—"

"I'm no longer a dick. I'm single and free and my resignation goes in now! I'm going to fight Cavallo, Steve, at his own game!"

"What do you mean?"

"Just what I said. I'm resigning from the Department. I'm going on my own and wipe out Cavallo and every one of his dirty gunmen! Richmond City is going to see one of the biggest gang wars in its history! When they killed Joe Hanley, they killed the wrong man, for my part! I'm going to fall on 'em like a ton of brick!"

"Jack, you can't do it!"

"Watch me!" chuckled Cardigan, his eyes glittering.

III

Men said Jack Cardigan was reckless and case-hardened—men meaning cops and reporters and Richmond City's generous sprinkling of gunmen. Something might be added; he was ruthless. As a detective, he'd been hated and feared by more crooks than perhaps any other man in the Department—inspectors, captain, lieutenants and all the rest included. Because he was hard—tough—rough on rats; rats being one of his favorite nicknames applied to a species of human being that shoots in the dark and aims for the back.

For three years Joe Hanley had been his partner, in the Department. In life, they'd been partners for years—and the bond of friendship had been welded firmly and topped off with the marriage of Cardigan's sister Marion to Joe. It was a far, long cry from that happy, flowered day to the day when Marion and Cardigan rode home from the cemetery, after the burial of Joe. Cardigan held his sister in his arms on the slow journey. There was nothing he could say to comfort her. Pity, condolence, make empty, meaningless words on such a tragic day. So he held her in his arms and let her sob.

His own face was a mask, grim and carven, the eyes dark and close-lidded. Home, he put her into the hands of their mother. No one spoke. Glances, gestures, conveyed far more. For a long while he sat alone, motionless and thoughtful. The funeral was over, but the dread pall of it still lingered. Even the house seemed to take on a personality of mourning—quiet and hollow and reverent.

A week later Cardigan sat in a speakeasy on the outer circle of Richmond City's theatrical district. He was sipping a dry Martini when Kennedy of the *Free Press* drifted in and joined him.

"What's the idea of shaking your job, Cardigan?"

"What's that to you?"

"Or were you *told* to resign?"

"Maybe."

Kennedy chuckled. "Sounds more like it. What you get for bringing in Clark. Lord, that was a joke! His lawyer was a sharp egg. Clark played the dope all through. Bet his lawyer spent nights drilling him how to act. Clark was just a hired chauffeur. How did he know the plates were stolen? He was hired a week before the mess out on Webster Road to drive a car. They gave him a car to drive. The whole thing was a joke, and the presenting attorney gave the defense every possible opening. What are you doing now?"

"Nothing. Taking life easy."

"Don't make me laugh!"

"Well, have it your way."

"Listen, Cardigan," said Kennedy. "You know a lot. The *Free Press* would sell its shirt to get some straight dope from you. That's no boloney. I mean it. I've got the whole thing figured out, but what we need is a story where we can omit the 'alleged' crap. Man, you can clean up!"

"Yeah?" Cardigan laughed softly. "Be yourself, Kennedy. Run along. You're wasting time on me."

"I don't know about that."

"Then learn."

Kennedy had a highball and went on his way. Alone, Cardigan took another drink, and looked at his watch. It was half-past eight at night. He looked across at the telephone on the wall. He drained his glass and lit a cigarette.

The telephone rang. He got up and beat the owner to it. "This is for me," he said, and took off the receiver. "You, Pete? . . . O.K. Be right over."

He hung up, paid for his drinks and shrugged into his dark overcoat. Outside, it was damp and cold, and automobiles hissed by over slushy pavements.

Cardigan did not walk toward the bright

glow that marked the beginning of the theatrical district. He bored deeper into the heart of Jockey Street. Where it was dirtiest and darkest, he swung in toward a short flight of broken stone steps, reached a large, ancient door, groped for a bell-button and pressed it. It was opened a moment later by a huge, beetle-browed negro.

"Pete Fink," said Cardigan. "He expects me."

"Who yuh are?" asked the negro.

"None of your damned business."

"I'll get Fink," said the negro and slammed the door in Cardigan's face.

"Takes no chances," muttered Cardigan. "Well, that's good."

Fink opened the door this time, while the negro hovered behind him, his face like shining ebony under the single gas-jet.

"Take a good look, big boy," Cardigan said, as he passed in.

And the negro said, "Got yuh, boss."

Fink led the way up a flight of crooked stairs that creaked under their footfalls. They reached the upper landing. Cardigan placed six doors in a row. One of these Fink opened, and they entered a large, square room, furnished cheaply with odd bits of furniture, no two pieces the same in make or design.

Cardigan stood with his hands in his coat pockets, idly running his eyes about the room.

Fink was leaning against the door he had closed. He was a big, rangy man, with one of his shoulders higher than the other. His nose was a twisted knot; a tawny mustache sagged over his mouth. He had a jaw like a snowplow, and eyes like ice—cold and steady and enigmatic. His hands were big and red and bony. He wore brown corduroy trousers, a blue flannel shirt, a wide belt with an enormous brass buckle. He looked like a tough egg. He wasn't a soft one.

Cardigan sighed and poured himself a drink. He downed it neat, rasped his throat, and looked at the empty glass.

"Good stuff, Pete."

"Cavallo sells the same."

They faced each other. Their eyes met and held and bored one into the other. At last Fink grinned and rocked away from the door, sat down at the table and lit a cigarette. Cardigan sat down opposite him, opened his overcoat and helped himself to one of Fink's cigarettes.

"Well, Pete? . . ."

Fink leaned forward, elbows resting on the table, his butt jutting from one corner of his mouth and an eye squinted against the smoke that curled upward.

"Six," he said. "I got six."

"Who are they?"

"Chip Slade, Gats Gilman, Luke Kern, Bennie Levy, Chuck Ward and Bat Johnson. All good guns."

"Yeah, I know. How do they feel about it?"

"Cripes, they're ripe!"

"They want to know who's behind you?"

"I said a big guy—somebody big, who's in the know."

Cardigan chuckled. "Remember, Pete, it stays that way. I'm—it sounds like a joke—the mystery man in this. The master mind!" He chuckled again, amusedly, then grew serious. "To come out in the open would be to shoot the whole works. I'm too well known as a gumshoe. But I'll manage this, Pete, and supply the first funds. I've got a measly two thousand saved up, but it's a starter. And I'm out to flop on the bums that got Hanley, my buddy. If everybody holds up his end, you'll all make money and Cavallo and his crowd will get washed out."

"You say the word, Jack. I'm takin' orders from you. The rest take orders from me and no questions asked."

"Good. I'll give you five hundred bucks to buy a second-hand car. Get a big touring. To hell with the looks of it; buy it for the motor—for speed. Buy half-a-dozen high-powered rifles and plenty of ammunition. Pick up some grenades if you can. How about a storehouse?"

"Got one picked—an old farmhouse out on Farmingville Turnpike."

"Sounds good. Rent it for a month."

"It's way out in the sticks," added Fink. "Off the main pike, way in on a lane, and no other house inside of a quarter mile. I can get it for fifty bucks a month."

"Get it. We've got to watch out for tapped wires, though. Here, I'm staying at the Adler House. You know that number. If things get hot and you've got to talk a lot, just call me up and say, 'I've got something to tell you.' I'll hang up and run down to the drug-store on the corner. There's a booth there and I'll get you the number. We'll choose booths all over the city where we can make calls, and we'll get the numbers."

"O.K."

"How about the dinge downstairs?"

"He owns a dump. Sees a lot and says nothin'."

Cardigan ground out his cigarette. "Then it's all set. Get me straight, Fink. Leave the cops alone. Tell your boys that. We're after Cavallo and his rats—not the cops. If the cops show up, run. I've got a grudge against that wop and the crowd he runs with. I'm playing my grudge to a showdown. If I make some jack out of it, all right. But I'm after rats first—not jack. You and your guns can clean up sweet in this racket, if you use your head and move how I tell you."

"I got you, Jack," nodded Fink.

"All right. Let me know when you're all set and I'll map out our first move. Get the rifles, ammunition, grenades. Get a fast car and see that the tires are good." He drew a wad of bills from his pocket. "There's a thousand as a starter."

Fink shoved the money into his pocket and poured another brace of drinks.

"You got guts, Jack," he said, "to chuck the Department—for this."

"Guts, my eye!" clipped Cardigan. "I've got a grudge, Pete, a whale of a grudge—against the dirty, rotten bums that killed the best friend I ever had." He raised his glass. "Down the hatch."

On that they drank.

IV

Two days later Cardigan was sitting in his room at the Adler House, when the telephone rang. It was the desk, and he said, "Send him up." Then he settled back again in his over-stuffed easy-chair. It was ten in the morning and he was still in pajamas and bathrobe. On a settee beside him was a detailed map of Richmond City and its suburbs. Here and there he had marked x's, or made penciled notations.

There was a knock on the door and he called, "Come in, Steve."

MacBride came in, closed the door and stood there stroking his chin and regarding Cardigan seriously.

"Sit down," said Cardigan. "Take the load off your feet, Steve. You'll find cigars in the box on the table. How's tricks?"

MacBride took a cigar and eased himself down on a divan. "My day off and I thought I'd drop in and see you."

"Is that all you came for, Steve?"

MacBride lit up and took a couple of puffs before replying. "Not exactly, Jack."

"Spill it."

"Oh, it's not much. Only I was worrying. You still thinking of butting in on Cavallo's racket?"

"What a question! Why'd you suppose I left the Department?"

"M-m-m," droned MacBride. "I wish you hadn't, Jack. You were the best man I had, and, Jack, old boy, you can't buck that crowd. It's madness. You'll get in trouble, and if you make a bad step, you'll get the Department on your neck. You haven't got politics behind you. You'd be out of luck. That's straight. How do you think I'd feel if it came to the point where you faced me as a prisoner?"

"I've been thinking about that, Steve," admitted Cardigan. "It's the one thing I'd hate."

"No more than I would." MacBride licked a loose wrapper back into place on his cigar. "Kennedy's been in to see me again. That guy's so nosey and so clever it hurts. Look out for him. *He's* got an idea you're up to something."

"I know. That bird's so sharp he's going to cut himself some day."

"Made any moves yet—I mean, you?"

"Some—getting things ready."

"What's up your sleeve anyway?"

"Steve—" Cardigan paused the flex his lips. "Steve, we've been mighty good friends. We are yet. But I can't tell you. I'm playing a game that can't have any air-holes. You understand?"

MacBride nodded. "I guess so. But I'm worrying, Jack. I've got a hunch you're going to get in wrong and somebody's going to nail you."

"Don't worry. Forget it. If I pull a bone I'll take the consequence. But I'm not counting on pulling a bone. This town is going to shake. Somebody's going to get hurt, and, Steve, before long some pretty high departmental offices are liable to be vacated so damned fast—"

"I'd go easy, Jack."

"I am—feeling my way."

MacBride shrugged and got up. They shook, and the captain went out, a little mournfully and reluctantly.

Ten minutes later the phone rang and Fink asked, "How soon can you come out?"

"Five minutes."

"I'll pick you up at Main and Anderson in the car."

Cardigan hung up and snapped into his clothes. Five minutes later he shot down in the elevator, strode through the lobby and out on to Main Street. Two blocks south was Anderson. He saw the big touring car idling along—the one that Fink had bought for five-fifty; five years old, but it could do seventy-five an hour. The curtains were on, all of them.

The door opened and he hopped in, settled down beside Fink. They pounded down Main Street, swung into a side street to avoid a traffic stop, and cut north until they struck Farmingville Turnpike.

Then Cardigan said, "Well?"

"I got the rifles and ammunition and some grenades," said Fink. "I want to show you the farmhouse. The boys are ripe to go, soon as you say the word."

It took them half an hour to reach the ramshackle farmhouse. It was quite some distance from the hub of the city. It stood well off the main highway, hidden behind an arm of woods and reached by a narrow lane where the snow still lay. Fink pulled up into the yard and they got out. He had keys and opened the kitchen door. They entered and Cardigan looked it over. Two big rooms and a kitchen downstairs. Three bed-rooms upstairs. Dust, the dust of long neglect, covered the floor. The windows were small and set with many little squares of glass. The place was old, years old. The walls were lined with brick, a relic of days when houses were built to last for more than one generation.

"Just the thing," nodded Cardigan. "Maybe we'll use it tonight."

"Huh?"

"Tonight. Cavallo keeps a lot of his booze on North Street. Know the old milk stables?"

"Yeah."

"That's the place. There are three in a row, all joined together. The one in the middle is our meat. It has sliding doors, and there's always a reserve truck inside."

"How do you know all this, Jack?"

"What do you suppose the Department does, sleep all the time?"

"Oh. . . . I gotcha. Yeah, sure."

"Get your map out."

Fink dived into his pocket, came out with a folder that opened to large dimensions. Cardigan also had his out.

"I've figured out the route you're to take," he said. "Mark these down now, so there'll be no slip up. The truck is a type governed to do thirty-five per and no more. Four speeds ahead. All right." And he proceeded to give Fink precise directions to follow, street by street to Black Hill Road which leads into Farmingville Turnpike. "Got the route all marked?" he asked, as he finished.

"Yeah, all marked."

"Who'll drive the truck?"

"Bat Johnson and—"

"No—Bat's enough. The rest of you drift along ahead in the touring car and lead the way. One man on a truck 'll cause no suspicion. More might. And get this. Maple Road runs parallel with North Street—behind the stables. You park on Maple Road and watch across the lots till you see three blinks from a flashlight. That will mean to come on and take things over. When Bat takes the truck out you boys beat it back across the lots, into the car and fall in ahead of the truck on Avenue C."

"Who's goin' to blink the lights?"

"I am."

"Huh?" Fink seemed incredulous.

"That's what I said. I'm going ahead to see if the road's clear. I'll take care of the watchman. If there's more there—the gang, I mean—we'll give up for the night. And mind this, if you don't see any flashes by ten o'clock, breeze. Be on Maple Road at exactly nine fifty, no sooner or later. If everything turns out all right, if you get the booze out to the farmhouse and away safe, call me up and just say, 'Jake'; that's all. And about the truck. Drive it back and abandon it on Black Hill Road."

"But, hell, Jack, why can't me and the boys bust in the stables and crash the place proper?"

"You would say that, Pete. That's just the way to ball up the whole works. We're not out to butcher our way if we can help it. That's the trouble with you guys. You don't use your head. That's the main reason why Cavallo and his rats are going to blow up. They're too damned free with their gats."

"Um—I guess you're right there, Jack."

"All right, then. Come on, let's breeze. Drive me to the bus line and drop me off."

An hour later Cardigan was eating lunch at his favorite haunt in Jockey Street, with a bottle of Sauterne on the side. It was one of fifteen restaurants circulated throughout the city and owned by a syndicate of brokers that paid a fat sum monthly to the authorities for the privilege. Four were in the financial district, six in the theatrical district, the rest scattered. More would open for business in time. You didn't need a card. The places were wide, wide open. Where the syndicate got the liquor, was nobody's business.

The Jockey Street place was managed by an ex-saloon keeper named Maloney. Cardigan had been a frequent visitor there since his resignation from the force, and they got on well. This day he called Maloney over and asked him to sit down.

He asked, "Between you and me, what does your outfit pay for good Scotch?"

"That's our business, buddy, if you know what I mean."

"I know what you mean. Come on, I'm *talking* business."

"You in the game?"

"I know somebody who is."

Maloney thought hard. "Sixty-five bucks a case."

Cardigan nodded. "You can get it for fifty-five. Work the deal with your boss and you'll get a rake-off of five bucks on the case."

"Your friend must be hard up."

"He's just starting in business."

"Oh. We'll have to sample it first."

"Sure. But are you on?"

"It sounds good. How—how many cases?"

"Maybe two hundred."

"Cripes!"

"Think it over. Speak to your boss. I'll see you again in a day or so."

He left ten minutes later, pretty certain that he had paved the way nicely. To kill the afternoon, he dropped in at a vaudeville theatre, and ate dinner at the hotel. Later he sat in his room smoking a cigar and going over his plan step by step, searching for a loop-hole. He couldn't see any. Tonight would start the ball rolling. His vengeance would be under way. They'd murdered Joe Hanley. Now they'd pay—pound for pound. It was law of his own making, a hard, raw law—fighting rats on their own ground with their own tactics. Yet he had one advantage; a reasoning, calculating mind, thanks to his service in the Department; strategy first, guns—if it should come to that means—later.

He had a hard crew under him. Pete Fink, a product of the bootleg age—one time in the prize ring, once a sailor. Cardigan knew that he was a tough customer, and he also knew that he could rely on him. The other guns; he relied on Fink to take care of them. He'd arrested Bat Johnson only a year ago for petty larceny. Chip Slade had once felt the rap of his blackjack.

"Hell," he mused, "if they only knew who was behind Fink!"

V

Eight-thirty came around. Cardigan put on his overcoat and shoved an automatic into his pocket. He took his time. He wandered leisurely out of the hotel, walked a couple of blocks down Main Street and boarded a bus bound for the suburbs. Half an hour later he got off, lit a cigarette and strolled north. He was a little ahead of time, so he went on at ease.

He reached Maple Road, and continued south. Houses were scattered, and fields intervened. Then, squatting dimly in the murk beyond a field of tall grass, the old milk stables, Cardigan paused behind an ancient oak tree and looked at the illuminated dial of his watch. It was nine-thirty-five. His hand slid into his pocket and gripped the butt of his automatic.

He slipped away from the tree, hunched over and weaved his way through tall weeds. His feet slushed through snow. At intervals he paused briefly, to listen. Then he went on, bit by bit, until he reached the old picket fence behind the stables. In this he found a gap and muscled through, and squatted still for a long moment.

From his coat he drew a dark handkerchief and fastened it about his face, just below his eyes. His hat brim he pulled lower.

There was a faint yellow glow shining from a window, and toward this Cardigan crept. A shade had been drawn down to within an inch or two of the bottom of the window. Smoke was drifting from a tin stove chimney. In a moment Cardigan was crouched by the window.

He saw two men sitting in chairs by a little stove. On the stove a kettle was spouting steam. A lantern stood on an empty box nearby. One of the men was asleep. The other was half-heartedly reading a newspaper; Cardigan recognized him, a huge brute of a man called "Dutch" Weber, with a record. The other he placed as Jakie Hart, sometimes called the Creole Kid, a one-time New Orleans wharf rat. A dirty pair, he mused.

Minutes were flying, and so much depended on chance. Cardigan bent down and felt around on the snow. He found a two-foot length of board, and hefted it in his left hand. His right hand still gripped the automatic. Again looking in, he raised the board, set his jaw and crashed the window. The shade snapped up. The man with the paper spun in his chair, clawed at his gun.

But Cardigan had him covered, his head and shoulders thrust through the window.

"Drop that gat, Dutch!" he barked. "You too, Jakie—drop it! Fast, you guys, or you'll get lead in your pants!"

The Creole Kid blinked bleary eyes. Dutch Weber cursed under his breath, his huge face flushing, murder in his gimlet eyes, his big hands writhing. But he dropped his gun, and the Creole Kid imitated him a moment later.

"Stand up—both of you," went on Cardigan. "Face the wall! Move out of turn and God help you!"

"You lousy bum!" snarled Weber.

"Can that crap, buddy! About face!" bit off Cardigan.

Sullenly they faced the wall, hands raised.

A moment later Cardigan was in the room. He yanked down the shade, picked up the men's discarded guns, thrust them into his pocket. And from his pocket he drew two pairs of manacles.

"Back up six paces, Dutch! Stay where you are, Jakie! Never mind looking, Dutch—just back up. Now put your hands behind your back. Don't get funny, either." In a flash he had the manacles on Weber. "Get over against the wall again. Move!" He jabbed the muzzle of his gun in Weber's back. "Now you, Jakie—back up!"

In a moment he had the other pair of bracelets on the Creole Kid, and forced him back against the wall. Then he took a small bottle of chloroform from his pocket and saturated a handkerchief.

"Back up again, Jakie! As you are, Dutch!"

He clamped his arm around the Creole Kid's neck, forced the handkerchief against his nostrils and into his mouth, held it there, while he still warned Weber to stay where he was. Presently the Creole Kid went limp, relaxed, and Cardigan let him fall to the floor, unconscious.

Then he soaked another handkerchief, approached Weber and planted his gun in the big man's ribs.

"Not a stir, big boy!"

His left hand shot out, smacked the saturated handkerchief against Weber's mouth. The big man struggled, but Cardigan reminded him of the gun.

"Damn your soul!" snarled Weber in muffled tones.

"Shut your trap!"

In a short time Weber joined the Creole Kid on the floor, muttering vaguely, his hands twitching slower and slower. Cardigan pocketed his gun, produced a coil of thin, strong wire and bound their ankles. Then he ripped away strips of their shirts and bound the handkerchiefs securely in their mouths. From Weber's pockets he took a ring of keys.

With his flashlight he started a quick, systematic search of the stables. The large, covered truck was in the main stable. Its tank registered seven gallons of gasoline. Under tarpaulins he saw case upon case of liquor—between two and three hundred. He also saw ten barrels of wine. These he tipped over and sprung the spigots, and the wine gurgled and flowed on the dirt floor.

Chuckling, he hurried into the back room, blew out the lantern and pulled up the shade on the window. He raised his flashlight and blinked it three times. Then he opened the back door, sped into the main stable and unlocked the big sliding doors, but did not open them.

He turned, jumped to a ladder and climbed up to a small loft, drew the ladder up after him. Then he lay flat on his stomach in the pitch gloom, waited and listened. After a few moments he heard a door creak, and then footsteps—saw the reflection of a flashlight in the back room.

"Huh," muttered a voice, "the Chief sure paved the way. Lookit the way them two babies is tied up!"

"Shut up, Bat. Come on, gang." That was Fink.

The beam of light jumped into the stable. Figures loomed in. The flash settled on the draining barrels. Someone chuckled.

"What he can't take he busts," said a voice. "This Chief knows his termaters, what I mean!"

The beam of light swept around the stable and found the stacked cases of liquor.

"*Ba-by!*" exclaimed someone, softly.

"Cut the gab!" hissed Fink. "Step to it! There's the truck! Come on, guys!"

Cardigan watched them spread out. They hauled off the tarpaulins. Two men jumped into the truck. The others leaped to the cases of liquor. They worked swiftly and for the most part silently, passing the cases to the pair in the truck, who stacked them rapidly.

One muttered. "Y' know, first off I thought this Chief was just a guy wit' brains an' no guts.

I mean, like he wanted us to do his dirty work—"

"Pipe down, Gats!" snapped Fink. "Y' see he's got guts, don't you now?"

"Sure. I'm all for him."

"You better be," muttered Fink. "Any one o' you guys that thinks he's ain't 's got a lot to learn."

"Where's he now?"

"None o' your business!" said Fink. "Prob'ly ridin' home in a bus or somethin'. Nemmine the talk. Step on it."

Cardigan smiled in the darkness. Yes, he could trust Fink; no doubt of it, now. Not even Fink knew he was up there in the loft, a silent watcher.

The minutes dragged by. Case after case went into the truck. The pile on the floor grew smaller and smaller. The men worked rapidly, and now silently. Cardigan looked at his watch. Half-past ten. He was stiff from holding his tense position.

"Cripes, what a load!" a voice said hoarsely.

"How many more?"

"Ten."

"That," said Fink, "'ll make two-hundred-and-forty-two."

"Ba-by!"

Cardigan saw the last case go in. Then Fink and two others spread tarpaulins over the rear and lashed them to the sides.

"All right, Bat," he said.

Bat Johnson climbed up into the seat, juggled the transmission lever. Another man grabbed the crank, heaved on it. The motor spat, barked, and then pounded regularly. Two men jumped to the doors, slid them back. They looked out, came back in and one said, "Clear! Let her go!"

Bat shoved into gear and the big truck rumbled out. The doors were pulled shut. The men bunched together and at a word from Fink slipped out through the back door.

Three minutes later Cardigan dropped from the loft. He strode into the back room, snapped on his flash, played its beam on the Creole Kid and Dutch Weber, still unconscious. Then he dropped their keys and guns beside them, snapped off his flash and made for the door.

With a brittle little chuckle he went out, crossed the fields and struck Maple Road. He sought the bus line by a different route than the one by which he had reached the stables. At a quarter to twelve he entered his room, took off his coat and dropped into an easy-chair. He lit a cigar and relaxed, a little weary after the strenuous night.

But deep within him there was a great calm. He thought of Joe, and of his widowed sister. He thought, too, of other cops who had met death in strange back-alleys at the hands of rats who always shot from the rear. What protection was a shield nowadays? Protection! He grimaced. More a target! But mainly it was Joe he thought of—mild-mannered, easy-going Joe. Joe with two bullets in him, out on Webster Road. . . .

At half-past one the telephone rang. He picked it up.

"Jake," said Fink.

"Jake," said Cardigan, and hung up.

VI

It did not get into the papers. Things like this don't. But the underworld rumbled ominously, and the echoes seeped into the Department, but got no further. The law-abiding element of Richmond City went about its daily tasks and pleasures as usual, all ignorant of the fact that in the world of shadows, wolves were growing and baring hungry fangs.

The very next afternoon MacBride dropped in to see Cardigan.

"Well, Jack," he said.

And Cardigan said, "Well?"

"M-m-m, you did it."

"You mean Cavallo?"

MacBride nodded.

Cardigan chuckled.

"We got a whiff of it this morning," went on MacBride. "Cavallo must have gone to his brother-in-law Diorio and I guess Diorio went to his friend Alderman Pozzo and then Pozzo had a chat with State's Attorney Mulroy. Jack, for God's sake, watch your step!"

"I am. Why, do they suspect?"

"No, but—" MacBride clenched his fists and gritted his teeth. "I shouldn't be telling you this, Jack. But—we're—old friends, and I'd like to see that dago wiped out. And I guess—if I was younger and single—and a buddy of mine—like Joe was to you—was bumped off, I'd do the same. Maybe I wouldn't. Maybe I wouldn't have the guts. But, Jack, I've got to tell you, for old times' sake. McGinley and Kline, of the State's Attorney's office, have been detailed to get the guys who flopped on Cavallo's parade!"

"Oh, yes?"

"Yes. For my sake, Jack, shake this racket. You can't beat it. You see what you've got against you?"

Cardigan nodded. "I know, Steve. But I've started, and I'm not going to let the thing just hang in the air. The more I think of Cavallo and Bert Geer and Monkey Burns and all that crowd, the more I want to blow up their racket. Imagine Pozzo for Alderman—a guy that can hardly speak English and calls himself a one hundred per cent American! Cavallo's bulwark! Mulroy having to take these wops' part because they put him in office, and getting a rake-off from their proceeds."

"I know, Jack, I know. But—"

"No, sir, Steve. I'm playing this to a showdown, and somebody's going to get hurt in the wind-up."

"It might be you, Jack."

"Here's hoping it won't."

"No one gets anywhere today trying to be a martyr."

Cardigan laughed shortly. "Martyr! You think *I'm* taking the godly role of a martyr? Hell, no! I'm just an ordinary guy who's sore as a boil. I'm a guy whose buddy got a dirty break, and I'm starting to go after these lads the only way they can be reached."

MacBride shrugged and remained silent. Then he got up, shook Cardigan's hand and went out.

A little later the phone rang and Fink said, "I got somethin' to tell you."

"All right," replied Cardigan briskly.

A few minutes later he walked into a drugstore on the corner, stepped into the booth and closed the door. A minute, and the bell rang.

"O.K., Pete," he said.

Fink explained. "Meet me in the dump on Jockey Street in half an hour. I've got a sample, and it's sure powerful stuff. I'll be waitin' outside the door there. Everything is jake, and the boys are feelin' good but wonderin' about their divvy."

"Be over," said Cardigan.

When, later, he strolled down Jockey Street, he saw Fink cross the street, pause on the steps of their rendezvous, look his way, and then pass inside. Cardigan swung up the steps and the door opened. He went in and Fink led the way up to the latter's room. The big man drew a pink flask from his pocket.

"They're all in pints," he explained. "Try it."

Cardigan took a pull on the bottle and let the liquor burn in. "Good," he nodded. "The best I've tasted."

Fink grinned. "If that stuff ain't come across the pond I don't know Scotch. It's the first time I ain't drunk dish water in a long time. D' you figger Cavallo's sore?"

"Sore!" echoed Cardigan, and laughed on it.

"Yeah," droned Fink, "I guess he'd lookin' to kill. Um. Now the stuff's out there in the farmhouse, what?"

"I'll know by tonight. Keep your shirt on."

"I ain't worryin'. The gang. They're achin' to see some jack and have a good time."

"You tell 'em to watch their step, Pete. It's hard lines for any guy pulls a bone. We're not through yet. It would be just like Chip Slade, for instance, to doll up in new duds, pick up a broad, get tight to the eyes and blabber. We've got to watch out for that, Pete."

"Yeah, I know, Jack. I been keepin' my eye on Chip."

"I'll see you here tonight, Pete."

Cardigan went out with the pint flask on his hip and dropped in to see Maloney in the speakeasy. He talked business to him, and let him take a drink from the bottle.

"Boy!" whistled Maloney. "That's *Scotch*, what I mean!"

"What's the news?"

"The boss says all right, if he likes the stuff. Fifty-five a case."

"I can get two-hundred-and-forty cases. He can have the lot or none, and he's got to act fast. This is no young stuff—"

"Hell, I know! Ain't I just tasted it? And me—I get my share, when?"

"When your boss pays, you get twelve-hundred bucks, and then forget about everything. There are no names necessary."

"Of course not," nodded Maloney. "How do you get the money?"

"Your boss'll send it to John D. Brown, at a post office box. You'll get the box number later. Send it in a plain package, with no return address. Thirteen thousand and two hundred dollars in one hundred dollar bills."

"Insure it?"

"Lord no! Just first class—that's the safest way to send stuff through the mails. It beats registered mail four ways from the jack. I never lost a first class letter, but I've lost 'em registered and I've lost insured packages. A man will pick up the letter at the post office." He thought for a moment. "Get the dope from your boss, and let's know where the booze goes."

"I ought to get my share first," demurred Maloney.

"I know. You think I'll skip. You'll get yours through the mail, too. That's the proposition. It's up to you."

"I'll take the chance." Maloney got up. "Come in at six."

Cardigan nodded and left. He took a box at a suburban post office under the name of John D.

Brown. When he met Maloney at six that night the ex-saloon keeper was flushed with elation. Everything was settled, and the liquor was to be delivered as soon as possible.

"That means tonight," put in Cardigan.

"The boss stores it at the Tumbledown Inn. Say the word and there'll be somebody there tonight to meet the truck."

"It'll be delivered sometime after midnight."

With that Cardigan went out and met Fink in the latter's hideout. He explained what had transpired, and Fink rubbed his hands in joyful anticipation.

"I know where I can get a truck, Jack. Leave it to me."

"I am," said Cardigan.

He explained in detail how the liquor should be transported, how Bat Johnson should drive the truck alone and the others ride in the touring car ahead. The Tumbledown Inn was on Farmingville Turnpike, four miles beyond the farmhouse where the liquor was stored at present.

"It's a cinch," said Fink.

"When it's all over, ring me up and say the O.K. word."

They parted, and Cardigan headed for the Adler House. He had proved a successful general on his first try. He believed he could repeat a second time, and then some more. He turned in at eight and set his alarm to wake him at one. He figured that he should get a report from Fink at about two.

When he got up at one a.m., he dressed, in the event of an emergency. He drank some hot black coffee from a thermos and ate some sandwiches which he had brought up before. Then he lounged on a divan with a cigar and watched the clock. The hands moved around the hour and passed two. They passed two-thirty and wheeled on toward three. At three, Cardigan sat up.

He looked grave, a bit tight-lipped. He stared at the telephone. It was black and silent. The hotel was silent as a tomb. Up from the street floated the sound of a lone trolley car rattling across a switch. He sat down, clasping his hands around one knee, tapping an impatient foot. Half-past three.

"Something's gone wrong," he muttered. He cracked fist into palm, cursed under his breath, bitterly.

Dawn came, and then the sun. And still no word from Pete Fink.

Cardigan put on his overcoat and went out. He bought a paper, thinking he might find some clue there, but he reasoned that if anything had happened in the early hours, the morning papers wouldn't have it yet. The next edition might. He ate breakfast in a dairy restaurant. Then, reasoning that he ought to be at his room in case Fink might call, he hurried back.

At nine Fink called. He said two words. "My room."

"Right," said Cardigan.

VII

Twenty minutes later he was striding down Jockey Street. The negro let him in and he climbed the rickety staircase. He knocked at Fink's door. There was a slow movement.

Then, "You, Jack?"

"Yes, Pete."

The door opened. Cardigan went in.

Fink was dropping back into a chair.

"Lock it," he muttered.

His face was haggard. His left arm was in a sling, and blotches of dry blood showed on the bandage.

"I thought so," said Cardigan.

"Yeah," nodded Fink, and forced a grin. "They got Bat."

Cardigan sat down. "Go on."

"They got Bat. It was all a accident. We delivered the booze and was on the way back. We took Prairie Boulevard. Bat wanted to bring back the truck. The tourin' car got a flat and we stopped to make a change. Bat went ahead slow all by his merry lonesome. We got the spare on, all right, and whooped it up to catch him. You know where Prairie Boulevard goes through them deep woods. It's pretty lonely there.

"Well, our headlights pick up Bat and he's stalled. But we see another car stopped in front of him, facing him. It looks phony, and we take it easy. We see some guys standin' around on the road, but they duck for the car. We stop our car and wait. We think maybe they're dicks, see. Then their car starts and roars towards us. It looks like they're goin' to crash us, but they cut around and slam by, scrapin' our mudguard. A lot of guns bust loose and I'm socked in the arm. Chip gets his cheek opened. Nobody else is hurt. Gats turns around and empties his rod at the back of it. I don't know who he hit, but the car kept goin'.

"I get out, holdin' my arm and Bennie tears off some of his shirt and sops up the blood. Chip is holdin' his cheek and cursin' a blue streak. Gats runs up to the truck and we go after him. Bat is layin' on the road, pretty still. Him and Gats were buddies, you know. You should hear Gats curse!

"Bat is dyin'. They'd busted his knob with a blackjack. He says he was ridin' along when this car stopped him. See, just by accident. Monkey Burns and Bert Geer and two others. They smell there was booze in the truck, and ask him what's he been doin'. He tells them where they can go. They wanter know who he's been runnin' booze for. He ain't talkin'. They sock him, but he don't chirp. That's Bat all over. More you sock him the worse stubborn he gets. Gawd, they batted hell outta him! Ugh! Then they see us. Bat croaks after he spiels us his story. Poor Bat. He was a good shuffer."

Cardigan stared at the floor for a long minute, his hands clenched.

Fink was saying, "I took the plates off the truck and disfiggered the engine number and the serial number with a couple o' shots. Then we drove to the farmhouse. The boys are there now. I got here alone, quick as I could. I could ha' sent one o' the boys to call you up, but I didn't want any o' 'em to know where you was."

"You're aces up in a pinch, Pete," said Cardigan, and he meant it.

"I did the best I could."

"I'll say you did. Did Monkey and his gang see you boys?"

"No. And Bat didn't tell 'em. But they know, like everybody else, that Bat was buddies with Gats, and they'll be huntin' Gats. And Gats has gone wild. He wants to go out gunnin' for them guys. He swears he'll do it. And Gats is the best damn gunman I know about."

"You've got to keep him under cover."

"Yeah. I got to get back to the farmhouse. Bandage this arm tight so I can put it in a sleeve. I can't go walkin' around too much with a sling. It'll hurt without it, but what the hell."

"Good man, Pete. Get out there, see how things are. I'll hang around the corner drugstore between two and three. Call me there from a booth and give me a line."

When he had bandaged Fink's arm, he patted the big man on the back and left him. Below, in the street, he ran into Kennedy, of the *Free Press*, leaning indolently against a lamp-post. He brought up short, his breath almost taken away.

"Hello, Cardigan," said the reporter in his tired way. "What's the attraction?"

"You trying to crack wise, Kennedy?"

"Who, me? No-o, not me, Cardigan. See this yet?" He handed Cardigan the latest edition of the *Free Press*.

RIVAL BOOTLEG GANGS CLASH

That was the headline. Something about an abandoned truck, empty, with license plates gone and engine number disfigured. Blood on the road. Empty cartridges. Nearby trees showing bullet marks. A farmer beyond the woods had heard the shooting about half-past one a.m.

No cops on the job. The farmer himself had come out to investigate and reported the abandoned truck. It looked like the beginning of a gang feud.

Cardigan looked up. "Well that's news, Kennedy."

"Is it?" Kennedy had a tantalizing way of smiling.

"I'm in a hurry," said Cardigan, and started off.

Kennedy fell into step beside him. "I'm not green, Cardigan. You ought to know that by this time. And I know that one of the gangs was Cavallo's. Now the other gang . . . Cardigan, be a sport."

"What do you mean?"

"Tell me about it."

"You're all wet, Kennedy."

"Oh, no I'm not. Listen, Cardigan. You're not pulling the wool over this baby's eyes. The Department knows who the guy was that was bumped off and then carried away by his buddies. They got the dope from Cavallo's friends—maybe Diorio to Pozzo to Mulroy. Then they tell the Department to get busy—just like that, and they're spreading for somebody. That riot squad's on pins and needles, waiting for another break. Now, it would take guts to head a gang to buck that outfit—you tell me, Cardigan."

Cardigan laughed. "Kennedy, you're funny. So long." He crossed the street and left Kennedy in perplexed indecision.

But he realized that Kennedy was one man he'd have to look out for. That news hound, in other words, knew his onions. He was nobody's fool.

After luncheon Cardigan went out to the suburban post office, opened his box and took out a solitary package. He thrust it into his pocket and returned to his hotel. There he opened it, and found thirteen thousand, two hundred dollars. Twelve hundred he put in a plain envelope and addressed it to Maloney. In each of five plain envelopes he placed a thousand dollars, for Pete Fink's boys. For Pete he placed aside two thousand. He lost no time in mailing Maloney's letter.

Later, he was at the booth in the corner drugstore to get Fink's prearranged call. Fink mentioned his room, but Cardigan objected, remembering Kennedy, and told Fink to pick him up at a street corner well out of the city. Then he hung up and took a bus out, got off at the street he had named, and waited for Fink. He did not have to wait long. The touring car came up, and Fink was driving with his one good arm. Cardigan got in and they rolled off.

"Gats," said Fink. "He slipped out on the boys. He's out gunnin' for the guys who got Bat Johnson."

"What!"

"Yup."

Cardigan saw his nicely made plans toppling to ruin. This was one of those things the best of tacticians cannot foresee. An accident. A bad break. Gats gone gun-mad because his buddy 'd been killed by the wops.

"We've got to get him," he said.

"Yeah, but where?"

Cardigan cursed the luck. Then he said, "Well, I've got the money. It's all here. A thousand each for the boys. Two thousand for you. Twelve hundred went to the go-between for the booze." He passed over the envelopes. "That'll make the boys feel better." After a moment he said, "The riot squad's ready for action."

"It won't take long, if we don't get Gats. He'll start the fireworks sure as hell."

"Drop me off when the next bus comes along. Look for Gats. Go to all the places you think he'd be. Ring me at the hotel and say 'Jake' if you get him. Then stay out at the farm—all of you— until this blows over."

A few minutes later he got out of the car, boarded a bus and went back to his hotel. He was very much on edge, and he mused that no matter how perfectly you lay a plan, something is liable to happen that will bring down the whole framework.

At four o'clock the telephone rang, and Fink said, "Jake."

"Jake," said Cardigan.

A great burden was automatically lifted from his mind. He even whistled as he got into his bath. He hummed while he shaved. Then he dressed, spent half an hour with a cigar and the evening paper, and at five-thirty put on his overcoat and went out. As he swung out of the hotel, he heard the scream of a siren. He looked up the street.

Three police cars were roaring down Main Street. Traffic scattered. People gathered on the curb. The three cars shot by the hotel doing fifty miles an hour. They were packed with policemen, and automatic rifles were clamped on the sides. The sirens snarled madly.

Cardigan's breath stuck in his throat. A chill danced up and down his spine. Then his jaw set and he crossed to a taxicab.

"Hit Farmingville Turnpike," he clipped, and jumped in.

He started to close the door, but something held it. He turned around. Kennedy was climbing in after him.

"Mind if I go?"

Cardigan sank into his seat, his fists clenched. But he managed to grin. "Sure. The old gumshoe instinct in me always follows a riot call. I'm anxious to see what this is all about."

"Yeah?" smiled Kennedy.

"Yeah. I'm in the dark, just like you."

Kennedy frowned after the manner of a man who wondered if after all he isn't wrong in what he'd been supposing.

VIII

Cardigan had a hard time masking his inner emotions. He said to the chauffeur, "Follow those police cars. It's all right. We're reporters."

Kennedy lit a cigarette. "You've got me guessing, Cardigan."

"Me? Same here, Kennedy. You've got me guessing, too."

"Have a butt."

"Thanks." It was casual, everything he said,

but inside of him there was turmoil. What was going on? What had happened to Fink and the boys? He'd formed a strange liking for Pete Fink. In his own way Pete had proved his fidelity, his worth.

The sirens went on screaming. People were still looking out of windows when the taxi shot past in the wake of the police cars. Pedestrians had gathered on street corners and were speculating. Some were talking to traffic cops, asking questions. The cops only grinned and shrugged and waved them away. Other cars were joining in the impromptu parade, breaking all speed laws. The people had been reading of a fresh outbreak in gangdom, of a bitter gang feud. They were obsessed now, rushing to get a bird's-eye view, for human nature is fundamentally melodramatic and its curiosity very close to the morbid.

It was already dark, in the early winter gloom. The taxi struck Farmingville Turnpike, fell into the stream of vehicles that pounded along. Horns tooted, and big, high-powered cars shot by so fast that the taxi seemed to be standing still. Mob curiosity was at its peak. Anything draws it—a fire, an accident, a soap-box orator, a brawl between school-boys, a man painting a flag-pole.

Then suddenly the cars began parking. In the gleam of the headlights two policemen with drawn nightsticks were shouting hoarsely, waving the people away.

"I guess we get out here," said Kennedy.

"Looks that way."

"Come on."

Cardigan paid the fare and they walked ahead. Kennedy showed his card and Cardigan went through with him. They strode briskly along the edge of the woods.

"Hear it?" asked Kennedy.

Cardigan heard it—the rattle of gun fire. Yes, the farmhouse. Alternate waves of heat and cold passed over him. The shadows in the woods were pitch black. Soon they could see the flash of guns, hear the brittle hammering of a machine-gun, firing in spasmodic bursts.

A figure in plainclothes loomed before them. "Hello, Mac," said Kennedy.

"Who's your friend?" muttered the captain.

"Cardigan."

"Oh-o!"

Kennedy pushed on. Cardigan stopped and MacBride came closer.

"Well, Jack, you see?"

Cardigan bit his lip. "What are you doing, blowing the place up?"

"Yes. Captain McGurk in charge."

"How'd it start?"

"Headquarters got a phone call about a lot of shooting going on out here."

Cardigan growled. "Can't you get 'em to offer a truce? God, Steve, it's pure slaughter!"

He was thinking of Pete Fink and the other boys, trapped in the house.

"There's no use. We came up in the bushes and let go with a machine-gun as a warning. A lot of rifle fire was our answer. This looks like the end."

"Cripes, Steve, stop it—stop it!" He lunged ahead.

MacBride grabbed him, held him in a grip of steel.

"Easy, Jack. You can't do a thing. Don't be a fool. You took the chance and this is the result."

"Let me go, Steve—let go!"

"No, dammit—no! By God, if you make a move I'll crack you over the head!"

"You will, will you?"

"So help me!"

Cardigan swore and heaved in MacBride's grasp. They struggled, weaving about, silent and grim. They crashed deeper into the bushes. Then MacBride struck, and Cardigan groaned and slumped down.

MacBride knelt beside him, white-faced and panting. "Jack, old boy, you hurt much? I didn't mean to hit so hard . . . Jack, but you can't do a thing. It's the breaks of the racket. God! . . ." He was rubbing Cardigan's head.

The battle was still on. Daggers of flame slashed through the dark. Lead drummed against the walls of the house, shattered the windows, pumped into the rooms. Spurts of flame darted from the house. A policeman crumpled. Another heaved up, clutching at his chest, and screamed.

"Oh, God!" groaned MacBride.

Captain McGurk, in charge, swore bitterly. He looked around. "That's three they got. We'll have to give 'em the works. Charlie, you got the grenades?"

"Yes, Cap'n."

"Go to it."

A machine-gun, silent for a moment, cut loose with a stuttering fusillade that raked every window in sight. Intermittent flashes came from the windows. Lead slugs rattled through the branches and thickets. The breeze of evening carried acrid powder smoke. The men in the bushes moved about warily.

Cardigan lay in a daze, conscious of the shots and the din, but in a vague, dreamy way. He wanted to yell out, and he imagined he was yelling, at the top of his lungs, but actually his lips moved only in a soundless whisper. His head throbbed with pain. MacBride had clipped him not too gently. And the captain was now bent over him, with one arm beneath him, rocking him.

The man called Charlie had worked his way closer, crawling on hands and knees, from tree to tree. Finally he stood up, and his arm swung. A small object wheeled through the dark, smacked on the roof of the house. There was a terrific explosion, and a sheet of ghastly flame billowed outward. Stones and bits of timber sang through space, clattered in the woods. The roof caved in, parts of the walls toppled in a smother of smoke and dust.

Out of the chaos groped a man, with hands upraised. He stumbled, sprawled and hit the earth like a log. He never moved once after that. Another crawled out of the ruins, turned over on his back and lay as still as the first. The policemen advanced out of the woods. Nothing stopped them now. They closed in around the house, entered here and there through torn gaps.

MacBride hauled Cardigan to his feet, put on his hat. "You've got to get out of this, Jack," he muttered.

Cardigan was able to stumble.

"It's all over," said MacBride.

He half-dragged him back through the woods to the road, walked him along it.

"Brace up!" he ground out. "I'll put you in a taxi. Look natural. Keep your hat down, your collar up. Get back to your hotel. Stay there, for God's sake. It's all over, you hear? There is no use making a fool of yourself."

They found a taxi and Cardigan got in. MacBride gripped his hand.

"Good luck, Jack!"

"Thanks, Steve."

Cardigan rode to his hotel in a sunken mood. He got out, paid his fare, and sagged up to his room. He locked the door and slumped into a chair. He groped for a cigarette and lit it, and stared gloomily into space. He muttered something old—something about plans of mice and men . . .

"Hell!" he mumbled, and sank lower.

Ten minutes later the telephone rang. He looked at it darkly. He didn't know whether he should answer it. But he got up, laid his hand on it, then took off the receiver.

"Hello," he muttered.

"Jack—my room," said Fink, and that was all.

Cardigan snapped out of his mood, sucked in a hot breath. He slammed down the receiver and dived for his overcoat.

IX

He climbed the rickety stairs in the ancient house in Jockey Street. He did not know what to expect. He paused a whole minute before the door until he knocked. Then he rapped. There was the sound of quick steps. Then the door swung open and Fink loomed there, grinning. He pulled Cardigan in, closed the door and locked it.

"Park your hips, Jack," he rumbled. "Have a drink."

Cardigan crossed the room, dropped to a chair and slopped liquor into a glass. He held it up. "I need this." He downed it neat. "Well?"

Fink rubbed his big hand along his thigh vigorously. "Well, Cavallo and his gang oughta be done for. Cripes, it was a great break for us! Well, I picked up Gats all right, and we drove back to the farmhouse. Then I figured maybe one o' Cavallo's guns was trailin' us. I seen a closed coupé follerin' all the way out, but I didn't let on. I swung in by the farm and I saw this coupé slow down and then shoot ahead.

"I put Gats in with the boys, and then I went out and hid in the bushes by the road. An hour later I see a big tourin' car stop down the road and a guy get out. It was Monkey Burns. I run back to the house and plan a trap. I pull down the shades and leave a light lit. Then me and the boys skin out and hide in the bushes with our rifles.

"Little later the bums sneak up. Monkey and Cavallo and Bert Geer and six others. They creep up on the house, and Monkey tries a door. It's open. He turns to his guns and whispers and they all bunch. Then they crash the door and go in shootin'. Before they know what's what, Gats busts loose with his gun and gets the last mutt goin' in. They see they're trapped and they slam the door.

"We surround the place. Then I explain things to the boys. Then I drive off in the car, get to a booth and call Police Headquarters and tell 'em a gunfight's goin' on out there. Then I drive back and park up the road a bit. The boys was takin' pot-shots at the winders now and then. I tell 'em what I done and then run back to the road. When I see a mob o' cars whoopin' down, I whistle and the boys beat it through the woods. We sit in the car until we hear guns goin'. Then we know the cops is at it, and Cavallo and his bums still thinkin' it's us. Then we drive off, and the boys scatter in the city. Just like that."

Cardigan regarded Fink for a long moment. Then he wagged his head. "Pete, you've got a sight more brains than I ever gave you credit for. Every man in that house was killed."

"Humph. What ammunition we saved. So the cops got 'em after all. Well, who has more right than the cops?"

Cardigan went back to his hotel with a light heart. He turned in, slept well, and got the whole thing in the morning extras. At ten MacBride came in to see him. The captain looked full of news.

"Well, you know it all by this time, eh, Jack?" he asked.

"Yes."

"No, you don't." MacBride sat down and took off his hat. "There's a big shake-up. Cavallo and all his rats were wiped out last night. But Cavallo's brother-in-law, Diorio, president of the Hard Club, goes wild this morning. He got in an argument with Pozzo, his friend, the alderman, and blamed him for it all. Claimed Cavallo was framed because he knew too much—framed by Pozzo and Mulroy. It wound up by Pozzo getting shot. Pozzo passed the buck and drew in State's Attorney Mulroy. Kennedy, that wiseacre reporter, crashed in on the row and got the whole story. What dirt they raked up! It's something nobody can hush. Diorio was pinched and he sprung the whole rotten story of graft and quashed criminal cases. Pozzo threatened to have him sent up for twenty years, but Pozzo can't do a thing. He's in the net. So is Mulroy. The governor's wires have been buzzing, and in a short time we're going to see a new state's attorney and a new alderman. It's the biggest shake-up in the history of the city. And you, Jack, in your own little way, caused it, thank God!"

Cardigan smiled. "Not me, Steve—exactly."

"Who, then?"

Cardigan shrugged. "Well, let it drop. A lucky break—and a certain friend of mine." He grew grave. "Now I'm satisfied. Joe Hanley, my buddy, is vindicated. I swore he would be. I was counting on some good breaks. For a while it looked like I was wrong. But the good ones came in the end."

MacBride nodded. "It's funny, there wasn't a trace of the gang that was riding Cavallo and his guns—not a trace."

Cardigan grinned. "I hoped there wouldn't be."

"M-m-m," mused MacBride. "Well, what are you going to do now?"

"That's a question," replied Cardigan. "I was thinking of starting a detective agency. I know the ropes, and I'm through with the Department, and I know where I can get a good right-hand man."

"Who's that?"

Cardigan chuckled. "You may meet him some day, Steve."

He was thinking of Pete Fink.

Dog Eat Dog

Frederick Nebel

A city where crime and politics are organized as one business; an honest, hard-fighting Police Captain who is bucking the crowd of graft-takers and their gunmen when his own daughter is caught in the slimy mesh

I

WHEN CAPTAIN MacBRIDE was suddenly transferred from the Second Precinct to the Fifth, an undercurrent of whispered speculations trickled through the Department, buzzed in newspaper circles, and traveled along the underworld grapevine.

It was a significant move, for MacBride, besides being the youngest captain in the Department—he was barely forty—was known throughout Richmond City as a holy terror against the criminal element. He was a lank, rangy man, with a square jaw and windy blue eyes. He was brusque, talked straight from the shoulder, and was hard-boiled as a five-minute egg. Now the Second Precinct is in the very heart of Richmond City's night-life, hence an important and busy station. The Fifth is out on the frontier, in a suburb called Grove Manor, and carries the somewhat humorous sobriquet of the Old Man's Home. Plenty of reasons, then, why MacBride's transfer should have been made matter for conjecture.

MacBride said nothing. He merely tightened his hard jaw a little harder, packed up and moved. To his successor, Captain O'Leary, he made one rather ironic remark: "Well, I'll be nearer home, anyhow." He had a bungalow, a wife and an eighteen-year-old daughter in an elm-shaded street in Grove Manor.

He landed in the Fifth in the latter part of August. It was a quiet, peaceful station, with a desk sergeant who played solitaire to pass the time away and a lieutenant who used his office and the Department's time to tinker around a radio set which he had made and which still called for lots of improvement. MacBride's predecessor, retired, had spent most of his time working out crossword puzzles. All the patrolmen, and three of the four detectives, were local men, and well on in years. The fourth detective had just been shifted from harness to plainclothes. Ted Kerr was his name; twenty-eight, sandy-haired, and a dynamo of energy and good-humor. He was ambitious, too, and cursed the luck that had placed him in the Fifth.

"Gee, Cap, it sure is a shock to see you out here," he said.

MacBride could remember when Kerr wore short pants. He grinned in his hard, tight way. "Forget it, Ted. Now that I'm here, though, I'm going to clean out a lot of the cobwebs. They say time hangs heavy on a man here. Too bad I haven't got a hobby."

"Why did they shift you, Cap?"

"Why?" MacBride creaked his swivel chair and bent over some reports on the desk, tacitly dismissing the subject.

A month dragged by, and the hard captain found ennui enveloping him. He was lounging in his tipped back chair one night, with his heels hooked on the desk, reading the newspaper account of a brutal night-club murder in his old district, when an old acquaintance dropped in—Kennedy, of the city *Free Press*.

"Oh, you," grumbled MacBride.

Kennedy helped himself to a seat. "Yeah, me. Gone to seed yet, Mac?"

"Won't be long now."

"What a tough break you got," chuckled Kennedy.

"Go ahead, rub it in. Pull a horse laugh, go on."

"I'll bet Duke Manola's laughing up his sleeve."

"That pup!"

Kennedy shrugged. "Serves you right for taking the law in your own hands. You birds can shake down a common sneak thief or a wandering wop that goes off on a gun spree coked to the eyebrows. But, Mac, you can't beat organized crime.

You can't beat it when it's financed by silent partners—and those silent partners"—he arched a knowing eyebrow—"on the inside, too."

"Man, oh, man, I'm going to get that greaseball yet!" MacBride's lip curled and his windy eyes glittered.

"Still got him on the brain, eh?" Kennedy lit a cigarette and spun the match out through the open window. "He's fire to fool with, Mac. He'll burn you surer than hell. Anyhow, you're out here in the sticks keeping the frogs and the crickets company, and you're not worrying Duke much. He's planted you where you'll do no harm. Oh, I know, Mac. There's a lot I know that the paper can't afford to print. When you raided the Nick Nack Club you stepped on Duke's toes. Not only his—but his silent partner's."

"Easy, Kennedy!"

"Easy, hell! This is just a heart-to-heart talk, Mac. Forget your loyalty to the badge when I'm around. You've kept a stiff upper lip, and you'll continue to. But just keep in the mind that here's one bird who knows his tricks. I know—see?—I know that Judge Haggerty is the Duke's silent partner in those three night-clubs he runs. Haggerty's aiming for Supreme Court Justice, and he needs lots of jack for his campaign. And he's not going to let a tough nut of a police captain get in his way."

MacBride bit the reporter with a keen, hard eye. After a long moment he swung his feet down from the desk and pulled open a drawer.

"Have a drink, Kennedy."

He drew out a bottle and a glass and set them down. Kennedy poured himself a stiff three fingers and downed it neat, rasped his throat.

"Good stuff, Mac," he said.

"Have another."

"Thanks."

Kennedy measured off another three fingers and swallowed the contents at a gulp, stared meditatively at the empty glass, then set it down quietly.

"Now, Mac," he said, looking up obliquely, while the ghost of a smile played around his lips. "I'll tell you what I came here for."

"Came to razz me, I thought."

"No. That's just my roundabout way of getting at things. One reason why I got kicked off the city desk."

MacBride felt that something important was in the wind. Sometimes he liked Kennedy; other times, he felt like wringing the news-hound's neck. Clever, this Kennedy, sharp as a steep trap.

"Well," he said, leaning back, "shoot."

"Just this, Mac. Maybe you're going to run up against Duke again."

"Go ahead."

Kennedy's smile was thin, almost mocking. "Duke's bought that old brewery out off Farmingville Turnpike."

MacBride's chair creaked once, and then remained silent. His stare bored into the lazy, whimsical eyes of the reporter. A sardonic twist pulled down one corner of his mouth.

"What's that wop up to?" he growled, deep in his throat.

"I've got a hunch, Mac. He's getting crowded in the city. He's going to make beer there—the real stuff, I mean. And gin. And—" he leaned forward—"he's going to rub it in—on you."

"He is, eh?" MacBride's voice hardened. "He'll take one step too many. He's getting cocky now. I never saw a wop yet who didn't overstep himself. Riding on my tail, eh? Well, we'll see, Kennedy. Let him move out of turn and I'll jump him. That wop can't kick me in the slats and get away with it. The booze I don't give a damn about. I wouldn't have cared how many speakeasies he ran in the city. But when he ran stud games in the back rooms and reached out for soused suckers I got sore. That's why I broke the Nick Nack Club. It was three in the morning, and among the bums in the back room were two guns from Chicago."

Kennedy chuckled. "That was when Captain Stephen MacBride pulled one of the biggest bones in his career. What a beautiful swan song that was! Hot diggity!"

MacBride rose to his lean, rangy height and cracked fist into palm.

"Boy, but I'm aching to meet that dago! I hope to hell he does make a bum move!"

"He put you out in the sticks; out," added Kennedy whimsically, "in the Old Man's Home.

And you're sore, Mac. I can foresee some hot stuff on the frontier, and Grove Manor on the map."

MacBride swung to face him, his feet spread wide. "Just that, Kennedy—just that. They shoved me out here to cool off and grow stale. But I'm not the guy to grow stale. Duke's cracking wise. Maybe he thinks that the transfer has shut me up. Maybe he thinks he can ride me and get away with it. Let him—that's all—just let him!"

There was a knock at the door, and then Sergeant Haley looked in, his beefy face flushed with excitement.

"Carlson's on the wire, Cap'n. There's been a smash-up out on Old Stone Road. Carlson was riding along in the patrol flivver when he saw a big touring car tangled up against a tree half in the bushes. There's a dead man in the car but Carlson can't get him out 'count of the wreckage."

MacBride snorted. "Is Carlson so hard up for company that he has to call up about a wreck?"

"No, but he says he thinks there's something fluky about it. He says there's a woman's footprints near the car, but he didn't see no woman."

"Maybe she walked home," put in Kennedy. "Lot of that going on these days."

"I'll speak to him," clipped MacBride, and sat down at his desk.

Sergeant Haley went out and switched over the call and it took MacBride only a minute to get the details. Then he hung up and, pouring himself a drink, corked the bottle and dropped it back into the drawer.

"The ride will do me good," he remarked as he slapped on his cap.

"Me, too," added Kennedy.

MacBride looked at him. "You're out of your territory, aren't you?"

"What the hell!"

On the way out MacBride told the sergeant, "When Kelly and Kerr drift in—God knows where they are now—tell 'em to hang around. Call up the nearest garage and tell 'em to send a wreckage crew out to Old Stone Road, about a mile north of Pine Tree Park. Buzz the morgue and tell 'em to send the bus to the same place. Tell 'em tonight, not sometime next week. When Lieutenant Miller gets fed up on monkeying with his radio, ask him to kindly take care of things till I get back. When you work out your present game of solitaire, I'd appreciate your getting those delinquent reports as near up to date as you're able. I won't be long."

Outside, he stopped on the curb to light a fresh cigar. Then he followed Kennedy into the police car, and said, "Shoot, Donnegan," to the man at the wheel.

II

Out of the hub of town, the car struck Old Stone Road and followed it past neat, new bungalows and later, past fields and intermittent groves of piney woods. Once through Pine Tree Park, the road became darker, lined by heavier woods, with not even an occasional house to relieve the gloom.

Donnegan, at the wheel, pointed to a pair of headlights far up the road, and when they drew nearer, MacBride saw a small two-seater flivver parked on the side and a policeman in uniform spreading his arms to stop them. Kennedy hopped out and MacBride followed him.

"There it is," said Carlson, and pointed to a tangled heap of wreckage against a tree alongside the highway. MacBride strode over, and Carlson followed, snapped on a flashlight and played its white beam over the ruined car.

"Three thousand bucks shot to hell," observed Kennedy. "And still insurance companies make money." He sniffed. "Who's the stiff?"

"Don't know," muttered MacBride and made a gesture which indicated that the man was so deeply buried beneath the wreck that they could not get him. He turned to Carlson. "You said something about footprints."

"Yeah, Cap. See?" He swung his flash down to the soft earth around the car. "Sure, a woman's."

MacBride nodded, then said, "But she never got out of this car after it struck."

The wreck offered mute evidence to that statement. Its radiator was caved in half the length of the long, streamlined hood, and the cowl and part of the hood were crushed up through the windshield frame. Beneath this, and

wedged in by the left side of the car, lay the man who had been at the wheel, face downward, the steering-wheel broken and twisted around his chest.

"I been wonderin' where the woman could have went," ventured Carlson.

"Whoever she was, she must have walked away," said MacBride. "Her footprints wouldn't show on the macadam." He added, after a moment, "At any rate, I'll bet my hat she wasn't in the car when it socked that tree."

Donnegan called out, "Guess this is the wrecker."

It was. The wrecking outfit from the garage rolled up, and two men in overalls got out.

"Hello, boys," greeted MacBride. "Before you haul this piece of junk away, there's a dead man inside. See if you can chop away some of the wreck."

The two men pulled axes from their car and set to work and hacked away at the snarled mass of metal. MacBride stood at one side, sucking on his cigar, offering no suggestion to men who knew their business and were doing the best they could. Presently he saw them lay down their axes, and he stepped over to help.

Bit by bit they hauled out the broken, blood-stained body, and laid it down on the ground. MacBride bent down on one knee and taking Carlson's flashlight, snapped on the switch. He grimaced, but gritted his teeth. A swarthy young face, the face of a boy in his early twenties.

"Hot diggity!" exclaimed Kennedy.

MacBride looked up. "What's eating you?

"Don't you know him?" cried Kennedy, his usually tired eyes alight with interest.

"Frankly, I don't."

Kennedy slapped his knee. "Duke Manola's kid brother!"

"Hell!" grunted MacBride, and took a swift look at the discolored face.

"He was always a sheik with the ladies."

"I've heard of him," nodded MacBride. "Now what the cripes kind of a stunt did he try to pull?"

"Simple," shrugged Kennedy. "Got fresh with some broad probably."

"But how did the broad shake the wreck? I

still say she wasn't in the car when it hit. Man alive, there'd been no chance of her walking after that!"

"The crack reporter of the *Free Press* agrees with the astute captain's common sense remark. But wait till Duke gets wind of it. You know these wops. Tweak the nose of a forty-eighth cousin and the whole shooting-match sharpens up their stilettos. Boy, don't I know!"

"Well, if he started playing around it's his tough luck. The trouble with a lot of these sheiks is that they're so used to the yes-girls that when they meet another kind they get sore—and nasty."

Kennedy rasped his throat. "Picture a decent gal trotting out with a marcelled sheik like Joe Manola! Don't tell me!"

MacBride shrugged as he stood up. He took his flashlight and mounted the wreck, shooting the beam down through the twisted metal. A moment later he stood up and held a short, stubby automatic in his hand.

"One shot fired," he said. "Not long ago, either." He had rubbed his finger across the muzzle, and looked at the black streak it left.

A siren screamed through the night, and two headlights came racing down the road. It was the morgue bus, and it pulled up behind the patrol flivver.

"What kind of a gun?" asked Kennedy.

"Thirty-two," shot back MacBride, and with a sudden movement crossed to the body and knelt down.

Kennedy trailed after him and bent over his shoulder. Then MacBride stood up, wiping his hands, a glitter in his eyes.

"He was shot, Kennedy. Shot through the right side."

"And then he hit the tree!"

"Exactly."

Kennedy whistled. "When the Duke hears this!"

MacBride turned to one of the man from the morgue bus. "You can take him. But there's a slug somewhere inside. I want it after the autopsy."

A few minutes later the bus shot off with its dead cargo, and MacBride turned to watch the wrecking-car tugging at the smashed machine.

Its derrick hoisted up the front end, and thus the rear wheels were in a condition to move.

"Keep it in the garage," said MacBride, "and I'll take care of your bill."

When the wreck had gone, with the rear red light winking in the distance, Kennedy made for the police car. "Well, let's be going, Mac. This'll be in the early editions."

MacBride started to follow, but turned and retraced his steps to where the wreck had lain. His flash played on the gashed tree and down on to the gouged ground. His eyes narrowed and he bent over, picked up something that shimmered in the white light.

In the palm of his hand lay an emerald pendant, attached to a thin gold chain that had been broken. His lips parted in a sharp intake of breath, and his hand knotted over the pendant.

"Oh, shake it up, Mac," called Kennedy.

MacBride turned and strode to the police car with hesitant steps. He climbed in and closed the door softly behind him. His hand, still holding the emerald pendant, slid into his pocket and remained there.

"Shoot, Donnegan," he clipped.

III

On the way back through town, MacBride had the car stop in front of a cigar store.

"Want to get some cigars," he told Kennedy, and strode into the store.

He bought half-a-dozen cigars, spent no more than a minute in a telephone booth, and then returned to the waiting car.

"Have one," he offered Kennedy.

"You were always a good-natured Scotchman," grinned Kennedy.

A couple of minutes later they walked into the station, and Kennedy made for the telephone, and shot the news into his office. Then he said, "Duty calls, Mac. Something tells me I'll be seeing you often."

"Don't make it too often," growled MacBride.

Kennedy waved and strolled out to catch a trolley back to the city.

MacBride tipped back his cap, revealing strands of damp hair plastered to his forehead by perspiration. His chiseled face looked a bit drawn.

He addressed Sergeant Haley huskily—"Call up the Nick Nack Club. Leave word to be delivered to Duke Manola that his brother was found dead at ten-thirty tonight—"

"Dead!" exclaimed Haley, who hadn't recorded a killing in his precinct in ten years.

"Don't butt in," recommended MacBride, lazily, as though deep within him he was very, very weary. "Do that. Found dead in a wrecked car on Old Stone Road, near Pine Tree Park. Tell 'em the body's at the morgue and may be reclaimed after the autopsy. No hint as to who shot him. No"—his teeth ground into his lower lip—"no clues. Make out your regular report and file it. Joseph Manola. We'll get his age and other incidentals later."

"Looks like murder, Cap'n!"

"Ye-es, it looks like murder," droned MacBride, sagging toward his office.

Ted Kerr came in briskly from another room, stopped short in the path of the captain.

"In here," said MacBride, and led the way into his office.

He sank into his chair, slammed his cap down on the desk and took a stiff drink.

"Hear you went out to investigate a wreck," ventured Kerr.

"Ye-es. And ran into a murder." MacBride's hand was in his pocket fingering the emerald pendant.

"Well!"

"Don't get worked up," dragged out MacBride.

"You look all in," said Kerr, seriously.

"Never mind me. What's on your mind?"

"Well, nothing much. Kelly and I were out to the Blue River Inn. You know there's been some complaints about raw parties being pulled off there. Pretty quiet tonight. Couple of drunken dames and a few soused college boys. And then—well. . . ." He hesitated, and looked away, his lips compressed.

"Well, what?"

"Oh, nothing much. Just. . . ." He paused again.

"Come on, Ted. Let's have it."

"Well, I just got a bit of a shock, that's all." His clean-cut face bore a vaguely hurt expression. "Well, Judith was there—"

MacBride snapped forward, his eyes keened. "Yes!"

"Why, what's the matter, Cap?"

"Keep talking. Judith was there. Who with?"

"Oh, hell, I shouldn't have said anything about it. But I've sort of liked Judith—"

"Don't say like when you mean love. And?"

"Well, she was there, that's all. Was another girl with her. Never saw the other girl. Kind of—well, brassy type. Chic looking and all that but brassy. And two fellows. The one with Judith was young and dark—looked like an Italian sheik. The other fellow was older—so was the girl. I didn't let on I saw them. They had a couple of drinks, then breezed in a big, classy touring car. Don't bawl Judith out, Cap. I shouldn't have told you, but—well, it just came out. Judith's a good girl. I guess I've got a nerve to think I ever had a chance—me just a dick. Promise me you won't say anything to her about it."

MacBride drew in a deep breath and held it trapped in his lungs for a long moment. Then he let it out, slowly, noiselessly, and followed it with a sigh.

"Ah-r- it's a rough, tough world, Ted, old timer."

Kerr attempted to change the subject. "But what about this murder, Cap?"

"It's going to start something—something big—big! Well, I've got my wish—but not in the way I'd expected." He was thinking of his wish that Duke Manola would face him again for a showdown.

"What wish, Cap?" asked Ted Kerr.

"No matter. Joe Manola was the bird got killed. He's Duke Manola's brother, and the Duke can call two dozen gunmen any time he wants to."

The telephone on the desk jangled. MacBride leaned forward, picking up the receiver and said, "Captain MacBride—"

"Yes, MacBride," came a voice with a hint of a nasal snarl. "This is your old playmate, Manola."

"The elder," supplemented MacBride.

"Be funny," snapped Duke Manola. "I just heard my kid brother was bumped off out in the sticks. What's the lay?"

"No lay yet, Duke. When I get the lay I'll send you an engraved copy of the report, autographed."

"Crack wise, big boy, crack wise."

"And—"

"You better snap on it, MacBride. I'm just telling you, get the pup or pups that winged the kid before I do. And don't get tough, either. Kind of a sock on your jaw, eh? You having to work for the guy gave you a buggy ride out to God's country!"

"Lay off that, Duke. And don't *you* get tough. You keep your hands out of this. And take a tip: Try to play around in this neck of the woods and I'll flop on you like a ton of brick. I'll handle this case, and I don't want any dirty greaseball getting in my light."

"I may drop in for tea soon, big boy."

"If I never saw you, Duke, that'd be years too soon. There's no Welcome sign hanging out here, and there's no good-luck horseshoe parked over the door. In short, I'm not entertaining."

"Whistle that, guy, and go to hell!" With that a sharp click indicated that Duke Manola had hung up.

MacBride slammed down the receiver, and Kerr offered, with a half-grin, "You men don't seem to get along so well."

"We get along worse every day," replied MacBride.

Kerr lit a cigarette. "Any clues on that murder, Cap?"

MacBride's hand was in his pocket, and it clenched the emerald pendant in sweaty fingers.

"No, Ted," he muttered.

IV

Mrs. MacBride was a woman of thirty-eight who still retained much of her youthful charm. The onyx sheen of her hair was not threaded by the slightest wisp of gray. Ordinarily, at breakfast time, she was a bright-eyed, animated woman, with a song on her lips and pleasant banter for her husband; and occasionally, as she passed back and forth from the kitchen, a kiss for the captain's cheek. Secretly, MacBride cherished this show of affection.

But something in his attitude that morning— or it may have been something in the heart of his wife—tended to eliminate this little by-play. There was a song on her lips, but it was in an unnatural, off-tone key.

When they sat down at the table facing each other, MacBride, without looking up from his morning paper, said, "Judith up yet?"

"Yes. She'll be right in, Steve." She went about sprinkling sugar on the grapefruit. "Grove Manor must have gasped this morning when they read the papers about—about—"

"Yes," nodded MacBride. "Haven't had a murder here in ten years."

"You'll be careful, Steve."

He glanced up. "Careful, Ann?"

"Well—you never can tell. I'm always worried."

"Oh, nonsense, Ann. You shouldn't worry—"

There was a step on the stair, and Judith came in, quietly. Ordinarily she entered at a skip, vivacious, animated. Her hair was jet black, and bobbed short, in the extremely modern manner. Likewise was her mode of dress extremely modern.

"Morning, dad. Morning, ma." Cheerful the tone, but with a faintly hollow ring.

As she crossed to the table she limped a trifle, but it escaped MacBride's eyes. His gaze was riveted on the newspaper.

"Morning, Judith," he said.

When she was seated, he folded his paper and laid it aside.

It seemed that Mrs. MacBride was holding her breath.

Hard on the outside, hard with men who were hard, he had always found it difficult to be hard at home. He wanted to eliminate a lot of preliminary talk. Somehow, he did not want to see a woman of his own crumpling bit by bit under a lightning parry and thrust of words.

He drew his hand from his pocket and laid the emerald pendant on the table.

"Yours, Judith?"

But the girl had already blanched. Mrs. MacBride sat stiff and straight, her hands clenched in her lap, the color draining from her tightly compressed lips.

"It was found," went on MacBride slowly, clumsily gentle, "beside a wrecked car on Old Stone Road last night."

"Oh!" breathed Judith, and looked to left and right, as if seeking an avenue of escape.

"Come, now, little girl," pursued MacBride. "Tell me about it. What happened?"

Judith jerked up from her chair, started for the stairs leading to her room.

"Judith!"

She dragged to a stop and turned.

"Please, Steve!" choked Mrs. MacBride. She got up and put an arm around her daughter.

"Ann, please stay out of this," recommended MacBride; and to the girl, "Judith, tell me about it. I know you were out in the company of the man who was murdered last night! I'll have to have an explanation!"

"I—I can't tell!" came her muffled, panicky voice.

"But you must!" he insisted sternly.

"No—no! I can't! I won't! Oh, please! . . ."

He crossed the room and laid his hand on her shoulder. "Do you realize the significance of this? I don't say you killed Manola. But you were out with him, and you know what happened on that road. Judith! Out with one of the worst rakes in the city—the brother of Duke Manola, the gang leader and—my enemy! My God, girl, what have you been thinking of? Isn't Ted Kerr good enough for you? Or does a classy car and a marcelled wop win you?"

She was crying now, but through it all she kept reiterating—"I won't tell! I won't tell!"

"Judith, so help me, you will!"

"No—no! I won't! You can beat me! You— can—beat—me! I won't tell! Oh-o-o-o! . . ."

"Steve," implored Mrs. MacBride, "don't— please!"

"Ann, be still! Do you think I enjoy this? How do you think I felt last night when I picked that pendant up by the wreck? God, it's a wonder the hawkeyed Kennedy didn't see me! Judith, listen to reason. You've got to tell me!"

She spun back, her hands clenched, a storm of terror in her moist eyes—tense, quivering, like a cornered animal, and defiant.

"No—no—never! You can't make me. Dear God, you can't!"

She pivoted and clawed her way up the stairs, fled into her room and locked the door.

Half-way up the staircase, MacBride stopped, turned and came down slowly, his face a frozen mask.

"To think, to think!" he groaned.

His wife touched him with her hands, and he took them in his own and looked down into her swimming eyes.

"Ann, I wish you could make me happy, but just now—you can't. I'm as miserable, as sunk, as you are."

Years seemed to creep upon him visibly. He picked up the pendant and dropped it into his pocket.

V

At five that evening MacBride was sitting at his desk in the precinct, when Ted Kerr breezed in, closed the door quietly and stood, wiping perspiration from his forehead.

"Well?" asked MacBride.

"I was out there. Kline, the bird that runs the Blue River Inn, acted dumb. He didn't remember the party of four. Had never seen them before. In short, didn't know them."

"Think he's on the level?"

"No." Kerr dropped to a chair. "I could see he was walking on soft ground, watching his step. It's my bet that he knows the two fellows." He paused. "How—how's Judith?"

"Still love her?"

"Well, God, Cap, she's in trouble—"

"Sh! Soft pedal, Ted!"

Kerr spoke in a husky whisper. "I don't believe she's done bad. She wouldn't. Just lost her head. Damn these oily birds with their flashy cars!"

"Listen. If you saw the guy who was with Manola again, would you recognize him?"

"Sure."

"Then take a trolley to Headquarters and look over the Rogues' Gallery. Call me up if you have any luck."

Kerr took his departure, and a little later Kelly entered and said, "Yup, Cap, there's men out in that brewery where you sent me. I heard some hammerin' goin' on like, and the windows on the third floor—that's the top, you know—them windows was open, they was. Then I seen two cars parked inside the fence, under the sheds where the beer used to be loaded on trucks. Classy cars—one a big sedan, all black—number A2260. The other was a sport roadster, C4002. Nobody was around them."

On his desk pad MacBride marked down the type and number of the two cars. He dismissed Kelly and then called up the automobile license bureau. The sport roadster, he found, belonged to a man named John A. Winslow. The sedan was owned by Judge Michael Haggerty.

MacBride sat back with a bitter chuckle. "That sounds like 'Diamond Jack' Winslow, the race-track kid. H'm. And Mike Haggerty. Cheek and jowl with Duke Manola."

He lit a cigar and looked up to find Detective-Sergeant O'Dowd, from Headquarters.

"Hello, O'Dowd."

"Hello, Mac. I just dropped in with a little order from the big cheese. Know that brewery out off Farmingville Turnpike?"

MacBride nodded.

O'Dowd said, "Well, don't let it worry you, Mac. They're making some good beer there, and orders are to leave 'em be."

"I've been waiting for those orders," said MacBride. "So long as they bust the Volstead Act and don't make any noise, it's O.K. by me. Anything else, though—"

"Let your conscience be your guide, Mac," grinned O'Dowd, and left.

The machinery of the underworld and politics, mused MacBride, was getting under way. Kerr called up a little later, and he had information.

"I'm sure it's the same guy, Cap," he said. "Chuck Devore. The records show he was arrested two years ago in connection with the shooting of a taxi driver named Max Levy. But he wasn't indicted."

"We're hot, Ted," shot back MacBride. "Devore is a gangster, and a pretty tough egg. He used to run with Duke Manola. In that killing two years ago we had the hunch that Manola tried to frame Devore to take the rap. Then they broke and Devore drifted. If he's back in town, there's a pot of trouble brewing."

"You mean a gang war?"

"Right. Dog eat dog stuff, and hell's going to pop or I miss my guess. All right, Ted. Hop a trolley home."

MacBride slammed down the receiver and sat back rubbing his hands. Devore back in town! But what had he been doing in the company of Duke Manola's brother? And who was the woman in the case—besides Judith? A chill shot through MacBride. His own daughter mixed up in an underworld feud!

He snapped up to his feet, changed from his uniform coat and cap into a plain blue jacket and a gray fedora. He strode out of his office, told Donnegan to get the car out, and left brief instructions with Sergeant Haley.

Outside, he climbed into the car and said, "Know the Blue River Inn?"

Donnegan said, "Yes."

"That's where we're going. Don't run right up to it. Park back a distance, out of sight."

The car shot off through town, hit Old Stone Road and followed it into Farmingville Turnpike. Half an hour later Donnegan pulled up on the side of the road, in the shadow of a deep woods. Up ahead they could see *Blue River Inn*, picked out in electric light bulbs.

"You wait here, Donnegan," said MacBride. "I won't be long."

The inn was large and rambling, two storied, with many windows. MacBride entered the large, carpeted room that served as a lobby, and the head-waiter, with a menu in his hand, bowed.

"I'm not eating," clipped MacBride. "Who runs this dump?"

"Sir?"

"Cut out the flowers, buddy. I'm from the precinct." He flashed his badge. "Snap on it!"

A short, rotund man in dinner clothes came strolling in from the main corridor, and the head-waiter, a little troubled, beckoned to him.

"You the owner?" asked MacBride. "What's your name?"

"Hinkle, owner and manager. What can I do for you?"

"I'm MacBride, from the precinct. There were two couples in here last night— *You!*" he suddenly shot at the head-waiter. "Stay here! Now," he went on, "who were the two men?"

"Of course," said Hinkle, "there are so many people come here, we cannot recall them. So many are transients."

"Look here," pursued MacBride. "One of those men was Joe Manola, who was later killed in a wreck last night. Now who was the other guy—the guy with him?"

Hinkle moistened his lips and his eyes shifted nervously. "I'm sorry. I don't know. Nor does my head-waiter."

The girl at the desk trilled, "Mr. Hinkle, telephone."

Hinkle went over to the desk, and MacBride followed, stood beside him. Hinkle picked up the telephone, and said, "Yes, Hinkle talking." And then his face blanched, and his lips began to writhe.

MacBride's gun came out of his pocket, jammed against Hinkle's adipose paunch. He tore the receiver from Hinkle's hand and clasped it to his own ear, heard—

". . . and get that, Hinkle. Act dumb, all the time, see. And if it gets too hot, call me on the wire. Got that number? Main 1808?"

MacBride's lips moved silently, forming the words, "Say yes, Hinkle."

"Yes, yes," said Hinkle, his face pasty white.

"O.K. then," was the reply, and the man at the other end hung up.

MacBride hung up, set down the telephone, a thin, hard smile on his face.

"Who was that, Hinkle?"

Hinkle wilted, blubbered, kept shaking his head.

"Chuck Devore, eh?" grinned MacBride, without humor.

"Oh, G–God!" choked Hinkle, gasping for air and reeling backward.

MacBride picked up the telephone and called the precinct. To Sergeant Haley he said, "Send a man out around to the telephone exchange. Tell the operators there to allow no calls incoming or outgoing from"—he looked down at the number on the phone—"Farmingville 664. Also, no calls to be connected, outgoing or incoming, to Main 1808. Until further notice from the station. Also, get me the address of Main 1808, quick, and ring me at Farmingville 664 before the order to shut off. Snap on it, sergeant!"

He hung up, stepped to the door and blew his whistle. When Donnegan came in on the run, MacBride said, "No hurry. Just stay here and keep your eyes on these two men till you get word from the precinct. Don't let them get out of sight. Go in the dining-room and tell all the guests to clear out."

There were only a dozen-odd persons in the dining-room, and they made an angry and protesting exodus. When they had gone, MacBride said to Donnegan. "Let no more in. See that no more cars leave."

The telephone rang, and he picked it up, listened. "All right, sergeant," he said. "I'll have to pass there on the way through. Tell Kelly and Kerr to be ready and I'll pick them up."

He turned from the telephone, looked at the group of waiters and at Hinkle and his steward. Then he looked at Donnegan. "Keep them salted, Donnegan, right in this room. You, Hinkle, have your sign shut off and all the lights in the house except in this room. You're temporarily closed for business."

"It's an outrage!" choked Hinkle.

"See if I care," chuckled MacBride; and to Donnegan, "I'll take the car."

VI

Kelly and Kerr were waiting outside of the precinct when MacBride drew up.

"Hop in, boys. We're going for maybe a little target practice."

Kelly shifted his chew and climbed in, and Kerr, eagerness sparking in his eyes, followed. MacBride stepped on the gas and they shot off.

"What's the lay, Cap?" asked Kelly.

"We're going to look up Chuck Devore, at a dump in lower Jockey Street. There may be a fight. You boys well heeled?"

They were. And as they drove on, MacBride explained about his pilgrimage to the Blue River Inn.

They made good time into the city. Traffic on Main Street, the artery of theatres and cabarets, held them up.

Presently MacBride turned into Jockey Street and followed it west. Near Main Street, small restaurants, Chinese or Italian, displayed their signs. Further along, it changed to blank-faced brick houses, old and peeling, with here and there a single globe of light marking out a speakeasy. The municipal lighting system was poor, and the way was dark.

MacBride pulled up in the middle of a block and said, "It's on the next block, but we'll leave the car here. Come on."

They got out and continued down Jockey Street with MacBride taking long strides in the lead. There was a noticeable jut to his teak-hard jaw and a windy look in his blue eyes. He was not the man to grow stale from sitting on his spine in a precinct office. The game on the outside still lured him—the somewhat dangerous game of poking into back alleys and underworld hideouts.

He slowed down, but did not stop. "This is the house, boys. Number 40. Don't stop. All dark except the third floor. Shades drawn there, but you can see the light through the cracks. I know this neighborhood. They have a lookout in the hall, and a man needs a password to get in. A red light dump without the red lights. We'll see if there's a way to it from the next street."

At the next block they turned south, and then east into the next street. Between the houses here they could see the backs of the houses on Jockey Street.

"There it is," pointed out MacBride. "That three-story place, taller than the others." He stopped. "Here's an alley. Come on."

They swung into a dark, narrow passageway that led between two wooden houses and on into a small yard criss-crossed with clothes-lines. Separating this yard from that of the one belonging to the house in Jockey Street was a high board fence. Behind this, the three paused and looked up. All floors were dark except the third and top-most.

MacBride gripped the top of the fence, heaved up and over, landed in soft earth. Kerr and Kelly followed and they stood hunched closely, whispering. MacBride pointed to the fire-escape.

"Up we go. You boys trail me. Easy!" he warned.

He led the way up the ladders, his gun drawn. Nearing the top story, he went more cautiously, more quietly, and turned once to recommend silence with a finger tapping his lips. At the third floor he stopped, hunched over. The window was open, a half-drawn shade crackling in the draft.

Slowly MacBride raised his head and peered in over the sill. Four men were sitting around a table in shirt-sleeves, their collars open. A bottle and glasses were on the table, and MacBride caught whiffs of cigarette smoke. He saw Chuck Devore in profile. Devore was a tall, smooth-shaven man of thirty, with curly brown hair and a cleft chin. His eyes were deep-set and peculiarly luminous. In repose, his face was not bad to look at—except for the strange, impenetrable eyes. MacBride had never seen the others, but all of them bore the stamp of hard, dangerous living. The most outstanding, besides Devore, was a huge bull of a man with flaming red hair and a heavy jaw.

"It will be a cinch," Devore was saying. "We can bust in about three a.m. and stick up the works, and you can take it from me, there'll be no small change. Not with Diamond Jack Winslow in on the show and a lot of big political guns. And they can't yap. That's where we've got them. They're playing a crooked game, and if the public got wind of it, Perrone would have about as much chance of getting in the aldermanic show as I would. And Haggerty'd land on his can, too."

"And won't Duke Manola get sore!" chuckled the red-head.

"Yes, the lousy bum!" snapped Devore. "Cripes, his kid brother spilled a lot of beans. Wild sheik, that bird was."

"Yeah—*was,*" nodded the red-head.

"I feel a draft," said Devore, and got up, coming toward the window.

He walked into the muzzle of MacBride's thirty-eight.

"Nice, now, Chuck!" bit off MacBride. "Up high."

He stepped in through the window, and Kerr was half-way through behind him, his gun covering the startled group at the table.

Then came Kelly, slit-eyed, dangerous.

"What's the meaning of this, Mac?" snarled Devore.

"Be your age, Chuck," said MacBride.

No one saw a hand sliding in through a door that led to another room. This hand, slim and white, felt for the light-switch, found it, and pressed the button.

The room was thrown into sudden darkness. Chairs scraped. A door banged.

A dagger of flame slashed through the gloom, and a man screamed, his body hit the floor with a thud.

MacBride found Devore on his hands, and the gangster was trying to twist the captain's gun arm behind his back.

"No, you don't, Devore!"

MacBride heaved with him, spun through the darkness, crashed into other struggling figures. He slammed Devore against the wall, and Devore tried to use his knee for a dirty blow.

MacBride blocked with his hip and banged Devore's head to the wall, again and again. Then Devore twisted and dragged out of the jam, but MacBride heaved against him and they crashed to the floor.

Struggling feet stumbled over their twisting bodies, and curses ripped through the darkness. Another shot banged out, went wild and shattered a light bulb in the chandelier. The table toppled, and somebody crashed over a chair.

Then the door leading to the hall was flung open and dim figures hurtled through it on the way out, their feet pounding on the floor. Devore planted his knee brutally in MacBride's stomach and the captain buckled, gasping for breath. Then Devore tore free, reeled about the room and dived for the open door.

But MacBride caught his breath, heaved up and lunged after him. Doors opened and banged, but nobody came out to get in the way. Somewhere far below MacBride heard a sharp exchange of shots. He catapulted after Devore who was racing down the staircase. Near the bottom, he leaped through space and landing on Devore's neck, crashed him to the floor.

Devore groaned and relaxed. MacBride straddled him, drew out manacles and settled Devore's status for the time being. He stood up, wiping blood from his face, shoving wet strands of hair back from his forehead. He heard footsteps rushing up from below and swung around with his gun leveled.

It was Ted Kerr, his clothes in tatters and a couple of blue welts on his face.

"They got away, Cap," he explained. "Through the back. Went through a door, slammed it and locked it. Kelly and I tried to bust it, but no can do. I came up to see if you were all right. One was wounded. Here's Kelly."

Kelly puffed up, his collar gone but his tie still draped around his neck.

"Take this guy," MacBride said, jerking a thumb toward Devore. "I'll be right down."

He went upstairs two steps at a time and entered the gang's quarters. He lit a match, found the light switch and snapped it. The room was in ruin, and the shade still clicked in the draft. He crossed to another door, stood to one side, then turned the knob and kicked the door open. A light was burning inside, and a breeze blowing through an open window.

Entering, MacBride set it down as a room used by a woman. There was a littered dressing table, and a bureau with several drawers half out and signs indicatory of somebody having made a quick getaway. A cursory examination revealed no tell-tale clues. MacBride turned out the lights, left the rooms, and descended the staircase.

Devore was standing up now, between Kerr and Kelly, and venom was burning in his strange, enigmatic eyes.

MacBride said, "Now for a little buggy ride, Devore."

"You're going to regret this, MacBride," the man snarled. "By cripes, you are!"

"Cut out the threats, you bum!"

"Cut out hell! Before you know what's what I'm going to have you tied by the heels."

"Should I sock him, Cap?" inquired Kelly.

"No. He'll get a lot of that later, where it's more convenient." MacBride's hand clenched, and his lips flattened back against his teeth.

Devore smiled, mockingly. "We'll see, MacBride—*we'll see!*"

VII

It was about half-past ten when the police car rolled into Grove Manor. Ted Kerr was at the wheel. Devore sat in the rear, between MacBride and Kelly.

"Looks like a crowd in front of the station," sang out Kerr.

" 'Swing into the next block," said MacBride. "Probably some photographers and—no doubt— that very good friend of mine, Kennedy, with his nose for news, and his wisecracks."

The car turned into a dark street several blocks this side of the police station and halted.

"What should I do, Cap?" asked Kerr.

MacBride was thinking. "Let's see. H'm. Drive around the back way, Ted. Park a block

away from the station. I'll run this bird in the back way, right into my office. You and Kelly drive up a little later. And don't spill any beans—keep your traps shut. Then you come in my office, Ted, and we'll see."

Kerr drove off slowly, cut around the back of the town and came up a dark, poorly paved street that ran back of the station. When he pulled up, MacBride hauled Devore out and marched him off. They took a path that led through a vacant lot and on up to the back of the station.

Here MacBride, using a key, opened a door and shoved Devore in, then followed and, locking the door, guided the gangster along a dark hallway that ended against another door. MacBride unlocked this and stepped into his office, relocked it quickly and crossing to the door that led into the central room, shoved shut the bolt. Then he turned with a sigh of relief, took off his cap and sailed it across his desk.

"Take the load off your feet, Devore," he droned, and pulling open a drawer in his desk, hauled out a bottle and downed a stiff bracer. He turned to Devore. "Dry?"

"I don't drink slops, thanks."

"You can go to hell," chuckled MacBride, slamming shut the drawer.

"Listen," jerked out Devore. "Let me use that phone. I gotta talk to my lawyer."

"Try setting that to music, guy. You're calling no lawyer. You're seeing no one. And the newspapers aren't going to know I've got you. I'm top-dog, you dirty slob, and you're going to come across!"

"About what?"

"Ask me another," scoffed MacBride. "About the killing of Joe Manola. Now don't try to hand me a song and dance, Devore. I was listening outside the window on the fire-escape. I heard you and your guns talking."

"How did you get the lay on me, MacBride?"

"Don't worry about that, Devore. The thing is, I've got you, and you're going to come across."

Devore leaned forward, his teeth bared, but not in a smile. "How about your kid daughter, big boy?"

"Yes, you pup, how about her?" exploded MacBride, a bad light in his eyes.

"Sound nice, won't it? Daughter of Captain MacBride linked up with gangsters. Think it over, MacBride."

"I'm thinking it over, Devore. It's a blow—a sock flush on the button, but I'll weather it. She'll have to talk, sooner or later, even though she is my daughter. But she's been framed somehow. And what I want to know is, who's the woman who was in the quartette last night at the Blue River?"

"Ah, wouldn't you like to know!" Devore snarled; and then snapped, "Try and find out, you big bum!"

There was a knock on the door. MacBride walked over and asked, "Who is it?"

"Ted."

He opened the door and Ted Kerr slipped in. MacBride snapped shut the bolt. Kerr scowled at Devore.

"Right at home, eh, Devore? You won't be," he threatened.

MacBride said, "Keep your eye on him, Ted. I'm going out and give the gang the air."

There was a sizable crowd waiting for news. Four reporters, three photographers. And Kennedy, with his whimsical smile.

"Ah, captain," he chortled, "and now you broadcast."

MacBride bored him with a keen stare. "You're wasting your time, Kennedy. On your way—all of you boys. No news tonight."

"But who's the bird you've got?" demanded a reporter from the city news association.

"You heard me," shot back MacBride. "No news. There's a trolley goes through here in five minutes. Take a tip. Hop it."

"Aw, for cripe's sakes," protested Kennedy. "Be a sport, Cap. Think of all the good breaks I've put in your way."

"Think of all the good drinks I've handed out," replied MacBride. "No use, Kennedy. Beat it, all of you. You're cluttering up the station."

The outer door opened and a man strolled in nonchalantly smoking a cork-tipped cigarette.

He was of medium height, slight in build, dressed in the acme of fashion. He wore a gray suit that could not have been made for less than a hundred dollars, a cream-colored silk shirt, a blue tie, and a rakish Panama hat. He carried a Malacca stick, and now he leaned on it, his hand aglitter with diamonds, a lazy, indolent look in his slitted brown eyes.

"Hello, MacBride," he droned through lips that scarcely moved.

"Aren't you late for tea, Duke?" asked the captain.

"Kind of. But I heard you've been shooting the town up. Where's the catch?"

"Rehearsing. No public showing just yet, Duke."

"Forget it. I got a right to a private interview."

MacBride shook his head. "That's a lot of noise. You've got no rights at all so far as I'm concerned. The door's behind you, Duke. The air'll do you good."

Duke Manola snarled, "Can that tripe, Mac. I didn't come out here to chin with you. I came out to see who you picked up. Cut the comedy!"

"Soft pedal, Duke. You're in bad company right now."

"Why, damn your soul, MacBride!—"

"Shut up!" barked the hard captain. "You might be a big guy in other circles, but just now, as far as I'm concerned, you're only a little dago shooting off a lot of hot air." He stepped to the outer door and yanked it open. "Now get the hell out!"

Manola's lips moved in a silent oath, and his eyes flamed behind lids that were almost closed. Then he shrugged. "All right, MacBride. Have your way. I see you're not tamed yet."

"Not by a damned sight, Duke!"

"Maybe—I'll try a little more—taming." With that he sauntered out, a leer on his dark, smooth face.

A moment later the newspapermen followed.

From then on until midnight MacBride sat in his office, behind locked doors, and raked Devore with a merciless third degree. But

Devore only taunted him. He made no confession. He gave no details. He weathered the gale with the hardness of his kind, and at midnight MacBride, worn and haggard, torn inwardly by emotions that he never revealed, called it a day.

"All right, Devore. That'll do for tonight. More later, buddy."

He called in a policeman and directed him to put Devore in a cell.

"Listen here, MacBride," the gangster protested on the way out of the office. "I want a lawyer. I want him mighty quick."

"Dry up. You're not getting out on bail while I'm alive."

Still protesting, Devore was dragged away to a cell.

Weary, sunk at heart, MacBride slumped back in his chair, his chin dropping to his chest, his tousled hair straggling down over his red-rimmed eyes. He was up against it. He dared not look ahead. There was no telling what the morrow would bring. But one thing was certain. His daughter would be drawn into the net, linked with a gangster's crime, her name and likeness published throughout the country. Judith MacBride, daughter of Captain MacBride, feared by the criminal element of Richmond City. A stickler for the law. A hard man against crooks. Possessed of an enviable record.

He shuddered; the whole, big-boned frame of him shuddered.

And then the telephone rang, and he picked up the receiver.

"Is this you, Steve?" came his wife's anxious voice.

"Yes, Ann."

"Steve! I don't know where Judith is. She went to a movie tonight—to—forget for a little while. She'd promised to go with Elsie, from the other end of town. You know the show's out at eleven. And she hasn't come home yet. I called up Elsie and she said they parted in front of the theatre at eleven and Judith started walking home.

"And Steve, listen. At about ten some woman called up and asked for Judith. I said she wasn't in, that she'd gone to the movies. Then she hung up. What do you suppose could have happened?"

Under the desk, MacBride's clenched fist pounded against his knee.

"I don't know, Ann. But don't worry. I'll be home right away. Don't worry, dear. I'll—be—home."

The color had drained from his face by the time he slipped the receiver back on to the hook. He sat back, his arms outstretched, the hands knotted on the edge of the desk, the eyes wide and staring into space. And then the eyes narrowed and the lips curled.

He heaved up, banged on his cap and strode out of the station. When he reached home his wife was sobbing, and she came to his arms. Hard hit as he was, he, nevertheless, put his arms around her and patted her gently.

"Buck up, Ann. That's a brave girl. Maybe it's nothing after all. Maybe—"

The ringing of the telephone bell interrupted him. Slowly, he approached the instrument, unhooked the receiver.

"Who is this?" grated a voice.

"MacBride."

"Get wise to yourself, MacBride. You see that Devore gets free by tomorrow midnight, or your daughter gets a dirty deal. This is straight. The gang's got her at a hide-out you'll never find. I'm calling from a booth in the railroad station. By tomorrow midnight, MacBride, or your daughter gets the works! Good-bye!"

A click sounded in MacBride's ear. He turned away from the telephone, met his wife's wide-eyed stare.

"Steve! Steve!" she cried.

"Judith's been kidnapped by Devore's gang. Devore's the man I've got in jail. His freedom is their price—for Judith."

"Oh—dear—God!"

Ann MacBride closed her eyes and swayed. The hard captain caught her, held her gently, carried her to a sofa and laid her down, kneeling beside her.

For the first time in his life MacBride prayed—for his daughter.

VIII

Next day he sat in his office, with the doors bolted, and Ted Kerr facing him.

"Ted, I'm cornered," he muttered. "I've got to pay through the nose."

"The skunks!" exclaimed Kerr. "God, can't we comb the city? Can't we run the pups down?"

"It would take two or three days. They demand Devore by midnight. I've got to swallow my pride and let him go."

"But, Cap, you can't let him just walk out."

"I know I can't. There must be another way. He must escape."

Kerr bit his lip, perplexed. "Escape? Can you imagine the razzing you'll get?"

MacBride nodded. "Yes, more than you can. I've been called a tough nut, Ted. Well, I won't deny it. And my pride's been one of the biggest things in me. Swallowing it will damn near choke me. But my daughter—my flesh and blood—is the price, and, by God, I can't stand the blow!"

"But can't it be fixed so the blame'll fall on me? Hell, Cap, you've got so much more at stake."

"No. I'm the guy pays through the nose. Devore must escape."

"What about those birds at the Blue River?"

"They're not in the know. I hauled Donnegan off last night. Devore was just their bootlegger. Hinkle came across. He said Devore warned him to close his trap and keep it closed, or wind up wrestling with a bullet. No, there's no alternative. Sometime tonight I've got to pull a bonehead move and let Devore blow. Afterwards, Ted, I'll clean him out. But Judith comes first."

"Suppose they double-cross you?"

"I'll take care of that before Devore goes."

The day dragged by, and at nine that night MacBride had Devore brought in from the cell. He dismissed the officer with a nod. Devore sat down—he was without manacles—and helped himself to a cigarette from a pack on the desk. He needed a shave, and he looked down at the mouth—and nasty.

"What a crust you've got, MacBride!

Dammit, I want a lawyer. I want to see something besides polished buttons. I gotta right to that, MacBride."

MacBride rocked gently in his swivel chair. "Pipe down. And listen. You're going to slide out of here tonight."

Devore looked up, suspecting a trick. "What d' you mean?"

"The rats you run with kidnapped my daughter last night. Their price is—your freedom. They've got me buffaloed, and I know they'd slit her open if I didn't come across."

"Told you I'd get you tied by the heels."

"Shut up. It's a bum break, and I'm not yapping. You slide out tonight."

Devore looked around. "Which way?"

"Not yet, buddy. You're going to call up your gang and tell 'em to let my daughter go."

"Do you see any green on me, Cap?" snarled Devore.

"You can take my word or leave it. I've never framed a guy yet, Devore. You ought to know that. Here's my proposition. You call up your gang and tell 'em it's all fixed. They let my kid go. You breeze. I'll give you twelve hours' grace. But after that I'm going after you. I'll know what number you call up, so don't hang around there after you're out. You're getting a lease on life, a twelve hours' lease. Grab it before I change my mind."

Devore leaned forward, his luminous eyes roving over the captain's face.

"Call Northside 412," he breathed.

MacBride reached for the telephone and put through the call. When he heard the operator ringing, he passed the phone over to Devore and watched him intently.

"Hell—hello," snapped Devore. "This you, Jake? . . . Yeah, this is Chuck. It's all fixed. Let the dame go—right away. Put her in a taxi and send her home. Then clear out and I'll meet you at Charlie's. . . . Of course, I mean it. For God's sake, don't act dumb! . . . Yeah, right away. S' long."

He hung up, his eyes narrowed. "Now, MacBride!"

MacBride pulled open a drawer and laid an automatic on the desk. "The gun you shot Joe

Manola with. It's empty. You grab it and cover me and beat it out the back way, through the lots, and run for three blocks. There's a main drag there, and a bus goes through to the city in five minutes."

Devore grabbed the gun, his eyes brilliant in their deep sockets, his lips drawn tight.

"Paying through the nose, eh, MacBride?"

"Shut up. When I meet you again, Devore, I won't be taking any prisoners. The morgue bus will gather up the remains. Breeze!"

Devore snapped to his feet, leered, and sped out through the rear door. MacBride sat still, his face granite hard, his fingers opening and closing, his teeth grinding together. For two minutes he sat there. Then he jumped up, ran to the door leading into the rear hall and banged it shut.

He spun around and dived for the door leading into the central room. Sergeant Haley was playing solitaire. Kerr was sitting at a table playing checkers with Kennedy, of the *Free Press*.

"Snap on it!" barked MacBride. "Devore's escaped! He pulled a fast one. Grabbed a gun lying on the desk. Come on!"

Kerr kicked back his chair. Two patrolmen came running from another room, drew their nightsticks.

MacBride led the way out, and on the street said, "We'll split." He directed the patrolmen to head for the trolley line. To Kerr he said, "We'll watch the bus line."

A moment later he and Kerr were running for the bus line, and when they reached the highway, MacBride pointed to a red light just disappearing around a bend.

"That's the bus," he said. "And Devore."

"So you did it, Cap."

"Hell, yes!"

IX

An hour later, MacBride and Kerr stopped in at the captain's house. Judith was weeping in her mother's arms and her mother was shedding tears of happiness.

"Judith just came in," she said.

MacBride took his daughter and stood her up, placing his hands on her shoulders. "Poor kid—poor kid. Now tell me, Judith, tell me—all you know."

Ted Kerr stood a little back, ill at ease.

"Oh, daddy, I've been a fool—a little fool. When I was walking home from the movies last night that girl drove up in a car, called to me—and then two men jumped for me, gagged me, and they drove off."

"What girl?"

"Arline Kane. I met her a month ago at a hairdressing parlor in the city. She said she was an actress, and marveled at my hair. She said I ought to go on the stage. She took me to lunch, and then promised to introduce me to some theatrical men. She was going with a man named Devore. I met him several times, and then the other night we went to the Blue River and there was another fellow—for me. Mr. Manola. I—I didn't like him. He—he drank too much.

"When we drove away from the Blue River, he wanted to park on a dark road. But I didn't want him to. He was pretty drunk, and he wanted to make love to me. I fought him off, and then he turned to the others and said, 'I thought you said I'd find a good time.' And Mr. Devore said, 'Don't crab, Joe. Drive on.' And Mr. Manola said, 'Nothing doing. I've got a mind to make you all walk. Go on, get out, all of you.' Well, he meant it, and he was pretty angry, too. And Mr. Devore got angry. They began swearing. Then Mr. Manola said, "You *will* get out, all of you!' And he drew his gun. But Mr. Devore, who was sitting in the back, jumped on him, and the gun went off, but it was twisted around so that the bullet struck Mr. Manola.

"He screamed, and then he shouted, 'I'll wreck all of you!' He seemed crazy, and threw into gear, and the car started. Then Mr. Devore yelled, 'Jump! We'll have to jump!' And we all did. And the car gathered speed, and Mr. Manola must have fainted, because it swerved to right and left and then hit a tree.

"We fled through the woods, after I'd gone to

the wreck to see if he was alive. But he wasn't. Then Mr. Devore told me to say nothing about what had happened. He threatened that if I did he'd wipe out my whole family. That's why I wouldn't tell you, dad. I've been terrible—a fool—a fool!"

"Yes, you have," agreed MacBride. "But did Devore and Manola talk about—well, business?"

Judith thought; then, "No. But I remember, at the Blue River, when Arline and I had come back to the table from the ladies' room, Mr. Devore was saying to Mr. Manola, 'And they think hooch is being made there! A good blind!" And then he laughed.'

MacBride stepped back, stroking his jaw. Judith threw Kerr an embarrassed look, but he came to her and took her hand. "It's all right, Judith. I'm awfully glad you're safe."

"I've been awful, Ted. And yet you're so kind." Feeling his arm about her, she laid her head on his shoulder. "I'll never—never do it again, Ted—never."

MacBride clipped suddenly, "Ted, I've got a hunch. That brewery. I wonder if something besides beer and hooch is being made there."

Kerr looked up from Judith. "What do you mean?"

"I don't know. But I'm going to find out. Come on."

Leaving Judith, Kerr flicked her cheek with his lips, and she pressed his hand.

But MacBride was calling him, and he hurried out at the captain's heels. They strode back to the station, and MacBride hauled out Donnegan and the police car.

"Drive to that old brewery," he clipped.

He sat back beside Kerr and lit a fresh cigar.

Kerr said, "I thought the orders were to lay off that place?"

"I said I'd lay off if they were busting the Volstead Act. But I've got a hunch something else is going on there."

"What, Cap?"

"That's what I'm going to find out. Shoot, Donnegan!"

Donnegan nodded, and as the car moved away from the curb, there were running feet on the sidewalk, and a moment later Kennedy was riding on the running-board.

"Mind if I tag along, Mac?" he grinned.

"You're like a burr in a man's sock, Kennedy. But get in beside Donnegan."

"What's the lay, Mac?"

"Stick around and see if you can find out. Here's a cigar. See if that'll keep your jaw shut."

"Thanks, Mac. Only I'm sore as hell that you didn't tell me beforehand it was Devore you had. Cripes, won't they hand you the razzberry! I shot the story right in. I said you were sitting with Devore alone in your office, with the automatic lying on the desk. You were trying to make him swear it was his gun, and in the heat of the argument Devore grabbed it and covered you. I had to make up a lot of fiction, but that was because you didn't explain. I ended up by saying that you were sure you'd recapture him, and all that sort of boloney."

"That's as good as anything," muttered MacBride. "Now jam that cheroot in your mouth and sign off."

Twenty minutes later they were driving along Farmingville Turnpike. The night was dark, and within the past ten minutes a chill Autumn drizzle had started, the kind of drizzle that is half rain and half mist—penetrating and clammy. The rubber tires hissed sibilantly on the wet macadam, and the beams of the headlights were reflected back from the gray vapor.

Presently Donnegan slowed down and swung in close to the side of the road, extinguished the lights.

"Can't you drive into the bushes?" asked MacBride. "We ought to get the car off the road and out of sight."

Donnegan tried this and succeeded. Then they all got out and stood in a group.

MacBride said, "We'll walk up. There's a lane a hundred yards on, leading into the brewery, which is a quarter of a mile off the Turnpike. You," he said to Kennedy, "better stay out of this."

"Try and do it, Mac. I didn't come out here to pick wildflowers."

MacBride growled, turned and plowed through the bushes. The others followed, and in short time they reached the lane. It led through vacant fields, fenced in, where in the old days horses belonging to the brewing company had grazed.

"Here comes a machine!" warned Kerr, and they dived into the tall grass by the fence.

Two beams of light danced through the gloom. The machine was bound in from the Turnpike, and presently it purred by—a big, opulent limousine. When its tail light had disappeared behind a bend, MacBride stood up, motioned to the others, and proceeded. The visor on his cap was beaded with the drizzle.

Gradually the buildings loomed against the blue-black sky—the big main plant, surrounded by stables and storehouses. Not a light could be seen. They reached the first outbuilding, and from where he stood MacBride could see a half-dozen automobiles parked near the main building, by the loading platform. Here and there he saw a faint red glow near the machines.

"Chauffeurs, smoking," he decided, and his gaze wandered up the dark face of the big three-storied building, which an ancient brewing company had evacuated three years ago.

"Something phony going on there, or I don't know my tricks," remarked Kennedy.

"Guess this is the time you do," replied MacBride. "Let's work around to the rear."

They retraced their steps a short distance and then began creeping around the outside of the building, weaving through tall grass and dried-out weeds. Ten minutes later they were at the off-side of the main building, deep in shadows. MacBride found a window with broken panes, nodded to the others, and crawled through. He dropped a few feet into a chill, damp cellar, black as pitch; stood waiting while Kerr, Kennedy and then Donnegan, followed.

"Your flash, Donnegan," he whispered, and felt the cylinder pressed into his hand.

He snapped on the light. The beam leaped through the clammy gloom, shone on stacks of dusty kegs, long out of use, and on stacks of bottles musty with cobwebs. The odor of must and mold seeped into the men's nostrils.

MacBride led the way, winding in and out between the rows of barrels. Further on he came to a small, heavy door which, swinging open under his hand, led into another section of the cellar. Here were more barrels, but they were standing upright, and the smell of new wine was prevalent. Barrels of it. Kennedy licked his lips, then pointed ahead.

The beam of light swung back and forth across stacked cases of liquor. The men crept closer.

"Hot diggity!" whispered Kennedy. "Look at the Dewar's, and the Sandy MacDonald. And—say! . . . Three Star Hennessy!"

"Pipe down!" snapped MacBride under his breath.

"Maybe you got a bum steer after all, Mac. If it's only liquor, and you dragged me all the way out here—"

"Nobody dragged you out here, Kennedy! Quit yapping!"

"I know, but—"

Bang! Bang!

Kerr tensed and his breath shot out with—"What's that?"

Bang! Bang!

MacBride had his gun out, his lips pursed, his eyes looking up toward the unseen regions above.

"One thing," he muttered. "It's not just target practice. Come on!"

X

Four shots, muffled by floors and walls but, nevertheless, somewhere in that building.

MacBride, with his flash sweeping around furiously, finally located a staircase that led up to the ground floor. At his heels came Kerr, trailed closely by Donnegan and Kennedy. MacBride paused to get his bearings.

Another shot rang out, echoes trailing, commingled with the sounds of banging doors and the shouts of men.

"This way!" clipped MacBride, espying another stairway.

He ascended two steps at a time, reached the next landing. He looked up into the gloom above just in time to see a slash of gun-fire rip through the darkness. In the sudden flare he saw a man with hands upthrown. Then there was a thumping sound, as the man fell.

MacBride's flash was out. His lips were set. He whispered to his men, "Watch it, boys! This place is a death trap! Stick close!"

A sudden exchange of shots burst out on the floor above, and the rebound of bullets could be heard intermingled with screaming oaths and pounding feet. Then, nearby, MacBride heard a body hurtling down the stairs. He jumped in that direction, caught a man in the act of scrambling to his feet. Heaving up, the man struck out and the barrel of a revolver whanged by MacBride's cheek and stopped against his shoulder.

MacBride struck back with his own thirty-eight and landed it on the stranger's skull. Then Donnegan was there to help him, gripping the man's arms from behind. They dragged him down the hall, felt their way into a room, and then MacBride snapped on his flash and looked at their catch.

It was the bull-necked red-head whom he had seen in Devore's hide-out in Jockey Street. The man was streaked with blood.

"What the hell are you doing here?" MacBride wanted to know.

"Playin' Santy Claus—"

"Cut out the wisecracks! What's going on upstairs?"

"Go up an' find out. Go on. Slugs are sailin' around up there like flies in the summer time."

"I'll tend to you later," bit off MacBride; and to Donnegan, "Get out your bracelets and clamp him to the water pipe on the wall."

This done, MacBride again led the way back up the hall. As they reached the foot of the staircase leading to the floor, they partly heard, vaguely saw, a knot of men milling down the steps.

MacBride squared off and pressed on his flash.

"Good cripes almighty!" exploded one of the men.

"As you are!" barked MacBride.

The man in the lead was carrying a canvas bag. The man was Chuck Devore, and behind him were six others. One of these snapped up his gun and fired. The shot smashed MacBride's flashlight, tore through his left hand that held it. He cursed and reeled sidewise, and Kerr's gun boomed close by his ear, and the slug ripped through the gang on the stair.

"Back up!" one of them called to his companions.

MacBride thrust his wounded hand into his pocket and fired at them.

"Come on!" he snapped, and leaped up the staircase.

Kerr passed him on the way up, and let fly with three fast shots. A gangster crumpled near the top, spun around and came crashing down. He reeled off MacBride and pitched over the railing. At the top, a gun spat and a bullet grazed Kerr's cheek, leaving a hot sting. Then they were on the top floor.

In a close exchange of shots Kennedy gasped and clutched at his left arm, and Donnegan stopped short, his legs sagging. His gun dropped from his hand and he crumpled. MacBride stumbled over him and sprayed the gloom with three shots. A man screamed and another flung out a bitter stream of oaths that died in a groan. MacBride plugged ahead, reeling over prone bodies, himself dazed with the pain of his wounded arm.

He saw a square of the night sky framed in a window, saw it blocked suddenly by a figure that stepped out to a fire-escape. The figure twisted and a slash of gun-fire stabbed the darkness. MacBride's cap was carried from his head. His own gun belched and the man in the window doubled over and fell back into the hall.

Then he brought up short, looked out and saw, vaguely, a couple of automobiles tearing away into the night. He spun around, expecting another enemy, but a dread pall had descended after that last shot. Kerr limped up to him, panting. Kennedy was swearing softly. MacBride snapped on his own flash and saw them, bloody and torn; Kerr with a gash on his cheek, Kennedy slowly sopping a wound in his arm. The beam picked out dead bodies on the floor. He swayed back and bent over Donnegan, then stood up, wagging his head.

"I'll never say, 'Shoot, Donnegan,' again," he muttered.

His light swung around and settled on the man he had shot by the window. It was Devore, still gripping the canvas bag. MacBride bent down and opened the bag, and saw a mass of bills—fives, tens, twenties. He gave the bag to Kerr, and moved on toward a door. He threw his light in here and saw a large, square room whose expensive furnishings were in ruin. He espied a light switch and pressed the button, and a big chandelier sprang to life.

"Hot diggity!" exclaimed Kennedy.

Dead men were here, too. But what had caused Kennedy's exclamation was the gambling layout. There was a roulette wheel. There was a faro table. There were a half dozen card tables, two of them overturned. There were cards and chips spread over the floor. The windows were covered by heavy curtains, and ventilators were in the ceiling.

"My hunch was right," nodded MacBride, bitterly.

"And look who's here!" cried Kennedy. "Duke Manola—dead as a doornail. And—oh, boy!—the late Judge Mike Haggerty—*late* is right. Where," he yelled, looking around, "oh, where is a telephone? What a scoop!"

There was a shot below, and MacBride whirled. He dived out into the hall, with Kerr at his heels, and went down the stairway on the fly. His flash leaped forth and spotted two figures running for the lower staircase.

"Stop!" he shouted.

His answer was a shot that went wild. But MacBride fired as he ran, and saw one of the figures topple. He kept going, furiously, and collided with the other.

"All right, Cap. You've got me."

His flash shone on the face of a woman.

The man lying dead on the floor was the redhead.

XI

"Well," said MacBride, "who are you?"

"Arline Kane, and what about it?"

"No lip, sister. What are you doing here?"

She laughed—a hard little laugh. "Came in to look around. I heard the fireworks from the road. I found Red tied to a pipe and I shot away the nice little bracelet."

"You come upstairs," directed MacBride, and shoved her toward the staircase.

Once in the hidden gambling den, Arline stood with her hands on her hips and looked around with lazy eyes.

"Hell," she said, "what a fine mess. Real wild West stuff. Jesse James and his boy scouts were pikers alongside these playboys. Well, there's Duke, the bum. Good thing."

"What do you mean?" asked MacBride.

She sat down and lit a cigarette. "Don't know, eh? Well, Duke used to be my boy friend, until he got hot over a little flapper not dry behind the ears yet. Gave me my walking papers. That was after he tried to frame Chuck Devore, and Chuck breezed for a while. But when Chuck came back, I looked him up and we consolidated our grudge against the wop.

"We got one good break. Duke and his kid brother were on the outs. The kid wanted more money, but Duke was nobody's fool. He told Joe where he got off. I understand they actually came to blows. Well, it was about that time I met Joe, and like a kid he handed me his sob story about Duke landing on him.

"I got him tight one night and he sprung his tongue for a fare-ye-well. Told me about Duke buying this brewery to make and store booze. But some politicians, and Diamond Jack Winslow—laying there, with the busted neck—were behind him. Diamond Jack installed the games here and Haggerty was to get a thirty percent split from Jack on the house winnings. Duke had some money in it, but he was mainly for the booze end. Haggerty promised protection, and Duke, in payment, promised three thousand votes for Haggerty's party.

"Well, Duke's kid brother was hard up for money, and Duke would never let him run with the gang. So Chuck and I got the kid one night and put it up to him: He could clean up by raiding this dump, by tipping us off when the games were running high. Then the other night, he got drunk and sore and—"

"Pulled a bone," put in MacBride, "on Old Stone Road. I know all about that. And then tonight Devore and his rats thought they'd pull a fast one—do what we'd least expect after their first fumble—jump this joint and clean out before we'd caught our breath. Well, they would have fooled me, sister. I *didn't* expect them. I came here on a hunch to look around, and found fireworks. And you—you're the last one."

"Out of luck again," she nodded.

"You could make some money," put in Kennedy, "writing a series of articles for the *Evening News* on 'How I Went Wrong.'"

"You would say that, ink fingers," she gave him, derisively. "But I'll do no writing. And because I'm the last straggler, I'll take no rap." She bit off the end of her cigarette and flung the other part away with a defiant gesture. "A pill was in the tip. Always carried one for just a tough break like this." Her eyes were glazed. "Not lilies, boys . . . something red . . . roses."

A day later MacBride sat at his desk in the station, his cap tipped back, one eye squinted against the smoke from his cigar while he read the *Free Press*' account of last night's holocaust. Sometimes he wagged his head, amazed at remarks which he was alleged to have made.

The city was shocked to the core. Election possibilities had turned more than one somersault during the past twelve hours. Big officials were making charges and counter charges. And MacBride, with his hunch, was mainly responsible for it.

He looked up to see Kennedy standing in the doorway. He put down the paper and leaned back. Kennedy's arm, like his own, was in a sling.

"Greetings, Mac. No end of greetings." He wandered in and slid down on a chair. "How do you like the writeup I gave you?"

"You're a great liar, Kennedy."

"Well, hell, I had to make up a lot of goofy stuff, sure. What's the biggest lie, Mac?"

"Where the account says, 'Captain MacBride, having received a tip from an unidentified person, probably a stoolie, that a certain gang was planning to raid the near-beer plant on Farmingville Turnpike last night, immediately drove out to forestall any such attempt.'" He jabbed the paper with a rigid forefinger. "That's the part, Kennedy."

Kennedy shrugged. "Yeah, you're right. When I got back to the office and wrote the thing up, I wondered how you *had* got the tip. Well, I was in a hurry, so I wrote in that—just that. It sounded all right, fitted all right—and look here, Mac. It just about cinches any chance of the big guns bawling you out. You were tipped off by a stoolie—a phone call—no name. You shot out there and the raid was under way. What developed later was not your fault. It's air tight!"

MacBride creaked his chair forward, sighed, and drew a bottle and glasses from his desk. He set them down.

"Have a drink, Kennedy."

Kennedy edged nearer the desk and, arching a weary eyebrow, poured himself a stiff three fingers. MacBride poured himself a drink, and leaned back with it.

"Kennedy," he said, "there have been times when I ached to wring your neck. You're a cynical, cold-blooded, snooping, wisecracking example of modern newspaperdom. But, Kennedy, you've got brains—and you're on the square. Here's to you."

Kennedy grinned in his world-weary way. "Boloney, Mac. No matter how you slice it, it's still boloney," he said.

The Law Laughs Last

Frederick Nebel

Captain MacBride and organized crime have a showdown

I

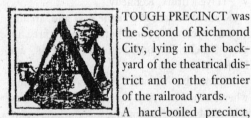

TOUGH PRECINCT was the Second of Richmond City, lying in the backyard of the theatrical district and on the frontier of the railroad yards.

A hard-boiled precinct, touching the fringes of crookdom's élite on the north—the con men, the night-club barons; and on the south, the dim-lit, crooked alleys traversed by the bum, the lush-worker and poolroom gangster. On the north were the playhouses, the white way, high-toned apart-

ments, opulent hotels, high hats, evening gowns. On the south, tenements, warehouses, cobblestones, squalor, and the railroad yards. The toughest precinct in all Richmond City.

Captain MacBride, back again in the Second, ran it with two fists, a dry sense of humor and a generous quantity of brass-bound nerve. He was a lean, windy-eyed man of forty. He had a wife and an eighteen-year-old daughter in a vine-clad bungalow out in suburban Grove Manor, and having acquired early in life a suspicion that he was going to die young and violently in the line of duty, he had forthwith taken out a lot of life insurance. He was not a pessimist, but a hard-headed materialist, and he rated crooks and gunmen with a certain species of rodent that travels by dark and frequents cellars, sewers and garbage dumps.

He was sitting in his office at the station house a mild spring night, going over a sheaf of police bulletins, when Kennedy, of the *Free Press*, strolled in.

"Spring has come, Mac," Kennedy yawned.

"Why don't you set it to poetry?"

"I got over that years ago." He drifted over to the desk, helped himself to a cigar from an open box, sniffed it critically. "Dry," he muttered.

"I like 'em dry."

"I always keep mine moist."

MacBride chuckled. "That's rich! First time I see you smoking a cigar of your own I'll buy you a box of Montereys. Well, what's on your mind?"

Kennedy looked toward the open window through which came the blare and beat of a jazz band muffled by distance.

"That," he said.

MacBride nodded. "I thought so. I'll bet if something doesn't bust loose over there you'll get down-hearted."

Kennedy shrugged, sank wearily to a chair and lit up. "And I'll bet you're happy as hell they're staging that political block-party. You look it, Mac."

"Don't I!" muttered MacBride, a curl to his lip. "Yes, Kennedy, I'm happy as a school kid when vacation time comes. Of all the dumb stunts I can think of, this block-party takes the cake. If this night passes without somebody getting bumped off, I'll get pie-eyed drunk and take a calling-down from my wife. A political campaign in Richmond City makes a Central American rebellion look comical."

"And how!" grinned Kennedy. "But I only hope Krug and Bedell get kicked out of office so hard they'll never get over it. As State's Attorney, Krug's made a fortune, and Alderman Johnny Bedell's his right-hand man. I'm all for Anderson for State's Attorney and Connaught for alderman of this district. They're square. But I wouldn't be willing to bet on the

outcome. The Mayor and his crowd are behind Krug.

"And here's the nigger in the woodpile. Connaught and Anderson are square men. They deserve to get in office. But there's a gang in this city that's taken it into their own hands to make things hot as hell for Krug and Bedell, and by doing this they're going to cramp the Anderson-Connaught square style. Connaught and Anderson don't want their support, but they've got to take it—through the nose, too."

"Say who you mean, Kennedy," broke in MacBride. "Come on and tell me you mean Duveen and his guns."

"Sure—Duveen. Duveen hasn't got a good break since Krug's been State's Attorney. But who has? Simple, Bonelio, the S.A.'s friend. And Bonelio is sure tooting his horn for the Krug-Bedell ticket. If Anderson gets in for State's Attorney he'll put a wet blanket on Bonelio's racket; and if Anderson sweeps Connaught in with him, it'll mean that Bonelio's warehouses this side of the railroad yards will be swept clean.

"And that's what Duveen wants, because he wants to run the bootleg racket in Richmond City, and so long as Bonelio has the present State's Attorney and the alderman for this district on his side, Duveen's blocked. What a hell of a riot this election is going to be!"

MacBride grunted, opened a drawer and pulled out a bottle of Three Star Hennessy.

"Have a drink, Kennedy," he said. "There are times when I'd like to kick you in the slats, but I admire your brains and the way you get the low-down on things."

Through the window came another burst of dance music. On Jackson Street couples were dancing, political banners were flying, ropes of colored lights were glowing. And policemen were on the walkout, idly swinging nightsticks, watching, waiting, prepared for the worst and hoping for the best.

MacBride lit a cigar and looked up to find Detective Moriarity standing in the doorway.

" 'Lo, cap. 'Lo, Kennedy." Moriarity was a slim, compactly built young man, short on speech, quick in action—one-time runner-up for the welterweight title.

"How do things look?" asked MacBride.

"Depends," said Moriarity. "Committeeman Shanz is a little tight. Bedell ain't there yet. Shanz expects him, though. Says Bedell's s'posed to speak at eleven."

"See any bums?"

"No. But pipe this. I just been tipped off that a crowd of Anderson-Connaught sympathizers from the Fourth Ward are making a tour of the town. About ten machines. Band and flags and all that crap. I figure this way. Ten to one all o' them have got some booze along, to make 'em feel better. They're mostly storekeepers and automobile dealers, but if they get tight they'll get gay. Like as not they'll wind up at the block-party and some wiseguy will haul off and talk outta turn."

MacBride doubled his fist and took a crack at the desk. "Just about that, Jake! All right. Get back on the job. Cohen with you?"

"Yeah, Ike's over there. Patrolmen Gunther and Holstein at one end the street. McClusky and Swanson the other. Things are running smooth so far. Don't see any o' Duveen's guns, or Bonelio's."

"That," said MacBride, "is what itches me. Bonelio ought to be there. He's Shanz's friend."

"He's not there. None of his guns, either. Tell you who is there, though, cap."

"Who?"

"Bonelio's skirt. That little wren he yanked from the burlesque circuit and shoved in his ritzy night-club on Paradise Street. Trixie Meloy. Ask me and I'll crack she still oughter be back in burlesque, and third rate at that."

"Who's she with?"

"Alone. High-hatting everybody. But she sticks close to Shanz."

"I got it!" clipped MacBride. "She's waiting for somebody, for Bonelio. Watch her, Jake. It's ten-thirty now. Bonelio should have been on hand long ago. He shows up at all of the district's balls and dances. Until he comes anything can happen. Tell the cops to keep their eyes open.

Tell Cohen to tend to business and quit trying to date up the gals. I know Ike. On the way out tell the sergeant to see the reserves are ready for a break. First time you pipe a Duveen gun on the scene, run him off. If he cracks wise, bring him over here.

"Remember, Jake, this precinct is just about as safe as a volcano. We've heard rumblings for the past month, and God knows when the top'll blow off. It's a tough situation. I'm all for the Anderson-Connaught ticket, as you know, but no rat like Duveen is going to get away with anything. He doesn't give a damn for the Anderson-Connaught combine. He's sore at the present State's Attorney and the greaseball Bonelio. Both of them ought to be in the pen, and before this election is over I've got a hunch one of them will be—if he doesn't get bumped off during the rush. On your way, Jake, and good luck."

Moriarity went out.

Kennedy said, "I'm going over and look around, too, Mac."

"You smell headlines for tomorrow's *Press*, don't you?"

"Yeah—the city of dreadful night. Hell, man, we ain't had a good hot story since that Dutch butcher tapped his frau on the knob with a meat ax. Years ago, Mac, old bean!"

"Two weeks ago last night," mused MacBride. "Ah-r-r, when will this crime wave stop? Wives killing husbands; husbands killing wives! College kids going in for suicide and double death pacts! Men braining little kids! Men willing to kill to get power!"

"That," said Kennedy, pausing in the doorway, "is what keeps the circulation of the daily tabloids on top. See you later."

Alone, MacBride stared into space for a long moment, his eyes glazed with thought. Then he sighed bitterly, flung off the mood with a savage little gesture, and continued looking over the collection of police bulletins.

Fifteen minutes dragged by. The dusty-faced clock on the wall ticked them off with hollow monotony.

Then the telephone rang.

MacBride picked up the receiver, said, "Hello."

"MacBride?"

"Yup."

"Bedell's slated to get the works tonight."

The instrument clicked.

"Hello—hello!" barked MacBride.

There was no use. The man behind the mysterious voice had hung up. MacBride rang the operator, gave his name.

"Trace that call," he snapped. "Fast!"

II

He pressed one of a series of buttons on his desk. The door opened. Lieutenant Donnelly tramped in wiping the cobwebs of a recent nap from his eyes.

"On your toes, lieutenant!" cracked MacBride. "Just got a blind call that Bedell's going to get bumped off. You'll take charge here tonight while I'm on the outside."

The telephone rang. MacBride reached for it, said, "Yes?" A moment later he hung up, snorted with disappointment. "Call was from a booth in the railroad terminal."

"Who d' you suppose it was, captain?" ventured Donnelly.

"How the hell do I know?" MacBride was on his feet, buttoning his coat. He reached for his visored cap, but changed his mind and slapped on a flap-brimmed fedora.

"I'll be over on Jackson Street," he told Donnelly crisply. "Bedell's supposed to pull a campaign speech at eleven. I'll put the clamps on that. Bedell's no friend of mine, but I'm damned if any bum is going to kill him in my precinct. If Headquarters wants me, give 'em the dope and tell 'em where I am."

He strode into the central room and shot brief orders to the desk sergeant. Then he drafted four policemen from the reserve room. They came out buttoning their coats, nightsticks drawn. The lieutenant, the sergeant, the four policemen—all were affected by the vigor, the spirit with which MacBride dived into the middle of things. No captain liked more to get out in the raw and the rough of crime than MacBride. The crack of his voice, the snap of his movement, made him a man whom others were eager to follow. Hard he was, but with the hardness of a man supremely capable of command. He had turned down a Headquarters job on the grounds that it was too soft—that he would stagnate and grow old before his time, grow whiskers and a large waistband.

He led the way out of the station house. His step was firm and resolute, and he carried himself with a definite air of determination. One block west, and two south, and they were at Jackson Street.

The band was playing a fox trot. The block was roped off at either end, and a hundred couples were dancing on the street pavement. On the sidewalks and the short stone flights before the tenement were a hundred-odd onlookers. Strung from pole to pole were rows of colored electric lights. Banners were waving; posters showing likenesses of Alderman Bedell and State's Attorney Krug emblazoned the houses and the poles. A temporary bandstand had been erected in the middle of the block, and from this, too, the candidates for re-election were expected to speak.

MacBride looked the place over critically. Detective Ike Cohen left a couple of girls to join the captain.

"Something up, Cap?"

"Maybe. See any old familiar faces around?"

"None that'd interest you. Here comes Moriarity."

At sight of the captain Moriarity frowned quizzically. "Huh?" he asked.

MacBride explained about the telephone call. Gunther and Holstein, the patrolmen stationed at that end of the block, mingled with the four reserves, all wondering what was in the wind.

"Where's Committeeman Shanz?" MacBride asked.

"I'll get him," said Moriarity, and faded into the crowd.

He reappeared in company with Shanz, district committeeman and chairman of the night's carnival. Shanz was a German-Jew, though he had more of the beer-garden look about him. A short, rotund man, beefy-cheeked and spectacled, with a jovial grin that was only skin deep.

"Well, well, captain," he boomed, waddling forward with his hand extended, "this is a pleasure."

MacBride shook and said, "Not so much, Shanz. You've got to bust up this picnic."

Shanz's grin faded. "How's this?"

"The ball is over," explained MacBride. "There's trouble brewing and it's liable to boil over any minute."

"But I got to make a speech," argued Shanz. "And Alderman Bedell is due here now." He looked at his watch. "He's going to make a speech, too."

"I don't give a damn! You're not going to broadcast and neither is Bedell. I tell you, Shanz, this block-party scheme is the bunk. It's the best way I know of to start a riot."

"Do you say that, heh, because you favor the opposition? Ha, I know where your sympathy lays, captain!"

"Don't be a fool! I just got a tip that Bedell's set to get bumped off, and it's not going to happen in my precinct."

Shanz leaned back and threw out his chest. "What is the police for? What are you for?"

"I've got a hunch I'm supposed to side-track crime. I'm no master mind, Shanz. I don't go in for solving riddles. I'm just a cop who tries to beat crime to the tape. Now don't stick out your belly and hand me an argument. I'm not in the mood."

Shanz was troubled. "I can't stop it. If I do that and Bedell can't make his speech he'll land on me. Wait till he comes. Talk to him. But I ain't going to call it off. We staged this so Bedell could make a speech."

MacBride, impatient, cracked fist into palm. "Cripes, I want to clear this crowd out before Bedell gets here! I told you he's not going to make a speech. I won't let him."

The dance number stopped. But from the distance came the sound of another band, with brass and drums in the majority. It drew nearer with the minutes, and then a string of cars appeared, flaunting banners that exalted the virtues of the Anderson-Connaught combine. Colored torches smoked from every machine, and the roving campaigners cheered their candidates lustily.

"What in hell is this?" roared Shanz, reddening.

"Competition," said MacBride.

The automobiles stopped, and the brass band attained new heights of noise commingled with the singing voices of the men. The carnival orchestra, not to be outdone, burst into action, hammering out a military march. The result was boisterous, maddening, and everybody began yelling.

The first symptoms of mob hysteria were apparent.

MacBride snapped quick orders to the policemen. "Chase this crowd! The dance is over!"

He pivoted sharply, set his jaw and plowed through the crowd on a beeline for the leaders of the parade.

"You move on!" he barked. "Come on, no stalling. Get out of here, and I mean now!"

"Aw, go fly a kite," came a bibulous retort. "Everybody havin' helluva good time. Who's all right? Hiram Anderson, the next State's Attorney's all right! Y-e-e-e-e!"

Others took up the cry. Somebody flung a bottle and it crashed against a house front, the glass spattering.

"Dammit," yelled MacBride, "you're starting a riot! Get a move on!"

One of the cars started moving. Others honked their horns. Many of the occupants had piled out and several of them, far gone with walloping liquor, hilarious as sailors on a spree, were trying to tear down the banners of the Krug-Bedell faction. The supporters of Alderman Bedell objected strenuously, and fists began flying about promiscuously. It was, now, anybody's and everybody's carnival. Admission fees were waived. The two bands continued to add to the din and clamor. The tempo of their combined efforts went far toward heightening the strain of hysteria that had taken hold of the mob. The streets were jammed with motor cars, and the horns honked and bleated.

Women screeched, and men began striking out without apparent provocation. The crowd surged this way and that, but never got anywhere. Nightsticks rapped more frequently on stubborn heads. Somebody heaved a brick that crashed through an automobile windshield and knocked the man at the wheel unconscious. The machine swerved, bounded and banged head-on into a doorway.

"Good God Almighty!" groaned MacBride.

He plunged through the mob, fought, pounded, hammered his way to the big touring car that carried the musicians. He leaped to the running-board, wrenched a trombone from the player's hand.

"Stop it!" he yelled. "I'll cave in the next mouth that pulls another toot!"

He silenced them.

He turned and weaved toward the bandstand, and on the way ran into Alderman Bedell.

"Who started this, MacBride? What is it? What's going on?"

"What the hell does it look like, a May party?"

"Don't get sore—don't get sore!"

"Listen to me, Bedell!" MacBride gripped his arm hard. "You're no friend of mine, but I'm giving you a tip. Get out of here! Jump in your car, go home and lock all the doors. Some pup is out to get you!"

"He is, eh?" snarled Bedell, a big whale of a man with gimlet eyes. "Let him!"

"Don't be a blockhead all your life! I tell you, man, you're in danger!" A whiff of Bedell's breath told him the man had been drinking. Drink always made Bedell cocky, and he spoke best from a platform when he was moderately soaked.

"I'm going to d'liver a speech here tonight, MacBride—"

MacBride snorted with disgust and went on

his way. He reached the bandstand and ripped the baton from the leader's hand. He kicked over the drum and shot out short, sizzling commands. He left a silenced bandstand.

The policemen had managed to club into submission the instigators of the riot. Swollen heads, black eyes and bruised jaws were in abundance. The best argument in a riot is a deftly wielded nightstick. A clout on the head is something a temporarily crazed man will understand.

The hysteria was dwindling. A dozen of the rioters were hastily escorted away from the scene by four policemen and taken to the station house. The crowd quieted, took a long breath generally, and waited.

MacBride climbed back upon the bandstand, rumbled the drum in plea for silence, and then raised his voice.

"Please, now, everybody go home!" he demanded. "The party is over. It's too bad, but nothing can be done." He waved his arms. "Clear out, everybody—now!"

A figure bulked at his elbow. It was that of Alderman Bedell, and before MacBride could get a word in edgewise, Bedell roared, "La-dies and gentlemen, it grieves me to see this sociable gathering break up because of the undignified actions of the hirelings—yes, hirelings, I say—of the party which is trying to drive me out of office. As alderman of this district, I want to say—I . . . ugh!"

He clapped a hand to his chest, swayed, then crumpled heavily at MacBride's feet.

"Heart attack," cried someone in the crowd.

MacBride knelt down, turned the alderman over, felt his chest, ran his hand inside the shirt. It came out stained with blood. Bedell twitched, stiffened, and was dead.

Cohen said over MacBride's shoulder, "Headlines, Mac, in the first edition. Hot diggity damn!"

III

An hour later MacBride stood spread-legged in his office at the station house. His coat was unbuttoned, his hair was tousled, and his lean cheeks looked a little drawn.

Among the others present were Committee-man Shanz, Trixie Meloy, Moriarity and Cohen, and the inevitable Kennedy. No one had been apprehended. No shot had been heard. Obviously a silencer had been used on the gun that sent Bedell to his death. Bedell's body was at the morgue being probed by the deputy medical examiner.

"Now look here, Miss Meloy," MacBride said. "You say you were standing on Jackson Street near Holly. You saw a man wearing a light gray suit and a gray cap drift down Holly, get into a car and drive off when Bedell was shot. Why didn't you yell out?"

"Does a lady go shoutin' out like that?" she retorted, tossing her peroxide bob. "Besides I didn't know what it was all about. I didn't know he was shot. I thought he fainted or something. I didn't connect the two up until I heard you yell he was killed. Then I thought of the other man."

"In that case, how does it happen you remember what he wore?"

"Well, I got an eye for nice clothes. He was dressed swell, that's why. A woman notices clothes more than a man does."

"Remember the car?"

"Not so good. It wasn't so near. It looked like a roadster."

"How about the man—besides his clothes?"

"I didn't see his face—only his back as he was walkin' away."

"I see. You're a friend of Tony Bonelio's, aren't you?"

"Yes. Antonio's a good friend of mine."

"My mistake. Antonio." He smiled drily. "How come Antonio wasn't at the dance with you?"

"He was at his night-club. I never seen a block party, so I come down to look it over. Mr. Shanz here invited me. He's a friend of Antonio's."

"Yes, that's right," put in Shanz.

"And listen," said Trixie, looking at her strap-watch. "I got to dance at the Palmetto Club tonight."

"All right, Miss Meloy. You run along. Keep in mind, though, that I may want to ask you more questions."

Shanz stood up. "I'll take Miss Meloy to the club in my car," he said.

"Suit yourself," shrugged MacBride. "Maybe this'll be a lesson to you about block parties."

"It cooks the Anderson-Connaught goose, too, captain," replied Shanz. "Connaught's a guy preaches a lot and then goes and hires gun-men."

"Careful how you talk," warned MacBride. "If it was a gunman of Connaught's I'll nail him. But I've got a hunch it wasn't."

"Then who was it?"

"If I could answer that right now, d' you think I'd be losing a night's sleep?"

"See you get him, anyhow. There's lots o' captains want this job here."

"That's my worry, Shanz, not yours."

"Well, I'm just telling you, see you get him."

"See you mind your own business, too."

Shanz and Trixie Meloy went out.

MacBride opened his desk and passed around the Hennessy. He downed a stiff bracer himself and lit a fresh cigar.

"Cripes," he chuckled grimly, "this'll mean one awful jolt to Connaught. It'll be hard to believe that the guy got Bedell wasn't on Connaught's payroll."

"If," said Moriarity, "we only knew who the guy was sent in that tip you got."

"That's the hitch, Jake," nodded MacBride. "The guy who called up is the key to who killed Bedell."

There was a knock on the door, and Officer Holstein looked in.

"Say, Cap, there's a Polack out here wants to see you. He lives on Jackson Street."

At a nod from MacBride, an old man came in, fumbling with his hat.

"Hello," said the captain. "What's your name?"

"Ma name Tikorsky. I got somet'in' to tell. See, I live number t'ree-twent'-one Jackson, up de top floor. I look out de window, watch de show, see. When de big fellar drop down, I hear"—he looked up at the ceiling—"I hear noise on de roof, like a man run, see."

MacBride jerked up. "You heard a man run across the roof?"

Tikorsky nodded.

"Is there a fire-escape back of where you live?"

"Yeah, sure."

MacBride reached for the phone, called the morgue. In a moment he was speaking with the deputy medical examiner. When he hung up he pursed his lips, and his eyes glittered.

"All right, Mr. Tikorsky," he said. "You can go home. Thanks for telling me. I'll see you again."

The Pole shuffled out.

MacBride looked at Kennedy. "Out, Kennedy. Go home and hit the hay."

"Ah, Mac, give a guy a break," said Kennedy. "What's in the wind?"

"A bad smell. Come on, breeze, now. When there's any news getting out, I'll let you know."

Kennedy got up, shrugged, and sauntered out.

Moriarity and Cohen regarded the captain expectantly.

MacBride said, "I just got the doctor's report. The bullet was a thirty-eight. It hit Bedell in the chest, knocked off part of his heart and lodged in his spine. But get this. The angle of the bullet was on a slant. It went in and *down*."

"Then," said Cohen, "it couldn't have been fired from the corner where the broad saw this guy she was beefin' about."

"No," clipped MacBride. "The Polack was right. He heard a guy on the roof. The guy who was on the roof bumped off Bedell."

"What about this guy in the gray suit?"

"I'm wondering. But we know he couldn't have done it. A bullet from him would have gone up and hit Bedell on the left somewhere." He tapped his foot on the floor. "Well, the show is on, boys. Bonelio, the late alderman's buddy, has a whale of an excuse to oil his guns and start a

war of his own. And Krug, the State's Attorney, will give him protection. Bonelio will suspect the same guy we do."

"Duveen," said Moriarity.

"Exactly. I know just what the greaseball will do."

"Let him," suggested Cohen, with a yawn. "Let the two gangs fight it out, exterminate each other. Who the hell cares?"

MacBride banged the desk. "You would say that, Ike. But I'm responsible for this precinct. I've got one murder hanging over my head as it is. Personally, I wouldn't care if these two gangs did mop each other up. But in a gang war a lot of neutrals always get hurt." He put on his hat. "Let's look over the Polack's roof."

The three of them went around to 321 Jackson Street, located the rooms where the old Pole lived, and then ascended to the roof. Moriarity had a flashlight. They discovered nothing to which they might attach some relative importance. They took the fire-escape down to a paved alley that paralleled the back of the row of houses and led to Holly Street.

"See here, boys," MacBride said. "Wander around and get the low-down on Duveen's gang. If you see Duveen, cross-examine him. Better yet, tell him I want to see him."

The two detectives moved off. MacBride headed back for the station-house and requisitioned the precinct flivver. A man named Garret was his chauffeur. After brief instructions on MacBride's part, they drove off.

Twenty minutes later they stopped on Paradise Street, uptown. It was a thoroughfare of old brownstone houses that, following the slow encroachment of the white lights, had been turned into tearooms, night-clubs and small apartments, patronized mostly by people of the theatre.

Garret remained with the flivver. MacBride entered the Palmetto Club, to which an interior decorator had tried his best to give a tropical air. The manager did not know him, and said so.

"That's all right," said MacBride. "I don't want to see you, anyhow. Where's Bonelio?"

A moment later he met Bonelio in a private room handsomely furnished. Bonelio was a chunky Italian of medium height, dressed in the mode. He had smooth white skin, dark circles under his eyes, and an indolent gaze.

"Sit down, MacBride. Rye or Scotch?" he asked.

MacBride noticed a bottle of Golden Wedding. "Rye," he said.

"Ditto." Bonelio poured the drinks, said, "Well, poor Bedell."

"What I came here about."

They looked at each other as they downed their tots.

"About what?" Bonelio dropped on to a divan and lit a cigarette.

"Just this," said MacBride. "I'm banking on the hunch that you suspect who's behind the killing. I'm asking, and at the same time telling you, to keep out of it. We've never been friends, Bonelio, and don't get it into your nut that I'm making any overtures. But I don't want any rough work done in my precinct. I'll handle it according to the law. You just stand aside and keep your hands off. You get me?"

"Sure. But let me tell you, MacBride, that the first pup gets in my way or monkeys around my playground, I'll start trouble and I don't give a damn whose precinct it's in. I'm sitting on top of the world in Richmond City and no guy's going to horn in."

"I'm telling you, Bonelio, walk lightly in my precinct. I'm giving you fair warning. I'm putting on the lid and I'm locking up any guy that so much as disturbs the peace. That goes for you and your gang as well as anybody else. You can sell all the booze you want. Much as I dislike you, I've never bothered your rum warehouses down by the railroad yards—"

"You were told not to. The big boys are my friends."

"Don't take advantage of it. I could be nasty if I wanted to. And I will, if you butt in in my precinct."

"Here's hoping you get Duveen for the murder of Bedell."

"Make sure *you* don't try to!"

MacBride banged out, hopped into the flivver and Garret drove him back to the station-house.

Moriarity and Cohen were playing penny-ante, half-heartedly.

"What news?" asked MacBride.

"None," said Cohen. "Duveen hasn't been seen for the past week."

"Hasn't, eh? All right, we want him, then. Sergeant," he called to the man at the desk, "ring Headquarters. General alarm. Chuck Duveen wanted. Ask Headquarters to spread the news and start the net working. I want Duveen before"—his lips flattened—"before somebody else gets him."

IV

Next day the papers carried big headlines. The sheets that were in sympathy with the current administration bellowed loudly and asked the public to consider the drastic measures used by the opposition to gain its own end. The others, among them the *Free Press,* employed a calmer, more detached tone, and pleaded with justice to get at the root of all evil. Both Anderson and Connaught, aspirants for the offices of State's Attorney and alderman of the Sixth Election District respectively, deplored the tragedy and promised all manner of aid in running down the person or persons who had murdered their opponent, the late Alderman Bedell. State's Attorney Krug promised quick action in the event the criminal was apprehended. Charges and counter charges ran rampant.

MacBride, having gone home at three in the morning, did not get back on the job until noon. He felt rested and his clean-clipped face glowed ruddily from recent contact with lather and razor. He had read the papers on the way in from Grove Manor with the attitude of a man who knows the inner workings of politics and news-paperdom. In short, a slight morsel of what he read was worthwhile, and the rest was bunk—salve for an outraged public.

The one item that drew his attention was anent the fact that Adolph Shanz was to run for alderman in place of the late Alderman Bedell. This made him chuckle bitterly. As committee-man Shanz had been, ever since he was elected, clay in the hands of Krug and Bedell. If elected for alderman, he would be one of Krug's most pliable tools.

The police net was spread for Duveen. The city was combed up, down and across. But the man was not caught. The only information available, gleaned as it was from old familiar hangouts of the gang boss, showed that Duveen had not been seen for a week. A day passed, and then two and three, with the man still at large.

Wherefore, on the fourth day, Captain MacBride was convened for a solid hour with the Commissioner of Police, a man who ran the Department and gave quarter nowhere. The meeting took place in the morning, and before noon MacBride was back in the station-house. There he held a brief consultation with his assistants.

In conclusion, he said to the sergeant at the desk, "When Kennedy, or any other of his breed drifts in, tell him I have a statement for the press."

Alone in his office, he drank his first bracer and started his first cigar of the day. He chafed his hands vigorously, paced the floor with a little more than his customary energy, trailing banners of excellent cigar smoke behind him. A beam of sunlight streamed through the open window. On the telephone wires that passed behind the old station-house, birds were swaying and chirping. MacBride's eyes were keen and narrow with thought.

An hour later, when he was writing at his desk, a knock sounded on the door.

"Come in," he yelled.

Kennedy came in. "What the hell's this I hear about—"

"Sit down. Glad to see something can work you up and make you look as if you weren't dying on your feet."

"Come on, spill it, Mac!"

"My wife's birthday."

"Cripes—"

"Should see the new spring outfit I bought her. Kennedy, she gets younger every day. Well"—he cleared his throat with a serio-comic air—"look who her husband is."

"For the love o' God, what's the matter, are you batty?"

MacBride grinned—one of his rare, broad grins that few people knew, outside of his wife and daughter.

"All right, Kennedy," he said. "I said I'd give you a break when I started broadcasting. I'm broadcasting. Tune in. Early this morning Detective Moriarity picked up a man for violating the state law regarding the possession of concealed weapons. This man was carrying an automatic pistol.

"He was cross-examined by Captain Stephen J. MacBride—don't omit the J. Intense questioning brought out certain interesting facts, in the light of which Captain MacBride hopes to apprehend—and don't insert 'it is alleged'—Captain MacBride hopes to apprehend the man who killed the late Alderman Bedell within the next twenty-four hours.

"For certain reasons known to the Department alone, the informant's name will not be divulged for the present. Suffice it to say that during the course of the cross-examination it was learned that this man was the one who phoned anonymously to Captain MacBride about one hour before Alderman Bedell was murdered, warning him that the murder was prearranged."

He rubbed his hands together. "How does that sound? Pretty good for a plain, ordinary cop, eh? And I never took a correspondence course, either."

"But who's this guy you picked up?" demanded Kennedy.

"You heard me, didn't you? He's under lock and key right here in the precinct. Put that in, too, Kennedy. He's locked up at the precinct. But who he is—that's my business for the time being. Headquarters is standing by me to the bitter end on that. Now pipe down and consider yourself lucky I've given you this much. Here, sink a drink under your belt and see that story gets good space."

Still curious, Kennedy, nevertheless, went out. Within the hour other reporters got the story. It would be on the streets at four that afternoon.

Moriarity dropped in, when MacBride was alone, and asked, "Think it will work, Cap?"

"Man, oh, man, I'm banking everything on it right now. It's a bluff—sure, a hell of a big bluff. And if it doesn't trap somebody or give me a decent lead I'll take the razz. Just now the underworld is stagnant, Jake. This will be the stone that stirs the water. We're supposed to have somebody here who knows who killed Bedell. Whoever killed him, will make a move. What that move will be, I don't know, but I'm ready to meet it."

Moriarity was frankly dubious. "Dunno, Cap. Maybe I'm short on imagination. You're taking a long chance giving out the news we got a mysterious somebody picked up and locked in."

"I'm willing to take it, Jake. It's a bluff—the biggest bluff I ever pulled in my life. Just play with me, Jake. Appear mysterious. All you've got to keep saying is that you picked a guy up— but no more. I've got all the keys to that cell and nobody, I don't care who he is, is going to see that it's empty."

"Gawd," muttered Moriarity, "I hope you don't get showed up."

"That's all right, Jake. Cut out worrying. Just play your part, and if the breaks go against us, I'll take the razz personally."

Moriarity wandered out, far from overjoyed.

At four the news spread. Quick work, mused many—an important prisoner in the hands of the police already, with the account of the murder still vivid in the city's mind. And the mysterious tone of it; that was intriguing, MacBride holding the man's name a secret.

MacBride read three different sheets.

The *Free Press* mentioned his name more than the others. That was Kennedy's work. Good sort, Kennedy, even though he did get on a man's nerves at times. Kennedy's column was well-written, concise, cool, almost laconic.

At four-thirty a big limousine pulled up before the station-house. State's Attorney Krug, a large, faultlessly groomed man, innately arrogant, strode into MacBride's office swinging his stick savagely.

"Look here, Captain," he rapped out, "what is the meaning of this? I refer to the late editions, and to this fellow Moriarity picked up."

"What does what mean?" MacBride wanted to know, unperturbed.

Krug struck the floor with his stick. "Why, as State's Attorney of this county, I think it is no more than pertinent that I should be informed of such important news before it comes out in the newspapers."

"Dark secret, Mr. Krug," said MacBride. "The Department's prisoner. When we get through with him, we'll turn him over to the State Attorney's office."

"But I should like to have a preliminary talk with the fellow, so that I may go about preparing briefs. I tell you, Captain, action is what is necessary."

"I agree with you. But as it is, Mr. Krug, the prisoner is still in the Department's hands."

"Nonsense! We can have just an informal little chat. I want to see the fellow. What is he called, by the way?"

MacBride shook his head. "The whole thing is a dark secret. When I spring it, everybody'll know."

"But dammit, man, I am State's Attorney! I demand to interview the prisoner!"

"I ought to add," put in MacBride, "that I have the backing of the Department. There's the phone if you care to call the Commissioner."

State's Attorney Krug departed in high heat, bewailing the fact that the Department was trying to double-cross the very efficient State's Attorney's office.

"You know why he's in such a hurry, Jake?" MacBride asked Moriarity.

"Sure. Stage a fast trial, get a quick conviction. It'd help him for re-election."

MacBride chuckled grimly. Moriarity drifted out, leaving the captain alone.

It was about half an hour later that the door swung open, and a tall, broad-shouldered man entered casually. He kicked the door shut with his heel, stood with his hands thrust into his coat pockets, a cigarette drooping from one corner of his mouth. His face was deeply bronzed, his eyes pale and hard as agate.

"My error," he said, "if I didn't knock. Thought I'd drop in and see why you've been looking for me."

"Sit down, Duveen."

"I'll stand."

MacBride leaned back in his chair. "Are you heeled?"

"No. Want to look?"

"I'll take your word. But you've got one hell of a lot of nerve to come in here."

"Open to the public, ain't it?" Duveen gushed smoke through his nostrils. "I want to know what's all this crack about you looking for me."

"Where have you been for the last ten days?"

"I don't see where that's any of your business. I was touring. I took a ride to Montreal. Get up on your dates, skipper. I've been gone two weeks. Scouting around for good liquor. Got two truckloads coming down for the election—and afterwards."

"Counting on Anderson and Connaught getting in?"

"Yup."

"Won't do you any good. Connaught's going to clean up this district, and you'll never be able to buy off Anderson."

"All I want is the bum Krug out. Well, you were looking for me. Here I am."

"About that Bedell killing."

"What about it?"

"You'll need a strong alibi to prove where you were on that night, Duveen."

"Talking of—arrest?"

"About that."

Duveen laughed. "Not a chance, MacBride.

Krug would frame me so tight I'd never have a chance. Guess again."

"Nevertheless. . . ." MacBride's hand moved toward the row of buttons on the desk.

Duveen snapped, "*Kid!*"

"Up high, Cap!" hissed a voice at the window.

MacBride swivelled. A rat-faced runt was leaning in through the open window, an automatic trained on the captain.

Duveen ran to the window, stepped out. There was an economy of words. With a leer, the rat-faced man disappeared.

MacBride yanked his gun, blew a whistle.

The reserves, Moriarity and Cohen came on the run. They swept out, guns drawn.

But the city swallowed Duveen and his gunman.

MacBride took the blow silently, choking down his chagrin.

"Did he wear a gray suit?" asked Moriarity.

"Yes," muttered MacBride. "Block all city exits, place men in the railroad station. Tell Headquarters to inform all outlying precincts and booths, motorcycle and patrol flivvers, Duveen's in town. What I can't understand is, why the hell he came strolling in here?"

"Crust, Cap. Duveen's got more gall, more nerve, than any bum I know of. Probably came looking for information."

"Yes, and I pulled a bone," confessed MacBride. "I should have played him a while, drawn him out. But seeing him here, I wanted to get the clamps on him right away. He had no gun—he's wise. But he had a gunman planted outside the window. If I can get him, get this Trixie Meloy gal to identify him as the man walked down Holly Street toward the roadster, we can crash his alibi. We know he couldn't have fired the shot, but it's likely one of his rats was planted on the roof, and Duveen was on hand to see things went off as per schedule."

An hour later the telephone rang.

"MacBride?"

The captain thought fast. "No. You want him?"

"Yes."

"Wait a minute."

MacBride dived into the central room, barked, "Sergeant, call the telephone exchange—quick—see where this guy's calling from."

The sergeant whipped into action, had the report in less than a minute. "Booth number three at the railroad waiting room."

"Good. Call the Information Desk at the railroad. Cohen's there. Tell him to nab the guy comes out of booth three. Fast!"

The sergeant put the call through, snapped a brief order to Detective Cohen.

MacBride was on the way back into his office. He stood before the desk, looked at his watch. He would give Cohen two minutes. The two minutes ticked off. He picked up the instrument, drawled "MacBride speaking."

"Just a tip, MacBride. Your station-house is going to be blown up. If you're clever, you'll get the guys. Sometime tonight."

That was all.

MacBride hung up, sat back, his fists clenched, his eyes glued on the instrument.

V

Who was the man behind the voice? Who was he double-crossing, and why?

MacBride went into the central room, called out four reserves. "Look here, boys," he said. "I've got a tip somebody's going to try to blow up this place. One of you at each end of the block, the other two in the back. Let no machines come through the street. No people, either. Make 'em detour. Anybody around the back, pick him up. Anybody tries to hand you an argument, get rough. All right, go to it."

He went back into his office, clasped his hands behind his back and paced the floor.

Twenty minutes later the door opened. Cohen came in with a man. The man was a little disarranged. His natty clothes were dusty and his modish neckwear was askew. His derby had a dent in it, and wrath smoldered in his black eyes.

Slim and lithe he was, olive skinned, with long, trick sideburns that put him in the category familiarly known as "Sheik."

Cohen's explanation was simple. "He tried to argue, Cap."

MacBride rubbed his hands together briskly. The mysterious informant was in his hands. His enormous bluff, recently put into print, that he had a valuable suspect in connection with the murder of Bedell, had worked out admirably.

"What's your name?" he asked.

"I'm not telling," snapped the high-strung stranger, struggling for dignity.

"I want to thank you for those tips," went on MacBride, "but I want to know more. Now cut out the nonsense."

"I'm not telling," reiterated the stranger. "It was a dirty trick, getting me this way. If those guys knew I'd been tipping you off, my life wouldn't be worth a cent."

"You tell me your name," proceeded MacBride, "and I'll promise to keep your name mum until the whole show is over."

"That's out. I don't want your promise. I didn't do anything. I'm not a gangster. I was just trying to help you out and keep my name out of it at the same time. It wouldn't do you any good to hold me. I've got no record. I didn't do anything."

MacBride told him to sit down, then said, "I'm sorry we had to grab you, buddy, but I've got a lot to answer for, and I've no intentions of getting tough with you. Just come across."

The man was losing his dignity rapidly. His black eyes darted about feverishly, his fingers writhed, his breath came in short little gasps. Fear was flickering across his face, not fear of MacBride, but of something or someone else. Mixed with the fear was a hint of anguish.

"Please," he pleaded, "let me go. My God, if I'd thought it would come to this, that I'd be picked up, have my name spread around, I'd never have tipped you off. Give me a chance, Captain. Let me go. I told you this place is going to be blown up tonight."

"Who's going to blow it up?"

"Don't make me tell that! God, don't. I guess I've been a fool, but I—I— Oh, hell!" He choked on a hoarse sob. "I told you what's going to happen. Lay for them. Get them when they try to blow you up. You'll learn everything then."

"Why have you been tipping me off?"

"I—for many reasons. A grudge, but behind the grudge—something else. It's been driving me crazy. Haven't been able to sleep. I was going to kill—but—I didn't." He raised his hands and shook them. "I'm lost, Captain, if you keep me, if you let loose who tipped you off. Dear God, give me a break—won't you?"

He leaned forward, extending his hands, pleading with his dark eyes, his face lined with agony.

MacBride bit him with an unwavering stare. What tragedy was in this fellow's life? He was sincere, that was certain. Something terrible was gnawing at his soul, making of him a shivering, palsied wreck, pleading eloquently for mercy.

"I don't want anybody to know I've been in this," he hurried on. "It's not only my life's at stake, it's something else—something bigger and deeper. Don't make me explain. I can't. Isn't it enough I warned you about this—this bombing?"

MacBride looked down at the desk, tapped his fingers meditatively. Then he looked up. "I'll give you a break," he said. "I'm going to lock you up for the night. If I get the men I want, you slide out quietly, and my mysterious informant remains a mystery. That's a promise. If Cohen here can find a Bible, I'll swear on it."

"Not a Bible in the whole dump," said Cohen.

The stranger was on his feet. "You promise, Captain? You will promise me that?"

"I've promised," nodded MacBride.

"Thanks. God, thanks! I've heard you were a hard-boiled egg. I—I didn't expect—"

"Pipe down. Ike," he said to Cohen, "lock him up and keep your jaw tight about what's just happened."

Cohen took the man out, and MacBride leaned back to sigh and light a fresh cigar, musing, "Maybe I ought to get kicked in the pants for making that promise. But I think the guy's hard-hit."

Half an hour later he was visited by State's Attorney Krug. Krug was pompous. "What are the latest developments, Captain?"

"Got some dope this joint is going to be blown up. You better get on your way."

Krug's eyes dilated. "Blown up!"

"Right."

"Then why don't you clear out?"

"See me clearing out for a lot of bums like that!"

"But this fellow you've got—this mystery man. Hadn't you better get him out of here? Don't you realize that it is possible they intend blowing up the place so that the man will be exterminated? Dead, he can give no evidence. I say, Captain, you ought to turn him over to me. Consider that I am eager to start a trial. We can use him, put the blame on him temporarily, at least make some headway. Come, now."

MacBride shook his head. "Nothing doing, Mr. Krug."

"This," stormed Krug, indignantly, "is monstrous!"

"If I were you, I'd get out of the neighborhood. Hell knows when these birds will show up. You don't want to follow in Bedell's footsteps, do you?"

"Damn my stars, you are impossible!" With that Krug banged out.

The echoes of his departure had barely died when Kennedy wandered in.

"How about some more news, Mac?"

"Thanks for mentioning my name so much in your write-up," replied MacBride. "When there's more news, you'll get it."

"Meaning there's none now."

"How clever you are!"

"Applesauce!"

"On your way, Kennedy."

"I'm comfortable."

"You won't be if you hang around here much

longer. Now cut out the boloney, old timer. I'm busy, there's no news, and you're in my way."

Kennedy regarded him whimsically. "When you talk that way, Mac, I know there's something in the wind. All right, I'll toddle along." He coughed behind his hand. "By the way, I intended buying some smokes on the way over, but—"

MacBride hauled out his cigar box, and Kennedy, helping himself to a cigar, sniffed it as he sauntered to the door.

"I wish you'd keep 'em a little moist, Mac," he ventured.

He was gone before MacBride could throw him a verbal hot-shot.

The captain put on his visored cap, strode into the central room, looked around and then went out into the street. At the corner he paused for a brief chat with the policemen stationed there.

"Everything okay, boys?"

"So far, Cap."

"Keep a sharp lookout. If it comes, it will come suddenly."

The men nodded, fingering their nightsticks gingerly. A street light shone on their brass buttons, on their polished shields. Beneath their visors, their faces were tense and alert.

MacBride made a tour of the block, and then through the alley in the rear. Everything was calm, every man was in readiness. They spoke in voices a trifle bated. They exuded an air of tense expectancy, peering keenly into the shadows, moving on restless feet.

As MacBride swung back into the central room he almost banged into the desk sergeant.

"Just about to call you, Cap," the sergeant puffed. "Holstein and Gunther just picked up a touring car with three guys, and a machine-gun and half-a-dozen grenades."

"Where?" MacBride shot back.

"Down near the railroad yards. They were coming north and stopped to fix a flat. Holstein and Gunther are bringing 'em in."

"Good!" exploded MacBride, and punched a hole in the atmosphere. "By George, that's good."

Moriarity and Cohen were grinning. "Looks like them guys got one bum break," chuckled Moriarity.

"Sure does, boys!"

MacBride strode up and down the room grinning from ear to ear. He kept banging fist into palm boisterously. He was elated.

A little later there was a big touring car outside, and a deal of swearing and rough-housing. MacBride went out, and found Holstein and Gunther manhandling three roughnecks. Kennedy was there, having popped up from nowhere.

"Knew something was in the wind, Mac," he chortled.

"You'll get plenty of headlines now, Kennedy," flung back the captain.

Patrolman Gunther said, "Nasty mutts, these guys, Cap. One of 'em tried to pull his rod and I opened his cheek."

"G' on, yuh big louse!" snarled that guy.

"I'll shove your teeth down your throat!" growled Gunther, raising his stick.

"All inside," clipped MacBride.

The roughs were bustled into the central room. A reserve carried in the grenades and the machine-gun. There was a noticeable lack of politeness on the part of the three gangsters. Also, there was noticeable lack of gentleness on the part of the policemen. One of the gunmen, a big, surly towhead, was loudest of all, despite the gash on his cheek. He started to make a pass at Gunther, but MacBride caught him by the shoulder, spun him around and slammed him down upon a chair.

"That'll be all from you, Hess," he ripped out warmly. "I guess we're near the bottom of things now."

"Who is he?" asked Kennedy.

" 'Slugger' Hess, Duveen's strong-arm man."

"Hot diggity damn!"

"Now where's Duveen?" MacBride flung at Hess. "I want that guy. Every damn gangster in this burg is going to get treated rough. Now you come clean or you get the beating of your life!"

"And I'd like to do it, Cap," put in Gunther.

"Yah, yuh big hunk of tripe!" snarled Hess.

"Can that!" barked MacBride. "Where's Duveen?"

Hess was not soft-boiled. Despite the roomful of policemen, he stuck out his jaw. "Go find him, Captain. You can't bulldoze me, neither you nor that pup Gunther!"

"Where's Duveen?" MacBride had a dangerous look in his eyes, and his doubled fists were swinging at his sides.

"You heard me the first time."

Gunther flexed his hands. "Should I sweat him, Cap?"

"Sweat the three of them," said MacBride. "In my office. Ike, Jake, you'll help," he added to Moriarity and Cohen.

Eager hands took hold of the three gangsters and propelled them toward MacBride's office.

But before they reached the door there was a terrific explosion, and the walls billowed and crashed.

VI

Stone, splinters, plaster, beams thundered down. Yells and screams commingled with the tumult of toppling walls and ceilings. Lights were snuffed out. The roof, or what remained of it, boomed down. There were cries for help, groans, oaths. Tongues of flame leaped about, crackling.

MacBride found himself beneath a beam, an upturned table, and an assortment of other debris. Near him somebody was swearing violently.

"That you, Jake?"

"Yeah, Cap . . . if I can get this damn hunk of ceiling off my chest. . . ."

MacBride squirmed, twisted, heaved. He jackknifed his legs and knocked aside the table. He brushed powdered plaster from his eyes, spat it from his mouth. The beam was harder. It was wedged down at both ends by other weighty debris, and MacBride could not shove it off.

But he twisted his body from side to side, backed up bit by bit, finally won free and stood up. His face was bloody, the sleeve of his right arm was torn from shoulder to elbow. He did not know it. He stumbled toward the pinioned Moriarity, freed him from the weighty debris pressing upon him and helped him to the sidewalk.

Going back in, he ran into Cohen. Ike was carrying a semi-conscious desk sergeant.

A crowd had already gathered. People came on the run from all directions. Somebody had pulled the fire-alarm down the block. The flames were growing. From a crackling sound they had been whipped into a dull roar.

Two battered but otherwise able policemen came out and MacBride sent them to chase away the crowd. Blocks away fire-engines were clanging, sirens were screaming. The policemen fought with the crowd, drove it back down the street. MacBride and Cohen were busy carrying out those they were able to pry from beneath the debris.

The first fire-engine came booming around the corner, snorted to a stop, bell clanging. Helmeted fire-fighters with drawn axes ran for the building. A couple of flashlights blinked. The big searchlight on the fire-engine swung around and played its beams on the demolished stationhouse. The firemen stormed into the mass of wreckage, hacked their way through to the pinioned men.

MacBride plowed back into the cell where the mysterious stranger had been placed a few hours before. He had trouble finding him. The man was deep beneath the wreckage. MacBride ran out, got an axe and came back to chop his way through. He carried out a limp dead weight.

Other engines came roaring upon the scene. There was a din of ringing bells, hooting motors, loud commands. Hose was being strung out. Streams of water began shooting upon the building, roaring and hissing. A grocery store down the street was used to shelter the injured men, all of whom had been taken from the building. An ambulance was on the way.

MacBride and Cohen were bending over the stranger. He was a mass of bruises, scarce able to breathe, let alone talk.

"Guess . . . I'm . . . dying," he whispered, his eyes closed, his body twitching with pain.

"The hell you are!" said MacBride. "We'll have an ambulance here in a minute."

"Don't . . . tell." He struggled for breath, then choked. "Two ten . . . Jockey Street. . . . Get 'em!" Then he fainted.

One of the gangsters was dead. The two others had escaped in the wild mêlée.

Kennedy was alive, though pretty much the worse for wear. He was hatless, covered with soot and grime, one eyes closed, a welt on his forehead. He limped, too, but he was not daunted.

"What next, Mac?"

MacBride turned. "God, Kennedy, you look rotten!"

"Feel rotten. I'd like to find the guy put his heel on my eye. I'm out of smokes. Who's got a butt?"

Moriarity had one.

The battalion chief for the fire department came up. "Hello, Mac. Bomb, eh? Yeah, I know. I've just been around. It was pitched through a window in the back." He looked up. "Good-bye, station-house, Mac!"

Even as he said this the front swayed, caved in with a smother of smoke, cinders and flame. Firemen rushed to escape the deluge. The hose lines pounded the place with water.

Detective Cohen appeared, with a bad wrist—his left hand.

"Where you been, Ike?" asked MacBride.

"Looking around. Guy in a cigar store around the corner said he was looking out the window a few minutes before the fireworks. Saw a big blue sedan roll by slow. He noticed because it's a one-way alley and classy machines don't often go through it. Runs back of the station-house, you know—Delaney Street."

"See here, boys." MacBride's voice was tense. "You all well heeled? Good. We're going to take a ride up to 210 Jockey Street, and I smell

trouble. There's something here I don't understand. We were caught napping. I'll say I was—I'm the dumb-bell. There I thought I had the case all ready to bake, and we were blown up."

He found Lieutenant Connolly and gave him brief orders. He gathered together six reserves and Moriarity and Cohen. They used the big touring car in which Hess and the other two gangsters had been brought to the precinct. Gunther drove, and as he was about to slide into gear, Kennedy came up on the run.

"Room there for me, Mac?"

MacBride groaned. Getting rid of Kennedy was like getting rid of a leech. But taking a look at Kennedy, seeing him all banged up but still ready to carry on, the captain experienced a change of heart.

"Hop in," he clipped.

The big machine lurched ahead. Once in high gear the eight cylinders purred smoothly.

Two left turns and a right, and they were on a wide street that led north. In the distance the reflection of the white light district glowed in the sky. Ten men were in the car. There was no room for comfort.

The white light district grew nearer.

MacBride and his men ignored traffic lights. They struck Jockey Street. Jockey Street is like a cave. At one end it is lit by the glare of the theatrical district. As one penetrates it, it becomes darker, narrower, and the street lamps are pallid. Two and three-story houses rear into the gloom, lights showing here and there, but not in abundance. Most of the doors are blank-faced, foreboding. It is a thickly populated section, but pedestrians are rare. More than one man has been killed in lower Jockey Street. Patrolmen always travel it in pairs.

The machine stopped.

"Two ten's on the next block," said MacBride. "We'll leave the car here. Gunther, you and Barnes go over one block south and come up in the rear. Hang around there in case anybody tries to get out. The rest of us will try the front."

They all alighted. Gunther and Barnes, their

sticks drawn, their pistols loose in their holsters, started off purposefully. MacBride, though he saw no one, had a vague feeling that eyes were watching him from darkened windows. People might have been curious in Jockey Street, like all humanity, but they differed materially in that they rarely came into the open to vent their curiosity.

As the men walked down the street, their footsteps re-echoed hollowly; a nightstick clicked against another. MacBride led the way, a jut to his jaw, his fingers curled up in his palms. Home, in peaceful Grove Manor, his wife was probably mending socks. Maybe his daughter was playing the piano; something about Spring from Mendelssohn or one of those Indian love lyrics. Well, he carried lots of insurance.

How about the men with him? Most of them married, too, with little kids. Moriarity, Cohen, Feltmann, Terchinsky, O'Toole, Pagliano. Gunther and Barnes in the back. Two hundred a month for the privilege of being a target for gunmen. They made far less—and paid double the life insurance premium—than many a man whose most important worry was a cold in the head or the temperature of his morning bath.

"This is it," said MacBride.

Kennedy said, "Dump."

"You stay out of it, Kennedy."

"If you've got a pen-knife I'll sit out here and play mumble-peg on the pavement."

In front of the house, which was a two-story affair built of red brick, was a depression reached by four stone steps that led down to the basement windows. At a word from MacBride, the men hid in this depression. A single step led to the front and main entrance, where there was a vestibule with glass in the upper half.

Alone, MacBride approached this, tried the door, and finding it locked, pressed a bell button. Somewhere distant he heard the bell ring. He took off his cap of rank and held it under his left arm, partly to hide his identity. His teeth were set, his lips compressed. He rang again.

Presently he heard a latch click. It was on the inner door. There was a long moment before a face moved dimly in the gloom behind the vestibule window. MacBride made a motion to open the door. The face floated nearer, receded, remained motionless, then came nearer again. Then it disappeared abruptly. The inner door banged. He heard running feet.

"We crash it, boys!" he barked in a low voice.

His revolver came out. One blow shattered the glass in the vestibule. He reached in, snapped back the latch. His men swarmed about him. He leaped into the vestibule, tried the next door. It was locked, built entirely of wood.

"All together, boys," he clipped.

En masse, they surged against the door. Again they surged. Wood creaked, groaned, then splintered. The door banged up under the impetus, and the law swept in. MacBride had a flashlight. It clicked into life, its beam leaped through the gloom. He turned.

"Holstein and Feltmann! Guard the front!"

"Yup, Cap!"

His flashlight swung up and down, back and forth, showed a stairway against one wall, leading to regions above. In the lower hall, he saw two closed doors.

"Bust these!"

He was the first to leap. The first door opened easily. The room was bare, unfurnished. He dived out and tried the next. It was unlocked. Empty. But it was meagerly furnished; a cot, a table, a rocking-chair, a gas stove.

"Lookout's room," he speculated. "Guy who came to the door."

Sentences, words, were clipped.

The flashlight's beam picked out the foot of the stairway.

"Up, boys!"

MacBride was off on the run. He led the way up the stairs.

Came two gun reports, muffled.

"Gunther and Barnes," he said. "These guys are trying for a break."

They were in the hall above. The first door they tried was locked. MacBride hurled his weight against it.

Bang!

A shot splintered the panel, passed the captain's cheek. He sprang back.

Moriarity, leaning against the bannister, shot from the hip. He plastered four shots around the doorknob. Pagliano put three more there. Then they waited, silent, all guns drawn. They listened. Men were moving inside the room. There was an undertone of voices.

MacBride turned to Cohen "Ike, go downstairs and get the chair in that room."

Cohen departed, returned carrying a heavy kitchen chair. MacBride took a chair, hefted it, then swung it over his head and dived with it toward the door. The chair splintered; so did the door. A couple of shots banged from the inside. MacBride felt a sting on his cheek. Blood trickled down his jaw.

Two policemen stood side by side and pumped bullets into the room. There was a hoarse scream, the rush of bodies, the pound of feet. Glass shattered.

Firing, MacBride and Moriarity hurtled into the room. Moriarity saw a dim figure going out through the window. He fired. The figure buckled and was gone.

"They've made the roof!" clipped MacBride.

He jumped to the window, out upon the fire-escape, up to the roof. He could see vague blurs skimming over the roof of the adjoining house. For a block these roofs were linked together, trimmed with chimneys, ventilating shafts, radio aerials.

Cohen went past MacBride in leaps and bounds, stopped suddenly, crouched and fired two shots. One knocked a man over. The other whanged through a skylight. Moriarity cut loose, missed fire.

Then the gunmen, near the end of the row of roofs, stopped and hid behind chimneys and the projections that separated one roof from another. They sprinkled the night generously with gunfire. Officer Terchinsky went down with a groan, came up again.

The policemen advanced warily, darting from chimney to chimney, crouching behind a skylight, wriggling forward. MacBride was mopping the wound on his cheek with a handkerchief. His gun was in the other hand. Moriarity was with him. A slug chipped off the corner of the chimney behind which they crouched.

Moriarity fired.

"Got that bum!" he muttered.

Both sides suddenly opened a furious exchange of shots. Lead ricochetted off the roof, twanged through aerial wires, shattered the glass in skylights. Shouts rose, sharp commands and questions. The policemen rose as one and galloped forward, firing as they ran.

The gunmen loomed up in the darkness—four, five, six of them. Guns bellowed and belched flame at close quarters. Terchinsky, already wounded, went down again, this time to stay. Guns empty, the men clashed, hand to hand, clubbing rifles. Nightsticks became popular.

Below, crowds were gathering, machines coming from other districts. Police whistles were blowing.

Gunther and Barnes came up from the rear, joined the fight. From then on it was short-lived. Every one of the six gunmen, rough customers to the last man, were beaten down, and most of them were unconscious.

The policemen were not unscathed, either. Terchinsky, of course, was dead. Cohen was on the point of collapse. MacBride was a bit dazed. They handcuffed the gangsters. MacBride looked them over, one by one, with his flashlight, and then went off to examine the ones who had been shot down. Moriarity was with him.

"Recognize anybody, Cap?"

"One or two, but can't place 'em. I'd hoped to find Duveen."

"Didn't you pot a guy going through the window? Maybe he fell down the fire-escape."

"That's right, Jake. Let's look."

MacBride gave brief orders to his men, told them to carry the prisoners down to the ground floor. Then he went off with Moriarity, descended the fire-escape, followed it down to the bottom.

Lying on the ground, face down, was a man dressed in a tuxedo. MacBride turned him over.

"Alive," he muttered, "but unconscious."

"Who is he?" asked Moriarity.

MacBride snapped on his flash, leaned over, his eyes dilating.

"*Bonelio!*" he muttered.

Kennedy was coming down the fire-escape.

VII

A day later MacBride stood in a large room in Police Headquarters. He was a little pale. His cheek was covered with cotton and adhesive tape. Moriarity was there, strips of tape over his right eye. And Cohen's left arm was in a sling.

Against one wall was a bench. On this bench sat Trixie Meloy, Adolph Shanz, and Beroni, manager of the Palmetto Club. All three were manacled, one to the other. Shanz was despair personified. Beroni was haggard. Trixie wore a look of contempt for everybody in the room.

Kennedy came in, sat down at a desk and played with a pencil.

MacBride said, "I have a letter here that I'm going to read. It will interest you, Miss Meloy."

He spread a sheet before him, said, "It was dictated to a stenographer at the hospital by a man named Louis Martinez."

Trixie bit her lip.

MacBride read, " 'To Captain Stephen MacBride: The man you want is Tony Bonelio. I worked in his club. I was Miss Meloy's dancing partner. We'd danced before, all over the country. I loved her. I thought she loved me. Maybe she did until Bonelio won her with money. It drove me crazy. I wanted to kill him. But I didn't. But I learned a lot. He killed Bedell. I heard the plans being made. Bedell was getting hard to handle. State's Attorney Krug and Shanz and Bonelio got together. Shanz was to get Bedell on the speaker's platform, so Bonelio could shoot him from the roof. Shanz and Krug staged the block-party just for that. When Bonelio read that you had a man prisoner who was in the know, I heard him phone Krug. Krug

promised to go down and get the man from you. Whoever he was, they were going to pay him a lot of money to take the rap. But when you wouldn't give him up, Bonelio told Krug there was only one way—blow the station up.

" 'I tipped you about all this because I wanted to see Bonelio get his. I wanted to win back Trixie's love. But I knew if she knew I'd done all that, she'd never look at me again. I was crazy about her. I was, but that's over. I was lying here, dying, and I called her up to come over. She told me to go to hell and croak. I've been a fool. I see what she is now. But go easy with her, Captain, anyhow. The only thing she did was to go to the block-party and say she saw a man in a gray suit walking away. She didn't see anybody. It was just a stall. That's all she did, except what she did to me. I don't know, maybe I still love her.' "

MacBride concluded, and you could have heard a pin drop. Then he said, "That was Martinez's death-bed confession."

"The damn sap!" snapped Trixie, her face coloring.

"What a fool he was to waste his time on a hunk of peroxide like you," observed Kennedy. "And what a dirty write-up I'm going to give you, sister."

"Rats for you, buddy," she gave him.

"Here's hoping you become a guest of the state. Don't forget to primp up and look pretty when the tabloid photographers get around. I don't even see what the hell Bonelio saw in you."

"Damn you, shut up!" she cried fiercely.

"Now, now," cut in MacBride, "that'll be enough. You, Shanz, are under arrest, and your trial won't come up till the new administration's in."

"Where's Krug?" he grumbled.

"Still looking for him," said MacBride. "He slipped out at three this morning. Moriarity was over to his house and saw signs of a hasty departure. Krug got cold feet when he heard we had Bonelio. He knew he couldn't help Bonelio, because the wop staged a gunfight with us. And he knew that if Bonelio knew Krug couldn't help him, then Bonelio would squeal. As a matter of fact, Bonelio has squealed. You'll go on trial in connection with the killing of Bedell. The net is out for Krug."

Even as he said this, the telephone rang. He picked it up.

"Hello," drawled a voice. "I want MacBride."

"You've got him."

"Well, MacBride, this is Duveen. I was sore as hell because you picked up Hess and the other two boys. They were on the way to blow up one of Bonelio's warehouses. Say, I hear you're looking for Krug."

"Yes, I am. He's wanted—bad."

"I've got him. I'm calling from up-State. He ran into me a little while ago with his car. I nabbed him. I'm sending him in with a State trooper. That's all, MacBride."

"Thanks. Drop in for a drink some time."

"I might, at that."

That was all.

MacBride rubbed his hands together. "And now we've got Krug," he said. "Krug, Shanz, Bonelio. And thank God, they'll go on trial when Anderson is State's Attorney."

Shanz groaned. A little man, a tool of others, he had tried to barter honor for power.

The three of them, including Trixie Meloy, were marched out and locked in separate cells.

The commissioner came in, a large, benign man, mellow-voiced, steady-eyed.

"Congratulations, MacBride," he said, and shook warmly. "It was great work. You've broken up an insidious crowd in Richmond City, and there's every possibility you'll be made inspector and attached to my personal staff."

"The breaks helped me," said MacBride. "I got a lot of good breaks toward the end."

"That may be your way of putting it. Personally, I attribute your success to nerve, courage and tenacity."

With that he left.

MacBride sighed, sat down, and felt his head. It hurt, there was a dull pain throbbing inside. He would carry a three-inch scar on his cheek for life. He felt his pockets.

"Thought I had a smoke. . . ."

Kennedy looked up, grinned, pulled a cigar from his pocket. "Have one on me, Mac."

MacBride eyed him for a moment in silent awe. Then he chuckled. "Thanks, Kennedy. I see where I have to buy you a box of Montereys."

"See they're good and moist, Mac," said Kennedy.

Law Without Law

Frederick Nebel

I

ENNEDY CHUCKLED. "So you're back in the Second, Mac."

"See me here, don't you?"

"Ay, verily!"

The old station-house blown up during the last election had been rebuilt, and the office in which Captain Stephen MacBride sat and Kennedy, the insatiable news-hound, stood, smelled of new paint and plaster. Something of the old atmosphere was lost—that atmosphere which it had taken long years to create: dust, age-colored walls decorated with news clippings, "wanted" bulletins, likenesses of known criminals.

Two days ago MacBride had been suddenly and inexplicably shifted from the suburban Fifth to the hectic Second. He was surprised, more than a little incredulous; and he suspected some ulterior motive behind the new Police Commissioner's leniency.

So did Kennedy. And Kennedy said, "This is funny, Mac."

"As a crutch."

"Now, if you'd asked me a week ago, I'd have said you were stuck in the Fifth for the rest of your term—or shoved farther out in the sticks. What did Commissioner Stroble say?"

"Said we ought to get on well."

"Was he nice?"

"Gave me a drink and asked about the health of my family."

"Hot damn!" Kennedy clasped his hands and with a serio-comic expression stared at the ceiling. "O, Lord what hath come over the powers that be in this vale of iniquity, Richmond City?"

"You jackass!"

"Mac, poor old slob—"

"Don't call me a slob!"

"Mac, my dear, what's up now? Why did the Commissioner suddenly put you in the precinct nearest your heart's desire?"

"Out of the pure and simple goodness of his heart."

"Amen!"

Kennedy sagged limply and supported himself with one extended arm against the wall.

"Of course, Mac," he said, "you know and I know that this is one awful lot of liverwurst."

"Then why ask?"

"Kidding you."

"Ho!"

"Getting your goat."

"Ho! Ho!"

Kennedy left the wall, crept dramatically across the floor and slid silently upon the desk. And in a hushed voice, with mock seriousness, he said, "Mac, somebody's trying to make a boob out of you!"

"How do you know?"

"I suspect, old tomato—I suspect. It's too sudden, Mac. Stroble has got something up his sleeve. He's brought you back into the town for a purpose."

"How big do you think he is?"

"Pretty big."

"Big enough to be the Big Guy?"

"Almost—and yet, not quite."

"Who is?"

"Beginning to get a faint idea. If I'm right, the Big Guy has been behind it all from the very beginning. The gangs have come and gone, but the Big Guy has succeeded in remaining hidden. If it's the bozo I think it is. . . ."

"Yes?"

"I don't think you'll reach him."

"Oh, go to hell, Kennedy! Listen, I'll get to him. Man alive, I *couldn't* lay off now! The thing's got in my blood. I've got to see it through. And I'm going to."

"Well, Mac, so far you've surprised me. Why you aren't occupying a snug grave in somebody's cemetery, is beyond me. But you've still got lots of opportunity of following in Jack Cardigan's footsteps. He was a poor slob."

"A martyr, Kennedy."

"Well, dignify it." Kennedy put on his topcoat. "I'm going places, Mac. Good-luck."

He wandered out, trailing cigarette smoke.

MacBride creaked back and forth in his chair, stopped to light a cigar, went on creaking. Damn new chairs, the way they creaked! The whole room was strange, aloof. Not like the old one, not as dusty—as intimate. Those three chairs standing against the wall—mission oak, bright and shiny, like the desk. Everything trim and spic and span—on parade. Even the clock was new, had a fast, staccato tick. He remembered the old one, a leisurely, moon-faced old chronometer, never on time.

A noise in the central room roused him. He raised his eyes and regarded the door. It burst open. Rigallo and Doran and a third man weaved in. The third man looked like a Swede, and was a head taller than either of the detectives. He slouched ape-like, great arms dangling, and his sky-blue eyes were wide and belligerent. He wore corduroy trousers, a blue pea-jacket.

"What's this?" asked MacBride.

Rigallo said, "Know him?"

"No."

The two detectives steered the man across the room and pushed him into one of the three chairs. He looked more the ape than ever—an ape at bay—sitting there with shoulders hunched, jaw protruding, huge hands dangling across his knees.

"Who is he?" asked MacBride.

"Says Alf Nelson," clipped Rigallo. "Me and Tim here were poking around the docks. We caught this baby trying to set a Tate & Tate barge adrift. He'd slipped the bow line and we caught him as he was on the stern."

"H'm," muttered MacBride. "That right, Nelson?"

"It ain't."

"He's a lousy liar!" snapped Rigallo.

"We saw him," supplemented Doran.

MacBride said, "Come Nelson, why did you do it?"

"I tell you, I didn't do nothin'." His Scandinavian accent was barely noticeable. "These guys are tryin' to frame me."

"Ah-r-r!" growled Rigallo. "Can that tripe, buddy! D' you think we waste time framin' guys? Come down to earth, you big white hope!"

"Look here, Nelson," said MacBride, rising. "This is damned serious. It's a rough night on the water, and that barge would have caused a lot of trouble. Riggy, was anybody on the barge?"

"Yeah, guy sleeping. We woke him up. Scoggins. He was scared stiff, and I'll bet he doesn't sleep a wink the rest of the night."

MacBride took three steps and stood over Nelson. "Did you have a grudge against Scoggins?"

"No. I tell you, I ain't done nothin'. I found the lines loose and was tryin' to fix 'em."

"Cripes!" spat Rigallo.

"Who's he work for, Riggy?"

"Dunno. Frisked him for a gat. Here it is. Thirty-eight."

MacBride said, "Who do you work for, Nelson?"

Nelson growled, pressed back in his chair. MacBride reached down toward his pockets. Nelson raised a hand to block him. Doran caught the hand and knocked it aside. MacBride went through the man's pockets.

"H'm. Badge," he said, "of the Harbor Towing. This guy's a barge captain. Here's his Union card. Name's right. Thirty-five. Unmarried, citizen. Listen, Nelson, come across now. Why the hell did you try to cut that barge loose?"

"I told you I didn't try to cut no barge loose," rumbled Nelson.

MacBride turned on Rigallo. "You're sure he did, Riggy?"

"Ask Tim."

"Sure he did, Cap," said Doran.

MacBride put Nelson's belongings in the desk and said, "Tim, plant him in a cell. I'm going down to the river. You come along, Riggy. There may be something in this, and there may not."

II

IT was cold and windy on the waterfront. The pier sheds loomed huge and sombre, and overhead the sky arched black as a cavern roof. And there was not a solitary star afield, not a vagrant moonbeam, not a patch of color against the black inverted bowl.

The river was a dark mystery moving restlessly toward the sea, and fringed sparsely with pier-head lights which probed its surface with thin, tremulous needles of radiance. And here and there, between the fringes, other lights—red, green, white—marked black shapes that moved through the thick gloom. The sound of bells, rung intermittently, skipped across the water with startling clarity.

MacBride and Rigallo strode down Pier Five and came to a barge moored at the end. Beneath them the water gurgled among the piles, and the barge thumped dully against the wharf. The tide was high, and they leaped to the barge without difficulty.

A man was standing in the doorway of a small, lighted cabin, smoking a pipe.

"Scoggins," said Rigallo.

"Hello, Scoggins," said MacBride. "Let's go inside."

They entered and Scoggins closed the door and leaned back against it. He was a small man, knotty in the framework, weather-beaten, steady-eyed.

MacBride said, "You know Nelson?"

"Yeah, years—from seein' him around the

docks and in the lunch-wagon sometimes. Works for the Harbor Towin'."

"Ever have a scrap with him?"

"Nope."

"Sure?"

"Yup. But I got a scare tonight, though!"

"You figure he tried to cut you loose?"

"Says he didn't. I ain't never had a line slip on me yet, and I been twenty years on the river."

"Well, look here, can you think of anything that might cause him to do it?"

Scoggins frowned thoughtfully and rubbed his jaw. "Gosh, I dunno. Of course, Tate & Tate, the comp'ny I work for, had a split with the Union, and they ain't hirin' Union men 'less they can help it. The Harbor Towin' 's all Union. Guys get in scraps over that sometimes. Day before yest'day Bill Kamp, who's on Number Three Barge, got in a fight with a Harbor Towin' guy. The guy called Bill a scab and Bill poked him."

"What caused this split with the Union?"

"Dunno. Just know they split. Young Mr. Tate was sore as hell over somethin'."

"Do you know what barge Nelson is on?"

"Number Three. Up at Pier Twelve now."

MacBride turned to Rigallo. "Come on, Riggy, let's snoop around."

They left Pier Five, reached the cobbled street and walked north. Fifteen minutes later they turned into a covered pier, met a watchman, flashed their shields and passed on down the vast interior.

On the south side of Pier Twelve they found a lighter flying a metal pennant numbered Three. A light shone in the little cabin. They leaped down from the wharf, pushed open the door and walked in.

A girl sat on the bunk. She was a large girl— not fat, but large, broad in the shoulders, wide at the hips. Her skin was fair, her hair light brown; and her cheek-bones were high, prominent; her mouth wide with lips full and frankly sensuous. Her clothes were cheap and not precisely in the mode, and she regarded the two intruders with a dull stare.

Rigallo smiled. "Hello, girlie."

"Hal-lo."

"Where's Alf?" asked MacBride.

"Ay don't know."

"H'm. We were supposed to meet him here tonight," lied Rigallo.

"Yes," nodded MacBride.

She shrugged her broad shoulders. "So vas I. Dat Alf iss neffer on time."

"Ah, he's a good guy, though," said Rigallo.

She regarded him stolidly for a moment, then grinned, showing large white teeth. "Yah, Alf iss good fal-ler. Ay vait. You fal-lers vaiting for Alf?"

"Sure," nodded Rigallo. "We're his friends. Eh, Mac?"

"You said it, Riggy."

"Alf's some guy," said Rigallo.

"Yah," nodded the girl, shedding some of her nerves. "Alf iss good fal-ler." She paused, meditated heavily, then laughed and slapped her knee. "Ay tal you, Alf is vun big guy. Dis Meester Braun he likes Alf much."

"Sure," said MacBride. "Mr. Braun's a good guy, too. But he should treat Alf better."

Still more of the girl's reserve vanished, and she leaned forward, waxing confidential. "Yah, like Ay tol' Alf. But Ay t'ank dis Meester Braun iss be sqvare by Alf. Alf he tal me he vill get lots dol-lars."

"Well, it's no more than right," put in Rigallo.

"Yah. Alf vill be rich fal-ler some day."

MacBride and Rigallo grinned at each other. Then they grinned at the girl, and MacBride said, "Gosh, miss, Alf's been holding back on us. Never told us he had a nice girl like you."

She dropped her eyes. "Yah, Ay t'ank Alf luffs me lot. Ay luff Alf lot."

"He'll invite us to the wedding, though, I hope," said MacBride.

"Sure," nodded Rigallo.

"Yah," said the girl.

MacBride tried. "When did Alf say he would be back?"

"Vun hour ago. But Ay vill vait."

"Yeah," said Rigallo. "Alf said something

about a job down on Pier Five. I wondered what he meant."

"Vass it Pier Five?" asked the girl.

"Yeah," said Rigallo.

"Ay vill go."

"No. You stay here," put in MacBride. "We'll look him up and tell him you're waiting. What did he say he was doing?"

"Alf didn't say. Alf ain't tal me much, but he say he be very busy dese nights soon."

MacBride stood up. "Well, if we see him, we'll tell him you're waiting. What did you say your name was?"

"Hilda. Hilda Yonson. Ay come from Oslo two year' ago."

"See you again," said MacBride.

"Yeah, see you again," said Rigallo.

"Yah," said Hilda Yonson.

MacBride and Rigallo climbed back to the wharf and strode through the pier-shed.

"Who is Braun?" asked Rigallo.

"Don't know. Probably one of the bosses. We'll ask the night watchman."

In a little office at the far end of the pier they found the watchman, and MacBride asked, "Who is Mr. Braun?"

"Manager. Yeah, he's the manager."

"Good-night," said MacBride, and steered Rigallo into the street.

"What now, Cap?"

"Nothing, until I see Braun."

"It looks as if Nelson is somebody's dope."

"What I think, Riggy. Flag that taxi."

MacBride went home that night, pounded his ear for eight hours and was back on the job at eight next morning. In plain clothes, he left the station-house and went down to the general offices of the Harbor Towing Company, which were located over Pier Nine.

Braun had evidently just arrived, for he was going through the morning's mail. He was a fat, swarthy man, nervous and shifty, with a vague chin.

"Oh, Captain MacBride," he said. "Ah, yes. Won't you sit down? Won't you have a cigar?"

MacBride sat down but refused the cigar.

"You probably know," he said, "that I've got one of your barge captains over at the station-house."

Braun's eyes squinted, and he licked his lips. "Why, no! That's too bad. Likely a drunken brawl, eh? Well, I suppose I'll have to bail him out—mark against his salary."

"Not quite," said MacBride. "He was caught trying to cut a barge adrift last night. Pretty serious."

"Well, I should say so! Can you imagine! Humph! You never know what these drunks will do."

"But Nelson wasn't drunk."

"Well, that *is* strange! Now why do you suppose he tried to do a fool thing like that, Captain?"

"Search me. Thought maybe you might know."

"Me?"

"Uhuh."

"But, Captain, I'm surprised, how should I know why these fool Swedes—"

"Aboveboard, now, Mr. Braun!"

"Why—um—why, what do you mean?"

"Don't make me go into detail."

"But I tell you, Captain, I don't understand—"

"Aboveboard, Mr. Braun!"

Braun pursed his lips, his eyes dilated. He looked amazed. "Really, Captain—"

"Oh, for God's sake, cut out this stalling!"

"I tell you, Captain, I'm in the dark. I don't know what you're driving at."

MacBride's lips curled. "There's something crooked somewhere."

"Well, if there is, I'd certainly like to know about it. If Nelson has been going wrong, I'll certainly fire him. Tell you what, I'll go down to the station-house and give him a talking. Let's see. It's nine now. I'll be there at ten, Captain."

MacBride stood up. "I'll be waiting there."

"Good! Won't you have a cigar?"

"No."

MacBride's exit was like a blast of wind.

III

Twenty minutes later he walked into the offices of Tate & Tate, and a boy piloted him into the sanctum of Hiram Tate, the younger and executive member of the firm. Tate was a lank, rock-boned man of forty-odd, with flashing dark eyes.

"I came over," said MacBride, "about that bit of business on Pier Five last night."

"Oh, you did? Good! I'll go right over with you and prefer charges against this bird you've got."

"What is your opinion?" asked MacBride. "Why do you suppose he tried to cut that barge loose?"

"Captain, my answer will be heavily prejudiced. You want to know what I think? I think that the Harbor Towing is trying to intimidate me. We're non-Union. I'll tell you why. Mike Tate, my old man, was double-crossed. And keep this under your hat. The Harbor Towing and Tate & Tate have always been rivals for the river trade.

"We've had more damned inspectors on our tail than I thought were in existence. What for? For little things. Unsanitary lavatories. Doors that opened in instead of out. Electric wiring. Unsafe barges. Condemned tugs. Ever since we kicked the Union in the slats.

"And what started it? The municipal pier at Seaboard Basin. It was offered for sale, and we wanted it. The Harbor Towing wanted it. We claimed it should come logically to us because we had no uptown terminal and did a lot of uptown business. The Harbor Towing carried it right to the Union. I was out of town. The old man rep-

resented us, and he's known for a convivial old souse. They got him tight at the board meeting, and he signed all the dotted lines he could find.

"Well, we couldn't retract. The whole mess was attested by a notary, and when the old man came to he discovered that the Harbor Towing owned the municipal pier. When I came back to town I found him raving mad. I got sore, too, and we told the Union what we thought of it, and dropped. What's the use of catering to an outfit that kowtows to big money? The Harbor Towing is a big outfit, and they get all the court decisions, too. It's damned funny. When we get a square deal, get at least one section of the municipal pier to unload and load freight, we'll go back into the fold. That's my story. Believe it or not."

"I'll think it over. If you want to press a charge against Nelson, we'll indict him."

"I'll press charges, all right!" Tate rose and put on his overcoat. "Have a cigar?"

"Go good. Thanks."

They drove to the station-house in Tate's private car, and as they entered the central room, they found Rigallo pacing up and down in something akin to rage.

"Hell, Cap, where have you been?" he snapped.

"What about it?"

"Bower came down from Headquarters and took Nelson up for a quiz."

MacBride tightened his jaw. "Why'd you let him?"

"How could I stop him. I'm only a dick."

"What's this?" put in Tate.

MacBride said, "Nelson's at Headquarters."

"I want to place that charge."

"All right," said MacBride; then to Rigallo, "You go along with Mr. Tate, Riggy."

They went out, and MacBride banged into his office. Kennedy was parked in his chair before his desk, immersed in solitaire.

"Out of my throne, Kennedy!"

"Just a minute, Mac. I've almost got this."

MacBride grabbed the back of the swivel chair, hauled it and Kennedy away from the desk, slid another into its place, and sat down. He studied the cards for a moment, made several swift moves, filled the suits and said, "Learn from me, Kennedy."

"That was good, Mac. How about two-handed poker."

"No. Busy."

"What doing?"

"Thinking."

"Bower came down and got Nelson."

"Don't I know it!"

Kennedy chuckled. "Bower's the Headquarters 'yes' man. Guess the Commissioner wanted to see Nelson, shake his hand, and tell him to go home."

"H'm." MacBride stood up, put on his coat and strode out.

Ten minutes later he entered Police Headquarters.

Commissioner Stroble regarded him through a screen of excellent cigar smoke.

"How about Nelson?" asked MacBride.

"We let him go," said the Commissioner.

"Let him go!" echoed MacBride.

"Why, certainly. No case at all, MacBride. We had a chap named Scoggins here, too. I weighed both testimonies. Scoggins was asleep. Nelson saw that one of the cables had slipped and was trying to fix it. Scoggins was vague. Don't bother with such small change, MacBride."

"Small change!" MacBride curled his lip. "If it was so small, why did Bower take Nelson from the precinct, and why did you bother with it?"

Stroble's eyes narrowed. "Remember, MacBride, I took you out of the Fifth, gave you another chance. Don't be a fool!"

"You're trying to make a fool out of me! I know the situation on the waterfront, and it's not small change. That guy Nelson is guilty as hell. And the outfit he works for is a damned sight guiltier!"

Stroble leaned forward, pursing his lips. "MacBride, I said it was small change. Now don't hand me an argument. Go back to your roost and forget about it. This interview is over."

MacBride went out with a low growl. He walked back to the station-house, certain now that trouble was breeding on the river. Small

change! He cursed under his breath. He was very near the end of his tether. Time and time again someone in the machinery of the city government had tried to balk him.

In his office that day he had moments of black depression. He wondered if after all he were not beating his head against a stone wall. What was he? Only a common precinct captain, with strong ideas of his own. How could he hope to carry out his own straightforward plans when the Department sidetracked him?

Yet there was the strain of the hard in his blood. To give up now, to fall in line with the long column of grafters, would be a tremendous blow to his conscience—and to his stubborn pride. Rigallo and Doran would razz him. And Kennedy! And a lot of other men who were aware of his single-handed struggle against graft and corruption.

No, there was no backing out now. He had built a structure of two-fisted justice, escaped death, release from the Force, by the skin of his teeth. The game at this stage was far too interesting. He had wiped out some of the most notorious gangs in Richmond City, had made the political racketeers squirm, had driven some right out of office.

But still he had not got to the roots. Had the Commissioner before his appointment, been the drive wheel in the racket? And now, being in a position of vital importance, would he rebuild all that MacBride had knocked down? How big was he? How far could MacBride push him? Why had he permitted Nelson's release on such short notice?

Small change! Hell!

It was strange that a month should pass without an untoward murmur on the river. At times MacBride wondered if after all Nelson had been innocent. But then it wasn't like Rigallo to make such a raw blunder. He was not a detective who usually went in for small game.

An interesting and significant bit of news drifted in one morning. Kennedy, the inevitable, walked in on MacBride and said:

"What do you think, Mac?"

"What?"

"A Tate & Tate barge sank last night. One of their oldest. Just foundered, so the report goes, off the coast. Sprung a leak. Went down with one hundred thousand dollars' worth of copper wire. The barge captain was saved. The tug *Annie Tate* was towing, and saved him. Read what the *News-Examiner* says."

He scaled a newspaper on the table, and MacBride conned a terse editorial:

Last night the Tate & Tate barge Number Two sank off the Capes. It is evident that this barge was sadly in need of repair. The sea was only moderately rough and the tug *Annie Tate* had good steerageway.

A cargo valued as $100,000 was lost in fifty fathoms, and the barge captain, Olaf Bostad, is in the City Hospital suffering from exposure. It seems to us that there is a deplorable lack of efficiency somewhere. Why the Number Two, one of the first barges built for Tate & Tate, was allowed to go to sea, is beyond us.

It seems incredible that a reputable company should place a man in jeopardy by sending him on a coastwise voyage in a barge of such ancient vintage. The company, of course, does not lose. The underwriters do. We no longer wonder why marine insurance is at such a premium, and why many underwriters refuse to insure coastwise barges.

"H'm," muttered MacBride.

"I wonder who paid for that," said Kennedy. "Tate & Tate are in hot water now, for sure. Watch the insurance company go into action!"

"And the waterfront bust wide open," said MacBride.

Indeed, the first rumble came on the following day, when not a single tug or barge of Tate & Tate moved. Captain Bower, of Headquarters, boomed into the station-house with orders from the Commissioner.

"MacBride, you've got to patrol the river," he said. "Use all your available men. Two cops on each pier where there's Tate & Tate shipping. The insurance company has refused to allow

Tate & Tate to move until every barge and tug has been inspected. The city is also sending its own inspectors, and there's a complete tie-up."

"All right," nodded MacBride.

He called on his reserves, dispatched them to six different piers, and himself went down to the Tate & Tate general offices.

Young Hiram Tate was in high heat. "What do you think of this, MacBride? By God, can you beat it? That barge was overhauled only two months ago and the underwriters O.K.'d it. Now we're tied up. Not a thing allowed to move. We've got thousands of dollars' worth of freight that has to move—has to make trains, ships—and some of it's perishable. Hell, we'll go bankrupt!

"What happens now? Consignees and consignors are bellowing. But we can't move. We lose our contracts, and the movement of freight is taken over by other companies. And what company mainly? The Harbor Towing. God, what a blow below the belt this is!"

"We're putting men on the piers to prevent trouble," said MacBride.

But trouble broke. When a Harbor Towing tug and three lighters warped into Pier Eight to move perishable freight from a Tate & Tate shed, a fight started. Fists flew, and then stones and canthooks. The police joined, and shots rang out, and one man was wounded before the outbreak was quelled.

But the feud had taken root and spread the length of the waterfront, and MacBride was here and there and everywhere, struggling for law and order.

The Commissioner called him and said, "Clamp the lid, MacBride. It looks as if Tate & Tate employ a lot of hoodlums. This can't go on. Pitch 'em all in jail if you have to."

MacBride had been up most of that night, and he was weary. "If you'd get the inspectors on the job and make that insurance company snap on it, this would stop. I'm doing the best I can."

"Keep up the good work, MacBride!" was Stroble's parting shot.

MacBride slammed down the receiver, whirled and stared at Rigallo. "Now I know why

I've been shifted here! I'm getting a beautiful kick in the slats! I'm told to ride Tate & Tate, and, Kennedy, way down in my heart I believe Tate & Tate is the goat!"

"Mac, I'm with you, you know. So is Doran."

"Thanks, Riggy. It's good to know."

Reports came in continually from the river. All the reserves were out. Fights occurred every few hours—uptown—downtown.

MacBride slept at the station-house that afternoon, awoke at six, had hot coffee and a couple of hamburgers sent up, and prepared for another night. Tate & Tate were at the breaking point. The inspectors were taking their time, and the first barge that was looked over was held up for some minor detail that was not yet settled among the inspectors.

On the other hand, the Harbor Towing Company was reaping a harvest, taking over all the freight that Tate & Tate could not handle. And the Union men of the Harbor Towing, old enemies of the non-Union crowd of Tate & Tate, took every opportunity to bawl insults at the men whom circumstances had forced to a standstill.

Hiram Tate called MacBride on the telephone and yelled, "Look here, MacBride! You've got a good name in this lousy burg. What am I going to do? These pups from the Harbor Towing are getting away with murder. You can't blame my men for fighting. I've bailed twenty out already. If this keeps up, if my floating equipment isn't allowed to move, we'll go bankrupt. It's dirty, MacBride. There's some underhand work somewhere. I tell you, if it keeps up, I'm going out on the river myself and bust the first Harbor Towing bum that opens his jaw!"

"Sit tight, Tate," said MacBride. "I've got to maintain law and order."

"Law and order, hell!" exclaimed Tate, and hung up.

Rigallo asked, "What's the matter, Cap?"

"Tate's sore. Can you blame him?"

"No."

"Riggy, this is getting worse. There's big money in it, and between you and me it looks as if the Harbor Towing is trying to wipe out Tate & Tate, their biggest competitors. And how they're doing it! That sunken barge was just what they needed. Graft all around. Ten to one the underwriters were bribed. The *News-Examiner* was bribed. The city is being bribed."

"D' you ever stop to think, Cap, that the barge might have been monkeyed with?"

"You know, I wonder!"

The hours dragged by, with more reports coming in, and at midnight came a staggering report from one of the patrolmen stationed at Pier Fifteen.

"We just found a stiff, Captain."

"Who?"

"Guy named Nelson. We heard a shot and ran down the dock and found him dead in his barge. Right through the heart."

"Hold everything, Grosskopf. I'll be over."

MacBride hung up and looked at Rigallo. "Riggy, somebody plugged Alf Nelson of the Harbor Towing."

"God help Tate & Tate!"

"Let's go!"

IV

FFICER TONOVITZ met MacBride and Rigallo at the entrance of Pier Fifteen.

"Grosskopf's on the barge," he said.

They strode down the covered pier, came out in the open, and saw Grosskopf standing outside the cabin door. MacBride and Rigallo jumped down to the barge.

Nelson was lying on the floor, flat back, one arm flung across his chest, the other extended straight from his shoulder. A chair was overturned.

"Fight," ventured Rigallo.

"Maybe not," said MacBride. "He might have been sitting on the chair, and jerked up when he was hit."

"Door and windows were closed," put in Grosskopf.

"Didn't find anything?"

"No."

MacBride went out and up to the dock, and found a knot of men hovering nearby, expectantly.

"You guys knew Nelson, didn't you?"

Most of them did.

"See anybody around here tonight?"

One replied, "I seen Gus Scoggins."

"Going or coming?"

"He must ha' been goin' to the barge. I seen him on this dock. Was about nine o'clock. He said, 'Hello, Joe.' And I said, 'Hello, Gus.'"

"You didn't see him go back?"

"Well, no. I didn't hang around. I was on the way to my own barge when I saw Gus."

"Who do you work for?"

"Harbor Towin'."

"Sure you're not tryin' to frame Scoggins?"

"Who? Me? No. I'm a' old timer. I know Gus for years. I don't figger he did anything."

"He might have," said another voice. "Him and Nelson ain't been good friends since Scoggins claimed Alf tried to cut him loose."

MacBride left the group and called Grosskopf. "Ring the morgue and have them get Nelson. Tonovitz, you stay on this barge. Riggy, come with me."

MacBride and Rigallo went to the float dispatcher for Tate & Tate and got from him the position of Scoggins' barge. It was at Pier four, and ten minutes later they found it. No lights shone. MacBride boarded, tried the door, found it padlocked from the outside.

"He should be on board," remarked Rigallo.

"He should," agreed MacBride. "Cripes, if Scoggins did this, Tate & Tate will be swamped!"

They climbed back to the pier and accosted the patrolman on duty, O'Toole.

"You know Scoggins? Have you seen him?"

"Saw him about eight-thirty, Cap, leaving."

"When he comes back, hold him and ring the station-house. If he doesn't show up by the time you leave, call me and tell your relief to watch for him, too."

"O.K."

MacBride and Rigallo shot back to the station-house. Rigallo went home, and MacBride hauled out a blanket and curled up on a cot in one of the spare rooms.

By morning he had the medical examiner's report. The bullet had gone through Nelson's heart aslant and lodged in his spine. A thirty-two.

O'Toole had rung in with no word of Scoggins. MacBride called the patrolman at Pier Four, and found that Scoggins was still absent. He hung up, went down to the pier, picked up the harbor master for Tate & Tate, and had him open the door to the little cabin. Everything was in order. Scoggins' suitcase, clothes, and other odds and ends, were still there.

MacBride went back to the pier, and found Hiram Tate, just arrived.

"What do you think about this killing, MacBride?"

"Looking for Scoggins. Somebody saw him around Nelson's barge last night."

"This is a rotten break, MacBride! Do you think it was Scoggins?"

"It looks as if it might be. He hasn't showed up all night."

They walked back to the street, and then MacBride made for the barge that had been Nelson's home. Officer Pallanzo was on duty, and he was having his hands full.

"I can't get rid of her, Cap," he complained.

MacBride stood with arms akimbo and stared at Hilda Yonson, who sat on the dock beside the barge. Her hands were clasped about her knees, and she was rocking back and forth and moaning. Her yellow hair blew in coarse wisps across her hueless face. Her hat was askew.

"Alf. . . . Alf. . . ."

She was dazed. When MacBride spoke, it seemed she did not hear him. She rocked on—and on, staring with red-rimmed eyes.

"Look here, Hilda," MacBride said, bending

down. "Come on. Don't sit around here. I'll take you home."

He shook her. She looked up, and her lips quivered. "You—you said you vass Alf's friend. All de time you had Alf in de station-house."

"Forget that. I was doing my duty. Come on, Hilda, I want to get the man who killed Alf. I want you to help me get him."

"Ay vill keel him!" She doubled a fist and squared her jaw.

"No, you leave that to me. Let's go." He took her arm, urged her.

She rose and permitted MacBride to lead her from the barge. She walked with a steady, purposeful tread, her face grim.

MacBride found a room at one corner of the warehouse, and they entered it, Rigallo close behind.

"When did you last see Alf, Hilda?" asked MacBride.

"Ay see Alf last night."

"What did he say?"

"Ay didn't talk. Ay go down by de dock und Ay see Alf iss playin' cards vit two fal-lers. So Ay don't go in. Ay go home."

"You know the men?"

"No. Vun vass dressed like vat you call sheik. Ay looked in by de vindow. De odder vun vas dat fal-ler Scoggins."

"About what time?"

"Vas maybe half-past nine."

MacBride turned to Rigallo. "This looks queer, Riggy—Nelson and Scoggins playing cards."

"With another guy—yeah."

"Ay vill keel him, whoever it vass dat keeled Alf. O-o-o-o, my poor Alf!" she moaned, rocking on the chair.

"Listen, Hilda," put in Rigallo, "buck up. And don't do any killing. Leave that to us. We'll get this bum and he'll burn for it."

"Ay vill bet it vass dat Scoggins."

They took her home, where she lived with an elder sister, and then went over to the station-house.

"The Commissioner's been calling you, Cap," said Sergeant Flannery. "Wants to talk to you."

MacBride took the phone and called Head-quarters, and the Commissioner said, "That Scoggins is a good lead, MacBride. Tail him and get him. He's the guy we want, all right."

"I'm not so sure," said MacBride.

"Get him, MacBride. Grill young Tate. Maybe Tate knows a lot about it. Maybe he knows where Scoggins is."

Hanging up, MacBride swore softly. "Riggy, they're sure out to crush Tate & Tate, and making no bones about it."

Sergeant Flannery knocked and came in. A little boy accompanied him.

Flannery said, "Kid, just came in with a note."

MacBride took a rumpled piece of brown wrapping paper, and read:

For Cap. MacBride, Second Police Pre-cinct. I been took here and held. Looks like these guys are going to kill me or something. Get me out of it. I can't write more now.
                    GUS SCOGGINS.

MacBride looked at the boy, who was standing on one foot, twisting a cap which he held in his hand.

"Where'd you get this, son?"

"I picked it up in the gutter on North Street."

"You know just where?"

"Yes."

MacBride stood up and put on his overcoat. "Come on, Riggy. Where's Doran?"

Flannery said, "Playing poker with the reserves."

"Call him."

MacBride and Rigallo pushed out into the central room and a moment later Doran appeared and joined them.

"We're going places, Tim. You heeled?"

"Yup."

"Then let's go. Come on, sonny."

V

acBRIDE flagged a taxi, and they all piled in. Ten minutes later they alighted and walked down North Street.

"It's on the next block," said the boy, "on the other side of the street. See that red brick house? I found it right in front of that, in the gutter."

"All right," said MacBride. "Here's a half-dollar. Run home."

The boy ran off and MacBride stopped. "Riggy, Tim, we've got to get Scoggins. The Commissioner wants him."

"I wonder if he really does," said Rigallo.

MacBride grinned. "I'll be doing my duty. He told me to get him."

They walked on, crossed the street and drew near the red brick house. An empty store was on the street level, windows soaped and pasted with *To Let* signs. Above this ranged two stories. North Street is a mongrel street. There are warehouses, garages, poolrooms, a few tenements.

"There's an alley," said Doran, pointing a few doors further on.

"Good idea," said MacBride. "We'll go around to the back."

They entered the alley, followed it to the rear, vaulted a couple of board fences and eventually found themselves in the yard back of the red brick house. A door that apparently led into the back of the store barred the way. There were two windows.

"We don't want to make any noise," said MacBride. "Cut the putty away from that top pane and we'll pry it out."

They used jack-knives, succeeded in removing the pane with a minimum of noise. MacBride reached in, unlocked the window, pushed it up. Then he crawled in. Doran and Rigallo followed, and they stood in an empty room littered with paper and old boxes.

"Upstairs, I guess," said MacBride, and opening a door, stepped into a musty hallway.

Each man carried one hand in his pocket, on his gun.

MacBride led the way up a flight of stairs. He stood on the first landing, looking around. Doran and Rigallo joined him. There were four doors along the side, and one at either end of the corridor.

MacBride whispered, "You guys park on the next stairway and watch. Quiet, now."

They nodded and cat-footed off.

MacBride stood alone, deliberating. Now that he was here, what should he do? The situation presented some difficulties. Where was Scoggins? What room? How much of a gang was here? Where was the gang? Why hadn't Scoggins been more explicit?

Questions? The answers would be arrived at only through action. He shrugged. Couldn't stand here all day. Supposed he picked a door at random and knocked?

Well, try it. He did. Squared his shoulders, assumed an innocent expression and rapped on the nearest door. Whom should he ask for? . . .

The door opened and a man in an undershirt and trousers looked out.

"Hello," said MacBride.

"Hello," grunted the man.

"I'm a tenement-house inspector," said MacBride. "I'd like to look through the rooms. Won't take long."

"What do you want to look for?"

"Just see about lights, fire exits. Won't take long. Few minutes. Hate like hell to bother you, but the boss has been riding me."

"Well, come in, then," grunted the man.

MacBride entered, wondering what tenement-house inspectors were supposed to do. He took out a pencil, however, and a batch of old envelopes from his pocket. He made a few lines, looked very thoughtful, went to each of the two windows in the room, opened and closed them. The man in the undershirt watched him closely.

"Well, this room's all right," said MacBride. "Now the next."

"Wait a minute," grumbled the man, and entered the next room, closing the door behind him. MacBride heard subdued voices during the brief moment the door was open.

He stepped to the hall door, swung it open, caught Rigallo's eye, and put a finger to his lip. Rigallo, hiding with Doran on the staircase, nodded and grinned. MacBride closed the door softly.

A second later the other door opened, and the man in the undershirt came back. With him was another man, a tall, slim, saturnine man smoking a cigarette through an ivory holder. He eyed MacBride with a cold stare.

"Who sent you here?" he clipped.

"My boss."

"Well, come around some other time."

"Can't. I'm taking this block today."

"Well, take this dump some other day."

"What's the idea?" shot back MacBride. "What do you suppose the boss will say if I take all the houses on this street except this one?"

"That's your lookout. Here's twenty-five bucks. Mark this place as okey."

"Sorry," said MacBride.

"Then clear out."

MacBride didn't know how tenement-house inspectors acted in such a case, but he knew how a cop acted. "Now look here, mister," he said. "My job is to look these places over, and I'm going to look it over. Don't get snotty, either, or I'll condemn the damned joint right off the bat."

"You will, eh?"

"You said it."

"Who cares?"

"I don't," shrugged MacBride.

"And neither do I. Can that crap and on your way, buddy."

"Well, all right, then, if you want to get mean about it," said MacBride. "I'll hand in a bum report."

"Sure. Go ahead. I don't care."

MacBride put away his pencil and paper and pulled open the door, shoved his hand into his pocket, and stood there.

"Now I'll get mean," he ripped out. "Just like this!"

His gun jumped into view, and the two men gasped.

"Raise 'em high!" snapped MacBride; and over his shoulder, "Come on, boys."

But Doran and Rigallo were already beside him. "Frisk 'em," said MacBride.

Rigallo entered the room and approached the man in the undershirt, relieving him of an automatic. The other man snarled:

"What the hell kind of a stunt is this?"

"Shut up!" said MacBride. "Get your hands up."

He snatched a gun from the man's pocket and put it into his own.

"It's a frame-up!" yelled the man.

"Damn you, close your trap!" barked MacBride.

The door to the next room swung open. He caught a momentary glimpse of a group of startled faces. Then the door banged, as Doran leaped toward it and tried to keep it open.

"Hold everything, gang!" yelled the saturnine man.

A shot crashed, splintered the door.

Doran stepped back, leveled his gun and put three shots through the lock.

Rigallo handcuffed the two men together. MacBride took another pair of manacles and secured them to a waterpipe.

"You guys are dicks!" cried the saturnine man.

"God, but you're bright!" chuckled MacBride.

Somewhere below, glass crashed. Doran reloaded his gun. Rigallo fired a couple of shots through the door.

Footsteps were pounding up the stairway. MacBride jumped into the hall, his gun leveled. Two policemen appeared, guns drawn.

"Take it easy, boys," called MacBride. "Stay here in the hall. We've got some bums bottled up."

Even as he said this a door further down the hallway burst open and men rushed out. Revolvers blazed, and one of the policemen went down. MacBride fired and Doran joined him. Eight men swept down upon them like an avalanche. Rigallo came hurtling out of the room.

Doran sank under a blackjack. MacBride put two shots through the head of the man who had wielded it. A clubbed revolver skimmed along his skull and thudded on his shoulder. He twisted and clubbed his own gun, and broke a man's nose. Blood splashed over him.

Somebody reeled, balanced on the balustrade, and then pitched down into the hallway below. Somebody else kicked MacBride in the stomach while he was trying to reload. He doubled and fell to the floor, and another foot cut open his left ear.

Rigallo, holding the doorway of the room wherein the two men were manacled, put a slug in the back of the man who was kicking MacBride's head. The man fell over the captain and never moved once, until MacBride shoved him over and staggered to his feet.

Two men rushed Rigallo, and one swore in Italian. Rigallo snarled, "As one wop to another, back up!" The man struck with his blackjack. Rigallo dodged and blew out the man's stomach.

"Cripes!" choked the other.

"Stay back," warned Rigallo, "or I'll spill your guts, too."

Two more policemen rushed up the stairs, met two gangsters at the head, forced them back. Suddenly the shots ceased, and the hallway was strangely quiet. Six men, one of them a policeman, lay on the floor, dead. Three gangsters stood with their backs against the wall, disarmed, breathing thickly, one with a broken and bloody nose.

Rigallo still stood in the doorway. MacBride lifted up Doran, shook him.

"You all right, Tim?"

"Yeah—sure," mumbled Doran.

"Hold him," MacBride said to one of the policemen.

Then he turned toward the door, laid his hand on Rigallo's shoulder. "Riggy, this was a hell of a blow-out!"

"Sloppy," nodded Rigallo.

MacBride entered the room and looked at the two men manacled to the water-pipe.

"Well, you satisfied?"

The man in the undershirt said nothing. The other said, "No, are you?"

"Not yet."

MacBride entered the other room. A table was littered with bottles and glasses. He looked around, rubbing his jaw. He crossed and opened another door, looked into a bedroom. It was empty. He backed up, called Rigallo.

"You and Doran hunt for Scoggins. He must be hidden somewhere. Go right to the roof, if you have to."

They went out, and MacBride sampled a bottle of Three Star Hennessy. It was good stuff, warmed him up. He noticed a closet door, and with the bottle still in his hand, walked over and grasped the knob. He pulled, but the door resisted, yet it was not locked. He dropped the bottle and drew his gun. Someone was in that closet, holding the door shut.

"Come out!" MacBride called.

There was not a murmur.

"Out, or I'll riddle the door!" said MacBride.

Still no answer.

"I'll count three," said MacBride. "Ready. *One!*" He marked time. *"Two!"* His gun steadied. *"Three!"*

His finger tightened on the trigger. He aimed low.

Bang! Bang!

Rigallo and Doran came in, with Scoggins between them.

"Found him, Cap," said Rigallo.

"Just a minute, Riggy," said MacBride. "I've found something else."

He waited. He saw the knob move.

"Atta boy!" he called. "Open it or I'll shoot higher. Ready!"

The door burst open and a wild-eyed man tottered out.

"Well!" exclaimed MacBride. "Greetings, Mr. Braun!"

"G-God!" stuttered Braun.

A new voice penetrated the room—"Is that Braun of the Harbor Towing, Mac?"

MacBride pivoted.

Kennedy of the *Free Press* was leaning in the doorway, tapping his chin with a pencil.

VI

Braun, that short, round, dark, nervous man, seemed to be swallowing hard lumps.

MacBride spoke to a policeman, "Ed, you shove those three bums in the hall into the next room with the other two."

"Right-o, Cap."

"Riggy and Tim, you stay in here with me," went on MacBride. "Kennedy, you can stay here on the condition that you don't publish anything unless you have my consent."

"Suits me, Mac."

MacBride rubbed his hands gingerly. "This will be interesting. Make yourselves at home, men—you, too, Braun, and you there, Scoggins. There's a bottle and glasses. Let's get clubby."

Braun was not in a clubby mood. He was emphatically nervous, and kept biting his thin red lips.

MacBride said, "Now, Scoggins, what happened?"

Scoggins had taken a drink. He wiped his mouth. "Gosh, I was scared. T' other afternoon me and Alf Nelson met in the lunchroom across from Pier Ten. I said, 'Hello, Alf.' And he said, 'Hello, Gus.' Then I said, 'Look here, Alf, we know each other for years. We worked together. What's the sense o' bein' mean? I know you tried to cut me loose t'other night, but I'm willin' to forget it.' And Alf said, 'I been a big bum, Gus.' And I said, 'You been a fool, Alf. You never had much brains. You're lettin' some big guys talk you into doin' things. You'll get in trouble, Alf, if you don't look out.' So Alf looked kinda guilty, and he said, 'Yeah, I been a big bum, Gus. I been wantin' to get some money ahead, so me and Hilda could get hitched. You

and me been friends for years, Gus.' And I said, 'We sure have, Alf. And like one friend to another, I'd warn you to look out for them big buys. If you get in Dutch, they ain't goin' to help you.' So he said, 'I guess you're right, Gus. I been a dumb-bell.' I said, 'You sure have, Alf.' And he nodded and then said, 'Gus, come over my barge tomorrer night and have a game of pinochle like old times.' So I said I would, and I did.

"So I went over. We played for an hour, and then some guy came in, and Alf said, 'This is a friend, Gus. Call him Pete.' So I called him Pete and he called me Gus, but I didn't like him. He wasn't a waterfront man. Along about 'leven o'clock I figgered I better go, and Pete said, 'Me, too. I got a motorboat out here. I'll take you upriver.' I said, 'Thanks,' and we went.

"There was another guy waitin' in the boat, and when we got out in the river they jumped me. I was knocked out. When I come to I was in a room upstairs. I was sore. I wonder if Alf double-crossed me."

"Alf is dead," said MacBride.

Scoggins squinted. "What!"

"Was killed about an hour after you left."

"Dead!"

"Uhuh."

"But who did it?"

"I don't know—yet." MacBride turned to Braun. "Maybe you know."

Braun started. His eyes blinked. He moistened his lips. "Captain, I seem in a peculiar position. Unfortunately, circumstances are against me. I believe I'll not say anything until I've thought things out more."

"Until you've seen a lawyer?" sneered MacBride.

"Until he's seen the Commissioner," sliced in Kennedy.

It was like dropping a bomb. MacBride swung on him. Braun shuddered, clenched his hands, pursed his lips. Rigallo tapped the floor with his toe. A long moment of silence enveloped the room. Kennedy smiled whimsically, one eyebrow slightly arched.

MacBride said to Rigallo, "Bring in those guys we hitched to the pipes inside."

Rigallo grinned, entered the adjoining room, returned a minute later with the saturnine man and the man in the undershirt. The saturnine man had tightened his dark face, and his eyes were two black slots of malevolence, his lips were flattened against his teeth.

Scoggins said, "That's the guy we played cards with. He's the guy took me for a motorboat ride."

"The guy that killed Nelson, eh?" put in Kennedy. "Know him, Mac?"

"Not yet."

"He's from Chicago, if I've got my mugs right. Pete Redmond."

"Well, what about it?" snarled the man.

"Soft pedal," said MacBride. "I'm going to plant you for a long while, buddy."

"Like hell you are!" snapped Redmond.

"Sh!" put in Braun.

Redmond turned to him. "What's the matter with you? You look yellow around the gills. Come on, tell this guy who we are. I can't hang around here all day. I got a date. Call the Commissioner on the telephone."

Braun turned a shade whiter. "Sh! Don't be a fool, Redmond!" he gulped.

"Well, then, let's go. He can't hold us. Telephone the Commissioner. I tell you, I got a date."

MacBride said, "Braun, do you want to make a telephone call?"

Braun shifted nervously, wore a pained look.

"Go ahead," urged Redmond. "Call him up."

Braun went over to the telephone, called a number. "Hello, George," he said. "Listen, George. . . . Huh? You know. . . . Well, what are you going to do? . . . Yeah, Pete is here. . . . Well, how could I help it? . . . Well, don't bawl *me* out, George. . . . All right."

He hung up, said, "He'll be right over."

Kennedy licked his lips. "Hot diggity!"

Braun was pale. Redmond scowled under MacBride's steady gaze and said, "Think you're wise, eh? I get a great kick out of you, big boy. I didn't think they came that dumb."

"You'll find how dumb I am," said MacBride.

"Wait till the Commissioner comes," smirked Redmond.

"Ah, just wait," said Kennedy.

So everybody waited. Thirty minutes passed, and then an hour.

Braun said, "I wonder what's keeping him."

"He'd better hurry," said Redmond. "I got a date."

"Oh, damn your date!" cried Braun.

"Yeah?" snarled Redmond.

MacBride took a drink and said, "Pipe down."

The telephone rang. Rigallo was nearest and took the call. When he hung up, he said, "We should all go over to Headquarters."

"Now why the hell should we go to Headquarters?" snapped Redmond. "I'm not going."

"Let's go," said MacBride.

"I don't savvy this at all," complained Redmond.

"It will be all right," soothed Braun.

"It better be," said Redmond.

MacBride called the morgue, said, "There are a lot of stiffs at 46 North Street. Better come up and collect 'em."

He went into the next room, and told one of the policemen to remain with the dead until the men from the morgue arrived. To the others he said, "We're taking the rest over to Headquarters."

MacBride, Rigallo and Doran and the three policemen gathered the six gangsters together and marched them down the stairs. All were handcuffed, including Braun, who stumbled as he walked. MacBride hauled him along roughly. Scoggins walked beside Kennedy.

Below, a crowd of people swarmed on the sidewalk outside the door. MacBride chased them as he led the way. Rigallo and Redmond were behind him. They marched down the street, two by two.

"I don't like this," complained Redmond. "I don't see why the hell we have to go to Headquarters."

"Be quiet," called back Braun.

"I tell you, guy, if—"

Bang!

VII

EDMOND sagged, belched blood.

Bang!

Braun stopped in his tracks, buckled, groaned.

"Duck!" yelled MacBride, and dragged Braun into the nearest hallway.

Rigallo lugged Redmond into a fruit store.

Four shots rang out, and the four gangsters behind crumpled.

Kennedy and Scoggins dodged into a hardware store as a shot smashed the window beside them.

MacBride had disengaged himself from Braun. Braun was dead.

Rigallo joined the captain and said, "Redmond's cooked, too. What the hell do you suppose happened anyway?"

"God knows, Riggy! Those shots came from that store across the way. Come on!"

He rushed into the street, blew his whistle. Doran came on the run, followed by the policemen. Doran said, "Every guy was picked off, Cap, and there was some straight shooting! That store—"

"Yeah. Let's go," clipped MacBride, and crossed the street on the run.

The store was empty, but they broke through the door and cascaded into the interior. The men bunched around MacBride.

"They've cleared out—through the back! Come on!" he said.

He led the way into the rear, and they found a back door open and thundered out into a yard. A fence barred the way, but they vaulted over it, crashed through the back door of another house and milled in a dark hallway.

MacBride rushed headlong, came to another door, yanked it open and looked out upon Jackson Street. He started to step out, when a machine-gun stuttered and the door frame splintered. Rigallo yanked him back, slammed the door.

"Don't be a fool, Mac!"

They heard the roar of a motor. It diminished in a few seconds. MacBride again opened the door, stepped out, looked up and down the street, said over his shoulder, "Come on."

His men came out warily. The street was empty—not a car, not a person in sight.

"Dammit!" muttered MacBride.

"Well, why worry?" asked a policeman. "One gang against another. That's a good way of getting rid of rats."

"It sure is," said another cop.

MacBride grumbled.

Kennedy said, "Come on, Mac. I've got several ideas."

"I'm going to Headquarters," growled MacBride. "Riggy, you and Doran go back to North Street and see the morgue bus gets those bums."

He turned on his heel and strode down the street. Kennedy fell in step beside him.

"Mac, we're near the end. It won't be long now. I figure you're just outside the Big Guy's doorstep."

MacBride made no comment. His jaw was hard, and his eyes glittered.

They entered Police Headquarters. Kennedy lingered at the desk while MacBride went on to the Commissioner's office. But the Commissioner was not in. MacBride rejoined Kennedy at the desk, prodded him and marched out.

"What's the matter?" asked Kennedy.

"He's not in."

"Where'd he go?"

"Left no word."

They stopped on the wide steps outside, and MacBride lit a cigar.

A big black limousine drew up, and Commissioner Stroble alighted. He stood speaking with someone who remained in the tonneau behind drawn curtains. Then he suddenly spun around and saw MacBride and Kennedy standing on the steps. He spoke hastily in an undertone and stepped back to the sidewalk.

The car started off. Kennedy ran down the steps, called, "Hey, how about a lift?"

The Commissioner looked startled. Kennedy jumped to the running-board, but the car jerked ahead, and he slipped, fell, rolled into the gutter.

Stroble mounted the steps, eyes narrowed. "What do you want, MacBride?"

"Just wanted to see you."

"Come up to my office."

As MacBride followed Stroble in, he turned and saw Kennedy standing on the sidewalk, grinning.

In the Commissioner's office, a tenseness became apparent. Stroble took off his overcoat and sat down.

"Well, MacBride."

"I thought you were coming over to North Street."

"I was. But when I reached the street there was a gun-fight going on. I'm too old for gun-fights, MacBride."

"Braun was killed. He was a friend of yours."

Stroble sighed. "Poor Charlie. Yes, he was a friend of mine, from school days. What kind of a mess did he get into?"

"I'm sure I don't know," said MacBride. "I caught him with a bad gang. A bird named Pete Redmond, from Chicago, and some other guns."

"My!" exclaimed Stroble. "That was strange. Charlie shouldn't have done that."

"He was sure you could help him," gritted MacBride.

"Yes, for old times' sake. Months ago he came to me and said Tate & Tate were riding him. Trade was falling off. He wanted more police protection. Well, I tried to make it easy for him. You'd do the same, MacBride, for an old friend. I didn't know he'd gone bad."

MacBride restrained himself with an effort. Deep in his heart he knew that Braun had been double-crossed, yet what could he do? There was no evidence.

Stroble was saying, "It was strange, too, how that other gang popped up. Why do you suppose they committed such wholesale slaughter?"

MacBride blurted out, "It looks to me like a double-cross."

Stroble blinked. "I say, now, do you really think so?"

"Yes."

"H'm. That is possible. Poor Charlie! He was a good chap, MacBride, but a bit of a fool. No clue to who did it?"

"No. All the cops ran to North Street when the shooting started. The gang, after they killed Braun, and the others, beat it through to Jackson Street and made a clean getaway. We tried to follow, but I damned near got plastered by a machine-gun. We had to hide."

"Sensible, MacBride—very sensible. Personally, I believe that in such a situation, you should be careful. Gangs often destroy each other, and take that task off a policeman's hands. Of course, we must spread an alarm. But poor Charlie! I didn't think he'd take advantage of me—of a good thing, MacBride."

"Scoggins, you know, was kidnapped and held by Braun's gang."

"Goodness, now why do you suppose they did that?"

MacBride leaned forward, barbed every word—"So that we'd think Scoggins killed Nelson. So that red tape would tie up Tate & Tate a little longer, drive them nearer to bankruptcy, give the Harbor Towing a big lead."

"Could that be possible!" exclaimed the Commissioner. "And there I was trying to do Charlie a good turn, for old times' sake! It wasn't fair of Charlie. Do you think so, MacBride?"

"I don't know."

"H'm. Well, run along. I've some work to do. File the report on this when you find time. Good luck."

MacBride almost lost control of himself. His fingernails dug into his palms. A grunt escaped his lips.

The Commissioner looked up. "Eh?"

MacBride snapped, "Good day," and banged out.

In the street he found Kennedy, and the reporter said, "You look fit to be tied, Mac."

"I am! I'm stumped!"

"Mac"—Kennedy took his arm and steered him down the street—"Mac, buck up. Before very long you're either going to get the Big Guy—or he'll get you."

"What do you mean, Kennedy?"

"I know things. Come on over to the station-house."

They tramped into MacBride's office. Kennedy closed the door and locked it. He rubbed his hands together, smiled his tired, whimsical smile. He slid upon the desk, and tapped the blotter in front of MacBride.

"Get this, Mac, and think it over," he said. "I've been keeping a few things under my hat. Yesterday I made a discovery. Why do you think Stroble was giving the Harbor Towing all the breaks?"

"Braun was a friend of his."

"Nonsense! Stroble is a big stockholder—silent one, you know—in the Harbor Towing."

"How do you know?"

"I found out. I went to that lousy broker-age firm of Weber & Baum. They used to handle Stroble's business, but he broke with them, and they got sore. In confidence Baum told me that Stroble practically owns the Harbor Towing. And look here. The Mayor owns the Atlas Trucking Corporation—under cover—and the one is practically linked with the other.

"I've got the whole thing doped out, Mac. Pete Redmond was head of Stroble's private gang, and Braun had to move as he was told. When they balled things up that way, and when you flopped on their big parade—and I turned up at the right moment—the Commissioner knew that he was cooked.

"You had Braun and Redmond cold. Even Stroble, with all his power, couldn't get them clear. So what did he do? Wiped them out! Double-crossed them! Got another gang to kill every one of them as you marched down the street."

"Good God!" groaned MacBride. "I believe you, Kennedy. I'm sure you're right. But the Mayor—man—the Mayor! You're sure he's mixed up in it?"

"I'll say this, Mac. I'll bet my shirt that the gang that wiped out Redmond was the Mayor's own. Stroble went to him, told him the fix he was in. The Mayor knew that if Braun and Redmond were caught, they'd squeal on the Commissioner and that Stroble would yap on the Mayor. So he lent Stroble his gang."

"But who is the Mayor's gang?"

"That's for you to find out."

"And you think the Mayor is the Big Guy?"

"If he isn't, I'm all wrong."

MacBride snorted. "Hell, Kennedy, it's incredible. I never thought much of him, but—"

"Look here, Mac," cut in Kennedy. "The Atlas Trucking Corporation has been having hard sledding, too. The Harbor Towing will have to shut up. Tate & Tate will get that concession at Seaboard Basin. But the Colonial Trucking Corporation is a subsidiary of Tate & Tate, and I'll bet that before long this trade war will be carried toward that end."

"If it is, Kennedy—"

"You'll find a hard nut to crack."

"I'll crack it or croak."

Kennedy lowered his voice. "I didn't tell you, Mac, who was in that limousine I tried to hop."

Their eyes met, MacBride's wide and blunt, Kennedy's narrowed and smiling.

"Who, Kennedy?"

"Don't you know?"

"You mean, the. . . ."

"Sure," nodded Kennedy. "The Mayor!"

Graft

Frederick Nebel

I

OLICE CAPTAIN Steve MacBride, elbow on desk, chin on knuckles, looked down along his nose at the open dictionary, and concentrated his gaze on the word "graft." Now graft is a word of various meanings, and the definitions, as MacBride discovered, were manifold. But the definition that attracted and held his eyes longest, was clean-cut, crisp and acutely to the point:

> Acquisition of money, position, etc., by dishonest, unjust, or parasitic means.

His lips moved. "Parasitic. Humph! That's what they are, parasites!"

He sighed, creaked back in his swivel chair, and stared absently at the night-dark window. Cold out. The panes rattled. The wind hooted through the alley. More distant, it keened shrilly over housetops, whinnied through the complicated network of radio aerials. Even the poor had radios—bought tubes and what-not and went without shoes.

But graft. Parasitic. Parasites in the Town Hall. Hell, why hadn't he taken up plumbing, after his father? You could straighten out a bent pipe, plug a leak. But, as a police captain, with a wife and a daughter to support, and three thousand still due on that new bungalow in Grove Manor. . . .

He banged shut Webster's masterpiece with a low growl, got up and took a turn up and down the room. Straight was MacBride—morally and physically. Square-shouldered, neat, built of whip-cord, hard bone, tough hide. His face was long, rough-chiselled, packed well around cheek and jaw. His mouth was wide and firm, and his eyes were keen, windy—they could lacerate a man to the core.

He ran the Second Police Precinct of Richmond City. His frontiers touched the railroad yards and warehouses, plunged through a squalid tenement district and then suddenly burst into the bright lights of theatres, hotels, nightclubs. It was the largest precinct territorially in Richmond City. It was also the toughest.

Beyond the rooftops, a bell tolled the hour. Midnight. MacBride looked at his watch. Home. He could catch the last street car out to Grove Manor. Stifling a yawn, he walked to a clothes tree and took down his conservative gray coat and his conservative gray hat. He had one arm in his coat when the door opened and Sergeant Flannery, bald as a billiard ball, poked in.

"Just a minute, Cap. Girl outside pestering me—"

"Why pass the buck?" MacBride had his coat on. "I'm going home, Sergeant."

"But I can't get rid of her. She wants to see you."

"Me? Nonsense. You'll do for a sob case, Flannery. I mind the last sob sister you pawned off on me. Was hard up for a drink, the little tramp. Widowed mother and all that crap. Bah!"

"This one's different, Cap. Married a little over a year. Left her kid, three months old, home with her old lady. Name of Saunders. Lives over on Haggerty Alley. Damn near bawling. Wants to see you."

"Well"—MacBride started to put on his hat, but changed his mind and flung it on the desk—"send her in."

Overcoat partly buttoned, he dropped into the swivel chair and sighed after the manner of a man who has to listen, day in and day out, to tales of woe, of stolen cats, strayed dogs, blackened eyes, and broken promises. Well, another wouldn't kill him. . . .

The girl came in timidly. She wore no hat, and her coat was a cheap thing, and she looked cold and forlorn and afraid. Pity—MacBride claimed there was not an ounce of it in his make-up—prompted him to say:

"Take that chair by the radiator. Warmer."

"Thank you."

Pretty kid. Young, pale, brown-eyed, hatless, and hair like spun copper. A mother. Haggerty Alley. God, what a draughty, drab hole!

"Well?"

"I came to you, Captain, because Jimmy—he's my husband—because Jimmy always says, 'MacBride, the gent runs the Second, is one reason why there ain't more killings in this neighborhood.'"

MacBride was on guard. He hated compliments. But, no, this wasn't salve. Her lower lip was quivering.

"Go on, madam."

"Well, I feel funny, Mr. MacBride. I feel scared. Jimmy ain't come home yet. I've been reading things in the newspaper about some trouble in the trucking business. Jimmy drives a big truck between Richmond City and Avondale—that's thirty miles. He leaves at one and gets back to the depot at nine and he's always home at ten. He's been carting milk from Avondale, you know—for the Colonial Trucking Company."

MacBride's eyes steadied with interest. He leaned forward. "What makes you afraid, Mrs. Saunders?"

"Well, I was reading the paper only the other night, about this trouble in the trucking business, and Jimmy said, he said, 'Wouldn't surprise me if I got bumped off some night.' You know, Mr. MacBride, only last month one of the drivers was shot at."

"H'm." MacBride's fingers tapped on his knee. "Don't worry, Mrs. Saunders. Everything's all right. Truck might have broken down."

"I phoned the depot, and they said that, too. But the drivers always phone in if they're broke

down. Jimmy ain't phoned in. The night operator was fresh. He said, 'How do I know where he
is?' So I hung up."

"Listen, you go right home," recommended
MacBride. "Don't worry. They don't always
break down near a telephone. Run home. Want
to catch cold chasing around the street? Go on,
now. I'll locate Jimmy for you, and send a man
over. Got a baby, eh?"

Her eyes shone. "Yes. A boy. Eyes just like
Jimmy's."

MacBride felt a lump in his throat, downed it.
"Well, chase along. I'll take care of things."

"Thank you, Mr. MacBride."

She passed out quietly; closed the door quietly. Altogether a quiet, reticent girl. He stood
looking at the closed door, pictured her in the
street, rounding the windy corner, with shoulders hunched in her cheap coat—on into Haggerty Alley, dark, gloomy hole.

Jerking himself out of the reverie, he grabbed
up the telephone, asked Information for the
number of the night operator at the Colonial
Trucking Company's River Street depot. He
tapped his foot, waiting for the connection.

"Hel-lo-o," yawned a voice.

"Colonial?"

"Yup."

"That driver Saunders. Heard from him yet?"

"Cuh-ripes!" rasped the voice. "Who else is
gonna call about that guy? No, he ain't showed
up, and he ain't called, and if you wanna know
any more, write the president."

"I'll come down there and poke you in the
jaw!" snapped MacBride.

"Aw, lay off that boloney—"

"Shut up!" cut in MacBride. "Give me the
route Saunders takes in from Avondale."

"Say, who the hell are you?"

"MacBride, Second Precinct."

"Oh-o!"

"Now that route, wise guy."

He picked up a pencil, listened, scribbled,
said, "Thanks," and hung up.

Then he took the slip of paper and strode out
into the central room. Sergeant Flannery was

dozing behind the desk, with a half-eaten apple
in his pudgy hand.

"Sergeant!"

Flannery popped awake, took a quick bite at
the apple, and almost choked.

"Chew your food," advised MacBride, "and
you'll live longer. Here, call the booth at Adams
Crossing. We're looking for a Colonial truck,
number C-4682, between Avondale and here.
Call the booths at Maple Street and Bingham
Center. Those guys have bicycles. Tell 'em to
start pedaling and ring in if they find any trace.
Brunner—you can locate him at the Ragtag Inn.
He hangs out there between twelve and one,
bumming highballs. Tell him to fork his motorcycle and start hunting."

He paused, thought. Then, "Where's Doran
and Rigallo?"

"Stepped out about eleven. Down at Jerry's,
shooting pool. Should I flag 'em?"

"No."

MacBride turned on his heel, entered his
office and kicked shut the door. He sat down, bit
off the end of a cigar, and lit up. He hoped everything was all right. Poor kid—baby three months
old—Haggerty Alley—eyes like Jimmy's. Bah!
He was getting sentimental. Did a man get sentimental at forty?

The door opened. Kennedy, of the *Free Press,*
drifted in. A small, slim man, with a young-old
face, and the whimsical, provocative eyes of the
wicked and wise.

"Cold, Mac. Got a drink?"

MacBride pulled open a drawer. "Help yourself."

Kennedy hauled out a bottle of Dewar's and
poured himself a stiff bracer—downed it neat.
He slid onto a chair, coat collar up around his
neck, and lit a cigarette. The cigarette bobbed in
one corner of his mouth as he said:

"Anything new about this trucking feud?"

"Not a thing."

Kennedy smiled satirically. "The Colonial
Trucking Company versus the Atlas Forwarding Corporation. Hot dog!"

"Take another drink and breeze, Kennedy."

"Cold out. Warm here. Say, Mac, look here. What chance has the Colonial against the Atlas when the Atlas is owned—oh, privately, sure!—by the Mayor? Funny, how those inspectors swooped down on the Colonial's garage last week and condemned five trucks as unfit for service and unsafe to be on the public highways. Ho—protecting the dear, sweet public! D'you know the Atlas is worth five million dollars?"

"Shut up, Kennedy!"

"Funny, how that driver was shot at last week. He was going to tell something. Then he turned tail. Who threatened him? Or was he paid? The new State's Attorney, good chap, could get only negative replies out of him. Hell, the guy got cold feet! Then he disappeared. This State's Attorney is ambitious—too clean for this administration. He'll get the dirty end, if he doesn't watch his tricks. So will a certain police captain."

MacBride bit him with a hard stare. Kennedy was innocently regarding the ceiling.

"Some day," he went on, "or some night, one of these drivers isn't going to get cold feet. I pity the poor slob!"

Sergeant Flannery blundered in, full of news.

"Brunner just rang in. Found the truck. Turned upside down in a gully 'longside Farmingville Turnpike. Milk cans all over the place. Driver pinned underneath. Brunner can't get him out, but he says the guy's dead. He's sent for a wrecking crew, nearest garage. Farmingville Turnpike, two miles west of Bingham Center."

MacBride was on his feet, a glitter in his windy blue eyes. Haggerty Alley—eyes like Jimmy's. Hell!

"Haul out Hogan," he clipped, "and the flivver." He buttoned his coat, banged out into the central room, fists clenched.

Kennedy was at his elbow. "Let's go, Mac."

"It's cold out, Kennedy," said MacBride, granite-faced.

"Drink warmed me up."

No use. You couldn't shake this news-hound. Prying devil, but he knew his tricks.

Outside, they bundled their coats against the ice-fanged wind, and waited.

The police flivver came sputtering out of the garage, and the two men hopped in.

MacBride said, "Shoot, Hogan!"

II

HAVE you ever noticed how people flock to the scene of an accident, a man painting a flagpole, or a safe being lowered from a ten-story window?

MacBride cursed under his breath as, the flivver rounding a bend on Farmingville Turnpike, he saw up ahead dozens of headlights and scores of people. A bicycle patrolman was directing traffic, and the flivver's lights shone on his bright buttons and shield. Automobiles lined either side of the road. People moved this way or that. One pompous old fellow, with a squeaky voice, remarked that truck drivers were reckless anyhow, and served him right for the spill.

MacBride stopped on the way by, glared at the man. "Did you see this spill?"

"No—oh, no, no!"

"Then shut your trap!"

The captain was thinking of Haggerty Alley, and his tone was bitter. He moved on, and Motorcycle Patrolman Brunner materialized out of the gloom and saluted.

"Right down there, Cap. Guy's dead, and the truck's a mess. Can hardly see it from here."

"How'd you spot it?"

"I went up and down this pike twice, and the second time I noticed how the macadam is scraped. The guy skid bad, and you can see the marks. Closed cab on the truck, and he couldn't jump."

"Wrecker here yet?"

"No—any minute, though. Hoffman's handling traffic."

"Give me your flashlight. Go out with Hoffman and get these cars moving."

"Right."

MacBride took the flash and started down the embankment. Kennedy, huddled in his overcoat, followed. The way was steep, cluttered with boulders, blanched bushes; and as they descended, they saw turned earth and split rocks, where the truck had taken its headlong tumble.

Then they saw the truck, a twisted heap of wood and metal. A ten-ton affair, boxed like a moving van. But the truck had crashed head-on into a huge boulder, and the radiator, the hood, the cab and the cargo were all jumbled together. And somewhere beneath this tangled mass lay the driver.

Kennedy sat down on a convenient stump and lit a cigarette. MacBride walked around the wreck, probing with his flashlight. The beam settled on an arm protruding from beneath the snarled metal. Bloody—the blood caked by the cold.

He snapped out the flash, stood alone in the chill darkness, quivering with suppressed rage. The wind, whistling across the open fields, flapped his coat about his legs. Probably that girl was still sitting up, with her slippered feet in the oven of the kitchen stove, and her wide, sad eyes fixed on the clock. Brutal thing, death. It not only took one, but stung others. He wondered if there were any insurance, and thought not. Good thing, insurance. He carried twenty thousand, double indemnity, in case of accident. Could a guy in the Second Precinct die any other way but through an accident? Or was getting a slug in your back by a coked wop, death from natural causes?

A broad beam of light leaped down into the rocky gully.

"Wrecker," said Kennedy.

MacBride nodded, watched while several men came weaving down the slope.

"Cripes!" muttered one, upon seeing the wreck.

Another said, "Hell, Joe, we can never haul this out. Need a derrick."

"Well," said MacBride, "you've got axes. Hack away enough junk so you can get the man out."

MacBride stood back, hands in pockets, chin on chest. Axes flashed, rang. Crow-bars heaved, grated.

Brunner came down and said, "Morgue bus just came, Cap."

They got the body out, and one of the men became sick at his stomach. Another—case-hardened—chuckled, said, "Hell, buddy, you should ha' been in the war!" War! This was war—guerrilla warfare! War of intimidation!

They put a blanket over the dead man, laid him on a stretcher, carried him up over the hill and slid him into the morgue bus.

"I want the report as soon as possible," MacBride said to the man from the morgue.

The bus roared off into the night.

MacBride and Kennedy climbed into the police flivver. It was a bleak, cold ride back to the precinct.

The captain, without a word, went straightway into his office, uncorked the bottle of Dewar's and downed a stiff shot. He rasped his throat, stood staring into space.

Kennedy drifted in, espied the bottle, rubbed his hands together gingerly. "B-r-r! Cold out."

MacBride turned, eyed him, then waved toward the bottle. "Go ahead."

"Thanks, Mac."

Alone, MacBride went out into the black, windy street, turned a corner, crossed the street and entered Haggerty Alley. He stopped before a drab, three-story dwelling. Aloft, one lighted window stared into the darkness. He drummed his feet on the cold pavement, then suddenly pushed into the black hallway, snapped on his flash, and ascended the worn staircase.

Third floor. One lighted transom. He knocked. The door opened. That pale young face, wide, questioning eyes. Shoulders wrapped in a plaid shawl.

"Come . . . in."

MacBride went in. Yes, the kitchen, and an old woman sitting before the open oven of the stove, and clothes drying on a line above the stove. Faded wallpaper, hand-me-down furniture, warped ceiling. Cracked oilcloth on the floor. Neat, clean—poverty with its face washed.

The girl knew. Oh, she knew! Her breath, bated for a long moment, rushed out.

"Is he . . . ?"

MacBride stood like an image of stone. "Yes. Bad wreck."

She wilted, like a spring flower suddenly overcome by an unexpected frost. The old woman moved, extended a scrawny arm.

"Betty!"

The girl reeled, spun, and buried her face in her mother's lap. The mother cradled her in ancient arms.

MacBride wanted to dash out. But he held his ground, and something welling from the depths of him melted the granite of his chiseled face. The old woman looked up, and though her eyes were moist, there was a certain grimness in her expression. Age is strong, mused MacBride. It meets fate with an iron jaw.

The old woman, looking at him, shook her head slowly, as if to imply that this was life, and we either died and left others to mourn, or mourned while others died.

MacBride put on his hat, backed toward the door, opened it softly. He bowed slightly, and without a word, departed.

He was a little pale when he reached the station-house. Doran and Rigallo, his prize detectives, and four or five reserves were hanging about the central room, and Kennedy, his coat collar still up to his ears, was leaning indolently against the wall and blowing smoke circles.

MacBride nodded to Doran and Rigallo and strode into his office. Kennedy tried to edge in but MacBride closed the door in his face. Doran hooked one leg over a corner of the desk and Rigallo stood jingling loose change in his pocket.

He said, "Trouble, eh, Cap?"

"Plenty!" MacBride bit off.

"Was the guy shot?"

"No telling yet. Too messed up to see. That's the morgue's job. We'll get news soon. But I'm willing to bet my shirt the guy's been done in. If

he has, I'm going to bust loose and drive the Atlas Corporation to the wall."

Doran grunted. "Fine chance, with that bum of a mayor back of it. How the hell did he ever get in?"

"Don't be dumb," said Rigallo "That last election was a farce. All the polls in the Fourth and Fifth wards were fixed. Guys voted twice, and the polls committee scrapped a lot of votes for the opposition because of some lousy technicality—illegibility, unreadable signatures and all that crap. Who votes in this city? The better element yap at conditions and turn up their noses and don't even go near the polls. The bums, the bootleggers, the blockheads and gunmen vote! And the New Party sends loud-mouthed guys to ballyhoo the mill and river bohunks during lunch-hour, and under-cover guys go around near the employment agencies, the bread-lines, and the parks. They find guys out of work and up against it, and they slip 'em a ten-dollar bill to vote. The Atlas Corporation employs eight hundred men, and they vote right or lose their jobs, and their wives, mothers and the whole damned family are dragged to the polls. Now d'you wonder why we have this bum of a mayor?"

MacBride said, "Sounds like Kennedy."

"It is," replied Rigallo. "Kennedy and I have the whole thing thrashed out."

The telephone rang. MacBride picked it up, muttered his name, and listened. When he put the instrument down, he sucked in his breath and curled his lip.

"Poisoned," he said. "Saunders, the driver, was poisoned. A stuff that he could drink and it wouldn't have any effect for an hour. Then it hits a man like a stroke of paralysis. That's how it hit Saunders."

Doran said, "Must have stopped at a roadhouse for a snifter and got poisoned liquor."

"Just that," nodded MacBride. "I'll find that roadhouse. Some pup is going to hang for this, just as sure as God made little green apples!"

"Remember, Cap, the mayor," put in Doran.

MacBride doubled his fist. "I'll bring it right to his doorstep if I have to, and I'd like to see the bum try to can me. I'm sick and tired of these conditions! I'm going to put a dent in the Atlas Corporation, and wipe out this graft, this dirty, rotten corruption."

"They'll bump you off, Mac."

"I'll take the chance! I'm insured for twenty thousand, and my plot in the cemetery is paid for!"

It took a tough man to run the Second.

III

NEXT day the noon edition of the *Free Press* gave the wreck and the death of Saunders a front-page column. It recited the details in its customary offhand manner, giving the place, the approximate time, name of the deceased, and financial loss. It wound up with the non-committal statement that the police were investigating the matter, but did not say why.

MacBride, reading it over his coffee, at his home in Grove Manor, was a little disgruntled at its apparently disinterested attitude. But, turning the pages, his eye rested on the editorial columns, and particularly on an item labeled,

CRIME—CORRUPTION

Crime. We've always had it. It is a disease, recurring every so often, like smallpox, diphtheria, and scarlet fever. It lays waste, like any and all of these diseases, and causes suffering, misery and despair.

And on the other hand, wealth, affluence, power. To whom? Why, to those, quite often in high place, who like parasites, feast avidly upon the meaty morsels gathered by vultures who swoop in the dark, kill from behind, and crow at the dawn.

What we need is a crusader. Not a preaching, scripture-quoting, holier-than-thou sort of fellow.

Not an altruist, nor a gavel-thumper. But a Man, and we capitalize that symbolically. A man somewhere in the rusty machinery of this municipality, who cares not a whoop for authority and is willing to stack the possibility of losing his job against the possibility of sweeping out the unclean corridors of intrigue and corruption, and satisfying the ego of his own morals and ethics.

A two-fisted, slam-bang, tougher-than-thou sort of man! The streets of Richmond City are more sordid than its sewers. They smell to high heaven. We need a chunk of brimstone to sterilize them. Amen.

"Whew!" whistled MacBride. "This will cause apoplexy in the Town Hall. The *Free Press* is out to ride 'em."

He was back in his office at the precinct at one, and Kennedy was sound asleep in the swivel chair. He kicked it, and Kennedy awoke.

"Hello, Mac."

"Hello. Pretty ripe, that editorial."

"Thanks."

MacBride looked at him. "You didn't write it."

"Yup. My name'll go down in posterity."

"If the Big Gang knew you did it, it would go down in the Deceased Column. Get out o' that chair."

Kennedy got out and sat on the desk, swinging his legs.

MacBride said, "I see, now, that you were shooting in my direction. Humph. Crusader!"

Kennedy smiled. "Would you, Mac."

"I am," snapped MacBride, "but there's nothing of the crusader about me. I'm sore, and I'll bust up this racket if it's the last thing I do. That poor kid, Kennedy—her name's Betty. . . . God Almighty! Government of the people, by the people and for the people! What a bromide!"

He pulled an empty cigar box from his desk, took a pen and a piece of paper, and on the paper printed, in large letters:

SPARE CHANGE, BOYS, FOR A HARD-HIT NEIGHBOR

This he pasted on the cover of the box, and said, "Dig down, Kennedy."

He himself dropped in a couple of dollars, and Kennedy added another and some odd change. Then MacBride carried the box into the central room and placed it on the desk, where none might pass without seeing it.

Still in plain-clothes, he shook Kennedy, and walked down to River Street. He found the Colonial depot, and from a number of drivers learned that, on cold nights, they usually stopped at the *Owl's Nest,* out beyond Bingham Center, on the pike, for a shot of rum. Reasoning that Saunders had lived, driven and drunk similarly, he took a trolley car to the outskirts of the city, alighted where Main crossed Farmingville Turnpike, and boarded an outbound bus.

It was a long ride, and they passed the shattered truck on the way. It still lay in the gully, but a derrick was at work, and one of the Colonial's trucks was gathering up the remains. At four-thirty he left the bus, and stood regarding the *Owl's Nest.* It stood well back off the highway, a low, rambling casino with many windows. The main entrance was decorated with colored light bulbs, but on one side was a sign, *Delivery Entrance,* and MacBride judged that this also was the logical entrance for truck-men in quest of a drink.

He pushed this door open and found himself in a hallway that turned sharply to the left. But directly in front of him was an open door leading into a small, shabby room containing two tables and a half dozen chairs, and a fly-specked electric light hanging from the ceiling.

MacBride sat down, and presently a man in shirt-sleeves entered.

"Rye highball," said MacBride.

The man, large, beetle-browed, hairy-armed, looked him over, then shook his head. "No drinks here, buddy."

"Tripe! I know."

"Not here, buddy."

"You the boss?"

"No."

"Flag the boss."

The man disappeared, and a few minutes later a short, fat, prosperous-looking man entered with a frown of annoyance. But the frown disappeared like a cloud and sunlight beamed.

"Oh, hello, Mac."

"Didn't know you ran this dump, Hen. Sit down."

Hen sat down, cheerful, twinkle-eyed, and said to the hovering waiter, "Make it two, Mike." And a moment later, to MacBride, "What *you* doing out this way, Mac?"

"Poking around."

"I mean—really, Mac."

"Trailing a clue. Hear about that truck smash-up?"

"Sure. Tough, wasn't it?"

"You don't know the half of it. And that's why I'm up here, Hen."

Hen's eyes widened perplexedly. He started to say something, but the drinks arrived, and he licked his lips instead. The waiter went out, and the two men regarded each other.

MacBride jerked his head toward the door. "How long has that guy been working here? What's his name?"

"A month. Mike Bannon."

"He serves all the drinks?"

"Ye-es."

"All the truck drivers stop in this room, I guess?"

"Sure."

MacBride took a drink and let it sink in. "Good stuff," he nodded, and then leaned across the table. "You're a white guy, Hen, and you're sensible. Fire that man."

"What's the matter?"

"Fire him tomorrow. If he gets sore, tell him the cops are tightening down on you, and you're cutting out the hooch for a month or more. I'm doing you a turn, Hen. You want to keep your hands clean, don't you?"

"Cripes, yes, Mac!"

"Then bounce him—tomorrow at noon."

"Okey, Mac."

MacBride was back in the precinct at seven.

He picked up Rigallo and Doran and they all went over the Headquarters and sought out the Bureau of Criminal Identification. This was a vast place, lined with rows of card-indexes, and on the wall were several huge metal books, attached by their backs, so that a man could swing the metal pages back and forth and scan the photographs of those men who, having stepped outside the law, were recorded therein, with further details of their crimes recorded in the surrounding files. MacBride, turning page after page, suddenly grunted and pointed.

"There's the guy, boys," he said.

He noted the number, gave it to the attendant, and while waiting, said to his prizes, "Working at the *Owl's Nest.*"

The attendant reappeared with a card and handed it to MacBride. MacBride scrutinized it. "H'm. Michael Shane, arrested for criminal assault against Rosie Horovitz, June 12, 1924. Indicted, June 13th. Acquitted July 2nd. Lack of evidence. And again: Arrested October 5, 1925. Charge, felonious assault with attempt to rob. Charge preferred by Sven Runstrom. Indicted October 6th. Sentenced October 15th, sixty days, hard labor."

"Let's go out and nab him," said Rigallo.

"No," said MacBride. "He's working as Mike Bannon. Come on."

They returned to the precinct, and in the privacy of his office, MacBride said, "This guy poisoned Saunders' liquor, but I'm after bigger game. He's a tough nut, and he'll hold his tongue until some shyster, retained by the gang, gets him out of our hands on a writ. What we want to know is, who's the boss of the gang, the mayor's right-hand man. *That* is the guy we want. We've got more to do than apprehend the actual murderer of Saunders. We've got to grab the mob and their boss, and prevent further killings, and when we do this we'll have the mayor against the wall. Shane is a stoical bum, and a rubber hose wouldn't work him. We've got to get the big guy—the one with the most brains and the least guts."

"What's your idea?" asked Rigallo.

"Just this. At tomorrow noon Shane gets his walking papers from Hen Meloy. You go out there tomorrow morning in a hired flivver, and when this guy gets a bus headed for town, tail him. He'll head for his boss, to report. Tail him that far and then give me a ring."

MacBride went home early that night, slept well, and was back on the job at nine next morning. He took the cigar box from the desk in the central room, went into his office, and counted out forty-two dollars and fifty cents. This he shoved into an envelope, with the brief message, "From the bunch at the Second Police Precinct." He called in a reserve, gave him the envelope and the Haggerty Alley address, and then, sitting back with a sigh, started his first cigar of the day.

Kennedy dropped in on his way to Headquarters, and said, "The municipal inspectors condemned two more Colonial trucks. Said Saunders death was caused by a faulty steering gear. Nobody knows the details? What did the morgue say, Mac?"

"Run along, Kennedy."

"Keeping it under your hat, eh? It's all right, Mac. I can wait. Here's another tip. The Colonial people aren't dumb, and there's a guard riding on all their night trucks now. They're die-hards, Mac. These guys liked Saunders, and they're primed to start shooting first chance they get."

Kennedy went out, and MacBride cursed him in one breath and complimented him in the next.

At two o'clock the telephone rang and MacBride grabbed it.

"Cap? Rigallo."

"Shoot, Riggy."

"Tailed him okey. Two-ten Jockey Street. I'm waiting in the cigar store on the corner. Come heeled."

MacBride hung up, slapped on his visored cap, and strode into the central room. "Six reserves, Sergeant! Ready, Doran!"

A windy look was in his eyes, and his jaw squared.

IV

JOCKEY Street is hell's own playground. You enter it from the theatrical center, and all is glittering, blatant and intensely alive. But as you bore deeper, riverward, the street lights become further apart, the chop suey joints disappear, and the houses, losing height, likewise lose color.

It was cold that afternoon, and fog smoked in from the river, damp and chill. The din of upper Jockey Street died to a murmur, and on its lower reaches few men were afield. Here or there you heard footsteps, and soon, dimly at first, then clearer, a pedestrian materialized out of the fog, swished by and gradually disappeared again, trailing his footsteps. Up the man-made causeway came the muffled rhythmic tolling of a pier-head fog bell.

Down it rolled a black, inconspicuous touring car, with drawn side-curtains. Nearing a side street, the door to the tonneau opened, and MacBride leaped out. The car rolled on, was swallowed up by the wet gray clouds.

MacBride strode toward a cigar-store. Rigallo came out, smoking a cigarette, looking unconcerned. They fell in step and strolled down the side street, leisurely.

"He hasn't come out, Riggy?"

"No. Came on the bus to Main and Farmingville. Took a taxi from there. Got off at Main and Jockey. Walked. I left the car there and walked, too. Saw him go in 210. There's a gray touring car parked outside—powerful boat."

"I'll crash the joint."

"They'll never open the door. Bet you need signals."

"Try my way."

They circumnavigated the block, and came out upon Jockey Street a block nearer the river. Here the police car was parked, the men still hidden inside. MacBride stood on the edge of the curb, spoke to the curtains.

"I'm aiming to get in 210. Two minutes after I leave here you boys get out and surround this block. It may be messy."

"Okey," came Doran's low voice.

MacBride said, "Come on, Rigallo," and they walked up the street. He explained. "We'll both climb the steps to the door. I'll knock. Somebody will come, but if he doesn't get the proper signals, he won't open. But he'll listen. Then you walk down the steps, hard as you can, and walk away. He may open then and peek out. I'll crash it."

"What then?"

"Hell knows!" MacBride's fists clenched. "Just let me get in that dump!"

They reached the four stone steps that led to the door of 210. They mounted them, and MacBride, one hand on the gun in his pocket, knocked with the other.

They waited, looking at each other. Presently they heard the padding of footsteps, then silence. MacBride knocked again, insistently. No, that wasn't the signal. He nodded to Rigallo. Rigallo nodded back, stamped heavily down the steps and walked off.

MacBride flattened against the doorframe, breath bated, gun half-drawn. The latch clicked. A hinge creaked. The door moved an inch, another inch. A nose appeared. Then two beady eyes, and a pasty, pinched face.

MacBride cannoned against the door, and knocked the look-out sprawling. The door, working on a spring, slammed shut. The captain was bent over the prostrate, speechless form, with the muzzle of his gun screwed into a sunken chest.

"Chirp and I'll bust you!"

The man writhed under the firm pressure of the gun. His mouth worked, gasping. His eyes popped.

"Cripes!" he moaned.

"Pipe down! Quick, now. What's the lay? Where's the gang?"

"Cripes!"

"Spill it!

"Cripes!"

Desperate, MacBride rapped his jaw with the gun barrel.

"Ouch!"

"Then talk!"

"Second floor, door t' back o' the hall. Cripes!"

"Open?"

"Uh—yup."

"How many?"

"Tuh—ten."

"Get up!"

MacBride hauled the runt to his feet, dragged him to the front door, opened it. Rigallo was on the curb. MacBride motioned to him, and Rigallo skipped up.

"Take this, Riggy!"

Rigallo grabbed the look-out, clapped on manacles. "Should I get the boys?"

"No. I'll start the ball. There are ten guys upstairs, and I feel ambitious. Besides, if we all crash it, it will be a mix-up and the boys might get hurt. One man can crash a room better than six. I'll blow when I need you. You hang here, and then blow for the boys."

"It's a long chance, Cap!"

"I carry heavy insurance. Don't let this door close."

MacBride turned and re-entered the hall. Gun drawn, he went up the stairway, paused at the first landing, listened, and then ascended the next flight. He was wary, alert, dangerous. There were captains on the Force who directed operations from the outside, smoking cigars on street corners, at a safe distance. MacBride was a man who never sent his men into a trap before first examining the trap himself. One reason why his wife lay awake nights, thinking.

Door in the rear. He stood at the stair-head, muscles tense, gun pointing toward the door. He advanced straight, light-footed, primed to go off. He stood before the door, the muzzle of his gun an inch from the panel.

His left hand started out, closed gently, carefully, over the knob. Some said you should turn a knob slow, bit by bit, until you could not turn it any more; then heave and rush. But sometimes you never got that far. A knob might creak. A wandering gaze on the other side might see it turning.

Turn, heave and rush all at once—that was it. MacBride did it. The door whanged open and he crouched on the threshold, poised and deadly.

A woman, alone, looked up from the depths of an overstuffed chair. She had been trimming her fingernails with a steel file, and she sat there, apparently unperturbed, the file, in her right hand, poised over the thumb of her left. She wore a negligée, pink and sheer. Her hair was peroxide treated, bobbed and fuzzy.

MacBride reached back and closed the door. The woman, with a shrug, went on trimming her nails, and said, in an offhand manner,

"Got your nerve, Cap, busting in on a lady."

"What's wrong with that sentence, Gertie?"

"Well, rub it in."

"Get dressed."

"I'm not going out."

"No?" He leaned back. "I'm waiting."

She rose, running her hands down her sides and lodging them on her hips, thumbs forward.

"Suppose I yell?"

"You'll be the first woman I ever killed."

"You would?"

"I sure would."

They stood staring at each other, the lynx and the lion.

"Think I can get dressed with you in the room?"

"I'm not particular. If you're too modest, put on that fur coat."

"I'm not modest. *Particular*, guy."

"Put on the coat."

She tilted her chin, cut MacBride with a brassy, withering look. Then she sauntered over to the coat, picked it up and slipped into it. She thrust her hand into a pocket.

"Careful!" warned MacBride.

She laughed, drew out a handkerchief, touched her nose and then shoved the handkerchief back into her pocket. A split second later flame and smoke burst through the fur, and hot lead ran up MacBride's gun arm. His gun clattered to the floor.

The woman leaped for the switch, threw off the lights. With his left hand MacBride, gritting his teeth with pain, recovered the gun. Another burst of flame slashed through the darkness, and a shot whanged by his ear. He dived, headlong, collided with the woman and knocked her over. Again her gun went off, wildly, and the shot banged through the ceiling.

With his wounded hand MacBride groped for hers—found it, wrenched away her gun, groaned with the pain of it. He heaved up, rushed to the door, shot home the bolt. Then he dived for the light switch, snapped it, and a dazzling radiance flooded the room.

The woman, on her feet, flung a Chinese vase. MacBride ducked and the vase crashed through a mirror. She crouched, quivering in every muscle, her breath pumping fiercely from her lungs, eyes wide and storming with anger.

"You—lousy—bum!" she cried.

"Pipe down!"

Fists hammered on the door, feet kicked it. Voices snarled.

The woman laughed hysterically. "The Gang! The Gang! They'll riddle you! They'll cut your dirty heart out!"

"Will they?"

MacBride drew his whistle, blew it.

V

ABRUPTLY, the scuffling and pounding stopped. A moment of silence, then retreating footsteps.

MacBride stood with his cap tilted over one ear and a slab of hair down over one eyebrow. His right arm hung down, blood weaving a red tracery on his hand, then dropping to the floor. His hand felt heavy as lead, dragging at wounded muscles. A thought struck him, and he shoved the hand into his coat pocket.

Footfalls sounded again, hammering up the stairs. Cops' shoes—heavy-soled, thick-heeled. Now they were out in the hall, moving about, whispering hoarsely. MacBride backed against the door, unbolted it, pulled it open.

Rigallo came in. "Hell, Gertie!" he chuckled, sarcastically.

Gertie thumbed her nose and wiggled her fingers.

"You trollop!" snapped Rigallo.

"Pst, Riggy," said MacBride. "Where's the look-out?"

"Doran's got him in the machine."

"Jake!" He looked into the hall. Six cops out there and two closed doors. They had the doors covered. "Take her downstairs, Riggy."

"Who's her boy friend?"

"That's what we'll find out. She's not talkative just now. Grab a dress, sister, and take it along."

"If you think I'll spill the boy friend's name, MacBride, you're all wet," she snapped.

"Take her, Riggy."

Rigallo grabbed a dress from a hanger and flung it at her. It draped across her shoulder. She left it there.

"Get out," he jerked.

She put one hand on her hip and sauntered leisurely. Rigallo took a quick step, gripped her by the arm and propelled her out not too gently. She cursed and added something relative to his maternity. He trotted her down the stairs.

MacBride joined his cops. "Let's bust this door."

Seven guns boomed, and seven shots shattered the doorknob and crashed through the lock. Patrolman Grosskopf, one-time leader of a German mudgutter band, hurled his two hundred and twenty pounds of beef against the door and almost ripped it from its hinges.

MacBride waved his men back and stepped in. The room was empty. His right hand was still in his pocket. His men did not know he was wounded. He came out in the hall and nodded at the other door.

Bang! Seven shots sounded as one.

"Now, Grosskopf."

Grosskopf catapulted, and the door capitulated.

The room yawned empty. It showed signs of some having made a hasty departure. Bureau drawers were pulled out, a chair was overturned. Glasses, some of them still containing liquor, stood on the table. A chair, also, stood on the table.

"Up there," said MacBride, pointing to a skylight. "To table, to chair, to roof."

He led the way up to the roof, and they prowled around, from one roof to another. Wind, fog, and emptiness. They came to a fire-escape in the rear.

"They skipped," he said. "Come on back."

Below, in the hall, they found Rigallo and the woman, Doran and the look-out. MacBride looked at the woman but addressed his men. "We've got an ace-in-the-hole now. Let's go."

They went out into the foggy street, and MacBride said to the look-out, "Thought you tricked me, eh? Ten men in the back room!"

The woman laughed. "Ten! That's head-quarters, Cap, not the barracks. What a joke! There was only three—in the front."

Rigallo said to the look-out, "Boy Scout, we will entertain you a while at the precinct. I have a nice new piece of rubber hose."

They piled into the police car. Its motor roared. It turned about and purred up Jockey Street, and at Main Rigallo got out and picked up his flivver, and the two cars proceeded toward the Second.

The prisoners were locked up in separate cells. Then MacBride, alone, went out and walked several blocks and entered a door above which was a small sign bearing the legend, Dr. O. F. Blumm, M.D.

"Oh, hello, Mac."

"Hello, Doc. Fix this." He drew his blood-soaked hand from his pocket, and the doctor frowned, murmured, "H'm," and added, "Take off the coat, shirt."

The bullet had struck just above the wrist, sliced open three inches of the forearm and lodged in the hard flesh just short of the elbow. MacBride, teeth clamped, his eyes closed, shed streams of sweat while the doctor probed for the

bullet and finally removed it. Then MacBride sank back, a little pale, very grim.

"It might have been worse," remarked the doctor.

"Sure," said MacBride, and breathed quietly while the wound was cauterized, stitched and bandaged.

"Most men take a little dope for this, Mac."

"Uh!" grunted MacBride through tight lips.

Through the fog, he returned to the station-house, his hand concealed in his pocket, his wound throbbing.

Kennedy was lounging in the office. "You look yellow around the gills, Mac."

"Liver," clipped MacBride, and took a drink.

"Hear you got Gertie Case and Midge Sutter."

"Um."

"How long do you suppose you can hold 'em?"

"Watch me."

"There'll be a writ of release here before you know it," said Kennedy. "How come you didn't get the gang?"

"Breeze, Kennedy! Dammit, I'm not in the mood!"

Kennedy shrugged and went out.

Alone, MacBride drew out his hand, laid it on the desk. God, how the arm throbbed! He heard a voice outside the door and slipped the hand back into his pocket. The door opened and a big, bloated man, with a moon-face, large fishy eyes, and an air of pompous importance, sailed in.

"Hello, Mac."

"Hello."

Captain Bower, plainclothes, a Headquarters "yes man," and the mayor's bodyguard. MacBride drew into himself, wary, on guard.

Bower deposited his indecent bulk in an arm-chair and sent a tobacco shot into the cuspidor. "This latest business, Mac. The Jockey Street fizzle."

"Fizzle?"

"Well, whatever you like. Anyhow it's out of your district, and Headquarters is going to han-dle it. Another thing. We're also handling the case of Saunders. Of course, there's nothing to it, and we'll dispose of it right off."

MacBride's jaw hardened. Graft again! Nothing to it! Bah! They knew he was out to riddle their racket. They were cornered, and playing a subtle game. They could not fire him immediately, could not shove him out in the sticks while this thing was hanging fire. But they *could* take a case out of his hands. Could they?

"It's my case, Bower," he snapped. "My men got the clues, did the tailing, and we've got Midge Sutter and that Case broad salted."

"On what charge?"

"Suspicion. That's enough for any cop."

"We'll work it out at Headquarters," said Bower, very matter-of-fact. "I'll take the pair along with me, now."

Color crept into MacBride's face. "Not before I indict 'em—tomorrow."

Bower frowned. "Don't be a goof. What can you indict 'em on?"

MacBride was in his last ditch, his back to the wall. He had hoped to conceal this, but—

He drew out his wounded arm, placed it on the table. "This, Bower. The woman potted me."

Bower's face dropped, and his mouth hung open. He stared at the bandaged hand. Then he drew his face back into place and got up.

"Good-bye," he sniffed, and pounded out.

MacBride waited a few minutes, then called in Rigallo. "Riggy, take Sutter in the sweat room. Sweat him."

"Right," nodded Rigallo, and went out.

MacBride sat back in his chair and lit a cigar. The pain pounded furiously, shot up and down his arm, reached his neck. Sweat stood out on his forehead, and muscles knotted on either side of his wide, firm mouth. An hour dragged by.

Then Rigallo came in, brushing his hands together. His hair, ordinarily neatly combed, was a bit disheveled.

"Well?" asked MacBride.

Rigallo shook his head. "No go. The guy is little but tough. He's been through it before. Knows if he squeals the gang will crucify him."

MacBride held up his wounded arm. Rigallo clicked his teeth.

"Hell, Mac. I didn't know."

"The broad got me. Look here, Riggy. You're the whitest wop I've ever known. My back is to the wall, and I need a guy who's willing to kick authority in the slats and play this game to a fare-three-well."

"Shoot, Mac."

"Take the broad and bounce her around from one station to another. They'll have a writ out for her, or some trick. The idea is, the writ mustn't find her. When they come here, I'll say she's over at the Third. Then I'll ring you and you take her to the Fourth and so on, and the guys at the Fourth will tell the runner you've taken her to the Fifth. Keep ahead of the runner. The precincts will play with us. They're good guys. Keep moving until tomorrow morning. Judge Ross will be on the job then, and he's the only judge we can depend on. He'll indict her. We'll get hell, Riggy, but we'll crash this racket."

"Right!"

Five minutes later Rigallo was headed for the Third with Gertie Case.

Ten minutes later a runner appeared with writs for Gertrude Case and Midge Sutter.

"Sutter's here," said MacBride, "and you can take him. But the Case woman's over at the Third."

And he telephoned the Third.

A little later a doctor from the Medical Examiner's Office, accompanied by Captain Bower, entered, and the doctor said:

"I'll look at your wound, Captain."

Grim, stony-faced, MacBride allowed his wound to be looked at.

The doctor said, "Bad, Captain. You can't carry on."

"The hell I can't!"

"Nevertheless—" The doctor sat down and affixed his signature to a document, scaled it across to MacBride. "You're released from active duty until I sign a health certificate of reinstatement. Signed by the Commissioner and attested by me. Go home and rest."

MacBride saw through a red haze. Vaguely, he heard Bower's words. "Your lieutenant will take charge until a captain can be sent over."

MacBride's heart sledge-hammered his ribs. The men went out, and he sat alone, like a man in a daze. Alone against graft, corruption and the very Department to which he had given eighteen years of his life! The blow should have crushed him, sent him storming out of the station in rage and righteous indignation. It should have driven him to ripping off his uniform, throwing his badge through the window, and cursing the Department to the nethermost depths.

But tough was MacBride, and a die-hard. He heaved up, swiveled and glared at the closed door. His lip curled, and challenge shone in his eyes.

"Home—*hell!*" he snarled.

VI

UT he went out, his slouch hat yanked over his eyes. Night had closed in, half-brother to the fog. And both shrouded the city. Street lights glowed wanly, diffusing needle-like shafts of shimmering radiance. Headlights glared like hungry eyes. Autos hissed sibilantly on wet pavements. Faces appeared, palely afloat, and then disappeared.

Cold and wet and miserable, and MacBride tramping the streets, collar up, hands in pockets, pain pumping through his arm. In minutes he aged years. Why not let things slide? Why go to all the bother? What reward, what price honour? Let Headquarters take 'em. Let Bower frame their getaway. Cripes, but Bower would get a nice slice of graft out of this! How could a single precinct captain hope to carry his white plume in this city of graft?

He dragged to a stop at an intersection. Well, Rigallo was standing by him. And the State's Attorney was a square-shooter.

"H'm."

He suddenly flagged a taxi, climbed in and gave an address. Out of the dark of the street another figure appeared, got into a second taxi.

Ten minutes later MacBride alighted in a quiet, residential street, told the driver to wait, and ascending a flight of brown-stone steps, pushed a bell-button. A servant appeared and MacBride gave his name. A moment later he was ushered from the foyer into a spacious library.

State's Attorney Rolland, thirty-eight, lean, blond, clean-cut in evening clothes, extended a hand. MacBride shook with his left, and though Rolland's eyes flickered, he said nothing.

"You look worn, Captain. Sit down. Cigar?"

"Thanks—no. Am I keeping you?"

"No. Dinner at eight." He leaned against the side of a broad mahogany table, arms folded loosely, eyes quizzical.

MacBride detailed, briefly, the fight in Jockey Street, the apprehension of Gertie Case and Midge Sutter; the release of Sutter on a writ, the game of hide and seek even now being played by Rigallo.

"I'll pick up Rigallo and the woman around dawn," he went on. "I'll get her indicted. I thought if you could be around there, to take her in hand before her lawyer gets to her— Hell, we've got to get the jump on these pups!"

"Don't know her man, eh?"

"No. That's why we've got to hold her. If she's faced with twenty years for shooting an officer, she'll think. She's thirty now, and no guy is worth enough in her eyes to take a twenty-year rap for him. She'll come across. Ten to one her boy friend realizes this."

"And you believe that Saunders chap was poisoned?"

"Yes. Bannon did it. He's been lying low for a couple years. Always lone-wolfed. That's why we can't connect him with the gang he must have hooked with. If the Case woman squeals, we'll get the gang, and getting the gang means—"

"Ah, yes," nodded Rolland.

It was politic, in the State's Attorney's rooms, not to mention the name both men had in mind.

Then Rolland said, "Good you have the woman. These gangsters laugh at a prison sentence. But a woman—and especially one of her type—looks upon prison as death. I'll be there in the morning. Take care of your wound."

They shook, and MacBride departed. The Regime thought they had picked soft clay in Rolland. What a shock when they had discovered cement instead, unpliable!

Entering the taxi, MacBride drove off, and further back, another taxi began moving.

He left his taxi at the Fourth, and discovered that Rigallo and the woman had gone on to the Fifth ten minutes before. He hung around, saw the runner with the writ rush in and start broadcasting to the desk. The sergeant told him where the woman had gone, and cursing, the runner went off and out like a streak.

MacBride followed from station to station, and at the Seventh, just after the runner had gone on, he met Bower.

"Look here, MacBride. What's your game?"

"What's yours, Bower?"

"Cut that boloney."

"Then cut yours."

Bower scowled. "You'll get broke for this. Stop that guy that's got the dame."

"I don't know where he is. What's more, Bower, I'm off duty. Got nothing to say. You find him—and try stopping him. Your job depends on that, Bower."

Bower worked his hands. He started to say something but bit his lip instead and stormed out.

A game was being played on the checkerboard of Richmond City's police stations. Rigallo moved from one to another, doubled back, moved across town, uptown, downtown. Midnight passed, and dawn approached, and still Rigallo kept the lead; and Bower blundered in his wake, fuming and cursing; and the man with the writ, worn to a frazzle by the chase, now tottered at Bower's heels.

MacBride, weary, haggard, sapped by the pain in his arm, sometimes dizzy, met Rigallo in the Eighth at four a.m. Gertie cursed and

protested at such inhuman treatment, but no one paid her any attention.

MacBride and Rigallo formulated plans, and then MacBride took the woman and carried on the game. When Bower caught up with Rigallo, the latter wasted half an hour of the other's time by stalling, kidding and then finally telling Bower that the woman was probably uptown. Bower saw the trick and bowled off in high heat.

When he caught up with MacBride, he discovered that the woman had again changed hands and was now probably downtown. Bower cursed a sizzling blue streak and was indiscreet enough to call MacBride an untoward name.

With his one good hand, MacBride hung a left hook on Bower's jaw and draped him over a table. Then he went out into the wet gray dawn, and felt a little better.

At half-past eight he met Rigallo in the Third, joined him and the woman in Rigallo's flivver.

"Cripes, I'll never get over this!" rasped Gertie.

"You said something, sister," nodded MacBride.

"You're a big bum, MacBride," she stabbed. "And you're another, Rigallo."

Rigallo spat. "Three of a kind, eh?"

"And your mother's another," she added.

Rigallo took one hand from the wheel and with the palm of it slapped her face.

She laughed, baring her teeth, brazenly.

A block behind, a taxi was following.

Ahead yawned the entrance to Law Street, and half way down it loomed the Court.

"Here's where you get indicted, sister," said MacBride.

"I'm laughing."

"You don't look that way."

On one side of the entrance to Law Street was a cigar store. On the other corner was a drugstore. As the flivver crossed the square, a man sauntered from the drug-store, and at the same time another sauntered from the cigar-store.

They looked across at each other, and both nodded and shoved hands into pockets.

Bang!—bang! Bang—bang!

VII

IGALLO stiffened at the wheel. Gertie screamed, clutched her breast. MacBride ducked, and the flivver leaped across the square, slewed over the curb and crashed into the drug-store window.

Pedestrians stopped, horrified, frozen in their tracks. The two well-dressed men who had stood on either corner joined and walked briskly up the street toward a big, gray touring car.

The taxi that had been trailing the flivver stopped, and Kennedy, leaping out, ran across to the demolished flivver. He reached it as MacBride, streaked with blood, burst from the wreckage.

"There's the car, Mac!" He pointed.

"Where's another?" clipped MacBride.

Kennedy nodded to the taxi, and they ran over.

"Nossir," barked the driver, "I ain't chasin' them guys." He climbed out. "You guys go ahead."

"I'll drive," said Kennedy casually.

"Kennedy," said MacBride, "you stay out of this."

"What! After tailing you all night! Coming?"

He was beside the wheel, shoving into gear. MacBride clipped an oath and hopped in, and the taxi went howling up the street.

He muttered, "Pups—got—Riggy! Step on it, Kennedy!"

"The broad?"

"Dead."

"They made sure you wouldn't indict her."

"Pups! *Watch that turn!*"

"Yu-up!"

Kennedy took the turn on two wheels, knocked over a push-cart full of fruit, and jammed his foot hard down on the gas.

"Applesauce!"

"And crushed pineapple!"

Bang!

A cowl-light disappeared from the taxi.

Bang—bang—bang! went MacBride's gun.

People scattered into doorways. Moving cars stopped. Heads appeared at windows.

The gray car swung into a wide street set with trolley tracks. It weaved recklessly through traffic, heading for Farmingville Turnpike, where speed would count. It roared past red traffic lights, honking its horn, grazing other cars, swerving and swaying in its mad, reckless flight.

The taxi hurtled after it no less recklessly. MacBride was leaning well out of the seat, twisting his left arm to shoot past the windshield. Kennedy swung the machine through startled traffic with a chilling nonchalance.

MacBride fired, smashed the rear window in the tonneau.

"Lower, Mac. Get a tire," suggested Kennedy.

"Can't aim well around this windshield."

"Bust the windshield."

MacBride broke it with his gun barrel. He dared not fire again, however. People were in the way, darting across the street in panicky haste. A traffic cop was ahead, having almost been knocked over by the gray touring car. MacBride recognized him—O'Day. He leaned out, and as they whanged by, yelled:

"O'Day—riot squad!"

The gray car reached Farmingville Turnpike, a wide, macadam speedway, and its exhaust, hammered powerfully. The taxi was doing sixty miles an hour and Kennedy had the throttle right down against the floor boards.

"Faster!" barked MacBride.

"Can't, Mac. This ain't no Stutz!"

Bang! No shot that time. The rear left had blown, and the taxi skidded, bounced, and dived along like a horse with the blind staggers. Kennedy jammed on his brakes as a big powerful car slewed around him and slid to a stop ten yards ahead. It was a roadster, and out of it jumped Bower.

"Well, MacBride, see what you've done!"

"Pipe down, Bower!" clipped MacBride, starting for the roadster. "Come on, Kennedy. This boat looks powerful."

Bower got in his way. "MacBride, for cripes' sake, lay off! You'll get broke, man!" His voice cracked, and he was desperate.

"Out of my way!" snapped MacBride.

Bower tried to grasp him. MacBride uncorked his left and sent Bower sprawling in the bushes. Then he ran toward the roadster and Kennedy hopped in behind the wheel.

"Step on it, Kennedy!"

Kennedy stepped on, and whistled. "Boy, this is *my* idea of a boat!"

Inside of three minutes he was doing seventy miles an hour. MacBride's hand dropped to the seat, touched a metal object. He picked it up. It was a pistol fitted with a silencer. Kennedy saw it out of the corner of his eye.

MacBride opened the gun. A shell had been fired.

"Now," said Kennedy, "you know how we got a flat."

MacBride swore under his breath.

Soon they saw the gray touring car, and Kennedy hit the gun for seventy-five miles an hour. They were out in the sticks now. Fields, gullies, occasional groves of sparse timber flashed by. Curves were few and far between. The road, for the most part, ran in long, smooth stretches.

The roadster gained. MacBride screwed open the windshield, fired, aiming low. He fired again. The touring car suddenly swerved, its rear end bounced. Then it left the road, hurtled down an embankment, whirled over and over, its metal ripping and screeching over stones and stumps.

Kennedy applied his brakes, but the roadster did not stop until it was a hundred yards beyond the still tumbling touring car. MacBride reloaded his gun, shoved the one with the silencer into his pocket, and started back. Kennedy was beside him. As they left the road

and ran through the bushes, they saw two figures staggering into the timber beyond.

MacBride shouted and fired his gun, but the figures disappeared in the woods. Kennedy brought up beside the shattered touring car. Four broken, twisted men were linked with the mangled wreckage.

"They're done for, Mac," he said.

"You stay here, Kennedy. I'm going after the others."

"So am I."

"Kennedy—"

"Let's go, Mac." He was off on the run.

MacBride galloped past him, dived into the timber. Somewhere ahead, two men were thrashing fiercely through the thickets. Five minutes later MacBride caught the fleeting glimpse of one. He yelled for the man to stop. The man turned and pumped three shots. Two clattered through the branches. A third banged into a tree behind which MacBride had ducked.

Kennedy, coming up at a trot, raised his automatic and blazed away. MacBride saw the man stop, throw up his arms, and buckle.

"Come on," said Kennedy.

They plunged ahead, reached the fallen man.

"Bannon!" muttered MacBride. "You finished him, Kennedy."

"Good."

Bang!

Kennedy and MacBride flung themselves into a convenient clump of bushes. They lay still, back to back, until they heard the sounds of continued flight up ahead.

"Let's," said MacBride, heaving up.

"Sure—let's."

MacBride started, hunched way over, darting from tree to tree, bush to bush. He stopped, to listen. Kennedy puffed up behind him.

"Come on," said MacBride.

"Sorry, Mac. . . ."

MacBride pivoted. Kennedy was sitting on the ground, holding his right leg.

"Hell, Kennedy!"

"Hell, Mac!"

MacBride bent down.

"Go on," grunted Kennedy. "Get the slob!"

"I'll get him," said MacBride, and started off. Dodging from tree to tree, he finally came to the edge of the timber. Before him lay a wide, marshy field, and the wind rustled in blanched weeds and bushes.

Bang!

MacBride's hat was shifted an inch, and the bullet struck a tree behind his head. His teeth clicked and he fired three shots into the weeds, then ducked. He crouched, breath bated, and listened.

The weeds crackled, and he heard a groan. Warily he crawled out into the weeds, worming his way over frozen puddles. A groan, and a rasped oath reached his ears. Sounded a bit to the right. He wriggled in that direction. He stopped, waiting. Five, ten minutes passed. Half an hour.

Then, ten yards from him a head appeared above the weeds, then a pair of shoulders. MacBride stood up.

"Drop it, guy!" He leaped as he said it.

With a snarl the man spun, but not completely. MacBride jabbed his gun in the man's side, and the latter regarded him furiously over one shoulder.

"Hello, Sciarvi."

Black and blue welts were on Sciarvi's face. He was hatless, and his overcoat was ripped in several places.

"Where'd I pot you?" asked MacBride, snatching his gun.

"In the guts," grated Sciarvi.

"Didn't know you had any."

"Get me to a doctor. Snap on it, and can the wisecracks. You don't worry me, MacBride."

"Get going." MacBride prodded him. "And lay off the lip, you lousy Dago! You're the guy I've been looking for, Sciarvi, and I'll see you to the chair!"

"Yeah? Laugh that off, MacBride. I got friends."

"I'll get your friends, too."

"That's a joke!"

"On you, Wop."

They passed into the timber, and came upon Kennedy leaning against a tree and smoking a cigarette.

"Sciarvi, eh?" he drawled. "Spats Sciarvi, the kid himself, the Beau Brummell of crookdom, the greasy, damn dago."

"Yeah?" sneered Sciarvi. "When I get out of the doctor's care I'll come around and pay you a visit."

"Tell me another bed-time story, Sciarvi!"

They moved along, Kennedy limping in the rear. They came upon Bannon, alias Shane, lying face down, quite dead. They walked past, rustled through the bushes, and came out near the wrecked car.

Half a dozen policemen and a sergeant looked up, and then Bower appeared, red-faced and bellicose.

"Oh," grumbled MacBride, "the riot squad. What did you do, come around to pick souvenirs?"

"We'll take the prisoner," rumbled Bower.

"You'll take hell!" said MacBride.

"Damn you, MacBride!" roared Bower.

MacBride pulled the gun with the silencer from his pocket, held it in his palm, looked at Bower. "Don't you think you'd better pipe down?"

Bower closed his mouth abruptly, stood swaying on his feet, his bloodshot face suffused with chagrin.

"Come on, Bower," snarled Sciarvi, "do your stuff."

Bower caught his breath, glared at Sciarvi with mixed hatred and fear. Then he stamped his foot and pointed a shaking finger at MacBride.

"You'll see—you'll see!" he threatened, but his tone was choked and unconvincing.

MacBride chuckled derisively, turned to the sergeant and said, "There's a stiff back in the woods. Better get him."

Then he pushed Sciarvi up the slope toward the road, and Kennedy limped after him. They reached the roadster and Kennedy eased in behind the wheel.

"Your leg," said MacBride.

"It's the right one, Mac. I'll use the hand-brake."

Sciarvi was shoved in and MacBride followed, and the roadster hummed back toward Richmond City.

"Now the big guy," said Kennedy.

"Now the big guy," said MacBride.

"Jokes!" cackled Sciarvi.

VIII

HE MAYOR paced the library of his opulent, fifteen-room mansion. He wore a beaver-brown suit, a starched, striped collar, a maroon tie and diamond stick-pin. He was small, chunky, with a cleft chin, a bulbous nose, and shiny red lips. He wore *pince-nez,* attached to a black-ribbon, and this, combined with the gray at his temples, gave him a certain *distingué* air. He was known for a clubable fellow, and a charming after-dinner speaker; and he went in for boosting home trade, sponsoring beauty contests, and having his picture taken while presenting lolly-pops to the half-starved kids of the South Side, bivouack of the bohunks.

He was not his best this morning. There was a hunted look in his usually brilliant eyes, and corrugated lines on his forehead, and he'd lost count of how many times he'd paced the room. He stopped short, to listen. There was a commotion outside the door, a low, angry voice, and the high-pitched, protesting voice of Simmonds, his man.

Perplexed, he started toward the door, and was about to reach for the knob when the door burst open. He froze in his tracks, then elevated chest and chin and clasped his hands behind his back.

MacBride strode in, kicked shut the door with his heel. He was grimy, blood-streaked, and dangerous. A pallor shone beneath his ruddy tan, and dark circles were under his eyes. He was weary and worn and the hand of his wounded arm was resting in his pocket. His coat collar was half up, half down, and his battered fedora, with Sciarvi's bullet hole in the crown, was jammed down to his eyebrows.

"Well?" said the Mayor.

"Well!" said MacBride.

And they stood and regarded each other and said not a word for a whole minute.

"Who are you?" asked the Mayor.

"MacBride. A common precinct captain you never saw before. But you know the name, eh?"

"Humph," grunted the Mayor. "I shall refer you to my secretary. I'm not in the habit of receiving visitors except by appointment."

MacBride lashed him with windy blue eyes, and a crooked smile tugged at his lips. "Mister Mayor, Spats Sciarvi's dying. He wants to see you."

The Mayor blinked and a tremor ran over his short, chunky frame.

"Sciarvi? Who is Sciarvi?"

"Better come along and see."

"I don't know him."

He turned on his heel and strode away.

MacBride put his hand on the knob. "Remember, Mister Mayor, I carried a dying man's wish. He's at 109 Ship Street."

The Mayor stopped, stood still, but did not turn.

MacBride left the room, and as he went out through the front door he ran into Bower. They stopped and stared at each other.

Bower snarled, "Where's Sciarvi? What did you do with him? He ain't at Headquarters. He ain't in none o' the precincts. He ain't in the hospitals."

"Ask the mayor," said MacBride, and passed on.

He got into a taxi, sank wearily into the cushions, and closed his eyes. Twenty minutes later the taxi jerked to a stop. The driver reached back, opened the door and waited. After a moment he looked around.

"Hey," he called.

"Um." MacBride awoke, paid his fare and entered a hallway.

The room he walked into was electrically lighted. Sciarvi lay on a bed, his face drained of color. Kennedy sat on a chair while a doctor was bandaging his leg. Another doctor hovered over Sciarvi.

"MacBride . . . ?" a question was in Sciarvi's tone.

MacBride shook his head. "Your friend wouldn't come. Never heard of you."

Sciarvi stared. "You're lyin', MacBride!"

"God's truth, Sciarvi!"

Their eyes held, and in the captain's gaze Sciarvi must have read the awful truth.

He closed his eyes and gritted his teeth. Then he glared. "Damn your soul, MacBride, why are you hidin' me here? Why didn't you take me to a hospital?"

MacBride said, "You started yelling for a doctor. This was the first M.D. plate I saw."

"Why the hell didn't you turn me over to Bower?"

"You're in my hands, Sciarvi, not Bower's. I've got two doctors here. You wanted your friend, and I went for him. He said he didn't know you. You've gotten a damned sight more than you deserve already. Quit yapping."

"Cripes, what a break!" groaned Sciarvi, relaxing, closing his eyes.

MacBride sat down, stared at Kennedy's bandaged leg. Kennedy looked sapped and drawn. But his cynical smile drew a twisted line across his jaw.

"I needed a vacation, Mac," he drawled.

"Hurt?"

"Hell, yes!" And still he smiled, eyes lazy-lidded, features composed.

The one doctor left Kennedy, and joined the other doctor and the two doctors put their heads together and conversed in undertones. Then they looked at Sciarvi, examined his wound, took his temperature. After which they went back to the window, put their heads together again, and mumbled some more.

The upshot of this was quite natural. One doctor said, "Captain MacBride, we have come to the conclusion that, for the sake of everyone concerned, this man should be removed to the City Hospital."

"Gawd!" groaned Sciarvi.

"Huh?" said MacBride.

"Gawd!" groaned Sciarvi.

All eyes looked toward him. He glared at the doctors. "City Hospital, eh? Why the hell don't you come right out and say I'm done for? I know the City Hospital. You saw-bones always send a dyin' guy there. It's just a clearin' house for stiffs. Come on, mister, am I done for?"

The doctor who had spoken before spoke again. "I will tell you frankly—you have one chance in a hundred of living."

"What odds!" cackled Sciarvi, sinking again. Then a shocked look came into his eyes, and he stared with the fierce concentration of those who are outward bound.

"MacBride!" he choked.

Kennedy drew a pencil and a couple of blank envelopes from his pocket.

MacBride stood at the bedside. "Yes, Sciarvi?"

"The Mayor—the pup! He hired me, at a thousand a month to wage a war of—whaddeya call it?—intimidation?—against the Colonial Trucking. He promised absolute protection in case I got in a jam. For the killing of Saunders—Bannon did it—I got a bonus of fifteen hundred. The Mayor supplied that special kind o' poison. He got it from the City Chemist. When you got Gertie, I wised him and he started working to nip an indictment in the bud. His right-hand man is Bower. Bower flopped, and two this mornin' I told the Mayor that if Gertie was planted in the State's Attorney's hands, we were done for. He turned white. He was in a hole, and he asked me what idea I had. I told him we could block off Law Street and get rid of Gertie. He said go ahead. We went ahead. Huh—and now the pup says he don't know me! Ugh. . . . Get a—ugh. . . ."

"Get an ambulance," said one doctor.

"He wants a priest," said MacBride, understanding.

"He won't die for half an hour," said the doctor. "And if we get him to the hospital—"

"He'll burn in the chair eventually," said MacBride.

"That's not the point," said the doctor, and took up a telephone.

When he put it down, Kennedy said, "I wrote it down, Mac. I've signed as a witness. You sign and then the doctors."

All signed, and then MacBride stood over Sciarvi. "Want to sign this, Sciarvi?"

"Read it."

MacBride read it. Sciarvi nodded, took the pen and scrawled his signature.

"Get a . . . ugh. . . ."

Five minutes later an ambulance clanged to a stop outside. Two men came in with a stretcher, a hospital doctor looked Sciarvi over briefly, and then they carried him out, and the ambulance roared off.

Kennedy hobbled out on MacBride's arm, and they entered a taxi. Twenty minutes later they drew up before an imposing mansion. Kennedy hobbled out and with MacBride's assistance climbed the ornate steps.

MacBride rang the bell and a servant opened the door. MacBride brushed him aside and helped Kennedy into the foyer.

The mayor was standing in the open door of his library, and his face was ghastly white. Toward him MacBride walked and Kennedy hobbled, and the mayor backed slowly into the room. MacBride closed the door. Kennedy sat down in a comfortable chair and lit a cigarette. The mayor stood with his hands clasped behind his back—very white, very still, very breathless. MacBride looked around the room, and then walked toward a table. He pointed to the phone.

"May I use it?"

The mayor said nothing. MacBride picked up the instrument and gave a number. A moment later he asked, "That Sciarvi fellow. What about him?" He listened, said, "H'm. Thanks," and hung up.

Then he drew an envelope from his pocket and handed it to the mayor. The mayor read, and moved his neck in his stiff collar, as though something were gagging him. His hand shook. Then he laughed, peculiarly, and scaled the letter on the desk.

"His dying confession," said MacBride, picking up the envelope.

"Confessions made at such times are often worthless. This Sciarvi was a little off. A dead man makes a poor witness."

MacBride nodded. "Yes. But, you see, Mister Mayor, he is not dead. He had one chance in a hundred, and he got it. They just told me he'll live. Of course, it will mean the chair."

The mayor drew a deep breath. MacBride bit him with keen, burning eyes, and nodded toward Kennedy.

"This," he said, "is Kennedy, of the *Free Press*. Of course, this confession will appear in the first edition."

He said no more. He shoved the envelope into his pocket and turned to Kennedy. "Come on."

They went out, arm in arm, and left the mayor standing transfixed in his ornate library.

MacBride went home that night, and his wife cried over his wounded arm, and he patted her head and chuckled and said, "Don't worry, sweetheart. It's all over now."

He had his wound dressed and went to bed and slept ten hours without so much as stirring once. And he was awakened in the morning by his wife, who stood over his bed with a wide look in her eyes and a newspaper trembling in her hands.

"Steve," she breathed, "look!"

She held the paper in front of him, and he saw, in big, black headlines, three significant words:

"MAYOR COMMITS SUICIDE."

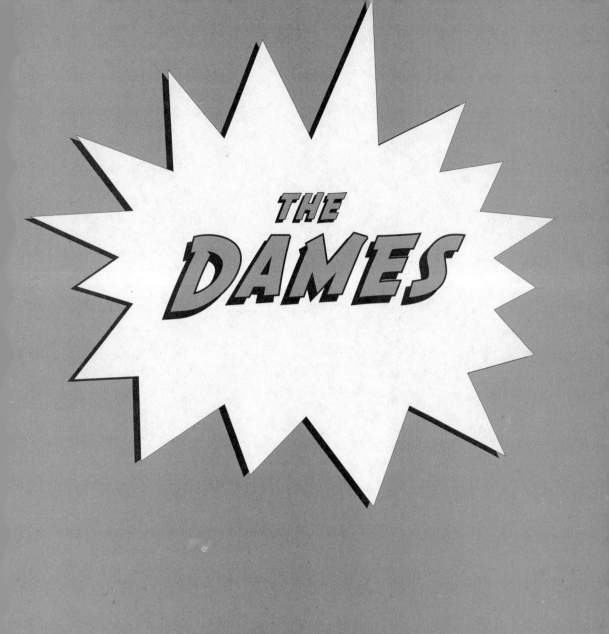

INTRODUCTION BY LAURA LIPPMAN

LATELY, IT SEEMS TO ME, there is a lot of hand-wringing about the lack of suitable role models for young people. Apparently, there was some halcyon period in U.S. history when everyone was good and pure, a time when rosy-cheeked boys and girls ate sandwiches made from Wonder Bread while choosing among an embarrassment of heroic riches. They were told that they could grow up to be presidents or astronauts or surgeons or firefighters. Now our young people watch something called celebutantes in homemade sex tapes on YouTube, and we are all going to hell in a handbasket. Or so I've heard. My Internet connection is too slow to watch videos.

At any rate, I simply cannot work myself into the requisite tizzy. You see, I actually came of age as feminism was dawning and what I remember is a dearth of female role models, good or bad. We were advised that any *boy* could grow up to be president; a girl had to set her sights on First Lady. A boy might train to be an astronaut, but a girl could aim no higher than stewardess—and, yes, that was the only term used at the time. If you scanned the textbooks of my grade-school days, virtually the only females you would find would be Pocahontas, Sacagawea, and Amelia Earhart. Granted, Earhart really did break the mold. But the mistakes she made in her final journey didn't do much to change all those jokes about women and their sense of direction.

The pop culture of the 1960s did not act as a corrective to the academic void. In the comics, we had Betty or Veronica fighting over the dubious prize of Archie Andrews. At the movies, all I remember is Julie Andrews, who seemed to find fulfillment in tending to others' children. On television, the highlight of the week was the June Taylor Dancers, spreading their legs in synch. (That's not a double entendre, but a perfectly literal description of the geometric patterns the dancers made when the camera switched to an overhead shot.) I thought it was marvelous, but I doubted I could ever perform such feats. Even then, I knew I wasn't a team player.

How desperate was I for a role model? Desperate enough to fixate on Lois Lane, as played by Noel Neill in all but one season of the *Adventures of Superman* television series with George Reeves. As I parsed it out, an extremely lucky girl might grow up to be a lady reporter and, occasionally, someone would kidnap her and gag her, and then Superman would show up. Also, one would wear a lot of hats. Fated, perhaps, by my double-L initials, like Lois, I did become a reporter, but a hatless one, and Superman never once put in an appearance.

The point is, I might have been better off with a steady diet of the pulps. Certainly, I wouldn't have been any worse. True, the pulps of the early-twentieth century will never be mistaken for proto-feminist documents. As Otto Penzler notes in his foreword, the motif of rescue is as prevalent here as it was in any *Superman* episode. Still, even if women seldom take the lead in these stories, there is just enough kink in these archetypes of girlfriend/hussy/sociopath to hint at broader possibilities for the female of the species.

Take Polly Knight in Randolph Barr's "The Girl Who Knew Too Much." She seems to be little more than a gang-girl Pocahantas, offering to sacrifice her rosy flesh—and we are frequently reminded of its pink perfection—for the sake of the newspaperman she has met by chance. Polly, as it turns out, is not quite the damsel in distress that she appears to be.

Creamy skin, along with jaw-dropping beauty, is a frequent motif in these stories, as are gray eyes, most notably in Dashiell Hammett's "The Girl with the Silver Eyes." Here, the Continental Op comes face to face with an old nemesis, and marvels at the effect this chameleon has on every man she meets. "Porky Grout, whose yellowness was notorious from Seattle to San Diego, standing rigidly in the path of a charging metal monster, with an inadequate pistol in each hand. . . . She had done that to Porky Grout, and he hadn't even been human!" The story is vintage Hammett—and provides a lovely inside joke, the red herring of a Baltimore address only a few blocks south from where Hammett lived as a boy.

Raymond Chandler's story here is also vintage, albeit an immature one, if you will. One doesn't need to be a Chandler scholar to spot some *very* familiar elements—an unsavory book dealer with a penchant for kinky photos, a wild-eyed thumb-sucker named Carmen, and a dead chauffeur. "Killer in the Rain" should be taught in college creative writing courses, if only as an object lesson in how a disciplined writer can reshape material, deepening its themes and expanding its possibilities.

The most dynamic female in these stories, for my money, is the avenging angel in Cornell Woolrich's "Angel Face." Although she requires a timely rescue in the end, her resourcefulness and bravery are beyond question. For the love of her brother, she withstands torture and risks death. But, as she tells us in the story's first paragraph when she refers to her makeup as war paint, she's being quite literal.

Of course, the reader inclined to pick up this volume is probably already steeped in the work of Chandler, Hammett, and Woolrich. Even for the pulp cognoscenti, there are multiple treasures to be unearthed, the style ranging from a little campy to downright classic. Your mileage may vary, as the kids say now, but I was particularly taken by Perry Paul's Dizzy Malone in "The Jane from Hell's Kitchen," piloting her plane above the Atlantic Ocean and surviving a fusillade of bullets. (Take *that,* Amelia Earhart!) And I feel as if I found a new friend in the acerbic, absurdly competent Sarah Watson, featured in D. B. McCandless's "He Got What He Asked For."

Around the time that I read this anthology, the United States was titillated—there is no other word—by the story of an astronaut who drove cross-country to confront a romantic rival. Determined to make good time on the 800-mile-plus journey, the astronaut wore an adult diaper. The items packed for the trip included a BB gun, a four-inch folding buck knife, a new steel mallet, black gloves, rubber tubing, and plastic garbage bags. We may never know exactly what was planned, for the intended victim foiled the attack and the assailant was arrested and charged with attempted murder.

The big twist was that the astronaut was a woman. But then, so was the quick-thinking victim. One could argue that this is progress of a sort, women seizing the initiative and taking action, with no men at all in the climactic confrontation. Or one could conclude that feminism is still a little spotty when women decide that eliminating other women is the way to resolve a romantic triangle. All I know is that I prefer the company of the dames within these pages, who parade before us in impeccable suits, filmy negligees, torn evening dresses, and—in the memorable case of Sarah Watson—a voluminous purple kimono worn over a corset. But not a diaper, never a diaper, thank God. Even the most venal among them have more class than that.

Angel Face

Cornell Woolrich

IN 1935, CORNELL WOOLRICH (1903–1968) submitted a story titled "Angel Face" to *Dime Detective,* which published it as "Murder in Wax" in its March 1, 1935, issue. A couple of years later, he sold a similar story about an avenging angel to *Black Mask,* who published it as "Face Work." This story has been reprinted often as the title Woolrich clearly wanted for it, "Angel Face," finally given to it by Frederic Dannay when he reprinted it in *Ellery Queen's Mystery Magazine* for December 1946. While it has the usual number of plot inconsistencies one expects from the great poet of darkness, it is quintessential Woolrich in all its noir glory. Both "Face Work" and "Murder in Wax" were the basis for one of the seven great novels in his memorable "Black" series, *The Black Angel* (1943).

In addition to its frequent reprints, "Face Work" enjoyed other incarnations. It was bought for the movies soon after publication—the first of numerous Woolrich stories to be filmed. Columbia made it into a weak fifty-eight-minute B movie titled *Convicted* in 1938. Although it starred a young Rita Hayworth and meticulously followed the story, even lifting much of the original dialogue, it is neither a noir film nor a memorable one. Twelve years later, it was aired as "Angel Face" on radio's famous *Suspense* series (May 18, 1950) with Claire Trevor as the good-hearted stripper who tries to save her brother from being convicted of a murder.

"Face Work" was first published in the October 1937 issue of *Black Mask.*

Beauty plus brains
makes a deadly weapon

Angel Face

Cornell Woolrich

HAD ON my best hat and my warpaint when I dug into her bell. You've heard make-up called that a thousand times, but this is one time it rated it; it was just that—warpaint.

I caught Ruby Rose Reading at breakfast time—hers, not mine. Quarter to three in the afternoon. Breakfast was a pink soda-fountain mess, a tomato-and-lettuce, both untouched, and an empty glass of Bromo Seltzer, which had evidently had first claim on her. There were a pair of swell ski slides under her eyes; she was reading Gladys Glad's beauty column to try to

figure out how to get rid of them before she went out that night and got a couple more. A Negro maid had opened the door, and given me a yellowed optic.

"Yes ma'am, who do you wish to see?"

"I see her already," I said, "so skip the Morse Code." I went in up to Ruby Rose's ten-yard line. "Wheeler's the name," I said. "Does it mean anything to you?"

"Should it?" She was dark and Salome-ish. She was mean. She was bad medicine. I could see his finish right there, in her eyes. And it hadn't been any fun to dance at Texas Guinan's or Larry Fay's when I was sixteen, to keep him out of the orphan asylum or the reformatory. I hadn't spent most of my young girlhood in a tin-seled G-string to have her take apart what I'd built up, just to see what made him tick.

I said, "I don't mind coming right out with it in front of your maid—if you don't."

But evidently she did. Maybe Mandy was on a few other payrolls besides her own. She hit her with the tomato-and-lettuce in the left eye as preamble to the request: "Whaddo I pay you for, anyway? Take Foo-Too around the block a couple of times!"

"I tuk him once already, and he was a good boy," was the weather report she got on this.

"Well, take him again. Maybe you can kid him it's tomorrow already."

Mandy fastened something that looked like the business-end of a floor mop to a leash, went out shaking her head. "You sho didn't enjoy yo'self last night. That Sto'k Club never do agree with you."

As soon as the gallery was out of the way I said, "You lay off my brother!"

She lit a cigarette, nosed the smoke at me. "Well, Gracie Allen, you've come to the wrong place looking for your brother. And, just for the record, what am I supposed to have done to him, cured him of wiping his nose on his sleeve or something?"

"He's been spending dough like wild, dough that doesn't come out of his salary."

"Then where does it come from?" she asked.

"I haven't found out. I hope his firm never does, either." I shifted gears, went into low—like when I used to sing "Poor Butterfly" for the customers—but money couldn't have dragged this performance out of me, it came from the heart, without pay. "There's a little girl on our street, oh not much to look at, thinks twelve o'clock's the middle of the night and storks leave babies, but she's ready to take up where I leave off, pinch pennies and squeeze nickels along with him, build him into something, get him somewhere, not spread him all over the land-scape. He's just a man, doesn't know what's good for him, doesn't know his bass from his oboe. I can't stand by and watch her chew her

heart up. Give her a break, and him, and me. Pick on someone your size, someone that can take it. Have your fun and more power to you—but not with all I've got!"

She banged her cigarette to death against a tray. "O.K., is the screen test about over? Now, will you get out of here, you ham-actress, and lemme get my massage?" She went over and got the door ready for me. Gave a traffic-cop signal over her shoulder with one thumb. "I've heard of wives pulling this act, and even mothers, and in a pitcher I saw only lately, Camilly it was called, it was the old man. Now it's a sister!" She gave the ceiling the once-over. "What'll they think of next? Send grandma around tomorrow—next week East Lynne. Come on, make it snappy!" she invited, and hitched her elbow at me. If she'd touched me, I think I'd have murdered her.

"If you feel I'm poison, why don't you put it up to your brother?" she signed off. And very low, just before she walloped the door after me: "And see how far you get!"

She was right. I said, "Chick, you're not going to chuck your job, you're not going to Chicago with that dame, are you?"

He looked at me funny and he said, "How did you know?"

"I saw your valise all packed, when I wanted to send one of your suits to the cleaners."

"You ought to be a detective," he said, and he wasn't pally. "O.K.," he said, "now that you mention it," and he went in and he got it to show me—the back of it going out the door. But I got over there to the door before he did, and pulled a Custer's Last Stand. I skipped the verse and went into the patter chorus. And boy did I sell it, without a spot and without a muted trumpet solo either! At the El-Fay in the old days they would have all been crying into their gin and wiring home to mother.

"I'm not asking anything for myself. I'm older than you, Chick, and when a girl says that you've got her down to bedrock. I've been around plenty, and 'around' wasn't pretty. Maybe you think it was fun wrestling my way home each morning at five, and no holds barred, just so—so. . . . Oh, I didn't know why myself sometimes; just so you wouldn't turn out to be another corner lizard, a sharpshooter, a bum like the rest of them. Chick, you're just a punk of twenty-four, but as far as I'm concerned the sun rises and sets across your shoulders. Me and little Mary Allen, we've been rooting for you all along; what's the matter with her, Chick? Just because her face don't come out of boxes and she doesn't know the right grips, don't pass her by for something that ought to be shampooed out of your hair with gasoline."

But he didn't have an ear for music; the siren song had got to him like Ulysses. And once they hear that. . . . "Get away from the door," he said, way down low. "I never raised a hand to you in my life, I don't want to now."

The last I saw of him he was passing the back of his hand slowly up and down his side, like he was ashamed of it; the valise was in the other one. I picked myself up from the opposite side of the foyer where he'd sent me, the place all buckling around me like seen through a sheet of water. I called out after him through the open door: "Don't go, Chick! You're heading straight for the eight-ball! Don't go to her, Chick!" The acoustics were swell. Every door in the hall opened to get an earful.

He just stood there a split-second without looking back at me, yellow light gushing out at him through the port-hole of the elevator.

He straightened his hat, which my chin against his duke had dislodged—and no more Chick.

At about four that morning I was still snivelling into the gin he'd left behind him, and talking to him across the table from me—without getting any answer—when the door-bell rang. I thought it was him for a minute, but it was two other guys. They didn't ask if they could come in, they just went 'way around to the other side of me and then showed me a couple of tin-heeled palms. So I did the coming-in—after them; I lived there, after all.

They looked the place over like they were prospective tenants being shown an apartment. I didn't go for that; detectives belong in the books you read in bed, not in your apartment at four bells, big as life. "Three closets," I mentioned, "and you get a month's concession. I'm not keeping you gentlemen up, am I?"

One of them was kind of pash looking; I mean he'd washed his face lately, and if he'd been the last man in the world, well, all right, maybe I could have overlooked the fact he was a bloodhound on two legs. The other one had a face like one of those cobblestones they dug up off Eighth Avenue when they removed the trolley tracks.

"You're Jerry Wheeler, aren't you?" the first one told me.

"I've known that for twenty-seven years," I said. "What brought the subject up?"

Cobblestone-face said, "Chick Wheeler's sister, that right?"

"I've got a brother and I call him Chick," I consented. "Any ordinance against that?"

The younger one said, "Don't be so hard to handle. You're going to talk to us and like it." He sat down in a chair, cushioned his hands behind his dome. He said, "What time'd he leave here this evening?"

Something warned me, "don't answer that." I said, "I really couldn't say. I'm not a train-despatcher."

"He was going to Chicago with a dame named Ruby Rose Reading; you knew that, didn't you?"

I thought, "I hit the nail on the head, he did help himself to his firm's money. Wonder how much he took? Well, I guess I'll have to go back to work again at one of the hotspots; maybe I can square it for him, pay back a little each week." I kept my face steady. I said, "Now, why would he go anywhere with anyone with a name like that? It sounds like it came off a bottle of nail-polish. Come to the point, gentlemen. What's he supposed to have done?"

"There's no supposition about what he's done. He went to the Alcazar Arms at eight-fifteen tonight and throttled Ruby Rose Reading to death, Angel Face."

And that was the first time I heard myself called that. I also heard the good-looking one remonstrate: "Aw, don't give it to her that sudden, Coley, she's a girl after all," but it came from 'way far away. I was down around their feet somewhere sniffling into the carpet.

The good-looking one picked me up and straightened me out in a chair. Cobblestone said, "Don't let her fool you, Burnsie, they all pull that collapsible concertina act when they wanna get out of answering questions." He went into the bedroom and I could hear him pulling out bureau drawers and rummaging around.

I got up on one elbow. I said, "Burns, he didn't do it! Please, he didn't do it! All right, I did know about her. He was sold on her. That's why he couldn't have done it. Don't you see, you don't kill the thing you love?"

He just kind of looked at me. "You go to bat for the thing you love too," he murmured. He said, "I've been on the squad eight years now. We never in all that time caught a guy as dead to rights as your brother. He showed up with his valise in the foyer of the Alcazar at exactly twelve minutes past eight tonight. He said to the door-man, "What time is it? Did Miss Reading send her baggage down yet? We've got to make a train." Well, she had sent her baggage down and then she'd changed her mind, she'd had it all taken back upstairs again. There's your motive right there. The doorman rang her apartment and said through the announcer, 'Mr. Wheeler's here.' And she gave a dirty laugh and sang out, 'I can hardly wait.'

"So at thirteen past eight she was still alive. He went up, and he'd no sooner got there than her apartment began to signal the doorman frantically. No one answered his hail over the announcer, so he chased up, and he found your brother crouched over her, shaking her, and she was dead. At fifteen minutes past eight o'clock. Is that a case or is that a case?"

I said, "How do you know somebody else wasn't in that apartment and strangled her just before Chick showed up? It's got to be that!"

He said, "What d'you suppose they're paying

that door-man seventy-five a month for? The only other caller she had that whole day was you yourself, at three that afternoon, five full hours before. And she'd only been dead fifteen to twenty minutes by the time the assistant medical examiner got to her."

I said, "Does Chick say he did it?"

"When you've been in this business as long as I have, you'd have their heads examined if any of them ever admitted doing anything. Oh, no-o, of course he didn't do it. He says he was crouched over her, shaking her, trying to restore her!"

I took a deep breath. I said, "Gimme a swallow of that gin. Thanks." I put the tumbler down again. I looked him right in the eye. "All right, I did it! Now how d'ye like that? I begged him not to throw his life away on her. When he walked out anyway, I beat him up to her place in a taxi, got there first, gave her one last chance to lay off him. She wouldn't take it. She was all soft and squashy and I just took a grip and pushed hard."

"And the doorman?" he said with a smile.

"His back was turned. He was out at the curb seeing some people into a cab. When I left, I took the stairs down. When Chick signaled from her apartment and the doorman left his post, I just walked out. It was a pushover."

His smile was a grin. "Well, if you killed her, you killed her." He called in to the other room, "Hey, Coley, she says she killed her!" Coley came back, flapped his hand at me disgustedly, said, "Come on, let's get out of here. There's nothing doing around here."

He opened the door, went out into the hall. I said, "Well, aren't you going to take me with you? Aren't you going to let him go and hold me instead?"

"Who the hell wants you?" came back through the open door.

Burns, as he got up to follow him, said off-handedly, "And what was she wearing when you killed her?" But he kept walking to the door, without waiting for the answer.

They'd had a train to make. I swallowed hard. "Well, I—I was too steamed-up to notice colors or anything, but she had on her coat and hat, ready to leave."

He turned around at the door and looked at me. His grin was sort of sympathetic, under-standing. "Sure," he said softly. "I guess she took 'em off, though, after she found out she was dead and wasn't going anywhere after all. We found her in pajamas. Write us a nice long letter about it tomorrow, Angel Face. We'll see you at the trial, no doubt."

There was a glass cigarette-box at my elbow. I grabbed it and heaved, beserk. "You rotten, lowdown—detective, you! Going around snoop-ing, framing innocent people to death! Get out of here! I hope I never see your face again!"

It missed his head, crashed and tinkled against the door-frame to one side of him. He didn't cringe, I liked that about him, sore as I was. He just gave a long drawn-out whistle. "Maybe you did do it at that," he said. "Maybe I'm underestimating you," and he touched his hatbrim and closed the door after him.

The courtroom was so unnaturally still that the ticking of my heart sounded like a cheap alarm-clock in the silence. I kept wondering how it was they didn't put me out for letting it make so much noise. A big blue fly was buzzing on the inside of the windowpane nearest me, trying to find its way out. The jurists came filing in like ghosts, and slowly filled the double row of chairs in the box. All you could hear was a slight rustle of clothing as they seated themselves. I kept thinking of the Inquisition, and wondered why they didn't have black hoods over their heads.

"Will the foreman of the jury please stand?"

I spaded both my hands down past my hips and grabbed the edges of my seat. My handker-chief fell on the floor and the man next to me picked it up and handed it back to me. I tried to say "Thanks" but my jaws wouldn't unlock.

"Gentlemen of the jury, have you reached a verdict?"

I told myself, "He won't be able to hear it, if my heart doesn't shut up." It was going bangetty-bangetty-bang!

"We have, your honor."

"Gentlemen of the jury, what is your verdict?"

The banging stopped; my heart wasn't going at all now. Even the fly stopped buzzing. The whole works stood still.

"We find the defendant guilty of murder in the first degree."

Some woman screamed out "No!" at the top of her lungs. It must have been me, they were all turning their heads to look around at me. The next thing I knew, I was outside in the corridor and a whole lot of people were standing around me. Everything looked blurred. A voice said, "Give her air, stand back." Another voice said, "His sister. She was on the stand earlier in the week." Ammonia fumes kept tickling the mem-branes of my nostrils. The first voice said, "Take her home. Where does she live? Anybody know where she lives?"

"I know where she lives. I'll take care of her."

Somebody put an arm around my waist and walked me to the creaky courthouse elevator, led me out to the street, got in a taxi after me. I looked, and it was that dick, Burns. I climbed up into the corner of the cab, put my feet on the seat, shuffled them at him. I said, "Get away from me, you devil! You railroaded him, you butcher!"

"Attagirl," he said gently. "Feeling better already, aren't you?" He gave the old address, where Chick and I had lived. The cab started and I couldn't get him out of it. I felt too low even to fight any more.

"Not there," I said sullenly. "I'm holed up in a cheap furnished room now, off Second Avenue. I've hocked everything I own, down to my vaccination mark! How d'you suppose I got that lawyer Schlesinger for him? And a lot of good it did him! What a wash-out he turned out to be!"

"Don't blame him," he said. "He couldn't buck that case we turned over to the State; Dar-row himself couldn't have. What he should have done was let him plead guilty to second-degree, then he wouldn't be in line for short-circuiting. That was his big mistake."

"No!" I shrilled at him. "He wanted us to do that, but neither Chick nor I would hear of it! Why should he plead guilty to anything, even if it was only housebreaking, when he's innocent? That's a guilty man's dodge, not an innocent man's. He hasn't got half-an-hour's detention rightfully coming to him! Why should he lie down and accept twenty years? He didn't lay a hand on Ruby Reading."

"Eleven million people, the mighty State of New York, say that he did."

I got out, went in the grubby entrance, between a delicatessen and a Chinese laundry. "Don't come in with me, I don't want to see any more of you!" I spat over my shoulder at him. "If I was a man I'd knock you down and beat the living hell out of you!"

He came on, though, and upstairs he closed the door behind him, pushing me out of the way to get in. He said, "You need help, Angel Face, and I'm crying to give it to you."

"Oh, biting the hand that feeds you, turning into a doublecrosser, a turncoat!"

"No," he said, "no," and sort of held out his hands as if asking me for something. "Sell me, won't you?" he almost pleaded. "Sell me that he's innocent, and I'll work my fingers raw to back you up! I didn't frame your brother. I only did my job. I was sent there by my superiors in answer to the patrolman's call that night, questioned Chick, put him under arrest. You heard me answering their questions on the stand. Did I distort the facts any? All I told them was what I saw with my own eyes, what I found when I got to Reading's apartment. Don't hold that against me, Angel Face. Sell me, convince me that he didn't do it, and I'm with you up to the hilt."

"Why?" I said cynically. "Why this sudden yearning to undo the damage you've already done?"

He opened the door to go. "Look in the mirror sometime and find out," was all he said. "You can reach me at Centre Street, Nick Burns." He held out his hand uncertainly, probably expecting me to slap it aside.

I took it instead. "O.K., flatfoot," I sighed wearily. "No use holding it against you that you're a detective. You probably don't know any better. Before you go, gimme the address of that maid of hers, Mandy Leroy. I've got an idea she didn't tell all she knew."

"She went home at five that day. How can she help you?"

"I bet she was greased plenty to softpedal the one right name that belongs in this case. She mayn't have been there, but she knew who to expect around. She may have even tipped him off that Ruby Rose was throwing him over. It takes a woman to see through a woman."

"Better watch yourself going up there alone," he warned me. He took out a notebook. "Here it is, One Hundred Eighteenth, just off Lenox." I jotted it down. "If she was paid off like you think, how you going to restore her memory? It'll take heavy sugar. . . ." He fumbled in his pocket, looked at me like he was a little scared of me, finally took out something and shoved it out of sight on the bureau. "Try your luck with that," he said. "Use it where it'll do the most good. Try a little intimidation with it, it may work."

I grabbed it up and he ducked out in a hurry, the big coward. A hundred and fifty bucks. I ran out to the stairs after him. "Hey!" I yelled, "aren't you married or anything?"

"Naw," he called back, "I can always get it back, anyway, if it does the trick." And then he added, "I always did want to have something on you, Angel Face."

I went back into my cubbyhole again. "Why, the big rummy!" I said hotly. I hadn't cried in court when Chick got the ax, just yelled out. But now my eyes got all wet.

"Mandy doan live her no mo'e," the colored janitor of the 118th Street tenement told me.

"Where'd she go? And don't tell me you don't know, because it won't work."

"She done move to a mighty presumptuous neighborhood, doan know how come all of a sudden. She gone to Edgecomb Avenue."

Edgecomb Avenue is the Park Avenue of

New York's darktown. Mandy had mentioned on the stand, without being asked, that Reading had died owing her two months' wages. Yet she moves to the colored Gold Coast right on top of it. She hadn't been paid off—not much!

Edgecomb Avenue is nothing to be ashamed of in any man's town. Every one of the trim modern apartment buildings had a glossy private car or two parked in front of the door. I tackled the address he'd given me, and thought they were having a housewarming at first. They were singing inside and it sounded like a revival meeting.

A fat old lady came to the door, in a black silk dress, tears streaming down her cheeks. "I'se her mother, honey," she said softly in answer to what I told her, "and you done come at an evil hour. My lamb was run over on the street, right outside this building, only yesterday, first day we moved here! She's in there daid now, honey. The Lawd give and the Lawd has took away again."

I did a little thinking.

Why just her, and nobody else, when she held the key to the Reading murder? "How did it happen to her? Did they tell you?"

"Two white men in a car," she mourned. " 'Peared almost like they run her down purposely. She was walking along the sidewalk, folks tell me, wasn't even in the gutter at all. And it swung right up on the sidewalk aftah her, go ovah her, then loop out in the middle again and light away, without nevah stopping!"

I went away saying to myself, "That girl was murdered as sure as I'm born, to shut her mouth. First she was bribed, then when the trial was safely over she was put out of the way for good!"

Somebody big was behind all this. And what did I have to fight that somebody with? A borrowed hundred and fifty bucks, an offer of cooperation from a susceptible detective, and a face.

I went around to the building Ruby Rose had lived in, and struck the wrong shift. "Charlie Baker doesn't come on until six, eh?" I told the doorman. "Where does he live? I want to talk to him."

"He don't come on at all any more. He quit his job, as soon as that—" he tilted his head to the ceiling, "—mess we had upstairs was over with, and he didn't have to appear in court no more."

"Well, where's he working now?"

"He ain't working at all, lady. He don't have to any more. I understand a relative of his died in the old country, left him quite a bit, and him and his wife and his three kids have gone back to England to live."

So he'd been paid off heavily too. It looked like I was up against Wall Street itself. No wonder everything had gone so smoothly.

No wonder even a man like Schlesinger hadn't been able to make a dent in the case.

"But I'm not licked yet," I said to myself, back in my room. "I've still got this face. It ought to be good for something. If I only knew where to push it, who to flash it on!"

Burns showed up that night, to find out how I was making out.

"Here's your hundred and fifty back," I told him bitterly. "I'm up against a stone wall every way I turn. But is it a coincidence that the minute the case is in the bag, their two chief witnesses are permanently disposed of, one by exportation, the other by hit-and-run? They're not taking any chances on anything backfiring later."

He said, "You're beginning to sell me. It smells like rain."

I sat down on the floor (there was only one chair in the dump) and took a dejected half-Nelson around my own ankles. "Look, it goes like this. Some guy did it. Some guy that was sold on her. Plenty of names were spilled by Mandy and Baker, but not the right one. The ones that were brought out didn't lead anywhere, you saw that yourself. The mechanics of the thing don't trouble me a bit, the how and why could be cleared up easy enough—even by you."

"Thanks," he said.

"It's the who that has me baffaloed. There's a gap there. I can't jump across to the other side. From there on, I could handle it beautifully. But

I've got to close that gap, that who, or I might as well put in the order for Chick's headstone right now."

He took out a folded newspaper and whacked himself disgustedly across the shins with it. "Tough going, kid," he agreed.

"I'll make it," I said. "You can't keep a good girl down. The right guy is in this town. And so am I in this town. I'll connect with him yet, if I've got to use a ouija board!"

He said, "You haven't got all winter. He comes up for sentence Wednesday." He opened the door. "I'm on your side," he let me know in that quiet way of his.

He left the paper behind him on the chair. I sat down and opened it. I wasn't going to do any reading, but I wanted to think behind it. And then I saw her name. The papers had been full of her name for weeks, but this was different; this was just a little boxed ad off at the side.

AUCTION SALE

Jewelry, personal effects and furniture belonging to the late Ruby Rose Reading Monarch Galleries Saturday A.M.

I dove at the window, rammed it up, leaned halfway out. I caught him just coming out of the door.

"Burns!" I screeched at the top of my voice. "Hey, Burns! Bring that hundred and fifty back up here! I've changed my mind!"

The place was jammed to the gills with curiosity-mongers and bargain-hunters, and probably professional dealers too, although they were supposed to be excluded. There were about two dozen of those 100-watt blue-white bulbs in the ceiling that auction rooms go in for and the bleach of light was intolerable, worse than on a sunny beach at high noon.

I was down front, in the second row on the aisle; I'd got there early. I wasn't interested in her diamonds or her furs or her thissas or her thattas. I was hoping something would come up

that would give me some kind of a clue, but what I expected it to be, I didn't know myself. An inscription on a cigarette case maybe. I knew how little chance there was of anything like that. The D.A.'s office had sifted through her things pretty thoroughly before Chick's trial, and what they'd turned up hadn't amounted to a row of pins. She'd been pretty cagy that way, hadn't left much around. All bills had been addressed to her personally, just like she'd paid her rent with her own personal checks, and fed the account herself. Where the funds originated in the first place was never explained. I suppose she took in washing.

They started off with minor articles first, to warm the customers up. A cocktail shaker that played a tune, a make-up mirror with a light behind it, a ship's model, things like that. They got around to her clothes next, and the women customers started "ohing" and "ahing" and foaming at the mouth. By the looks of most of them that was probably the closest they'd ever get to real sin, bidding for its hand-me-downs.

The furniture came next, and they started to talk real money now. This out of the way, her ice came on. Brother, she'd made them say it with diamonds, and they'd all spoken above a whisper too! When the last of it went, that washed up the sale; there was nothing else left to dispose of but the little rosewood jewel case she'd kept them in. About ten by twelve by ten inches deep, with a little gilt key and lock; not worth a damn but there it was. However, if you think an auctioneer passes up anything, you don't know your auctioneers.

"What am I offered for this?" he said almost apologetically. "Lovely little trinket box, give it to your best girl or your wife or your mother, to keep her ornaments in or old love letters." He knocked the veneer with his knuckles, held it outward to show us the satin lining. Nothing in it, like in a vaudeville magician's act. "Do I hear fifty cents, just to clear the stand?"

Most of them were getting up and going already. An over-dressed guy in my same row, across the aisle, spoke up. "You hear a buck."

I took a look at him, and I took a look at the box. "If you want it, I want it, too," I decided suddenly. "A guy splurged up like you don't hand a plain wooden box like that to any woman that he knows." I opened my mouth for the first time since I'd come in the place. "You hear a dollar and a quarter."

"Dollar-fifty."

"Two dollars."

"Five." The way he snapped it out, he meant business.

I'd never had such a strong hunch in my life before but now I wanted that box, had to have it, I felt it would do me some good. Maybe this overdressed monkey had given it to her, maybe Burns could trace where it had been bought. . . .

"Seven-fifty."

"Ten."

"Twelve."

The auctioneer was in seventh heaven. "You're giving yourself away, brother, you're giving yourself away!" I warned my competitor silently.

We leaned forward out of our seats and sized each other up. If he was giving himself away, I suppose I was too. I could see a sort of shrewd speculation in his snaky eyes, they screwed up into slits, seeming to say, "What's your racket?" Something cold went down my back, hot as it was under all those mazdas.

"Twenty-five dollars," he said inexorably.

I thought: "I'm going to get that thing if I spend every cent of the money Burns loaned me!"

"Thirty," I said.

With that, to my surprise, he stood up, flopped his hand at it disgustedly, and walked out.

When I came out five minutes later with the box wrapped up under my arm, I saw him sitting in a young dreadnaught with another man, a few yards down the street.

"So I'm going to be followed home," I said to myself, "to find out who I am." That didn't worry me any; I'd rented my room under my old stage name of Honey Sebastian (my idea of a classy tag at sixteen) to escape the notoriety attendant on Chick's trial. I turned up the other way and hopped down into the subway, which is about the best bet when the following is to be done from a car. As far as I could make out, no one came after me.

I watched the street from a corner of the window after I got home, and no one going by stopped or looked at the house or did anything but mind his own business. And if it had been that flashy guy on my tail, you could have heard him coming from a block away. I turned to the wrapped box and broke the string.

Burns' knock at my door at five that afternoon was a tattoo of anxious impatience. "God, you took long to get here!" I blurted out. "I phoned you three times since noon."

"Lady," he protested, "I've been busy, I was out on something else, only just got back to Headquarters ten minutes ago. Boy, you threw a fright into me."

I didn't stoop to asking him why he should be so worried something had happened to me; he might have given me the right answer. "Well," I said, "I've got him," and I passed him the rosewood jewel case.

"Got who?"

"The guy that Chick's been made a patsy for."

He opened it, looked in, looked under it. "What's this?"

"Hers. I had a hunch, and I bought it. He must have had a hunch too—only his agent— and it must have been his agent, he wouldn't show up himself—didn't follow it through, wasn't sure enough. Stick your thumb under the little lock. Not over it, down below it, and press hard on the wood." Something clicked, and the satin bottom flapped up, like it had with me.

"Fake bottom, eh?" he said.

"Don't be an echo. Read that top letter out loud. That was the last one she got, the very day it happened."

" 'You know, baby,' " Burns read. " 'I think too much of you to ever let you go. And if you ever tired of me and tried to leave me, I'd kill you first, and then you could go wherever you want. They tell me you've been seen going around a lot lately with some young punk. Now, baby, I hope for his sake, and yours too, that when I come back day after tomorrow I find it isn't so, just some more of my boys' lies. They like to rib me sometimes, see if I can take it or not.' "

"He gave her a bum steer there on purpose," I pointed out. "He came back 'tomorrow' and not 'day after,' and caught her with the goods."

"Milt," Burns read from the bottom of the page. And then he looked at me, and didn't see me for once.

"Militis, of course," I said, "the Greek night-club king. Milton, as he calls himself. Everyone on Broadway knows him. And yet, d'you notice how that name stayed out of the trial? Not a whisper from beginning to end! That's the missing name all right!"

"It reads that way, I know," he said undecidedly, "but there's this: She knew her traffic signals. Why would she chuck away the banana and hang on to the skin? In other words, Milton spells real dough, your brother wasn't even carfare."

"But Militis had her branded—"

"Sure, but—"

"No, I'm not talking slang now. I mean actually, physically; it's mentioned in one of these letters. The autopsy report had it too, remember? Only they mistook it for an operation scar or scald. Well, when a guy does that, anyone would have looked good to her, and Chick was probably a godsend. The branding was probably not the half of it, either. It's fairly well known that Milton likes to play rough with his women."

"All right, kid," he said, "but I've got bad news for you. This evidence isn't strong enough to have the verdict set aside and a new trial called. A clever mouthpiece could blow this whole pack of letters out the window with one breath. Ardent Greek temperament, and that kind of thing, you know. You remember how Schlesinger dragged it out of Mandy that she'd overheard more than one guy make the same kind of jealous threats. Did it do any good?"

"This is the McCoy, though. He came through, this one, Militis."

"But, baby, you're telling it to me and I convince easy, from you. You're not telling it to the Grand Jury."

I shoved the letters at him. "Just the same, you chase out, have 'em photostated, every last one of them, and put 'em in a cool, dry place. I'm going to dig something a little more convincing to go with them, if that's what's needed. What clubs does he own?"

"What clubs doesn't he? There's Hell's Bells—" He stopped short, looked at me. "You stay out of there."

"One word from you . . ." I purred, and closed the door after him.

"A little higher," the manager said. "Don't be afraid. We've seen it all before."

I took another hitch in my hoisted skirt, gave him a look. "If it's my appendix you want to size up, say so. It's easier to uncover the other way around, from up to down. I just sing and dance. I don't bathe for the customers."

"I like 'em like that," he nodded approvingly to his yes-man. "Give her a chord, Mike," he said to his pianist.

"The Man I Love," I said. "I do dusties, not new ones."

> *"And he'll be big and strong,*
> *The man I love—"*

"Good tonsils," he said. "Give her a dance chorus, Mike."

Mike said disgustedly, "Why d'ya wanna waste your time? Even if she was paralyzed from the waist down and had a voice like a frog, ain't you got eyes? Get a load of her face, will you?"

"You're in," the manager said. "Thirty-five, and buy yourself some up-to-date lyrics. Come around at eight and get fitted for some duds. What's your name?"

"Bill me as Angel Face," I said, "and have your electrician give me an amber spot. They take the padlocks off their wallets when I come out in an amber spot."

He shook his head, almost sorrowfully. "Hang on to that face, girlie. It ain't gonna happen again in a long time!"

Burns was holding up my locked room-door with one shoulder when I got back. "Here's your letters back; I've got the photostats tucked away in a safe place. Where'd you disappear to?"

"I've landed a job at Hell's Bells. I'm going to get that guy and get him good! If that's the way I've got to get the evidence, that's the way. After all, if he was sold on her, *I'll* have him cutting out paper dolls before two weeks are out. What'd she have that I haven't got? Now, stay out of there. Somebody might know your face, and you'll only queer everything."

"Watch yourself, will you, Angel Face? You're playing a dangerous game. That Milton is nobody's fool. If you need me in a hurry, you know where to reach me. I'm right at your shoulder, all the way through."

I went in and stuck the letters back in the fake bottom of the case. I had an idea I was going to have a visitor fairly soon, and wasn't going to tip my hand.

I stood it on the dresser-top and threw in a few pins and glass beads for luck.

The timing was eerie. The knock came inside of ten minutes. I'd known it was due, but not that quick. It was my competitor from the auction room, flashy as ever; he'd changed flowers, that was all.

"Miss Sebastian," he said, "isn't it? I'd like very much to buy that jewel case you got."

"I noticed that this morning."

He went over and squinted into it.

"That all you wanted it for, just to keep junk like that in?"

"What'd you expect to find, the Hope diamond?"

"You seemed willing to pay a good deal."

"I lose my head easy in auction rooms. But, for that matter, you seemed to be willing to go pretty high yourself."

"I still am," he said. He turned it over, emp-tied my stuff out, tucked it under his arm, put something down on the dresser. "There's a hundred dollars. Buy yourself a real good one."

Through the window I watched the dread-naught drift away again. "Just a little bit too late in getting here," I smiled after it. "The cat's out of the bag now and a bulldog will probably chase it."

The silver dress fitted me like a wet compress. It was one of those things that break up homes. The manager flagged me in the passageway leading back. "Did you notice that man all by himself at a ringside table? You know who he is, don't you?"

If I hadn't, why had I bothered turning on all my current his way? "No," I said, round-eyed, "who?"

"Milton. He owns the works. The reason I'm telling you is this: You've got a date with a bottle of champagne at his table, starting in right now. Get on in there."

We walked on back.

"Mr. Milton, this is Angel Face," the manager said. "She won't give us her right name, just walked in off Fifty-second Street last Tuesday."

"And I waited until tonight to drop around here!" he laughed. "What you paying her, Berger?" Then before the other guy could get a word out, "Triple it! And now get out of here."

The night ticked on. He'd look at me then he'd suddenly throw up his hands as though to ward off a dazzling glare. "Turn it off, it hurts my eyes."

I smiled a little and took out my mirror. I saw my eyes in it, and in each iris there was a little electric chair with Chick sitting strapped in it. Three weeks from now, sometime during that week. Boy, how they were rushing him! It made it a lot easier to go ahead.

I went back to what we'd been talking about—and what are any two people talking about, more or less, in a nightclub at four in the morning? "Maybe," I said, "who can tell? Some night I might just feel like changing the scenery around me, but I couldn't tell you about it, I'm not that kind."

"You wouldn't have to," he said. He fooled with something below table-level, then passed his hand to me. I took it and knotted my handkerchief around the latch-key he'd left in it. Burns had been right. I was a dangerous game, and bridges were blazing and collapsing behind me.

The doorman covered a yawn with a white kid glove, said, "Who shall I announce?"

"That's all been taken care of," I said, "so you can go back to your beauty sleep."

He caught on, said insinuatingly, "It's Mr. Milton, isn't it? He's out of town tonight."

"You're telling me!" I thought. I'd sent him the wire that fixed that, signed the name of the manager of his Philly club. "You've been reading my mail," I said, and closed the elevator in his face.

The key worked, and the light switch worked, and his Filipino had the night off, so the rest was up to me. The clock in his two-story living room said four-fifteen. I went to the second floor of his penthouse and started in on the bedroom. He was using Ruby Rose Reading's jewel case to hold his collar buttons in, hadn't thrown it out. I opened the fake bottom to see if he'd found what he was after, and the letters were gone, probably burned.

I located his wall safe but couldn't crack it. While I was still working at it, the phone downstairs started to ring. I jumped as though a pin had been stuck into me, and started shaking like I was still doing one of my routines at the club. He had two phones, one downstairs, one in the bedroom, which was an unlisted number. I snapped out the lights, ran downstairs, picked it up. I didn't answer, just held it.

Burns' voice said, "Angel Face?" in my ear.

"Gee, you sure frightened me!" I exhaled.

"Better get out of there. He just came back, must have tumbled to the wire. A spotter at Hell's Bells tipped me off he was just there asking for you."

"I can't, now," I wailed. "I woke his damn doorman up getting in just now, and I'm in that silver dress I do my number in! He'll tell him I was here. I'll have to play it dumb."

"D'ja get anything?"

"Nothing, only that jewel case! I couldn't get the safe open but he's probably burned everything connecting him to her long ago."

"Please get out of there, kid," he pleaded. "You don't know that guy. He's going to pin you down on the mat if he finds you there."

"I'm staying," I said. "I've got to break him down tonight. It's my last chance. Chick eats chicken and ice-cream tomorrow night at six. Oh, Burns, pray for me, will you?"

"I'm going to do more than that," he growled. "I'm going to give a wrong-number call there in half an hour. It's four-thirty now. Five that'll be. If you're doing all right, I'll lie low. If not, I'm not going to wait, I'll break in with some of the guys, and we'll use the little we have, the photostats of the letters, and the jewel case. I think Schlesinger can at least get Chick a reprieve on them, if not a new trial. If we can't get Milton, we can't get him, that's all."

"We've got to get him," I said, "and we're going to! He's even been close to breaking down and admitting it to me, at times, when we're alone together. Then at the last minute he gets leery. I'm convinced in my own mind he's guilty. So help me, if I lose Chick tomorrow night, I'm going to shoot Milton with my own hands!"

"Remember, half an hour. If everything's under control, cough. If you can get anywhere near the phone, cough! If I don't hear you cough, I'm pulling the place."

I hung up, ran up the stairs tearing at the silver cloth. I jerked open a closet door, found the cobwebby negligee he'd always told me was waiting for me there whenever I felt like breaking it in. I chased downstairs again in it, more like Godiva than anyone else, grabbed up a cigarette, flopped back full length on the handiest divan and did a Cleopatra—just as the outside door opened and he and two other guys came in.

Milton had a face full of storm clouds—until he saw me. Then it cleared and the sun came up in it. "Finally!" he crooned. "Finally you wanted a change of scenery! And just tonight somebody had to play a practical joke on me, start me on a fool's errand to Philly! Have you been here long?"

I couldn't answer right away because I was still trying to get my breath back after the quick-change act I'd just pulled. I managed a vampish smile.

He turned to the two guys. "Get out, you two. Can't you see I have company?"

I'd recognized the one who'd contacted me for the jewel case, and knew what was coming. I figured I could handle it. "Why, that's the dame I told you about, Milt," he blurted out, "that walked off with that little box the other day!"

"Oh, hello," I sang out innocently. "I didn't know that you knew Mr. Milton."

Milton flared, "You, Rocco! Don't call my lady friends dames!" and slapped him backhand across the mouth. "Now scar-ram! You think we need four for bridge?"

"All right, boss, all right," he said soothingly. But he went over to a framed "still" of me, that Milton had brought home from Hell's Bells, and stood thoughtfully in front of it for a minute. Then he and the other guy left. It was only after the elevator light had flashed out that I looked over and saw the frame was empty.

"Hey!" I complained. "That Rocco swiped my picture, right under your nose!"

He thought he saw a bowl of cream in front of him; nothing could get his back up. "Who can blame him? You're so lovely to look at."

He spent some time working on the theory that I'd finally found him irresistible. After what seemed years of that, I sidestepped him neatly, got off the divan just in time.

He got good and peeved finally.

"Are you giving me the runaround? What did you come here for anyway?"

"Because she's doublecrossing you!" a voice said from the foyer. "Because she came here to frame you, chief, and I know it!"

The other two had come back. Rocco pulled my picture out of his pocket. "I traced that dummy wire you got, sending you to Philly. The clerk at the telegraph office identified her as the sender, from this picture. Ask her why she wanted to get you out of town, and then come up here and case your layout! Ask her why she was willing to pay thirty bucks for a little wood box, when she was living in a seven-buck furnished room! Ask her who she is! You weren't at the Reading trial, were you? Well, I was! You're riding for a fall, chief, by having her around you. She's a stoolie!"

He turned on me. "Who are you? What does he mean?"

What was the good of answering? It was five to five on the clock. I needed Burns bad.

The other one snarled, "She's the patsy's sister. Chick Wheeler's sister. I saw her on the stand with my own eyes."

Milton's face screwed up into a sort of despairing agony; I'd never seen anything like it before. He whimpered, "And you're so beautiful to have to be killed!"

I hugged the negligee around me tight and looked down at the floor. "Then don't have me killed," I said softly. It was two to five, now.

He said with comic sadness, "I got to if you're that guy's sister."

"I say I'm nobody's sister, just Angel Face that dances at your club. I say I only came here 'cause—I like soft carpets."

"Why did you send that fake telegram to get me out of town?"

He had me there. I thought fast. "If I'm a stoolie I get killed, right? But what happens if I'm the other kind of a doublecrosser, a two-timer, do I still get killed?"

"No," he said, "because you were still a free-lance; your option hadn't been taken up yet."

"That's the answer, then. I was going to use your place to meet my steady, that's why I sent the queer wire."

Rocco's voice was as cracked as a megaphone after a football rally.

"She's Wheeler's sister, chief. Don't let her ki—"

"Shut up!" Milton said.

Rocco just smiled a wise smile, shrugged, lit a cigarette. "You'll find out."

The phone rang. "Get that," Milton ordered. "That's her guy now. Keep him on the wire." He turned and went running up the stairs to the floor above, where the other phone was.

Rocco took out a gun, fanned it vaguely in my direction, sauntered over.

"Don't try nothing, now, while that line's open. You may be fooling Milton, you're not fooling us any. He was always a sucker for a twist."

Rocco's buddy said, "Hello?"

Rocco, still holding the gun on me, took a lop-sided drag on his cigarette with his left hand and blew smoke vertically. Some of it caught in his throat, and he started to cough like a seal. You could hear it all over the place.

I could feel all the blood draining out of my face.

The third guy was purring, "No, you tell me what number you want first, then I'll tell you what number this is. That's the way it's done, pal." He turned a blank face. "Hung up on me!"

Rocco was still hacking away. I felt sick all over. Sold out by my own signal that everything was under control!

There was a sound like dry leaves on the stairs and Milton came whisking down again. "Some guy wanted an all-night delicatess—" the spokesman started to say.

Milton cut his hand at him viciously. "That was Centre Street, police headquarters. I had it traced! Put some clothes on her. She's going to her funeral!"

They forced me back into the silver sheath between them. Milton came over with a flagon of brandy and dashed it all over me from head to foot. "If she lets out a peep, she's fighting drunk. Won't be the first stewed dame carried outa here!"

They had to hold me up between them, my heels just clear of the ground, to get me to move at all. Rocco had his gun buried in the silver folds of my dress. The other had a big handkerchief spread out in his hand held under my face, as

though I were nauseated—in reality to squelch any scream.

Milton came behind us. "You shouldn't mix your drinks," he was saying, "and especially you shouldn't help yourself to people's private stock without permission."

But the doorman was asleep again on his bench, like when I'd come in the first time. This time he didn't wake up. His eyelids just flickered a little as the four of us went by.

They saw to it that I got in the car first, like a lady should. The ride was one of those things you take to your grave with you. My whole past life came before me, in slow motion. I didn't mind dying so terribly much, but I hated to go without being able to do anything for Chick. But it was the way the cards had fallen, that was all.

"Maybe it's better this way," I said to myself, "than growing into an old lady and no one looks at your face any more." I took out my mirror and I powdered my nose, and then I threw the compact away. I'd show them a lady could die like a gentleman!

The house was on the Sound. Milton evidently lived in it quite a bit, by the looks of it. His Filipino let us in.

"Build a fire, Juan, it's chilly," he grinned. And to me, "Sit down, Angel Face, and let me look at you before you go." The other two threw me into a corner of a big sofa, and I just stayed that way, limp like a rag doll. He just stared and stared. "Gosh, you're swell!" he said.

Rocco said, "What're we waiting for? It's broad daylight already."

Milton was idly holding something into the fire, a long poker of some kind. "She's going," he said, "but she's going as my property. Show the other angels this, when you get up there, so they'll know who you belong to." He came over to me with the end of the thing glowing dull red. It was flattened into some kind of an ornamental design or cipher. "Knock her out," he said, "I'm not that much of a brute."

Something exploded off the side of my head, and I lost my senses. Then he was wiping my mouth with a handkerchief soaked in whiskey, and my side burned, just above the hip, where they'd found that mark on Ruby Rose Reading.

"All right, Rocco," Milton said.

Rocco took out his gun again, but he shoved it at the third guy hilt first. The third one held it level at me, took the safety off. His face was sort of green and wet with sweat. I looked him straight in the eyes. The gun went down like a drooping lily. "I can't, boss, she's too beautiful!" he groaned. "She's got the face of an angel. How can you shoot anything like that?"

Milton pulled it away from him. "She double-crossed me just like Reading did. Any dame that doublecrosses me gets what I gave Reading."

A voice said softly, "That's all I wanted to know."

The gun went off, and I wondered why I didn't feel anything. Then I saw that the smoke was coming from the doorway and not from Milton's gun at all. He went down at my feet, like he wanted to apologize for what he'd done to me, but he didn't say anything and he didn't get up any more. There was blood running down the part of his hair in back.

Burns was in the room with more guys than I'd ever seen outside of a police parade. One of them was the doorman from Milton's place, or at least the dick that Burns had substituted for him to keep an eye on me while I was up there. Burns told me about that later and about how they followed Milt's little party but hadn't been able to get in in time to keep me from getting branded. Rocco and the other guy went down into hamburger under a battery of heavy fists.

I sat there holding my side and sucking in my breath. "It was a swell trick-finish," I panted to Burns, "but what'd you drill him for? Now we'll never get the proof that'll save Chick."

He was at the phone asking to be put through to Schlesinger in the city. "We've got it already, Angel Face," he said ruefully. "It's right on you, where you're holding your side. Just where it was on Reading. We all heard what he said before he nose-dived anyway. I only wish I hadn't shot him," he glowered, "then I'd have the pleasure of doing it all over again, more slowly."

Chosen to Die

Leslie T. White

LESLIE TURNER WHITE (1901–1967) was born in Ottawa, then moved to California, where he was a lifelong member of the law enforcement community. He became a largely self-taught expert in fingerprinting, electronic eavesdropping, photography, trailing suspects, and other nascent tools of crimefighters.

He had headline-making experiences in the tong wars, battles with communists, and numerous other major criminal activities in California, all recounted in his autobiography and fictionalized in such novels as *Homicide* (1937), *The River of No Return* (1941), and his most important book, *Harness Bull* (1937), which included a four-page glossary of "S'language"—terms used among members of law enforcement organizations. The novel served as the basis for the famous motion picture *Vice Squad* (1953), released in Great Britain as *The Girl in Room 17,* directed by Arnold Laven with a screenplay by Lawrence Roman; it starred Edward G. Robinson.

In "Chosen to Die," private investigator Duke Martindel is married to Phyllis, a smart lawyer he met while she was a law student and he was still a member of the police department. They got married the day she passed her bar exam. Phyllis, though still young, has largely retired, mainly taking on a case only when her husband gets in trouble.

"Chosen to Die" was first published in the December 1, 1934, issue of *Detective Fiction Weekly.*

The trussed-up body fell at his feet

Chosen to Die

Leslie T. White

It was the prettiest murder frame Martindel had ever found himself in—gilt-edged, steel-barred and time-locked against cracking. But those who had stuck him there hadn't taken into consideration the fact that their dupe's wife was the smartest criminal lawyer in town—and just enough in love with her husband to play mouthpiece for him and not double-cross or chisel in the usual way.

CHAPTER ONE
ROBBERS' PLEA

PHYLLIS MARTINDEL WAS jerked from the depths of a sound sleep with an abruptness that left her breathless and moist with perspiration. She cocked her head, listening, but the apartment seemed all too silent, like a morgue peopled with the dead. Propped upon one elbow, she sought to force her eyes to pierce the darkness but the tarnished silvery glow that seeped through the single window mellowed into opaque shadows before it reached the bedroom door. She leaned over and touched the broad shoulders of her husband and seemed to absorb some of his great strength from the contact. Her heart ceased its mad fluttering as she tried to recall what had awakened her.

Then she felt, rather than heard, the door swing open!

The limp hand suddenly became a bony talon that tightened on her husband's flesh. "Hey! What's the idea?" he grumbled thickly.

She shrank against him. "Duke! There is—there is someone in the apartment!"

He gave her a playful bunt with his head and then his lazy voice drawled out of the darkness beside her. "Say, Phyl, just because you're married to a detective don't be so damn suspicious. Oh, well, if there's anyone here tell 'em to g'wan away and come back at a decent—" He stopped abruptly as the sudden glare of a flash blinded him.

"Keep your hands away from that pillow, Duke!" a tense voice commanded from the shadows behind the source of light. "Get 'em in plain sight on top the covers!"

Duke Martindel arched his neck and blinked into the beam. Very slowly he spread his big hands on top of the counterpane, then shot a sidelong glance at his wife. "Darling," he grinned wryly, "is this guy calling on you or me?"

A shadow moved across the wan light of the window. The shades were carefully drawn, then a wall-switch clicked and the room was flooded with light. Martindel pushed himself erect and stared at his guests.

They both had guns on him, but there the similarity ceased. The big man at the foot of the bed had apparently dressed hurriedly for his visit, for even the up-turned collar of his black topcoat failed to hide the fact that he wore no tie. Close-cropped gray hair bristled from the brim of a derby that shaded his tiny close-set eyes—eyes that reminded Martindel of twin bullet holes in a cantaloupe. His square jaw and heavy jowls were tinted a deep purple by a stubble of beard and he carried a scar that coursed upward from the corner of his thin mouth to the criss-crossed sack under his right eye. It was the first

time Duke Martindel had ever seen stark fear in Sam Skuro's eyes.

"Get up, Duke!" growled Skuro. "You're goin' places."

Martindel felt the convulsive clutch of his wife. He turned his head and looked at the man who had drawn the window shade.

"Well, Gus Nuene! Since when have you and Sam gone into the kidnaping racket?"

The man addressed as Nuene gave his neck a nervous jerk. He was very tall and very thin like a giant crane and the angled bridge of his hooked nose made it seem as though he were perpetually sighting a shotgun. He was all straight lines and angles.

"This isn't a snatch, Duke," he announced. "We got a job for you."

Martindel chuckled without pleasantry. "I maintain an office, boys."

Sam Skuro made an impatient gesture with his gun. "Pile out, Duke," he growled. "We're in one hell of a hurry. This is on the level."

Duke Martindel glanced at his wife and a thrill of pride suffused him. She looked very young and very cool lying there with her round blue eyes fastened on Skuro's gun muzzle. Brown hair tumbling around her bare shoulders made her look like a school girl rather than a clever lawyer and the wife of a well known detective. Duke grinned in spite of himself.

"Phyl," he said in an audible stage-whisper, "you're the legal brains of the family. What would you advise in a situation like this?"

Phyllis Martindel was scared—Duke could tell that by the way the nostrils on her little turned-up nose quivered—but she prided herself that she could match her husband's cool wit, so she tried it now. "Darling, they seem to be clients of yours."

The detective's quick laughter brought a dark scowl to the swarthy features of Sam Skuro. "Listen, Duke, this is no time for wise-crackin'. There's big dough in this for you."

Nuene took a step nearer the bed. "Ten gran', Duke! That's more than you private dicks can make in a year on a straight job."

Martindel chuckled. "Straight job? Now that's a word I didn't think you boys included in your vocabulary; you, Gus Nuene, the slickest con-man in town, and Sam Skuro the veteran peterman! Why, Sam, you must be well over fifty! You were cracking cribs when I was in short pants."

Skuro leaned over the foot of the bed. "Duke, you got a reputation in this town. Everybody that knows you at all knows you left the police department and went into private practice because the department went crooked."

"Part of it did," Martindel admitted.

Skuro nodded vigorously. "All right, then, part of it; the biggest part. Well, you wouldn't sit by an' see them frame an innocent man, frame an' hang him, would you?"

The detective drew up his knees and locked his hands around them. "Sam, you old fraud, you couldn't be innocent of anything."

Nuene said: "You know Harry Washburn, Duke?"

Martindel nodded. "Sure. He's the grand jury investigator. We teamed on the force when I was in harness."

Sam Skuro's gun sagged. "Listen, Duke, before my God, I didn't kill Washburn!"

The detective stiffened slightly. "Well, who said you did?"

Skuro opened his mouth as if to say something, apparently changed his mind and, swiveling, walked over to a small radio near the bed. With trembling fingers he rotated the dial. Then he stepped back and listened as the cool, impersonal voice of the police announcer droned out of the instrument.

". . . railway stations, apartments, rooming houses and small hotels. Repeating general order to all cars. Description of wanted men as follows: Sam Skuro, age fifty, six foot one, two ten, gray, close-clipped hair, bullet head, dark complection, scar running from right corner of mouth to right cheek-bone. Skuro is a three-time loser, dangerous criminal. Gus Nuene, confederate, probably holed up together. Nuene five eleven, thirty-eight, gaunt and angular,

dark and sleek, well dressed, thin hawk-face, cold gray eyes. Take no chances in arresting these men as they are wanted for murdering investigator Harry Washburn. All cars will patrol their—"

Sam Skuro switched off the instrument. Both men kept their eyes on Martindel's sober features.

Duke spat: "Cop-killers!"

Skuro caught the bed post. "We didn't, Duke! I'm tough, I've cracked a lot of cribs in my day, slugged a lotta guys, but before my God, Duke, I never drilled a guy." He paused and amended the statement by adding, "I never drilled a guy in the back!"

Martindel's voice was cold. "What did you come to me for?"

"We're bein' framed, Duke. With our records any jury in the world would sink us. We're innocent, we need help."

Martindel gave a dry laugh that lacked mirth. "What you birds need is a lawyer, not a detective. You better speak to my wife."

Nuene shook his head. "No, Duke, a lawyer can't help us out of this spot."

"Have you got an alibi?" Martindel asked.

The two visitors exchanged glances. Nuene answered through tightened lips. "We can't use it, Duke."

Nuene shot another glance at Sam Skuro. The latter gave his head a perceptible nod. Nuene turned back to the detective.

"Duke, we'll lay our cards on the table—cold. But first we want your word that under no circumstances will you tell the law."

Martindel shook his head. "I can't give my word on that. If they subpoena me into court, I'll have to talk." He smiled sardonically. "However, if you boys hired a good lawyer and told her your troubles, she would be able to protect your confidences by the laws of privileged communications."

Phyllis swung around. "Darling! I don't want—"

"Go on, boys," Duke interrupted. "Tell the attorney your troubles."

Nuene nodded to Sam Skuro; Sam began to talk. "Harry Washburn was diggin' up a lot of graft dope—"

"Skip it," Duke cut in. "We know all about Washburn's activities."

"Well, he knew too much so he got bumped at five minutes after twelve."

"Ask him who bumped him?" Duke suggested to his wife.

Skuro answered before Phyllis had a chance to repeat the query. "I don't know that. It was framed to look like Gus an' me did it."

"How do you mean—framed?" asked Phyllis.

Skuro shrugged helplessly. "Phoney evidence—I don't know just what. A friendly stoolie tipped me off just in time to the raid or we'd have been—" He ended with a shudder.

"They want us—dead," contributed Nuene.

"Where were you at five minutes after twelve?" Phyllis Martindel wanted to know.

Both men hesitated, then Sam Skuro heaved his shoulders. "In the main vault of the County and Suburban Bank!"

Martindel laughed harshly. His wife gasped.

"They were cracking the bank, darling," the detective told her drily, "when Washburn was murdered."

"Couldn't you prove that?" Phyllis asked. "It would be better than being charged with murder!"

"Not much better," Duke put in. "Sam and Gus are both old offenders, if memory serves me right they each have three convictions behind them."

"That's right," Nuene admitted wearily.

"And that means they'll get life even if convicted for cracking the bank."

"It means," Nuene corrected drily, "that unless you prove us innocent we'll both be killed by the cops. We heard they don't aim to make any arrests in this case; they don't want to chance it to a jury in case anything slips up. It's a frame, I tell you, Duke!"

"But how," protested the charming lawyer, "can we prove you innocent when you are guilty of something else?"

Skuro bit his lip. "Your husband will know how to handle that, ma'm."

"You tell me," suggested Martindel.

Nuene spoke: "For ten gran', Duke, we want you to frame us innocent!"

Duke Martindel whistled softly and dropped his feet over the edge of the bed. "That's a new one," he mused aloud. "They are guilty of one crime and want to be framed innocent on one they did not commit." He shook his head. "I don't want any part of it, boys. You're a couple of bad eggs that should be frying up in the big house."

His wife caught his arm. "But, Duke, if they didn't kill Washburn, you wouldn't want to see them—" She stopped, embarrassed.

"They robbed a bank," he reminded her. "I'll be compounding a felony if I monkey with that or try to cover it up."

Nuene interrupted. "We thought of that, Duke, so we got a counter proposition. Suppose we give you the dough we got out of that crib— fifty thousand, it was—and you go and make a deal with the manager. It's a small, independent bank and I don't think the manager would want any publicity about the job if he could recover his dough on the quiet."

"Any damage done?"

Nuene shook his head. "Not much. We stuck up the watchman and gagged him with tape. Sam opened the vault like it was a can of sardines." He glanced at his wrist watch. "It's not three yet. If you beat it out to the manager's house, offer to return the dough and pay for any damages, I think he'll listen to reason. We're on the level about this, Duke, we don't want to dangle for something we didn't do."

Skuro contributed: "The manager's name is Mayhew Henderson. He lives at Two Sixty Carthay Circle. He's home tonight—we checked all those angles."

"The money?" Duke asked.

"We'll leave it on your back door step."

"Where will you boys be?"

Skuro shook his head decisively. "You don't need to know that, Duke. We'll get in touch with our"—he gave Phyllis Martindel a glance—"our attorney when the time comes."

"How do you know I won't run out on you with the money?"

"Two reasons," Nuene replied. "First, you're a square dick; second, you'll want to know who knocked off Washburn by shooting him in the back."

Sam had already backed out of the room and now Gus Nuene followed. As the door closed, Martindel grinned at his wife.

"Well, Mrs. Martindel, how would you like to go to Europe on sixty thousand—"

"No thank you, Mr. Martindel. Now will you be on your way to Carthay Circle?" She placed a tiny foot in the small of his back and prodded him out of the bed.

CHAPTER TWO
MURDER FRAME

Duke Martindel brought his roadster to a stop diagonally across the street from a large, brick mansion. He turned the beam of his spotlight onto the white numerals painted on the curb, saw they were 260. Then he climbed out and approached the darkened house.

It took considerable argument to convince the sleepy butler who answered the door that the matter was of sufficient importance to disturb the slumber of his master. But the sounds of the verbal exchange succeeded where the reasoning had failed, for a stubby little man appeared at the head of the stairs and demanded to know what the trouble was. Before the servant could speak, Martindel cut in.

"Mr. Henderson, I am a detective. I have some very urgent business to discuss with you relative to your bank."

Henderson gave an astonished grunt and padded down the stairs, his slippers clap-clapping on the polished surface. He dismissed the butler with an imperious wave of his hand, tightened his robe around his full figure and led the way into a small reception room off the

hallway. Without sitting down, he faced the detective.

"Now, sir," he demanded. "What business have you to discuss?"

Martindel let his eyes sweep the banker in a cold, appraising stare. To him, every man was a subject to be dealt with differently and he wondered how best to approach the rather delicate matter he had to discuss. Henderson, he readily surmised, was not a man that would have any sympathy for others; there was a tightness around his small, thin mouth, set as it was in his chubby face, that suggested cruelty. He stared at his visitor with a haughty frown, but Duke saw a tremor of fear in the depths of his eyes and it heartened him. He made his approach accordingly.

"Mr. Henderson, if your bank was burglarized, your vault rifled, it would be rather awkward from a business point of view, would it not?"

The banker's eyes bulged. "Burglarized? Why, what are you trying to say?"

"Your bank was burglarized last night. The vault was cleaned!"

Henderson collapsed into a chair. "Are you from the police?" he gasped.

Martindel shook his head. "No, I am a private detective."

"You represent the insurance?"

"I," the detective put in flatly, "represent the burglars."

Henderson gave a startled grunt, then groped for the telephone. Before he could lift the receiver, Martindel pinned his hand down.

"Wait a minute," he suggested quietly. "You would do well to hear me out."

"You can't blackmail me!" blustered the banker.

"I'm not trying to blackmail you. I have with me the entire amount stolen and enough extra to make good any damages incurred by the entry. It is a most unusual circumstance, but I want to return the money on behalf of the criminals on the one condition that you make no report of the incident. I believe, if you will consider the matter from all angles, you would be well advised to agree. If your clients knew that your vault could be opened like"—he grinned as he recalled Gus Nuene's apt simile—"like a can of sardines, you would lose a lot of business."

Henderson hesitated and his hand slowly came away from the instrument. "What about Chris Foy, the watchman?" he queried huskily.

"Foy is all right, so I understand," Duke assured him. "I'm confident he will keep his mouth shut under the circumstances. He is now bound and gagged at the bank."

"You have the money with you?"

"In my car. I suggest that you dress and come with me. We will liberate the watchman, return the money to the vault and let the matter drop."

Henderson squinted at Martindel. "I don't understand why you are doing this. Do you expect a reward?"

"No. I expect nothing—from you. My reasons, on the other hand, are no concern of yours. Are you going to come, or not?"

Henderson ran a chubby hand across his moist forehead as though the matter was too much for his comprehension.

"How do I know this isn't some trick to get me to open the bank?" he asked defensively.

Martindel shrugged. "You don't know, but you cannot afford to take a chance that I might be right. If someone discovers the burglary before we get this money back, you know what will happen to your depositors. They'll walk out on you. I'd suggest that you pile into some clothes and make it snappy."

Henderson nodded. "I'll be ready in five minutes," he promised and hurried from the room.

He was ready in six minutes by Martindel's watch. He came into the room dressed in a conventional serge suit, but a too obvious bulge in his right coat pocket warned the detective that he was armed. Duke frowned impatiently. It irritated him when untrained men carried guns. With a curt nod, he led the way out of the house and across the street to his roadster.

Henderson hesitated before entering. "Where is the money?" he demanded.

Martindel swore softly, walked to the rear of the machine and unlocked the turtleback. He opened the portmanteau and held the beam of a small pocket flashlight on the contents. It was bulging with currency and negotiable bonds.

"Satisfied?" he growled.

Henderson bobbed his head, edged into the seat and sat warily in one corner. The detective stretched his lanky frame under the steering wheel, depressed the starter and tooled the machine into motion.

The ride was made in silence. The banker crouched on the extreme end of the seat and it was quite apparent that he did not trust his companion. But Duke Martindel was indifferent to that. There was nothing he had to discuss with Mayhew Henderson and he wanted time to mull over the strange situation in which he found himself.

Perhaps he was a plain damn fool. He knew he could trust neither Gus Nuene nor Sam Skuro as far as he could throw them with a broken wrist; he was too experienced a veteran to believe that quaint old fairy tale about honor among thieves; that was plain hooey. He sought to mentally marshal his facts, slim as they were. First, Nuene and Skuro were scared—they had to be plenty terrified to return fifty thousand in loot. Both men were veteran criminals, but they were the old-time craftsmen, not the modern, back-shooting assassin of today. Duke nodded to himself—yes, he was inclined to believe the precious pair when they said they did not kill Washburn. If they had killed Washburn in looting the bank—they would hardly be willing to return the loot. It would appear logical for them to use the money in making a get-away.

But Harry Washburn was dead! Duke had heard that officially from the police broadcast, and Skuro and Nuene were accused and suspected of the crime. Yet it was easy to find a motive why certain people and factions might want the relentless investigator out of the way. Duke had worked with Harry Washburn back in the days when he was in harness and even then, Washburn was a cold-blooded, tenacious man-hunter. There was something about the way he tore into a case that chilled even his co-workers. But he was a smart dick, uncompromisingly honest, and he had risen rapidly, although cordially disliked by his associates, and when the grand jury picked him out of the entire force to investigate certain underworld activities in the city, dislike turned to fear.

Duke knew what it was to be feared and disliked. He had chucked the police force when things became too raw for his taste and opened a private bureau. He had made good on several well paying cases and wisely invested his surplus. Honest coppers, like old "Skipper" Dombey, grizzled pilot of the detective bureau, favored him, gave him tips and did what they could to help him along. But the department was under the thumb of Inspector Egan of the uniformed men. Egan hated two things—Duke Martindel was both of them.

A cheerful grin stole over Duke's tanned features as he recalled Phyllis booting him out of the bed. What a girl! Even after some three years of marriage, Duke continued to marvel at his luck in winning her. They had met when she visited the police department as a member of a law class studying criminal procedure. The day she passed her bar examination they were married. Since that time, she had only practiced law when it was necessary to extricate her adventurous husband from some escapade. Yet Duke invariably insisted that she was the real business head of the family and that he merely worked for her. It tickled him immensely when she begged him to quit the detective business, with its attendant dangers, and then the first case that looked as though some innocent party might be in trouble, she insisted that he take it and straighten it out.

The sudden looming up of the County and Suburban Bank before him broke up his reverie. He stopped the car at the curb in front of the building and switched off the engine.

"All right," he grunted at Henderson. "Let's go."

The other hesitated, moistening his lips. "I warn you," he jerked huskily. "If anything is—"

"Don't be a damn fool!" cut in Martindel. He opened the door and stepped to the sidewalk.

Henderson followed reluctantly. He paused, glanced suspiciously up and down the deserted street, then hurried across the sidewalk and keyed open the front door. He started to enter, changed his mind and stepped aside for the detective to precede him.

Duke gave an impatient snort, knuckled open the big door and strode inside. The foyer was dimly illumined by a night-light that bathed the empty cages in pale shadows. The thick marble pillars, cold and stark, reminded Duke of a mausoleum. Some strange unfamiliar dread began to come over him. He glanced around but could see no sign of the watchman. Casting a quick look over his shoulder, he found Henderson watching him through narrowed eyes.

"Where's the vault?" he asked.

The banker jerked his head toward the rotunda. As Duke passed the end of the cages, he saw the vault door ajar. He pushed aside a brass rail and strode over. He shot another glance at Henderson, then gripped the big handle and swung the door outward. He jumped backward with an unwitting gasp of surprise.

For the trussed-up body of a man tumbled out of the dark recess of the vault and fell at his feet!

Martindel rasped a curse, whipped out his flash and turned the light on the features of the man on the tiled floor. One quick glance was sufficient; the man was dead.

"Foy!" choked Henderson.

Martindel dropped to one knee beside the corpse. The watchman had been beaten about the head until it was but a pulpy mass. Ropes wrapped around his body held him mummy-like and the dirty strips of adhesive tape across his dead lips added a grim touch to the horror of it all. The detective's jaw tightened and the veins along his temples swelled. He pushed slowly erect and turned to Henderson.

"I don't understand—" he began, then stopped abruptly as he found himself staring into the tremulous muzzle of the banker's gun.

"You dirty crook!" rasped Henderson. "Don't move or I'll kill you!" His rotund little body was doubled into a half-crouch as he backed toward a desk.

Martindel stiffened. "Be careful of that gun," he suggested drily. "It might go off."

"It will go off if you move before the police get here!" promised Henderson. He put his left hand behind him and patted the desk as he searched for the instrument.

Duke Martindel bit his lip. He was in probably the worst predicament of his eventful career. If the police caught him now—he shuddered. He turned his attention to Henderson. The latter was just picking up the receiver.

Duke gauged his distance. Henderson stood about ten feet away. The gun was aimed in the general direction of the detective's broad chest but the muzzle wavered in a restless arc. Duke heard the receiver make metallic noises, saw Henderson open his mouth to speak, then he jumped—

He went feet first like a player sliding for a base. The gun roared over his head—the marble foyer amplifying the sound. Then his feet struck Henderson's legs and with a terrified bleat, the banker flopped on top of him.

Duke's powerful arm closed around Henderson's throat, choking the cry before it was born. He rolled over, came to his knees then releasing his strangle hold, he caught the other by the tie and jerked him into a sitting position. Henderson made one futile attempt to cry out just as Duke's fist reached his jaw. The bleat turned into an indifferent *whoosh* as the air left the tubby body and Mayhew Henderson cradled his head on the mosaic floor and temporarily lost all interest in the encounter.

Martindel combed his fingers through his hair and stood up. The telephone lay on its side, the receiver squawking imperiously. With a soft

oath, he pronged the thing and recovered his crush felt. He jammed it on the back of his head, carefully wiped the handle of the vault door so as to eradicate any fingerprints, and moved swiftly toward the front of the bank.

He was directly in the middle of the foyer when the barred front door suddenly swung inward and three blue-coated figures barged inside. The pale moonlight glinted on blued steel. A cold, venomous voice knifed the stillness. "Hold it, Martindel!"

Duke Martindel froze immobile. He rasped the one word: "Egan—" and made a run for it.

A gun belched in his face. His head exploded and he went down—cold.

CHAPTER THREE
FRENCH LEAVE

Daybreak filtering through the grimy little window of the headquarters' interrogation room, fell in wan splashes on the weary features of Duke Martindel. With clothing disheveled, his shirt front stiff with dried blood and a turban of bandages crowning the upper portion of his head, he sprawled in a hard-backed chair in the center of the battered room. There were four other men present, but Martindel's eyes were focused unwaveringly on the tall, gaunt figure that stood before him, silhouetted by the tiny window.

Inspector Egan was a thinnish man whose gauntness was deceptive. Like a puma, his muscles were so evenly divided over his frame as to be unnoticeable. His face was long and narrow and the features sharp, fox-like, and his salt-and-pepper brows, when he frowned, formed a straight unbroken line across the upper part of his face. This tended to thrust his colorless eyes into a pocket of shadow and give to them a metallic luster that was disconcertingly impersonal. No man on the department had ever seen him smile. He was shrewd and intuitive; he seemed to smell a situation before it was possible to know by any other means. Few men liked him personally, but he had the knack of winning the respect and blind obedience of his men. It was rumored that he was the real power behind the city government, but such rumors were always whispered furtively, for Wyatt Egan was not the type of man to oppose unless one was prepared to prove his accusation.

"Talk?" he asked Martindel.

Duke shrugged. "Sure. I didn't kill Chris Foy."

Egan tugged at his nose. It seemed to lengthen in his hand. "It was a two-man job—who was your partner."

"I didn't have a partner, Egan; I didn't need one."

"That your story?"

"Part of it."

"What's the rest of it?"

"I didn't crack that vault."

One of the other cops laughed. Egan rocked on his heels meditatively. When he spoke, his voice was low, controlled as though he were holding himself back.

"You killed Chris Foy, Martindel, then tried to put one over on Henderson. Don't forget, we found fifty thousand bucks in the turtle-back of your roadster. How do you explain that?"

Duke shook his head. "I'm not going to try," he said wearily.

"You had ten thousand dollars in your pocket," Egan went on. "You know where that came from, don't you?"

"Sure, but you don't."

"Wrong," corrected Egan drily. "We checked the serial numbers of those bills and found they were part of the loot stolen from the Seaside National Bank last month. Talk yourself out of that one."

Duke Martindel swore softly and covered his chagrin by gingerly patting the bandage around his head. From the neck up he was just one big ache; a slug from Egan's gun had creased his skull and come, literally, within a hair's-breadth of killing him. And now, with throbbing head, he found the predicament almost too much for him. The evidence was damning—he could not dispute that fact.

He tried to reason it out in his mind. Although satisfied that Sam Skuro and Gus Nuene had deliberately framed him for the burglary and the murder of the watchman, Foy, he could see no point in explaining the matter to Inspector Egan. In the first place, he had been caught red-handed and would be, in any case, considered an accomplice of Skuro and Nuene. As such, his testimony would be worthless in court and he would be regarded equally guilty with the other pair. Then, too, the police were perfectly satisfied that Skuro and Nuene were the murderers of Washburn; they neither would be, nor could be, induced to change that theory.

A sharp commotion in the corridor outside broke in on his musing. Egan scowled and started across the floor when the door swung open and a woman darted into the room. Her eyes settled for an instant on the group, then with a little cry, she ran to the prisoner and threw her arms around him.

"Duke! Are you hurt, darling?" she whimpered.

Martindel jumped to his feet. "Phyllis!" Then he grinned ruefully. "No, Phyl, Egan shot me in the head where it couldn't do any damage." He cast a glance over his shoulder where the inspector was growling at a desk sergeant.

The latter was fuming embarrassedly. "I couldn't stop her, Inspector!" he apologized. "She walked right past me an' headed for this room."

Egan swung around. "You'll have to get out, Mrs. Martindel," he snapped.

Phyllis Martindel drew herself up to her full five feet. "I will not!" she retorted.

"The hell she does, Egan," put in Duke. "She's my attorney, in case you don't know."

Phyllis slapped a folded document on the table. "Here is a writ for Duke's release."

Egan pushed it away from him. "You keep a supply of those damn things all filled out?"

The girl gave him an icy stare. "I think you will find it in perfect order."

Egan picked it up. Without unfolding it, he turned to Martindel. "Duke, I happen to know that you had two visitors earlier this morning: Sam Skuro and Gus Nuene. We want those two. Where are they?"

"Haven't the slightest idea," Duke told him.

Egan tugged at his nose. "We know definitely that they came to see you. After they left, you went out. Now I want to know what business they had with you that prompted that. You're in a bad spot, Duke, so you better talk. In any case, I can take you before a magistrate, put you under oath and either force you to talk or put you in the position of an accomplice, because the only excuse you could give for not talking is that it might tend to incriminate you."

Martindel grinned maliciously. "I'm only a dumb private dick, Egan; I work for my lawyer. Skuro and Nuene came up to see her because she's their attorney as well as mine. They didn't tell me a damn thing."

The inspector's eyes retreated into a deeper socket of shadow. "I'll make her talk," he growled.

Phyllis shook her head. "I don't think you will!" she challenged him testily. "If you know anything about legal procedure at all, you know that an attorney cannot be forced to testify to any conversation with a client. That is a privileged communication, you murdering old crook!"

Egan sniffed; it was the nearest he ever came to laughter. "You make a fine pair—a shyster mouthpiece in skirts and a crooked, double-crossing, gum-shoe. That's like marrying a jackal and a skunk."

Duke smiled thinly. "You're well up on zoology, Egan, but then, that's natural. Now, how about this writ?"

Inspector Egan turned slowly and walked over to the window where he stood straddle-legged, his hands behind him, staring into the street below. Finally, after a moody silence that lasted for nearly five minutes, he swung around and shook the crumpled writ at the Martindels.

"You win this round," he growled. "I'm not ready to tip my hand yet. This case has a lot of angles and if I resisted this writ, I'd have to go into court and show my evidence right now.

When I'm ready, I'll have you picked up, Duke, but in the meantime, don't either of you try to leave town. You can beat it now."

Phyllis sniffed disdainfully and proffered a pack of cigarettes to her husband. Duke came slowly to his feet, paused with irritating nonchalance to light his smoke, then with a cynical grin for the somber-faced coppers, he turned and limped out of the room.

They tramped down the dingy stairs in silence. At the front door of the station-house, she gave his arm a squeeze.

"Drive, darling?"

Duke grinned, shook his head. "You drive, Phyl. I want to think." He crossed the sidewalk and opened the door of his wife's coupé.

Phyllis slid under the wheel and Duke lolled beside her, his head resting against the top of the cushion. As his wife tooled the little car into the early-morning traffic, she laughed.

"I'll bet you're thinking what a smart little wife you have," she chided. "I don't know what you would do if I didn't keep yanking you out of tight spots all the time, you big baby."

Duke grinned. "It would be mighty dull, Phyl. You invariably yank me out of one spot, all right, but you drop me into the middle of a tighter one."

"Meaning—"

Duke tried a smoke ring—and failed. "Darling," he asked, "do you look good in black?"

"Hideous! Why?"

"Then you better watch your step unless you want to be wearing a widow's garment."

A tinge of terror crept into Phyllis' voice. "What do you mean, Duke?"

"I mean that something's up," he told her drily. "Why do you suppose Egan turned me loose?"

She hesitated. "Why, the writ—"

"Nope, darling, wrong. Old Egan could beat that writ without half trying. All he had to do was to show to any magistrate that I was captured in a bank in the wee morning hours with a dead man and fifty thousand bucks in my car and—" he made an eloquent gesture with his hands.

"Then why did he turn you loose?" she protested.

Duke shrugged. "Egan tried to kill me; he wants me—dead. Perhaps it is just his personal animosity, perhaps it is something else."

"You think he knows you had nothing to do with the bank robbery—"

Martindel sighed. "I'm not sure. Did you hear from Skuro or Nuene?"

"Sam Skuro called; he left a number where we could reach him in an emergency." She fished a slip of paper out of a pocket and handed it to him.

"When was that?"

"Just before I left for the station."

Duke flipped his cigarette stub into the street. "By the way, how did you know I was down at headquarters?"

"Somebody telephoned. They told me you were in a jam and needed an attorney—they should have said a nurse. I didn't recognize the voice." Anxiety crept into her tone. "You didn't tell me why Egan turned you free, Duke."

Duke pushed himself erect in his seat. "I can't answer yet, except to say that there must be a damn good reason, otherwise he wouldn't have done it. Don't underestimate old Egan, he makes a fox look like a moron by comparison." He reached up and adjusted the rear-view mirror so that he could see behind without turning his head.

"Don't drive so fast, darling," he suggested.

"Why—" Phyllis asked, startled. "I always drive—"

"Because you're making it tough for those dog-faced flatfeet of Egan's to stay on our tail."

She whistled softly. "You mean they are following us, Duke? Shall I lose them?"

"*Uh-uh.* I know a better way. We don't want them cluttering up our own apartment, so drive to Chelsea Street. I know a nice quiet family hotel. You remember it, darling; I took you there for a couple of days right after I gave you that nice mink coat."

Phyllis shot him a malicious glance. "You know very well I never had a mink coat."

Duke chuckled. "Pardon me. I got us confused with two other people."

Phyllis Martindel brought the coupé to a stop before a small hotel that was sandwiched in between two austere apartment houses. A bellhop ran across the sidewalk and yanked open the door.

Duke handed him a dollar. "Put this bus in a safe place, son. We don't want it for several hours; I need some sleep." He left the hop in charge of the coupé and crossed the sidewalk. As he pushed open the door of the hotel, he glanced over his shoulder and saw a sedan drift slowly past.

"I don't understand how you can talk of sleep at a time like this," sighed his wife. "I never felt less like sleeping in my life."

Duke chuckled. "Well, Phyl, keep it a secret then," he whispered as they approached the desk.

After exchanging the usual greetings with the hotel clerk, Duke picked up the pen and wrote *Mr. and Mrs. Duke Martindel* in bold letters across the registry card. "And now," he told the clerk, "we want a room with a southern exposure. I am very particular about rooms."

The clerk picked up a key ring. He signaled to an assistant to take his place and then he circled the counter. "The only rooms we have with a southern exposure, Mr. Martindel, face on an alley at the rear," he said doubtfully. "I'll be glad to show you what we have." He led the way to the elevator. As the lift started to rise, he told the operator to stop at the sixth floor.

Duke interrupted him. "That's too high. My wife has a very poor heart; she likes something nearer the ground than that. Don't you, darling?"

Phyllis gave him a quick grimace. "Of course," she acquiesced.

At the clerk's command, the elevator paused at the second floor and they got out. The clerk showed them a room on the southwest side.

"How do you like this, Mrs. Martindel?" he inquired.

Before Phyllis could reply, Duke cut in. "No, this won't do. How about something on the other side of the hall?"

The clerk shrugged and led the way across the hall. As they passed through the door, Phyllis whispered: "Have you gone completely crazy?"

Duke winked. "Don't forget, I was shot in the head."

The next room seemed to please the detective, although it appeared identical with the other one. But the clerk was used to cranky customers, so he politely inquired if there was anything else they wanted.

Duke nodded. "Yes, I want perfect quiet." He tapped his bandaged head significantly. "I had a slight accident and I intend to get a little rest. Please put a *Do Not Disturb* sign on the door and a plug in the phone. Under no circumstances do I wish to be bothered. If there are any visitors or phone messages, kindly get the name or numbers. Is that plain?"

"Certainly, sir," agreed the clerk. "I will see that you are not interrupted."

Duke handed him a bill. "Since we had no baggage, I will pay in advance for the room. Put the receipt in my mail box." He dismissed the clerk with a wave of his hand.

As the door closed, Phyllis sank on the bed and made a weary little gesture with her hands. "Crazy! Crazy as a loon! A murder charge hanging over your head, the police trying to kill you and you come to a respectable hotel and act like an old maid on her honeymoon."

"No such thing," he corrected her, "as an old maid on a honeymoon."

"Be serious, Duke," Phyllis begged. "What in the world made you do this? Why, you said yourself that the police were following you. They will be sitting down in the street waiting for you."

"Exactly, darling. That's what I'm counting on. Do you know why I didn't take that room across the hall? Well, this room has a fire escape,

the other did not. I am very timid about fires, you know."

Phyllis grimaced. "Oh, you fool! I see it now. You went to all the trouble of renting this room and telling those monstrous lies, just to sneak out of here and lose the police. I could have lost them in five minutes."

He kissed her. "Remarkable, Watson! But I don't want to lose them; I want them sitting out front and I want head-quarters to believe I'm holed up here asleep. You can bet your sweet little life that right this very minute, a scared desk-clerk is repeating my orders to a couple of Egan's bloodhounds."

"So what?"

"So I take French leave through that window and get in touch with that double-crossing Sam Skuro. After that, well, who knows."

Duke hurried into the bathroom. He carefully unwound the bandage and found that the wound had caked over. He gingerly adjusted his hat and came back into the bedroom. Phyllis still sat on the edge of the bed looking very crestfallen.

"Oh Duke, why did you get mixed up in this terrible affair? Let's take a boat to Europe, or someplace."

"I offered you that, Mrs. Martindel," he reminded her with a grin, "but you chased me into this, literally kicked me headlong into it. Now I've got to get out of it. Bye." He brushed her cheek with his lips, crossed the room and raised the sash.

The alley appeared deserted. The fire escape was the type that descends with weight, so Duke eased his bulk through the window and, turning, blew a kiss to his wife. "I'm glad you have a weak heart, darling. Hope it's over me."

Phyllis wrinkled up her pert little nose at him. "Conceited idiot!" she jeered as he softly closed the window behind him and disappeared.

Once on the alley level, Duke swung west. At the first street that intersected the alley, he turned south until he located a drug store. Inside, he found a phone booth, dialed headquarters and asked for Captain Dombey. When he finally heard the low, quiet voice of the veteran detective on the wire, he said: "Hello, Skipper. This is Martindel."

Dombey grunted in surprise. "I wasn't expectin' a call from you, Duke."

"I imagine not. Are you working on the Washburn case, Skipper?"

"We're all workin' on it, in a way," Dombey replied cautiously. "The dragnet's out for Skuro an' Nuene."

"Preferably dead, eh?"

Dombey gave another noncommittal grunt. "I heard somethin' like that," he admitted drily.

From his pocket, Duke fished out the memo his wife had given him. "I think I can locate that pair, Skipper," he said, "but I have reasons for wanting them taken alive. How about it?"

The copper agreed. "That's all right with me, Duke. What's the angle?"

"Call the telephone company and get the address on this telephone number." He tilted the slip of paper so that the light fell across it. "Hempstead Two-four-two-o-six. Then pick up an extra gun for me and meet me alone."

"Where?"

"Drive down Market. Go slowly after you pass Glendale Avenue. I'll hop aboard if everything is O.K."

"I'll be there in twenty minutes," the copper promised and hung up.

CHAPTER FOUR
TRAP FOR RATS

Captain Dombey looked just what he was—a straight cop. Nature had molded him for the task; years in harness had sculptured his character in deep, seamed lines. He was broad and strong, built close to the ground, with powerful neck and ham-like fists, the better to fight when the going was rough. His crag of a jaw might represent bull-headed aggressiveness, or perhaps just strength of character.

Time had mellowed nature's work by carving deep channels along his leathery old face, by

crowning his massive head with thick silvery hair, and by giving to his voice a low richness that stirred the listener. Through twenty years of departmental intrigue, of crime, of hatred and tragedy, old Skipper Dombey had gone his quiet, sure way, doing his work as best he could, sticking, helping, fighting.

As Duke Martindel swung onto the running board of the Skipper's machine, he felt all those things in one quick rush of confidence.

Dombey wasted no words in idle greeting. "That number you gave me—it's a roomin' house on Chester Street. Want to go there?"

Martindel slipped into the seat, nodded. "Who killed Washburn, Skipper?"

Dombey grunted. "I'll bite. It was supposed to be Sam Skuro an' Gus Nuene."

"Couldn't have been. They got an alibi."

Dombey glanced sideways. "How do you know, Duke? You were supposed to be robbin' a bank."

Martindel nodded grimly. "Sam and Gus framed me on that, Skipper." He briefly recounted the series of events that had transpired since the moment he was awakened to find Skuro and Nuene in his room.

Dombey remained silent. At length he shook his head deliberately. "Nuene might pull that, but it don't sound like Sam Skuro. Sam has slugged too many men to make a mess of it like you say Foy was."

"That's the rub," Duke growled. "Foy was either beaten to death and then gagged, which would be silly, because any fool could have seen he was finished, or else he was bound and gagged and then battered, which would be needless brutality."

"That's what I can't figger," Dombey contributed. He took a gun out of his coat pocket and pushed it toward his companion. "I don't think you'll need this; I've pinched Sam a dozen times an' never had to use one."

Duke tested the balance of the revolver, flipped open the cylinder and checked the load, then shoved it into his pocket. He was about to speak, when Dombey suddenly slowed the machine.

"What's this?" he growled. "There's the dead wagon in front of the roomin' house I was headin' for."

Duke felt a queer, unfamiliar tightening around his diaphragm as he glanced through the windshield. A crowd stood in a great semi-circle around the coroner's small black truck, and uniformed policemen were seeking to clear a path for traffic.

"Looks like we was late," Dombey commented morosely. He pulled over to the curb and stopped. "You wait here, Duke. I'll mosey over an' prowl the joint." He slipped out to the sidewalk and melted into the excited throng.

Duke slumped in his seat, jerked his hat down until the brim rested on the bridge of his nose and lighted a cigarette. Intuitively he knew the answer, but when Dombey came back to the car five minutes later, he verified it.

"Sam an' Gus got it," he grunted laconically. "Resistin' arrest."

Duke felt a little sick. It came to him suddenly that he had not eaten since the day before. As though the veteran read his mind, Dombey suggested:

"Let's get a cup of coffee, kid." Without waiting for a reply, he piloted the car around the first corner and drove until he came to a small, counter lunchroom.

Coffee warmed him, stirred him out of his apathy. "I counted on Sam," Duke mused glumly. "He was my one alibi. Now Egan's got a fine set-up; he cleans up the Washburn killing by fastening it onto Skuro and Nuene and then bumping them off. I'm the goat on the murder of Chris Foy."

"It's bad," Dombey admitted.

"Bad, hell!" Duke retorted with a rueful grin. "It's terrible. Now I see why Egan turned me loose; he wanted me to lead him to Skuro. With them out of the way, I'll be next. They'll try to knock me off for resisting arrest!"

Dombey shook his head slowly. "Listen, Duke, nobody'll knock you off while you're with me."

"Thanks, Skipper, but you can't be with me always."

"That's what I was thinkin', Duke," Dombey said quietly. "The safest place for you right now is in jail as my prisoner. Why not let me book you on suspicion, then take over the case an' have my boys prove you didn't do it."

Duke laughed without pleasantry. "Skuro and Nuene tried to let some one prove them innocent, Skipper. They got a free ride in the official meat-wagon. No, I'll go it alone for—" He stopped as the waiter paused in front of him.

"Say, mister," said the waiter, "you're wanted on the phone."

Duke frowned. "You must have made a mistake. No one knows I am here. What name did they ask for?"

The waiter shrugged. "It's a dame. She didn't ask for you by name. She said there was a tall, good-looking young guy sittin' in here with a cop."

Dombey sniffed. "G'wan, Duke, that must be for you."

Martindel rose, walked to the rear of the lunchroom and picked up the receiver that dangled from a wall phone. Clapping it to his ear, he growled: "Hello?"

"It's your shyster mouthpiece," came the familiar voice of his wife. "I just thought you might be interested to know that two men have been following you."

Duke started. "Where are you, Phyl?"

"Across the street, in a drug store, you idiot. Knowing you need a wet nurse, I followed you after you left the hotel. This pair picked you up when you met Captain Dombey."

"Cops!"

"I don't think so, darling. They are young and sleek-looking. One—the tall one—walks with a limp in his left leg. The other is squat and tubby. He seems to walk on his heels."

"Where are they now?"

"Sitting in a green sedan halfway down the block. Now, you fool, will you go to Europe with me?"

Duke grinned wryly. "Can't just now, darling, I've got a business engagement, but will you please go home and quit playing detective!"

"Who is your engagement with, Mr. Martindel?"

"Two mugs in a green sedan, Mrs. Martindel," said Duke, as he pronged the receiver.

Duke's first impulse was to repeat to Dombey what Phyllis had told him, but by the time he reached his stool, he changed his mind. The copper gave him a quizzical, sidelong glance.

"Someone you know?" he inquired.

Duke shrugged. "A dame who saw us enter. She tried to date me up. Called from the drug store across the street."

"That's the hell of bein' good-lookin'," grunted Dombey, then changed the subject by asking: "Well, what did you decide to do?"

Duke lighted a cigarette before answering, finally gave his decision. "I'm not going to risk my life in a courtroom, Skipper; I'll take my chances outside where I can do my own fighting. As it stands right now, I'm framed for a bank job and a murder, neither of which I committed. I know that Sam Skuro and Gus Nuene didn't kill Washburn. They're a pair of crooks, I'll admit, and they're better off dead, perhaps, but they did not murder Washburn."

"All of which doesn't help you," Dombey put in drily.

"Admittedly, but it does explain things. For instance, I committed a crime—compounded a felony when I sought to square that bank job by returning the money. Even a regular city cop has to break the law many times in order to get around some legal red tape in settling a more serious offense, but when a private dick gets tripped up, he's in a jam."

"You haven't any evidence as to who did kill Washburn," Dombey pointed out.

Duke shook his head. "Not yet."

"That 'yet' is the trouble," Dombey grunted. "If your hypothesis is correct, if the reason they released you was so you would lead 'em to Skuro and Nuene, then you've served your purpose an' your number is up about now. You won't have a chance even to get started, Duke. No, you better come in with me."

Martindel grinned, but shook his head. "By the way, Skipper, do you know a couple of mugs, one tall—that walks with a limp in his left leg, the other short, squat and gives the impression of walking on his heels?"

Dombey frowned, massaged his forehead with gnarled fingers. "Sounds like Louis Nagel an' Tubby Arnison. Nagel's a tall flashy-lookin' wop from St. Louis. Arnison used to be a stoolie for Egan before he graduated into the money rackets."

"Arnison still stool?"

Dombey snorted. "You tell me, kid."

"Guns?"

"Yeah—Nagel anyhow. Tubby's just a dirty little rat that started out snatchin' purses."

Duke pushed to his feet, jockeyed a coin down the counter and faced the copper. "Thanks, Skipper. My appreciation and all that. I'll be seeing you."

The old man shoved erect. "Wait a minute, kid, I'll tag along awhile."

Duke gave his head a decisive shake. "Thanks, but I'd prefer to go it alone. There's a lot of angles to this and there's no use of you risking your pension on a losing bet. You can do me one favor, though—if the breaks go against me, keep an eye on Phyl."

Dombey grunted. "I'll marry her myself the day she's a widder." He gave the younger man a friendly punch on the chest. "You're just a head-strong damn fool, Duke."

Martindel grinned, swung around and, leaving Dombey staring after him, barged outside. He cast a quick glance across the street, but could see no sign of Phyllis. A whimsical smile twitched the corner of his mouth, then he let his gaze wander casually down the block. The green sedan was parked within a hundred yards of where he stood. His smile vanished. His hand brushed against the hard lump in his pocket where the gun reposed and he felt the impulse to run amuck. He felt stifled, as though a great unseen web were slowly tightening around him. The sacrificial goat! But why? What was back of it all? Why were these mugs tailing him? How did they know where to pick him up? No one knew that but Dombey and himself. For a brief moment he felt the urge to charge the green sedan and gun out the pair, but almost immediately reason prevailed. That would be suicide and get him no place, except, perhaps, the morgue.

A cruising cab offered a chance to meditate. The driver caught his signal and a moment later he was comfortably ensconced in the tonneau. Up until the moment that the driver asked him where he wanted to go, Duke had been undecided, but when the question was suddenly propounded, he gave directions for reaching a small cottage in the mountains just back of the city. As the driver turned back to his task of piloting the swaying cab, Duke risked a hasty glance out the rear window. The green sedan had swung in line behind.

He had no plan. The tiny cottage suggested itself because of its isolation; he wanted to get these two hoods alone someplace where he was not likely to be disturbed. It was situated on the edge of a small lake; Duke and Phyllis had spent their honeymoon there.

He wanted first to know why these men were tailing him and who sent them. He fished a cigarette out of his pocket and tapped it musefully against the window. Abruptly the possible answer came to him: Egan! Egan had released him on a writ when he might well have been held; Egan had sent his flat-feet to follow him, and now two hoods magically appear on his tail. That was too coincidental especially since one of the pair was a stoolie of Egan's. There was only one possible explanation—Egan, knowing that Duke was friendly with Dombey and often called when he was in trouble, had tapped the wires on all the Skipper's calls. That would explain the appearance of the two mugs at the rendezvous.

A grim, cynical smile twisted the corner of Martindel's mouth. He could use more direct methods in dealing with two known criminals than with the police. His fingers slipped into his coat pocket and massaged the checkered butt of the gun Dombey had given him. Perhaps Tubby Arnison could be induced to wag his tongue.

The cab suddenly swung into a clearing and stopped before the little cottage. Duke stepped out and handed the driver a bill.

"Want I should wait, mister?" asked the man at the wheel.

Martindel grinned, shook his head. "No. I'm expecting friends." He waved the cab away and mounted the steps to the wide veranda that encircled three sides of the little cabin. He opened the front door, walked swiftly through the dust-covered living room and let himself out a rear door. A short run brought him to the fringe of trees that formed a hedge around the cottage. He took out his gun and padded in a great arc until he came to a spot where he commanded a view of the front of the cabin.

CHAPTER FIVE
DUKE MAKES A KILLING

The cab was gone. For a few moments he could see no sign of human life, then his sharp eyes picked up the outline of a man standing in the shadow of a tall tree. Even as Duke watched him, a second man—a short, fat fellow—eased out of the brush and joined his taller companion.

They held a whispered consultation, but their words did not reach the detective. However, their meaning was obvious, for both drew guns, examined them briefly and slipped them into convenient pockets.

Duke sized them up. The tall one—Nagel, if Dombey was correct—was swarthy, and vicious-looking. His close-set eyes, thin mouth and the way he carried his head low, like a bull, suggested that he would be a tough nut to crack. His squat companion, on the contrary, had a moon-face that looked soft and flabby. He had eyes that could easily cradle fear. Coupled with a killer of Nagel's type, Tubby Arnison might conceivably commit murder, but if left to his own devices, Duke surmised that he would slide into rackets that carried with them a lesser chance of physical liability.

Nagel suddenly stepped into the clearing and approached the cottage; Arnison drew his gun, braced it against the tree and covered the veranda.

Duke's teeth bared in a cold smile. So that was it? Nagel was going to lure him out while Arnison shot him from ambush! He melted back into the trees and silently made his way to a spot directly back of the stubby little gunman. Then he eased forward—

Tubby Arnison's first indication of misfortune came when Duke pressed the cold muzzle of his revolver against his well-rolled neck.

"Not a sound!" Martindel reached forward and removed the gun from the tremulous fingers. "Now call to your partner and tell him to come back here!" He increased the pressure of the gun on Arnison's neck. "Any tricks, mug, and I'll part your hair from the inside!"

Arnison nodded, terror-stricken. He lifted his voice and jerked huskily, "Hey, Louis, come here a minute!"

Nagel glanced back, hesitated and then started to retrace his steps. When he reached a point about halfway across the clearing, he suddenly jerked to a stop. Perhaps some animalistic instinct warned him of danger, for his hand suddenly streaked toward his pocket.

Martindel saw it coming. He took a quick swing at Arnison's head with one gun. As the squat hood toppled into the brush with a squeal of pain and terror, he jumped into the open.

"Don't try it, Nagel!" he warned.

The St. Louis gunman flung a curse at him and brought his gun up shooting. Duke's first shot was high. Before he got in a second, a slug from Nagel's gun tore into his leg, turned him halfway around and dropped him on his hands and knees. He rolled over, braced one elbow on the ground and fired twice in quick succession.

Nagel was dead before he hit the ground!

Duke rolled over hastily, expecting trouble from Arnison, but the tubby little assassin was clinging groggily to a tree, trying to wipe the blood out of his eyes. Duke inched over to a sapling, pulled himself erect and tested his leg. It was numb now and refused to hold his weight.

He dropped Arnison's gun into his pocket, picked up his own, and turned the muzzle on the fat man. "Snap out of it, Tubby," he rasped harshly. "Amble out there and grab hold of your boy friend. Drag him into the bushes here. We may be having company. Step lively."

Arnison wavered, wet his thick lips and looked at the gun. Duke let his thumb toy with the hammer. That decided the gunman. He mumbled something unintelligible and swayed across the clearing. He hesitated a long time before he could bring himself to touch his dead confederate, but at last he caught Nagel by the ankles and dragged him into the surrounding trees.

"Now," commanded Duke, "we'll go into the house where we can have a nice, quiet chat. Get going, mug!"

Arnison moved with surprising alacrity. Duke broke off a branch to serve as a walking cane and hobbled after him. It was painful work limping up the four steps to the veranda for he had to keep his eyes fastened on the waddling bulk of his prisoner. But at last he made it and, pushing into the cottage for the second time since his arrival, dropped into a chair near the door. He let his eyes settle musefully on the other's flabby features.

Arnison stood with his back to a small table in the center of the room. He was a man close to forty with watery eyes that shifted constantly. His red, bulbous nose was criss-crossed with little purple veins and his puffy cheeks seemed to drag down the skin under his eyes like a St. Bernard's. Periodically he opened his mouth as if to speak, but no words came.

It was Martindel that broke the stillness.

"Arnison, I'm not going to fool with you. I'm going to ask you some questions and I want smart answers. First, who sent you after me to make this kill?"

The prisoner wagged his head. "We weren't goin' to bop you, fella. You got us all wrong. This was just a heist, see! We saw you pass down the state highway an' tailed you—"

The roar of Martindel's gun drowned his words. He gave a shrill bleat of terror, clawed at the fleshy part of his leg and toppled on his face.

Duke's voice was chilled. "That didn't hurt you much, Arnison, but it's a sample of what you can expect if you keep on with those lies. Now I happen to know you picked up my trail down in the city about the time I met Captain Dombey. Who sent you after me, Arnison?"

The hood sobbed, dragged himself to his hands and knees and crawled toward the detective like a cur dog. "S'help me, I don't know," he whined. "Nagel got the orders from somebody, but I don't know who. Nagel's dead now an'—"

Duke leaned forward. He cupped the gun in the palm of his hand and struck the hood across the side of the head. Arnison yelped and fell on his face, grovelling.

Martindel straightened. "I know different, Tubby. Talk, or I'll shred you to ribbons. I've no compunction about killing you; none whatever. For the last time—who sent you two guns after me?"

Arnison slowly lifted his head and stared at Duke through a veil of blood. "I can't, s'help me! He'd kill me—"

Duke raised his gun to the level with the other's battered countenance. "O.K., Tubby, if you'd rather have it now." He thumbed back the hammer.

Arnison hesitated until he heard the second click of the gun, then terror seized him. "Wait!" he bleated. "I'll talk!" His head fell forward into his arms and he sobbed out the name so huskily that Martindel had to lean forward to catch it.

"Egan—"

Duke's mouth contracted. "Why?" he rasped.

"He wanted you dead for the bank job!" choked Arnison.

Duke grunted, leaned back and contemplated the man on the floor. So his guess was correct—Egan had made a deal with these two rats to remove him. His scowl deepened. What good was this information? If he returned Arnison to the city, the stool-pigeon would deny his accusation the moment he was under the protection of the police. Even if he didn't, it would be the word of a known criminal against a police official; Duke knew he could not get to court with anything as slim as that.

Duke pulled himself erect, hobbled across the room and picked up a telephone. He pulled it as far as the cord would allow, then placed it on the floor.

"Tubby," he commanded grimly. "I want you to make a call, a very important call."

Arnison lifted his head and stared. The detective canted his head toward the instrument. "Crawl over to it, Tubby. Call Inspector Egan, tell him Nagel shot me, but that he got it as well. Suggest that you found something of vital importance and ask him to come out here. The idea is, Tubby, that unless Egan comes to this cottage, you're going out the hard way."

Arnison choked. "You want me to lure Egan here? My God, guy, you don't know what you're askin'!"

Duke squinted along the barrel of his gun. "Have you ever seen what happens when they take you to the morgue, Tubby? How they rip you open down the middle, stick a water-hose into you to wash out your insides? If I shoot you in the head, for instance, they'll cut off your skull to see where the bullet went. They'll—"

"Cut it!" screamed the gunman. "Cut it, I tell you!"

"There's the phone, Tubby," Duke suggested drily.

Arnison inched toward the instrument on his stomach. His tremulous fingers fumbled with the receiver as he sought to remove it.

"Easy, Tubby, easy," cautioned Martindel. "I'll hold you responsible if Egan doesn't show up, so don't let him smell a rat."

Arnison sobbed aloud, shuddered convulsively, then took down the receiver. In broken sentences he jerked out the number of headquarters, but by the time he got the inspector on the wire, his voice was reasonably cool.

"Arnison, chief. I don't want to talk over the phone, see, but can you come up here right away?" He shot a sidelong glance at Duke, then shut his eyes as though to blot out the vision of the gun muzzle. "We—Nagel got him, chief, but you better come. I found somethin', see. I—yeah, we're up in a cottage on Bear Mountain." He choked out the directions for reaching the cabin, then slowly cradled the receiver.

Duke grinned cynically. "He's coming?"

Arnison shuddered. "He's comin'!" he sobbed and dropped his head in his arms.

When the noise of a car reached the cabin about a half hour later, the stage was set. Duke Martindel stood back of the entrance door, leaning on the top of a chair. Tubby Arnison, still trembling with terror, crouched on another straight-backed chair beside the center table, facing the front door. Brakes ground outside, then the motor died. A car door slammed.

Arnison mumbled something. Duke wagged the gun. "Easy, Tubby," he whispered. "Easy."

Steps pounded up across the veranda, paused a moment, then the door swung open. Egan strode into the room.

"Well, Arnison, where is he?" demanded the inspector. Duke reached out and slapped the door shut with his free hand. "Right here, Egan! No, don't reach for that gun. You can't make it!"

The uniformed man swiveled like a cornered hobo. For a brief instant he seemed undecided whether to go for his gun, then he slowly elevated his hands.

"What is this?" he snapped.

"This," Duke told him drily, "is a showdown. Arnison here has been telling me some interesting things, Inspector, things that corroborate some old-time suspicions of mine."

Egan flashed a venomous glance at the quaking stoolie, then turned back to Martindel. "You're a damn fool, Duke!" he commented. "Put down that gun!"

"You're right, Egan, I am a damn fool," Duke admitted. "But I'm not going to put down this gun until we settle a few points of interest. First, I'd like to know what excuse you have for putting a couple of hoods on me!"

Egan shrugged. "You're crazy. You can't prove a thing."

"Who said anything about proving it? I'm curious, that's all, damn curious. For instance, I'm curious to know how it happened that Harry Washburn was murdered at the exact moment that Skuro and Nuene were cracking the County and Suburban Bank, how you appeared at the bank just as I was leaving." His mocking smile vanished into a scowl. "And, lastly, Egan, I'd like to know why you deliberately shot at my head."

"We don't take bank robbers alive," growled Egan, "not after they kill a watchman."

Duke sniffed. "But you weren't supposed to know that Foy was dead when you walked in there. That's another point I'd like cleared up, Egan—the killing of Foy. Sam and Gus didn't kill him, I didn't, so who did?"

"You can't talk your way out of this mess," Egan threatened.

Duke grinned sardonically. "I'm not going to do the talking, Inspector. Tubby here, for instance, knows a lot of interesting things."

Egan ponderously swung his head. Arnison winced before the cold glitter of those colorless eyes. "S'help me, chief, I ain't—" he choked to a stop.

Duke hefted his gun. "Well, Tubby, make up your mind. Don't be bashful—this is a nice, chummy get-together. Now what do you know about this business?"

Arnison pulled himself erect, his fingers tightened around the back of his chair. "My God, you wouldn't murder a man in cold blood?"

"Don't be a fool!" rasped Egan. "He's bluffing you."

Duke smiled, but said nothing. His thumb dragged back the hammer of his revolver and in the silence of the dusty room, two distinct clicks were audible. Arnison's voice rose to a shriek.

"Bluffin' hell! I ain't gonna die, I ain't, I tell ya."

Martindel had hoped to provoke an argument between his two captives and thus glean some of the truth back of the tangled mess. He well knew Egan's vicious temper and he counted on Arnison's fear of death to form a verbal explosion of some sort. But he was hardly prepared for what followed.

Arnison was trembling from head to foot. "You got me into this, Egan!" he shrilled. "He'll shoot me down like a dog. I won't die—s'help me, I won't, I tell ya—"

Duke swung his eyes to Egan to see how the latter was taking it, when Arnison flung the chair!

With one leg injured and unable to bear his weight, Duke had propped himself against the chair in front of him. Arnison's wild fling struck the chair, knocked it from under him and he fell headlong to the floor. As he went down, he tried to swing his gun, but Egan kicked it from his hand and it bounced across the room.

Duke cursed his own carelessness, rolled over and tried to drag himself erect. Then he paused. He saw Arnison swing and pounce toward the revolver. Just as the crook reached it, a gun roared. Arnison gave a startled yelp, pirouetted once and sprawled in a corner.

Duke jerked his eyes away, brought them back to Egan. The inspector was lowering his own service revolver and a faint dribble of smoke curled from the muzzle.

"There goes a perfectly good witness," Duke drawled cynically.

Egan turned. "You won't need any witnesses," he growled. "Not where you're going."

Duke gave up trying to pull himself to his feet. He sat back on the floor and looked into the relentless features of the policeman. "So it's like that, Egan?"

The inspector nodded. "Just like that." He stepped sideways so that he could get a clear, unobstructed shot at the man on the floor.

Duke sighed. "Just one question. Why was I framed on that bank job?"

Egan drew back the hammer of his gun. "You can ask Arnison that when you meet him in hell."

Abruptly a gun thundered into the silence. Duke's first impression was that Egan had fired. The inspector stood with his arm still outstretched, but now his gun had vanished and his hand was dripping blood.

Duke called on his waning strength to drag himself erect. He jerked around to face the hoodlum, but Arnison still lay inert where he had fallen.

Then a door opened and Captain Dombey and Phyllis came into the room. Dombey covered Egan. Phyllis gave a little whimper and ran toward Duke, arms outstretched. He swayed forward to meet her. The floor rose suddenly. He went out.

Duke recovered consciousness in the hospital to find Phyllis sitting on the edge of the bed, holding his hand. "Take it easy, darling," she whispered, and he saw that she smiled through her tears.

"How'd I get here?" Duke wanted to know.

A familiar voice answered from the foot of the bed. "They started to put you in the meat wagon," Dombey growled, "but your wife wouldn't stand for it. Was afraid they'd get their loads mixed, I guess, so you made the trip in an ambulance."

Duke winced as he tried to move his leg. "Say, where's Egan? Did you kill him?"

"Naw," grumbled Dombey. "We're savin' him to hang. I'll try to get passes for us all—we can make a day of it."

Phyllis shuddered. "Not the Martindels," she assured the grinning copper. "They are going to Europe."

Duke groaned. "They can't hang him without more evidence than we got. Gosh, what a lousy shame you didn't show up before Arnison was killed." He frowned at them both. "Say, how did you two happen to show up?"

Dombey chuckled. "Well, it's a long story, but I figured as long as you didn't want the date with the swell-lookin' jane in the drug store, I'd mosey over. I dated her up myself an' we ambled up here. By a strange coincidence, you was here."

Duke scowled at his wife. "So," he sneered, "you don't trust me? You follow me—"

"Oh, shut up!" Phyllis said.

"About Arnison," Dombey butted in, "he ain't dead. Egan's slug creased his skull, but it didn't do him no damage. However, me 'n the doc made him think he was slated for the long trail. Did he talk? Ha! Plenty. First, he says—" Dombey stopped as a physician motioned him to silence.

"Our patient has had enough, I'm afraid, Captain," the doctor said firmly. "The details can wait until—"

"The hell they can!" shouted Duke. "I want to know why Egan framed me!"

Dombey turned at the door. "O.K. You was in the way. Egan wanted a goat for the Washburn kill, so his stoolies tipped him off to the fact that Sam Skuro an' Gus Nuene were set to crack the bank at midnight. Egan set a watch on the bank job and sent Arnison an' Nagel out to bump Washburn. According to Arnison, Nagel did the actual kill. Egan had Skuro and Nuene followed so that they couldn't establish an alibi, but some-body tipped Sam off by telephone and he an' Gus beat it over to your place."

"Humph!" grunted Duke thoughtfully. "I'm beginning to see through it. Who killed Foy?"

"Egan. They followed you to Henderson's home, guessed what you was goin' to do, so Egan figgured it a good chance to frame you proper an' so have a sucker for the bank job. He gave Foy the works. Arnison saw him do it. Egan began to get restless when he knew you was working against him, so he decided to let the boys polish you off. Well, so long." He closed the door.

The doctor took Phyllis by the arm and gently propelled her to the door. "No more questions for this young man," he announced firmly.

"Just one," shouted Duke. "Just one, Doc."

"And that is—"

"How soon can a guy travel to Europe with a leg like this?"

A Pinch of Snuff

Eric Taylor

ERIC TAYLOR was a frequent, though not prolific, contributor to various pulps in the 1920s and 1930s, notably to *Black Mask, Dime Detective,* and the lower-paying *Clues.*

While the seal of approval that came with being published in the Golden Age of *Black Mask*—in the years in which it was publishing Hammett, Whitfield, Cain, Nebel, and its other major stars—would normally have given an author greater opportunity for success, this seems to have eluded Taylor. He never published a novel and never even had a single short story collected in an anthology.

Some of this may be due to the fact that he eschewed the traditional path of most pulp fiction writers, which was to produce a series detective. In the seven stories published in *Black Mask,* for example, three were about different detectives and three were about thieves, including the story collected here.

Another reason that Taylor may not have enjoyed the financial and critical success of many of his fellow pulpsters is his melodramatic style. The impossibly pitiful early years of the heroine of "A Pinch of Snuff" would have been an embarrassment to producers of stage plays at the turn of the last century, at which audiences were encouraged to hiss at the villain as he twirled his mustache while throwing a waif out of her home to freeze in the winter snow.

"A Pinch of Snuff" was originally published in the June 1929 issue of *Black Mask.*

A Pinch of Snuff

Eric Taylor

*A small thing, but it leads to a murderer,
vengeance, and a strange discovery*

I N MONTREAL they like to show you the view from the top of Mont Royal. To the south, church spires like gracile mile posts guide the eye to the green St. Lawrence, panting here from its fierce flight over the Lachine Rapids, widening for its majestic march to the sea. Beyond the river lies a great plain that meets the sky near the hills along the American border. To the north, the Laurentian Mountains hide uncountable lakes that lie like verde antiques, cool and inscrutable as they await a sportsman's rod. To the west, gay red roofs peer through the verdant screen of maples, while to the east . . . But Montreal might prefer that you didn't look to the east.

A family of five brooded in a single room apartment in an East End flat. The room was hot, steaming, fetid with the snow that melted on Armand's coat and the baby wash that hung on a length of twine.

Armand sat sullen, his right hand stroking a nearly-empty bottle. He glanced across the room toward his youngest brat and thought it droll that the gin and milk should end simultaneously. His eyes wandered over to Gabrielle. He saw the ugly lines that poverty had etched across the fragile beauty of youth. She had cheated him, he thought. Bony, hollow-chested, with bent shoulders, reproachful eyes, and mute lips—a hag at thirty! Could this be the dancing-eyed, cream-skinned beauty he had wed thirteen years ago?

Irène moved across the room toward the table. Armand scowled. A doctor down at the clinic had informed Armand that Irène was undernourished. A thin arm crossed Armand's vision and raised the cover of a thin metal box. A savage blasphemy burst from Armand's lips. His hand struck out. One of Irène's pale cheeks flushed crimson as she jumped back. Gabrielle turned with a furious protest on her lips. But something she saw in her husband's eyes choked back the words.

"She knows there is no bread in the box," Armand said after a minute.

At nine o'clock Armand went out. At a corner grocery, where his credit had been stopped, Armand halted to beg an empty sack. With this beneath an arm he struck south to a district of small wholesale produce merchants.

Before a window, Armand stood in deep thought for a long time. The flakes of snow that were falling grew larger. A few drops of rain fell, and Armand's decision was made. This mild winter was starving the poor. Mid-January and the river was still unfrozen despite the supplications of a thousand women who prayed for cold that their men might work at the ice-cutting.

Armand broke the window and crawled into a small warehouse. A few minutes later Armand thrust the filled sack through the window he had broken. He dropped to the street and raised the sack to his shoulder.

But recently there had been other raids on the wholesale provision houses. A keen-eyed detective with a reputation to make was watching the district.

At the detective's first cry to halt, Armand threw down the sack and ran. Armand was lean and fleet, and the detective had less at stake. At the detective's third cry, Armand's heart lifted. He was escaping the law. Then the detective fired. Something reached up from behind and gripped Armand's leg. He staggered forward painfully, dragging this leg that seemed to be caught in a trap. He turned down an alley. His leg felt free now, but very heavy. He climbed a fence, fell to the ground and lurched forward. Twenty minutes later he reached his room weak and panting.

Gabrielle cried out her fear when she saw him. She ran to lock the door. Irène raised a small head from a heap of blankets that lay on the floor. Panic stifled her crying as a heavy pounding shook the door.

Armand glanced down and saw the blood that dripped from his soaked trousers. The hammering on the door increased. Gabrielle was holding him close. She was sobbing her anguish and kissing him. He must not leave her. For God's sake, no! She and the little ones—they would starve!

The soft wood door seemed to bellow inward. Armand kissed her once. He bent for an instant to drop a tear on the face of Irène. Then he seized an empty gin bottle and slid to the door.

The door crashed and Armand struck. The bottle shattered. The detective fell forward into Armand's arms. Armand's fingers closed on the man's throat. The detective tried to speak, but Armand choked back his words. And then a great blast shook the room. The low jet of gas was blown out.

The room was heavy with rancid smoke and escaping gas. Someone came in who shut off the gas and later lighted it. There were two men on the floor. One of them, the detective, rose slowly.

Gabrielle crossed the floor to her man. She stood above him—ominously calm, immobile. Then a long-drawn scream echoed the anguish of the woman in despair. She clutched at her breast and pitched forward across the body of Armand.

Neighbors and strangers swarmed into the room. Irène's frail little body shook with the chill of terror. The detective, with a gun in his hand, shouted fierce orders.

Irène crept from her blankets. The detective angrily waved back the intruders pressing in the doorway. The child slipped into the throng and was pushed with the rest from the room.

She stood in the doorway watching when the ambulance attendants brought stretchers into the room. She saw the doctor bend over her mother and heard him pronounce her dead. She saw him turn from her father and shake his head hopelessly. She was jostled roughly out of the way when the stretchers were carried from the room.

Irène shrank back further as a giant policeman carried her two baby sisters, one in each arm, from the room.

The dark hall was a swirling vortex of the morbidly curious. Men and women swarmed the place and fought for a glimpse into the room of tragedy. Police threw them back roughly. Children clung to their mothers' skirts crying out their fear. Irène shrank from sight in a corner.

In time the police herded the neighbors into their own quarters, and quiet reclaimed the building.

Irène crept fearfully down the hall. A policeman guarded the door to Armand's room. Irène stood there for a minute gazing dully, dry-eyed, at the door. The policeman waved an enormous nightstick and ordered her to be gone.

Irène walked slowly to the street door. She flung a last startled glance over her shoulder and fled down the street. Her spindling legs revealed amazing fortitude and carried her miles from that East End flat.

That night she fell in with a crippled beggar. Outcast, nearly helpless, the discovery of a bit of humanity more wretched than himself was flattering. The beggar took Irène to a basement. She made peasoup for him, and he rewarded her with two blankets.

Irène told him her story and the beggar reciprocated with the tale of a thrilling flight from a crime that had ended when a freight train ground off his two legs. He told her further tales of glorious days and nights in the underworld. He promised to learn the name of the detective who had killed Armand and murder him.

Irène took courage from his brave tales.

"*Non!*" she exclaimed passionately, "you find the name, and I will kill him!"

There were no truant officers to evade. Irène cooked peasoup for "Sticks" Grady until he died of acute alcoholism three years later.

Irène was sixteen, but looked twenty. She was tall, too thin, but pretty in a hard way. Her eyes were smoldering bits of repressed hate. Her cheek bones were too prominent, and her lips were thin and straight. Sticks Grady had trained her well, and Irène was ready for crime.

She experimented with shop-lifting, snatching purses, and picking pockets, then tried burglary and found it most profitable. She could move through a house with the fleet grace of a shadow. Against the hazards of capture she carried a small stiletto—a weapon essentially feminine, but with the deadly possibilities of a cobra. The blade was a scant three inches in length and came to the point of a needle. Irène meant one day to strike that point to the heart of a detective named Jean Duret, who, Sticks Grady had informed her, was the slayer of her father.

In time her life drew Irène into contact with other thieves. She was cunning and ambitious and organized a band. Irène lived with her companions in an old three-story stone building on St. Paul Street. The house was two hundred years old and ran back to an ancient cobbled street named St. Amable. The windows were few and narrow. They had originally been protected with thick iron shutters to withstand the arrows and bullets of the Iroquois. Fragments of these shutters still clung to rusted hinges.

Irène rented the two upper floors and professed to run a lodging house for sailors. For fifty years the ground floor had been occupied by a snuff manufacturer, but now that part of the building stood vacant, giving Irène's band the run of the whole place. The cellar was a deep, dark pit that smelled foully of the river. A small section of the flagged floor of the cellar was a trapdoor that opened down into a tunnel which Irène had heard was once part of the early fortifications of the city. Irène marked that tunnel for the tomb of the detective, Jean Duret.

Her band of thieves held up ships' officers on the dimly-lighted streets leading to the river. They occasionally lured drunken seamen to the grim, iron-shuttered house on St. Amable; robbed them, and threw their senseless bodies into deserted alleyways or abandoned warehouses. With one or two of the more skillful, Irène swept uptown on forays on the rich. She was surprisingly lucky, and the gang prospered.

It was on a night that Irène sat in her room weaving mental webs to ensnare the detective, Jean Duret, that a stranger hammered on the St. Amable Street door.

Irène's eyes peered through the perforations in a rust-eaten iron shutter. She saw a big man, wide of shoulders, but not stout. He was dressed in a pair of cord trousers and a blue flannel shirt. She could not see his face.

A frown of perplexity crossed Irène's forehead. It was not some fool thinking to rent a room, because the only lodging sign was an inconspicuous one on the St. Paul Street side of the house. The knocking on the door persisted. Irène was alone. She drew the stiletto from her breast and swiftly descended the foot-worn stairs.

"Who is there?" she demanded.

"It is I, Le Loup. I come from Desfarges!"

" 'Le Loup,' " Irène repeated. "I don't know you."

"You know Desfarges. Desfarges, of the Black Water Tavern?"

"Yes."

"Then open this cursed door! Is it not enough that Desfarges has sent me?"

Irène opened the door doubtfully. The tall stranger entered and closed and locked the door. "My card, miss!"

Irène looked deep into the man's eyes. Her glance dropped uncomfortably. The lines of that long, lean face were ruthlessly hard. A knife slash that began near the right ear ended at the fellow's mouth. There was a sardonic twist to the other side of his mouth. Thick cords stood out upon his neck. His cleft chin was outthrust in swagging bravado. "My card, miss!" he repeated with a distorted grin.

Irène reached forward and accepted a sheet of folded paper. She opened the paper slowly, her eyes still more upon her curious visitor than upon what he had offered as his card.

"Read," the man laughed.

Irène's eyes dropped to the paper. She drew back startled, then a smile flitted across her lips. He was droll, this Apache. What he offered as his card was a police bulletin from Paris bearing his photograph, his fingerprint classification, and his Bertillon measurements. Beneath these details was the printed information that Emil Desjardins, alias Le Loup, was wanted for the savage murder of an old woman.

Irène glanced from the photograph to the man. "The scar?" she asked.

"It was acquired since that episode," Le Loup laughed.

"And what do you want of me?" Irène demanded.

"Desfarges told me that I could trust you—else I would not have offered my *card*. I have placed my life in your hands. I want shelter. The police may be looking for me here; though I got clean away from France." He leaned close to Irène. "Desfarges told me of your cellar; he told me, too, of the old tunnel that leads to the fortifications. I want shelter, protection, Miss, and a chance to escape if necessary. But I expect to earn it!"

Desfarges was the gang's fence. Irène was under obligations to him. She dared not send this Apache away.

She took Le Loup through the house. She showed him the two-foot thickness of the stone walls. With a flashlight she guided him to the cellar and showed him the trap in the flagged floor that opened into the tunnel.

Le Loup and Irène stood silent while the Apache gazed approvingly at the closed trap. There was not a sound in the cellar but their breathing. Then from beneath their feet came the faint squeal of rats.

Le Loup grinned, but Irène drew back with a shudder. "The tunnel is alive with them," she explained. "New wharves of cement are being built and the rats have been driven back from the waterfront. They have little chance to find food now, and Jules, one of my men, tells me they will eat each other until none but a few remain. It is not a nice place, down there, but it it better than the gallows, or the guillotine, eh! And there is small danger that you will have to use it."

At first Irène's band received Le Loup with suspicion. But he was a spectacular figure and his endless bragging caught the fancy of these unimaginative rouges. By day the Apache amused himself in the practice of knife-throwing in the old quarters of the snuff manufacturer. He appeared to be a careless braggart, but Irène noticed he was always careful to wipe away the particles of dust or snuff that might have clung to his knife during this sport. At night Le Loup drank enormous quantities of gin and talked. He swaggered about the hideout, voicing opinions and offering advice in a manner that alarmed Irène.

A night when he and Irène happened to be alone in the house, Le Loup threw open her door without knocking.

Irène jumped to her feet and faced the Apache. He stood on the threshold, his great body filling the doorway. His eyes glittered menace; his torn mouth was distorted in a grin.

Irène struck a hand to her breast. "Get to your quarters!" she cried.

Le Loup stepped toward her. A stiletto flashed into Irène's hand. Her arm swept downward and struck. But Le Loup was swifter. His hand shot forward. Blood spurted from his palm, but he held Irène's wrist. Le Loup laughed hysterically. His teeth ground in a frenzy. Irène felt an enormous pressure on her wrist. Her arm was bending at the elbow. The stiletto came up in her hand guided by the powerful arm of Le Loup. Irène's eyes dilated with horror. Her face was a mask of fear. But she uttered no cry.

Le Loup forced her wrist backward until the stiletto was a scant inch from her throat. Irène's left hand shot forward and her nails clawed at Le Loup's eyes. The Apache grinned and gripped that wrist in his left hand. Irène retreated until

her back was pressed hard against the wall. Still the stiletto drew nearer. She felt its sharp point graze on her flesh. Her skin was pierced, Irène screamed when she felt a short, hot flash in her throat. Le Loup laughed and dropped her wrist.

"Another time, my vixen, it will not be a scratch!"

He reached down and tore a great piece of silk from her dress. This he bound around his bleeding palm.

Irène stood silent, the stiletto dangling from her limp hand. Le Loup looked contemptuously from the dagger to Irène's eyes. But Irène had forgotten the stiletto. She was looking at Le Loup with new interest. For in the Apache, Irène suddenly saw the weapon with which she would destroy Jean Duret, the killer of her father.

Two of the band entered the house and the tension was broken. Le Loup walked from her room and Irène closed and locked her door.

She could hear Le Loup and the others laughing in another room. Their talk grew boisterous and Irène knew they were drinking. A loud scraping of chairs reached Irène's ears, then came the clump of heavy feet descending the stairs. Le Loup had gone out for the first time since his arrival.

It was hours later when Irène was awakened by a soft rap on her door.

"Who is there?" she called quietly.

"Joe."

Irène arose and opened the door. A pale, trembling wretch slid into her room.

"*Mon Dieu*, Joe, what is it?"

"Le Loup," Joe whispered hoarsely. "Godin and I drank with him. We went out at midnight. There was a lone sailor on St. Paul Street. We crept into a doorway. When he passed, I stepped out with my gun. He raised his hands and Godin emptied his pockets. Le Loup stepped forward and counted the haul. 'Here, young fellow,' Le Loup shouted, 'let this be a warning to you to carry a fuller pocket in the next world!' With that he struck the sailor to the heart. It was awful.

Then as we came home, the madman boasted that he kills on every job. We must flee, Irène, or he will hang us all!"

Irène laughed softly. "You are upset, Joe. Here is money. Take Godin and go to the country for a rest. Stay away for some weeks, and when you return go to Desfarges before you come here. Where did you leave this sailor?"

"We dragged him into the passage by Dionne's warehouse."

Irène dressed quickly, then waited in her room until she heard Godin and Joe steal down the stairs. She slipped on a pair of kid gloves and stepped into the hall. She paused at Le Loup's door and heard him deep in an alcoholic sleep. Irène laughed softly and went downstairs.

She paused in the old snuff factory long enough to scoop up a pinch of dust from a corner, then she stepped out into St. Amable Street. The narrow, cobbled street was silent and deserted. Irène skirted the block and came to St. Paul Street. The old stone buildings, old as the city, and once the homes of early adventurers from Old France, loomed up in great black shadows. Irène moved swiftly under the protecting shield of the darkness. Soon she came to the passage by Dionne's warehouse. She listened for a full minute, then crept toward the victim of Le Loup's knife.

They had placed him in a doorway and he sat with knees drawn up and head thrown forward. He looked like a drunken man asleep, but the flesh on his face was cold to the touch.

Irène bent over him and found the wound where his coat was wet. She opened his coat, then drew her stiletto and dipped its point into the pinch of dust she had taken from the snuff factory. She threw a startled glance along the passage. Her breath came in short gasps. The stiletto point sank easily into the open wound. Irène withdrew the blade and wiped it carefully on the man's coat. Again she dipped its point in the dust in her gloved hand, and this time touched the blade lightly along the rent Le Loup's knife had made in the sailor's coat.

Half an hour later the dagger was washed clean, the gloves were destroyed, and Irène was back in her room.

In the morning she told her band singly of Le Loup's killing and warned them to scatter.

It was noon when Le Loup, sullen and dishevelled, came from his room. "Where are the others?" he demanded abruptly.

"Pah!" Irène exclaimed in disgust. "The cowards have run! They are fools. This is the safest place in the city—in the country, for that matter. What detective would look for a murderer within a hundred yards of the murder?"

Le Loup winced at the word murderer. He seemed to have lost some of his bravado. "What about this detective Duret? Joe was telling me something of him."

Irène laughed lightly. "*Mon brave,* you are nervous this morning. Does Le Loup fear Duret? Come have a drink!"

"I fear no one!" Le Loup blustered. "But they tell me—"

"I will tell you of Duret," Irène said quickly. "He is gun-shy. There was an episode years ago. Duret killed an innocent. Since that day he has been gun-shy. When he gets into a tight corner, he will draw his pistol, but he will hesitate and hold his fire. I tell you Duret is not to be feared. He is ambitious. He has been on homicides for three years now. When he can, Duret will work alone to gather all the glory. And other detectives do not care about working with him because in a corner, he is uncertain. Why are you afraid? Last night you were so strong—so heroic."

Le Loup's face broke into a smirk. Like a mask removed, the fear was struck from his countenance.

"But come," Irène said. "I must watch at the windows so that if Duret should come you will have time to hide."

Irène left Le Loup with a bottle of gin and spent the afternoon moving between the windows on St. Amable and St. Paul streets.

As five o'clock drew near Irène's vigilance increased. The body of the sailor, she knew, must have been discovered at seven o'clock when Dionne's warehouse was opened. At nine it would have been placed in the hands of the coroner. Before that time the enterprising Duret would be engaged on the case. Duret and the coroner would discover the dust in and about the dead man's wound. Dr. Leclaire the famous *medicin-legiste,* would take the dust to his laboratory. Some hours later he would pronounce the dust to be snuff.

Duret's theory would be that the murderer was addicted to snuff. But then the clever Leclaire would point out that from the depth and width of the wound it was obvious that the weapon was too large to be a clasp knife, therefore it was improbable that the knife was carried in a pocket. Leclaire would offer the suggestion that the murder was committed in some place where there was a large quantity of snuff, and that later the body was carried to the passage where it was found. From that point it would be a matter of minutes until Duret appeared at the old snuff factory. And Irène knew that Duret would make his first investigation of the old stone house alone.

It would have been simpler for Irène to have lured Duret to the house with a telephone call notifying him of the whereabouts of Le Loup. But then Duret would have descended on the place in force.

At twenty minutes to six Irène's heart quickened as she glimpsed the familiar figure of the man who had killed her father. The detective was on the opposite side of St. Paul Street. A shadow crossed Irène's face as she saw Duret walk casually down the block without a side glance. In a moment he had passed beyond her vision and Irène regretted that she had not made some signal to attract him. But then he might have called for help before entering the place.

When Duret disappeared, Irène crossed the building and watched through the perforations of a rusty iron shutter on St. Amable Street.

In a few minutes the detective loomed into sight. Irène's face glowed. Duret had stopped. A bell jangled noisily.

"Le Loup! Le Loup!" Irène called quickly,

"to the cellar and into the tunnel! Duret has come. He is alone! You can work the trap?"

"Yes," Le Loup answered, as he stole down the stairs.

The bell rang again. Irène descended the stairs and opened the street door. Duret, tall, handsome, well-fed, stood upon the threshold. Irène's eyes met his. She swayed uncertainly for an instant while a little room fetid with the smell of drying clothes swam before her eyes. She saw Armand her father limp into that room, his foot dripping blood. She saw this man who stood before her burst in and grapple with her father. She heard again the screams of her mother. Her ears seemed to burst with the crash of gunfire. Then her nostrils were drenched with the stench of powder and the room was dark.

As though through a mist she saw Duret again. She recovered with a start.

Duret was gripping her arm; he was searching deep into her eyes. He relinquished his hold slowly. "Pardon, madame, I thought you were about to faint."

Irène smiled weakly. "You remind me of my father!" she said.

Duret bowed gravely and said nothing.

"What do you wish. It cannot be that you want one of my rooms," Irène said, glancing significantly at Duret's well-fitting clothes.

"No, madame, I came to look over this factory, but the doors are locked. I thought perhaps there might be an entrance from your hall."

"There is," Irène admitted readily, "and it is open because I have permission to use the cellar beneath to store my lodgers' boxes. You have seen the agent?"

"Of course, madame."

"Then come in."

Irène opened the door that led into the old snuff factory. Duret stepped into the large room. His eyes searched into dark corners and satisfaction glowed on his face. He turned abruptly to Irène. "I understood the place has not been used for some time, yet upon the floor I see signs of recent occupancy."

"It is my lodgers, *m'sieu.* Some of them have

been with me for years and they keep their boxes in the cellar. They have to pass through here to reach the cellar stairs."

"What do your lodgers do, madame?"

"They work on the docks—that is, all but one!" Irène leaned toward Duret and her voice grew guarded. "That one is a strange fellow. I have considered mentioning the matter to the police. He has been with me only a week. He does not work and he does not leave the house— at least during the day. Today, whenever the bell rang, he went to the cellar before I had time to open the door. Do you think I should report him to the police, m'sieu?"

Duret looked shrewdly into Irène's eyes. She returned his gaze evenly.

"Listen, madame, I come from the police. Where is this fellow now?"

"You are a detective?" Irène asked with awe in her voice. "Come, m'sieu, I will show you. He went down the cellar as I came to answer your ring."

Irène led the detective across the snuff factory to the cellar door. She descended the stairs boldly. Duret thought for a second that perhaps he should call for assistance. But this woman went so coolly, he drew his revolver and flashlight and followed.

They saw no one in the cellar. Duret peered behind rubbish-filled packing cases and small trunks. The detective noticed a piece of strange mechanism. He was about to speak of it when Irène gestured toward a mark on the flagged floor. "See, m'sieu, is that not a footprint?"

Duret stepped forward. He reached the spot on the floor Irène had indicated. He turned suddenly as he heard a subdued laugh behind him. Then the floor dropped beneath his feet and Duret was plunging through space.

Irène ran to the edge of the trap. She flashed a torch into the black pit. The detective was on his feet now, groping for the torch he had dropped in falling.

The dark shape of Le Loup appeared suddenly in the zone of light. Irène switched off the torch and left them in darkness. A red glow flashed from the tunnel three times and the floor rocked with the concussion of shots. Irène heard a sharp scream that did not come from Le Loup. She knew then that the Apache's knife had found its mark in the dark. "Papa! Papa!" she cried hysterically.

The killer of her father was dead! But Irène was reminded suddenly of the second object of her vengeance. She ran forward to the short lever that controlled the trapdoor. Her moment of ecstasy over Duret's scream had cost her dear. The lever stuck in her hands when the trap was half closed. Irène threw her weight wildly against the iron bar. A gasp of exhaustion escaped her lips. Suddenly the lever moved freely. Irène jammed it home with a cry of exhaltation. And then she heard the mocking laugh of Le Loup at her side.

His right arm wound around Irène's side, binding her arms as he drew her against his body with the strength of a boa constrictor. Le Loup's left hand manipulated the trap lever. He turned swiftly, raised Irène in his two arms and tossed her into the tunnel.

Irène struck hard on the tunnel floor. She lay stunned for an instant but came to quickly with Le Loup's mad laughter in her ears. She looked up and light dazzled her eyes. Le Loup had found the flashlight Irène had dropped. Irène was conscious of a writhing movement at her feet. She glanced down and saw Duret clutching at a knife that was buried in his thigh. The knife came from the wound and Le Loup backed from the edge of the trap. The detective arose on one knee.

Irène saw the head and shoulders of Le Loup as he bent over the lever to close the trap. She screamed and grasped frantically at the edge of the lifting door. The trap was closing. With horror in her heart Irène saw she would be pinned by her hands between the closed trap and the cellar floor. She released her hold and dropped back into the tunnel. As she fell a faint breath of air struck her gently on the cheek. Something that gleamed bright whizzed past her head. Scream after scream came from Le Loup above. Then the trapdoor dropped. The tunnel was in utter darkness and the cries from Le Loup came faintly as from a great distance.

Irène stood listening. Slowly the cries of Le Loup receded into silence. Irène could see nothing. But now she could hear the sharp squealing of many rats.

"Duret! Duret! You killed him?"

The detective did not answer.

Panic seized Irène and she crawled about the tunnel groping for the detective. Her hand struck something and she heard a soft moan.

"Duret! Duret!"

She wondered fearfully if the detective were dead. Her hands went into his pockets and at last found a box of matches. She struck one and looked into the detective's face. He was ghastly in the wan light of the match. She clutched at his wrist and cried out her joy when she felt the beat of life. The match end burnt her fingers and she struck another. Off to one side Irène caught a gleam of nickel. She reached out and found the flashlight the detective had dropped.

Irène switched on the light and looked at the detective's leg. She ripped off lengths of her skirt and fastened a tourniquet above the wound. Then she bound the wound itself. She worked over the detective with frenzied solicitude. The ironic thought that this was the man she had sought to kill did not cross her mind. She knew only that she was in terror of being alone. When she had bound Duret's wound, Irène sat down beside him.

She thought of the flashlight battery. That must be conserved.

HOURS later, it seemed, Duret recovered consciousness and asked for water. Irène recalled him to their predicament.

The detective looked at her strangely, but said nothing. He ran a hand to his bandaged leg and looked more mystified than before. "Tell me," he said at last, "is there a way to raise the trap from below?"

Irène shook her head hopelessly. "No. The trap can be worked only from above. Once open, it may be set to close itself, but there is no way to raise it. One of my—my lodgers told me that arrangement was a precaution against thieves or an enemy getting into the tunnel. The tunnel is as old as Montreal. Most of it has been blocked up and built over. I suppose there was once some central place where the trap could be worked from below. I have never been down here before, but I understand there is only a small section of the tunnel now in existence."

"Then come," Duret said, "we will investigate. I can walk on one foot if you will permit me to lean a little upon your shoulder."

They moved slowly down the littered passage. Rats scuttled beyond the range of their flashlight. As the light advanced, the squealing of the rats increased. Then in a few more minutes, they heard no more of the rats and the tunnel ended abruptly against a cement wall.

Duret stood in deep thought. "The rats have gone," he said slowly. "And they did not pass through this wall of cement!"

The detective lowered himself to the ground and crawled back along the tunnel, examining the walls. The rats had dug many galleries, but they were nothing more than black holes.

He was nearly halfway back to the trapdoor

beneath the stone house when he shouted to Irène.

She ran forward and dropped to her knees beside him.

"Look!" he cried.

Irène peered through a rat hole and saw twilight ahead. The detective put his mouth to the hole and shouted for help. He called until he was exhausted. But there was no answering cry from the world beyond.

Irène drew the detective aside. "It is nearly night," she said, "there is no one about these streets. It can be only a short distance. I can dig."

Irène went to work on the wall with her stiletto. The earth flew back from the rapid knife thrusts, but it was tedious work and at the end of an hour, though her fingers were raw from tearing away the loosened earth, she had progressed only a short distance.

Duret lapsed into unconsciousness after his violent shouting for help and Irène toiled on alone. She stopped from time to time for a brief rest, and during one of these intervals tightened the tourniquet and replaced the sodden bandage on Duret's leg.

At last the wall before her crumbled and the dislodged earth fell outward. A great rush of fresh air nearly overwhelmed Irène. She widened the opening quickly and crawled through.

The sky was lightening in the east and Irène saw that she was in the excavation for a new building that was being erected two blocks from the house on St. Amable Street.

She was free. And with her safety her mind recalled the motive that had led up to this adventure in the tunnel. The primitive tourniquet and bandage she had wrapped around Duret's wound would not stanch the flow of blood much longer. She had only to abandon him and her vengeance would be complete.

Strangely enough, the thought gave Irène little satisfaction. Some subtle change had come over her in those first moments of terror in the tunnel. She recalled suddenly the throb of joy that had pulsed through her when she felt the feeble stirring of life in Duret's wrist when she had believed him dead.

Her mind reverted across the years to that night in the East End flat. For the first time she saw clearly the inevitability of the whole affair. Duret, her father, and her mother, all toys of the same malignant fate. Her father wrought up to insane resistance by the hysterical fears of her mother. Duret, entering the house to make a simple arrest, suddenly struck upon the head and seized in a death grip. With amazing clarity she saw the ruin the lust for vengeance had made of her own life. And now that it lay within the hollow of her hand, what an empty mockery that vengeance was.

Irène dropped slowly to her knees and crawled back through the hole. She tried to rouse Duret. Failing this, she began to drag him through the narrow passage. The pain of movement, or the rush of fresh air to his lungs, aroused the detective to consciousness as Irène drew him clear of the hole.

Duret looked about him in surprise. His eyes turned up to look deep into Irène's. Her gaze dropped.

"You came back for me," he said tenderly. His tone changed. "Listen, go to the cellar. And go with caution. See if Le Loup is there. Put on a coat to cover your torn dress, then come back to me."

Irène ran up the ramp to the sidewalk and went swiftly to the hideout. She climbed the stairs and procured a coat and flashlight from her room. Back downstairs, she crept into the cellar. She saw Le Loup doubled over the lever by the trapdoor, the handle of his own great knife protruding from his stomach.

Irène ran back to Duret. The detective seemed surprised, and smiled at her return.

"He is dead!" she said quietly.

The detective nodded. He lifted his eyes whimsically. "Now tell me, why did you do that thing to me?"

She flushed and turned away.

"And why did you later save my life?" he added.

Irène laughed harshly. Words surged from her heart and she told him of her band of thieves. She told him, too, of her identity, of the pinch of snuff, and of her plot to kill him.

"Then why did you not let me bleed to death?" Duret demanded.

"Ah, give me no credit for that. Alone I would have gone mad in that place!"

"Why did you wander off from your father's room that night?" Duret asked.

She shrugged her shoulders. "My mother was dead; my father was dead; the police took away my two baby sisters, and I was afraid they would come back and take me. I went far that night. I was in St. Henri shivering on a corner when a crippled beggar came upon me. He took me to his cellar. Later this beggar told me it was a detective named Duret who had shot my father. I swore to kill this Duret."

Duret's face blazed with anger. "This beggar, what did he want of you?"

"Nothing. He was kind to me. He provided me with food, shelter, and clothes, and he taught me the tricks of the underworld. I cooked for him. He was old, and I relieved his loneliness."

"He did you an awful wrong!" Duret said fiercely. "There is a pencil and notebook in my pocket. Thank you."

Duret wrote rapidly. "Go now to the hotel in the market-place and telephone for help to be sent me. Then go to this address. There you will find your father and your sisters. He was not killed, but dangerously wounded that night. . . ."

A convulsive sob shook Irène. She cried, "Papa! Papa!" and swayed upon her feet.

Duret looked alarmed. "Get help for me quickly!" he said in a sharp voice. Irène steadied, and Duret continued. "Later, we found your father steady work; he is well and prosperous. We combed the city for you at that time, but your beggar had hid you well!

"Stay with your father and say nothing of this business. The police will not question you. My report will deal only with the snuff factory and the cellar. Later I shall come to see you and we may discuss your future. Now leave me and send help quickly. I am weak and tired."

"And you mean, Duret, that you do not arrest me?"

Duret smiled whimsically. "Arrest you over a trifling pinch of snuff? Hardly!"

Killer in the Rain
Raymond Chandler

THE FOURTH SHORT STORY published by Raymond Chandler (1889–1959), "Killer in the Rain" was never reprinted during his lifetime. As with "Curtain," which had its magazine appearance the following year, Chandler had "cannibalized" the story for his first novel, *The Big Sleep*. Six characters and much of eleven chapters in the novel were lifted in whole or in part from "Killer in the Rain," generally being fleshed out to provide more fully developed characters.

Names were changed. None of Chandler's short stories featured Philip Marlowe, the hero of all seven of his novels, though whether named Carmody, Dalmas, Malvern, Mallory, or unnamed, as in the present story, they were interchangeable with his famous creation.

The wild young woman who is the catalyst for all that transpires in both the novel and this story is named Carmen Dravec here, but she is Carmen Sternwood in *The Big Sleep*. Drug-addicted, alcoholic, perhaps a bit dim, almost certainly a sociopath, the beautiful Carmen was played by the now-forgotten Martha Vickers in the 1946 Warner Bros. movie that starred Humphrey Bogart as Marlowe. The novel added a sister who tried to protect the reputation of her younger sibling by getting the detective to end his investigation.

"Killer in the Rain" was originally published as a novelette in the January 1935 issue of *Black Mask*.

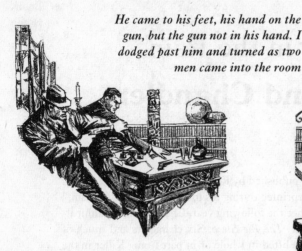

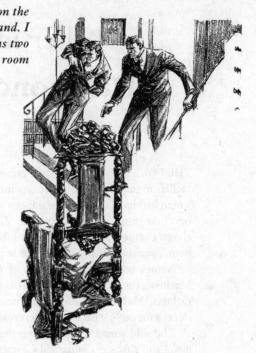

He came to his feet, his hand on the gun, but the gun not in his hand. I dodged past him and turned as two men came into the room

Killer in the Rain

Raymond Chandler

I

E WERE SITTING in a room at the Berglund. I was on the side of the bed, and Dravec was in the easy chair. It was my room.

Rain beat very hard against the windows. They were shut tight and it was hot in the room and I had a little fan going on the table. The breeze from it hit Dravec's face high up, lifted his heavy black hair, moved the longer bristles in the fat path of eyebrow that went across his face in a solid line. He looked like a bouncer who had come into money.

He showed me some of his gold teeth and said:

"What you got on me?"

He said it importantly, as if anyone who knew anything would know quite a lot about him.

"Nothing," I said. "You're clean, as far as I know."

He lifted a large hairy hand and stared at it solidly for a minute.

"You don't get me. A feller named M'Gee sent me here. Violets M'Gee."

"Fine. How is Violets these days?" Violets M'Gee was a homicide dick in the sheriff's office.

He looked at his large hand and frowned. "No—you still don't get it. I got a job for you."

"I don't go out much any more," I said. "I'm getting kind of frail."

He looked around the room carefully, bluffing a bit, like a man not naturally observant.

"Maybe it's money," he said.

"Maybe it is," I said.

He had a belted suede raincoat on. He tore it open carelessly and got out a wallet that was not quite as big as a bale of hay. Currency stuck out of it at careless angles. When he slapped it down on his knee it made a fat sound that was pleasant to the ear. He shook money out of it, selected a few bills from the bunch, stuffed the rest back, dropped the wallet on the floor and let it lie, arranged five century notes like a tight poker hand and put them under the base of the fan on the table.

That was a lot of work. It made him grunt.

"I got lots of sugar," he said.

"So I see. What do I do for that, if I get it?"

"You know me now, huh?"

"A little better."

I got an envelope out of an inside pocket and read to him loud from some scribbling on the back.

"Dravec, Anton or Tony. Former Pittsburgh steelworker, truck guard, all-round muscle stiff. Made a wrong pass and got shut up. Left town, came West. Worked on an avocado ranch at El Seguro. Came up with a ranch of his own. Sat right on the dome when the El Seguro oil boom burst. Got rich. Lost a lot of it buying into other people's dusters. Still has enough. Serbian by birth, six feet, two hundred and forty, one daughter, never known to have had a wife. No police record of any consequence. None at all since Pittsburgh."

I lit a pipe.

"Jeeze," he said. "Where you promote all that?"

"Connections. What's the angle?"

He picked the wallet off the floor and moused around inside it with a couple of square fingers for a while, with his tongue sticking out between his thick lips. He finally got out a slim brown card and some crumpled slips of paper. He pushed them at me.

The card was in gold type, very delicately done. It said: "Mr. Harold Hardwicke Steiner," and very small in the corner, "Rare Books and De Luxe Editions." No address or phone number.

The white slips, three in number, were simple I.O.U.s for a thousand dollars each, signed: "Carmen Dravec" in a sprawling, moronic handwriting.

I gave it all back to him and said: "Blackmail?"

He shook his head slowly and something gentle came into his face that hadn't been there before.

"It's my little girl—Carmen. This Steiner, he bothers her. She goes to his joint all the time, makes whoopee. He makes love to her, I guess. I don't like it."

I nodded. "How about the notes?"

"I don't care nothin' about the dough. She plays games with him. The hell with that. She's what you call man-crazy. You go tell this Steiner to lay off Carmen. I break his neck with my hands. See?"

All this in a rush, with deep breathing. His eyes got small and round, and furious. His teeth almost chattered.

I said: "Why have me tell him? Why not tell him yourself?"

"Maybe I get mad and kill the————!" he yelled.

I picked a match out of my pocket and prodded the loose ash in the bowl of my pipe. I looked at him carefully for a moment, getting hold of an idea.

"Nerts, you're scared to," I told him.

Both big fists came up. He held them shoulder high and shook them, great knots of bone and muscle. He lowered them slowly, heaved a deep honest sigh, and said:

"Yeah. I'm scared to. I dunno how to handle her. All the time some new guy and all the time a punk. A while back I gave a guy called Joe Marty five grand to lay off her. She's still mad at me."

I stared at the window, watched the rain hit it, flatten out, and slide down in a thick wave, like melted gelatine. It was too early in the fall for that kind of rain.

"Giving them sugar doesn't get you anywhere," I said. "You could be doing that all your life. So you figure you'd like to have me get rough with this one, Steiner."

"Tell him I break his neck!"

"I wouldn't bother," I said. "I know Steiner. I'd break his neck for you myself, if it would do any good."

He leaned forward and grabbed my hand. His eyes got childish. A grey tear floated in each of them.

"Listen, M'Gee says you're a good guy. I tell you something I ain't told nobody—ever. Carmen—she's not my kid at all. I just picked her up in Smoky, a little baby in the street. She didn't have nobody. I guess maybe I steal her, huh?"

"Sounds like it," I said, and had to fight to get my hand loose. I rubbed feeling back into it with the other one. The man had a grip that would crack a telephone pole.

"I go straight then," he said grimly, and yet tenderly. "I come out here and make good. She grows up. I love her."

I said: "Uh-huh. That's natural."

"You don't get me. I wanta marry her."

I stared at him.

"She gets older, gets some sense. Maybe she marry me, huh?"

His voice implored me, as if I had the settling of that.

"Ever ask her?"

"I'm scared to," he said humbly.

"She soft on Steiner, do you think?"

He nodded. "But that don't mean nothin'."

I could believe that. I got off the bed, threw a window up and let the rain hit my face for a minute.

"Let's get this straight," I said, lowering the window again and going back to the bed. "I can take Steiner off your back. That's easy. I just don't see what it buys you."

He grabbed for my hand again, but I was a little too quick for him this time.

"You came in here a little tough, flashing your wad," I said. "You're going out soft. Not from anything I've said. You knew it already. I'm not Dorothy Dix, and I'm only partly a prune. But I'll take Steiner off you, if you really want that."

He stood up clumsily, swung his hat and stared down at my feet.

"You take him off my back, like you said. He ain't her sort, anyway."

"It might hurt your back a little."

"That's okay. That's what it's for," he said.

He buttoned himself up, dumped his hat on his big shaggy head, and rolled on out. He shut the door carefully, as if he was going out of a sick-room.

I thought he was as crazy as a pair of waltzing mice, but I liked him.

I put his goldbacks in a safe place, mixed myself a long drink, and sat down in the chair that was still warm from him.

While I played with the drink I wondered if he had any idea what Steiner's racket was.

Steiner had a collection of rare and half-rare smut books which he loaned out as high as ten dollars a day—to the right people.

II

It rained all the next day. Late in the afternoon I sat parked in a blue Chrysler roadster, diagonally across the Boulevard from a narrow store front, over which a green neon sign in script letters said: "H. H. Steiner."

The rain splashed knee-high off the sidewalks, filled the gutters, and big cops in slickers that shone like gun barrels had a lot of fun carrying little girls in silk stockings and cute little rubber boots across the bad places, with a lot of squeezing.

The rain drummed on the hood of the Chrysler, beat and tore at the taut material of the top, leaked in at the buttoned places, and made a pool on the floorboards for me to keep my feet in.

I had a big flask of Scotch with me. I used it often enough to keep interested.

Steiner did business, even in that weather; perhaps especially in that weather. Very nice cars stopped in front of his store, and very nice people dodged in, then dodged out again with wrapped parcels under their arms. Of course they could have been buying rare books and de luxe editions.

At five-thirty a pimply-faced kid in a leather windbreaker came out of the store and sloped up the side street at a fast trot. He came back with a neat cream-and-grey coupé. Steiner came out and got into the coupé. He wore a dark green leather raincoat, a cigarette in an amber holder, no hat. I couldn't see his glass eye at that distance but I knew he had one. The kid in the windbreaker held an umbrella over him across the sidewalk, then shut it up and handed it into the coupé.

Steiner drove west on the Boulevard. I drove west on the Boulevard. Past the business district, at Pepper Canyon, he turned north, and I tailed him easily from a block back. I was pretty sure he was going home, which was natural.

He left Pepper Drive and took a curving ribbon of wet cement called La Verne Terrace, climbed up it almost to the top. It was a narrow road with a high bank on one side and a few well-spaced cabin-like houses built down the steep slope on the other side. Their roofs were not much above road level. The fronts of them were masked by shrubs. Sodden trees dripped all over the landscape.

Steiner's hideaway had a square box hedge in front of it, more than window-high. The entrance was a sort of maze, and the house door was not visible from the road. Steiner put his grey-and-cream coupé in a small garage, locked up, went through the maze with his umbrella up, and light went on in the house.

While he was doing this I had passed him and gone to the top of the hill. I turned around there and went back and parked in front of the next house above his. It seemed to be closed up or empty, but had no signs on it. I went into a conference with my flask of Scotch, and then just sat.

At six-fifteen lights bobbed up the hill. It was quite dark by then. A car stopped in front of Steiner's hedge. A slim, tall girl in a slicker got out of it. Enough light filtered out through the hedge for me to see that she was dark-haired and possibly pretty.

Voices drifted on the rain and a door shut. I got out of the Chrysler and strolled down the hill, put a pencil flash into the car. It was a dark maroon or brown Packard convertible. Its license read to Carmen Dravec, 3596 Lucerene Avenue. I went back to my heap.

A solid, slow-moving hour crawled by. No more cars came up or down the hill. It seemed to be a very quiet neighborhood.

Then a single flash of hard white light leaked out of Steiner's house, like a flash of summer lightning. As the darkness fell again a thin tinkling scream trickled down the darkness and echoed faintly among the wet trees. I was out of the Chrysler and on my way before the last echo of it died.

There was no fear in the scream. It held the note of a half-pleasurable shock, an accent of drunkenness, and a touch of pure idiocy.

The Steiner mansion was perfectly silent when I hit the gap in the hedge, dodged around the elbow that masked the front door, and put my hand up to bang on the door.

At that exact moment, as if somebody had been waiting for it, three shots racketed close together behind the door. After that there was a long, harsh sigh, a soft thump, rapid steps, going away into the back of the house.

I wasted time hitting the door with my shoulder, without enough start. It threw me back like a kick from an army mule.

The door fronted on a narrow runway, like a small bridge, that led from the banked road. There was no side porch, no way to get at the windows in a hurry. There was no way around to the back except through the house or up a long flight of wooden steps that went up to the back door from the alley-like street below. On these steps I now heard a clatter of feet.

That gave me the impulse and I hit the door

again, from the feet up. It gave at the lock and I pitched down two steps into a big, dim, cluttered room. I didn't see much of what was in the room then. I wandered through to the back of the house.

I was pretty sure there was death in it.

A car throbbed in the street below as I reached the back porch. The car went away fast, without lights. That was that. I went back to the living-room.

III

That room reached all the way across the front of the house and had a low, beamed ceiling, walls painted brown. Strips of tapestry hung all around the walls. Books filled low shelves. There was a thick, pinkish rug on which some light fell from two standing lamps with pale green shades. In the middle of the rug there was a big, low desk and a black chair with a yellow satin cushion at it. There were books all over the desk.

On a sort of dais near one end wall there was a teakwood chair with arms and a high back. A dark-haired girl was sitting in the chair, on a fringed red shawl.

She sat very straight, with her hands on the arms of the chair, her knees close together, her body stiffly erect, her chin level. Her eyes were wide open and mad and had no pupils.

She looked unconscious of what was going on, but she didn't have the pose of unconsciousness. She had a pose as if she was doing something very important and making a lot of it.

Out of her mouth came a tinny chuckling noise, which didn't change her expression or move her lips. She didn't seem to see me at all.

She was wearing a pair of long jade ear-rings, and apart from those she was stark naked.

I looked away from her to the other end of the room.

Steiner was on his back on the floor, just beyond the edge of the pink rug, and in front of a thing that looked like a small totem pole. It had a round open mouth in which the lens of a camera showed. The lens seemed to be aimed at the girl in the teakwood chair.

There was a flash-bulb apparatus on the floor beside Steiner's out-flung hand in a loose silk sleeve. The cord of the flash-bulb went behind the totem pole thing.

Steiner was wearing Chinese slippers with thick white felt soles. His legs were in black satin pyjamas and the upper part of him in an embroidered Chinese coat. The front of it was mostly blood. His glass eye shone brightly and was the most lifelike thing about him. At a glance none of the three shots had missed.

The flash-bulb was the sheet lightning I had seen leak out of the house and the half-giggling scream was the doped and naked girl's reaction to that. The three shots had been somebody else's idea of how the proceedings ought to be punctuated. Presumably the idea of the lad who had gone very fast down the back steps.

I could see something in his point of view. At that stage I thought it was a good idea to shut the front door and fasten it with the short chain that was on it. The lock had been spoiled by my violent entrance.

A couple of thin purple glasses stood on a red lacquer tray on one end of the desk. Also a pot-bellied flagon of something brown. The glasses smelled of ether and laudanum, a mixture I had never tried, but it seemed to fit the scene pretty well.

I found the girl's clothes on a divan in the corner, picked up a brown, sleeved dress to begin with, and went over to her. She smelled of ether also, at a distance of several feet.

The tinny chuckling was still going on and a little froth was oozing down her chin. I slapped her face, not very hard. I didn't want to bring her out of whatever kind of trance she was in, into a screaming fit.

"Come on," I said brightly. "Let's be nice. Let's get dressed."

She said: "G-g-go—ter—ell," without any emotion that I could notice.

I slapped her a little more. She didn't mind

the slaps, so I went to work getting the dress on her.

She didn't mind the dress either. She let me hold her arms up but she spread her fingers wide, as if that was very cute. It made me do a lot of finagling with the sleeves. I finally got the dress on. I got her stockings on, and her shoes, and then got her up on her feet.

"Let's take a little walk," I said. "Let's take a nice little walk."

We walked. Part of the time her ear-rings banged against my chest and part of the time we looked like a couple of adagio dancers doing the splits. We walked over to Steiner's body and back. She didn't pay any attention to Steiner and his bright glass eye.

She found it amusing that she couldn't walk and tried to tell me about it, but only bubbled. I put her on the divan while I wadded her underclothes up and shoved them into a deep pocket of my raincoat, put her handbag in my other deep pocket. I went through Steiner's desk and found a little blue notebook written in code that looked interesting. I put that in my pocket, too.

Then I tried to get at the back of the camera in the totem pole, to get the plate, but couldn't find the catch right away. I was getting nervous, and I figured I could build up a better excuse if I ran into the law when I came back later to look for it than any reason I could give if caught there now.

I went back to the girl and got her slicker on her, nosed around to see if anything else of hers was there, wiped away a lot of fingerprints I probably hadn't made, and at least some of those Miss Dravec must have made. I opened the door and put out both the lamps.

I got my left arm around her again and we struggled out into the rain and piled into her Packard. I didn't like leaving my own bus there very well, but that had to be. Her keys were in her car. We drifted off down the hill.

Nothing happened on the way to Lucerne Avenue except that Carmen stopped bubbling and giggling and went to snoring. I couldn't keep

her head off my shoulder. It was all I could do to keep it out of my lap. I had to drive rather slowly and it was a long way anyhow, clear over to the west edge of the city.

The Dravec home was a large old-fashioned brick house in large grounds with a wall around them. A grey composition driveway went through iron gates and up a slope past flower-beds and lawns to a big front door with narrow leaded panels on each side of it. There was dim light behind the panels as if nobody much was home.

I pushed Carmen's head into the corner and shed her belongings in the seat, and got out.

A maid opened the door. She said Mister Dravec wasn't in and she didn't know where he was. Downtown somewhere. She had a long, yellowish, gentle face, a long nose, no chin and large wet eyes. She looked like a nice old horse that had been turned out to pasture after long service, and as if she would do the right thing by Carmen.

I pointed into the Packard and growled: "Better get her to bed. She's lucky we don't throw her in the can—drivin' around with a tool like that on her."

She smiled sadly and I went away.

I had to walk five blocks in the rain before a narrow apartment house let me into its lobby to use a phone. Then I had to wait another twenty-five minutes for a taxi. While I waited I began to worry about what I hadn't completed.

I had yet to get the used plate out of Steiner's camera.

IV

I paid the taxi off on Pepper Drive, in front of a house where there was company, and walked back up the curving hill of La Verne Terrace to Steiner's house behind its shrubbery.

Nothing looked any different. I went in through the gap in the hedge, pushed the door open gently, and smelled cigarette smoke.

It hadn't been there before. There had been a complicated set of smells, including the sharp memory of smokeless powder. But cigarette smoke hadn't stood out from the mixture.

I closed the door and slipped down on one knee and listened, holding my breath. I didn't hear anything but the sound of the rain on the roof. I tried throwing the beam of my pencil flash along the floor. Nobody shot at me.

I straightened up, found the dangling tassel of one of the lamps and made light in the room.

The first thing I noticed was that a couple of strips of tapestry were gone from the wall. I hadn't counted them, but the spaces where they had hung caught my eye.

Then I saw Steiner's body was gone from in front of the totem pole thing with the camera eye in its mouth. On the floor below, beyond the margin of the pink rug, somebody had spread down a rug over the place where Steiner's body had been. I didn't have to lift the rug to know why it had been put there.

I lit a cigarette and stood there in the middle of the dimly lighted room and thought about it. After a while I went to the camera in the totem pole. I found the catch this time. There wasn't any plate-holder in the camera.

My hand went towards the mulberry-colored phone on Steiner's low desk, but didn't take hold of it.

I crossed into the little hallway beyond the living-room and poked into a fussy-looking bedroom that looked like a woman's room more than a man's. The bed had a long cover with a flounced edge. I lifted that and shot my flash under the bed.

Steiner wasn't under the bed. He wasn't anywhere in the house. Somebody had taken him away. He couldn't very well have gone by himself.

It wasn't the law, or somebody would have been there still. It was only an hour and a half since Carmen and I left the place. And there was none of the mess police photographers and fingerprint men would have made.

I went back to the living-room, pushed the flash-bulb apparatus around the back of the totem pole with my foot, switched off the lamp, left the house, got into my rain-soaked car and choked it to life.

It was all right with me if somebody wanted to keep the Steiner kill hush-hush for a while. It gave me a chance to find out whether I could tell it leaving Carmen Dravec and the nude photo angle out.

It was after ten when I got back to the Berglund and put my heap away and went upstairs to the apartment. I stood under a shower, then put pajamas on and mixed up a batch of hot grog. I looked at the phone a couple of times, thought about calling to see if Dravec was home yet, thought it might be a good idea to let him alone until the next day.

I filled a pipe and sat down with my hot grog and Steiner's little blue notebook. It was in code, but the arrangement of the entries and the indented leaves made it a list of names and addresses. There were over four hundred and fifty of them. If this was Steiner's sucker list, he had a gold mine—quite apart from the blackmail angles.

Any name on the list might be a prospect as the killer. I didn't envy the cops their job when it was handed to them.

I drank too much whiskey trying to crack the code. About midnight I went to bed, and dreamed about a man in a Chinese coat with blood all over the front who chased a naked girl with long jade ear-rings while I tried to photograph the scene with a camera that didn't have any plate in it.

V

Violets M'Gee called me up in the morning, before I was dressed, but after I had seen the paper and not found anything about Steiner in it. His voice had the cheerful sound of a man who had slept well and didn't owe too much money.

"Well, how's the boy?" he began.

I said I was all right except that I was having a little trouble with my Third Reader. He laughed a little absently, and then his voice got too casual.

"This guy Dravec that I sent over to see you—done anything for him yet?"

"Too much rain," I answered, if that was an answer.

"Uh-huh. He seems to be a guy that things happen to. A car belongin' to him is washin' about in the surf off Lido fish pier."

I didn't say anything. I held the telephone very tightly.

"Yeah," M'Gee went on cheerfully. "A nice new Cad all messed up with sand and seawater . . . Oh, I forgot. There's a guy inside it."

I let my breath out slowly, very slowly. "Dravec?" I whispered.

"Naw. A young kid. I ain't told Dravec yet. It's under the fedora. Wanta run down and look at it with me?"

I said I would like to do that.

"Snap it up. I'll be in my hutch," M'Gee told me and hung up.

Shaved, dressed and lightly breakfasted I was at the County Building in half an hour or so. I found M'Gee staring at a yellow wall and sitting at a little yellow desk on which there was nothing but M'Gee's hat and one of the M'Gee feet. He took both of them off the desk and we went down to the official parking lot and got into a small black sedan.

The rain had stopped during the night and the morning was all blue and gold. There was enough snap in the air to make life simple and sweet, if you didn't have too much on your mind. I had.

It was thirty miles to Lido, the first ten of them through city traffic. M'Gee made it in three-quarters of an hour. At the end of that time we skidded to a stop in front of a stucco arch beyond which a long black pier extended. I took my feet out of the floorboards and we got out.

There were a few cars and people in front of the arch. A motor-cycle officer was keeping the people off the pier. M'Gee showed him a bronze star and we went out along the pier, into a loud smell that even two days' rain had failed to wash away.

"There she is—on the tug," M'Gee said.

A low black tug crouched off the end of the pier. Something large and green and nickeled was on its deck in front of the wheelhouse. Men stood around it.

We went down slimy steps to the deck of the tug.

M'Gee said hello to a deputy in green khaki and another man in plain-clothes. The tug crew of three moved over to the wheelhouse, and set their backs against it, watching us.

We looked at the car. The front bumper was bent, and one headlight and the radiator shell. The paint and the nickel were scratched up by sand and the upholstery was sodden and black. Otherwise the car wasn't much the worse for wear. It was a big job in two tones of green, with a wine-colored stripe and trimming.

M'Gee and I looked into the front part of it. A slim, dark-haired kid who had been good-looking was draped around the steering post, with his head at a peculiar angle to the rest of his body. His face was bluish-white. His eyes were a faint dull gleam under the lowered lids. His open mouth had sand in it. There were traces of blood on the side of his head which the sea-water hadn't quite washed away.

M'Gee backed away slowly, made a noise in his throat and began to chew on a couple of the violet-scented breath purifiers that gave him his nickname.

"What's the story?" he asked quietly.

The uniformed deputy pointed up to the end of the pier. Dirty white railings made of two-by-fours had been broken through in a wide space and the broken wood showed up yellow and bright.

"Went through there. Must have hit pretty hard, too. The rain stopped early down here, about nine, and the broken wood is dry inside. That puts it after the rain stopped. That's all we know except she fell in plenty of water not to be banged up worse; at least half-tide, I'd say. That would be right after the rain stopped. She showed under the water when the boys came down to fish this morning. We got the tug to lift her out. Then we find the dead guy."

The other deputy scuffed at the deck with the toe of his shoe. M'Gee looked sideways at me with foxy little eyes. I looked blank and didn't say anything.

"Pretty drunk that lad," M'Gee said gently. "Showin' off all alone in the rain. I guess he must have been fond of driving. Yeah—pretty drunk."

"Drunk, hell," the plain-clothes deputy said. "The hand throttle's set half-way down and the guy's been sapped on the side of the head. Ask me and I'll call it murder."

M'Gee looked at him politely, then at the uniformed man. "What you think?"

"It could be suicide, I guess. His neck's broke and he could have hurt his head in the fall. And his hand could have knocked the throttle down. I kind of like murder myself, though."

M'Gee nodded, said: "Frisked him? Know who he is?"

The two deputies looked at me, then at the tug crew.

"Okay. Save that part," M'Gee said. "I *know* who he is."

A small man with glasses and a tired face and a black bag came slowly along the pier and down the slimy steps. He picked out a fairly clean place on the deck and put his bag down. He took his hat off and rubbed the back of his neck and smiled wearily.

" 'Lo, Doc. There's your patient," M'Gee told him. "Took a dive off the pier last night. That's all we know now."

The medical examiner looked in at the dead man morosely. He fingered the head, moved it around a little, felt the man's ribs. He lifted one lax hand and stared at the fingernails. He let it fall, stepped back and picked his bag up again.

"About twelve hours," he said. "Broken neck, of course. I doubt if there's any water in him. Better get him out of there before he starts to get stiff on us. I'll tell you the rest when I get him on a table."

He nodded around, went back up the steps and along the pier. An ambulance was backing into position beside the stucco arch at the pier head.

The two deputies grunted and tugged to get the dead man out of the car and lay him down on the deck, on the side of the car away from the beach.

"Let's go," M'Gee told me. "That ends this part of the show."

We said good-bye and M'Gee told the deputies to keep their chins buttoned until they heard from him. We went back along the pier and got into the small black sedan and drove back towards the city along a white highway washed clean by the rain, past low rolling hills of yellow-white sand terraced with moss. A few gulls wheeled and swooped over something in the surf. Far out to sea a couple of white yachts on the horizon looked as if they were suspended in the sky.

We laid a few miles behind us without saying anything to each other. Then M'Gee cocked his chin at me and said:

"Got ideas?"

"Loosen up," I said. "I never saw the guy before. Who is he?"

"Hell, I thought you was going to tell me about it."

"Loosen up, Violets," I said.

He growled, shrugged, and we nearly went off the road into the loose sand.

"Dravec's chauffeur. A kid named Carl Owen. How do I know? We had him in the cooler a year ago on a Mann Act rap. He run Dravec's hotcha daughter off to Yuma. Dravec went after them and brought them back and had the guy heaved in the goldfish bowl. Then the girl gets to him, and next morning the old man steams downtown and begs the guy off. Says the kid meant to marry her, only she wouldn't. Then, by heck, the kid goes back to work for him and been there ever since. What you think of that?"

"It sounds just like Dravec," I said.

"Yeah—but the kid could have had a relapse."

M'Gee had silvery hair and a knobby chin and a little pouting mouth made to kiss babies with. I looked at his face sideways, and suddenly I got his idea. I laughed.

"You think maybe Dravec killed him?" I asked.

"Why not? The kid makes another pass at the

girl and Dravec cracks down at him too hard. He's a big guy and could break a neck easy. Then he's scared. He runs the car down to Lido in the rain and lets it slide off the end of the pier. Thinks it won't show. Maybe don't think at all. Just rattled."

"It's a kick in the pants," I said. "Then all he had to do was walk home thirty miles in the rain."

"Go on. Kid me."

"Dravec killed him, sure," I said. "But they were playing leap-frog. Dravec fell on him."

"Okay, pal. Some day you'll want to play with *my* catnip mouse."

"Listen, Violets," I said seriously. "If the kid was murdered—and you're not sure it's murder at all—it's not Dravec's kind of crime. He might kill a man in a temper—but he'd let him lay. He wouldn't go to all that fuss."

We shuttled back and forth across the road while M'Gee thought about that.

"What a pal," he complained. "I have me a swell theory and look what you done to it. I wish the hell I hadn't brought you. Hell with you. I'm goin' after Dravec just the same."

"Sure," I agreed. "You'd have to do that. But Dravec never killed that boy. He's too soft inside to cover up on it."

It was noon when we got back to town. I hadn't had any dinner but whiskey the night before and very little breakfast that morning. I got off on the Boulevard and let M'Gee go on alone to see Dravec.

I was interested in what had happened to Carl Owen; but I wasn't interested in the thought that Dravec might have murdered him.

I ate lunch at a counter and looked casually at an early afternoon paper. I didn't expect to see anything about Steiner in it, and I didn't.

After lunch I walked along the Boulevard six blocks to have a look at Steiner's store.

VI

It was a half-store frontage, the other half being occupied by a credit jeweler. The jeweler was

standing in his entrance, a big, white-haired, black-eyed Jew with about nine carats of diamond on his hand. A faint, knowing smile curved his lips as I went past him into Steiner's.

A thick blue rug paved Steiner's from wall to wall. There were blue leather easy-chairs with smoke stands beside them. A few sets of tooled leather books were put out on narrow tables. The rest of the stock was behind glass. A paneled partition with a single door in it cut off a back part of the store, and in the corner by this a woman sat behind a small desk with a hooded lamp on it.

She got up and came towards me, swinging lean thighs in a tight dress of some black material that didn't reflect any light. She was an ash-blonde, with greenish eyes under heavily mascaraed lashes. There were large jet buttons in the lobes of her ears; her hair waved back smoothly from behind them. Her fingernails were silvered.

She gave me what she thought was a smile of welcome, but what I thought was a grimace of strain.

"Was it something?"

I pulled my hat low over my eyes and fidgeted. I said:

"Steiner?"

"He won't be in today. May I show you—"

"I'm selling," I said. "Something he's wanted for a long time."

The silvered fingernails touched the hair over one ear. "Oh, a salesman . . . Well, you might come in tomorrow."

"He sick? I could go up to the house," I suggested hopefully. "He'd want to see what I have."

That jarred her. She had to fight for her breath for a minute. But her voice was smooth enough when it came.

"That—that wouldn't be any use. He's out of town today."

I nodded, looked properly disappointed, touched my hat and started to turn away when the pimply-faced kid of the night before stuck his head through the door in the paneling. He went back as soon as he saw me, but not before I saw some loosely packed cases of books behind him on the floor of the back room.

The cases were small and open and packed any old way. A man in very new overalls was fussing with them. Some of Steiner's stock was being moved out.

I left the store and walked down to the corner, then back to the alley. Behind Steiner's stood a small black truck with wire sides. It didn't have any lettering on it. Boxes showed through the wire sides and, as I watched, the man in overalls came out with another one and heaved it up.

I went back to the Boulevard. Half a block on, a fresh-faced kid was reading a magazine in a parked Green Top. I showed him money and said:

"Tail job?"

He looked me over, swung his door open, and stuck his magazine behind the rear-vision mirror.

"My meat, boss," he said brightly.

We went around to the end of the alley and waited beside a fire-plug.

There were about a dozen boxes on the truck when the man in the very new overalls got up in front and gunned his motor. He went down the alley fast and turned left on the street at the end. My driver did the same. The truck went north to Garfield, then east. It went very fast and there was a lot of traffic on Garfield. My driver tailed from too far back.

I was telling him about that when the truck turned north off Garfield again. The street at which it turned was called Brittany. When we got to Brittany there wasn't any truck.

The fresh-faced kid who was driving me made comforting sounds through the glass panel of the cab and we went up Brittany at four miles an hour looking for the truck behind bushes. I refused to be comforted.

Brittany bore a little to the east two blocks up and met the next street, Randall Place, in a tongue of land on which there was a white apartment house with its front on Randall Place and its basement garage entrance on Brittany, a story lower. We were going past that and my driver

was telling me the truck couldn't be very far away when I saw it in the garage.

We went around to the front of the apartment house and I got out and went into the lobby.

There was no switchboard. A desk was pushed back against the wall, as if it wasn't used any more. Above it names were on a panel of gilt mail-boxes.

The name that went with Apartment 405 was Joseph Marty. Joe Marty was the name of the man who played with Carmen Dravec until her papa gave him five thousand dollars to go away and play with some other girl. It could be the same Joe Marty.

I went down steps and pushed through a door with a wired glass panel into the dimness of the garage. The man in the very new overalls was stacking boxes in the automatic elevator.

I stood near him and lit a cigarette and watched him. He didn't like it very well, but he didn't say anything. After a while I said:

"Watch the weight, buddy. She's only tested for half a ton. Where's it goin'?"

"Marty, four-o-five," he said, and then looked as if he was sorry he had said it.

"Fine," I told him. "It looks like a nice lot of reading."

I went back up the steps and out of the building, got into my Green Top again.

We drove back downtown to the building where I have an office. I gave the driver too much money and he gave me a dirty card which I dropped into the brass spittoon beside the elevators.

Dravec was holding up the wall outside the door of my office.

VII

After the rain, it was warm and bright but he still had the belted suede raincoat on. It was open down the front, as were his coat, and vest underneath. His tie was under one ear. His face looked like a mask of grey putty with a black stubble on the lower part of it.

He looked awful.

I unlocked the door and patted his shoulder and pushed him in and got him into a chair. He breathed hard but didn't say anything. I got a bottle of rye out of the desk and poured a couple of ponies. He drank both of them without a word. Then he slumped in the chair and blinked his eyes and groaned and took a square white envelope out of an inner pocket. He put it down on the desk top and held his big hairy hand over it.

"Tough about Carl," I said. "I was with M'Gee this morning."

He looked at me emptily. After a little while he said:

"Yeah. Carl was a good kid. I ain't told you about him much."

I waited, looking at the envelope under his hand. He looked down at it himself.

"I gotta let you see it," he mumbled. He pushed it slowly across the desk and lifted his hand off it as if with the movement he was giving up most everything that made life worth living. Two tears welled up in his eyes and slid down his unshaven cheeks.

I lifted the square envelope and looked at it. It was addressed to him at his house, in neat pen-and-ink printing, and bore a Special Delivery stamp. I opened it and looked at the shiny photograph that was inside.

Carmen Dravec sat in Steiner's teakwood chair, wearing her jade earrings. Her eyes looked crazier, if anything, than as I had seen them. I looked at the back of the photo, saw that it was blank, and put the thing face down on my desk.

"Tell me about it," I said carefully.

Dravec wiped the tears off his face with his sleeve, put his hands flat on the desk and stared down at the dirty nails. His fingers trembled on the desk.

"A guy called me," he said in a dead voice. "Ten grand for the plate and the prints. The deal's got to be closed tonight, or they give the stuff to some scandal sheet."

"That's a lot of hooey," I said. "A scandal sheet couldn't use it, except to back up a story. What's the story?"

He lifted his eyes slowly, as if they were very heavy. "That ain't all. The guy says there's a jam to it. I better come through fast, or I'd find my girl in the cooler."

"What's the story?" I asked again, filling my pipe. "What does Carmen say?"

He shook his big shaggy head. "I ain't asked her. I ain't got the heart. Poor little girl. No clothes on her . . . No, I ain't got the heart. . . . You ain't done nothin' on Steiner yet, I guess."

"I didn't have to," I told him. "Somebody beat me to it."

He stared at me open-mouthed, uncomprehending. It was obvious he knew nothing about the night before.

"Did Carmen go out at all last night?" I asked carelessly.

He was still staring with his mouth open, groping in his mind.

"No. She's sick. She's sick in bed when I get home. She don't go out at all. . . . What you mean—about Steiner?"

I reached for the bottle of rye and poured us each a drink. Then I lit my pipe.

"Steiner's dead," I said. "Somebody got tired of his tricks and shot him full of holes. Last night, in the rain."

"Jeeze," he said wonderingly. "You was there?"

I shook my head. "Not me. Carmen was there. That's the jam your man spoke of. She didn't do the shooting, of course."

Dravec's face got red and angry. He balled his fists. His breath made a harsh sound and a pulse beat visibly in the side of his neck.

"That ain't true! She's sick. She don't go out at all. She's sick in bed when I get home!"

"You told me that," I said. "That's not true. I brought Carmen home myself. The maid knows, only she's trying to be decent about it. Carmen was at Steiner's house and I was watching outside. A gun went off and someone ran away. I didn't see him. Carmen was too drunk to see him. That's why she's sick."

His eyes tried to focus on my face, but they were vague and empty, as if the light behind them had died. He took hold of the arms of the chair. His big knuckles strained and got white.

"She don't tell me," he whispered. "She don't tell me. Me, that would do anything for her." There was no emotion in his voice; just the dead exhaustion of despair.

He pushed his chair back a little. "I go get the dough," he said. "The ten grand. Maybe the guy don't talk."

Then he broke. His big rough head came down on the desk and sobs shook his whole body. I stood up and went around the desk and patted his shoulder, kept on patting it, not saying anything. After a while he lifted his face smeared with tears and grabbed for my hand.

"Jeeze, you're a good guy," he sobbed.

"You don't know the half of it."

I pulled my hand away from him and got a drink into his paw, helped him lift it and down it. Then I took the empty glass out of his hand and put it back on the desk. I sat down again.

"You've got to brace up," I told him grimly. "The law doesn't know about Steiner yet. I brought Carmen home and kept my mouth shut. I wanted to give you and Carmen a break. That puts me in a jam. You've got to do your part."

He nodded slowly, heavily. "Yeah, I do what you say—anything you say."

"Get the money," I said. "Have it ready for the call. I've got ideas and you may not have to use it. But it's no time to get foxy. . . . Get the money and sit tight and keep your mouth shut. Leave the rest to me. Can you do that?"

"Yeah," he said. "Jeeze, you're a good guy."

"Don't talk to Carmen," I said. "The less she remembers out of her drunk, the better. This picture—" I touched the back of the photo on the desk, "—shows somebody was working with Steiner. We've got to get him and get him quick—even if it costs ten grand to do it."

He stood up slowly. "That's nothin'. That's just dough. I go get it now. Then I go home. You do it like you want to. Me, I do just like you say."

He grabbed for my hand again, shook it, and went slowly out of the office. I heard his heavy steps drag down the hall.

I drank a couple of drinks fast and mopped my face.

VIII

I drove my Chrysler slowly up La Verne Terrace towards Steiner's house.

In the daylight, I could see the steep drop of the hill and the flight of wooden steps down which the killer had made his escape. The street below was almost as narrow as an alley. Two small houses fronted on it, not very near Steiner's place. With the noise the rain had been making, it was doubtful if anyone in them had paid much attention to the shots.

Steiner's looked peaceful under the afternoon sun. The unpainted shingles of the roof were still damp from the rain. The trees on the other side of the street had new leaves on them. There were no cars on the street.

Something moved behind the square growth of box hedge that screened Steiner's front door.

Carmen Dravec, in a green and white checkered coat and no hat, came out through the opening, stopped suddenly, looked at me wild-eyed, as if she hadn't heard the car. She went back quickly behind the hedge. I drove on and parked in front of the empty house.

I got out and walked back. In the sunlight it felt like an exposed and dangerous thing to do.

I went in through the hedge and the girl stood there very straight and silent against the half-open house door. One hand went slowly to her mouth, and her teeth bit at a funny-looking thumb that was like an extra finger. There were deep purple-black smudges under her frightened eyes.

I pushed her back into the house without saying anything, shut the door. We stood looking at each other inside. She dropped her hand slowly and tried to smile. Then all expression went out of her white face and it looked as intelligent as the bottom of a shoe box.

I got gentleness into my voice and said:

"Take it easy. I'm pals. Sit down in that chair

by the desk. I'm a friend of your father's. Don't get panicky."

She went and sat down on the yellow cushion in the black chair at Steiner's desk.

The place looked decadent and off-color by daylight. It still stank of the ether.

Carmen licked the corners of her mouth with the tip of a whitish tongue. Her dark eyes were stupid and stunned rather than scared now. I rolled a cigarette around in my fingers and pushed some books out of the way to sit on the edge of the desk. I lit my cigarette, puffed it slowly for a moment, then asked:

"What are you doing here?"

She picked at the material of her coat, didn't answer. I tried again.

"How much do you remember about last night?"

She answered that. "Remember what? I was sick last night—at home." Her voice was a cautious, throaty sound that only just reached my ears.

"Before that," I said. "Before I brought you home. Here."

A slow flush crept up her throat and her eyes widened. "You—you were the one?" she breathed, and began to chew on her funny thumb again.

"Yeah, I was the one. How much of it all stays with you?"

She said: "Are you the police?"

"No. I told you I was a friend of your father's."

"You're not the police?"

"No."

It finally registered. She let out a long sigh. "What—what do you want?"

"Who killed him?"

Her shoulders jerked in the checkered coat, but nothing changed much in her face. Her eyes slowly got furtive.

"Who—who else knows?"

"About Steiner? I don't know. Not the police, or someone would be here. Maybe Marty."

It was just a stab in the dark, but it got a sudden, sharp cry out of her.

"Marty!"

We were both silent for a minute. I puffed on my cigarette and she chewed on her thumb.

"Don't get clever," I said. "Did Marty kill him?"

Her chin came down an inch. "Yes."

"Why did he do it?"

"I—I don't know," very dully.

"Seen much of him lately?"

Her hands clenched. "Just once or twice."

"Know where he lives?"

"Yes!" She spat it at me.

"What's the matter? I thought you liked Marty."

"I hate him!" she almost yelled.

"Then you'd like him for the spot," I said.

She was blank to that. I had to explain it. "I mean, are you willing to tell the police it was Marty?"

Sudden panic flamed in her eyes.

"If I kill the nude photo angle," I said soothingly.

She giggled.

That gave me a nasty feeling. If she had screeched, or turned white, or even keeled over, that would have been fairly natural. But she just giggled.

I began to hate the sight of her. Just looking at her made me feel dopey.

Her giggles went on, ran around the room like rats. They gradually got hysterical. I got off the desk, took a step towards her, and slapped her face.

"Just like last night," I said.

The giggling stopped at once and the thumb-chewing started again. She still didn't mind my slaps apparently. I sat on the end of the desk once more.

"You came here to look for the camera plate—for the birthday suit photo," I told her.

Her chin went up and down again.

"Too late. I looked for it last night. It was gone then. Probably Marty has it. You're not kidding me about Marty?"

She shook her head vigorously. She got out of the chair slowly. Her eyes were narrow and sloe-black and as shallow as an oyster shell.

"I'm going now," she said, as if we had been having a cup of tea.

She went over to the door and was reaching out to open it when a car came up the hill and stopped outside the house. Somebody got out of the car.

She turned and stared at me, horrified.

The door opened casually and a man looked in at us.

IX

He was a hatchet-faced man in a brown suit and a black felt hat. The cuff of his left sleeve was folded under and pinned to the side of his coat with a big black safety-pin.

He took his hat off, closed the door by pushing it with his shoulder, looked at Carmen with a nice smile. He had close-cropped black hair and a bony skull. He fitted his clothes well. He didn't look tough.

"I'm Guy Slade," he said. "Excuse the casual entrance. The bell didn't work. Is Steiner around?"

He hadn't tried the bell. Carmen looked at him blankly, then at me, then back at Slade. She licked her lips but didn't say anything.

I said: "Steiner isn't here, Mister Slade. We don't know just where he is."

He nodded and touched his long chin with the brim of his hat.

"You friends of his?"

"We just dropped by for a book," I said, and gave him back his smile. "The door was half open. We knocked, then stepped inside. Just like you."

"I see," Slade said thoughtfully. "Very simple."

I didn't say anything. Carmen didn't say anything. She was staring fixedly at his empty sleeve.

"A book, eh?" Slade went on. The way he said it told me things. He knew about Steiner's racket, maybe.

I moved over towards the door. "Only *you* didn't knock," I said.

He smiled with faint embarrassment. "That's right. I ought to have knocked. Sorry."

"We'll trot along now," I said carelessly. I took hold of Carmen's arm.

"Any message—if Steiner comes back?" Slade asked softly.

"We won't bother you."

"That's too bad," he said, with too much meaning.

I let go of Carmen's arm and took a slow step away from her. Slade still had his hat in his hand. He didn't move. His deep-set eyes twinkled pleasantly.

I opened the door again.

Slade said: "The girl can go. But I'd like to talk to you a little."

I stared at him, trying to look very blank.

"Kidder, eh?" Slade said nicely.

Carmen made a sudden sound at my side and ran out through the door. In a moment I heard her steps going down the hill. I hadn't seen her car, but I guessed it was around somewhere.

I began to say: "What the hell—"

"Save it," Slade interrupted coldly. "There's something wrong here. I'll just find out what it is."

He began to walk around the room carelessly—too carelessly. He was frowning, not paying much attention to me. That made me thoughtful. I took a quick glance out of the window, but I couldn't see anything but the top of his car above the hedge.

Slade found the potbellied flagon and the two thin purple glasses on the desk. He sniffed at one of them. A disgusted smile wrinkled his thin lips.

"The lousy pimp," he said tonelessly.

He looked at the books on the desk, touched one or two of them, went on around the back of the desk and was in front of the totem pole thing. He stared at that. Then his eyes went down to the floor, to the thin rug that was over the place where Steiner's body had been. Slade moved the rug with his foot and suddenly tensed, staring down.

It was a good act—or else Slade had a nose I

could have used in my business. I wasn't sure which—yet, but I was giving it a lot of thought.

He went slowly down to the floor on one knee. The desk partly hid him from me.

I slipped a gun out from under my arm and put both hands behind my body and leaned against the wall.

There was a sharp, swift exclamation, then Slade shot to his feet. His arm flashed up. A long, black Luger slid into it expertly. I didn't move. Slade held the Luger in long, pale fingers, not pointing it at me, not pointing it at anything in particular.

"Blood," he said quietly, grimly, his deep-set eyes black and hard now. "Blood on the floor there, under a rug. A lot of blood."

I grinned at him. "I noticed it," I said. "It's old blood. Dried blood."

He slid sideways into the black chair behind Steiner's desk and raked the telephone towards him by putting the Luger around it. He frowned at the telephone, then frowned at me.

"I think we'll have some law," he said.

"Suits me."

Slade's eyes were narrow and as hard as jet. He didn't like my agreeing with him. The veneer had flaked off him, leaving a well-dressed hard boy with a Luger. Looking as if he could use it.

"Just who the hell are you?" he growled.

"A shamus. The name doesn't matter. The girl is my client. Steiner's been riding her with some blackmail dirt. We came to talk to him. He wasn't here."

"Just walk in, huh?"

"Correct. So what? Think we gunned Steiner, Mister Slade?"

He smiled slightly, thinly, but said nothing.

"Or do you think Steiner gunned somebody and ran away?" I suggested.

"Steiner didn't gun anybody," Slade said. "Steiner didn't have the guts of a sick cat."

I said: "You don't see anybody here, do you? Maybe Steiner had chicken for dinner, and liked to kill his chickens in the parlor."

"I don't get it. I don't get your game."

I grinned again. "Go ahead and call your friends downtown. Only you won't like the reaction you'll get."

He thought that over without moving a muscle. His lips went back against his teeth.

"Why not?" he asked finally, in a careful voice.

I said: "I know you, Mister Slade. You run the Aladdin Club down on the Palisades. Flash gambling. Soft lights and evening clothes and a buffet supper on the side. You know Steiner well enough to walk into his house without knocking. Steiner's racket needed a little protection now and then. You could be that."

Slade's finger tightened on the Luger, then relaxed. He put the Luger down on the desk, kept his fingers on it. His mouth became a hard white grimace.

"Somebody got to Steiner," he said softly, his voice and the expression on his face seeming to belong to two different people. "He didn't show at the store today. He didn't answer his phone. I came up to see about it."

"Glad to hear you didn't gun Steiner yourself," I said.

The Luger swept up again and made a target of my chest. I said:

"Put it down, Slade. You don't know enough to pop off yet. Not being bullet-proof is an idea I've had to get used to. Put it down. I'll tell you something—if you don't know it. Somebody moved Steiner's books out of his store today— the books he did his real business with."

Slade put his gun down on the desk for the second time. He leaned back and wrestled an amiable expression on to his face.

"I'm listening," he said.

"I think somebody got to Steiner too," I told him. "I think that blood is his blood. The books being moved out from Steiner's store gives us a reason for moving his body away from here. Somebody is taking over the racket and doesn't want Steiner found till he's all set. Whoever it was ought to have cleaned up the blood. He didn't."

Slade listened silently. The peaks of his eyebrows made sharp angles against the white skin of his indoor forehead. I went on:

"Killing Steiner to grab his racket was a dumb trick, and I'm not sure it happened that way. But I *am* sure that whoever took the books knows about it, and that the blonde down in the store is scared stiff about something."

"Any more?" Slade asked evenly.

"Not right now. There's a piece of scandal dope I want to trace. If I get it, I might tell you where. That will be your muscler in."

"Now would be better," Slade said. Then he drew his lips back against his teeth and whistled sharply, twice.

I jumped. A car door opened outside. There were steps.

I brought the gun around from behind my body. Slade's face convulsed and his hand snatched for the Luger that lay in front of him, fumbled at the butt.

I said: "Don't touch it!"

He came to his feet rigid, leaning over, his hand on the gun, but the gun not in his hand. I dodged past him into the hallway and turned as two men came into the room.

One had short red hair, a white, lined face, unsteady eyes. The other was an obvious pug; a good-looking boy except for a flattened nose and one ear as thick as a club steak.

Neither of the newcomers had a gun in sight. They stopped, stared.

I stood behind Slade in the doorway. Slade leaned over the desk in front of me, didn't stir.

The pug's mouth opened in a wide snarl, showing sharp, white teeth. The redhead looked shaky and scared.

Slade had plenty of guts. In a smooth, low, but very clear voice he said:

"This heel gunned Steiner, boys. Take him!"

The redhead took hold of his lower lip with his teeth and snatched for something under his left arm. He didn't get it. I was all set and braced. I shot him through the right shoulder, hating to do it. The gun made a lot of noise in the closed room. It seemed to me that it would be heard all over the city. The redhead went down on the

floor and writhed and threshed about as if I had shot him in the belly.

The pug didn't move. He probably knew there wasn't enough speed in his arm. Slade grabbed his Luger up and started to whirl. I took a step and slammed him behind the ear. He sprawled forward over the desk and the Luger shot against a row of books.

Slade didn't hear me say: "I hate to hit a one-armed man from behind, Slade. And I'm not crazy about the show-off. You made me do it."

The pug grinned at me and said: "Okay, pal. What next?"

"I'd like to get out of here, if I can do it without any more shooting. Or I can stick around for some law. It's all one to me."

He thought it over calmly. The redhead was making moaning noises on the floor. Slade was very still.

The pug put his hands up slowly and clasped them behind his neck. He said coolly:

"I don't know what it's all about, but I don't give a good ———— damn where you go or what you do when you get there. And this ain't my idea of a spot for a lead party. Drift!"

"Wise boy. You've more sense than your boss."

I edged around the desk, edged over towards the open door. The pug turned slowly, facing me, keeping his hands behind his neck. There was a wry but almost good-natured grin on his face.

I skinned through the door and made a fast break through the gap in the hedge and up the hill, half expecting lead to fly after me. None came.

I jumped into the Chrysler and chased it up over the brow of the hill and away from that neighborhood.

X

It was after five when I stopped opposite the apartment house on Randall Place. A few windows were lit up already and radios bleated discordantly on different programs. I rode the automatic elevator to the fourth floor. Apartment 405 was at the end of a long hall that was carpeted in green and paneled in ivory. A cool breeze blew through the hall from open doors to the fire escape.

There was a small ivory push-button beside the door marked "405." I pushed it.

After a long time a man opened the door a foot or so. He was a long-legged, thin man with dark brown eyes in a very brown face. Wiry hair grew far back on his head, giving him a great deal of domed brown forehead. His brown eyes probed at me impersonally.

I said: "Steiner?"

Nothing in the man's face changed. He brought a cigarette from behind the door and put it slowly between tight brown lips. A puff of smoke came towards me, and behind it words in a cool, unhurried voice, without inflection. "You said what?"

"Steiner. Harold Hardwicke Steiner. The guy that has the books."

The man nodded. He considered my remark without haste. He glanced at the tip of his cigarette, said:

"I think I know him. But he doesn't visit here. Who sent you?"

I smiled. He didn't like that. I said:

"You're Marty?"

The brown face got harder. "So what? Got a grift—or just amusin' yourself?"

I moved my left foot casually, enough so that he couldn't slam the door.

"You got the books," I said. "I got the sucker list. How's to talk it over?"

Marty didn't shift his eyes from my face. His right hand went behind the panel of the door again, and his shoulder had a look as if he was making motions with a hand. There was a faint sound in the room behind him—very faint. A curtain ring clicked lightly on a rod.

Then he opened the door wide. "Why not? If you think you've got something," he said coolly.

I went past him into the room. It was a cheerful room, with good furniture and not too much

of it. French windows in the end wall looked across a stone porch at the foothills, already getting purple in the dusk. Near the windows a door was shut. Another door in the same wall at the near end of the room had curtains drawn across it, on a brass rod below the lintel.

I sat down on a davenport against the wall in which there were no doors. Marty shut the door and walked sideways to a tall oak writing-desk studded with square nails. A cedarwood cigar box with gilt hinges rested on the lowered leaf of the desk. Marty picked it up without taking his eyes off me, carried it to a low table beside an easy chair. He sat down in the easy chair.

I put my hat beside me and opened the top button of my coat and smiled at Marty.

"Well—I'm listening," he said.

He stubbed his cigarette out, lifted the lid of the cigar box and took out a couple of fat cigars.

"Cigar?" he suggested casually, and tossed one at me.

I reached for it and that made me a sap. Marty dropped the other cigar back into the box and came up very swiftly with a gun.

I looked at the gun politely. It was a black police Colt, a .38. I had no argument against it at the moment.

"Stand up a minute," Marty said. "Come forward just about two yards. You might grab a little air while you're doing that." His voice was elaborately casual.

I was mad inside, but I grinned at him. I said:

"You're the second guy I've met today that thinks a gun in the hand means the world by the tail. Put it away, and let's talk."

Marty's eyebrows came together and he pushed his chin forward a little. His brown eyes were vaguely troubled.

We stared at each other. I didn't look at the pointed black slipper that showed under the curtains across the doorway to my left.

Marty was wearing a dark blue suit, a blue shirt and a black tie. His brown face looked somber above the dark colors. He said softly, in a lingering voice:

"Don't get me wrong. I'm not a tough guy—

just careful. I don't know hell's first thing about you. You might be a life-taker for all I know."

"You're not careful enough," I said. "The play with the books was lousy."

He drew a long breath and let it out silently. Then he leaned back and crossed his long legs and rested the Colt on his knee.

"Don't kid yourself I won't use this, if I have to. What's your story?"

"Tell your friend with the pointed shoes to come on in," I said. "She gets tired holding her breath."

Without turning his head Marty called out: "Come on in, Agnes."

The curtains over the door swung aside and the green-eyed blonde from Steiner's store joined us in the room. I wasn't very much surprised to see her there. She looked at me bitterly.

"I knew damn' well you were trouble," she told me angrily. "I told Joe to watch his step."

"Save it," Marty snapped. "Joe's watchin' his step plenty. Put some light on so I can see to pop this guy, if it works out that way."

The blonde lit a large floor lamp with a square red shade. She sat down under it, in a big velours chair and held a fixed painful smile on her face. She was scared to the point of exhaustion.

I remembered the cigar I was holding and put it in my mouth. Marty's Colt was very steady on me while I got matches out and lit it.

I puffed smoke and said through the smoke: "The sucker list I spoke of is in code. So I can't read the names yet, but there's about five hundred of them. You got twelve boxes of books, say three hundred. There'll be that many more out on loan. Say five hundred altogether, just to be conservative. If it's a good active list and you could run it around all the books, that would be a quarter of a million rentals. Put the average rental low—say a dollar. That's too low, but say a dollar. That's a lot of money these days. Enough to spot a guy for."

The blonde yelped sharply: "You're crazy, if you—"

"Shut up!" Marty swore at her.

The blonde subsided and put her head back against the back of her chair. Her face was tortured with strain.

"It's no racket for bums," I went on telling them. "You've got to get confidence and keep it. Personally I think the blackmail angles are a mistake. I'm for shedding all that."

Marty's dark brown stare held coldly on my face. "You're a funny guy," he drawled smoothly. "Who's got this lovely racket?"

"You have," I said. "Almost."

Marty didn't say anything.

"You shot Steiner to get it," I said. "Last night in the rain. It was good shooting weather. The trouble is, he wasn't alone when it happened. Either you didn't see that, or you got scared. You ran out. But you had nerve enough to come back and hide the body somewhere—so you could tidy up on the books before the case broke."

The blonde made one strangled sound and then turned her face and stared at the wall. Her silvered fingernails dug into her palms. Her teeth bit her lip tightly.

Marty didn't bat an eye. He didn't move and the Colt didn't move in his hand. His brown face was as hard as a piece of carved wood.

"Boy, you take chances," he said softly, at last. "It's lucky as all hell for you I didn't kill Steiner."

I grinned at him, without much cheer. "You might step off for it just the same," I said.

Marty's voice was a dry rustle of sound. "Think you've got me framed for it?"

"Positive."

"How come?"

"There's somebody who'll tell it that way."

Marty swore then. "That—damned little ————! She would—just that—damn her!"

I didn't say anything. I let him chew on it. His face cleared slowly, and he put the Colt down on the table, kept his hand near it.

"You don't sound like chisel as I know chisel," he said slowly, his eyes a tight shine between dark narrowed lids. "And I don't see any coppers here. What's your angle?"

I drew on my cigar and watched his gun

hand. "The plate that was in Steiner's camera. All the prints that have been made. Right here and right now. You've got it—because that's the only way you could have known who was there last night."

Marty turned his head slightly to look at Agnes. Her face was still to the wall and her fingernails were still spearing her palms. Marty looked back at me.

"You're cold as a night watchman's feet on that one, guy," he told me.

I shook my head. "No. You're a sap to stall, Marty. You can be pegged for the kill easy. It's a natural. If the girl has to tell her story, the pictures won't matter. But she don't want to tell it."

"You a shamus?" he asked.

"Yeah."

"How'd you get to me?"

"I was working on Steiner. He's been workin' on Dravec. Dravec leaks money. You had some of it. I tailed the books here from Steiner's store. The rest was easy when I had the girl's story."

"She say I gunned Steiner?"

I nodded. "But she could be mistaken."

Marty sighed. "She hates my guts," he said. "I gave her the gate. I got paid to do it, but I'd have done it anyway. She's too screwy for me."

I said: "Get the pictures, Marty."

He stood up slowly, looked down at the Colt, put it in his side-pocket. His hand moved slowly up to his breast-pocket.

Somebody rang the door buzzer and kept on ringing it.

XI

Marty didn't like that. His lower lip went in under his teeth and his eyebrows drew down at the corners. His whole face got mean.

The buzzer kept on buzzing.

The blonde stood up quickly. Nerve tension made her face old and ugly.

Watching me, Marty jerked a small drawer open in the tall desk and got a small, white-handled automatic out of it. He held it out to the blonde. She went to him and took it gingerly, not liking it.

"Sit down next to the shamus," he rasped. "Hold the gun on him. If he gets funny, feed him a few."

The blonde sat down on the davenport about three feet from me, on the side away from the door. She lined the gun on my leg. I didn't like the jerky look in her green eyes.

The door buzzer stopped and somebody started a quick, light, impatient rapping on the panel. Marty went across and opened the door. He slid his right hand into his coat pocket and opened the door with his left hand, threw it open quickly.

Carmen Dravec pushed him back into the room with the muzzle of a small revolver against his brown face.

Marty backed away from her smoothly, lightly. His mouth was open and an expression of panic was on his face. He knew Carmen pretty well.

Carmen shut the door, then bored ahead with her little gun. She didn't look at anyone but Marty, didn't seem to see anything but Marty. Her face had a dopey look.

The blonde shivered the full length of her body and swung the white-handled automatic up and towards Carmen. I shot my hand out and grabbed her hand, closed my fingers down over it quickly, thumbed the safety to the on position, and held it there. There was a short tussle, which neither Marty nor Carmen paid any attention to. Then I had the gun.

The blonde breathed deeply and stared at Carmen Dravec. Carmen looked at Marty with doped eyes and said:

"I want my pictures."

Marty swallowed and tried to smile at her. He said: "Sure, kid, sure," in a small, flat voice that wasn't like the voice he had used in talking to me.

Carmen looked almost as crazy as she had looked in Steiner's chair. But she had control of her voice and muscles this time. She said:

"You shot Hal Steiner."

"Wait a minute, Carmen!" I yelped.

Carmen didn't turn her head. The blonde came to life with a rush, ducked her head at me as if she was going to butt me, and sank her teeth in my right hand, the one that had her gun in it.

I yelped some more. Nobody minded that either.

Marty said: "Listen, kid, I didn't—"

The blonde took her teeth out of my hand and spat my own blood at me. Then she threw herself at my leg and tried to bite that. I cracked her lightly on the head with the barrel of the gun and tried to stand up. She rolled down my legs and wrapped her arms around my ankles. I fell back on the davenport again. The blonde was strong with the madness of fear.

Marty grabbed for Carmen's gun with his left hand, missed. The little revolver made a dull, heavy sound that was not loud. A bullet missed Marty and broke glass in one of the folded-back French windows.

Marty stood perfectly still again. He looked as if all his muscles had gone back on him.

"Duck and knock her off her feet, you damn' fool!" I yelled at him.

Then I hit the blonde on the side of the head again, much harder, and she rolled off my feet. I got loose and slid away from her.

Marty and Carmen were still facing each other like a couple of images.

Something very large and heavy hit the outside of the door and the panel split diagonally from top to bottom.

That brought Marty to life. He jerked the Colt out of his pocket and jumped back. I snapped a shot at his right shoulder and missed, not wanting to hurt him much. The heavy thing hit the door again with a crash that seemed to shake the whole building.

I dropped the little automatic and got my own gun loose as Dravec came in with the smashed door.

He was wild-eyed, raging drunk, beserk. His big arms were flailing. His eyes were glaring and bloodshot and there was froth on his lips.

He hit me very hard on the side of the head without even looking at me. I fell against the wall, between the end of the davenport and the broken door.

I was shaking my head and trying to get level again when Marty began to shoot.

Something lifted Dravec's coat away from his body behind, as if a slug had gone clean through him. He stumbled, straightened immediately, charged like a bull.

I lined my gun and shot Marty through the body. It shook him, but the Colt in his hand continued to leap and roar. Then Dravec was between us and Carmen was knocked out of the way like a dead leaf and there was nothing more that anybody could do about it.

Marty's bullets couldn't stop Dravec. Nothing could. If he had been dead, he would still have got Marty.

He got him by the throat as Marty threw his empty gun in the big man's face. It bounced off like a rubber ball. Marty yelled shrilly, and Dravec took him by the throat and lifted him clean off his feet.

For an instant Marty's brown hands fought for a hold on the big man's wrists. Something cracked sharply, and Marty's hands fell away limply. There was another, duller crack. Just before Dravec let go of Marty's neck I saw that Marty's face was a purple-black color. I remembered, almost casually, that men whose necks are broken sometimes swallow their tongues before they die.

Then Marty fell down in the corner and Dravec started to back away from him. He backed like a man losing his balance, not able to keep his feet under his center of gravity. He took four clumsy backward steps like that. Then his big body tipped over backwards and he fell on his back on the floor with his arms flung out wide.

Blood came out of his mouth. His eyes strained upward as if to see through a fog.

Carmen Dravec went down beside him and began to wail like a frightened animal.

There was noise outside in the hall, but nobody showed at the open door. Too much casual lead had been flipped around.

I went quickly over to Marty and leaned over him and got my hand into his breast-pocket. I got out a thick, square envelope that had something stiff and hard in it. I straightened up with it and turned.

Far off the wail of a siren sounded faintly on the evening air, seemed to be getting louder. A white-faced man peeped cautiously in through the doorway. I knelt down beside Dravec.

He tried to say something, but I couldn't hear the words. Then the strained look went out of his eyes and they were aloof and indifferent, like the eyes of a man looking at something a long way off, across a wide plain.

Carmen said stonily: "He was drunk. He made me tell him where I was going. I didn't know he followed me."

"You wouldn't," I said emptily.

I stood up again and broke the envelope open. There were a few prints in it and a glass negative. I dropped the plate on the floor and ground it to pieces with my heel. I began to tear up the prints and let the pieces flutter down out of my hands.

"They'll print plenty of photos of you now, girlie," I said. "But they won't print this one."

"I didn't know he was following me," she said again, and began to chew on her thumb.

The siren was loud outside the building now. It died to a penetrating drone and then stopped altogether, just about the time I finished tearing up the prints.

I stood still in the middle of the room and wondered why I had taken the trouble. It didn't matter any more now.

XII

Leaning his elbow on the end of the big walnut table in Inspector Isham's office, and holding a burning cigarette idly between his fingers, Guy Slade said, without looking at me:

"Thanks for putting me on the pan, shamus. I like to see the boys at Headquarters once in a while." He crinkled the corners of his eyes in an unpleasant smile.

I was sitting at the long side of the table across from Isham. Isham was lanky and grey and wore nose-glasses. He didn't look, act, or talk copper. Violets M'Gee and a merry-eyed Irish dick named Grinnell were in a couple of round-backed chairs against a glass-topped partition wall that cut part of the office off into a reception room.

I said to Slade: "I figured you found that blood a little too soon. I guess I was wrong. My apologies, Mister Slade."

"Yeah. That makes it just like it never happened." He stood up, picked a malacca cane and one glove off the table. "That all for me, Inspector?"

"That's all tonight, Slade." Isham's voice was dry, cool, sardonic.

Slade caught the crook of his cane over his wrist to open the door. He smiled around before he strolled out. The last thing his eyes rested on was probably the back of my neck, but I wasn't looking at him.

Isham said: "I don't have to tell you how a police department looks at that kind of a cover-up on a murder."

I sighed. "Gunfire," I said. "A dead man on the floor. A naked, doped girl in a chair not knowing what had happened. A killer I couldn't have caught and you couldn't have caught—then. Behind all this a poor old roughneck that was breaking his heart trying to do the right thing in a miserable spot. Go ahead—stick it into me. I'm not sorry."

Isham waved all that aside. "Who did kill Steiner?"

"The blonde girl will tell you."

"I want you to tell me."

I shrugged. "If you want me to guess—Dravec's driver, Carl Owen."

Isham didn't look too surprised. Violets M'Gee grunted loudly.

"What makes you think so?" Isham asked.

"I thought for a while it could be Marty, partly because the girl said so. But that doesn't mean anything. She didn't know, and jumped at the chance to stick a knife into Marty. And she's a type that doesn't let loose of an idea very easily.

But Marty didn't act like a killer. And a man as cool as Marty wouldn't have run out that way. I hadn't even banged on the door when the killer started to scram.

"Of course I thought of Slade, too. But Slade's not quite the type either. He packs two gunmen around with him, and they'd have made some kind of a fight of it. And Slade seemed genuinely surprised when he found the blood on the floor this afternoon. Slade was in with Steiner and keeping tabs on him, but he didn't kill him, didn't have any reason to kill him, and wouldn't have killed him that way, in front of a witness, if he had a reason.

"But Carl Owen would. He was in love with the girl once, probably never got over it. He had chances to spy on her, find out where she went and what she did. He lay for Steiner, got in the back way, saw the nude photo stunt and blew his top. He let Steiner have it. Then the panic got him and he just ran."

"Ran all the way to Lido pier, and then off the end of that," Isham said dryly. "Aren't you forgetting that the Owen body had a sap wound on the side of his head?"

I said: "No. And I'm not forgetting that somehow or other Marty knew what was on that camera plate—or nearly enough to make him go in and get it and then hide a body in Steiner's garage to give him room."

Isham said: "Get Agnes Laurel in here, Grinnell."

Grinnell heaved up out of his chair and strolled the length of the office, disappeared through a door.

Violets M'Gee said: "Baby, are you a pal!"

I didn't look at him. Isham pulled the loose skin in front of his Adam's apple and looked down at the fingernails of his other hand.

Grinnell came back with the blonde. Her hair was untidy above the collar of her coat. She had taken the jet buttons out of her ears. She looked tired but she didn't look scared any more. She let herself down slowly into the chair at the end of the table where Slade had sat, folded her hands with the silvered nails in front of her.

Isham said quietly: "All right, Miss Laurel. We'd like to hear from you now."

The girl looked down at her folded hands and talked without hesitation, in a quiet, even voice.

"I've known Joe Marty about three months. He made friends with me because I was working for Steiner, I guess. I thought it was because he liked me. I told him all I knew about Steiner. He already knew a little. He had been spending money he had got from Carmen Dravec's father, but it was gone and he was down to nickels and dimes, ready for something else. He decided Steiner needed a partner and he was watching him to see if he had any tough friends in the background.

"Last night he was in his car down on the street back of Steiner's house. He heard the shots, saw the kid tear down the steps, jump into a big sedan and take it on the lam. Joe chased him. Half-way to the beach, he caught him and ran him off the road. The kid came up with a gun, but his nerve was bad and Joe sapped him down. While he was out Joe went through him and found out who he was. When he came around Joe played copper and the kid broke and gave him the story. While Joe was wondering what to do about it the kid came to life and knocked him off the car and scrammed again. He drove like a crazy guy and Joe let him go. He went back to Steiner's house. I guess you know the rest. When Joe had the plate developed and saw what he had he went for a quick touch so we could get out of town before the law found Steiner. We were going to take some of Steiner's books and set up shop in another city."

Agnes Laurel stopped talking. Isham tapped with his fingers, said: "Marty told you everything, didn't he?"

"Uh-huh."

"Sure he didn't murder this Carl Owen?"

"I wasn't there. Joe didn't act like he'd killed anybody."

Isham nodded. "That's all for now, Miss Laurel. We'll want all that in writing. We'll have to hold you, of course."

The girl stood up. Grinnell took her out. She went out without looking at anyone.

Isham said: "Marty couldn't have known Carl Own was dead. But he was sure he'd try to hide out. By the time we got to him Marty would have collected from Dravec and moved on. I think the girl's story sounds reasonable."

Nobody said anything. After a moment Isham said to me:

"You made one bad mistake. You shouldn't have mentioned Marty to the girl until you were sure he was your man. That got two people killed quite unnecessarily."

I said: "Uh-huh. Maybe I better go back and do it over again."

"Don't get tough."

"I'm not tough. I was working for Dravec and trying to save him from a little heartbreak. I didn't know the girl was as screwy as all that, or that Dravec would have a brainstorm. I wanted the pictures. I didn't care a lot about trash like Steiner or Joe Marty and his girl friend, and still don't."

"Okay. Okay," Isham said impatiently. "I don't need you any more tonight. You'll probably be panned plenty at the inquest."

He stood up and I stood up. He held out his hand.

"But that will do you a hell of a lot more good than harm," he added drily.

I shook hands with him and went out. M'Gee came out after me. We rode down in the elevator together without speaking to each other. When we got outside the building M'Gee went around to the right side of my Chrysler and got into it.

"Got any liquor at your dump?"

"Plenty," I said.

"Let's go get some of it."

I started the car and drove west along First Street, through a long echoing tunnel. When we were out of that, M'Gee said:

"Next time I send you a client I won't expect you to snitch on him, boy."

We went on through the quiet evening to the Berglund. I felt tired and old and not much use to anybody.

Sally the Sleuth

Adolphe Barreaux

ADOLPHE BARREAUX (1899–1985) studied at the Yale School of Fine Arts and the Grand Central Art School. He created "Sally the Sleuth" for *Spicy Detective,* one of the sleaziest of the pulp magazines, in November 1934, with a little two-page strip titled "A Narrow Escape." The material published in this pulp was generally produced by the worst writers of the era, mainly when they failed to sell their work to the better-paying, higher-end books. All the stories included illustrations of scantily clad women, frequently in bondage—all so racy that the magazines were kept under the counter at most newsstands and sold only to adults. These illustrations were provided by Majestic Studios, a tiny art shop owned by Barreaux from 1936 to 1953. He was also the owner of Trojan Publishing from 1949 to 1955. Although he worked for a few other pulps from the 1930s to the 1950s, most of his work went to *Spicy,* for which he drew the "Sally the Sleuth" strip until 1942, when other artists took it over. Barreaux went on to work for many of the major comic book publishers, including DC ("Magic Crystal of History"), Dell ("The Enchanted Stone"), Ace ("The Black Spider" and "The Raven"), and Fox ("Flip Falcon" and "Patty O'Day").

These episodes of "Sally the Sleuth" appeared in *Spicy Detective.*

SALLY THE SLEUTH

LEDA MARMON WAS UNDOUBTEDLY BITTEN BY AN ASP. YET - THOUGH SHE WAS APPEARING IN AN EGYPTIAN PLAY, THERE WERE NO SNAKES USED IN THE PRODUCTION

THERE MUST BE ONE, CHIEF. LET'S GRILL THE REST OF THE CAST

ACT I SCENE 6

WELL, NONE OF YOU SEEM TO BE IMPLICATED, SO YOU MAY GO

FOLLOW THE SWARTHY FELLOW WITH THE CANE. HE'S FAZIL HUSSEIN, A REAL EGYPTIAN. I HAVE A HUNCH...

I WONDER IF HE DID IT. HE CAN'T CARRY A POISONOUS ASP AROUND IN HIS POCKET

SO HE LIVES IN THIS OLD THEATRICAL BOARDING-HOUSE. IT SHOULDN'T BE DIFFICULT TO GET A LINE ON HIM HERE

!!!

SPYING, EH! WELL, YOU'LL TAKE NO TALES BACK TO THE DETECTIVE!

OOH!

· 845 ·

Matinee Murder

"HAWAIIAN SPY HUNT"

THERE'S OUR GREAT BASE AT PEARL HARBOR. IT'S ENDANGERED BY A SPY RING DIRECTED BY A MASTER MIND UP IN THE HILLS. TOMORROW, WE START OUT TO LOCATE HIM.

NEXT DAY

WE'LL JUST PRETEND TO BE TOURISTS AND KEEP OUR EYES AND EARS OPEN. IF ANYTHING HAPPENS, I HAVE A WAY TO CONTACT THE ARMY AT ONCE. THEY WILL BE WATCHING...

THAT'S SWELL, ISN'T IT, CHIEF?

I'LL BET YOU COULD DO BETTER, YOURSELF.

BUT ALREADY THEY AROUSE SUSPICION AS A RUNNER STREAKS UP THE SIDE OF AN EXTINCT VOLCANO.

A MILE FURTHER ON — CHIEF AND SALLY ARE TAKEN PRISONERS.

THEY REACH THE MASTER SPY'S HIDEOUT

SO YOU THINK YOU COULD FOOL SANTOS, EH? I KNEW ALL ABOUT YOU TWO AS SOON AS YOU GOT OFF THE BOAT.

CHIEF IS LOCKED UP, BUT SALLY IS FORCED TO ENTERTAIN SANTOS.

I'M TIRED OF THOSE NATIVE HULA DANCERS. YOU PUT THIS ON AND SHAKE A HIP.

SALLY IS MADE TO ACT AS A WAITRESS.

YOU NEED MORE EXERCISE. GO FETCH SOME FIREWOOD.

YOU BUM!

SUCH A LEETLE BIT! GET MORE — MUCH MORE!

SO YOU FAINT, EH? I KNOW THAT TRICK!

OH!

I BRING YOU TO - QUEEK!

YOU STOLE A KNIFE FROM THE KITCHEN, EH? BUT YOU DO NOT FOOL SANTOS!

TIE HER OUTSIDE. THE NIGHT CHILL WILL COOL HER TEMPER A BIT

BRRRH! IT'S CHILLY. I WONDER WHAT THEY'VE DONE WITH THE CHIEF---

MEANWHILE, THE CHIEF MAKES A ROPE OUT OF HIS BLANKET...

...AND FASHIONS A SNARE OUTSIDE HIS WINDOW.

THE UNWARY GUARD STEPS INTO THE NOOSE -- IS YANKED OFF HIS FEET AND IS KNOCKED COLD.

AH, THE KEYS -- THIS IS LUCK.

PSST- SALLY!

CHIEF!

SOMEONE'S COMING!

IT'S SANTOS!

ANOTHER THRILLING ADVENTURE NEXT MONTH

A Shock for the Countess
C. S. Montanye

CARLTON STEVENS MONTANYE (1892–1948), an active writer in the early
years of pulpwood magazines, appears to have had an exceptional fondness for
criminals as protagonists.

Although he wrote for many different periodicals, he achieved the peak of any
pulp writer's career by selling numerous stories to *Black Mask*, beginning with
the May 1920 issue and continuing through the issue of October 1939. Most
were about various crooks, including an old-fashioned Monahan, a yegg, Rider
Lott, inventor of the perfect crime, and the Countess d'Yls, an old-fashioned
international jewel thief: wealthy, beautiful, brilliant, and laconic, the female
equivalent of his most famous character, Captain Valentine, who made his *Black
Mask* debut on September 1, 1923, with "The Suite on the Seventh Floor," and
appeared nine more times in two years, concluding with "The Dice of Destiny"
in the July 1925 issue. The gentleman rogue was also the protagonist of the novel
Moons in Gold, published in 1936, in which the debonair Valentine, accompanied
by his amazingly ingenious Chinese servant Tim, is in Paris, where he has his eye
on the world's most magnificent collection of opals.

Montanye was also one of the writers of the Phantom Detective series under
the house name Robert Wallace.

"A Shock for the Countess" first appeared in the March 1923 issue of *Black
Mask*.

A Shock for the Countess

C. S. Montanye

According to Joe Taylor, BLACK MASK'S *own ex-bandit, the little unexpected things rather than the watchfulness of the authorities prevent a crook's success. The Countess never heard of Joe Taylor, but, after her adventures in this story, she is of the same opinion.*

FROM THE TERRACES of the Château d'Yls, the valley of Var was spread out below Gattiere, threaded with the broad bed of the River Var, swirling over its stony reaches from its cradle in the Hautes-Alpes. The snow-crowned mountains frowned ominously down but in the valley summertime warmth prevailed—quietude disturbed only by the song of birds and the voice of the river.

On the shaded promenade of the Château, the pretty Countess d'Yls stared thoughtfully at the unwinding river of the dust-powdered highway, twisting off into the dim distance. Beside her, a tall, well-built young man in tweeds absently flicked the ash from his cigarette and tinkled the ice in the thin glass he held.

Once or twice he surreptitiously considered the woman who reclined so indolently in the padded depths of a black wicker chair. The Countess seemed rarely lovely on this warm, lazy afternoon.

Her ash-blond hair caught what sunshine came in under the sand-colored awning above. Her blue eyes were dreamy and introspective, her red lips meditatively pursed. Yet for all of her abstraction there was something regal and almost imperious in her bearing; a subtle charm and distinction that was entirely her own.

"I do believe," the Countess remarked at length, "we are about to entertain visitors."

She motioned casually with a white hand toward the dust-filled road. The man beside her leaned a little forward. A mile or less distant he observed an approaching motor car that crawled up the road between clouds of dust.

"Visitors?"

The Countess inclined her head.

"So it would appear. And visitors, *mon ami*, who have come a long way to see us. Observe that the machine is travel-stained, that it appears to be weighted down with luggage. Possibly it is our old friend Murgier," she added almost mischievously.

The face of the man in tweeds paled under its tan.

"Murgier!" he exclaimed under his breath.

The Countess smiled faintly.

"But it is probably only a motoring party up from Georges de Loup who have wandered off the main road, Armand."

The man in tweeds had torn the cigarette between his fingers into rags. As if held in the spell of some strange fascination he watched the motor grow larger and larger.

"There are men in it!" he muttered, when the dusty car was abreast the lower wall of the Château. "Four men!"

The woman in the wicker chair seemed suddenly to grow animated.

"*Mon Dieu!*" she said in a low voice. "If it is *he*, that devil!"

The man she addressed made no reply, only the weaving of his fingers betraying his suppressed nervousness. The hum of the sturdy motor was heard from the drive, way among the terraces now.

There was an interlude—voices around a bend in the promenade—finally the appearance of a liveried automaton that was the butler.

"Monsieur Murgier, madame."

The man in tweeds stifled a groan. The Countess turned slowly in her chair.

"You may direct Monsieur Murgier here, Henri."

The butler bowed and turned away. The man in tweeds closed his hands until the nails of them bit into the palms.

"God!"

The Countess laid a tense hand on his arm.

"*Smile!*" she commanded.

The Monsieur Murgier who presently sauntered down the shaded promenade of the Château was a tall, loose-jointed individual with a melancholy mustache and a deeply wrinkled face. A shabby, dusty suit hung loosely and voluminously about his spare figure. A soft straw hat was in one hand; he was gray at the temples.

When he bowed over the slender fingers of the Countess there was a hidden glow in his somber eyes.

"To be favored by the presence of the great!" the woman murmured softly. "Monsieur, this is

an honor! May I make you acquainted with the Marquis de Remec?"

She introduced the visitor to the man in tweeds, who bowed stiffly. Somewhere back around the corner of the promenade the drone of the voices of those who had been in the car sounded faintly.

"A liqueur, m'sieu?" the Countess asked. "A cigar?"

Her visitor shook his head, gazed on the peaceful panorama of the valley of the Var.

"Thank you, no. My time is limited. My journey has been a long one and I must make a start for Paris with all due haste. You," he explained courteously, "and the Marquis will put yourselves in readiness with as much rapidity as possible. You are both my guests for the return journey!"

The man in tweeds whitened to the lips. His startled glance darted to the Countess. The woman had settled herself back in the black wicker chair again and had joined her fingers, tip to tip.

"Accompany you to Paris?" she drawled. "Are you quite serious?"

The wrinkled face of Monsieur Murgier grew inflexible, brass-like!

"Quite serious," he replied. "You are both under arrest—for the theft of the de Valois pearls!"

For a week, intermittently, Paris had known rain—the cold, chilly drizzle of early springtime. Because of the weather cafés and theatres were crowded, fiacres and taxis in constant demand, omnibuses jammed and the drenched boulevards deserted by their usual loungers.

From Montmartre to Montparnasse, scudding, gray clouds veiled the reluctant face of the sun by day and hid a knife-edged moon by night.

The steady, monotonous drizzle pattered against the boudoir windows in the house of the Countess d'Yls, mid-way down the Street of the First Shell. Within, all was snug, warm and comfortable. A coal fire burned in a filigree basket-grate, the radiance of a deeply shaded floor lamp near the toilette table, where a small maid hovered like a mother pigeon about the Countess, diffused a subdued, mellow glow.

The evening growl of Paris came as if from faraway, a lesser sound in the symphony of the rain.

"Madame will wear her jewels?"

The Countess turned and lifted her blue eyes.

"My rings only, Marie, if you please."

The maid brought the jewel casket, laid it beside her mistress, and at the wardrobe selected a luxurious Kolinsky cape which she draped over an arm. The Countess slipped on her rings, one by one—flashing, blue-white diamonds in carved, platinum settings, an odd Egyptian temple ring, a single ruby that burned like a small ball of crimson fire.

When the last ring glinted on her white fingers she dropped the lid of the casket, stood and turned to a full-length cheval mirror back of her.

The glass reflected the full perfection of her charms, the sheer wonder of her sequin-spangled evening gown, the creamy luster of her bare, powdered arms, shoulders and rounded, contralto throat. Standing there, the soft light on her hair, she was radiant, incomparable, a reincarnated Diana whose draperies came from the most expert needles of the Rue de la Paix.

"I think," the Countess said aloud, "those who go to fashionable affairs to witness and copy will have much to occupy their pencils on the morrow. My gown is clever, is it not, Marie?"

"It is beautiful!" the maid breathed.

With a little laugh the Countess took the Kolinsky cape.

"Now I must hasten below to the Marquis. Poor boy, it is an hour—or more—that I have kept him cooling his heels. Marie, suspense, they say, breeds appreciation but there is such a thing as wearing out the patience of a cavalier. The really intelligent woman knows when not to overdo it. You understand?"

"Perfectly, madame," the maid replied.

The Countess let herself out and sought the stairs. She moved lightly down steps that were made mute by the weight of their waterfall of gorgeous carpet. Murals looked down upon her progress to the lower floor, tapestries glittered with threads of flame, the very air seemed somnolent with the heaviness of sybaritic luxury.

Humming a snatch of a boulevard *chansonette*, the Countess turned into a lounge room that was to the right of the entry-hall below. The aroma of cigarette smoke drifted to her. When she crossed the threshold the Marquis de Remec stood, a well-made, immaculately groomed individual in his perfectly tailored evening clothes.

"Forgive me, Armand," the Countess pleaded. "Marie was so stupid tonight—all thumbs. I thought she would never finish with me."

The Marquis lifted her fingers to his lips.

"How lovely you are!" he cried softly. "Ah, dear one, will you never say the word that will make me the happiest man in all France? For two years we have worked together shoulder to shoulder, side by side—for two years you have been a star to me, earth-bound, beautiful beyond all words! Two years of—"

The Countess interrupted with a sigh.

"Of thrills and danger, Armand! Of plots and stratagems, plunder and wealth! I think, *mon ami*," she said seriously, "if we are successful tonight I will marry you before April ends. But wait, understand me. It will be a secret. I will still be the Countess d'Yls and you will remain the Marquis de Remec to all the world but me. Then, my friend, if either of us suffers disaster one will not drag the other down. You see?"

She seated herself beside the Marquis, considering him wistfully.

"But *tonight?*" he said in a stifled voice. "The de Valois affair is the hardest nut we have yet attempted to crack! Tonight we will need all of our cunning, all of our wits!"

The Countess lifted airy brows.

"Indeed?"

The Marquis leaned closer to her.

"There is not," he explained rapidly, "only Monsieur Murgier of the Surete to consider—the knowledge that he has been blundering after us for months—but the Wolf as well! An hour ago only, François picked up some gossip across the river, in some dive. The Wolf steals from his lair tonight *questing the de Valois pearls!* Do you understand? We must face double enemies—the net of Murgier, the fangs of the animal who sulks among the Apache brigands of the river front. And this is the task you give to set a crown upon my every hope!"

The Countess d'Yls touched his hand with her pretty fingers.

"Does the threat of Murgier and the presence of the Wolf pack dismay you?" she questioned lightly. "You, the undaunted! You who have been the hero of so many breathless adventures! Armand, you—you annoy me."

De Remec stood.

"But this is different!" he cried. "Here I have something at stake more precious than gold or jewels—your promise! I—I tremble—"

The Countess laughed at his melodrama.

"Silly boy! We shall not fail—we will snatch the famous pearls from under the very noses of those who would thwart and destroy us. *Voilà!* I snap my fingers at them all. Come now, it grows late. Had we not better start?"

The other glanced at his watch.

"Yes. François is waiting with the limousine—"

When they were side by side in the tonneau of the purring motor, the Countess glanced at the streaming windows and shivered.

"Soon it will be late spring," she said quietly. "Soon it will be our privilege to rest city-weary eyes on the valley of the Var. I intend to open the Château in six weeks, *mon ami*. It will seem like heaven after the miserable winter and the rain, the rain!"

The car shaped a course west, then south. Paris lifted a gaudy reflection to the canopy of the frowning clouds, flashing past in its nightly pursuit of pleasure. The Countess eyed the traffic tide idly. Her thoughts were like skeins of silk on a loom that was slowly being reversed. She thought of Yesterday—of the little heap of jewels in the boudoir of the villa at Trouville that had been the scene of that week-end party, of herself stealing through the gloom to purloin them—of the Marquis bound on the same errand—of their meeting—surprise—their pact and the bold, triumphant exploits they had both planned and carried out.

The red lips of the Countess were haunted by a smile.

It had all been so easy, so exciting, so simple. True, the dreaded Murgier of the Law had pursued them relentlessly but they had always outwitted him, had always laughed secretly at his discomfiture, rejoicing together over their spoils.

Now, tonight, it was the de Valois pearls—that famous coil the woman had had strung in Amsterdam by experts. Tomorrow Madame de Valois would be bewailing its loss and the necklace—the necklace would be speeding to some foreign port, safe in the possession of the agent who handled all their financial transactions.

"The Wolf!" the Countess thought.

Surely there was nothing to fear from the hulk of the Apache outlaw—a man whose cleverness lay in the curve of a knife, the slippery rope of the garroter, the sandbag of the desperado. How could the Wolf achieve something that required brains, delicate finesse? It was only the chance that Murgier might upturn some carefully hidden clew that was perilous—

"You are silent," the Marquis observed.

"I am thinking," the Countess d'Yls replied dreamily.

A dozen more streets and the motor was in the Rue de la Saint Vigne, stopping before a striped canopy that stretched from the door to the curb that fronted the Paris home of Madame de Valois. The windows of the building were brightly painted with light. The whisper of music crept out. Set in the little, unlighted park that surrounded it, the house was like a painted piece of scenery on a stage.

A footman laid a gloved hand on the silver knob of the limousine door and opened it. The Marquis de Remec assisted the Countess to alight. Safe from the rain under the protection of the awning, they went up the front steps and entered the house.

"You," the Countess instructed cautiously, "watch for Murgier and I will take care of the Wolf whelps! If the unexpected transpires we will meet tomorrow at noon in the basement of the Café of the Three Friends. François has been instructed?"

"He will keep the motor running—around the corner," the Marquis whispered.

Then, pressing her hand: "Courage, dear one, and a prayer for success!"

To the Countess d'Yls it seemed that all the wealth and beauty of the city had flocked to the ballroom which they entered together.

Under the flare of crystal chandeliers Fashion danced in the arms of Affluence. Everywhere jewels sparkled, eyes laughed back at lips that smiled. Perfumes were like the scents of Araby on a hot, desert breeze. Conversation blended with the swinging lilt of the orchestra on the balcony—the shuffle of feet and the whisper of silks and satins filled the room with a queer dissonance.

Separating from the Marquis, the Countess, greeting those who addressed her with a friendly word, a smile or bow, promptly lost herself in the crush. Murgier's assistants she left to the attention of de Remec. She decided, first, to mark the presence of Madame de Valois and the pearls— after that she would seek the Wolf or his agents in the throng.

After some manoeuvering the Countess discovered the location of Madame de Valois. The woman was dancing with a gray-bearded Senator—an ample, overdressed burden from whose fat neck the famous rope of pearls swayed with every step. The Countess watched the woman drift past and then turned to seek the footprints of the Wolf.

In and out among the crowd she circulated, disregarding those she knew, scanning anxiously the faces and appearance of those she had never before seen. An hour sped past before she believed she had at last discovered the man she sought. This was a beardless youth in shabby evening attire who lingered alone in a foyer that adjoined the south end of the ballroom.

Watching, the Countess touched the elbow of a woman she knew, discreetly indicated the youth and asked a question.

"That," her friend replied, "is a Monsieur Fernier. He is a young composer of music from

the Latin Quarter. Madame de Valois invited him tonight so that he might hear the orchestra play one of his own dance compositions. He is so melancholy, do you not think?"

"From the Latin Quarter," the Countess told herself when she was alone again. "I will continue to watch you, Monsieur Fernier!"

A few minutes later the Marquis de Remec approached.

"Three agents of Murgier present!" he breathed, drifting past. "The doors are guarded. Be cautious, dear one!"

Another sixty minutes passed.

It was midnight precisely when the Countess saw the putative student from the Latin Quarter make his first move. The youth took a note from his pocket and handed it to a footman, with a word of instruction. The servant threaded a way among the crowd and delivered the message to Madame de Valois. The woman excused herself to those about her, opened the note, read it, and after several more minutes began to move slowly toward the ballroom doors. The Countess, tingling, tightened her lips. A glance over her shoulder showed her that Fernier had left the foyer.

What was the game?

A minute or two after Madame de Valois had disappeared through the doors of the ballroom the Countess had reached them. She looked out in time to behold the other woman crossing the entry-hall and disappearing through the portieres of the receptionroom beyond. There was no one in evidence. Certain she was on the right trail and filled with a growing anticipation, the Countess waited until the portieres opposite ceased to flutter before moving swiftly toward them.

The metallic jar of bolts being drawn, a scraping sound and then a damp, cool current of air told the Countess that without question the long, French windows in the receptionroom, opening out on a balcony that overlooked one side of the park, had been pushed wide. She parted the portieres cautiously and looked between them.

The chamber was in darkness—Madame de

Valois was a bulky silhouette on the balcony outside—voices mingled faintly.

On noiseless feet the Countess picked a stealthy way down the room. Close to the open windows she drew back into a nest of shadows, leaned a little forward and strained her ears.

There came to her the perplexed query of Madame de Valois:

"But why do you ask me to come out here? Who are you? What is the secret you mention in your note?"

A pause—the suave, silky tones of a man:

"A thousand pardons, Madame. This was the only way possible under the circumstances. My secret is a warning—unscrupulous people are within who would prey upon you!"

"You mean?" Madame de Valois stammered.

"I mean," the man replied, "your pearls!"

Another pause—plainly one of agitation for the woman on the balcony—then the man again:

"Madame, allow me to introduce myself. Possibly you have heard of me. Paris knows me as the Wolf! Madame will kindly make neither outcry nor move—my revolver covers you steadily and my finger is on the trigger! I will take care of your pearls and see that no one takes them. Madame will be so kind as to remove the necklace immediately!"

Madame de Valois's gasp of dismay followed hard on the heels of a throaty chuckle. Came unexplainable sounds, the words:

Thank you. Adieu!

—then the woman tottering in through the open windows, a quivering mountain of disconcerted flesh, making strange, whimpering sounds.

Madame de Valois had hardly reached the middle of the reception room before the Countess was out on the balcony and was over its rail. A single glance showed her the shadowy figure of the Wolf hastening toward the gates at the far end of the park that opened on the avenue beyond.

With all the speed at her command the Countess ran to the other door in the street wall that was to the right of the house. The door was unlocked. She flung it open and surged out onto the wet pavement, heading toward the avenue, running with all speed while her fingers found and gripped the tiny revolver she had hidden under the overskirt of her evening creation.

She reached the gates at the northern end of the park at the same minute footsteps sounded on the other side of them. They gave slowly, allowing a stout, bearded man to pass between them. The Countess drew back and waited until he turned to close the gates after him.

Then she took two steps forward and sank the muzzle of her weapon into the small of his back.

"Do not trouble yourself to move, Monsieur Wolf," she said sweetly. "Just keep facing the way you are and I will help myself to the pearls without bothering you."

She could feel the quiver of the man's back under the nose of the gun.

"You will die for this!" the Wolf vowed.

The Countess found the smooth, lustrous coil of Madame de Valois's necklace in his side pocket and stuffed it hastily into her bodice.

"Possibly," she agreed amiably. "But this is no time to discuss the question. Pay attention to what I say. If you move before two minutes elapse I will shoot you down in your tracks! Continue to keep your face glued to the—gates—and—"

Dropping her weaponed hand, the Countess surged around the turn of the wall where the avenue joined the side street and raced across the petrol-polished asphalt toward François and the waiting limousine. Hazily aware of the growing tumult in the house itself, the Countess was stunned by the sudden crack of a revolver, the whistle of a bullet flying past her, the hoarse bellow of the Wolf's voice:

"Police! . . . Police! . . . Thieves! There she goes! . . . In that car . . ."

Pausing only to fire twice at the howling Apache, the Countess, sensitive to the fact that a machine was rolling down the street toward her, climbed into the limousine.

"Quick!" she cried breathlessly. "Off with you, François!"

Like a nervous thoroughbred, the car sprang

toward the junction of the avenue beyond. The Countess pressed her face to the rear window. The other motor was a thousand rods behind, a car with pale, yellow lamps—a police car—one of the machines of the Surete.

"Across the river!" the Countess directed through the open front glass of the limousine. "We will shake them off on the other side of the Seine!"

Across a bridge—over the night-painted river—past cafés and then into a district of gaunt, silent warehouses, the limousine panted. Twice more the Countess looked back. The pale, yellow lamps behind followed like an avenging nemesis.

"Round the next corner and slow down," the Countess commanded crisply. "The minute I swing off, speed up and head for the open country—"

On two wheels the limousine shot around into the black gully of a narrow, cobble-paved side street. Its brakes screamed as it slowed for a minute before lunging forward again. Shrinking back behind a pile of casks that fronted one of the warehouses, the Countess laughed as the second car whirled past.

"The long arm of Murgier!" she sneered. "What rubbish!"

Still laughing a little, she moved out from behind the casks—to stiffen suddenly and dart back behind them again. A motorcycle had wheeled into the silent street and a man was jumping off it.

The Countess, frantic fingers clutching the pearls of Madame de Valois, knew it was the Wolf even before his level tones came to her.

"Mademoiselle," the Apache said. "I know you are there. I saw the shimmer of your gown before you stepped back behind those casks. You cannot escape me. *Hand the necklace over!*"

"The theft of the de Valois pearls?" the Countess d'Yls cried softly. "Monsieur is joking!"

Murgier, on the shaded promenade of the Château, touched the tips of his disconsolate mustache.

"There is really," he said almost wearily, "no use in pretending surprise or indignation. Four days ago we bagged the Wolf—he made a full and complete confession . . ."

The sunlit quiet of the promenade was broken by the throaty cry of the Countess d'Yls. She jumped up, her blue eyes cold, blazing stars.

"Yes, you devil!" she said unsteadily. "Yes, Monsieur Ferret, we took the pearls—*I* took the pearls! The Wolf did not get them! No one else shall! I have hidden them well! Take me, take us both—jail us—you will never find the necklace—no one ever will!"

Murgier snapped his fingers twice. The men who had come up the dusty road in the travel-stained motor rounded the corner of the walk. The Countess laughed insolently at the man who faced her.

"In a measure," Murgier said quietly, "your statement is true. No one will ever reclaim the de Valois pearls. Let me tell you something. When the Wolf made his appearance that night at the warehouse, you saved the necklace from him by dropping it into the mouth of an open cask. Is that not correct? You marked this cask so you might distinguish it again. When you foiled the Wolf your agent began a search for the cask. It had been stored away in the warehouse—there were difficulties—so far your aid has not been able to locate it—but you have hopes. Madame Countess, it is my duty to disillusion both you and—" he nodded toward de Remec "—your husband. There was one thing you over-looked—the contents of the cask in question—"

The Countess drew a quick breath, leaning forward as if to read the meaning of the other's words.

"The contents?"

Murgier smiled.

"The cask," he explained, "we found to be half full of vinegar. The pearls are no more—eaten up like that! Pouf! Let us be going."

Snowbound

C. B. Yorke

HAROLD B. HERSEY, the publisher who created *Gangster Magazine*, wrote in his memoir, *Pulp Editor* (1937), that this was the magazine "that enabled me to lose money in that enterprise until the depression wiped out the business." He had also created *Racketeer Stories, Mobs, Gun Molls,* and *Gangland Stories.* The American public had become enthralled with gangsters and their luxurious lifestyle, so vividly reported in the nation's newspapers. While ordinary people suffered privation as the country plunged into what is now referred to as the Great Depression, they took solace and guilty pleasure from reading about the fun gangsters enjoyed as they partook of music, wine, beautiful women, fast cars, and so on. Little of it was true, but it made for good reading. Tastes change, and soon it was the FBI and the G–Men, those who captured or killed the criminals, who suddenly became the heroes, killing off the gangster publications.

Many of these pulps came to an abrupt end as the Roaring Twenties drew to a close. During their brief lives, they had failed to seduce the top writers into working for them, and most of the bylines appearing in their pages are unknown today. It is entirely possible that many of the stories were produced by popular writers using pseudonyms on their lesser work that appeared in less prestigious publications. Nothing could be discovered about C. B. Yorke.

"Snowbound" was first published in the October 1931 issue of *Gangster Stories.*

Snowbound

C. B. Yorke

Queen Sue was the toughest moll that ever pulled a gat this side of Hades—she was in the rackets for what she could get out of 'em—But peddlin' snow was entirely out of her line, and not even Garland's "persuasive" methods could make this baby change her mind!!

CHAPTER I

OVER HER HEAD

SHE WAS NERVOUS from the moment she entered my apartment. I didn't blame her much. Suds Garland had given her a tough job.

"Here's the money," she said, fumbling in her purse with trembling hands. "Five grand, cash."

I laughed softly. The girl looked up at me with wide eyes. Something in her gaze told me she feared more than what I might do to her.

"Chicken feed," I said, still smiling.

"Seven thousand?" she countered.

"That's funny!"

"Ten grand? That's a lot of money."

Perhaps ten thousand was a lot to her. She looked like a kid who wasn't accustomed to dealing in big figures when it came to cold cash. But as for me, ten thousand dollars didn't even get me interested in her proposition, and I told her so.

"Well," she went on, her thin voice shaking slightly from excitement and nervousness, "I'll give you fifteen thousand. Suds will go that high just to get you—"

"Make it fifty grand," I told her sharply.

A little gasp escaped her. I knew she didn't have fifty grand with her, and in all probability Suds wouldn't consider that price. It made no difference to me. So when she got over the shock of the figure I'd named I gave it to her straight.

"Listen, kid," I explained quietly. "I was just kidding about that fifty grand limit. No matter what—"

"Then you'll take fifteen grand?" she interrupted.

"No. Now listen closely. No matter what Suds Garland offers I'm not accepting it. See? Not even fifty grand in cash could tempt me to tie up with him in the dope racket. And that's final. What's your name?"

The girl looked at me with troubled eyes. She had come to my apartment that afternoon to try to get me to change my mind. I'd already told Suds that I wasn't interested in dope, wouldn't be interested, and couldn't be interested. He had sent the girl over to my place to see if money talked louder than words.

That had been a smart move on his part, but not smart enough. Had he known the real Queen Sue he wouldn't have wasted his time. Sure, I could probably supply much needed brains in his racket, but dope is one thing I don't touch, not even the racket angle of it.

Apparently the girl hadn't heard much about me, either. The kid figured I needed cash and would take anything she offered, gladly. Now when I asked for her name she snapped her purse shut and started to get up.

"Sit still," I told her gently. "There's nothing to get excited about. You've done your part, and you can't help it if I refuse the offer you've made. So now, just as one woman to another, let's have a little talk. Smoke?"

When we had cigarettes going she seemed to forget her nervousness. But she still watched me with sort of a sidewise glance as though she expected a couple of guns to appear around the corners of the rug and begin shooting. Perhaps she had heard something about me.

"Tell me your name," I went on presently.

"Kate Travers," she said softly.

"All right, Kate," I continued. "You know who I am, and now that we're acquainted I'm going to tell you something. You look like a nice sort of girl to be mixed up in this dope business. Just how—"

"Oh, I don't use it myself," she broke in quickly.

"I didn't think so," I responded, smiling faintly. "You're just playing along with Suds for what you can get out of it. That right?"

Kate Travers nodded and dragged at her cigarette. I framed my next speech carefully.

"I'm going to tell you something, Kate. Maybe you know it already, and maybe you don't. It doesn't matter much. I just want you to know that I'm not the least bit interested in Suds Garland, personally or financially. Feel better now?"

"But you—"

"Sure," I broke in swiftly. "Suds and I teamed up against Buzz Mallon. That was business, but I didn't take a cent from Suds. Partners in a business arrangement aren't necessarily friends. Suds and I worked together to protect ourselves. But that's all over now."

"Then you won't consider my proposition at all?"

I pitied the kid. She asked that question out of sheer ignorance. She was in the middle of something she didn't know a thing about, just acting as a cat's paw for Garland.

"No," I answered, moving my head slowly from left to right. "The proposition doesn't interest me. We're talking as friends now."

"But what will I tell—"

She stopped suddenly and stared at the cigarette in her hand with frightened eyes. She knew she had said too much, but it was too late to take back her words.

"You've got an out, Kate," I explained. "A good out. Suds can't blame you if I won't agree to throw in with him. I'll put it in writing if you want me to. I don't want to get you into trouble."

"Kind of you," she murmured.

I paused a moment and during the brief silence I wondered why I was being so lenient with the kid. I should have tossed her out the minute she tried to bribe me to join Suds Garland's mob. But I didn't.

Perhaps I saw in her a vision of myself a few years ago—young, slightly innocent of certain phases of gang life, and a little fearful of everybody and everything. Well, I was still young, but no longer innocent. And I was entirely without fear of physical forces. I'd managed to take care of myself, had fought my way up to the top of a big mob, and had seen it crumble under me.

Now I was lone-wolfing it, freelancing in crime for what I could get out of it. But I wasn't taking part in a dope racket, and anything Suds Garland had to offer was connected with dope. I had the Club Bijou, and was making money. For the moment that was all I wanted.

Later, perhaps, I would start building another mob. If I could find the right men to work with I'd do that. But it was all in the future. The loss of Dan Reilly, Biff Brons and Blimp Sampson, who had died in my fight with the cops, was still too recent to raise my hopes of ever finding men who could take their places.

So while I looked at the pathetic, frightened figure of Kate Travers I felt sorry for her. I did the best I could, but it wasn't much. Her troubles were not mine. She was sitting in with Suds Garland and there was nothing I could do about it. But I told her something I thought she should know.

"I'll be frank with you, Kate," I said finally. "You've probably heard that Queen Sue, Sue Carlton, was the toughest mob leader that ever pulled a rod. Well, I am hard sometimes. You've got to be in this life. But there's a time and place for everything. So you've got nothing to worry about now. How long have you been with Suds?"

"Two weeks, but I've known him—"

"No matter about that, Kate," I interrupted. I didn't want her life history. "He expecting you back right away?"

"I'm seeing him tonight to give him your answer."

"Fine. Now, I'll tell you what you do. Got a boy friend?"

Kate looked up, then nodded slowly. I went on.

"Well, run around and see him for a while. I'll get in touch with Suds myself and deliver my message in person. Then when you see him tonight there won't be a chance for him to get sore at you. Okay?"

"That's awfully kind of you, Queen," the girl said tremulously, "but Suds said I'd have to arrange things with you or—"

"Don't worry about that. Suds won't have anything to say, won't do anything to you." I smiled my assurance and she brightened. I honestly believed at that moment I was telling the truth. "So just run along now. It's not quite three o'clock. Have dinner with the boy friend and I'll fix everything with Suds."

After again thanking me, the kid moved to the door. I saw her to the elevator and then went back to my apartment and watched her leave the front entrance of the building a few minutes later. Suds should have known better than to pick a kid like her to talk to me about joining a racket.

When the kid passed out of sight along the street I turned away from the window, went over to the telephone, and called Suds Garland's number. There was no answer, so I made a mental note to call him later and dismissed the frightened little Kate Travers from my mind.

I had other work to do, what with managing a night club, arranging for liquor deliveries, entertainment, and a lot of other details, and it wasn't until almost an hour later that I remembered I had to call Garland and arrange for a meeting with him.

I'd just lifted the receiver when the door-bell rang. I got up, moved across the room, opened the door and got a real surprise.

Standing in the doorway, his soft felt hat pushed back off his brow, was Sid Lang, the big detective from the District Attorney's office who had broken me as a mob leader. I hadn't seen him since that night in Cincinnati when I had trapped him in my room and had purchased my freedom by sparing his life.

Since then the indictments against me had been quashed. So I put a big smile on my face, knowing full well there was nothing to fear.

"Come in, Sid," I said, not stopping to wonder why he was calling on me. "Certainly is nice to see you again. How's the D.A. and all your flat-footed playmates?"

The broad face of Sid Lang didn't relax in a smile. His cold eyes held mine steadily as he stepped into the room. He kept his hands in plain sight so I didn't make any moves toward the gun on my right leg.

"'Lo, Queen," he said laconically when the door was closed. "Heard the news?"

"The D.A. after me again?" I laughed.

"No. I'm not with the District Attorney's office any more. I'm working for an agency now—private dick."

"Trying to drum up business with me?"

"Cut it, Queen!" he said sharply. "I just heard something I thought you ought to know."

"Nice of you, Sid," I nodded, wiping the smile from my face. "When did you start playing on my side of the fence?"

"Don't be funny," he continued. "A kid by the name of Kate Travers was gunned out a while ago, a half dozen blocks from here."

My heart stopped.

"I got it straight," Sid Lang went on slowly, his voice sounding strangely hollow, "that she left you a few minutes before she got it. She was running with Suds Garland's mob. I happen to know that he wants you to join up with him."

Lang paused. I wasn't telling him anything, so I merely said, "Yes?" and waited. A moment later Lang added:

"The cops found fifteen thousand in marked bills in her purse. I'm interested because Kate Travers was—my girl friend!"

CHAPTER II
CLEVER—BUT NOT ENOUGH

Red rage gripped me as I heard Sid Lang's words. For a moment I didn't think about him or his feelings. I saw only the clever plot that Suds Garland had tried to trap me with.

It was all plain enough now. Perhaps Garland had really wanted me to join his mob at first, but my refusal had angered him. So when I wouldn't change my mind he wanted me out of the way. Perhaps it wasn't just business that was on his mind, and in turning down his business proposition I had unconsciously insulted his amorous intentions.

Well, it was too late to worry about what had brought on all the trouble. Kate Travers was dead. But I saw his whole plan.

Not for a minute had Garland expected me to refuse the money that Kate had offered. He had taken it for granted that I had taken the money. Then he had the girl killed so I would get into a pile of trouble.

And trouble it would have been. The cops would have swarmed all over me, for Suds Garland would have tipped them quietly that I'd taken money from the kid and then had had her killed so it wouldn't become known that Queen Sue could be bought.

Yes, it might have worked out that way. Suds Garland had planned carefully. The only hitch in his plans had been the fact that Queen Sue is her own boss. I never sell out to the side with the most money.

In the midst of my thoughts I was suddenly brought back to the present. Sid Lang stepped in close to me and gripped me hard with a big hand on either shoulder.

"What d'you know about the kill, Queen?" he demanded, icy points of cold rage appearing in his blue eyes. "Better talk fast because I'm going—"

"You're going to do—nothing!" I snapped.

"I'm going to kill you just as sure as I'm standing here! You put Kate on the spot and—"

My harsh laugh brought back his common sense. Looking him in the eye, every muscle in my small body steeled against the pain of that iron grip on my shoulders, I gave him glare for glare. Physically I didn't have a chance against him, but I won that silent clash of wills.

"Sorry, Queen," he muttered brokenly a moment later, taking his hands from my shoulders and flopping into a chair. "I guess I—lost my head."

"Forget it, Sid," I said quietly. "We all think we're pretty tough until something comes along that hits right at our hearts."

He nodded slowly. "Kate meant a lot to me. You wouldn't know how much."

A bitter smile curled my lips. In a low voice I said:

"I know exactly how you feel. Remember Chick Wilson and Dan Reilly? Well, you can't tell me a thing about sorrow. I've been there myself. You're just getting a dose of what I felt when you helped gun out Dan and Blimp and—"

"But I had to do—"

"Sure," I broke in quickly. "There was nothing personal in it. I know that. You just happened to be on the side of the law. I wasn't. If it would have done me any good I'd have killed you long before this. But that wouldn't bring Dan or Chick back. Neither will killing me give Kate a new lease on life. How did she happen to tie up with Suds?"

"Don't know—unless it was the money in it. We were going to be married as soon as I got enough money saved. But you don't put aside much in my work and—"

"Yes, she was just the type that would try to help her man. I'd have done the same myself. She probably thought she could step out of it after she'd made a couple of thousand. What did you let her do it for?"

"I couldn't stop her, Queen. She was in with Suds before I knew it. Then when I found out about it I didn't know how to go about telling her that she was making a mistake. You see—"

"Of course I see," I answered in a tired voice. "You men are all the same; great big stone brutes who can lick their weight in wildcats, but you're afraid of a little woman who might get angry with you. Kate didn't know what it was all about—didn't realize what she was doing. Listen."

I told Sid Lang how the kid had tried to buy me. That part of it I told quickly so he wouldn't get another idea that I'd had anything to do with the killing. Then I explained what had been behind her murder.

When I finished, Sid Lang took off his hat, ran broad fingers through his thin blonde hair, and looked at me with bleak eyes.

"God only knows why, Queen, but I believe you. See you later."

He got up and moved quickly toward the door. But I was quicker. "Calm down, bright guy," I ordered, turning the key in the lock and slipping the piece of metal down the neck of my dress. "You're not leaving here until you cool off."

"Give me that key before—"

He never finished that sentence. As his big hands reached for me again I sidestepped away from in front of the door. At the same instant my right hand shot under the hem of my dress and came out with my gun in my fingers.

"Back up, Sid!" I snapped. "You're not such a bad guy for being a dick, and you're not going to make a damned fool of yourself. Sit down—before I send you to the hospital with a slug in your leg. You'll be safe there."

For a moment I thought my argument wasn't going to work. I've never seen a guy with more nerve than Sid Lang has, but he knew I meant every word I said. He'd learned by experience that Queen Sue doesn't bluff.

When he was seated in the chair again I gave him some advice.

"I didn't want to do this, Sid, but I had to. You don't mean a thing in my young life, but listen anyway. If anything happens to Suds Garland now, the cops will come looking for you. You aren't on the force now. You're just an agency man—a private dick. And you might end up in the electric chair. Get it?"

He got it all right, but he didn't nod immediately. Behind his cold eyes I could see that his brain was working again.

"That's fine," I continued. "Perhaps in a way I was partly responsible for what happened to Kate, but you can't go around shooting a guy just because you know he's guilty of a dirty trick. You've got to have proof."

"I'll get it, and then I'll—"

"You listen to me! Get yourself a good alibi and sit tight. Remember, the cops will look you up if anything happens to Suds Garland."

"You mean you are going to—" Lang half rose to his feet in his eagerness.

"Sit down, Sid. That's better. I'm saying nothing about what I'm going to do or not going to do. I'm just giving you some good pointers. You happen to be a dick and I happen to be—well, a gang girl. We've always been enemies, but we're calling a truce for the next few days or weeks."

"I guess we are," nodded Lang resignedly. "But I'm not letting you fight my battles. I see the point in what you've been talking about, and I'll take it easy. Think I'll go now."

There was no use of talking to him any longer, so I went over, unlocked the door, and then stepped aside as I put my gun back on my leg. Sid Lang paused at the threshold and looked down at me with a faint smile.

"Thanks, Queen, for not letting me go off half-cocked," he said quietly. "I'll remember that."

Yes, he would remember that I'd done him a favor, but he didn't fool me. I knew as well as though he'd told me in so many words that he was going to kill Suds Garland, regardless of what I had said. And after I'd closed the door behind him I did some fast brain work.

Then a few minutes later I stepped to the telephone and called Suds Garland's number again. This time I got him on the wire. After that I didn't waste time.

"Don't ask who's calling," I said quickly. "This is just a friendly tip. You're on the spot!"

Before Suds could say a word I hung up. He had been clever in trying to frame me for the killing of Kate Travers, but not clever enough to outwit Queen Sue. My telephone message would give him something to worry about.

CHAPTER III
STRAIGHT TALK

Don't get the idea I was playing stoolie for anybody. No, nothing like that. I just didn't like the way things were shaping up.

There was a lot more to this whole business than surface indications showed. In the first place, Sid Lang's explanation of how Kate Travers happened to be in with Suds Garland's mob was very weak. But right at the moment I wasn't arguing the point.

My best bet was to play a waiting game, and I did just that. With Sid Lang thinking that I believed his story I figured something would break. Of course, I was taking a big chance that I wouldn't get in a jam, but I can usually take care of myself.

So far as Lang wanting to kill Suds Garland was concerned, I knew it was true. Garland had gunned out the girl and ought to pay for it. But for no reason at all both Garland and Sid Lang were trying to get me into the fight.

That's why I tipped Garland that he was on the spot. I didn't want anything happening to him until I found out just why and how I figured in his plans. I knew something would happen if I let things run their course. And it happened, but not as I'd expected.

I was sitting in my private office at the Club Bijou two nights later when there was the sound of scuffling outside my door. It was long past midnight and with a big crowd in the dining room I thought it was just a couple of drunks who'd found their way back into the corridor that led past my office.

A moment later I discovered what it was all about. The door opened and Francis, my head waiter, and one of the bouncers dragged in a small man who was sniveling and begging for mercy. I took one look at the three of them, then got up and closed the door behind them, locking it.

"What's up, Francis?" I demanded, frowning at the little man who suddenly became silent when he saw me.

Francis was nothing like his name sounded. He was more than two hundred pounds of bone and muscle packed into six feet of height. In the dining room, bowing and smiling to the patrons of the club, he looked and spoke like a gentleman. Out of character, he was the best muscle man I had.

So when I asked that question Francis scowled, jerked the little man around in front of him and snapped:

"Caught this guy peddling dope—snowbird himself."

I took a moment to think that over. The Club Bijou is on the lower East Side and in that district nobody but Suds Garland sells the stuff that makes old men out of younger men quicker than anything else in the world. So I figured this was another of Garland's bright ideas.

"What's your name, buddy?" I asked.

The little man cringed and looked up at Francis and the bouncer like a whipped dog. Then he babbled:

"I ain't done nothing! These birds just framed me—"

"Search him," I ordered, not wanting to hear his sob story.

"Already did it, Queen," replied Francis. "Here's what he had left."

He took a number of small folded papers from a side pocket of his tuxedo jacket and tossed them on my desk. I gave them only a glance and then looked back at the little man.

"So they framed you, eh?" I said quietly.

The little man nodded vigorously.

"Like to sniff a deck? Fix you up—steady your nerves," I continued, and almost smiled at the little man's reaction.

He looked at the folded papers on the desk, licked his lips with a nervous tongue, and frowned with indecision. He didn't know whether I was kidding him or not. I didn't wait for him to make up his mind.

"Sock him once, Francis," I instructed, "and toss the rat out into the alley. He won't come back."

Francis and the bouncer dragged the little guy out before he could squeal. A few minutes later I picked up the bindles of coke, went into the ladies' room, and washed them down a toilet. Then I went out to the main room and looked over the crowd.

Had the guy really been peddling the stuff in the club, or was he just trying to hide it? I didn't know, but I wouldn't have been surprised if Suds Garland had made a plant and then tipped the narcotic agents to raid me.

But there was nothing to gain by trying to figure things out by mere headwork. Francis had spotted the fellow before he could do any harm. So I dismissed the incident from my mind and sat down at one of the tables with some friends.

An hour later I was still there, laughing and chatting after the floor show had played its last turn of the night, when Francis gave me the high sign from the side of the room. I excused myself and went over to him.

"Suds Garland just went back to your office," he whispered rapidly. "I couldn't stop him without raising a row and that would have been bad for business."

"Anybody with him?" I inquired. Things were beginning to move faster. I like speed.

"Two bodyguards. What'll I do?"

"Get a couple of the boys and hang around the corridor. No gunplay unless I give the word. Don't want to ruin business. See?"

Francis nodded and I started to move toward the corridor that led to my office in the rear of the building. I'd taken two steps when Francis caught me by the arm.

"Where are you going?"

"To my office," I answered quietly. "Any objections?"

"No—but I don't want you to get hurt."

I smiled. "Thanks, Francis. Save your sympathy for Suds."

With that I moved on. It seemed like old times again to have somebody worrying about my safety. But it wasn't unusual. I pride myself on picking men who are loyal to me through thick and thin. And Francis was proving me right.

Once out of sight of the crowd in the main room I got the gun from the holster on my leg. Then with the comforting feel of steel in my palm I moved quickly down the corridor.

At the door of my office I paused for a moment and listened. Little sounds of movement came from the room, but there was no talking. Suds was apparently looking over the place before he settled down to wait for me. I didn't give him time to get impatient.

Turning the knob with my left hand, I opened the door a few inches, and slipped silently into the room. The next moment I had the door closed again, my gun up at my hip, and my back to the wall.

"Looking for me, Suds?"

The three men whirled at the sound of my voice. At the moment I had entered the room they had been crowded around my desk with their backs to the door.

None of them had their guns out. But as I spoke one of the bodyguards, a young fellow with a smooth, beardless face, raised his right hand toward an armpit holster.

"I wouldn't!" I snapped, and the youngster froze.

"What's the meaning of this?" demanded Suds.

I narrowed my eyes slightly while I smiled at his weak attempt to bluff my play. His tall, thin body was stooped in a half-crouch as though he

was going to leap across the room at me. His black eyes were expressionless, but the sight of my gun had caused the blood to drain from his ruddy face, leaving his skin the color of dirty milk.

"Sit down, all of you," I ordered. "You, Garland, squat at the desk, hands on the glass where I can see them. Snap into it!"

Suds Garland didn't argue. He seated himself in the chair in front of the desk and flattened his hands, palm downward, on the top like I'd ordered. The two bodyguards flopped into a couple of chairs along the wall at the right of the desk.

"Hands on your knees—and keep them there!" I continued.

They didn't need to be told twice. My smile broadened as I looked at each of the three men for a moment in silence. Then abruptly I wiped the smile from my face, bent slightly, replaced my gun in the holster on my leg, and then straightened.

"Think you're pretty tough, eh?" I sneered as the three held their poses. "Dealing with a woman is usually soft pickings for hard guys like you. Well, here's your chance to prove how tough you are. Reach for your gats!"

For perhaps all of ten seconds none of the three men moved a muscle. Maybe they knew I wasn't bluffing when I put my gat back on my leg. I knew I could beat them to the draw and none of them wanted to take the chance. Where I only had inches to move my hand they had feet, and covering distance in split seconds counts on the draw.

Finally Suds Garland shifted his eyes to the men along the wall and shook his head slightly. I laughed harshly.

"Bright guy, Suds," I snorted. "Telling the boys not to draw when they've already made up their minds to be good. I guess my reputation isn't so bad!"

Suds spread his lips in a sickly smile. "We're just making a friendly call, Queen. You beat up Johnny's brother and—"

"Who's Johnny?" I wanted to know.

Garland nodded toward the beardless fellow

who looked like a kid alongside the other muscle man who had a scarred lip and a broken nose.

"Okay," I said. "Go on with your song and dance."

"Well, you beat up Johnny's brother and—well, I just wanted to know what the idea was," Suds finished lamely.

"And I'll tell you," I returned in a harsh voice. "Dope peddling—or planting—is out at the Club Bijou. Get that straight! The next time I catch one of your punks around here you pick him up at the morgue. See?"

"But, Queen, I thought we were friends?" whined Garland.

For a moment I didn't know whether to laugh or call Francis and the boys and have the three of them thrown out. But I did neither. I just nodded slowly.

"I'm going to talk straight," I said quietly. "I think I was right when I guessed that you thought you were going to have an easy time fighting a woman. Now, I'm going to tell you something, Suds, and your two trained seals can listen in for future reference."

I paused a moment, but Garland had nothing to say. So I went on.

"A month ago when we were both fighting Buzz Mallon we played ball together. But if you got the idea we were friends you were mistaken. I told you then I didn't like dope and wouldn't join your racket. You, Suds, came into power after the cops wrecked my old mob and I had to leave town. You only know Queen Sue from what you've heard about her. If you were bright, you'd have learned something from what I did to Mallon."

"Didn't I help you get rid of Mallon?" Suds asked in a thin voice.

"You did, but I also helped you and that squared our account," I shot back quickly. "And from now on you'd better watch your step, or you'll think Mallon had an easy time of it. Maybe I'm not running a big mob like I used to, but I'm still Queen Sue. That's not boasting. That's a fact. Remember it."

"Ah, you're just nervous about something, Queen," shrugged Garland.

"Not half as nervous as you," I pointed out, smiling at the way Suds and his henchmen were holding the pose I'd given them. "You're walking out of here like good little boys, unless you want a skinful of lead. Move!"

The three of them got slowly to their feet. Keeping their arms at the sides they moved slowly towards the door. I backed off to one side, kept my back to the wall, ready for anything. But nothing happened that time.

Suds paused at the door and the other two crowded around him.

"Sorry we can't be friends, Queen," he said.

"I'm not," I replied. "Just because you had an easy time of rubbing out one woman you don't have to think all of them are that easy. And don't try to plant any more kills on me."

Suds arched thin eyebrows in feigned surprise. "Me—tried to plant a kill?"

I laughed again. "Forget it, Suds. It didn't work. But don't make the same mistake twice. By the way, better get a couple of guys with nerve. Bodyguards that let a woman bluff them don't amount to much."

Garland didn't reply to my taunt. He swung open the door and ran smack into Francis in the corridor. The other two crowded out after him and I smiled at my head waiter who looked at me for instructions.

"Take them out the front way," I said. "Just a little friendly call, but give them the works if there's any funny business. Scram."

Suds gave me a parting glare. My little talk hadn't accomplished much, but I knew it would serve to bring matters to a head. And it did, even sooner than I expected.

CHAPTER IV
FOOLISH BUSINESS

Dawn was breaking when I finally left the night club. I hadn't given Suds Garland and his mob a second thought since I'd seen him go down the corridor with Francis and the boys.

There had been no trouble at all about their leaving. But the moment I stepped out of the Club Bijou into the first faint light of a new day I had the uneasy feeling that something was going to happen. Perhaps it was just the eery half-light between night and day that affected me that way, but I was taking no chances.

A slight fog had settled over the city and now hung in shifting ribbons that swirled along the street like ghosts hurrying to escape the rising sun. I noticed those little details unconsciously because I wasn't interested in the beauties of a new day at the moment.

Across the pavement from the entrance of the club a cab waited. There was nothing unusual in that because the doorman or Francis always ordered a cab for me when I left in the morning, and any cab they ordered was safe.

So with scarcely a glance to either side I walked across the sidewalk and stepped into the cab. Then just as I seated myself I caught a glimpse of moving figures in the fog beyond the entrance of the club.

Before I could say a word the doorman, who was on duty late that morning, slammed the door and the driver let in the clutch. The figures in the fog grew plainer as they approached the cab, heads down, hands sunk deep in the side pockets of their coats.

I didn't wait to see more. The cab started to move as I opened the door on the far side and stepped out into the street. Shielded by the slowly moving cab from the figures on the side-walk, I slipped across the street and was partly concealed by the fog.

I hadn't acted too soon, for as I reached the opposite curb guns crashed across the street. A man cursed, and the cab stopped with a sudden squeal of brakes. I counted five quick shots. Then the slap of running feet on pavement came to me.

Straining my ears to keep the running men within earshot, I started along the street after them. A moment later the fog parted and I got a brief view of two men. Instantly my gun was in my hand, but even as I raised it the fog closed in again and the men were lost in the half-light.

Then as I started to cross the street again I heard the low purr of a powerful motor behind me. At the same time there was a chorus of shouts from the Club Bijou as Francis and some of the late diners and drinkers piled out on the street.

Almost before I knew it a long sedan slid past me in the fog and swung in toward the curb. The sound of running stopped.

Thinking fast, I sprinted across the few yards that separated me from the big car and swung up on the trunk rack that jutted out over the gas tank in the rear as the car gathered speed.

Minutes passed while the car swung around several corners, putting plenty of distance between it and the Club Bijou. I had all I could do to keep my balance on my precarious perch during the first few moments of that ride, but finally the car settled down to a steady run.

A few minutes later the protecting wisps of fog became thinner and finally vanished. But the hour was early and the few persons that were on the street didn't give me a look.

Then after about ten minutes of fast riding the car slowed down and slid in alongside the curb on one of the side streets uptown. I watched my chance and slipped off the trunk rack just before the car stopped.

I'd just gained the shelter of the doorway of a small apartment house when a rear door of the car opened and two men hit the sidewalk, moving fast. I raised my gun, then changed my mind.

They thought they'd got me in the taxicab. It wouldn't hurt anything to let them continue to think that for a while.

The house before which the car had stopped was a two-story brick structure. The first floor was vacant, so I figured the boys were to meet Suds Garland on the second floor. He had lost no time in repaying the courtesy I'd shown him at the Club Bijou.

But I couldn't tip my hand in broad daylight with no means for a getaway. So I put my gun back on my leg and watched the men go into the house. A moment later the car pulled away from the curb and disappeared around the next corner.

Five minutes later I was walking fast across town. I'd recognized one of the men who had tried to get me as the young fellow who'd been with Garland, but after being up all night I needed sleep more than anything else. I was going to have a lot of work to do that night.

Presently I caught a cab and twenty minutes later I was at my apartment. I had the driver wait for me while I packed a bag, and then went up to a hotel in the theatrical district.

It was almost three o'clock in the afternoon when I got up, bathed, dressed, and had breakfast sent up to my room. Then I phoned Francis at his apartment.

"God, Queen!" he exclaimed when he heard my voice. "I thought they'd taken you for a ride."

"Almost did," I admitted, "but I'm still alive and kicking. Get a couple of the boys and meet me at the club at five-thirty sharp. I've got work for you."

Well, that was that, I thought while I ate breakfast and then took a cab across town to Simon Grundish's office. I was going to need some airtight protection, and perhaps an alibi, and Grundish was the man who could fix it for me.

The political power behind the throne at City Hall didn't keep me waiting. He met me at the door of his private office right after I'd sent in my name. His wizened face and pale eyes seemed almost joyful when I greeted him and closed the door.

"What have you been up to now?" he asked quietly, knowing that I didn't waste time with social visits during business hours.

"Nothing much," I smiled. "Suds Garland tried to gun me out this morning. That was foolish business on his part. Understand?"

"I think I do," returned the little old man who had been instrumental in seeing that the old indictments against me had been dismissed. "Remember what I told you about Garland a month ago? Well, I still think he's bad company. It won't be any great loss if he—"

"Think you can fix it for me if there's a flareback after I get done with him?"

Grundish frowned for a moment, then nodded.

"Good," I smiled. "Seems like a lady can't even run a night club around this city any more without having some guy think he owns her. I don't like it. I think I'll have to branch out into something bigger just to keep the small-timers away from me."

"Suds Garland isn't a small-timer."

"No, and he's not so big, either. He thinks he's tough just because he makes a lot of money out of the racket. Maybe he was tough once, but money and good living have made him soft. It's ruined more than one good man, and dope doesn't draw good men."

"Well, Queen," Grundish shrugged, "you branch out any way you want to. I'd be careful of Garland, though."

"From now on I'm going to be," I admitted. "Just pass the word along to the cops that I know nothing about the dope business. See?"

Grundish smiled his thin smile which was as near as he ever came to genuine mirth. I left him a few minutes after that, knowing that even if some bright cop did want to ask questions he wouldn't get far. Grundish would see to that.

It was almost five-thirty when I reached the Club Bijou. Francis and four of the bouncers at the club were already there, waiting for me to give them the office. I did, starting first with the address of the house where the two men from the car had holed up.

"Drop out there after it gets dark," I ordered, "and smoke the boys out. It's a fairly quiet neighborhood so don't make too much noise."

"Leave it to us, Queen," promised Francis. "Anything else?"

"I think that will be enough for one night," I replied, and didn't smile when I said it. That business wasn't any joking matter, but I knew those two punks would never squeeze another trigger.

And they didn't. Francis and the boys returned to the club around ten o'clock that night. I listened quietly while Francis told me how they'd trapped the pair in the upper apartment. Maxim-silenced guns had done the rest.

I figured that incident would make Suds Garland think twice before he tried any more funny stuff with me. The killing of Kate Travers had ceased to be of importance in my mind, because to me the quarrel with Suds Garland was nothing but a personal grudge fight.

So I paid off on that job and when the club opened for business at midnight Francis and the boys were on deck as usual.

Everything went along quietly that night for the first hour or so, and then in the midst of the floor show, shortly after one-thirty, Suds Garland pulled the most foolish stunt of his career.

I was standing at the doorway of the corridor that led back to my office when it happened. The orchestra was playing a snappy little number and the chorus was cavorting across the floor when suddenly there was a stunning roar of an explosion.

Instantly the lights went out. Glass crashed at the front of the club and was lost in the crescendo of splintered wood, hurtling bricks and falling plaster. One guess was enough to know what had happened.

Suds Garland's mob had tossed a pineapple into the entrance hall!

CHAPTER V
THE QUEEN ACTS

Fighting my way blindly through the darkness and the crush of the mob that tried to rush the front entrance, I finally gained the main door. By that time tiny flames were crackling in the wreckage of what had been a hall, and were gaining headway fast.

The crowd of diners and dancers didn't get far. The whole front corridor was a shambles. Then over the shouts of the crowd sounded the bellowing voice of Francis, directing them to the rear corridor which led to an alley in the back.

With one accord the crowd rushed the narrow hall. It didn't take five minutes for them to jam themselves out of the main room. By that time I'd found a fire extinguisher in the darkness and was trying vainly to stem the tide of the flames.

Francis and some of the boys were lighting the place as best they could with flashlights. Other waiters were working more fire extinguishers and making no progress. Then suddenly in the distance I heard the clang of fire bells and the wail of police sirens.

"No talking, boys," I ordered, shouting to make myself heard. "I'll deal with the cops."

A chorus of agreement came to me out of the semi-darkness of what a few minutes before had been a brilliantly lighted spot of night life. I thought of the checkroom girl and wondered whether any guests had been caught by the blast.

For the first few minutes the battalion chief and the sergeant in charge of the emergency squad of cops had their hands full with the fire and the crowds that gathered in the street. Then when the flames were under control both the chief and the sergeant looked me up.

"Well, young lady," began the grizzled fire fighter, "what have you got to say for yourself?"

"Who tossed the bomb?" shot in the sergeant,

another veteran of bulldozing tactics which were usually effective.

"One at a time," I said quietly. "Suppose we go back to my office. It's still in one piece."

When I had a cigarette going in the back room and had rubbed most of the sweat and grime from my face and hands, I looked the two men in the eyes. They'd been firing questions at me continually, but they hadn't been able to break down my pose of ignorance.

"Listen," I said finally. "If I knew who did this, I'd tell you. Right at the moment this night club happens to be my only means of making a living. It's going to cost money to make repairs, but that's my worry. That's all I know. The blast get anybody?"

The two men exchanged a quick glance. Then the sergeant cleared his throat and said:

"Killed the checkroom girl and injured a man. That's all we've found so far."

"Who was the man?"

Why I asked that question, I don't know. Right at the minute I really wasn't interested in who the man might be, but the question popped out before I could stop it. A moment later I was glad I'd asked.

"The man was a private detective," said the sergeant. "Name of Sid Lang."

I didn't move a muscle as I heard those words, but my brain was working hard. What had Sid Lang been doing at the Club Bijou? Had he suspected that I'd had the two men, Suds Garland's bodyguards, rubbed out? I didn't know.

So I kept my face expressionless while I said:

"That's tough. Tell the guy I'll stand good for his hospital expenses and those of anybody else who was hurt. I don't want to have it said that Queen Sue doesn't take care of her friends. Tough about the checkroom girl. She was a nice kid."

"And you don't have any idea of who might have tossed that bomb?" persisted the battalion chief.

"None at all. You might scout around and see whether any of the neighbors saw anybody

they'd recognize just before it happened. I wasn't paying anybody protection and wasn't asked to. I just don't know who might have wanted to ruin my business."

"That's a lie, Queen Sue!"

I opened my mouth to deny that accusation, but I didn't speak. The voice had sounded strangely familiar, but had not come from the sergeant or the fire chief. Suddenly I caught my breath as I looked past them.

Swaying in the doorway, big hands braced doggedly against the jambs, his head swathed in bloody bandages, was Sid Lang!

"What are you doing here?" demanded the sergeant. "You ought to be—"

"That's—all right," gasped Lang, waving the sergeant's objections down while he crossed the room unsteadily and stopped in front of me.

For a moment none of us spoke. Hovering outside the door, I could see the dim form of Francis. Then I looked up and met Sid Lang's boring gaze.

"Get out, you," mumbled Lang. "I want to talk—to the girl—alone."

Slowly the two older men moved to the door and closed it after them. In the light of the flash that was propped up on one corner of the desk Lang's blood-streaked face was ghastly. I expected him to collapse any moment, but when I placed a chair for him he merely shook his head and remained standing.

"Sorry, Queen," he said slowly with a great effort, his voice nothing but a hollow whisper. "Didn't mean—to spoil your play."

"You didn't," I assured him. "You ought to be in the hospital."

"Going there—soon." He paused, laboring for breath. Finally he went on. "Listen, Queen. I'm out of this—for a while. I'm going to tell you something. I didn't give it to you straight—on Kate Travers."

"I know you didn't," I responded. "Come clean this time."

"Yes, do that. Kate was an undercover agent. Wasn't working for the agency—just for me.

Swaying in the doorway, his head swathed in bloody bandages, was Sid Lang!

She thought she could get more than I could. I told you straight about—what she meant to me. I'm hired to bust Suds for some rich guy. Garland made a snowbird out of his son. And so far Suds has made a bum—out of you. Get it?"

"Better rest up in the hospital," I said quietly. "You're off your head."

"Want me to—tip your play to the cops?"

"Spill and be damned!" I snapped. "I'm taking orders from no dick—not even a private flattie! Beat it!"

My heart stopped as Sid Lang turned slowly, laboriously toward the door. I wasn't fighting his battles, and he knew it. He had hoped to enlist my aid against Garland by giving me the straight story on Kate Travers.

Perhaps under ordinary circumstances I might have been impressed. As it was, I was fighting my own battles. I had a lot to settle with Suds Garland and his dope racket, but I wasn't giving Sid Lang any definite indication of what I was going to do to Garland. After all, Sid Lang was on the side of the law. I wasn't.

I'd played a lone hand this far, but as Lang started towards the door I thought sure he was going to spoil my play. Then I sighed with relief as he opened the door and said:

"I was wrong, sarge. The girl's okay. God— I'm tired."

As he finished speaking in a hoarse whisper, Sid Lang stumbled. Only the strong arms of the sergeant and the battalion chief kept him from crashing to the floor. Instantly I was at his side.

He opened his eyes for a moment. A faint smile wreathed his pallid lips as he looked up at me. Then he relaxed and lay still.

"Just fainted," grunted the sergeant. "Hey, somebody! Give us a light!"

I caught up the flash from the desk and led the way down the corridor to the alley. Silently I paid tribute to the sheer nerve that had kept Sid Lang on his feet until he had set me straight on the Kate Travers business. Perhaps that was what he had come to the club to do in the first place. It didn't make much difference now.

When Lang had been carted away in an ambulance the sergeant turned to me.

"A real man, that one," he said with genuine admiration. "He did great work while he was with the D. A.'s office."

"I know it," I said softly, and let it go at that.

The sergeant looked at me hard for a moment. Then he nodded.

"I guess you do," he agreed, remembering how Sid Lang had smashed my old mob. Then he added, "Well, I'll leave a police guard here, young lady, till morning. If you hear anything about who did this, let us know."

Thanking him quickly, I made my way back into the club and found Francis. By some strange means he had managed to avoid ruffling even a hair of his shiny head, and his dinner clothes were still as immaculate as though he had just come on duty. That suited me fine.

I'd been doing a lot of headwork in the spare moments I'd had between arguing with the sergeant and the battalion chief. I meant to pay my debt to Suds Garland in no uncertain way, but first I was going to play havoc with certain parts of his racket. So I gave Francis his instructions quickly.

"Get four or five of the boys who are still presentable. I'll meet you a couple of blocks away, corner of Severn and Leistner, in twenty minutes. We've got a lot to do, so make it fast."

Watching my chance, I slipped out the back way again. A few minutes later I was at an all-night garage, renting a sedan. I drove the car myself and picked up Francis and the boys right on schedule.

During the time Suds and I had been fighting Buzz Mallon, Suds had made the mistake of showing me what he called "spots of gold." In reality they were nothing but high-class apartments in the swankier districts of town where those who could afford to pay plenty were privileged to indulge their dope habits unmolested.

Suds furnished protection for the places and maintained them for his high-class clientele. I meant to smash at least three of the places that I knew existed.

Perhaps this bit of sabotage sounds like a childish prank, but it wasn't. Suds had struck at my pocket-book through bombing the Club Bijou. I meant to cut into his bankroll by smashing his expensive joints. Loss of money in a racket hurts worse than having a couple of punk gunmen killed.

So when I picked up Francis and the boys I explained the situation to them rapidly. They were all for the idea immediately and were in high spirits as I started uptown.

For my part, I wasn't exactly light-hearted. Anything can happen when you start out on a job like that, and right at the moment I didn't want anything to happen to me before I got to see Suds Garland personally.

He had a lot to answer for, and I meant to make him do it. Still, I've never been able to send my men into a place that was too tight for me to go myself. And I always lead the way when there's work to be done.

This time was no exception. When I pulled up at the corner above a tall apartment house twenty minutes later I cautioned the boys to go easy with the gats, and then piled out of the car.

Francis had a gun equipped with a silencer so I had him follow close behind me while we walked down to the entrance of the building, a half block away. The four other men paired off behind us.

Only one mug was on duty in the lobby. I gave him a bright smile as I walked towards the elevators, and then as I passed him I turned quickly, slipped out my gun, and jammed it against his back.

"Quiet!" I warned, and the guy wilted. Suds didn't seem to have luck in picking gunmen.

Francis pushed the signal bell at the elevator and a moment later the car stopped at the ground floor. It was one of those automatic affairs and it crowded us considerably as we all piled into it. I didn't take my gun from the mug's back for a moment.

On the way up to the tenth floor Francis relieved the guy of his rod and turned him over to the boys. Then as the elevator stopped, Francis and I stepped out while the rest of the boys held back. So long as the door was open the elevator couldn't be called to any other floor.

Walking towards the rear of the building, we didn't see anybody in the corridor. When I came to the door of apartment 1014 I pushed a bell button.

Almost immediately the door opened. Francis jammed his foot in the opening and followed it with a massive shoulder as he dug his gun into the belly of a guy with a long, thin face. After that there was no trouble at all.

I signaled the boys in the elevator and they came trooping back to the apartment. Half a dozen couples and two unattached men were lounging around the lavishly furnished rooms in various stages of helplessness. There had been a larger crowd earlier in the evening, I knew, because of the heavy reek of opium smoke that was still in the air.

We had a little trouble herding the people into one of the back rooms with the guards. Two of the women had to be carried, but after that the

boys had the place to themselves. In less than ten minutes it was one sweet wreck. Then we left.

We visited the other two places before we called it a night. At the third one Francis had to put a bullet through one guard's belly before he'd listen to reason, but there was no other trouble. Then I felt better.

Back in the car again, I told the boys to call at my hotel the next day for their pay, and then promised them a vacation while the Club Bijou was being remodeled. I let them out at one of the better hot spots, and then returned the car to the garage.

It was only a few minutes past three when I left the garage. I had intended to return to the hotel and catch up on some sleep, but after I'd caught a cab I decided to drop around to my apartment and get another dress. Crawling through that wreckage hadn't helped the looks of my evening gown much.

After that bit of work I figured Suds Garland would be plenty busy for a few hours, listening to the stories his guards would tell. I didn't know then that he still had another card up his sleeve.

I'd been dragging on a cigarette, very much pleased with myself, but when the cab came in sight of my apartment house I got a shock. Several cars were parked along the curb and a large crowd was gathered around the entrance of the building.

A crowd at that time of night meant just one thing. The cops were staging a raid, and something told me they were looking for me.

CHAPTER VI
IN THE BAG

Quickly I leaned forward in the seat, rapped on the glass partition, and told the driver to swing around the next corner and stop. While he followed those instructions I did some fast headwork.

By the time the cab halted alongside the curb I'd decided to see for myself what all the excitement was about. So I paid the driver and let him go. Then I started down the street towards the crowd.

If the cops were looking for me, I knew it wouldn't be a bad idea to find out what I was wanted for before they found me. There was enough of a crowd in the street to give me a chance to look around and ask some questions without being too conspicuous. And that's just what I did.

At first I tried to piece together the comments of the spectators that I overheard, but except for a lot of excited chatter about nothing in particular nobody was volunteering real information. Finally I moved in beside a man at the edge of the crowd.

"What happened, buddy?" I inquired, smiling my sweetest. "Raid a disorderly house?"

The man smiled at my sally. Then he became very blasé.

"Maybe that's what it is," he answered. "There's nothing to see here. I'm going home and get some sleep."

I was all set to crack wise at him when suddenly I felt a hand close over my left arm. Turning my head, I looked into the pale eyes of Simon Grundish. So I didn't say a word, just responded to the pressure on my arm and followed him down the street, away from the crowd.

When we were alone he took his hand from my arm. Grundish wasn't much of a night owl, and at his age when he was on the street at that hour I knew it was serious. But I waited for him to open the conversation.

"I just heard about it, Queen," he said a moment later, "and came right down to see what I could do. Lucky I found you."

"Yes, it is lucky," I admitted, "but I don't know what it's all about. What do the cops want me for now?"

"You don't know?"

"I don't. I just arrived before you found me."

"Well, Queen, this is pretty serious. The men who raided your place were Federal narcot agents."

"What!" I stopped and looked hard at Grundish.

"That's right, Queen," he continued. "They found a large quantity of dope—cocaine, I think it was—in your apartment. We're going to have a devil of a time beating the rap on that charge. I'll do what I can, but I can't promise—"

"Jeeze, what a lousy break that is!" I interrupted. "Snowbound, and no way of explaining that dope in my apartment!"

"No way at all that I know of. Looks like Suds Garland has played his ace."

"Yeah, but I'll beat the rap." I said that impulsively, not having the faintest idea of how I was going to do it. Then I got an idea. "Let's walk."

We walked, and I did some hard thinking. Presently I thought I had things doped out enough to give Grundish my idea.

"Listen," I began, speaking slowly in a low voice, "remember Sid Lang, the big detective who used to work for the district attorney? You know, the guy who smashed my liquor mob."

"Yes, I know who you mean. I don't think I ever met him, but—"

"Well, you're going to meet him. He's in the Mercy Hospital with a cracked head. That blast at the club caught him—killed my checkroom girl at the same time. He's a private dick now and has been working quietly on breaking Suds Garland's racket."

"Did he put the Federal agents on you?"

I shook my head. "No, nothing like that. Suds thinks he's clever, but he isn't. He planted that dope in my place—not Lang—and then passed along the tip for the raid. Remember the girl who was killed several days ago shortly after leaving my place?"

Grundish nodded.

"Well," I continued, "she was Sid Lang's sweetheart. That's something he's got to settle with Suds himself. So I want you to see Lang as early as you can. Explain the situation to him. Tell him I'm going to do him a favor and expect one in return."

"But what can he do that I can't, Queen?"

"Just this. He's been on the prod against this

dope racket. He knows who's at the head of it and probably was all set to make the pinch when he got smacked by that blast. I could use his testimony if the Feds get me and bring me to trial. See?"

"Bright idea, Queen," said Grundish admiringly. "I could probably fix the case, but it would take time and might cause a lot of questions to be asked. It isn't as though it were merely a liquor charge."

"Okay, then. You do that for me. Also see my lawyer and send him around to the hotel later today. You might drop around yourself and tell me what Sid Lang says. I think he'll come through. He's a pretty white guy for a dick. And thanks a lot for showing up when I needed you most. See you later."

"Where are you going now?"

"Me?" I put on a good act of being surprised. Then I smiled slightly and added, "I'm getting under cover where it's safe."

"Do that," said Grundish in parting.

My smile became bigger while I turned and watched Grundish walk off down the street, his short, thin body looking very frail in the darkness. And I had good reason to smile.

I wasn't going under cover just yet. I was going to settle the score with Suds Garland in the only way he seemed to be able to understand—with guns.

It was still more than an hour before daylight, and I figured I had time enough to call upon Garland in person that night. The weight of the gun on my leg gave me added confidence as I hailed a cab a few minutes after Grundish left me.

Giving the driver an address that would bring me within a block of Suds Garland's place, I lighted a butt and settled back to enjoy the ride. Fifteen minutes later I left the cab and waited until the car moved away again, getting down to the business at hand.

The apartment house where Garland was living was a six-story structure, situated on a corner. Along one side ran an alley that showed the faint outline of fire escapes up the side of the building in the darkness. The other side of the building was adjoined by a small brownstone front.

I didn't waste any time trying to climb up the fire escape. Suds lived on the fourth floor and that was too much of a climb for the time I had to spare. I went right to the main entrance and looked over the array of bell buttons and name cards, among which was one plainly labeled Garland.

But I didn't push the bell under that card. I selected two apartments on the sixth floor and held down the buttons for a full minute of steady ringing.

The street door was one of those safety latch things that can be opened from any apartment in the building. Somebody in one of the two apartments I was ringing would almost certainly release the latch, late though it was. And they did.

With the first click of the latch I was in the building. The main corridor was dimly lighted by widely spaced bulbs. I found the stairs and climbed fast, ignoring the automatic electric elevator opposite the steps. Too much noise might warn Suds of my visit.

At the fourth floor landing I paused. Not a sound came to me. As yet the people at the top floor didn't suspect they were receiving no visitors and had not opened their doors to investigate.

Silently I moved along the corridor until I stopped at the door of Suds Garland's apartment. Then after a final glance along the hall I got my gun in my right hand and pressed the doorbell with my left forefinger.

I was taking a big chance, and I knew it. I wasn't certain that Garland was home, and if he was I wanted to be ready for anything. I was.

After a couple of minutes there was the sound of a key turning in the lock. Then several bolts were shot back. Keeping off to one side of the door, my back flattened against the wall so that I was out of sight, I waited.

I felt rather than saw the door swing open on silent hinges. For a long breathless moment I thought my plan wasn't going to work. Then, curiosity aroused, Suds Garland himself put one foot over the threshold and looked out along the corridor.

My gun hit his belly and stayed there.

"Inside!" I breathed, increasing the pressure of the gun as Garland recoiled from its touch. "Keep your hands high!"

His eyes went wide with sudden terror, but he raised his hands without a murmur. The next moment I was on the other side of the door and had kicked it shut and locked it.

"Got company?" I asked.

Suds shook his head. I didn't believe him.

"You lead the way. I want to talk to you, but if you're lying I'll give you the business pronto. Move!"

He walked steadily enough into the living room. There I found a couple of softly shaded lights burning. Garland was in his shirt sleeves, and had apparently come in only a few minutes before I arrived. His hat and coat were lying on a chair as though he had just taken them off.

So far as I could see he hadn't been lying after all about not having company. From the living room I could see into a small dining room. Beyond that I knew was a bedroom, and both rooms were in darkness.

But I didn't take any chances with Garland. The boy was tricky, and before I faced him again I relieved him of a snub-nosed .38 revolver that bulged plainly in his hip pocket. Then with a gun in each hand I backed around in front of him and made him sit down on a divan. I remained standing.

"Suppose we cut the talk short," I opened, noticing that Suds had regained his composure. If I hadn't been so mad I might have known that his confidence spelled trouble.

"Just as you say, Queen," he answered evenly. "You didn't have to come busting in here like that. I'd have let you in."

"Yes, you would!" I jeered. "I'm finished with playing nice with you, Suds. I'm going to show you how tough a lady can be."

"You and who else?"

"We won't argue the point," I went on. "I

want a signed confession from you that you planted that snow in my apartment."

"What snow?"

His pose of innocence was funny. But I didn't laugh.

"You've got a pencil in your vest pocket," I continued. "Get that newspaper off the floor in front of you. Write the confession on the margin. I'll dictate it."

"I'm a hard man to deal with, Queen," he stated with a great show of nerve. "A hard man. You just think I'm soft because I've been easy with you. Now I'm going to show you just how tough I am."

"Can the chatter!" I snapped. "Get that pencil in your hand!"

I gestured with the gun in my left hand. Suds Garland laughed softly, derisively.

"You little fool!" he blazed, leaning forward while he looked up at me with flashing black eyes. "You've been covered ever since I sat down. Give it to her, Gus, if she moves a muscle!"

For a moment I didn't know whether he was merely bluffing or really meant that speech. The business of getting you to look behind you for an attack from the rear was old stuff. So I hefted the guns in my hands and watched Garland closely.

Suddenly I froze.

"Right," drawled a voice behind me.

Suds Garland had not been bluffing. The single word told me that a gunman was concealed in the darkness of the dining room. Just when I thought I had Garland in the bag I had been trapped myself!

CHAPTER VII
NOT SO TOUGH

For a full minute I remained perfectly motionless. Not a sound could be heard, save the hoarse breathing of Suds Garland and the man behind me.

The strain was terrific, but I've been in a lot of tight places and my nerves can stand plenty. This time was no exception. If I could prolong the suspense either Garland or the fellow called Gus would break under the nervous torture. But I wasn't doing nothing while I waited.

I was thinking—hard!

Finally as Suds moistened his lips with the darting point of his tongue I raised my left thumb and slowly pulled back the hammer of the .38. There was a sharp click as the hammer settled into the full cock position.

That slight sound only served to increase the tension. Garland's black eyes narrowed to slits. The muscles of his lean face became rigid as he sought to control his features. I might be in a tight place, but he certainly wasn't having a picnic.

"Well?" I said softly, and in that intense silence it sounded as though I had shouted at the top of my voice.

I wasn't making a grandstand play. Pulling back the hammer of the .38 had been straight business. I figured that if it came to a showdown with the man behind me I could get in at least one shot that would keep Garland with me when I went down under a bullet.

But I really didn't want to kill Suds Garland—yet. I wanted him to live long enough to write that confession and sign it. After that I would kill him with his own gun and make it look like suicide. That would give him the best out he could get.

When there was no answer to my single question I knew Garland and the guy behind me were uncertain about their next move. They had expected me to drop my guns and be a good girl, but they didn't know Queen Sue.

After another minute or so of silence I got tired of waiting. It was evident enough that both men knew what would happen if the guy in the dark took a shot at me. But waiting was getting me nothing. I wanted action.

"Take plenty of time to think it over, Suds," I advised in a sneering voice. "If you're the hard mug you think you are, tell your buddy to squeeze lead or drop the gun."

"You—you don't have a chance, Queen," he stammered after a moment. Little beads of sweat oozed from his face and formed bigger drops that ran down his cheeks and the sides of his nose unheeded. "You can't get out of here alive."

"Speaking for yourself?" I threw back coolly.

But I wasn't as cool as I sounded. I'm only human after all and with a guy like Garland I couldn't tell how this battle of wills was going to turn out.

My last crack floored Garland for a moment. Then he looked past me and did things with his eyes.

I guessed what he meant, and raised the gun in my right hand slightly. Then I shifted the .38 slightly to the left where it would be handier for a quick shot without interfering with the movement of my right arm.

Suds' work with his eyes had meant only one thing. The man behind me was to close in and overpower me without risking the chance of Garland getting shot.

The next moment soft-soled shoes slithered over the floor behind me. But I didn't turn immediately. I waited until I figured the man behind me was almost within reach. Then I went into action.

Raising my right hand swiftly, I brought the nose of my automatic down hard on Suds Garland's mouth. Simultaneously I whirled towards the left, brought the .38 in the open away from my body, and squeezed the trigger once.

I hadn't been a moment too soon. The guy behind me had raised the gun in his right hand to club me down. The bullet from Garland's gun caught him in the center of the throat under the chin, passed upward through his head, and knocked plaster from the ceiling.

The impact of the bullet lifted him up on his toes. Then while the roar of the shot still seemed to fill the room he started to fall.

I shot a quick glance at Garland. The guy who claimed he was so tough was grovelling on the divan from the blow on the mouth that had brought blood spurting to his smashed lips. I started to talk fast, but something that wasn't on the schedule took the words out of my mouth.

The guy who'd tried to slug me hit the floor with his face. At the same instant his gun exploded as his right hand thumped the rug, throwing the muzzle of the gun upward.

He wasn't six feet from the divan when he fell. The bullet plucked at the skirt of my dress and slammed into Suds Garland's chest. The guy called Gus must have used hollow-nosed slugs, for that hunk of lead made a gaping hole as it tore through flesh and bone.

I didn't wait to see more.

Slipping my automatic back into the holster on my leg, I quickly wiped the butt of the .38 with a corner of my dress and tossed the gun down beside Suds. I didn't try to remove all traces of fingerprints. It would look more natural if they were only smeared so they couldn't be recognized.

One look was enough to know that trying to get a confession from Garland was useless. He was still alive, but that slug had ripped a lung wide open. Already bloody froth bubbled to his lips.

I didn't wait to see the end. Less than a minute had passed since I'd fired that first shot, but voices in the corridor told me that I didn't have a moment to spare.

Moving swiftly, I passed through the dining room and into the bedroom. Another moment and I had the window up, and stepped out on the fire escape. A police siren moaned plainly as my feet touched pavement again, and I was a block away when the cops rushed into the building.

Yes, Suds Garland thought he was pretty tough. Maybe he was. But all men—and women, for that matter—look alike to a hunk of lead.

The cops put Suds Garland's death and that of Gus down as a duel over gang affairs, and I didn't tell them any different. On the advice of my lawyer I gave myself up and stood trial on the dope charge.

But I didn't stay snowbound long. Sid Lang's testimony about the dope ring resulted in my acquittal, and I wondered what Suds thought of me beating the rap with the aid of a dick.

The Girl Who Knew Too Much
Randolph Barr

NOT TOO SURPRISINGLY, the author of this rather formulaic story is unknown, as Randolph Barr was a house name, used by many of the hacks willing to work for one of the *Spicy* publications. Published by Culture House (perhaps named ironically), the minor empire included *Spicy Detective*, which was issued from April 1934 to December 1942; *Spicy Adventure* (July 1934–December 1942); *Spicy Mystery* (July 1934–December 1942); *Spicy Western* (November 1936–December 1942); and *Spicy Movie Tales* (one issue only in October 1935). Because of the racy covers and interior illustrations, plus the content of the stories, public pressure caused the publisher, now Trojan Publishing Co., to change titles to *Speed Detective*, *Speed Mystery*, etc., and reduce the provocative nature of its contents. But don't get your expectations too high. What was racy, spicy, snappy, and saucy in the 1930s will seem rather tepid today. "The Girl Who Knew Too Much" is one of the better stories to be found behind the garish covers of the *Spicy* books, which does not make it Shakespeare, or Chandler, either, since the magazine paid much less than its contemporaries. While *Black Mask* and *Dime Detective* were paying two cents a word, and lesser periodicals half that, *Spicy* paid only a half cent a word—the bottom of the barrel for writers struggling to pay the rent. As is true of most of the stories in *Spicy*, we meet our heroine with her dress ripped down to her waist. This is what passed for titillation in April 1941, when "The Girl Who Knew Too Much" was first published.

The Girl Who Knew Too Much

Randolph Barr

He shoved the girl back and brought up his gun

THERE WASN'T ANY particular reason for my being way down on the East Side. It was a warm Spring night, and I was taking a walk, not paying much attention where my feet strayed. It was nearly two o'clock when I looked at my watch, wondering if I shouldn't be turning back and thinking again about going to bed.

I looked around. Deep in thought, I'd wandered all the way to Second Avenue and Second Street. That part of town was, curiously, almost deserted.

Then from up a side alley I heard the clicking heels of a running girl. I turned. She came like a miracle of beauty out of that dingy cul-de-sac of warehouses and manufacturing lofts. Her skirt was bunched in her hand above her knees to facilitate her speed, and white flesh gleamed in the dim light.

I stood stock still, just around the corner of the building where she'd come out on the avenue. Her black dress had been ripped to her waist, and the remnants of a pink silk slip barely held together at one shoulder.

She reached the mouth of the alley and I stepped suddenly in front of her, blocking her way. I studied her in the winking lights of the Little Albania, Louis Russo's third-rate night club. I said, "What's the hurry? Something scare you?"

Her breasts were heaving from her running,

and she fairly panted when she spoke. "Let me alone! Look out! For God's sake!" She darted suddenly to the side and tried to compress herself into a doorway.

I didn't know what it was all about, but she hadn't been fooling when she spoke. I squeezed in beside her and followed suit in trying to keep out of sight.

Then there were other footsteps coming up the unlighted alley. This time they were made by a man, a man who was trying to move soundlessly.

I chanced a look.

There was a black shape creeping around the corner of the building to the street. It hugged the wall.

Out of the alley came a flash of orange flame. There was the report of a gun that was like a sharp cough, and the crouching figure tumbled in a heap, legs in the alley, head and outflung arms on the sidewalk of the avenue.

The girl and I remained flattened in the doorway—even when unseen hands caught the ankles of the fallen man, and we heard the gruesome sound of his body being dragged over the rough cobblestones back into the darkness.

My forehead had an uncomfortable clammy feeling as I peered out again and saw the little pool of blood and the man's hat near the curbstone. As a newspaper man, I'd seen my share of violent death, but this was giving me the jitters.

The street itself had become morgue-quiet. The only sound was the faint sobbing of violin strings, the occasional pulse of a drum, and the wail of a saxophone from the Little Albania's shuttered windows.

The girl came to life. She said, "You'd better scram fast, mister!" She caught up her skirt again and started to run north up Second Avenue, sticking closely to the shadows. Automatically I followed.

A couple of blocks up, she halted in a vestibule and confronted me. "Will you keep out of this? Haven't you seen enough? Do you want to be laid out on a slab beside that other man back in the alley?"

I caught her arm. "I'm a newspaperman, sister. Give!"

Her eyes widened. "You'd better not print anything you've seen tonight! Russo's mob doesn't like reporters. Anyway, I'm in a hurry!"

"That's okay with me," I told her. "I've got a lot of time. And I'm sticking with you."

She smiled wanly. It looked as if she were going to lose the slip when she shrugged, but she caught it and pulled the tatters of her clothes together. "If I can't shake you, let's go. The farther we get away from here, the better!"

At the next corner I whistled for a cab. I asked, "Where do you live?"

"Not far away. But I'm not going home tonight! It might not be healthy."

She shivered against me as I helped her into the cab. I slid an arm around her, and she didn't object. Speculatively, I gave the driver the address of my own Grove Street apartment.

She didn't demur, even when we pulled up at my place and I asked her in for a drink.

The first sip of her highball went far in helping her to relax. We sat side by side on my divan, and she smiled when I put an arm around her shoulders. "Feel like loosening up?" I asked her.

She misunderstood me and snuggled closer, but I didn't mind. I kissed her warm, moist, inviting mouth. But a minute later I laughed. I said, "I really meant do you feel like telling me what it's all about?"

She reddened prettily. "You mean about Dick Tobin's shooting. He wasn't really a bad guy—" She stared straight ahead as if deciding how much to tell me. "Both Dick and the big fellow—"

"You mean Russo?"

"Yes. They both wanted me. The mob considered me Dick's girl. Louis intended to bump Dick anyway. I'm not sure just why he had it in for Dick, but he used me as an excuse to get rid of him."

I pointed to the silk dress which hung in jagged strips. Through the tatters her flesh was pink and smooth and warm-looking.

She colored again, and tried to cover herself better. "Russo did that. He had me in his office, and was getting rough. I managed to fight him off, and slipped out the back way. He sent Dick Tobin after me—"

I nodded. "And then he himself came out—"

"Yes. And I'm scared! I know he wants me now, but he'll kill me when he tires of me! I know too much about his mob."

She seemed as pitiful as she was lovely, sitting there in my living room. I looked into her great dark eyes, and wondered what I could do for her. I said, "You've got a hell of a good story, but it would be dynamite to handle. At least, without a lot of substantiation." She was cuddled against me so that I could feel the vibrancy of her slender, exquisite form. I hugged her against me so tightly that her breasts flattened on my chest, but she strained even harder. . . .

Breathless, she pushed away. She said, "Now that you've got me here, what are you going to do with me? I don't dare go home."

"What about a hotel?"

"At this time in the morning? And looking like this?" She indicated her ruined dress.

I said, "Well—?"

"You haven't even thought of inviting me to stay here?"

I grinned. "It's okay with me. It ought to be safe enough."

She caught my arm when I picked up the telephone. "What are you going to do?"

"My job, baby." I brushed her arm off and dialed the *Courier*. I talked to the desk briefly, then turned back to the girl. "That's that," I said. "Tomorrow the paper will carry a short paragraph saying that a gangster named Dick Tobin was killed near the Little Albania. By the way, you haven't told me your name."

"Polly Knight. And where can I sleep?"

I pointed to the bed. "Such as it is, it's all yours. I'll see if I can find you a pair of pajamas."

When I turned back from the bureau, she was seated on the edge of the bed, peeling off her stockings. The picture was tempting, but I forced myself to think of my job. I should be reporting at the office. I picked up my topcoat.

"Where are you going?" Polly asked, her eyes showing panic again. I told her, and she caught at my arm. "No! No! You can't leave me! You've already called in. If there was anything important for you, they would have told you!"

I studied her. And her terror wasn't faked.

She said, "I didn't like the way that taxi-driver stared at me. He might be one of Russo's men. Please don't go!"

I hung up my coat. While she watched me, I got my automatic from my desk and put it in a hip pocket. I saw that the key in the lock was turned so that it wouldn't easily fall out. For extra precaution I wedged a chair under the knob. I said, "That ought to cover everything."

Much calmer, Polly slipped out of her torn dress. While she got into the pajama jacket, I fought to keep from sweeping her into my arms. All that saved her, I think, was her atmosphere of utter helplessness.

She said, "You're being awfully decent. And me, I'm just a gangster's girl! Funny, isn't it?"

I took off my coat and vest and shoes and sprawled in the morris-chair. When I looked at Polly again, she was under the covers.

Her voice was a gentle murmur. "I feel like a heel—chasing you out of your bed."

I knew how I felt, but I didn't tell her. I said, "Don't worry. In case we should have visitors—" I switched off the lights, and tried to make myself comfortable.

It seemed like a long while, but couldn't have been more than half an hour, when I heard the shuffling footsteps outside down the corridor. I was wide awake in an instant. I got silently to my feet. I tiptoed to the bed.

A small soft hand caught mine. Polly was sitting up in bed, trembling.

The steps came nearer. I took out my automatic, and stared through the gloom toward the door. But the footsteps shuffled past and grew fainter.

Relieved, I stuck the gun back in my pocket.

"It was a drunk, trying to find his room," I whispered. I patted Polly's shoulder.

"Stay here beside me for a little while," she pleaded. "When I can't see you or touch you, I get the willies."

Tired and sleepy, I leaned back. . . .

It seemed like ten seconds, but it was daylight when I opened my eyes. Dressed in my over-size pajamas, Polly was seated in the morris-chair, examining her ruined dress. She smiled ruefully. "I don't suppose you'd have a needle and thread?"

I wouldn't and I told her so. I had a better idea. "Tell me where you live, give me your key, and I'll get you something to wear. None of Russo's crowd knows me."

She assented. "Before you go," she said, "I'd like to tell you that, in spite of what they all said, I never really was Dick Tobin's sweetheart. None of Russo's crowd ever actually touched me."

She was a little wistful, and I don't think she really expected me to believe her. Curiously, I did, and my heart was strangely light as I fitted her key into her door.

The apartment was nicely furnished, done with restraint and in good taste—not at all the sort of place you would have expected a gang girl to have.

I headed for a closet, had a sudden apprehension of danger, turned, and caught the full weight of whatever it was that hit me squarely on the head. . . .

Coming back to consciousness was an agonizing experience. My head had bells in it, and was all but cleft in two, anyway. Then I discovered that my hands were tied behind me and that my ankles were roped together. I was in Polly's apartment. Louis Russo sat in a chair across from me.

He leered at me. "So you tried to butt in!" he sneered. "I was waiting for Polly. If I keep on waiting, she should be along anyway. I'm in no hurry." He blew smoke in my face.

I recognized the truth of what he said, but there was nothing I could do about it.

He grinned. "I'll take care of you later," he said. "When I get through with Polly, I'm not going to leave you where you can talk about it."

There were icicles in my blood.

Russo must have heard the step outside before I did, for he jumped up suddenly, caught me by the collar, and literally dragged me across the floor to the bathroom. He left the door open a crack—probably due to his haste—and I could see into the other room without being easily seen.

The knob of the door to the corridor turned, and the door opened. It was Polly Knight. Her mouth made an explosive gasp as Russo suddenly appeared from behind the door. He jammed the muzzle of a gun into her side.

Without a word he reached out, caught her torn dress at the neckline and ripped it all the way down. Then he stood off and surveyed her. He said, "Get into another rig! That thing might attract too much attention where I'm going to take you."

While she, helplessly, took another dress from a hook and slipped it over her shoulders, he said, "I thought you'd be along when your boy-friend didn't come back to you." All the time, his eyes were licking at her alluring loveliness.

When she had dressed, he flung the door to the bathroom wide. I glared at him and tried to flash some sort of encouragement to Polly. I'm afraid that, bound up as I was, I couldn't have helped much.

Louis Russo grinned unpleasantly. "We'll have to leave this one. If we took him in the car, it might attract too much attention. We'll send some one to take care of him soon." He turned to the girl. "You walk ahead of me. And don't forget the gun in my pocket!"

When they had gone, I continued my struggle against my bonds. The only result was to make them bite more deeply and painfully into my flesh. Nevertheless, realizing that Russo's men might arrive at any moment, I didn't relax my efforts.

My eye lingered on the glass shelf over the wash bowl. One end had been splintered and looked as if it might provide a cutting edge.

Sweating, I edged across the floor, nudged a

stool along with me. After half a dozen tries I got onto the stool and worked my wrists up to the jagged edge of the shelf.

My wrists were lacerated and bloody before my hands were free. It was a matter of seconds then to release my ankles.

My muscles still felt cramped and my head was dizzy when I reached the street. A long black sedan was edging in to the curb. Certain that the car was driven by Russo's men, I kept my head down and hurried my steps to the drugstore on the corner.

I stumbled into a phone booth and dialed police headquarters. My pal, Inspector Daly, wouldn't be in for a couple of hours. I cursed. But, knowing pretty well what my answer would be, I talked to his relief, Lieutenant Finger. He said, "*What?* You want us to raid the Little Albania! And the only reason you can give us is your word that a girl is being held prisoner!

"Listen, newshound! Louis Russo's too smart to be playing with that kind of stuff. Before we tangle with him, we're going to need a little more to go on. Besides, the police department wasn't established to build up the circulation of your lousy paper. Better lay off the pipe, and tell your boss the same thing!" He hung up.

It had been about what I'd expected, but that didn't make me feel any better. Whatever I did, I'd have to do alone—and in a hurry.

I flagged a taxi and gave an address a block away from the Little Albania. The alley that led to the back entrance was deserted. I edged down it and found that the door was locked. There was an open window on the third floor.

The alley was only a few feet wide and the open window gave me an idea. Across from Russo's place was an abandoned warehouse, most of its windows shattered.

I slid into the warehouse and picked my way up stairs jammed with refuse. On the third floor I found a long plank lying among dust-covered heaps of rusty, outmoded machinery. I dragged the plank to the window and eased it across the

alley. It reached the sill on the other side with a foot to spare.

Cautiously, giddy with fear, I worked my weight out on the sagging plank. I had reached the other side when the thing canted sideways. I caught at the open sash as the far end of the plank slipped clear, slapped at me, and crashed thirty feet down to the cobbled court. Weak as water, I half fell over the window sill.

The room I was in was evidently a storeroom. Cases of all sizes, crates, and boxes crowded all but an aisle to a door. I opened it noiselessly and looked into a private banquet room. A thug-like porter was mopping the floor.

I kept back behind the door until he had worked around to where I waited. Then I leaped. Both my hands got him around the throat. He was gasping for breath when I released him a second and swung my Sunday punch to the point of his jaw. He went limp.

I devoted precious minutes to knotting a twisted table-cloth about his wrists and ankles, and gagging him with a napkin. By the time I'd dragged him under a table, I was sure that he wouldn't be able to bother me for a while.

There was the sound of voices from a door that I took to be Russo's office. I tried the knob silently and found the door locked. Now I could make out the words. It was Russo speaking. "You can yell your head off, sweetheart. Nobody will hear you. Up here we are very safe."

I tiptoed toward the front of the place, entered a cloakroom, and followed it through to a door on the other side. I came out on the landing of a stair-case. And, as luck would have it, there was another entrance to Russo's office! Prayerfully I tried the knob. Thank God, Russo hadn't thought it necessary to lock this door!

I had it open a fraction of an inch when I froze. Voices came from the banquet room. Hands rattled the door I had found bolted. "You there, boss? We went to the dame's apartment, and the guy wasn't there."

"He wasn't there?" It was Russo's unbelieving bellow. "I will be with you in ten minutes. You mugs wait downstairs until I call you."

Feet shuffled away.

And I made my move. I opened the door wide.

Louis Russo was bending Polly back over a table. The dress she had changed to was now more tattered than the one in which I had first seen her. The gangster ran his tongue over thick lips—

He hadn't even looked around when I started my charge. But the man was quick. Before I was half way across the floor, he'd whirled and snatched for his shoulder holster. The flame of the gun seared my shoulder as I tackled him. My hand clamped down on his wrist.

For a little while it was touch and go. I threw my weight into bending his arm back in an attempt to get the gun. Russo was plenty husky. The gun exploded again and its lead ploughed a furrow in my ankle.

I redoubled my pressure and heard the crack of a bone. The gun dropped. Russo writhed like an eel. His teeth closed in one of my wrists as he lunged for the gun with his good arm. I kicked it out of his reach, wrenched free, and leaped for it myself.

Coming up with the gun, I found that Russo had been as quick as I. He held Polly in front of him as a shield. "Shoot if you dare!" he gritted. Then, "Tony! Joe! Smash the door down! Come in!"

The door shook as powerful bodies lunged against it. I fired twice as the lock gave way, then snapped the trigger and heard the hammer click on an empty cylinder.

Two guns bored into my kidneys. I was backed against the wall and held in impotence. Once again my hands and wrists were tied expertly.

Russo grinned. "Now leave him here, and you boys go outside until I call you."

Leering like a madman, Russo waited until his men had left. Then once more he turned to Polly who cringed away from him. His brutal hand reached out and snatched even more of her few remaining garments from her.

A red film of hate and rage blinded me. Bound as I was, I tried to dive for the man. He turned from the girl and began methodically to beat me with his revolver. Blood poured from my lacerated scalp, from my torn face, but still he raised the gun and brought it down. At any moment he could have knocked me out, but that was not his intention. In cold blood he hacked and cut, and I could do nothing but take it.

Eventually he tired of his sport. He slipped a cartridge into the gun. "You've been asking for it," he said. "You're going to get it!"

I could actually see his finger grow white as it tightened on the trigger.

At that instant Polly Knight came out of her semi-conscious state. Half-naked, she hurled herself in front of Russo. "Stop! Don't kill him!" she begged.

Russo shoved her away, slapped her face brutally. He brought up the gun again toward me. . . .

A fusillade of shots hammered in from the banquet room. One of Russo's men lurched over the threshold and fell, blood gushing from his throat.

Russo fired once toward the door, then squealed and pitched to the floor under a hail of lead.

The film cleared from my eyes and I saw Inspector Daly come into the room followed by two men in uniform. Polly Knight, ignoring her state of nudity, knelt beside me, loosening the knots that held me.

Daly grinned at me. "That fathead Finger, my relief, told me about your call. Technically, he may have been within his rights, but I thought I'd better look into the matter!" He smiled down at Polly. "I'll take the boys and wait outside until the young lady has had a chance to cover herself up a little."

I gave her my coat and sat patiently while she wiped blood from my face. "Was it worth it—all for a gangster's girl?" she whispered.

I put an arm around her, not caring how much the effort hurt. "I don't care what kind of girl you are," I told her. "It was worth it!"

There was a devil dancing in her eyes. "As a matter of fact, I'm not a gangster's girl. And my name isn't Polly Knight. Don't you remember 'God's Good to the Irish'?"

I stared at her in amazement. "You're Polly Day!" I gasped. "You played the lead in the show!"

She nodded. "But the show folded. I was broke and I got a job for a private detective agency. I was sent down here because there were indications that Russo's mob was behind a series of hold-ups. I went to work in the Little Albania as a hostess. I was trying to get something on the gang—"

I stopped her explanations with a kiss. "That'll be enough for now," I said. "You can give me installment two of your story when we get back to my apartment."

The Corpse in the Crystal &
He Got What He Asked For
D. B. McCandless

AN ELEMENT OF a great deal of pulp fiction that correctly prevents it from being regarded as serious literature is the absurd reliance on the reader to accept virtually any far-fetched coincidence or series of events. The suspension of disbelief is often pushed to the very brink of fantasy.

The Sarah Watson stories of D. B. McCandless are a case in point. They are humorous and charming, and the protagonist runs against stereotypes. She is not a sexy redhead in tight, low-cut sweaters who has every man she encounters eating out of her hand. She is, instead, middle-aged, heavy, dowdy, and relatively charmless. This element of originality, as well as a fast-paced narrative, combine to make the stories among the most readable of their kind—so much so that two tales of "The Female She-Devil" have been included in this collection. Do not, however, judge the stories based on credibility, as they will fall somewhat short. Even allowing for the difference of era between the 1930s and the present day, railroad and airplane travel had little in common with the events related in the second of these adventures.

"The Corpse in the Crystal" and "He Got What He Asked For" (January 1937) were originally published in *Detective Fiction Weekly*.

The Corpse in the Crystal

D. B. McCandless

"You know everything—
and it's just too bad for you."

A MASSIVE individual in blue and brass marched resoundingly down a tiled corridor and halted before a door. Scabby gilt letters on the door said: "Watson Detective Agency." The massive individual pounced upon the door knob, wrenched it and swung himself into the office beyond.

A long, languid young man with red hair let his feet thump from his desk to the floor, sat upright, said: "Cheese it, the cops!" and relaxed again, grinning.

The massive individual, standing spread-legged and stroking a black eyebrow thick enough to have served as a mustache for a daintier man, greeted the young man.

"'Lo, Ben Todd. Where's your boss?"

"'Lo, Sergeant. Sarah Watson has gone out."

"I can see that, even if I am a cop. Where's she gone?"

"Crazy, I guess. She said she was going to consult a crystal gazer."

Sergeant O'Reilly cried out and shook his fists at the ceiling.

"Damn Sarah Watson!" he exclaimed. "A crystal gazer, eh! I might have known she'd get ahead of me!"

O'Reilly sat down heavily in the chair beside Sarah Watson's roll-top desk. He reached a thick arm and laid heavy fingers upon a newspaper lying there. He lifted the paper and stared at a square hole cut neatly therein. He took a square clipping from his pocket and fitted it into the hole in the newspaper.

"Read this, Ben Todd."

Ben Todd shambled across, lounged over the Sergeant's shoulder and read. The clipping fitted into the empty space in Sarah's newspaper, under "Letters from Readers." It read:

Dear Editor: People say all fortune tellers, mediums and crystal gazers are fakes. Two weeks ago, I sat before a crystal ball and the most wonderful seer in the world looked into the crystal and saw the body of a certain well known wealthy young man laying dead in a marsh, with cat-tails drooping over him and a bone-handled knife in his heart. That was two weeks ago, and the next day, the body of that same well known, wealthy young man was found dead, laying in a marsh, just exactly as the wonderful seer had seen it in the crystal. Now that young man lays in his grave and the police can't find his murderer. And then people say crystal gazers are fakes!

Yours respectfully,
Lily Tarrant

"A certain well-known, wealthy young man," Ben Todd whistled, went on. "Found in a swamp . . . with a bone-handled knife in his heart . . . *Alexander Courtwell!*"

"The same!" O'Reilly agreed. "I wonder if this wonderful seer saw the ring when he saw the corpse in the crystal?"

"Ring?"

"The ring we found under the corpse. The big onyx ring with the two big diamonds in it. The ring we knew belonged to Honest Jim Carson."

"Well, for Pete's sake, O'Reilly, if you knew, why isn't Honest Jim Carson in jail for the Courtwell killing?"

"Honest Jim Carson," said O'Reilly, "is in his grave. He was there, of unnatural causes, three days before Courtwell was killed."

"Oh!" said Ben Todd.

O'Reilly got to his feet, cast the crumpled newspaper from him, and shook his fist again at

Sarah's roll-top desk. Ben Todd said, thoughtfully:

"So . . . a crystal gazer saw Alexander Courtwell dead before he was found dead . . . and Sarah's gone to consult a crystal gazer!"

"Damn her brains! There's ten thousand dollars reward for the apprehension of Courtwell's murderer, Ben Todd, and that Watson woman had to set her eagle eye on that clipping before I . . . Wait!"

O'Reilly grabbed the 'phone on top of the roll-top desk. He shouted a number, glared at Ben Todd.

"*Evening Star?* O'Reilly. Yeah, the cop. Gimme Watkins. You, Watkins? Listen, you made one bad boner, letting that Tarrant woman's letter get into print. You made another bad boner not calling the papers off the street quick enough after I ordered you to. Let's see, now if you've made another boner? Anybody get the Tarrant woman's address out of you since that paper went on the streets? What? They did? *She* did? I might have known! I might have . . . Oh, God!"

O'Reilly slammed up the 'phone and whirled on Ben Todd.

"That Watson woman is a liar and a thief," he roared. "She called up the *Star* and told 'em she was assisting me on the Courtwell case. She asked for that Tarrant woman's address and she got it."

"She would."

"She got it. Which means she's probably with the crystal gazer now, picking his brains dry, and she'll have that ten thousand dollars reward in her damn, thieving fists before I . . ."

"Listen," said Ben Todd. "I don't allow anybody to damn Sarah Watson. She may be an old battle-axe and an old liar but she's not a damn old thief."

"She is a damn old thief!" shouted O'Reilly, thrusting his blue jaw close to Ben Todd's: "I came here with every intention of sharing that reward with her if she'd help me by going to that crystal gazer and picking his brains dry before we closed in on him. Now she's got the jump on me, and she'll cop the whole reward!"

Ben Todd yawned and said:

"Well, you're giving her a good start, anyway, O'Reilly, while you stand here, sizzling in your own grease. Listen, O'Reilly! I just thought of something! If the crystal gazer knew about the murder before the murder was done, then he's involved, and if he's involved . . ."

"*If* he's involved! Of course he's involved! What else do you think I've been thinking? What I should have done was to close in on him first and sweat him after, instead of thinking of conniving with Sarah to pick his brains first . . ."

Ben Todd reached for his hat and took a long stride toward the door.

"The old girl may be with him now!" he cried. "If he gets wise to what she's after, then Sarah's in . . ."

O'Reilly reached over Ben Todd's shoulder and opened the door.

"Of course she's in danger!" he admitted. "What else do you think I've been thinking? If you don't move quicker, Ben Todd, I'll grind down your heels."

At just about the moment that Sergeant O'Reilly first made his entrance into the office of the Watson Detective Agency, Sarah Watson herself was leaning upon the rickety stoop railing of a certain flathouse, conversing with a janitress perfumed with gin.

The thick shaft of Sarah's sturdily corseted body was wrapped in nondescript, rusty black garments. Her antique headgear was set at a hurried angle on her straggling gray hair. There was a slight, unaccustomed tinge of hectic red on the high cheek bones under her grey, bristling-browed eyes. There was, however, no hint of excitement in the hoarse, downright voice with which she fired questions at the vague and wavery target of the janitress.

"She left in a hurry, eh? In a big, black car with red wheels? Walking between two men, eh? Did you get a look at those two men?"

"Well, now." The janitress ran a soiled hand over her mouth. "Well, I tried to get a look, because it seemed kind of queer, Mrs. Tarrant going off with two strange men like that and her a new widow woman that's always trying to communicate with her dead husband through the spirits and such, but the men walked awful fast. Seems to me they was both dark and one of 'em had his lip puckered down at the side by a scar, sort of, and the car was the swellest thing on four wheels I ever seen, four red wheels . . ."

"What time? Think, woman! Remember I'm paying you to think."

"Am thinking. Fifty cents will buy . . . Well, don't glare at me that way, missus. They left right before twelve, because I remember, I was wiping up the halls right after and I smelled something in Mrs. Tarrant's kitchen and her door was open and I edged in and the smell was beans—burnt to a crisp."

"Burnt to a crisp, eh? Mrs. Tarrant must have left in a hurry! Well, here's your fifty cents and take my advice and put it in the bank and not down your gullet."

Sarah Watson started briskly down the stoop, wheeled abruptly and transfixed the janitress with a glinting eye.

"By the way, what's the name of the crystal gazer Mrs. Tarrant goes to?" she asked. "I might find her there . . ."

"You might. She's been running there enough, trying to see her dead husband in heaven, but it's my opinion she's been looking in the wrong place for him . . . Don't growl, missus. It's Charlot she goes to. Charlot, his name is, and his place is on Green Street, Number . . ."

Sarah took a little black notebook from her capacious handbag and noted down the address.

A ramshackle vehicle which faintly resembled an automobile chugged to a stop at a corner on Green Street. Sarah Watson stepped out and strode down the street.

Halfway down the block, she passed a dirty first-floor window with a sign in it which said: "Charlot." She strode by the window, about-faced suddenly, and disappeared down an odorous alley which led to a backyard.

Five minutes later, she mounted the first flight of an iron fire escape ladder and was sitting, bolt upright, on the top step of the ladder, gazing calmly through a rift in the dirty curtains on the open back window of Charlot's flat.

There was no one in the kitchen beyond the curtains but something was sizzling on the stove. The nostrils of Sarah's beak quivered appreciatively as a little breeze blew the fragrance out.

Presently, a door in the kitchen opened. For a moment, the aroma of cooking was diluted by the heavy odor of incense and the room beyond the kitchen showed dimly. Then, a swarthy man in a white robe and white turban closed himself into the kitchen, ripped off his white wrappings, flung them on the floor, yanked off his dark, pointed beard, slung it at a chair, kicked at the discarded robe and turban and bent over the sink. Outside on the fire escape, Sarah Watson nodded grimly.

The man turned from the sink suddenly, facing the window. Sarah edged closer to the wall of the building. The man was clothed in dark trousers and undershirt. He was towelling vigorously. His face was no longer swarthy. It was white, very white—and young.

A fuzzy grey kitten rolled out from under the kitchen table and dabbed at the fringes of black beard protruding from the edge of the chair. The man threw down his towel, picked the kitten up by its scruff, grinned at it, and thrust its soft body under his chin. With the kitten cuddled between his collar bone and his jaw, the man bent over a pan on the stove and expertly flipped over a sizzling steak. He bent over another pan, stirring . . .

A square door in the wall between the man at the stove and the window where Sarah Watson watched began to open, very slowly, very silently. Sarah edged closer to the curtain. The stubby fingers of her right hand began to slide into her handbag . . .

Suddenly the opening door flew wide, revealing the black hole of a dumbwaiter shaft. A man

leaped noiselessly through the door and into the kitchen. He was dark and his profile showed a mouth drawn down by a puckered scar. Before his feet hit the oilcloth, he had placed a gun between the shoulder blades of the man bending over the stove.

The man at the stove stiffened but did not move. The kitten clawed at his shoulder and dropped to the floor, squealing.

"Take it now, snitcher—!" the man with the gun snarled.

A gun blasted. The man with the scar dropped his gun, clawed at his back, slid slowly to the floor. The man at the stove bent over the prostrate man, straightened and looked up at the billowing curtains at the back window. There was smoke still wreathing out of the rift in those curtains, but nothing else.

A few minutes later, a brilliant female in rusty black strode along Green Street and climbed into the ancient automobile parked at the corner. For a moment or so, she sat behind the wheel, her hard bosom rising and falling hurriedly, her stubby fingers wiping away the moisture that beaded the incipient mustache upon her upper lip.

Then the old car coughed and chugged down Green Street. Halfway down the block, it slowed. There was a car parked opposite the window in which Charlot's sign appeared. It was a fine car, black, with red wheels.

Sarah Watson's car snorted on a few more yards and stopped. Sarah got out.

The man sitting behind the wheel of the black car sat up suddenly, taking his eyes off the dingy entrance to Charlot's flathouse and transferring them to the woman standing with her elbow resting on the edge of the open window at his left.

"No use waiting," she said. "He's not coming out." She jabbed her elbow viciously into his neck just below the chin. Something in her right hand cracked down upon the back of his head. His slid, his lids fluttering down over amazed eyes.

Sarah Watson drew a hairpin from the knob

of grey hair under her hat. She thrust the pin into the button in the center of the steering wheel. The horn began to blow.

Sarah leaned over the man slumped under the wheel and peered into the back of the car.

"It's all right, Mrs. Tarrant," she soothed the frightened woman. "The cop will come running when he hears the horn and the cop will take the ropes and bandages off you. I haven't time."

Sarah withdrew her head, gazed sternly for a moment at the unconscious man behind the wheel, then strode away.

As she mounted the steps of the tenement which housed Charlot, a horn was still blowing behind her, and a ruddy cop was tearing around the corner and down Green Street toward the black car with red wheels. Sarah stepped into the vestibule of the tenement, opened a door into the hall, pressed a firm finger on the bell under Charlot's name and kept the finger there.

The horn of the black car ceased blowing suddenly. Sarah took her finger off Charlot's bell. A smell of burned steak permeated the hall.

The door opened two inches. A man's voice said: "Charlot is not receiving."

Sarah leaned on the door and said, hoarsely:

"Charlot's receiving me, if he knows what's good for him," and she wedged her common-sense shoe into the two-inch opening.

"Madam, if you wish a reading, you must return later. The crystal is clouded. Charlot cannot—"

"Listen," Sarah interrupted fiercely, wedging her foot farther in, "the crystal may be clouded, but it ain't too clouded for me to see that there's a corpse in Charlot's kitchen . . ."

The voice behind the door gasped. Sarah pushed through, stepped into the dimly lit room beyond, slammed the door shut behind her, locked it, and faced a white-robed man whose white turban was over one ear and whose dark, pointed beard was slightly askew.

"Charlot," Sarah declared, "I got a premonition we ain't got much time. Now talk. I want to know how you were able to tell that fool Tarrant woman just where and how the body of Alexander Courtwell would be found, and I want to know quick."

The man in the tipsy turban looked down at the gun in Sarah's stubby fingers.

"Who . . . ? What . . . ?" he stuttered.

"And what have you done with the man shot down in your kitchen?" Sarah asked.

"My God! You know about that . . . You think I killed him?"

"Young feller, you're in a mess and if you want to get out of it, you'd better talk. Sit down here by your glass ball. I'll sit here on the other side, where your fool clients sit. I'll look into the crystal myself, young feller, and see what I see. I see you, Charlot, without that brown stain on your skin and without that beard. You're peaked and white . . . prison white . . ."

"Prison! How did you know . . . ?"

"I saw it in the crystal, young man. Yes, you've been in jail. Maybe you didn't belong there . . ."

"I didn't. I was . . ."

"Half of 'em don't belong there—so they say. You've been in jail, Charlot, and somehow, either there or after you got outside, you found out just how and why Alexander Courtwell was going to be killed, and you blabbed it to one of your gullible woman customers. Why?"

"I had to. I had to tell her something. She kept tormenting me, kept coming here every day, begging me to see something in the crystal. I kept seeing things, of course, things I thought she wanted me to see. But I kept thinking of that poor fellow, Courtwell. I kept thinking of how I'd heard those two planning in the next cell, planning to stick him in the heart with the bone-handled knife one of 'em owned, and planning to throw his body in the swamp.

"I kept thinking how I'd heard them whispering about what Courtwell had done to 'em, how he'd cheated 'em out of some big gambling debt. I kept thinking about it, I tell you, and when the Tarrant woman kept nagging me to see something, I kept seeing Courtwell's body in a swamp with a bone-handled knife sticking out of the heart, and one night, before I knew I'd done it, I blabbed. I didn't mean to. I didn't think she'd ever tell anybody, 'til I saw that letter in the paper today, and then I knew something was going to happen—something like that dead man in the kitchen—something like you . . ."

"Young man," said Sarah, "worse things could happen to you than me. Now, I'm looking in the crystal I see two men, planning and plotting in a cell. What do they look like?"

"I don't know."

"What?"

"I was released the morning after they came in. I never saw them. I only heard their voices."

"Damn," said Sarah and leaned over the crystal. "Wait! I'm beginning to see . . . One of them had a scar on his chin . . ."

"No," Charlot shivered, twisted in his chair. "That one spoke to me before he fell down with a bullet in his back. I'd have known the voice, if he'd been one of them."

"Drat it, man," Sarah explained. "You can't hang a murderer on a voice. Think, now! You must have heard those two say something definite, something that would identify them?"

"I heard their names."

Sarah Watson stood up. She waved her gun under Charlot's nose.

"At last we're getting some place," she said, hoarsely. "Their names, young feller! What were their names?"

A bell shrilled suddenly, went on ringing, filling the dim room with clamor. Charlot sat erect, staring into Sarah's glinting eyes. Someone began to bang lustily upon the flimsy door to the hall.

"The cops!" Sarah cried. "You've got one chance, Charlot. Scuttle down the fire escape. Take my car outside—License 4738. In the side pocket, you'll find the keys to my flat and the address. Get there quick—and stay there 'til I come. It's your one chance, Charlot. There's a dead man in your kitchen and your fingerprints are all over the place and you've been to jail . . ."

Charlot got up, still staring at Sarah.

"Leave that white nightgown in the kitchen,"

she said, "and take the kitten with you. It might starve before you get back here again."

Charlot looked into her grim eyes a moment longer, then turned and fled. Sarah got up and opened the door. O'Reilly and Ben Todd stood outside.

"Too late, boys," she lied. "The swami's evaporated . . . climbed up a rope and disappeared . . . magicked himself into thin air or something. There's a man in the kitchen and you might ask him, but I don't think he'll answer. He's dead."

The police car sped through the night, O'Reilly at the wheel, Sarah Watson bolt upright beside him, Ben Todd lounging in the rear.

"A little speed, please, Sergeant," Sarah urged. "I'm used to speed."

"You'll have to get unused to it, then," O'Reilly chuckled. "Your racing car is gone and Charlot, alias Eddie Danville, has gone with it."

"You know, Sergeant," said Sarah, dreamily, "Charlot—Eddie Danville, I mean—didn't look like a boy that would steal a poor old woman's car."

"Whadya know about how he looked?"

"I saw his prison picture, didn't I? A nice looking feller. Didn't look like he belonged in jail."

"He don't," admitted O'Reilly. "He belongs in a nice comfortable chair, wired for electricity."

"All men are alike," said Sarah. "They jump to conclusions. Just because Eddie left a dead man in his kitchen and just because Eddie's fingerprints showed he'd been in jail . . . Listen, O'Reilly. Anybody could have shot that man. I could have shot him."

"You!" O'Reilly laughed. "You couldn't hit a clay pigeon in a shooting gallery, woman."

"No, but men make better targets than clay pigeons—bigger targets, I mean. Now, O'Reilly, you can let me off at this next corner. I've got to . . ."

"I'm taking you right to your door, Sarah Watson. You're tired, woman, hanging around with a bunch of cops all afternoon. It must have been a shock to you, too, woman, when you came on that dead body in Charlot's kitchen."

"It would have been a greater shock if the body hadn't been dead. You slow up, O'Reilly. Stop at the next corner. Stop, I say! Let me off here. I've got to . . ."

The car swept past the corner with Sarah grabbing the door handle beside her. It swung into Sarah's street, slid halfway down the block. O'Reilly shouted:

"Glory be! Look what's out in front of your door, Sarah Watson. Look! Your car!"

"Stop!" Sarah shouted. "Don't run into it. My car! What a coincidence! O'Reilly, I told you that Eddie Danville wasn't all bad. Maybe he stole my car to make a getaway in, but he found my name and address in it, and left it here for me, before he went wherever he was going . . ."

O'Reilly put on the brakes. He turned slowly in his seat and stared hard at Sarah.

"Woman, I'm beginning to understand why you were so anxious to stop at that corner . . ."

Ben Todd poked his head out of the open rear window and twisted his neck to look up.

"Sarah," he yelled, "somebody's in your flat. There's a light . . ."

"Of course there's a light," Sarah agreed. "There's always a light. You know that, Ben Todd, you crazy squirt. You know I always turn a light on in the morning, so I won't have to come home to a dark place. You know . . . O'Reilly, turn this car around!"

O'Reilly did not stir. His black brows were gathered, his eyes glaring at Sarah's craggy countenance.

"Woman," he began, but choked suddenly, as Sarah reached across him, put one foot on the starter, and kicked his shins viciously in an effort to put her other foot on the clutch.

"Woman," O'Reilly repeated, giving her a dig with his elbow which sent her bouncing back to her own side. "I'm taking you to that corner, but if you was a man, I'd . . ."

The car whirled into a U-turn and sped back toward the corner.

"Thank you, Sergeant. I have to stop at the

corner to buy milk. I've got a new cat in my flat."

Sarah Watson sat on the edge of her bed. The bed was in a cubbyhole between the front room and the rear room of her railroad flat. The window of the cubbyhole looked out on a dark, narrow airshaft. Both doors of the cubbyhole were closed.

On a straight chair, facing the bed, sat Charlot, whose real name was Eddie Danville. He was still in trousers and undershirt and his face was whiter, if possible, than it had been when Sarah first saw it.

"Now, Eddie, we're safe here for a few minutes," Sarah began. "I've got a premonition there will be a big mick cop stamping through the premises soon. Let's have them now, Eddie, the names I've been waiting all afternoon to hear."

Eddie Danville looked around the room. He wet his lips and whispered:

"One of 'em was named Jake."

"Jake what?"

"Jake. That's all I know."

"Jake! There are ten thousand Jakes. What was the other one's name. Come now, Eddie. Hurry!"

"Tony. That's all I know. Tony."

"You're a big help. Tony! Ten thousand Tonys! Wait a minute . . . that man with the scar who died in your kitchen . . . you ever see him before this time?"

"No."

"His name was Chinny Downs. A killer, according to the cops. Now, Eddie. We know that Chinny Downs was mixed up with Jake and Tony somehow, because he came to your place to do their dirty work for them, and get you before the cops got you. If we could find out who else Chinny Downs was mixed up with . . . Drat it! There's the bell! Remember what I told you, Eddie, about the fire escape . . ."

The bell in Sarah's kitchen went on ringing. It rang furiously, first in frenzied spurts, then long, loud, and insistently. Presently, Sarah swished into the kitchen, silencing the bell by the simple method of jabbing a button in the kitchen wall. As she jabbed, her eyes roved over the kitchen. Suddenly, she ceased jabbing, dashed to the table, grabbed one of the two used coffee cups there, rinsed it and set it back in the cupboard. A moment later, she was at the door which opened from her parlor to the main hall.

"Sergeant," she greeted the man puffing up the last flight, "why, I never expected to see you . . ."

Sergeant O'Reilly did not answer. He came on up the stairs, rounded the banister, pushed past Sarah, strode into the little parlor, strode into the cubbyhole bedroom, peered under the bed, jerked open a closet door, yanked at a yellow rubber raincoat and some dangling black garments, then strode back into the kitchen.

"What is this? A raid?" Sarah asked.

"You know what it is. Where is he?"

"Where's who?"

"Charlot. Eddie Danville."

"Heavens, O'Reilly! You don't mean you think that jail bird . . . that . . . er . . . murderer . . . is here?"

"You know I think he's here and you know why. Ten thousand dollars is why, Sarah Watson. You'd do anything for ten thousand." His eyes shifted to the window. "What's that outside that window? Glory be! She's got him on the fire escape!"

O'Reilly dashed to the kitchen window, his gun ready. The shade flew up revealing a dark form on the fire escape.

"Don't shoot, Sergeant," the fellow pleaded. "It's Ben Todd. I'm here for the same reason you are. I came back because I got a hunch the old gal was up to something . . ."

Ben Todd jumped down into the kitchen. Sarah Watson stepped between him and O'Reilly, her hands on her broad hips, her bristling brows tied in a knot.

"O'Reilly," she said, hoarsely, "I might have expected this from you, but you, Ben Todd . . ." She whirled on the long-legged, red headed young man standing just inside the open window. "You, you young addlepate. Who do you think you're working for, anyway? Me, or O'Reilly?"

"I'm working for you, Sarah."

"Not any more, you ain't."

"I'm working for you, Sarah, and when I got a hunch that jail bird might be here with you . . . . Well, I just had to come back to protect you, old girl."

"Any time I need protection from any man, I'll ask for it! Now, git! No, you stay, Ben Todd. You and me are going to have a talk. O'Reilly, you git! And next time you come here to go through my personal belongings and look under my bed, you bring a search warrant."

The door banged on O'Reilly's broad back. Before the echoes died away, Sarah was at her front window, peering down. A few moments later, she returned to the kitchen.

"Now," she said to the young man sitting on the window sill, "we can talk, Ben Todd. We can talk about what's going to become of you, poor soul, now that you're out of a job."

Ben Todd grinned. He twisted about on the window sill, reached out a long arm, and dragged into the kitchen a white-faced young man in undershirt and dark pants.

"Sarah," Ben chuckled, "what do you think would have become of you, poor soul, if I hadn't been out on that fire escape to create a little diversion for Sergeant O'Reilly?"

Sarah Watson looked at Eddie Danville, then grinned at Ben Todd.

"Bennie, I wouldn't have given you credit for that much brains!" she said. "Bennie, meet Eddie—a nice feller, even if he has been in jail, and he's kind to animals and knows how to cook. Drat it! I let the Sergeant get away without asking him . . ." Sarah wheeled and charged out of the kitchen door.

Sarah barked a number into the 'phone on her parlor table.

"O'Reilly back yet?" she asked. "Good. O'Reilly? Listen. That dead feller in Charlot's kitchen. You said you recognized him—that he was called Chinny Downs. Now listen, O'Reilly. Chinny Downs was a gangster. What gang was he mixed up in?"

"I thought of that, too, you old war horse," boomed O'Reilly's voice. "But it's no soap. Chinny was a punk in Big Smiley's gang, just joined up recent. There are a hundred punks just like him lined up with Smiley . . ."

"What's a hundred punks to a bull like you? Get the whole hundred rounded up. Take 'em under the light . . . Listen, O'Reilly. What about the man you found unconscious in the car with that fool Tarrant woman? Maybe he'd spill something?"

"Maybe he would, if he knew something. He says he don't, and I believe him. He says Chinny Downs knew something, but Chinny Downs is dead."

"Somebody made a mistake," said Sarah. "If Chinny had been allowed to live, he might have talked. Oh, well, sometimes it ain't good to be too impulsive."

"What's that?"

"Nothing, Sergeant. I was just thinking you've made some headway, anyway, toward collecting that ten thousand reward. You know the Courtwell murderer is connected somehow with the Smiley mob. Now, you'd really have that ten thousand reward cinched, Sergeant, if you just knew the name of the murderer, even the first name . . ."

The 'phone clanked in Sarah's ear. She hung up, smiling grimly.

Sarah Watson stalked back into her kitchen. She found Ben Todd with a gun pointed at Eddie Danville, who stood with his back to the wall.

"Bennie, you're being childish," Sarah said.

"I ain't. This guy is trying to tell me that you put that bullet in Chinny Downs."

"He's trying to tell you the truth."

"Sarah! What the devil? Why—"

"If I hadn't, Chinny would have put a bullet in Eddie. I didn't want to see murder done, Bennie, especially when the murderer was liable to be worth ten thousand to you and me."

Ben Todd sank into his chair, his gun and his mouth both slack. Sarah shoved Eddie Danville into a chair.

"Now, Eddie, tell us," she asked. "Do you know the Smiley outfit?"

"Do I know it? Smiley's the guy who framed me into the pen, because I—"

"Never mind what you did to him, Eddie. Whatever it was, he deserved it. Now, when you knew the Smiley mob, Eddie, was there maybe a Jake connected with it—a Tony?"

Eddie Danville jumped to his feet and held on to the edge of the table.

"Jake Benner and Tony Corelli!" he cried. "Why didn't I think of them before? What a blasted fool I am!"

"Of course," agreed Sarah. "Sit down, Eddie. You need food. We all need food. We've got work to do before morning, bloody work, maybe. We need red meat."

Sarah Watson stepped out on her front stoop and peered up and down the dark, sleeping block. She made a dash down the steps, across the sidewalk, and into the battered wreck waiting at the curb.

Two young men ran after her, one of them hatless and enveloped in a voluminous yellow raincoat. The car door slammed. The machine snorted away from the curb.

"Sarah, for Pete's sake, tell us what we're up against," Ben Todd pleaded. "If you're planning to break into Smiley's roadhouse hangout, we wouldn't have a chance, the three of us . . ."

"If we break into Smiley's roadhouse," said Sarah, swerving the car around a corner, "we'll break in because I know we have a chance."

"Sarah, for Pete's sake, stop being cryptic . . ."

Sarah Watson slowed the car, stopped it in front of an all-night drug store.

"Cryptic? What's that mean?" she asked, then got out of the car and stalked into the drug store.

Sarah Watson stood wedged into a telephone booth, the receiver clamped to her car.

"Hello? This Smiley's roadhouse? Want to speak to Jake. Jake or Tony."

Sarah waited. She waited a long time. She heard some one step into the booth next to hers. She put out a tentative hand to pull open her door and peer out. Just then, a voice spoke into her ear.

"Yeah? This is Jake."

"Tony there, too?"

"Who wants to know?"

"Listen, Jake. Smiley don't know it yet but Chinny Downs got his today. He got it in Green Street. Yes, Green Street. And the cops found Jim Corker knocked-out in a car with the Tarrant skirt tied up in the back. They found Jim Corker on Green Street, too. Jim's down at Headquarters now, sweating. Yes, I said sweating. Now listen, Jake. The feller Chinny Downs was after is sneaking back to-night to Green Street. Never mind who I am, Jake. I'm no fool, and neither are you."

Sarah hung up, tore open the door and peered into the adjoining booth. A red headed young man peered back at her, through smudged glass, then opened the door and stepped out.

"Dumb-ox!" she cried. "Suppose Eddie's got nervous and skeedaddled while you've been in here, spying on me?"

"Double-crosser," muttered Ben Todd. "You never had a job yet that you didn't double-cross somebody. You've double-crossed O'Reilly and now you're going to double-cross Eddie. You old female snake! If Eddie has made a getaway, so much the better for Eddie . . ."

Sarah did not answer, but stalked out of the drug store. Ben Todd followed. At the curb, Sarah peered into the rear of her car and gave a satisfied grunt. She slid in under the wheel, reached out and yanked Ben Todd in by his long arm.

"Bennie," she said, "you had one bright flash of intelligence to-night when you stalled off O'Reilly. I suppose I oughtn't to expect anything more of you. Shut up, now. I'm going to talk to Eddie. Eddie, we're going back to your crystal gazing den right now . . ."

"No," shouted Ben Todd. "We can't. There'll be at least one cop on duty there. Maybe two."

"If there's three," said Sarah, "there's three of us."

"Eddie," Ben Todd warned, "you take my

advice and get out of this car now, while you can."

"Be quiet," commanded Sarah. "Eddie, we're going back to Green Street because if Jake and Tony are as dumb as I think they are, we're going to have callers there."

"Sarah," apologized Ben Todd, "forgive me. But I still don't . . ."

"You ought to apologize," said Sarah, complacently. "You ought to grovel."

"I will," Ben Todd agreed, "if I'm able to, after the cops at Eddie's place get through with us."

"Don't worry about a few paltry policemen," Sarah insisted. "The thing to worry about now is whether we can beat Jake and Tony to Green Street."

The old car plunged around a corner and rattled into amazing speed.

"But, Sarah," Ben Todd asked, "even if you get this Jake and this Tony, how are you going to hang the Courtwell murder on 'em so it sticks? You've only got Eddie's word, and Eddie's word . . ."

"Ain't worth a hoot," Sarah finished for him. "I know. But there's no use worrying about more than one thing at one time. You leave things to me, Ben Todd."

Three figures stole down an odorous alley at the side of a tenement in Green Street and stopped in deep shadows. One figure whispered:

"Look's like our company ain't here yet, but we can't be sure. Eddie, you go back into this alley and wait 'til I call you. Cops are too dangerous for you."

"Listen, old girl," whispered another one of the figures, "if you're going to mess up with cops . . ."

"Who said I was going to mess up with cops? Come along, Ben Todd. Keep your hand off that gun and don't get any bright ideas of your own."

Sarah Watson moved down to the mouth of the alley. She surveyed the street, then charged swiftly out of the alley and up the front stoop of the tenement, with Ben Todd behind her. A long, sleek car was just turning the corner.

Sarah and Ben went through the vestibule door and into the hall. A cop sitting on the bottom step of the stairs roused suddenly, stood up.

"Quick, officer!" Sarah yelled. "Get inside and turn the lights off in that flat. Eddie Danville's on his way here. Sergeant O'Reilly sent us . . ."

"The hell he did!" roared the cop, reaching for his holster. "Sergeant O'Reilly is inside that flat . . ."

Sarah Watson lurched suddenly. The cop staggered under the onslaught and sat down again on the bottom step with Sarah on his lap. Sarah's stubby fingers gripped the cop's right wrist.

"Move, Bennie. Take his gun," she ordered.

Ben Todd snatched at the gun, backed with it in his hand. The cop heaved suddenly, throwing Sarah back, sprawling. The cop charged at Ben Todd. Sarah got to her knees, straightening her hat.

"Officer," she warned, "if you don't behave, I'll tell Sergeant O'Reilly a woman disarmed you."

The door to Eddie Danville's flat swung out. Sergeant O'Reilly stood framed in the dim light from the swinging lanterns beyond.

"What's this?" he asked.

"Misunderstanding," Sarah answered. "Get those lights off in there, O'Reilly, and get this competent cop stowed away somewhere where he won't be seen. Eddie's coming home."

Sarah pushed by O'Reilly and into the room beyond, reaching up and switching off the hanging lanterns as she went. O'Reilly remained rigid a moment, then crooked a hairy finger at Ben Todd and the cop and followed Sarah.

Sarah was at the window, the heavy curtains parted in her stubby fingers.

"Two," she whispered. "One of 'em coming up the stoop. One of 'em going around the back way. Lord! Eddie's out back, I've got to . . ."

She wheeled, saw the dim forms of the three men.

"All of you hide," she commanded. "Somewhere . . . anywhere, and don't move, whatever

happens . . . Get in back of those curtains hanging on the wall, the three of you . . ."

"Say!" O'Reilly's voice was husky. "Who's giving the orders around here, anyway?"

"I am," said Sarah. "And if you know what's good for you, O'Reilly, you're taking 'em."

Sarah strode out of the room and through the kitchen, which was dark. She poked her head out of the window and called softly:

"Eddie!"

No answer. A faint scuffling, a deep groan. Sarah got on the fire escape, peered down.

"Eddie!"

Two forms in the shadows below, struggling. Sarah went down swiftly. The two wrestling figures fell, rolled on the asphalt at her feet.

"Eddie! Which is you?"

A groan answered her. She bent, caught hold of a slippery garment which gleamed faintly yellow in the darkness.

"I'd like to watch a good battle, but there ain't time," she said, smashing the butt-end of her gun down on the skull of the man straddling Eddie.

Sarah and Eddie dragged a recumbent figure through the kitchen window, laid it on the floor in the darkness. Sarah whispered:

"Which one, Eddie?"

"Jake, I think."

"Leave Jake lay. I've got to see what Tony is up to . . ."

Sarah stole to the door which led into the front room, and inched the door open. The room on the other side was dark and still. Dimly, Sarah could discern bulges in the dark stuff which curtained the walls, three bulges. In the silence there came a faint clicking of metal against metal. It seemed to come from the door to the hall.

Sarah turned back into the kitchen.

She whispered a warning. "Eddie, you stay here."

"No. That's Jake at that door, Sarah. He's a killer."

"You stay. No nonsense. Wait a minute! Where's that white nightgown of yours . . . ?"

Sarah stepped into the front room and closed the kitchen door firmly behind her. She moved silently in the darkness, reached up and switched on a lantern which hung directly over the crystal ball. The dim rays of the lantern revealed her swathed in a white robe and wearing a white turban well down over her bushy brows. A snort came from one of the bulges in the curtains. Sarah looked at the bulge.

"O'Reilly," she whispered, "I've got one of the Courtwell killers in the kitchen and the other one is coming through that door. You stay put and don't snort . . ."

Sarah walked to the hall door and threw it open. The man outside straightened suddenly, reached for his hip.

"Why didn't you ring the bell?" Sarah asked. "I don't often look into the crystal this late, but if you want a consultation . . ."

Sarah backed into the room. The man followed, shutting the door with his foot. He kept his hand on his hip.

"Where's this guy Charlot?" he rasped.

"Charlot? I don't know. At least, my conscious mind don't know, mister. Maybe if I looked in the crystal I might see him. Of course, it's late, and my fee would be double . . ."

The man shoved his face close to Sarah's, stared at her under the eerie rays of the lantern.

"So that's it? How much?" he asked.

"Twenty," Sarah replied. She stalked to the table which held the crystal globe and sat down.

The man hesitated, then lowered himself into the seat opposite.

"Come on now," he ordered. "No use stallin' with the fortune tellin' stuff. You know where Charlot is and you're willin' to spill for twenty. Spill, or . . ."

He drew his hand from his hip and showed the gun in it to Sarah. Sarah glanced at it, then bent her head over the crystal globe.

"Charlot!" she muttered. "I can almost see him. I can see him! He's near, very near. Wait! There's something else swimming into the crystal . . ."

"Can that stuff! Where's Charlot?"

"In a minute. It's coming clear. I see a man's figure . . . lying down . . . very still . . . there are cat-tails swaying over him . . . there's a dark stain on his breast . . . there's something in his breast . . ."

The man with the gun jumped out of his chair, then sat down again. He ran his left hand over his forehead. "You can't pull that. That's a lot of—"

"Ah!" Sarah went on. "I see it now. It's sticking out of his heart. It's still quivering in his heart. It's a knife, a bone-handled knife . . ."

"Hey!" cried the man on the other side of the table.

"Wait! It's going. Charlot! I see Charlot. Something is between his face and mine. Something black with two sparkling circles in it. Ah! A ring, an onyx ring with two diamonds . . ."

The man with the gun leaped up again. His gun arm came up. He said:

"O.K. You know everything. I don't know whether you see it in that ball, or whether you don't. You know it. You know about the ring I took off Honest Jim Carson's stiff and lost the night I croaked Courtwell. You know it, and it's just too bad for you! Look into your damned crystal and see if you see yourself with wings, lady, because you're going—"

Two guns spurted fire—one from the curtained wall, one from the gun in front of Sarah Watson. At the same moment, Sarah pitched the crystal ball through the air. It struck, splintered, crashed. The man who had shot at Sarah crashed with it.

Lights flashed on. Three men—O'Reilly, Ben Todd, and the cop, dashed to the writhing figure on the floor. He was surrounded by jagged, bloody glass.

Sarah Watson clasped stubby fingers over an arm which was beginning to seep red into the white of her robe.

"Meet Tony, boys," she said. "Too bad I had to break Eddie's crystal."

O'Reilly straightened, turned and faced Sarah.

"Eddie! Eddie Danville!" he bellowed. "You said he was coming . . . ?"

"He's come," said Sarah. "He's in the kitchen, guarding Jake—Tony's helper in the Courtwell killing. When Jake and Tony are able to talk some more, O'Reilly, you might get 'em to talk a little about how Eddie was railroaded to jail. I'd like to see Eddie cleared, because I want him to buy a new crystal. I want to look into a crystal, O'Reilly, and see future events. I want to see myself handing part of the ten thousand dollars reward for Courtwell's murderers to Ben Todd and part to Eddie Danville . . ."

"Part!" shouted O'Reilly. "It will be a small part indeed you'll hand out to anybody, Sarah Watson."

"And part," said Sarah, "to Sergeant O'Reilly. It will have to be a small part, of course, because I'll have to divide the ten thousand dollars four ways."

He Got What He Asked For

D. B. McCandless

Sarah and Ben were
doubly cautious

CRIME
F
D W
SHORT

The Theft and Getaway Were
Perfect—All Detective Sarah
Watson Had to Do Was to Find
the Missing Diamond Necklace
and Turn It Into Paste!

I

THE HEAVY FRONT DOORS of the Citizens'
Saving Bank swung in. A woman in rusty black
entered the cloistered silence of the main banking room, strode purposefully across the tiled
floor and halted at one of the depositors' windows. The woman had a savings bank book in
her black-gloved fingers, with some soiled bills
folded inside it. The outside of the savings book
said, "Sarah Watson."

She shoved the book and the money under
the elaborate wicket, put an elbow on the marble shelf of the window and swung the thick,
rigidly corseted column of her body around,
waiting and staring from under bristling iron
gray eyebrows.

The clerk behind the wicket made haste to
enter her deposit, murmuring polite nothings.
She paid no attention to the nothings. She was
watching the door. The armed guard stalking

from marble column to marble column bowed respectfully to her. Her gray eyes glinted on him a moment, and returned to the door.

The door swung in. A long, lank young man with red hair and gingersnap freckles entered. The woman's craggy chin grew a trifle more prominent. She reached around, took her savings book from the clerk, thrust it into her shabby, capacious black handbag, and bore down upon the young man.

"Ben Todd!" she said in a voice which echoed hoarsely back from the vaulted ceiling. "Thought you'd be along, feller. Which are you going to do—put or take?"

The young man grinned sheepishly. He said: "Whadya think?"

"How much you got left, squirt?"

"Nine dollars and two cents. Not that it's any of your damn business. Just because I'm a ground down underling in your measly detective agency is no reason . . ."

Sarah Watson adjusted her ancient black headgear more firmly upon her hard knob of gray hair. She said: "You put your bank book back in your pants, young man.

"We're going to see the president of the bank."

"Good Lord! You don't think the president of this mausoleum is going to take pity on my plight?"

"From what I know of him, he never took pity on anything," said Sarah, grasping the young man's arm firmly, "but we're going to see him, because he telephoned and asked us to see him. After we've seen him, maybe you won't need your piddling nine dollars. Come on."

Two minutes later, Sarah Watson and Ben Todd were behind the door which said, in gold letters, "Adolph A. Hecker, President," and Sarah was being bowed into a chair by Mr. Adolph A. Hecker himself.

"Mr. Hecker," said Sarah, leaning forward stiffly from the waist, "meet Mr. Todd, my assistant. We came as soon as possible. Of course we have a great press of work at the office . . ."

"Quite," said Mr. Hecker, nodding grudg-ingly at Ben Todd and settling himself behind his large mahogany desk. Mr. Hecker had some difficulty settling himself, because the distance between the edge of the desk and the edge of Mr. Hecker's pot belly had to be nicely judged.

Mr. Hecker made a steeple of his thin white hands and turned his bleak eyes upon Mrs. Watson. He said: "Quite! Mrs. Watson, I will state the case frankly and concisely. I find myself in need of an agent upon whose discretion I may rely. I make it a practice, as you know, to be informed regarding each and every depositor in my bank . . ."

"The case, please," said Sarah.

"And so," said Mr. Hecker, "knowing you, Mrs. Watson, and your excellent reputation, I—ah—that is to say—Mrs. Watson, what would your fee be for recovering a stolen diamond necklace belonging to my wife?"

"Ten per cent of the value of the necklace," said Sarah promptly.

"Ten per cent? I had no idea! Does that not seem excessive, my dear lady?"

"Ten per cent," said Sarah, firmly.

"Ten per cent. Well—ah—perhaps in that case, you would not care to undertake my—ah—job. The necklace I wish recovered is, you see, only paste. A very clever imitation, but paste. The value is relatively small—not more than two thousand dollars."

"Ten per cent," said Sarah, "and expenses, of course."

"Ah? The expense would be slight in this case. I happen to know the—ah—young person who stole the necklace. I happen to know where—ah—she will be at a certain time this evening."

Sarah Watson got to her feet, stood looking down at the square toes of her black shoes. She said: "A case for the police, Mr. Hecker. Too simple for us."

"Sit down, Mrs. Watson, pray. It is not simple at all. I—ah—wish it were. Let me explain. I will be frank. This is confidential, of course. Quite! The necklace—the paste necklace, Mrs. Watson—was taken under peculiar circumstances. The young lady who took it was calling on me at the time at my apartment.

"My wife—ah—happened to be travelling abroad."

"Quite," said Sarah.

"What? Oh! Yes, yes. Well, Mrs. Watson, I was showing the young lady my wife's collection of jewels, among them the imitation diamond necklace which my wife keeps for most functions. The real one, which is the famous Gautier necklace, remains in our safe deposit box practically all the time. Now, the—ah—young lady managed to abstract the necklace—the imitation necklace, Mrs. Watson, and shortly afterward, she departed with it, believing that I would be in no position to accuse her of theft . . ."

"Was she right?" said Sarah.

Mr. Hecker's pale eyes wandered away from Sarah's. After a moment, he said: "She was."

"Quite," said Sarah. "Well now, Mr. Hecker, while I never object to picking up a bit of small change even so small a bit as I would pick up on this job, it doesn't seem to me that it's worth it to you to hire us. If the necklace the young lady removed was simply an imitation, it would be simpler and easier for you to have another imitation made, and—"

"Ah, Mrs. Watson, there you have me. I cannot have an imitation made, for this reason. It was yesterday morning that I discovered the theft of the paste necklace and it was yesterday morning that my wife returned from abroad. I had just time to go to our safe deposit box, remove the real necklace and place it in my wife's safe at home, where the imitation had been. It is there now, and there isn't a chance in the world of my extracting it again in order to have an imitation made without my wife's knowing, so . . ."

"I see," said Sarah, staring intently at Mr. Hecker, "and of course, there's the fact, too, Mr. Hecker, that if we steal back this necklace for you—"

"Mrs. Watson! I beg you—not steal—recover!"

"Steal," said Sarah, firmly. "If we steal back this necklace for you, Mr. Hecker, it will cost you only two hundred dollars, plus expenses, whereas, if you were to have an imitation made, it would cost you two thousand dollars. Eh, Mr. Hecker?"

"Quite," said Mr. Hecker. "I have considered that angle, naturally. A banker always considers . . ."

"Let's get down to brass tacks," said Sarah. "What's the young lady's name? What's she look like? Where is this place that you know she'll be this evening? How have you any guarantee that she'll have the necklace with her?"

"She will be on the eight o'clock train to Chicago tonight. She has lower berth number 3, car Number 654," said Mr. Hecker. "I am sure she will have the necklace with her, because I have information that she has quit the theatrical production with which she was connected and has—ah—closed her books definitely in this city."

"Mr. Hecker," said Sarah, "did you get all that data yourself?"

"I did."

"You'd make a good detective," said Sarah. "What's the young female's name?"

Mr. Hecker's thin lips writhed a trifle as though he were about to swallow a dose of astringent. He said: "Her name is Dolores Flores."

"That describes her," said Sarah. "Now, if you'll advance some expense money, Mr. Hecker, about two hundred dollars to start with, we'll get ready to steal your necklace."

Sarah Watson and Ben Todd stepped out of the bank and into the sunshine. Sarah said: "You've got two hundred dollars in your pants, Bennie, and all afternoon. You might get the tickets. Be sure to get in Car 654, and be sure you get me a lower, young feller. You might drop my ticket at the office. Then you might check up on this Dolores Flores female and make sure she is taking that train. You might get a look at her, if you can, but not too long a look, Bennie. I know men! Then you might interview somebody that knows jewels and find out what the Gautier necklace looks like and how much the real one is worth, and then you might . . ."

"Listen, slave driver," said Ben Todd, "after I do all that, there won't be any *then*. What are you doing in the way of work yourself this afternoon, old girl?"

"Bennie," said Sarah solemnly, "I'm going to a tea—a Republican tea."

"Republican? I thought you were a Democrat?"

"What if I am? It ain't branded on my forehead, is it? I'm going to a Republican tea, Bennie, because Mrs. Adolph A. Hecker is giving the tea, in her own apartment.

"Listen, you old wench! You're not beginning your double-crossing tricks already?"

"Fiddlesticks! I'm merely interested to see the woman who could bear Adolph as a husband. Bennie, do ladies wear diamond necklaces at tea parties?"

"Not ladies," said Ben Todd. "Sarah, you're up to something. Now listen, you stalking tigress, Adolph may only be going to pay us a coupla hundred—"

"And expenses . . ."

"But a coupla hundred would pay my salary for four weeks, Sarah, so for hell's sake, stick to Adolph."

"Bennie, you know me. I have yet to betray the confidence of a client. Good-by. I'll see you on the train."

II

Sarah Watson stalked down the ramp beside which the Chicago train waited. She was dressed as she had been dressed that morning. She held firmly a large yellow suitcase of the cardboard variety and ignored, as she stalked, the three pestiferous red caps who pursued her.

Halfway down the long train, her steps slackened. There was a young man lounging there, with one foot on the lowest step of a car. He was a red-headed young man and he was deep in converse with a slinky young person who was aggressively female from the black velvet hat perched on her platinum curls to the black velvet bows on her spike heeled slippers.

Sarah took longer strides. She stopped abruptly beside the conversing couple. She said: "Young man, is this car 654?"

The young man stared blankly at her a moment, then his wide mouth grew wider. He said: "Well, if it ain't Aunt Sarah! Auntie, you're early. I want you to meet my friend, Miss Dolores Flores."

Miss Flores extended a drooping hand which dripped ruby red at the fingernails. She said: "Charmed!"

Sarah Watson grunted. She gave a nod which set her ancient headgear to quivering. She turned her back and mounted the steps. At the top of the steps, she paused. Ben Todd's red head was close to the platinum blonde curls. Ben Todd was whispering and the young lady was giggling. Sarah peered down at them and made a horrible face.

The conductor was bawling his last warning when Miss Dolores Flores made her entrance into car 654, followed by Ben Todd. The young lady's progress down the aisle was marked by a small flurry among the seated passengers, particularly the males. Only the woman in Section 4 remained oblivious, and she kept her rugged countenance bent over a printed circular until the pair passed. The circular said: "Twenty Reasons why American Ladies Should Vote Republican." One sheet of the circular was devoted to the photograph of a lady whose nose and bosom were both prominent. The photograph was inscribed in flowing ink, "With regards to Mrs. Sarah Watson, from Mrs. Adolph A. Hecker."

Ben Todd slid into seat 4, beside Sarah. Sarah lifted her eyes from the circular and fixed them on the elaborate curls which covered the back of Miss Flores' head. Sarah said: "If you've got the necklace, Bennie, we've still time to get off?"

"Got the—! Whatya think I am, woman, a professional dip?"

"I think you're a damn fool," said Sarah. "If you ain't got the necklace, what was the idea of all the billing and cooing?"

"Listen, horse-face," whispered Ben Todd, leaning closer, "I—er—happened to scrape an acquaintance with the charmer in the course of my investigations this afternoon and . . ."

"I'll bet you didn't have to scrape very hard!"

"No. She likes auburn hair. Now listen, and no more cracks, old lady. This is biz. The charmer's afraid. She's asked me to protect her. There's a naughty, bad man with dark hair and slimey eyes and a wart on his chin . . ."

"And two hairs growing out of the wart," said Sarah. "I know. I saw him on the observation platform as I came by. And I've seen him somewhere before, but I can't think where. He looks like a bad 'un. Now, I wonder who sicked him on Dolores?"

"Hell knows. You say he was on the observation . . . ?"

"He was, but he ain't now. Look!"

Ben Todd followed the lift of Sarah's gray eyes. A dark individual was sliding into the seat directly opposite theirs.

"Bennie," said Sarah, "I've got a premonition we have competition. We've got to look spry. It might not be a bad idea for you to go and bill and coo some more with Dolores. Buy her new magazines and things and charge 'em to Mr. Hecker. Stick with her—No! Wait—"

Sarah had risen abruptly. The young lady with the platinum tresses was making her way forward toward the door marked "Ladies." Sarah stepped over Ben Todd's long legs and into the aisle. The train began to move. Sarah lurched forward toward the door marked "Ladies."

Five minutes later, Miss Flores was back in her seat and Sarah was back in hers.

"Ben," whispered Sarah, "when that girl bleached her hair, she bleached out all her brains. She's got that necklace in her handbag, crammed in with all the face paint and lip paint and the cigarettes and the rest of it. I saw it—the Gautier necklace!"

"The imitation of the Gautier necklace."

"I was forgetting," said Sarah. "Well, the imitation's worth two thousand, ain't it? The girl's an imbecile. Go on up, now, Bennie, and sparkle for her. Keep your eye on her purse but don't put your hand in it. When the time comes for snitching, I'll snitch."

"Well, when is the time coming for snitching? That's a little detail we ain't worked out, yet, old girl."

"*We* ain't but *I* have. It won't be until after dinner anyway, Bennie. I never steal except on a full stomach."

The train sped on. Sarah sat with her head back against the green plush, her hands folded over her prominent abdomen. Two hours passed. A black man with a white smile and a white coat came down the aisle, beating a musical gong. Sarah stirred. Ben Todd came down the aisle, behind him, Miss Dolores Flores. They stopped at Sarah's seat.

"If you don't object, Auntie," said Ben Todd, "Miss Flores and I are going to dine togeth—"

"Delighted," said Sarah, rising. "Love to eat on trains. Lead the way, nephew."

After dinner was over, Ben Todd squired Dolores into the club car at the end of the train for a cigarette. Sarah returned to car 654, and was occupying the seat opposite her own, while the porter made up her lower and the upper above it—reserved for Ben Todd. Sarah wore the complacent and reminiscent look of one who has relished good food.

A long-legged young man charged suddenly into the almost empty car and gripped Sarah by the shoulder. He said: "Listen. There's a stop in five minutes. I saw you fingering the girl's purse. If you've got the goods, let's hop off and . . ."

Sarah shook his fingers off. She half rose from the seat and pushed her face close to his. She said: "You go back and stick with the fool girl, Ben Todd. She's in danger as long as she's got that thing in her bag. I've just remembered where I saw the gent with the wart last—Go!"

Ben Todd waited a moment, staring. Then he wheeled and charged back down the aisle. In the doorway he collided with a gentleman who also seemed in haste. The gentleman had a wart on his chin.

Sarah settled back in her seat and closed her eyes. A few moments passed. Someone again laid a hand on her shoulder. She started, looked up into a pair of slimey, dark eyes. She said: "Mercy! I'm afraid I'm sitting in your place, mister. The porter's making up my bed. If you don't mind, I'll just—" She slid over to make room for the owner of the seat.

The gentleman with the wart sat down.

Sarah said: "You know, I've seen you some place before, mister."

The gentleman with the wart looked her over. He said:

"Old stuff! You ain't."

"Maybe it was a picture of you I saw," said Sarah thoughtfully. "I see a lot of pictures of people—"

The porter said: "All ready, Madam."

Sarah rose. She glanced down at the face with the wart. She crossed the aisle and disappeared between the green curtains of her berth.

For five minutes thereafter, Sarah's hoarse voice grunted and groaned behind her curtains. Then, she emerged, swathed in a purple crêpe robe, and lurched up the aisle toward the Ladies' Room. When she returned, the gentleman with the wart had vanished. There was no one in the car to notice that Sarah was still thoroughly corseted and shod under her kimono.

An hour passed—two hours—three hours. The berths were all made up and the car dark, except for the dim lights at either end. Someone fell against the curtains of Sarah's berth. She opened them with a gun in her hand. She saw a ladder and a pair of long legs ascending the ladder, and she lay back. She kept the curtains slightly parted with one hand, and her eye fixed to the opening.

More hours passed, hours filled with the hooting of the train's whistle and the rattling of the train's wheels. Sarah opened her curtains wide and surveyed the empty aisle. She drew back into her cubicle and tapped smartly on the ceiling above her.

"Huh?" said a sleepy voice. Sarah tapped again. She put her feet into the aisle and stood up. She was still wrapped in her purple kimono.

The curtains of the upper berth parted. A rumpled red-head appeared in the opening. Sarah said, very softly:

"Time! Ring for the porter. Keep him busy this end."

The red-head nodded. Its eyes blinked. Sarah strode up the aisle. At the other end of the car, the porter's bell began to ring, insistently. It was then three a.m.

Two minutes later, Sarah thrust her head out of the Ladies' Room door and peered down the car. Deserted. Not a sound but the faint wailing of the train.

Sarah began to walk down the aisle toward her own section. She paused before she got there, her hand gripping the curtains of the lower occupied by Miss Dolores Flores.

III

In the men's washroom, Ben Todd took his head out of his hands and looked up into the anxious face of the porter. Ben Todd said:

"I feel better now, George. What time is it?"

"Three fifteen, suh."

"Um. So we been in here ten minutes, huh? Well, George, that was sure nifty liquor you gave me. It did the trick. Here!"

Ben Todd thrust a bill into the porter's ready fingers and stood up.

He said: "Don't bother any more about me, now, George. Just stay and finish up that bottle."

Ben Todd swayed down the aisle toward section 4. The car was dark, silent. The ladder was still in place in front of his berth.

Ben Todd climbed up. Someone had switched the light on over his bed. Someone had left a slip of paper stuck into his pillow with a large safety pin. The determined script on the paper was Sarah Watson's. It said: "Next stop 3:25. Get ready. The girl is dead."

There was no signature. There was a smudge of red near the ragged lower edge of the note.

Ben Todd sat hunched up, staring. His freckles began to take on a darker hue against the whitening of his face. Presently, the paper began to shake a little in his hand.

It was sixty seconds before he began frenziedly adjusting the few garments he had removed that night. He was badly handicapped by the jerkiness of his breathing and the fumbling of his fingers.

At 3:24, he was sitting cross legged on his berth, gripping his valise. There was no sound from the berth beneath him.

At 3:25, the train stopped. Still no sound from below.

At 3:25½, there was a stir in the aisle. Ben Todd peered down, saw a man dashing into the vestibule of the car.

At 3:26, the conductor's whistle blew from the platform outside the train, and the train gave a preliminary lurch.

Sarah Watson erupted from her berth, charged down the aisle. Ben Todd swung his long legs over at the same instant, ignored the ladder, leaped, followed her, caught up with her in the vestibule. The conductor was just mounting the steps. Sarah put a hand on his chest and shoved. She went by him like a blast.

The conductor leaped back on the moving train, cursing. Ben Todd slid into the next vestibule and jumped. He landed sitting down on the dark platform, the few scattered lights of the town beyond the station pinwheeling in his head.

A firm hand hauled him up. A hoarse voice said: "Stop resting, feller. I've got a car waiting."

Together, they dashed around the dark bulk of the station, dived into the lone car waiting in the dreary street beyond. The taxi began to move. There was only one other car in sight, its tail light rapidly diminishing. Ben Todd said: "Sarah! That poor girl! How—?"

Sarah lifted her black gloved hands. She crooked the fingers suggestively. She said: "This is the way it happened, Bennie."

"God!" breathed Ben Todd. "Strangled! Sarah, what in the name of hell are we going to do now?"

"We're going to keep quiet if you know what's good for you," said Sarah, with a glance at the driver's back. "This is no place to discuss—"

Sarah broke off and leaned toward the driver. She said:

"This flying field, young man. It is the only one hereabouts? You're sure? Good! Now, listen, young feller, a lot depends on this. You sure there ain't a single solitary private plane to rent at that field, for love nor money?"

The taxi driver kept his head over the wheel and nodded. They were making speed. The tail light of the single car ahead was growing larger.

Sarah said: "Then you're damn sure, young man, that there ain't a plane of any kind or description flying out of this place until the regular passenger plane comes through at four a.m. and takes off again?"

The driver nodded. He said, "You can stake your life on it."

"Maybe I am," said Sarah, quietly, and leaned back against the cushions.

Ben Todd spent the next ten flying minutes hunched in his corner, staring at Sarah Watson's rugged profile, which looked white in the flash of occasional street lamps, dark and brooding in the intervals between.

The taxi swerved on to a dirt road, bumped to a stop in front of a fenced field. There was a gate in the fence, and beyond the fence, a square, boxlike structure.

Ben Todd reached for the door handle on his side of the car. Sarah gripped his arm. She said: "Wait!"

The man standing just inside the gate of the flying field moved on, passed into shadows, emerged again and walked through the door of the square building beyond the gate.

Sarah said: "All right, now," thrust a crumpled bill into their driver's hand and got out. They passed through the gate and halted, Sarah's fingers digging into Ben Todd's arm, in their ears, the diminishing sound of the car they had come in. Sarah Watson said: "We've got about fifteen minutes to wait, if the plane's on time. Don't spend any of 'em in the light, Ben Todd, and don't go near that waiting room, until the last minute, and then get our tickets. If you can change your appearance any while you're hanging around in the dark, do it. And give me your valise. I need the duds in it."

"Sarah!" Ben Todd's voice sounded as though rust had attacked his vocal chords. "Sarah, you're not going to try to get into my clothes? They won't fit you and you couldn't get away with it anyway, old girl. Listen! I'd do anything to get you clear of this terrible thing, Sarah, but . . ."

"Idiot! Give me that bag. Remember, keep out of sight 'til the last minute. I'll meet you just before the plane leaves the ground."

Sarah Watson grabbed Ben Todd's valise from his nerveless hand and strode away and was lost in the shadows at the far side of the field.

Ben Todd located the spot where the plane would settle down to discharge and admit passengers. Thereafter, he skulked in shadows, his forehead beaded with perspiration in spite of the cool wind of approaching dawn. Once or twice, he thought he saw the dark bulk of Sarah's figure melt into the darker bulk of the shadowed side of the waiting room structure. Several times, he was sure he saw a flashlight darting there, close to the ground. Then, the distant drone of a big plane came to his ears and he lifted anxious eyes. The stars were fading out and gray was washing into the ceiling above him.

Like a monstrous, murmuring white bird, the plane rested in the white path of the runway. The trim stewardess stood at one side of the rear door, the collar-ad co-pilot at the other side, watch in hand. Faces peered out of the windows of the plane; waiting.

The co-pilot snapped his watch shut, grinned at the stewardess, put his foot on the first of the two little steps up to the plane's door.

A woman ran out from behind the waiting room, carrying a man's valise in one hand, a yellow cardboard suitcase in the other. An enveloping, bright yellow rain coat flapped as she ran. The bags smacked against her thighs as she came on.

She slowed. She lifted the hand with the valise in it and straightened the exotic creation of black velvet and nodding violets which had slid forward off her grey hair and was threatening to blind her. She came to a full stop, set the valise down, and adjusted the polka-dotted veil which hung from the hat, drawing it well down and over her prominent chin.

A long legged young man shot out from the waiting room door and joined her. She thrust the bags into his hands.

"Here," she said. "You handle it. Tell 'em we know the suitcase weighs too much, but your valise don't weigh anything, because it's empty now. Tell 'em to divide the weight of the suitcase between us, because we're travelling together. Don't bollix it, feller. It's important—"

Sarah Watson charged on, thrust a ticket under the co-pilot's handsome nose and entered the plane. She went in with no more sound than the rattling of her stiff yellow raincoat, and she took a seat at the rear.

The seats were brown leather, four seats on each side of the aisle. A man and woman sat on one side, rather white and tense. In front of them, an elderly gentleman, evidently a person of means, read a book.

On the other side, Ben Todd sat in the last seat, with his back against a walled-off cubicle labelled "Stewardess." In front of him, sat Sarah Watson. In the front seat on that side of the aisle, just behind the glass partition which separated the passengers from the pilots, a man sat. All that was visible of the man from the rear was a section of dark hair and a soft felt hat.

The plane soared. The squares of dark and light on the earth beneath grew smaller, then began to take form in the growing light. Here and there, sunlight glinted on a steeple.

Sarah Watson turned in her seat. Ben Todd leaned forward. Sarah said, through her veil: "Well, we made it. But I can't say I think much of your ideas of disguise. Any fool can turn up his coat collar and pull down his hat. Couldn't you have rustled a false mustache or something, Bennie? Not that it matters now. We're on and nobody can get off this thing until—"

"Sarah, listen! You can't get away with it, old

girl! The cops will be waiting for you at the next stop."

"Waiting for me?" Sarah thrust her proboscis close to Ben's. "Waiting for *me?* Ben Todd, do you mean to say you've been thinking that I—do you mean to say that you've been thinking that poor girl is dead because I—?"

Ben Todd stared into the eyes behind Sarah's dotted veil. For a long time, neither of them moved, except to sway slightly with the swaying of the plane. Ben Todd said, slowly: "I've been a damn fool, old girl. But you've got to admit you acted like you had something damn unpleasant to run away from."

"Not from," said Sarah, hoarsely. "After! Look ahead, Bennie. Ain't there something familiar about the back of that head?"

Ben Todd stared at the dark hair resting on the leather cushions of the seat up the aisle. He stared at the soft felt hat on top of the hair. Presently, Ben Todd said, very quietly:

"Wart face!"

"Exactly," said Sarah.

"But listen—if you mean you think he killed—"

"I know he killed her."

"Well, then, why the hell all the dramatics? Why the hell didn't we get him at the landing field?"

"You're forgetting we also want to get the necklace."

"What of it? If he killed her, he's got the necklace. We'd have got it. You could simply have claimed it for old Hecker."

"And had the cops hold it as evidence for months? Listen, Bennie. I set out to steal that necklace, and I'm going to steal it, for reasons of my own. Bennie, in which of a man's pockets do you think he'd be likely to hide a diamond—a necklace he thought was diamonds?"

"Listen, you damn fool woman. If that guy has the necklace, let him keep it. He's dangerous!"

"Bennie," said Sarah, "don't worry about me. Now, think! Where'd he be likely to put that necklace?"

"God knows. The Gautier necklace is pretty bulky, so the imitation must be, too. He might hide it in his luggage, far as that goes."

"He has no luggage. He must have hopped that train in a hurry, must have learned at the last minute that the necklace was on board. Think, now, Bennie! Which pocket?"

"Wait a mo," said Ben Todd, slowly. "I'm remembering something—in the dining car, while you were shovelling in grub, I was watching. I saw that guy take his wallet out to pay. He took it out of an inside coat pocket, left hand side. The pocket seemed to have some special kind of zipper arrangement on it."

"Bennie, you're worth your wages, sometimes! Let's see, now. The next landing is in three quarters of an hour. In about half an hour, Bennie, I'm going to be sick."

"Sick? Whad'ya mean, sick?"

"Sick. Lots of people get sick on planes. I never rode on a plane before, and I'm a sensitive nature, Bennie. I'm not only going to be sick, but I'm going to get hysterical. I'm going to do some staggering and some screeching. I'm going to stagger up front and then I'm going to stagger back."

"Listen, Sarah, for hell's sake! That fellow's a killer. He's dangerous."

"After I stagger back, Bennie, I'm going to stagger into that little cubbyhole right behind you. Your job is to see that that little snip of a stewardess don't follow me in there. After I'm in, Bennie, just let things take their course . . . just let things take their course."

Sarah turned squarely around. She became absorbed in peering out of her window. Ben Todd regarded the grey, rocky knob of hair on the back of her head for a long time. His lips moved silently. A lip reader reading those lips would have blushed.

Presently, Ben Todd relaxed and stared down from his window. Below, the earth revolved, slowly. Above, the thin, pink tinted clouds raced.

Sarah Watson stirred. She glanced at the small, plump watch pinned on her bosom. She rose.

Sarah gulped dangerously as she stood up. She gulped again and lurched into the aisle. She made some loud, unintelligible noises. She began to sway up the aisle.

The alert stewardess started down the aisle to meet her. Sarah stumbled, knocked the stewardess sidewise, went on with a rush. Sarah was screeching now, loud, thin screeches from which words were beginning to emerge.

"Stop the plane! I'm scared! I'm scared stiff! Something's going to happen—"

Ben Todd was in the aisle, racing after the stewardess. The stewardess was racing after Sarah. Sarah was now at the glass partition which separated the pilots from the passengers. Sarah was banging on the glass with clenched fists. She was yelling her terror.

The stewardess reached Sarah, clawed at the yellow rubber which covered Sarah's broad back. Sarah went on yelling, went on pounding.

Ben Todd reached the stewardess. He put firm hands on the stewardess. He said: "The old lady's scared into a fit. You can't handle her. Let me."

Sarah Watson wheeled suddenly. She staggered. One of her thick arms went out in a wild, wide sweep. The fist at the end of the arm struck Ben Todd on the point of the chin. Ben Todd staggered. His long arms sawed the air. One of the arms struck the stewardess.

With a last weird yell, Sarah Watson collapsed. She collapsed over the dark gentleman sitting directly behind the glass partition. The dark gentleman and Sarah became a conglomerate, moving mass of waving arms and legs, a mass slipping and sliding over the leather seat, a mass vocal with grunts and gasps.

The stewardess recovered. She leaped into the fray. She clawed indiscriminately at portions of Sarah's anatomy and portions of the dark gentleman.

Ben Todd gripped the edge of the dark gentleman's seat. Ben Todd swung out a long arm and curved it about the slender waist of the stewardess. Ben Todd lifted the stewardess up and out into the aisle. He said:

"I told you I could handle her. Lay off!"

Suddenly, Sarah Watson was on her feet. She was sagging against Ben Todd. She was pulling down her veil as she sagged. She was moving rapidly toward the rear of the plane, moaning as she moved, and taking Ben Todd with her.

The dark-haired gentleman was straightening himself. He was gulping in deep breaths. He was putting his hand to his left side. He was rising from his seat.

Sarah reached the door of the little cubicle marked "Stewardess." She opened the door. She said, loudly:

"No! Leave me alone! I want to be alone! Oh, I'm so ashamed!" and she slammed the door of the little cubicle shut in Ben Todd's face.

The stewardess was at Ben Todd's shoulder. The stewardess was reaching past Ben Todd, trying to open the door of the little cubicle.

Ben Todd closed his fingers about the wrist of the stewardess. He said: "Leave the poor old thing alone. She just got scared, and now she's ashamed."

A new voice rose over the tumult, the voice of the dark haired gentleman:

"I've been robbed!" he screamed. "Robbed!" The dark haired gentleman was in the aisle now, facing the rear, his arms raised, his wart revealed to all who cared to look. "Robbed!" he screamed again.

The door of the little cubicle burst open. Sarah Watson came out of the cubicle with a rush, covering her veiled face with her hands.

"A man in there!" she howled. "A man! He hit me. Oh, my! He hit me and he jumped out of the window in there. He jumped and he's going down with one of those parasol things!"

The passengers were all on their feet now, swaying and jerking, momentarily in danger of entangling with each other in the center of the aisle. As Sarah's screech reached them each followed with his eyes the direction of Sarah's stubby, pointing finger, and each scrambled into a seat, peered out a window.

"Look! A man—she's right—his parachute's

stuck—no, it's unfolding—he hit her—he must have been hid in there all the time!"

The dark haired man got back into the aisle again. He raised an arm and pointed it at Sarah. He yelled:

"I've been robbed! That woman robbed me!"

"What?" Sarah's answering yell was hoarse. "You've been robbed? You're accusing me—me? Look down there, man. Look! There goes your thief!"

"I've been robbed!" yelled the dark haired man. "She took them. She took the diamonds—my diamonds! She . . . that woman . . ."

"Diamonds?" said Sarah hoarsely. "My dear man! Just look out of the windows, as everybody else is looking!"

The passengers ceased staring with popping eyes at Sarah and the man with the wart. The passengers pressed their faces again against the windows:

"Look! He said diamonds—wait—the wind is carrying the parachute this way. What's that shining down there in the man's hand? Diamonds—he said diamonds—there's something shining in that man's hand. He's got away with the diamonds—he must have been hiding in there all the time. It's a blessing we're not all dead!"

The man with the wart got out into the aisle again. He raised his arms and shook his fists. He cried:

"That man's got my diamonds! That man! Stop the plane! That thief has my diamonds. He's going to land any minute! Stop the—"

And suddenly the man with the wart ceased yelling and crowded to a window and fixed his eyes avidly on the figure slowly drifting down, drifting now very close to earth, near the wide spread of a red factory's roofs!

The plane tilted, began to point its nose toward the earth. The man with the wart lost his balance on the slippery seat upon which he had been kneeling. He slid, he clawed at the seat, he banged his head against the back of the seat in front, and he fell.

The stewardess ran to him and said, "The plane's stopping very soon now, anyway, sir—the regular stop. And you must have seen where that thief landed with your diamonds—"

Sarah Watson settled in her seat and folded her hands complacently. She turned her head and Ben Todd leaned toward her.

"Bennie," she said, close to Ben Todd's ear, "Bennie, I've always said that all men were alike, but the one that just landed under that parachute is different, Bennie, because I made him myself. I had a hell of a time finding enough scrap iron about that airport to weigh him down, and a hell of a time stealing a parachute there, too, and, of course, there's a good suit of yours gone to pot to clothe him, but we can charge the suit to Mr. Hecker."

A hand touched Sarah on the shoulder. She turned, looked up through her veil at the face of the gentleman with the wart.

"Madam," said the gentleman, "I wish to apologize for accusing you of stealing my diamonds. I was wrong!"

"That," said Sarah, "is perfectly all right, perfectly all right."

The man with the wart leaned closer. He stared down into the face behind the polka dots of Sarah's veil. He said: "Madam, I—" and suddenly wrenched the veil away, brushing aside the clutch of Ben Todd's fingers.

The man with the wart stared down into the eyes under Sarah Watson's bristling brows. He said, very slowly, and lingeringly:

"Ah!"

Sarah said nothing. The thin lips under her incipient mustache curved slightly.

The gentleman with the wart began to talk with a rush of words. He said:

"I see! I remember you! I know you now! You took them and you passed them over to him back here and he jumped with them. What a dummy I've been!—A *dummy!* I see it all now! A *dummy!* Not a man, but a—"

The plane bumped. Dust fanned past its windows from the whirring propeller. There was another bump.

The man with the wart took one more moment

to glare balefully into Sarah's eyes. He said: "You think you're damn smart, yes, but I'll outsmart you yet, you old harridan."

And then he rushed to the door at the rear of the plane, wrenched it open, and leaped while the plane was still gliding down the runway. In the silence which followed the cessation of movement and sound, Sarah Watson's voice said hoarsely: "The gent who lost his diamonds seems to be in a hurry to get some place."

The car carrying Sarah Watson and Ben Todd away from the airport sped along the wide, white boulevard. Ahead of it, another car sped— far ahead.

Ben Todd took his clenched hands off his knees for a moment and turned to Sarah. He said: "He may make it yet. If he's as smart as I am, he knows just about where that dummy landed."

Sarah Watson unfolded her hands, opened her capacious handbag, stared at herself in the bag's mirror. She said: "Becoming hat, this. It's my Sunday hat."

"Sarah, for the love of—listen, that guy with the wart is gaining. He's going to get there long before we do. He's going to get there and he's going to find that dummy, and he's going to get that necklace. Sarah, you've got to think of something!"

"I am thinking of something," said Sarah, snapping her bag shut. "I'm thinking we'd better tell the driver to slow up a bit."

"Listen, you! You gone batty? Can't you see that guy is eating up the road?"

"Bennie," said Sarah calmly, "some day you're going to have a nervous breakdown. Now listen. You may think you know just where that dummy landed and probably the gent with the wart thinks he knows, too, but things look different from the air, Bennie, and I'm betting the gent with the wart is going to spend a long time searching for that necklace . . ." Sarah broke off and leaned forward to the driver.

"Driver," she said. "Take the next turning, please. And don't go so fast. My partner's a bit nervous."

"Who wouldn't be nervous!" yelled Ben Todd, "with an idiot woman like you! Slow up and let me out of here, driver. I'm going to get another car and go after that guy . . ."

"You're going to stay right in this car," said Sarah firmly. "Take the next crossing, driver— the one that leads to the police station."

IV

Sarah Watson strode into police headquarters, her fingers on Ben Todd's arm. Ben Todd's pallor was excessive and his forehead was dewed with sweat.

"Captain," said Sarah to the man behind the desk, "I'm Sarah Watson. Here's my card. This is my assistant. We're here to put you on the trail of the murderer of Dolores Flores."

"Already?" said the man behind the desk. "We just got it over the wire that they'd found that dame dead on the train to Chi."

"Let me talk, Captain. I'm in a hurry. I was on that train. I had the berth opposite the murderer's. I meant to keep my eyes on him all night because I knew who he was. I'd seen his photo in the police files at home. Wait, let me talk, Captain.

"I meant to watch him, but my eyes got stuck together for a few minutes and when I opened them, I saw the murderer sneaking back into his berth from somewhere. He was in his shirt sleeves. He had something red on his cuff, his right cuff. It'll be there yet, when you get him."

"Blood, eh? Where is this guy?"

"Not blood, captain. There was no blood. The girl was strangled to death. When I found her, dead, in her berth, her handbag was lying open beside her. There was a lipstick in it, blood red, and uncapped. The metal case of the lipstick had printing on it that said the lipstick was made special for Dolores Flores. Your chemists will be able to match that lipstick up with the red smudge on the murderer's cuff, Captain, when you get him."

"Say listen, where is this guy? Where do we get him?"

"Let me talk, Captain. The murderer got that smudge on his cuff, of course, when he put his thieving hand in the girl's purse to steal her valuables. I would have got the same smudge on my own—er—hand, if I had put it in. But of course, I didn't. Fingerprints, you know, Captain. Now, Captain, if you'll just send a squad car out with a half dozen men with guns. There's a big red brick factory about ten miles southwest of the airport here."

"The Furness factory," said the Captain.

"The name don't matter," said Sarah. "The point is, you'll probably have to beat the woods that lie south of the factory. The murderer will be in those woods, doing some beating himself, for something he lost. You'll catch him easy, Captain. Those woods are big and they're thick, and the murderer don't know just where to look. He's a dark man, the murderer, with black eyes, and a wart on his chin with two hairs sprouting out of it and—"

"Warty Capruccio! He's been up for murder before, and slipped clear."

"The same, Captain. Well, Captain, you've got my card and you can reach me if you want to, though you won't have a smidgin of trouble convicting Warty without me, I'm sure. I'm in a hurry now, Captain, because I'm on a job, and it ain't finished yet."

Sarah Watson and Ben Todd emerged from the building which housed the local police. Ben Todd was not only perspiring, he was gnawing his nails.

"Sarah, here comes a cab. I don't know what in hell's name you were up to in there, wasting time, setting the cops on that guy's trail."

"Time," said Sarah, sententiously, "is never wasted when it's used to bring a criminal to justice."

"You should talk about criminals! Listen, you imbecilic old battle-axe, we may have time yet to repair the damage you've done. If we hire a plane, we can get there before the cops get there . . . Sarah, stir your stumps! We've got to get that necklace . . ."

"Bennie," said Sarah, "you can go hire a plane if you want to. But it ain't worth it, especially as we couldn't charge it to Mr. Hecker's expense. The necklace that dummy took down to earth came from the five and ten, Bennie, and it cost me a dollar. It ain't worth retrieving, because it's already charged to Mr. Hecker, anyway. I had it ready to drop in that poor girl's purse, in case I managed to steal the string she had."

"Sarah! Do you mean to say you fumbled getting the imitation string from the murderer?"

"I never fumble anything, young man," said Sarah, and opened her purse.

Ben Todd stared down at the coiled, glittering thing in the bottom of Sarah's purse. He had put his hand out toward the purse. Sarah snapped the purse shut. She advanced to the curb and signalled a taxi. She said: "The thing to do now, Bennie, is to get the first train out of here for home. I've got a date with Mrs. Adolph A. Hecker."

"Mrs. Hecker! Why you damn, double-crossing old . . ."

"Mrs. Hecker," said Sarah, "is a very fine woman, even if she is married to Mr. Hecker. Mrs. Hecker has promised me ten thousand dollars for this necklace, Ben Todd."

Sarah Watson stepped into the cab. Ben Todd stepped after her and flopped on the seat. Ben Todd took his head in his hands. He said:

"My head, my poor, poor head! I knew before this thing was over you'd have us tied up in a mess of double-crossing, triple-crossing knots!"

"Bennie," said Sarah, firmly. "You wrong me. I engaged to do a job for Mr. Hecker and I intend to do it. Of course, Mr. Hecker shouldn't have lied to me. If you had eyes in your head, Bennie, you'd have seen him lying. Ten per cent seemed excessive to him, Bennie, until he happened to remember that the necklace he wanted to recover was paste, nothing but paste. Oh, well, all men are alike! Let's see now . . . Ten thousand from Mrs. Hecker, and two hundred from Mr. Hecker, and expenses from both of them."

D. B. MCCANDLESS

"Sarah Watson! How in hell are you going to collect two hundred from Mr. Hecker when you haven't got a necklace to turn over to him—when you're turning the necklace over to his wife?"

"Simple," said Sarah. "Mrs. Hecker is turning the imitation over to me, Bennie, when she pays me the ten thousand. The imitation has been in Mrs. Hecker's wall safe ever since Mr. Hecker put it there, after Dolores Flores—poor girl—stole the real necklace under Mr. Hecker's eyes. Let's see now . . . ten thousand and two hundred and . . ."

The doors of the Citizens' Savings Bank swung open, letting in morning sunshine. A woman in rusty black strode across the tiled floor and halted at a depositors' window. A long legged young man entered behind her and strode to another depositors' window. With perfect timing the two shoved bank books and sizeable wads of bills under the wickets of their respective windows.

A door at the side of the banking room slammed. The slam echoed against the vaulted ceiling. Sarah Watson turned, leaning her elbow on the sill of the window. Her bristling brows lowered over her eyes as she watched the pompous figure of the bank's president come toward her across the tile floor.

The president came very close. His pale eyes lifted and regarded Sarah bleakly. He said:

"Mrs. Watson, that necklace you returned to me an hour ago—that necklace for which I've already paid you two hundred dollars and an exorbitant expense account—that necklace, Madam, is nothing but—"

"Nothing but paste," said Sarah. "A clever imitation, but paste. Well, Mr. Hecker, that's what you asked for, and that's what you got."

The clerk shoved Sarah's bank book through the wicket.

He peered around Sarah's bulky figure and addressed himself, in a loud and cheery voice, to the president of the bank.

"Mr. Hecker," he said, "I thought you'd like to know. Mrs. Watson has just made a very nice deposit, very nice indeed. Mrs. Watson must have put over a very shrewd piece of business this time, I think."

Gangster's Brand

P. T. Luman

LIKE MOST OF the authors who worked for *Gun Molls* magazine, nothing is known of P. T. Luman, except in the negative. He never published a novel, his name appears in no reference book, and no information could be gleaned from the Internet, where there were numerous references to P. T. Barnum, with whom it seems unlikely that there was a connection.

His pulp publisher did think enough of his story to feature it on the cover of the magazine, where it also is first in the table of contents.

While it would be untrue to compare its literary quality to that of Hammett, Chandler, Woolrich, or the other great pulp writers of the era, "Gangster's Brand" has a narrative that never slows for an instant. Since the author presumably was paid the standard rate for this lower-rung magazine, which was a quarter-of-a-cent a word, he may have been tempted to do a little padding to earn just a little more (as Charles Dickens, in another era, was famous for doing), but, if so, he obviously resisted the temptation.

"Gangster's Brand" was first published in the August 1931 edition of *Gun Molls* magazine.

Gangster's Brand

P. T. Luman

TWO SMALL, TRIM FEET, then shapely legs in sheer silk, swung below the fire-escape in the dim light of the areaway. They swung only for an instant and then dropped, ten feet to the concrete pavement below. The girl staggered from the shock, and then, picking herself up, swung back into the shadow of the big apartment building, hugging the wall as she regained her breath.

A wicked-looking gat glistened in her right hand as her snapping black eyes riveted on the iron door above her through which she had reached the fire-escape and safety.

Carlotta Wynn, active member of "Mort" Mitchell's mob, waited expectantly for the opportunity to plug the guy or guys who had spoiled one of the prettiest lays the gang had had for many a month.

A shadow moved behind her, far back in the

areaway in which she stood. The gat in the girl's hand swung around like lightning.

"Stick 'em up," she said through gritted teeth, or I'll—!"

"Out of here, quick, kid," responded a guarded but agitated voice, and Mort Mitchell himself motioned the girl to his side. With Mort leading, the rod and the moll stole through the shadows to a doorway in the wall surrounding the court and slipped through as Mitchell threw the door open cautiously.

They were in the alley behind the big apartment. A half-block away was their getaway car, planted there a half-hour before with "Needle" Sam Schwartz at the wheel and with the engine running. They hustled to the corner of the alley and looked around the protecting wall cautiously. The car was there, and Barry Crandall, the fourth of the mob, was stepping into the front seat with the driver.

"Take the right-hand side of the street and hit for that car as fast as you can make it," whispered Mort, "I'll take the left-hand side—and watch!"

The girl's gat was hidden under her light coat now and she walked quickly to the car. Mort hopped into the seat beside her just as Needle Sam stepped on it and the big car jumped away from there.

There was cursing a-plenty as the car dashed through side streets where traffic cops would not bother them. For the third time in two weeks Mort Mitchell's mob had been within an inch of grabbing off some of the softest-looking hauls in their history. And for the third time, just as everything was right for the heist, something had gone wrong. The fall guy was wised up— and Mort and his mob had gotten nothing for their carefully laid plans.

Mort and his mob were being double-crossed and every one of them knew it. After the curses came silence as the minds of the four recalled the mysterious jinx which seemed to have fastened itself upon the mob. Three times—and every one the same. Even as the roaring car sped toward their hideaway the four looked at each other curiously and askance. Suspicion, even between

members of the mob against each other, was growing. The same thought came to all. Somebody in the mob—or somebody in a position to know their movements—was a rat!

Mort Mitchell, thinking deeply, was puffing feverishly on his cigarette as the car pulled into the garage in back of "Dapper" Dan's speakie, where the gang hung out.

"In the back room," Mort said curtly as they climbed from the car, and the four slipped through the passageway between the garage and the farthest back room of Dan's. Mort Mitchell was going to find out, and that very night, too, if he could, just who was putting his mob over the jumps of failure. He sat at the end of the table and nodded to Dapper Dan, who appeared at the signal which came with their entrance.

"Send a bottle of rye and some soda, Dan," said Mort grimly, "and then go out and forget we're here. Don't let anybody disturb us, for this ain't no mass meeting. This is a secret party that may end seriously for somebody!" His dark eyes snapped as he looked into the faces of his mobsters. The bottles were brought and the door snapped shut behind Dapper Dan. Mort poured himself a stiff shot of rye and shoved the bottle down the table to the others. They poured and drank, and Mort, throwing his hat on the nearby desk, faced them again.

Mort didn't look the part of the mobster any more than Carlotta Wynn looked the rôle of a moll. He was tall and thin, but of a deceptive thinness which concealed his tremendous strength. His hair was dark brown and his eyes almost black, with a particular snap and keenness. His clothes were of expensive material and conservative cut; clothes such as a broker might select.

The girl could have walked into the Ritz on his arm and seemed perfectly in place. She was of medium height and slender, but sinuous figure. Her features were small and regular, set in skin of marked smoothness and whiteness. The whiteness of her skin was emphasized by her silky black hair and eyebrows and black flashing eyes, which were large, almost round, giving her an appearance of innocence, of surprise.

Needle Sam and Barry Crandall, the other two at the table, however, looked their parts. Sam's face was fat, with close-set eyes. His suit was flashy, of extreme cut. The first and second fingers of his right hand were stained deeply by the cigarettes he smoked in every waking moment. Sam was a chauffeur par excellence—nothing else. He thought he was a hard rod, but he wasn't. He just was about the best driver in the city, for he knew every short cut in traffic, he drove like a charioteer and he never had accidents. They didn't pay in his business.

And Barry Crandall was a rod who had graduated from a lowlier beginning. There had been days when he did not scoff an opportunity to lift a wallet or even bend a lead pipe over an unsuspecting head. Now, however, he was in faster company and was Mort Mitchell's right hand—and Mort wasn't a piker.

Mort's handsome face was turned on the other three.

"Well," he asked, sarcastically, "who spilled it?"

None answered.

Mort's expression grew hard and ominous, as he went on:

"One slip-up can happen. Two *might* happen, but three times means—" He looked intently into the faces of the moll and the two other rods. "Three slips—and each one almost spelling curtains for me—mean *a rat!*"

The moll's eyes flashed dangerously.

"Don't insinuate that I'm a rat, Mort," she said evenly, but the tiny muscles at the corners of her mouth tightened and her small hands clenched. "I'm no rat and you know it. I'd go to hell for you, and the boys would, too. Maybe *you've* talked too much in your off moments. Remember, you're mingling in *society* now!" Her voice was bitter and jealousy showed in the tone of that word "society."

"Never mind what I'm doing," retorted Mort, angrily, "I'm not monkey enough to talk where there's going to be a comeback at me."

He turned to face the girl squarely.

"Let's start from the beginning," he said grimly, "and maybe we can find the leak. You got the tip-off from the Hag, didn't you?"

"Yes."

"When?"

"The night 'Carmen' was sung at the Metropolitan," answered the moll. "She was doing her usual stuff, whining around the automobiles near the entrance, with that tooth sticking down on her lower lip and that mole on her cheek sticking out over her coat collar. She slipped me the signal and I watched my chance to step up to her and drop four-bits into her tin-cup.

" 'The Vanderpools on Wednesday night, girlie,' she said in that whine of hers. 'It's a pipe. I heard 'em talkin' as they dropped me a dime from the carriage window. All of 'em will be away Wednesday night, except the old dame, herself, and she'll be home taking a backgammon lesson from a girl sharp. And the old woman wears her diamonds for dinner every night, even in her home. It's a pipe, girlie. Tell Mort—an' I want my cut.' "

"Anybody see you getting the info from her?" asked Mort.

"What if they did see me talking to her?" retorted the moll. "Who'd think she was tipping us to a job? I was just an opera-goer to the crowd on the pavement. Everybody talks to her—she's the Hag of the Opera to everybody. Never misses the carriage door on opera nights. All the society folk know her whining story; she was Dolores, the dancer, she tells them as she begs. Dolores the famous ballet dancer. How she gets away with it with that fang sticking out over her lower lip from her upper jaw and that mole, I don't know. Figure her as a dancer! But they listen to her and slip her change—and she's the best lookout and tipster *this* mob ever had, until now!"

"Yes," agreed Mort, reluctantly, "but she gave us the bum steer on the Stickney job, too, didn't she? And she sent us out on Hark Island for that bust in the Longmans' home that pretty near put me back of the walls."

"She's tipped us to plenty. She doesn't get her cut unless we click."

"Yes," responded Mort grimly, "but maybe

she's changed her racket. Anyway . . ." He paused and looked into the anxious faces before him. "Anyway, either the Hag—or somebody here in this room—tipped off the Vanderpools tonight and we came damned near to dissolving this mob when that roomful of private dicks stepped on our feet. Now, suppose some one of you tries to answer that!"

"She's playin' with the Orange mob, maybe," suggested Barry, " 'Blackie' Rango and his gorillas been knockin' off some sweet jack without no trouble while we're sticking our throats out for the knife."

"Yes," added Carlotta vengefully, "and Blackie Rango is a hog so greedy that he'd send us to hell in a minute, if he could. It gives him violent cramps if he hears any other mob's grabbed a few dollars. He wants it all himself."

"Yes," responded Mort, grimly. "Some day Blackie and I are going to argue that little matter out—especially if I find he's back of this business of steering us into jams!"

Mort Mitchell straightened himself in his chair. He turned to the moll, who now was watching him admiringly.

"Baby," he said, "this looks like your job. The Hag has been playing with us—and getting plenty for it. But, maybe she's *getting more* to double-cross us now. You find out—and maybe when you do find out it'll have some bearing on your private grudge."

As he spoke the moll's hand went involuntarily to her right shoulder and a spasm of hatred crossed her face.

"If it does," she answered grimly, "I'll want no more of any mob's takings. I'll be happy."

"Watch the Hag," warned Mort earnestly. "When's the next opera?"

"Friday night. It's 'Lucia' with Stephanie and Bendi in the cast. All the box-holders will be there."

"You go, as usual with that music hound from the *Village*—and watch the Hag for her signal. And watch her close, *before and after you talk to her*. Maybe she's spilling her chatter for

Blackie and his rats, and if she is, she's trying to put the finger on us!"

Mort pushed back his chair and rang for Dapper Ben again.

"Mort," interrupted the moll anxiously, "are you coming over to my place with me?"

"No!" His tone was abrupt and he avoided looking the moll in the eyes.

"Society man again!" The girl snapped the words. "I guess—"

"Never mind about my business, baby," Mort replied menacingly. "I'll go with who I please. Your job is to watch the Hag, and bring the dope to me. I'm running this mob yet!"

The moll stifled her anger. She threw down another generous drink and stepped to the door. Her voice was cold now, despite the glitter in her eyes.

"I'll see the Hag Friday night," she said, "and if she's got any stuff I'll get it and bring it here to the Big Society Man—if he's not too busy drinking tea and eating lady-fingers to accept it!"

She stepped through the door and slammed it behind her before Mort could reply. Barry and Sam grinned, for they knew the reason for her anger. Deeply in love with the handsome Mort, Carlotta knew that a mysterious woman, a strikingly beautiful woman with flaming hair and star-like eyes who haunted the better supper clubs and mingled freely with Park Avenue pleasure-lovers, was claiming every spare moment that the handsome Mort could give her. Their grins, however, were wiped from their faces by the grave words of Mitchell.

"Lay low for a few days," he cautioned them. "That moll is smart and she may be able to smell out the rat who's trying to put the finger on us. And, if she doesn't, well— Then, it looks to me as though this mob is through. Blackie Rango is trying to hog every racket in the city, and he'll do it, too, unless the jane spoils his plans before they work any further."

Mort Mitchell left them abruptly. He hurried to his rooms to dress, for he was going to step out that night to one of the city's snootiest supper clubs where he knew he would meet and have at least a few words with the woman whose flaming beauty had fascinated him, the red-haired, glorious Vi Carroll, mystery woman of the night clubs and associate of those who moved in the faster set of Society with the capital S.

Perhaps Mort Mitchell would not have been so eager for the smiles of the flashing Vi had he known of the scene which was being enacted at the time he was dressing for his night's pleasure. For the dazzling Vivian, her face unsmiling now and her musical voice harsh in emphasis, was talking angrily and excitedly, not with one of her society friends, but with Blackie Rango himself, the greedy mob leader, who seemed perfectly at home amid the luxuries of Vi's apartment.

And Blackie Rango was no sheik. He puffed from the exertion of crossing one fat leg over the other and his language seemed very much out of place in the tasteful surroundings. His beady eyes peered from beneath thick, bushy brows in a beetling forehead that wrinkled as he talked. Vi's anger he passed unnoticed.

"You messed it up again, didn't you, broad?" he asked, interrupting her. "Everything set to give the works to Mort Mitchell, his frail with him an' all his mob an' instead o' him gettin' his'n he's still around, gettin' in my hair."

"Yes! He's still around because you and your gorillas didn't have the guts to take him when I put him right in your hands!"

"Maybe," answered Blackie, evenly, "an' then again, maybe not. Now, see here, broad." His gimlet eyes glowed as he thrust his ugly face closer to hers. "It's got to be me or Mort Mitchell. They ain't room in this town for his mob an' mine, an' mine ain't goin' to be the one to go out."

He reached over and grabbed the red-haired moll by the wrist.

"Get this," he said, and there was murder in his tone. "I'm puttin' up for you. There ain't no limit. You can play this society gag an' you sock away plenty of jack. Yes, I know you're doin' it, but I don't care, so long as you're on the level with me. Your job is to frame Mort Mitchell—

he's got to go. An' don't think I don't know how friendly you are with him, too!"

The moll started as Blackie's eyes bored into hers. She started to speak, but he went on:

"An' when Mort goes, you'd better see to it that his frail goes, too. Maybe you don't know her. An' maybe you do. Anyhow, she's with him on all his jobs an' she's a fightin' fool. Carlotta Wynn, that's what they call her. But that ain't her name. She ain't no ordinary moll. Nobody knows where she come from, but she's a moll for a reason—and nobody but her knows why."

"What do I care about his moll?" asked Vi angrily.

"Maybe you don't, but you're monkeyin' with her man, an' she looks like poison to me. Anyway, get this through your skull. Three times now you've slipped info to the Hag to send Mort Mitchell and his mob into a jam. An' three times you've made a fine mess of it. Now, dame—"

Blackie's manner was menacing and he twisted the moll's wrist to emphasize his words.

"*Get that guy!* Tell the Hag to slip him a certain one, a tip he won't pass up—an' leave the rest to me. I'll see they's a load o' hot lead waitin' for him when he steps into it. An', broad, don't miss *this time!* Make it right, so Mort and his whole mob will go, includin' the moll, for if you don't—"

"Well, if I don't?" challenged the girl defiantly.

"Here's your answer," replied Blackie ominously, "that moll Carlotta, in swimmin' suit or evenin' clothes, *never was known to bare her right shoulder!* Does that mean anythin' to you?"

Vi Carroll cried out hoarsely. There was terror in her eyes.

"What's her name?" she screamed. "Tell me, you big ape—what's her name?"

"You guess it," replied Blackie brutally, with a half-smile. "She come from Chi, too."

Horror was written on the white face of Vivian Carroll. Her hands shook and the words she tried to speak would not come. Blackie laughed loudly.

"Maybe you'll follow orders now, eh, kid?"

he asked. He wheezed from the deep chair and balanced his fat body on his feet. "Better forget your yen for that pretty boy, Morton," he added, "an' play along with the guy who's been right with you. Get me, frail?"

The girl nodded. Finally she regained her composure.

"I'll frame him, Blackie," she said with visible effort. "I'll frame him *if you promise me you'll get that moll, too.* My life isn't worth a nickel if that girl ever recognized me. Don't worry. I'll play a hundred per cent with you now!"

"Atta baby, Vi," answered Blackie, and he pulled on his coat with the help of the girl and waddled from the room. His soul was at peace as he waited for the elevator which took him to the street, and, as he rode away in his armored car with his gat bodyguard, Blackie Rango saw himself seated soon on the throne of gangdom. With the menacing Mort Mitchell and his mob out of the way, none in the underworld would dare dispute his leadership.

"An' that there Vi," Blackie said, half audibly, as he mused, "I'll keep her around. She's pretty easy on the eyes—an' besides, I got the deadwood on her. She oughta pay dividends!"

Despite her valiant efforts to appear natural Vi Carroll plainly was suffering from some repressed emotion that night. Her companions in the gay party which went to the ultra-fashionable Club Meta to see the new floor show and hear the reigning tenor noticed it. They joked with her; in mock solicitude they inquired gravely whether her dampened spirits were due to Wall Street, to a love affair, to the loss of a dear friend, or what else?

Then the floor show engaged their attention and she had a moment's peace from their banter. She fingered the thin-stemmed glass before her and looked through the crowd anxiously. She was looking for the handsome Mort Mitchell, the striking-looking, mysterious Mort, who held such a subtle attraction for her and the man she was pledged to frame. Her usual complacency was gone when she saw his tall figure appear.

She was agitated when he bowed to her and exchanged a greeting.

"Let's dance," she said as the orchestra struck up a number. "I'm blue tonight, I'm depressed."

They danced silently for a round of the small floor and then the girl said abruptly:

"Morton, I want to talk to you. Let's walk out on the balcony, so we can be alone. Try to cheer me up. I feel morbid, almost afraid."

The mob chieftain laughed. What in the world, he thought, could this glorious girl, with wealth, social position, and beauty, have to worry about? They leaned over the balcony rail together, looking out on the lights of the city. When Vivian spoke, she tried to conceal the eagerness in her voice.

"I've been hearing things about you, Morton," she said.

"What were they, Vi?"

"You're the man of mystery to all my friends," she went on. "They like you, but they do not know your antecedents—and, as a matter of fact, neither do I."

"Just a fellow lucky to have a little bit of money," Mort said, "and a business which takes care of itself. I'm a consulting engineer, if you must know, but my duties are not confining."

Vi turned to him with an air of frankness.

"I'm not questioning you, Mort," she said, "and I don't care what the crowd thinks of you. But—" She hesitated, and then went on with a burst of apparent frankness. "Mort, who is the beautiful girl, the beautiful black-eyed girl I've heard is in your company pretty often? Frankly, I'm a bit jealous of her."

Mort laughed heartily.

"You jealous?" she scoffed. "I just wish you cared enough about me to be jealous. The other girl? Just an employee, Vi, a girl who has worked in my office, an efficient stenographer, that's all. We have no social contact. She's been in my car, of course, but only in the line of her duties."

"Who is she, Morton?"

"Just a girl who came here from Chicago a year ago. I really don't know her first name. Miss Wynn, that's all the name I know."

Vi's voice was strained as she persisted in her questioning.

"This girl, Morton. Has she particularly large, black eyes?"

"Yes, she has."

"Did she—" Vi hesitated, then she went on, speaking almost desperately. "Morton, did this girl ever have an accident? Was she ever hurt badly, was—?"

Mort looked at the agitated Vivian curiously.

"Why all this interest in an office working girl, Vi?" he asked. "I don't know anything more about her. How would I know whether she ever suffered injury?"

"Forgive me, Morton," said Vi. "I've heard this girl described, and—and the description fitted a girl I once knew in the West. I thought, maybe—" She broke off with a laugh, a relieved laugh. "Let's forget about the girl and rejoin the party," and she led the way back to the dining-room with the attentive, but slightly puzzled, Mort behind her.

From that moment Vi Carroll's manner changed. Her spirits rose, she laughed gayly, she seemed determined to still any disquieting thoughts with an excess of gaiety. "It can't be the same girl," she said to herself as she tripped through a dance with Mort. "Only a chance in a million it's the same, and my luck is good."

Mort left the party comparatively early, for he had troublesome things on his mind. That matter, that vital matter of Blackie Rango, wouldn't be brushed from his recollection by the bright lights and gaiety. He left before the party broke up, managing a few whispered words again with Vi before leaving.

"Shall I see you tomorrow night, Vi?" he asked anxiously.

"Tomorrow," replied the flushed girl—"let's see, tomorrow's Friday. No, Morton, but I'll see you Saturday. Tomorrow night's the opera, you know, and I'm going with the Elberts, and then out to the island for the night."

She smiled fondly at Mort's disappointment and squeezed his hand tightly as he said adieu. A qualm came to her heart as she watched his tall figure moving toward the door. God, but he was a fine-looking fellow to be marked for Death! Why did he have to be the one?

Friday night and the opera, with favorites singing the principal roles and the diamond horseshoe ablaze with celebrities and color. Outside the forbidding opera house the stream of automobiles, the crowds of curious, fascinated by the jewels and scintillating frocks of society. And along the line of crawling automobiles, slowly approaching the entrance to disgorge their cargoes of dressed-up and bejeweled folks, croaked the Hag of the Opera, the bunchy figure of that wreck of a woman who whined for her alms at the automobile windows. Her slovenly body was swathed in the ground-length, dingy coat which came high on her neck, to her chin. Over her head the inevitable dirty shawl. Beneath the shawl peered the beady eyes, the gnarled sallow skin of the Hag, whining and showing the long discolored tooth, more like a fang, which reached from the front of her upper jaw down over her lower lip as she pleaded with the richly-gowned opera patrons for alms. Adding to her hideousness was a blemish—a huge, hairy mole—on her right cheek, which moved up and down as she whined.

Dirty, hideous, repulsive was the Hag of the Opera, yet she had her clientele. Women in shining automobiles shrank from her dirty extended paws, yet they besought their escorts to help her.

"Help Dolores," the Hag cried, "help the old woman who once knew so well the plaudits of the crowd. Dolores of the Imperial ballet—I, Dolores, who danced for kings. Now I need crusts. Help me, good people."

And, as she begged her acute ears were attuned, not for words of sympathy, but for the intimate talk inside the vehicles, the chatter about social engagements, anything that might mean an unguarded mansion, a particularly fine display of gems at some social gathering—some target for the mob's arrows!

Receiver of their largess, the Hag of the Opera was betraying their secrets to the banditti! Long had it been her trade, with no suspicion directed at her. She had played into the hands of Mort Mitchell and to those who had gone before him in command of the same mob. Now, however, the Hag had extended the scope of her double-crossing. Her greed aroused by the calculating Blackie Rango, the Hag was getting the heist info for Blackie while purporting to be co-operating with Mort, and was acting as the go-between to arrange the frame-ups against Mort's mob which Blackie engineered!

The Hag was watching closely the faces in the cars as they approached the entrance. She was looking for the flaming hair and the face of Vi Carroll, the bearer of instructions, and she wandered up and down the row of cars until she saw Vi's signal. She hobbled to the side of the handsome limousine and approached the window through which Vivian's brilliant opera cape showed.

"Alms, good folks," the Hag cried, leaning close to the window, and Vi lowered it, compassionately, turning to her escort as she did so.

"Give me some money for this miserable creature," Vivian said, and a man of the party thrust a bill in her hand. Vi's daintily gloved hand stretched through the auto's window as the Hag whined her thanks. Her mumbled words, however, merely were a cover for the whispered words which Vi directed to her.

"The Horton Place on the Sound, Monday night!" Vi said, and the Hag winked acknowledgment of the words.

The shiny limousine moved forward toward the opera house entrance with Vi Carroll chatting laughingly with her companions as the Hag moved away. The first step in the trap set for Mort Mitchell and his mob had been taken. Within a half-hour the deceiving message would be on its way to pave the road for destruction. The Hag would relay the false information to Carlotta Wynn, emissary of the Mitchell mob!

The Hag moved down the line of carriages, ready to relay the frame-up message. She now was looking for Carlotta, the moll from Mitchell's mob. She did not know that Carlotta, hidden in the milling throng on the sidewalk, had been almost at her elbow when Vi Carroll whispered her message—and further than that, the keen-eyed Carlotta, seeing through a changed appearance in the beautiful Vivian, had recognized the society-minded moll as the enemy she was stalking so desperately!

Carlotta Wynn, her teeth clenched and her hands doubled into small fists, gloried in the triumph she foresaw over the woman who had sent her into the underworld on her adventure into vengeance. That smiling beauty with the flaming hair now, apparently, a society favorite, only two years before had done the irreparable wrong to the black-eyed girl who stood in the opera crowd and planned her revenge!

The moll forgot the presence of the "music-loving kid" who always accompanied her to the opera performances. He was a harmless sort; he did not know that he was a pawn in the machinations of a mob. He went to the opera with the pretty girl who seemed pleased to enjoy the music with him.

Everything except revenge was forgotten by the black-haired moll. She moved forward as Vi's auto moved toward the entrance.

"I could kill her now—!" she spoke aloud and the music-loving kid startled.

"Who could you kill, Carlotta?" he asked in astonishment. The girl recovered her poise.

"No one, Robbie," she replied, "I was just joking." She saw the Hag approaching and she knew the crone sought her, to relay the death-trap message to Mort Mitchell.

"There's the Hag," Carlotta said, pushing toward her. "I always give her a little change. Isn't she horrible looking? I feel as though I had to help her."

She drew a few coins from her small purse and stepped to the side of the Hag, dropping the coins into the outstretched tin cup. The Hag leaned close to her, the repulsive, hairy mole almost touching the girl's face.

"The Horton Place, on the Sound—on Monday night, girlie," the Hag whispered. "Tell Mort it's a pipe—and not to forget me."

She turned from the girl, whining her plea for alms to others as Carlotta and her escort walked to the entrance.

Blackie Rango's message to trap Mort Mitchell and his mob to death was delivered—but it was delivered through a moll who knew that the Hag had turned on her former benefactors and was plotting with their enemies for their deaths!

The beautiful strains of "Lucia" meant nothing to Carlotta that night. She sat through the performance with the lad because she did not know where to reach Mort until late in the night. And before her eyes, instead of the singers and the brilliant audience, was the picture of Vi Carroll, the woman the moll was determined should feel the weight of her vengeance.

The moll dismissed her escort quickly as the throng poured from the house of music. She raced to a taxicab and hurried to Dapper Dan's, where she felt sure she would find Mort at midnight. She entered the speakie through the garage and the rear door, and waited for Mort in the secret chamber.

The moll was on her feet, pacing the room, when Mort entered.

"I've got the works, Mort," she cried. "It's a cold frame, set up by Blackie Rango. Here's the message from the Hag: 'The Horton Place, on the Sound—Monday night!' It's phony! It's—"

"How do you know it's phony?" demanded Mort.

"Because I overheard the message slipped to her, Mort, I heard it slipped to her by the very woman I've been hunting, the jane I've sworn to find and to repay a certain debt."

"And who," asked Mort, eagerly, "was Rango's messenger? Did you spot her?"

"Yes, I spotted *her!*" responded the moll, and her eyes were blazing. "And maybe you'll be interested to know just who she is! You've been playing around with your society friends—with a red-headed woman who's got you dizzy, haven't you?"

"Never mind that. It's my business where I go and—"

The moll blazed at him angrily:

"Well, maybe this is your business, too. The red-headed moll who gave the Hag the tip that's set to put you under the grass went to the opera with the Elberts, your society friends, and is the crookedest snake that ever wore woman's clothes!"

Mort Mitchell's amazement held him speechless.

"Not Vi, not Vi Carroll!" he ejaculated. "It can't be—"

"Fall for the tip, then, sap," retorted the moll, "but I won't. If you go near the Horton Place Monday night, Mort, you'll die from hot lead poisoning. I know!"

Mort grabbed the moll by the wrist and swung her around until she was looking up right into his eyes. His voice was low, but it was full of menace.

"Damn you," he snarled, "are you on the level, or are you framing Vi Carroll, just to—"

The moll twisted away from him furiously.

"Take it or leave it, you sap," she snapped, "but I'm going to get HER! And I'll make you believe it. Listen, Mort, will you believe your red-headed vamp is crossing you before it's too late? Will you believe me if I prove it to you?"

"Yes," he answered sullenly, "if you prove it. But, how are you going to do it?"

An inspiration came to the moll.

"I've got it, Mort," she cried excitedly. "You'd kidnap the Hag of the Opera, wouldn't you—to save yourself?"

"No, but why?"

"Because," replied Carlotta, "I want her out of my way on the next opera night—because that night I'LL BE THE HAG OF THE OPERA!"

"What?" asked Mort, bewildered.

"Just that," replied the moll. "Act just as though we're falling for that bum tip on the Horton Place, but stay away from there. Then, on the next opera night, grab the Hag, so I can get her clothes. I'll do her whining act and I'll get the tip-off from your red-headed friend who's trying to put the finger on you!"

"You can't do it, kid," responded Mort, "you

can't impersonate the Hag. There's no other like her. Look at that fang which hangs down her lip—that mole!" He almost shuddered when he recalled the evil face of the Hag.

"I'll do it, Mort," cried the moll, her eyes snapping. "I'm entitled to a chance this time, for I've got a score to even and then, maybe—" Her voice caught, but she went on. "Maybe, Mort, you won't think so badly of me. Does my scheme go?"

"Yes," he replied. "We'll stay just about a thousand miles away from that Horton Place and, then—" His eyes gleamed ominously. "Then, if your dope is right, we'll see how Mr. Blackie Rango likes lead for supper! It's up to you, kid!"

He squeezed her arm and the girl stepped closer to him, expectantly. But his mind wasn't on the moll. He was wondering whether he could successfully fight against the power of Blackie Rango. He left her absently, and walked to the front of the speakie. The girl, her face showing her disappointment, walked from the speakie and went to her room. She slept little, for she was laying her plans, not only to thwart Blackie Rango's plot against the Mitchell mob, but also to satisfy her ancient feud against the brilliant Vi Carroll.

Mort Mitchell and his mob stayed severely away from the country place of the Hortons on the Sound that Monday night. It was well they did, for hidden in the shrubbery a quarter-mile up the private road which led to the estate was a band of a dozen rods in the employ of Blackie Rango, ready to mow them down. And Blackie Rango was a sadly disappointed vice king when he got the word of the failure. He called Vi Carroll on the telephone and told her in no uncertain words that her job was in peril—that she must make good on her next attempt.

So it was a perturbed Vi who rode with friends slowly toward the opera house entrance on the next opera night. She had her instructions from Blackie and they were explicit. She was to tell the Hag to lure the Mitchell mob to an uptown apartment building with an exciting story of unguarded jewels and an absent family and the following Friday night was to be the time for the massacre.

Again, on this occasion, Vi was a guest of the Elberts. She chatted nervously with Elbert and his wife and another guest as their car approached the glittering opera house. But her mind was not on the small talk. She was watching anxiously for the Hag of the Opera—for she simply had to make good now. Morton Mitchell had to be sacrificed. Her eyes wandered through the crowd as the car approached the entrance. God! Would that damnable Hag never appear? At last she saw the tottering, repulsive figure. It hurried to the side of the Elberts' auto and Vi lowered the window, coins in her hand to cover the few words she must exchange with the repulsive croon.

The Elberts and their guests looked in wonder as Vi leaned nervously from the car window. Why did Vivian pay so much attention to that pest, that wreck of a woman with the revolting face? But Vi was oblivious to them.

"Dolores," she whispered vehemently, "they've *got* to fall for this; tell them the Donaghan jewels, a half-million dollars worth, will be absolutely unguarded Friday night. The approach is through the areaway beside the apartment. *Make* them fall for it."

She peered intently into the wrinkled face before her. She saw the loathsome fang denting the Hag's lower lip. She shuddered as she looked at that horrible mole on the crone's right cheek.

"Yes, dearie," whined the Hag, accepting the coins Vi handed to her. "They'll go, all right. I'll fix that. Now, here's something for Blackie, and tell him it's a chance of a lifetime. Mrs. Alex Wilson's pearls, the great Wilson pearls, will be delivered to their country place Thursday night by automobile, a car with only the Wilson butler and one guard in it. The car will get there at seven o'clock in the night—and if Blackie don't get them he'll never get another such a chance at them."

The Hag was creeping alongside the slowly moving car. Vi heard the message leaning from the window. The Elberts and their other guests wondered at the whispering between the glittering Vi and the loathsome Hag. The Hag, however, leaned close to Vi again.

"Tell Blackie it won't be easy; tell him to have the whole mob, but for God's sake not to miss this one!"

She fell back into the crowd as Vi turned back to her hosts apologetically.

"I'm sorry," she said as their car neared the opera entrance, "but the Hag insists upon my hearing her troubles. I've tried to help her; to get her off the street in this pitiful begging, but she insists upon haunting the opera."

Vi accepted the arm of an escort and the Elbert party moved under the marque to the foyer of the opera house, Vi in possession of two things she cherished—belief that she had set the trap for Mort Mitchell's mob, and information that would make her even more solid with Blackie Rango.

Hardly had the Elbert party disappeared into the interior of the opera house, however, when the Hag of the Opera House, for the first time in a decade, lost all interest in the opera-going crowd. With surprising quickness for one of her age and dumpy figure, she slipped through the crowd on the pavement, and away from the opera. Ignoring her former benefactors who might still be mulcted, she disappeared down a cross street and boarded an automobile which waited there.

"Quick, Sam," she snapped to the chauffeur, and Needle Sam did his stuff, taking the short cuts to Dapper Dan's speak. At the garage, she left the car and traversed the secret way to Dan's furthest back room and entered. Mort Mitchell was waiting there. He jumped from his chair as the Hag entered. It MUST be the Hag, that dumpy, uncouth figure, that revolting fang which dented her lower lip; that mouse-like mole which blemished the right side of her face.

"Hell!" Mort ejaculated, "I thought—"

The dumpy figure of the Hag straightened and a quick hand pulled the dirty shawl from the head. Another quick motion and Carlotta Wynn, the fake Hag of the Opera, pulled from her mouth an odd dental plate to which was attached the fang which protruded from her mouth. Another pull wrenched from her face the "mole," the imitation such as marked the face of the real Hag. Quickly she wiped the grease paint from her face—and Carlotta, the moll, stood before the mob leader in the Hag's habiliments. With an expression of disgust, she ripped the Hag's rags from her body and stood before Mort in her undies.

"Had to get that filth off me before I could think or talk," she said calmly. She slipped into a suit which she had left in the speakie room, ordered a drink by pressing a button and turned to face Mort, the mob leader and more than that to Carlotta.

"The trap's set, Mort," she said quietly. "Blackie Rango's greed will not let him pass up a chance at the Alex Wilson's pearls. If you don't get him and his gorillas Thursday night, you'd better knuckle to Blackie's orders—for you'll never again get such a chance."

Carlotta explained the set-up "tip" she got from Vivian—and her face contorted with hate as she told it.

"You get Blackie and his apes, Mort," she said, vindictively, "and while you're doing it, I'll pay off my score."

"You'll lay off that dame," Mort replied, angrily, "I'm not satisfied that she's not regular. Hands off—till I give the word!"

Carlotta laughed—a bitter laugh.

"All right, Mr. Society-Man-About-Town," she said sarcastically. "I'll promise you this; I won't harm a red hair of her head—until I tell you about it first."

The moll gathered up the discarded clothing of the Hag and threw them into a suitcase. She turned to Mort.

"What'll you do with the Hag?"

"Keep her prisoner until I decide," he responded shortly. "Anyway, I'll hold her till after Thursday. Don't worry about her."

"Good night, Mort," said the moll, moving toward the speakie door, "don't you want to come over to my place for a while and have a nightcap with me? I'm tired and I've got some Scotch such as Dapper Dan never dreamed of." The moll's voice was pleading, but it drew no response from the handsome mob leader. His thoughts, despite Carlotta's expose of Vi's perfidy, still were on the red-haired siren.

"No, kid," he answered absently. "See you some other time."

Carlotta slammed the door and went out into the night. More than ever she was determined to "get" the red-haired Vivian Carroll.

Thursday night in that secret back room of Dapper Dan's speakie. There was an air of tenseness as Mort Mitchell explained for the last time the plans for the night.

"We'll reach the Wilson place road a half-hour before Blackie's gang," Mort said slowly, "and Sam, you'll hide the car in the cross-road, pointed for a quick getaway. The big tree at the proper spot has been cut so deeply that a push will send it across the road. That's your job, Barry. When you get the signal, you and Sammy give the tree a shove. It can't fall, except across the road.

"Our Tommy-guns will be beside that same tree trunk. When the tree falls, you, Barry, and Sam grab them and step to the side, where you can rake Blackie's car. If his car withstands your fire—I'll have a surprise package for him. That's my part of the job. I'll attend to that and you attend to yours. But, above all else, *don't go near Blackie's car* until I give the word!" Mort turned to Carlotta.

"And you," he said emphatically, "you're going along! You'll sit in the car and wait for us until—"

"But," interrupted the moll heatedly, "I won't do anything of the kind—for I won't be there!"

"Where will you be?" The question came in a snarl from Mort.

"I'll be calling on your red-haired society girl friend," mocked Carlotta, "and I'll be waiting for you in her apartment." Her voice grew biting with scorn, as she continued:

"You still think she's on the level, don't you? You poor sap! You believe her, but you won't believe me. Do this, then. Settle your score with Blackie Rango. I was smart enough to plant that job for you and to save your neck! Then, when you've done your job, drive back to your redhead's place. I'll be waiting for you there. I won't hurt her before you come. I'll merely set the stage for the show which is going to make you see that one of us is crooked and the other straight. Are you game for that?"

The moll's eyes were snapping in her challenge.

"I won't hurt the dear thing before you come," she mocked as he hesitated. "You've my promise. Answer, big boy, are you game?"

"Yes," he snapped angrily. "Remember, no fireworks till I get back!"

The mobsters rose from the table and prepared to go to the garage for their car.

"Happy trip, boys," said the moll. "I hope, when you return, there'll be fewer snakes in the world."

As the gorillas passed from the room, the moll helped herself to a man-sized drink from the bottle on the table. She had stern work before her and she welcomed the scorching liquor as it warmed her throat. The moll walked swiftly from the rear door of the speakie, just as Mort Mitchell's big black car slid away from the garage door on its errand of death.

Silently through the twilight the big car swept, through the outskirts of the city and into the fashionable residence area. Hardly a word was spoken, for the route was well-mapped and the trip timed to the minute. Finally it drew up in the shadows of the small cross-road outside the Wilson estate and the gangsters took up their stations.

Ten minutes before the time they looked for the car of Blackie Rango and his apes, its dimmed lights appeared far down the smooth road leading to the Wilson country mansion. Smoothly and menacingly the armored car of Rango approached through the semi-darkness. They recognized its lines, even at a distance.

Mort gave his last order.

"When they get opposite the big pine on the right," he whispered, "over with the tree—and then grab your Tommy-guns and open up on the car. And, remember, STAY AWAY FROM THAT CAR if you fail to penetrate his armor!"

Closer came the Rango car as Mort and Sam and Barry crouched in the protecting foliage at the roadside. Sweeping up the road, the big car approached almost before they were hidden. It seemed right upon them when the shoulders of Sam and Barry leaned against the big tree which already was cut for falling. With a muffled roar, the tree plunged across the road, hardly a dozen feet in front of the rival gangsters' auto!

There was a screeching of brakes—but not in time. Blackie Rango's automobile, carrying the eager Blackie and three of his gorillas, plunged into the tree's foliage just as the Tommy-guns of Mort Mitchell's gorillas spat flames!

The lead hail played a tattoo against the sides of the heavy armed car, and in a minute Rango and his rod men had picked themselves from the floor and were replying to the fire through slits in the body of the car.

Despite his trap, Mort Mitchell found Rango, his enemy, apparently safe in his fort-like automobile embedded in the foliage of the felled tree.

"Back!" yelled Mort, and there was a momentary silence as the Tommy-guns of Sam and Barry stopped. "Back into the woods," yelled Mort—and he dived to a depression beneath a distant tree. As he dived, his hand stretched out and struck a plunger—a plunger such as is used in dynamiting. The pressure on the plunger completed the electric contact he had set.

There was a flash and a roar—and the road beneath Blackie Rango's enmeshed automobile opened up in a devastating blast.

The mine which Mort Mitchell had set in the road had done the work the Tommy-guns could not do through the thick armor of the Rango car. Struck from below, its vulnerable spot, the big

armored car flew apart as though the explosion came from within itself. As the echoes of the blast died away, a heavy pall of smoke hung over the spot. And as it cleared, nothing remained except a huge crater in the once smooth road, a few broken and twisted bits of metal.

The stunned Sam and Barry rushed for their car as Mort joined them.

"Out of here, quick," Mort commanded. "That blast will bring every dick and every motorcycle cop from miles around. Back to the city, Sam—and by the back road."

The car leaped ahead under the skilled hands of Sammy, with Mort urging him to more speed. A gripping fear came to Mort as the car swept on. Carlotta! Would she keep her promise not to molest the rival moll, Vi Carroll, until Mort returned? Through gritted teeth, Mort ordered Sammy to drive to Vi's apartment. As they swept into the city proper, he said:

"Drop me at the corner and you three hit it for Danny's. I'll join you there as soon as I can."

The car merely slowed for him. He leaped to the street and the car swept away, leaving Mort a scant half-block from the imposing apartment building on fashionable Park Avenue where Vi Carroll lived among her friends of society. Mort entered the elevator, scorning the suspicious looks of the attendant at his dusty and disheveled clothing. He left the car and hurried down the quiet corridor on the fifth floor, reaching the door of Vi's home.

No sound came through the door and Mort tried the door knob. The door opened to his touch and he stepped inside, peering through the dim light of the reception room. He saw no one. Silently he walked to a door on his left. That door, he knew, led to Vi's sumptuous boudoir. That door, too, was closed. He turned the knob softly and the door half opened. He peered into the room.

There, facing him in negligée, sat Vivian Carroll, a look of horror on her face, facing someone else in the room, directly opposite her. A look showed Mort the reason for the fright of the red-haired beauty. Her "caller" was Carlotta Wynn, the gun moll, who sat quietly toying with a shiny gat pointed toward Vi's body!

"Drop that gat!" Mort's voice brought a subdued scream from Vi and Carlotta sprang to her feet. "What's this stuff?" he demanded.

"Hands off, Mort," retorted Carlotta quietly, but her eyes were snapping dangerously. "You've had your party and this is MINE! Come in and shut the door." She waved the gat toward the red-haired siren and said elaborately:

"Mr. Mitchell, let me introduce Miss Vivian Carroll, alias 'Chicago Red' Hardy, the red-haired Siren of The Loop and a few other names! And, also, Mr. Mitchell, the moll who has been trying to put the finger on you for weeks as a small favor for her good friend, the late Mr. Blackie Rango!"

"You lie!" snapped Vi, looking to Mort for protection. "I've never been in Chi—"

"Put that gat down, moll," snapped Mort. "I know this girl and you're all wrong about her!"

Carlotta laughed sardonically. She threw the gat from her and it clattered on the polished floor, as she faced Mort.

"Mort, you poor fool," she said, bitingly, "will you never be convinced? That red-headed moll was head of one of the most cruel, savage mobs that Chi ever knew. She blew here because Chi got too hot for her—and she's making saps out of people here just as she did before. But, I KNOW HER!"

The moll's eyes flashed with bitter hatred as she spoke and her voice rose shrilly. "I know her—and I'll never forget her, the snake that she is."

She turned again passionately to the confused Mort.

"You won't believe? Then I'll show you!"

With a quick gesture she seized the right sleeve of her dress and tore it away, exposing her arm. Again she tore at the dress, ripping it open at the shoulder. As the fabric tore she pointed dramatically to the white skin of her upper arm and body.

"Look there," she cried vengefully, "there's the mark put on me by that hell-car, that vampire!"

And as Mort looked and Vi stifled the involuntary sob which came, Carlotta bared to them an angry-looking fiery-red brand on her white shoulder—a vivid brand of the *fleur de lis*, the ancient French brand for a thief!

"Look at that, Mr. Mitchell," cried the moll. "That's what your society girl-friend did for me. She laughed while her gorillas put the hot electric needle to my flesh and drew that design there, drew it because that red-headed bum thought I'd stolen the dirty little hop-head she claimed as her 'Man'! That's what I owe her."

She turned on Mort vengefully.

"And you want to save her, to protect her, the moll who put the finger on you! All right, then, take my gat—and I hope the two of you will be happy. I won't drill her. She'd poison a decent bullet!"

She stopped and looked from the disconcerted Mort to the now relieved Vi. Her voice was lowered and she apparently had expended her anger.

"I'll go," she said sadly. She wiped her eyes with her handkerchief and took from her bag a small, silver vanity case. "Might as well go," she went on monotonously to the two silent ones, and she dabbed at her face with a small powder puff from the compact. She turned to Vi as she used the puff.

"Before I go," she went on, stepping closer to Vi's side, "there's one thing I want to say—" She put the small powder puff back into the vanity case and absently took another small puff from the receptacle, holding it poised in her hand. "Just one thing—!"

She stood facing the now reassured Vivian, the little puff half way to her face.

"You branded me, Vi Carroll," she cried, quietly, "and I've spent time and money to track you down to punish you." She paused again. Then her voice came like a whip lash.

"AND I'M GOING TO DO IT!"

There was a flash of a bared white arm, and the small powder puff from Carlotta's compact smacked firmly against the left cheek of the red-haired woman. Vi screamed and Mort Mitchell grabbed the now violent Carlotta.

"We're even!" Carlotta Wynn's voice was triumphant now. She looked without pity at the suffering and horrified Vi, who was clawing at the left side of her face, which was turning a blotchy red and then purple.

"I've branded you, you hell-cat," she went on. "Branded you with acid—you rat!"

She turned to the astonished Mort and asked:

"Do you want her or do you want me? She branded me and she double-crossed you. Look at her and see whether I speak the truth!"

They looked, and the sobbing, hysterical Vi answered for Mort.

"Yes," she said, "I branded you because I hated you—and I hate you, too," she blazed at the confused mobster. "I'll get the pair of you. I'll get you—"

Mort Mitchell interrupted her. He seemed to come to himself, as though recovering from the influence of some insidious drug. He reached out to the little black-eyed moll, Carlotta, and pulled her close to him. He held her coat as she slipped it over her scarred, exposed arm and the two of them, the rod and his moll, moved toward the door. At the threshold Mort turned to the acid-marked Vivian. There was nothing lover-like in the tone of his voice now. It was cold as steel.

As Carlotta hung on his arm, he said:

"Get out of town in two hours, red-head! If you don't—I'll be back here to put MY mark on the OTHER cheek—and I don't want to have to bother to do that, for I'm going to be busy, squaring myself with my own moll. Eh, baby?"

He smiled at Carlotta as he asked the question—and the smile he got in return indicated the answer.

Dance Macabre

Robert Reeves

ONE OF THE forgotten authors of the pulp era is Robert Reeves (1911 or 1912–1945), largely because he came to the game late and because his career was cut short by World War II. His first short story was not published in *Black Mask* until 1942, his last in 1945. Altogether, there were nine stories in *Black Mask*, two others in *Dime Detective*, and three novels. His major creation was Cellini Smith, a private eye who appeared in all three of his novels: *Dead and Done For* (1939), *No Love Lost* (1941), and *Cellini Smith: Detective* (1943), as well as in seven of his eleven short stories. Three additional stories featured Bookie Barnes, who got his nickname, not for making books, but because he attended college and actually read books—rare for pulp characters. "Dance Macabre," Reeves's second story, is the only one he wrote that did not feature one of his series heroes. It is darker than his other tales since none of his principal characters fall into the standard pulp mode of being tougher or smarter or funnier than everyone with whom they come into contact. The mousy Firpo Cole, a former petty thief and pickpocket, hangs around a nightclub because of a crush he has on one of the dime-a-dance girls, the all–American-seeming Ruth Bailey.

The author served in World War II in the 500th Bombardment Squadron in the Army Air Corps, and it is believed he died in action only a month before the war ended. He was buried in a common grave with four other GIs, probably having been in the same plane.

"Dance Macabre" was first published in the April 1941 issue of *Black Mask*.

Dance Macabre

Robert Reeves

*There was nothing too tough for that little lunger to take—even acting as a walking
checkroom for a gunsel's gat—so long as he could be near his three-for-a-dime dance-hall
mouse. And the night she was shived there was nothing left for him to do but cash in
the life he'd been hoarding—to settle the score with her killer.*

CHAPTER ONE

SWOLLEN FEET

UTSIDE, the neon sign styled Jugger Callahan as the *King of Swing* but since Jugger owned the Tango Palace and had conferred the title on himself, not many people believed it. The sign also described the forty-eight hostesses as glori-ous, glittering, glamorous, and *that,* absolutely nobody believed—not even the girls.

Inside, Jugger Callahan kicked off the beat to the *Smiling Troubadours.* They played mechanically, with that automatic, pounding, unvarying rhythm that experienced jazz bands acquire, and, belying their name, they were unsmiling. It was nearing the closing hour of one a.m. and they were tired.

The tinted baby spots that were set in the ceiling revolved and played amber, red and blue over the dance floor. The place was large and ramshackle—the kind of second-story loft where you get natty, credit clothing—and it was just as much a fire trap as the taxi joint that had burned down on Jugger two months before. Nevertheless, the Tango Palace was a thriving enterprise aiming at that thin item of change known as the "dime." The dances were three for a dime and most of the customers stayed on a dime through all three of them.

The hostesses who waited for trade, chatted behind the frayed velvet rope that encircled the dance floor. Their low-cut evening gowns were creased and soiled, their eyes heavy-lidded with mascara and no sleep. Yet when a customer seemed inclined to switch partners, smiles appeared on vermilion lips, hips undulated sensuously and swollen, tired feet suggestively beat time to the music. Out of every dime ticket theirs was two and a half cents.

Ephraim Tuttle, who served as business manager, accountant and general factotum for Jugger Callahan, wandered back and forth, keeping a nervous eye on the girls and the ticket chopper. He was a tall, gaunt man with a bony skeleton-face. His treatment of the girls was always scrupulously fair and they respected him. They could not even accuse him of showing favoritism to Evelyn Dorn, his flame of the moment.

He made a mental calculation of the swaying couples on the dance floor and found that business was only fair for a Friday night. He decided that they'd better pass out some more handbills on Spring and Main streets and approached a man quietly sitting on one of the settees that lined a wall.

"Firpo, have you been messing around in my office?"

Firpo Cole looked up at Ephraim Tuttle. "No. Why should I?"

"Someone stole my letter opener," responded Tuttle.

"That's bad," said Firpo. "If you get a letter now you'll have to open it with your fingers."

Ephraim Tuttle pulled a five-cent stogie out of his vest, carefully split the end and lit it before replying. "It's funny," he mused, "how the squirts always act the toughest. If I'd spit at you you'd drown, yet you like to throw your weight around."

"Just leave me alone," said Firpo. "When somebody loses a night's sleep around here they right away think I took it."

"Firpo, you don't appreciate the break we're giving you. We let you mooch a few bucks around here instead of letting you go back to picking pockets on the street. But remember, it's only because Ruth Bailey's a nice girl and she wants us to give you a break."

"Thanks."

"I don't know what you want from the Bailey kid anyway, Firpo. You'll never get to first base and—"

Ephraim Tuttle broke off as he noticed Firpo Cole's face. He didn't like what he saw there. "God, but you're touchy about that skirt," he muttered and walked away.

With expressionless eyes, Firpo Cole watched the business manager retreat. He didn't know that his face, which always showed an unhealthy pallor, was now even whiter and more strained than usual. He was a youngish, frail man with spindle-legs, chicken-breast and sunken cheeks, and he had once been facetiously dubbed "Firpo" by someone who was supposed to be as funny as a card.

He found a loose cigarette in his pocket and lit it. As he did so, he forgot to make his customary salute to the medical profession by thumbing his nose. The medicos had told him that each cigarette took one month of his life. Like oil and water, cigarettes and lungers don't mix.

Jugger Callahan and his boys wound up the quickie trio of dances and immediately started on another set of three. The hostesses collected tickets from the men and slipped into their arms for another few minutes of those curious, swaying gyrations that passed for dancing.

Firpo Cole took a pad out of his pocket and marked down the figure 8. Then he leaned back

*Rocco whipped out his handkerchief
and carefully wiped the gun*

to watch a man and a girl sitting and talking on a sofa in a far corner. He didn't like to have Ruth Bailey sitting out dances. It was a funny thing, he reflected, but he didn't at all mind when Ruth Bailey was being pawed by some ten-dollar millionaire out on the floor. It was her job. At first, his stomach used to tighten up from jealousy but even that had stopped. You get used to those things. What he did mind, though, was to have her talking with some man through eight dances and not get the tickets for them. She was an easy mark for chiselers. But he'd see to it that this baby got away with nothing. He could do nothing if Ruth preferred some other guy to him, but at least he'd see to it she wasn't rooked out of her rights.

On the band platform, Jugger Callahan broke into *Ain't Misbehavin'* and Mona Leeds, the outfit's torch singer, took over the mile. A hush settled over the place. The voice was rich and husky and, like her face and figure, possessed a torrid beauty. She sang into the mike but faced Jugger Callahan—as if to let the world know who her man was.

Mona Leeds finished her number and the dance hall echoed with appreciative whistles and stomping feet. Next to Firpo Cole, a voice said: "That's the kind of chicken they should have in every pot."

Firpo looked up to find Rocco Pace standing beside him. Rocco was one of the city's moderately successful racketeers. He dressed according to color charts, seemed pleasant and mild-mannered, but, if occasion demanded, could be dangerous.

Firpo said: "Yeah, Mona's all right."

Rocco nodded toward Ruth Bailey who still talked with the stranger. "But nothing like her, eh?"

"Nobody's like her," said Firpo in a flat, emotionless voice.

"Has she still got that yen for Jugger?"

Firpo Cole nodded.

"How come you take it laying down, Firpo? Me, I'd blow a fuse."

"Jugger's a good-looking guy. I don't blame her. I'm just going to see she gets them dealt from the top of the deck."

Rocco Pace shrugged. Certain things were beyond his Latin comprehension. He slipped a flat .32 automatic out of a shoulder holster and handed it to Firpo Cole who dropped it in his pocket. It was a service for which Firpo usually made four bits. Rocco had long ago discovered that he couldn't hold the girls the way he liked if he sported an eighteen-ounce piece of metal over his chest.

Rocco Pace waved to Firpo and walked toward the barrier. The hostesses made a beeline for him. They liked this smiling, pleasant racketeer who gave big tips and who really came to dance.

Firpo Cole saw the stranger in the corner stand up and nod a farewell to Ruth Bailey. He didn't hand her any tickets. Firpo waited till the man got near him, then stood up and blocked his path.

"Well?" asked the stranger. He was middle-aged and asthmatic.

Firpo Cole said: "What are you trying to get away with?"

"Anything I can," replied the stranger pleasantly.

"Well, I'm here to see that you don't, mister."

"Get out of my way, son."

"Not till you pay her, chiseler."

"Pay Miss Bailey?" The stranger sounded puzzled. "Maybe you got me mixed up with Santa Claus."

"You owe her ten tickets," said Firpo, figuring the extra two as a tip. "That'll be one buck."

"For the last time, get out of my way."

Firpo Cole knew it was coming but he did nothing to prevent it. Ruth Bailey was worth a beating any day in the week. It never occurred to him to draw the flat automatic in his pocket.

The stranger's arm came around in a wide arc that sent the frail Firpo spinning over the floor for fifteen feet. Firpo saw the stranger leave with unhurried steps, then a sudden attack of vertigo seized him and he passed out.

IRPO COLE came to on a couch in Ephraim Tuttle's office. Mona Leeds, the torch singer, was swabbing his forehead with a damp rag and, from behind his desk, the business manager regarded them sourly.

Tuttle said: "Firpo, for a guy who couldn't lick a butterfly you certainly like to throw your weight around."

"Stop riding him," snapped Mona Leeds.

The door opened and Ruth Bailey came in. "Firpo, they told me you were in a fight. Are you all right?"

Firpo Cole struggled into a sitting posture. "Nothing happened. I'm fine."

Ruth seemed to notice the torch singer for the first time. The corners of her mouth twisted. "Well, well, if it isn't our little thrush trying to cut in on Firpo."

"Now, Ruth," said Firpo weakly. "She was just trying to help me."

Mona Leeds stood up and walked over to the hostess. The two women faced each other: Mona Leeds, in all her beautiful, slithering, scented allure, and Ruth Bailey, refreshing and young in a simple gown with a gold brooch at the neck. The one, a night life beauty with a duco finish, the other, a breath of fresh air too rare in a taxi-joint.

Ruth Bailey's voice had a faint hint of hysteria. "Why aren't you satisfied with Jugger? You got him solid—why do you want more? Firpo would be a pretty miserable addition to your collection. Why don't you leave him alone?"

"You —," said the torch singer.

Ruth's hand snapped out and slapped Mona Leeds squarely over the face.

Ephraim Tuttle's warning shout was lost as the torch singer sprang for Ruth Bailey, her claws spread like a cat's. Mona's hands tore into Ruth's face and hair and the hostess clutched at the singer's dress. In a moment they were on the floor, scrabbling in mute fury. Paralyzed with the fascination of the spectacle, the two men simply watched.

With a yank, Ruth ripped apart the front of Mona's dress and the torch singer sank sharp, white, translucent teeth into the hostess's shoulder. Long, lacquered nails clawed, fists pummeled, slipper-shod feet kicked. The wildcats rolled over the floor and, with squeals of rage, tore at hair, face, clothing.

The door opened and Rocco Pace appeared. He said, "What the hell," and leaped to separate the fighting girls.

Their fury subsided as suddenly as it rose and they stood up, appraising the damage they had done each other.

"That's a lousy way to act in my office," complained Ephraim Tuttle.

"Oh go add up some numbers," said Mona Leeds calmly. She pulled her torn dress together and left.

Ruth Bailey anxiously scanned her face in a compact mirror.

"Girls will be girls," philosophized the racketeer. "I used to have one who tried to kill me every time I went to sleep."

Ruth Bailey picked up the brooch that had been ripped from her gown. It was a simple item of jewelry, with what seemed to be a pale-blue piece of glass set in the center.

"Say, don't that belong to Mona?" asked Tuttle.

"Even if it did," replied Ruth Bailey smoothly, "I wouldn't give it to her." Then she walked out.

"There's life in those girls," said Rocco Pace. He turned to Firpo Cole. "I came for my persuader."

Firpo returned the automatic. The racketeer tossed him a half dollar and bade them good-bye.

Tuttle snorted and hunted for a cigar. "This place is getting to be a regular nuthouse. First somebody steals my letter opener and now this. Did you hook that opener, Firpo?"

Firpo Cole was feeling a little better. The stranger hadn't hit him very hard. He said: "Don't bother me."

Ephraim Tuttle's Adam's apple bobbed up and down. "Listen, you lousy pickpocket, I'm just asking nicely if you took it. It was pretty valuable. It had an onyx handle with silver edging."

Firpo said, "The hell with you and your letter opener," got up and left.

It was after one already and the customers had gone. On the bandstand, Jugger Callahan and his boys were putting away their instruments, though Monkey Harris, a drummer, still banged on the skins as if to relieve his pent-up weariness.

Firpo Cole made his way to the back, entered a large dressing-room and sat down in a corner to wait for Ruth Bailey. The hostesses were hanging their gowns in a closet and changing into street clothes. Some sat quietly and rested their swollen feet in pans of hot water. None paid the slightest attention to Firpo.

Ruth Bailey changed her stockings, which had snagged during the fight, and touched up a blackened eye with powder. Ephraim Tuttle came in and asked whether anyone had seen his letter opener. No one had and he left. Ruth Bailey finished making up and she and Firpo Cole quit the dressing-room and went out to the street.

These nightly walks, when he took her home, were usually full with the talk and gossip of the Tango Palace, but tonight, it was some time before Ruth Bailey finally broke the heavy silence between them.

"Firpo, I'm afraid."

"Forget it, Ruth. Mona won't get you fired. She's too white for that."

"I'm not talking about the fight," she said. "I just forgot myself when I saw her by you and she was mad about this." She touched the brooch at her throat.

"What has that got to do with it?"

"Well, you remember the night the old ballroom burned down? I went back for my purse which I'd forgotten and there was a light in Jugger's office. I went inside and there was no one there but I saw a jewel case on his desk. It had this inside of it."

"You shouldn't of taken it."

"Maybe, but all I knew was that Jugger bought it for Mona and I guess I got jealous. I started wearing it a few days ago. Jugger's seen it but he's too much of a gentleman to say anything. But Mona knows it belongs to her and that's what she was really fighting about with me."

"You've got to give it to her, Ruth."

"I will. Tomorrow. She's beautiful—I don't blame Jugger for preferring her to me."

"Jugger may be a nice guy but he's a damned fool for wanting Mona Leeds instead of you."

They reached her rooming house and halted.

"You know, Firpo, it's funny how I'm sick about Jugger and you about me. It seems like such a damned shame that life never—"

"I know all about it," he cut in harshly. "You didn't tell me what you're afraid of."

"Firpo, someone—I don't know who—put five hundred dollars in my purse tonight."

He whistled. "That's a lot of money."

She reached into her coat pocket. "This is what the money came in."

He took a plain, white envelope from her hand and read the typewritten line on it: *This better be enough.*

Under a lamplight, Firpo Cole's prematurely weazened face was lost in thought. After a while he returned the envelope to her and said: "You better hold on to this and the dough. You didn't see anyone messing around with your purse tonight?"

"No—but of course anyone could have gotten at it in the dressing-room."

"Has anything like this happened before?"

"No."

"Well, all I can figure, Ruth, is that someone's mixing you up with somebody else. I'll try and check tomorrow."

"There's another thing, Firpo. You know that man you had a fight with today?"

"What about him?"

"He said not to tell anybody but he's a detective from an insurance company. They think that fire wasn't an accident. He knows I came back that night after everyone was gone and he asked me a lot of questions about it."

Firpo Cole shrugged. "If that fire's faked it's Jugger's worry—not yours. He got the insurance dough from it."

"I know Jugger wouldn't do a thing like that. Something's wrong, Firpo. I'm afraid."

"Forget it, Ruth."

She leaned over and kissed him full on the lips. "You're swell, Firpo. I'm sorry we don't hit it off together."

"Sure," said Firpo Cole. "I'm swell." He turned abruptly and made for his own lodgings.

CHAPTER TWO
DEAD FEET

HERE was hard and insistent rapping on the door panel. After some time, the steady pounding had its effect. Firpo Cole stirred uneasily in his sleep, then awoke with a start.

He groped for the light chain above his bed and the light revealed a small, unkempt, five-dollar-a-week room. He knuckled his eyes, then peered at a clock on the dresser but found that he had forgotten to wind it. Through the window he could see the first streaks of dawn. The pounding on the door did not let up.

Firpo Cole disentangled himself from the bed covers, worked his feet into straw slippers and opened the door. Two men entered. He knew one—a plainclothes police dick named Simms. The other was a uniformed cop.

Simms said, "Go to it, Max," and the uniformed cop began a somewhat perfunctory search of the room. The dick sat down on the bed. "How you getting along, Firpo?"

"Fine," replied Firpo Cole. "And you?"

"Just dandy, thanks. Have you been picking pockets lately, Firpo?"

"No."

"That's swell. Your record ain't so good on the blotter, is it?"

"I lost once."

"I remember, Firpo. Meatball rap. Two years in college, wasn't it?"

"One year. What is this, Simms—a frame?"

The police dick shook his head. "Nope. I've just been checking on you, Firpo. I'm glad

you're going straight. What time did you check in last night?"

"I came home around two or a little after."

"Go out again?"

"No."

"How do you pay for your room and grits, Firpo?"

"I do odd jobs around the Tango Palace."

Simms nodded sagely. "So I hear. I also hear you're carrying a torch for one of the dames that works there—a Ruth Bailey—and that she won't give you a tumble because she got a yen for Jugger Callahan."

"What are you driving at, Simms?"

Max was finished with his cursory examination of the room. "Nothing," he grunted.

Simms shrugged. "There's nothing to find anyway. It's open and shut." He turned to Firpo again. "I'll tell you what I'm driving at. That Ruth Bailey of yours was murdered a couple of hours ago."

"If you're being funny," said Firpo Cole tonelessly, "I'll kill you, Simms."

Simms said: "Sure I'm being funny. Me and Max come here only to have tea and crumpets."

Firpo's eyes searched the police dick's face. He saw that Simms was speaking the truth. Suddenly he felt sick. He got up and stumbled through the door, across the hallway, to the washroom. He kneeled over the bowl and the fleshless body shook and strained convulsively.

Simms cautioned, "Don't let the guy pull any fast one," and Max walked over to the open door and watched till Firpo returned.

Simms said: "I figure it this way, Firpo. Tell me if I get the details wrong. You were after Ruth Bailey but there was no sale because she was hot for this Jugger Callahan. So you got fed up with the whole business and went and killed her."

"I didn't kill her." He began to tremble and a fit of coughing seized him. He covered his mouth with a towel and when he took it away there were flecks of blood on it. "I didn't kill her," he repeated.

Simms said: "It probably just slipped your mind, Firpo. I guess we can make you remember again. Get some duds on that gorgeous torso of yours and come along."

The prowl car stopped at the rooming house of the late Ruth Bailey. The sun was already showing itself and supplanting the coolness of a Los Angeles night with a dry desert heat.

Simms, Max and Firpo Cole went up the two flights of groaning steps and entered Ruth Bailey's small apartment. The place had already been dusted and photoed and the few department men who remained sat around yawning and wishing they were home in bed. A couple of bored reporters were handicapping the Caliente races and exhibiting a complete disinterest in this murder of a taxi dance hall hostess.

The body lay on the floor where it had fallen. Simms yanked off the bed sheet that covered it and said: "Come here."

Firpo Cole walked over and stared down on Ruth Bailey. He thought he would be sick again but the feeling passed. She wore the same dress, and the brooch that Jugger had bought for Mona Leeds was still clasped at her neck. The steel point of Ephraim Tuttle's stolen letter opener was buried deep in her heart.

But Firpo was looking neither at the brooch nor the murder weapon. His eyes were fastened on the dead lips and the heavy coloring of lipstick over them—and on the strange shading of tangerine.

As if from a great distance, Firpo heard Simms' matter-of-fact voice saying: "Take a good look at what you done and then see if you still got the crust to deny it."

Firpo Cole gave a queer, strangled gasp and sank down on his knees beside the body. His hand went out and caressed Ruth Bailey's neck and he bent over and kissed her on the forehead. Behind him, a flashlight bulb exploded.

After a while, Firpo stood up. His eyes were dry and had a strange glint of understanding in them and the white, unhealthy face was set with rocky determination.

Simms said: "You did a pretty messy job, didn't you? Do you feel like talking about it now?"

"I didn't do it."

"No? Then who did?"

Firpo Cole was sure he knew. Jugger Callahan! It couldn't be anyone else. But his face gave no inkling of his thought. He would get at the truth—and when he did, no one but he would have the pleasure of dealing with the murderer. He said: "I didn't do this, Simms. I would of killed myself for even thinking of doing it."

Max gave a yell and pointed at the body. "It's gone!"

They followed the cop's fingers. The brooch that had been clasped at Ruth Bailey's neck was missing.

"Kee-rist!" roared Simms. "You lousy pickpocket, what the hell do you think you're pulling off here?"

The police dick grabbed at Firpo Cole and began to bounce him up and down like a cocktail shaker. "You wouldn't kill her!" he shouted. "Why you even rob her dead body to get a two buck hunk of jewelry!"

"I didn't take it," Firpo gasped as well as he could.

"No one else was near her," snorted Simms. His hands plunged into Firpo's pockets—and came up empty. Bewilderment spread over his beet-face as he ran his hands over Firpo's clothes. "What the hell did you do with it?"

"I didn't touch it," said Firpo.

"Take your duds off!"

Firpo Cole shed his clothes till he stood completely naked. Simms carefully felt and looked over each item of clothing and even ran his hands through Firpo's hair and looked in his mouth. The brooch was not on him. Simms gave the shivering Firpo permission to dress.

Then the department men carefully combed the room for any possible hiding place. The search did not reveal the missing jewel. Simms scratched at his chin, puzzled.

"Sure as hell that thing was on her neck when we come in here," he said.

Max asked: "Are you sure it was there when Firpo touched her?"

They looked at each other uncertainly, even suspiciously. Finally, Simms said: "Well, we know that Firpo hasn't got it." He jerked a finger at the reporters. "Search those crumbs down to their drawers. If it ain't on them you better take this room apart till you find it!"

Simms grabbed Firpo by the arm and pushed him toward the door. He never felt Firpo's sensitive, experienced fingers as they dipped into his jacket pocket to retrieve the missing brooch.

ALONE in a small cell in the city jail, Firpo Cole hid the brooch in one of his shoes, then lay down on the iron cot and waited. He tried not to think of the dead body. It would just make him sick again and he couldn't afford that now. Afterwards it would be all right but first there was work to do.

Several hours passed and it was nearing ten before a guard came along and roused Firpo out of his dull, lethargic sleep. He blinked as he was taken into a sunlit, cheerful room. Simms sat behind a desk talking with Jugger Callahan and Ephraim Tuttle. There were a few cops there, including Max, and a male secretary was taking notes on a stenotype. The guard pushed Firpo into a chair and left.

Jugger was saying: "I didn't see her after she left with Firpo. Firpo used to walk her home every night so it was nothing out of the ordinary. Lots of crumbs hang out in front of every dance hall and she never liked to go home alone."

Simms asked: "Didn't you have another joint which burned down a couple of months ago?"

"Yes. I have a new place now. What of it?"

"Nothing. I just remembered. Was Ruth Bailey on the weed?"

"Not that I know of."

"The autopsy'll show anyway." Simms absently tore at a blotter. "It still looks like Firpo did it. He was nuts about Ruth Bailey but she passed him up for you."

Jugger's words came clipped and precise. "Ruth Bailey and I were friends and nothing more. Understand?"

Simms shrugged. "It makes no difference what you call it. Any way you slice it the motive is still jealousy. Last night Firpo got particularly jealous when he saw some guy talking to her through a few dances. Afterwards he picked a fight with the guy and got poked. He was mad clear through so he stole the letter opener and took her home and let her have it."

"That don't hold water," Ephraim Tuttle intruded. "My letter opener was missing *before* Firpo had that fight."

Simms carefully dropped the shreds of the blotter into a waste basket. "Before-after-sooner-later. What's the difference so long as he hangs for it?"

"I still think you're all wet about Firpo," said Jugger Callahan. "I'll be glad to stand the bail for him if he's held."

Simms pushed his chair back. "There ain't no bail in a first degree homicide charge."

Jugger Callahan and Ephraim Tuttle moved for the door. The band leader said to Firpo, "Take it easy," and they left.

Simms came from behind the desk and planted himself in front of Firpo. Max and one of the other cops moved in closer.

Simms spoke persuasively, almost with a note of regret: "It's open and shut, Firpo. If you get a good shyster you'll probably be able to beat it with an insanity plea. Sick guys like you who don't rate with the dames often get violent about it. You suddenly got tired of playing second fiddle to Jugger Callahan with the Bailey frill so you stole the letter opener. You had a chance to steal it any time because you were always around the Tango Palace. You walked her home, went up to her room and killed her."

Simms went over to a water cooler and drank three times from a lily cup.

Max said: "Firpo thought he wiped his prints off that letter opener but we'll bring 'em up with a special process."

Simms returned. "It had to be you, Firpo," he continued, "because anyone coming along later would have found Bailey in bed and she was wearing her street clothes when she was killed. What makes the whole thing worse is that you stole the letter opener beforehand so that makes it premeditated murder. Why don't you plead guilty, Firpo, and we'll let you cop an insanity plea?"

Firpo Cole didn't reply. The dick's words made him wonder why Ruth was still wearing her clothes when she was murdered. Ordinarily, she would have gone to bed right away. She was tired enough. Did she stay up to wait for Jugger? Did she go out to visit him and then come back?

Simms sighed. He said: "I hate to do this." He slapped Firpo squarely over the mouth and someone behind Firpo hit him over the ear. "Are you gonna look at this sensibly?" asked Simms.

The stenotypist left. The brooch was cutting into the sole of Firpo's foot but he was glad to feel it there. That cheap piece of jewelry which Jugger Callahan had bought for Mona Leeds would yet prove his guilt.

Simms hit Firpo over the mouth again and repeated his question. Blood from a broken tooth choked Firpo and he could only shake his head in reply. Somebody gave him a sharp, clipping blow over the nape of his neck, the chair tilted and the broadloom rug seemed to rush up at him.

"Like hitting an old woman," commented Max disgustedly.

When Firpo Cole regained consciousness, he found himself lying on the cot in his cell. The tooth socket had stopped bleeding. He did not know how long he stayed there. Somebody brought him a tin platter full of some mush but he didn't touch it. A drunk in the next cell tried to find out from Firpo what had caused the Yankees to slump.

After a while, the guard came along and he was taken up to that cheerful room again. Simms, Max and the other shams were there but this time the outsider was the stranger who had sat through eight dances with Ruth and who had subsequently biffed Firpo.

"Sit down, Firpo." Simms sounded friendly.

He indicated the stranger. "This is Mickey Hymer."

"I met him," responded Firpo through bruised lips.

"So you did. How come you tried to step on Mr. Hymer last night?"

"He wouldn't pay Ruth Bailey her tickets."

"As it turned out, Firpo, she didn't need them. Mr. Hymer is an investigator for Easternstates Insurance and he wants to ask you a few questions."

Mr. Hymer reached over and extended a hand to Firpo Cole. "First how about letting bygones be bygones?"

Firpo ignored the outstretched hand.

"Have it your way," shrugged the insurance dick. "Firpo, I'll be frank with you. We think that was no accidental fire that burned down the Tango Palace. Jugger Callahan had a pretty heavy policy on it and the whole business stinks."

Firpo Cole felt a sudden surge of panic. Jugger Callahan in jail for incendiarism and insurance fraud was the last thing he wanted. Jugger had to be kept free—and very accessible. He said: "That fire was on the level."

"What makes you think so, Firpo?"

"Jugger had over twelve hundred bucks in his desk when the place burned down. It was the take for three days and he was going to deposit it the next morning. If he would have started that fire he wouldn't have left that much dough there."

Mr. Hymer nodded. "That's the story I heard, Firpo, but Callahan had a heavy property policy on the place and that more than made up for the money that burned. Besides," he added with careful emphasis, "outside of Jugger Callahan's business manager, we have no proof that the money was really left there."

"What stinks about the fire?" asked Firpo.

"We found what looks like the remains of a few empty oil cans in the basement. In addition, it was a very profitable fire for Callahan. But what I'd like to know from you is where Ruth Bailey came in on it."

"Don't think you can frame her because she's dead," said Firpo tensely.

"Keep cool," soothed Mr. Hymer. "I got as much respect for the dead as the next man. Only I know she was the last one in the dance hall before it burned down and I thought maybe she told you something she forgot to say to me."

"She told me nothing you don't know. When she got home that night she found out that she forgot her purse at the dance hall so she had to go back."

"Why couldn't she get it the next day?"

"Because the key to her apartment was in it," said Firpo.

"I see. What's the rest of her story?"

"When she got back the place was empty and outside of a couple of lights someone left on, she saw nothing suspicious. She got her purse and went home. That's all she had to do with it."

Firpo wondered what the insurance dick would say if he knew that Ruth had taken that brooch from Jugger's office. Did it prove that Jugger Callahan had also come back after the others were gone and forgotten it on his desk?

Mr. Hymes picked at his nose thoughtfully. "That's the same story she—the deceased—told me last night." He stood up. "I guess I'll mosey along."

 HEN the door was closed behind the insurance dick, Simms turned to Firpo. "It still looks like you're the murderer," he informed him cozily.

"I didn't do it," said Firpo Cole for the sake of the secretary's record.

"My men have been checking all morning and they can't find anyone who saw Ruth Bailey go out after you took her home last night. So you must have gone up to the apartment with her and killed her before she had a chance to get her clothes off and go to bed."

Suddenly, Firpo Cole knew the meaning of the lipstick on the dead woman's mouth. It was something no one could have noticed but he. He knew the kind of lipstick she always used—a deep carmine brand named *Machavelli*. On those rare occasions that Ruth had kissed him, he had never wiped it off. But the lipstick on her, when she was murdered, had a tangerine coloring—the kind that Mona Leeds, the torch singer, used. It could mean only that Ruth had gone out again to see Mona.

Firpo hadn't been listening to Simms' persuasive arguments for appointing him the murderer. He said: "Go jump in a sewer."

Simms and Max came around to where Firpo sat. The stenotypist left the room. Firpo braced himself.

Simms sighed. "This is a hell of a case. I wish I knew what happened to that jewelry that was on Bailey's neck." Then he began to hit Firpo methodically, with semi-clenched fists.

A spasm of coughing shook Firpo's spare body. The contents were heavy and deep from the lungs.

Max moved away. "Watch those damned germs," he complained. "You oughta learn enough to cover your mouth."

Firpo knew he was going to faint again. He struggled against it, for a few moments, then gave way.

When Firpo Cole came around, he found himself lying on a cot in the dispensary. He could see through an unshaded window ahead of him. It was dark outside. He must have been out for several hours.

The doctor who was bending over Firpo stood up and faced Simms and Max. "He's all right now but if you give him another shellacking I'm not responsible."

"Shellacking!" exclaimed Simms. "We hardly touched the guy. We just gave him a few slaps to help his memory and—"

"I'm not interested," cut in the doctor. "All I say is that another memory course might bring on a much worse hemorrhage, so don't try it." He snapped his bag shut and stalked over to a desk to fill in a report.

"And that's what you call cooperation," muttered Max.

Firpo sat up on the edge of the cot and buttoned his shirt. The telephone jangled and Max took it. He listened a moment, then tendered the receiver to Simms. "It's for you. The autopsy report on the Bailey woman."

"Yes?" said Simms. He glanced covertly toward Firpo. "You say that Ruth Bailey was opened by the usual mid-line incision? . . . You're some cut-up, ha, ha, ha . . . Now forget that scientific bull—tell me in plain, everyday American . . . I see . . . And how about her guts? . . . I see . . . Aha—the liver and spleen . . . and the markings on the body? . . . Good-looking, eh? . . . O.K., send up the report."

Simms cradled the receiver and turned to Firpo. "That sawbones just hasn't got any feelings."

"I know," said Firpo. "It's the psychological angle, so forget it."

"Wise guy. Well, what do you think about this? Ruth Bailey was gonna have a kid."

Firpo found some kind of medicine bottle within his reach and threw it.

Simms ducked. "A lie like that," he said darkly, "don't give you the right to throw things at me. Watch your step or I'll forget myself and give you the shellacking of your life. Now beat it."

"Beat it?" said Firpo stupidly.

"Yeah. Get out of here. We know damned well you did the murder but we can't prove it—yet. We're just giving you rope, Firpo."

Max emitted a sudden guffaw. "Maybe," he explained, "we'll give him more rope later—around the neck!"

CHAPTER THREE
REQUIEM IN JAZZ

EAVING the Hall of Justice, Firpo Cole cut across to old Chinatown. He dodged into a dark alley and pressed himself against the wall. He waited thus for fifteen minutes before he felt assured that he was not being followed. The cops didn't even have enough on him to put a shadow on his tail.

He removed his shoe and took out the brooch.

The sole of his foot was criss-crossed with cuts and his cotton sock was caked with blood. He bound the foot with a soiled handkerchief and proceeded up Main Street.

Some ten minutes later he reached a pawn shop just as the owner was closing up for the night. He put the brooch on the counter.

"I want you to look at this, Saul."

"Firpo, when will you guys learn I don't handle hot stuff?"

"I only asked you to look at it."

The short, bald-headed man picked up the brooch and studied it. Finally, he said: "I wouldn't touch it, Firpo, but it's worth two or three hundred dollars."

Firpo started. "For that little gold and a little piece of glass? Are you sure?"

"Not for the gold, Firpo. It's for what you think is a piece of glass." Saul held it back to let the light of a lamp fall on it. Small white rays seemed to radiate from a flaw in its sparkling sky-blue center.

"It's a fair example of a star sapphire," continued Saul, "and if it wasn't hot you'd even be able to get up to four and a half hundred for it."

Firpo took the brooch from Saul's hand and walked out. This gave Jugger Callahan an even stronger motive to murder Ruth Bailey. The brooch was worth real dough—all the more reason for Jugger to be thoroughly enraged over its theft.

Firpo saw a clock over a bus depot. It was already after ten. He wasn't at all hungry but he hadn't eaten since the previous evening and he knew that he should have something. He found some loose change in his pockets and entered a cafeteria. With swollen lips he sipped a glass of buttermilk through a straw, and then he headed straight for the Tango Palace.

The taxi dance hall was going full blast. On the platform, Mona Leeds was giving her all to the *Basin Street Blues* and extra hostesses were on the floor to take care of the large, Saturday night trade.

Firpo Cole sank into the settee and his eyes automatically searched among the dancers for Ruth Bailey. Then he remembered. Some of the girls walked over to tell him that Ruth had been a good kid and that if they could do anything . . .

To one side, Simms was grilling the hostesses by turns. He saw Firpo and came over to him.

"I hope there's no hard feelings, Firpo."

"Who found the body, Simms?"

"The apartment door was left open and some tenant who came in at three thirty saw her on the floor."

"O.K."

"You don't look so good, Firpo. You're as white as a baby's behind. Why don't you go home?"

"Why don't you leave me alone?"

"Now don't take it that way, Firpo. Just regard me as a plainclothes dick who has to do his job."

Firpo said: "I love you with an overwhelming passion."

Simms snorted. "If you didn't do the murder a guy would think you'd try to help me find who did. But everybody in this stinkhole thinks I'm their enemy." He stalked off.

Mona finished her number and left the stand. Ephraim Tuttle scurried back and forth settling arguments when he found them and creating them when he didn't. He stopped by Firpo Cole.

"I heard you were out, Firpo. I tried to tell those dopes that you couldn't have done a thing like that to her."

"Thanks."

The business manager regarded Firpo's battered face and clucked sympathetically. "That's a hell of a way to treat you. As if you would have touched a hair of her head."

"We won't talk about it, Tuttle."

"Sure. She'd want us to forget it."

"That's right. Shut up."

Ephraim Tuttle muttered something under his breath and left. Firpo buried his face in his hands and sobs seemed to rack his body, but when his hands dropped away, his eyes were dry. Rocco Pace, dressed to the hilt, came by and sat beside him.

The racketeer asked: "Are you still a checking-room?"

"Sure."

Rocco Pace slipped his gun out of the shoulder holster and handed it to Firpo. "I see that the shams gave you the lumps, pal."

Firpo Cole nodded.

"Don't let it worry you, Firpo. You'll get used to it—after a while." He patted Firpo's back and went out on the dance floor. In a moment, he was dancing a wild waltz, to the beat of a fox trot, whirling in and out among the unmoving couples.

 IRPO COLE ran fingers over the automatic in his pocket. He caressed its smoothness and put down the safety. He stood up and pushed his way through the dancers and idlers, down the length of the hall. He went through a curtained archway that led backstage to the band platform and knocked on the dressing-room off the right wings.

Mona Leeds said: "Come in."

He entered the small dressing-room. The torch singer was buffing her nails before the mirror.

"I'm glad they let you go, Firpo." The rich, husky voice sounded strained.

He took a cigarette from a case on a table and sat down. "They had to. They didn't have anything on me."

"You shouldn't smoke cigarettes, Firpo. They're not good for you."

He laughed.

"I know," she said rapidly. "You feel you don't give a damn any more. I'd feel that way if something happened to Jugger but it's wrong, Firpo. I don't know how to tell you but—" She floundered for the right words. "You can't know how sorry I am about the quarrel I had with Ruth last night. It was just a crazy fit of jealousy."

"Don't let it worry you, Mona. You couldn't help it and even Ruth wasn't mad about it."

"Firpo, if only we could find out who did it."

"Don't let that worry you either, Mona. What'd you tell the cops?"

"Just what happened," she replied. "I had

that argument with Ruth and I never saw her again."

"That's a lie," said Firpo Cole deliberately. "I took Ruth home about one thirty. She probably went right out again and visited you. She didn't bring her purse along and before she left you she probably said that she looked like the wrath of God and—"

"Those were her exact words," uttered Mona Leeds softly.

He gave a wry grin. "Don't be surprised. I know Ruth. Anyway, you loaned her your powder and lipstick and she came home. That couldn't have been later than three in the morning. Somebody was either waiting for her at the apartment or followed her home and killed her. What I want to know is why you keep that visit to you a secret."

"You won't like it, Firpo. That's why I kept it to myself."

"I'm not a very sensitive plant. Go on."

"Well, she came to tell me she was sorry about our fight—and that she was a thief. She said she went back to the dance hall the night the old place burned down and found a piece of jewelry that Jugger had bought for me."

Firpo produced the brooch and showed it to the torch singer. "Is this what Ruth was talking about?"

"Yes—but she was wearing it on her dress. How did you get it?"

"That's a trade secret. Go on."

"Ruth took it from Jugger's desk," continued the torch singer, "and she came over last night to give it to me. I wouldn't take it."

"Why not?" he asked.

"Because it wasn't mine. Jugger might have bought it for me but he never mentioned it, so I told her to keep it—a sort of peace offering for that fight we had. I guess Jugger thinks it got lost in the fire."

Firpo Cole shook his head. "Jugger must have seen her wearing it."

"I guess so," replied Mona Leeds. "That's the way Jugger is. If he figured that she wanted it enough to steal it, he'd let her keep it."

"It's worth four or five hundred bucks, Mona, so I doubt it. You know, the Easternstates Insurance thinks the fire wasn't an accident."

The torch singer's hand went to her mouth in a frightened gesture. "No. Jugger wouldn't do a thing like that."

"How do you know?"

"But it's crazy, Firpo. He had a lot of money in his office—the receipts of a couple of days—that burned down, too."

"The insurance money more than made up for it. Besides, they're not so sure the money was there in the first place. They only have Jugger's and Tuttle's word for it."

"But why should he take such a chance for a few dollars, Firpo? He's doing fine the way he is."

"I don't know but I'll damned well find out." He stood up. "You're O.K., Mona. Don't take it too hard if I find out that Jugger killed Ruth."

He left her staring after him with wide-eyed apprehension.

IRPO COLE entered on the right wings of the band platform, found a meeting chair and sat down. From where he was, he could watch Jugger Callahan fronting the band.

Jugger caught sight of Firpo, snapped his fingers to the boys and the music trailed off. He spoke into the mike.

"Ladies and gentlemen, last night one of our beloved hostesses met a tragic end and out of respect to her I'd like everybody to keep thirty seconds of real silence."

He bowed his head and checked his wristwatch. Throughout the semi-dark hall, couples waited with their arms twined around each other. Some girl in the back giggled and said: "No."

The thirty seconds were up. Jugger Callahan's toes beat a tattoo and he snapped his fingers. "All right, boys. A one-a, a two-a, a three-a, scratch!" The band began *Potato Head Blues* and the couples started to sway again like puppets whose wires had suddenly been jerked.

Jugger walked over to Firpo. He patted his greased-back hair, obviously pleased that he had done the right thing by Ruth.

"Firpo," said the band leader, "we already got sixty-two bucks collected. How much can you chip in?"

"For what?"

"Ruth's funeral, of course," replied Jugger.

"I'm not interested in Ruth's funeral. There's somebody else's funeral I want to see about."

"Uh-huh. I get you, Firpo, but you ought to leave that to the cops. You probably never even met the guy who did it."

Firpo's bloodshot eyes fixed themselves on the band leader's face. "I won't have far to go. That letter opener was stolen from here."

"Say, that's right, isn't it? Ephraim come to me around eleven thirty last night and asked me if I'd taken it so it must have been stolen earlier."

Firpo's hands were in his pockets. There was something friendly and comforting about the feel of the automatic. He said: "We'll talk about it later."

"Sure, Firpo," said Jugger, not too heartily. "Sure."

The band leader returned to his post. The music ground on. Twenty sets, of three melodies each, every hour. Sixty dances in as many minutes with only an occasional break to give the customers a chance to buy more tickets.

The Smiling Troubadours never stopped playing, though every once in a while a musician left the stand. And, as the hours wore on and they became more tired, the music became faster and more frenzied.

Firpo stayed in his chair, watching the band leader. He didn't intend letting Jugger out of his sight—not till he could trap him some way and prove to himself that here was the murderer of Ruth Bailey.

Simms reached backstage in the course of his investigations. He seemed as much in a fog as ever. He asked Firpo whether Ruth had had any jewelry on her dress when he'd seen the body. Firpo couldn't remember and the police dick left.

The time went by and Firpo sat unmoving, watching Jugger Callahan with lackluster eyes. He tried to think of the murder of the only person he had ever cared for. What had Ruth said? That she was afraid? Of what?

Suddenly, it hit Firpo Cole like a ton of dynamite. Where was the five hundred dollars that had found its way into Ruth Bailey's purse and where was the envelope that read *This better be enough*?

The police hadn't said anything about the money or envelope so the murderer must have stolen both. There was no reason why the killer shouldn't have taken the money but the envelope was a different matter. That typewritten sentence on it meant something to the murderer. Someone in the Tango Palace had probably thought that Ruth Bailey was blackmailing him. That very envelope had probably been written on one of the office typewriters.

Firpo frowned and the swollen lips pursed in thought. His job was to find out who had typed that envelope.

 T two in the morning, the *Smiling Troubadours* gradually, almost reluctantly, stopped playing. There seemed to be a kind of weary excitement among them after the long grind. Customers filed out, spotlights went off and hostesses sat down to nurse their feet.

Firpo Cole fell into step beside Jugger Callahan as the band leader talked to friends, visited the washroom and finally went to his office. Jugger did not object. He imagined that Firpo felt lost—that he needed friendship. Firpo was like a dog that had lost its master and was trying to attach itself to someone else.

After Jugger had finished checking the night's receipts with the business manager, he turned to Firpo. "We're having a tea party tonight. How about coming along? A couple of reefers might do you good."

Tea parties were a custom of long standing on every Saturday night at Jugger Callahan's apartment. Any other time, Firpo Cole would have felt highly honored by the invitation, for these parties were attended only by the elite of the Tango Palace.

"I wouldn't miss it for the world," said Firpo.

Ephraim Tuttle locked up the books, said he'd see them later and went to pay off the girls. Firpo and the band leader left the dance hall. They walked down Main, then turned up Sixth.

"Jugger," asked Firpo Cole, "can you typewrite?"

"One finger stuff. Why?"

"It's not important. Is there a file up in the office listing the girls' addresses?"

"Of course."

"Then anyone at the Tango could find out where Ruth lived."

"I guess so, Firpo, but—"

"You could find out, too, couldn't you?" cut in Firpo.

"What the hell are you getting at?"

"Forget it, Jugger."

The band leader started to say something but stayed his reply. They turned in to an all-night drugstore. Here, for a fiver, the clerk forgot the narcotic laws and gave Jugger a twelve-ounce bottle of *cannabis indica*. The band leader then bought a carton of cigarettes and some brown cigarette paper.

They went outside and hailed a taxi.

CHAPTER FOUR
PAID IN FULL

UGGER Callahan's apartment was large and comfortable. Most of the boys from the band were already there. Mona Leeds and Evelyn Dorn, Ephraim Tuttle's current doll, were making and serving sandwiches to the guests. Jugger lolled in an overstuffed chair and Firpo sat right beside him watching the preparations.

Monkey Harris and a few of the other boys had sliced open the cigarettes from the carton and emptied the tobacco into a wide, shallow pan. Now they took the bottle of *cannabis indica* and poured the greenish-brown liquid into the pan. They allowed the tobacco to soak in the poisonous drug for several minutes, then put a match to it—which served both to burn up the excess alcohol and to dry the tobacco. This done, they began to wrap the residue in the brown cigarette paper. They worked diligently and the heap of these homemade marihuana cigarettes grew steadily.

Jugger said to Firpo Cole: "These give a much better kick than the ready made kind."

"I never tried them," replied Firpo. "When did you first start?" He wanted to hear Jugger talk—to wait for that mistake, that slip of the tongue which would point the finger of guilt at him.

Jugger Callahan was in an expansive mood. He said: "Back in Chi, in the Capone days. A bunch of us muggle-hounds would get together and play hot music long before the word 'swing' was ever invented. Today the high school punks have taken over. They call themselves jitterbugs and if we send good we're out of this world. They call the clarinet a licorice stick, a trombone a grunt iron, the bass fiddle a doghouse—and most of the time I don't know what the hell they're talking about."

"Yeah," said Firpo. "Those sure were the good old days, all right, in Chi."

"The only thing that flowed freer than money," continued the band leader reminiscently, "was blood. We used to have classy apartments and buy a lot of jewelry for our women."

Firpo suddenly reached into his pocket and held the brooch out. "You mean like this thing you bought for Mona?"

Jugger Callahan didn't bite. "I bought that for Mona? What you getting at, Firpo?"

"Haven't you ever seen it before?" asked Firpo Cole.

"No—yes, I think Ruth Bailey wore something like that."

Firpo frowned. Jugger was too old a hand to be caught that crudely. He said: "This is a star sapphire. It's pretty valuable."

Evelyn Dorn was hovering over them with a sandwich tray. Her doe eyes bulged. "Geeze! A star sapphire." She took it and examined it reverently. "That's what I always wanted to get—a star sapphire." She sighed. "But I guess I ain't got what it takes. Nobody's given me any—not even one yet."

"I'd still like to know what you were getting at, Firpo," said the band leader.

Firpo retrieved the brooch. "Let's drop it."

Evelyn Dorn suddenly snapped her fingers. "Hell, Firpo, I forgot to tell you!"

"What?"

"That gangster—that Rocco Pace is on the warpath after you. You better watch out."

"What's the matter now?" asked Jugger.

"That's all right," said Firpo. "It's nothing to worry about. I just stole Rocco's gun."

Jugger Callahan looked at him queerly but made no comment. Evelyn Dorn wandered off. Firpo leaned back and closed his eyes. An idea was stirring within him.

Turnip Billings, who played tenor horn, called out: "All finished, boys. Jugger Callahan and his Twelve Shtoonks will now get high."

He tossed a few reefers to Firpo Cole and Jugger Callahan.

Jugger Callahan was a breather and it was not long before a quiet contentment seemed to come over him. After a while, he fixed glazed eyes on Firpo and said: "You're not running after me because you like my mustache. You think I killed Ruth Bailey."

Firpo Cole, who was bluffing his smoke, nodded.

"What'll you do about it?"

"When I make sure, I'll kill you." Firpo's voice was dispassionate but as certain of itself as a pile driver.

Jugger Callahan laughed. His good humor was not even ruffled. "You two-bit grifter, you talk big. How come you think I killed your Ruth Bailey?"

"She was in love with you, Jugger—really in love—the way a bum like you couldn't understand."

"I liked Ruth, but that's all, Firpo. I never two-timed on Mona."

"I know," replied Firpo. "I would of made you marry Ruth if you had."

The band leader laughed again. "Pickpocket to marriage broker. That's good. But you haven't told me how you think I come to kill Ruth."

They were talking in low tones. The others around them still laughed and shouted boisterously. The drug had not yet begun to take effect.

Firpo said: "I figure it this way. You put a lot of insurance on the old Tango Palace and then faked a fire by soaking the drapes and everything else in oil and gasoline."

"You better keep those ideas to yourself," said Jugger Callahan a little more seriously.

"I don't have to. An insurance dick thinks that. He found what used to be oil cans in the ruins. You also forgot that stone I showed you on your desk, because Ruth had to go back to the Palace that night and she saw it there. You must have been fixing for the fire about that time and you probably saw her take it."

"So now you're calling Ruth Bailey a crook."

Firpo's hands began to tremble and he waited a few moments before replying. "She took it because she knew you bought it for Mona and she was jealous. She started wearing it every day after that, Jugger, just to get Mona's goat but you thought it was her way of saying that she knew you started that fire."

"Not so fast, Firpo. I lost over twelve hundred dollars in cold cash during the fire and you don't think I'd be crazy enough to leave it up there if I burned the place down."

"I know that angle too, Jugger, but there's no proof you left the dough to burn and that it isn't in your pocket right now."

"Well, I'll be damned," the band leader uttered softly. "And what do you think I did after the fire?"

"Ruth was wearing that thing and you thought she was blackmailing you so you tried to buy her off. You slipped five hundred bucks into her purse with a note saying that it better be enough. But she kept wearing the brooch and you thought she wanted more sugar so you stole

Tuttle's letter opener, figuring that anyone at the Palace could be blamed. Then you killed her with it. It had a sharp point. It must have been easy."

"That's a lot of shtush, Firpo, and you know it. You're just excited about the killing. When you have a good night's sleep you'll decide you couldn't prove a thing."

"That's the only reason you're still alive, Jugger."

Ephraim Tuttle had come in and walked over to them in time to hear the last sentence. "What's going on?" he asked.

"Firpo's puking about some kind of star sapphire and that I killed Ruth Bailey," responded Jugger.

"Oh, he's just weed-wacky," pronounced the business manager. "I don't know why the hell we let him louse up the place around here." He walked away.

HE doorbell to the apartment rang. Mona Leeds came in from the kitchen and said: "See who it is, Firpo." He went through the vestibule. It was Rocco Pace standing at the door.

"I thought I'd find you here," said the racketeer.

"Do you want to come in?"

"That ain't what I'm here for. I get a plenty good jag with dago-red."

"Then what did you want?" asked Firpo.

"Why'd you hook my gat?"

"I want to borrow it for a while, Rocco."

Rocco Pace gave a vague smile. "You liked that jane a lot, didn't you, Firpo?"

"Yes."

"I see. And you have to go gunning with my rod."

"I'll give it back to you after, Rocco."

"Let's have it now."

"I said I want to keep it for a while."

Rocco Pace's voice was silken. "You know better than to give me any backtalk, Firpo. Let's have it."

Firpo Cole hesitated a moment, then surrendered. "O.K.," he said bleakly and handed the automatic to the racketeer.

Rocco Pace whipped a polka-dotted handkerchief out of his breast pocket and carefully wiped the gun. Then he returned it to Firpo. "You ought to know better than to sport a rod with my prints on it." He started off, then paused. "I don't know if it'll help you, Firpo, but one of the guys up at the Tango Palace has been plunging pretty heavily with a bookie I know. It's practically bankrupted him. You can have it for what it's worth."

"Who is it?"

"I blowed my whistle plenty. It ought to satisfy you."

"Thanks, Rocco. You're white."

"Think nothing of it," said the racketeer breezily.

Firpo Cole returned to the living-room.

The tea party was in full session. All the lights were out but for a small, red bulb in a floor lamp. Firpo could distinguish the figures as they moved only to lift the reefers to their mouth for short, quick puffs. Mona Leeds reclined next to Jugger, in the easy chair that Firpo had vacated.

An expensive phonograph was playing repeats of a swing record as slowly as it was able. The record was Armstrong's version of *Knockin' a Jug* and in one corner Monkey Harris was beating an accompaniment on a tom-tom. His slim, yellowed fingers beat rapidly. The test of a good musician, on these occasions, was the number of beats and variations the player could get in, between two chords—and Monkey Harris was rated highly.

The effect was weird as the disk revolved and the tom-tom beat. The record was played slowly and the reefers themselves tended to slow and dull everything—thereby providing for a full appreciation of the music. And every so often a musician grunted or delivered an "Oh" or an "Ah" as he caught some new nuance in the music that he'd never before heard.

The air was heavy with those pungent, cloying fumes and Firpo Cole began to cough. He didn't have to look at his handkerchief to know it was becoming smeared with red. But he didn't care. At last he knew what was what. That small item of information from Rocco Pace had done the trick. The coughing became worse and he walked into the kitchen.

Evelyn Dorn was wolfing minced ham sandwiches. "I'd rather eat here than get sick in there," she explained.

Firpo Cole said: "Inside you were raving about star sapphires. Did you ever ask Tuttle to give you one?"

"Sure. It don't harm to ask—but I never got it."

"That's what I thought. Tuttle did buy it for you, Evelyn, only he forgot it at the old place when it burned down."

"No kiddin'?"

"He's bought you a lot of stuff, hasn't he?"

"Some," she said coyly. "Ephraim ain't a tightwad."

"That's what I figured—and on top of that he's been playing the horses. That's why he set that fire and later killed Ruth."

Evelyn Dorn stopped eating for a moment. "You mean it?"

Firpo nodded. "He stole twelve hundred bucks in receipts from Jugger and then burned the joint down. He figured rightly that Jugger would think the money burned with the building and that he was making enough profit on insurance not to investigate too much."

"Well, what do you know?" marveled Evelyn.

Firpo's voice became bitter. "When Tuttle stole that dough from Jugger's office he accidentlly left that brooch which he bought for you on Jugger's desk—and that's where Ruth found it. He made a too-big stink about losing his letter opener and then killed Ruth with it. He thought she was blackmailing him about the fire

and wasn't satisfied with a five-hundred-buck payoff."

"You can never tell about someone," she commented. "Can you?"

The double-hinge door swung open and Simms, the police detective, Max and Ephraim Tuttle came in.

"All right, Firpo," said Simms. "I know you got that jewelry you stole from Bailey's body. Let's have it."

The automatic appeared in Firpo's hand. The safety catch was still off—the way he wanted it. "Stick your mitts up and line against the wall."

The three men did as they were bid. Evelyn Dorn gave a squeal and fled. They could hear the apartment door slam shut.

"Now look here, Firpo," Simms' voice was hoarse. "This ain't gonna help. If you just take it easy—"

"Can it," interrupted Firpo. "I suppose Tuttle told you I had the brooch."

Simms nodded.

Tuttle said quickly: "I didn't mean anything, Firpo. I just heard it was stolen and then when Jugger said you was talking about it I thought I better call the cops."

Firpo's voice was as calm and as steady as the hand that held the gun. "Tuttle, all you figured was that you'd pin the killing on me and get out of it yourself. But there's no chance of that because you're paying for it now." He took a bead on the pit of Ephraim Tuttle's stomach.

"Now watch it," said Simms rapidly. "Let us take care of it, Firpo. If he did the killing he's entitled to a trial but sure as hell you'll swing if you try it yourself."

"I know I will," said Firpo Cole, "and this'll be one condemned man that'll really eat a damned hearty breakfast."

Then he sighted carefully and pulled the trigger six times.

The Girl with the Silver Eyes
Dashiell Hammett

"THE GIRL WITH THE SILVER EYES" seems to be a story about the Continental Op, the unnamed private eye who stars in most of Hammett's best short fiction as well as in his first two novels, *Red Harvest* and *The Dain Curse*. It is actually the story of the very beautiful young woman with long, lush brown hair who calls herself Jeanne Delano; in a previous adventure, "The House in Turk Street," she was Elvira, with bobbed red hair. A lot of people died in the first story, and more deaths followed in the second. It is Jeanne and her scheme that sets into motion the events that bring about the involvement of the Continental Detective Agency and its fat but very tough operative. Like many of the women in the stories by Hammett (1894–1961), she is young, very pretty, feminine, an inveterate liar, and utterly without conscience. She is a chameleon, changing from a desirable kitten to someone so cold-blooded that she will allow, even encourage, the slaughter of innocent people for her own selfish and greedy ends. Think of Brigid O'Shaughnessy in *The Maltese Falcon* and you know all you need to know about Hammett's femmes fatales and, in fact, just about every sexy girl in every noir book and motion picture.

"The Girl with the Silver Eyes" is connected to "The House in Turk Street" in that it features Jeanne/Elvira as the catalyst for the ensuing action. It was originally published in the June 1924 issue of *Black Mask*. "The House in Turk Street" had been in the April 1924 issue.

The Girl with the Silver Eyes

Dashiell Hammett

A BELL JANGLED ME into wakefulness. I rolled to the edge of my bed and reached for the telephone. The neat voice of the Old Man—the Continental Detective Agency's San Francisco manager—came to my ears:

"Sorry to disturb you, but you'll have to go up to the Glenton Apartments on Leavenworth Street. A man named Burke Pangburn, who lives there, phoned me a few minutes ago asking to have someone sent up to see him at once. He seemed rather excited. Will you take care of it? See what he wants." I said I would and, yawning, stretching and cursing Pangburn—whoever he was—got my fat body out of pajamas into street clothes.

The man who had disturbed my Sunday morning sleep—I found when I reached the Glenton—was a slim, white-faced person of about twenty-five, with big brown eyes that were red-rimmed just now from either sleeplessness or crying, or both. His long brown hair was rumpled when he opened the door to admit me; and he wore a mauve dressing-robe spotted with big jade parrots over wine-colored silk pajamas.

The room into which he led me resembled an auctioneer's establishment just before the sale—or maybe one of these alley tea rooms. Fat blue vases, crooked red vases, vases of various shapes and colors; marble statuettes, ebony statuettes, statuettes of any material; lanterns, lamps and candlesticks; draperies, hangings and rugs of all sorts; odds and ends of furniture that were all somehow queerly designed; peculiar pictures hung here and there in unexpected places. A hard room to feel comfortable in.

"My fiancée," he began immediately in a high-pitched voice that was within a notch of hysteria, "has disappeared! Something has happened to her! Foul play of some horrible sort! I want you to find her—to save her from this terrible thing that . . ."

I followed him this far and then gave it up. A jumble of words came out of his mouth—"spirited away . . . mysterious something . . . lured into a trap"—but they were too disconnected for me to make anything out of them. So I stopped trying to understand him, and waited for him to babble himself empty of words.

I have heard ordinarily reasonable men, under stress of excitement, run on even more crazily than this wild-eyed youth; but his dress—the parroted robe and gay pajamas—and his surroundings—this deliriously furnished room—gave him too theatrical a setting; made his words sound utterly unreal.

He himself, when normal, should have been a rather nice-looking lad: his features were well spaced and, though his mouth and chin were a little uncertain, his broad forehead was good. But standing there listening to the occasional melodramatic phrase that I could pick out of the jumbled noises he was throwing at me, I thought that instead of parrots on his robe he should have had cuckoos.

Presently he ran out of language and was

holding his long, thin hands out to me in an appealing gesture, saying:

"Will you?" over and over. "Will you? Will you?"

I nodded soothingly, and noticed that tears were on his thin cheeks.

"Suppose we begin at the beginning," I suggested, sitting down carefully on a carved bench affair that didn't look any too strong.

"Yes! Yes!" He was standing legs apart in front of me, running his fingers through his hair. "The beginning. I had a letter from her every day until—"

"That's not the beginning," I objected. "Who is she? What is she?"

"She's Jeanne Delano!" he exclaimed in surprise at my ignorance. "And she is my fiancée. And now she is gone, and I know that—"

The phrases "victim of foul play," "into a trap" and so on began to flow hysterically out again.

Finally I got him quieted down and, sandwiched in between occasional emotional outbursts, got a story out of him that amounted to this:

This Burke Pangburn was a poet. About two months before, he had received a note from a Jeanne Delano—forwarded from his publishers—praising his latest book of rhymes. Jeanne Delano happened to live in San Francisco, too, though she hadn't known that he did. He had answered her note, and had received another. After a little of this they met. If she really was as beautiful as he claimed, then he wasn't to be blamed for falling in love with her. But whether or not she was really beautiful, he thought she was, and he had fallen hard.

This Delano girl had been living in San Francisco for only a little while, and when the poet met her she was living alone in an Ashbury Avenue apartment. He did not know where she came from or anything about her former life. He suspected—from certain indefinite suggestions and peculiarities of conduct which he couldn't put in words—that there was a cloud of some sort hanging over the girl; that neither her past nor her present were free from difficulties. But he hadn't the least idea what those difficulties might be. He hadn't cared. He knew absolutely nothing about her, except that she was beautiful, and he loved her, and she had promised to marry him. Then, on the third of the month—exactly twenty-one days before this Sunday morning—the girl had suddenly left San Francisco. He had received a note from her, by messenger.

This note, which he showed me after I had insisted point blank on seeing it, read:

Burkelove:

Have just received a wire, and must go East on next train. Tried to get you on the phone, but couldn't. Will write you as soon as I know what my address will be. If anything. [These two words were erased and could be read only with great difficulty.] *Love me until I'm back with you forever.*

YOUR JEANNE

Nine days later he had received another letter from her, from Baltimore, Maryland. This one, which I had a still harder time getting a look at, read:

Dearest Poet:

It seems like two years since I have seen you, and I have a fear that it's going to be between one and two months before I see you again.

I can't tell you now, beloved, about what brought me here. There are things that can't be written. But as soon as I'm back with you, I shall tell you the whole wretched story.

If anything should happen—I mean to me—you'll go on loving me forever, won't you, beloved? But that's foolish. Nothing is going to happen. I'm just off the train, and tired from traveling.

Tomorrow I shall write you a long, long letter to make up for this.

My address here is 215 N. Stricker St. Please, Mister, at least one letter a day!

YOUR OWN JEANNE

For nine days he had had a letter from her each day—with two on Monday to make up for the none on Sunday. And then her letters had stopped. And the daily letters he had sent to the address she gave—215 N. Stricker Street—had begun to come back to him, marked "Not known." He had sent a telegram, and the telegraph company had informed him that its Baltimore office had been unable to find a Jeanne Delano at the North Stricker Street address.

For three days he had waited, expecting hourly to hear from the girl, and no word had come. Then he had bought a ticket for Baltimore.

"But," he wound up, "I was afraid to go. I know she's in some sort of trouble—I can feel that—but I'm a silly poet. I can't deal with mysteries. Either I would find nothing at all or, if by luck I did stumble on the right track, the probabilities are that I would only muddle things; add fresh complications, perhaps endanger her life still further. I can't go blundering at it in that fashion, without knowing whether I am helping or harming her. It's a task for an expert in that sort of thing. So I thought of your agency. You'll be careful, won't you? It may be—I don't know—that she won't want assistance. It may be that you can help her without her knowing anything about it. You are accustomed to that sort of thing; you can do it, can't you?"

I turned the job over and over in my mind before answering him. The two great bugaboos of a reputable detective agency are the persons who bring in a crooked plan or a piece of divorce work all dressed up in the garb of a legitimate operation, and the irresponsible person who is laboring under wild and fanciful delusions—who wants a dream run out.

This poet—sitting opposite me now twining his long, white fingers nervously—was, I thought, sincere; but I wasn't so sure of his sanity.

"Mr. Pangburn," I said after a while, "I'd like to handle this thing for you, but I'm not sure that I can. The Continental is rather strict, and, while I believe this thing is on the level, still I am only a hired man and have to go by the rules. Now if you could give us the endorsement of some firm or person of standing—a reputable lawyer, for instance, or any legally responsible party—we'd be glad to go ahead with the work. Otherwise, I am afraid—"

"But I know she's in danger!" he broke out. "I know that— And I can't be advertising her plight—airing her affairs—to everyone."

"I'm sorry, but I can't touch it unless you can give me some such endorsement." I stood up. "But you can find plenty of detective agencies that aren't so particular."

His mouth worked like a small boy's, and he caught his lower lip between his teeth. For a moment I thought he was going to burst into tears. But instead he said slowly: "I dare say you are right. Suppose I refer you to my brother-in-law, Roy Axford. Will his word be sufficient?"

"Yes."

Roy Axford—R. F. Axford—was a mining man who had a finger in at least half of the big business enterprises of the Pacific Coast; and his word on anything was commonly considered good enough for anybody.

"If you can get in touch with him now," I said, "and arrange for me to see him today, I can get started without much delay."

Pangburn crossed the room and dug a telephone out from among a heap of his ornaments. Within a minute or two he was talking to someone whom he called "Rita."

"Is Roy home? . . . Will he be home this afternoon? . . . No, you can give him a message for me, though . . . Tell him I'm sending a gentleman up to see him this afternoon on a personal matter—personal from me—and that I'll be very grateful if he'll do what I want . . . Yes . . . You'll find out, Rita . . . It isn't a thing to talk about over the phone . . . Yes, thanks!"

He pushed the telephone back into its hiding place and turned to me.

"He'll be at home until two o'clock. Tell him what I told you and if he seems doubtful, have him call me up. You'll have to tell him the whole thing; he doesn't know anything at all about Miss Delano."

"All right. Before I go, I want a description of her."

"She's beautiful! The most beautiful woman in the world!"

That would look nice on a reward circular.

"That isn't exactly what I want," I told him. "How old is she?"

"Twenty-two."

"Height?"

"About five feet eight inches, or possibly nine."

"Slender, medium or plump?"

"She's inclined toward slenderness, but she—"

There was a note of enthusiasm in his voice that made me fear he was about to make a speech, so I cut him off with another question.

"What color hair?"

"Brown—so dark it's almost black—and it's soft and thick and—"

"Yes, yes. Long or bobbed?"

"Long and thick and—"

"What color eyes?"

"You've seen shadows on polished silver when—"

I wrote down *gray eyes* and hurried on with the interrogation.

"Complexion?"

"Perfect!"

"Uh-huh. But is it light, or dark, or florid, or sallow, or what?"

"Fair."

"Face oval, or square, or long and thin, or what shape?"

"Oval."

"What shaped nose? Large, small, turned-up—"

"Small and regular!" There was a touch of indignation in his voice.

"How did she dress? Fashionably? Did she favor bright or quiet colors?"

"Beaut—" And then as I opened my mouth to head him off he came down to earth with: "Very quietly—usually dark blues and browns."

"What jewelry did she wear?"

"I've never seen her wear any."

"Any scars, or moles?" The horrified look on his white face urged me to give him a full shot. "Or warts, or deformities that you know?"

He was speechless, but he managed to shake his head.

"Have you a photograph of her?"

"Yes, I'll show you."

He bounded to his feet, wound his way through the room's excessive furnishings and out through a curtained doorway. Immediately he was back with a large photograph in a carved ivory frame. It was one of these artistic photographs—a thing of shadows and hazy outlines—not much good for identification purposes. She was beautiful—right enough—but that meant nothing; that's the purpose of an artistic photograph.

"This the only one you have?"

"Yes."

"I'll have to borrow it, but I'll get it back to you as soon as I have my copies made."

"No! No!" he protested against having his lady love's face given to a lot of gumshoes. "That would be terrible!"

I finally got it, but it cost me more words than I like to waste on an incidental.

"I want to borrow a couple of her letters, or something in her writing, too," I said.

"For what?"

"To have photostatic copies made. Handwriting specimens come in handy—give you something to go over hotel registers with. Then, even if going under fictitious names, people now and then write notes and make memorandums."

We had another battle, out of which I came with three envelopes and two meaningless sheets of paper, all bearing the girl's angular writing.

"She have much money?" I asked, when the disputed photograph and handwriting specimens were safely tucked away in my pocket.

"I don't know. It's not the sort of thing that one would pry into. She wasn't poor; that is, she didn't have to practice any petty economies; but I haven't the faintest idea either as to the amount of her income or its source. She had an account at the Golden Gate Trust Company, but naturally I don't know anything about its size."

"Many friends here?"

"That's another thing I don't know. I think she knew a few people here, but I don't know who they were. You see, when we were together we never talked about anything but ourselves. There was nothing we were interested in but each other. We were simply—"

"Can't you even make a guess at where she came from, who she was?"

"No. Those things didn't matter to me. She was Jeanne Delano, and that was enough for me."

"Did you and she ever have any financial interests in common? I mean, was there ever any transaction in money or other valuables in which both of you were interested?"

What I meant, of course, was had she got into him for a loan, or had she sold him something, or got money out of him in any other way.

He jumped to his feet, and his face went fog-gray. Then he sat down—slumped down—and blushed scarlet.

"Pardon me," he said thickly. "You didn't know her, and of course you must look at the thing from all angles. No, there was nothing like that. I'm afraid you are going to waste time if you are going to work on the theory that she was an adventuress. There was nothing like that! She was a girl with something terrible hanging over her; something that called her to Baltimore suddenly; something that has taken her away from me. Money? What could money have to do with it? I love her!"

R. F. Axford received me in an office-like room in his Russian Hill residence: a big blond man, whose forty-eight or -nine years had not blurred the outlines of an athlete's body. A big, full-blooded man with the manner of one whose self-confidence is complete and not altogether unjustified. "What's our Burke been up to now?" he asked amusedly when I told him who I was. His voice was a pleasant vibrant bass.

I didn't give him all the details.

"He was engaged to marry a Jeanne Delano, who went East about three weeks ago and then suddenly disappeared. He knows very little about her; thinks something has happened to her; and wants her found."

"Again?" His shrewd blue eyes twinkled. "And to a Jeanne this time! She's the fifth within a year, to my knowledge, and no doubt I missed one or two while I was in Hawaii. But where do I come in?"

"I asked him for responsible endorsement. I think he's all right, but he isn't, in the strictest sense, a responsible person. He referred me to you."

"You're right about his not being, in the strictest sense, a responsible person." The big man screwed up his eyes and mouth in thought for a moment. Then: "Do you think that something has really happened to the girl? Or is Burke imagining things?"

"I don't know. I thought it was a dream at first. But in a couple of her letters there are hints that something was wrong."

"You might go ahead and find her then," Axford said. "I don't suppose any harm will come from letting him have his Jeanne back. It will at least give him something to think about for a while."

"I have your word for it then, Mr. Axford, that there will be no scandal or anything of the sort connected with the affair?"

"Assuredly! Burke is all right, you know. It's simply that he is spoiled. He has been in rather delicate health all his life; and then he has an income that suffices to keep him modestly, with a little over to bring out books of verse and buy doo-daws for his rooms. He takes himself a little too solemnly—is too much the poet—but he's sound at bottom."

"I'll go ahead with it, then," I said, getting up. "By the way, the girl has an account at the Golden Gate Trust Company, and I'd like to find out as much about it as possible, especially where her money came from. Clement, the cashier, is a model of caution when it comes to giving out information about depositors. If you could put in a word for me it would make my way smoother."

"Be glad to."

He wrote a couple of lines across the back of a card and gave it to me; and, promising to call on him if I needed further assistance, I left.

I telephoned Pangburn that his brother-in-law had given the job his approval. I sent a wire to the agency's Baltimore branch, giving what information I had. Then I went up to Ashbury Avenue, to the apartment house in which the girl had lived.

The manager—an immense Mrs. Clute in rustling black—knew little, if any, more about the girl than Pangburn. The girl had lived there for two and a half months; she had had occasional callers, but Pangburn was the only one that the manager could describe to me. The girl had given up the apartment on the third of the month, saying that she had been called East, and she had asked the manager to hold her mail until she sent her new address. Ten days later Mrs. Clute had received a card from the girl instructing her to forward her mail to 215 N. Stricker Street, Baltimore, Maryland. There had been no mail to forward.

The single thing of importance that I learned at the apartment house was that the girl's two trunks had been taken away by a green transfer truck. Green was the color used by one of the city's largest companies.

I went then to the office of this transfer company, and found a friendly clerk on duty. (A detective, if he is wise, takes pains to make and keep as many friends as possible among transfer company, express company and railroad employees.) I left the office with a memorandum of the transfer company's check numbers and the Ferry baggageroom to which the two trunks had been taken.

At the Ferry Building, with this information, it didn't take me many minutes to learn that the trunks had been checked to Baltimore. I sent another wire to the Baltimore branch, giving the railroad check numbers.

Sunday was well into night by now, so I knocked off and went home.

Half an hour before the Golden Gate Trust Company opened for business the next morning I was inside, talking to Clement, the cashier. All the traditional caution and conservatism of bankers rolled together would but be one-two-three to the amount usually displayed by this plump, white-haired old man. But one look at Axford's card, with "*Please give the bearer all possible assistance*" inked across the back of it, made Clement even eager to help me.

"You have, or have had, an account here in the name of Jeanne Delano," I said. "I'd like to know as much as possible about it: to whom she drew checks, and to what amounts; but especially all you can tell me about where her money came from."

He stabbed one of the pearl buttons on his desk with a pink finger, and a lad with polished yellow hair oozed silently into the room. The cashier scribbled with a pencil on a piece of paper and gave it to the noiseless youth, who disappeared. Presently he was back, laying a handful of papers on the cashier's desk.

Clement looked through the papers and then up at me.

"Miss Delano was introduced here by Mr. Burke Pangburn on the sixth of last month, and opened an account with eight hundred and fifty dollars in cash. She made the following deposits after that: four hundred dollars on the tenth; two hundred and fifty on the twenty-first; three hundred on the twenty-sixth; two hundred on the thirtieth; and twenty thousand dollars on the second of this month. All of these deposits except the last were made with cash. The last one was a check."

He handed it to me: a Golden Gate Trust Company check.

Pay to the order of Jeanne Delano, twenty thousand dollars.

(Signed) *Burke Pangburn*

It was dated the second of the month.

"Burke Pangburn!" I exclaimed, a little stupidly. "Was it usual for him to draw checks to that amount?"

"I think not. But we shall see."

He stabbed the pearl button again, ran his pencil across another slip of paper, and the youth with the polished yellow hair made a noiseless entrance, exit, entrance, and exit. The cashier looked through the fresh batch of papers that had been brought to him.

"On the first of the month, Mr. Pangburn deposited twenty thousand dollars—a check against Mr. Axford's account here."

"Now how about Miss Delano's withdrawals?" I asked.

He picked up the papers that had to do with her account again.

"Her statement and canceled checks for last month haven't been delivered to her yet. Everything is here. A check for eighty-five dollars to the order of H. K. Clute on the fifteenth of last month; one 'to cash' for three hundred dollars on the twentieth, and another of the same kind for one hundred dollars on the twenty-fifth. Both of these checks were apparently cashed here by her. On the third of this month she closed out her account, with a check to her own order for twenty-one thousand, five hundred and fifteen dollars."

"And that check?"

"Was cashed here by her."

I lighted a cigarette, and let these figures drift around in my head. None of them—except those that were fixed to Pangburn's and Axford's signatures—seemed to be of any value to me. The Clute check—the only one the girl had drawn in anyone else's favor—had almost certainly been for rent.

"This is the way of it," I summed up aloud. "On the first of the month, Pangburn deposited Axford's check for twenty thousand dollars. The next day he gave a check to that amount to Miss Delano, which she deposited. On the following day she closed her account, taking between twenty-one and twenty-two thousand dollars in currency."

"Exactly," the cashier said.

Before going up to the Glenton Apartments to find out why Pangburn hadn't come clean with me about the twenty thousand dollars, I dropped in at the agency, to see if any word had come from Baltimore. One of the clerks had just finished decoding a telegram. It read:

BAGGAGE ARRIVED MT. ROYAL STATION ON EIGHTH. TAKEN AWAY SAME DAY. UNABLE TO TRACE. 215 NORTH STRICKER STREET IS BALTIMORE ORPHAN ASYLUM. GIRL NOT KNOWN THERE. CONTINUING OUR EFFORTS TO FIND HER.

The Old Man came in from luncheon as I was leaving. I went back into his office with him for a couple of minutes.

"Did you see Pangburn?" he asked.

"Yes. I'm working on his job now—but I think it's a bust."

"What is it?"

"Pangburn is R. F. Axford's brother-in-law. He met a girl a couple of months ago, and fell for her. She sizes up as a worker. He doesn't know anything about her. The first of the month he got twenty thousand dollars from his brother-in-law and passed it over to the girl. She blew, telling him she had been called to Baltimore, and giving him a phony address that turns out to be an orphan asylum. She sent her trunks to Baltimore, and sent him some letters from there—but a friend could have taken care of the baggage and could have remailed her letters for her. Of course, she would have needed a ticket to check the trunks on, but in a twenty-thousand-dollar game that would be a small expense. Pangburn held out on me; he didn't tell me a word about the money. Ashamed of being easy pickings, I reckon. I'm going to the bat with him on it now."

The Old Man smiled his mild smile that might mean anything, and I left.

Ten minutes of ringing Pangburn's bell brought no answer. The elevator boy told me he thought Pangburn hadn't been in all night. I put a note in his box and went down to the railroad company's offices, where I arranged to be notified if an unused Baltimore–San Francisco ticket was turned in for redemption.

That done, I went up to the *Chronicle* office and searched the files for weather conditions during the past month, making a memorandum of four dates upon which it had rained steadily day and night. I carried my memorandum to the offices of the three largest taxicab companies.

That was a trick that had worked well for me before. The girl's apartment was some distance from the street car line, and I was counting upon her having gone out—or having had a caller—on one of those rainy dates. In either case, it was very likely that she—or her caller—had left in a taxi in preference to walking through the rain to the car line. The taxicab companies' daily records would show any calls from her address, and the fares' destinations.

The ideal trick, of course, would have been to have the records searched for the full extent of the girl's occupancy of the apartment; but no taxicab company would stand for having that amount of work thrust upon them, unless it was a matter of life and death. It was difficult enough for me to persuade them to turn clerks loose on the four days I had selected.

I called up Pangburn again after I left that last taxicab office, but he was not at home. I called up Axford's residence, thinking that the poet might have spent the night there, but was told that he had not.

Late that afternoon I got my copies of the girl's photograph and handwriting, and put one of each in the mail for Baltimore. Then I went around to the three taxicab companies' offices and got my reports. Two of them had nothing for me. The third's records showed two calls from the girl's apartment.

On one rainy afternoon a taxi had been called, and one passenger had been taken to the Glenton Apartments. That passenger, obviously, was either the girl or Pangburn. At half past twelve one night another call had come in, and this passenger had been taken to the Marquis Hotel.

The driver who had answered this second call remembered it indistinctly when I questioned him, but he thought that his fare had been a man. I let the matter rest there for the time; the Marquis isn't a large hotel as San Francisco hotels go, but it is too large to make canvassing its guests for the one I wanted practicable.

I spent the evening trying to reach Pangburn, with no success. At eleven o'clock I called up Axford, and asked him if he had any idea where I might find his brother-in-law.

"Haven't seen him for several days," the millionaire said. "He was supposed to come up for dinner last night, but didn't. My wife tried to reach him by phone a couple times today, but couldn't."

The next morning I called Pangburn's apartment before I got out of bed, and got no answer.

Then I telephoned Axford and made an appointment for ten o'clock at his office.

"I don't know what he's up to now," Axford said good-naturedly when I told him that Pangburn had apparently been away from his apartment since Sunday, "and I suppose there's small chance of guessing. Our Burke is nothing if not erratic. How are you progressing with your search for the damsel in distress?"

"Far enough to convince me that she isn't in a whole lot of distress. She got twenty thousand dollars from your brother-in-law the day before she vanished."

"Twenty thousand dollars from Burke? She must be a wonderful girl! But wherever did he get that much money?"

"From you."

Axford's muscular body straightened in his chair. "From me?"

"Yes—your check."

"He did not."

There was nothing argumentative in his voice; it simply stated a fact.

"You didn't give him a check for twenty thousand dollars on the first of the month?"

"No."

"Then," I suggested, "perhaps we'd better take a run over to the Golden Gate Trust Company."

Ten minutes later we were in Clement's office.

"I'd like to see my canceled checks," Axford told the cashier.

The youth with the polished yellow hair brought them in presently—a thick wad of them—and Axford ran rapidly through them until he found the one he wanted. He studied that one for a long while, and when he looked up at me he shook his head slowly but with finality.

"I've never seen it before."

Clement mopped his head with a white handkerchief, and tried to pretend that he wasn't burning up with curiosity and fears that his bank had been gypped.

The millionaire turned the check over and looked at the endorsement.

"Deposited by Burke," he said in the voice of one who talks while he thinks of something entirely different, "on the first."

"Could we talk to the teller who took in the twenty-thousand-dollar check that Miss Delano deposited?" I asked Clement.

He pressed one of his desk's pearl buttons with a fumbling pink finger, and in a minute or two a little sallow man with a hairless head came in.

"Do you remember taking a check for twenty thousand from Miss Jeanne Delano a few weeks ago?" I asked him.

"Yes, sir! Yes, sir! Perfectly."

"Just what do you remember about it?"

"Well, sir, Miss Delano came to my window with Mr. Burke Pangburn. It was his check. I thought it was a large check for him to be drawing, but the bookkeepers said he had enough money in his account to cover it. They stood there—Miss Delano and Mr. Pangburn—talking and laughing while I entered the deposit in her book, and then they left, and that was all."

"This check," Axford said slowly, after the teller had gone back to his cage, "is a forgery. But I shall make it good, of course. That ends the matter, Mr. Clement, and there must be no more to-do about it."

"Certainly, Mr. Axford. Certainly."

Clement was all enormously relieved smiles and head-noddings, with this twenty-thousand-dollar load lifted from his bank's shoulders.

Axford and I left the bank then and got into his coupé, in which we had come from his office. But he did not immediately start the engine. He sat for a while staring at the traffic of Montgomery Street with unseeing eyes.

"I want you to find Burke," he said presently, and there was no emotion of any sort in his bass voice. "I want you to find him without risking the least whisper of scandal. If my wife knew of all this— She mustn't know. She thinks her brother is a choice morsel. I want you to find him for me. The girl doesn't matter any more, but I suppose that where you find one you will find the other. I'm not interested in the money, and I don't want you to make any special attempt to recover that; it could hardly be done, I'm afraid, without publicity. I want you to find Burke before he does something else."

"If you want to avoid the wrong kind of publicity," I said, "your best bet is to spread the right kind first. Let's advertise him as missing, fill the papers up with his pictures and so forth. They'll play him up strong. He's your brother-in-law and he's a poet. We can say that he has been ill—you told me that he had been in delicate health all his life—and that we fear he has dropped dead somewhere or is suffering under some mental derangement. There will be no necessity of mentioning the girl or the money, and our explanation may keep people—especially your wife—from guessing the truth when the fact that he is missing leaks out. It's bound to leak out somehow."

He didn't like my idea at first, but I finally won him over.

We went up to Pangburn's apartment then, easily securing admittance on Axford's explanation that we had an engagement with him and would wait there for him. I went through the rooms inch by inch, prying into each hole and hollow and crack; reading everything that was written anywhere, even down to his manuscripts; and I found nothing that threw any light on his disappearance.

I helped myself to his photographs—pocketing five of the dozen or more that were there. Axford did not think that any of the poet's bags or trunks were missing from the pack-room. I did not find his Golden Gate Trust Company deposit book.

I spent the rest of the day loading the newspapers up with what we wished them to have; and they gave my ex-client one grand spread: first-page stuff with photographs and all possible trimmings. Anyone in San Francisco who didn't know that Burke Pangburn—brother-in-law of R. F. Axford and author of *Sand-patches and Other Verse*—was missing, either couldn't read or wouldn't.

This advertising brought results. By the following morning, reports were rolling in from all directions, from dozens of people who had seen the missing poet in dozens of places. A few of these reports looked promising—or at least possible—but the majority were ridiculous on their faces.

I came back to the agency from running out one that had—until run out—looked good, to find a note asking me to call up Axford.

"Can you come down to my office now?" he asked when I got him on the wire.

There was a lad of twenty-one or -two with Axford when I was ushered into his office: a narrow-chested, dandified lad of the sporting clerk type.

"This is Mr. Fall, one of my employees," Axford told me. "He said he saw Burke Sunday night."

"Where?" I asked Fall.

"Going into a roadhouse near Halfmoon Bay."

"Sure it was him?"

"Absolutely! I've seen him come in here to Mr. Axford's office often enough to know him. It was him all right."

"How'd you come to see him?"

"I was coming up from further down the shore with some friends, and we stopped in at the roadhouse to get something to eat. As we were leaving, a car drove up and Mr. Pangburn and a girl or woman—I didn't notice her particularly—got out and went inside. I didn't think anything of it until I saw in the paper last night that he hadn't been seen since Sunday. So then I thought to myself that—"

"What roadhouse was this?" I cut in.

"The White Shack."

"About what time?"

"Somewhere between eleven-thirty and midnight, I guess."

"He see you?"

"No. I was already in our car when he drove up."

"What did the woman look like?"

"I don't know. I didn't see her face, and I can't remember how she was dressed or even if she was short or tall."

That was all Fall could tell me. We shooed him out of the office, and I used Axford's telephone to call up "Wop" Healey's dive in North Beach and leave word that when "Porky" Grout came in he was to call up "Jack." That was a standing arrangement by which I got word to Porky whenever I wanted to see him, without giving anybody a chance to tumble to the connection between us.

"Know the White Shack?" I asked Axford, when I was through.

"I know where it is, but I don't know anything about it."

"Well, it's a tough hole. Run by 'Tin-Star' Joplin, an ex-yegg who invested his winnings in the place when Prohibition made the roadhouse game good. He makes more money now than he ever heard of in his piking safe-ripping days. Retailing liquor is a sideline with him; his real profit comes from acting as a relay station for the booze that comes through Halfmoon Bay for points beyond; and the dope is that half the booze put ashore by the Pacific rum fleet is put ashore in Halfmoon Bay.

"The White Shack is a tough hole, and it's no place for your brother-in-law to be hanging around. I can't go down there myself without stirring things up; Joplin and I are old friends.

But I've got a man I can put in there for a few nights. Pangburn may be a regular visitor, or he may even be staying there. He wouldn't be the first one Joplin had ever let hide out there. I'll put this man of mine in the place for a week, anyway, and see what he can find."

"It's all in your hands," Axford said.

From Axford's office I went straight to my rooms, left the outer door unlocked, and sat down to wait for Porky Grout. I had waited an hour and a half when he pushed the door open and came in. "'Lo! How's tricks?" He swaggered to a chair, leaned back in it, put his feet on the table and reached for a pack of cigarettes that lay there.

That was Porky Grout. A pasty-faced man in his thirties, neither large nor small, always dressed flashily—even if sometimes dirtily—and trying to hide an enormous cowardice behind a swaggering carriage, a blustering habit of speech, and an exaggerated pretense of self-assurance.

But I had known him for three years; so now I crossed the room and pushed his feet roughly off the table, almost sending him over backward.

"What's the idea?" He came to his feet, crouching and snarling. "Where do you get that stuff? Do you want a smack in the—"

I took a step toward him. He sprang away, across the room.

"Aw, I didn't mean nothin'. I was only kiddin'!"

"Shut up and sit down," I advised him.

I had known this Porky Grout for three years, and had been using him for nearly that long, and I didn't know a single thing that could be said in his favor. He was a coward. He was a liar. He was a thief, and a hop-head. He was a traitor to his kind and, if not watched, to his employers. A nice bird to deal with! But detecting is a hard business, and you use whatever tools come to hand. This Porky was an effective tool if handled right, which meant keeping your hand on his throat all the time and checking up every piece of information he brought in.

His cowardice was—for my purpose—his greatest asset. It was notorious throughout the criminal Coast; and though nobody—crook or not—could possibly think him a man to be trusted, nevertheless he was not actually distrusted. Most of his fellows thought him too much the coward to be dangerous; they thought he would be afraid to betray them; afraid of the summary vengeance that crookdom visits upon the squealer. But they didn't take into account Porky's gift for convincing himself that he was a lion-hearted fellow, when no danger was near. So he went freely where he desired and where I sent him, and brought me otherwise unobtainable bits of information.

For nearly three years I had used him with considerable success, paying him well, and keeping him under my heel. *Informant* was the polite word that designated him in my reports; the underworld has even less lovely names than the common *stool-pigeon* to denote his kind.

"I have a job for you," I told him, now that he was seated again, with his feet on the floor. His loose mouth twitched up at the left corner, pushing that eye into a knowing squint. "I thought so." He always says something like that.

"I want you to go down to Halfmoon Bay and stick around Tin-Star Joplin's joint for a few nights. Here are two photos"—sliding one of Pangburn and one of the girl across the table. "Their names and descriptions are written on the backs. I want to know if either of them shows up down there, what they're doing, and where they're hanging out. It may be that Tin-Star is covering them up."

Porky was looking knowingly from one picture to the other. "I think I know this guy," he said out of the corner of his mouth that twitches. That's another thing about Porky. You can't mention a name or give a description that won't bring that same remark, even though you make them up.

"Here's some money." I slid some bills across the table. "If you're down there more than a couple of nights. I'll get some more to you. Keep in touch with me, either over this phone or the under-cover one at the office. And—remember this—lay off the stuff! If I come down there and find you all snowed up, I promise that I'll tip Joplin off to you."

He had finished counting the money by now—there wasn't a whole lot to count—and he threw it contemptuously back on the table.

"Save that for newspapers," he sneered. "How am I goin' to get anywheres if I can't spend no money in the joint?"

"That's plenty for a couple of days' expenses; you'll probably knock back half of it. If you stay longer than a couple of days, I'll get more to you. And you get your pay when the job is done, and not before."

He shook his head and got up. "I'm tired of pikin' along with you. You can turn your own jobs. I'm through!"

"If you don't get down to Halfmoon Bay tonight, you *are* through," I assured him, letting him get out of the threat whatever he liked.

After a little while, of course, he took the money and left. The dispute over expense money was simply a preliminary that went with every job I sent him out on.

After Porky had cleared out, I leaned back in my chair and burned half a dozen Fatimas over the job. The girl had gone first with the twenty thousand dollars, and then the poet had gone; and both had gone, whether permanently or not, to the White Shack. On its face, the job was an obvious affair. The girl had given Pangburn the *work* to the extent of having him forge a check against his brother-in-law's account; and then, after various moves whose value I couldn't determine at the time, they had gone into hiding together.

There were two loose ends to be taken care of. One of them—the finding of the confederate who had mailed the letters to Pangburn and who had taken care of the girl's baggage—was in the Baltimore branch's hands. The other was: Who had ridden in the taxicab that I had traced from the girl's apartment to the Marquis Hotel?

That might not have any bearing upon the job, or it might. Suppose I could find a connection between the Marquis Hotel and the White Shack. That would make a completed chain of some sort. I searched the back of the telephone directory and found the roadhouse number. Then I went up to the Marquis Hotel. The girl on duty at the hotel switchboard, when I got there, was one with whom I had done business before. "Who's been calling Halfmoon Bay numbers?" I asked her.

"My God!" She leaned back in her chair and ran a pink hand gently over the front of her rigidly waved red hair. "I got enough to do without remembering every call that goes through. This ain't a boarding-house. We have more'n one call a week."

"You don't have many Halfmoon Bay calls," I insisted, leaning an elbow on the counter and letting a folded five-spot peep out between the fingers of one hand. "You ought to remember any you've had lately."

"I'll see," she sighed, as if willing to do her best on a hopeless task.

She ran through her tickets.

"Here's one—from room 522, a couple weeks ago."

"What number was called?"

"Halfmoon Bay 51."

That was the roadhouse number. I passed over the five-spot.

"Is 522 a permanent guest?"

"Yes. Mr. Kilcourse. He's been here three or four months."

"What is he?"

"I don't know. A perfect gentleman, if you ask me."

"That's nice. What does he look like?"

"He's a young man, but his hair is turning gray. He's dark and handsome. Looks like a movie actor."

"Bull Montana?" I asked, as I moved off toward the desk.

The key to 522 was in its place in the rack. I sat down where I could keep an eye on it. Perhaps an hour later a clerk took it out and gave it to a man who did look somewhat like an actor. He was a man of thirty or so, with dark skin, and dark hair that showed gray around the ears. He stood a good six feet of fashionably dressed slenderness.

Carrying the key, he disappeared into an elevator.

I called up the agency then and asked the Old Man to send Dick Foley over. Ten minutes later Dick arrived. He's a little shrimp of a Canadian— there isn't a hundred and ten pounds of him— who is the smoothest shadow I've ever seen, and I've seen most of them.

"I have a bird in here I want tailed," I told Dick. "His name is Kilcourse and he's in room 522. Stick around outside, and I'll give you the spot on him." I went back to the lobby and waited some more.

At eight o'clock Kilcourse came down and left the hotel. I went after him for half a block—far enough to turn him over to Dick— and then went home, so that I would be within reach of a telephone if Porky Grout tried to get in touch with me. No call came from him that night.

When I arrived at the agency the next morning, Dick was waiting for me. "What luck?" I asked.

"Damnedest!" The little Canadian talks like a telegram when his peace of mind is disturbed, and just now he was decidedly peevish. "Took me two blocks. Shook me. Only taxi in sight."

"Think he made you?"

"No. Wise head. Playing safe."

"Try him again, then. Better have a car handy, in case he tries the same trick again."

My telephone jingled as Dick was going out. It was Porky Grout, talking over the agency's unlisted line. "Turn up anything?" I asked.

"Plenty," he bragged.

"Good! Are you in town?"

"Yes."

"I'll meet you in my rooms in twenty minutes," I said.

The pasty-faced informant was fairly bloated with pride in himself when he came through the door I had left unlocked for him. His swagger was almost a cakewalk; and the side of his mouth that twitches was twisted into a knowing leer that would have fit a Solomon.

"I knocked it over for you, kid," he boasted. "Nothin' to it—for me! I went down there and talked to ever'body that knowed anything, seen ever'thing there was to see, and put the X-rays on the whole dump. I made a—"

"Uh-huh," I interrupted. "Congratulations and so forth. But just what did you turn up?"

"Now le'me tell you." He raised a dirty hand in a traffic-cop sort of gesture. "Don't crowd me. I'll give you all the dope."

"Sure," I said. "I know. You're great, and I'm lucky to have you to knock off my jobs for me, and all that! But is Pangburn down there?"

"I'm gettin' around to that. I went down there and—"

"Did you see Pangburn?"

"As I was sayin', I went down there and—"

"Porky," I said, "I don't give a damn what you did! Did you see Pangburn?"

"Yes. I seen him."

"Fine! Now what did you see?"

"He's camping down there with Tin-Star. Him and the broad that you give me a picture of are both there. She's been there a month. I didn't see her, but one of the waiters told me about her. I seen Pangburn myself. They don't show themselves much—stick back in Tin-Star's part of the joint—where he lives—most of the time. Pangburn's been there since Sunday. I went down there and—"

"Learn who the girl is? Or anything about what they're up to?"

"No. I went down there and—"

"All right! *Went down there* again tonight. Call me up as soon as you know positively Pangburn is there—that he hasn't gone out. Don't make any mistakes. I don't want to come down there and scare them up on a false alarm. Use the agency's under-cover line, and just tell whoever answers that you won't be in town until late. That'll mean that Pangburn is there; and it'll let you call up from Joplin's without giving the play away."

"I got to have more dough," he said, as he got up. "It costs—"

"I'll file your application," I promised. "Now beat it, and let me hear from you tonight, the minute you're sure Pangburn is there."

Then I went up to Axford's office. "I think I have a line on him," I told the millionaire. "I hope to have him where you can talk to him tonight. My man says he was at the White Shack last night, and is probably living there. If he's there tonight, I'll take you down, if you want."

"Why can't we go now?"

"No. The place is too dead in the daytime for my man to hang around without making himself conspicuous, and I don't want to take any chances on either you or me showing ourselves there until we're sure we're coming face to face with Pangburn."

"What do you want me to do then?"

"Have a fast car ready tonight, and be ready to start as soon as I get word to you."

"Righto. I'll be at home after five-thirty. Phone me as soon as you're ready to go, and I'll pick you up."

At nine-thirty that evening I was sitting beside Axford on the front seat of a powerfully engined foreign car, and we were roaring down a road that led to Halfmoon Bay. Porky's telephone call had come.

Neither of us talked much during that ride, and the imported monster under us made it a short ride. Axford sat comfortable and relaxed at the wheel, but I noticed for the first time that he had a rather heavy jaw.

The White Shack is a large building, square-built of imitation stone. It is set away back from the road, and is approached by two curving driveways, which, together, make a semi-circle whose diameter is the public road. The center of this semi-circle is occupied by sheds under which Joplin's patrons stow their cars, and here and there around the sheds are flower-beds and clumps of shrubbery. We were still going at a fair clip when we turned into one end of this semi-circular driveway, and—

Axford slammed on his brakes, and the big machine threw us into the windshield as it jolted into an abrupt stop—barely in time to avoid smashing into a cluster of people who had suddenly loomed up.

In the glow of our headlights faces stood sharply out; white, horrified faces, furtive faces, faces that were callously curious. Below the faces, white arms and shoulders showed, and bright gowns and jewelry, against the duller background of masculine clothing.

This was the first impression I got, and then, by the time I had removed my face from the windshield, I realized that this cluster of people had a core, a thing about which it centered. I stood up, trying to look over the crowd's heads, but I could see nothing.

Jumping down to the driveway, I pushed through the crowd.

Face down on the white gravel a man sprawled—a thin man in dark clothes—and just above his collar, where the head and neck join, was a hole. I knelt to peer into his face. Then I pushed through the crowd again, back to where Axford was just getting out of the car, the engine of which was still running. "Pangburn is dead— shot!"

Methodically, Axford took off his gloves, folded them and put them in a pocket. Then he nodded his understanding of what I had told him, and walked toward where the crowd stood around the dead poet. I looked after him until he had vanished in the throng. Then I went winding through the outskirts of the crowd, hunting for Porky Grout.

I found him standing on the porch, leaning against a pillar. I passed where he could see me, and went on around to the side of the roadhouse that afforded most shadow.

In the shadows Porky joined me. The night wasn't cool, but his teeth were chattering. "Who got him?" I demanded.

"I don't know," he whined, and that was the first thing of which I had ever known him to confess complete ignorance. "I was inside, keepin' an eye on the others."

"What others?"

"Tin-Star, and some guy I never seen before,

and the broad. I didn't think the kid was going out. He didn't have no hat."

"What *do* you know about it?"

"A little while after I phoned you, the girl and Pangburn came out from Joplin's part of the joint and sat down at a table around on the other side of the porch, where it's fairly dark. They eat for a while and then this other guy comes over and sits down with 'em. I don't know his name, but I think I've saw him around town. He's a tall guy, in fancy rags."

That would be Kilcourse.

"They talk for a while and then Joplin joins 'em. They sit around the table laughin' and talkin' for maybe a quarter of an hour. Then Pangburn gets up and goes indoors. I got a table that I can watch 'em from, and the place is crowded, and I'm afraid I'll lose my table if I leave it, so I don't follow the kid. He ain't got no hat; I figure he ain't goin' nowhere. But he must of gone through the house and out front, because pretty soon there's a noise that I thought was a auto backfire, and then the sound of a car gettin' away quick. And then some guy squawks that there's a dead man outside. Ever'body runs out here, and it's Pangburn."

"You dead sure that Joplin, Kilcourse and the girl were all at the table when Pangburn was killed?"

"Absolutely," Porky said, "if this dark guy's name is Kilcourse."

"Where are they now?"

"Back in Joplin's hang-out. They went up there as soon as they seen Pangburn had been croaked."

I had no illusions about Porky. I knew he was capable of selling me out and furnishing the poet's murderer with an alibi. But there was this about it: if Joplin, Kilcourse or the girl had fixed him, and had fixed my informant, then it was hopeless for me to try to prove that they weren't on the rear porch when the shot was fired. Joplin had a crowd of hangers-on who would swear to anything he told them without batting an eye. There would be a dozen supposed witnesses to their presence on the rear porch.

Thus the only thing for me to do was to take it for granted that Porky was coming clean with me. "Have you seen Dick Foley?" I asked, since Dick had been shadowing Kilcourse.

"No."

"Hunt around and see if you can find him. Tell him I've gone up to talk to Joplin, and tell him to come on up. Then you can stick around where I can get hold of you if I want you."

I went in through a French window, crossed an empty dance-floor and went up the stairs that led to Tin-Star Joplin's living quarters in the rear second story. I knew the way, having been up there before. Joplin and I were old friends.

I was going up now to give him and his friends a shake-down on the off-chance that some good might come of it, though I knew that I had nothing on any of them. I could have tied something on the girl, of course, but not without advertising the fact that the dead poet had forged his brother-in-law's signature to a check. And that was no go.

"Come in," a heavy, familiar voice called when I rapped on Joplin's living-room door. I pushed the door open and went in.

Tin-Star Joplin was standing in the middle of the floor: a big-bodied ex-yegg with inordinately thick shoulders and an expressionless horse face. Beyond him Kilcourse sat dangling one leg from the corner of a table, alertness hiding behind an amused half-smile on his handsome dark face. On the other side of the room a girl whom I knew for Jeanne Delano sat on the arm of a big leather chair. And the poet hadn't exaggerated when he told me she was beautiful.

"You!" Joplin grunted disgustedly as soon as he recognized me. "What the hell do *you* want?"

"What've you got?"

My mind wasn't on this sort of repartee, however; I was studying the girl. There was something vaguely familiar about her—but I couldn't place her. Perhaps I hadn't see her before; perhaps much looking at the picture Pangburn had given me was responsible for my feeling of recognition. Pictures will do that.

Meanwhile, Joplin had said: "Time to waste is one thing I ain't got."

And I had said: "If you'd saved up all the time different judges have given you, you'd have plenty."

I had seen the girl somewhere before. She was a slender girl in a glistening blue gown that exhibited a generous spread of front, back and arms that were worth showing. She had a mass of dark brown hair above an oval face of the color that pink ought to be. Her eyes were wide-set and a gray shade that wasn't altogether unlike the shadows on polished silver that the poet had compared them to. I studied the girl, and she looked back at me with level eyes, and still I couldn't place her. Kilcourse still sat dangling a leg from the table corner.

Joplin grew impatient: "Will you stop gandering at the girl, and tell me what you want of me?" he growled.

The girl smiled then, a mocking smile that bared the edges of razor-sharp little animal-teeth. And with the smile I knew her!

Her hair and skin had fooled me. The last time I had seen her—the only time I had seen her before—her face had been marble-white, and her hair had been short and the color of fire. She and an older woman and three men and I had played hide-and-seek one evening in a house in Turk Street over a matter of the murder of a bank messenger and the theft of a hundred thousand dollars' worth of Liberty Bonds. Through her intriguing, three of her accomplices had died that evening, and the fourth—the Chinese—had eventually gone to the gallows at Folsom Prison. Her name had been Elvira then, and since her escape from the house that night we had been fruitlessly hunting her from border to border, and beyond.

Recognition must have shown in my eyes in spite of the effort I made to keep them blank, for, as swift as a snake, she had left the arm of the chair and was coming forward, her eyes more steel than silver.

I put my gun in sight.

Joplin took a half-step toward me. "What's the idea?" he barked.

Kilcourse slid off the table, and one of his thin dark hands hovered over his necktie.

"This is the idea," I told them. "I want the girl for a murder a couple of months back, and maybe—I'm not sure—for tonight's. Anyway, I'm—"

The snapping of a light-switch behind me, and the room went black.

I moved, not caring where I went so long as I got away from where I had been when the lights went out.

My back touched a wall and I stopped, crouching low.

"Quick, kid!" A hoarse whisper that came from where I thought the door should be.

But both of the room's doors, I thought, were closed, and could hardly be opened without showing gray rectangles. People moved in the blackness, but none got between me and the lighter square of windows.

Something clicked softly in front of me—too thin a click for the cocking of a gun—but it could have been the opening of a spring-knife, and I remembered that Tin-Star Joplin had a fondness for that weapon.

"Let's go!" A harsh whisper that cut through the dark like a blow.

Sounds of motion, muffled, indistinguishable . . . one sound not far away . . .

Abruptly a strong hand clamped one of my shoulders, a hard-muscled body strained against me. I stabbed out with my gun, and heard a grunt.

The hand moved up my shoulder toward my throat.

I snapped up a knee, and heard another grunt.

A burning point ran down my side.

I stabbed again with my gun—pulled it back until the muzzle was free of the soft obstacle that had stopped it, and squeezed the trigger. The crash of the shot. Joplin's voice in my ear, a curiously matter-of-fact voice: "God damn! That got me."

I spun away from him then, toward where I saw the dim yellow of an open door. I had heard no sounds of departure. I had been too busy. But I knew that Joplin had tied into me while the others made their get-away.

Nobody was in sight as I jumped, slid, tumbled down the steps—any number at a time. A waiter got in my path as I plunged toward the dance-floor. I don't know whether his interference was intentional or not. I didn't ask. I slammed the flat of my gun in his face and went on. Once I jumped a leg that came out to trip me; and at the outer door I had to smear another face.

Then I was out in the semi-circular driveway, from one end of which a red tail-light was turning east into the country road.

While I sprinted for Axford's car I noticed that Pangburn's body had been removed. A few people still stood around the spot where he had lain, and they gaped at me now with open mouths.

The car was as Axford had left it, with idling engine. I swung it through a flower-bed and pointed it east on the public road. Five minutes later I picked up the red point of a tail-light again.

The car under me had more power than I would ever need, more than I would have known how to handle. I don't know how fast the one ahead was going, but I closed in as if it had been standing still.

A mile and a half, or perhaps two—

Suddenly a man was in the road ahead—a little beyond the reach of my lights. The lights caught him, and I saw that it was Porky Grout!

Porky Grout standing facing me in the middle of the road, the dull metal of an automatic in each hand.

The guns in his hands seemed to glow dimly red and then go dark in the glare of my headlights—glow and then go dark, like two bulbs in an automatic electric sign.

The windshield fell apart around me.

Porky Grout—the informant whose name was a synonym for cowardice the full length of the Pacific Coast—stood in the center of the road shooting at a metal comet that rushed down upon him. . . .

I didn't see the end.

I confess frankly that I shut my eyes when his set white face showed close over my radiator. The metal monster under me trembled—

not very much—and the road ahead was empty except for the fleeing red light. My windshield was gone. The wind tore at my uncovered hair and brought tears to my squinted-up eyes.

Presently I found that I was talking to myself, saying, "That was Porky. That was Porky." It was an amazing fact. It was no surprise that he had double-crossed me. That was to be expected. And for him to have crept up the stairs behind me and turned off the lights wasn't astonishing. But for him to have stood straight up and died—

An orange streak from the car ahead cut off my wonderment. The bullet didn't come near me—it isn't easy to shoot accurately from one moving car into another—but at the pace I was going it wouldn't be long before I was close enough for good shooting.

I turned on the searchlight above the dashboard. It didn't quite reach the car ahead, but it enabled me to see that the girl was driving. While Kilcourse sat screwed around beside her, facing me. The car was a yellow roadster.

I eased up a little. In a duel with Kilcourse here I would have been at a disadvantage, since I would have had to drive as well as shoot. My best play seemed to be to hold my distance until we reached a town, as we inevitably must. It wasn't midnight yet. There would be people on the streets of any town, and policemen. Then I could close in with a better chance of coming off on top.

A few miles of this and my prey tumbled to my plan. The yellow roadster slowed down, wavered, and came to rest with its length across the road. Kilcourse and the girl were out immediately and crouching in the road on the far side of their barricade.

I was tempted to dive pell-mell into them, but it was a weak temptation, and when its short life had passed I put on the brakes and stopped. Then I fiddled with my searchlight until it bore full upon the roadster.

A flash came from somewhere near the roadster's wheels, and the searchlight shook violently, but the glass wasn't touched. It would be their first target, of course, and . . .

Crouching in my car, waiting for the bullet that would smash the lens, I took off my shoes and overcoat.

The third bullet ruined the light.

I switched off the other lights, jumped to the road, and when I stopped running I was squatting down against the near side of the yellow roadster. As easy and safe a trick as can be imagined.

The girl and Kilcourse had been looking into the glare of a powerful light. When that light suddenly died, and the weaker ones around it went, too, they were left in pitch unseeing blackness, which must last for the minute or longer that their eyes would need to readjust themselves to the gray-black of the night. My stockinged feet had made no sound on the macadam road, and now there was only a roadster between us; and I knew it and they didn't.

From near the radiator Kilcourse spoke softly:

"I'm going to try to knock him off from the ditch. Take a shot at him now and then to keep him busy."

"I can't see him," the girl protested.

"Your eyes'll be all right in a second. Take a shot at the car anyway."

I moved toward the radiator as the girl's pistol barked at the empty touring car.

Kilcourse, on hands and knees, was working his way toward the ditch that ran along the south side of the road. I gathered my legs under me, intent upon a spring and a blow with my gun upon the back of his head. I didn't want to kill him, but I wanted to put him out of the way quick. I'd have the girl to take care of, and she was at least as dangerous as he.

As I tensed for the spring, Kilcourse, guided perhaps by some instinct of the hunted, turned his head and saw me—saw a threatening shadow.

Instead of jumping I fired.

I didn't look to see whether I had hit him or not. At that range there was little likelihood of missing. I bent double and slipped back to the rear of the roadster, keeping on my side of it. Then I waited.

The girl did what I would perhaps have done in her place. She didn't shoot or move toward the place the shot had come from. She thought I had forestalled Kilcourse in using the ditch and that my next play would be to circle around behind her. To offset this, she moved around the rear of the roadster, so that she could ambush me from the side nearest Axford's car.

Thus it was that she came creeping around the corner and poked her delicately chiseled nose plunk into the muzzle of the gun that I held ready for her.

She gave a little scream.

Women aren't always reasonable: they are prone to disregard trifles like guns held upon them. So I grabbed her gun hand, which was fortunate for me. As my hand closed around the weapon, she pulled the trigger, catching a chunk of my forefinger between hammer and frame. I twisted the gun out of her hand; released my finger.

But she wasn't done yet. With me standing there holding a gun not four inches from her body, she turned and bolted off toward where a clump of trees made a jet-black blot to the north.

When I recovered from my surprise at this amateurish procedure, I stuck both her gun and mine in my pockets, and set out after her, tearing the soles of my feet at every step.

She was trying to get over a wire fence when I caught her.

"Stop playing, will you?" I said crossly, as I set the fingers of my left hand around her wrist and started to lead her back to the roadster. "This is a serious business. Don't be so childish!"

"You are hurting my arm."

I knew I wasn't hurting her arm, and I knew this girl for the direct cause of four, or perhaps five, deaths; yet I loosened my grip on her wrist until it wasn't much more than a friendly clasp. She went back willingly enough to the roadster, where, still holding her wrist, I switched on the lights. Kilcourse lay just beneath the headlight's glare, huddled on his face, with one knee drawn up under him.

I put the girl squarely in the line of light.

"Now stand there," I said, "and behave. The first break you make, I'm going to shoot a leg out from under you," and I meant it.

I found Kilcourse's gun, pocketed it, and knelt beside him.

He was dead, with a bullet-hole above his collar-bone.

"Is he—" her mouth trembled.

"Yes."

She looked down at him, and shivered a little.

"Poor Fag," she whispered.

I've gone on record as saying that this girl was beautiful, and, standing there in the dazzling white of the headlights, she was more than that. She was the thing to start crazy thoughts even in the head of an unimaginative middle-aged thief-catcher. She was—

Anyhow, I suppose that is why I scowled at her and said:

"Yes, poor Fag, and poor Hook, and poor Tai, and poor kid of a Los Angeles bank messenger, and poor Burke," calling the roll, as far as I knew it, of men who had died loving her.

She didn't flare up. Her big gray eyes lifted, and she looked at me with a gaze that I couldn't fathom, and her lovely oval face under the mass of brown hair—which I knew was phony—was sad.

"I suppose you do think—" she began.

But I had had enough of this; I was uncomfortable along the spine.

"Come on," I said. "We'll leave Kilcourse and the roadster here for now."

She said nothing, but went with me to Axford's big machine, and sat in silence while I laced my shoes. I found a robe on the back seat for her.

"Better wrap this around your shoulders. The windshield is gone. It'll be cool."

She followed my suggestion without a word, but when I had edged our vehicle around the rear of the roadster, and had straightened out in the road again, going east, she laid a hand on my arm.

"Aren't we going back to the White Shack?"

"No. Redwood City—the county jail."

A mile perhaps, during which, without looking at her, I knew she was studying my rather lumpy profile. Then her hand was on my forearm again and she was leaning toward me so that her breath was warm against my cheek. "Will you stop for a minute? There's something—some things I want to tell you."

I brought the car to a halt in a cleared space of hard soil off to one side of the road, and screwed myself a little around in the seat to face her more directly.

"Before you start," I told her, "I want you to understand that we stay here for just so long as you talk about the Pangburn affair. When you get off on any other line—then we finish our trip to Redwood City."

"Aren't you even interested in the Los Angeles affair?"

"No. That's closed. You and Hook Riordan and Tai Choon Tau and the Quarres were equally responsible for the messenger's death, even if Hook did the actual killing. Hook and the Quarres passed out the night we had our party in Turk Street. Tai was hanged last month. Now I've got you. We had enough evidence to swing the Chinese, and we've even more against you. That is done—finished—completed. If you want to tell me anything about Pangburn's death, I'll listen. Otherwise—"

I reached for the self-starter.

A pressure of her fingers on my arm stopped me.

"I do want to tell you about it," she said earnestly. "I want you to know the truth about it. You'll take me to Redwood City, I know. Don't think that I expect—that I have any foolish hopes. But I'd like you to know the truth about this thing. I don't know why I should care especially what you think, but—"

Her voice dwindled off to nothing.

Then she began to talk very rapidly—as people talk when they fear interruptions before their stories are told—and she sat leaning slightly forward, so that her beautiful oval face was very close to mine.

"After I ran out of the Turk Street house that

night—while you were struggling with Tai—my intention was to get away from San Francisco. I had a couple of thousand dollars, enough to carry me any place. Then I thought that going away would be what you people would expect me to do, and that the safest thing for me to do would be to stay right here. It isn't hard for a woman to change her appearance. I had bobbed red hair, white skin, and wore gay clothes. I simply dyed my hair, bought these transformations to make it look long, put color on my face, and bought some dark clothes. Then I took an apartment on Ashbury Avenue under the name of Jeanne Delano, and I was an altogether different person.

"But, while I knew I was perfectly safe from recognition anywhere, I felt more comfortable staying indoors for a while, and, to pass the time, I read a good deal. That's how I happened to run across Burke's book. Do you read poetry?"

I shook my head. An automobile going toward Halfmoon Bay came into sight just then—the first one we'd seen since we left the White Shack. She waited until it had passed before she went on, still talking rapidly.

"Burke wasn't a genius, of course, but there was something about some of his things that— something that got inside me. I wrote him a little note, telling him how much I had enjoyed these things, and sent it to his publishers. A few days later I had a note from Burke, and I learned that he lived in San Francisco. I hadn't known that.

"We exchanged several notes, and then he asked if he could call, and we met. I don't know whether I was in love with him or not, even at first. I did like him, and, between the ardor of his love for me and the flattery of having a fairly well-known poet for a suitor, I really thought that I loved him. I promised to marry him.

"I hadn't told him anything about myself, though now I know that it wouldn't have made any difference to him. But I was afraid to tell him the truth, and I wouldn't lie to him, so I told him nothing.

"Then Fag Kilcourse saw me one day on the street, and knew me in spite of my new hair,

complexion and clothes. Fag hadn't much brains, but he had eyes that could see through anything. I don't blame Fag. He acted according to his code. He came up to my apartment, having followed me home; and I told him that I was going to marry Burke and be a respectable housewife. That was dumb of me. Fag was square. If I had told him that I was ribbing Burke up for a trimming, Fag would have let me alone, would have kept his hands off. But when I told him that I was through with the graft, had 'gone queer,' that made me his meat. You know how crooks are: everyone in the world is either a fellow crook or a prospective victim. So if I was no longer a crook, than Fag considered me fair game.

"He learned about Burke's family connections, and then he put it up to me—twenty thousand dollars, or he'd turn me up. He knew about the Los Angeles job, and he knew how badly I was wanted. I was up against it then. I knew I couldn't hide from Fag or run away from him. I told Burke I had to have twenty thousand dollars. I didn't think he had that much, but I thought he could get it. Three days later he gave me a check for it. I didn't know at the time how he had raised it, but it wouldn't have mattered if I had known. I had to have it.

"But that night he told me where he got the money; that he had forged his brother-in-law's signature. He told me because, after thinking it over, he was afraid that when the forgery was discovered I would be caught with him and considered equally guilty. I'm rotten in spots, but I wasn't rotten enough to let him put himself in the pen for me, without knowing what it was all about. I told him the whole story. He didn't bat an eye. He insisted that the money be paid Kilcourse, so that I would be safe, and began to plan for my further safety.

"Burke was confident that his brother-in-law wouldn't send him over for forgery, but, to be on the safe side, he insisted that I move and change my name again and lay low until we knew how Axford was going to take it. But that night, after he had gone, I made some plans of my own. I did like Burke—I liked him too much to let him be the goat without trying to save him, and I didn't have a great deal of faith in Axford's kindness. This was the second of the month. Barring accidents, Axford wouldn't discover the forgery until he got his canceled checks early the following month. That gave me practically a month to work in.

"The next day I drew all my money out of the bank, and sent Burke a letter, saying that I had been called to Baltimore, and I laid a clear trail to Baltimore, with baggage and letters and all, which a pal there took care of for me. Then I went down to Joplin's and got him to put me up. I let Fag know I was there, and when he came down I told him I expected to have the money for him in a day or two.

"He came down nearly every day after that, and I stalled him from day to day, and each time it got easier. But my time was getting short. Pretty soon Burke's letters would be coming back from the phony address I had given him, and I wanted to be on hand to keep him from doing anything foolish. And I didn't want to get in touch with him until I could give him the twenty thousand, so he could square the forgery before Axford learned of it from his canceled checks.

"Fag was getting easier and easier to handle, but I still didn't have him where I wanted him. He wasn't willing to give up the twenty thousand dollars—which I was, of course, holding all this time—unless I'd promise to stick with him for good. And I still thought I was in love with Burke, and I didn't want to tie myself up with Fag, even for a little while.

"Then Burke saw me on the street one Sunday night. I was careless, and drove into the city in Joplin's roadster—the one back there. And, as luck would have it, Burke saw me. I told him the truth, the whole truth. And he told me that he had just hired a private detective to find me. He was like a child in some ways: it hadn't occurred to him that the sleuth would dig up anything about the money. But I knew the forged check would be found in a day or two at the most. I knew it!

"When I told Burke that, he went to pieces. All his faith in his brother-in-law's forgiveness went. I couldn't leave him the way he was. He'd have babbled the whole thing to the first person he met. So I brought him back to Joplin's with me. My idea was to hold him there for a few days, until we could see how things were going. If nothing appeared in the papers about the check, then we could take it for granted that Axford had hushed the matter up, and Burke could go home and try to square himself. On the other hand, if the papers got the whole story, then Burke would have to look for a permanent hiding-place, and so would I.

"Tuesday evening's and Wednesday morning's papers were full of the news of his disappearance, but nothing was said about the check. That looked good, but we waited another day for good measure. Fag Kilcourse was in on the game by this time, of course, and I had had to pass over the twenty thousand dollars, but I still had hopes of getting it—or most of it—back, so I continued to string him along. I had a hard time keeping off Burke, though, because he had begun to think he had some sort of right to me, and jealousy made him wicked. But I got Tin-Star to throw a scare into him, and I thought Burke was safe.

"Tonight one of Tin-Star's men came up and told us that a man named Porky Grout, who had been hanging around the place for a couple of nights, had made a couple of cracks that might mean he was interested in us. Grout was pointed out to me, and I took a chance on showing myself in the public part of the place, and sat at a table close to his. He was plain rat—as I guess you know—and in less than five minutes I had him at my table, and half an hour later I knew that he had tipped you off that Burke and I were in the White Shack. He didn't tell me all this right out, but he told me more than enough for me to guess the rest.

"I went up and told the others. Fag was for killing both Grout and Burke right away. But I talked him out of it. That wouldn't help us any, and I had Grout where he would jump in the ocean for me. I thought I had Fag convinced, but— We finally decided that Burke and I would take the roadster and leave, and that when you got here Porky Grout was to pretend he was hopped up, and point out a man and a woman—any who happened to be handy—as the ones he had taken for us. I stopped to get a cloak and gloves, and Burke went on out to the car alone—and Fag shot him. I didn't know he was going to! I wouldn't have let him! Please believe that! I wasn't as much in love with Burke as I had thought, but please believe that after all he had done for me I wouldn't have let them hurt him!

"After that it was a case of stick with the others whether I liked it or not, and I stuck. We ribbed Grout to tell you that all three of us were on the back porch when Burke was killed, and we had any number of others primed with the same story. Then you came up and recognized me. Just my luck that it had to be you—the only detective in San Francisco who knew me!

"You know the rest: how Porky Grout came up behind you and turned off the lights, and Joplin held you while we ran for the car; and then, when you closed in on us, Grout offered to stand you off while we got clear, and now . . ."

Her voice died, and she shivered a little. The robe I had given her had fallen away from her white shoulders. Whether or not it was because she was so close against my shoulder, I shivered, too. And my fingers, fumbling in my pocket for a cigarette, brought it out twisted and mashed.

"That's all there is to the part you promised to listen to," she said softly, her face turned half away. "I wanted you to know. You're a hard man, but somehow I—"

I cleared my throat, and the hand that held the mangled cigarette was suddenly steady.

"Now don't be crude, sister," I said. "Your work has been too smooth so far to be spoiled by rough stuff now."

She laughed—a brief laugh that was bitter and reckless and just a little weary, and she thrust her face still closer to mine, and the gray eyes were soft and placid.

"Little fat detective whose name I don't know"—her voice had a tired huskiness in it, and a tired mockery—"you think I am playing a part, don't you? You think I am playing for liberty. Perhaps I am. I certainly would take it if it were offered me. But— Men have thought me beautiful, and I have played with them. Women are like that. Men have loved me and, doing what I liked with them, I have found men contemptible. And then comes this little fat detective whose name I don't know, and he acts as if I were a hag—an old squaw. Can I help then being piqued into some sort of feeling for him? Women are like that. Am I so homely that any man has a right to look at me without even interest? Am I ugly?"

I shook my head. "You're quite pretty," I said, struggling to keep my voice as casual as the words.

"You beast!" she spat, and then her smile grew gentle again. "And yet it is because of that attitude that I sit here and turn myself inside out for you. If you were to take me in your arms and hold me close to the chest that I am already leaning against, and if you were to tell me that there is no jail ahead for me just now, I would be glad, of course. But, though for a while you might hold me, you would then be only one of the men with which I am familiar: men who love and are used and are succeeded by other men. But because you do none of these things, because you are a wooden block of a man, I find myself wanting you. Would I tell you this, little fat detective, if I were playing a game?"

I grunted non-committally, and forcibly restrained my tongue from running out to moisten my dry lips.

"I'm going to this jail tonight if you are the same hard man who has goaded me into whining love into his uncaring ears, but before that, can't I have one whole-hearted assurance that you think me a little more than 'quite pretty'? Or at least a hint that if I were not a prisoner your pulse might beat a little faster when I touch you? I'm going to this jail for a long while—perhaps to the gallows. Can't I take my vanity there not quite in tatters to keep me company? Can't you do some slight thing to keep me from the after-thought of having bleated all this out to a man who was simply bored?"

Her lids had come down half over the silver-gray eyes, her head had tilted back so far that a little pulse showed throbbing in her white throat; her lips were motionless over slightly parted teeth, as the last word had left them. My fingers went deep into the soft white flesh of her shoulders. Her head went further back, her eyes closed, one hand came up to my shoulder.

"You're beautiful as all hell!" I shouted crazily into her face, and flung her against the door.

It seemed an hour that I fumbled with starter and gears before I had the car back in the road and thundering toward the San Mateo County jail. The girl had straightened herself up in the seat again, and sat huddled within the robe I had given her. I squinted straight ahead into the wind that tore at my hair and face, and the absence of the windshield took my thoughts back to Porky Grout.

Porky Grout, whose yellowness was notorious from Seattle to San Diego, standing rigidly in the path of a charging metal monster, with an inadequate pistol in each hand. She had done that to Porky Grout—this woman beside me! She had done that to Porky Grout, and he hadn't even been human! A slimy reptile whose highest thought had been a skinful of dope had gone grimly to death that she might get away—she—this woman whose shoulders I had gripped, whose mouth had been close under mine!

I let the car out another notch, holding the road somehow.

We went through a town: a scurrying of pedestrians for safety, surprised faces staring at us, street lights glistening on the moisture the wind had whipped from my eyes. I passed blindly by the road I wanted; circled back to it, and we were out in the country again.

At the foot of a long, shallow hill I applied the brakes and we snapped to motionless.

I thrust my face close to the girl's.

"Furthermore, you are a liar!" I knew I was shouting foolishly, but I was powerless to lower my voice. "Pangburn never put Axford's name on that check. He never knew anything about it. You got in with him because you knew his brother-in-law was a millionaire. You pumped him, finding out everything he knew about his brother-in-law's account at the Golden Gate Trust. You stole Pangburn's bank book—it wasn't in his room when I searched it—and deposited the forged Axford check to his credit, knowing that under those circumstances the check wouldn't be questioned. The next day you took Pangburn into the bank, saying you were going to make a deposit. You took him in because with him standing beside you the check to which *his* signature had been forged wouldn't be questioned. You knew that, being a gentleman, he'd take pains not to see what you were depositing.

"Then you framed the Baltimore trip. He told the truth to me—the truth so far as he knew it. Then you met him Sunday night—maybe accidentally, maybe not. Anyway, you took him down to Joplin's, giving him some wild yarn that he would swallow and that would persuade him to stay there for a few days. That wasn't hard, since he didn't know anything about either of the twenty-thousand-dollar checks. You and your pal Kilcourse knew that if Pangburn disappeared nobody would ever know that he hadn't forged the Axford check, and nobody would ever suspect that the second check was phony. You'd have killed him quietly, but when Porky tipped you off that I was on my way down you had to move quick—so you shot him down. That's the truth of it!" I yelled.

All this while she watched me with wide gray eyes that were calm and tender, but now they clouded a little and a pucker of pain drew her brows together.

I yanked my head away and got the car in motion.

Just before we swept into Redwood City one of her hands came up to my forearm, rested there for a second, patted the arm twice, and withdrew.

I didn't look at her, nor, I think, did she look at me, while she was being booked. She gave her name as Jeanne Delano, and refused to make any statement until she had seen an attorney. It all took a very few minutes.

As she was being led away, she stopped and asked if she might speak privately with me.

We went together to a far corner of the room.

She put her mouth close to my ear so that her breath was warm again on my cheek, as it had been in the car, and whispered the vilest epithet of which the English language is capable.

Then she walked out to her cell.

The Jane from Hell's Kitchen
Perry Paul

WHILE THE BETTER pulps offered a pretty good living to those writers who could work fast and produce hundreds of thousands of words a year, there was a definite hierarchy, well known to the top guns of the fiction world—as well as to the least of the hacks, the beginners, and the wannabes.

Black Mask was the gold standard, but a few other magazines, like *Argosy* and *Dime Detective*, as well as such "hero" pulps as *The Shadow* and *Doc Savage*, paid equally well. Down at the bargain basement level were such trashy publications as *Gun Molls* magazine. Literary quality was pretty much nonexistent, though stories usually galloped along at a blazing pace, substituting action and violence for subtlety and characterization.

Major writers would send them stories only when they had been rejected by the better pulps. Lesser writers never could crack the top publications and generally failed to earn a living at their chosen profession. They vanished as quickly as they appeared, and they are largely unremembered today. Perry Paul is such a figure. A former crime reporter who created two series for *Gun Molls*, the other being "Madame," a mystery moll of the underworld, nothing else could be discovered about him.

"The Jane from Hell's Kitchen" first appeared in the October 1930 issue of *Gun Molls*.

*"Somebody'll get it in the neck," said Dizzy, "and don't forget
I told you to keep your eyes off the ground!"*

The Jane from Hell's Kitchen

Perry Paul

*Things happen quickly to
Dizzy Malone—because Dizzy
was a real gun moll—a jane
with a purple paradise and a red
past—but a sport*

CHICAGO PROSECUTOR VANISHES IN NEW YORK

MYSTERIOUS KIDNAPER DEMANDS HUGE RANSOM

LOCAL DISTRICT ATTORNEY SCOUTS

GANGSTER VENGEANCE MOTIVE

CHAPTER I
DIZZY MALONE

The grizzled district attorney stood over a news-paper spread out on his desk, scare heads staring up at him in crude challenge.

The district attorney, scourge of New York's underworld, glanced nervously from the head-lines to the watch on his wrist and showed his teeth in a smile of cynical satisfaction.

Behind him the door opened noiselessly—a flash of chiffon and silk—the door closed and a girl backed her quivering body against it, her mouth open, panting.

Her high, pointed heels ground into the heavy

rug as she struggled for self-control. Her lithe, supple body tautened. Her lips hardened into a thin scarlet line. The grey eyes, shadowed by a tight-fitting crimson bit of a hat, tempered to the glitter of new steel.

Sensing an alien presence, the district attorney's head came up sharply.

" 'Local D.A. scouts gangster vengeance motive!' " the scarlet lips jeered.

The man sprang round to face the door with the agility of a jungle beast of prey.

"Dizzy Malone," he gasped, "the same, gorgeous body and all!"

The girl swung her slender hips across the room until she faced the man.

James Mitchell, veteran district attorney of New York, looked down at her lovely blonde bravado with the expression of a man charmed against his will by some exotic yet poisonous serpent.

Dizzy Malone was like that. She went to men's heads. Her moniker was a stall. They called her Dizzy because she most decidedly wasn't any way you looked at it.

"Well, when did you get back to your purple paradise in Hell's Kitchen?" the district attorney demanded. He was a tough baby. He knew all the dodges. He talked gangster talk and every crook in New York feared him. "I thought you lammed it to Europe with the Ghost when he finished his rap up the river."

The girl's sensitive nostrils quivered.

"Yeah? You *thought* so!" she sneered. "Well, I didn't. The Ghost saw to it that I missed the boat. He'd decided to change his luck, I guess. Anyway, Spanish Lil went with him. Her hair is black, mine's blonde. And that's why—"

"Say, wait a minute!" Mitchell interrupted. "I'm not running any lovelorn bureau. What's the idea? How did you get in here, anyway?"

"That's my business!" she flared. "Now collapse, stuffed-shirt, while I put on the loud speaker!"

The D.A. opened his mouth—and closed it again. When Dizzy made up her mind to talk, she talked, and everyone else listened.

"Now, get a load of this," Dizzy snapped. "It's about that guy Burke, the D.A. from Chicago, that's disappeared. I gotta hunch who lifted him."

It was Mitchell's turn to sneer.

"So you want to squeal, huh, Dizzy?"

"Squeal?" Dizzy panted. "You—you—!"

She crouched like a feline killer ready to spring. Coral-tipped fingers that could tear a man's face to ribbons, tensed. Her lips curled back from her teeth in a fighting snarl of defiance.

"Now calm down, Dizzy. Calm down."

The girl's rage did a quick fade-out, leaving in its place a cold, calculating grimness that was a sure danger signal.

"No more cracks like that then, big boy." Her voice grated slightly on a note of savage restraint. "Get this through your smart legal mind—I came here to make you a proposition, not to turn anyone up. Get that straight!"

"All right, Dizzy," the D.A. growled, glancing hastily at his watch. "Shoot."

"You gotta job to do, Mitchell. I gotta job to do. You help me. I help you. See?"

The district attorney waited.

"Now about this D.A. from Chicago. His disappearing act puts you in a tough spot, doesn't it? Looks like a smart game to me. He gets a phoney wire to come see you. He hops the Century and walks into this office the next morning. You don't know what it's all about. You didn't send any wire. Burke walks outa here and disappears. You get a letter demanding a big ransom for his return. Your job is to get Burke back and turn up the guy that pulled the job. Right?"

"Right, Dizzy."

"My job's a little different. A guy—yes, it was the Ghost—put the double-x on me. I was his moll. We worked a good racket. We piled up a stake, a big one. We were all set to beat it for the sticks, get married and settle down respectable, and forget about rackets. My man was clever, he never let the coppers get anything on us. Then some fly dick framed a rap on him."

"Oh, yeah?"

"*Yeah!* I said *framed.* My man went stir-bugs

up there in the Big House, and no wonder. Baldy Ross, his partner, and a straight-shooting guy, gets lit out in Chi with a cokie that's a rat. A copper gets bumped off and the rat turns state's evidence to save his stinking hide. Baldy swings because my man's in stir and can't spring him."

Her pink fists clenched.

"The cokie that *shot* the copper's dead now—they put him on the spot for the rat he was."

The girl's grey eyes narrowed.

"Then what happens? Well, if there's one guy the Ghost's crazy about, it's his kid brother. The Kid's a wild one but my man can hold him. He keeps him outa the racket, sends him to college. While the Ghost's in the 'Can' some wise yegg gets the Kid coked up and they pull a job. A watchman gets knocked off. You got nothing on the Kid but circumstantial evidence, but you send him up the river and he fries, across the court from where the Ghost is raving in a strait-jacket.

"The Ghost's already a little nuts from the bullets he gets in his head when that German ace shoots him down in France—but he's a genius just the same. He comes outa the Big House completely bugs. What they did to Baldy and the Kid turns him into a mad killer.

"I been waiting for him, not touching our stake. I figure if I can get him to Europe I can nurse that killer streak outa him.

"Then what happens? That black-haired flossie, Spanish Lil gets her hooks into him and he takes the stake I'd helped him make, and lams it with her. She takes him for the wad and the Ghost is flat, and more bugs than ever."

"Well, what of it, Dizzy?" the D.A. cut in impatiently, shooting a hurried look at his watch.

"Just this, big boy. The Ghost taught me all he knows. He taught me how to fly, among other things, and how to work rackets the flatties never heard of. And I can spot the Ghost's technique through a flock of stone walls. Just about now he's got two things on his mind—dough and revenge.

"Listen! Someone will pay handsome to get this D.A. from Chi back. And don't forget—he prosecuted Baldey Ross—*he's the guy that swung Baldy!*"

She paused a moment to let her words sink in.

"This is the Ghost's work all right. You'll never find him but I think I can. And I can spring this bozo Burke for you, and *get* the guy that double-crossed me. But I want to do it legal. All I ask is a plane, a fast one, with a machine-gun on it, and your say-so to go ahead."

The district attorney's laugh grated through the silence of the room.

"For once I think you're really dizzy," he said.

His sarcasm cut the girl like the flick of a whip. Her face went white.

"Then you won't—"

"Take it easy for a minute, Dizzy, and let me talk," the big man interrupted not unkindly. The beaten look in the girl's eyes touched him in spite of himself. "In the first place the Ghost is still in Europe. I'd have been tipped off the moment he stepped off a boat."

"I think you're wrong there, big boy, but—go on."

The man took another surreptitious glance at his watch.

"It won't be long now, Dizzy, so I don't mind telling you a few things," he went on. "We've got this Burke business on ice."

He took an envelope from his pocket and drew out a soiled sheet of paper.

"Here is the ransom letter. For once we outsmarted the newspaper boys. They know it exists but they *don't* know what it says. Listen!"

He read:

"UNLESS HALF A MILLION DOLLARS IS FORTHCOMING BURKE WILL NEVER BE SEEN ALIVE AGAIN. FOLLOW THESE DIRECTIONS. THE MONEY, IN GRAND NOTES, IS TO BE TIED SECURELY IN A MARKET BASKET PAINTED WHITE. PLACE MONEY AND BASKET IN THE EXACT CENTER OF VAN CORTLANDT PARK PARADE GROUND AT 7:30 P.M. TODAY AND

CLEAR A SPACE FOR A QUARTER OF A MILE AROUND IT. IF THERE IS A PERSON WITHIN THAT AREA BURKE WILL BE PUT ON THE SPOT AT ONCE. THE MONEY WILL BE CALLED FOR AT 7:55 AND BURKE WILL BE DELIVERED AT THE CITY HALL ALIVE AT 8:00 IF DIRECTIONS ARE FOLLOWED IMPLICITLY. ONE FALSE MOVE QUEERS THE GAME."

Mitchell looked up and grinned.

"We followed the directions all right, but there's a cordon of police around the park that a midget louse couldn't get through. They wait for a flash from us and make the pinch, exactly at the moment Burke is being returned to City Hall. Furthermore, the money in the basket is phoney and there's a ring of plainclothesmen for five blocks each way around City Hall. Whoever made way with Burke won't stand a show. We'll nab them for sure."

"Clever, all right," Dizzy admitted, "but you can't outsmart the Ghost. He's a genius, I tell you, a crazy genius. And there's only one person can put the skids under him, and I'm that baby."

"Okay, okay, Dizzy," the man replied genially, "but whoever pulled this Burke coup is going to get it in the neck in a few minutes."

The girl hunched her shoulders.

"*Somebody'll* get it in the neck, all right," she said cryptically. "And don't forget I told you to keep your eyes off the ground."

Her remark went unheeded, however, for a rap sounded on the door and the next instant it was flung open admitting the slick, dark head of Tom Louden, the D.A.'s shrewd young assistant.

"Seven forty-five, Chief," he reminded Mitchell. "'Most time for the show to start."

"All right, Tom. Is the car ready?"

"Yes, sir."

"Good. Come on, Dizzy. You offered to help us so we'll let you in on the pay-off."

The girl followed them to a low, black police car that waited at the curb in front of the Tombs. She took her place in the back seat between Mitchell and the assistant D.A. without a word.

A sign from the district attorney and the car purred down Centre Street.

Mitchell rubbed his hands with keen anticipation. A suspicion of doubt drew Louden's lips down in a faint frown. Dizzy's face was a blank.

The car swung into Chambers Street and stopped opposite the rear entrance to City Hall. They were out and hurrying around the grimy, outmoded building.

The plaza in front wore a peculiarly deserted appearance. Walks and benches were empty. The statue of Civic Virtue thrust its marble chest upward, unwatched by newsboy or tattered bench-warmer.

Broadway and Park Row were still literally sprinkled with homeward-bound workers, but they shunned the plaza as though it bore a curse. An atmosphere of tense expectancy hung over it, brooding, sinister, almost palpable in the gathering summer dusk.

Dizzy found herself on the broad steps before City Hall in the midst of a group of grim, tight-lipped men.

The district attorney held his watch in his hand.

"Seven fifty-five," he muttered. "Five minutes to go."

The familiar sounds of traffic came to them in a muted murmur as though muffled by the wall of silence that ringed them in.

"Fifty-seven."

Bodies tautened.

"Fifty-nine."

Keen eyes swept the approaches to the plaza—right hands flicked furtively to bulging pockets.

Dizzy's shoulders slumped forward in a nonchalant slouch, her eyes rose in slow boredom toward the darkening heavens.

A low rumble impinged upon the silence, like the growl of distant thunder. Into it burst the first booming note of the clock in the tower.

The rumble increased to a roar, filled the air

with a howl of sound, snuffed out the metallic clang of the clock's second note. The screaming drone of wind through wires.

Eyes snapped upward.

Then it came.

Sweeping in low over the Municipal building hurtled a black shadow—a low wing, streamline racing monoplane. It banked sharply as though to give its pilot a view of the square below him, then disappeared behind the Woolworth building.

The watchers stood petrified.

Once more the black ship swung into their range of vision, lower this time, banked, and circled the cramped area like a hovering eagle.

No one moved.

Suddenly the pilot pulled his somber-hued bus into a steep zoom above the Municipal Building, fluttered up into a graceful reversement and hurled his crate across the plaza again directly at the grey Woolworth tower. Swooping down he pulled the screaming ship up into a sharp inside loop that almost scraped the walls and reached its apex directly above the huddled group on the steps.

As it hung there for an instant, upside down, a black shape dropped like a plummet from the auxiliary cockpit. The pilot brought his plane out of the loop and scudded out of sight toward the south.

The black object fell writhing. A flutter of black sprang from it, mushroomed out, breaking the swift descent with a jerk.

"A parachute!"

The cry broke like a single word from the lips of the stunned watchers, a moan of mingled surprise and relief.

The thud, thud of running feet as the nucleus of a crowd closed in.

Slowly, silently the 'chute floated down through the windless dusk, the figure suspended beneath it swinging back and forth in an ever-lessening arc.

The group on the steps scattered from beneath it.

A flash of sudden enlightenment burst upon the district attorney. His cry split the silence like the shrill of a siren.

"Burke!"

The kidnaper had kept his word.

A ragged cheer rose. It changed to a gasp of horror, an instant later, as the 'chute deposited its burden with a dull crash on the stone plaza and its black silken folds crumpled slowly over it.

There it lay in a huddled heap, unmoving.

The D.A. sprang toward it, followed closely by his men. Hands tore eagerly at the enveloping silk. A cordon of police appeared as if from nowhere to hold back the milling crowd.

Dizzy Malone stood unnoticed in the excitement, watching slit-eyed.

The black silk came away disclosing the still figure of a man crumpled on the pavement.

It was Burke, district attorney of the city of Chicago.

"He's stunned by the fall!" Louden cried. "Broken bones, maybe! Call an ambulance!"

Mitchell bent over the huddled body, fingers probing deftly.

He straightened up again.

"No need," he said, simply. "Burke is dead—hung."

A spasm of rage swept him. He shook his fists at the sky overhead and cursed the vanishing plane and its pilot with blasting, withering oaths.

"Hung him, the carrion!" he shrilled. "Burke was alive when he dropped. His body's still warm. The parachute was attached to a noose around his neck. When it opened it hung him—hung him by the neck until he was dead!"

He covered his face with his hands.

An examination of the corpse proved that he was right.

It was a clever job and timed to the second.

The shrouds of the 'chute had been fastened to a rope which ended in a noose. The noose circled the dead man's neck, a knot like a hangman's protruding from beneath one ear. His hands were wired together.

When the plane went into a loop and hung

there bottom side up, the man had been catapulted downward from his seat. The 'chute opened automatically and snapped his neck with the dispatch of a hangman's sprung trap.

An ambulance jangled up.

From Centre Street came the roar of a motorcycle. A police-runner elbowed his way to the district attorney.

"Flash from Van Cortlandt Park, Chief. At 7:55, a black plane swooped down over the parade ground and scooped up the basket with the ransom. Got into the air again before anyone could get near him."

The D.A.'s big shoulders drooped.

"And then he got wise to how we'd tried to frame him," the big man mumbled. "Poor Burke. My God! Oh, my God!"

His shoulders quivered spasmodically.

In the confusion, Dizzy Malone edged her way in until she stood beside him.

Her words dripped across his numbed mind—measured, stinging, calculated to cut with the bite of a steel-tipped lash.

"Yes, hung by the neck until he was dead—*like he hung Baldy Ross on a frame-up!*" The voice went on, its words searing themselves across the district attorney's soul. "And remember, big boy, *you sealed the death warrant that sent the Kid to the Big House to fry!*"

CHAPTER II
THE MOLL PAYS A VISIT

Dizzy Malone nodded her way between the huddle of tables that shouldered each other for space around the El Dorado's gleaming dance floor. With a crooked grin and a toss of her smoothly-waved blonde hair she dismissed half a dozen offers of parking space at as many tables.

She wanted to be alone—to think—and it was in the strident, blaring heart of a night club that her mind worked best. About her beat waves of flesh-tingling, erotic sounds—rising and falling rhythmically from brazen throats, from tense, stretched strings, from the quivering bellies of drums—the swirling, clamoring pulse of Broadway's night life.

Dizzy loved it.

She chose a table in the corner and sat down facing the writhing mass of lights and color.

Against its bizarre background the scene in the district attorney's office and the mad happenings in front of the City Hall that afternoon passed rapidly in review.

The job had all the ear-marks of the Ghost. She snarled the name hatefully into the drunken medley of sound. The Ghost must be back then, and broke.

Yes, it all fitted in perfectly. A quick recoup of the stake—part of it hers—that he'd thrown away on that flossie, Spanish Lil—and—revenge. A double-barreled goal that would eat into his twisted mind like acid.

It was like the Ghost to combine business with—revenge.

First this bird Burke who had convicted Baldy, and then—

A waiter with a broken nose and a livid scar that stretched from lip to ear bent over her solicitously, yet with an air of being in the know, of belonging.

"Scotch," Dizzy said, automatically.

The waiter disappeared.

Dizzy's shrewd mind pieced together the scattered bits of the puzzle. With Burke out of the way who would be next? Who, but—

The waiter again.

He placed the drink before her, bent close to her ear as he smoothed the rumpled tablecloth.

"I hear Spanish Lil is back."

Dizzy stiffened.

"Where?"

The words seemed to slip out of the corner of her mouth. Her lips did not move.

"At Sugar Foot's in Harlem, throwin' coin around like a coked-up bootlegger."

"Thanks."

The grapevine! System of underworld news.

The waiter moved away.

Dizzy made a pretense of drinking, smiled woodenly at a shrill-voiced entertainer, and rose.

Where Spanish Lil was, there the Ghost would be.

Outside the El Dorado, Dizzy climbed into a low, nondescript hulk of a roadster. There was class about the roadster. Its dull, grey finish gleamed in the lamp light. Its nickle fittings were spotless.

When she stepped on the starter, the car's real class became apparent, for under her hand pulsed the steady flow of a V-16 Cadillac. The long, grey hood covered a sixteen-cylinder motor mounted on the very latest in chassis.

The gears meshed and the iron brute rolled away with scarcely a sound.

Dizzy swung the wheel and they turned south into Seventh Avenue, then west to skirt the uppermost extremity of Times Square, south on Ninth, then west again and the grey snout of the roadster buried itself deep into the heart of the sink of gangland—Hell's Kitchen.

Before an inconspicuous brownstone front in the odd Forties the car drew up. The motor hissed into silence.

Dizzy climbed the battered stone steps and let herself into an ill-lit hallway. Two steep flights of stairs—another door. It yielded to her key and she stepped into her purple paradise and snapped on the lights. Behind her the door swung to with the solid clang of steel meeting steel and the snap of a double lock.

The room was a perfect foil for Dizzy Malone's blonde, gaming beauty, and truly a purple paradise. It ran the gamut of shades of that royal color, from the light orchid of the silk-draped walls to the almost-violet of the deep, cushion-drenched divans that lined three walls. Into the fourth was built a miniature bar whose dark, blood-purple mahogany gleamed dully in the subdued light of innumerable silken-covered lamps.

Cigarette tables on tall, slender legs flanked the divans; a massive radio was half-concealed by an exquisite Spanish shawl, worked with intricate mauve embroidery and surmounted by a silver vase holding a gigantic spotted orchid. There was not a book to be seen—not even "Indian Love Lyrics," acme of chorine literary taste and attainment; or Nietzsche's "Thus Spake Zarathustra" which is now considered passé by Broadway beauties; or Durant's "History of Philosophy," displayed, but never read.

Dizzy's purple paradise was, indeed, an institution.

She crossed its thick, soft carpet with a hurried step and entered the bedroom.

It was done entirely in the same color-scheme as the outer room, but, unlike it, was strictly private.

Dizzy tossed her hat on the square, purple bed that stood on a raised dias in the center of the room. From two wardrobes that squatted against the wall she took the flimsy garments she figured to need and spread them in readiness on the chaise-lounge stretching in luxurious abandon beneath the heavily-shaded casement window.

Then the clothes Dizzy had on fell at her feet in a crumpled shower and she stood, stretching her arms above her head, in provocative marble-pink nakedness.

But not for long. There was work to be done.

Throwing a smock about her slender shoulders, she sat down before a make-up table that would have done credit to the current reigning dramatic favorite, and switched on the blinding frame of electrics that threw its mirror into a pool of dazzling brilliance.

For several minutes her gaze concentrated on the reflected image of herself, then she rubbed the make-up off with cold cream and set to work.

Dark shadows blended in skillfully around her eyes, made their grey depths even deeper, faint penciled lines gave them a slanting oval appearance. She blocked her eyebrows out with grease paint and drew fine, arching ones over them. Deft dabs of rouge close up under the eyes and flanking her nose aided in completely changing the round, youthful contour of her face. It was the long, smouldering, passionate countenance of the Slav. She clinched the impression by drawing out her lips in two, thin crimson lines.

Dizzy gazed at the reflection and grinned. Even she failed to recognize herself. The make-up was perfect.

To complete the illusion, she combed the smooth waves of her blonde bobbed hair flatly down on her little head, then searched through the drawers until she found a flaming red wig.

It was a work of art, that wig, and so expertly made as to defy discovery of its artificiality.

Carefully Dizzy fitted it into place.

An exclamation of delight slipped between her lips.

Perfect, indeed!

Satisfied, Dizzy dressed slowly, choosing a scanty gown that hinted broadly at the palpitating curves beneath. Its vivid, jealous-eyed green threw into hot relief the flaming flower of her hair.

Throwing a light wrap about her, she descended the stairs to her roadster, eased in behind the wheel and gunned the grey hulk toward the river. She swung north on deserted lower West End Avenue, breezing along easily. There was no hurry and she had no desire to run into the drunken crush that marked the three o'clock closing hour of most of Broadway's night clubs.

The blocks slipped past.

At Cathedral Parkway she turned right, passed Morningside Park, and left into Lenox Avenue, the great pulsing artery of Harlem.

Into the maze of side streets the roadster nosed and came to a stop at last before a row of lightless, grimy stone fronts.

Dizzy climbed out and walked around the corner to where an awning stretched across the sidewalk.

In its shadow towered an ebony doorman.

He scrutinized her closely but at the mention of the name she snarled into his ear, he began to bow and scrape frantically. Flinging the locked doors behind him open, he admitted her to deep-carpeted stairs.

Down them she went, and at the bottom there rushed to meet her the hot music, the din, the flashing movement and color that was the underworld's basement-haven—Sugar Foot's.

Her eyes swept the crowded room in the split second before it was plunged into darkness punctured by a spotlight that picked out a brown-skinned girl in the center of the dance floor. The orchestra throbbed into a barbaric African rhythm and the girl flung herself into a writhing, shuddering dance.

Under cover of it, Dizzy threaded her way to an empty corner-table near the door, which she had spotted in that brief instant, before the lights went out.

When the lights flooded on again she was seated behind the table facing the room. She leaned one elbow negligently on its checked calico-top and joined in the applause. To all appearances she had been there for hours.

A boisterous waiter came and hung over her shoulder.

"Scotch!" Dizzy snapped.

There was that in her tone which sent him away on the jump, respectful, in spite of the aura of flaunted lure that clung about her.

In a moment he was on his way back, skipping, sliding, weaving his way across the dance floor in perfect time to the music. He lowered his tray and placed the drink before her, a tall glass, soda, ginger ale, a bowl of cracked ice, and melted away again.

Slowly, lingeringly, Dizzy mixed the drink, sipped it and settled to the business of looking over the crowd that jammed the stifling room to capacity.

Everyone was there—sporting gents flush from the race-track; sinister underworld figures, suave, shifty-eyed; a heavyweight contender with his wizened-faced manager; a florid police sergeant from the tenderloin; the principals of a smash colored review; a sprinkling of tight-lipped gamblers and individuals who fitted into no particular category. All their women—good, bad, and so-so.

But nowhere on the dance floor could Dizzy find the sunken, grey, cadaverous face of the Ghost, or the long, gangling stretch of his emaciated limbs. He would surely be there. He loved to dance, almost as much as Dizzy herself.

The saxophones sobbed their quivering "That's All!" and the dancers made for their tables.

The lights went out—the spotlight fell upon a black Amazon in a glittering, skin-tight gown. Swaying sensuously to the beat of the music, she broke into a wailing, throbbing blues. Wild applause.

Lights again—the beat of the music quickened—couples left the tables for the dance floor and locked themselves in shuddering embraces to the fervent tempo of the band.

Dizzy's eyes swept the tables.

There—ah! Dizzy's fists clenched. The pink nails went white.

At the ringside table sat Spanish Lil, high-bosomed, languorous, drunk.

The shimmer of new steel gleamed out from the slits that were Dizzy's eyes. They probed at each of the faces that swarmed around Spanish Lil, each one a worthless hanger-on scenting dough. For an instant they paused at a bloated face faintly reminiscent of the Ghost.

Her heart flopped over and beat wildly.

But no! The man's nose was small and straight, nothing like the Ghost's colorless, almost transparent hooked beak. His shoulders were square, not round and sloping; his eyes puffed and bleary.

A keen stab of disappointment tore at her throat.

Her eyes passed on.

Everywhere she met hot stares, pleading, offering, suggesting unmentionable things. Her own swept them coldly.

A pie-eyed newspaper reporter slouched over her table and began to talk. Dizzy knew him, but to add authenticity to her changed character she sent him away with a stinging rebuff that made even his calloused sensibilities writhe.

Darkness and the spotlight again. A dusky chorus hurled itself into an abysmal jungle dance. A roar of applause.

Lights.

Dizzy rose and made her way toward the ladies' room, taking care to pass close to the table where Spanish Lil and her satellites clustered.

The man with the bloated face looked up and caught her eye for an instant as she went past.

On the way back he was waiting for her. When she came abreast of the table he swayed to his feet.

"Dance, kid?" he mumbled thickly.

Something made Dizzy hesitate instead of brushing quickly by him. Misinterpreting it for assent he insinuated his hand under her elbow.

Spanish Lil leaped to her feet.

"Lay off that, you—you—!" she shrilled.

Her eyes burned with anger and liquor as she seized the man's arm and dragged him away.

"Come on, we're going home."

Dizzy eased out of the jam and returned to her table. She sat down watching every move of Spanish Lil and the man with the bloated face as they stumbled toward the door.

Suddenly, with a half-stifled cry, Dizzy sprang upright.

There was no mistaking that shuffling gait, that gangling length of limb. A plastic surgeon could chisel away the hooked beak, booze and coke could bloat the sunken, cadaverous face, a tailor could pad the round sloping shoulders; but nothing could disguise that shuffling, long-legged gait.

It was the Ghost.

Dizzy flung a bill down on the table and plunged after them, fighting her way through the crowd, taking the stairs two at a time.

As she burst through the outer door to the sidewalk faint streaks of dawn were silvering the sky.

Spanish Lil and the Ghost were in the back of a waiting taxi. The driver slammed the door and spurted away.

Dizzy dashed round the corner, wrap trailing—scrambled into the grey roadster without opening the door—clawed the ignition switch—kicked the starter.

The iron brute leaped ahead—swung—backed into the curb—hurtled ahead once more—bumped over the opposite curb—and took the corner into the avenue with a screaming skid.

A red tail-light was just visible in the distance.

Dizzy booted the accelerator to the floor and the sixteen cylinders responded with a lurching burst of speed.

The red light drew rapidly nearer and she eased off the terrific pace.

A slit-lipped grin broke across her face, mirthless, cruel.

She was on the trail of the Ghost at last, the only man who had ever double-crossed her.

"There's only one person that can put the skids under him," she muttered through clenched teeth. "*And I'm that baby!*"

CHAPTER III
IN THE DISTRICT ATTORNEY'S OFFICE

It was well into the afternoon before Dizzy finally slid her roadster to the curb before the brownstone front in the Forties that masked her purple paradise.

A drizzling summer rain fell steadily.

She climbed out and looked the iron-gutted monster over affectionately. It was spattered with mud and one of the rear tires was flat, cut to ribbons. Like its owner it seemed to droop with the fatigue of a sleepless night and almost continuous driving.

As Dizzy turned wearily toward the house a smile of grim satisfaction creased the corners of her mouth.

She knew all that she needed to know—now! It *was* the Ghost!

Stiffly she plodded up the stairs and let herself into the purple salon. Slamming the door behind her, she crossed to the bedroom leaving a trail of sodden garments in her wake. Her white body disappeared into the bathroom to

be followed almost instantly by the hiss of a shower.

She came out in a few minutes, fresh, almost radiant, all traces of her character of the night before completely removed.

It was a 100 per cent Dizzy Malone again who chose a quietly expensive street dress from a wardrobe and drew it on over her head.

When she stepped into the purple salon once more she was as modishly dressed, as cool and collected, as any millionaire broker's private secretary. And probably infinitely more beautiful. She looked, indeed, as though she had stepped out of the proverbial bandbox.

But then, Dizzy was Dizzy, and just at the moment she was ravenously hungry.

From the refrigerator behind the bar she salvaged half a grapefruit; set a percolator brewing coffee and made toast in a complicated electrical gadget.

When breakfast was ready she disposed of it with neatness and dispatch. Into the second cup of coffee she poured a generous slug of cognac and sipped it leisurely. Then she lit a cigarette.

At last Dizzy Malone was herself again and ready for whatever the day would bring, which, she figured, would be plenty.

And in that she was right, as she usually was, although things did not begin to happen as soon as she expected.

Calmly, at first, she sat smoking cigarettes and waiting while the rain dripped dolefully outside. Then she got up and began pacing the room, smoking with short nervous puffs.

Finally the break came.

An ominous rapping on the door.

Dizzy started, pulled herself together and ground the cigarette into an over-full ash-tray.

"Who is it?" she called.

"Horowitz and Rourke from Headquarters. The D.A. says you should take a walk to see him."

"Just a second, boys."

The expected had happened.

Dizzy straightened her hat in front of a mirror and opened the door. Outside were two plainclothes men.

"Hello, Dizzy."

Dizzy grinned.

Together they descended the stairs and made a dash through the rain for the black sedan with the P.D. shield on its radiator that was parked behind her roadster.

Instantly the police chauffeur was on his way, siren shrieking.

"What's the big idea of the ride?" the girl asked.

The dicks shrugged.

"We don't know ourselves."

And it was obvious to her that they didn't, although it was evident, too, that they were laboring under an over-dose of suppressed excitement. But they offered nothing and Dizzy asked no questions.

The remainder of the ride to the grim building on Centre Street was accomplished in silence. Once there she was conducted immediately to the office where she had had the futile conference exactly twenty-four hours before.

The district attorney sat at his desk, Tom Louden beside him.

"Fade!" the D.A. snapped at the plainclothes men and they backed out, closing the door behind them.

Dizzy stood in the middle of the room, waiting, watching.

Mitchell looked up at her out of eyes deep-sunken and blood-shot. His face showed lines of worry and strain. Even his grizzled hair seemed a trifle greyer. It was a cinch that his nerves were keyed close to the breaking point.

What had happened to the big boy, Dizzy wondered. It would surely take more than that business in front of the City Hall to throw a veteran like himself so completely haywire.

His eyes bored into her and a flush slowly rose to his cheekbones.

"You damned little punk!" he roared, suddenly, springing to his feet.

"But, Chief—"

"Shut up!" he snarled at his assistant. "Let me handle this!"

Seizing the girl's arm he twisted it savagely.

"Now come clean! What do you know about that Burke job?"

Dizzy looked him in the eye.

"I told you what I knew yesterday," she said coldly. "I made you a proposition purely on a hunch. The offer still holds. Give me a plane, a fast one, with a machine-gun on it, and your say-so to go ahead, and maybe I can get the Ghost for you. And when I say 'get' I mean '*get*'! That's all."

"It is, huh?"

The D.A. dragged her roughly to the desk.

"Well, what about *this?*"

He snatched a sheet of paper from its top and thrust it in front of her eyes.

It was in the same handwriting as the Burke ransom letter and on the same type of paper.

Dizzy read it hurriedly.

"You see what happens when you try to double-cross us, Mitchell! Don't try to chisel again. Unless you announce through the papers that you will comply with our demand for $500,000 as we shall direct, you will be dead by midnight!"

"Well?"

The district attorney pointed to a newspaper scare head.

DISTRICT ATTORNEY DEFIES BURKE KILLERS

"Now what have you got to say?" he asked fiercely.

"My proposition is still open. And remember, big boy, you prosecuted the Ghost's kid brother. *You sent him up to fry in the chair.*"

"Is that all?"

"Yes."

The D.A. stood over the girl threateningly.

"Listen, baby, you know plenty and you're going to spill it. Now are you ready to talk nice?"

Dizzy shrugged.

"You heard me the first time, big boy."

Mitchell's big hand shot out and clamped over her slim arm.

"You're gonna come clean with what you know, see, baby!" he snarled. "Or else I'll give you the works!"

"I'm no squealer!" Dizzy spit the words in his face.

The D.A. flung her savagely into a chair.

"All right, then, you little punk, *I'll just sweat it out of you!*"

"Good Heavens, Chief! Can't you see she'd had enough?" Tom Louden's voice quivered. "Lay off her. She won't talk."

The D.A. turned his back on the crumpled heap that lay whimpering piteously in the chair.

"All right, Tom. Jug her then for safe keeping. She's dangerous."

"Oh, go easy, Chief! Don't do that. I'll be personally responsible for her. I don't think she's in the know anyway."

Dizzy looked up gratefully at the young assistant D.A. out of a face that had become pinched and drawn. Racking sobs shook her, but she bit her lips to keep them back.

Mitchell gave tacit consent to his assistant's plea by ignoring it.

"Well, guess I'll call it a day," he said gruffly, pulling out his watch. "Eleven-thirty. The buzzards have got half an hour yet to keep their promise, *but they won't get me!*"

Mitchell turned abruptly on his heel and left the room.

When the door closed Louden crossed to the shuddering heap in the chair.

"I'm sorry, kid," he said with real emotion. "Feeling better?"

Dizzy nodded and tried to smile.

"Good, kid. Now promise that you won't take it on the lam and I'll run you home in my car."

"I won't lam it—now!"

"Let's go then, Dizzy," Tom urged as he helped her gently to her feet. "We'll just trail along behind the Chief to see that *he* gets home all right, then I'll chance Hell's Kitchen and drop you at your door."

Dizzy gulped her thanks and clung to his arm for support as they hurried to the street.

What amounted to a riot squad had been called out to escort the D.A. to his home. It roared away from the big grey building while Dizzy and Tom climbed into his modest sedan. An armored motorcycle preceded and followed Mitchell's limousine. On the seat beside him sat a pair of plainclothes men.

Mitchell had boasted that the buzzards who knocked off his colleague from Chicago wouldn't get him, but he was taking no chances.

Tom Louden's sedan stuck its nose into the drizzle of rain and scampered after the cavalcade as it streaked away northward.

Into Fifth Avenue they raced, sirens shrieking; past red lights and green alike, the smooth wet asphalt flowing behind them like a black ribbon.

Forty-second Street slid by and the rain-drenched statue of General Sherman dripping in its tiny park at Fifty-ninth.

A few blocks further on they turned right, bumped across the car tracks at Madison Avenue, past the great church on the corner of the Park. It was dark except for the illuminated dial of the clock on its steeple whose hands quivered on the edge of midnight.

Half way up the block the cavalcade stopped before the private residence of the D.A.

Louden pulled in behind the limousine. The coppers leaped to their stations, guns drawn. The D.A. stepped out, chuckling, and headed for his door, waving aside the proffered umbrella of the plainclothes men who walked beside him.

"The buzzards won't get me," he gloated. "Not tonight they won't."

He reached the door and stood on the mat, regardless of the pelting rain, drawing out his key.

The first stroke of midnight clanged hollowly from the church on the corner.

"I fooled 'em this time," the D.A. laughed.

He thrust the wet key in the lock.

As it touched, a point of blue flame appeared, sputtered into a glow that ran hissing across his hand and up his arm. The D.A.'s body stiffened. Blue sparks cascaded from his feet. His bulky frame writhed in spasmodic jerks, thin spirals of smoke rising from his seared flesh. His features convulsed in agony.

Then, its work done, the burning wave of electricity flung the charred body of New York's district attorney shuddering to the sidewalk.

When his bodyguard bent over him, Mitchell was dead.

In Tom Louden's sedan Dizzy's white lips framed scarcely audible words—"He fried— just like the Ghost's kid brother!"

CHAPTER IV
ANOTHER DEMAND

Dizzy Malone threw off the purple coverlet of her bed and reached for the morning papers. There was one thing she wanted to find out— how the trick had been turned.

The papers exposed the ingenious device in detail. She lapped them up as she munched rolls and drank coffee prepared by her cleaning woman.

A man had called at the D.A.'s house with the forged identification card of an inspector for the Electric Light Company. He wished to inspect the meter. He was admitted without question by an unsuspecting servant.

The meter was out of order, he said. He would fix it. As well as the servant could remember he had mentioned something about the wiring of the doorbell fouling the house current.

The bogus inspector set to work.

What he really did was to install a transformer which stepped-up the house current to a deadly degree. Ingenious wiring of the metal door frame and the steel door mat completed the trap, which was set by simply connecting a wire outside the door. An apparently innocent passerby could stoop over and make the connection. That done the victim stepped on the mat, inserted the key and completed the circuit that electrocuted him. The rain, of course, aided the design materially.

Dizzy shuddered at its utter hellishness.

It smacked lustily of the Ghost, but a Ghost goaded by homicidal mania, a Ghost stooping to the exhibitionism born of illusions of grandeur, a Ghost whose twisted mind was disintegrating in a final burst of fiendish bravado.

If it *was* the Ghost he had gone stark mad. And as such he was doubly dangerous.

But even Dizzy had no real evidence to pin the two killings on her former partner. From long experience with his methods she sensed, however, that he would have executed them in practically the same manner as the unknown. And then, too, there was the element of poetic justice in the two slayings that she had hunched in the very beginning.

She was two points up on the police any way you looked at it—she knew the Ghost was in New York and she knew his hideaway. And those two bits of information she intended to keep to herself, to be used to bring to a successful ending her vendetta of hate.

She would put the bee on the Ghost, and she would do it herself—that was her right—but she was smart enough to realize there must be a semblance of legality about it or it would be bars, and possibly the chair, for her.

The next move was up to the Ghost.

It came even as she wondered what it would be.

The faint buzz of the telephone.

Dizzy snatched for the French phone in its recess under the bed.

Tom Louden, acting district attorney for the city of New York, was on the wire. Mr. Louden's compliments and would Miss Malone be so kind as to come to Headquarters immediately?

Miss Malone would.

She held the hook down for a few seconds, then called the garage around the corner for her car. Tumbling out of bed she made a hurried toi-

lette and dashed down the stairs. The grey roadster was waiting at the curb, motor running.

Dizzy craved action and she got plenty of it
from the crowds of early bargain-shoppers on
the drive to the big grim building on Centre
Street.

It was the third time in three days that she had
crossed the threshold of the district attorney's
office, but this time she entered with a perky
smile and a jaunty step, for she realized that she
was master of the situation. It was her turn to
dictate.

Tom Louden greeted her with a harassed
smile.

"There's hell to pay, Dizzy," he said, running
his hand wearily through his hair. "Look!"

She took the extended sheet of paper, recognizing with an ominous shiver the soiled foolscap
of the two previous ransom letters.

"This just queers everything," Tom Louden
groaned. "Read it."

Dizzy's eyes swept back and forth across the
paper.

*"You see we mean business! The ante is
raised to $1,000,000. Follow these instruc-
tions exactly. Wrap the dough (grand notes
only) in a bundle and attach same to an automatically opening parachute. A pilot is to
take a single-seater up from Roosevelt Flying
Field with the dough and parachute today at
2 p.m. and head due east out over the ocean,
flying 100 miles an hour at 5,000 feet. Plane
is to be plainly marked with alternating black
and white stripes. When pilot sees a yacht
whose decks are similarly painted he is to
descend, drop the parachute and return. Bets
are off if any attempt is made to follow plane
or discover yacht. No tricks this time! We see
all, know all!*

*"If these directions are not followed to the
letter within twenty-four hours we will bump
off Jake Levine!"*

A cry of horror burst from Dizzy's lips at sight of
the sinister name.

Jake Levine—Boss Fixer of gangland, human
octopus in whose tentacles danced dip and judge
alike, maker and breaker of politicians, super-
fence, master blackmailer, banker for anything
from petty larceny to murder if the return was
not less than fifty per cent, chiseler and double-
crosser feared from the lowest sink in the tenderloin to the highest holder of the public trust.

"You see what I'm up against on my first job,
Dizzy," Tom growled hopelessly. "Levine got a
duplicate of this letter. He's been down here
already—he's here yet. Says he'll blow the lid
off, knock the legs out from under the administration—and he will, too—if something isn't
done. The party leaders have been on my neck
since daylight, and I'm half crazy."

He looked up to the girl appealingly.

"What I heard of that dope of yours about the
Ghost sounded pretty sensible and I'd like—"

The door of the office burst open and an
undersized, rat-faced man burst into the room.

"What the hell you going to do about this,
Louden?" he demanded, his voice high pitched
with panic.

He was trembling violently. The sickly sallow pallor of fear showed through his natural swarthiness. His eyes, beady and set close
together, jerked furtively about the room. The
aggressive loudness of his clothes even had lost
their swagger and he stood revealed as the yellow
rat he was.

"You've gotta do something, I say!" he almost
screamed. "Listen, you heel! When I got that letter I fixed it so there'll be hell to pay for *certain
parties*"—he emphasized the words slyly—"if
anything happens to me, and they know it. Have
they come through with the dough that bum
wants?"

"Why—a—not yet, Mr. Levine," Louden
stalled. "You see—"

"The hell I see! That guy means business.
Look who he's bumped off already. He ain't
fooling, and if you don't do something for me
damn soon I'll start talking and break every punk
in this administration."

His yellow teeth showed in a snarl.

"And don't make a false play either, boy.

Remember—if I go on the spot, I wreck the grafters just the same. Nobody ever made a heel outa Jake Levine. Now what kinda protection you givin' me?"

"I can lock you up in a cell, Mr. Levine," Louden suggested. "You would be safe there."

"In a cell—a cell!" the man shrieked. "Listen to him! Maybe that bum's got somebody planted to get me there—some lousy screw maybe. I don't trust nobody."

He paused a moment.

"I know where I'll go!" he burst out again. "I'll stick to one of those *certain parties* until he gets me out of this."

Turning abruptly he flung himself through the door.

"Well, it won't be long now before the axe falls," Tom muttered.

"And it won't be long before the time set by that letter is up, too," Dizzy cut in from where she had flattened herself against the wall. "It's almost noon now."

The acting D.A.'s eyes lit up hopefully.

"Oh, yes. That dope of yours about the Ghost—what was it?"

Dizzy gave him the same story she had Mitchell. It was all good hunching, she knew, but not tangible enough evidence on which to make a pinch. She even told Louden that she had positively seen the Ghost the night before, but she carefully refrained from any mention of having trailed him. It was too late to nail him at his hideaway, and even if she *had* been a squealer.

"And my proposition remains practically the same," she finished. "Let me fly that striped ransom plane from Roosevelt's Field at two o'clock this afternoon. Be sure it's a fast one and have a machine-gun mounted on it—and *I'll get the Ghost* for you."

Suspicion flashed squint-eyed across Louden's face.

"Say!" he demanded sharply. "How do I know *you're* not in on this game too? You were his moll."

Hot hate flushed Dizzy's face which changed,

gradually, to the amused expression she might have worn when watching the helpless squirming of a newborn puppy.

"Listen, stupid," she laughed. "I don't carry any dough. You weigh the 'chute with a flock of bricks. Everything's like it should be except for that, and the machine-gun, and Dizzy Malone flying the ship."

Louden considered.

"No, no, Dizzy," he burst out petulantly. "It's impossible. I can't take upon myself the responsibility of sending you of all people. It's a job for the police. Your proposition is absurd. I've a Boeing pursuit plane out at the field ready and waiting. It's camouflaged to look like an old crate that's about ready to fall to pieces, and it's striped black and white. The parachute is waiting for its load of a million dollars."

He laughed harshly.

"A million dollars! And I'm sitting here doing nothing. Why, look here! The thing to do is to lay a trap for the boat that's to pick up all that money."

"Don't be dumb!" Dizzy snapped. "I know the way the Ghost's mind works. He's a racketeer and a flier. He don't play with rowboats. I know him like a book and I'm the only one who can get him. Give me a chance!"

The peremptory jangling of the telephone cut in on the voice that had become low and pleading.

Louden picked up the receiver. His face went white as he listened.

"Yes, sir. Yes, sir . . . I'm doing the best I can . . . No, nothing definite yet . . . I'll give you a ring . . . Yes."

His hands trembled violently as he replaced the receiver.

"Come on, Tom." Dizzy was at him again. "Take a chance. Stall those certain parties off. Tell them someone's come through with the dough and you've sent it out. Call the field about the machine-gun. It's the Ghost—I know it's the Ghost and I'll get him so he won't bother anyone again. If I don't get him I won't come back," she finished simply.

Louden's eyes fixed themselves despairingly

on hers and slowly a look almost of relief came into them.

He stood up and squared his shoulders with decision.

"I'll do it!"

Dizzy was across the room. Her arms went around his neck and she pressed a red kiss full on his lips. Before he knew what had happened she was half way through the door. There she turned.

"Plenty gas in the Boeing and two motorcycle cops to shoot me through traffic," she shouted with a wave of the hand.

Then she tore.

Louden stood there, stunned, his mouth open.

"Gas—cops—" he mumbled, nodding his head dumbly.

But when Dizzy reached her grey roadster, two red motorcycles were coughing impatiently beside it. Their drivers were looking with some disdain at the unpromising hulk, but before they had gone two blocks they were pleasantly disillusioned.

Then, sirens shrieking, they proceeded to do their stuff and, for the first time in her life, Dizzy looked at a copper with favor. The baby in front of her could ride, and he did so.

Through traffic they wailed their way, screamed across crowded Queensborough Bridge and on to Long Island.

There, Dizzy gunned the V-16, worrying the heels of the man in front. In the mirror she could see the man behind grin as he hung on doggedly.

Then all three went raving speed-mad.

It was with fifteen minutes still to spare that they whined through the entrance to Roosevelt Field.

The coppers flung wearily off their busses and kicked them into their rests. But they stood to attention and brought their fingers to their caps with real admiration when Dizzy stepped jauntily to the ground and hurried to where she saw a battered-looking crate, striped black and white, being warmed up on the line.

A field official stepped forward.

"The ship is ready," he said, waving his hand.

"Gas?" Dizzy snapped.

"Full tanks."

"Cruising radius?"

"A thousand miles."

"Good!"

Dizzy stepped into the flying suit he held toward her and adjusted helmet and goggles.

She waved aside the parachute straps he started to buckle about her with a grim: "That won't do *me* any good!"

It was to be a battle to the death.

Dizzy climbed aboard and the man explained the manipulation of the machine-gun that had been hastily geared to the motor and camouflaged and showed her where the auxiliary belts of ammunition were nested in the cockpit.

"This is a regulation army pursuit ship," he said, "with complete equipment Very pistol and lights, earth inductor compass—"

"Okay, okay!"

The girl checked the details as he pointed them out and shot a glance at her wrist watch.

Two o'clock!

She revved the motor, thrilling to the smooth precision of its whining roar as the man snapped the buckles of the safety-belt.

"Money 'chute!" she cried.

The man brought it and stowed it away within easy reach.

"Bricks!" he shouted with a grin.

Dizzy nodded.

"Let's go!"

The chocks were pulled from the wheels. She gave it the gun and the crate rolled into the runway, hurtled forward. A slight pull on the stick and it catapulted into the air.

Climbing in a tight spiral she watched the altimeter—a thousand feet, two, three, four, five. Then she leveled off and threw the ship into a series of intricate maneuvers. She had been taught by a master—the Ghost—and had proved a more than apt pupil. The Boeing responded to the slightest touch on rudder and stick. Never had she flown such a ship.

She leveled off again and, putting the blazing disc of the sun at her back, set her course by the compass dead into the east. Full gun she watched the speed indicator climb to its maximum, then throttled down to an easy hundred miles an hour. No need to figure drift—not a breath of air stirred.

Long Island slid out from under her and the Boeing nosed out over the Atlantic.

Dizzy dipped her left wing and scanned the smooth blue expanse of water. No yacht with striped deck met her eager gaze; in fact, there was no boat of any sort to be seen, no smudge of black smoke, even, on the horizon ahead. She wormed round in the cockpit as far as the safety-straps would permit and scanned the air.

Nothing.

The scorching sun beat blindingly into her eyes.

A sense of utter loneliness settled depressingly about her.

She shot the moon to warm her guns, quivering with a throb of power at their chattering death-talk.

An hour spun round on the dial of her watch.

The sea below her was a round blue waste circled by a shimmering heat haze.

Another hour—

She dispelled a growing uneasiness with a screaming burst of the guns.

The sun settled slowly behind her. The Boeing roared on into the east.

Another hour—

The ship, perceptibly lightened of its load of gas, floated easily in the air. She flew left-wing low, now, searching the water for a striped-deck yacht.

Still nothing. The sea was as barren as a deserted mill-pond. She searched the sky above and behind. Nothing but the red round of the sun, slowly sinking.

The vague restlessness of fear shuddered along her nerves that the staccato of the guns failed to dispel. The gas was almost half gone and still the bare, tenantless reach of water stretched below her.

Where was the yacht?

The suspicion born in the D.A.'s office that it was only a stall grew into a certainty. Real fear gripped her. What was this all about? Should she turn back?

No! She remembered her boast and screamed it into the surrounding void.

"Damn the Ghost! I'll get him or I won't come back!"

As if in answer to her screamed challenge a black shadow seemed to sweep out of the sun.

Her eyes jerked to the side, her body went rigid.

Beside her floated a low-winged black Lockheed Sirius monoplane.

Her gaze probed through the pilot's goggles, locked with the pale smoldering eyes of—the Ghost!

He waggled his wings and motioned over the side with a long-armed gesture.

Dizzy held up the readied 'chute.

The Ghost nodded and she flung it clear.

A cold dash of warning from some seventh sense sent her up in a steep zoom and she fell off on one wing.

And none too soon for a spatter of holes ripped through the doped linen of one wing. The Ghost was heeled too.

She banked to see the man pull his ship out of a zoom that had been intended to rake her bus from prop to tail assembly, and dive for the opened 'chute. He caught it deftly on a hook suspended from the undercarriage and hauled it rapidly aboard.

Dizzy rammed forward on the stick, the wind droned through the wires as she dropped down and threw a burst of steel into the Sirius. It dropped off clumsily on one wing and pulled itself up heavily.

With that maneuver the insane daring of the Ghost's final gesture came clear. The Sirius with its cruising radius of 4,300 miles was fueled to capacity. The Ghost gambled to blast the ransom plane out of the sky with a single burst, pick up the money 'chute and head for Europe.

Dizzy thrilled in spite of herself at the very audacity of the thing, its colossal bluff.

Then the red mantle of hate dropped over her.

She dropped the Boeing down out of the sky and swept alongside the black ship. This would be a fair fight and to the death. She would get him, if she could, and on the level.

Dizzy tore off goggles and helmet, noting with satisfaction the cringe of recognition that swept across the Ghost's face.

She shook her fist at him and motioned him to dump his gas.

He accepted the challenge and a sheet of spray gushed downward. The black ship, lightened of its load, leaped upward.

They were on even terms now.

Dizzy tripped her guns and the man answered the salute—the salute of death, for one of them at least and perhaps both.

They flung their ships at each other, guns flaming.

Steel seared Dizzy's cockpit, rocking the Boeing. She dove, zoomed up in a loop and stood on her head pumping chattering hail into the Sirius.

The Ghost wing-slipped out of the way and they clawed down the sky to get at each other's bellies, then roared upward, guns raving.

Dizzy's instrument-board went to pieces. Stunned, the Boeing slipped into a spin, the Ghost on its heels waiting to rip in the coup de grace.

The girl threw the stick into neutral and, when her crate steadied, sat on her tail and clawed for altitude.

Sirius steel tore into the Boeing. Dizzy pulled into a reversement and for an instant the black crate was glued to her ring-sights. She pressed the trips. Steel gutted the black ship.

It wabbled. She was under it, ripping, tearing.

The Sirius nosed over into a spin, flame streaming behind.

The Boeing nosed in for the kill, wires screaming, guns raving.

A black wing collapsed and the Sirius spun faster, down, down.

Dizzy leveled off, banked and leaned over the side.

Below her a flaming ball cometed down through the dusk to be extinguished, suddenly, in a mighty geyser of spray—

Dizzy was limp and trembling when she pulled back on the stick and gunned the Boeing into a staggering climb. The motor missed, caught again and roared on as she leveled off and stuck its nose into the faint afterglow that streaked upward into the gathering darkness.

She rode the air alone, sky-victor in a riddled ship. Ominous metallic growlings broke the smooth beat of the motor from time to time. The instrument-board was shot away, but she realized that her gas must be running low.

The compass needle wabbled perilously on its luminous dial.

She nursed the game crate on—on.

The motor began to miss badly. Her eyes strained into the blackness below, but she remembered the deserted sea and gave up hope of distinguishing a light. A thin, complaining whine from the iron guts of the motor.

Bullet through the oil tanks, she thought. This can't last much longer.

But she kept on, content to take death as it should come, but still fighting. The score was even—victory hers even though she would never enjoy its spoils.

The whine of the motor was rising in a screaming crescendo—she felt the Boeing settle.

Her hands unloosed the buckles of the safety-belt, grazed the butt of a Very pistol. Her fingers closed about it and tore it out of its holster.

Pointing the Very gun over her head a rocket of light shot upward, burst in a shower of colored stars.

With a final shrill of protest the motor clanked into silence.

She nosed the ship down in a long easy glide.

The face of Spanish Lil sneered up out of her mind. Dizzy gritted her teeth. That score would have to go unsettled.

The Very pistol spurted another streamer of light that rocketed into twinkling stars.

The ship nosed down, a darker blackness rising to meet it. Wave crests slapped at the undercarriage, a spurt of spray dashed upward from the dead prop and the Boeing settled gently in the arms of the sea.

Uncomprehendingly, at first, Dizzy Malone's eyes took in the little white room, the stiffly-uniformed nurse, the white iron bed; came to rest on the face of the man bending over her—Tom Louden.

Realization filtered gradually into her mind.

Tom grinned.

"Feeling better?"

Dizzy nodded feebly.

"I may get myself into a jam for—ah—commandeering that sea sled but—it was worth the chance. And I was just in time."

"Thanks," she whispered. "You took a chance for me, huh? Well, I'm just dizzy enough to take one myself—now. I'll chance the straight and narrow, if you—think—"

Tom Louden's face bent closer—closer—.

The Duchess Pulls a Fast One
Whitman Chambers

THE AUTHOR OF MORE THAN twenty crime and mystery novels, as well as an active screenwriter, Whitman Chambers (1898–1968) is surprisingly neglected today. He created several private eye characters for the pulps and novels; perhaps the failure to produce an especially engaging series character has militated against his continuing popularity.

Among his most successful works are *The Come-On* (1953), which was filmed in 1955; he was the cowriter of the screenplay with Warren Douglas. A good and complex film noir, it starred Anne Baxter and Sterling Hayden; Russell Birdwell was the director. Hayden also starred in *Manhandled*, filmed in 1949, which also featured Dan Duryea as the quintessential small-time hood and Dorothy Lamour; Lewis R. Foster directed the Paramount feature. In 1960, Chambers wrote a novelization based on his own screenplay.

Among the many pulp stories Chambers wrote in the 1930s, he created Katie Blayne, known as "the Duchess," for *Detective Fiction Weekly*. Unlike many of her contemporaries, Katie was no one's assistant, wife, secretary, or partner. A reporter for *The Sun* who dated a man on a rival newspaper, she investigated crimes while digging out facts for her articles. She is good-looking and aggressive but often relies on intuition to solve a mystery; it was said that she could "produce hunches faster than a cigarette machine turns out coffin nails."

"The Duchess Pulls a Fast One" first appeared in the September 19, 1936, issue of *DFW*.

The Duchess Pulls a Fast One

Whitman Chambers

*Bergstrom directed them
toward the closet*

*Katie Blayne's Bluff Forces
a Mysterious Insurance
Murderer into the Open*

THE THREE OF US, Spike and Katie Blayne and I, were alone in the City Hall press room. It was six thirty of a dark and rainy evening. I'd just taken over the beat from Spike, for the *Telegram*, and Katie was waiting for the *Sun*'s night police reporter to come on the job.

"Duchess," Spike Kaylor beefed, "why don't you scram out of here and go home?"

"Spike, why don't you give yourself up?" the Duchess retorted, smiling.

"Pinky, doesn't she get in your hair the way she hangs around and hangs around, all the time?" Spike persisted.

I didn't say anything. I didn't want to be drawn into their quarrel which, for seven months, had kept the press room on pins and needles. In the first place, Spike Kaylor is my best friend. And in the second place, Katie Blayne—well, never mind about Katie Blayne.

The fire alarm gong tapped out 236. Spike strode over to the card tacked on the bulletin board. "Fifth and Chesnut." He looked more cheerful. "Our City Hall apparatus will roll on the deuce."

"And you, dear little boys, I suppose, will

take a ride on the big old fire engine," Katie jeered. "Won't that be just ducky!"

"Well," I said, "it's some consolation to be able to do something that you can't do."

Katie's blue eyes twinkled. "Maybe you think I can't."

"Skip it," I said. "You're not going kiting around on any fire truck. Not the way these lunatics drive."

At that instant the second alarm clanged in. "There's the deuce!" Spike shouted, and leaped toward the door.

I was on his heels and I realized, unhappily, that Katie was on mine. We tore down the corridor and into the fire house. The big pumper was just starting to roll. The three of us caught the hand rail and swung onto the running board. Two firemen up beside the driver looked back and yelled at Katie. The roar of the powerful engines drowned their words and the Duchess looked the other way.

As the pumper turned into the street with a breath-taking skid and roared away with bell clanging and siren wailing, Katie swayed toward me and shouted happily: "I've always wanted to do this."

"It's just the little girl in you," I growled.

We saw the red glow in the sky while we were still blocks away from the fire. Huge clouds of yellow smoke were rolling upward.

"Kurt Bergstrom's chemical plant is at Fourth and Chesnut," I yelled.

"Fine!" Spike shouted. "And if Bergstrom is going up in smoke with his chemicals, I'll buy the drinks."

Which is the way most newspaper men feel about Kurt Bergstrom. The head of the Bergstrom Chemical Company is an inventor, a nationally known chemist, a man of wealth and substance. But! He'll stool to any gag, short of murder, to get his name in the papers. And reporters do not like publicity hounds.

The pumper pulled up a block from the fire. Katie and Spike and I piled off and started down the street as one of the firemen yelled: "Hey, Duchess! Next time you want to go to a fire, hire a cab!"

"Thanks for the buggy ride," Katie called sweetly, and blew him a kiss.

The fire, we discovered with some disappointment, was confined to the north wing of the two-story brick building. It was evidently already under control, despite the billowing clouds of acrid smoke which rolled out of the shattered windows.

"Not much to this," I remarked.

Then we saw an elderly man talking excitedly to Battalion Chief Murphy. We pegged him for the night watchman and ran over.

"He was in the chem lab in the north wing when I come on at six," the old man was saying. "He was alone, workin' on some experiment. I goes over the plant and I'm down in my room makin' some coffee, when I smell smoke. That's about a half hour later. I runs upstairs and the whole chem lab is in flames. I never seen him go out. His car's right there in front of the office where he parked it, but he ain't nowheres around."

"Who?" Spike bellowed. "Who?"

The watchman blinked at us. "Mr. Hamlin. Mr. John Hamlin. He's Mr. Bergstrom's assistant in the lab."

Chief Murphy grunted. "Well, we'll find out if he's in there in a few minutes. I'll send in a couple of men with gas masks."

A little later they found the body, or what was left of it. They didn't even try to carry it out. They left that grisly job to the coroner. In the confined space of the laboratory the heat had been intense.

We cleaned up as many angles of the story as we could and then Spike called a cab. The Duchess, as usual, was right on our heels. She climbed into the taxi with us and sat down calmly between Spike and me.

Spike stared straight ahead as the cab pulled away from the curb. "My nose tells me it's still with us," he commented acidly.

"My Christmas Night perfume," Katie said blandly. "Don't you adore it?"

"I'd adore to drop you down a manhole," Spike groused.

She let that pass. "Are you by any chance going to the Hotel Drake?" she asked. "Because if you are, I'll go with you and we'll interview Kurt Bergstrom together."

Spike groaned, but didn't argue.

The clerk at the Drake directed us to the dining room and the head waiter told us Bergstrom was eating alone in the south alcove. Spike started off, then checked himself. A cagey look came into his eyes as he asked casually: "How long has Mr. Bergstrom been in the dining room?"

"Since a little after six, sir."

As we paraded through the room, a bit damp and sooty and bedraggled, Katie asked:

"Now what was the occasion for that question?"

"Did you ever hear, my little cabbage, of the crime called arson?"

"Yes," Katie said promptly, "and I've also heard of the crime called murder. But if you're thinking of them in connection with Kurt Bergstrom, you'd best forget them. Mr. Bergstrom is a wealthy man. He had no reason to stoop to arson, much less to murder."

"That mugg would stoop to anything to get his name in the papers."

Bergstrom rose when he saw us coming. He was a heavy-set chap of fifty, with very pink cheeks, keen blue eyes and close-clipped blond hair.

"Goot evening, gentlemen. Goot evening, Miss Blayne." He knew every reporter in the city. "There is something I can do for you?"

"There sure is," Spike said. "Who is John Hamlin?"

"Hamlin is my assistant in the laboratory."

"Not any more he isn't your assistant." Spike never beat around the bush. "The north wing of your plant was just gutted by fire. Hamlin was burned to death, or so the watchman believes. Anyway, the firemen found a body in the lab. Hamlin's car is out in front but Hamlin is missing."

Bergstrom took it calmly but that didn't prove anything. He's the type who never shows emotion.

"Now about this man Hamlin," Spike hurried on. "Was he married?"

"Yes. He lived with his wife at 17 Bay Terrace."

"Why was he down there after hours?"

"An experimental chemist," Bergstrom proclaimed, "has no hours. He was working nights on an experiment of his own. Only during the day did he help me with one of my inventions."

"Which is?"

Bergstrom brightened. "An inexpensive device for recording sound on motion picture film. An attachment for the home movie camera, selling for only a few dollars, which—"

"Give the details to the advertising department," Spike broke in. "We're not handing out any free publicity for your invention." He paused, looked the big German straight in the eye. "Do you believe, Mr. Bergstrom, that the body found was John Hamlin's?"

Bergstrom shrugged, said cautiously: "You say Hamlin iss missing und a body was found in the laboratory. Surely you, as a brilliant young newspaper man, should be able to draw the obvious conclusion."

"But perhaps," Spike said slowly, "the conclusion is too *damned* obvious!" He glared at the bristling Bergstrom. "Have you stopped to think of that?"

"I haff hardly had time," Bergstrom retorted stiffly, "to think of anything. Und now if you excuse me please, I run oud to the plant."

We followed him out of the dining room. In the lobby Katie asked: "Are you going out to see Mrs. Hamlin?"

"Yes, *darling!*" Spike shot back. "And I suppose you'd like to tag along."

"Yes, *dear!* I'd love it. You know how I enjoy your company."

We found Mrs. Hamlin dry-eyed and calm, though we knew immediately when we saw her that she had been informed of her husband's death. She was a tall, big-boned woman with black hair that looked dyed and dark, close-set eyes.

She invited us into the living room and asked us to sit down. "I knew that those experiments would end in tragedy," she told us calmly. "You see, my husband was developing a high explosive."

"So far as anyone knows," Spike pointed out, "there was no explosion."

"The chemicals he used were highly inflammable."

"I see." Spike didn't look as though he saw at all. "Did your husband come home for dinner tonight, Mrs. Hamlin?"

"He came home, yes. He ate an early dinner, as always, and rushed back to the laboratory. He must have got there a little before six. I did my dishes and sat down and tried to read. I had planned to go to a movie. But, somehow, I didn't dare leave the house. I was sitting here on the Chesterfield when the coroner phoned. I was neither surprised nor shocked. You see, I have been expecting this." She wiped her dry eyes with a folded handkerchief. "I suppose you will want pictures?"

She turned to a table, picked up three large snapshots and handed them to me. "They were taken a year ago today. Our wedding day."

Well, it should have been pretty pathetic, but somehow it wasn't. I looked at the pictures. Mr. and Mrs. John Hamlin on somebody's lawn. A little guy with a head too big for his stooped shoulders, his thin arm held in the possessive grip of a smirking, over-dressed Amazon.

Spike asked quietly: "Did Mr. Hamlin carry any insurance?"

"Yes. He took it out before we were married."

"A large amount?"

"Eighty thousand dollars."

Spike peered around the room.

"Quite a sizable policy for a man in his circumstances, wouldn't you say?"

I could see her stiffen as she glared at Spike. "Considering the dangers of his work, no. He wished me to be provided for if anything happened."

"Well, we'll hope his wish is granted," Spike said, rubbing a smile off his lips. "Although insurance companies sometimes get tough about things like this. Any further questions—children? If not,

that will be all, Mrs. Hamlin. Sorry to trouble you, and thanks for the pictures."

We filed out, climbed into our cab and started back to the Hall.

"What a story, what a story!" Spike chortled. "If we can only crack it!"

"You mean this poor woman's losing her husband on their wedding anniversary?" Katie asked.

Spike moaned. "Brilliance. That's it. Positive brilliance. Duchess, don't you know a Schwartz when one jumps up and spits in your face?"

"A Schwartz?"

"Tell her, Pinky. She was still in kindergarten when the Schwartz case broke."

"This Schwartz was a chemist and inventor too," I said. "He had a laboratory out in Walnut Creek where he was working on a process of manufacturing artificial silk. One night there was an explosion and the joint burned down. They found a man's body in the ashes. Everybody thought, of course, that Schwartz had cashed his checks. His wife put in for the hundred grand insurance he carried.

"Then it developed that the body wasn't Schwartz's at all. The dead guy was an itinerant preacher whom the chemist had lured into the laboratory and knocked over the head. Schwartz, in the meantime, had holed up in an apartment he'd rented weeks before he pulled the hoax. The dicks got on his trail and were closing in on him when Schwartz put a .45 slug between his eyes. Since then, Katie, an insurance hoax of that type has been known as a Schwartz."

The Duchess took one of my cigarettes and lit it with hands that weren't very steady. "And you think this is an insurance hoax?"

"Cinch," Spike declared flatly.

"Why?"

"Because it's too damned pat and because that guy Hamlin carried too much insurance."

"And who was the man they found in the laboratory?"

"Some hobo who'll never be missed. Hamlin got him in there on the pretext of giving him a job, slapped him over the conk and fired the joint. Simple, Duchess."

"And you think Kurt Bergstrom was in on the hoax?" Katie pursued.

"Cinch." Spike nodded gleefully. "The way I dope it, the time of the fire was prearranged to put Bergstrom in the clear. John Hamlin is a weak sister and the whole plot was cooked up by Bergstrom and Mrs. Hamlin. Hamlin is safely holed up somewhere, and when the heat is off he and the dame'll scram to South America with forty grand."

"And the other forty grand?"

"Into Kurt Bergstrom's sock. Well, what do you think of it, Duchess?"

"I think the whole thing," Katie promptly retorted, "is a silly machination of a disordered brain."

When we got back to the press room I called the beat while Spike and the Duchess phoned their offices. Then, on a hunch, I rang the morgue and by sheer good luck got hold of the coroner himself.

"Pinky Kane," I said. "Look, coroner. About that man who was burned to death in the Bergstrom fire. Have you got around to a p.m. yet?"

"We've made a cursory examination at the request of Captain Wallis."

"What'd you find?"

"Perhaps you'd better ask Wallis. He ordered me not to give out any details."

Katie and Spike were still in the phone booths as I impatiently jiggled the hook, got the operator and asked for the Captain of Detectives. Wallis came on almost immediately.

"This is Kane, skipper. Understand you ordered a post mortem on Hamlin's body."

"That's right, Pinky."

"What'd you find out?"

"Well, his height and build approximate that of John Hamlin. He carried a gold watch on which Hamlin's initials are still discernible. He wore a full denture—not a tooth in his head. Same as Hamlin. And that, Kane, is about the works."

"Come on, skipper. Kick in."

"I said that was the works."

"Now look here. You were on that Schwartz case and so was I. And I haven't forgotten it. Now what else did your medical examiner discover when he went over that body? Tell me everything."

"Well," Captain Wallis sighed, "you'll get it sooner or later, so I might as well give it to you now. The man's skull had been fractured."

"Uh-huh, I thought you were holding out something like that. Hamlin's skull couldn't have been cracked in the fire, could it?"

"Chief Murphy said nothing fell on him and if he had a fractured skull he must have got it before the fire broke out."

"Well, what do you think?" I asked.

"I don't know how you spotted it, Pinky, but I think you're on the right track. Another Schwartz."

"How about Bergstrom? Do you think he's in on it?"

"If I answered that question I'd be guessing. So let's pass it."

"And Mrs. Hamlin?"

"I've only talked to her on the phone. She may be a party to the hoax and she may not. Probably not. Schwartz's wife wasn't, you know. He planned to contact her after the pay-off and, as the saying goes, tell all. Anyway, I've just sent out an all-state teletype with Hamlin's description. I've ordered him held."

"On what charge, skipper?"

"Murder, my boy. Murder," Captain Wallis said cheerfully.

I hung up, a bit breathless all of a sudden.

The Captain certainly had been working fast.

Katie came out of the *Sun* booth. "You've been talking to Bodie Wallis, haven't you?" she said, smiling.

"Bodie did most of the talking. I listened. He's sent out an all-state teletype to pick up John Hamlin."

Katie's laugh told me what she thought of Bodie Wallis. "John Hamlin has already been picked up. In a basket, by a couple of coroner's deputies."

"Captain Wallis doesn't think so."

"String with Captain Wallis, Pinky, and you'll sleep in the street," she said airily.

Spike tumbled out of the telephone booth bellowing:

"Hey, Pink! The office just got a flash from Duke Wayland on the lower beat. Captain Wallis—"

"I know. I was just talking to him."

"That guy had a fractured skull!" Spike exclaimed excitedly.

"Yeah," I said.

Katie's jaw dropped as she looked from Spike to me. "What guy had a fractured skull?" she asked in a small voice.

"The guy they picked up in a basket. The guy you were dumb enough to think was John Hamlin."

Katie sat down abruptly. Spike and I stood looking at her, gloating a little. It wasn't often that the Duchess put her money on the wrong number.

"Well, muh frand?" Spike grinned at last.

She shrugged. "It looks bad but it isn't hopeless. I'm banking on one thing: the integrity of Kurt Bergstrom. I've known him for several years and I can't see him getting mixed up in an insurance hoax involving murder. And I can't see that meek and mild person, John Hamlin, hitting a man over the head and burning his body."

"That's logic for you," Spike jeered. "Kurt Bergstrom looks too honest to go in for murder. And John Hamlin looks too meek to kill anybody. Forget, for a minute, the looks of those two guys and where are you? Well, I'll tell you. You're stringing along with Pinky and me and Captain Wallis."

"Three," Katie said sarcastically, "of the most brilliant minds in the city. Well, if you three are brilliant, I'm a low moron. Good night."

Katie breezed, slamming the door.

Spike chuckled. "Did we get the little lady's goat, all right. But I'd much rather get John Hamlin."

"And maybe you think we won't. Now look.

It's a ten to one shot the guy never left the city. His best bet was to establish a residence in some quiet apartment house. He's probably had the apartment for weeks, just like Schwartz did. All right. So what?"

"I'll bite."

"We smoke him out."

"You and me?"

"Don't be a sap. We got a staff, haven't we. We got three or four cubs sitting over there in the office wearing out the seats of their pants, haven't we? Oke! Tomorrow morning early we turn 'em loose, along with anybody else Andy can spare. We contact every hotel and apartment and rooming house in the city."

"The dicks will be doing just that," I pointed out.

"What of it? We can put as many men on the job as Bodie Wallis. We got just as good a chance as he has of turning up Hamlin. And if we get a break—well, will Katie's face be red? Dunt esk!"

We went to work the next morning. It was house-to-house stuff and it was tiring. But we didn't care. Spike and I felt, the whole *Telegram* staff felt, that we were on the right track.

As we read John Hamlin's mind, he never expected any hue and cry. He thought the corpse would be accepted as his, and the pay-off would be a pushover. He'd made only one mistake. He'd hit the poor devil he'd hired to double for him too hard a blow. The body wasn't wholly consumed, as he'd expected it to be, and the skull fracture showed up in the post mortem. John Hamlin, we reasoned, must have got quite a shock when he read the papers in the morning and learned that every law enforcement officer in the state was looking for him.

It was a long hard day and we found no trace of John Hamlin. Something, however, was in our blood. The thrill of the chase. We felt, Spike and I and the cubs, as though surely we'd locate him in the next apartment house, the next hotel. We kept doggedly at it all day, all the day following, all the day after that.

At five in the afternoon of the third day, dead

on my feet, I strolled into the City Hall press room. The reporters on the afternoon papers had gone home and Katie, looking fresh and spruce and more than a little like a million dollars, was all alone.

"You looked dragged out, Pinky," she smiled. "Where have you been all day?"

"Hunting John Hamlin," I said, slumping into a chair.

"Why, don't you read the papers? Hamlin was buried today. I covered the funeral."

I sighed. "You don't really think that was Hamlin, do you? I know you're silly, Duchess, and I know your judgment isn't very good. But you're not that silly, are you?"

She looked at me hard for a long minute. Then:

"See here, Pinky Kane. I don't like that. I don't like it even a little bit. You can call me almost anything else, but I draw the line at being called silly. I was going to spare you this, but on second thought I won't. I'll go out of my way, for once, just to show you how silly *you* are. Will you meet me at the Drake Hotel at eight tonight?"

"What for?"

"For the pay-off," Katie said.

The door had opened and Spike Kaylor stood on the threshold. "Where's the pay-off?" he demanded.

"At the Drake, tonight," the Duchess told him. "You're invited.

"Thanks," Spike grinned. "Will this affair be formal, or shall I—"

"Wear tails, by all means," Katie shot back, and left the room.

"What's the kid got on her mind?" Spike asked.

"You can't prove anything by me."

"Do you really think she has a hot lead?"

"I wouldn't put it beyond her."

"But what is it? She hasn't found John Hamlin, has she?"

"No. She insists Hamlin is dead and buried."

"But maybe that's just to throw us off the track." Spike eased into a chair. "Pay-off, huh? Pay-off," he mused. "Pink, there's something

screwy about this picture. If she was ready to crack this story, would she invite us to the party? Not any! She'd tell us something was due to pop and let us stew in our own juices until two o'clock tomorrow morning when the final edition of the *Sun* comes out."

"That's what you'd think, all right. So what?"

"So we take her up. What the hell else can we do?"

We found the Duchess, sitting off by herself, in the lobby of the Drake at eight o'clock.

"Well, keed, when does the curtain go up?" Spike asked.

"Almost any minute," Katie returned shortly. "Just keep your shirts on and your mouths shut."

She lit a fresh cigarette off a glowing butt.

Her hands were shaking and I saw that the palms were moist. Her eyes were bright, feverish, as she kept watching the door.

"Our little pal seems a bit nervous," Spike grinned.

"We can do without your puerile mouthings for a while, Mr. Kaylor," the Duchess told him.

Then Kurt Bergstrom strode into the lobby and Katie rose. The chemist spotted her and came over. He looked keyed up and he didn't smile as he bowed perfunctorily over her hand.

"These are your friends?" he asked, looking at Spike and me with cold and fishy eyes.

"Not my friends, but they'll do as witnesses."

"Goot! Bring them up in ten minutes."

Bergstrom turned and walked briskly toward the elevators. Katie sat down and lit another cigarette. She was plenty nervous.

I began to feel restive myself. Even Spike, who is almost irrepressible, didn't have anything to say. We watched ten slow minutes tick off on the clock over the desk. Then Katie stood up.

"When we go up to Bergstrom's room," she said, "you two will do as you're told and ask no questions. Have you got that straight?"

"Oke, kid," Spike nodded. "Lead the way."

Bergstrom received us in the living room of his suite. He waved Katie to a chair and then stood for a minute eyeing Spike and me. You could see he didn't like us. You could see he wished we were a long way from there. Finally he said:

"I hope we can trust them, Miss Blayne."

"They'll do as they're told and like it," the Duchess said.

"That all depends," Spike said, "on what you tell us to do."

Bergstrom threw open a door to a clothes closet. "You will go in there und stay there und keep quiet," he said crisply. "You will leaf the door oben two or three inches, joost enough so you can see und hear what goes on. You will nod come oudt until you are told to come oudt. All right?"

"All right," Spike agreed.

"I will tell you when to go in. In the meantime, please to sit down und be comfortable."

We sat down diffidently. So help me, I couldn't get the angle. I couldn't make head or tail of the layout. Spike caught my eye, while Bergstrom paced briskly up and down the room, and signalled: "Watch yourself. I don't trust this guy." I didn't trust him either.

After a time the telephone rang. Bergstrom took it up, listened a moment, ordered: "Show him up at once."

Spike started to rise.

"No, no. Nod yet," Bergstrom said irritably. "It iss only Captain Wallis."

Spike sat down again, looking a bit deflated. Bodie Wallis came in after a few minutes. In his quiet blue serge business suit, he didn't look much like a detective.

He nodded to Katie and Bergstrom, grinned at Spike and me.

"You two boys don't miss anything, do you?" he chuckled.

"Not if we can help it," Spike admitted, a bit boastfully.

"I might point out," Katie remarked, "that they are here at my invitation. And anything they see or hear won't be reported in the *Telegram* until it has appeared exclusively in the *Sun*. Right, Mr. Kaylor?"

"Wrong, Miss Blayne!" Spike bristled. "That wasn't part of the bargain."

"It's part of the bargain now."

"Sister, it takes two to make a bargain. And as long as I have two legs and can run to the nearest telephone—"

The phone buzzed at that instant and Bergstrom raised his hand authoritatively. "Silence, if you please!" He picked up the instrument, and after a moment: "Show her up at once."

He turned and waved us toward the closet. We got up and went in and closed the door to a two-inch crack. Spike jammed his foot against the door and I pulled on the knob, to hold it steady open. Spike, kneeling at the crack, whispered:

"It's a funny one, Pink. You got any ideas?"

"No ideas, but I got a good hunch," I whispered. "Bergstrom is on the spot. With Katie's unwitting help, he's trying to slide out from under."

"Yeah. That's the way I dope it. He's about to pull a fast one. And when it comes down the groove, we'll pole it over the right-field fence for a home run. How's about it?"

"That's okey by me."

We didn't say any more, because Bergstrom had stepped to the hall door and was admitting—Mrs. John Hamlin! She wore black and she looked tense and watchful and cool. Bergstrom was saying:

"Miss Blayne you haff met, I believe. Und this, Mrs. Hamlin, iss Mr. Wallis."

Mister Wallis! Well, why not? The whole situation was cockeyed anyway.

"Please to sit down, Mrs. Hamlin," Bergstrom said, helping her to a chair with great solicitude. "We haff wonderful news for you. Your husband, my dear, iss *alive!*"

Mrs. Hamlin sat on the edge of her chair, stiffly, blinking up at him. She said carefully: "I buried my husband this afternoon."

Bergstrom smiled down at her gently, shook his head. "The man you buried vas nod your husband. John iss alive. He vas badly burned in the fire und he sustained a severe injury to the head. He hass been suffering from amnesia ever since. In fact, even now he iss delirious. But the doctor assures me that his chances for pulling through are excellent."

The woman never moved but I could see the last of the color in her cheeks fade out.

Spike whispered: "Amnesia! Did I tell you a fast one was coming down the groove? Amnesia!"

Well, it was easy enough for a couple of smart reporters to dope the play. I saw it this way: When Bergstrom and Hamlin realized their hoax wasn't going over, they got together and devised this amnesia gag. Burned Hamlin with a little acid, probably. Cooked up a good story. "I don't remember anything that happened till I woke up in the hospital." That sort of thing—it's pulled every day.

Yes, it was all pretty smart. Just about the type of stuff you'd expect a bright lad like Herr Bergstrom to pull. Having Captain Wallis there on the job was just the right touch. It showed the supreme confidence and egoism of the chemist.

"I feel certain there has been some mistake," Mrs. Hamlin said slowly, gripping the arms of her chair. "I did not see John's body. I did not want to look at it. But I knew, as I sat there staring at the coffin this afternoon, that my husband was in it."

"But," Bergstrom pointed out calmly, "there iss no way you *could* know, Mrs. Hamlin. No way in the world, because—John iss in bed in the next room. Alive. Delirious, seriously burned, very ill—but *alive!*"

He shouted that last word in a way that sent a chill down my spine—even though I'd suspected all along that Hamlin wasn't dead.

And then all at once I was conscious of a voice from the room on the far side. Someone in there had been talking for quite a while, talking very softly. And now, as Spike and I and the people in the living room listened, the voice grew louder. We could catch a word or two: "Valence of three . . . calcium chloride . . . neutralized . . ."

What a shock to that woman who was sitting there so white and rigid. A voice, literally, from the dead!

I felt my hair standing on end. I heard Spike's

fast and unsteady breathing. I could feel his body shaking with the tension of nerves about to snap. Let me tell you, it was electric!

Bergstrom stepped to the other door. He threw it open. The room was dark but we heard that rasping voice going on monotonously: ". . . carbon union in the aliphatic hydrocarbons has apparently the same effect on the boiling point as two hydrogen atoms. But as I was telling you, Kurt, an acetylenic or triple linkage is associated with a rise in the boiling point. However . . ."

Mrs. Hamlin was on her feet, staring into the darkened room. She screamed: "No! No!"

Bergstrom said patiently, gently: "But yes, Mrs. Hamlin. Surely you recognize John's voice."

The woman caught the arm of a chair, steadied herself. "I tell you," she cried hysterically, "John is *dead!*"

"No. John iss very much alive."

Bergstrom reached inside the door, flipped the switch. The bedroom was bright with light. Looking straight across the living room, I could see a figure in the bed. I caught a glimpse of a head swathed in bandages. I saw lips moving. I heard the deadly monotonous voice going on and on.

". . . true of the fatty acid series, Kurt, and the corresponding ketones and . . ."

Then the bedroom door was blocked by the angular figure of Mrs. Hamlin. She swayed against the frame, caught herself, screamed: "No, no, I tell you! It can't be true! He can't be alive! I killed him myself with a hammer. I got into the plant with a key to the back door. I've had it for months: I crept up behind him. I knocked him down. I poured gasoline over him and struck a match. I saw him burn. *I saw him burn!*"

All this in a wild screech that sent icy chills up and down my spine. John Hamlin's voice went on:

". . . although, Kurt, the correlation of melting point with constitution has not . . ."

The tall woman covered her face with her

angular hands. She screamed through her bony fingers: "*I tell you I killed him!*"

Then she dropped in a dead faint.

". . . symmetry of the resulting molecule may exert such a lowering effect that the final result . . ."

"Westoby!" Bergstrom yelled, "Ged out uf bed und turn that damn' thing off. If I haff to listen to John Hamlin's voice one minute longer I shall haff hysterics!"

Well, after Mrs. Hamlin had snapped out of her faint and Captain Wallis had taken her away, we were all pretty limp. Bergstrom brought out a bottle and some ice, and we all sat down and tried to come back to Earth. The chemist remarked finally:

"Fortunately, Hamlin had been helping me with my sount devize. I suppose I haff a mile or two uf film on which his voice iss recorded."

Westoby, who is one of the chemist's lab men, added: "Lucky, too, the film was stored in the physical laboratory in the south wing, which the fire didn't touch."

The Duchess was smiling. "And speaking of luck, wasn't it a break that I brushed against Mrs. Hamlin's coat in her hallway the other night?"

"Huh?" Spike grunted. "What's Mrs. Hamlin's coat got to do with it?"

"It was wet, darling," Katie said pleasantly. "There were beads of rain on the fur collar. And Mrs. Hamlin had told us she hadn't left the house that evening."

"Look here!" Spike snorted. "Do you mean to tell me you had the play doped from the beginning?"

"I had it doped, as you put it, within an hour or two after I brushed against that wet coat."

"Well, Duchess, I got to hand it to you. You're the top." He drained his glass and stood up. "Bergstrom, you've put on a grand show and we'll give your sound recorder a million dollars' worth of publicity. Now I've got to hit a phone with the story. Okay to use yours?"

"No," Bergstrom said steadily. "It iss most decidedly nod okay to use mine."

"Huh?" Spike gasped. "Wha-zat?"

Bergstrom, still smiling, bowed to Katie. And the Duchess rose.

"Mrs. Bergstrom has ordered the operator to accept no out-going calls," she informed us. "So if you want to give your office the story, Spike, you'll have to find another telephone."

She moved toward the door, adding over her shoulder: "If you can, and that will be quite a job!"

"If I can!" Spike bellowed, and started after her. "While I've got the use of my legs, I guess—"

Katie threw open the door. Lounging in the hall outside I caught a glimpse of half a dozen of the toughest looking punks I ever saw outside of a penitentiary—or a morning paper's circulation department. Spike stopped in his tracks.

"Keep them here, boys, until midnight," the Duchess ordered cheerfully. "And try not to hurt them too badly if they make a break."

"We won't hurt 'em, Miss Katie," a big bruiser grinned. "Not *much!*"

Well, they didn't hurt us—because we didn't make a break. We stayed there till midnight, drinking very good whiskey with Kurt Bergstrom and wondering where we ever got the idea that the Duchess was silly, and dumb, and slow on the pick-up.

Mansion of Death &

Concealed Weapon

Roger Torrey

IT WAS RUMORED that Roger Torrey's real name was Torres, but he insisted he was of Irish descent and apparently tried to prove it by giving most of his cops and private detectives Irish names. And with so many other pulp writers, famous and not-so-famous, he was a heavy drinker of such mythical stature that he found the perfect woman for him—in a bar. Also a hard-drinking writer, she moved into his hotel room and they established a system of producing fiction that seems to have worked for them. He sat at one desk, she at another, with a bottle of booze nearby. The first person to finish the story on which they were working was permitted to drink while the other had to finish the story before being allowed to have a nip. Torrey, a veteran of the pulps, wrote faster, so generally finished first, then drank and mocked her while getting smashed. A prolific as well as gifted short story writer, Torrey produced fifty stories for *Black Mask* alone, writing for many other publications as well. He wrote only one novel, *42 Days for Murder*, published by the unprestigious house of Hillman-Curl in 1938.

In "Mansion of Death," Torrey has produced the most atypical story one could imagine in the pages of a pulp: a little old lady takes a hard-boiled detective and leads him around by the nose. It was originally published in the *Detective Fiction Weekly* issue of May 25, 1940. "Concealed Weapon" is a more common story of a private eye with an invaluable female assistant, first published in the December 1938 issue of *Black Mask*.

I fired then—
into his shin bone

Mansion of Death

Roger Torrey

Miss Conklin didn't have anything
against detectives; she simply liked
to solve murders her own way

I LIKED THE OLD LADY the first time I saw her . . . but then, I've always gotten along better with old ladies than with the young ones. Though maybe that's because I've never worried about the old ones as much. Anyway, she came in the office and held out her hand as if she expected me to bow over it, and said:

"I'm Miss Conklin! I talked with you over the telephone, young man."

I bowed, though I hadn't intended any such foolishness, and told her I was glad to meet her in person. And she twinkled her bright little blue eyes at me and shook her finger at me and said:

"Now young man! You're glad to see me because I'm a customer."

And then she perched on the edge of the chair I'd bounced around the desk and brought up for her.

She was really cute. She looked like an old-fashioned grandmother dressed up in Fifth Avenue clothes. They fitted her beautifully and undoubtedly had cost her a lot of money. But she didn't seem to belong in them. She should have been wearing a lot of ruffles with lace around her neck and a poke bonnet. And Congress gaiters instead of high-heeled shoes. I sat down on my own side of the desk and asked:

"What was it, Miss Conklin?"

"I've been robbed," she said calmly. "And I don't like it. I don't like the feeling of not being able to trust my own household."

I said that was understandable. She went on: "There was $1,864 taken from my desk drawer. There was an envelope containing slightly more than $50,000 in negotiable bonds directly beside the money, but that wasn't touched. No one had broken in the house and it's self-evident that some one in the house itself is guilty of the theft. I don't wish to have the police tramping over my house and asking innocent people a lot of silly questions, but I *do* want to catch the thief."

"Suppose I find the guilty person. Will you turn him—or her, if that's the way it turns out—over to the police?"

She shook her head and said: "I will not. I have an odd household, Mr. Shay. If you'll ride up to the house with me, I'll explain that remark on our way."

I took my gun from its place in the upper desk drawer and started to slip it in the clip under my arm—and she frowned and said:

"You will not need a weapon, Mr. Shay. I'm sure there'll be no necessity for one."

So I put the gun back and reached for my hat instead. She hadn't talked about payment for what I was or wasn't going to do, and I thought I'd better look over things before bringing the subject up.

I wasn't worried; people who leave eighteen-hundred-odd dollars loose in desk drawers can usually pay a private cop's starvation wages.

Her chauffeur was an ugly bird that looked as though he'd just got out of jail. And the funny part of it was he just had. She told me all about it on the way up to the house. She said:

"My house is staffed with people who have been . . . well, let us say in houses of correction. I believe they should be given a helping hand and

a chance to earn an honest living, once they have paid their debt to society."

"And you keep eighteen hundred dollars, loose, in a desk drawer. Along with fifty thousand dollars worth of bonds that could be hocked with any fence."

She said: "I have never been robbed, young man. Never."

"What about now?"

She sounded stiff and old-ladyish now. "There is some mistake, young man. Of that I am sure. One of my people must have faced a problem that only money could solve. Something he or she couldn't come to me about."

I told her I faced the same sort of a problem every rent day and listened to more. She had a nephew and niece with her, besides the jail help. And then I got a shock. She said:

"My nephew is George Lawrence, Jr. His sister is Frances Lawrence. I understand they are fairly well-known among the younger set."

"I know Georgie, Miss Conklin," I said. "If you have your driver stop, I'll get out here and go back to my office."

She asked me what was the matter and I told her. I said: "I had the pleasure of knocking young Georgie almost over the *Black Cat Club's* bar, just night before last. I'm surprised you didn't hear about it—the newspapers had a lot of fun with the thing."

"I know all about it," she said placidly. "In fact, that's one reason I came to you. George has had that coming to him for some time. He came home with a black eye, after my lawyer bailed him out of jail, and told me all about it."

"What did he say?"

She twinkled her eyes at me and said: "You can depend on it not being the truth. But I asked questions and found out the truth. That should happen oftener to the boy."

"You're not sore about it?"

"My goodness no! I'm grateful to you, Mr. Shay. You'll find George isn't the kind to cherish a grudge, Mr. Shay. . . . Just forget all about the episode."

Personally I thought young Georgie would

carry a grudge until the day he died, but I didn't care a whoop whether he did or not. He was one of those loud-mouthed freshies that grates on me, and I was perfectly willing to knock him over a bar whenever we met. A bar was the logical place to look for young George. The kid was a society swack and they don't come any swackier than that.

And then we pulled into the driveway and up to her house.

It could have been turned into a library without much trouble; it had the lines and the size. An old place and very dignified. I helped her, judging her to weigh not over eighty pounds wringing wet and with lead in her shoes, and as we watched the chauffeur swing the car on and around toward the garage, she cautioned me:

"Now use tact, Mr. Shay! I want none of my people worried. The innocent shouldn't suffer for the thoughtlessness of one."

Then the butler opened the door and we went in.

I got a break right off the bat. Fresh from the griddle. The butler was Preacher Toomey, who usually did his time for slipping up on some confidence racket. Of course he'd taken one jolt for armed robbery and another for assault with intent to kill, but they were outside of his regular field of endeavor.

"Why hello, Preacher," I said.

He bowed and looked at me out of mean little eyes.

"Good afternoon, Mr. Shay."

Little Miss Conklin twinkled her eyes at both of us and marveled: "Well, isn't this nice. You know each other then?"

"You might say a professional acquaintance, eh, Preacher?" I said.

Preacher said: "Yes, sir."

And then Miss Conklin and I went in the library and found the maid.

She hadn't been dead long . . . and her name had been Mary Morse. At least that was one of them. She'd done time for everything from shoplifting on up. Somebody had caved in her right temple with something that hadn't broken the skin at all. The skull bone there is not much thicker than paper and it was crushed in all right, but there was no blood. Just a sort of darkening, where blood vessels below the skin had broken.

Miss Conklin and I had walked in on her together, and I turned to catch the old lady when she fainted, but she just caught the corner of the desk to steady herself.

"My goodness sake!"

"I'll call the police," I said.

She waved her hand, palm up, in front of her, but didn't speak for a moment. And then she said: "Not for a little while, please. I ask that, Mr. Shay."

"It's the law, Miss Conklin. They have to be notified at once."

"Not for a little while, please. I can handle any trouble resulting from your not calling them at once, I can assure you."

I thought the moment I got a chance at a phone I'd call, so didn't argue. Just looked at the dead girl.

She'd been pretty. She was maybe twenty-five or twenty-eight, not over that, and she'd been a good-sized wench. Probably around a hundred and thirty, though she didn't look half that big lying there.

Dead people never do look their weight—they seem to shrink.

There was no sign around of anything she could have been hit with; I decided it was probably a shot-filled sap, though it could have been some home-made affair, filled with sand or anything like that. She was right by the desk, and the drawer above her was half open, as though she might have been searching in it. She was dressed in a neat little black and white outfit—the kind that has a little apron all frilled at the edges and a cap to match.

The cap was still on her head, but it was riding a little cock-eyed.

"This is murder, Miss Conklin, and the first thing to do is call the police."

"I know exactly what to do, Mr. Shay," she said. "Please don't ask any questions now. Just come with me."

We went out in the hall then and found Preacher Toomey still puttering around there. Miss Conklin said:

"Toomey, have there been any visitors?"

"Why no, Miss Conklin," he told her. "Mr. Franks is here calling on Miss Lawrence, but that is all that I know of."

"Is Mr. Lawrence in?"

"Yes, ma'am."

"You haven't been out, have you, Toomey? You'd surely know if there's strangers here?"

"I've been here all afternoon, ma'am."

"Noticed anything wrong?"

"Why no, ma'am."

She told him that was all and we went back to the library. She said then, in a tired voice: "Well, I wanted to be sure. I'll call the police now. . . . It was possible somebody else had killed poor Mary, but now it's surely someone in the house. Toomey would say if there'd been anybody else here."

"Would he know for sure?"

She said: "If he knew this had happened, he'd have said that various unknown people had been in and out. Toomey is no fool, Mr. Shay; he would realize that he and everyone else in the house would be under immediate suspicion. Because of their past lives, you know."

That made sense. Then there was a knock on the door and Toomey followed it, stopping just inside where he couldn't see the dead girl's body.

"Might I have a few words, Miss Conklin?"

She said he could. He looked at me and said: "Of course I know Mr. Shay is here investigating the robbery, Miss Conklin. I'd just like to say I know nothing about it. I want to tell both you and Mr. Shay that I'm innocent, that I'm leading a decent life."

"I'm sure you are, Toomey," she said. "But I'd like to know just how you knew about the robbery. I told no one."

"Morse told me of it, ma'am. I'm sure I don't know how she knew. . . . She informed me it was confidential, but all of us seem to know of it."

He bowed then and left, and Miss Conklin said: "I told no one about the robbery but

George and his sister. Do you suppose one of them could have told poor Mary?"

I didn't know the sister but I knew George, and the way he chased girls. And I knew that Mary had just adored being chased—and had never run very fast when pursued. And she'd still been a good-looking gal and young George had money. I got the answer right away, but I only said:

"I'm sure I don't know."

"I'll call the police now," she sighed. "I *do* wish this hadn't happened. The police will certainly be most abrupt with my people—there's nothing I can do to prevent it."

I thought her using "abrupt" as a description of what the police would be with her collection of jailbirds was a miracle of understatement, but I let that go along with the other. She picked up the telephone and I wandered out in the hall.

Toomey was waiting for me. He beckoned me away from the door, and when I followed he said:

"Look, shamus! That's gospel that I gave in there. I haven't done a thing."

"I believe you," I said, "that's the funny part of it. If it had been you, you'd have taken the bonds along with the dough. You'd have gone hook, line, and sinker—and left the town because you couldn't take that along too. Okay! *Now* what?"

"I didn't want you picking at me all the time, is all. Maybe I'm no lily, but I'm clear on this deal."

"I get it, Preacher. You were holding off—waiting to get a chance at a *real* killing. Who's this guy Franks you told Miss Conklin was here?"

"He's the gal's sweetie. He tags her all around. He comes here every day."

"What kind of a guy is he?"

He shrugged. "*She* likes him. She's going to marry him."

I went back in the library and Miss Conklin hung up the phone and said: "The police tell me they will be here at once. Oh my goodness! The trouble my poor people will have."

I grinned and she saw it. She said sharply:

"Mr. Shay! These poor unfortunate victims of our society are entitled to decent treatment, once they have made penance. There's no reason why they shouldn't be treated as any decent citizen should be. I want you to think of that."

I thought of Preacher Toomey and the cut-throat that had driven us to the house—and the Lord knows what other specimens she had around—and said:

"You think of it, Miss Conklin. I'd as soon live in a cage with wild tigers as here."

"That is very unfair," she said.

I waved toward the desk that shielded the dead Mary Morse and said: "If Mary could talk, I'll bet she wouldn't agree with you."

The cops came and there was merry hell to pay. They lined up the help and of all the collection I ever saw they won in a walk. They'd have made the average police line-up look like a meeting of the Ladies Aid. The chauffeur had served time in Dannemora and Joliet. One gardener had taken a course at McAlester, in Oklahoma, and a P.G. at Folsom, in California. The other one had graduated from Leavenworth, which is a Federal pen. The cook was an old gal who'd killed her husband with a frying pan and had done seven years for the trick. The two other maids were about in the dead Mary Morse's class, though they didn't own the looks she'd had.

And then there was young George Lawrence, who was a worthless bum if one ever walked. He was half drunk, and when he saw me he wanted to pick up the argument where we'd left it off two nights before.

The cops stopped him quick on that—telling him they'd do all the fighting necessary.

Franks, the Lawrence girl's fiancé, was a thin-faced, dark young fellow. He seemed to be okay. I didn't know anything about him, but I wondered how a honey like the Lawrence girl could go for him. She could have done better, with what she had to work with, which was practically everything it takes.

She was small and blonde, and had that wide-set appealing stare that makes you want to pick

'em up and cuddle 'em and tell 'em everything will be all right.

Nobody had any alibi—the cops found that out right away. Nobody had any notion about who didn't like Mary Morse. Or said they hadn't. And then I got a break. The cops were ganged up, talking to one of the gardeners, and Preacher Toomey caught my eye and beckoned me over to him. He said, so no one else could hear it:

"Listen, Shay! I'll do you a favor and maybe you can do one back for me. The kid, young Georgie, was mixed up with the gal. She was clipping him for all the dough he could get his hands on."

"You sure?"

"Certain. She bragged about it."

"Did his aunt know about it?"

"Listen, Shay! If there's one single, solitary thing goes on in this house that she don't know about, I'll put in with you. She's so smart it's painful."

"Nuts!" I said. "If she was, she'd never have a bunch like she's got here around her. Was the kid still playing around with the Morse dame?"

"Sure. But she was taking him for dough and he was sore about it. He beat the hell out of her three weeks ago. . . . His aunt kept her from calling the cops in on it. That'll give you an idea of how much she knows about it. You going to tell the cops?"

"Why don't you?"

He said gloomily: "That'd make 'em think I was trying to pass the buck to somebody else. The best thing I can do is keep my mouth shut."

I told him I thought it a very good idea . . . and I did the same. I figured there'd be plenty of time to tell it later.

It ended right there. The Captain in charge, Chick Williams, grumbled to Miss Conklin: "And what can I do about it? I tell you I'll take your crew down to the station for questioning and you tell me that you'll have 'em out on a writ of habeas corpus as soon as you can get in touch with your lawyer. What can I do, lady?—You tie my hands."

"I know very well what would happen to

them at the station," Miss Conklin said primly. "They would be brow-beaten, if not physically beaten. They have told you what they know."

"Every damned one of them has stood in front of me and lied by the clock."

"Can you prove that, officer?"

Williams admitted he couldn't. Miss Conklin said: "Then I certainly wouldn't make the statement. These people look to me for protection and I intend to see they have it."

Williams went away, growling about making a check on everybody in the place and on the dead girl's past life. And as soon as he left I told Miss Conklin what Toomey had told me. She gave me a queer stare and said:

"But you didn't tell the police?"

I said that I hadn't as yet. . . .

"Give me a couple of days, Mr. Shay. If I don't think of a plan by that time, you and I will go together, taking Toomey with us, and see he tells his story to the police. I naturally don't want my nephew in jail if he's innocent, though if he's guilty that's the place for him."

I said: "Will you tell me honestly what you think about it?"

"I don't think George is guilty—I can tell you that much," she said, pursing her lips and looking like a grandmother making up her mind about how many jars of pickles to put up. "No, I really don't."

"Why not?"

"He hasn't the nerve, Mr. Shay. He's too dependent on me to do a thing like that. Rather than kill the girl, he'd have come to me and made a clean breast of the matter."

"He did—once. When he beat the girl up and you went to the front for him and kept her from calling in the cops."

"Toomey told you that, too?"

"You bet."

She smiled then. "Doesn't that support my theory, Mr. Shay? If he'd had murder in his mind, wouldn't he have committed it then, rather than just abuse the girl? He knew then I'd find it out."

"People can change," I told her. "Sometimes

a man can be driven just so far. And then he'll back up."

She admitted that maybe I was right and that she'd get in touch with me at my office in a day or so. And I left, wondering why I didn't tell the cops what I knew and have them take the young punk down to the station and sweat a confession out of him.

He was my customer for the killing and there wasn't a doubt in my mind about it. And the only thing holding me back from turning him in was the old lady. In my business, a client's always right, at least until proved a mile wrong. She was a client and so I went along with her on the two days of grace she asked for. I couldn't see it, but there was an outside chance of somebody else having done the killing—and it was just possible that she had an idea who it was.

And, after all, the cops could pick up young Lawrence just as well two days later as then.

She came in two days later, looking even smaller and more fragile. She gave me her pretty, anxious smile and said:

"I have thought it all out, Mr. Shay. There is absolutely no way to prove who killed that girl. Nor who took my money."

"That's ridiculous," I told her. "The cops could take the whole bunch down to the station, and they'd have a confession in twenty-four hours. You know that."

"It wouldn't be fair to the ones that didn't do it," she said stubbornly. "I have a deep feeling about such things. Now I have worked out a plan and I'm sure it will be successful. But I need your help."

I said I was still working for her, as far as I knew.

So then she told me what she wanted—and I finally said I'd do it. I'd argued two hours and hadn't won a point, before I caved.

"Then I'll depend on you," she finished. "I'm supposed to be playing bridge this afternoon, and I'm not expected back until around eight. As I told you, I told George and Toomey that I knew who'd killed Mary Morse and that I intended to tell the police about it tomorrow. I can depend on Toomey telling the others about it."

"They'd think it was funny you not telling the police right then," I said.

"Oh no! I told them I was waiting for certain proof," she said. "And that I'd find that out tomorrow. But that there was no doubt in my mind right then. So you see I've thought of everything."

"I'm beginning to think you have," I said.

I got into the house easily enough. . . . She'd given me the key to a side door that opened into the library, and it was just a question of making sure no one was in the room and then walking in. I moved a couch, at the corner of the room, far enough out to climb behind it, then got it back in place. It made a snug little nest. If I sat down naturally, the thing was just low enough for me to see over, and if I ducked my head a little, I was entirely out of sight.

And then I waited.

Miss Conklin came in a little after nine and never even looked toward where I was. She had that much will power. She was humming to herself, as though she hadn't a care in the world. She got a book from a shelf and sat down in a big chair that almost hid her. Her back was to the door. I could hear pages rustle as she turned them. . . . Then there was a knock on the door, and she called "Come in!" without looking around.

It was young Georgie. And he looked bad with the black eye I'd given him. I slid my gun out of its clip and got ready to go into action. He passed around in front of her and stood.

"Aunt Alice," he said, "I've got to talk to you."

"Go ahead, George."

And then I got a shock. "I heard what you told Frances," he said, "and she told me you'd told Toomey the same thing. That you knew who killed Mary."

"That's right," she said. "I intend to notify the police tomorrow. As I told Frances, there's one little detail I want cleared up and I can't do that until tomorrow."

Then came the pay-off. The kid said: "I'm going to stay right here with you, Aunt Alice. Don't you realize that you're in danger? The same person who killed Mary knows by now that you know who he is. He's liable to try to silence you. I'm going to stay right here with you."

Miss Conklin said: "No, George. I'm perfectly all right. But I thank you for the thought. Now run along—don't waste your time talking to an old lady."

"I'm going to stay, Aunt Alice."

The old lady didn't raise her voice, but it now had a snap in it. She just said: "George!"

"All right, Aunt Alice, you know best."

He marched out of the room, just barely giving me time to duck out of sight. Then the old lady said, as if she were talking to herself:

"Nice boy, George."

So there was my number one suspect cleared. . . . I was just getting over the shock of that when there was another knock and the niece came in. Looking like a million dollars! She bounced over in front of her auntie and knelt down and said:

"Oh, Aunt Alice! Aren't you afraid? You know this is Toomey's night off."

Miss Conklin said: "Yes, I've thought of that."

"But aren't you frightened, Aunt Alice?"

I didn't hear what Aunt Alice said because I was too busy ducking back out of sight. The hall door was opening—very quietly and softly—and I wanted to be out of sight until whoever it was had passed me.

And he did. It was young Franks, the girl's fiancé. He was walking on his toes and he was swinging a sap in his left hand. The girl looked over her aunt's head at him and said to the aunt:

"I just thought I'd better stay with you, Aunt Alice. Just in case of—"

I shot young Franks then, taking him just below the knee, where I had a lot of brittle shin bone to aim at. A slug from the kind of gun I shoot will wreck bone structure of that kind and leave a man crippled for life . . . and I was thinking of that. The girl stood and screamed. It cut through the roaring thunder the big gun made in the room. And Miss Conklin got up from her big chair and peered down at Franks, who was rolling around on the floor and making a lot of noise.

"It's as I thought," Miss Conklin said calmly. "Mr. Shay, will you telephone for the police. I'm going to be very busy for a few minutes."

She didn't pay any more attention to me, but went over to a drawer built in the bookcase. She pulled out a heavy riding whip. And then she went back to the girl and said:

"Now, you little sneak! I'm going to take the hide right off your damned back. You ungrateful little—!"

And then, by heaven, she did. She had a nice command of language and every time she gave the girl a new title she came down with the whip.

I didn't want to interfere, but finally I had to.

"You don't want to kill her, do you?" I said.

She stopped then.

"Did you call the police?" she asked.

I said I hadn't but would right away. And then somebody said, from the door doorway: "I did, ma'am!"

We turned and looked that way. And here was the cook, the chauffeur, and the two maids staring in. The chauffeur said:

"I called when I heard the shot, ma'am. Then I came in to help."

I said to Miss Conklin: "You going to turn the girl over to the cops?"

"Certainly not," she snapped. "I can take care of her very well. The man, the sneak, he will certainly go to prison, if he doesn't hang."

"He'll limp when he goes down that hall to the scaffold," I told her. "Did you think it was him all the time?"

"Of course," she said.

And then the cops came.

She came down to see me the next afternoon again. Just as nice as though nothing had happened. She even blushed a little when she asked me how much money I wanted. And I blushed even more when I told her—because all I'd done was what she'd told me to do. She'd supposedly

hired a detective and then she'd done all the detective work. She gave me a check.

"Miss Conklin," I said, "I don't like to appear too dumb, but what made you think it was young Franks who'd killed the maid? You told me you had that idea right along. Of course we know now why he did it—she'd seen him swipe the dough from your desk. She started to blackmail him, the same as she was already blackmailing your nephew. Of course not for the same reason. But I'd like to know why you picked him as the guilty one, instead of George, or Preacher Toomey, or that thug chauffeur or those gardeners?"

She twinkled her eyes at me and said: "Why it just *had* to be him, Mr. Shay. I knew that none of my people would steal—and of course I knew my nephew wouldn't. Not that I'd put it past the boy, but there was no need for him to steal; all he had to do was ask me for the money and I'd have given it to him. So that left only Frances and her friend. And do you know, I've never trusted that young man since the first time I met him."

"But you'd trust that collection of jailbirds you've got?"

"Why, of course," she said pensively. "You see, I know their peculiar psychology. And then I had another reason for thinking young Mr. Franks the murderer. You see, poor Mary had been struck on the right temple—that showed me a left-handed man had struck the blow. Just try it—you're right-handed, and you'll notice if you strike another person on the temple it will invariably be on the left side. This was just reversed. And, of course, my nephew, and all the others in the house, happen to be right-handed. Young Mr. Franks is the only left-handed one. But I really didn't need that proof—and it isn't the sort of thing that would stand up in court."

She went out then and left me trying to figure things out. Not the left-handed angle—that's one of the simple things you overlook because it is *so* simple.

It was the old gal herself. Here she'd acted like one of the nicest ladies I'd ever met—up to the time she'd found out for sure her niece was in the plot to kill her. And even then she didn't turn the girl over to the police. Instead she gave her a beating, and kept her where she could keep an eye on her.

And then the language she'd used was hardly the thing a lady knows.

And to top the whole thing off—having that collection of thugs around her and actually protecting them from the police.

It was all by me.

It stayed that way until I met Chick Williams, the police captain, who'd been in charge of the case. I ran into him on the street and he laughed and said:

"You still working for the Conklin woman?"

I told him I'd like to have her for a partner . . . that she'd shown more brains in the thing than either he or I had. He didn't like this so well and told me that if he'd had his way, and taken the whole bunch down to the station and sweated them, that he'd have had the answer before the old lady had it.

I agreed. And then he laughed again and poked me with a finger and said: "You know who that old gal *is?* I just happened to mention her to one of the old-timers, who dropped in the office . . . and he remembered her."

I said I didn't know who she was, other than she seemed like a nice, old gal with a lot of money. Then he poked me again and winked and said:

"She's *the* Miss Conklin. The one that scragged her sweetie, over forty years ago, and did sixteen years in the pen for it. Cold-blooded murder it was, according to the old boy. He said it was a wonder they *ever* let her out. She'd fell into a bunch of dough while she was doing time, and that probably had something to do with that angle. Ain't that a kick, Shay?"

I said it was very funny and felt a lot better. It solved the puzzle. Here I'd been wondering why she'd looked after her convict help and claimed to understand 'em. Why shouldn't she?

And it explained the language she'd used to the girl and the whip act. They talk rough and they handle their own problems in the women's wards in jails.

I left Williams. I was thinking that it would be a good bet the jail was glad to see her go. I'm willing to bet the warden slept better.

Because I had the notion that Miss Conklin would be top dog wherever she was. . . . She was one client of mine that had been right on every count.

Concealed Weapon

Roger Torrey

*McCarthy hits and runs
after a hit and run driver*

THE MAN CAME weaving down the hall of the office building and McCarthy said to Marge Chalmers: "Jeez! That guy's got seven dollars' worth of start. What a load!"

McCarthy turned and slammed his office door and the spring lock took hold with a click. The stranger in the hall lurched into Marge and would have fallen if she hadn't held him up with a short but sturdy arm. McCarthy said pleasantly enough:

"Hey, guy! Take it some place else. You better go some place and sleep it off."

The man's face was a dingy white. Even with Marge's support he was standing bent and twisted. He muttered something and McCarthy said tolerantly:

"All right, guy! I didn't hear you. But you ain't the first to get this way."

Marge said, not tolerantly: "*You* should tell him that! You, of all people!" And then, with a total change in tone: "Pat! The man's hurt!"

The man proved it by quietly falling on the floor in spite of Marge's attempt at holding him erect. He went down in a loose and sodden pile, and Marge looked up from him and snapped: "Pat!"

McCarthy was already in action. He was stooping and tearing the man's coat open, and when he saw the blood mottling the white shirt he said:

"Oke, kitten! We won't move him. Call the ambulance and the cops. Quick! If we move him, it might make it worse."

"What is it, Pat?"

McCarthy pointed out a half-dozen holes in the bloody shirt. "Maybe an ice pick, I don't know. But they're in his belly, and that means he shouldn't be moved. Get going."

wounded man, and that smart young man said to him:

"Maybe we're in time. Unless the fellow gets a transfusion inside the next few minutes he'll be shaking hands with Saint Peter."

"How bad, Doc?" McCarthy asked.

Marge took his keys and opened the office.

The police came, after a little while, cars full of them, as did the ambulance. McCarthy watched Doctor Solari straighten up from the

Solari had a smooth and unlined face. He looked to be about twenty—but he had ten years and a reputation of being an authority on the sort of violence police are faced with added to the innocent look. He stared up at the ceiling, as though looking at something new and different, and said:

"Well, he's been pierced, through and through, with something. I'm not prepared to say exactly just what, but if this had happened down in colored town I'd say the weapon was an ice pick. They favor that down there; ice picks don't come under the head of concealed weapons. Now this man has twelve wounds in his abdomen and has lost some blood. The shock was slight, owing to the nature of the wound. He will most certainly have peritonitis as his intestines are most certainly pierced through and through. He may get through it if he isn't too far along to react to a transfusion. Now does that answer you, Mr. McCarthy?"

McCarthy said, "In a big way, Doc. It means the guy's got a chance, don't it?"

"If he gets a transfusion immediately. I'm having him removed to the hospital at once."

Two husky white-coated men came in with a stretcher. They lifted the now unconscious man on this with Dr. Solari assisting, and then there came an outraged bellow from the outer office. A voice came out distinctly with:

"Hey! Miss Marge! I got to see the Chief."

McCarthy muttered, "That damn Benny!" and went through the knot of policemen and into the outer office.

Benny Cohn, McCarthy's pet cabbie, was at the door. He apparently didn't want to stay there but two policemen, who had him by the arms, were winning the argument about just where Benny was going. Or staying. Benny saw McCarthy and stopped struggling and said:

"Hey, Chief! I come up to see you and it seems I can't. They tell me I got to stay outside, they do, Chief."

McCarthy said, "Let him go."

Marge, who'd been awaiting the doctor's report, said, "Personally, I think one of us ought to see about a transfusion for this man. He fell into our arms in front of your office. How is he?"

"He might make it. . . . What d'ya want, Benny? I'm busy."

Benny said, "And so am I busy, Chief. Like I say, these cops won't let me in and see you. I got to see you, Chief. No fooling, I got to see you."

"What about?"

Marge broke in with: "Does the doctor think he'll live if he gets a transfusion?"

Benny brightened and broke away from the two policemen. He said to McCarthy, "Hey

now, Chief! If it maybe is the guy needs the same kind of blood that I got, maybe you can fix it for me. I took the test—they give you thirty-five bucks for it and I got my name on the list for giving it. Maybe you can fix it for me, Chief; I got to have the dough."

"What d'ya want to see me about?"

"That's it, Chief. Dough."

McCarthy said, "Then I certainly will try to fix it. If you can earn it, it's better than me having to give it to you."

Marge said, "But, Lord, what will the harvest be? With the man full of Benny's blood!"

 cCARTHY fixed it with no trouble. The wounded man's blood was typed, in a hurry, and found to match that of Benny's. McCarthy and Marge left the hospital, McCarthy grinning, and he said:

"That's the easiest thirty-five bucks I ever made in my life. I'd have had to give it to him if he hadn't made it this way."

"Why?"

McCarthy said uncomfortably, "Well, you know how Benny is. He never makes any dough out of his hack and now he's jammed."

"How?"

McCarthy sounded even more uncomfortable. "Well, he's been running around with some gal. He got in a little argument with her and slapped her. And she says unless he pays for the three teeth he knocked out she'll have him thrown in the sneezer."

"Swell kid, Benny is."

"Hell, baby, if Benny thought I wanted somebody's teeth knocked out he'd do it for me just as quick as he would for himself. He's that way."

"That's just it," Marge said warmly. "He's always getting you in trouble over things like that. You know he is."

McCarthy led the way into a Bar and Grill and changed the subject quite effectually. He fanned out five brand new hundred dollar bills and said nothing. Neither did Marge for a moment. Her blue eyes bulged and she finally gasped:

"Pat! Where did you get that?"

McCarthy said, in a complacent voice, "From the guy, kitten. Before the cops came—before they took him into my office. He had five hundred and forty bucks in his wallet, beside a few cards, and I left him the forty bucks and the wallet. I told the hospital I'd guarantee his bill, though, so it won't be all clear profit."

"But, Pat! It isn't your money?"

McCarthy looked injured and dragged out some cards. He held one out to her and she took it and read: Billy Tucker's Roadhouse. She said:

"What has a man named Billy Tucker got to do with you taking the stabbed man's money?"

"Turn it over, kitten."

Marge did this. The card had McCarthy's name scrawled in pencil on it, as well as his office address. He said:

"See! It's got my name on it. The guy was probably on his way up to see me when he got stabbed. So this is my retainer; I can't be expected to work for nothing. And anyway, he can't use it right now and I can."

Marge shook her head and said, "Let's look over the rest of the cards. What d'ya suppose he wanted to see you for?"

"Probably to keep from getting stabbed," McCarthy said, spreading out the cards.

There was one that read: The Silver Slipper— Dine and Dance. One of a chop suey place and another advertising a particularly poor brand of bourbon and a bar that sold it. The Silver Slipper card had a telephone number written on it and an explanatory note that read: "Small; blonde; drinks Scotch; Marie." McCarthy grinned at this and said:

"The guy's got an idea. Card-indexing his women."

He put the card down by the one bearing his address and name, then frowned. He pointed out: "Hey, look! The same man didn't write 'em both. Look!"

The writing was decidedly different and

Marge agreed that this was so. She said, "What difference does it make?"

"Probably none. Maybe the blonde wrote her name and number for him."

"She wouldn't have gone into details about the Scotch if she had, Pat."

McCarthy shrugged and looked at more cards. One was of Ira A. Halstead, Attorney-at-Law, and this was new and unsoiled. Another, equally new, was that of James R. S. Wilson. And then there were two more bar cards, which McCarthy discarded after looking them over for more telephone numbers and descriptions of girls. He studied the lawyer's card and that of Wilson and said:

"This Wilson is a big shot broker. Very strict church member and the rest of that stuff. And this lawyer Halstead has something to do with him, but I can't remember just what."

"Why not ask him?"

McCarthy said, "Maybe he wouldn't tell me. I'll get a guy from a newspaper and ask *him*."

HET MORRIS was the newspaper man McCarthy picked for an information bureau. He was short, fat, and almost bald, and he had a notorious passion for checked and wildly patterned suits. McCarthy opened up with:

"Hi, Chet! That's new, ain't it?"

Morris looked down at the plaid affairs that made him look even more roly-poly than ever and said, "It's half paid for, anyway."

"It looks good."

Abe Goldstein, who worked the police beat for a rival paper, snickered and said: "It looks good, hell! It looks just gorgeous. Just too simply gorgeous."

Morris managed a sickly grin for McCarthy. He gave Goldstein a cold and haughty look and said, "Yah! Well, it cost me sixty bucks, anyway."

The unimpressed Goldstein said that the tailor had certainly seen Mr. Morris coming from a distance and recognized him as the chump he was. He also said his brother-in-law, who was in that business, could duplicate the plaid job for not a cent over thirty-five dollars but that the said brother-in-law ran a quality store and would not have a piece of goods with a pattern like that in the shop. Morris gave up the argument and said hastily to McCarthy, sniffing the press room:

"You want to see me, Pat? Let's go outside. I got to get fresh air, every so often around here."

Goldstein's voice followed him out with: "That's quite a breeze you got on your back, Chet, and you can't get an argument against it from the next five guys you meet."

"What d'ya know about Mr. James R. S. Wilson? A big shot, as I remember about him," McCarthy asked.

Morris took off horn-rimmed glasses and started a polishing job. He said, "Right. A very big shot. Chairman of the Community Chest drive last year. Selectman of the Trinity Church. President of Wilson, Marks and Linehan, Investment Brokers. A very big shot to be sure."

"What about a lawyer named Ira A. Halstead?"

"Another big shot. A different kind. He's the people's friend, if you know what I mean."

"I don't, Chet."

"Well, he takes damage cases against railroads and such. On contingency, of course. Some people might call it a form of blackmail but as long as it's a big company that's stuck, who cares? The jury always goes for the poor devil who's suing the heartless corporation, don't they? So that makes him the people's friend, because he doesn't ask for a retainer when he takes that kind of a case."

"What does he get?"

Morris put his glasses back on and wiped his bald spot with the handkerchief he'd used to polish them with. "Well, usually half the damages the jury gives the victim. Less expenses, of course. But he gets big damages for his clients and very often there's a few bucks left over for them. A very few though, I'd say."

"A nice guy, I can see."

"Not in trouble with him, are you, Pat?"

"Not yet, anyway."

Morris's round, good-natured face showed worry. "He's got connections, if you know what I mean. We lay off him in the sheet. If that means anything."

"It does, Chet. Thanks a lot."

"Is that what you wanted to know?"

McCarthy said, "Yeah. It made me remember something. It made me remember that Halstead is the lawyer for some guy that's suing Wilson over a car accident. I remembered it when you said he took damage cases."

"Wilson is the sort of bird he likes to tackle," Morris agreed. "I don't keep up with things on this damn police beat. It's all I can do to keep up with the cops."

"And Goldstein," McCarthy suggested. "Abe can take the hide off a man's back with that tongue of his."

Morris said sadly, "Worse than that! He just about took this suit off my back a minute ago and the thing is brand new."

"I still say it looks good," said McCarthy, and left.

McCarthy went from the police press room to the paper Morris honored with his services. There he looked over the clippings on the car accident James R. S. Wilson was involved in, and he looked these over thoughtfully. He finally grumbled:

"My stabbed man can be either William Bowes or he can be Antonio Giovanni. And he didn't look Italian."

He left the newspaper morgue for a drugstore phone booth and telephoned the hospital. He said, "I'm McCarthy. What about the man who was stabbed in my office building?"

He held the phone, far from patiently, for ten long minutes before he got the doctor in charge of the case. The doctor said:

"He's doing as well as might be expected, Mr. McCarthy. The police are here now, waiting for the man to recover enough to make a statement. This in spite of my telling them the man will be in no shape to talk for at least twenty-four hours."

"They don't know who he is yet?"

"Apparently not. That fact seems to worry them, I might say."

McCarthy said, disagreeably, "It always worries the police when a man is stabbed. They're paid to worry about such things." He consulted the phone book and got Ira A. Halstead's address and telephone number and studied the phone thoughtfully for a moment. Finally he grumbled:

"Might as well go; he wouldn't tell me anything over the phone, anyway."

And then went hunting for a cab.

ALSTEAD'S law offices looked stately and dignified but Halstead looked like a boy barely out of college— like a boy who'd majored in athletics. He shrugged his bulky shoulders, lifted calm brown eyes from McCarthy's card, and said: "My secretary told me it was about one of my clients, Mr. McCarthy. Will you explain?"

"I'm trying to identify a man," McCarthy explained. "He had nothing in his pockets but your card and I thought possibly you might be a help. He's a man of about forty and he weighs around one fifty. He's got sandy hair and eyebrows and when I last saw him he needed a shave. In fact, he'd needed one for the last couple of days. He wears a brown suit and hat and white shoes. The shoes needed cleaning. He has a scar along his jawbone, not very long but still noticeable. Can you think who that might be?"

Halstead studied the problem and then shook his head. "I don't recall any client who that describes. You say he had my card in his pocket?"

"And that's all he had," McCarthy lied, leaving out all mention of Wilson's card and the five new hundred dollar bills.

"I'm afraid I can't help you, Mr. McCarthy."

"It wouldn't be Antonio Giovanni, would it?"

Halstead laughed. "Antonio Giovanni is at least fifty. He isn't over five feet tall and he must weigh at least two hundred pounds. He talks broken English, very broken English. He's been in this country thirty years or more but he acts like an immigrant to this day."

"What about William Bowes?"

McCarthy was watching Halstead's hands and he thought one of them tightened almost imperceptibly. And when he looked up he noted Halstead's eyes had lost their warm frankness and now looked wary. Halstead said, as though surprised:

"Now I never thought of him. Bowes *does* answer that description to an extent. By George, it might be Bowes at that."

McCarthy said, "I thought it might be."

"Is the man in trouble? He's my witness in a rather important case that's coming to trial shortly. As a matter of fact, the Giovanni case. By George, that's why you spoke of Giovanni! You associated the two in some way! Where is the man now?"

"In the hospital. He was stabbed."

Halstead shook his head and said, "Poor fellow. If he dies, it will be too bad for my client, I am afraid. I was depending on his testimony to show negligence on the part of the driver who killed his son."

"You mean Wilson."

Halstead nodded and smiled. The warm look was back in his eyes. He leaned forward and said, "That was an unfortunate thing. Mr. Wilson was driving along and struck young Giovanni, killing him instantly. Two days after that this man you speak of, William Bowes, got in touch with the elder Mr. Giovanni and told him he'd witnessed the accident. I may add that Mr. Wilson got in a panic immediately after the accident and drove around some time before reporting the matter to the police. You understand that makes him technically liable to a hit and run charge. Bowes insisted Mr. Wilson was entirely at fault."

"How? How was he wrong on it?"

Halstead said, in as friendly a voice, "Mr. McCarthy, I am a lawyer. I can't ethically answer your question. I don't understand your interest in the matter unless you should be investigating the matter for Mr. Wilson. Mr. Wilson is opposed to my client and I can't very well tell you our case against him. I hope you will understand."

McCarthy got to his feet. "I'm not investigating it for anybody but myself. At least not as yet. But this man Bowes was stabbed in front of my office door, and there was a reason back of it. I'm naturally interested in it. Well, thank you, Mr. Halstead."

Halstead stood also. "Is the man in bad shape, Mr. McCarthy? Will he recover?"

"The medicos don't know yet. He's at the Sisters of Mercy Hospital; you can keep in touch with them."

"I'll certainly do that," Halstead said, following McCarthy to the door. "And thank you, Mr. McCarthy, for telling me this. As I said, Bowes is the backbone of our case. If he should die, I'm afraid we haven't one."

McCarthy shook hands and left the office. He stood on the sidewalk for a moment, then headed for another phone booth. He got the Central Station and Detective Lieutenant Shannon, and told that big Irishman:

"I think the guy that got stabbed in front of my place is named Bowes. William Bowes. You might do a little checking on it. He's a witness in a damage case against Mr. James R. S. Wilson, if that means a thing to you."

Shannon whistled and said, "He's flying high, Pat. I'll look into it. How'd you get it?"

"From Halstead, the lawyer who's suing Wilson. The lawyer this Bowes is a witness for. And Shan, here's something funny. I didn't crack about where the guy was or what had happened to him or a thing that would tip Halstead off. But I talked as though something had happened to him and Halstead let it go. He seemed to think the guy was dead. Then he caught himself on it and changed it to asking questions. Does that mean anything?"

"What should it mean?" Shannon asked cautiously.

"Well, it should mean you should keep a police guard on this Bowes, if it's him, until he's out where he's got a chance to fight for himself.

This Halstead is supposed to be a smart baby, that's why I talked to him the way I did."

"He's smart, all right."

"He's too damn smart," said McCarthy. "I don't trust these baby-faced boys that don't look as though they'd ever spoken out of turn in their life. They're the kind I watch because they're too good to be true. I'll be seeing you, Shan."

"Why are you angling around on it, Irish?"

McCarthy said bitterly, "Well, I think the guy was coming to me for help when he got the shiv in him. I don't like to lose clients that way, even if I haven't really got 'em at the time. And then I'm a Socialist or something—the poor guy didn't have any money and everybody else that seems interested in him has. Wilson and this lawyer Halstead, both. I want to see the guy get a break."

"What do you get out of it?"

"Well, exercise, at least," McCarthy said. "And maybe practice."

BENNY COHN was waiting for McCarthy by the time he got back to his office. And Benny's nose was swollen out of shape and his left eye was a lovely green and adhesive tape held down a plaster on his left cheekbone. McCarthy stared at him and said:

"What the hell happened?"

"Didja ever see one of these iron things like they press pants with, Chief?" Benny asked, in a plaintive voice. "Well, I take the thirty-five smackers I get at the hospital and I go down to pay off this gal I was telling you about and, Chief, guess what happens."

McCarthy said, "I don't have to guess. I know. She clouted you with the iron."

"Wrong, Chief, wrong. I dodge the iron, except for it bouncing off the wall and falling against my neck, sort of. But when I duck the iron, Chief, she unbuckles herself and comes at me with the ironing board thing and she lands with it. I run like hell, Chief, and no mistake."

"Did you give her the thirty-five?"

"I never had a chance. She started in throwing that iron thing when I put my head in the door and say to her 'Hi, sweetheart.' Right then she starts. I mail that thirty-five to her, Chief, I mail it. And I get another thirty-five from you tomorrow or the next day, the Doc says."

"From me!"

"The Doc says you're paying the shot, Chief, and that I should come to you for the dough. So I'll be here."

McCarthy estimated how long five hundred dollars would last if the man in the hospital had a daily transfusion at thirty-five dollars a copy. He groaned. Benny said helpfully:

"He must be a pal of yours for you to pay off like that. The Doc says he may be in there for the next six months, on account of his guts being all cut to hell. I bet it costs you a pretty penny, Chief, a pretty penny."

"Will you get out?" McCarthy said.

Benny went out. He poked his head around the door a moment later, however, and said, "Hey! I get thinking about getting smacked in the puss with that iron board arrangement and I forget. You're to call Miss Marge. See, Chief! Your phone it rings and it's her and she says to call her up."

"How long ago was this?"

"Just now, Chief."

Benny left for the second time, and McCarthy called Marge's number. She said in a rush, as soon as she heard his voice:

"Oh, Pat! I've been trying to get you. It's Chet Morris. He tried to get you and when he couldn't he called me. He went up to see that Wilson man and told him you were checking on that accident thing or something."

"I didn't tell him that."

"He said that after he talked to you he got thinking and remembered that lawyer was suing Wilson. And that he thought there might be a story in it and went up to see about it. He said Wilson was very nice, but that he got telephoned at the paper, almost as soon as he got back from seeing Wilson, and that somebody told him to lay off and keep out of what didn't concern him.

He thinks that means you, too. He said he didn't want to see you get in trouble."

"Little Mother Morris," said McCarthy, sourly. "Why did he have to tell Wilson I was looking around?"

"He said he didn't think it made any difference."

"Well, it probably doesn't," McCarthy said, and made a dinner date for eight that evening.

Marge said, "Why not at seven? I'm hungry now."

"I've got to see this Giovanni guy that's suing Wilson first, hon. It may take me a little time to find him."

"I see. You be careful, Pat. It worries me about what Chet Morris said."

McCarthy laughed and said, "You and Chet would make a good pair. You both worry."

NTONIO GIOVANNI owned a small and messy vegetable store in the center of Italian town and it was there McCarthy found him. Antonio was on the floor and on his face and he'd apparently been trying to crawl under a long tray-like metal affair that held vegetables beneath a spray-like arrangement. The tray, possibly four feet wide, sloped down toward the front of the store for a display, and Antonio was sprawled partly under this and looking like a large and very dead frog.

Water from the spray had seeped through on him and washed part of the blood around him away, but there was still plenty left. He'd had long sweeping mustaches and one was soaking in blood while the other hung like a brush toward the floor.

McCarthy, without touching anything, knelt and looked—and thought he'd never seen such a pitifully ridiculous corpse. He saw three small, round, and purple holes in the cheek turned toward him, saw another in the part of fat neck in view. He cursed, silently and viciously and stood, and then a voice from behind him said:

"Hey! Where's Tony?"

McCarthy turned fast. He saw a small and dirty boy of around ten with black curly hair and bigger and blacker eyes than McCarthy thought were possible. He gulped and said:

"Tony isn't here right now. You run along and come back by and by."

The boy said, "Ma says for him to come to supper. She says she won't wait, that it'll spoil. Where is Tony?"

"He's out right now."

The boy said reflectively, "Ma'll raise hell with him when he comes home. She says all he does is run along and talk to lawyers and that the store ain't run right any more."

"Is he your dad?" asked McCarthy, going a little sick. There was no resemblance between the dead man and the boy but he got the answer he dreaded.

"Sure! I'll go back and tell Ma he ain't here. If you see him, tell him supper's ready."

McCarthy said he'd surely do that and watched the boy swagger out. He decided that Tony had been an indulgent father and that the children had rather taken things into their own hands—basing this on the good nature still showing in the dead man's face and on knowledge of other decent, kindly, honest Italian people he'd met. He went out of there, head down and deciding he would not be the one that broke the news of Tony's death to his family.

He called the station and told Shannon what he'd found, and Shannon cursed luridly and asked him to go back and stand guard until he could get a radio car on the scene.

And McCarthy did, praying the youngster wouldn't be back looking for his father.

Chet Morris was at Marge's apartment when McCarthy got there. He was again polishing his glasses and his mild, near-sighted eyes peered up at McCarthy as he said:

"I'm sorry, pal! I guess I spoke out of turn to that big, stuffed shirt. How was I to know he'd take it the way he did?"

"You told him I'd talked to you about him? That it?"

"Yeah! I didn't stop to think a thing about it." He put his glasses back on and this cleared his vision. He looked McCarthy over and said, in a different tone:

"What's the matter with you, Pat? You look sick."

McCarthy said: "I *am* sick. Marge, honey, how's about a drink? I thought I could take it but I guess I can't."

Marge brought the drink and said anxiously, "What's the matter, Pat? What's the matter with you?"

"I want to kill a man. This bird with the ice pick. Him or the man who hired him. That's all. I didn't know I could get so crazy mad that I'd be sick."

Morris asked, "What's happened?" and McCarthy told them both. Morris started toward the phone, saying: "I'll telephone it in. With the guy in the hospital getting it the same way, it's a story. They may not get the connection."

McCarthy said, with no inflection: "You touch that phone, Chet, and I'll beat you to a pulp. I'm praying God that nobody will see there *is* a connection. That other business didn't rate much of a spread and maybe nobody will add 'em together. I'll work it my own way, Chet. Let the other boys handle it. You're off shift."

Morris said, "If you say so, Pat! But give me a break when the thing smashes."

"If it smashes," McCarthy said bitterly. "It's going to be hell to lay it on that guy. You don't accuse men like Wilson of having murder done unless you can prove it. And he's got no motive."

Marge said: "Chet told me all about it. This Italian man was suing Wilson for damages. If he was dead, he couldn't sue, could he? That's why that other man was stabbed, too. They tried to kill him so he couldn't testify. It stands to reason, Pat."

McCarthy said wearily, "Oh, use your head, Marge. Giovanni was asking for twenty-five grand, claiming Wilson was driving carelessly. Wilson is very wealthy and what's twenty-five grand to a man like that? He'd pay it in a second rather than have anybody killed. It ties up some way, but we haven't caught the angle yet."

The phone burred and Marge answered it and then said, "It's for you, Pat. It's Lieutenant Shannon." McCarthy took it and said, "Yeah, Shan?" and Shannon blurted out:

"You called the turn on it, Irish! You sure did. I had a man on guard up at the hospital and two guys came in and tried to kill that Bowes guy. One of them even got in the room. That's the one that got away, down the fire-escape. I should have seen that they put him some place where he was easier watched."

"What happened?"

"Well, this man, his name's Dugan, was sitting out in the hall. He admits he was talking to some nurse, or maybe it wouldn't have gone as far as it did. Two men come up the stairs and walk down to Bowes room and Dugan finally gets wise to himself and asks 'em what they want. One of them pulls a gun and starts using it and Dugan kills him. The other ducked in Bowes' room and down the fire-escape and Dugan missed him three times hand running. He's going to put more time in on the range or get off the force and I told him so."

"Was Bowes hurt?"

"Hell, no! They've got him doped up so he won't roll around and tear himself up any more and he didn't even know anything happened."

"Has he talked yet?"

"He can't. And the doctors wouldn't let him if he could."

"Who was the man the cop killed?"

"Some bird named Weeks. Just a hired hand."

"Did Dugan see the one that got away well enough to identify him?"

"No. He was talking to that nurse, like I said. He wasn't paying any attention to what he was supposed to be working at. I'm going to see he gets a month's suspension without pay if I have to resign to get it. . . . You coming down?"

McCarthy said not that evening and then he asked if the man the policeman had killed had happened to have an ice pick on his person, and found he hadn't. And then he said to Marge and Chet Morris:

"Let's eat! Chet, why don't you come with us?"

Morris said, "Don't think I'm not. I'm sticking close until this thing's settled. I'm scared, Pat, and I'm not fooling."

Marge said, "I'm afraid about Pat."

And McCarthy said, "And I'm afraid the cops will get to the ice-pick guy before I do. I want to be first."

IT TOOK McCarthy the best part of a week to find that Mr. James R. S. Wilson was maintaining a small apartment in a discreet apartment house. And a small blond girl who fitted the apartment. The small girl's name was Mrs. Martha Abott, or at least that name was accepted. Her husband was Mr. James Abott, supposedly a traveling man, but his travels only extended from the Wilson brokerage firm or the Wilson house to the apartment.

It took twenty-five dollars of what was left of the five hundred for McCarthy to get details but he thought it money well spent. He said to Marge and to Chet Morris, who was arrayed in something new that shocked the eye:

"The guy's keeping her all right, but in this day and age that's no crime. And I'm damned if I can see that he's doing anything else. I've tagged him back and forth, from his house to his office, from there to this apartment, and I haven't seen him do one thing that would tie him up to any of the rough stuff.

"Of course I can't tell just who he sees in his office, but he's too cagy an old turkey to meet some hoodlum there where the help could spot it. I've got a boy on the day shift and another one on the night shift to tell me if he meets anybody there at this apartment and they say he doesn't."

Morris asked, "Does he know you're following him?"

"If he does, he hasn't done anything about it."

Marge said firmly, "He's a nasty old man. Or he wouldn't be doing things like that."

Morris said, "Did you ever see his wife?"

"No. Why?"

"Well, I did. When I went to see him. I don't blame him a bit. She'd drive a man to drink."

McCarthy asked what woman wouldn't and Marge slapped half-heartedly at him. She said, "What are you going to do now, Pat?"

"Keep after him, of course. He's bound to make contact with his hired killers before long and I want to see 'em. He's the only lead to them I've got."

"I wish you'd drop it. After all, it's none of your business."

McCarthy said, "You didn't happen to see old man Giovanni stretched out like I did. You didn't see this poor kid of his. You didn't go to the old man's funeral."

"Pat! You didn't go to the funeral!"

Chet Morris said, "Pat and some of the cops, mostly Shannon, and some of the boys on my paper paid for it, Marge. Even Abe Goldstein came in for ten bucks and the guy thinks money is something to hide in a bank. All of them had seen the family the guy left and it seems he'd given Halstead all the money he could raise to prosecute Wilson for running over his oldest boy. He'd mortgaged the shop he had and they took it away from the family before they could even have his funeral."

Marge said, "Oh, the poor people."

There was a knock on the door and Marge opened it for Benny. He came in, grinning, and said, "Another thirty-five bucks you owe me, Chief. I'm running you into dough—that's five of 'em."

"You always cost me," McCarthy said sourly.

"But not any more, Chief. It seems that I'm getting amnesia or something like that and the docs say I'm no good any more and that they're going to get another boy until I get fat again. Jeez, Chief, I lose ten pounds, but it's seventeen and a half a pound the way I figure it and that buys a lot of groceries."

"I'd rather pay you than some other mugg."

"Thanks, Chief, thanks. I like that."

McCarthy explained, "If I pay you, you don't have to borrow from me. If I pay somebody else I'm stuck with you again."

"Jeez, Chief, that ain't right. Don't I always kick it back to you?"

"You haven't yet."

"Well, I never had it yet. When I'm in the dough I will."

McCarthy looked at his watch and asked, "You got the hack downstairs?"

"Sure."

"I'll ride with you then."

He said to Marge and Chet Morris: "I'll start after Wilson some more. He gets out of his office in half an hour; he's as regular as the old maid putting the cat out. See you some more."

Marge went to the door with him. She said earnestly, "You be careful, Pat! I've got a funny feeling about this."

"Forget it, kid! He'll lead me to the right guys sooner or later. He has to—they'll contact him some time. And then I'll step in on him and them both."

Benny said, from where he was waiting in the hall: "Hey, the guy talked today. When I was doing my stuff with the docs and him. But all he wanted was a priest. He said he wanted to confess."

"Shannon know this?"

"Sure. But the guy wouldn't talk to him. He wanted a priest is all, Chief."

McCarthy said, "I'll put Wilson to bed, either at his house or at his apartment, and then I'll see Shannon and we'll talk to the doctors. If the guy can talk to a priest he can talk to the cops. And he knows things we have to know to get any place."

"Is he getting along all right?" Marge asked.

"According to the doctors he is."

He said good-by again and Marge watched him follow Benny down the hall with quick strides. She went inside and said to Chet Morris:

"This has Pat down. I never saw him get upset about anything like that before."

Morris said slowly, "Well, here was a case of the innocent bystander being the victim. Worse than that. That killing was so senseless, and there was no reason for the attack on Bowes.

Twenty-five thousand dollars means little to Wilson—and the death of his oldest boy hit Giovanni pretty hard. From what his wife said, he only wanted the money for his family. And then he gets killed and leaves five kids, none of them over ten. Twenty-five thousand isn't worth that."

Marge said, "Maybe Pat's after the wrong man. Maybe he didn't do it or have it done."

Morris shrugged his gaily covered shoulders and said, "Don't be silly. If it wasn't Wilson back of it, why should the one witness against him be almost killed? Why should the man making the charge be killed? It doesn't make too much sense, but he's the only connecting link between the two happenings."

"I wonder where the man Bowes got the five one hundred dollar bills."

Morris said, "I didn't know he had any," and Marge told of them. She defended Pat with: "He just took them so he'd have money to care for the man in the hospital. That was all."

"Sure," said Morris, with no conviction in his tone.

Marge said, "Poor Pat! I've got the oddest feeling about him. I'm really worried."

"If the cops find out Pat took the five hundred you'll have something to worry about," Morris told her.

cCARTHY walked a hundred feet behind the sedate-looking James R. S. Wilson. But Wilson was alone and McCarthy wasn't. A thin, very dark man was on one side of him and a heavy but equally dark man was on the other. The heavy man was saying:

"Go ahead, shamus. You been following him and he didn't know it and we been following you and *you* didn't know it. Now we're all going to get together and get acquainted."

The heavy man had a hand in a side coat pocket and the pocket lumped out with more than hand. His thin partner was just as close to

McCarthy and his pocket bulged in the same manner. He had a high whiny voice and he said:

"You're a stupid, shamus! You might've known we was keeping watch on him. You're stupid."

McCarthy admitted it with: "I've been told so before. By better men than you two punks will ever be."

"Sing high, sing low," the heavy man said. "But if you do it out loud I'll smear you all over the town. You guys out here think you know something but you're made to order."

The thin man said, "Yeah, tailor-made."

Wilson turned into the apartment house, first glancing suspiciously up and down the street, and McCarthy said, "Now what?"

"We go in. Just act right."

McCarthy acted right. He went inside and to the elevator as though expected, and the clerk looked at him casually and turned away. They rode up to 3C and the heavy man said:

"You know, Mike, I don't blame the guy for going with the gal here. She's a honey. I don't blame him for going for her."

The thin partner said, "Why should you? He's paying for it, ain't he?"

"And how!" the heavy man agreed. He said to McCarthy: "Just you knock on his door. When he opens it you just walk in like you owned the place. No funny stuff now."

The thin man said, "Hey, wait!" and reached over and snapped McCarthy's heavy gun from its shoulder sling. He stuck this in the waistband of his trousers and said, "O.K. now. Go to it."

McCarthy knocked. He heard fluttering sounds inside and then a girl's voice said, "What is it?" McCarthy got a warning gun jabbed in his short ribs and held silent.

The heavy man said, "Electrician, ma'am!"

There was more fluttering and then the door opened. The small and blond and supposedly Mrs. Abott stood framed in it, a black silk negligée wrapped around what appeared to be herself and nothing else. The thin man jammed his gun into McCarthy's ribs and said:

"In!"

McCarthy went in, accompanied by a small shriek from the blond girl. The heavy man said in an approving voice:

"Now that's nice, lady. That's the way to yelp. If you'd made any more noise than that somebody might have heard you and then there'd have been hell to pay for this chump."

She said, "Who are you? What do you want?"

Wilson's voice said, from inside: "What is it, darling?"

The girl didn't answer, just backed into the room where Wilson was, staring at the three men and the two guns that followed her. Wilson jumped to his feet, his face suddenly white, and the heavy man said:

"Don't have kittens, mister. We're friends. And I'll prove it to you." He said to his partner: "You watch 'em, Mike," and headed toward the French phone by the window.

Wilson said, "Why, what—" and the heavy man grinned back at him over one shoulder and said:

"Don't get in a lather, dad. I'm going to call Halstead. I'll get him to come up and we can sort of talk things over."

McCarthy said, "You'd better call the cops, Wilson. This has gone far enough."

Then the thin man hit him on the back of the head with his gun and McCarthy went ahead and on his face. And completely out.

He came back to life in time to hear Halstead say, "This is going to complicate things, Wilson. This man possibly has somebody working with him. This is going to cost money to hush up."

McCarthy opened his eyes just wide enough to take in the room. He saw Halstead sitting composedly in a chair with the heavy man standing back of it and leaning on it. Wilson was standing in front of him and looking very unhappy. The girl was sitting on a couch, swinging and admiring an arched instep that held a high-heeled bedroom slipper. The thin man was at the window and looking directly at McCarthy. He said:

"Hey! Ain't it about time Sleeping Beauty woke up? I didn't rap him hard, Halstead. I just slapped him a little."

Halstead said to Wilson: "You're in this too far to back out now, Wilson. If Bowes gets a police guard, which he is very apt to do, there'll be hell to pay all the way around."

The thin man said, "We'll take him and his copper guard if we have to, Halstead. I never liked cops anyway." He walked over to McCarthy and kicked him in the ribs, and McCarthy took it with a lax body and still half-opened eyes. It took what will power he had to do it but the thin man turned and walked back satisfied and McCarthy thought the effort worth it.

Halstead said, "You didn't do so well at the hospital, Mike. If that cop had been a better shot, you wouldn't have done well at all."

The thin man spat on the rug and the girl flared at him with: "Damn you! Don't do that. You're not in a barn now."

The thin man told her where he was, using good old English words, and the girl glared at him and used language equally strong. Wilson looked even unhappier and Halstead grinned and said to the girl:

"Shut up, Martha. I'll handle this. As I say, Wilson, it will cost you money. It cost money to buy Bowes off. If he'd gotten on the stand with his yarn, you'd have been tarred and feathered and chased out of town."

The girl said, "Yes, Daddy! Think of my reputation. It would have ruined me."

The thin man, who didn't seem to think a great deal of the girl, snapped, "Hagh! That'd be a day."

Halstead said thoughtfully, "There's only one thing to do. Let Mike and Jerry take the fellow out the back way while he's still out. If they meet anybody they can pretend he's drunk and that they're taking care of him."

"And then what?" Wilson asked.

Halstead said, "What can we do? He's wise to the setup. You're wrecked if we don't get rid of him for you. That was the reason for taking care of old man Giovanni. Bowes had told him the story and you couldn't afford to have him telling it around, could you?"

Wilson said miserably, "I—I didn't know what you were going to do."

Halstead waved his hand and said, "You're in it just as deep, whether you knew it or not. And I'll never think you didn't know what was going to happen. Now do you pay for us taking this man out or shall we let him stay here with you? Think fast—he won't be out like that very much longer."

Then Benny said, from the hallway: "You're damn right he won't."

Benny was behind McCarthy and the shock of hearing Benny's voice brought his head around. Benny was in the center of the door, crouching a little and holding an iron jack handle in one big hand. Chet Morris crowded up behind him, holding a small gun, and he menaced the room with this and quavered:

"Hands up!"

That started it. The thin man went for the gun he carried under his arm and Benny went for the thin man with the jack handle. The heavy man jerked at his pocket and Morris closed both eyes and pulled the trigger of his little gun three times.

McCarthy was watching the heavy man and lunging to his feet at the same time, but Halstead's head was in his line of vision. He saw a black dot spring out at the side of Halstead's forehead and saw Halstead put his head down on his knees. And then the heavy man got his gun clear of his pocket and McCarthy hit him at the knees.

The man had a big gun and it drowned out the echo of Morris's small one when it exploded. But the man was falling backward when this happened and the slug smashed into the ceiling. The heavy man clubbed the gun at McCarthy, who was hanging stubbornly to his knees, and McCarthy took the blow on the shoulder and let go of knees with an arm gone numb. Then he heard a crunching sound about him and heard Benny say:

"Leave him go, Chief. I bopped the—"

McCarthy released the heavy man, who showed no further interest in the affair and whose face was now oddly shaped. He heard a

screeching sound from the door and turned and saw the blonde pounding at Chet Morris with her high-heeled slipper and saw Morris fending her away and not doing well at all. The girl was crying out:

"You shot Ira! You shot Ira!" and her voice was a high thin scream that didn't sound sane.

And then McCarthy looked for Wilson and didn't see him and heard a door slam above the noise of the girl's keening. He got to his feet and went to the thin man and saw he was lying with his head twisted in a line with his shoulder. He got his own gun from where the thin man had put it in his waistband and when he got to the hallway he reached out and caught the blond girl by the hair and threw her back by it clear across the room.

Then he crowded past Morris and out into the hall in time to see Wilson dancing up and down in front of the elevator opening. He set himself sidewise, as though preparing to shoot at a target, and then called harshly:

"*Wilson!*"

And when Wilson stopped his mad hopping and turned, McCarthy shot him through the knee.

Later McCarthy told Marge: "We're celebrating tonight, lamb. Chet Morris and Benny have already started it. They were plastered early this afternoon. They're to meet us here."

Marge said, "I can see the reason for celebrating but that's about all I see. I haven't seen you since it happened."

"I had to be with the cops, hon. I couldn't get away. There was a lot to explain—for that matter the cops are still investigating. I asked Shannon to come along, too, and he's too busy."

"What happened?"

McCarthy told her what had happened, dwelling with emphasis on Benny's work with the jack handle and on Morris's poor marksmanship.

He said, "At that it was a good thing. The guy was a good enough lawyer to maybe slide out of it. He can't slide off a morgue slab, even if Morris put him there by mistake. You should have seen that little hell cat of a Martha go for Morris with a slipper, hon, it was really good. Benny and Morris saved the day when they followed me and came in."

"So Halstead was bleeding Wilson all the time? Halstead was back of it all?" Marge asked.

"In a way. Halstead had found out Wilson was running around with this tart of a Martha. It was his business to find out those things—he made most of his money by blackmailing. When Wilson ran over the young Giovanni kid the girl was with him, and he was afraid of the scandal and ran away. Halstead got to the girl and she told him the truth—she fell hard for him. He was a nice-looking guy, honey."

Marge said automatically, "Nobody'll ever say that about you, Pat," and then: "Go on."

"That's about all. Halstead hired Bowes to say he saw the thing. He had to have a witness if he was going to shake down Wilson in a big way. Then Bowes got cold feet on the deal and started to back out. Then Halstead put him out of the way. Or had Mike, one of his two thugs, do it. This Mike used an ice pick, because they can be carried wrapped up and they can't be classed as a dangerous weapon if you're stopped by a cop. Get it?"

"I guess so. But why did they kill that poor Mr. Giovanni?"

"They had to tell him Bowes was a witness before the old man would consent to start suit. Bowes, when he got cold feet—he calls it religion, but he finally talked to both the priest and the cops, so you can take your pick—went to Giovanni and confessed it was a frame. So they had to kill Giovanni, too. Now is it all straight?"

"I guess so. I'm glad it's over, Pat."

McCarthy said gloomily, "It got over too soon to suit me, hon. I wanted that little thin guy that was so handy with the ice pick all to myself. Benny got to him first. I'll admit Benny did a good job—he broke his neck. The big guy'll hang and Halstead's dead and Wilson will be laughed out of town as soon as he gets out of the hospital."

"Why did you shoot him? You didn't have to do that."

McCarthy said indignantly, "Hell, kid! If he'd been a man and faced the music, none of this would have happened. If he hadn't been drunk and out riding around with that chippy he'd have never run over the Giovanni boy. If he'd have stood the scandal like a man, the old man wouldn't have been killed. I should have aimed center instead of just crippling him a bit. He started the whole thing. . . . I take that Giovanni thing pretty hard, kid."

Marge said soberly, "I see what you mean." And then her eyes widened and she said, "My heavens! It isn't possible."

McCarthy turned and saw Benny and Chet Morris almost at the booth. They were both very drunk. Benny had a severe and formal Homburg perched exactly center on his head and this didn't go well with a shabby sweater and grease-stained slacks. He carried a pair of yellow gloves proudly in his right hand. His left held a half-full whiskey bottle.

Morris looked even more spectacular. He wore a cap on the side of his head and the suit he wore had been made for a taller, much thinner man. The green trouser cuffs dragged four inches on his shoes, which were an ugly yellow. The coat hung almost to his knees. He held two glasses and was saying to Benny:

"Le's stop an' have 'ittle drinkie. Thirsty, I am."

McCarthy said, under his breath to Marge: "Look at the poor—face. That's what the gal did with that high heel."

Morris' face was blotched and lumpy and both eyes were black. He looked as though he'd fallen down several flights of stairs.

Marge gasped, "And him so fussy!"

Then Morris looked up and saw them. He waved happily, almost falling down while doing so, and came to a halt in front of the booth. He beamed at them and said:

"Hi! What d'ya think of the new outfit?"

"Ain't it something, huh?"

Marge said, "I'd never deny it."

Benny came to a halt alongside Morris and said, "I got me a hat at the same place, Chief. Hey, look at me, too, Chief."

McCarthy said, "I can't help it."

Chet Morris said, in a confidential voice:

"Like this, Pat, m' frien'. Benny and I we bust into Abe Goldstein down at the station while you was busy with the cops. Abe's got a brother-in-law who has a clothing store. So Benny and I and Abe take a couple of snorts or so and go down to get a new outfit. Abe says his brother-in-law's got the best stock in the city and he helped us pick this outfit out. Didn't cost us nothin' at all. How's it look, pal?"

McCarthy said, "Gorgeous! Simply gorgeous! Will you do me a favor, Chet?"

"Sure."

"Then let me be with you when you see Abe in the morning."

"Why? He won't take our clothes back. He *gave* 'em to us. S'funny, too, with him so stingy, but—"

McCarthy said, "Let's not spoil our fun tonight, guy. But there's reasons and you'll realize it tomorrow. Believe me you will."

Marge giggled and said, "It would be bad enough to look at that at any time. But with the hangover Chet'll have, it's liable to be fatal."

McCarthy agreed with: "Yeah, fatal to Abe."

The Devil's Bookkeeper

Carlos Martinez

GUN MOLLS MAGAZINE had a brief and unexciting life. The first issue was published in October 1930 and appeared monthly for only eighteen additional months, folding after the issue of April 1932. Examining the list of contributors fails to elicit a single recognizable name, even to pulp experts who have devoted the major portion of their professional lives to the scholarly study of what was at one time a major element of American literature. Carlos Martinez is such an author—possibly the pseudonym of another hack trying to pay the rent at the rate of half a cent a word, which is what this publication paid.

Gun Molls and such sister publications as *Gangland Detective Stories, Racketeer Stories, Gangster Stories,* and others similarly titled did not offer literary prose nor enduring works of fiction. Characterization has no more depth than spray paint, and stylistic nuance is as rare as a humble politician. The villains are utterly odious; they would be loved neither by their mothers nor their dogs. The molls, unless they are working undercover or hopelessly in love with the wrong man, are still more sinister than the thugs with whom they share adventures. Nonetheless, even the worst of these publications offered exactly what their readers demanded: nonstop action, snappy dialogue, blazing guns, automobiles careering around corners with the cops in hot pursuit, and other standard scenes from the cheap B movies of the era and the least of the pulps.

"The Devil's Bookkeeper" first appeared in the August 1931 issue of *Gun Molls.*

The figure gyrated maddeningly before them

The Devil's Bookkeeper

Carlos Martinez

Clerical Clara kept records for gangdom, and therefore she knew plenty. But even an auditor can be wrong.

ACROSS THE ROOF-TOP, a dim shadow slipped silently to a barred window, like a dull gray wraith that merged perfectly with the curling fingers of fog drifting in from the lake.

It made no sound in its ghost-like approach, and was visible only when the clouds across the crescent moon allowed a faint ghoulish light to filter for a moment upon the roofs of the sleeping city.

A pale hand attached a small piece of cloth to the glass of the window, on which was smeared a bit of fast drying cement. Then the scratch of a diamond cutting a circle on the glass, a snapping tap as the inner oval fell loose and was withdrawn by the attached piece of cloth.

Came a hissing intake of breath, unmistakably a woman's, as the still form of a man was revealed lying on a small bed within the darkened room. Again that pale hand in the shimmer of greenish moonlight; two dull clicks from the blue metal in his fist; a convulsive jerk from the figure on the bed, and when the clouds again cleared across the crescent moon, the dirty rooftop was empty and silent.

Detective Sergeant Dan Conley was talking to his chief. His Irish face was twisted into a puzzled frown as he hitched his shoulder holster to a more comfortable position, and took a chair opposite the captain.

" 'Mugs' Brandon was bumped off last night," he began.

"Where did they get him?" asked Captain Steele.

"In that roof-top apartment of his," said Conley. "No fingerprints. The gun that did for Mugs cut out a circle of the window with a diamond, and let him have it with a .45. Must have used a silencer!"

"Mugs put up a fight?" asked the captain.

"Never knew what hit him," said Conley. "Got him while he was asleep!"

"Hell!" blazed the captain. "Get out of here and bring somebody in. The commissioner has been threatening to fire every man in the precinct the next time there was a killing. We got to make a showing!"

"I got a tall hunch about this killing," said Conley slowly.

"Sez you!" sneered Steele. "What's the big idea this time?"

"There was one footprint on the roof under that window," said Conley. "It was made by the rubber-sole from a woman's shoe!"

"One of Mugs' old molls," said Steele. "Check up on those Clancy Street dames he used to play around with. Some hallway baby, maybe!"

"I got a hunch," said Conley, stubbornly.

"Mind letting me in on it?" asked the captain with heavy sarcasm.

" 'Clerical Clara,' " said Conley. "It looks like her work!"

The captain looked at the detective for a moment while his heavy face grew red with exasperation. He spat viciously at the brass cuspidor which is a part of every police captain's office furniture.

"You thimble-wit!" he roared. "Clerical Clara!

You know dam' well that dame ain't never been mixed up in this booze racket, and you've made us all look like dam' fools half a dozen times. Now you get out on the East Side, and bring in some of those Clancy Street trollops!"

"Yes, sir!" Detective Sergeant Conley saluted, swung on his heel, and left the room with his great hands clenched to control his rising anger. He stepped into a squad car, jammed in the shifting lever and roared out of the small courtyard with exhaust wide open.

In a neat little office on the fourth floor of a side street building a blonde beauty was carefully sorting a list of accounts receivable, and making figures on a pad with machine-like accuracy.

Her hair was combed straight back in a mannish bob, and the carefully penciled brows were drawn together in a frown of concentration. Her age might have been anything between twenty-five and thirty-five, according to her mood.

Soft and hard by turns; cold and warmly yielding, whichever best suited her purpose and the business at hand. The sign on her door said: "Clara Beaumont, Accountant. Income Taxes and Collections."

She looked up as the handle of the door turned, and then smiled as she motioned lazily to a chair.

"Hello, Conley," she drawled. "Can I help you with your income tax?"

"Can the comedy," said Conley. "You know dam' well I don't have any grafts that make me pay taxes."

"More fool you," she answered. "What's on your mind?"

"Mugs Brandon," said Conley. "When did you last see him?"

"Don't know the gent," said the girl. "That is, not personally."

"He was bumped off last night," said Conley, watching her carefully. "Some dame did for him."

"How interesting," she sneered. "But then, I specialize in income taxes."

"And collections," said Conley.

"And I always collect," said the girl.

"I know that," said Conley. "You either collect—or else—"

"What do you mean—or else?" The girl shot the question at him viciously.

"Just what I said, and Mugs Brandon never paid anything he could get out of," said Conley.

He looked critically at her well-shaped legs, and then allowed his eyes to drop to her shoes. He noted that the thin slippers she was wearing were at least two sizes smaller than the print of the rubber-soled shoe he had measured on the roof of Brandon's apartment.

"You dicks make me sick," she said with disgust.

"Pardon my asthma," he said. "I'll be moving along."

"Wait a minute." She watched him with puzzled eyes. "You got nothing on me."

"That's what I said," he agreed. "I'll be shoving along."

For ten minutes after he had taken his abrupt departure she sat motionless, trying to figure out what the detective had meant. Then she returned to her accounts. It took brains to swindle the government out of taxes, and she was one of the best in the game.

"Clerical Clara in the flesh!"

She started as the smooth feminine voice addressed her, and looked up to see a quietly dressed girl standing just inside the door. As though reaching for a paper, her hand started to slide inside an open drawer.

"Hold it!"

The order shot out like the snap of a whip, as the stranger moved her hand out from her side, a wicked little automatic clenched in the tiny fist.

"I ain't on the kill for sugar, but you make a funny pass at me and I'll fan you a heavy dose of lead poisoning," she articulated slowly. "You know who I am?"

"I don't go to cheap shows," sneered Clara. "But on a bet I'd say you were Chorus, back row!"

For a moment it seemed as though the stranger would turn her rod on her tormentor.

She was a dark slender girl of about twenty-two, with the regal high-breasted carriage that speaks of breeding in any language.

"I am Premier Dancer at Brandon's Club, and you know it," she said quietly. "And Mugs stopped two slugs last night while he was sound asleep. You are good at figures, so I thought maybe you could figure that one out."

"Why, you cheap boop boop a doop, I'll burn you down so quick—"

"Stay put!" snapped the dancer. "I'd like to let you have it right now, but first I want to see you turn yellow like the sneakin' rat that you are!"

"Put up that rod and give me a break," begged Clara. "I'll fan a heat on you so dam' fast that you will think you are up against a Baby Thompson."

For a moment it looked as though the stranger would comply with the request. Then she sighed and backed toward the door. Never for an instant did she take her gun from the other.

"Not this time, old sister," she drawled. "But next time we meet, start doing your stuff with your lead atomizer. I'm giving you a break; that's more than you ever gave anyone."

The door slammed behind her with a bang, and for five minutes Clara sat motionless. She knew the ways of gangdom. They might wait five minutes outside to plug you if you got reckless and followed, or then they might beat it right away, and have five minutes start to the good. Either way, you never could tell for sure.

Two days later, Mugs Brandon was put away in style. His casket was the most expensive that money could buy, and three cars loaded with flowers followed the hearse. His friends sent them because they regretted his demise, and his enemies were as profligate in the expenditures, to signify their satisfaction.

Weeping women were at the church; the girls from Clancy Street. But there were two who did not weep, though the eyes of one were dry with a burning hate that glittered like the fires of hell, as they looked across the casket at another woman who was coolly looking down upon the pale chiseled features of the corpse.

Clerical Clara looked up from her inspection, and glanced insolently at the woman on the other side of the bier.

"He looks so natural," she sighed. "As though he had paid all his debts, and had a clear conscience."

"Yes," whispered the other as softly. "He rests content. He knows *all* his debts will be paid."

The gangsters in line shoved them along with gentle pressure, and they parted one on each side of the casket, and passed down opposite walls of the little church.

From a nearby pew, Detective Sergeant Conley had observed the little by-play between them. As the stranger left the church he was close behind her, and followed until she turned in at the Club Brandon.

"Carmen Ryan!" he whispered to himself. "I heard that she was Brandon's real moll, but about those Clancy Street dames?"

He sighed heavily as he turned toward Headquarters to make his report to Captain Steele. Sometimes he wished he had listened to the voice of graft. He was not so young any more, and a detective's pay—

Sergeant Conley could not have told you what prompted him to return to the apartment where Mugs Brandon had been killed, and as he stood in the large living-room with its bizarre furnishings, his eyes strayed to a large desk in one corner beneath a massive floor lamp.

He seated himself in the heavy chair behind the desk, and opened the various drawers with the keys taken from the effects of the slain gangster. In a secret compartment in the rear of the large center drawer, he found a small japanned box, and fitted a tiny key from the ring in his hand.

On top of a small account book were fifty bills of one-thousand-dollar denomination, and in the book were accounts that would incrimi-nate many prominent men. Beneath the book were several pages written in a neat feminine hand. The work of Clerical Clara!

"Jake Cling, $5,000."

"Soapy Taylor, $5,000."

"Toad Wilson, $3,000."

Conley's eyes grew wide with understanding as he scanned the three cards. The three men had been enemies of Mugs Brandon, and each had been shot and killed in some mysterious way. Soapy had been killed while he slept. His mind pieced the puzzle together as accurately as if he had seen the killings take place.

Clerical Clara had done her work, and had then rendered her bill for the service. Mugs Brandon had refused to pay her, and he had remembered Clara's boast that she *always* collected—or else—

So absorbed was he in his thoughts that he failed to hear the slight click of the door as it opened on its well-oiled hinges.

"You find anything, Dick?"

He started to jump to his feet, and then sank back again as he looked into the muzzle of the gun held upon him in the steady hand of Clerical Clara. Her blue eyes were fastened upon the tell-tale slips on the desk before him.

"Hold that pose, please, and keep both hands on the desk where I can see them!"

Keeping him covered, she walked slowly to the desk, and reached for the papers. Before her hand could take them up, another soft voice purred gently over her shoulder.

"As you are, and don't move! Now drop that gat on the desk!"

As the automatic clattered to the mahogany desk, Carmen Ryan jammed the muzzle of her own rod into the back of her enemy.

"Hands high, and swing around," she ordered.

As Clara obeyed her blue eyes were filled with venom that shook her frail body like the ague.

"I'll get you for this, you cheap hussy!" she hissed through clenched teeth.

Like a steel spring the arm of the dancer shot out, and mashed the lips of the killer woman. All the pent-up anger of the past two weeks went into that one blow that made the dancer careless for a moment.

Before Detective Sergeant Conley could interfere, Clara's right foot shot out, and the automatic flew from the hand of the dancer and went spinning across the room. In the same breath the killer snatched up her own heavy automatic from the desk and swung around on the man and woman with the threat of death in her savage eyes.

"Take those papers out of your pocket and hand them to me!"

As she snapped the words, the detective stiffened. He gazed steadily into the hate-filled eyes before him, and slowly shook his head.

"You have fooled me a dozen times," he said. "Now I have enough on you to swing you into hell!"

"You must think I'm a fool," she sneered. "Thirty seconds, and then I start shooting."

The dancer made a movement, and the eyes of the killer swept toward her for a brief instant as she swung the muzzle of her rod around with the movement of her body. In that split second, Conley threw his body forward and down against the desk.

Even as he fell, Clerical Clara wheeled and threw a slug across the desk which was overturning. He slid to the floor, the desk falling on top of him. As the dancer started forward, Clara faced her with the smoking rod.

"I never miss," she said quietly. "Another move from you and I'll burn you down, too."

Watching the dancer closely, she leaned over and attempted to reach into the breast pocket of the fallen detective, but the heavy desk covered his chest like a shield. The telephone lay where it had fallen, and a series of sharp clicks warned her that some one was listening in.

"Take hold of that desk and help me move it, or I'll drill you," she ordered the dancer.

As the girl started to obey, a sharp knock sounded on the hall door. Then a heavy body smashed against the panels. The killer looked quickly about, and backed toward the window.

She slid a slender leg over the sill, and climbed onto a fire-escape. There she paused.

"Take that!"

But even as she fired, the dancer had flung herself sideways behind the desk. Then the hall door crashed down, and two uniformed police rushed in with drawn weapons. One of them covered the crouching girl, while the other hurried to the fallen detective.

"They got Sergeant Conley," he said.

"You're a liar!"

At the drawling words, the policeman bent over and looked into the twinkling eyes of the detective. Then he smiled with relief.

"Don't stand there," said Conley. "Lift this dam' dead wood off of my chest."

The next moment he was on his feet, and as he pressed a hand to his side he winced with pain. The girl ran to him.

"She shot you! I saw her," she cried. "Are you hurt bad?"

"Naw! I got a bullet-proof vest on," grunted Conley. "Just knocked me out for a while. Where did that dam' killer go?"

"She took it on the lam out the window, just as these cops broke down the door," said the dancer. "Threw a shot at me from the sill, but I did a dive behind the desk-top, and she missed. I think she went over the roof."

"She knows the way," said Conley. "She came over that same roof when she did for Brandon."

At his words the girl began to sob. He patted her shoulder with clumsy gentleness.

"There now," he comforted. "We will be catching her soon, and I'll see to it that you have a seat right up in front when they spring the trap under her."

He picked up the telephone and reported to Headquarters. Ten minutes later the net was set to tighten about the fleeing killer, and the apartment of the slain gangster chief was once more deserted and silent.

A day and a night went by, and Clerical Clara had not been taken. A score of gangsters and politicians had been questioned about their connection with Mugs Brandon, but they denied any knowledge of his activities, and Detective Conley was about ready to throw the little account book away as worthless.

He was idly thumbing its pages when he came upon a notation on the last page which aroused his interest. He looked closer, and then cursed himself silently for not having recognized the significance of those few penciled words before.

"C.C.," it read. "Terry T is heavy."

It came to him like a flash. So far as he could learn, Clerical Clara had no man in her life. Trust a man like Brandon to know, he ruminated. Brandon's notation meant that Terry T. was her man.

That was funny, too. He knew that Terry Train was a gunman, but had never been able to pin anything on the dapper gangster. It was a well-known fact that Train had no moll, and here was Brandon's notation that Train was *heavy* with Clara!

Conley called to Dick Trent, his running mate, and after explaining his latest hunch, they started for the building where Train leased an apartment. He knew that the gangster would not be expecting a call from the police, but once in the squad car he looked carefully at his gun, and advised Trent to do the same.

Arriving at the apartment building, they walked quickly through the ornate lobby and entered the elevator. Conley turned to the colored operator and snapped his number before the other could voice the protest that showed on his ebony face.

"Fifth floor, and keep your mouth shut!"

As the car stopped, he threw open the door and ran quickly to Apartment 36, with Trent close at his heels.

"Take that window, and watch that no one ducks through to the roof," he told Trent.

As Trent posted himself at the window which commanded the roof, Conley rang the buzzer of Train's apartment. After a brief pause he rang again.

"Open up!" he called.

The knob was turned slowly, and just as the door swung back, a shot sounded from the roof, and Trent fell to the floor. Like a flash Conley stepped in, his service gun in his hand.

"Get 'em up!" he snapped.

The slender, well-dressed man before him raised his hands, and lifted his eyebrows in simulated surprise. He was evidently just about to leave the apartment when Conley rang his bell.

"Well, what's it all about?" he asked in a quiet voice.

Conley stepped in and clicked a pair of cuffs about the upraised wrists.

"Get in there," he ordered gruffly. "I want to see who fired that shot."

Herding the prisoner before him into the back room, he ran to the closed window and quickly raised it. Leaning out, he scanned the roof which ran just under the windows along the entire side of the building. No one was in sight, and as he turned back into the room, Trent entered from the hall.

"Get you?" asked Conley.

"Just a bare scratch," said the other detective. "It was a woman," he added.

"So Clara has been hiding out here," said Conley.

"I don't know any Clara," said the prisoner.

"You better come clean," said Conley. "We know that Clerical Clara was your moll. You both kept it pretty shady, but Mugs Brandon knew it, and left word where it would do the most good. One of his cards said you were mixed up in that Toad Wilson killing."

"The dam' double-crossing punk." The exclamation seemed to explode from the lips of the dapper gangster before he could control himself. Then he bit his lip and turned furiously on the detective.

"Don't kid me," he snarled. "I know you bulls, and you haven't got a thing on me."

Conley was smiling as he turned to Trent.

"Take him down and book him on suspicion," he said. "I'll be down in an hour, so wait for me."

As Trent drove away with the prisoner, Conley hailed a taxi and gave the address of Carmen Ryan. He phoned to her from the house phone in the hall, and she pressed the buzzer that admitted him.

"You working tonight?" he asked without preamble.

She nodded without speaking. Her eyes were swollen as though she had been weeping, and in their sullen depths he could see the same hatred that had been there the day of Brandon's funeral.

"You'd like to see this Clara get hers, wouldn't you?" he asked.

"If the cops don't get her soon, I'll get her on my own," snapped the girl. "Mugs Brandon might not have been so much, but he was good to me, and I loved him. She shot him while he was asleep, like the lousy rat that she is!"

"He left fifty grand that comes to you as his common-law wife," said Conley.

"The Club is in my name," said the girl. "I'm going to run it myself."

"If you will do what I tell you, I think we can land this Clara dame tonight," said Conley.

"What can I do?" asked the girl. "I should have burned her down when I had her under my rod."

"And you'd have got the hot seat," reminded Conley. "I got a hunch that she will be paying you a visit tonight, and my hunches have been working lately."

"What do you want me to do?" asked the girl. For twenty minutes Conley talked earnestly, coaching the girl in the part she was to play. Then he left her and hurried to Headquarters.

The "Club Brandon" was having a formal reopening. The interior had been decorated according to the whims of the new owner, and was a combination of silver and old gold, with panel bands of somber black contrasting the two.

On a raised dais at the far end of the main room, a ten-piece orchestra was playing the latest dance arrangements. Unlike most orchestras, each man was carrying an automatic under the perfectly fitting dinner coats. They were called "Brandon's Army." And Carmen Ryan had seen them in action and had decided to keep them.

Huge bouquets of flowers stood along the walls, representing the good wishes of her friends, and those who would like to be. The tables were well filled with guests, and the waiters moved constantly about with silent efficiency.

At the entrance to the main room just inside the grilled iron doors, Detective Conley was sitting behind a small palm, watching each newcomer. Four men were posted in other places around the room, unknown to any one but Conley and Carmen Ryan.

They mingled with the guests, chatting as affably as though they were part of the reception. Messenger boys rushed in with telegrams of congratulations, and new floral pieces were being added to the masses of blossoms along the walls.

At ten minutes to twelve, a glittering truck drew up in front of the entrance and unloaded a mass of roses built on a small platform mounted on iron casters. Four men carried it carefully up the stairs, wheeled it through the grilled iron doors and placed it in the center along one of the walls.

A gasp of admiration went up from the assembled guests as one of the attendants pushed a wall socket, and a glitter of colored incandescents flashed out from the mass of roses. They were of the deepest red, and were so placed as to make the entire piece resemble a huge blood-red rosebud.

A small card was fastened to one corner. It read:

"Good luck. Hope you get yours. You deserve it!"

A small gong struck the hour of midnight, and with the last stroke the brilliant lights faded out, to be replaced with soft reflections from the coves which ran around the walls just under the ceiling. They were of different colors, changing from rose and lavender to amber and gold in soft lambent waves.

The orchestra started playing softly, and a strange hush came over the crowd which had been so noisy but a moment before. From the four corners of the room shafts of colored lights shot out, and focused on the very center of the polished floor. The beat of the muffled drums sounded like tom-toms from deep in some savage forest, mingling with the barbaric cadences of the muted instruments.

Another gasp went up from the crowd as the center of the floor opened upward and a silver and gold fountain came into view. Streams of water splashed against the sparkling crystal which formed the lesser ornaments, and changed to cascades of leaping fire as the vari-colored lights played upon their revolving facets.

The beat of the tom-toms became louder as the orchestra was heard playing some wild song of the desert. From above, a brilliant floodlight of amber suddenly cast its glow upon the large figure in the very center of the fountain, and breaths were held as the semi-nude goddess became a woman of living gold.

For just an instant she poised on the lip of the fountain shell, and then leaped lightly to the floor. As the lights from the four corners followed her, she began a slow dance to the strains of the half-savage music, which seemed to blend with the shades of colored lights, and made them seem like a part of the very air.

The crowd grew tense as the strange witchery of sound and light crept into their blood. Hearts pounded and hands clenched with passion as the desire to become primitive cast its insinuating spell upon them.

Not a sound was heard as the music went on, and that silent, beautiful figure of gold gyrated maddeningly before them; no sounds except the raking intake of breath in bodies reverting to the abysmal.

Like a wild creature of the forests the dancer began to move in a creeping glide that carried her ever nearer to the tinkling fountain, and then, in one crashing crescendo from the orchestra hidden in the shifting shadows, she leaped onto the fountain and froze into statuesque immobility.

Before the crowd could relax, a staccato blur

of shots rang out from the center of the farthest wall, and as the spitful orange flames cut the semilighted shadows of color, the statue toppled from her pedestal and fell into the shallow water with a sodden splash.

At the same instant the lights went on, and from five different places in the crowded room, a fusillade of shots was directed toward the huge bouquet of deep red roses. The hidden lights were shot out, and clipped roses flew from the frame as the bullets from the guns of the detectives chopped their way into the heart of that massive rosebud.

The crowd stood still, holding their breaths with the surprise of it all, wondering whether it were a part of the entertainment, or whether some new debt of gangdom were being paid.

From behind the grilled doors Dan Conley came in at a crouching run, his gun held at his side as he approached that mutilated offering of roses.

From the far end of the room came the orchestra, spread out fan-wise as every man held a rod ready before him. In the center of the room a dripping figure was climbing out of the splashing fountain, and then the fountain sank again below the level of the floor, as the dancer disappeared behind a group of palms.

Conley and his men ripped the large floral rose to shreds, and deep in the heart of that token of love and good wishes they found nothing— except six brass shells from an automatic, and the rubber print of a woman's shoe!

Again the waiters took up their task of serving the crowd, and again the orchestra played the latest number for the dance. The spell had passed, and the crowd was once again occupied with the business of having a good time in their separate ways.

Behind the palm by the grilled doors Conley sat with Trent, trying to figure out where he had slipped. He felt sure that he could not be wrong, and he was glad that he had insisted that Carmen wear the thin suit of gilded chain armor for her dance. It cost plenty to get that costume, but if they had trapped the murderer it would have been worth it. Even at that, her body would wear the bruises of those bullets for weeks.

From behind the orchestra came a brilliant figure clad in a gown of deepest red that accentuated the contours of her flawless figure with artistic perfection. The only relief to that deep rosebud red was a narrow trimming of black around the bodice.

"Carmen!" The crowd shouted the one word.

She held up her hand for silence, as she reached the exact spot where the fountain had been. And strangely enough, she faced the mutilated rosebud of roses.

"Thank you all," she said simply. "I hope you liked the show. It is not over yet, but it will soon be finished."

She crouched as she spoke, her eyes never leaving that emblem of love along the wall. Without warning, the flood-lights from two corners of the room were focused on that shattered token, and the crowd missed the lightning move of the dancer in the center of the room.

Her right hand flashed to her leg, and came away spitting blood-colored flashes of flame into the heart of that huge rosebud. A figure seemed to emerge from the heart of the rose, and sagged through the crushed flower, to drop on the polished floor.

The crowd gasped. A messenger boy!

Detective Conley started as he turned over the still figure, and closed the glazing eyes. Then he pushed back the small uniform cap and disclosed the blond mannish bob of—"Clerical Clara!"

"I saw a messenger boy when the lights went out!" he muttered half to himself.

"I saw a footprint," said Carmen. "I knew she wouldn't resist trying it again. We wouldn't be looking for it. And now the devil has a dam' good bookkeeper to keep his records straight."

Black Legion

Lars Anderson

COSTUMED HEROES in the pulp era were pretty thick on the ground, largely due to the enormous success of the Shadow, who was soon followed by crime-fighters using sobriquets that made them sound more villainous than heroic: Doc Savage, The Spider, The Phantom, The Whisperer, The Ghost, The Black Bat. What was decidedly unusual was a female masked avenger. The Domino Lady in her real life was Ellen Patrick, a gorgeous twenty-two-year-old who swore vengeance on criminals after her father was murdered. She has curly blond hair, penetrating brown eyes, is tall, and has a stunning figure. Her modus operandi generally finds her at a party or social gathering in a thin, low-cut, backless dress that clings to her every curve. When she discovers the item that she came to steal from her adversary, she slips into a bedroom or closet, peels off her dress and dons another one (both dresses so gossamer that they fit in a small handbag), puts on a mask, and returns to the party. Her disguise apparently works, just as Clark Kent's removal of his glasses appears to make him unrecognizable. When successful, she leaves a card bearing the inscription: "Compliments of The Domino Lady." There were only six stories about her, five of which appeared in *Saucy Romantic Adventures* and one in *Mystery Adventure Magazine*. Little is known of the author, whose career appears to have lasted only about four years (1935–1938), and all of whose stories were published in the second-level pulps.

"Black Legion" was first published in the October 1936 issue of *Saucy Romantic Adventures*.

Black Legion

Lars Anderson

CHAPTER ONE
THREATENED

ELLEN PATRICK, radiantly youthful and possessed of that intangible something which lends allure to some fortunate women, rose from the crimson *chaise longue.*

Pink-nailed fingers patted her perfect suntouched coiffure and straightened the blue silken kimono that she wore. She smiled up into the dark, good-looking features of a man.

"You must be very careful, Paul," she breathed softly, "I'm afraid this is more than a mere threat. That Black Legion wouldn't hesitate to kill you, you know."

She laughed nervously, stepped closer to his side. The man could see the tiny fires of interest blazing deep in her great brown eyes, and he laid a caressing hand upon the heated velvet that was her rounded shoulder.

Paul Cathern flashed white teeth in an engaging grin. He was of medium height, slender, wiry, and possessed more than his share of vibrant magnetism. Astutely fearless, he was known as one of the most successful special investigators working out of the sheriff's office. His deep voice was low, passionate.

"You're sweet, Ellen!" he told her, his gray eyes frankly admiring her sensuous figure, set off as it was by the filmy kimono. Lovely bosom, lithe thighs, slender calves, trim ankles, dainty feet.

His grin widened.

"Of course, I'll be careful, honey. It's part of my job. But they can't scare or bluff me off! I'm out to get the goods on this outfit, and I'm not quitting cold when success is in sight! Why, the information on the Obispo rendezvous alone gives me a swell chance of rounding up some of the ringleaders."

Ellen quivered within the depths of her being. Paul Cathern had long been an intimate friend, and more. She admired him greatly, loved him not a little. Now, the mysterious Black Legion threatened his life because of his activities as investigator into their atrocities along the Pacific Coast! Theirs was no idle threat.

Already two detectives had been cruelly tortured by black-hooded creatures. Another had mysteriously vanished without a trace. And judging from their cowardly ultimatum delivered to Cathern's apartment a few hours previously, the young sleuth was to be next on their list!

Ellen's brown eyes were filmed with worry as she walked to the door with her caller. There, she lifted her moist, red lips for his goodnight kiss. As Cathern bent his dark head to the pale oval of her face, he clasped her in his arms. She laughed softly at his hungry zeal.

"You're sweet, Ellen!" he repeated, huskily, gazing into her eyes. The little adventuress thrilled to the touch of his hands and the caress of his long fingers.

She couldn't resist liking the possessive embrace of his arm about her pliant waist as Cathern drew her close to him. Her ductile curves were flattened against him, and she experienced an emotion that was strangely new to her! She returned the kiss as his lips were pressed to the ripe contours of her cerise mouth.

"I'll be seeing you in a couple of days, Ellen," he whispered as he reluctantly released her, and opened the door.

"As soon as I've investigated that hide-out a bit further, I'll have some good news for you, I hope. Keep sweet, honey." And he was gone.

Ellen did not move for a little while. Her agile brain was clicking rapidly over the details of the disclosures concerning the Black Legion which Paul Cathern had given her.

Her piquant face was grim as she moved sensuously over the deep-piled rug, procured a cigarette from a black and silver box which stood on an end table, and lighted it. Filling her lungs with the fragrant smoke, she began to pace back and forth with feline grace, her racing mind sorting and filing the information she had obtained.

Ellen Patrick, known in certain circles through California as The Domino Lady, was nearing twenty-three.

Just tall enough to be majestic, with a figure whose curves set men's pulses hammering, her beautiful rounded features, crowned by a coronet of silky, golden curls, often graced the rotogravure supplements of the Sunday newspapers as one of the Southland's prettiest debs. Yet no one connected Ellen Patrick with the notorious Domino Lady!

Her father, Owen Patrick, had been the czar of California politics at one time.

A murderer's cowardly bullet had cut him down in his prime some three years before. Rumor was that the killer had been an employee of the state political machine. A small trust fund, and a wealth of wit and courage, had been his bequeathal to his lovely, orphaned daughter.

Previous to her father's brutal slaying, Ellen had lived a life of comparative ease as befitted the only child of Owen Patrick.

She had graduated at Berkeley, spent several glorious months in the Far East, and then an assassin's slug had robbed her of the one who meant more to her than life itself! Small wonder that her life had been dedicated to a campaign of vengeance against the murderers of her parent!

Ruthless, roguish, Ellen at times accepted almost impossible undertakings simply for the sake of friendship and an inordinate craving for adventure! For example, her recent exploits in Santa Anita, in which she had matched wits and daring with the notorious Kilgarlin gang, and emerged victorious.

At other times she was coldly involved in hazardous schemes, aimed at the discomfiture and embarrassment of the authorities whom she blamed for her father's death, at the same time earning a princely income, most of which was donated to a worthy charity.

Oft-times, her adventures were so arranged as to encompass both the friendship and vengeance angles, and those were the ones in which she gloried, particularly.

Only a short time ago, she had retrieved a packet of compromising letters for a friend in a daring raid upon the penthouse apartment of Rob Wyatt, aspirant for political honors, and at the same time had bluffed the big game hunter and politician into a state of oblivion!

A unique black and white, or white and black ensemble was widely recognized as The Domino Lady's costume, and mention of it in certain circles was always productive of inward shudders! No vulpine politician or unscrupulous crook in all California wanted any part of The Domino Lady!

Now, as she moved back and forth about the beautifully-furnished apartment, Ellen was prodding her keen mind, searching for some method by which she could aid Paul Cathern in his struggle with the Black Legion, and perhaps save his life.

The special investigator had confided in Ellen, never dreaming that he was betraying secrets to the formidable Domino Lady! Without a doubt, leading politicians (some of them Ellen's sworn enemies) were members of the feared organization, according to Cathern, and especially was he convinced that this was true in the case of J. Riggs Saint, the district attorney.

Saint, campaigning for reelection, was loud in his vociferations against the Black Legion. His newspaper editorials were heated protests against their reputed outlawry and murder.

He cried long and loud for some scrap of evidence with which to push prosecutions, knowing full well that there was scant possibility of any such damaging material coming to light. In fact, the very storm of his indignation and threats was the moving factor behind Cathern's conviction of the district attorney's implication!

Two days previously, the special investigator had chanced upon a Black Legion rendezvous in the Obispo country; a wild spot well-suited to their campaign of torture and death.

He had kept the fact strictly to himself, but had called the district attorney for another detective to aid him in his Legion investigation, dropping the hint that he expected results, shortly. Then, he had received the anonymous death threat, commanding him to cease all operations immediately, and get out of the state!

With typical courage, the young sleuth had squared his craggy jaw, and ignored the cowardly ultimatum! All these facts harassed Ellen as she pondered the dilemma. What an opportunity to clean up the state, expose crooked politics, if Cathern's information was correct! And Ellen felt sure that it was.

A frown puckered her lovely features, and a chain of cigarettes overflowed from the ashtray as she paced the floor. The frown was still there as she peeled the kimono from her shapely body, and stepped into pajamas. And, when Ellen retired for the night, long moments passed before she drifted off to her usual dreamless sleep.

CHAPTER TWO
A DARING VENTURE

The odds-and-ends closet was small, really nothing more than a locker built into one corner of the garage.

Slightly stooped, Ellen Patrick found it exceedingly uncomfortable. Although the door was open a few inches, it was stuffy and unbearably close within the cramped quarters. Perspiration bedewed her smooth white forehead and pert upper lip. From one beautifully-shaped hand protruded the ominous snout of a small, black automatic.

The upper part of her face was covered by a domino mask of black silk. A form-fitting backless frock of white satin covered her shapely figure, the scanty bodice caught in a halter neck across the creamy expanse of her lovely bosom. The cape of black silk concealed bare, kissable shoulders, and her hands were gloved.

For some hour and a half, Ellen had been waiting like this.

She was beginning to wonder if she had guessed wrong. Raising a gloved hand, she wiped the perspiration from her forehead with a tiny wisp of lace. Then a tight little smile curved the corners of her red mouth.

"He should be along any minute now!" she reassured herself, silently. "And I'll get things straightened out, or give him a dose of his own medicine!"

There was no thought of failure in the little adventuress' mind. For two nights, she had checked on J. Riggs Saint and his movements. He always arrived home at the same hour, and alone. It shouldn't prove difficult to get the drop on the district attorney, she mused.

Forty-eight hours before, Paul Cathern had disappeared, vanished from his apartment and usual haunts. The sheriff's office had hunted feverishly for their ace sleuth, but to no avail. The disappearance had spurred Ellen into action.

Cautious inquiries on her part had been in vain. Immediately, she had thought of the Black Legion warning. Was her good friend to vanish as had other victims of the hooded organization?

Not if The Domino Lady could help it, she decided. In consequence, she had decided upon the boldest move of her daring career; the snatching of the unscrupulous district attorney

· 1048 ·

whom she was convinced was a ring leader in Legion affairs!

The hour was nine o'clock, and it was very quiet in the residential section of town. Flattened within the tiny locker, Ellen prayed for quick action to ease the strain on her aching body and quivering nerves.

Abruptly the purr of a powerful engine came to her keen ears, and the whisper of rubber on concrete.

A yellow glow of headlights shone through the frosted glass panels of the doors, dimly illuminating the inner confines of the spacious garage.

It was impossible for Ellen to be sure that this was J. Riggs Saint, but her nerves snapped taut and her slender fingers tightened about the corrugated butt of the automatic. Her mouth was suddenly dry. This was one of the most crucial moments of her career! An overwhelming desire for a cigarette assailed her, but she dared not risk it. Her presence must not be suspected at this stage of the game.

Came the sound of footsteps outside the garage doors, and a key gritted in the lock. The big doors swung gratingly open a moment later, and Ellen shot a surreptitious glance from her place of concealment. J. Riggs Saint, dapper, slender, was outlined in the glow of the headlights as he walked back to a powerful sedan! Her zero hour was at hand!

The big car purred smoothly as it rolled into the garage. Through the crack in the door, Ellen looked closely at the district attorney.

His features were refined, but hardened, his blue eyes icy, flint-hard. A half sneer played about his thin-lipped mouth, giving him a sinister look.

In the narrow confines of the closet, Ellen caught and held her breath. A feeling of vague apprehension went through her soft body as she thought of the gigantic task that confronted her.

Not only might Saint be a dangerous man to tackle, even with the automatic and other equipment with which she was armed, but subsequent moves would be double perilous! She shook off the apprehension, grimly.

The district attorney slid from the driver's seat. He was carrying a bulky briefcase which he handled carefully, placing it on the running board beside his feet. He reached within the car, drew the ignition key from the dash, prepared to slam the door. Abruptly, he tensed.

"Reach high!"

The cold, high-pitched command knifed through the garage as Ellen slid swiftly up behind the unsuspecting politician.

The muzzle of her weapon formed an icy ring of menace against Saint's neck. His hands were trembling as they shot upward over his head.

"Who—who're you?" he managed, struggling for composure, "and what do you want here?" His tones betrayed a mixture of astonishment and rising rage.

Ellen laughed softly, but there was little of mirth in the sound. "Do you still desire evidence against the Black Legion, Saint," she snapped, quickly, "so that you may prosecute? Or is it all pre-election bluff?"

Saint snorted.

"Everyone knows where I stand on that subject! I'm ready to prosecute whenever I get material evidence, not hearsays! But what has that to do with this high-handed outrage? Don't you know I'll get you a stretch in Tehachipi for this, you fool?"

Again Ellen's mocking laughter. "I don't bluff worth a peso, Saint!" she gritted. "So you might as well save yourself the effort! I'm going to see to it that you get the evidence you've been crying for! In fact, unless I'm badly mistaken, you'll wish you'd never heard of the Black Legion before the light of another day shines upon you, my friend!"

"I'm afraid I don't understand," began the district attorney, weakly.

"You're a member of that Legion, Saint!" snapped Ellen, boldly.

Saint laughed, uglily. "You're taking a lot for granted!" he said. "And I wouldn't want the job of proving such an accusation!"

"Well, that's exactly what I'm intending to do

before I'm finished, Saint!" she returned, coolly. "Not only prove it, but see to it that you're put where you belong! You're a traitor to the honest citizens who put you in office!"

Saint edged slowly forward, his crafty eyes riveted on Ellen's automatic. "The Domino Lady is very much wanted by a great many men in this city." He sneered. "I'd advise you to tend to your own business."

Suddenly he lunged, his hand outstretched. For a moment it seemed as though he'd overpowered her. Her gun hand grasped in his own hand, he catapulted with her to the floor.

For once Ellen had been taken unawares. In the uncertain light she had failed to notice his forward movement. In the moment he leaped she fired. Her bullet going, as she thought, wild.

For she had scarce time to aim in that split second.

Springing lithely to her feet Ellen stared at the form of J. Riggs Saint on the stone floor. He lay inert, strangely still . . . dead.

For a moment panic seized her.

Murder. Something she had always steered clear of. Murder. A vision of the gallows flitted across her remorseful mind. She noticed a trickle of blood seep from his temple onto the hard floor.

A feeling of nausea swept over her. She reeled and, had it not been for her nervy will, would have slipped to the floor, unconscious.

A harsh breath escaped the figure on the floor. Ellen bent, her hand retrieving the little automatic which but a moment before had slipped from her nerveless fingers. One little hand slid beneath his shirt front. He lived! His breathing was regular, though rapid.

In another moment her fingers had flecked at the smear of blood on his temple. Only a scalp wound, a crease. But it had been that perhaps, that had saved The Domino Lady from prison.

Swiftly her fingers dipped into a tiny pocket inside her cape, drew forth a small object which glittered in the indirect light. It was a little hypodermic syringe, previously loaded with a quick-acting drug. The drug, though harmless, was sufficiently strong to render the victim unconscious for several hours.

A deft motion and the sharp needle sank home, its fluid finding a place beneath his skin. Ellen Patrick was coolness personified, now. Her movements were precise, and executed with a deftness that was truly amazing.

She picked up the briefcase, opened it, and hurriedly scanned its contents. Her features lit up with an exultant smile as she read, briefly, here and there, before replacing the contents back in the case, which she tossed in the front seat of the car.

Working with incredible speed and precision, she produced a roll of cord from the garage locker and proceeded to bind the hands and feet of the insensible man. Bending, she cut a heavy strip of adhesive from a roll taken from her handy wrist bag. This was carefully applied across Saint's mouth.

It was quite a task for Ellen to get the bound figure into the rear of the sedan.

He was not a large man, but his drugged body was a limp, dead freight, and it required all the strength in her hundred-and-twenty-pound frame to accomplish the task. She was panting softly when she had finished and closed the door.

She backed the big car noiselessly from the garage, consumed precious moments in shutting the garage doors.

Although her heart was churning madly from exertion and excitement, she was as cool as a Winter's breeze as she swung the sedan about in the street, and trod the accelerator. A laugh of triumph burst from her lips as she removed the domino mask, the big car leaped forward into the night.

CHAPTER THREE
DANGER TRAIL

The night was dark, moonless, and wisps of yellow fog had drifted in from the nearby Pacific.

A good night for her venture, mused Ellen, as she throttled the sedan to a higher speed. Paul

Cathern's directions emblazoned on her mind, she felt no fear of missing her destination. A moment after she had crossed the city line, a new concrete highway stretched before her.

Along this she roared at sixty miles an hour. After five miles, she slowed the car, went forward more cautiously. Suddenly, she swung the wheel, switched on to a narrower macadam road which ran off to the left into open country.

Driving slowly, a half mile brought a winking eye of light to her attention. She cut off the sedan headlights, idled the engine to a noiseless purr. Moments later, she cut the engine off entirely, braked to a standstill. All was ominously quiet in the blackness of the foggy night.

Ellen climbed from the sedan after a quick glance assured her that her captive still slumbered. She hesitated beside the car, drew the tiny black mask again up about her eyes. The automatic again in hand, she set off in the direction of the light.

She moved soundlessly through the darkness. If this were indeed the Obispo rendezvous of the Black Legion, she might expect a guard lurking in any of the darker spaces, she knew.

And this would hold doubly true if her guess concerning the whereabouts of the missing detective was well-founded. Outwardly, she was calm, but her heart was racing, blood pounding wildly through her veins as her crisis approached.

At closer view, Ellen made out the outlines of a rather ramshackle building. It was but one story in height and possessed three rooms. The room on her left was lighted, the remainder of the structure being darkened.

She crept toward the lighted side, every sense alert to her danger. At the mere cracking of a twig under foot, she paused for precious moments, pulse pounding, and a prayer for safety on her quivering lips.

So much depended upon her this night—she just couldn't fail. It would be tonight or never! Failure now would mean tasting Saint's vengeance.

Abruptly, a dark figure loomed between her and the light which filtered from the window!

A sentry!

The man seemed to be leaning against the wall near the corner of the building, unmoving. Ellen tensed, catching her breath sharply. She hadn't tried to fool herself; these were desperate men—if she were caught, it would mean torture, death, or worse!

Many another might have faltered at the obstacle now confronting her. But the little adventuress was made of sterner stuff. The sight of a guard only added to her determination to follow through with her plans.

To one of her temperament, there was but one means of procedure. She must move directly, court the element of surprise to her favor, overcome the sentry by physical means, and as quietly as possible! She tensed, moving an inch at a time upon the unsuspecting man, the automatic reversed in her fist!

The black-hooded sentinel was half-asleep at his post. He snapped to attention a moment too late to miss the white-clad figure which hurtled upon him from out of the blackness.

A hurried motion toward his left armpit, a sucking intake of breath for a cry of warning and Ellen lunged forward, every ounce of her athletic frame behind the move, her right arm swinging in the arc of a swift half circle as she leaped.

The solid shank of the automatic whammed against the side of the guard's head. The force of her charge carried them both to the ground, this time Ellen atop the heap. She rose immediately, dusting dried grass from her clothing, and smiling grimly at the recumbent figure.

She had come prepared for such an emergency. The large roll of adhesive was put into use, sealing the man's lips, and securing his hands and feet against his possible awakening, she quickly rolled the limp figure into a dark corner near a rickety fence to prevent early discovery.

For a full minute, Ellen paused, tense, brown eyes straining in the direction of the lighted window.

Her great orbs were agleam. Here was the work that she loved, and it was being performed in the cause that meant more to her than life itself.

Adventure was her meat and danger her dessert.

Gone were the hours of planning and fuming. Action loomed ahead on the danger trail! Ellen's adventurous spirit leaped at the thought, confident, exultant!

Swiftly, yet noiseless as a night shadow, she gained the side of the window. A purr of voices came to her keen ears from within the building. A ragged shade was but partly drawn, and a view of the room was easily obtained.

Carefully avoiding the light which filtered through the panes, she looked within. She glimpsed three hooded figures seated at a table a few feet away. They were big fellows, but she could not see their features.

A rough table and several rickety chairs went to make up the furnishings of the bare room. There was a brown bottle and glasses on the table, and the men drank occasionally as they waited, conversing in low tones, inaudible to the watching girl. *The Black Legion!*

One man drinking more freely than the others was quite audible to Ellen's straining ears.

"Say, Chenville," he bellowed, maudlinly, "why not get things going and get 'em over with? No use waitin' on the others. Old Gorsh always was a slow poke. He'll hold the others up, and we won't get this job done before daylight! I'm for—"

The one addressed as Chenville interrupted with a wave of a gloved hand, but Ellen couldn't make out his words. She imagined he was reasoning with the other man. The latter laughed raucously, and poured another drink which he tossed off at a gulp.

"Yeah?" he sneered, loudly, wiping his loose mouth with the back of a gloved hand. "That's what you say, Chenville! But I say different. I think we could do with less politics in this outfit. I never did like politics or politicians! They can't be trusted! And when it comes time to do a little job, or a little bump, it ought to be hurried along. Waitin' is only invitin' trouble to come along! Now take this snoopin' Cathern mug. He's been

here for hours, waitin' for Gorsh to arrive, and superintend the job. He oughta been taken care of hours ago."

Ellen tensed in the darkness.

Her hunch had been right!

Paul Cathern was in the hands of these men, awaiting a fate she knew not what, and with no hope of rescue save through her own efforts!

And the man's words confirmed her belief that the politicians of the state machine were behind the depredations of the notorious Black Legion!

She saw no point in waiting and listening to further disclosures. Time was speeding; any moment might be too late! She must locate Paul Cathern, save him, and at the same time keep her true identity from him. There was no time to lose if her plans were to be carried out with half a chance for ultimate success!

She tested the catch of her automatic, gripped it firmly, and moved silently through the darkness toward the other side of the house.

Obviously the thing to do was to get to Cathern as quickly as possible. She found the window on the right side of the house without difficulty, paused and listened intently. She could hear the ticking of her tiny baguette in the stillness of the night.

The little adventuress removed a compact folding jimmy from her wrist bag, opened it into a slender sliver of steel. With this handy implement, she began jimmying the window. Using utmost caution, it required several pries to snap the cast-iron fittings. With the fifth effort, they snapped brittlely, and Ellen slid the window upwards.

"Say!" she called in a sibilant whisper. "Is anyone there?"

A slight, muffled groan was the only answer, but it sent a quick thrill through Ellen's soft body. At the moment, she realized just how alarmed she had really been about the young special investigator!

It was but the work of an instant for her to swing herself upon the sill, and agilely lower herself into the interior of the darkened room. Then, a pencil flash gave her a glimpse of the bare confines of Cathern's prison, and of the sleuth, himself.

Paul Cathern was tightly bound, a handkerchief mask over the upper part of his face, his mouth tightly sealed by a wide strip of adhesives. He had been tossed into a corner of the room to await torture and possible doom!

With a reassuring whisper, Ellen sank to her knees and labored at the cramping gyves. It required three minutes of concentrated effort to free his hands and feet, and a moment to remove the tape from his mouth. A word of thankfulness seeped from his lips as they were freed from the adhesive.

"You took a devil of a chance," he whispered, grasping her arm, "in coming here like this. Those men were going to torture me—lash me—burn me with white-hot irons! I owe my life to you! I'm Paul Cathern, investigator with Sheriff Bonsill. Who're you, anyhow?"

Ellen hesitated, briefly. "No time for introductions now," she snapped. "But I can assure you I'm a friend! We must move fast! Everything's clear at the moment. Let's go!"

Abruptly, the little adventuress tensed in the darkness. Her hand went to Cathern's lips as she caught and held her breath. A chair had scraped within the adjoining room, and heavy footsteps were approaching the connecting door!

Her nerves jerked taut as a hand twisted the knob and swung the portal halfway open, yellow lamplight streaming across the rough flooring of the room! The automatic bristled viciously, as she aimed it at the doorway and waited!

"Get away from that door, Lucas!" snapped someone whom Ellen imagined to be the leader, Chenville. The intruder swung about to face the giver of the command, while Ellen's heart churned, madly. Would the drunken brute ignore the other man, and enter to discover her in the act of freeing her prisoner? What mercy might she expect at his hands if he did?

The queries were answered a moment later when the fellow turned again toward the prison room.

"Aw, nuts, Chenville!" he flung back over his massive shoulder. "I'm goin' to see if the snooper's okay, that's all!"

Ellen's finger tightened upon the trigger, her heart sinking as the big man lunged forward through the doorway!

CHAPTER FOUR
A FRAMER FRAMED

A coolness settled upon Ellen Patrick as she faced one of the most crucial situations of a lifetime of adventure.

Her lovely bosom rose and fell with her accelerated breathing beneath the black cape which she had tightly drawn about the white frock.

Great eyes were fixed in an unwinking stare upon the doorway. Her slender fingers trembled a little as they contacted the safety catch of the automatic to be sure it was down. She was prepared to shoot it out with the black-hooded devils, no matter what the ultimate outcome!

But the drink-drugged intruder was spared a quick end.

Chenville was evidently the man in charge, and a subordinate's disregard of orders infuriated him. As Lucas came through the doorway, a heavy hand was clamped on his shoulder, and he was roughly jerked back into the other room.

A push sent the big man spinning across the floor.

"Damn you, Lucas!" snarled the leader, harshly.

"You'll obey orders or take the consequences! I'm in charge here, and don't forget it! One more funny move out of you, and you'll get what Gorsh gives the others!" His outburst was cut short as he slammed the door behind him, leaving Ellen and the investigator in darkness again.

Ellen heaved an immense sigh of relief. "Whew! That was a bit too close for comfort!" she breathed, as she helped Paul Cathern to his feet.

"You said it!" agreed the sleuth, softly. "I thought for a moment we were goners. You're one nervy little person."

Paul Cathern staggered and would have fallen but for her steadying arm, so cramped were his limbs from long hours beneath the bindings.

She helped him to the window, across the sill, and joined him a moment later. Outside, she leaned close to him, and he caught his first glimpse of her costume and the identifying mask.

"The Domino Lady!" he exclaimed, wonderingly.

"At your service!" she returned, evenly, her soft voice tempered to a lazy, disguising drawl for Cathern's benefit. "And having a crack at the Black Legion, and its unscrupulous political backers! I've tried to help you, Paul Cathern; will you help me in return?"

"Name it!" he said, quickly, earnestly, "and the life you've saved will be risked in its accomplishment if necessary!"

She laughed softly in the darkness.

"The help I ask," she said, "will bring about the downfall of the Black Legion and the complete ruin of the higher-ups in this state, Cathern! We must move fast! Come—"

Without another word, Ellen Patrick set out in the direction of the road, and Paul Cathern followed after her.

As the rear door of the sedan swung open, and Ellen's pencil flash sprayed the interior with white light, Paul Cathern's lips curved in a pleased grin. He stood for a moment looking down upon the bound figure of J. Riggs Saint without a hint of compassion in his gray eyes.

Then he shot a questioning glance at The Domino Lady.

"The Black Legion owes much to this man," drawled Ellen in explanation. "He's one of the higher-ups who provide protection! It's my idea that he should pay as they have made other victims pay!"

"Just what is your idea?" whispered Cathern, meaningly.

Ellen laughed, liquidly. "Have you noticed the similarity in size and coloring between you and Saint?"

The investigator started. "You're right!" he exclaimed, "though I'd never noticed it before! Just what—"

"They were going to torture you," she interrupted, evenly, "and this scoundrel had assured them of immunity! What could be more appropriate than a quick switch of clothing, plant Saint in your place, and his brutes do as they will with him! By the way they looked tonight, I have a feeling that they'll fail to recognize him. And J. Riggs Saint will get a sound flogging; a dose of his own medicine."

The special investigator grinned. "All the way!" he cried, softly, "and then some! Let's get busy!" He began peeling off his coat.

Ellen busied herself with the bulky briefcase she had taken from the politician.

By the dashlight, she gave its contents closer attention than before. She was astounded by the scope of damaging evidence it contained. Evidently the district attorney had been an active organizer and a charter member of the Black Legion in the state!

His intimate papers went into detail, mentioned prominent names, some of them political figures of highest power!

She turned at the sound of Cathern's voice to find him garbed in the district attorney's natty tweeds, his own rumpled worsted gracing the figure of the politician.

The latter was now conscious, and his eyes rolled in fear from one to the other of his captors. Cathern had again bound him, securely.

The tape prevented him from speaking, but he squirmed frantically about, struggling with his bonds.

The investigator bent, placed the handkerchief mask upon the upper part of the attorney's face. Thus rigged, no one could possibly tell the politician from the young detective!

And, since the Legion usually bound and taped a masked prisoner before torturing him, it looked as though J. Riggs Saint was in for a dose of his own medicine!

It wasn't far to the window. Cathern was small but wiry, with spring steel rippling along shoulders and legs. He had no particular difficulty in lifting the flabby form of the district attorney to his shoulders. Guided by Ellen, he moved noiselessly toward the house with his burden.

Sounds of maudlin singing came from the lighted room as they hefted the figure over the sill, and into the interior of the prison. Evidently, the heavy drinking Lucas had reached a state of inebriation where song alone could express his feelings. Ellen was glad.

The sounds of their movements were masked completely by the off-key bellowing of the drunken Legionaries!

They placed the still squirming form of the politician in the exact spot where Paul Cathern had lain.

A moment later, they were again outside the building, the window closed. They hurried toward Saint's sedan. Ellen would have liked to remain in the vicinity to witness the surprising denouement when Saint's men discovered that their victim was the district attorney himself, but the need for retreat was pressing.

Too much depended upon a quick return to the city, and safe disposal of the incriminating evidence to think of tarrying for the sake of pleasure!

So it was that she backed the car in a noiseless half circle, and allowed it to glide toward the distant concrete highway without engine power.

Once at a distance from the torture house, she throttled the engine to a steady, mile-eating pace, headed for the city.

There was little conversation between them as they hurtled along through the night. Ellen thought she understood why Paul Cathern was so quiet.

He was an employee of the sheriff's office, and The Domino Lady was reputedly outside the law. She had saved his life, and he couldn't very well question her or attempt to establish her identity!

He looked out of the window, away from her, his long fingers testing the toughness of a two-day growth of dark beard on his lean cheeks.

As they crossed the city limits, and neared a cab stand, Ellen laughed swiftly, and slowed the sedan.

"Obviously, you must leave me here," she told him in the assumed drawl, "since I must remove the mask before driving farther into the city. And I must ditch Riggs Saint's car, you know! You should have no difficulty in getting a taxi to your apartment."

For the first time in minutes, he looked at her, intently.

"Certainly!" he returned, quickly.

"I understand! But before we part, let me assure you of my undying gratitude for this night's work! I've heard some pretty awful things about The Domino Lady in the past."

She interrupted. "And you believed them, of course?"

Cathern grinned.

"Perhaps I did," he admitted, "but never again! You're aces with me! If I can ever help you in any way, please call upon me. I owe a lot to you."

Again Ellen interrupted, as she drew the sedan to the curb.

"Forget it!"

And then, "It was all in the night's work. I'm amply repaid if you're convinced that I'm not the creature my enemies would have everyone believe. But there is one favor you can grant me, if you will."

"Just name it!" he said, eagerly.

Ellen held out the briefcase to him.

"Take this," she said, "and see that it gets into the right hands. It contains a lot of vital information which will help to break up the Black Legion in California. It contains dates, rituals, and a complete list of political office holders who are secretly members of the clan."

"But the credit?" interpolated Paul Cathern, soberly.

She gestured with gloved hands, briefly. "Who cares about that? It was only to defeat the political machine that I became interested. If you will take this evidence I'll be more than satisfied. As an officer, the credit will set well on your shoulders."

He had climbed from the car, briefcase in hand, but now he leaned through the window, and grasped her hand. Her red lips pursed a charming:

"Goodbye."

"Til we meet?" he breathed, with an engaging grin.

"*Quien sabe?*"

She meshed the gears, rolled from the curb, pulling the domino from her round cheeks as soon as she was out of range of his vision. It was one o'clock when she parked the sedan, got out and walked away. Twice she looked behind her, fearful that some prowl car might connect the abandoned Saint car with her. But her fears were groundless; the streets were deserted. A short time later, she had descended from a cab and entered the exclusive apartment house which she called home.

CHAPTER FIVE
THE DOMINO LADY TRIUMPHANT

It was evening of the following day when Ellen Patrick moved across the heavy Boukhara of her living room and opened the outside door. Paul Cathern entered the room. He carried a folded newspaper, and he was grinning, widely. He took off his gray felt as he closed the door, then followed Ellen to the center of the room.

The powder-blue negligee she affected set off her shapely rounded body to perfection, and Cathern's eyes were freighted with frank admiration as he followed the intoxicating undulations of her figure as she sank down upon a crimson *chaise longue*. She smiled, motioned him to sit beside her.

"Suppose you give an account of yourself, big boy?" she said, pertly, brows arched in interrogation. "Haven't seen you around."

Paul Cathern had such an engaging grin, and it broadened to show his white teeth as he dropped down beside Ellen. He unfolded a late edition of the *Express*, handed it to her.

"Perhaps this will explain," he said.

Ellen feigned complete amazement as she looked at the paper. Little sounds of excite-ment and pleasure escaped her ripe lips as she read the information emblazoned upon the front page:

BLACK LEGION DEFINITELY DOOMED!
CHARTER MEMBERS FLEEING AFTER EXPOSÉ BY ACE SLEUTH FROM SHERIFF'S OFFICE. INDICTMENTS OUT FOR LEADING POLITICAL FIGURES; J. RIGGS SAINT, DISTRICT ATTORNEY, IS MYSTERIOUSLY MISSING!

June 7. Following a startling exposé of Black Legion activities in the state, by Paul Cathern, special investigator from Sheriff Bonsill's office, indictments have been sworn out for some of the leading politicians, including J. Riggs Saint, District Attorney, and Leo U. Gorsh, State Representative.

Saint has handed in his written resignation, but cannot be reached for a statement. One report has it that he is confined in a private hospital, suffering from mysterious injuries that threaten his life. Another that he is taking an extended sea voyage for his health. Mr. Gorsh is reported as flying to Mexico City on business. In any event, both gentlemen will find a warm welcome awaiting them when they are located and turned over to the newly-appointed District Attorney, Mr. John Smithson. This is one of the most startling exposés in the history of the state, and politicians both big and small are leaving for parts unknown by rail, water and air. Mr. Smithson, interviewed at his office today, promises a thorough clean-up, and in taking every step to apprehend the fleeing higher-ups of the Black Legion . . .

There were columns more of lurid details, but Ellen turned to her visitor without reading them. Her great eyes were gleaming. Her plans had worked out to perfection! This was her most successful and far-reaching master stroke against the state machine which had brought about the death of her father! It all seemed too marvelous to be true and she leaned toward Paul Cathern, lovely bosom tossing with emotion.

"Oh, Paul! It's wonderful!" she cried softly. "Almost too good to be true! It's simply great to think that you accomplished so much where all others have failed." She leaned closer, kissed him lightly upon the cheek. He grinned.

"It's great, all right, honey!" he told her, enthusiastically, "but I'd never have accomplished anything without help. In fact, if it hadn't been for the timely interference of a mysterious lady, I wouldn't be alive now!"

Ellen looked at Cathern, intently. "A mysterious lady?" she repeated softly, "I don't understand, Paul. It fails to mention her in the news."

The investigator's gray eyes focused upon her piquant face, the grin fading. "Last night," he said, slowly, "I was a prisoner of the Black Legion, facing torture, or worse. A fearless woman, The Domino Lady, seized the D.A., rescued me from under the noses of my guards, and substituted Riggs Saint in my place! That no doubt accounts for his 'mysterious injuries' referred to in the *Express*! The Domino Lady likewise turned over to me incriminating documents she had taken from Saint. Those documents furnished the exposé you've been reading about, yet she insisted that I take full credit, and leave her name out of it! Don't you agree that I owe the lady much, Ellen?"

She smiled, "Why, yes, of course, Paul. But I thought The Domino Lady was wanted by the police? How could you permit her to go free?"

Cathern's eyes softened. "Ellen," he said, "I recognized The Domino Lady!"

The little adventuress' body went rigid. With a great effort she fought down the panic that welled within her slender frame. She raised guileless eyes to meet his probing glance.

"So what?" she managed, precisely.

For a moment his eyes held hers, in an effort to read her calm gaze.

"Don't you see I couldn't betray her, honey," he murmured, "after she'd saved my life, and accomplished so much good for the state? Besides," he went on, grinning again, "the credit she bestowed upon me has assured me a fancy promotion! If the authorities wait on me to reveal the identity of The Domino Lady, they're going to have a mighty long wait!"

She breathed a deep sigh of relief, leaned against Cathern. She smiled at him, her great eyes filled with admiration for the conquering male.

"You're tops, Paul!" she breathed. "A grand person! Any woman would be lucky to have you for a friend, I'm so glad of your success and promotion, darling! Shall we drink a toast to them?"

Paul Cathern smiled, understandingly, and manipulated the decanter. He handed a drink to Ellen, then dropped down beside her again, glass in hand. They touched glasses, lifted them high.

"To the future!" she toasted, softly, brown eyes starry.

"Of The Domino Lady!" added Paul Cathern, meaningly.

He rose, replaced the glasses upon their taboret without looking at her. Then he turned. Ellen Patrick laughed throatily as she went to his open arms.

Three Wise Men of Babylon
Richard Sale

STRANGELY FORGOTTEN today, Richard Sale (1911–1993) was one of the most successful pulp writers of the 1930s and '40s, known as "the Dumas of the pulps," and then enjoyed even greater success in Hollywood. At the peak of the pulp era, his work was in such demand that he averaged a story a week for *Argosy, Detective Fiction Weekly, Dime Detective*, and most other top magazines while also writing novels, producing a million words a year for a decade. His first novel, *Not Too Narrow, Not Too Deep* (1936), about tough prisoners attempting to escape from Devil's Island, was filmed as *Strange Cargo* in 1940 with his screenplay. Two of his best, most enduring, and quirkiest novels were set in Hollywood. *Lazarus #7* (1942) involves a movie star with murderous intentions and leprosy, and a studio doctor who raises dogs from the dead. *Passing Strange* (1942) tells the story of a doctor shot dead while performing a Cesarean on a famous movie star.

Sale's most famous pulp creations were Joe "Daffy" Dill, a tough-talking wiseguy who appeared in *Detective Fiction Weekly* with regularity, and Dinah Mason, his outrageously gorgeous colleague at the New York *Chronicle*. She is not one of the boys. She looks like a Petty girl, only better, and is a good reporter but gets sick at the sight of a corpse. In a running sidebar to the mysteries they get involved with, for years Dill ask Dinah to marry him.

"Three Wise Men from Babylon" was first published in the April 1, 1939, issue of *DFW*.

*Murder was on the make—and I was
yelling into a dead phone*

Three Wise Men of Babylon

Richard Sale

*Gotham's wackiest scribe, Daffy Dill,
puts a small brown fox on the trail
of a dog-eared murderer*

IT WAS A FRIDAY when the holocaust began. I remember that because Friday was never a good day for me. I don't like fish, black cats bother me, and the Friday issue of the *Chronicle* is always, for some reason, the kind that runs a guy ragged around the arches. So it was a Friday, and when I say holocaust, I don't mean a casual massacre.

I was sitting at my desk in that dark and dingy corner of the city room which I call home because nobody else will, and I was writing a follow-up on the suicide of a guy named Milton Swan, when a Western Union boy popped into the city room and began to call my name. McGinty at the sports desk showed the boy over to me, and I signed for the wire and did not tip him.

"Well, well," Dinah Mason said, "wires from Garbo, hah? I knew I never should have let you go cover that screwy case in Hollywood. I don't care if Candid Jones did go with you, he's a pal of yours and if you told him to say that you didn't carry the torch for any—"

"Did Candid say I'd been a good boy? Bless his little heart," I said. "And how do you get that way, Angel-Eyes? Don't you trust me?"

"Sure," Dinah said. "Like I trust king cobras."

"You've got a nerve," I said. "You won't marry me, so why should you worry what cutie I parade in the Tinsel Town? Confidentially, my hollyhock, time goes on, you get older, silver threads among the gold, and your chances may not be so good. You'd better grab me now while you can still handle a husband. And lay off trying to pump Candid on my movie-town activities . . . Well?"

"Well, what?" Dinah said, preening her platinum hair as she sat there on the edge of my desk. "If you mean will I marry you, the answer is hmm."

"Nix," I snapped, irked. "I mean, what are you hanging around for? Can't you see I'm busy?"

"Yes, darling," she said. "But you also have not opened that telegram and I'm just dying to see what kind of a sap would spend the mazuma to send you a message via the wires when it would only cost three cents to write the same thing. Open up and let's have a look."

I stared at her. "You uncommon buzzard," I said. "No wonder you got so interested and came over to sling words with me. This wire."

"From Hollywood," she said. "Who sent it? Come on."

I opened the wire and I looked at the date line. It was Babylon, Iowa, and I told her so. That fixed it. "Babylon, Iowa," Dinah snorted. "Well, personally, I wouldn't care what it said after that name for a town. It's all yours and you can have it."

Well, as it turned out, Dinah did the right thing. It *was* all mine and I was stuck with it. The telegram said:

DAFFY DILL
N Y CHRONICLE
NEW YORK N Y
   WILBUR PENN PROMINENT BABY-
LON CITIZEN SHOT AND KILLED BY
UNKNOWN ASSAILANT TONIGHT AT
TEN PM STOP HAVE ATTEMPTED TO
REACH PENNS BROTHER NAMED MAR-

TIN PENN SOMEWHERE IN NEW YORK
CITY BUT AM UNABLE TO LOCATE
HIM STOP APPRECIATE IT IF YOU
COULD FIND HIM AND GET STATE-
MENT FROM HIM CONCERNING MUR-
DER OF HIS BROTHER STOP WILL
SPLIT NEWS ON CASE WITH YOU IF
YOU HELP STOP WIRE CHARGES
COLLECT
           JOHN HARVEY
   EDITOR BABYLON GAZETTE

Well, that was a hot one. I was to go out and scour New York looking for some punk named Martin Penn to get a statement out of him about a murder in a hick town in Iowa, and the editor of the town rag, Mr. Harvey, was going to be big about it and split news with me concerning his gigantic murder case. As if the readers of the New York sheets would give two hoots about murder in Babylon (Iowa). The picture of me roaming the wintry streets looking for a statement was not at all appealing.

I would have tossed the telegram in the waste basket, if I hadn't had a conscience. Wilbur Penn shot tonight. That meant the night before and that meant I was holding a night letter, not a straight telegram and that meant Mr. Harvey was a cheap skate.

So I took the telegram in to the Old Man who was sitting forlornly in his doghouse, his green eyeshade hiding his eyes and accentuating the glistening prairie of hairless dome that covered his skull. I dropped the thing on his desk and I said, "Rural editor asks collaboration. How do you like them berries?"

"Don't bother me," said the Old Man. "Can't you see I'm reading?"

He had a copy of *How to Make Friends and Influence People* in his lap, and I tsk-tsked and shook my head. "Come on, come on," I said. "You're too far gone for that book to do you any good. Take a look at this thing and grab a laugh. They're few enough nowadays."

The Old Man picked up the wire and read it, and he didn't laugh.

When he had finished it, he said, "What's so funny about it? Just because it's a hick town? A hick paper? There's nothing funny in that. We didn't all begin in New York, Mr. Dill, like yourself. Some of us were small-town scribes for years before we got a break and came on here. Do you know where I came from before I hit New York? Wipe that smile off your face. The name of the town was Punxatawney, Pa . . . So go ahead and cover for John Harvey."

"Go ahead—and cover—for him?" I said. "You mean you're going to waste me on this guy's Babylon killing?"

"I've always made it a policy," replied the Old Man severely, "to cast my bread upon the waters. When a man wires me for help from out of town, I give. Don't be a sap, Daffy. The day might come when you would wind up in Babylon, Iowa, needing a stake, an 'in,' or just plain help. And having helped this guy once, he'll help you twice."

"I have no intention of ever going to Babylon," I said. "The Bible told me it was a sinful, wicked place. It should have said that there was a moocher in the place too."

"Never mind the wisecracks," said the Old Man wearily. "Cover for this guy. And just to make sure you do, let me see Milton Penn's—"

"Martin Penn," I said sarcastically.

"You let me see his statement before you wire it. It would not be unlike you to forge a statement from Daffy Dill, Esk., rather than go out and find this other guy. Snap into it."

When I came out of the doghouse, Dinah met me and shook her head. "Boy, you look low."

"I am low," I said. "Out of seven and a half million people in this burg, I've got to find one guy to ask him for a statement."

"Far be it from me to simplify your existence," Dinah said, patting my cheek. "But did you ever think of looking up the lug in a telephone book and asking for his statement via Alexander Bell's marvelous invention?"

I said, "Wonderful! At rare intervals you show genius."

"A mere nothing, my dear Watson."

I went through a Manhattan telephone directory and found one Martin Penn as easily as falling off a log. *Martin Penn*, it said, *107 Beeker Place r. CRawford 2-2399.*

I buzzed the number, but after a few clicks the operator said, "Sorry, sir, your party does not answer. I will call you again in twenty minutes."

Well, that was all right. But when five p.m. rolled around and the party still had not answered, I knew that I was going to have to go up there and interview the guy when he got home from work, and that it was all kind of a nuisance. Dinah made a date for dinner, but I agreed only on condition that she went up to Beeker Place with me. She must have been hungry because she accepted the stipulation without a howl.

So off we went to cover the man from Babylon, Iowa, little knowing what we were letting ourselves in for . . .

Martin Penn was not home. He lived in a small apartment house in Beeker Place and we rang his doorbell for ten minutes before we gave it up as a bad job. I was just as glad but Dinah, the little nimbus cloud, only said, "Hi-ho, it only means you have to come back tomorrow and try, try again. Let's eat at the Hideaway Club. I haven't seen Bill Latham since they put Santa Claus' whiskers back among the moth-balls."

That was all right with me. We took a cab over to Broadway where the Hideaway Club failed to live up to its name by advertising its location in no uncertain neon lights.

Bill Latham greeted us at the door with a broad grin. "Well, well," he said, "the Fourth Estate in person. Are you following Poppa Hanley around or did he tell you to meet him here?"

"Is that galoot here?" Dinah sighed. "Oh great gouts of blood—now he and Daffy will discuss death and detection all night. It's like going out to dinner with a signal 32 ringing in your ears. I'll bet you five fish, Bill, that they get a call before dessert."

"I'll take it," Latham grinned. "Things have been pretty quiet, Poppa was telling me, so the chances are you'll lose. He's over there in a wall booth, down by the band."

We wended our way past the jitterbugs on the dance floor and reached the red leather booth where Poppa was sitting, mangling a half a dozen oysters and looking pompously dignified.

When he saw us, he leaped to his feet and looked happier. Poppa is one homely man, when you come right down to it. He was all dressed up, but that didn't keep his long ears from sticking out like an elephant's flappers, and his face, always brick red, was holding its own. "Golly," he said, "this is a pleasure, Dinah. If only you could have left the runt at home. Oh well, a guy can't have everything. Sit down."

... Dinah won the five bucks. We had finished the beefsteaks and were waiting for the salad when Bill Latham came over and slipped a fin in Dinah's bag and said, "Telephone call for you, Lieutenant. Will you take it here?"

Poppa looked grim and nodded. They brought a telephone to the booth and plugged it in.

"Wow," I said, "so you've been to Hollywood, Bill, eh? This is the way they do it in the Brown Derby and Sardi's out there. Guys go to eat in those joints and tell their butlers to give them a ring, just so they'll be paged and get the eye from the other customers."

Poppa said, "Hello? This is Hanley . . . Oh, hello, Babcock. I'm eating dinner. I told you not to call unless it was something important . . . eh? . . . Oh . . . Hell . . . All right. What's the address again? . . . I've got it. I'll meet you there. You pick up Claghorn and Louie, and tell Dr. Kyne to come running. I think he's over in Bellevue. I'll see you there."

He hung up and took a deep breath and sighed and looked at me.

Dinah groaned, "The march of crime."

"A guy," Hanley said to me. "Bumped off. Want to come?"

"Who is it?" I said. "Of course I'll come. If I didn't come, the Old Man would beat my pride into the dust, grrr!"

"Guy named Fenwick Hanes," said Poppa. "Babcock got the call through Telegraph Bureau.

Someone telephoned in and said that this guy had been found in the Hotel Metronome on West 45th. That's not far from you. Let's go see. Just up Broadway a couple of blocks. You heard what I said."

"Well," Dinah said sourly, "I'll be a rootin' tootin' hillybilly if I get left here alone with the check. I'm coming too, boys, and don't argue with a woman. *Garsong! L'addition* for these gentlemen!"

We got out of there and walked north, the three of us, until Dinah got a stitch in her side from the pace. "Take it easy," she said. "That meal is having its troubles. The fellow is dead. Why the rush?"

"Listen, Angel-Eyes," I said. "The last time you saw a corpse, you passed out on me. I think you'd better go home."

"Not me," Dinah said grimly. "I've got a date with you and not even a murder is going to make me a wall-flower."

We reached the Metronome a few minutes later and found Detective Claghorn waiting for us in the lobby downstairs. We shook hands with him and then we went up.

Claghorn said, "I came right up, Chief, when I heard the news. Did Babcock telephone you? I guess he's on the way with the stuff and the M.E. I happened to be home when he buzzed me and I don't live far from here myself. The manager is upstairs and I don't think we're gonna get a lead from what he said."

On the seventh floor, we found the manager, a man named Horace Wilson, who was pastyfaced and nervous. "These things are always bad publicity for the hotel," he groaned, "but what can we do about them? They always happen."

"Let's have a look-see," Hanley grunted noncommittally.

We opened the door and went in. Dinah took one look and opened the door and went out again. "I'll wait downstairs," she said. "I'll tell the other boys where to come. But as for me, I just had dinner and I don't want to waste the money you all spent on it. See you anon."

Dinah is a sissy, but I like her for it. These women who can look a stiff in the eye without flinching are too hard-boiled for Daffy. It wasn't that Mr. Fenwick Hanes was a mess, for he wasn't. He had been murdered very neatly indeed, and there was little blood.

Fenwick Hanes had been shot to death. One shot. He was lying in his bed with his shoes and his coat and vest off.

"Mr. Hanes left a message at the desk that he was to be awakened at eight o'clock," the manager explained. "Apparently he decided to take a nap. He was in from out of town and had been running around quite a bit and was tired. At eight p.m., the elevator boy heard a shot. He called me and I came in and found him like that."

"Hmm," said Hanley. "Looks like a .32 . . ." He stared at the manager. "You mean that's all there is? You didn't see anyone in here?"

"Yes."

I went over and picked up a small alarm clock which Hanes had set by his bed. It said eight-thirty. I looked at it sharply and I said, "Boy, if this could only talk."

The elevator boy showed up then along with Dr. Kerr Kyne and Babcock and the police fotog. Hanley went to work on the boy and the gist of it was that the boy had been going by the floor when he heard a shot. He instantly came back to the seventh floor and stepped out. He said he heard a bell ringing. Then he went for the manager. He did not see anybody.

Big help. I could see the disappointment in Hanley's face.

Well, it was one of those things. I wasn't particularly interested in the killing and I didn't see where the *Chronicle*'s readers would be. Just a hotel knock-off. That is, until I asked for some dope on Fenwick Hanes himself.

"We don't know anything about him," said the manager. "He checked in three days ago and signed the register Fenwick Hanes, Babylon, Iowa—" The manager stopped short because of the way I gaped at him.

"Babylon, Iowa!" I said.

"That's right."

I grabbed the telephone and then set it down again. I was that excited. Then I took up a telephone book and looked up the apartment in Beeker Place and telephoned the superintendent. "This is the police department," I growled at the super while Hanley watched me as though he thought me half cracked. "I want you to go right up to Mr. Penn's apartment and open it and have a look at it. We have a tip that there's been foul play and we're checking on it. You telephone back and tell me what you find." And I gave him the number. "Ask for Lieutenant Hanley, room 706."

"All right," said the super. "I'll take a look right away."

Ten minutes later he telephoned back and I grabbed the handset and listened while he roared shrilly, "Murder! Murder! Mr. Penn is been murdered!"

I hung up instantly and I turned to Poppa Hanley and said, "Three wise men, all of Babylon, all dead. Come on, Poppa. The thing is really beginning to get hot."

Wilbur Penn had been killed in Babylon. Martin Penn had been killed the day before we found him. Fenwick Hanes had been killed at eight p.m. this very night.

What had started with a routine inquiry from Iowa had suddenly blossomed into three exceedingly dead corpses. Which goes to show that life is still full of little surprises.

Poppa and I sent Dinah home and we left Babcock and Claghorn over at the Metronome and took Dr. Kerr Kyne with us. "I want it clearly understood," Dr. Kyne said to me with sarcasm as we drove to Beeker Place, "that you never call me Buzzard again. For if anybody ever made me look like an amateur when it comes to hovering over the dead, you are that man, Mr. Dill, and it gives me great pleasure to say that I can practically scent the smell of graveyards all over and around you."

I let him go on. I couldn't help smiling because it was about time he got a chance to crow a little. We reached Beeker Place in nothing flat and were greeted at the door by the superintendent who was almost hysterical with fright. He took us right up to the apartment where Dinah and I had previously rung the bell to no avail. He unlocked the door and we trooped in.

Dr. Kerr Kyne went right to work. Martin Penn was dead, all right. You didn't have to be the chief M. E. of New York County to gather that much. He was a thin, sharp sort of man with a shrewd face, this corpse which sat comfortably in a chair. No bullet in the head this time, as in the case of Fenwick Hanes. This bullet had struck Martin Penn directly over the heart. From the expression on the dead man's face, it was plain that he had seen his killer, perhaps even talked with him. For there was hate in Martin Penn's face and no fooling.

We had better luck here, though. Dr. Kyne said that Penn had been dead for at least thirty-six hours and that the slug was a .32, and undoubtedly the same gun which killed Hanes had killed Penn. I reminded myself to check with John Harvey of the *Babylon Gazette* on the slug which had killed Wilbur Penn. There was an avenging angel on the trail somewhere and it would be a good idea if we stopped him. Murder is a habit when you do too much of it, the killer might easily leave a line of dead behind him, getting scared and more scared on the way. It's fear that makes murder, in one way or another.

Martin Penn had been a shrewd man, so shrewd that even in death he had pointed out a clue to the identity of his killer.

Sitting in that chair, with a bullet in his body, he had not died at once. This isn't strange, for I have seen men shot through the heart with a high-power copper-jacket still stumble on and fire several shots, although they were already dead. In man, there is sometimes an unconquerable will which makes him perform even after a mortal wound has been inflicted. In any case, with his own finger, dipped in the blood of his own wound, Martin Penn had traced something upon the maple arm of the chair in which he sat.

It was a flat-sided arm, wide enough to take a pad for sketching, and the blood had dried black upon the wood, leaving his handiwork quite plain there by his right hand.

It was the sketch, crude and macabre, of an ear. Just one ear.

But it was enough to start me thinking and I remembered the alarm clock and suddenly I said, "Poppa, I think I get it."

"You're a smarter guy than I am if you do," Poppa said sourly.

"An ear," I said. "Well, what about an ear? It would just be guessing if we had this killing alone. But we've got the Fenwick Hanes murder too, and to me, the distinctive thing about that one was the alarm clock. Did you know that the alarm had run down on the thing? And the alarm hand was set for eight o'clock. Now it's my guess—guess, mind you—that Hanes wanted to make an evening performance at eight-thirty in some theater. He told the desk to wake him at eight. He didn't trust them, but set the clock for eight himself. Everything happened at eight. There was a killer in there who shot him. The elevator boy heard the bell ringing even when the shot was fired. Which would mean the alarm went off before Hanes was killed. *And it was allowed to run down!* Now, Poppa—look me in the eye and imagine me a killer. I'm standing here and I'm going to bump you off. Just as I'm getting up nerve, an alarm clock goes off. What do I do?"

"You instinctively turn off the alarm because it's noisy and you're afraid of two things: You're afraid it'll wake up your victim and you're afraid it will attract outside attention."

"Fine," I said, "and right. I never saw a man yet who didn't dive for an alarm clock to turn it off when it started to holler. Yet this killer stood there, heard the alarm, shot Hanes, then scrammed, and the alarm kept going to advertise things. What does that mean to you?"

"It means," said Hanley heavily, "that the killer was deaf."

"It sure does," I said. "And Martin Penn didn't sweat out his last seconds drawing this ear for no other reason but that."

Hanley grunted. "Well, you don't have to

look so pleased about it. I still don't see how it gives us a lead. All we have to do is find a guy with a .32 caliber gun which fits these bullets, the guy being deaf. Huh. That's *all* we have to do."

"I think," I said, "that when you get a line on the Penns and Hanes, it will narrow down your choice considerably. But as for now, I see nothing to keep me from returning to the gay white way. So long, Pater, I'm to pick up Dinah and see the sights. Tomorrow I'll buzz John Harvey in Babylon and see what he has to offer on the murder of Wilbur Penn."

At the city room of the New York *Chronicle*, next morning at ten a.m., I gladdened the Old Man's heart by pounding out the dope on the stories of the night before, and then I telephoned the *Babylon Gazette* out in Iowa—at the *Chronicle*'s expense—and asked to speak with John Harvey. I got a man named Wooley who apparently worked on the sheet and he said, "Gosh, Mr. Dill, it's funny you should call him. He's not here. He left for New York yesterday morning and he'll be arriving on the Golden Arrow sometime this morning in Pennsylvania Station. This murder out here is raising a lot of fuss, and when he didn't hear from you in answer to his telegram, he decided to go on to New York himself and see Wilbur Penn's brother. There are some folks here think Martin Penn shot his own brother, and John wants to be first on the spot to make sure. He said he'd go see you and maybe you could help him find Martin Penn. I think the train gets in at eleven."

"I can show him Martin Penn all right," I said. "Mr. Penn is now residing in the morgue. There's a headline for your rag. Martin Penn was shot and killed two days ago in his New York apartment. He was killed before his brother Wilbur was, only nobody knew it. I'll meet Harvey at the train. So long."

How I was going to pick John Harvey out of the welter getting off the Golden Arrow I didn't know, but I made a try. I went up to Pennsy and tipped a porter to page John Harvey when the crowd came off the ramp. But I didn't locate him in the crowd and no one answered the name. I

had lunch at a drugstore fountain and then went downtown again.

When I got there, Mr. Harvey was waiting for me.

He was a little man in an old suit, his hair touched with gray, and he smoked cigarettes without touching them. The one I saw just hung in his mouth and he handled it wonderfully with his lips. He had a big mole on the right cheek.

"Sure am glad to meet you, Mr. Dill," John Harvey said. "I guess you don't know how out-country editors kind of idolize the way you do things. When that Penn murder broke I said to myself, what a break it would be if Daffy Dill could help us out on the New York end."

"Well, I was helping you," I said. "I didn't wire you but I got out on the rounds and I telephoned you this morning and got Woolsey. Then I went up to the station to meet you."

"You went up to meet me?" he said. "I didn't see you, and I'd have recognized you from your pictures, I think. I went out the cab way and got right in a cab. I've still got my luggage with me here."

I glanced down and saw he had two bags with him.

"Well," I said, "I suppose you've heard the news."

"I just arrived. I've heard nothing."

"Martin Penn is dead, shot and killed before your friend Wilbur ever was. Did you know a man named Fenwick Hanes?"

"Of Babylon? Certainly I did. Nasty old coot. Used to hang around with Wilbur and Martin Penn and Maxwell Green. The four of them pulled together quite a while."

"He's in New York," I said. "Dead too."

Harvey stared at me. "Dead in New York? I saw him in Babylon on Wednesday."

"At the morgue," I persisted grimly. "With a tag on his toe."

"My God," he said huskily.

"Now listen," I said, "you're supposed to go over to Police Headquarters. Lieutenant William Hanley wants to talk with you. He thinks you can give him some dope on the backgrounds of these corpses, and I think you can too. We need help. We're stymied." I watched him light a cigarette and he glanced down at the match as he did so, and I said, "The little brown fox jumped over the big high fence."

"Well," said Harvey, looking up, "I'll run down there then and help them out, and then I want to see you again, and get the story on this for my own paper. Will I find you here?"

"You will," I said, "as soon as you come back."

"May I leave my things here? I'll put up at a hotel when I come back. I don't know New York at all. Never been here before in my life."

"They'll be right here," I said.

As soon as he had left, I telephoned TWA airlines and I said, "Did you have a plane leaving from Babylon, Iowa, yesterday morning at ten a.m.?"

"No," they said. "But the Des Moines plane left at ten a.m. and Des Moines is only twenty miles from Babylon. If you wanted to fly to New York, you'd run over to Des Moines and get the plane there."

"When did that ship come in?"

"Three yesterday afternoon."

"Thanks very much." I hung up and Dinah came over. I pointed at the grips and I said, "A very careless guy, my hollyhock. For instance, how would you get a TWA tag on your luggage if you'd come east on the Pennsy's Golden Arrow?"

"Simple, dolt," she said. "It's a tag from a previous trip."

"Could be," I said, "but ain't for one reason. Guy says he's never been to New York before in his life. Tag says *Destination N.Y.* So?"

"You've got something there," Dinah said. "And you can have it."

"The little brown fox jumped over the big high fence," I said.

"Have you gone crazy?" Dinah said. "What has the fox got to do with the high cost of living?"

"Not a thing," I said. "But when I told John Harvey about the little fox, he didn't seem to worry about it at all. Never even noticed I said it."

"Maybe he's just polite."

"And on the other hand, maybe the laddy is deaf. He spoke with me all the time, watching my lips carefully. I gave him the fox business when his eyes were off my face, and he never heard it. He's deaf. He reads the lips. He didn't come in on the Golden Arrow. He came in on the Sky Chief yesterday, in time to bump off Fenwick Hanes last night at eight bells. And I'll bet you dough he's only sticking around to grab off someone else. He knocked off Wilbur Penn himself, and I'll bet you a fin he was in town two days ago on Tuesday to slip the slug into Martin Penn up in Beeker Place. How? We see now."

I telephoned the *Babylon Gazette* again long distance and got hold of Woolsey once more. "This is Daffy Dill again," I said. "I want some info, my friend, and for it I'll promise to hand you the biggest scoop your rag ever printed, and you'll have it on the streets before the Des Moines papers ever see it. Tell me one thing: where was John Harvey on Tuesday? He wasn't in town, was he?"

"Oh no," Woolsey said. "John left Sunday afternoon to take a little fishing trip up in Michigan. He likes to go after muskellunge up there. He got back here Wednesday morning."

"Does a Maxwell Green live in Babylon?"

Woolsey hesitated.

"He used to, but he lives in New York now. Him and Martin Penn are lawyers together, somewhere in New York."

"That's all I wanted to know," I said. "Thanks." I hung up.

"All right, brainstorm," Dinah Mason said dryly. "What's up?"

"Get me a telephone book," I said, "and we'll soon see."

Dinah threw hers over and I looked up Maxwell Green. He was there all right. He lived on West 56th Street and I gave him a ring.

"Hello?" a voice said.

"Maxwell Green?"

"Yes."

"Of Babylon, Iowa?"

"That's right," he said. "Who is this? Harvey?"

"Yes." I said it on the spur of the moment to see what would come.

"Look here, Harvey," Maxwell Green said heavily, "I told you I'd see you at eleven-thirty and it's nearly that now. You said it was important enough for me to remain at home. Now you'd better get here and get here fast with your important matter. I haven't got all day to waste on you." He slammed up.

Victim number four. And he didn't even know it. "Hello, Poppa," I said a few minutes later. "Is Harvey still there?"

"Still here?" Poppa Hanley said. "He hasn't been here yet."

Oh yes, I saw the gag nicely. Never been in New York before. Must have got lost. But meanwhile John Harvey was on his way to 56th Street to kill a man.

"Hanley!" I snapped. "Get over here fast. Pick me up. Bring a rod. We're going to stop another one! Now make it fast, Poppa, we've got no seconds to lose!" I gasped. "No—wait a minute, Poppa. No time. You haven't time to pick me up. Meet you there!"

I gave him the address, hung up and called Maxwell Green back. "Listen, Mr. Green," I snapped, "and get it straight the first time. This is Daffy Dill of the New York *Chronicle*—"

"No statement," he snapped and hung up.

The damned old fool. I rang him again but he wouldn't answer.

I got my faithful old grave-scratcher out of the drawer, tore downstairs and grabbed a cab. I waved a bill under the driver's nose and we went north like a bat out of hell. We took the west side express highway up to 52nd and cut off and then doubled back. We made it damned fast. When we pulled up in front of the building I saw that I had beaten Poppa Hanley there and I went in like a Roman ram.

The doorbells said that Maxwell Green lived on the fourth floor. I tried the vestibule door but it was locked, so I broke the glass with my gun

butt and opened the door from the inside. I went up the stairs like a madman, and I heard Poppa Hanley's siren approaching down the street. It was a nice thing to hear, believe me.

When I reached the fourth floor I was in a blind panic. I went from door to door looking for the name *Green* and finally found it and tried the knob. The door was locked.

From across the hall I charged at that door and hit it with my shoulder. I weigh one eighty and I was glad of it then because I knocked that lock clean out of its socket, split that door in half and nearly rooked my shoulder.

I didn't fall. I was careful not to fall. I balanced my weight when I hit the door so that I was standing in a fixed position with my gun hand ready when I came to a stop.

I was right.

John Harvey was standing there. He had forced Mr. Maxwell Green into a chair and in Harvey's hand was a .32 caliber Colt revolver with the hammer back and his index finger flexing on the trigger.

I think if John Harvey had been able to hear, he might have shot me dead when I hit that door. But he couldn't hear. He saw the expression on Maxwell Green's face, and only because of that did he know something was amiss. By the time he turned, he was rattled, and when he saw me, he was more rattled.

He fired twice at me before he had his gun all the way around. He put two bullets through the window, only one of them had an urn in front of it and there was a hell of a crash.

I didn't want to kill that guy because he knew too much that Hanley wanted to know in the way of explanation, but what can you do when someone is throwing lead at you? You don't aim carefully down the barrel and then break a kneecap. You just keep fanning the trigger and aiming low from instinct and hoping your next one will put him down. But he stands there too long; you think he's never going to fall. He stands there and you see the red spit of his gun and a bullet cracks by your ear. Close, that means. They only crack when they're close to your ear. Otherwise, it's a buzz and that means it's away from you.

Harvey went to one knee after my third shot and I was already down, hit in the side. It was as though the dog had bit the hand that fed it, for Harvey had not hit me. Maxwell Green had. He picked up a book end and flung it at Harvey and missed and hit me. He nearly broke a pair of ribs.

The next thing I knew Harvey was limping past me and had reached the door. I couldn't do a thing about it. I was trying to get a breath into my lungs and couldn't. The damned brass book end had knocked the wind clean out of me and I just couldn't manage to get a breath of fresh air.

Harvey made the door at exactly the same time that Poppa Hanley made it. They were both going in opposite directions. I tried to yell to Poppa to stop the lug, but you don't have to tell Poppa what to do. He can scent trouble very easily, and he can scent a killer even more facilely.

Poppa just pulled up without a word and rapped Harvey across the jaw with a gun barrel and then followed it with a lovely left hook which dropped the Babylon editor right in my lap where I rapped him one more for not getting in the way of that book end and getting clipped with it instead of me, who is frail and fragile when it comes to such things.

That was the business. Harvey wasn't out and he made a try at his gun, tried to jam it into his ear and pull the trigger, but Poppa kicked it out of his hand and growled, "Can't face the Musica, eh?"

Which, I thought later, was really a very good crack, and I told Dinah so when I saw her. Maxwell Green seemed to know what it was all about.

"Yeah," Poppa Hanley told him, "the first one he knocked off was Martin Penn. He came to New York on Tuesday instead of taking a fishing trip as he said, and he bumped Martin. Then he went back home and bumped Wilbur Penn, Martin's brother. He telegraphed Daffy merely to insure his being in Babylon when the body was discovered. Having done that, he told his assistant he was taking the train for this town. Instead, took the plane, got here early, knocked off Fenwick Hanes, and he planned to knock you off this morning."

"Why, he called me last night and made an appointment with me this morning," Green exploded. "To kill me!"

"That's right," I said, "and you're a lousy shot with a book end, incidentally."

"Knowing all that," Poppa Hanley said, "have you got any ideas on why this deaf plug-ugly was pulling this round robin of homicides? Not just to keep the police department on its toes, certainly."

Maxwell Green sat back in his chair and sighed. "Yes," he said. "I think I know the answer."

"Then give, mister. I want to wrap this thing up for the D.A. before this guy thinks up some excuse a dumb jury will like."

Maxwell Green said slowly, "Wilbur Penn was the man whom Harvey wanted to get."

"All right," I said. "But you and Martin Penn and Fenwick Hanes were all too smart. I mean, you knew that Harvey would be the one to kill Wilbur. Three wise men of Babylon. So to kill Wilbur Penn, John Harvey had to kill four men."

Green nodded. "But I don't doubt he would have enjoyed the extra work involved," he said bitterly. "Four years ago, John Harvey and Wilbur Penn were in love with the same woman, but she married Harvey. Well, that was all right. They had a youngster, a little girl, cute little trick. But it seems that Margaret Harvey, John Harvey's wife, came into some money. Her uncle left her nearly one hundred thousand dollars. And Harvey began to run around with other women.

"Next thing, Margaret Harvey was found dead. Gas in the kitchen. Wilbur was county attorney at Babylon then, and when he found Margaret, he also found a live canary in the same kitchen. Now, a canary doesn't live through a gassing that kills a grown woman.

"Wilbur could have put Harvey in the electric chair, but he didn't. He didn't because of

Margaret's daughter. Wilbur got quite fond of her. And Margaret's will left her money to her daughter, so John Harvey had outfoxed himself.

"Wilbur told Harvey the truth, told him that if he ever stepped out of line again, or ever tried to regain custody of the daughter—whom, incidentally, Wilbur took over, with Harvey's consent, of course—he, Wilbur, would prosecute Harvey to the full extent of the law. And if anything happened to Wilbur, the rest of us, all former law partners, would take up the task."

"I get the setup," I said. "This little rat without any hearing got desperate for money. He wanted to get his daughter back, contest the will, and get some of the mazuma. To do that, he had to knock off Wilbur, but he also had to knock off the three men Wilbur Penn had put wise to the mess."

Green nodded.

Well, it was easy to prove. I had to make a trip to Babylon and it wasn't as bad a town as it sounds. Harvey's daughter, little Meg, was a cute trick, and she was too young to know what was going on. She's living now with Uncle Maxwell, as she says, and John Harvey is only a memory.

Dinah still kids me about the allergy I have for book ends, but if you've ever been cracked in the ribs with a well-flung one—or maybe you're happily married—you'll bear with me and understand.

The Adventure of the
Voodoo Moon
Eugene Thomas

DETECTIVE FICTION WEEKLY, one of the most successful of the mystery pulps, liked to run two or three true crime stories each issue. Easily one of the most popular featured a female spy named Vivian Legrand, who was no sweetheart. Beautiful, intelligent, and resourceful, she was also a liar, blackmailer, and thief who was responsible for her own father's death. Her exploits, which were reported by Eugene Thomas (1894–?), began to appear so regularly that doubt was cast upon their veracity—with good reason. Without apology, *DFW* continued to run stories about the woman dubbed "The Lady from Hell," now acknowledging that the tales were fictional. Were any of the stories true? Was there really a woman named Vivian Legrand? There is little evidence either way, but only the most gullible would accept the notion that all the stories published as true had any genesis in reality.

Thomas, the author of five novels, created another series character, Chu-Seng, typical of many other fictional Yellow Peril villains. A Chinese deaf-mute with paranormal abilities, he works with the Japanese in their espionage activities against the United States in *Death Rides the Dragon* (1932), *The Dancing Dead* (1933), and *Yellow Magic* (1934). He is thwarted by Bob Nicholson, an American agent, Lai Chung, a Mongol prince, and a team of lamas who counteract Chu-Seng's powers with their white magic.

"The Adventure of the Voodoo Moon" first appeared in the February 1, 1936, issue of *DFW*.

And then she saw Wylie.
He was tied to a post in the clearing.

The Adventure of the Voodoo Moon

Eugene Thomas

Undaunted in the Face of Outlawed
Death, Vivian Legrand Makes
Strange Magic—and Beats a
Rascal at His Own Game

CHAPTER I
CROOKS ON HOLIDAY

THE LADY FROM HELL was standing on the upper deck of the little inter-island steamer as it neared the coast of Haiti. Her crown of flaming red hair was beaten back from her smooth forehead and her white dress modeled tightly to her body by the strong trade wind.

She and her companion in crime, Adrian Wylie, had just completed one of the most amazing coups in their whole career, and were now on a vacation. The Lady from Hell had been emphatic on that point before leaving Havana.

"Nothing is to tempt us into mingling business with pleasure," she had told Wylie. "Not even if we stumble across the vaults of a bank wide open and unguarded."

Now, the second day out from Havana, the sun was just rising over the blue bubbles dreaming on the horizon that were the mountains of Haiti, and still she could not account for the vague sense of disquiet, the little feeling of apprehension that had been growing in her ever since the steamer passed between Morro Castle and its smaller counterpart on the other side of Havana harbor.

No one on the little steamer dreamed that she was the notorious Lady from Hell, whose fame had already filtered even to the West Indies. And if they had, it would have seemed incredible that this graceful, beautiful woman could have started her career by poisoning her own father; could have escaped from a Turkish prison—the only time in her career that the net of the law had closed about her; could have held up and robbed the Orient Express, a deed that had filled the press of the world, although her part in it had never even been suspected.

The daring coup in Havana that had added a large sum to the bank account of Adrian Wylie, her chief of staff, and herself had not been brought to the attention of the Cuban police. And, although the police of half a dozen European countries knew her well and swore when her name was mentioned, there was not a single thing with which she could be charged, so cleverly had her tracks been covered, so adroitly her coups planned.

She turned away and began to stride up and down the deck. More than one passenger turned to stare at her as she passed with a rippling grace of motion, a little lithe stride that told of perfect muscles and the agility of a cat.

A sound made her turn as a passenger came up behind her and fell into step with her.

"Good evening, Mrs. Legrand," he said in English, with the faintest of accents. "You are up early."

"I was eager to catch a sight of Haiti," Vivian responded with a smile. "The mountains there are lovely."

"They are lovely," he responded, "Even though Haiti is my home I never tire of seeing her mountains grow about the horizon line." Then he added, "We dock in a few hours. See that headland there," and he pointed to an amethyst bulk that thrust itself out into the sea. "That is Cap St. Feral. The port is just beyond it."

There was an impression of power, perfectly controlled, about Carlos Benedetti that was perfectly evident to Vivian Legrand as she surveyed him for a fleeting instant through narrowed eyes. His face was unhealthily pale, the nose slightly crooked, the black eyes very sharp and alert beneath the close-cropped and sleek black hair. He had the air of one to whom the world had been kind, and from it he had learned assurance and a kind of affability.

But behind his assurance—this affability—the Lady from Hell sensed something that was foreign to the face he presented to the world, something that made her cautious.

"Do we dock?" she queried. "I thought that we landed in small boats."

"The word was incorrectly used," he admitted. "I should have said that we arrive. Cap St. Feral is not modern enough to possess a dock for a ship of this size, small as the vessel is." He hesitated a moment. "I assume that you are not familiar with Cap St. Feral."

"No," Vivian said. "This is my first visit to Haiti."

The man's oblique stare was annoying her. Not that she was unaccustomed to the bold stare that men give beautiful women. But this was different. Had the man been wiser he might have taken warning at the hard light that lay in the depths of her greenish eyes.

But he went on suavely:

"To those of us who know the island it offers little in the way of entertainment," he said, "but to a stranger it might be interesting. If you care to have me, I should be glad to offer my services as a guide while you are in port."

A casual enough courtesy offered to a stranger by a native of a place. Vivian thanked him and watched, with a calculating eye, as he bowed and walked on down the deck. The man was sleek, well groomed and obviously wealthy. His spotless Panama was of the type that cannot, ordinarily, even be bought in Equador, where they are woven. A hat so fine and silky that usually they are reserved as gifts to persons in high position. And the white suit that he wore had not come from an ordinary tailor.

It was made of heavy white silk—Habatui silk that in the East sells for its weight in gold, literally.

Adrian Wylie found Vivian on deck. In a few swift words she told him of the invitation and of the intuitive warning she had felt.

Wylie nodded slowly. "That explains something that had been puzzling me," he said. "For an hour last night the purser insisted on buying me drinks in the smoking room and casually asking questions about the two of us. And hardly five minutes after he left me I saw him talking earnestly to Benedetti at the door of the purser's office. Evidently the man hunted you up for the first thing this morning, after his talk with the purser."

Benedetti, they knew from the ship's gossip, was an exceedingly wealthy sugar planter, who owned the whole of an exceedingly fertile island called Ile de Feral, not far from the port of Cap St. Feral. The Haitian Sugar Centrals— actually the sugar trust, so ship gossip ran—had attempted to drive him out of business, and failed miserably. Despite a price war, he had managed to undersell the trust and still make a profit. Then he had been offered a staggering sum for the island, and had refused. The offer was still open, so she had been told, and any time he cared to sell the sugar trust would be only too eager to buy him out.

A little smile formed on Vivian's lips. Benedetti, she suspected, was accustomed to having his own way where women were concerned. And the Lady from Hell knew full well her own attractiveness as a woman.

But even the Lady from Hell, astute as she was, could not have fathomed the dark reason that lay behind Benedetti's advances.

CHAPTER II
DANGER'S WARNING

The faint sound of drums somewhere in the distance; a regular, rhythmic beat, as though a gigantic heart, the heart of Black Haiti, were beating in the stillness of the blazing moon, hung over the little city of Cap St. Feral as the Lady from Hell, Wylie and Benedetti rode through the sun-washed streets.

The heat that hung about them like a tangible thing seemed to be intensified and crystallized by the monotonous beating of the lonely drums.

The Lady from Hell turned to Benedetti with a question, the brilliant sunlight through the trees overarching the road catching her hair and turning it into a halo of flame about her exquisitely lovely face.

"Voodoo drums," he said. "The night of the Voodoo Moon is approaching. The drums will keep on sounding until the climax of the Snake Dance. They're beating like this all over the island, even in Port-au-Prince. Worshipers in the cathedral can hear the sound of the drums from the hills outside the city drifting through the intoning of the mass. Then, almost as if they had been silenced by a gigantic hand, they will all stop at the same moment—the climax of the Snake Dance."

Vivian stole another glance at the people along the roadside as their car passed. Voodoo. It was something out of a book to her, something a little unsettling to come so closely in contact with. And it seemed difficult to believe that the happy, smiling faces were the faces of people who had run mad through the streets of Port-au-Prince, so history said, tearing President Guillaume Sam to bloody bits while he still lived.

Benedetti caught the thought in her mind.

"You have not lived here, Mrs. Legrand," he said quietly. "You cannot understand the place that Voodoo holds in these people's lives; the grip it has upon them. And you are not familiar with the effect of rhythms upon the nerve centers. It does strange things to blacks, and to whites things stranger still."

He leaned forward and flung a few words in Creole French at the driver—words that Vivian Legrand, fluent as her French was, could barely follow. The car stopped before a long, rambling structure, of gleaming white *coquina*, half hidden behind crimson hibiscus bushes.

"I brought you here for lunch," he said. "It would be unbearably hot on the ship and there is no hotel at which you would want to eat, even if you could, in the town itself. This is a little house that I maintain, so that I may have a comfortable place to stay when necessity or business compels me to be in town. I took the liberty of assuming that Dr. Wylie and yourself would have lunch with me here."

Vivian looked about her curiously as their host opened the little gate and ushered them into the flower garden that surrounded the house.

From the whitewashed, angular, stone walls of the old house, almost smothered in pink Flor de Amour, her eyes went to the table set beneath a flowering Y'lang-y'lang tree in the center of the close-cropped lawn. An old woman stood beside it, an ancient crone with more than a trace of white blood in her, one of those incredibly ancient people that only primitive races can produce. Her face was a myriad of tiny wrinkles and her parchment skin had the dull, leathery hue and look that is common in the aged of the Negro race.

The woman turned slowly as the trio approached and her eyes fastened on Vivian. In her cold, yellow eyes was a look almost of fear. Something that was like lurking terror coiled in the depths of those alert, flashing eyes and rendered them stony, glassy, shallow.

And then, as Benedetti and Wylie went on past her she made a gesture, an unmistakable gesture for Vivian to halt, and her voice, lowered until it was barely a sibilant whisper, came to Vivian's ears in French.

"Do not stay here," she said. "You must not stay."

There was definite horror in her eyes, and fear also, as her glance flitted from Vivian toward Benedetti. Despite the whisper to which her voice had been lowered there was fear to be distinguished in her tones also.

Her face was impassive as she turned away. Only her eyes seemed alive. They were cold, deadly bits of emerald. The Lady from Hell abhorred the unknown. All through her criminal career the unsolved riddle, the unsolved personality, the unexplained situation, inflamed her imagination. She would worry over it as a dog worries a bone.

And how her mind hovered over this problem with relentless tenacity, her brain working swiftly, with smooth precision. Her intuition had been right, after all. The feeling of danger, of disquiet, of apprehension that had haunted her ever since the coast line of Haiti came in sight over the horizon had not been wrong. She knew now, beyond a shadow of doubt, that danger hovered over her like a vulture.

The fear that she had glimpsed in the old woman's eyes, Vivian reasoned, was fear for herself should she be caught warning the white woman. But what was the danger against which she was warned, and why should this old woman, who had never seen her before, take what was obviously a risk to warn her against it?

Luncheon was just over when a long hoot sounded from the steamer.

"The warning whistle," Benedetti told her. "A signal to the passengers that the steamer will sail in an hour."

He turned to Vivian.

"My roses," he said, "are so lovely that I took the liberty of requesting Lucilla to cut an armful of them for you to take back to the ship as a remembrance."

There was a distinct warning in the old woman's veiled eyes as Vivian stretched out her hands for the big bunch of pale yellow roses that Lucilla brought; not only warning, but that same terror and fear that had stood starkly in them a short time before. Instinctively Vivian stiffened and looked about her, her nerves tense. Was the danger, whatever it was, ready to spring? But the scene seemed peaceful enough.

"How lovely they are!" she exclaimed, and wondered if it could be her imagination that made the old woman seem reluctant to part with the flowers. Then she gave a little exclamation of pain as she took them from Lucilla. "Like many other lovely things, there are thorns," she said ruefully, gazing at the long, thorny stems, still slightly damp from standing in water.

"That is true," Benedetti said, and there seemed to be an expression of relief in his eyes. "Our Haitian roses are lovely, but there have longer and sharper thorns than any other roses I know."

"Don't you think we had better be leaving?" Vivian queried, glancing at her watch. The shimmering heat haze that covered everything seemed to have blurred her vision, and she had to peer closely at the little jewelled trinket to make out the time. "It's a long drive back to the ship."

"There is still plenty of time," Benedetti assured her. "The warning whistle is supposed to sound an hour before sailing time, but it always is nearer two hours." Then he gave a little exclamation of concern. "But you are ill," he said as Vivian swayed a little.

"Just the heat," she said. "I am not yet accustomed to it."

The flowers she had been holding tumbled to the table and thence to the ground. The long-stemmed yellow blossoms gave no hint of the fact that from the moment Benedetti's message had been delivered to the old woman until the moment before they had been placed in Vivian's hands their stems and thorns had been soaking in a scum-covered fluid brewed by Lucilla herself.

"You must go inside for a few moments. You must rest," Benedetti said sharply. "I should

have realized that you were not accustomed to heat. It might be fatal for you to drive back to the ship in this sun without a rest."

Wylie, a look of concern on his face, took Vivian's arm and helped her to her feet. Even then, with her vision blurred and an overpowering drowsiness creeping over her, the Lady from Hell did not realize that she had been drugged. It was not until she reached the threshold of the room to which she had been guided that the truth burst upon her dulled senses with the force of a thunderbolt.

Stacked neatly against the whitewashed walls of the room was the baggage she had left in her cabin on the steamer!

Dizzily, clutching at the door for support, she turned . . . just in time to see a short heavy club descend with stunning force on Wylie's head. And then, even as her companion crumpled to the stone flooring, blackness flooded her brain.

CHAPTER III
VIVIAN LEGRAND TRAPPED

Dusk had fallen with tropic swiftness before Vivian awoke. She had not been conscious of her journey, wrapped in coco fiber matting from the house where she had been drugged, to Benedetti's launch, nor of the subsequent trip to the man's home on the Ille de Feral.

Now, anger smoldering in her greenish eyes, she faced him across the dining room table. In the dim room the table floated in a sea of amber candlelight. Barefooted black girls passed in and out, their voices keyed to the soft stillness, a thing of pauses and low voices. The whole thing, to Vivian, seemed to take on a character of unreality—a dream in which anything might happen.

She waited for Benedetti to speak after the slender black girl drew out her chair for her. But the man did not, so finally she broke the silence herself.

"What do you hope to gain by this?" she queried.

"Won't you try your soup?" he said bitterly. "I am sure that you will find it very good."

He halted as one of the girls stopped beside his chair and said something in Creole in a low voice. He rose to his feet.

"Will you pardon me?" he said. "There is someone outside, with a message. I shall be gone only a moment."

He disappeared through the door beside the staircase, the door that Vivian imagined led to the rear of the house.

Swiftly she beckoned the black maid to her, slipped the glittering diamond from her finger, and folded the girl's hand about it.

"Come to my room tonight," she whispered tensely, "when it is safe. No one will ever know. And in Port-au-Prince or Cap St. Feral you can sell that ring for sufficient to live like a *blanc* millionaire for the rest of your days."

The girl's face paled to a dusky brown, she glanced furtively from the glittering jewel in her hand to the pale face of the woman who had given it to her. Vivian caught the hesitation.

"I have others in my room," she urged desperately. "You shall choose from them what you want—two—three—when you sell them there will never have been another girl in Haiti as rich as you will be."

"I will come," the girl said in a whisper and stepped back against the wall. A moment later Benedetti returned.

"I regret to have been so poor a host as to leave you alone for even so short a time," he said.

"Please," Vivian said shortly, and there was in her manner no indication of the triumph that filled her breast. "Why dissemble. You've brought me here for a purpose. Why not tell me what it is?"

Already a scheme was forming in that agile mind of hers. When the girl came to her room that night she would persuade her to find weapons—guide Wylie and herself to a boat so that they might escape. But was Wylie still alive?

Benedetti's answer interrupted her thoughts.

"It is not so much what I hope to gain, as what I hope to keep," he said smoothly. He paused, and through the silence there came to her ears that queer rise and fall of notes from drums that had followed her ever since she arrived in Haiti—the drums of the Voodoo Moon, Benedetti had called it. He leaned forward.

"You might as well know now," he said abruptly. "You have until tomorrow midnight to live."

"Unless?" Vivian queried meaningly. She was very sure that she knew what the man meant.

Benedetti calmly placed the spoon in his plate and pushed it aside.

"There is no proviso. I know nothing of your personal life—of your finances. They are no concern of mine. You may be extremely rich, or completely poor—that does not enter into the matter at all. You have nothing that I care to buy. All I know is that you are young and extremely beautiful." He studied her with a cold dispassionate interest, then sighed, a bit regretfully, it seemed. "That is the reason you must die tomorrow night."

The thing was utterly fantastic. Vivian listened in amazed fascination. She could hardly bring herself to believe that she had heard correctly. So sure had she been that the man's interest in her rose from the fact that he was attracted to her that the thought there might be another, more sinister motive behind the drugging and kidnaping had not occurred to her.

Her green eyes narrowed a trifle—only that, but there was the impression of a steel spring tightening. Then she said quietly:

"Why must I die?"

"Because," he answered, "tomorrow night is the night of the Voodoo Moon—the night when the Papaloi and the Mamaloi present Ogoun Badagri, the Bloody One, with the Goat Without Horns."

"The Goat Without Horns?" Vivian repeated, uncomprehendingly. "What is that?"

"You," the man said tersely. "Tomorrow at midnight, when the Voodoo Moon is fullest, you will be offered as a sacrifice to Ogoun Badagri, the snake god."

For a moment the Lady from Hell stared at him, a chill feeling clutching at her breast. Then an alert look came into her eyes, a look that she quickly veiled. She was listening intently.

"You're not actually in earnest?" she asked quietly. Every nerve was strained to catch that sound again—the drone of an airplane engine that had come faintly to her ears. It was louder now. "You are trying to frighten me, to trap me into something. You will find that I am not easily frightened or trapped."

The sound of the plane was louder now. She shot a furtive glance at Benedetti. Could aid be on the way? Could Benedetti's plans have gone wrong, and a search be underway for them?

"I am very much in earnest," the man opposite her said. "You see, that is the secret of my successful defiance of the sugar trust, the secret of why my laborers never leave me, the secret of why I can manufacture sugar at a cost that the sugar trust cannot possibly equal and still make a profit. Once a year I present the Papaloi and the Mamaloi, the high priest and priestess of Voodoo, with a human sacrifice—a white man or woman—and in turn these two guardians of the great snake see to it that my laborers do not leave, and are kept content with the lowest pay scale in the island of Haiti."

He broke off and smiled.

"You may relax, Mrs. Legrand," he said. "That plane that you hear will not land here. It is the marine mail plane that passes over the island every night between eleven thirty and twelve o'clock."

Vivian looked at him blankly. "Plane?" she said vaguely. "Oh, yes, that is a plane, isn't it? Quite honestly, I had not noticed the sound before you spoke."

It was so well done that it fooled him. She picked up the slender silver fruit knife that lay on the table in front of her, twisting it so that it shone in her fingers, a pale, metallic splinter of light. She regarded him with eyes that had turned mysteriously dark, and leaned forward a little. Her voice, when she spoke, was very soft, and it held a quality of poignancy.

"You seem to live alone here," she said, and her eyes regarded him warmly. "Don't you ever become—lonely?"

There was a world of promise and invitation in the soft tone, in the alluring lips.

He looked at her and tightened his lips.

"That is useless," he said. "You are beautiful, one of the most beautiful women that I have ever seen, but a dozen such women as you could not make up to me for the loss of my plantation. No, my dear, your charm is useless."

"But you wouldn't dare," she said. "A woman cannot simply disappear from a steamer without inquiries being made. This is not the Haiti of twenty years ago. The Americans are in control—they are the police . . ."

Benedetti shook his head. "Do not raise false hopes. You sent the purser of the steamer a note saying that you had unexpectedly found friends in Cap St. Feral and were breaking your voyage here. The same man who brought the note took yours and your companion's baggage off the ship. By now he has probably forgotten your existence.

"There is nothing to connect you with me, and if inquiries should be made it will simply be assumed that you either left the island or were murdered by a wandering Caco. And as for an Haitian, who might know something of your disappearance, aside from the fact that the secrets of Voodoo are something that are never discussed, there is an island saying: '*Z affaires negres, pas z'z affaires blancs.*' And you will find that the affairs of the Negroes are not the affairs of the whites. And then," his voice was bland as he made the significant statement, "there is rarely any proof—left—when the great green snake god has completed his sacrifice."

"And my companion—Dr. Wylie—what have you done with him?" Vivian queried steadily. A bright spark glowed in her narrowed green eyes for a moment. It died slowly.

"He is safe, quite safe," Benedetti assured

her, "for the time being. He also will be a sacrifice to Ogoun Badagri."

He said it with simple, sincere ruthlessness; undisguised, but neither vindictive nor cruel.

"You are quite sure of yourself," Vivian said softly, and had Wylie been there he would have recognized the meaning of that tone; the threat of that greenish glow at the back of her eyes. He had seen that cold light in her eyes before. But Benedetti, even had he glimpsed it, would not have known that it was like the warning rattle of a snake before it strikes.

Now, with a swift movement she flung the silver fruit knife she held at the gleaming shirt front of the man opposite her. Her aim was deadly, for few people could throw a knife with the skill and precision of the Lady from Hell.

But Benedetti had caught the glitter of the candlelight on the metal a split second before she launched the knife. His agile mind perceived her intention and he flung himself to one side just in time. The knife thudded into the high back of the chair in which he had been sitting and rested there, quivering.

"You are a fool," the man commented curtly. Striding to the French windows he flung them wide, letting moonlight stream into the room. The sound of the drums came in louder, a barbaric rhythm beating in strange tempo with the pulse in her wrist.

"Look at that," he said, flinging out an arm.

At the edge of the veranda, which ran along the front of the house, lounged a white cotton-clad Haitian, a three-foot cane knife clasped in his fist. Further along, at the edge of the beach, another man leaned against the bole of a coconut tree, and the glitter of the moonlight on steel betrayed the fact that he also was armed with a cane knife.

"Even if you had killed me," he said quietly, "you would have been no better off. You could not escape from the island. There are no boats here. Even the launch on which you arrived has been sent away and will not return until after the ceremony. And if you had attempted to swim, the sea swarms with sharks."

It was after midnight when Vivian went upstairs to her room again. Benedetti escorted her to the door.

"I am locking you in," he told her. "It is really quite useless to do so. You could not escape. There is absolutely no possibility of success. But it is a precaution I always take with my annual—visitors."

Then he drew from his pocket the diamond ring that Vivian had, earlier in the evening, given to the little black maid.

"You will find," he said with a smile, "that it is useless to attempt to bribe my servants. The fear of the Voodoo in them is greater than the greed for money."

With a slight bow he closed the door, leaving her staring at the blank panels with a sinking feeling in her heart. She was a prisoner in a prison without walls, and yet the sea that girdled the land was a barrier as effective as stone ramparts and iron bars. Instead of one jailer she had dozens—perhaps hundreds—for she realized that every laborer on the island was a potential guard, alert to halt any attempt to escape. She did not attempt to deceive herself by thinking that every native of the place did not know of her presence and the fate for which she was destined.

She wondered what prompted the old woman—Benedetti's servant—to take her life in hand and warn her, back there in Cap St. Feral? The woman had, of course, realized Benedetti's purpose in bringing her here, since it had been she who had prepared the drugged rose stems. It was not for a long time, and then only by accident, that Vivian was to discover that in a Haitian the desire for revenge can transcend even the fear of Voodoo, and that it was to avenge what she considered a wrong that the old woman had warned her.

Vivian turned her thoughts back to her position. She believed she knew where Wylie was being held. On her way down to the dining room a little earlier she had encountered one of the black maids with a tray; had noted the door through which the girl had passed. That, she reasoned, must be the room in which Wylie was held prisoner, unless there were other prisoners in the house of whom she knew nothing.

She smiled a trifle grimly at the thought of being locked in her room. If Benedetti only knew of how little importance a lock—particularly an old-fashioned one such as this—was to her. Opening her suitcase she took out a hand mirror with a long handle. Unscrewing the handle, she removed from the hollow interior a long slender rod of thin steel. This she forced slowly into the thin opening between door and jamb. The rod scraped on metal. She worked it up and down, slowly pressing inward. Bit by bit the sloping tongue of the lock was forced back into its sheath, until the blade slipped through. A twist of the door handle and Vivian was peering out into the corridor.

Darkness hung before her eyes. It was as if a curtain of some impenetrable texture hung before her. She knew nothing of the floor plan of the big, rambling house, but she knew that the room she had seen the girl entering was the last on her side of the corridor, and accordingly she made her way cautiously in that direction, feeling her way, finger-tips trailing the wall, listening intently every step or so for some sound that might warn her of the presence of another person.

Her hand trailing along the wall touched a door—the fifth one she had passed. This was the door she sought. Gently she tried the knob. It was locked. A few minutes' work with the thin steel rod and the door swung inward with only the faintest of sounds. But even that was sufficient to betray her presence to Wylie's alert ears.

"Who is it?" he queried.

"Shhh," she whispered warningly, and, closing the door, crossed swiftly toward the chair where he sat beside the window.

In low, tense whispers she told him of her conversation with Benedetti and of the fate that was in store for both of them.

"We've got to get away tonight," she fin-

ished. "It's our only chance. There must be some way—perhaps we can make a raft. At least we can try."

CHAPTER IV
THE FIRST VICTIM

With Wylie by her side she made her way to the door; peered cautiously outside. By diligent practice the Lady from Hell had long ago acquired the chatoyant eye—the cat's—good for prowling about and seeing things in the dark, but here in the corridor the blackness was intense, with a tangible quality that was numbing to the senses. The utter opacity was tactile, half fluid, like fog. She crept down the hallway with feline assurance, passing her fingers delicately over objects that came into her path with a touch light enough to stroke a butterfly's wing. The house was a sea of silence, and on its waves the slightest noise made long and screeching journeys.

To Vivian's hearing, sandpapered by suspense, the slight give of the polished boards of the staircase beneath their slow steps produced a terrific noise. By making each step a thing of infinite slowness, they crept forward safely. Each downward step was a desperate and long-drawn-out achievement, involving an exactly calculated expenditure of muscular energy, an unceasing, muscular alertness.

Once, as they reached the bottom of the stairs, there came from the dining room in which they stood the rattle of a clock preparing to ring out a quarter hour. It struck Vivian's tense nerves as a thing of abominable violence—like countless, swift hammer strokes on the innumerable frayed ends of her nerves. She had the sensation of being driven into the woodwork of the floor upon which she stood, of being crushed under an immense and lightning-like pressure.

After what seemed an eternity they reached the further side of the dining room. Under her careful manipulation the latch of the door slipped slowly back. The door moved silently, slowly. A brilliant line of moonlight appeared. Vivian caught her breath sharply.

Standing there in the open ground in front of the veranda stood a Haitian, alert, watchful, armed with a machete.

There was no escape that way. Weaponless, they were helpless before the menace of that shining three-foot length of steel, even if they could cross the moonlit space that lay between the veranda and the man without being detected.

"The back of the house," Vivian whispered to Wylie, her voice barely perceptible.

She knew that the door to the kitchen was beside the staircase they had descended. That much she had observed during her interview with Benedetti earlier in the evening. By locating the staircase first in the blackness, she found the door she sought and opened it. A passageway opened before them, dimly illuminated by a shaft of silver that poured through a half opened door at its further end.

Silently they made their way down the passage and cautiously peered through the partly opened door. Another disappointment.

It was a small room, one wall covered with shelves, boxes and bags stacked high on the other side with a single window, half way up the wall, through which moonlight poured. A storeroom of some sort.

Vivian reached out and caught Wylie's arm, drew him silently into the little room and closed the door.

"There may be weapons here," she said. But she was mistaken. The nearest approach was a broken kitchen knife used, probably, to slash open the burlap bags which stood against the wall.

It was a poor substitute for a weapon, but Vivian took it thankfully. And then she gave a gasp. Her hand, exploring a shelf, had come in contact with something clammy and sticky that clung and would not be shaken off. Her first thought was that it was some monstrous tropical insect. It seemed alive, it clung so persistently, despite her efforts to shake it loose.

Then, as Wylie snapped his cigarette lighter into flame, the tiny glow illuminated an oblong of sticky fly paper fastened to her hand. There was a pile of the sheets upon the shelf. Despite the tenseness of the situation she almost laughed at the uncanny feeling the thing had given her there in the darkness.

In the dim flame of Wylie's lighter they searched again for anything that might prove of assistance to them in their predicament. Bags of flour. Bags of potatoes. Kegs of pig tails and pig snouts in brine—evidently food for the laborers. A half-emptied case of bacale—dried codfish, a staple article of diet in the West Indies—and a can of phosphorescent paint. Also row after row of canned food. But nothing that might be of assistance to them.

Climbing upon a box Vivian peered through the window, then turned back to Wylie, excitement in her voice.

"We can get out this way," she whispered. "There is the limb of a tree almost against the window and shrubbery around the tree."

"Anybody in sight?" Wylie queried.

"No one," Vivian said, and pried the latch of the window with her broken knife blade. It came open with a tearing shriek that sounded like thunder in the silence. Disregarding the noise Vivian slipped through the window and swung on to the limb of the tree. Wylie followed her, and in a moment they stood on the ground in the midst of dense shrubbery.

"We will have to keep in the shadow," she said as they crept silently through the bushes, only an occasional rustling leaf marking their passage. "The moment we step in the moonlight we'll be seen, if anyone is watching."

Even there in the bushes the brilliant moonlight illuminated the ground about them. A faint drumming ebbed to them through the brilliance, faintly touching the dark membrane of the night as they emerged on what seemed to be a well-defined path leading toward the beach.

A sudden opening in the trail, a burst of moonlight, and they stood on a strip of white sand with breakers creaming softly in front of them.

"There," Vivian said, still keeping her voice

low. "See that pile of driftwood. We'll make a raft of that. Drag it to the water's edge while I cut vines to lash it together."

Feverishly they worked, Wylie dragging the heavy logs into position, lashing them firmly together with the vines that Vivian cut from the jungle's edge, until at last a crazy-looking affair bobbed up and down in the ripple at the edge of the beach. Makeshift, clumsy, but it would float and it was an avenue of escape, the only avenue that had presented itself.

Vivian returned from a final trip to the jungle, dragging behind her three bamboo poles.

"We can use two of these to shove the thing with, until we get into deep water," she said. "The other we can lash upright as a mast and use my dress as a sail."

At that instant, from the path behind them, came the sound of voices. Vivian flashed a frantic glance at the jungle rearing up behind them, and then leaped on board the raft. Wylie followed. It dipped and swayed, but held their weight. The voices came nearer. Desperately Vivian braced her pole against the sandy bottom and shoved. Wylie followed suit. Sluggishly the clumsy craft moved away from the shore—five feet—ten feet—and than half a dozen men poured through the opening in the jungle and raced across the sand, splashed through the shallow water and surrounded the little craft, gleaming machetes raised threateningly.

Vivian did not see Benedetti when they returned to the house with their captors that night, nor was he visible when she awoke the next morning after a night spent in futile speculation and planning, and descended to the dining room.

A black girl served them breakfast. Golden sunlight poured through the wide French windows, beyond which they could see the beach and the green cove. Nowhere was there evidence of the fate that hung over them. But both knew, and the fact of that knowledge was evident in their eyes, in their short jerky words, that Death's wings were already casting their shadows across them.

The sun was well up when they went on to the veranda. There should have been the click of machetes in the cane fields and the low, lazy laughter of the workers. But everything was still, and that stillness held an ominous meaning.

Wylie was frankly without hope—more so as the day wore on, and Vivian, although she had never admitted defeat, admitted to herself that she saw no way out of the impasse. Benedetti, she saw now, had made no mistake when he told her that escape was impossible.

The day wore on, and still Benedetti did not put in an appearance. Once Vivian asked one of the maids where he could be found and received in answer a queer jumble of Creole French that held no meaning. Later, they essayed a walk to the Sugar Central, whose smokestacks rose on the other side of the cane fields, but one of the ever-present natives stepped slowly in their path, his machete openly in evidence. From the corner of her eyes Vivian could see others, alert, ready, at the edge of the jungle. Their captors were taking no chances.

On the far side of the cleared space Vivian could see a break in the jungle where a path ended. From this path men kept coming and going, and this, she surmised, must lead to the place where they were scheduled to die that night.

It was after dinner when Benedetti made his appearance, and with him stalked tragedy.

Vivian and Wylie were on the broad veranda, walking up and down. Something—some sixth sense—warned Vivian of danger, even before she heard the quick, catlike tread behind her. She made an attempt to swing around an instant too late. Someone leapt on her. A strong arm was locked about her throat. A hand was clamped over her mouth. A knee dug into the small of her back. She wrenched, tore at the gripping hands, even as she saw other hands seizing Wylie; she was aware of Benedetti's face, his features hard as stone. In the same second something dropped over her head and blotted the world into darkness.

How long she was held there motionless on the veranda she did not know. Then came a quick gabble of Creole in Benedetti's voice and the smothering hand was removed.

She flashed a glance around. The place was deserted save for herself, Benedetti and one tall native who stood beside the veranda steps, the ever-present machete in evidence. Obviously a guard.

The man interpreted her look.

"Your companion is gone. You will never see him again," he said, and his voice was indifferent. He might have been speaking of some trivial object that had disappeared. He turned back toward the dining room, where candlelight made a soft glow. Vivian followed. The house seemed curiously still, as if all life had departed from it save these two.

"Gone—you mean—" She could not finish the sentence.

Benedetti nodded and selected a cigarette from a box on a little side table; lit it at one of the candles.

"He will be the first sacrifice to Ogoun Badagri. When the great green snake god has finished with him they will come for you. You will be the climax of the ceremony," he told her brutally.

"You mean that you—a white man—will actually permit these men to make a sacrifice of us?" she queried. She knew, before she said it, that any appeal to him would be useless, but her mind was going around frantically, seeking a method of warding off the death that was imminent.

"What is your life and that of your companion to me?" he asked. "Nothing—not so much as the ash from the cigarette—compared with the fact that your death means that I keep my plantation a year longer. I refused close to half a million dollars from the sugar trust for the island. Do you think, then, that I would permit a little thing like your life to rob me of it?"

CHAPTER V
VOODOO DEATH

Vivian did not answer. Her eyes roamed around the room, although already every article in it had been photographed indelibly on her retina. A fly had alighted on the border of the sticky fly paper that lay in the center of the mahogany table. It tugged and buzzed, but the sticky mess held it too firmly.

"You may comfort yourself with the thought," Benedetti went on, "if the fact is any comfort, that you are not the first. There have been others. The little dancing girl from the Port-au-Prince cabaret, a Spanish girl from Santo Domingo . . ."

He was not boastful, purely meditative as he sat there and smoked and talked, telling Vivian of the victims whose lives had paid for his hold on his sugar plantation. Vivian's eyes were fastened on the feebly fluttering fly on the sticky paper. They, too, were caught like flies in a trap, and unless she could do something immediately—she faced the fact calmly—it would be the end.

Abruptly she leaned forward. There was a stillness in her pose, a stillness in her opaque eyes. Her hands coiled like springs. She found it difficult to keep her detached poise as the scheme began to unfold and take shape in her brain.

She smiled thinly. The air was suddenly electrical, filled with the portent of danger. Benedetti caught the feel of it, and peered at her suspiciously for a moment. The Lady from Hell knew that it was a thousand to one that she would lose. But, if her scheme worked, she could save Wylie's life and her own, and Benedetti might be made to pay for the thing he had attempted—pay as he had never dreamed that he would have to pay.

Reaching out one hand she moved the candle in front of her, so that its glow fell more on Benedetti's face than her own. Her voice, as she spoke, was quiet, almost meditative. But her eyes told a different story.

"How much time have I to live?" she said.

The man glanced at his watch.

"Roughly, two hours," he said. He might have been estimating the departure time of a steamer, his voice was so calm. "It might be a trifle more or less—the time of my workers is not accurate. When the drums stop they will come for you. And when they start again—well, you will be there then."

She rose to her feet, leaning lightly on the table.

"If I am to die," she said hysterically, "I will die beautiful." Then she added as an explanation, "My makeup is in my room."

But he was on his feet too, alert, wary. "You must not leave my presence," he said. "I cannot permit it. The sacrifice must go to the arms of Ogoun Badagri alive, not a corpse."

His dark eyes held no recognition of the fact that she was a very beautiful woman. Vivian sensed, and rightly, that to him she was merely a woman who might thwart his plans. But she caught the implication in his last sentence.

"I shall not take poison," she said. "You may come with me—watch me, if you wish."

She took a step or two and groped blindly at the table for support. Instinctively he stretched out a hand to steady her.

That was the moment for which she had planned, the instant for which she had been waiting. Benedetti made the fatal mistake that many men had made with the Lady from Hell as an opponent—of underestimating her as an adversary.

Like a striking snake her hand darted to the table, seized one of the heavy candlesticks. Before Benedetti could interfere, had even divined her purpose, the heavy metal fell across his forehead with stunning force. He crumpled to the floor without a murmur.

Leaving him where he had fallen, Vivian ran to the door and peered out. The gigantic black on guard at the veranda steps had heard nothing. He was still standing there, unaware of the drama being enacted within the dining room.

Swiftly she turned back and her slender fingers searched the drawers of the carved mahogany sideboard against the wall until she found what she sought—a heavy, sharp carving knife. She balanced it speculatively in her hand. It would do, she decided.

The man was still standing there when she peered out the door again. He never saw the slender blade as it flew through the air, sped by a hand that had learned its cunning from the most expert knife thrower in Shanghai. The blade went through, sinking into the flesh at the base of his throat as though it had been butter. He died without an outcry.

Now she must work fast, if she were to escape and save Wylie too. Benedetti she bound and gagged and rolled against the sideboard where he was out of the way. But first she had taken his revolver from his side pocket.

Trip after trip she made, first to the flat tin roof of the house, and then to the front of the house. Finally she was satisfied with what she had done, and, snatching up a flashlight from the sideboard, fled toward the path in the jungle that she knew led to the place of sacrifice.

A tropical squall was rising out of the sea beyond the little cove. A cloud, black in the light of the moon, was rising above the horizon. She glanced at it anxiously. Then she plunged into the jungle.

The valences of the palms were motionless against the moonlit sky. The atmosphere, as she pushed her way along, seemed saturated with mystery, dew dripping, bars of green moonlight between the trunks of the trees; the cry of night birds, the patter of something in the dark mystery of the tree roof overhead, the thudding of the drums that had never ceased. Out of that familiar hollow rhythm of drums that had begun to emerge a thread of actual melody—an untraditional rise and fall of notes—a tentative attack, as it were, on the chromatic scale of the beat. A tentative abandonment of Africa. It was a night of abandonment, anyhow, a night of betrayal and the peeling off of blanketing layers down to the raw.

Once she stopped short with a sudden emptiness in her chest at sight of what she thought was a man in the path ahead. But it was only a paint-daubed, grinning skull on a bamboo stake planted in the ground—a voodoo *ouanga*. Then she went ahead again. Evidently there were no guards posted. With every inhabitant of the island concerned in the ceremony in one way or another there would be no need for guards to be posted now.

The rapid sequence of events had edged Vivian's nerves, and the boom of the drums—heavy, maddening, relentless—did nothing to soothe them. That passage through the jungle was galling, fraying the nerve ends like an approaching execution.

A red glow came to her through the trees, and seemed to spread and spread until it included the whole world about her in its malignancy. The drums, with that queer rise and fall of notes that it seemed impossible to achieve with taut skins stretched over drum heads, beat upon her senses, pounded until the air was filled with sounds that seemed to come from the earth, the sky, the forest; dominated the flow of blood with strange excitations.

She had formulated no plan for rescuing Wylie. She could not, until she reached the spot and saw what she had to contend with. She had the gun she had taken from Benedetti, but six cartridges against a horde of drum-maddened blacks—that was only a last resort.

And then she stood on the edge of a clearing that seemed sunk to the bottom of a translucent sea of opalescent flame.

Something that was age-old was happening in that crimson-bathed clearing, something old and dark, buried so deeply under the subtleties of civilization that most men go through life without ever knowing it is there, was blossoming and flowering under the stark madness of those thudding drums.

Coconut fiber torches, soaked in palm oil, flaring red in the blackness of the night lit up the space in front of her like a stage, the torchlight weaving strange scarlet and mauve shadows. Tall trees, lining the clearing opposite her, seemed to shelter masses of people, darker shadows against the red glow of the burning torches.

Two enormous drums, taut skins booming under the frenzied pounding of the palms of two drummers, stood on one side. A dozen, two dozen dancing black figures, male and female,

spun and danced in the center of the clearing, movements graceful and obscene—animal gestures that were identical with similar dances of their ancestors hundreds of years before in Moko or the Congo.

And then she saw Wylie. He was tied to a post in the center of the clearing, and the dancers were milling about him. Beside him stood a woman whom Vivian instinctively knew must be the Mamaloi, the priestess of whom Benedetti had spoken.

Now and then the priestess gave vent to a sound that seemed to stir the dancers to greater activity—to spur the slowly humming throng of watchers to a point of frenzy; a sound such as Vivian had never heard before and never hoped to hear again. When she stopped, it would hang, incredibly high-pitched, small, like a black thrill in the shadow. It was shocking and upsetting out of that ancient thin figure.

Her eyes shifted from the aged figure to the sky line above the trees. The black cloud that, a short time before had been no larger than the palm of her hand on the horizon, was visible through the branches of the trees now. Even as she looked a faint flicker of heat lightning laced through it.

And then, as if at a conductor's signal, more torches flowered on the edge of the clearing, and in their light the Lady from Hell saw half a dozen men staggering forward with an enormous thing of bamboo—a cage—and in that cage was a great snake; a boa constrictor, perhaps, or a python, although neither of them, she seemed to remember, was native to Haiti.

CHAPTER VI
WHITE MAN'S VOODOO

They placed the cage in the center of the clearing, and Vivian saw that it had been placed so that a small door in the cage was directly opposite Wylie's bound figure. The significance of that fact went through her like a breath of cold wind. If she failed, she also would be bound to that stake. Mentally she could see the little door in the cage opening, the great triangular head of the snake gliding slowly . . .

Swiftly she bent over and caught up a handful of the black leaf mold underfoot, smeared it over her face, her arms, her neck, her shoulders. A section of the dress she was wearing was ripped off and made into a turban that hid the flaming crown of her hair. More earth was rubbed onto the white of her dress.

Then, with swift leaps, she was on the outer fringe of the dancers, and the chaos of moving arms and legs caught her up and swallowed her as a breaking wave on the beach swallows a grain of sand.

It was a mad thing to do, a desperate thing. She knew that, normally, her crude disguise would not have fooled the natives. The Haitian black seems to have the ability to almost smell the presence of a *blanc,* much as an animal can smell the presence of another. But, in that flickering torchlight, the crudeness of disguise would not be so apparent, and in that unceasing madness of drums that went on like a black echo of something reborn, she hoped that her alien presence would pass unnoticed long enough for her to accomplish her object.

Slowly she worked her way through the writhing, dancing mass of figures toward the center. She knew that her time was short—that the lesser ceremony was approaching its height. Even as she reached the inner ring of dancers she saw the ancient Mamaloi joining in the dance, while the others kept a respectful distance from her. Monotonously, maddeningly, the priestess twisted and turned and shivered, holding aloft a protesting fowl. Faster and faster she went, and while all eyes were fastened on that whirling figure Vivian managed to reach Wylie's bound figure.

A swift slash with the knife she had hidden beneath her dress and his hands were free.

"Keep still . . . don't let them see that you're not bound," she whispered. Another motion and the bonds that fastened his ankles to the post were free.

Vivian moved about Wylie with graceful motions, imitating the movements of the blacks about her, and her voice came to him in broken, desperate whispers:

"Signal . . . you'll recognize it . . . don't move until then . . . dead tree by the edge of the clearing . . . that's the path . . . I'll be waiting there . . . it's only chance . . ."

Then she was gone, breasting her way through the black figures that danced like dead souls come back from Hell in the evil glow of the sputtering torches. And then came a great shout as the Mamaloi caught the chicken she held by the head and whirled it around and around.

Throom . . . throom . . . throom. The drums were like coalescing madness. A moan went up from the onlookers and a chill went through Vivian.

She knew from what Benedetti had told her that the chicken was the prelude of what would happen to Wylie. Next, the old woman would slash Wylie's throat . . . let his life blood spurt into a bowl with which the dancers would be sprinkled. Then would come the lesser ceremony, while the guard at the house would start with her for the ceremony that would end with the door in the great snake's cage being opened . . .

Vivian snatched a torch from the hands of one of the dancers. The man did not even seem to be aware of the fact that it had been taken away. From beneath her dress she took a stick of dynamite with fuse attached—part of her loot from the storeroom—and touched the fuse to the flame of the torch.

It sputtered and she hurled it with all her strength at her command toward the overhanging tree beneath which the drummers sat, then fled for the bare naked branches of the dead tree that stood where the path entered the clearing— the spot where she had told Wylie she would meet him.

She had barely reached the spot when there came a tremendous concussion that shook the earth, and a gush of flame. The thing was as startling, as hideously unexpected to the drum, maddened Haitians as a striking snake. Scream after scream—long, jagged screams that ripped red gashes through the dark, were followed by a swift clacking of tongues, a terrified roar as dancers and onlookers milled about, black bodies writhing in the light of the remaining torches. A black tide, rising, filled the clearing with terrified clamor. A moment later there was the sound of running feet and Wylie was at her side.

"This way," she whispered, and guided him into the path.

Both of them knew that it would be only a moment before the startled natives recovered their wits and discovered that their victim was gone. Then they would take up their trail again immediately.

"Where are we going?" Wylie asked her as he ran behind her along the winding jungle trail.

"The house," she answered tersely.

"The house?" He almost halted in his amazement. "But Vivian—that's the first place they'll make for. Even if you've found weapons we can't hold them off forever."

"Wait," she said. "No time to explain now . . . But if things work out, we'll be off this island before morning, safe and sound."

From behind them a quavering yell rose on the air and the two fugitives knew that Wylie's escape had been discovered. It was a matter of yards and of minutes now. Then they burst from the shadow of the jungle into the moonlight clearing.

"Follow me," she said quickly. "Don't take the path," and he followed her footsteps as she twisted and twined about the space toward the steps.

At the steps he halted a moment in wonder at what he saw there, and then, in spite of the gravity of the situation, a chuckle broke from his panting lips.

"So that's it," he said, and Vivian nodded.

"That's it. Be careful. It's a slim enough chance, but there is just a chance it'll work—the only chance we've got."

"But even that," he said, a thought striking him, as he threaded his way carefully up the steps to the veranda, "will only be temporary. Even if it holds them at bay until dawn—when daylight comes . . ."

"I know," she said a trifle impatiently, "but

long before then—" She broke off suddenly as their pursuers appeared, breaking out from under the palms, just as a flash of lightning came.

"They're here," he whispered. "If the scheme won't work, then it's all up with us."

"It will work," Vivian said confidently.

But, although her tone was cool, confident, there was anxiety in her eyes as she watched the black figures pouring out of the jungle. Vivian knew that her own and Wylie's lives were hanging by the slenderest margin in their criminal career.

The Papaloi, the giant Negro with the white lines and scar ridges criss-crossing his muscular torso, was the first to see them as another flash of lightning illuminated the veranda where they stood. He uttered a single bellow, a stentorian cry, which seemed to shake the house, and bounded toward the stairs. Behind him came part of his followers, while others rushed for the other pair of stairs.

The Papaloi leaped for the steps, his men close behind him. His feet landed in something that slid quickly under him, that clung to his soles. He lost his balance, fell asprawl, his followers in a momentary confusion that quickly increased to panic—the panic of the primitive mind confronted with something unseen that it cannot understand.

The hands of the gigantic black Papaloi were glued now to squares of sticky fly paper that he could not shake off—the fly paper that the Lady from Hell had taken from the storeroom and spent so much precious time placing upon the steps and around the veranda without encountering it, save along the narrow, tortuous trail along which Vivian had led Wylie.

There was a square of fly paper on the Papaloi's face now, clinging there, flapping a little as if alive, persistent as a vampire bat. There were more on the side of his body where he had slipped. He struck at them and accumulated more.

The Mamaloi, that ancient crone, was in trouble also. She had slipped and, in falling, had a sheet of fly paper plastered squarely across her eyes. She was uttering shrill cries of distress as she pawed at her face with hands that were covered with sticky fly paper and glue. All about the two men and women were struggling, shouting in alarm. The silent attack had materialized out of nothing with such appalling swiftness, and continued with such devastating persistence that it robbed them of every thought save alarm.

Robbed of their spiritual leaders, terror was striking at the hearts of the voodoo worshipers. At the edge of the veranda, black men writhed in horror, snatching at one another for support, tearing at the horrible things that clung as if with a million tiny sucking mouths. Their machetes, covered with glue and flapping fly paper, had been dropped, forgotten in the confusion. Torches had dropped underfoot, forgotten, so that the struggle was in darkness, illuminated only by the light of the moon through the clouds and the flashes of lightning. Fly paper in their hair, across their eyes, clinging, hampering, maddening them with the knowledge that some frightful voodoo, stronger than their Papaloi or Mamaloi, had laid hands upon them.

A flare of lightning slashed from the very center of the storm cloud that was now hanging overhead. Its brilliance illuminated, for a moment, the figure of the Lady from Hell, standing at the edge of the veranda, her arms uplifted as if calling down the wrath of the heavens upon them. A shattering blast of thunder followed and a gust of wind swept across the clearing.

That gust of wind was the crowning touch, the straw that was needed to break the camel's back of resistance in that struggling, milling black throng. It set all the loose ends of the fly paper fluttering, where it was not fastened to bodies. And, more than that, it caught up the sticky squares that were still unattached and sent them dancing through the air.

There rose a howl of fear. The demons of these *blancs*, not content with lying in wait and springing out upon them, were now flying through the air; attacking them from the heavens, sucking from their bodies all their strength.

What use to resist when even the magic of the Papaloi and the Mamaloi was not sufficient to fight off the demons.

They bolted headlong, fly paper sticking to every part of their anatomy. They fell, scaled with the awful things, and promptly acquired more. Women fell and shrieked as they were trampled upon, not from the pain of the trampling feet, but from the fear that they might be left behind at the mercy of the demons. Men, blinded by the sticky things, ran in circles and clutched at whatever they came in contact with.

Then came the low drone of an airplane engine in the distance, flying low because of the storm. Turning, Vivian ran back into the dining room, where Benedetti still lay, bound upon the floor, his eyes glaring hatred at her. Calmly she sat down and wrote upon one of his letterheads which she found in the desk there. Then she snatched off the gag that muffled his mouth.

"The danger is all over," she told the man, "for us. But for you trouble is just beginning."

"You can't escape," he raved at her viciously. "I don't know what you've done, but you won't be able to leave the island. In an hour, two hours—by daylight at least—they will return, and what they will do to you won't be pleasant."

Vivian smiled. The invisible plane seemed to be circling the house now. She waved the paper she had written to dry the ink.

"What the American authorities in Port-au-Prince do to you will not be pleasant, either," she told Benedetti. "Voodoo is forbidden by law. You have not only aided and abetted voodoo ceremonies, but you have also procured human sacrifices for the ceremonial. There was the little French girl from the Port-au-Prince cabaret, and the girl from Santo Domingo—you should not have boasted. For you murdered them as surely as if you had driven a knife in their hearts, and the law will agree with me."

"You'll never live to tell the Americans, even if they believed the tale," he scoffed.

"Oh, yes I will," she mocked. Her voice was as dry and keen as a new ground sword. "Within an hour I shall be on my way to Cape Hatien. Hear that," and she raised an admonitory hand. In the silence the plane could be heard. She threw open the French windows. From where he lay Benedetti could see a Marine plane slanting down toward the comparatively sheltered waters of the little cove.

"In less than ten minutes," she said, "the plane will have taxied up to the beach and the Marine pilot and his observer will be in this room, asking if we need aid. You see," and her smile was completely mocking and scornful now, "you yourself brought about your own downfall—planted the idea in my brain when you told me that the plane passed overhead every night at about this time. There was a can of luminous paint in your storeroom. I saw it, and there he is coming to see what it's all about—and to take you to Cape Hatien—unless . . ."

"Unless what?" he queried eagerly.

"Unless you sign this memorandum. It deposes that I have purchased this plantation from you—that you have received the purchase price—and that proper legal transfer to it will be made later."

There was a calculating gleam in the man's eyes as he made assent. His gaze flickered out through the open door to where the plane had already landed on the surface of the cove.

Vivian had caught that gleam. "Of course," she went on smoothly, "we will have the Marine officers sign it as witnesses in your presence. Then you can accompany us back to Cape Hatien in the plane, and the lawyers of the Haitian Sugar Central will be glad to see that memorandum is put in proper legal form before I, in turn, resell the plantation to them. I shall not refuse the price they are willing to pay—and it will not matter to the sugar trust whether you or I are the owner." She gazed at him for a moment. "Well, do you agree?—or do you go to Cape Hatien a prisoner?"

Benedetti shot a glance at the trim, uniformed figure coming cautiously up from the beach. Feverishly he scribbled his name at the bottom of the memorandum.

Brother Murder

T. T. Flynn

MORE FAMOUS AS A WRITER of Western fiction for the pulps, the prestigious *Saturday Evening Post,* and in book form, Thomas Theodore Flynn (1902–1978) was also a prolific author of mystery fiction, producing a story, "The Pullman Murder," for the very first issue of *Dime Detective* (November 1931).

He led the type of macho life that many male writers thought helpful in learning about the world, spending time as a hobo and working as a carpenter, door-to-door salesman, clerk, traveling salesman, and in a shipyard, steel mills, on ships in the engine and fire rooms, and in a railroad shop, inspecting locomotives.

He published five Western novels with Dell between 1954 and 1961, one of which, *The Man from Laramie,* was filmed starring James Stewart and directed by Anthony Mann.

Flynn's only two mystery novels were paperback originals published in Great Britain by Hector Kelly, *It's Murder* (1950) and *Murder Caravan* (1951).

His mystery pulp stories tended to be humorous and cheerful, as exemplified by the series featuring Mike Harris and Trixie Meehan, both of whom work for the Blaine International Agency. Mike is tough, redheaded, and wise-cracking; Trixie is cute and pert and, while depending upon her partner if a fight breaks out, is also smart and inventive when necessary.

"Brother Murder" first appeared in the December 2, 1939, issue of *DFW.*

Father Orion was the Prophet of Truth,
with Death as the greatest Truth of all—
but Mike and Trixie were unbelievers

Brother Murder

T. T. Flynn

CHAPTER I
GIRL IN A COFFIN

I WAS DOING SIXTY-EIGHT on the Ventura highway, north of Los Angeles, when the siren wailed behind me—and you could have had all the fun for a kippered herring.

Sixty-eight on that smooth open highway through the orange groves—and when I heard the siren and looked in the rear-view mirror, the motorcycle cop was coming like a bee to a flower.

"Whoa, Mike," says I, and stood the long fast coupé halfway on its nose at the edge of the pavement.

He rolled alongside, killed the engine and wanted to know sarcastically: "Going somewhere?"

"Points east," says I. "Did the sunshine make me reckless for a moment?"

"It made you murderous at that speed!" he snapped. "Name, please!"

"Harris," says I.

"First name?"

"Michael Harris."

"Red hair," says he, peering in at me. "Sawed-off and wisecracking."

"Is this a beauty contest?" I gave him.

"It's a pinch," he informed me coldly. "We'll go down the road and get it over with. I came out here looking for you."

"Not me," I told him. "No one knew I'd be along this stretch of road."

He was glancing in a small notebook.

"Blue Packard coupé," he read off. "New York tags. Sawed-off redhead named Mike Harris driving." He pocketed the book and grinned nastily. "If I hadn't been out this way looking for you, I wouldn't have caught you splitting the road open. Which makes us even for my trouble. Over sixty-five—and that'll cost you huckleberries, young feller."

"Okay," I said sourly. "Huckleberries it is. But why look for me?"

"The Los Angeles office of the Blaine International Agency want you to telephone," he said. "Drive on."

So I drove on—and they took huckleberries away from me. When I put a call through to Lew Ryster, manager of our Hollywood office, I was fit to tie.

Lew sounded relieved when he heard my voice. "So they got you, Mike! I wasn't sure what road you were taking out of the state, and your next address being New York, I put out a general call for you."

"They *got* me all right," I said through my teeth. "And try to explain my fine on your expense sheet, wise guy! *I'm* not taking the rap for it!"

"What fine?" says Lew.

"The cop who came out looking for me slapped a speed charge on me!"

Lew haw-hawed.

"Cackle like a Death Valley jackass!" I said. "I'm heading on to New York. We'll settle my fine from there."

"Wait, Mike!" Lew yelled. "Your vacation's canceled! I telephoned New York. And now you've been formally notified!"

"You Judas!" I howled. "*You* had my vacation *canceled?*"

"I've got a job for you," says Lew. "It's important, Mike. Murder, I think."

"There'll be murder if I get near you!"

Lew said: "Get back here fast. I'm waiting for you, Mike."

I slammed the receiver down and blistered the phone booth. But when you worked for the Blaine Agency you were in harness. The Agency had discipline and a tradition of breaking cases fast. An assignment to a case put you to work fast or else.

So I drove back to Los Angeles to meet murder.

There's a cold-blooded touch to murder. Crooks, thieves and swindlers are mostly ordinary people with ordinary weaknesses. A lot of us would like to collect from life the easy way.

But we're all born knowing murder is out of bounds. And you never know what angles a murder case will turn up. Dangerous angles sometimes. Two murders can't draw much worse penalty than one murder. Long ago I'd decided that after the first murder, a second one comes easier—so look out for murder, Mike.

Lew Ryster was waiting in the Hollywood office, big and pink-faced as ever, with the usual striped collar, natty suit and expansive confidence that clicked with the Hollywood trade, which was mostly theft, blackmail and body-guarding.

"What's on your mind, Rat?" I asked as I shoved a paper cup under the water cooler.

Lew grinned. "I had to do it, Mike. No hard feelings, I hope."

"Later," I said, "we'll settle that. Who murdered whom?"

Lew stood up and took his Panama from the desk.

"I've an appointment, Mike, and I was hoping you'd get here in time to come along. Let's shove off."

So we shoved off from Hollywood and Vine in my car—and over on Sunset Boulevard, Lew ordered me to stop before the Greek-colonnaded front of J. Conwell Smythe's Sons, Morticians.

"Did you read my mind?" I growled as we got out. "A funeral parlor is exactly where I'd like to leave you!"

Lew chuckled. "Kid, you'll thank me for this before you're through. Did I tell you there was a two grand reward for anyone who broke this case?"

"You wouldn't," I said, "if you could figure a way to collar the dough . . . And what does the score have to read before the reward is paid?"

We were inside by then. A long, lean, lugubrious lassie of some forty winters met us.

"Yes?" she said, and thawed visibly as Lew grinned.

"I have an appointment here with Mr. Farnson," Lew beamed in his best Hollywood manner. "Ryster is the name."

A faint flush appeared in her pallid cheeks.

"Mr. Farnson is in Room Three, with two other gentlemen. He is expecting you, Mr. Ryster. If this other gentleman will have a seat, I will show you to Room Three."

"He's here to meet Farnson also," says Lew carelessly, and when he grinned again her doubtful look vanished and we all went back to Room Three.

The heavy scent of flowers filled the small room into which we walked. Three men in there had been talking in low tones; and one of them—the tallest—said: "I was wondering if you'd come."

"Sorry if I'm late, Mr. Farnson," says Lew—and I saw the old Hollywood chuckle start and freeze off as Lew realized where he was.

Two floor lamps in the back corners of the room dusted indirect light against the ceiling and down in subdued dimness, down over the flower sprays and the pinkish coffin resting just beyond the men . . .

She might have been sleeping in the coffin—that girl whose peaceful, life-like face rested there on a satin pillow surrounded by a chaste froth of lace.

They had dressed her in what might have been a wedding gown of white satin, and she was heart-stoppingly natural, even to the little splash of good-natured freckles still luring along the bridge of a small tippity nose. Her mouth had once been built for laughter—and now it never would again smile.

But the spell of her was there in the room, even on the mortician's lean lady, who lingered inside the door eyeing the coffin for a moment, and whispered: "*So* lovely—and we have *never* brought out a face so well."

Farnson, whose mustache was a white military line against his heavy, full-blooded face, snapped: "Enough, Madam! This meeting is *not* an exhibit of your skill!"

She faded out in pallid silence and closed the door and the stocky-chested man on Farnson's left speared me with a disagreeable stare, jerked his head at me and grunted: "Who's this guy?"

A cop. He was smeared with copper from sparse, sandy hair to thick-soled shoes—and he didn't like us. He didn't like Lew Ryster who could handle a tight spot coolly when he had to. And who did now.

"This," said Lew suavely, nodding at me, "is Mike Harris, one of our best operatives. Mike, this is Jake Dennis, from Homicide—*and* Larry Sweet, who helps Jake think."

"Never mind the cracks," Jake Dennis put in belligerently.

"Hold it, Jake," said Larry Sweet mildly. His light-blue eyes were amused.

I liked this Larry Sweet, who was small, slim and almost too good-looking in a careless way to be a homicide cop. Sweet belonged over on the other side of the Hollywood fence, under the Kleig lights.

And Jake Dennis held it, biting down on his lower lip as he scowled at Lew.

"What," said Farnson, "is all this about? I was not expecting these gentlemen from the police again, Mr. Ryster. They will be going soon."

He was a fine figure of an old gentleman, all of six feet, prosperous and a little on the stern side, now trying not to be be angry. And behind all of it showing a bewilderment and hurt which left him almost childishly helpless.

Jake Dennis took a deep breath and spoke through throttled emotions.

"Maybe we'll be going an' maybe we won't. You didn't tell us you'd called the Blaine Agency in on this."

Farnson's face hardened.

"You did not ask me. I did what I thought was proper. I am not interested in your opinions of what I do."

"Now listen," said Jake Dennis, getting red.

"Hold it, Jake," Larry Sweet said mildly, and automatically, as if it were a habit with him.

Sweet smiled apologetically at Farnson. "We understand that, Mr. Farnson. No offense meant. Dennis is trying to suggest that he's surprised you aren't satisfied with our investigation of this matter."

I caught Lew's sour grin. So did Jake Dennis. It was meant for Dennis, and he got redder above the collar.

Sweet must have had eyes in the side of his head. "Hold it, Jake," he suggested casually, without looking around.

Farnson missed all that. His high forehead had furrowed with emotion. He looked at the girl in the coffin, swallowed and was husky as he answered Sweet.

"I will not be satisfied until I know exactly why my niece is dead. You tell me it was suicide or an accident. I don't believe you. Why should such a sweet girl want to kill herself? She was happy. Only last week she wrote my wife in Boston, saying how happy she was in her work here, and how much she was enjoying the visit of Nancy Cudahy, who used to be her best friend. And—and the next word we had was the telegram saying she was dead."

Farnson shook his head emphatically. "No! I do not believe it!"

Jake Dennis opened his mouth to say something, and Larry Sweet beat him to it, soothingly and argumentatively.

"We only suggested suicide, Mr. Farnson. These carbon monoxide cases are hard to pin down. Folks drive into small garages and stay in there for some reason or other with the motor running and the doors closed—and before they know what's happening it's all over."

"No," said Farnson flatly. "Frances was not so careless. She was always careful. How could she have done so well as a script girl in the moving pictures if she was careless? She has written us how careful she must always be in her work. Every little detail must be considered. And now you tell me she did something that everyone who drives a car knows must not be done."

Jake Dennis muttered under his breath and rolled his eyes helplessly. Larry Sweet gave him a warning look and went on in the same patient manner.

"We've thought of all that. But we've checked on your niece at NGN, and among her friends outside. She had no love troubles. She was getting ahead at NGN and on the verge of moving into the writing end on a contract. They tell us her voice didn't register well or she'd have had a chance at the acting end. No troubles—and more important, she had no enemies. Doesn't leave much choice but accidental death, does it?"

"This Cudahy girl who was visiting her from the East says it couldn't have been anything else but an accident," Jake Dennis grunted, and his look at Lew Ryster and me was a scowl. "So you're wasting any money you pay the Blaine Agency. They'll charge you plenty, an' tell you in the end just what we've told you."

"That," said Farnson stiffly, "is my business, gentlemen."

Jake Dennis lifted his hands helplessly. Larry Sweet asked patiently: "Is there anything you've forgotten to suggest to us? Anything we may have overlooked before you leave for the East with your niece's body?"

Farnson was hurt and helpless, but he was stubborn too.

"I am not taking Frances back East until I know why she was murdered," he stated heavily.

I thought Jake Dennis was going to explode. Larry Sweet stared at him for a moment, and then nodded smoothly.

"You understand, Mr. Farnson, that we're anxious to do everything we can. Perhaps it would be better if we worked with the Blaine people too. No objections to that, I suppose."

Lew Ryster grinned.

"Glad to have you help, Sweet—for what it's worth—and as long as we get credit for what we do. Jake, that's agreeable, I suppose?"

"What do you think?" Jake Dennis growled. "And now you've got that settled, what are you going to do that we ain't done?"

Lew looked solemn.

"We're going to bring all the facilities of our organization to bear on this, Dennis. With our usual success, I hope. Suppose you two drop around to the office late this afternoon for a conference. Mr. Harris has some matters to check, and then we'll be in a position to collaborate on any steps that we may be taking."

Larry Sweet's lip curled slightly in amusement. Jake Dennis looked his disgust at the smear of Hollywood oil Lew had given them. But Farnson was pleased.

"Just what I want, gentlemen," he said eagerly. "I will be at the Ambassador waiting for any word from you."

So that was our interview. I took a last look at the dead girl as we all went out. She made our cross-talk seem poison and useless. And I was scathing when I drove Lew away.

"So you dragged me back for a carbon monoxide case that probably was an accident like the police have decided. Any mug on your payroll could handle this."

"But not satisfy Farnson," said Lew cheerfully. "He's a Boston investment banker and lousy with money. He'll spend high to prove he's right about this. That girl meant more to him than a daughter. He and his wife reared her. And if he thinks it's murder, we might as well try to prove that it's murder."

"Maybe you *are* a rat!" I snapped. "You've been around Hollywood too long. You know damn well the Blaine Agency never chisels for money if they're sure there's not a case. And to think I let you scramble my vacation on a play like this!"

Lew chuckled.

"Jake Dennis is a headline hog, Mike. Never give that guy a break or he'll break you. I've done business with him before. And Larry Sweet is so smooth he'll be around you before you know it." Lew pursed his lips. "I only hope Larry really believes it is suicide and thinks we're giving Farnson a run-around for his money."

"Aren't you?" I said disgustedly.

"Maybe," said Lew. "You saw the dead girl and heard most of the fact. She made a try for pictures, and when her voice didn't click, she tossed society life back in Boston overboard, rolled up her sleeves out here and went to work with the lower third. Was making good on it too, and then yesterday morning she was found dead in her coupé at the bungalow court where she lived. Garage doors closed, car windows open, the girl behind the steering wheel with her hat on, cigarette between her first and second fingers, just as if she'd driven in and sat there smoking and thinking and forgetting to cut the motor off.

"I guess, Mike, you didn't notice it there in the coffin, and I didn't want to point it out with Dennis and Sweet around. There was a mark on her finger where the cigarette had burned down against the flesh."

"I didn't notice it," I said. "So what?"

Lew grinned.

"If you'd looked close, Mike, you'd have seen that there was the slightest sign of cigarette stain on the other side of her second finger, and on the inside of her third finger. She had an awkward way of holding a cigarette, between her second and third fingers, instead of the usual first and

second fingers. And yet she died, holding a cigarette the usual way. As near as I can figure it, Kid, that little fact is going to turn you into a screwball and make you a disciple of the Great Truth, Father Orion."

CHAPTER II
PEACE, BROTHER

A truck cut over in front of me and I stood the coupé on its nose, and shaved a wreck and said violently:

"Somebody around here is a screwball—and it's not me! What kind of tripe is this about the Great Truth, Father Orion? And how do you know so much about cigarette stains on that girl's fingers?"

"I'm good," says Lew smugly. "The body was found by the girl friend, Nan Cudahy—who's due to inherit a couple of million one of these days, if that makes her any more attractive."

"It doesn't," I said. "What's the dope on the cigarette stains?"

"You know me," says Lew. "Always on the spot at the right time. When Farnson retained me, I ducked around for a talk with this Nan Cudahy. She was taking it hard and didn't have any more to tell me than Sweet and Dennis know. But she let slip one thing. She'd been thinking, she said, how terribly symbolic it was that her friend should have been holding a cigarette between the first and second fingers when all the girl friends had teased her so much about the awkward way she had always smoked. Wasn't it symbolic, the Cudahy gal asked, with her eyes big and round, that Miss Farnson should have changed an old habit that way just when she died? Crossing the threads of the subconscious like that just as the threads of life got all tragically mixed. The Great Truths of existence, Miss Cudahy said tearfully, get all tangled up like that unless they are interpreted right. And maybe if the dead girl had been a little more of a believer in some things, the terrible accident wouldn't have happened."

"I'm dizzy but able to stand more," I said. "What kind of a screwball is this female?"

"Tut-tut," says Lew. "You're talking about two million bucks. She's a poor little girl who came out to Hollywood on a visit and got on the track of the Great Truths of Life."

"Yeah?"

"Heaven knows," said Lew more seriously, "I'd have thought two million dollars could keep its head. But I've seen bigger ones tumble. Miss Cudahy never saw anything like this village, Mike, and before she could catch her breath she went Hollywood nuts. That's the only explanation I can make. Not that I gave a damn after her crack about the dead girl holding a cigarette between the wrong fingers. And the cigarette staying there until it burned into the skin! Get it?"

"It can't be kosher," I said. "The cops would be howling bloody murder. If true, it means that someone shoved a lighted cigarette between the wrong fingers after the girl was dead, and left her there in the car with the motor running to cover up."

"Now," says Lew brightly, "we see all, know all. So it gets murder and I thought fast and hauled you back here. Miss Two Million Bucks didn't tumble she'd said anything that mattered. She had just thought of the cigarette while talking to me. I'm the only one who knows about it. She's been questioned by the police and newspaper men, and has testified at the inquest, and had her picture taken, and her soul is harrowed with grief, and all she wants now is to Get Away From It All, and let the Great Truths of Life assuage the tragedy of losing her best friend."

I had the car parked near Hollywood and Vine by then, and I sat there with a hand on the door eyeing Lew warily.

"Are you nuts?" I wondered. "Or was Miss Millions feeding you a line? It's been a long time since I'v heard such addled talk. And that brings me back to your crack about screwballs and someone called The Great Truth, Father Orion."

Lew was enjoying himself.

"Name your brand of nut and I'll pick it off the Hollywood tree," he offered. "Father Orion hangs up on one of the top branches, out near the tip. He doesn't go in for publicity, but I run across his name now and then. His Shrine of Truth is located away out in the hills beyond Laurel Canyon. He's got plenty of acres inside a burglar-proof fence out there, and his buildings and land are worth money. Some of the people who go for his line would rate headlines in any newspaper. And they're not all local folks. Disciples make pilgrimages here. He's got guest houses on the place for the ones who rate lodging while they're hanging around getting injections from the fountain of wisdom itself."

"What is it, a yoga racket?"

"Heaven knows," said Lew. "But it's profitable. You can tell me more about it after you come back from the joint."

"Say that again."

"You've going to be a disciple of The Great Truth, Father Orion," Lew informed me.

"Like hell I am!"

Lew was in fine fettle as he lighted a cigarette and sat there grinning at me.

"You'll arrive from the East with a pocketful of money, Mike. And if we're lucky, you'll get into the inner circle around Father Orion and inspect the skeletons in the closet. I've got it all figured out."

"When you figure anything out, it's time to run," I cracked back. "Why should I get next to this Father Orion?"

And for the first time Lew grew serious.

"That girl was murdered, Mike. Her contacts and life around Hollywood don't offer a reason. It wasn't even robbery. Her purse with money in it was beside her on the seat. I don't think this Cudahy girl knows anything. But from the way she talked, I gathered the dead girl wasn't in favor of her interest in Father Orion. Is that a motive for murder?"

"Is it?"

"You'll have to find out," says Lew, still serious. "And don't think if we pin this murder on someone after the police have called it accidental death or suicide, that it won't mean plenty of local business for the Blaine Agency."

"*If*," I repeated sarcastically. "And you had to plaster the job on me. All right—how do I become a disciple of this Father Orion?"

Lew grinned broadly again. "That's why I wanted you on this, Mike. I've done my share. The rest is up to you."

So I thought it over, grabbed an east-bound plane, and in the morning was at Chicago Police Headquarters with Brophy, one of the Blaine vice-presidents.

I framed the telegram that went out from the Missing Person's Bureau to Father Orion, Los Angeles.

AMNESIA VICTIM CARRYING LOS ANGELES AIRLINE TICKET AND CONSIDERABLE SUM OF MONEY ON PERSON IN CUSTODY OF THIS BUREAU AND UNABLE TO REMEMBER ANYTHING BUT DESIRE TO SEE FATHER ORION AT LOS ANGELES. PERSON UNABLE TO REMEMBER WHETHER CATHOLIC OR NOT. PLEASE ADVISE COLLECT TELEGRAM ANY KNOWLEDGE YOU MAY HAVE OF PARTY.
LIEUTENANT HOWELL

And in less than two hours the Lieutenant had a wire back.

PLACE AMNESIA VICTIM ON LOS ANGELES PLANE AND WIRE HOUR OF ARRIVAL. FATHER ORION WILL ASSUME RESPONSIBILITY.
JOHN PAIGE,
SECRETARY TO FATHER ORION.

"Hook, line and sinker," says I, in Lieutenant Howell's ofice. "Who could resist an amnesia victim with a pocketfull of cash?"

The Lieutenant, a gray-haired fatherly-looking man, scratched his head.

"It ain't according to the rules," he informed Brophy and me. "We'd usually investigate further before we let an amnesia case go off to strangers."

Brophy was more than dubious. He was worried. "Take good care of that money, Harris. I don't like to see so much of the Agency's cash being exposed to risk. I don't know why I let you talk me into this."

"You never can tell what'll happen in an amnesia case," I cracked, and back I went to the airport and headed west again with eight thousand dollars and some extra bills in my pocket and amnesia on my mind.

How does amnesia feel? I wouldn't know. L.A. was a vast blanket of sparkling lights when the big silver plane eased out of the late evening sky and settled on the airport. And the pretty little stewardess who gave me a parting smile and I walked down the portable steps into the blaze of light beside the plane.

Nine of us left the plane. Three were movie stars, and they walked into waiting photographers, flash bulbs and friends surging to greet them. And I walked past all that with a glassy look, wondering who was going to meet me and could I put this over.

A hand touched my arm. A smooth voice intoned: "Father Orion sends his greeting, Brother."

I said, "Ahhhh . . ." and then almost strangled as I caught sight of two men well off to one side who had stopped and were staring at me.

Jake Dennis and Larry Sweet if I never had a bad dream. Sweet's hand was on his stocky companion's arms. I could almost hear him saying: "Hold it, Jake."

Meanwhile Father Orion had sent his greetings.

Sweet and Dennis had caught me offguard. I didn't know what my face had revealed to the man who had touched my arm.

He was a head taller than I, a jolly, well-fed

young man with pink smiling cheeks and a stare that took me apart.

"I'm John Paige, Father Orion's secretary, Brother. I've never seen you before, have I?"

I shook my head and mumbled: "I was hop- ing you'd know me. Will Father Orion know me?"

The hand he put to my elbow wore a curious jade ring. His manner was cheerfully confident. "This way, Brother. Father Orion knows all Truth."

Dennis and Sweet were still watching as we walked away. I was in a sweat as to whether they'd hail me, and in another sweat as to whether they'd follow us.

"Everything went blank . . ." I mumbled to Paige.

"Yes, yes," he said soothingly. "But Father Orion has the light. Here's the car, Brother."

At least Father Orion gave the faithful good taxi service. Paige stowed me into the front seat of a big blue Cadillac sedan and we rolled away. I tried to see if we were being followed and had no luck. But those two flat-feet from Headquarters would at least get the license number.

"How long have you followed the Master?" Paige inquired.

"There's a—a wall in my mind," I said for- lornly. "In Chicago all I could remember was the name of Father Orion. I asked the police and— and they put me on the airplane."

"Quite right," Paige approved. "Strangers might have taken advantage of you. Remember any more now?"

"No." And I groaned: "It's terrible being like this!"

Paige dropped his hand on my arm. "You're with friends, Brother. Perhaps we'd better make sure you haven't any identifying papers on you. Let's see your billfold."

He parked at the curb, and I let him have the billfold and watched closely while he looked inside. Paige whistled softly at the hundreds and five hundreds Brophy had reluctantly turned over to me.

"A lot of money to be carrying around, Brother."

"There was more," says I vaguely. "The safe deposit box was almost full. I think I always keep money ready in the deposit box. But I—I can't remember where the box is. Will Father Orion tell me?"

"The Master knows all Truth," Paige stated. "Were you bringing this money, Brother, as a Love Offering?"

"I can't remember," I told him helplessly as I reached for the billfold.

So there we were without any secrets, as we rolled into the high wooded hills beyond Hollywood . . .

Lew Ryster had prepared me for Orion's Shrine. But Lew hadn't told all. Maybe Lew wouldn't have believed it himself. A side road led us to stone gate towers flanked by a high, close-meshed fence topped by strands of barbed wire.

"The top wire is electrified," Paige remarked casually as we paused in the glare of floodlights on the gate posts.

A guard unchained the gates and, as we rolled through, called: "Welcome, Brothers!"

And I gandered at the fellow and moved up another notch on the Hollywood nut tree. That big guard wore sandals on bare feet and a white cloak resembling a Roman toga. He had a curly brown beard and the bulging muscles and build of a ham wrestler. And the air of a wild-eyed fanatic.

The whole lay-out was getting a little more unbelievable as I came closer to Father Orion.

"Electricity?" I mumbled.

"Lots of electricity, Brother," Paige assured me cheerfully.

"But—but—"

"The Shrine, Brother, is guarded from dese-cration by all unbelievers and scoffers." Paige delivered the statement with a solemn manner and a deeper voice.

I said: "Ahhhh . . ."

Paige said nothing. The silhouette of his face was sterner, as if his manner at the station had been for the outside world.

There was nothing screwball about the muscles of that guard at the gate and the electrified fence. It made you wonder what would happen if Father Orion decided not to like a pilgrim. The eight grand cash inside my coat was folding money in any language. And if there did just happen to be murder in the background and Mike Harris stubbed his toe and got in bad—then what?

I'd have felt better with a gun tucked under my armpit or inside my shirt. But it wouldn't have looked kosher for Brother Amnesia to show up packing a rod. So I sat watchful and wary as we rolled up the winding driveway to the Shrine.

Here were broad smooth lawns and narrow paths to small rustic outbuildings haphazardly scattered back against the trees. A few dim bulbs on poles showed the paths and the driveway, and made clear and startling the big white, temple-like building that dominated the center of the broad lawns.

They called it a shrine and it looked like a pillared temple, with softly lighted windows and a wide flag-stone terrace all around. Our headlights picked out several figures on the terrace clad in the flowing white togas.

Paige turned the big car into a narrow side drive that skirted the trees and the small outbuildings. We stopped before one of the small buildings.

"You will live here, Brother," Paige said, getting out.

Not so bad. It was a snug little cabin built of peeled cedar logs, with screened windows, flower beds and a trellised vine.

"Is Father Orion here?" I wanted to know doubtfully.

"Father Orion," Paige said as he entered the cabin and switched on a light, "is now supervising the Evening Circle of Felicity. After you change into your robe and sandals, I'll take you into the Circle."

"Robe?" says I, eyeing the white garment Paige took from a hook and tossed on a narrow bed.

"I'll change also and come back for you," Paige nodded.

"B-but I'm dressed," I protested weakly.

Paige was stern. "Father Orion only sees those who put aside all things of the world. I'll return in fifteen minutes, Brother."

CHAPTER III
THE WOMAN IN BLACK

He drove off and under my breath I damned Lew Ryster again. Mike Harris in one of those Roman nightgowns! If someone I knew ever caught me out in that harness I'd never live it down.

But if I balked, I'd probably get no closer to Father Orion.

Outside in the night something was softly throbbing, throbbing.

It sounded like a drum, muted, beating a lazy irregular rhythm. I switched off the light, opened the door and traced the sound to the looming mass of the Shrine off there across the lawns.

More hocus-pocus. It stopped as I buckled on the sandals and stood up in the white toga, feeling like a fool.

They'd saved the day with a roomy inside pocket where I could carry the billfold. Brophy, back in Chicago, would have had a spasm if he'd known the company his eight grand was keeping now.

I lighted a cigarette and was wondering what gives next when Paige returned. He had changed into a white toga. One look and he snatched my cigarette and stamped it under a sandaled foot.

"Tobacco would desecrate the Shrine, Brother," he reproved. "This way."

So I smothered an impulse to slug Brother Paige and slap-slapped after him in the leather sandals.

Dew got on my feet. The cold night air blew up my bare legs under the toga. We looked like a couple of lost ghosts as we moved toward the Shrine, crossed the terrace and passed inside.

The lazy drumming had started again, and the soft rhythm was there at the other end of a big crowded patio which we had entered.

Shaded wall lamps filled the place with soft light. Men and women were moving about and sitting on couches, backless chairs and benches. Long ones, short ones, fat and thin, young and old, talking, laughing. All wore white togas and robes. Incense curled from small braziers toward the open sky and stars overhead.

Paige led me toward a dais at the far end. A thin, mystic-faced Oriental was seated cross-legged at one corner of the dais, head thrown slightly back, eyes closed as his hand beat out that lazy, irregular rhythm from a small drum.

And then the huge, white-bearded, patriarchal old man who stood up on the dais caught all my attention.

He had been sitting on a backless couch talking to a small group of men and women. They remained seated as he drew a flowing white toga close and stepped down off the dais to meet Paige. His voice was a dreamy rumble.

"Brother, we have been waiting for you. Is this the troubled one you went to greet?"

Paige gestured solemnly toward me. "Come from the shadows to seek the Truth, Master." And to me Paige said: "Where there is truth, there is peace. Father Orion greets you."

So I mumbled: "Ahhhhh . . ."

The drummer had paused. Voices had lowered as those near us took a gander at the newcomer. And I stood there in my bare gams and wondered what one did next.

He looked older than the hills and wiser than the Encyclopedia. A big arched nose like a beak came out of the center of the beard and his eyes had a dreamy fixed stare.

He held out a hand as if expecting it to be kissed. I shook it. The big fingers were long and supple, and they returned to toy slowly with the fringes of the beard.

In that dreamy rumble which made you wonder what his shout was like, Father Orion said: "Welcome, Brother, to the House of Truth."

"Truth," I breathed, half-closing my eyes.

He rumbled: "Your name is?"

"The name hasn't been remembered yet," Paige answered for me.

A big hand lifted in a benign gesture.

"Wordly names are put aside here anyway. We shall call him Brother Rudolph."

I started to protest and he cut me off in a dreamy chant.

"Brother Rudolph, you come seeking the great Truths of the past. The old forbidden secrets of the sacred lamas of Lhasa and the teachings of the sages long lost amid the blindness and ignorance of men. You have been seeking that which could not be found. What is it, Brother, for which you grope?"

I looked away for a moment. His manner had almost made me dizzy. I should have known that anyone who could run a show like this had something on the ball.

"My name," I told him meekly. "I want to know my name and where can I find my deposit box?"

Father Orion looked at me like a sleepwalker. "The Truth will be opened up to you. In your heart will be peace. Join our Circle of Felicity now, Brother, and open your heart to Peace."

Neat, eh, but not obvious. Paige didn't help it any by turning to the crowd and saying:

"I give you Brother Rudolph, a new seeker of Truth. Surround him with Felicity."

The drumming started again. They surrounded me, long ones, and fat ones, old ones and young ones, pushing heads at me from the togas and robes, clapping me on the shoulder, beaming, smiling, calling me Brother, giving me great bunches of Felicity as I edged through and kept a hand of Brophy's eight grand inside my toga.

And suddenly I gritted my teeth and swore under my breath as a foot kicked my bare shin bone. Then I froze as a voice cooed sweetly at my elbow.

"Welcome, Brother. Welcome, Brother Rudolph."

You can't guess! But I knew. Only one soft

cooing little voice in all the world could set my nerves quivering like this. I looked and I was right.

Trixie Meehan stood at my elbow with a leer on her lovely little face. The others probably thought Trixie was smiling. They didn't know the gal. They didn't know Trixie Meehan.

And who is Trixie Meehan? Brother, Trixie Meehan also works for the Blaine Agency. Pert and sweet, soft and cuddly, harmless as a kitten and luscious-looking to all big strong men— that's Trixie if you don't know her.

But I knew her. Trixie was smart, shrewd, fearless and tireless on a case. And her temper would make a scorpion blush and her little tongue could peel the hide off a brass-bound monkey. And when Trixie and I crossed trails on a case, it was usually *my* hide that took the peeling.

Under her breath Trixie said: "Brother! Oh, *Brother!*" And behind her hands she giggled: "If I could only get your picture, Brother!"

A fat lady was pouring garlic-scented Felicity in my ear and inviting me to sit on a couch.

"Madam," I said, "the young lady will tell me about Truth—and nothing but the Truth."

She forgot Felicity and Father Orion long enough to give Trixie a dirty look and crack back: "Where I come from, they don't call it Truth!"

But I already had Trixie's arm and was shoving her toward the other end of the patio.

"Listen, Ape, you're twisting my arm off!" Trixie said angrily under her breath. "And someone will see that we know each other!"

"I'd like to twist your little neck off!" I gritted. "Where did you come from?"

"We're on the same case, Mike."

"Who said so?"

"Lew Ryster sent me."

"I'll kill that doublecrossing so-and-so! He didn't say anything about you."

"And why should he? Let go my arm or I'll scream."

She would have too. The things Trixie Mee-

han would do if pushed hard enough would curdle your blood. I released her arm.

Trixie snapped: "Lew didn't say anything because he knew you'd have a spasm. And if you think *I* cried for the chance to work with the world's greatest ego, they haven't slipped you the proper dose of truth yet!"

Trixie glared at me—and in the midst of it suddenly began to giggle again. "Mike, have you looked in a mirror yet?"

"I have not," I said. "You'd fit in a Roman bath scene yourself. How long have you been here?"

"Since yesterday," says Trixie, ducking over to a couch where we could have a little privacy. "And Mike, I'm scared."

Trixie looked at me soberly. And I looked back, thinking that she was one of the few women in the place who looked appealing and sweet in the graveyard uniforms they issued.

"Afraid of what?" I asked.

Trixie shrugged slightly. "Nothing—and everything. This place is guarded like a prison farm."

"So I noticed."

"Look at them," said Trixie. "They're fanatical. They've turned their minds over to that old man."

"How many of them had a mind to start with?"

"Scratch deep enough," said Trixie, "and you'll find that most of them have a bank account. They weren't swept up out of the gutter to be loaded with Truth and Felicity."

"Somebody has to pay for the overhead," I said. "Look at me. I brought eight grand cash money along, and I've got more in a safe deposit box if I can ever recover from my attack of amnesia and think where it is."

"Does Father Orion know about the money?" Trixie asked quickly.

"Sister, the Master—knows all!"

"I'm trying to be serious, Mike!"

"Eight grand is always serious," I grinned. "What's wrong with the Master?"

"I'm afraid of him," Trixie said without hesitation. "Mike, these people *believe* in him!"

"Does Paige?"

"I don't know."

"Both of us are foggy then," I admitted. "The more I see of all this, the less sure I am—" I broke off, staring across the patio, and whistled softly in amazement.

"Don't mug," I said under my breath. "But get a load of that thin fellow with the black hair moving along the wall over there? He was looking at us."

"I knew talking to me this way was a fool stunt!" Trixie snapped.

"He's easing up for a gab fest with Father Time," I said. "Know him?"

"I'm not the local directory," says Trixie nastily. "I've only been here a day myself."

"He's dropped some weight," I said. "But four-five years ago in Philly he was a con-man just paroled. Eddy Voss was his name. Haggerty, who was in our Philadelphia office then, had helped send him up several years before."

"Did he see you with Haggerty?"

"I wish I knew."

"A stir-bird," says Trixie under her breath. "And now he's a crackpot with the rest of them. I don't believe it."

"They bait a mean hook around here for suckers, Baby."

"Nuts," says Trixie. "Do you see any more familiar faces?"

I was looking, and I was more uneasy about Voss than I let Trixie see. If he remembered me, what then? At the least I'd be tossed out on my ear. And I wondered what kind of dice he was throwing in this crowd.

"I can't spot anyone else," I told Trixie. "If you see Lew Ryster before I do, have him get Voss' record since the parole."

Trixie nodded.

"How did you crash the gate here?" I asked.

"I pretended I worked at the studio with Nancy Cudahy's dead friend," Trixie said wryly. "Nancy was loaded with Father Orion, and was telling me about him before we'd been together fifteen minutes. I asked for more. It wasn't hard to get her to bring me here."

"Where is the Cudahy girl?"

"Up there on the platform with Father Time," says Trixie. "That lumpy brunette with too much weight."

"That?" I said. "*That* worth two million bucks?"

"That," Trixie said.

I decided: "For a million bucks and a pair of smoked glasses I'd take a chance on her myself. Is she as big a fool as I hear?"

"Not as big a fool as most men who'd do anything for a pretty face or a bank account," Trixie said acidly. "She's bad enough. Tutors, guardians, servants and guards have insulated her from a lot she ought to know. That dumb-looking face hasn't helped her any. In a way I'm sorry for her."

"Poor kid."

"Like hell," says Trixie. "Not with millions. And don't make any passes at her. She tells me she's secretly engaged."

"Who's the lucky speculator?"

"She wouldn't say. It's a great big breathless secret. What are you going to do now, Mike?"

"Keep away from you and keep my fingers crossed."

"We'll both be happy then!" Trixie snapped. "Keeping away from you is one of life's pleasures!"

Trixie flounced away with a swirl of her white robe.

And I sat there trying to make two and two into five. How could you tie all this into a slick murder? The dead girl hadn't been one of this bunch. Father Orion had a neat enough racket. Why should he want anyone killed? And to add a little frosting to the cake, why was Eddy Voss here?

Meanwhile I had eight grand inside my robe and Felicity all around. And as I got up from the couch, the woman in black came in out of the night.

I was near the entrance to that big roofless patio. I was one of the first who saw that her pale face was molded in tragedy. I think I was the first to sense that her spirit was feeding on inner fires of suffering.

"Here's trouble, Mike!" I decided—and I drifted across the patio after her to see what would happen.

She wore the somber black of mourning. She was in her thirties, plain-looking, uninteresting. Probably like the others for she seemed to be at home here.

But now she stood out sharply from the rest of the gathering. She came in slowly, one hand clutching a black purse to her bosom. She traversed the long patio toward Father Orion with the same heavy steps.

Those who became aware of her stopped talking and watched as I was watching.

A few moved toward the dais after her as I did.

Father Orion saw her. He stood up, hesitated, and stepped slowly off the dais and waited for her.

By now most of the talk had died away. You could feel the quick tenseness, like the quiet before a storm. Eddy Voss left the side of the dais in a stealthy manner.

Father Orion toyed with his beard in that dreamy manner as the woman stopped before him. She did not speak loudly, but in the quiet her brittle voice sounded loud.

"He killed himself," she said. "He killed himself after they took the last of his money and kept on threatening him. He's dead. *You* know why he's dead. No one but *you* could have known. I've come all the way back here to settle with you."

Her voice gave no further warning. She was still talking when she snatched a gun from her black purse. The first blasting shot broke the tension.

Women screamed, men yelled. They fled in all directions and became a milling, helpless mob. And the woman stood there and emptied her gun at Father Orion.

I had leaped on a couch to see better. Her black-clad figure did not move as the small automatic in her hand blasted shots directly into Father Orion's chest.

There wasn't anything I could do. He didn't have a chance. It wasn't pretty to watch. A bloody execution never is particularly pretty.

Father Orion did not try to save himself. I saw it. He stood there with that big white beard over his chest and his arms half-lifted as if he might be blessing her while she poured bullets into his body.

The ripping roar of explosions was over in seconds. All the patio was in an uproar. And I stood frozen on a couch waiting for Father Orion to fall.

Eddy Voss dived in from one side, caught her gun hand and jerked her around to him. He hit her in the jaw. She dropped. And I jumped off the couch and pushed and shoved toward the spot.

Voss was trying to lift the woman's limp figure when I reached them. I caught her feet to help. And once more froze as the unbelievable happened.

Father Orion had stepped back on the dais and lifted his arms. His big hooked nose and half-closed eyes, his bushy white beard and uplifted arms made him like a prophet out of the old books. His voice came in a dreamy, awesome boom above the panic and the noise.

"Peace! Peace, Brothers! The Truth lives. The Great Truth lives undying."

A woman screamed. "It didn't hurt him! Master, they can't kill you!"

Guess who! Miss Two Million Bucks screamed that.

Other voices caught her up. "Master, they can't kill you!"

"Praise the Truth! Praise the Master!"

I almost shivered. They were like animals yapping with fanatical joy. And so help me that huge old man stood there on the dais, unharmed, unhurt.

I was close. I could see two of the bullet holes in the outer cloth of his robes. The holes were over his chest. He should have been dead, dying at least. And I could see no blood, no hurt, no break in the dreamy, unearthly manner.

Voss' eyes were black slits as he snarled:

"Pick her up! Pick her up! Toward that door back of you!"

The crowd was surging toward the dais as we started to carry the woman away. They weren't even thinking of her. Voss had slipped the gun into his pocket. I thought of her purse and didn't see it.

John Paige appeared beside me and snapped: "I'll take her!"

"She isn't heavy," I panted.

"I'll take her!" he snapped again, and elbowed me aside.

So I let him have her and started to follow them.

Paige was excited. His voice broke at me. "We don't need you. Go on back!"

"Scram!" Eddy Voss threw at me. His eyes were black coals. He looked like he might start shooting himself.

So I turned back. Starting a fight with those two wouldn't get Mike Harris any information.

I pushed back toward the dais hoping to find the woman's purse. No sign of it. I looked again to make certain Father Orion was all right. He was.

By now I was thinking again. You don't do tricks with bullets from modern automatics, even if it is small. But you can stop 'em with bullet-proof vests.

And bullet-proof vests mean that someone expects to get shot at now and then. People don't shoot because they're taught the Great Truth of Life.

Trixie Meehan hauled at my elbow.

"I've got her purse, Mike!"

"Slip me!" I said quickly. "Find out where Paige and Voss are taking that woman. See what they do with her. They ran me away. It'll look suspicious for me to watch them now!"

Trixie gave me the black purse and hurried off like the little trouper she was in a pinch. And for once I was thankful for the bedsheet I was wearing. Under cover of the robe I emptied the purse into the pocket where my money was. Back in the crowd again I dropped the purse on the floor.

As near as I could tell from a quick look, my haul was some paper money and coins, a Pullman check, vanity, nailfile, a little memorandum book, a crumpled envelope and a small handkerchief.

She had spoken of a man who had killed himself, had charged Father Orion with the responsibility. The idea was hot enough to sizzle. A plain trail of death pointed to Orion! And if once, why not twice? Like, say, Frances Farnson? Well, why not?

So we had more mystery. Ideas began to rattle in my mind. A nebulous thought took form, so startling that I almost shrugged it off.

The woman in black could have settled the idea in a few minutes. But would I have a chance to talk with her? I would not. Paige and Voss' manner had left no doubt that I wasn't wanted around her.

I wondered if they suspected me? But why should they? What cop would turn up carrying eight thousand dollars?

Would they turn her over to the police? Don't be silly. By now I could see that this guarded estate in the hills north of Hollywood could settle its own troubles.

I smiled at the thought of Larry Sweet and Jake Dennis. They'd give something to be in on this. Chances were that Jake Dennis was still profanely wondering why I'd appeared on that Chicago plane.

Trixie came back. "They took her through that door, Mike. It's locked."

"What's beyond the door?"

Trixie shrugged.

"Will the Cudahy girl know?" I asked.

"Maybe."

"Ask her. But first, you'd better get outside and see if they're taking her away."

Trixie nodded. "Where are you staying, Mike?"

"Fourth—no, fifth cabin—to the right of the driveway."

"We're two cabins from the eating pavilion. Sometimes Nancy spends the night. And the more I see of this the less I like it," Trixie said as she turned away.

CHAPTER IV
HITTING THE PIPE

Paige was back on the dais a moment later, leaning close as he spoke to Father Orion. The old man nodded. Paige lifted his voice for quiet.

And when he had quiet, Paige called: "The woman dropped her purse. Who has it?"

"Here, Brother." A reedy eager little man pushed forward with the purse.

Paige solemnly lifted his hand.

"You have seen. The woman is mad. The Master orders that there be no mention of this."

"No mention," Father Orion boomed dreamily.

"Another day ends," Paige told them. "There will be no ceremonies tonight. The Master gives you Peace and Truth."

"Peace and Truth!" Father Orion intoned.

So we were eased out, and I had to leave also. Voss hadn't appeared. Outside I made a circuit of the big white building. Trixie wasn't in sight.

The woman had fainted, Paige had said. Fooey. I wondered what Paige would think when he found the purse empty.

The brethren and sistern were scattering. I headed for my cabin to shuck out of the white sheet. I'd left my suit over the foot of the bed with a few flakes of cigarette ash scattered where they'd do the most good. The little gray flakes had vanished from the suit fabric.

So my clothes had been frisked. I lighted a cigarette and was reaching for the loot inside my robe when Paige knocked and entered hurriedly.

"I'll lock your money in the safe tonight," he told me.

"Don't bother," I said. "It's safe with all that electricity around and Father Orion near." And I added: "Brother, I'm afraid I'll forget where *this* money is if I lock it up anywhere."

"Nonsense," Paige said.

"Tomorrow, Brother, I'll look for the Truth about it."

"Take my advice in this," Paige insisted.

"Tomorrow," I promised. "Tomorrow, Brother."

Paige looked as if he were not sure whether he was being kidded or not. A slight smile followed.

"Tomorrow," he agreed. "We'll settle everything tomorrow. Remember, Brother, no smoking near the Master."

He left as abruptly as he entered—and I hadn't been so near a chill in years.

Father Orion, Paige and the disciples were funny on the surface. The guarded estate and fantastic Shrine of Truth were good for a laugh. But some crackpots are only a hair-line from an asylum. And a madhouse can have its horrors.

Paige had just called me "Brother." His changed manner had suggested "Sucker." I switched off the light and got into my clothes fast.

And when the money went back inside my coat I damned myself for thinking of such a stunt. But then I hadn't thought it possible to walk into a situation like this.

The purse loot was next. I drew the curtains before I switched on the light to take inventory.

The money came to fourteen dollars and some coins. The Pullman check didn't tell me much at the moment. A Philadelphia pawnshop ticket made out to Mrs. H. Mossman dropped out of the memorandum book. The crumpled letter was postmarked Bridgeport, Connecticut, and was addressed to Mrs. Harry Mossman, at a North Side address in Philadelphia.

Dear Mae:

I can't loan you any more. And I don't see how you and Harry can need so much cash. Last year when you folks came back from Los Angeles and bought the garage, you were well fixed. For that matter I never could see why Harry sold out and came back. He was doing well and liked the Coast. If business is so bad, Harry had better sell out and take a job somewhere. We're all well here. We'd like you two to come up and visit us.

Your Affct. Brother,

SAM

The memorandum book held bridge scores, a housewife's small notation, some addresses, mostly in the East, several in Los Angeles.

But I had my information. She'd come from Philly. She'd been to a pawnshop just before she left, evidently to get rail-road fare.

Fourteen dollars wouldn't take her back. She hadn't been thinking of going back. I had seen her, heard her. There wasn't any doubt in my mind that the woman had been obsessed with the one idea of getting to L.A. and emptying a gun into old Orion. After that it didn't matter.

She'd lived in Los Angeles. She'd been one of the disciples. For some reason her husband had moved to Philadelphia. If you asked Mike Harris, the husband might have gone to Philly to get his wife away from these lunatics.

Suddenly the husband had begun to need cash money. His wife had borrowed from her brother. When the money was all gone, the husband had shot himself. Only a hockshop had gotten the woman back to Father Orion.

All that I knew now. But I didn't know why the husband had bankrupted himself without a squawk and finally shot himself.

The woman could tell me. But could I talk to her in the privacy I had to have? Would she be alive that long? Would I be alive that long?

Sounds jittery, doesn't it? Well, I had Brophy's eight grand, and Father Orion's madhouse all around, and a dead girl down the hill in Hollywood and a dead man in Philadelphia. I'd witnessed an automatic spitting bullets at Father Orion.

A little cool thought about the situation was enough to lift the hair on a sane man's head.

So I tucked the contents of the purse under the mattress, switched the light off again and opened the door quietly.

The local disciples had been driving automobiles off the estate. When I stepped outside, the grounds seemed pretty well deserted. The Shrine was dark. Most of the overhead lights along the paths had been turned off. Here and there I could see the dim-lit windows of occupied cabins. The white shape that suddenly appeared at the corner of my cabin made me jump and swear violently.

"Iss forbidden," I was sternly informed.

"Forbidden hell!" I said, mad because he'd surprised me out of a week's growth. I needed growth at the moment. This toga-clad fellow was almost as big as the guard at the gate. "What's forbidden?" I asked.

"Go out," he said in an accent thick enough to slice.

"Yeah?" I said. "Who's forbidden and who said so?"

"Everyone—you," he told me. "Father Orion orders."

"The hell with Father Orion," I started to say—and didn't. Such talk wouldn't do me any good around here. "Where's Paige?" I snapped.

"Don' know."

"Where's Father Orion?"

"Don' know. You sleep now, huh?"

"Yeah?" I said. "Oh, sure, I'll sleep."

He was big and the white toga made him look bigger. He was carrying a stick. I couldn't see whether he had a gun.

"You go back," he said.

"Sure," I said.

What else? His yell would have brought others. I might have ducked into the woods, reached the fence and gotten outside the guarded gate some way. But I didn't think so. Back inside the dark cabin I began to fumble around as quietly as I could.

Ten minutes it took me, maybe a little more. When I finally looked past the edge of the window shade, the white toga was still out there a few feet from the front door. And for once I could have said a kind word for the sheet-wrapped brigade. They were easy to see at night.

The door hinge creaked. He was turning around when I started out, so I talked fast.

"Look," I said. "I've got to see Father Orion."

"Tomorrow," he said stolidly.

"Tonight," I said, walking up to him.

"What iss?" he asked suspiciously, looking down at my left hand.

"Money," says I, holding it out. "I found it in the cabin. Look, Brother, look."

He took the money instinctively. Maybe I'd have done the same. And I slugged him with the twisted pillow cases in my right hand and he went down with a funny grunting sound.

I forgot to say that the two pillow covers, one inside the other for strength, had a heavy doorknob knotted in the end. I'd used my knife point for a screwdriver to get the knob off. It was almost as good as a blackjack. For a moment I was afraid I'd caved his skull.

But I hadn't. He was breathing heavily when I dragged him inside, turned the light on and began to tear sheets to tie and gag him. When I was through, he was through too, bound, gagged, helpless on the floor.

His eyes opened. He struggled, made sounds behind the gag and glared up at me.

I hefted the wooden club, which felt like it was loaded with lead in the end, and grinned at him.

"Brother," I said, "it's forbidden. You sleep now, huh—or I'll bust you one with this bat you were carrying."

He was silent and glaring when I turned the light off again and slipped out.

The estate was weird now in its quiet. Many of the cabins had gone dark. I wondered if more of the guards were creeping around. And I wondered where the woman in black was, and where Trixie Meehan was, and would it be safe to go to the cabin that Trixie was occupying with the Cudahy girl.

I decided to take a chance. Second cabin from the eating pavillion, Trixie had said.

The cabin was lighted. A small radio was playing softly inside. When I knocked cautiously the light went out, the music stopped.

"That's Trixie, all right," I thought. "And she doesn't know anything or she'd have looked me up. So what now?"

And the door opened, a girl slipped out and threw her arms around me, crying softly: "Darling! Sweetheart!"

"Wrong number, sister," I said, trying to untangle her from my neck.

She'd already discovered that. She uttered a little scream as she jumped back.

"I thought you were John!" she stammered.

Lightning does strike now and then. Miss Two Millions made a bull's-eye with her confused comment—and I knew something I'd been wondering about. I thought fast before I spoke.

"Paige is busy just now," I said. "He wanted me to tell you to—er—wait for him."

"I didn't think he could get back from town so quickly," she babbled. "Who—who are you?"

"I've a message for Miss Meehan."

"She isn't here."

"Where is she?"

"I don't know. She—she didn't come back from the Felicity Circle."

"That's funny," I said calmly. "I wonder where she could be?"

Inside I wasn't calm. I was suddenly afraid for Trixie. The night was too quiet, too ominously quiet. Paige had made a quick night trip into town for some reason—and Trixie was the first reason I thought of. Could she have been carried helplessly off the estate? And would Trixie's body be found tomorrow somewhere down in the city, accidentally dead?

"Paige didn't tell me where he was going," I said. "Do you know any way I could get hold of him quickly?"

She said, "No," and it sounded suspicious. So did the question that followed. "Who are you? I don't believe I know you."

"I'm Mike Harris," I said. "Hasn't John told you about me?"

"No."

"He will, Miss Cudahy," I promised, chuckling. "He'll have a lot to say about me. I'll look around for Miss Meehan. If she comes back, tell her I'm looking for her."

I left before she could think to turn on the light. One look and she'd have me spotted as Brother Amnesia. And she wouldn't be dumb enough not to smell a rat about my sudden familiarity with Paige's secrets.

And so Paige was her sweetheart, her darling. Smooth, eh? Smoother than I had thought. Sweetheart and darling to millions! Who said there wasn't any profit in being a crackpot?

But there wasn't any profit in Mike Harris wandering around Father Orion's zoo. Everything that happened was making the situation worse. And what about Trixie?

I was afraid—afraid for Trixie Meehan as I walked toward the big white shrine, the loaded club swinging in my hand and growing anger seething inside. Crackpots or no crackpots, if any harm came to Trixie I'd take the whole place apart.

The building was dark and seemed deserted. I skirted the terrace on the damp grass and made a circle of the shrine. Not a light, not a sound.

The patio entrance was open. I slipped inside and felt my way to the door through which Eddy Voss and Paige had carried the woman.

The door was unlocked. A dark hall was on the other side. Dark? It was an inky solid, with a tiled floor underfoot and rough plastered walls on either side. And the silence of a tomb.

I was wasting time. This wasn't finding Trixie, wasn't getting anywhere. I was sniffing unconsciously before I realized what I was doing.

The sickly pungent odor that tainted the air was familiar. Then I got it. Marijuana. So I wasn't alone. Somebody was dragging on the weed close by. A slight draft was moving against my face and I followed it up, and almost walked into a blank wall as the passage made a sudden left-hand turn.

The marijuana fumes were stronger. A partly opened door around the passage turn let out a beam of sickly light, and a voice was mumbling in a dreamy, monotonous monotone. Hefting the club, I crept to the door and looked in.

You could have knocked me over with a marijuana weed. Father Orion was doing the mumbling. Across the room he sat cross-legged with his back to a heap of gay silk pillows. The white toga had been put aside, sandals and bullet-proof vest were gone. He wore a white loin cloth, sat cross-legged like an Oriental, holding the mouthpiece of a water pipe.

A shaded lamp on the floor showed his eyes set in a fixed dull stare. His dreamy monotone was directed into space, and the words were strange and unfamiliar.

A thousand years ago the Egyptians had smoked marijuana like this bony, rather terrible old man across the room. Only the Egyptians had called it hashish.

They too had had their fantastic dreams swirling lazily through drugged minds. And so had Father Orion. You could see it on his face. He'd been partly doped out there in the patio. Hashish gave him that piercing, dreamy stare, that remote manner.

Now he half-turned to suck at the mouthpiece. His back and chest were criss-crossed by livid weals that seemed to be scars left by whips. You could only wonder what gruesome experiences he had lived through far back in the past.

He began to mumble again as I pushed the door open.

I was inside the room before I saw the thin Oriental who had been beating the drum out in the patio. He sat back in the shadows to the right, cross-legged on the floor also, watching, listening as if in a trance.

But he wasn't in a trance. He turned his head. For a long moment we stared at each other. His eyes were like dark bright buttons. He seemed to shrink in on himself and tense as I took a step toward him.

"What's the idea?" I asked, jerking my head toward the old man.

The fellow was dark-skinned, wiry, middle-aged. He might have been thirty or fifty. His thin-lipped face held no expression as he stared.

Father Orion mumbled into space without noticing us.

I wanted to swear. My pulses were jumping. The white loin cloth looked brilliant against the dark, oily skin. His torso muscles had tightened, ridged, until he seemed poised with threat as he sat there cross-legged and silent to my question.

A master mind might have bluffed it out easily. But tonight I wasn't master-minding. I was only Mike Harris, with a club in my hand and seething anger suddenly wild and reckless as I faced discovery, alarm and the blow-up of everything I was trying to do.

"Which one of you talks first?" I said.

I had started toward him when he jumped at me. One instant he was sitting cross-legged; the next he was flying through the air in an uncanny leap, white teeth gleaming and his hand flashing up from the loin cloth with a knife.

No time to talk, to dodge. I didn't want to dodge anyway. I swung at his knife hand, hit it, smashed the hand aside. He landed like a cat, fighting and clawing. And the biggest claw was the knife which he had grabbed with the other hand.

The blade slashed my arm as I tried to parry the blow. I dropped the club and slugged him in the face with my fist. He staggered back on his heels and I jumped after him and hit him again.

He could use a knife but he didn't savvy fists. He tried to dodge, but I'd softened him into stumbling awkwardness. His chin turned just right. I hooked one to the button—and he dropped the knife and went down, glassy-eyed and cold.

Panting, I snatched the knife and club and turned to Father Orion. And still he hadn't noticed us, hadn't stopped mumbling. It was enough to give you the creeps.

He started to suck on the mouthpiece of the water pipe again, and I shoved the end of the club through the middle of the beard and pushed him back against the pillows.

"Come out of it, you dope!" I panted. "Can you understand me?"

He shook his head dazedly and his eyes cleared a trifle. "Truth," he mumbled. "Truth, Brother."

"Truth hell!" says I. "Where did John Paige go? What did he do with that woman who shot at you?"

"Brother," he said vaguely. "What do you desire, Brother?"

"Absolutely nuts!" I said through my teeth.

"And people who ought to be sane are looney because of you! Come out of the clouds, damn you!"

His eyes had already closed. He mumbled inaudibly as he sank back on the pillows. I knew it wasn't any use. He was off on a nod and man nor beast couldn't get sense out of him. I swore at him, wondering what I could do now.

Trixie Meehan's cry of warning took care of that.

"*Look out, Mike!*" Trixie's faint cry sounded somewhere outside the room.

CHAPTER V
CAT O'NINE TAILS

I whirled around with the club and knife—and saw the man inside a doorway across the room. He was in the shadows. I saw the gun before I recognized the face behind it.

He thought I was coming at him. Maybe I was. Trixie's voice had set me wild for the moment, and I'd gone too far now to back out.

The lick of fire from the gun muzzle, the roaring reverberations of the report, the numbing shock that paralyzed my left shoulder and arm and side, all seemed to come at once.

I staggered back and couldn't help it. Father Orion's companion was sprawled on the floor behind me. His hand clamped on my ankle and jerked me in a sprawling fall such as I had given him.

The floor didn't seem hard. Maybe my mind was numb too. Trying to fight both men off a moment later was like a slow-motion picture. I couldn't do what I wanted to do. And I was waiting for the second shot and wishing I had Father Orion's bullet-proof vest. Eddy Voss was behind the gun and I thought he was going to finish what he had started.

He didn't. The gun muzzle tapped my head and made me foggier—and then they both yanked me to my feet.

"You want another?" Eddy Voss was snarling. "Keep quiet or I'll blow your damn face off!"

So I kept quiet as they held me. Warm blood was crawling sluggishly down my left arm. I was dizzy, gasping for breath, sick and weak with the shock and the pain that was beginning to replace the numbness.

"Bring him in here!" Eddy gritted.

Beyond the door was a short, windowless corridor, dimly lit by a single bulb. The floor was carpeted, the walls seemed to be covered with leather over some kind of padding. There were five doors on each side of the corridor. I counted them. Ten doors, covered as the walls were. One stood partly open, and it was as thick and massive as an icebox door.

The little cell-like room inside was padded also; and as Eddy Voss jerked the door wide I saw Trixie sitting on an iron-framed couch in the center of the tiny room.

"Mike!" Trixie said, and then gasped as she saw the blood that had smeared down over my wrist and hand. "Oh, Mike, what did he do to you?"

Eddy Voss sneered at her. "I oughta finished him off in there. So you two know each other? Ain't that interesting?"

Trixie was pale, tiny and pretty in her helplessness as she sat there in the white robe with one of her wrists fastened to a corner of the bed by a short chain.

Chains and handcuffs hung from the other three corners of the beds, so that a person could be spread-eagled there helplessly. The low-ceilinged room seemed to crowd in and smother. Even our voices sounded flat and muted.

I felt cold enough to shiver through the pain as I realized that with the massive door closed all sounds would probably be smothered in the windowless, padded room.

"I met the lady tonight," I said. "We talked a little. What the hell's the idea of putting her in here?"

"Just met her tonight?" Voss said.

"That's right."

"So she lets out a yell when she thinks something is going to happen to you. Just met her— and she knows your voice clear from the other room. And she's ready to faint when she gets a look at you."

"He's bleeding!" Trixie said unsteadily. "Why don't you stop it before he's lost too much?"

"Look at her," Voss said to me. "A hard-boiled little tramp like she's been the last half hour, getting all washy about you. Do I look dumb?"

"Damn dumb," I said. "How much of this do you think you can get by with?"

"Plenty," Voss told me, and he spoke to Trixie. "Maybe if we hold him here until he bleeds long enough, you'll talk."

"I doubt it," said Trixie, and I could have patted her on the back for the way her chin went up and her eyes flashed at him.

We weren't talking like crackpots now. Eddy Voss didn't look like one, although he still wore the toga and sandals. His thin face was hard, sneering, intent as he looked from Trixie to me and back to Trixie.

"She was snooping around here trying to see what she could discover," Voss said. "And now you show up doing the same thing. I heard you asking about that fool woman who popped off tonight. And you're the guy who lost his memory and didn't know what it was all about."

"I'm learning," says I, seeing that the amnesia role was washed up.

"Hold him, Ali," he said.

Ali could understand English all right. He nodded and clung to my right arm while Voss frisked me and found the fat billfold.

"Christ!" Voss said under his breath when he got a look at the money. "No wonder Paige said you were his private sucker." Voss spat and grinned as he put the billfold inside his toga. "This'll teach him a lesson."

Blood was dripping off my finger tips. I caught Trixie's eyes watching it. "I'm all right," I said.

But I wasn't. Trixie knew it. So did Voss. He grinned again as he looked at the arm.

"You won't last long if that isn't fixed," he said.

"So what?" I said.

He hit me in the face. Ali held my good arm while Voss knocked me reeling against the padded wall with blow after blow. I heard Trixie cry out, but Voss was yelling at me in a sudden fury.

"I'll fix you, you redheaded little squirt! I'll have you chained in a cell and let Ali work on you with one of his whips! Who else is with you? What are you here for? I'll find out who you are and what the money's for! Will you talk? *Will you talk?*"

His nerves weren't any better than mine had been before I found Father Orion. He had me, but he was afraid of what he didn't know. He spoke of whips—and I thought of Father Orion's whip-scarred body and these sound-proofed cells fitted up to chain people helplessly for any kind of torture.

Father Orion and his cultists were grotesque, unreal—but this was a look into depths more horrible than I could have suspected. And if I'd get what Voss was shouting, what would Trixie get? What would happen to us both if Voss was sure we were detectives?

I knew. I guess Trixie knew too. Voss probably already had his mind made up. We'd seen too much, we knew too much. There wasn't a chance even now of either one of us getting down into Hollywood to tell our stories.

So I fainted. It's always a good gag, whether the girls use it or Mike Harris tries it in a tight spot. Back against the padded wall I slumped with Ali still holding my arm. Eddy Voss dropped his fist.

"Damn him!" he gasped. "I—"

My foot caught him in the stomach when he got that far. Never mind Ali, never mind Eddy's gun; braced against the wall I had the leverage I needed. The shoe went deep in his middle and hurled him back over the bed where Trixie was held.

"The gun!" I yelled. "Get the gun, Trixie!"

She didn't need the order. Little Trixie could think faster than most men. She had the whipcord muscles of an adagio dancer. She was already grabbing at Voss as he tumbled off the bed on the other side.

Trixie had the full length of her arm and the short chain to move in. Voss' coat ripped as she caught it and yanked. He had hardly struck the floor when Trixie was off the bed and down on her knees catching at him.

Ali uttered a gobbling, unearthly cry as he released my arm and dived toward her. I tripped him and grabbed at him. His slippery arm went out of my fingers as he fell on all fours.

I couldn't see what Trixie was doing as I lurched down on Ali. He bounced up from under me like a ball of buttered muscles—and in the same instant Trixie raised up with the gun in her hand.

It was good to see the business-like look on Trixie's face and to know that she could handle any gun like an expert. Ali must have sensed it, must have realized that he didn't have a chance with the gun so close. He whirled with the startling rapidity which had surprised me in the other room and darted toward the door.

Trixie fired at him, high deliberately, and he streaked out the door and vanished.

"Hurry, Mike!"

Trixie crouched at the foot of the bed with the gun covering Eddy Voss. When I staggered to her side, Voss was holding his middle and weakly trying to sit up. He looked sick, dazed.

"Keys are in his right trousers pocket, Mike!"

I had them a moment later.

"That littlest one, Mike!"

A moment later Trixie was free and on her feet. She handed me the gun, caught Voss' wrist, and had it in the steel bracelet before Voss could resist.

"Good work, Sweetness," I told her.

And only then did Trixie's voice break, quaver as she came to me.

"Mike, dear, are you badly hurt? Here, let me see!"

My lip was bleeding. My face felt like it had been jumped on. The pain had been there in my shoulder but I'd been too busy to notice it. Now I did. With clenched teeth I let Trixie get my coat off, jerk my shirt off.

The arm wasn't pretty to look at. Trixie used the shirt for a swab.

"Can you use the arm, Mike?"

"Yes—fingers too," I groaned after trying.

"Not as bad as I thought," says little Trixie briskly. "The bleeding is slowing up too. I'll wrap it quickly."

"We've got to get out of here, Baby! That bird in the breech clout will have the whole place around our ears!"

Trixie ripped half of Voss' toga off with one pull and tore strips off the edge.

"Only a minute, Mike. And that woman's in the room across the hall. We can't leave her. They'll kill her."

"I'd like to take Voss," I said as Trixie hastily bandaged the shoulder.

Voss' head jerked up in surprise at hearing me mention his name.

"Yes, you louse, I know you," I said. "And the next time you won't draw a parole. What's the racket here?"

His face had gone pasty. He was afraid, and defiant too, like a rat in a corner.

"That'll do for a little," said Trixie. "Hurry, Mike. Maybe we've waited too long now."

I stopped and grabbed my billfold back from the remnant of Voss' toga.

"If we turn up without *this*," I said, "we might as well keep going."

"That damn money!" Trixie exclaimed. "If you ever do a trick like that again, I'll—I'll—"

"I'll do it for you," I promised.

We were across the hall by then and I was trying keys in the door. The third one made it. The door swung out.

"Come on, lady," I said. "We're taking you out of here."

She was on the floor by the bed, as if she'd rolled off and hadn't moved after she landed. I had a premonition. Trixie beat me to it. She was pale and shaken as she looked up from the woman.

"Dead, Mike!" Trixie exclaimed.

"Murdered?" I said.

Trixie picked a little pill box off the floor and held it up so I could see the poison label.

"She killed herself, Mike."

"I'd call it murder, anyway," I said. "Hell, what a joint they've been running here right under the noses of all Hollywood. Let's get out of here while the getting is good."

I was afraid again, mostly for Trixie. What chance would she have if they caught her now? For that matter what chance had she had chained in that padded cell? At least we had a gun now, with a few cartridges left.

I lingered long enough to lock Eddy Voss in, and the woman too. If no more keys were handy, it would be a long time before anyone beat the police to them. And I wanted the police now. Jake Dennis, Larry Sweet and a squad of big-footed dicks would have looked sweeter than taffy on a stick.

I know! I hadn't solved the murder that Lew Ryster had tossed in my lap. But I'd done something bigger. I'd smashed this whole vicious, gruesome mess wide open. That was enough work for one night.

And there was still more to do. There was Nancy Cudahy. A fool she might be. But also she was a dumb innocent kid with dollars stacking the cards against her.

What chance did she have against men like Eddy Voss, Paige and Father Orion? She'd lost her head in Hollywood, she'd taken a dizzy tumble, she'd fallen in love. Maybe love had thrown her off balance. They say a woman in love is just a woman, or something like that. I wouldn't know.

"Hurry, Mike," says little Trixie unsteadily.

"Hold it," I said. "I want to see what's in a couple of these other rooms. I've got a hunch."

"You idiot!" says Trixie, half-crying. "Can't you *ever* forget you're a detective? You're half-dead now! Please come on, Mike! I can't have anything more happening to you!"

"What's happening to me—and who cares?" I said as I unlocked another door and opened it.

No soap. Unoccupied.

"One more," I said to Trixie, who was all but hanging on my bad arm to get me started.

"Mike!" Trixie wailed. "Can't you see what this is doing to me?"

"You sound worse than a woman in love," I cracked. "Buck up, baby. It isn't as bad as that. I'll get you out of here all right."

"Oh!" says Trixie. "Why you insuffer-able—"

"*Holy cow!*" I yelped. "*Now* will you shut up?"

I'd turned across the padded corridor and unlocked a door on the other side. Trixie cried out in pity. I felt a little sick myself as we forgot everything else but the man who was spread-eagled and handcuffed face down on the narrow bed in the center of the room.

A leather cat-o-nine-tails hung on the wall. The man's back was covered with bloody weals. He lay there like dead—but the sound of my voice brought his head up with a convulsive jerk and a whimpering cry of fear.

He was young, unshaven, rough-looking and powerful. He might have been a dock-worker at one time, or a sailor. His arms were tattooed. But he had starved, suffered; ribs showed plainly and his face was haggard, hollow-eyed as he stared at us.

"All right, fellow," I said. "We're going to take you out of here. Tell us about it later."

He wasn't telling anything. He was like a man who'd had fear beaten into his heart and soul and was expecting more. I'll never forget the fearful look of his eyes as he watched me free his hands. And the unbelieving, smoldering look as his hands came free and I moved to his feet.

I saw him eyeing Trixie and the gun she was holding as I unlocked the last ankle.

"We're detectives," I said quickly. "We're tak-ing you down to Hollywood to the police. Don't get us wrong and make a grab for that gun."

He shuddered and seemed to relax and all but collapse as he swung his feet to the floor. He hadn't spoken; his voice was husky and strained as he stood up.

"Police? You're *police?*"

"That's right," I said. "Come on. We may have to fight our way out of here. They're wise to us. Can you run? How'll you be in a scrap?"

He flexed his arms. The muscles bulged.

"God! Can I fight?" he gulped thickly as we started to the door. "All I want is that brown devil who whipped me every day and that old man who watched and mumbled like it was church service. I'll kill 'em both! I'll kill 'em with my bare hands!"

My club and knife were still on the floor of the room where Father Orion lay back on the pillows breathing stertorously. I was stooping for them when our man saw old Orion and jumped at him with an animal-like cry.

Trixie gasped: "Mike, he'll kill him!"

And he would have too. His hands had plunged through the white beard and grabbed the throat. He was shaking that bony, drugged old carcass in a frenzy when I reached him.

"The cops'll get him!" I snapped. "Come on!"

He wouldn't listen. He was in a frenzy. Maybe he didn't even hear me.

"I'll shoot him!" says little Trixie. "Come on, you big baboon! You're making trouble for us!"

Trixie got to him where I'd have failed. He looked at her angry little face and the gun she was holding on him, and batted his hand across his eyes and laughed sheepishly.

"I shoulda counted ten first," he mumbled, looking down at the half-strangled heap of beard and bones he had dropped. "Come on."

That inky black passage I led them into was like a trip through a macabre nightmare. The breech-clouted brown man had had time enough to call an army. The shrine might have held twenty men by now, waiting for us at any step. And I didn't have much fight left. I was weak, wobbly and beginning to feel light-headed.

But the door at the end was there as I'd shut it. The starlight in the silent patio was bright by comparison. And when we were outside on the terrace I sucked in the cool night air thankfully.

"If we could get an auto," I said, "it'd be easier. Paige is in town. Might be we could get the cops back here before he returns—or meet him on the road somewhere. Or if we could find a telephone around the joint. Trixie, know where the phone is?"

"No," says Trixie. "In the shrine there somewhere, I think. I didn't have a chance to see much. I was looking around outside when that Eddy Voss slipped up on me. He and that gobbling mute who got away from us were looking around out there as if they expected someone to come along."

"Paige!" the boy with us growled. "That's the name of the fellow who got me into this! Picked me up on Pershing Square and said he had a job working around his estate. Brought me up here himself—and I was locked up before I knew what was happening."

"I don't get it," I said. "What's the idea?"

"I dunno," he said. "I thought they were all crazy—and then I thought I'd go crazy when I found what was happening to me. That old man talking to me by the hour about his dirty heathen gods, and how he'd been to India and Egypt and Tibet and Africa and learned all there was to know about everything. And how the great crystal springs of truth could only come from eternal pain and punishment. And then he'd stand there with his eyes wild and talk and yell stuff I couldn't understand while that brown-skinned devil whipped me! Ten days I'd been there and only fed half the time—and I got the idea from things he said that there'd been others before me and if I died there'd be others after me. I was going nuts. A day or two more was about all I could have lasted. I knew I didn't have a chance. I was just Joe Clark, on the bum and nobody even knowing I'd drifted into California. Mister, what's all this about anyway?"

"Joe," I said, "I'm not sure about it all myself. After we get out of here, we can sit down and put the pieces together."

"We'll get out now! Hell, we're as good as out!"

"There's a fence around here that a monkey would have a hard time climbing over," I said.

"And the top wire is charged with electricity, I was told. Or warned. The gates are chained and guarded. Figure the percentage yourself."

"What sort of a place is this? Ain't there any law around here?"

"Sure there is," I said. "If we can get past that fence and down the mountain to Hollywood. Keep your fingers crossed until then."

We had been talking under our breath as we hurried across the smooth clipped lawns toward the cabin I'd occupied. The gate was in that direction. I didn't want to get any further away from the gate. And I looked around for a parked automobile that we might have a chance of taking.

It was Trixie who said huskily: "Over there, Mike! Running towards us!"

I looked over to the left and saw ghosts!

CHAPTER VI
THE GREAT TRUTH

They looked like ghosts at any rate. Half a dozen of them running across the lawns toward us. They'd evidently been heading for the shrine when they spotted us. They were coming without warning other than their white togas against the night.

"Scram!" I jerked out. "Toward the gate! It's the only way out I know! If there's only one man there we can handle him very easy! Save the cartridges in the gun!"

We were already running. Thank heaven, Trixie's sharp eyes had spotted them soon enough to give us some start. I expected them to start shooting; but they didn't; and then I remembered the club the guard had carried around my cabin and decided they didn't go armed with guns. Maybe someone thought the brand of fanatics around the place weren't to be trusted with guns. Clubs would do just as well most of the time—and they wouldn't be heard outside the estate by strange curious ears.

We ran. I ran too, weak and wobbly as I was. The idea of being caught and locked up in one of the padded cells was enough to bring double strength.

"Don't leave him!" Trixie panted to Joe Clark. "He's wounded and almost helpless!"

That to a man who'd been through ten days of hell as had this Joe Clark. But he didn't have any idea of leaving us.

"Gimme that club!" he blurted at me.

So I gave him the club. I had the knife left. Trixie had the gun. That only made the odds two to one against us—if you could forget we were a woman and two half-dead men.

Down through the black, lonesome shadows under the trees, with the crunch of our steps the only sounds.

They made no noise; they didn't even shout; but twice when I looked back the flutter of their white togas was there in grim ghostly pursuit.

Then the gate, with the floodlights glaring from the stone gate posts and the stout iron gates closed. The guard was there, the same big guard with the bulging muscles and curly brown beard.

He had heard us coming or was expecting us. He stood there before the gates in the full glare of the floodlights, holding a club ready for trouble.

"Gun!" I gasped to Trixie.

She shook her head. By the way her eyes had kept turning to me, she expected me to fall any step.

Joe Clark sprinted ahead. It might have been fear or fury; he went ahead anyway despite all he'd been through. He charged that burly guard as if it were all in the day's work.

They came together swinging clubs. I swore helplessly as Joe Clark reeled aside from a blow on the head.

"Don't try it, Mike!" Trixie cried.

But I'd have tried anything. I had the knife. I kept going.

So did Trixie. She darted in front of me and brought the gun up before I realized what she was doing.

He was a bearded, fanatical, challenging figure as Trixie ran in close and pulled the trigger. And he screamed and collapsed like a sawdust dummy that had lost stuffing.

Trixie had shot his knee—little Trixie who

went to target practice two and three times a week when she had the chance. I'd kidded her about it—and look now.

The guard was howling, writhing on the ground when I reached him. The gate key on a length of thin chain was attached to his belt. I tore it away.

Trixie had turned and fired a shot as I whirled to the chain and lock that held the gates. Joe Clark had jumped to her side on unsteady feet.

My hand was shaking so that I had to try twice to get the key in. Trixie fired another shot. Maybe it was the last one in the gun. I hadn't looked at the clip. And when we were outside the gate—then what?

Hollywood and help were miles away. What chance did we have after all? I wouldn't be able to stagger another quarter of a mile.

Trixie fired a third shot as I got the lock open . . .

Joe Clark howled: "Keep back or we'll shoot every damn one of you!"

"Come on!" I yelled as the gates swung open.

And I looked back over my shoulder and saw four of them scattered out and coming after us. And Trixie's voice was agonizing in its helplessness.

"The gun's empty, Mike! What can we *do?*"

"Run!" I said. "Duck off in the woods beyond the light! Clark and I will hold 'em!"

"No!" Trixie gasped, and I knew she meant it.

One of them yelled in triumph as they burst through the gate after us. We were almost out of the lighted area when Joe Clark's hoarse cry of despair drove sick helplessness right through me.

"More of 'em ahead!"

I saw the two figures charging up the road toward us.

"Get over in the trees!" I cried . . . and a moment later I yelled: "Wait! They're not trouble!"

Lew Ryster had been wrong. I had been wrong. Jake Dennis and Larry Sweet were the finest fellows in the world. I loved them—I'd always love them after that moment when I recognized them running up the road toward us, guns in their hands and looking for trouble.

Jake Dennis fired a shot in the air and waved the gun threateningly as they came close.

"What the hell's going on here? Hands up!" And then Dennis recognized me and bawled: "It's that doublecrossing little Blaine guy! Look at him! So help me I never seen—"

"Hold it, Jake!" Larry Sweet snapped. He turned to me. "What's all this about? Who are those comics who ran back through the gate?"

"Turn in a riot call and collar the whole bunch!" I panted. "It's murder and torture, kidnapping, blackmail and God only knows what! It's big—and you'll have to move fast to get everyone!"

"It's a laugh by the way you three look!" Jake Dennis sneered. "I knew Ryster was stalling when he said he'd work with us. I knew he had a slick trick up his sleeve. And when you flew to Chicago I had a buddy in the department there pick you up and keep an eye on you. What d'you think of that?"

"Fast work," I grinned, breathing easier and wanting to slap that big red-faced dick's back and shake his hand.

"We give you a chance to let us in on it," Jake Dennis blared indignantly. "And did you hand Sweet an' me a tumble when you stepped off that plane tonight?"

"I wondered how the hell you happened to be there," I admitted.

"So we hadda tail you up here in the mountains," Jake Dennis snorted. "We had to hang around down there in the bushes slapping at the bugs and wondering what the hell all this was about! All because of a dirty—"

"Hold it, Jake!" Larry Sweet broke in. "Who are these two, Harris?"

"Miss Meehan, from my agency," I said. "And Joe Clark, who was kidnapped and tortured in there. I've got Eddy Voss, an ex-con, locked up, and there's a dead woman who seems to have taken poison, and the old he-goat of the whole outfit was out on a marijuana nod when we left. The guard at the gate there is shot through

the knee. I left another fellow tied up. Miss Meehan shot a couple more times. I don't know whether she knocked anyone over or not. It was a close squeak."

"It sounds like a lunatic party!" Larry Sweet exclaimed.

"It was," I said. "And you better get help fast."

"There's a car coming," Jake Dennis said, looking down the road.

"Paige!" says I. "I'll bet it's John Paige, Father Orion's secretary! We want him bad! He's in the center of all this!"

"We'll get him," Dennis snapped. "Get back off the road!"

Headlights were flashing beyond the next turn as we faded into the underbrush. The car came into view fast and slowed for the gates.

Jake Dennis waited until it was almost to us and leaped out into the road waving his gun. The car surged ahead. Dennis was expecting it. Give that big cop credit; he knew what to do. He swung on the runningboard with an arm hooked through the front window, and his bellow reached us.

"You're under arrest! Stop this car!"

A gun crashed—and it wasn't Jake's. Then his gun blasted twice before he fell off the running board. He stumbled, sprawled, staggered up a moment later as the big Caddy that had brought me from the airport swerved and hit one of the stone gate posts.

Jake Dennis was running unsteadily toward it when we caught up with him.

"He flashed a gun on me! I hope I killed the dirty rat!" Dennis cried hoarsely. "Shot me in the arm!"

Well, he hadn't killed the man. The smash hadn't either. John Paige was feebly trying to get out from behind the wheel when we pulled him out.

His face was gashed and bleeding, he had a bullet hole through his chest and a line of pink froth was on his lips as he choked and breathed hard.

"What's this?" Larry Sweet said, jerking open the back door.

He dragged out a brown-haired young woman whose head lolled limply and whose eyes were wide and sightless.

"Dead!" Larry Sweet said in a flat voice. "It must have broken her neck." He laid her on the ground and turned to Paige. "Who is she?"

"My wife," Paige said. His eyes had been rolling at me with a wild, questioning stare. He hesitated before making the admission, and then broke into a fit of coughing that brought more of the bloody froth to his lips.

Then he saw Joe Clark, unshaven, gaunt and menacing, and he cowered against the ground.

"His wife," I said. "And there's a girl in there who's ready to marry him. And she's lousy with money. What would he do with a wife who stood in his way of getting his hands on that money?"

I was thinking aloud and stooping over the dead girl on the ground at the same time.

"Sweet," I said, "did you see this?"

Larry Sweet's handsome face went hard and he cursed under his breath as he followed my pointing finger. She had been a pretty girl with fair delicate skin and a slender neck. The ugly, purple fingerprints on her neck might have been painted there.

"Killed her—murdered her!" Sweet said in a hard voice.

"Murdered her," I said, "like he murdered the Farnson girl. Both women were in his way. They would have queered his marriage to a couple of million dollars. Eh, Paige? You wanted the money bad, didn't you? Worse than you wanted my eight grand?"

He coughed, breathing with harsh rattles. "Damn you—who are you?" he gasped.

"A cop," I said. "So is the young lady here who came with Nancy Cudahy. See this fellow you turned over to old Orion? Eddy Voss is locked up. It's all over. I doubt if you'll last until we get you to a doctor. Why did you think you had to kill the Farnson girl?"

I thought he was dying and it didn't matter much. He thought the same. Keeping his mouth shut wouldn't help now.

"She knew I was married," he got out with an effort. "She'd known my wife at one of the studios where they worked together. She had me meet her and told me she'd tell Nancy about the wife if I didn't make Nancy forget Orion and me and start back East. Had to get rid of her. She'd have ruined everything."

"Who runs this joint—Orion or you?"

"Me," Paige mumbled. "Good business. They eat it up. He believes in himself and they believe in him. Never was anything like it. He didn't have a dime when I found him. I made him famous. They do anything for him, tell anything . . ."

"Hell, what a story this'll make in the papers tomorrow!" Jake Dennis said prayerfully. "Watch everything, Larry, while I get the car." His voice came back to us as he started at a run down the road. "What a story—*what* a story . . ."

Lew Ryster thought so the next morning, in the Blaine Agency office in Hollywood, after he heard all the details and read the papers.

"But I told you," Lew yelped, almost purple-faced, "that those two pirates would steal the shirt off your back when it came to getting credit for a case." Lew slapped the papers on his desk. "Look at 'em! Read it and weep. You have to be a good guesser to find anything about *us* in these papers."

Little Trixie Meehan, pale and pretty, sweet and soft in a white summer dress and hat, said: "Nuts, Lew. Mike would have cashed in if those two cops hadn't appeared. Let them have the glory. This man Farnson has promised Mike the two thousand reward, hasn't he?"

"All right," Lew surrendered. "Mike takes a thousand, you get a thousand, and I hold the bag. There's just one thing that'll make me happy. What is this Great Truth that was being taught to everyone up there?"

"I never found out," I confessed; and suddenly I grinned as I stood up and reached for my hat. "But I've got an idea," I said. "Never give a sucker an even break. And when we split Farnson's reward money, I'll keep you in mind. Lew."

"Swell, Mike—that's decent of you. I didn't expect it."

"That's right," I said. "I've had a shot of the Great Truth myself since you busted up my trip to New York. I'll keep you in mind while this shoulder is healing and I'm spending the reward money."

I stopped at the door and grinned at Lew.

"So long, Sucker," I said.

Kindly Omit Flowers

Stewart Sterling

IT WAS NOT AT ALL uncommon for pulp writers to be prolific, considering how little they were paid for their work, but some went to extremes, and Prentice Winchell (1895–1976), whose best-known pseudonym was Stewart Sterling, was at the front of that group. In addition to hundreds (about four hundred seems the best estimate, as there may have been unrecorded pseudonyms) of short stories, he also wrote and produced more than five hundred radio programs, as well as journalism and numerous literary efforts for film and television. Like many other pulp writers, he created detective characters with unusual occupations, most notably a tough fire marshal (Ben Pedley, who appeared in forty stories and nine novels), a hotel dick (Gil Vine, the protagonist in eight novels), and a department store detective (Don Cadee, in nine novels, all written under the Spencer Dean pseudonym). For *Black Mask*, he created an innovative series of nine novelettes headlined as "Special Squad" stories, covering the activities of the Bomb and Forgery Squad, the Harbor Patrol, the Pickpocket and Confidence Bureau, the Air Police, the Pawnshop Detail, Emergency, Safe-and-Loft, and, twice, Homicide. In the present story, Sergeant Helen Dixon, generally a member of the Policewoman's Bureau, is temporarily assigned to the Homicide Division. Although there were few women cops or private eyes in *Black Mask*, Dixon stood out for, well, not standing out. She was ordinary-looking, a useful characteristic for a policewoman.

"Kindly Omit Flowers" was first published in the March 1942 issue of *Black Mask*.

The Herald of Happiness *was the answer to an old maid's prayer. To its clarion call hearkend one ecstatic victim after another—till Sergeant Helen Dixon of the Policewomen's Bureau was summoned by the siren tones to keep a blind date with death.*

The blow knocked Lieutenant Teccard senseless before his knees started to buckle

Kindly Omit Flowers

Stewart Sterling

CHAPTER ONE

A GRUESOME EXHIBIT

IEUTENANT TECCARD rocked back in his swivel chair. His fingers gripped the shiny oak arm-pieces tightly. It was an instinctive movement to get as far away as possible from the thing on his desk. Ordinarily, his office in the headquarters building seemed large enough. Now, suddenly, it was oppressively small and close. He kept his eyes away from the long, glass tray on the flat-top, as he reached for the phone.

"O.K. for Sergeant Dixon."

The woman who came in wouldn't have been noticed in the average Manhattan lunch-hour crowd. She was pretty, but she hadn't worked hard at it. A man might not have paid particular attention to her as he passed her on the street, unless he happened to meet her glance. Her eyes were gray and curiously calm—as if they had seen a lot they hadn't found amusing.

She wrinkled up her nose. "My God, Jerry! A man can live without food for three weeks and without water for three days! But you can't last three minutes without air!"

Jerry Teccard shoved his brown felt back off a harassed forehead. "Light a cigarette if it gets you, Helen." He indicated the roll of checkered oil-cloth resting in the photographic tray. "You don't have to turn yourself inside out, gandering at this. You can take the medical examiner's word for it."

Acting Detective-sergeant Helen Dixon, second grade, regarded him grimly.

"After that year I put in at the Forty-seventh Street station, it'll take something to turn my stomach," she declared.

He lifted one corner of the oilcloth cylinder. "What's left of a woman's thigh. After the wharf rats worked on it awhile."

Her lips compressed a little, but none of the color left her face.

"Where'd it come in?"

"Twenty-third precinct. East Hundred and Fourth." He consulted a report sheet. "James Boyle, probationer, found a child trying to salvage the oilcloth that had been tied around it with some string. Boyle's beat takes him along the Harlem docks, foot of Ninety-eighth. This thing was on the tide flat at the side of the Ninety-eighth Street pier."

"When was this, Jerry?"

"This a.m. Quarter past ten. Doc says it's been lying there, or under the head of the pier, more'n a week. Some *pupae* of flies in the end of the bone. Eggs must've been laid seven, eight days ago, anyway."

Helen Dixon bent over the tray. She didn't peer at the discolored bone, her finger pointed to brown shreds of fiber which clung to the outside of the oilcloth.

"You said it was tied with string?" she asked.

Teccard pointed to a soggy tangle of frazzled gray in one corner of the tray. "Was. Doesn't mean a thing, though. Million yards of that stuff used every day."

"But these look like rope strands to me."

He squinted at them. "I noticed those. I'm going to send 'em up to the lab, for a microscopic. But the reason I sent for you—".

"You figure this might be one of the *Happiness* cases?" She moved past his chair to the window, opened it from the bottom a few inches, stood staring down into Centre Street.

"There's better than an even chance. That's why I asked the Policewomen's Bureau to send

you up here. I know you've been plugging like hell on that assignment. If Crim. Ident. can help, maybe you and I can work together on it. Like old times, when you were playing Big Sister to the floozies we picked up on Sixth Avenue." He swung around toward her. "My office wouldn't want any credit."

She touched his shoulder lightly for an instant, spoke without turning around.

"Damn the credit! If I could only break the case. I've been running around in circles for three weeks, hoping it's just another flock of old maids forgetting about friends and families because wedding bells are still ringing in their ears. But if this," she inclined her head toward the tray, "is one of them, it means the very nastiest kind of murder."

Teccard nodded. "Never knew a suicide to cut off her leg. It's pretty obvious."

"Any special reason to think she was one of this matrimonial agency's customers?"

He lifted his chin, ran a finger around under his collar uncomfortably. "Remember what you said that day we had lunch at the Savarin? About the kind of heels who have to find their females through an ad? Especially when they pick on dames who've had the lousy luck to be disfigured or crippled?"

Her voice was bitter. "I'm not likely to forget. Every one of those five appeals for inquiry come from friends or relatives of women who have some physical disability—or some facial blemish that would put them at a disadvantage in the national pastime of husband-hunting. Of course those poor lonely lambs could be led to the slaughter, by some unscrupulous devil who flattered them and promised them . . . whatever he promised."

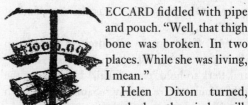ECCARD fiddled with pipe and pouch. "Well, that thigh bone was broken. In two places. While she was living, I mean."

Helen Dixon turned, perched on the window sill.

"The left leg?"

"Yair. Wasn't there one of those dames . . . ?"

"Ruby Belle Lansing." The sergeant eyed the oilcloth with repugnance. "Spinster. Thirty-six. Grade-school teacher in Tannersville. Hip broken in automobile accident, October 1939. Double fracture, set at Catskill Memorial Hospital. Entered into correspondence with the *Herald of Happiness* in August 1941. Came to New York, October sixth, after being introduced, by mail, to Philip Stanton, then of 4760 Madison Avenue, this city."

The lieutenant consulted his report sheet. "Length of femur, 18.1 inches. Let's see—factor for women is three and six-tenths. About sixty-five inches tall. Would this Lansing—"

"She was just five feet, five, Jerry. By the Tannersville Board of Education records. What must have been more important to Stanton, Ruby Belle had a little more than two thousand dollars in the savings bank at Phoenicia. Three days after her arrival, she had this deposit transferred to the Emigrant Bank here. On October tenth, the next day, it was withdrawn, except for ten dollars. Since then, there hasn't been a trace of her. Or of Stanton!"

"Any description of him?"

Helen shrugged. "Nothing to count. He never went to Tannersville. Her uncle—the one who asked us for a check-up—said he saw a snapshot of Stanton. But all he remembers is, the fellow was good-looking and had a mustache."

"That's a great big help!" Teccard called for a policeman to take the thigh-bone back to the morgue. "What about the people where Stanton lived?"

"A rooming house. Man who runs it's nearly blind. Stanton didn't seem to use the room much, anyway. Half the time the bed wasn't disturbed. Best I could get was, he was kind of dark."

"Ah! Send out an all-borough to pick up dark guys with mustaches! And reserve Central Park to hold 'em in! Yair! How about the other four who're missing? Same skunk, each time?"

Helen bent over the oilcloth, peered at the brown fiber again. "I wish I could remember what that stuff makes me think of. About the men in the other cases—I'm up against one of those things, Jerry. The disappearances were strangely similar. In every instance, the man resided in New York. The woman involved always lived in some small town, upstate. And every time the man sent the woman a ticket to come to the big city. What's more, flowers were invariably sent. Can you tie that? A bouquet for the unseen bride! Also, every one of the five dropped out of sight within three or four days—after sending for their home-town funds."

"All cut from the same pattern!"

"I thought so, at first. But the men in each of the cases had different names. Different addresses."

"What the hell! A crook of that kind could pick out a new alias or a new address as easy as you choose a blue plate!"

"I saw some of the letters these men wrote. In the agency files. The handwritings don't bear any resemblance."

"He could fake them. Or get someone else to write them for him."

"Not usual, is it? A murderer taking someone into his confidence? Unless it's a gang. Which it might be, from the varying descriptions of the men—according to the photos. There was always a snapshot, you see. One of the *Happiness* rules. One man had a beard. Another was partly bald. One was around fifty. The fellow in the Schwartz case couldn't have been more than twenty-five, the victim's brother claims. You wonder I've been stymied?"

Teccard spread his hands. "We'll have to go at it from this end. That oilcloth probably came from the five-and-dime—be tough to trace. But if this killer chopped the Lansing woman up, there'd have been more than a thigh bone to dispose of. Not so easy to get rid of a cadaver. And he slipped up this once. If he was careless again, we'll get somewhere. I've put a crew from the precinct on that. They'll sift that whole damn waterfront through a sieve, if necessary."

The sergeant sauntered toward the door. "I hope you beat me to it, Jerry. I haven't been sleeping so well, lately. Thinking about some other poor, lonely fool on her way to meet a murderer. If this guy—or this gang—has gotten away with it five times, there won't be any stop now. It's about time for another one. They've been spaced about a month apart."

Teccard frowned. "I thought you said you were up a blind alley on it. What do you mean, beat you to it?"

She smiled, tightly.

"I didn't say I was licked. I still have a card to play."

"If we're going to work together—"

"That would be all right with me. But this is something you couldn't very well come in on. I'm entered in Cupid's Competition."

He jumped to his feet. "Now what in the hell!"

She nodded, calmly. "Current issue of the *Herald of Happiness,* Meeting Place of the Matrimonial Minded Department. 'Miss Mary Lownes, single, thirty-one. Of Malone, New York. Pleasant disposition. Capable housewife, though suffering from slight spinal complaint. Occupation, nurse.' I was, you know, before I turned policewoman. 'Anxious to meet amiable, sober businessman under fifty.' That ought to get him, don't you think?"

"Just because you were assigned to an investigation doesn't mean you're supposed to risk running up against a killer, Helen."

"After the slimy specimens I've been running up against, a murderer'll be a relief. This chasing up and down subways and elevateds to trap exhibitionists, those hours of stting through double features to nab mashers in the act—that's not only hard work, it kind of gets you to thinking half the world's made up of perverts."

"Yair. But that's the sort of stuff only a woman can handle. Homicide isn't for the Women's Bureau, it's a man's job."

"It's my job to put a stop to any matrimonial agency that's doing business like this—to see that love-hungry women don't get murdered when they figure on getting married."

"You find the man. We'll put a stop to it—without your getting into it."

"That would suit me swell. But it might not work. I may have to get into it, to find the evidence necessary to convict."

The lieutenant put his fists on his hips and glared. "Hey! You don't mean you'd go so far as to marry the murdering so-and-so?"

"I'll go as far as I have to, Jerry. Maybe you've forgotten I had a sister who fell for a slimy snake like this Stanton. Alice turned on the gas one night—without lighting it. I found her body. I hate men like that worse than those phoney abortionists I rounded up this spring. At least those girls knew they were taking a terrible chance. These poor, misguided love-seekers don't even realize their danger until it's too late." There was a dull, hurt look in the gray eyes. "But so far, there's been no proof that any of these women wound up with any legal certificates. No record of any licenses at City Hall, even."

"God's sake, Helen! You know the regulations forbid any infraction of ordinances in attempting to trap a criminal!"

"Nothing criminal about getting married, is there, Jerry?"

He opened his mouth, shut it again, glared at her. When he spoke, it was in the tone of a commanding officer. "You let me know before you go through with any damn nonsense like that, hear?"

She saluted, stiffly. "Yes, Lieutenant."

He wasn't more than a minute behind her in leaving the office. The police clerk by the rail in the outer room spoke out of the corner of his mouth to a plainclothesman one-fingering on a typewriter. "Geeze! The Lieutenant musta just swallowed a cup of carbolic or something."

"Teccard? He always looks like that when the Dixon dame gives him 'No' for an answer. He's been carryin' the torch for her so long, he sleeps standin' up, like the Statue of Liberty."

CHAPTER TWO
HERALD OF HAPPINESS

HE detective-lieutenant drove his department sedan up Broadway to Twenty-eighth, studied the directory board in the lobby of a ten-story office building, pushed into the elevator.

The *Herald of Happiness* was housed in a single room at the rear of the third floor. The door was locked, but there was a bulky shadow moving against the ground glass. He rapped.

The man who let him in was fat. Tiny purple veins laced the end of a bulbous nose. The eyes that searched the lieutenant's were slightly bloodshot.

"You the proprietor of this agency, mister?"

"I am, sir. T. Chauncey Helbourne, if I can be of service to you. You are a subscriber?"

"I'm from police headquarters."

"What, again? I've already put up with a distressing amount of annoyance from a Miss Dixon . . ."

"You'll be putting up with a prison diet, if you're not careful."

"Prison! You can't frighten me, sir. I run a legitimate business."

"Nuts! You come close to being a professional panderer. Don't tell me you have a license, it doesn't cover complicity in fraud!"

Helbourne's neck reddened. "I won't be bulldozed by any such tactics, officer!"

"Lieutenant. Lieutenant Teccard." He surveyed the cheap furniture, the unpainted rack of pigeonholes along one wall.

"It makes no difference to me if you're the commissioner, himself. I have influential connections at City Hall, too. And my records are always open for inspection by authorized parties."

"O.K. I'm an authorized party. I'll have a look at any letters that've come in here the last week or so."

The fat man waved vaguely at the row of green-painted files. "Help yourself. It would take me a couple of months to locate 'em. I don't file by dates."

"I'll make a start at it." Teccard pulled out a steel drawer marked *L.* He ran his thumb along the tabs until he came to one with the letters *LO,* took out all the folders in that section. "How many letters you rake in, per day, mister?"

"You mean the preliminaries?"

"What the hell is a preliminary?" There was a folder with the name *Mary Lownes* at the top. It was empty, except for an envelope in Helen's handwriting, addressed to *Herald of Happiness*— and a clipped-out advertisement.

Helbourne picked up a proof-sheet of a page. "Subscribers are allowed one free advertisement to each subscription, plus as many answers to other advertisements as they wish. Our only restriction is, these replies to ads must be addressed to the box-number of the *Herald.*" He pointed to one. "Any letters coming in, addressed to that box-number, are copied and sent along to the advertiser, no charge. Without the name or address of the sender, naturally."

Teccard slid the folders back in place. "The old come-on. What do you tap them for giving out with the address?"

The proprietor of the *Herald* frowned. "Our fee is five dollars."

"At each end of the transaction? Five from the snappy skirt who wants the address of some dope who's given her a line of mush? And another five from the dope himself, if he wants to get in touch with her direct?"

"I don't like the way you put it, Lieutenant."

"Catch them coming and going, don't you! Next thing you know, you'll catch five years in the pen." Teccard drifted toward the rack of pigeonholes. There were letters and folded carbon copies in most of them. Under each space was pasted a copy of some *Herald* advertisement.

Helbourne watched him sullenly. "I'm not responsible for what my subscribers do after I've performed an introduction."

"Hell you aren't! You're wide open for prosecution. You were warned some New York crut has been rooking old maids from upstate, using you as a go-between." There was a cubbyhole with two letters, over an advertisement reading:

YOUNG LADY OF BREEDING

seeks companionship of amiable, sober businessman, under fifty, with quiet tastes. One who would appreciate a better-than-average table and a comfortable home. Not wishing to be supported, as have slight means of own. Able and active, though slight spinal injury. Brunette, thirty-one, former trained nurse. Box LL27.

Helen was a brunette—the age and the references to the spinal injury and having been a nurse clinched it. Teccard reached for the letters.

The fat man caught his arm. "You'll have to get a court order, if you're going to ransack my mail, Lieutenant."

Teccard disengaged the pudgy fingers. "One side, mister. A minute ago you told me to help myself. I am. You want any trouble, I'll see you get plenty." He crackled the letters open. The first one read:

Dear Miss Box LL27.
   Your ad made a great deal of an appeal to me. I am a farmer, widower five years now, age forty-six. It's a seventy-acre fruit farm, paying good, too. I have a piano, radio, Chevrolet, nice furniture. The part about better than average cooking appealed to me. Do you play the piano? Hoping to hear from you,
                    Very sincerely yours,
                    HERMAN SCHICHTE
                    Rural Route Six
                    Pathanville. N.Y.

The lieutenant stuck it back in the pigeonhole. "Park your pants in a chair, mister. It makes me nervous to have anyone reading over my shoulder."

Helbourne sat down. His mouth was open and he was panting as if he'd been climbing stairs. He kept rubbing his palms on his knees while he watched Teccard run through the other letter.

Your message in the Herald *was like music heard far off over the water at night. Perhaps I am wrong, dear LL27, but I sense in your heart an aching desire for the finer things which life too often denies those best fitted to enjoy them. If I have understood you rightly, your appeal for companionship strikes a very sympathetic chord in my own soul. I am thirty-five, dark and, though no Adonis, not bad to look upon, I have been told. I have a comfortable business and am fond of travel, theater and books. Possibly you would care to write me so we could exchange photographs and perhaps—quien sabe—perhaps, some day, rings to symbolize even more than companionship!*
                    With eager anticipation,
                    Your friend,
                    HAROLD WILLARD
                    971 East 88th Street
                    New York City

Teccard put the letter in his pocket. East Eighty-eighth wasn't so far from the pier where that grisly bone had been found.

"This Harold Willard," he said. "Let's see the other letters you've had from him."

Helbourne shook his head quickly. "That's the only one. I never heard of the man before. I can't keep track—"

"Yair. I heard that one. You recognize his signature?"

"No. Not at all."

"You sent the copy of this drool along to Box LL27?"

"Not yet. It was going out today," Helbourne said.

"Don't send it. And don't send out copies of *any* letters that come to you from New York City. Not until I've had a look at them. Understand?"

"Yes, sir." Helbourne held his head sideways, as if he expected the lieutenant to take a punch at him. "Is there—ah—any cause for you to believe the writer of that letter—has been involved in these—ah—irregularities you are investigating?"

Teccard stuffed a copy of the *Herald* into his coat pocket. "Only that he writes phoney as hell. You ought to have your butt booted for handling that kind of sewage. And if I find you've passed on any more of it, I'm coming back and rub your nose in it."

I T WAS dusk when the sedan reached the Twenty-third Precinct station house. Teccard was glad to get out of the chill wind whistling across Harlem from the river.

"Cap Meyer around?" he inquired of the desk sergeant.

"You'll find him in the muster room, with a couple boys from Homicide, Lieutenant."

Teccard strode into the back room. Four men stood about the long table under a green-shaded bulb. Three were in plain-clothes, the fourth was in uniform. There was a black rubber body-bag at the one end of the table, at the other a piece of wax paper with as grisly a collection as the Identification man had ever seen.

"What you got, Meyer?"

The captain turned. His face was a curious greenish-yellow in the cone of brilliance. "I wouldn't know, Teccard. But whatever it is, you can have it."

One of the Homicide men finished tying a tag to the third finger of a skeleton hand. "All we're sure of, it was an adult female."

His partner stripped off a pair of rubber gloves. "That's all you'll ever establish, for certain. Person who hacked this woman up was pretty tricky." He indicated the cracked and flattened end of the finger bones. "Mashed the tips to prevent any print-work."

Meyer tongued around his stub of cigar. "Wasn't really necessary, though. The rats took care of that."

The uniformed man spoke up. "All this mess had been dumped under the shore end of that Ninety-eighth Street pier, Lieutenant. There was a loose plank there, somebody must of ripped it up. It was near covered by muck, but we shoveled it out and used the hose on it, well as we could."

"Including that thigh bone, we got everything but one foot now," the first Homicide man said. "But it wouldn't do any good to try a reconstruction. All the teeth were hammered out of that head, before it was dropped in the mud."

Teccard bent over the yellowish skull, stained with dirty, grayish mold. "Parts of some fillings left. Jaw still shows where she had some bridgework done. We can check the dentists, up around Tannersville."

Captain Meyer exclaimed: "You got a line on her, already?"

"Yair. Schoolteacher who thought she was coming to town for her wedding ceremony. *'Till death do ye part.'* It parted her, to hell and gone, didn't it?" He turned away. "How about letting me have one of your men who knows the Eighty-eighth Street beat? In the nine hundreds."

Meyer and the uniformed man looked at each other. The captain gestured. "Patrolman Taylor, here, had that beat up to a month ago. How long you need him?"

"Depends. Bird we're after may have flown the coop already."

"O.K. You're relieved, Taylor. And if you have any trouble when it comes to putting the arm on the crut who did this," the captain jerked his head toward the table, "do me one favor."

The policeman touched the rim of his cap. "Yuh?"

"Shoot him a couple times where it'll really hurt. All he'll feel, if he goes to the chair, will be a few seconds' jolt. Way I feel, that'd be letting him off easy . . ."

Out in the car, Taylor pulled a folded-up newspaper from his hip pocket. "That kid who found the leg this morning squawked all over the neighborhood. We warned him to keep his puss shut—but the papers got it just the same."

Teccard didn't read it. "They can't print

much, if they don't know any more than we do, Taylor. What you know about number 971?" He pulled up half a block away.

The patrolman craned his neck. "Nine-seven-one? The old brick house? Nothing much. Just four- or five-buck-a-week furnished rooms. No apartments."

"Who runs it?"

"Old dodo named Halzer. Him and his wife. They got 969, too—operate 'em together. He's harmless, stewed about half the time."

"Yair? You ever hear of a guy, name of Harold Willard, in this parish?"

"Harold Willard. Harold Willard. I don't recall it, Lieutenant. What's he look like?"

"Dark, about thirty-five years old. That's all we've got to go on. My guess is he fancies himself for a double of one of the movie stars. Likely to be a flash dresser."

"I can't seem to place him. Maybe he's just moved in. They keep coming and going in a joint like this."

"Yair. If he happens to be in now, we'll keep him from going."

"We can do that, Lieutenant. There's no rear doors on this side of the block."

"You go on ahead, then. Go into 969. Find out from Halzer what room Willard has. When you know, stand in the door of 969 and wait for me to come past. You can give me the high sign without anyone watching you from one of the windows next door," Teccard explained.

"Check."

"And after I go in, nobody comes out. I mean nobody. Until I say so."

"Got you, Lieutenant." The patrolman strolled away, idly twisting his night-stick.

Teccard stood on the curb, tamping out his pipe. He gazed curiously up at the lighted windows of 971. What kind of murderer could it be who took such care to hack his victim to pieces—only to attempt to hide all the remains in one spot? There had been other instances of dismembered corpses in the records of the Criminal Identification Bureau but, so far as Teccard could remember, limbs and head and torso had invariably been strewn far and wide, to prevent any reconstruction of the body. Was he up against one of those unpredictable, pathological cases of sadism—where mutilation gives the killer a diabolical satisfaction? That didn't seem to match up with the carefully planned disposition of the victim's funds . . .

Taylor's club showed, in the areaway of 969. The lieutenant walked along, briskly.

"Third floor rear," the policeman whispered hoarsely. "Room J."

Teccard didn't turn his head, or answer. He marched up the steps to 971. The front door was unlatched. There was a row of battered, black-tin mailboxes. He paused just long enough to make sure one of them bore a piece of paper with the penciled scrawl: *Harold M. Willard.* Then he went in.

The hallway smelled of cooking grease and anti-septic, the carpeting on the stairs was ragged. Somebody was playing a radio. A baby squalled. There was a sound of running water from a bathroom somewhere on the second floor.

Over the sill of room J was a thread of yellow light. Someone was moving about in the room, but Teccard, with his ear to the panel, heard nothing else. He transferred his gun from his left armpit to the right pocket of his coat, kept his grip on the butt.

He knocked and, without waiting, raised his voice.

"Telegram for Mister Willard."

The movement behind the door ceased. There was a pause, then: "Slide it under the door."

Teccard kept his voice high. "You got to sign a receipt, mister."

"Shove your receipt book under, too. I'll sign it." The answer came from halfway down the door—the man inside was evidently trying to look through the keyhole.

"The book won't go under. You want the telegram, or not?"

Another pause.

"Wait a second. I'm not dressed."

"O.K." Teccard tried to make it sound weary.

"Where's the wire from?" The man had moved away from the door, but the tone was strangely muffled.

"We ain't allowed to read telegrams, mister. If you don't want to accept it—"

The door opened.

The man was in his underclothes. He stood sideways, so Teccard couldn't get a good look at him. His black hair was rumpled, he held a towel up over his mouth and the side of his face, as if he'd just finished shaving.

"Is there anything due—" He reached out with his other hand.

The lieutenant stepped in, fast.

"Yair. You're due, mister. Put down—"

There was a faint "*Hunh!*" from behind the door, the uncontrollable exhalation of breath when a person exerts himself suddenly.

Teccard whirled.

The blow that caught him across the top of the head knocked him senseless before his knees started to buckle!

CHAPTER THREE
MURDER IN ROOM J

AYLOR poured a tumbler of water over Teccard's head. "Take it easy, now. Amby'll be here any second."

The lieutenant rolled over on his side. "Quit slopping that on my head." The floor kept tilting away from him, dizzily. "Lemme have it to drink."

The cop filled the glass from a broken-lipped pitcher. "You been bleeding like a stuck pig."

Teccard paused with the tumbler at his lips. Was that a pair of shoes lying on the floor behind the patrolman? He shook his head, to clear away the blurriness. "Who in the hell is that?" he cried.

Taylor's jaw went slack. "That's the lad you was battling with. You fixed his wagon, all right!"

"I wasn't fighting with anybody! Someone slugged me from behind that door, before I could even get my gun out." The lieutenant got his elbows under him, propped himself up. The man on his back was T. Chauncey Helbourne— and his skin was a leaden blue.

The officer nodded sympathetically. "A crack on the conk will do that, sometimes. Make you forget what's been goin' on, when you snap out of it."

Teccard felt of the back of his neck. His fingers came away wet and sticky, the ache at the top of his skull was nauseating. "I didn't kill him, you dope!"

"Geeze! You had a right to drop him, didn't you! He was resistin' arrest, wasn't he?"

Teccard crawled on hands and knees to the dead man's side. There was an irregular dark blot on Helbourne's vest, just inside the left lapel; in the center of the blot something gleamed yellow-red, under the naked bulb overhead. The lieutenant touched the fat man's face. It was still close to normal body temperature.

"You got him first clip out of the box." Taylor pointed to the gun on the floor, by the side of the iron cot.

Teccard stood up shakily, sat down again, suddenly, on the sagging edge of the cot. Taylor, the corpse on the floor, the barren furnishings of the room—all seemed oddly far away. He bent over to let the blood get to his head again. "Where's the other gent who was in here? The one in shorts?"

The uniformed man squinted as if the light hurt his eyes. "The only lug I saw is this stiff, Lieutenant."

Teccard closed his eyes to stop the bed from shimmying. "He let me in here. How'd he get downstairs, past you?"

Taylor put up a hand to cover his mouth, his eyes opened wide. "Now I swear to God there wasn't a soul on them stairs when I come up. If there'd been a guy with his pants off—"

"How'd you happen to come up, anyway?"

"Why, geeze, Lieutenant. When this dame comes scuttling down to the front door, yelling for 'Police' naturally I hotfoot over from next door."

"A woman? What kind of a woman?" Teccard demanded.

"Why, just an ordinary mouse like you'd expect to find in one of these joints. Kind of blond and plump—I don't know."

"What'd she say?"

"She says, 'Officer, come upstairs quick. There's a couple of men fighting and making a terrible racket right over my room.' She says, '*Hurry!*' So I figure it's you subduing this Willard and maybe needing a hand. I come up on the jump."

Teccard started to shake his head, thought better of it. "Where is she now? Bring her here."

The policeman pounded out in the hall, downstairs. He left the door open. There was an excited hum of voices from the corridor.

Teccard took a pencil out of his pocket, stuck it in the barrel of the pistol, lifted it off the floor. He wrapped his handkerchief carefully about the butt, broke his weapon. Only one chamber had been fired from the .38. The bullet hole in Helbourne's chest would be about right for that caliber.

Taylor came clumping upstairs. "She put one over on me. That room underneath ain't even occupied. And she's scrammed, anyway."

"So has the jerk who was half undressed." The lieutenant put down the revolver, poured himself another drink of water. "That's over the dam, don't get gidgety about it. You were right, according to the way you figured it."

The cop wiped sweat off his forehead. "It's all balled up in my mind. Was this Willard the one who shot the fat boy, here?"

"Might have been. The gun was still in my pocket when I went down. Somebody took it out and used it on T. Chauncey Helbourne. Somebody else. Not me." Teccard gazed grimly around the room. "The worse of it is, I couldn't absolutely identify Willard, even now. He was covering his smush with a towel and he sort of kept his back to me, anyhow."

He didn't bring up the point that bothered him most—it was a cinch Willard hadn't been the one who crowned Teccard from behind that door. Maybe his unseen assailant had been Helbourne. In any case, what was the proprietor of the *Herald of Happiness* doing up here, when he had claimed complete ignorance of Willard!

A siren wailed, out in the street.

"Holler down to the doc, Taylor. Tell him all he needs to bring up is a few stitches for my scalp."

"You'd ought to go to the hospital, Lieutenant. Have an X-ray, to be sure there ain't any fracture."

Teccard went over to the closet door, opened it. "There's nothing more the matter with my head than's been wrong with it for thirty-seven years. Did you buzz the station, too, Taylor?" he said.

"Yes, sir. Cap Meyer is coming right over, himself, with a couple of the boys." Taylor went out into the hall, shouted down the stairwell.

The lieutenant sniffed at the empty closet. The only things in it were a few coat hangers and a sweet scent that made him think of church. Queer thing to find in a place like this, probably came from clothing that had been hung up here.

He looked around the room for the weapon with which he had been slugged. There wasn't anything heavier than a cane wastebasket. The wastebasket was empty, too, except for a crumpled piece of cellophane stripped from a pack of cigarettes. He fished it out with the point of his fountain-pen, put it on the bureau.

HE interne arrived, went to work with needle and sutures. Meyer and two plainclothesmen came up. While the doctor jabbed the needle through his scalp, Teccard told the captain what was wanted.

"Box up that cellophane, run it down to my office. There might be prints on it. Get a photographer up here from Homicide. Have him powder the knobs, the bureau drawers, the iron part of the bed, those hangers in the closet. Run a vacuum over the floor, ship the dust down to the lab for examination."

Meyer crouched over the fat man. "Who's this guy, Lieutenant?"

"Crumb who ran a matrimonial agency. That's what's back of those bones your boys dug up today. Go through his pockets, will you? And mark someone down for going through the house, here, to see what they can get on Willard. Taylor, you learn anything about him from the landlord?"

The patrolman scratched his head. "Not much. Oh, one funny thing. He must have a night job. Because he only comes here in the day-time. And he must write a lot of letters, because practically the only thing old Halzer remembers his having up here, outside his clothes, is a box of writing paper and a bottle of ink."

"Yair? See can you find if he threw any of his scribbling in the wastebasket. Maybe some of it is still in the trashcan."

Meyer said: "Not much dough, but plenty of unpaid bills, on this fella. He's been hitting the high spots, you ask me. Here's a credit-jewelry store summons for non-payment on a diamond wristwatch. And a bunch of duns from depart-ment stores and an automobile company." He tossed the sheaf of papers on the bed. "Eleven fish and some chickenfeed, a cheap ticker, two nickel cigars, a silk handkerchief stinking of whiskey, and a bunch of keys."

"No weapon?"

"Not even a pen-knife, Lieutenant. You're pretty positive he wasn't the fella cut up that girl's body?"

"He'd have been well-padded with folding money, in that case, Cap. No. You rustle around, get a description of Harold Willard."

Teccard waited until the doctor growled: "Kind of a patchwork job, Lieutenant. You'd be smart to take a couple days' sick leave. That's an ugly gash."

"If that stuff about the stitch in time is on the up and up, you must have saved about ninety-

nine of 'em. Thanks. I'll be around, for you to rip them out again." He picked up the keys. "I might use these, Cap."

"Want Taylor to go with you?"

"No." Teccard examined his hat. There was a right angle cut where the brim joined the crown. He smoothed the felt thoughtfully. "You might let me have a gun, though. Mine'll have to go to Ballistics."

Meyer brought out an automatic. "You can take Betsy, if you don't mind a big caliber."

The corners of Teccard's mouth curled up. "A forty-five is just the ticket."

"You after big game?"

"Yair." Teccard checked the magazine to make sure it was loaded. "You ever go after moose, Cap?"

"Moose? Hell, no. Duck is my limit."

"Well, when a guy goes after moose, he uses a horn that makes a sound like a female moose. The bull comes a-running—and the hunter does his stuff."

A puzzled scowl wrinkled Meyer's forehead.

"I'm going to get me a horn, Cap. But there's nothing in the book says for the rest of you to stop hunting."

He went downstairs.

The night elevator man in the building housing the *Herald of Happiness* regarded Teccard coldly. "Who you want to see on the third, mister?"

"Just giving the premises the once-over." The lieutenant held his badge out on his palm. "Snap it up. I haven't got all night."

"Ain't anyone up on that floor."

"That's why I'm going up. Do I push the lever myself?"

The car started. "I can't have people going in and out alla time. I'll lose my job."

"Don't worry about it. Everything's strictly copacetic."

The elevator door clanged loudly. Teccard swung around the corner of the corridor into the ell where Helbourne's office was located—and stopped short. Somewhere ahead of him a light had been suddenly extinguished. He stood still, listening. There were none of the noises to be expected when an office is being closed for the night. No door opened.

He balanced the heavy automatic in his left hand, held the keys in his right, tightly, so they wouldn't rattle. Quietly, on the balls of his feet, he moved to the *Herald*'s door. Still he heard nothing, except the faraway roar of Broadway. He tried the key which showed the most signs of use. The latch turned. He stepped aside swiftly to the right, kicked the door open.

If there was anyone inside, the only target would be Teccard's hand, holding the pistol. He snaked his wrist around the jamb of the door, fumbled for the light switch he knew must be there. It clicked. The office flooded with brilliance.

There was a laugh.

"Kamerad!"

He swore under his breath, stepped out into the doorway. She was sitting back in Helbourne's chair, her feet cocked upon the desk. There was a pile of letters in her lap, a flashlight in one hand and a short-barreled .32 in the other.

"Imagine meeting you here," he said dryly. "I phoned the Policewomen's Bureau for you. They knew from nothing!"

Sergeant Dixon took her high heels off the desk. "I've been using the super's passkey every night for the last two weeks. How'd *you* get in?"

He jangled the keys. "Property of T. Chauncey Helbourne. For the evidence clerk."

She looked at him sharply. "Evidence? Is Helbourne . . . dead?"

Teccard sat down on the edge of the desk. "That's what happens when you take a slug under the fourth rib."

"Who shot him, Jerry?" The sergeant tossed the letters on the desk, stood up.

"There seems to be a general impression I did. The bullet came from my Regulation, all right. But I'd say the killer was the same one who did away with Ruby Belle."

She saw the bandage on the back of his head. "Jerry! You were in it! You're hurt!"

"Yair." He managed a lop-sided grin. "That was no love-tap. Somebody dropped the boom on me, but good."

She reached up, lifted his hat off gently. "That was close, Jerry."

"They meant to kill me, at first. Changed their minds when they fished through my pockets, found my badge."

"They? Were there two of them?"

The lieutenant nodded. "One K.O.'d me while I was putting the gun on the other one. I went bye-bye before I got a square look at either of them. They both scrammed. Now they know we're closing in, they'll be foxier than ever. If they've got anything on fire, they may try to pull it off before they do the vanishing act. But we'll have to move fast, if we're going to catch up with them. That's why I came down here, to see if there might be any other poor boobs readied up for the kill."

"You might have asked me. Just because I spent two years putting fortune tellers out of business and running around to disorderly dance halls, doesn't mean I've forgotten how to use my mind." She held up a sheet of pink notepaper. "I dug this out of Helbourne's private postoffice, there. It has all the earmarks. Box KDD. A Miss Marion Yulett, seamstress of Algers. Thirty-three. Possesses certain means of her own. Has a cheerful, homeloving disposition, yet is full of pep. Miss Yulett encloses five dollars to secure the address of a certain Peter Forst who's apparently been giving her a buildup about his charms."

"He live in New York City?"

"Can't find any folder for Mr. Forst. Peculiar. Not even any letters to him—or from him."

 ECCARD chewed on his pipe-stem. Was Forst another one of Willard's aliases? Had Helbourne been putting one over when he claimed to know nothing about other letters from the mysterious individual who always wrote

from Manhattan? "When did this deluded dame come through with Helbourne's fee?"

"Week ago today."

The lieutenant reached for the phone. "Hustle me through to your super, pal. Supervisor? This is Lieutenant Jerome Teccard, New York Police Department, Criminal Identification Bureau. Talking from Bryant 3-2717. Yair. Get me the chief of police of Algers, New York, in a hurry, will you? Algers is up near Whitehall. Yair . . . I'll hang on . . ."

While he was waiting, Teccard tried the only flat key, from Helbourne's bunch, on the locked middle drawer of the desk. It fitted. In the drawer was an empty cigar carton, some paper matchbooks, an overdue bill from one printer and a sheaf of estimates from another, a half-full flask of *Nip-and-Tuck Rye*, and a torn, much-folded plain-paper envelope, addressed to the *Herals of Happiness, Box KDD!*

The envelope was postmarked three weeks ago, from Station U, New York City.

Helen looked up Station U. "East One Hundred and Sixth Street, Jerry."

"Same precinct as the bones. And friend Willard. One will get you ten that's where we find brother Forst, too."

There was a voice in the receiver. Teccard held it to his ear, muttered "Yair" a few times, added "Much obliged, Chief," racked the receiver.

"Too late. Sucker Yulett left Algers on the morning train."

Helen punched the files with her fist, angrily. "For New York?"

"Didn't know. Southbound, anyway."

The hurt look came into her eyes again.

Teccard shoved his hands into his pockets, gloomily. "All he did know—she had her suitcase, and the station agent said she was wearing a corsage."

She showed teeth that were clenched. "Those damned flowers again!"

"They'll probably last just long enough to be used on her casket," Teccard brooded. "Wait, though. We might still be in time."

"It wouldn't take her all day to get to New York!"

"It might. Station master didn't tell the chief what time the train left, this a.m. Might have been late morning. And those trains up north of the capital run slower than a glacier. If the Yulett girl had to change at Albany, and wait . . ."

Helen got the phone first, called train information. It was busy. The sergeant kept pounding the desk with her fist until she got her connection.

Before she hung up, Teccard was asking: "Can we stop her?"

"Only train making connections from Algers to New York arrives at Grand Central, eight forty. Gives us about twenty minutes."

He caught her arm. "Hell it does. We'll have to burn rubber to make it. We can't wait until she gets off the train. We'll have to find her, convince her we're on the level, tip her off what she's to do. Chances are, Forst'll be waiting for her. We'd scare him off before we spotted him."

She was streaking down the corridor toward the elevator. "We catch the train at a Hundred and Twenty-fifth, come in with her?"

"If she's on it. If we can locate it. And if she'll listen to reason. That's a hell of a lot of 'ifs.' "

 HE department sedan zoomed over to Park and Thirty-fourth—went through the red lights with siren screeching. They didn't stop to park at a Hundred and Twenty-fifth, sprinted up the stairs as the conductor gave the "Boa-r-r-d!"

The sergeant saw the bunch of lilies-of-the-valley first. "That sweet-faced one, in the dark blue coat and that God-awful hat, Jerry."

"Yair. You better break the ice. She'll be suspicious of a man."

Helen dropped into the empty seat beside the woman in the unbecoming hat. The lieutenant stayed a couple of paces in the rear.

"Miss Yulett?" the sergeant inquired, softly.

"You're Miss Marion Yulett, from Algers, aren't you?"

The woman smiled sweetly, opened her bag, produced a small pad and a pencil.

Swiftly she wrote: *Sorry. I am hard of hearing.*

Teccard smothered an oath. It wouldn't have mattered if she'd been crippled or scarred up—Helen would have been able to fix it so the Yulett woman could step into a ladies' room, somewhere, and give her instructions to handle the man she was going to meet. But there wouldn't be time to write everything out in longhand, without arousing "Forst's" suspicions. And if the killer had an accomplice, as the lieutenant believed, this deaf woman couldn't hear what "Forst" and the other would be saying to each other—and that might prove to be the most important evidence of all!

Helen scribbled away on the pad. Teccard sidled up alongside so he could read.

I am Sergeant Dixon from the N.Y. Police-women's Bureau. Are you Marion Yulett?

The woman shrank back in her seat.

"Yes. Why do you want me?" Her voice shook.

The pencil raced in Helen's fingers.

Only to save you unhappiness. Maybe worse. You plan to meet a man named Peter Forst?

"Yes. Is anything wrong?"

The sergeant held the pad out, again.

We believe he's a killer who's murdered several women who became acquainted with him through the Herald. Have you a picture of him?

Miss Yulett fumbled nervously in her bag, produced a small, glossy snap-shot. Teccard's forehead puckered up. This couldn't be a photo of Willard, by any possibility! The man in the snap-shot was round-faced and pudgy-cheeked. He had a neatly trimmed goatee and his hair receded at the temples, from a high forehead!

Helen wrote: *How will Forst recognize you?*

"I had my picture taken, too. I sent it to him day before yesterday." Miss Yulett bit her lip to keep from crying. "I'm afraid it wasn't a very good likeness—I don't photograph well. But I was wearing this hat and these beads," she touched a necklace of imitation pink jade, "and

I'm wearing his flowers, too." Tears began to stream down her cheeks, she turned her face toward the window. "You must be mistaken about Peter, his letters were so sweet and kind. I can't imagine his . . . hurting anybody."

The train began to slow for the track intersections in the upper yard. There was no time for softening the blow, with sympathy.

Helen made the pad say: *If he's the man we're after, he doesn't intend to marry you at all. If you have any money, he'll wheedle it away from you and then— Did he mention anything about money?*

The words came out between convulsive sobs: "Only that he had a small and prosperous business. With a partner who wasn't . . . quite honest, perhaps. If Peter and I . . . got . . . along . . . he said I might want to buy out this other man's interest. So my . . . my husband and I . . . could be partners."

The pencil moved so swiftly Teccard could hardly follow it.

Brace up now, Marion. We're getting in. Take off your hat. And your beads.

Miss Yulett dried her eyes on a tiny handkerchief, did her best to smile. "You're going to meet him, with me—so he can have a chance to explain?"

No, I'm going to meet him. As you. Wearing your hat and beads. Unpin those flowers, too.

"But, please! Please let me—"

Don't waste time arguing. If he looks all right to me, I'll let you meet him later. I'll take your bag, too. You take mine. And wear my hat.

The disturbed woman unclasped her beads. "But what on earth am I to *do*? Where will I *go*? I don't know anybody but Peter—"

The gentleman standing behind us is Police Lieutenant Teccard. He'll see that you get to a hotel. Stay where he tells you to until I can get in touch with you.

Teccard gripped Helen's shoulder. "No you don't. You take Miss Yulett to the hotel. I'll meet pal Peter."

Sergeant Dixon looked up at him. "What evidence do you think you'd get out of him, Jerry?

He's not the same man you ran into uptown, is he? As things stand, you haven't a thing on him."

"I'll sweat the evidence out of him, all right."

"Maybe you couldn't. There's always the possibility this fellow's on the level. If he is, I turn him over to Miss Yulett. If he isn't, I'll be able to give first-hand testimony as to how he operates. This is a job only a policewoman can handle effectively."

Teccard grimaced. "Put your gun in her bag, then. And don't be dainty about using it. Another thing: I'm going to turn Miss Yulett over to one of the pick-pocket squad in the terminal and tail you and your intended."

"All right, as long as he doesn't spot you." Helen adjusted the ridiculous brim of the hat, snapped the beads around her neck. Hastily, she used the pad once more.

Did Forst tell you where you were to stay in New York? Or how soon you'd get married?

"As soon as we could get the license." Tears glistened in the woman's eyes again. "He said I could stay with his family. But I don't know just where they live."

"I bet Peter doesn't, either," Teccard muttered, beneath his breath. He watched Helen go through the contents of Miss Yulett's bag—the little leather diary, the packet of envelopes like the one in Helbourne's desk drawer, the savings bank book.

The train slid alongside the concrete platform, redcaps kept pace with the slowing cars.

 ELEN put her arm around Miss Yulett's shoulders, hugged her lightly. Teccard pulled down the worn, leather suitcase from the overhead rack. "I'll get a porter for you."

"Don't be silly." The sergeant hefted the bag, easily. "*She* wouldn't spend a quarter that way. So I won't." She nodded cheerfully at the woman, joined the procession in the aisle.

Teccard got out his notebook, penciled: *I'm going to get a detective to take you to the Com-*

modore Hotel. Right here in the station. Register and stay right in your room until Sergeant Dixon comes for you. Don't worry about your bag, or expenses. We'll take care of them. Understand?

She didn't hide her fear. "Yes. But I'm afraid."

He patted her shoulder. "Nothing to be scared of—" he said before he realized she wasn't reading his lips. He followed her out to the platform, located one of the boys on the Terminal Squad, told him what he wanted done. "Keep her here on the platform for a while, too. Better take her out through one of the other gates—in case the man we're after is still waiting there. Phone my office and tell them her room number. Notify the desk at the hotel to route all calls to her room through the office of one of the assistant managers."

He tipped his hat to Miss Yulett, left her staring blankly at the bandage on the back of his head. The poor soul must be scared stiff, he knew. Well, better than *being* a stiff . . .

He had managed to keep sight of Helen's abominable hat, thirty or forty yards ahead. He put on steam to catch up with her. She was playing the part of the timidly anxious woman, to the hilt—searching the faces of the crowd lining the gate-ropes with just the right amount of hesitancy.

Teccard couldn't see anyone who resembled the snapshot. He was completely unprepared for what happened. A young man of thirty or so stepped abruptly out of the thinning crowd and took the suitcase out of the sergeant's hand.

Except for the exaggerated sideburns, his thin, clean-cut features could have been called handsome, in a sinister sort of way. If it hadn't been for the cream-colored necktie against the extravagantly long-pointed soft collar of his mauve shirt, he might have been considered well-dressed. There was no goatee, none of the full roundness of the face in Miss Yulett's snapshot. Yet Teccard was sure he recognized the man. He had only seen those dark eyebrows in side view—the deeply cleft chin had been covered with a towel when the lieutenant had pointed a gun at him. But this would be Harold Willard, beyond much doubt.

Teccard couldn't get too close to them. "Willard" or "Forst," or whatever his name was, would be certain to recognize the man who had crashed the room on Eighty-eighth Street! How could the lieutenant shadow them without being spotted himself?

Evidently "Willard" knew that Miss Yulett was deaf, he showed no surprise when Helen offered him the pad. But apparently there was some difference of opinion going on. The sergeant was shaking her head, as if she were bewildered.

When her escort took her arm and led her across the great central lobby, toward the subway entrance, she evidently protested. She made her way to one of the marble shelves alongside the ticket windows, pointed vehemently to the pad. "Willard" began to write, furiously . . .

Teccard bought a newspaper, unfolded it, kept it in front of his face so he could just see over the top. He edged, unobtrusively, within a dozen feet.

"But I don't understand." Helen gazed at "Willard" in obvious fascination. "You're so much better-looking. Why did you send me the other man's photograph?"

The youth favored her with a dazzling smile, proffered her a sheet from the pad.

She read it, crumpled it, seemed to thrust it into the pocket of her jacket. "I would have liked you even more, Peter—if you had trusted me— told me the truth."

They moved on toward the Lexington Avenue subway. Willard was having difficulty holding up his written end of the conversation. He kept setting the bag down, scribbling rapidly, then seizing her arm and rushing her along again.

Teccard followed them through the stile, downstairs to the uptown platform. They boarded the rear of one crowded car. The lieutenant squeezed onto the front platform of the car behind. He saw Helen's hand release the crumpled paper, before she was pushed into the

car. People surged in like a mob pressing to the scene of a fire. Teccard struggled through the door over the car-couplings, into the space Helen had just vacated. He stooped, retrieved the paper.

He held it down at his side, unfolded it.

I wanted to be certain you were not attracted to me merely because of my looks, darling. That's why I sent you the other picture. Now I am sure you will love me, for what I really am—not merely what I seem to be. Is that not better, dear one?

Teccard spat out a sibilant, jammed the paper in his pocket. The doors closed, the train rumbled out of the station.

He searched the crowded car aisle, ahead. They must have found seats somehow.

He unfolded the paper again, elbowed his way slowly forward.

They were nowhere in the car. Long before the brakes had screamed for the Eighty-sixth Street stop, he knew they were nowhere on the train.

CHAPTER FIVE
PRIMROSE PATH

ECCARD was in a cold rage as he shoved through the throng and up to Eighty-sixth Street. "Willard" had made a sucker of him with the old on-agin, off-agin, Finnegan—gone in the rear door, made his way, with Helen in tow, up by the side door at the middle of the subway car and— at the last instant—stepped off to the platform while the lieutenant was perusing the note Helen had dropped.

Of course, the sergeant couldn't have stopped the man without giving her hand away. Of course, also, "Willard" must have caught a glimpse of Teccard. Now, the make-love-by-mail guy would be on his guard—and likely to suspect Helen. Teccard had dragged her into this mess, by requesting her assignment from the Policewomen's Bureau. Now she was literally in the hands of a cold-blooded killer!

By force of habit, he called the Telegraph Bureau first, to get the alarm out for the dark-haired youth. The description was complete now. Teccard was good at estimating weight, height, age. Long experience in the Criminal Identification Bureau made him remember points that the average policeman wouldn't have noticed. "His ears are funny. Kind of pointed, at the top of the helix. He brushes his hair to cover them as much as he can. And his chin looks as if somebody had started to drive a wedge into it. And don't forget, this man is sure to be armed and dangerous."

Then he called Captain Meyer, repeated the description.

"Send a car around to check every man on beat, will you, Cap? Odds are good he hangs out in this parish somewhere. Have 'em keep an eye out for Sergeant Dixon, she'll be with him."

He had half expected to find a report from her, waiting for him when he called his office. He was wrong about that. The office didn't have much—there hadn't been any prints on the cellophane, too many on the knobs and furniture in the Eighty-eighth Street room. They hadn't been able to find any of record, though.

Talking with the Telegraph Bureau had given him an idea. He called Western Union, located the night traffic manager. "There was a bunch of flowers wired from this city to Miss Marion Yulett in Algers, upstate, sometime this a.m. Chances are, they went through Floral Telegraph Delivery. Find out what shop put in the order, will you? Buzz me back."

He fumed and stewed in the drugstore phone booth for what seemed like an hour. When he passed the clock over the soda fountain, on his way out, he found it had been seven minutes.

The address the telegraph company had given him was only a few blocks away. He didn't bother with a cab, but went on the run. Over to Second, up to Eighty-seventh. There it was, next to the undertaker's place in the middle of the block.

THE REMEMBRANCE SHOP.

Potted ivy and cactus in the window, flanked by lilies and dried grasses in tin vases—inside, a glass-front icebox with cut flowers, roses and carnations.

Carnations! Now he knew why that fragrance in the closet had reminded him of church, there had always been a big bunch of white carnations in front of the pulpit, when he was a kid. "Willard" must have had a carnation in the buttonhole of the coat he hung up in the closet . . .

A girl stood talking to the shirt-sleeved man behind the counter. As Teccard walked in she was saying: "You'll send those wreaths over to the sexton right away? He's waiting for them."

The florist nodded impatiently. "I'll get 'em right over, right away." He turned inquiringly toward the lieutenant. "What can I do for you, sir?"

Teccard drew a deep breath. This was the man in the snapshot! Round face, goatee, receding hair! "You can tell me who ordered some lilies of the valley wired to a lady up in Algers, New York."

"Was there some complaint?" asked the florist.

"Just checking up on the person who sent them. I'm from the police department."

The girl paused, on her way out, to stare at him out of stolid blue eyes set deep in a square, pleasant face.

"Police! What's the matter the police should come around?" The man waved his arms, excitedly.

Teccard said softly: "You have a duplicate record of your F.T.D. orders. Let's see it."

The florist ran stubby fingers through his hair, dug a flat, yellow book out of the debris on a bookkeeping desk. He ruffled the pages. "It ain't against the law, sending flowers like this!"

The carbon copy of the wired order wasn't helpful. All it indicated was that Peter Forst had paid two dollars and fifty cents to have a corsage delivered to Miss Marion Yulett at Algers.

"Who took the order?"

"Nobody. The envelope was under the door when I'm opening the shop this morning. With the cash. What's the matter, eh?"

Teccard's hand clamped on the other's wrist. "*You* sent those posies yourself, Mr. Forst."

"Forst! What's it, Forst?" The man's eyes narrowed. "I'm George Agousti, I run this business, no nonsense. I pay taxes."

The lieutenant's grip remained firm. "Then someone's been framing you, Agousti."

"Framing me? For what!"

"Murder." Teccard spoke quietly.

Agousti recoiled as from a blow. "It's terrible mistake you making. So much as a single flea, I ain't ever hurt."

"You don't know this Peter Forst?"

"The first time I ever hear his name, so help me!"

"What about Harold Willard? Heard of him?"

The florist shook his head.

"You don't feel like talking, do you? Maybe you'd feel more like it if you came down to headquarters with me."

Agousti shrugged. "I'm telling you. There ain't nothing on my conscience. I ain't afraid to go anywhere you like."

Teccard made one more try. He described the man Helen had gone with.

"Know *him?*"

Recognition crept into the florist's eyes. "I ain't dead sure. But from how you putting it, this one might be Stefan."

"Who's Stefan?"

"Stefan Kalvak. He's no good, a low life, sure."

"Yair, yair. Who is he? What's he do? Where's he live?"

"He's Miss Kalvak's brother, she really owns this shop. I run it for her. She's O.K., fine. But Stefan's a bum, a stinker. Always stealing dough out the cash register when I don't watch. Or getting girls into trouble, you know."

"He's done his best to get you in trouble. He sent your picture to this girl up in Algers—so she'd come to New York to get married."

"Holy Mother!"

"Where's he live?"

"You got me. His sister threw him out of her apartment. But you could phone her—"

A freckle-faced boy burst into the shop. "My pa sent me for the ivy for ma's birthday, Mr. Agousti."

"All right, Billy. Excuse me, one second." The florist whisked out of sight, back of the showcase.

The boy jingled seventy-five cents on the counter, an elevated roared overhead—and Teccard began to sweat, thinking of Helen Dixon and Stefan Kalvak.

The youngster called. "Pa says you needn't bother to wrap it up, Mr. Agousti."

There was no answer from the rear of the shop, though the sound of the elevated had died away.

Teccard stepped quickly around the glass case.

Agousti was leaning, face down, over a wooden bench—his head under the spreading fronds of a potted palm. There was a dark puddle on the boards of the bench, it widened slowly as drops splashed into it from the gash in the florist's neck.

 SHARP-bladed knife that had evidently been used to cut flower stems lay with its point in the glistening disk of crimson. There was blood on Agousti's right hand, too. Teccard lifted the limp wrist, saw the slash across the base of the fingers.

That settled it! A man didn't cut his hand that way, when he slashed his own throat! The florist had been attacked from behind, while he was putting the ivy in a flowerpot. He had tried to block off the blade that was severing his jugular—and had failed.

Not five feet from the dead man's back was a rear delivery door, with a wire screen nailed over the glass. The door was closed, but not locked.

Teccard tore a piece of green, glazed paper from the roll fixed to the end of the bench, wrapped it around the knob and twisted it. Then he opened the door.

A narrow alley ran behind the two-story building. It was floored with cement. There wouldn't be any footprints on it—and there wasn't anyone in sight.

He came inside, shut the door. He stuck his nailfile through the oval handle of the key, turned it until the bolt shot home.

The boy stuck his head around the corner of the glass case. Teccard stepped quickly between him and the body.

"Is he sick?" the youngster began.

"Yair. You go home, tell your father the ivy will be over later."

"O.K., mister. Gee, I'm sorry—"

"Wait a minute, son. You seen Stefan Kalvak around tonight?"

The boy made a face. "Naw. Steve ain't never around, except with girls. I don't like him, anyways—"

"You know where he lives?"

He jerked a thumb toward the ceiling. "I guess he lives right up over the flower store, here."

Teccard was startled. "That so?" Maybe the kid didn't know about the sister tossing Stefan out on his ear . . .

The boy ran. When he'd gone, the lieutenant felt in the pockets of the dead man, without disturbing the position of the body. There was a leather container, with four Yale keys. He took them.

One of the keys fitted the front door. He used it, from the street. Then he stepped into the entrance-way to the second floor stairs.

There was only one mailbox, a big brass one with a mother-of-pearl push button and a neatly engraved card: *Vanya Kalvak, Floriculturist.*

He went up the stairs, noiselessly.

There were two doors opening off the second-floor hall. The one nearest the front of the building had another of the engraved cards tacked to it.

He heard voices. They came from the room behind the door at the head of the stairs.

The tones of the girl who'd asked Agousti to deliver the wreaths were very distinct.

"Why do you come here, anyway, Miss Yulett?"

"Your brother brought me here," Helen answered. "He said it was all right."

Teccard's heart skipped a couple of beats. What was Helen doing, *talking?* She must have been startled out of her wits by this other woman and been caught off guard. He put his ear to the panel.

"I'm very sorry for you, Miss Yulett."

"I don't understand! Why should you be?" The sergeant was still playing her part. "Peter said he would be back in a moment. He'll explain."

"Peter!" The girl's tone was one of disgust. "His name is Stefan. Stefan Kalvak."

"It all seems very queer. I can't imagine why he lied to me about his name. But you ought to know, since you're his sister."

The girl laughed harshly. "You stupid idiot! He is my husband."

"What!" The sergeant didn't have to fake that exclamation, Teccard thought.

"It is the truth. I am his wife, God forbid." The girl spat out the words. "I know what he told you. The same as he told those others."

"You're just trying to drive me away from him."

Teccard decided they were in the kitchen of the apartment. One of them kept moving about restlessly—probably Mrs. Kalvak.

"I'm trying to save your life. You don't know Stefan. He's a fiend, absolutely. After he's taken your money—have you already given it to him?"

"No," Helen answered. "Tomorrow after we get the license, we will talk over buying the business."

"Tomorrow, you will be dead—if you do not let me help you get away."

"I should think you'd—hate me, Mrs. Kalvak. But honestly, I didn't know Peter—Stefan—was married."

"I don't care about you one way or the other. The reason I'm praying to God for you to get away quickly is that I don't want him caught."

"No . . ."

"I know what would happen to him, if the

police got him. My eyes haven't been closed all these months. Stefan hasn't earned the money he's been spending. Nevertheless—" she hesitated—"nevertheless, I love him."

A phone bell jangled in the front room. Mrs. Kalvak stalked away to answer it. Teccard waited until he heard her answering in monosyllables, then he tried the door. It was locked.

"Helen," he whispered as loudly as he dared. "Helen!"

The sergeant didn't hear him.

Mrs. Kalvak was storming back into the kitchen. "*You* talk of lying!" she cried. "You . . . trickster!" Mrs. Kalvak's voice rose in anger. "That was Stefan on the phone."

"He's coming back, then?"

"Sooner than you like, *my fine deaf lady!*"

"Wait—"

"You're no country innocent, Miss Yulett. I know who you are. You're a detective—trying to trap my man. And all the time I was sorry for you, thinking you were caught in his net!"

Helen screamed, once. Teccard heard a thud. He lunged at the panel. "Helen! Get the door open!"

There was no answer.

He pointed the muzzle of Meyer's automatic an inch from the edge of the jamb, at the lock.

Before he could pull the trigger he felt something, like the end of a piece of pipe, jab painfully into the small of his back. A suave voice murmured: "Use my key! It will be easier."

CHAPTER SIX
CUPID TURNS KILLER

HE lieutenant held the pose. A hand came around his side and relieved him of the .45.

"Come on, Vanya! Open up!"

The door swung wide. The girl stared, white-faced. "I didn't know you were out here, Stefan. I heard him—trying to get

in." She held a heavy, cast-iron skillet at her side.

"I came upstairs while he was bellowing like a bull." Kalvak prodded Teccard between the shoulder-blades with the muzzle of the automatic. "Get inside, there."

Helen sprawled on the floor beside the refrigerator. Her hat lay on the floor beside her, the wide brim crushed by the fall. The sergeant's head rested on a brown-paper shopping bag, her hair over her forehead.

Kalvak whistled, softly. "You killed her, Vanya!"

"She's only stunned." The girl lifted the skillet. "When I found she was a detective, I *could* have killed her."

"We've enough trouble, without having a cop-murder to worry about. Did you search her?"

Vanya kicked the sergeant sullenly. "There's no gun on her. What are you going to . . . do with them?"

Kalvak snarled at her. "I'll take care of them." He dug a spool of adhesive out his pocket. "Sit down in that chair. Grab the back with your hands. Close your eyes."

"Hell! You're not going to tape us, are you?"

"You think I want you to follow us, you—!"

Teccard saw a peculiar bulge inside the lining of Miss Yulett's hat. He couldn't be certain what it was—but it might be worth a gamble. "If you don't want to fret about a cop-murder, you better call a doc for her."

"She'll snap out of it, all right."

"Damn it! I tell you she's dying!" Slowly and deliberately, so Kalvak couldn't mistake his intention, Teccard moved a step closer to Helen—dropped down on one knee beside her.

The weapon in Kalvak's hand swiveled around to follow the lieutenant's movement. "Leave her alone."

Teccard rested his weight on one hand, close to the hat brim. The other he put on Helen's forehead. "She's like ice—if you don't get her to a doctor, fast—" His hand touched cold metal under the loose lining of the big hat.

Kalvak sensed something wrong. "Keep away from that hat!"

Teccard fired without drawing the stubby-barreled .32 out from under the hat-lining where Helen had hidden it. It was an angle shot and risky as hell—but the lieutenant knew the risk he and Helen were running, if he didn't shoot. The bullet hit Kalvak about three inches below his belt buckle. It doubled him over and spoiled his aim with that automatic. But the heavy slug ripped across the lieutenant's hip. It felt as if molten metal had been spilled all along the thigh. He lifted the .32—hat and all—emptied three more chambers. The first bullet missed its mark. The second one caught Kalvak under the V-cleft in his chin. The third wasn't needed.

Vanya sprang, caught him as he fell. She slumped on the floor, held his head in her arms, whimpering.

Helen struggled to sit up. "You and the U.S. Cavalry, Jerry," she mumbled.

He helped her to stand. "I was a sap to lose you, there in the subway."

Helen pressed her hands on top of her head, winced. "Peter—I mean Harold—or Stefan—Gone?"

"Thanks to your hiding that .32 in the Yulett dame's bonnet."

Vanya whined, wretchedly: "I know you're glad he's dead. I ought to be glad, too. After all the terrible crimes he's committed. But I'm not, I'm not."

The lieutenant limped over to her. "It was a good act, while it lasted, Mrs. Kalvak. But it couldn't last forever. You can take off the disguise."

She stopped rocking. "You mean I knew about Stefan's having committed murder? Yes, I knew. When it was too late to prevent them."

"I'll say you knew." He picked up Meyer's pistol. "The one who didn't know—for sure, anyway—was Stefan!"

Helen said, "What?"

The girl sat there, as if stupefied.

"All right. O.K. See what that innocence stuff gets you after Patrolman Taylor identifies you as the woman who ran downstairs at Eighty-eighth Street to tell him there was a fight going on over your room. Why'd you chase over there after your husband, anyway? Because you'd read that story in the newspaper about the kid finding the Lansing girl's bones?

"That'd be my guess. You were up there in the room Stefan had rented as Harold Willard, so he could get his hooks into another dame," he waved ironically toward Helen, "and you were packing up the clothes he had in the closet, or maybe just arguing with him so he wouldn't think you knew too much about those bones under the pier. Then who should ride up on his charger but T. Chauncey Helbourne. When he heard about the disappearing dames and the dough that vanished along with them, he wanted a cut of that, too. And he went to the right place to get it."

ANYA laid her cheek against the bloodless one in her lap. "You do not really believe such horrible things. No one could believe them."

Helen was at the sink, using cold water. She held up a small camp hatchet. "Could it be this Boy Scout meat axe? Somebody's been scouring it with steel wool."

"The head of it would fit the gash in my fedora just ducky," Teccard answered. "But it didn't kill Helbourne. It knocked him cold. He was shot after I'd had *my* light put out. *You* shot him, Mrs. Kalvak—so I'd either get blamed for bumping him myself or think Helbourne was the rat responsible for the *Happiness* murders."

"I was there at Eighty-eighth Street." Vanya stroked the corpse's forehead. "I did hear the fight. I told the truth to the policeman. You shot that man yourself."

"No cop shoots a man lying down, lady. The blood stain on Helbourne's vest was round, with the bullet hole in the center. If he'd died on his feet—the way it would have been if he was shot in a fight—the blood stain would have been tear-shaped—with the point down. How'd you beat it out of the house? Rush your husband down to that bathroom on the second floor—have him wait there, while you murdered Helbourne with-out Stefan's knowing it? And then take a powder after the patrolman ran up to the third floor?"

The sergeant went over to pick up what was left of Miss Yulett's hat. She picked up the brown-paper market basket at the same time. "Don't tell me this girl cut up that Lansing woman, all by herself, Jerry!"

"Yair. Probably did it all with her little hatchet."

"But why?" The sergeant held the bottom of the market bag up to the light. "If Stefan got the money out of these women, with his honeyed words . . . ?"

"Stefan wheedled it out of them—and turned the cash over to Mrs. Kalvak. She's the sort of skirt who wouldn't mind her hus-band monkeying with other femmes, if it paid enough."

Vanya kissed the corpse on the lips. "Darling! Listen to the hideous lies they make up about me!"

"Talk about lies, Mrs. Kalvak! You must have lied plenty to your husband. You'd probably promised to get the lovelorn out of his way after he'd garnered in the gold." Teccard turned his back to inspect the wound on his hip. "Maybe he thought you scared them off by that 'he's-a-married-man—I'm-his-wife' line. I don't know. But I'm damned certain *you* thought the easy way to keep the suckers quiet was to plant them. Why you had to hack them to pieces—"

Helen held up the market bag, by its brown-twine handle. "Recognize those brown fibers that clung to the oilcloth, Jerry? From this twine. Goes through the bottom of the bag to give it strength. She used this to carry . . . them . . . in."

"Yair. Yair. That's why she had to axe them in small hunks. So she could carry the pieces out of here and down to the wharf, without being conspicuous!" He went over, hauled the girl to her feet. "Or maybe it's you just like cutting up people. Like Agousti."

Vanya touched the wound in Stefan's neck, as if she couldn't believe her eyes. "Stefan went to . . . see Agousti. I know nothing of that."

"Don't, eh? Then it won't be your prints on that stem-cutter or the doorknob downstairs, eh? You didn't decide Agousti'd have to be shut up before he prevented your getaway, then?"

Mrs. Kalvak looked up at him. There was murder in her eyes.

Helen hurried to the front room. "I'm going to call the wrecking crew, to take over here."

"I've had all of this *I* want," Teccard agreed. "And I'll sure be glad when you don't have to muck around in this kind of slop."

"Man works from sun to sun," the sergeant twiddled the dial, "but woman's work is never done. In the police department."

"Far as that goes," he got out his twisters, "one cop is enough . . . in any one family. Don't you think?"

CONTRIBUTORS NOTES

Otto Penzler is the founder of New York's Mysterious Bookshop and The Mysterious Press. He has now edited ten annual editions of *The Best American Mystery Stories*. He lives in New York.

Harlan Coben has topped bestseller charts the world over with novels such as *The Innocent, Just One Look, No Second Chance, Tell No One,* and *Gone for Good.* He is the first author ever to win all four major crime-writing awards in the USA. He lives in New Jersey with his wife and four children.

Harlan Ellison is renowned in the fields of science fiction, fantasy, and crime fiction for his dry, cutting writing. He is the author of *Rumble (Web of the City)* and *The Sound of a Scythe.* He has won numerous awards, including two Edgars. He lives in Los Angeles with his wife.

Laura Lippman was born in Atlanta, Georgia, and raised in Baltimore, Maryland, where she now lives. She is the acclaimed author of *By a Spider's Thread, No Good Deeds,* and *What the Dead Know,* featuring her series character, Tess Monaghan. She has won numerous awards, including an Edgar for *Charm City* and the Anthony Award for *In Big Trouble.*

PERMISSIONS ACKNOWLEDGMENTS

and conservator of the respective copyrights, and successor-in-interest to Popular Publications, Inc.

"The Cat Woman" by Erle Stanley Gardner from *Black Mask Magazine*, February 1927. Copyright © 1927 by Erle Stanley Gardner. Reprinted by permission of Hobson & Hughes LLP on behalf of the Erle Stanley Gardner Trust.

"The Dilemma of the Dead Lady" by Cornell Woolrich. Copyright © 1936 by Cornell Woolrich. Originally published as "Wardrobe Trunk" in *Detective Fiction Weekly*, July 4, 1936. Copyright © by JP Morgan Chase Bank as Trustee for The Claire Woolrich Memorial Scholarship Fund a/w of Cornell Woolrich R 671100, June 24, 1936. Reprinted by permission of JP Morgan Chase Bank and The Firm on behalf of the Claire Woolrich Memorial Scholarship Fund.

"The Invisible Millionaire" by Leslie Charteris from *Black Mask Magazine*, June 1938. Copyright © 1938 by Leslie Charteris. Reprinted by permission of Gelfman Schneider Literary Agents for the author.

"You'll Always Remember Me" by Steve Fisher for *Black Mask Magazine*, March 1938. Copyright © 1938 by Pro-Distributors, Inc.; renewed 1955 by Popular Publications, Inc. Reprinted by special arrangement with Keith Alan Deutsch (keithdeutsch@comcast.net; www.blackmaskmagazine.com) proprietor and conservator of the respective copyrights, and successor-in-interest to Popular Publications, Inc.

"Faith" by Dashiell Hammett. Copyright © 2006 by the Dashiell Hammett Literary Property Trust, reproduced with permission; with thanks to the Joy Harris Literary Agency.

"Pastorale" by James M. Cain. Copyright © 1938 by James M. Cain; renewed 1965 by James M. Cain. Reprinted by permission of Harold Ober Associates. First published in *The American Mercury*, March 1938.

"Finger Man" by Raymond Chandler from *Black Mask Magazine*, October 1934. Copyright © 1934 by Raymond Chandler. Reprinted by kind permission of the Estate of Raymond Chandler and Ed Victor Ltd.

"The Monkey Murder" by Erle Stanley Gardner from *Detective Story Magazine*, January 1939. Copyright © 1938 by Street & Smith; renewed 1966 by Erle Stanley Gardner. Reprinted by permission of Hughes & Hobson LLC on behalf of the Erle Stanley Gardner Trust.

"Pigeon Blood" by Paul Cain from *Black Mask Magazine*, November 1933. Copyright © 1938 by Pro-Distributors, Inc.; renewed 1950 by Popular Publications, Inc. Reprinted by special arrangement with Keith Alan Deutsch (keithdeutsch@

comcast.net; www.blackmaskmagazine.com) proprietor and conservator of the respective copyrights, and successor-in-interest to Popular Publications, Inc.

"Killer in the Rain" by Raymond Chandler from *Black Mask Magazine,* January 1935. Coypright © 1935 by Raymond Chandler; renewed 1963. Reprinted by kind permission of the Estate of Raymond Chandler.

"A Shock for the Countess" by C. S. Montayne form *Black Mask Magazine,* March 15, 1923. Copyright © 1923 by Pro-Distributors, Inc.; renewed 1951 by Popular Publications, Inc. Reprinted by special arrangement with Keith Alan Deutsch (keithdeutsch@comcast.net; www.blackmaskmagazine.com) proprietor and conservator of the respective copyrights, and successor-in-interest to Popular Publications, Inc.

"The Corpse in the Crystal" by D. B. McCandless from *Detective Fiction Weekly,* 1937. Copyright © 1937 by Pro-Distributors, Inc.; renewed 1965 by Popular Publications, Inc. Reprinted by special arrangement with Keith Alan Deutsch (keithdeutsch@comcast.net; www.blackmaskmagazine.com) proprietor and conservator of the respective copyrights, and successor-in-interest to Popular Publications, Inc.

"He Got What He Asked For" by D. B. McCandless from *Detective Fiction Weekly,* January 16, 1937. Copyright © 1937 by Pro-Distributors, Inc.; renewed 1965 by Popular Publications, Inc. Reprinted by special arrangement with Keith Alan Deutsch (keithdeutsch@comcast.net; www.blackmaskmagazine.com) proprietor and conservator of the respective copyrights, and successor-in-interest to Popular Publications, Inc.

"Dance Macabre" by Robert Reeves from *Black Mask Magazine,* April 1941. Copyright © 1941 by Pro-Distributors, Inc.; renewed 1969 by Popular Publications, Inc. Reprinted by special arrangement with Keith Alan Deutsch (keithdeutsch@comcast.net; www.blackmaskmagazine.com) proprietor and conservator of the respective copyrights, and successor-in-interest to Popular Publications, Inc.

"The Girl with the Silver Eyes" by Dashiell Hammett from *Black Mask Magazine,* June 1924. Copyright © 1924 by Dashiell Hammett; renewed 1952 by Dashiell Hammett. Reprinted by permission of the Literary Property Trust of Dashiell Hammett. Reprinted in *The Continental Op* by Dashiell Hammett, Copyright © 1974 by Lillian Hellman, Executrix of the Estate of Dashiell Hammett. Used by permission of Random House, Inc.

"The Duchess Pulls a Fast One" by Whitman Chambers from *Detective Fiction Weekly,* September 19, 1936. Copyright © 1936 by Pro-Distributors, Inc.; renewed 1964 by Popular Publications, Inc. Reprinted by special arrangement with Keith Alan Deutsch (keithdeutsch@comcast.net; www.blackmaskmagazine.com) pro-